The Penny Parker Collection: 15 Complete Novels

By

Mildred A. Wirt

Cover Photograph: Aussiegall & VinothChandar

ISBN: 978-1-78139-367-3

© 2013 Oxford City Press, Oxford.

Contents

Danger at theDrawbridge

CHAPTER 1 - AN ASSIGNMENT FOR PENNY 3

CHAPTER 2 - REPORTERS NOT WANTED 6

CHAPTER 3 - GIFT TO THE BRIDE 9

CHAPTER 4 - BEHIND THE BUSHES 12

CHAPTER 5 - THE MISSING BRIDEGROOM 15

CHAPTER 6 - A RING OF WHITE GOLD 18

CHAPTER 7 - THE FORBIDDEN POOL 21

CHAPTER 8 - PARENTAL PROTEST 24

CHAPTER 9 - A SOCIETY BAZAAR 27

CHAPTER 10 - A THROWN STONE 30

CHAPTER 11 - QUESTIONS AND ANSWERS 33

CHAPTER 12 - FISHERMAN'S LUCK 36

CHAPTER 13 - TWO MEN AND A BOAT 39

CHAPTER 14 - THE STONE TOWER 42

CHAPTER 15 - A CAMEO PIN 46

CHAPTER 16 - GATHERING CLUES 49

CHAPTER 17 - A SEARCH FOR JERRY 53

CHAPTER 18 - OVER THE DRAWBRIDGE 56

CHAPTER 19 - A DARING RESCUE 59

CHAPTER 20 - AN IMPORTANT INTERVIEW 61

CHAPTER 21 - THE WHITE CRUISER 63

CHAPTER 22 - TRAPPED IN THE CABIN 65

CHAPTER 23 - AT THE HIDE-OUT 68

CHAPTER 24 - SECRET OF THE LILY POOL 71

CHAPTER 25 - VICTORY FOR PENNY 75

Behind the Green Door

- CHAPTER 1 - TROUBLE FOR MR. PARKER 81
- CHAPTER 2 - A RIVAL REPORTER 85
- CHAPTER 3 - TRAVELING COMPANIONS 88
- CHAPTER 4 - PINE TOP MOUNTAIN 91
- CHAPTER 5 - OVER THE BARBED WIRE 94
- CHAPTER 6 - PENNY TRESPASSES 97
- CHAPTER 7 - THE GREEN DOOR 100
- CHAPTER 8 - A CODED MESSAGE 103
- CHAPTER 9 - A CALL FOR HELP 106
- CHAPTER 10 - LOCKED IN THE CABIN 109
- CHAPTER 11 - A NEWSPAPER MYSTERY 113
- CHAPTER 12 - THE GREEN CARD 116
- CHAPTER 13 - AN UNKIND TRICK 119
- CHAPTER 14 - A BROKEN ROD 122
- CHAPTER 15 - IN THE TOOL HOUSE 125
- CHAPTER 16 - A PUZZLING SOLUTION 127
- CHAPTER 17 - STRANGE SOUNDS 130
- CHAPTER 18 - QUESTIONS AND CLUES 133
- CHAPTER 19 - PETER JASKO SERVES NOTICE 135
- CHAPTER 20 - VISITORS 138
- CHAPTER 21 - OLD PETER'S DISAPPEARANCE 142
- CHAPTER 22 - THE SECRET STAIRS 145
- CHAPTER 23 - RESCUE 148
- CHAPTER 24 - HENRI'S SALON 151
- CHAPTER 25 - SCOOP! 154

Clue of the Silken Ladder

- CHAPTER 1 - DOUBLE TROUBLE 159
- CHAPTER 2 - A ROPE OF SILK 163

CHAPTER 3 - SOCIETY ROUTINE 167
CHAPTER 4 - A TURN OF FORTUNE 170
CHAPTER 5 - THE MAN IN GRAY 173
CHAPTER 6 - AN APARTMENT BURGLARY 176
CHAPTER 7 - MARK OF THE IRON HOOK 179
CHAPTER 8 - PSYCHIC SIGNS 182
CHAPTER 9 - MRS. WEEMS' INHERITANCE 185
CHAPTER 10 - OUIJA BOARD WISDOM 188
CHAPTER 11 - THE CELESTIAL TEMPLE 191
CHAPTER 12 - A MESSAGE FOR MRS. WEEMS 194
CHAPTER 13 - COUSIN DAVID'S GHOST 197
CHAPTER 14 - WET PAINT 200
CHAPTER 15 - HIDDEN MONEY 203
CHAPTER 16 - OVER THE WINDOW LEDGE 206
CHAPTER 17 - KANO'S CURIO SHOP 209
CHAPTER 18 - THE BELL TOWER 212
CHAPTER 19 - PENNY INVESTIGATES 214
CHAPTER 20 - INSIDE THE CABINET 216
CHAPTER 21 - STARTLING INFORMATION 218
CHAPTER 22 - SCALING THE WALL 220
CHAPTER 23 - A PRISONER IN THE BELFRY 222
CHAPTER 24 - THE WOODEN BOX 225
CHAPTER 25 - EXTRA! 229

The Secret Pact

CHAPTER 1 - ABOARD THE GOODTIME 235
CHAPTER 2 - THE RIVER'S VICTIM 238
CHAPTER 3 - THE OCTOPUS TATTOO 241
CHAPTER 4 - A PROSPECTIVE TENANT 244
CHAPTER 5 - COBWEBS AND RUST 247

CHAPTER 6 - HEADLINES AND HEADACHES 250
CHAPTER 7 - PETER FENESTRA 253
CHAPTER 8 - THE STORM CAVE 256
CHAPTER 9 - A FALLEN TREE 259
CHAPTER 10 - A WORD TO THE WISE 262
CHAPTER 11 - MR. JUDSON'S DAUGHTER 265
CHAPTER 12 - OLD HORNEY 267
CHAPTER 13 - PAPER PROBLEMS 270
CHAPTER 14 - AN EMPTY BEDROOM 273
CHAPTER 15 - INFORMATION FROM TILLIE 276
CHAPTER 16 - BEHIND THE LILACS 279
CHAPTER 17 - THE ART OF TATTOO 282
CHAPTER 18 - PAULETTA'S EXPLANATION 285
CHAPTER 19 - MRS. WEEMS' REPORT 289
CHAPTER 20 - PICNIC BY MOONLIGHT 292
CHAPTER 21 - ELLIS SAAL'S CUSTOMER 295
CHAPTER 22 - GHOSTS OF THE PAST 298
CHAPTER 23 - PENNY'S PLIGHT 301
CHAPTER 24 - A BARRIER OF FLAMES 304
CHAPTER 25 - SAILORS' REVENGE 307

The Clock Strikes Thirteen

CHAPTER 1 - SANDWICHES FOR TWO 313
CHAPTER 2 - NIGHT RIDERS 317
CHAPTER 3 - A BLACK HOOD 320
CHAPTER 4 - A NEW CARETAKER 323
CHAPTER 5 - OLD SETH 327
CHAPTER 6 - TALL CORN 331
CHAPTER 7 - MR. BLAKE'S DONATION 334
CHAPTER 8 - PUBLICITY BY PENNY 337

CHAPTER 9 - JERRY'S PARTY	340
CHAPTER 10 - IN THE MELON PATCH	343
CHAPTER 11 - PENNY'S CLUE	347
CHAPTER 12 - ADELLE'S DISAPPEARANCE	350
CHAPTER 13 - AN EXTRA STROKE	353
CHAPTER 14 - THROUGH THE WINDOW	356
CHAPTER 15 - TRACING BEN BOWMAN	359
CHAPTER 16 - A FAMILIAR NAME	362
CHAPTER 17 - FALSE RECORDS	365
CHAPTER 18 - ADELLE'S ACCUSATION	369
CHAPTER 19 - TRAILING A FUGITIVE	372
CHAPTER 20 - CLEM DAVIS' DISCLOSURE	375
CHAPTER 21 - A BROKEN PROMISE	378
CHAPTER 22 - THE MAN IN GRAY	381
CHAPTER 23 - A TRAP SET	384
CHAPTER 24 - TIMELY HELP	387
CHAPTER 25 - SPECIAL EDITION	391

Wishing Well

CHAPTER 1 - AN OLD HOUSE	395
CHAPTER 2 - BY THE COVERED WELL	398
CHAPTER 3 - CHICKEN DINNER	402
CHAPTER 4 - A RECORD ON ROCK	404
CHAPTER 5 - STRANGERS FROM TEXAS	408
CHAPTER 6 - A WISH FULFILLED	411
CHAPTER 7 - PENNY'S DISCOVERY	414
CHAPTER 8 - A MOVING LIGHT	417
CHAPTER 9 - MYSTERIOUS PROWLERS	420
CHAPTER 10 - BENEATH THE FLAGSTONES	423
CHAPTER 11 - JAY FRANKLIN'S TRICKERY	426

CHAPTER 12 - NO ADMITTANCE	429
CHAPTER 13 - A SILKEN LADDER	432
CHAPTER 14 - NIGHT ADVENTURE	435
CHAPTER 15 - OLD BOTTLES	438
CHAPTER 16 - INSIDE THE MANSION	441
CHAPTER 17 - THE MARBOROUGH PEARLS	444
CHAPTER 18 - SIGNBOARD INDIANS	447
CHAPTER 19 - PUBLICITY PLUS	450
CHAPTER 20 - RHODA'S PROBLEM	453
CHAPTER 21 - MRS. MARBOROUGH'S LOSS	457
CHAPTER 22 - THE MISSING NECKLACE	460
CHAPTER 23 - GRAND BALL	464
CHAPTER 24 - RIVER RISING	467
CHAPTER 25 - PRECIOUS CARGO	470

Saboteurs on the River

CHAPTER 1 - TROUBLE AFLOAT	475
CHAPTER 2 - FRONT PAGE NEWS	479
CHAPTER 3 - STRAIGHT FROM THE SHOULDER	483
CHAPTER 4 - AN UNWARRANTED ATTACK	486
CHAPTER 5 - HELD ON SUSPICION	489
CHAPTER 6 - OLD NOAH	492
CHAPTER 7 - ARK OF THE MUD FLATS	495
CHAPTER 8 - THE GREEN PARROT	498
CHAPTER 9 - A JOB FOR MR. OAKS	501
CHAPTER 10 - SALVAGE AND SABOTEURS	504
CHAPTER 11 - PURSUIT BY TAXI	507
CHAPTER 12 - JERRY'S DISAPPEARANCE	510
CHAPTER 13 - A VACANT BUILDING	513
CHAPTER 14 - TEST BLACKOUT	516

CHAPTER 15 - A DRIFTING BARGE	519
CHAPTER 16 - DANGER ON THE RIVER	522
CHAPTER 17 - A STOLEN BOAT	525
CHAPTER 18 - PENNY'S PLAN	529
CHAPTER 19 - STANDING GUARD	532
CHAPTER 20 - A SHACK IN THE WOODS	536
CHAPTER 21 - THROUGH THE SKYLIGHT	539
CHAPTER 22 - A SEARCHING PARTY	541
CHAPTER 23 - HELP FROM NOAH	544
CHAPTER 24 - A MESSAGE IN THE BOTTLE	547
CHAPTER 25 - A BOW IN THE CLOUD	550

Ghost Beyond the Gate

CHAPTER 1 - LOST ON A HILLTOP	557
CHAPTER 2 - AT THE LISTENING POST	560
CHAPTER 3 - AN UNPLEASANT DRIVER	563
CHAPTER 4 - STOLEN TIRES	565
CHAPTER 5 - AN IMPORTANT INTERVIEW	568
CHAPTER 6 - FRONT PAGE NEWS	571
CHAPTER 7 - QUESTIONS WITHOUT ANSWERS	574
CHAPTER 8 - A FEW CHANGES	576
CHAPTER 9 - AN OPEN SAFE	580
CHAPTER 10 - TALE OF A GHOST	583
CHAPTER 11 - BY A CEMETERY WALL	586
CHAPTER 12 - FLIGHT	589
CHAPTER 13 - A BLACK MARKET	592
CHAPTER 14 - A FAMILIAR FIGURE	595
CHAPTER 15 - GHOST IN THE GARDEN	599
CHAPTER 16 - A DOOR IN A BOX	602
CHAPTER 17 - ADVENTURE BY MOONLIGHT	605

CHAPTER 18 - THROUGH THE CELLAR WINDOW	608
CHAPTER 19 - A BAFFLING SEARCH	611
CHAPTER 20 - ACCUSATIONS	613
CHAPTER 21 - MRS. BOTTS' REVELATION	616
CHAPTER 22 - A PARK BENCH	618
CHAPTER 23 - FORGOTTEN EVENTS	621
CHAPTER 24 - TRICKERY	625
CHAPTER 25 - FINAL EDITION	630

Hoofbeats on the Turnpike

CHAPTER 1 - OLD MAN OF THE HILLS	635
CHAPTER 2 - PLANS	638
CHAPTER 3 - INTO THE VALLEY	641
CHAPTER 4 - A STRANGER OF THE ROAD	644
CHAPTER 5 - SLEEPY HOLLOW ESTATE	648
CHAPTER 6 - GHOSTS AND WITCHES	651
CHAPTER 7 - BED AND BOARD	655
CHAPTER 8 - A RICH MAN'S TROUBLES	659
CHAPTER 9 - STRAIGHT FROM THE SHOULDER	662
CHAPTER 10 - BARN DANCE	665
CHAPTER 11 - THE HEADLESS HORSEMAN	668
CHAPTER 12 - PREMONITIONS	671
CHAPTER 13 - RAIN	673
CHAPTER 14 - A MOVING LIGHT	676
CHAPTER 15 - INTO THE WOODS	680
CHAPTER 16 - A FRUITLESS SEARCH	683
CHAPTER 17 - ACCUSATIONS	685
CHAPTER 18 - FLOOD WATERS	689
CHAPTER 19 - TRAGEDY	692
CHAPTER 20 - EMERGENCY CALL	695

- CHAPTER 21 - A MYSTERY EXPLAINED 699
- CHAPTER 22 - WANTED—A WIRE 702
- CHAPTER 23 - TOLL LINE TO RIVERVIEW 705
- CHAPTER 24 - A BIG STORY 707
- CHAPTER 25 - MISSION ACCOMPLISHED 709

Voice from the Cave

- CHAPTER 1 - AN UNINVITED GUEST 715
- CHAPTER 2 - STORMY WEATHER 718
- CHAPTER 3 - A JADE GREEN CHARM 721
- CHAPTER 4 - NO CAMPING ALLOWED 724
- CHAPTER 5 - OVER THE AIR 728
- CHAPTER 6 - BREAKFAST BLUES 730
- CHAPTER 7 - THE BEARDED STRANGER 733
- CHAPTER 8 - KEEPER OF THE LIGHT 736
- CHAPTER 9 - A SURPRISE FROM THE SKY 739
- CHAPTER 10 - HELP FROM MR. EMORY 742
- CHAPTER 11 - A MAN OF MYSTERY 745
- CHAPTER 12 - CAUGHT BY THE TIDE 748
- CHAPTER 13 - A HIDDEN PACKAGE 751
- CHAPTER 14 - VOICE FROM THE CAVE 754
- CHAPTER 15 - AFTERGLOW 757
- CHAPTER 16 - SUSPICION 760
- CHAPTER 17 - VISITORS NOT PERMITTED 763
- CHAPTER 18 - INSIDE THE LIGHTHOUSE 766
- CHAPTER 19 - A LOCKED DOOR 769
- CHAPTER 20 - NYMPHS OF THE SEA 772
- CHAPTER 21 - THE CARDBOARD BOX 775
- CHAPTER 22 - UNFINISHED BUSINESS 778
- CHAPTER 23 - NIGHT ADVENTURE 781

CHAPTER 24 - OUT OF THE SEA	784
CHAPTER 25 - A SCOOP FOR UNCLE SAM	788

Guilt of the Brass Thieves

CHAPTER 1 - ADRIFT	793
CHAPTER 2 - THE BRASS LANTERN	796
CHAPTER 3 - A "PROBLEM" BOY	799
CHAPTER 4 - THROUGH THE WINDOW	802
CHAPTER 5 - UNWANTED ADVICE	805
CHAPTER 6 - SWEEPER JOE INFORMS	807
CHAPTER 7 - NIGHT SHIFT WORKER	810
CHAPTER 8 - OVERHEARD IN THE GATEHOUSE	813
CHAPTER 9 - SALLY'S HELPER	816
CHAPTER 10 - OVERTURNED	820
CHAPTER 11 - A QUESTION OF RULES	823
CHAPTER 12 - NIGHT PROWLER	826
CHAPTER 13 - THE STOLEN TROPHY	830
CHAPTER 14 - TRAPPED	833
CHAPTER 15 - UNDER THE SAIL	836
CHAPTER 16 - SILK STOCKINGS	839
CHAPTER 17 - BASEMENT LOOT	842
CHAPTER 18 - OVER THE BALCONY	845
CHAPTER 19 - FLIGHT	848
CHAPTER 20 - A DESPERATE PLIGHT	851
CHAPTER 21 - RESCUE	853
CHAPTER 22 - CAPTAIN BARKER'S COURAGE	856
CHAPTER 23 - FIRE!	859
CHAPTER 24 - DREDGING THE RIVER	862
CHAPTER 25 - THE RACE	865

Signal in the Dark

CHAPTER 1 - HELP WANTED	871
CHAPTER 2 - EXPLOSION!	874
CHAPTER 3 - SPECIAL ASSIGNMENT	877
CHAPTER 4 - THE MISSING PLATES	880
CHAPTER 5 - SHADOW ON THE SKYLIGHT	883
CHAPTER 6 - BEN'S STORY	886
CHAPTER 7 - MAN OVERBOARD!	889
CHAPTER 8 - A SWINGING CHAIN	892
CHAPTER 9 - THE METAL DISC	895
CHAPTER 10 - COUNTRY SKIES	898
CHAPTER 11 - A FAMILIAR CAR	901
CHAPTER 12 - THE PROFESSOR'S HELPER	904
CHAPTER 13 - BEHIND OFFICE DOORS	907
CHAPTER 14 - A NOTE FROM BEN	910
CHAPTER 15 - THE DEMONSTRATION	913
CHAPTER 16 - SUSPICION	916
CHAPTER 17 - MAJOR BRYAN	919
CHAPTER 18 - A SECOND TEST	921
CHAPTER 19 - THE LANTERN SIGNAL	924
CHAPTER 20 - A CROOK EXPOSED	927
CHAPTER 21 - IN SEARCH OF WEBB	930
CHAPTER 22 - SALT'S MISSING CAMERA	933
CHAPTER 23 - ESCAPE BY NIGHT	935
CHAPTER 24 - A RAID ON THE SNARK	938
CHAPTER 25 - PICTURE PROOF	941

Whispering Walls

CHAPTER 1 - THE PLUMED SERPENT	947
CHAPTER 2 - AN UNEXPLAINED DISAPPEARANCE	951

CHAPTER 3 - A THATCHED ROOF COTTAGE	954
CHAPTER 4 - BEHIND THE BUSHES	956
CHAPTER 5 - AN EVIL CHARM	959
CHAPTER 6 - MATCHES AND STRING	962
CHAPTER 7 - WHISPERING WALLS	965
CHAPTER 8 - GHOST OF THE DARK CORNERS	969
CHAPTER 9 - JERRY ENTERS THE CASE	972
CHAPTER 10 - CHEAP LODGING	976
CHAPTER 11 - THE WOODEN DOLL	980
CHAPTER 12 - SUPERSTITION	983
CHAPTER 13 - MISSING FROM THE CHEST	986
CHAPTER 14 - STORM WARNINGS	989
CHAPTER 15 - MRS. RHETT'S ILLNESS	992
CHAPTER 16 - AN OPEN WINDOW	996
CHAPTER 17 - THE STOLEN WILL	998
CHAPTER 18 - THROUGH THE WINDOW	1001
CHAPTER 19 - RISING WIND	1004
CHAPTER 20 - TWELVE STEPS DOWN	1008
CHAPTER 21 - CEREMONIAL CAVE	1011
CHAPTER 22 - STRANGER IN THE STORM	1014
CHAPTER 23 - IN THE PRESSROOM	1017
CHAPTER 24 - THE GRINNING GARGOYLE	1020
CHAPTER 25 - ON THE BALCONY	1024

Swamp Island

CHAPTER 1 - THE BEARDED STRANGER	1029
CHAPTER 2 - ALERTING ALL CARS	1031
CHAPTER 3 - UNFINISHED BUSINESS	1034
CHAPTER 4 - A TRAFFIC ACCIDENT	1037
CHAPTER 5 - THE RED STAIN	1040

CHAPTER 6 - AMBULANCE CALL	1043
CHAPTER 7 - AN EMPTY BED	1046
CHAPTER 8 - IN SEARCH OF JERRY	1049
CHAPTER 9 - THE WIDOW JONES	1051
CHAPTER 10 - INSIDE THE WOODSHED	1054
CHAPTER 11 - AN ABANDONED CAR	1057
CHAPTER 12 - A JOB FOR PENNY	1061
CHAPTER 13 - INTO THE SWAMP	1064
CHAPTER 14 - A CODE MESSAGE	1067
CHAPTER 15 - BEYOND THE BOARDWALK	1070
CHAPTER 16 - TREED BY A BOAR	1073
CHAPTER 17 - RESCUE	1075
CHAPTER 18 - WANTED—A GUIDE	1078
CHAPTER 19 - PENNY'S PLAN	1082
CHAPTER 20 - TRAILING HOD HAWKINS	1085
CHAPTER 21 - THE TUNNEL OF LEAVES	1088
CHAPTER 22 - HELP FROM TONY	1091
CHAPTER 23 - LOST IN THE HYACINTHS	1094
CHAPTER 24 - UNDER THE FENCE POST	1097
CHAPTER 25 - OUTWITTED	1100

The Cry at Midnight

CHAPTER 1 - MIDNIGHT AT THE GATE	1107
CHAPTER 2 - "NO TRESPASSING"	1110
CHAPTER 3 - STRANGER OF THE STORM	1113
CHAPTER 4 - VANISHING FOOTPRINTS	1116
CHAPTER 5 - A CRYSTAL BALL	1120
CHAPTER 6 - CREAKING WOOD	1123
CHAPTER 7 - A WARNING	1125
CHAPTER 8 - INTO THE CREVASSE	1128

CHAPTER 9 - A CALL FOR HELP 1131
CHAPTER 10 - MR. ECKENROD'S SECRET 1133
CHAPTER 11 - MAP OF THE MONASTERY 1135
CHAPTER 12 - THE LOCKED DOOR 1138
CHAPTER 13 - OLD JULIA'S WARNING 1142
CHAPTER 14 - AN ASSIGNMENT FOR PENNY 1145
CHAPTER 15 - FOOTPRINTS IN THE SNOW 1149
CHAPTER 16 - THE KITCHEN CUPBOARD 1152
CHAPTER 17 - THE CULT CEREMONY 1155
CHAPTER 18 - ELEVEN BOWLS 1158
CHAPTER 19 - A DORMITORY ROOM 1160
CHAPTER 20 - TRICKERY 1163
CHAPTER 21 - SNATCHED FROM THE FLAMES 1166
CHAPTER 22 - THE CANOPIED BED 1169
CHAPTER 23 - DESCENT INTO THE CRYPT 1172
CHAPTER 24 - CHAMBER OF THE DEAD 1175
CHAPTER 25 - THE STAR SAPPHIRE 1179

DANGER AT THE DRAWBRIDGE

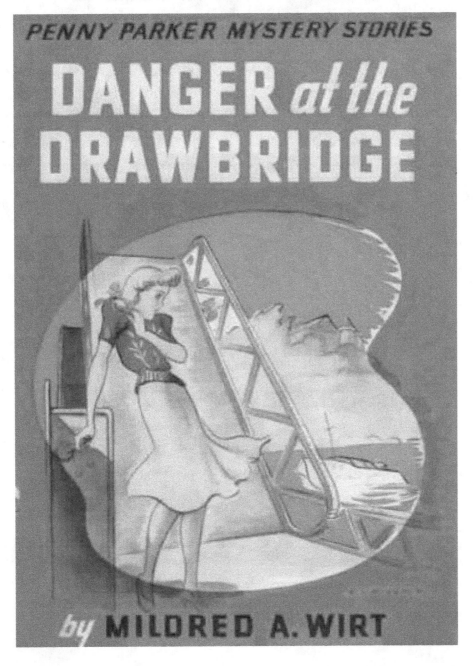

DANGER AT THE DRAWBRIDGE

The speeding automobile careened down the bank.

CHAPTER 1 - AN ASSIGNMENT FOR PENNY

Penny Parker, leaning indolently against the edge of the kitchen table, watched Mrs. Weems stem strawberries into a bright green bowl.

"Tempting bait for Dad's jaded appetite," she remarked, helping herself to the largest berry in the dish. "If he can't eat them, I can."

"I do wish you'd leave those berries alone," the housekeeper protested in an exasperated tone. "They haven't been washed yet."

"Oh, I don't mind a few germs," laughed Penny. "I just toss them off like a duck shedding water. Shall I take the breakfast tray up to Dad?"

"Yes, I wish you would, Penny," sighed Mrs. Weems. "I'm right tired on my feet this morning. Hot weather always did wear me down."

She washed the berries and then offered the tray of food to Penny who started with it toward the kitchen vestibule.

"Now where are you going, Penelope Parker?" Mrs. Weems demanded suspiciously.

"Oh, just to the automatic lift." Penny's blue eyes were round with innocence.

"Don't you dare try to ride in that contraption again!" scolded the housekeeper. "It was never built to carry human freight."

"I'm not exactly freight," Penny said with an injured sniff. "It's strong enough to carry me. I know because I tried it last week."

"You walk up the stairs like a lady or I'll take the tray myself," Mrs. Weems threatened. "I declare, I don't know when you'll grow up."

"Oh, all right," grumbled Penny good-naturedly. "But I do maintain it's a shameful waste of energy."

Balancing the tray precariously on the palm of her hand she tripped lightly up the stairway and tapped on the door of her father's bedroom.

"Come in," he called in a muffled voice.

Anthony Parker, editor and owner of the *Riverview Star* sat propped up with pillows, reading a day-old edition of the newspaper.

"'Morning, Dad," said Penny cheerfully. "How is our invalid today?"

"I'm no more an invalid than you are," returned Mr. Parker testily. "If that old quack, Doctor Horn, doesn't let me out of bed today—"

"You'll simply explode, won't you, Dad?" Penny finished mischievously. "Here, drink your coffee and you'll feel less like a stick of dynamite."

Mr. Parker tossed the newspaper aside and made a place on his knees for the breakfast tray.

"Did I hear an argument between you and Mrs. Weems?" he asked curiously.

"No argument, Dad. I just wanted to ride up in style on the lift. Mrs. Weems thought it wasn't a civilized way to travel."

"I should think not." The corners of Mr. Parker's mouth twitched slightly as he poured coffee from the silver pot. "That lift was built to carry breakfast trays, but not in combination with athletic young ladies."

"What a bore, this business of growing up," sighed Penny. "You can't be natural at all."

"You seem to manage rather well with all the restrictions," her father remarked dryly.

Penny twisted her neck to gaze at her reflection in the dresser mirror beyond the footboard of the big mahogany bed.

"I won't mind growing up if only I'm able to develop plenty of glamour," she said speculatively. "Am I getting any better looking, Dad?"

"Not that I've noticed," replied Mr. Parker gruffly, but his gaze lingered affectionately upon his daughter's golden hair. She really was growing prettier each day and looked more like her mother who had died when Penny was a little girl. He had spoiled her, of course, for she was an only child, but he was proud because he had taught her to think straight. She was deeply loyal and affectionate and those who loved her overlooked her casual ways and flippant speech.

"What happened to the paper boy this morning?" Mr. Parker asked between bites of buttered toast.

"It isn't time for him yet, Dad," said Penny demurely. "You always expect him at least an hour early."

"First edition's been off the press a good half hour," grumbled the newspaper owner. "When I get back to the *Star* office, I'll see that deliveries are speeded up. Just wait until I talk with Roberts!"

"Haven't you been doing a pretty strenuous job of running the paper right from your bed?" inquired Penny as she refilled her father's cup. "Sometimes when you talk with that poor circulation manager I think the telephone wires will burn off."

"So I'm a tyrant, am I?"

"Oh, everyone knows your bark is worse than your bite, Dad. But you've certainly not been at your best the last few days."

Mr. Parker's eyes roved about the luxuriously furnished bedroom. Tinted walls, chintz draperies, the rich, deep rug, were completely lost upon him. "This place is a prison," he grumbled.

For nearly a week the household had been thrown completely out of its usual routine by the editor's illness. Overwork combined with an attack of influenza had sent him to bed, there to remain until he should be released by a doctor's order. With a telephone at his elbow, Mr. Parker had kept in close touch with the staff of the *Riverview Star* but he fretted at confinement.

"I can't half look after things," he complained. "And now Miss Hilderman, the society editor, is sick. I don't know how we'll get a good story on the Kippenberg wedding."

Penny looked up quickly. "Miss Hilderman is ill?"

"Yes, DeWitt, the city editor, telephoned me a few minutes ago. She wasn't able to show up for work this morning."

"I really don't see why he should bother you about that, Dad. Can't Miss Hilderman's assistant take over the duties?"

"The routine work, yes, but I don't care to trust her with the Kippenberg story."

"Is it something extra special, Dad?"

"Surely, you've heard of Mrs. Clayton Kippenberg?"

"The name is familiar but I can't seem to recall—"

"Clayton Kippenberg made a mint of money in the chain drug business. No one ever knew exactly the extent of his fortune. He built an elaborate estate about a hundred and twenty-five miles from here, familiarly called *The Castle* because of its resemblance to an ancient feudal castle. The estate is cut off from the mainland on three sides and may be reached either by boat or by means of a picturesque drawbridge."

"Sounds interesting," commented Penny.

"I never saw the place myself. In fact, Kippenberg never allowed outsiders to visit the estate. Less than a year ago a rumor floated around that he had separated from his wife. There also was considerable talk that he had disappeared because of difficulties with the government over income tax evasion and wished to escape arrest. At any rate, he faded out of the picture while his wife remained in possession of *The Castle*."

"And now she is marrying again?"

"No, it is Mrs. Kippenberg's daughter, Sylvia, who is to be married. The bridegroom, Grant Atherwald, comes from a very old and distinguished family."

"I don't see why the story should be so difficult to cover."

"Mrs. Kippenberg has ruled that no reporters or photographers will be allowed on the estate," explained Mr. Parker.

"That does complicate the situation."

"Yes, it may not be easy to persuade Mrs. Kippenberg to change her mind. I rather doubt that our assistant society editor has the ingenuity to handle the story."

CHAPTER 1 - AN ASSIGNMENT FOR PENNY

"Then why don't you send one of the regular reporters? Jerry Livingston, for instance?"

"Jerry couldn't tell a tulle wedding veil from one of crinoline. Nor could any other man on the staff."

"I could get that story for you," Penny said suddenly. "Why don't you try me?"

Mr. Parker gazed at his daughter speculatively.

"Do you really think you could?"

"Of course." Penny spoke with assurance. "Didn't I bring in two perfectly good scoops for your old sheet?"

"You certainly did. Your Vanishing Houseboat yarn was one of the best stories we've published in a year of Sundays. And the town is still talking about Tale of the Witch Doll."

"After what I went through to get those stories, a mere wedding would be child's play."

"Don't be too confident," warned Mr. Parker. "If Mrs. Kippenberg doesn't alter her decision about reporters, the story may be impossible to get."

"May I try?" Penny asked eagerly.

Mr. Parker frowned. "Well, I don't know. I hate to send you so far, and then I have a feeling—"

"Yes, Dad?"

"I can't put my thoughts into words. It's just that my newspaper instinct tells me this story may develop into something big. Kippenberg's disappearance never was fully explained and his wife refused to discuss the affair with reporters."

"Kippenberg might be at the wedding," said Penny, thinking aloud. "If he were a normal father he would wish to see his daughter married."

"You follow my line of thought, Penny. When you're at the estate—if you get in—keep your eyes and ears open."

"Then you'll let me cover the story?" Penny cried in delight.

"Yes, I'll telephone the office now and arrange for a photographer to go with you."

"Tell them to send Salt Sommers," Penny suggested quickly. "He doesn't act as know-it-all as some of the other lads."

"I had Sommers in mind," her father nodded as he reached for the telephone.

"And I have a lot more than Salt Sommers in *my* mind," laughed Penny.

"Meaning?"

"Another big story, Dad! A scoop for the *Star* and this for you."

Penny implanted a kiss on her father's cheek and skipped joyously from the room.

CHAPTER 2 - REPORTERS NOT WANTED

In the editorial room of the *Riverview Star* heads turned and eyebrows lifted as Penny, decked in her best silk dress and white picture hat, clicked her high-heeled slippers across the bare floor. Jerry Livingston, reporter, stopped pecking at his typewriter and stared in undisguised admiration.

"Well, if it isn't our Bright Penny," he bantered. "Didn't recognize you for a minute in all those glad rags."

"These are my work clothes," replied Penny. "I'm covering the Kippenberg wedding."

Jerry pushed his hat farther back on his head and grinned.

"Tough assignment. From what I hear of the Kippenberg family, you'll be lucky if they don't throw the wedding cake at you."

Penny laughed and went on, winding her way through a barricade of desks to the office of the society editor. Miss Arnold, the assistant, was talking over the telephone, but in a moment she finished and turned to face the girl.

"Good morning, Miss Parker," she said stiffly. An edge to her voice told Penny more clearly than words that the young woman was nettled because she had not been trusted with the story.

"Good morning," replied Penny politely. "Dad said you would be able to give me helpful suggestions about covering the Kippenberg wedding."

"There's not much I can tell you, really. The ceremony is to take place at two o'clock in the garden, so you'll have ample time to reach the estate. If you get in—" Miss Arnold placed an unpleasant emphasis upon the words—"take notes on Miss Kippenberg's gown, the flowers, the decorations, the names of her attendants. Try to keep your facts straight. Nothing infuriates a bride more than to read in the paper that she carried a bouquet of lilies-of-the-valley and roses while actually it was a bouquet of some other flower."

"I'll try not to infuriate Miss Kippenberg," promised Penny.

Miss Arnold glanced quickly at her but the girl's face was perfectly serene.

"That's all I can tell you, Miss Parker," she said shortly. "Bring in at least a column. For some reason the city editor rates the wedding an important story."

"I'll do my best," responded Penny, and arose.

Salt Sommers was waiting for her when she came out of the office. He was a tall, spare young man, with a deep scar down his left cheek. He talked nearly as fast as he walked.

"If you're all set, let's go," he said.

Penny found herself three paces behind but she caught up with the photographer as he waited for the elevator.

"I'm taking Minny along," Salt volunteered, holding his finger steadily on the signal bell. "May come in handy."

"Minny?" asked Penny, puzzled.

"Miniature camera. You can't always use the Model X."

"Oh," murmured Penny. Deeply embarrassed, she remained silent as the elevator shot them down to the ground floor.

Salt loaded his photographic equipment into a battered press car which was parked near the loading dock at the rear of the building. He slid in behind the wheel and then as an afterthought swung open the car door for Penny.

CHAPTER 2 - REPORTERS NOT WANTED

Salt seemed to know the way to the Kippenberg estate. They shot through Riverview traffic, shaving red lights and tooting derisively at slow drivers. In open country he pressed the accelerator down to the floor and the car roared down the road, only slackening speed as it raced through a town.

"How do you travel when you're in a hurry?" Penny gasped, clinging to her flopping hat.

Salt grinned and lifted his foot from the gasoline pedal.

"Sorry," he said. "I get in the habit of driving fast. We have plenty of time."

As they rode, Penny gathered scraps of information. The Kippenberg estate was located six miles from the town of Corbin and was cut off from the mainland on three sides by the joining of two wide rivers, one with a direct outlet to the ocean. Salt did not know when the house had been built but it was considered one of the show places of the locality.

"Do you think we'll have much trouble getting our story?" Penny asked anxiously.

"All depends," Salt answered briefly. He slammed on the brake so suddenly that Penny was flung forward in the seat.

Another car coming from the opposite direction had pulled up at the side of the road. Penny did not recognize the three men who were crowded into the front seat, but the printed placard, *Ledger* which was pasted on the windshield told her they represented a rival newspaper in Riverview.

"What luck, Les?" Salt called, craning his neck out the car window.

"You may as well turn around and go back," came the disgusted reply. "The old lady won't let a reporter or a photographer on the estate. She has a guard stationed on the drawbridge to see that you don't get past."

The car drove on toward Riverview. Salt sat staring down the road, drumming his fingers thoughtfully on the steering wheel.

"Looks like we're up against a tough assignment," he said. "If Les can't get in—"

"I'm not going back without at least an attempt," announced Penny firmly.

"That's the spirit!" Salt cried with sudden approval. "We'll get on the estate somehow if we have to swim over."

He jerked the press card from the windshield, and reaching into the back seat of the car, covered the Model X camera with an old gunny sack. The miniature camera he placed in his coat pocket.

"No use advertising our profession too early in the game," he remarked.

Twelve-thirty found Penny and Salt in the sleepy little town of Corbin. Fortifying themselves with a lunch of hot dog sandwiches and pop, they followed a winding, dusty highway toward the Kippenberg estate.

Presently, through the trees, marking the end of the road, an iron drawbridge loomed up. It stood in open position so that boats might pass on the river below. A wooden barrier had been erected across the front of the structure which bore a large painted sign. Penny read the words aloud.

"'DANGEROUS DRAWBRIDGE—KEEP OFF.'"

Salt drew up at the side of the road. "Looks as if this is as far as we're going," he said in disgust. "There's no other road to the estate. I'll bet that 'dangerous drawbridge' business is just a dodge to keep undesirables away from the place until after the wedding."

Penny nodded gloomily. Then she brightened as she noticed an old man who obviously was an estate guard standing at the entrance to the bridge. He stared toward the old car as if trying to ascertain whether or not the occupants were expected guests.

"I'm going over to talk with him," Penny said.

"Pretend that you're a guest," suggested Salt. "You look the part in that fancy outfit of yours."

Penny walked leisurely toward the drawbridge. Appraisingly, she studied the old man who leaned comfortably against the gearhouse. A dilapidated hat pulled low over his shaggy brows seemed in keeping with the rest of his wardrobe—a blue work shirt and a pair of grease-smudged overalls. A charred corn-cob pipe, thrust at an angle between his lips, provided sure protection against the mosquitoes swarming up from the river below.

"Good afternoon," began Penny pleasantly. "My friend and I are looking for the Kippenberg estate. We were told at Corbin to take this road but we seem to have made a mistake."

"You ain't made no mistake, Miss," the old man replied.

"Then is the estate across the river?"

"That's right, Miss."

"But how are guests to reach the place? I see the sign says the bridge is out of commission. Are we supposed to swim over?"

"Not if you don't want to," the old man answered evenly. "Mrs. Kippenberg has a launch that takes the folks back and forth. It's on the other side now but will be back in no time at all."

"I'll wait in the car out of the hot sun," Penny said. She started away, then paused to inquire casually: "Is this drawbridge really out of order?"

The old man was deliberate in his reply. He blew a ring of smoke into the air, watched it hover like a floating skein of wool and finally disintegrate as if plucked to pieces by an unseen hand.

"Well, yes, and no," he said. "It ain't exactly sick but she sure is ailin'. I wouldn't trust no heavy contraption on this bridge."

"Condemned by the state, I suppose?"

"No, Miss, and I'll tell you why. This here bridge doesn't belong to the state. It's a private bridge on a private road."

"Odd that Mrs. Kippenberg never had it repaired," Penny remarked. "It must be annoying."

"It is to all them that don't like launches. As for Mrs. Kippenberg, she don't mind. Fact is, she ain't much afraid of the bridge. She drives her car across whenever she takes the notion."

"Then the bridge does operate!" Penny exclaimed.

"Sure it does. That's my job, to raise and lower it whenever the owner says the word. But the bridge ain't fit for delivery trucks and such-like. One of them big babies would crack through like goin' over sponge ice."

"Well, I rather envy your employer," said Penny lightly. "It isn't every lady who has her own private drawbridge."

"She is kind of exclusive-like that way, Miss. Mrs. Kippenberg she keeps the drawbridge up so she'll have more privacy. And I ain't blamin' her. These here newspaper reporters always is a-pesterin' the life out of her."

Penny nodded sympathetically and walked back to make her report to Salt.

"No luck?" he demanded.

"Guess twice," she laughed. "The old bridgeman just took it for granted I was one of the wedding guests. It will be all right for us to go over in the guest launch as soon as it arrives."

Salt gazed ruefully at his clothes.

"I don't look much like a guest. Think I'll pass inspection?"

"Maybe you could get by as one of the poor relations," grinned Penny. "Pull your hat down and straighten your tie."

Salt shook his head. "A business suit with a grease spot on the vest isn't the correct dress for a formal wedding. You might get by but I won't."

"Then should I try it alone?"

"I'll have to get those pictures somehow," stated Salt grimly.

"Maybe we could hire a boat of our own," Penny suggested. "Of course it wouldn't look as well as if we arrived on the guest launch."

"Let's see what we can line up," Salt said, swinging open the car door.

They walked to the river's edge and looked in both directions. There were no small boats to be seen. The only available craft was a large motor boat which came slowly downstream toward the open drawbridge. Penny caught a glimpse of the pilot, a burly man with a red, puffy face.

Salt slid down the bank toward the water's edge, and hailed the boat.

"Hey, you, Cap'n!" he called. "Two bucks to take me across the river."

The man inclined his head, looked steadily at Salt for an instant, then deliberately turned his back.

"Five!" shouted Salt.

The pilot gave no sign that he had heard. Instead, he speeded up the boat which passed beneath the drawbridge and went on down the river.

CHAPTER 3 - GIFT TO THE BRIDE

"Perhaps he didn't hear you," said Penny, peering after the retreating boat.

"He heard me all right," growled Salt as he scrambled back up the high bank.

Noticing a small boy in dirty overalls who sat at the water's edge fishing, he called to him: "Say, sonny, who was that fellow, do you know?"

"Nope," answered the boy, barely turning his head, "but his boat has been going up and down the river all morning. That's why I can't catch anything."

The boat rounded a bend of the river and was lost to view. Only one other craft appeared on the water, a freshly painted white motor launch which could be seen coming from the far shore.

"That must be the guest boat now," remarked Penny, shading her eyes against the glare of the sun. "It seems to be our only hope."

"Let's try to get aboard and see what happens," proposed the photographer.

They walked leisurely back toward the guard at the drawbridge, timing their arrival just as the launch swung up to the landing. With a cool assurance which Penny tried to duplicate, Salt stepped aboard, nodded indifferently to the wheelsman, and slumped down in one of the leather seats.

Penny waited uneasily for embarrassing questions which did not come. Gradually she relaxed as the boatman took no interest in them and the guard's attention was fully occupied with other cars which had driven up to the drawbridge.

A few minutes later, two elderly women, both elegantly gowned, were helped aboard the boat by their chauffeur. One of the women stared disapprovingly at Salt through her lorgnette and then ignored him.

"We'll get by all right," Salt whispered confidently.

"Wait until Mrs. Kippenberg sees us," warned Penny.

"Oh, we'll keep out of her way until we have our story and plenty of pictures. Once we're across the river it will be easy."

"I hope you're right," muttered Penny.

While Salt's task of taking pictures might prove relatively simple, she realized that her own work would be anything but easy. She could not hope to gather many facts without talking to a member of the family, and the instant she admitted her identity she likely would be ejected from the grounds.

"I boasted I'd bring in a front page story," she thought ruefully. "I'll be lucky if I get a column of routine stuff."

The boat was moving slowly away from the landing when the guard at the drawbridge called in a loud voice: "Hold it, Joe!"

Penny and Salt stiffened in their chairs, fearing they were to be exposed. But they were both greatly relieved to see that a long, black limousine had drawn up at the end of the road. The launch had been stopped so that additional passengers might be accommodated.

Salt nudged Penny's elbow.

"Grant Atherwald," he contributed, jerking his head toward a tall, well-built young man who had stepped from the car. "I've seen his picture plenty of times."

"The bridegroom?" Penny turned to stare.

"Sure. He's one of the blue-bloods, but they say he's a little short on ready cash."

The young man, dressed immaculately in formal day attire, and accompanied by two other men, came aboard the launch. He bowed politely to the elderly women and his gaze fell questioningly upon Penny and Salt. But if he wondered why they were there, he did not voice his thought.

As the boat put out across the river Penny watched Grant Atherwald curiously. It seemed to her that he appeared nervous and preoccupied. He stared straight before him, clenching and unclenching his hands. His face was colorless and drawn.

"He's nervous and worried," thought Penny. "I guess all bridegrooms are like that."

A sharp "click" sounded in her ear. Penny did not turn toward Salt, but she caught her breath, knowing what he had done. He had dared to take a picture of Grant Atherwald!

She waited, feeling certain that the sound must have been heard by everyone in the boat. A full minute elapsed and no one spoke. When Penny finally glanced at Salt he was gazing serenely out across the muddy water, his miniature camera shielded behind a felt hat which he held on his knees.

The boat docked. Salt and Penny allowed the others to go ashore first, and then followed a narrow walk which wound through a deep lane of evergreen trees.

"Salt," Penny asked abruptly, "how did you get that picture of Atherwald?"

"Snapped it through a hole in the crown of my hat. It's an old trick. I always wear this special hat when I'm sent out on a hard assignment."

"I thought a cannon had gone off when the shutter clicked," Penny laughed. "We were lucky you weren't caught."

Emerging from behind the trees, they obtained their first view of the Kippenberg house. Sturdily built of brick and stone, it stood upon a slight hill, its many turrets and towers commanding a view of the two rivers.

"Nice layout," Salt commented, pausing to snap a second picture. "Wish someone would give me a castle for a playhouse."

They crossed the moat and found themselves directly behind Grant Atherwald again. Before the bridegroom could enter the house a servant stepped forward and handed him a sealed envelope.

"I was told to give this to you as soon as you arrived, sir," he said.

Grant Atherwald nodded, and taking the letter, quickly opened it. A troubled expression came over his face as he scanned the message. Without a word he thrust the paper into his pocket. Turning, he walked swiftly toward the garden.

"Salt, did you notice how queerly Atherwald looked—" Penny began, but the photographer interrupted her.

"Listen," he said, "we haven't a Chinaman's chance of getting in the front door. That boy in the fancy knickers is giving everyone the once over. Let's try a side entrance."

Without attracting attention they walked quickly around the house and located a door where no servant had been posted. Entering, they passed through a marble-floored vestibule into a breakfast room crowded with serving tables. Salt nonchalantly helped himself to an olive from one of the large glass dishes and led Penny on toward the main hall where many of the guests had gathered to admire the wedding gifts.

"Now don't swipe any of the silver," Salt said jokingly. "I think that fellow over by the stairway is a private detective."

"He seems to be looking at us with a suspicious gleam in his eyes," Penny replied. "I hope we don't get tossed out of here."

"We'll be all right if Mrs. Kippenberg doesn't see us before the ceremony."

"Do you suppose Mr. Kippenberg could be here, Salt?"

"Not likely. It's my guess that fellow will never be seen again."

"Dad doesn't share your opinion."

"I know," Salt admitted. "We'll keep watch for him, but it would just be a lucky break if it turns out he's here."

Mingling with the guests, they walked slowly about a long table where the wedding gifts were displayed. Penny gazed curiously at dishes of solid silver, crystal bowls, candlesticks, jade ornaments, tea sets and service plates encrusted with gold.

"Nothing trashy here," muttered Salt.

"I've never seen such an elegant display," Penny whispered in awe. "Do you suppose that picture is one of the gifts?"

CHAPTER 3 - GIFT TO THE BRIDE

She indicated an oil painting which stood on an easel not far from the table. So many guests had gathered about the picture that she could not see it distinctly. But at her elbow, a woman in rustling silk, said to a companion:

"My dear, a genuine Van Gogh! It must have cost a small fortune!"

When the couple had moved aside, Penny and Salt drew closer to the easel. One glance assured them that the painting had been executed by a master. However, it was the subject of the picture which gave Penny a distinct start.

"Will you look at that!" she whispered to Salt.

"What about it?" he asked carelessly.

"Don't you notice anything significant?"

"Can't say I do. It's just a nice picture of a drawbridge."

"That's just the point, Salt!" Penny's eyes danced with excitement. "A drawbridge!"

The photographer glanced again at the painting, this time with deeper interest.

"Say, it looks a lot like the bridge which was built over the river," he observed. "You think this picture is a copy of it?"

Penny shook her head impatiently. "Salt, your knowledge of art is dreadful. This Van Gogh was painted ages ago and is priceless. Don't you see, the drawbridge has to be a copy of the picture?"

"Your theory sounds reasonable," Salt admitted. "I wonder who gave the painting to the bride? There's no name attached."

"Can't you guess why?"

"I never was good at kid games."

"Why, it's clear as crystal," Penny declared, keeping her voice low. "This estate with the drawbridge was built by Clayton Kippenberg. He must have been familiar with the Van Gogh painting, and had the real bridge modeled after the picture. For that matter, the painting may have been in his possession—"

"Then you think the picture was presented to Sylvia Kippenberg by her father?" Salt broke in quickly.

"Yes, I do. Only a person very close to the bride would have given such a gift."

"H-m," said Salt, squinting at the picture thoughtfully. "If you're right it means that Clayton Kippenberg's whereabouts must be known to his family. His disappearance may not be such a deep mystery to Mamma Kippenberg and daughter Sylvia."

"Oh, Salt, wouldn't it make a grand story if only we could learn what became of him?"

"Sure. Front page stuff."

"We simply must get the story somehow! If Mrs. Kippenberg would just answer our questions about this drawbridge painting—"

"I'm afraid Mamma Kippenberg isn't going to break down and tell all," Salt said dryly. "But buckle on your steel armor, little girl, because here she comes now!"

CHAPTER 4 - BEHIND THE BUSHES

A large, middle-aged woman in rose-colored silk, crossed the room directly toward Salt and Penny. Her pale blue eyes glinted with anger and there were hard lines about her mouth. She walked haughtily, but with grim purpose.

"Unless we do some fast talking, out we go!" muttered Salt. "It's Mrs. Kippenberg, all right."

They stood their ground, knowing they had been recognized as intruders. But before the woman could reach them she was stopped by a servant who spoke a few words in a low tone. For a moment Mrs. Kippenberg forgot about Penny and Salt as a new problem presented itself.

"I can't talk with anyone now," she said in an agitated voice. "Tell them to come back later."

"They insist upon talking with you now, Madam," replied the servant. "Unless you see them they say they will look around for themselves."

"Oh!" Mrs. Kippenberg drew herself up sharply as if from a physical blow. "Where are they now?"

"In the library, Madam."

Penny did not hear the woman's reply, but she turned and followed the servant.

"Saved by the bell," mumbled Salt. "Now let's get away from here before she comes back."

They pushed through the throng and reached a long hallway. Mrs. Kippenberg had disappeared, but as they drew near an open door they caught sight of her again. She stood just inside the library, her back toward them, talking with two men who wore plain gray business suits.

Penny half drew back, fearing discovery, but Salt pulled her along. As they went quietly past the door they heard Mrs. Kippenberg say in an excited voice:

"No, no, I tell you he isn't here! Why should I try to deceive you? We have nothing to hide. You are most inconsiderate to annoy me at such a time!"

Penny and Salt did not hear the reply. They reached an outside door and stepped down on a flagstone terrace which overlooked the garden at the rear of the grounds.

"Who were those men, do you suppose?" Penny whispered, fearful that her voice might betray them.

"Officers of the law, I should guess," Salt replied in an undertone.

"Government men?"

"Likely as not. I don't believe the locals would bother her. Anyway she's got the wind up and you can tell she's scared silly in spite of all her back talk."

"You know what I think they're after?" Penny said thoughtfully.

"Well, if I had just one guess," Salt replied, "I'd say they are after Mr. Kippenberg."

"I agree with you there."

"Sure, why else would they come sleuthing around at a time like this? The answer is simple. Daughter gets married. Papa wants to see his darling do it. Therefore, boys, we'll spread a net for Daddy and he might plump right into it."

"So that's the way a G man's mind works?" laughed Penny.

"But I would take it that Kippenberg is no fool," Salt went on. "If they really have a 'man wanted' sign hung on him he would be too cagey to come around here today."

They were standing beside the stone balustrade which bounded the terrace. Below them the green foliage of the gardens formed a dark background for the playing fountains. A cool breeze drifted in from the river and rattled a window awning just over their heads.

"We're in an exposed place here," observed Salt uneasily. "Maybe we ought to find a hole somewhere."

CHAPTER 4 - BEHIND THE BUSHES

"We'll never learn anything in a hole," Penny objected. "In fact, we're not making much progress in running down any sort of story. I do wish we could have heard more of that conversation."

"And get thrown out on our collective ear before we even have a chance to snap a picture of the blushing bride!"

"Pictures! Pictures!" exclaimed Penny. "That's all you photographers think about. How about poor little me and my story? After all, you can't bring out a paper full of nothing but pictures and cigarette ads. You need a little news to go with it."

"You like to work too fast," complained Salt. "Right now the thing to do is to keep out of sight. I'm telling you the minute Mrs. Kippy finishes with those men she'll be gunning for us."

"Then I suppose we'll have to go into hiding."

"First, let's mosey out into the rose garden," Salt proposed. "I'll take a few shots and then we'll duck under somewhere and wait until the ceremony starts."

"That's all very well for you," grumbled Penny, "but I can't write much of a story without talking to some member of the family."

Salt started off across the velvety green lawn toward the rose arbor where the service was to be held. Penny followed reluctantly. She watched the photographer take several pictures before a servant approached him.

"I beg your pardon," the man said coldly, "but Mrs. Kippenberg gave orders no pictures were to be taken. If you are from one of the papers—"

"Oh, I saw her in the house just a minute ago," Salt replied carelessly.

"Sorry, sir," the servant apologized, retreating.

Salt finished taking the pictures and slipped the miniature camera back into his pocket.

"Now let's amble down toward the river and wait," he said to Penny. "We'll blossom forth just as the ceremony starts. Mrs. Kippy won't dare interrupt it to have us thrown off the grounds."

They walked down a sloping path, past a glass-enclosed hothouse and on toward a grove of giant oak and maple trees.

"It's pleasant here when you're away from the crowd," Penny remarked, gazing up at the leafy canopy. "I wonder where this path leads?"

"Oh, down to the river probably. With water on three sides of us that's a fairly safe guess."

"Which rivers flow past the estate, Salt?"

"The Big Bear and the Kobalt."

"The same old muddy Kobalt which is near our town," said Penny in surprise. "I'll always think of it as a river of adventure."

"Because of Mud-Cat Joe and his Vanishing Houseboat?"

Penny nodded and a dreamy look came into her eyes. "So much happened on the Kobalt, Salt. Remember that big party Dad threw at the Comstock Inn?"

"Do I? Jerry Livingston decided to sleep in Room Seven where so many persons had disappeared."

"And then he was spirited away almost before our very eyes," added Penny. "Days later Mud-Cat Joe helped me fish him out of this same old Kobalt. For awhile we didn't think he'd ever pull through or be able to tell what had happened to him."

"But as the grand finale you and your friend, Louise Sidell, solved the mystery and secured a dandy story for the *Star*. Those were the days!"

"You talk as if they were gone forever," laughed Penny. "Other good stories will come along."

"Maybe," said Salt, "but covering a wedding is pretty tame in comparison."

"Yet this one does have interesting angles," Penny insisted. "Can't you almost feel mystery lurking about the place?"

"No, but I do feel a mosquito sinking his stinger into me." Salt slapped vigorously at his ankle.

They followed the path on toward the river, coming soon to a trail which branched off to the right. Across it had been stretched a wire barrier and a neatly lettered sign read:

NO ADMITTANCE BEYOND THIS POINT.

"Why do you suppose the path is blocked off?" Penny speculated.

"Let's find out," Salt suggested with a sudden flare of interest. "Maybe we'll run into something worth a picture."

Penny hesitated, not wishing to disregard the sign, yet eager to learn what lay beyond the barrier.

"Listen," said Salt, "just put your little conscience on ice. We're here to get the 'who, when, why and where.' You'll never be a first class newspaper reporter if you stifle your curiosity."

"Lead on," laughed Penny. "I will follow. Only isn't it getting late?"

Salt looked at his watch. "We still have a safe fifteen minutes."

He started to step over the wire, only to have Penny reach out and grasp his hand.

"Wait!" she whispered.

"What's the idea?" Salt turned toward her in astonishment.

"I think someone is watching us! I'm sure I saw the bushes move."

"Your nerves are jumpy," Salt jeered. "It's only the wind."

Even as he spoke the foliage to the left moved ever so slightly and a dark form could be seen creeping stealthily away along the ground.

CHAPTER 5 - THE MISSING BRIDEGROOM

Salt acted instinctively. Leaping over the wire barrier he dived into the bushes. Hurling himself upon the man who crouched there, he pinned him to the ground. The fellow gave a choked cry and tried to pull free.

"Oh, no, you don't," Salt muttered, coolly sitting down on his stomach. "Snooping, eh?"

"You let me up!" the man cried savagely. "Let me up, I say!"

"I'll let you up when you explain what you were doing here."

"Why, you impudent young pup!" the man spluttered. "You're the one who will explain. I am Mrs. Kippenberg's head gardener."

Salt's hand fell from the old man's collar and he apologetically helped him to his feet. Penny, who had reached the scene, stooped down and recovered a trowel which had slipped from the gardener's grasp.

"It was just a little mistake on my part," Salt mumbled. "I hope I didn't hurt you."

"No fault of yours you didn't," the old man snapped. "A fine howdydo when a person can't even loosen earth around a shrub without being assaulted by a ruffian!"

The gardener was a short, stout man with graying hair. He wore coarse garments, a loose fitting pair of trousers, a dark shirt and battered felt hat. But Penny noticed that his hands and fingernails were clean and there were no trowel marks around any of the shrubs.

"Salt isn't exactly a ruffian," she said as the photographer offered no defense. "After all, from where we stood it looked exactly as if you were hiding in the bushes."

"Then you both need glasses," the man retorted rudely. "A person can't work without getting down on his hands and knees."

"Where were you digging?" Penny asked innocently.

"I was just starting in when this young upstart leaped on my back!"

"Sorry," said Salt, "but I thought you were trying to get away."

"Who are you anyway?" the gardener demanded bluntly. "You're not guests. I can tell that."

"You have a very discerning eye," replied Salt smoothly. "We're from the *Riverview Star*."

"Reporters, eh?" The old man scowled unpleasantly. "Then you've no business being here at all. You're not wanted, so get out!"

"We're only after a few facts about the wedding," Penny said. "Perhaps you would be willing to tell me—"

"I'll tell you nothing, Miss! If anything is given out to the papers it will have to come from Mrs. Kippenberg."

"Fair enough," Salt acknowledged. He glanced curiously down the path which had been blocked off. "What's down there?"

"Nothing." The gardener spoke irritably. "This part of the estate hasn't been fixed up. That's why it's closed."

Penny had bent down, pretending to examine a shrub at the edge of the path.

"What is the name of this bush?" she inquired casually.

"An azalea," the gardener replied after a slight hesitation. "Now get out of here, will you? I have my work to do."

"Oh, all right," Salt rejoined as he and Penny moved away. "No need to get so tough."

They stepped over the barrier wire and retraced their way toward the house. Several times Penny glanced back but she could not see the old man. He had slipped away somewhere among the trees.

"I don't believe that fellow was a gardener," she said suddenly.

"What makes you think not?"

"Didn't you notice his nice clean hands and fingernails? And then when I asked him the name of that bush he hesitated and called it an azalea. I saw another long botanical name attached to it."

"Maybe he just made a mistake, or said the first thing that came into his head. He wanted to get rid of us."

"I know he did," nodded Penny. "Yet, when he found out we were from the *Star* he didn't threaten to report us to Mrs. Kippenberg."

"That's so."

"He was afraid to report us," Penny went on with conviction. "I'll bet a cent he has no more right here than we have."

Salt had lost all interest in the gardener. He glanced at his watch and quickened his step.

"Is it two o'clock yet?" Penny asked anxiously.

"Just. After all the trouble we've had getting here we can't afford to miss the big show."

Emerging from the grove, Salt and Penny were relieved to see that the ceremony had not yet started. The guests were gathered in the garden, the minister stood waiting, musicians were in their places, but the bridal party had not appeared.

"We're just in time," Salt remarked.

Penny observed Mrs. Kippenberg talking with one of the ushers. Even from a distance it was apparent that the woman had lost her poise. Her hands fluttered nervously as she conferred with the young man and a worried frown puckered her eyebrows.

"Something seems to be wrong," said Penny. "I wonder what is causing the delay?"

Before Salt could reply, the usher crossed the lawn, and came directly toward them. Penny and Salt instantly were on guard, thinking that he had been sent by Mrs. Kippenberg to eject them from the grounds. But although the young man paused, he did not look squarely at them.

"Have you seen Mr. Atherwald anywhere?" he questioned.

"The bridegroom?" Salt asked in astonishment. "What's the matter? Is he missing?"

"Oh, no, sir," the young man returned stiffly. "Certainly not. He merely went away for a moment."

"Mr. Atherwald came over on the same boat with us," Penny volunteered.

"And did you see him enter the house?"

"No, he spoke to one of the servants and then went toward the garden."

"Did you notice which path he took?"

"I believe it was this one."

"We've just come from down by the river," added Salt. "We didn't see him there. The only person we met was an old gardener."

The usher thanked them for the information and hurried on. When the man was beyond hearing, Salt turned to Penny, saying jubilantly:

"Say, maybe we'll get a big story after all! Sylvia Kippenberg jilted at the altar! Hot stuff!"

"Aren't you jumping to swift conclusions, Salt? He must be around here somewhere."

"It's always serious business when a man is late for his wedding. Even if he does show up, daughter Sylvia may take offense and call the whole thing off."

"Oh, you're too hopeful," Penny laughed. "He'll probably be here in another minute. I don't believe he would have come at all if he had intended to slip away."

"He may have lost his nerve at the last minute," Salt insisted.

"Atherwald did act strangely on the boat," Penny said reflectively. "And then that message he received—"

"He may have sent it to himself."

"As an excuse for getting away?"

"Why not?"

"I can't see any reason for going to so much unnecessary trouble," Penny argued. "If he intended to jilt Miss Kippenberg how much easier it would have been not to come here at all."

"Well, let's see what we can learn," Salt suggested.

Their interest steadily mounting, they went on toward the house and stationed themselves where they could see advantageously. It was evident by this time that the guests suspected something had gone amiss. Significant

CHAPTER 5 - THE MISSING BRIDEGROOM

glances were exchanged, a few persons looked at their watches, and all eyes focused upon Mrs. Kippenberg who tried desperately to carry off an embarrassing situation.

Minutes passed. The crowd became increasingly restless. Finally, the usher returned and spoke quietly to Mrs. Kippenberg. They both retired to the house.

"It looks as if there will be no wedding today," Salt declared. "Atherwald hasn't been located."

"I won't dare use the story unless I'm absolutely certain of my facts," Penny said anxiously.

"We'll get them, never fear."

Mrs. Kippenberg and the usher had stepped into the breakfast room. Posting Penny at the outside door, Salt followed the couple. From the hallway he could hear their conversation distinctly.

"But he must be somewhere on the grounds," the matron argued.

"I can't understand it myself," the young man replied. "Grant's disappearance is very mysterious to say the least. Several persons saw him arrive here and everything seemed to be all right."

"What time is it now?"

"Two thirty-five, Mrs. Kippenberg."

"So late? Oh, this is dreadful! How can I face them?"

"I know just how you feel," the young man said with sympathy. "If you wish I will explain to the guests."

"No, no, this will disgrace us," Mrs. Kippenberg murmured. "Wait until I have talked with Sylvia."

She turned suddenly and reached the hall door before Salt could escape. Her eyes blazed with wrath as she faced him.

"So here you are!" she cried furiously. "How dare you disregard my orders? I will have no reporters on the grounds!"

"I'm only a photographer," Salt said meekly enough. "Sorry to intrude but I've been assigned to get a picture of the bride. It won't take a minute—"

"Indeed it won't," Mrs. Kippenberg broke in, her voice rising higher. "You'll take no pictures here. Not one! Now get out."

"A picture might be better than a story that the bridegroom had skipped out," Salt said persuasively.

"Why, you—you!" Mrs. Kippenberg's face became fiery red. She choked as she tried to speak. "Get out, I say!"

Salt did not retreat. Instead he took his camera from his pocket.

"Just one picture, Mrs. Kippenberg. At least of you."

Realizing that the photographer meant to take it whether or not she gave permission, the woman suddenly lost all control over her temper.

"Don't you dare!" she cried furiously. "Don't you dare!"

Whirling about, she seized an empty plate from the tall stack on the serving table.

"Hold that pose!" chortled Salt, goading her on.

The woman hurled the plate straight at him. Salt gleefully snapped a picture and dodged. The plate crashed into the wall behind him, splintering into a half dozen pieces.

"Swell action picture!" he grinned.

"Don't you dare try to use it!" screamed Mrs. Kippenberg. "I'll telephone your editor! I'll have you discharged!"

"See here," offered the usher, taking out his wallet. "I'll give you ten dollars for that picture."

Salt shook his head, still smiling broadly.

The sound of the crash had brought servants running to the scene.

"Have this person ejected from the grounds," Mrs. Kippenberg ordered harshly. "And see that he doesn't get back."

Just outside the house, Penny huddled against the wall, trying to make herself as inconspicuous as possible. She had heard everything. As Salt backed out the door he did not glance at her but he muttered for her ears alone:

"You're on your own now, kid. I'll be waiting at the drawbridge."

An instant later two servants seized him roughly by the arms and escorted him down the walk to the boat landing.

CHAPTER 6 - A RING OF WHITE GOLD

Penny waited anxiously, but Mrs. Kippenberg did not come to the outside door. Nor had it occurred to the two servants that the girl was connected in any way with the photographer.

"On my own," she repeated to herself. "On my own with a vengeance."

Salt had his picture and it was up to her to get a good story. Until now she had depended upon his guidance. With all support withdrawn she suddenly felt uncertain and incompetent.

Penny waited a few minutes before gathering sufficient courage to enter the long hallway. One glance assured her that the breakfast room was deserted.

"Mrs. Kippenberg probably went upstairs to talk with her daughter," she reasoned. "I'd like to hear what they say to each other."

With the guests assembled in the garden, only a few persons lingered in the house. No one paid heed to Penny as she moved noiselessly up the spiral stairway.

A bedroom door stood slightly ajar. Hearing a low murmur of voices, Penny paused. Framed against the leaded windows she saw Sylvia Kippenberg talking with her mother. Despite a tear-streaked face the girl was very lovely. She wore a long flowing gown of white satin and the flowers at the neckline were outlined with real pearls. Her net veil had been discarded. A bouquet of flowers lay on the floor.

"How could Grant do such a cruel thing?" Penny heard her sob. "I just can't believe it of him, Mother. Surely he will come."

Mrs. Kippenberg held the girl in her arms, trying to comfort her.

"It is nearly three now, Sylvia. The servants have searched everywhere. A man of his type isn't worthy of you."

"But I love him, Mother. And I am sure he loves me. It doesn't seem possible he would do such a thing without a word of explanation."

"He will explain, never fear," Mrs. Kippenberg said grimly. "But now, we must think what has to be done. The guests must be told."

"Oh, Mother!" Sylvia went into another paroxysm of crying.

"There is no other way, my dear. Leave everything to me."

Before Penny realized that the interview had ended, Mrs. Kippenberg stepped out into the hall. Her eyes focused hard upon the girl.

"You are a reporter!" she accused harshly. "I remember, you were with that photographer!"

"Please—" began Penny.

"I'll tell you nothing," the woman cried. "How dare you intrude in my home and go about listening at bedroom doors!"

"Mrs. Kippenberg, if only you will calm yourself, I may be able to help you."

"Help me?" the woman demanded. "What do you mean?"

"I may be able to give you a clue as to what became of Grant Atherwald."

The anger faded from Mrs. Kippenberg's face. She came close to Penny, grasping her arm with a pressure which hurt.

"You have seen him? Tell me!"

"He came over in the same boat."

"How long ago was that?"

CHAPTER 6 - A RING OF WHITE GOLD

"Shortly after one o'clock. He was stopped at the front door by a servant who handed him a note. Mr. Atherwald read it and walked down toward the garden."

"I wonder which one of the servants spoke to him? It was at the front door, you say?"

"Yes."

"Then it must have been Gregg. I'll talk with him."

Forgetting Penny, Mrs. Kippenberg hastened down the stairway. She jangled a bell and asked that the manservant be sent to her. Unnoticed, Penny lingered to hear the interview.

The man came into the room. "You sent for me, Mrs. Kippenberg?" he inquired.

"Yes, Gregg. You were at the door when Mr. Atherwald arrived?"

"I was, Madam."

"I understand you handed him a note which he read."

"Yes, Madam."

"Who gave you the note?"

"Mrs. Latch, the cook. She told me it was brought to the kitchen door early this morning by a most disreputable looking boy."

"He had been hired to deliver it for another person, I suppose?"

"Yes, Madam. The boy told Mrs. Latch that the message came from a friend of Mr. Atherwald's and should be given to him as soon as he arrived."

"You have no idea what the note contained?"

"No, Mrs. Kippenberg, the envelope was sealed."

Sensing that when the interview ended Mrs. Kippenberg's wrath might again descend upon her, Penny decided not to tempt fate. While the woman was still talking with the servant, she slipped out of the house.

"Atherwald might have had that note sent to himself, but I doubt it," she told herself. "Either he is still on the estate, or the boatman would have had to take him back across the river."

She walked quickly down to the dock and was elated to find the guest launch tied up there. The boatman answered her questions readily. He had not seen Grant Atherwald since early in the afternoon. Salt was the only person he had taken back across the river.

"Have you noticed any other boat leaving the estate?" inquired Penny.

"Boats have been going up and down the river all day," the man answered with a shrug. "I didn't notice any particular one."

Penny glanced across the water. She could see Salt perched on the drawbridge waiting for her. But she was not yet ready to leave the estate.

Ignoring his shout to "come on," she turned and walked back toward the house. Deliberately, she chose the same path which she and Salt had followed earlier in the afternoon.

A swift walk brought her to the forbidden trail with the barrier sign. Penny glanced around to be certain she was not under observation. Then she stepped boldly over the wire.

Passing the place where she and Salt had talked with the gardener, she noticed his trowel lying on the ground. There was no evidence that he had done any work.

However, all along the path flowering shrubs were well trimmed and tended.

"So this part of the estate isn't fixed up," Penny mused. "It's much nicer than the other section in my opinion. I wonder why that gardener told so many lies?"

The path led deeper into the woods. Rustic benches invited one to linger, but Penny walked rapidly onward.

Unexpectedly, she came to a little clearing, and saw before her a large, circular pool. From a gap in the trees, warm sunshine poured down upon the bed of flowers which flanked the cement sides, making a circle of brilliant color.

"So this is where the path leads," thought Penny. "No mystery here after all."

She was at a loss to understand why this portion of the estate had been closed to visitors for certainly it was the most beautiful part. Yet there was a quality to the beauty which the girl did not like.

As she stood staring at the pool, she was fully aware of an uneasy feeling which had taken possession of her. It was almost as if she stood in the presence of something sinister and unknown. The gentle rustling of the tree leaves, the cool river air blowing against her cheek, only served to heighten the feeling.

She drew closer and peered down into the blue depths of the pool. She could not see the bottom plainly for the water was choked with a tangle of feathery plants. A few yellow lilies floated on the surface.

Penny absently reached out to pluck one. But as the stem snapped off, she gave a little scream and dropped the flower. She had seen a large, shadowy form slithering through the water beneath her.

Penny backed a step away from the pool. From among the lily pads an ugly head emerged and a broad snout was raised above the surface for an instant. Powerful jaws opened and closed, revealing jagged teeth set in deep pits.

"An alligator!" Penny exclaimed aloud. "Such a horrid, ugly creature! And to think, I nearly put my hand in that water."

She shivered and watched the movements of the alligator. Its head scooted smoothly over the water for a short distance. Then with a swish of its tail, the reptile submerged and the pool was as placid as before.

"Eight feet long if it's an inch," estimated Penny. "Why would any person in his right mind keep such a creature here? Why, it's dangerous."

She felt enraged, thinking how close she had come to touching the alligator. Yet justice compelled her to admit that she had only herself to blame. Deliberately, she had disregarded the warning not to explore the forbidden trail.

"The Kippenbergs keep nice pets," she thought ironically. "If anyone fell into that pool it would be just too bad."

Now that her curiosity was satisfied, Penny had not the slightest desire to linger near the lily pool. With another glance down into the murky depths she turned away, but she had taken less than a dozen steps when she paused. Her attention was held by a bright and shiny object which lay in the dust at her feet.

With a low cry of surprise she reached down and picked up a plain band of white gold. Obviously, it was a wedding ring.

"Now where did this come from?" Penny turned it over on the palm of her hand.

Startled thoughts leaped into her mind. She felt certain Grant Atherwald had taken this same path earlier in the afternoon. It was logical to believe that the ring had been his, intended for Sylvia Kippenberg. Had he lost the band accidentally or deliberately thrown it away?

Slowly, Penny's gaze roved to the lily pond. She noted that the coping was so low that one who walked carelessly might easily stumble and fall into the water. It made her shudder to think of such a gruesome possibility, yet she could not avoid giving it consideration. For that matter, Grant Atherwald might have been lured to this isolated spot. The mysterious message—

Penny delved no deeper into the problem for suddenly she felt someone grasp her arms. With a terrified cry she whirled about to face her assailant.

CHAPTER 7 - THE FORBIDDEN POOL

A wave of relief surged over Penny as she saw that it was the old gardener who held her fast.

"Oh, it's only you," she laughed shakily, trying to pull away. "For a second I thought the Bogey Man had me for sure."

The gardener did not smile.

"Didn't I tell you to keep away from here?" he demanded, giving her a hard shake.

"I'm not doing any h-harm," Penny stammered. She kept her hand closed over the white gold ring so that the old man would not see what she had found. "I just wanted to learn what was back in here."

"And you found out?"

The gardener's tone warned Penny to be cautious in her reply.

"Oh, the pool is rather pretty," she answered carelessly. "But I've seen much nicer ones."

"How long have you been here?"

"Only a minute or two. I really came to search for Grant Atherwald."

"Atherwald? What would he be doing here?"

"He disappeared an hour or so ago," revealed Penny. "The servants have been searching everywhere for him."

"He disappeared?" the gardener repeated incredulously.

"Yes, it's very peculiar. Mr. Atherwald arrived at the estate in ample time for the wedding. But after he read a note which was delivered to him he walked off in this direction and was seen no more."

"Down this path, you mean?"

"I couldn't say as to that, but he started this way. I know because I saw him myself."

"Atherwald didn't come here," the gardener said with finality. "I've been working around the lily pond all afternoon and would have seen him."

Penny's fingers closed tightly about the white gold ring which she kept shielded from the man's gaze. In her opinion the trinket offered almost conclusive proof that the bridegroom had visited the locality. Because she could not trust the gardener she kept her thoughts strictly to herself.

The man stared down at his feet, obviously disturbed by the information Penny had given him.

"Do you suppose harm could have befallen Mr. Atherwald?" she asked after a moment.

"Harm?" he demanded irritably. "That's sheer nonsense. The fellow probably skipped out. He ought to be tarred and feathered!"

"And you would enjoy doing it?" Penny interposed slyly.

The gardener glared at her, making no attempt to hide his dislike.

"Such treatment would be too good for anyone who hurt Miss Sylvia. Now will you get out of here? I have my orders and I mean to enforce them."

"Oh, all right," replied Penny. "I was going anyway."

This was not strictly true, for had the gardener not been there she would have made a more thorough investigation of the locality near the lily pool. But now she had no hope of learning more, and so turned away.

Emerging from among the trees, she glanced toward the rose garden. Nearly all of the wedding guests had departed. Penny considered whether or not she should speak to Mrs. Kippenberg about finding the ring. Deciding against it, she joined a group of people at the boat dock and was ferried across the river.

Salt awaited her at the drawbridge.

"I just about gave you up," he complained. "It's time for us to get back to the office or our news won't be news. The wedding is definitely off?"

"Yes, Atherwald can't be found."

"We'll stop at a drug store and telephone," Salt said, pulling her toward the car. "Learn anything more after I left?"

"Well, I found a wedding ring and was nearly chewed up by an alligator," laughed Penny. "It seemed rather interesting at the time."

The photographer gave her a queer look as he started the automobile.

"Imagination and journalism never mix," he said.

"Does this look like imagination?" Penny countered, showing him the plain band ring.

"Where did you find it?"

"Beside a lily pond in the forbidden part of the estate. I feel certain it must have been dropped by Grant Atherwald."

"Thrown away?"

"I don't know exactly what to think," Penny replied soberly.

Salt steered the car into the main road which led back to Corbin. Then he inquired: "Did you notice any signs of a struggle? Grass trampled? Footprints?"

"I didn't have a chance to do any investigating. That bossy old gardener came and drove me away."

"What were you saying about alligators?"

"Salt, I saw one swimming around in the lily pool," Penny told him earnestly. "It was an ugly brute, at least twelve feet long."

"How long?"

"Well, eight anyway."

"You're joking."

"I am not," Penny said indignantly.

"Maybe it was only a big log lying in the water."

Penny gave an injured sniff. "Have it your own way. But it wasn't a log. I guess I can tell an alligator when I see one."

"If you're actually right," Salt said unmoved, "I'd like to have snapped a picture of it. You know, this story might develop into something big."

"I have a feeling it will, Salt."

"If Atherwald really has disappeared it should create a sensation!"

"And if the poor fellow had the misfortune to fall or be pushed into the lily pool Dad wouldn't have headlines large enough to carry it!"

"Say, get a grip on yourself," Salt advised. "The *Riverview Star* prints fact, not fancy."

"That's because so many of Dad's reporters are stodgy old fellows," laughed Penny. "But I'll admit it isn't very likely Grant Atherwald was devoured by the alligator."

The car had reached Corbin. Salt drew up in front of a drug store.

"Run in and telephone DeWitt," he said, opening the door for her. "And remember, stick to facts."

Penny was a little frightened as she entered the telephone booth and placed a long distance call to the *Riverview Star*. She never failed to feel nervous when she talked with DeWitt, the city editor, for he was not a very pleasant individual.

She jumped as the receiver was taken down and a voice barked: "City desk."

"This is Penny Parker over at Corbin," she began weakly.

"Can't hear you," snapped DeWitt. "Talk up."

Penny repeated her name and DeWitt's voice lost some of its edge. Gathering courage, she started to tell him what she had learned at the Kippenberg estate.

"Hold it," interrupted DeWitt. "I'll switch you over to a rewrite man."

The connection was made and Penny began a second time. Now and then the rewrite man broke into the narrative to ask a question.

"All right, I think I have it all," he said finally and hung up.

Penny went back to the car looking as crestfallen as she felt.

CHAPTER 7 - THE FORBIDDEN POOL

"I don't know what they thought of the story," she told Salt. "DeWitt certainly didn't waste any words of praise."

"He never does," chuckled the photographer. "You're lucky if you don't get fired."

"That's one consolation," returned Penny, settling herself for the long ride home. "He can't fire me. Being the editor's daughter has its advantages."

The regular night edition of the *Riverview Star* was on the street by the time they reached the city. Salt signaled a newsboy and bought a paper while the car waited for a traffic light. He tossed it over to Penny.

"Here it is! My story!" she cried, and then her face fell.

"What's the matter?" asked Salt. "Did they garble it all up?"

"They've cut it down to three inches! And not a word about the alligator or the lost wedding ring! I could cry! Why, I told that rewrite man enough to fill at least a column!"

"Well, anyway you made the front page," the photographer consoled. "They may build the story up in the next edition after they get my pictures."

Penny said nothing, remaining in deep gloom during the remainder of the ride to the *Star* office. Salt let her out at the front door. She debated for a moment whether or not to go on home, but finally entered the building.

DeWitt was busy at his desk as she walked stiffly past. She hoped that he would notice how she ignored him, but he did not glance up from the copy before him.

Penny opened the door of her father's private office and stopped short.

"Why, Dad?" she cried. "What are you doing here? You're supposed to be home in bed."

"I finally persuaded the doctor to let me out," Anthony Parker replied, swinging around in his swivel chair. "How did you get along with your assignment?"

"I thought I did very well," Penny said aloofly. "But from now on I'll not telephone anything in. I'll write the story myself."

"Now don't blame DeWitt or the rewrite man," said Mr. Parker, smiling. "A paper has to be careful in what it publishes, especially about a wedding. Alligators are a bit too—shall we say sensational?"

"You made a similar remark about witch dolls," Penny reminded him.

"I did eat my words that time," Mr. Parker admitted, "but this is different. If we build up a big story about Grant Atherwald's disappearance, and then tomorrow he shows up at his own home, we'll appear pretty ridiculous."

"I guess you're right," Penny said, turning away. "Well, I'm happy to see you back in the office again."

Mr. Parker watched her speculatively. When she reached the door he inquired: "Aren't you forgetting something?"

"What, Dad?"

"Today is Thursday." The editor took a sealed envelope from the desk drawer. "This is the first time you have failed to collect your allowance in over a year."

"I must be slipping." Penny grinned as she pocketed the envelope.

"Why don't you open it?"

"What's the use?" Penny asked gloomily. "It's always the same. Anyway, I borrowed two dollars last week so this doesn't really belong to me."

"You might be pleasantly surprised."

Penny stared at her father with disbelief. "Dad! You don't mean you've given me a raise!"

Eagerly, she ripped open the envelope. Three crisp dollar bills fluttered into her hand. With a shriek of delight, Penny flung her arms about her father's neck.

"I always try to reward a good reporter," he chuckled. "Now take yourself off because my work is stacked a mile high."

Penny tripped gaily toward the door but it opened before she could cross the room. An office boy came in with a message for Mr. Parker.

"Man to see you named Atherwald," he announced.

The name produced an electrifying effect upon both Penny and her father.

"Atherwald!" Mr. Parker exclaimed. "Then he hasn't disappeared after all! Show him in."

"And I'm staying right here," Penny declared, easing herself into the nearest chair. "I have a hunch that this interview may concern me."

CHAPTER 8 - PARENTAL PROTEST

In a few minutes the office boy returned, followed by a distinguished, middle-aged man who carried a cane. Penny gave him an astonished glance for she had expected to see Grant Atherwald. It had not occurred to her that there might be two persons with the same surname.

"Mr. Atherwald?" inquired her father, waving the visitor into a chair.

"James Atherwald."

The man spoke shortly and did not sit down. Instead he spread out a copy of the night edition of the *Star* and pointed to the story which Penny had covered. She quaked inwardly, wondering what error of hers was to be exposed.

"Do you see this?" Mr. Atherwald demanded.

"What about it?" inquired the editor pleasantly.

"You are holding my family up to ridicule by printing such a story! Grant Atherwald is my son!"

"Is the story incorrect?"

"Yes, you imply that my son deliberately jilted Sylvia Kippenberg!"

"And actually he didn't?" Mr. Parker inquired evenly.

"Certainly not. My son is a man of honor and had a very deep regard for Sylvia. Under no circumstance would he have jilted her."

"Still, the wedding did not take place."

"That is true," Mr. Atherwald admitted.

"Perhaps you can explain why it was postponed?"

"I don't know what happened to Grant," Mr. Atherwald said reluctantly. "He left our home in ample time for the ceremony, and I might add, was in excellent spirits. I believe he must have been the victim of a stupid, practical joke."

"Well, that suggests a new angle," Mr. Parker remarked thoughtfully. "Did your son have friends who might be apt to play such a joke on him?"

"No one of my acquaintance," Mr. Atherwald answered unwillingly. "Of course, he had many young friends who were not in my circle."

Penny had listened quietly to the conversation. She now arose and came over to the desk. From her pocket she took the white gold wedding ring.

"Mr. Atherwald," she said, "I wonder if you could identify this."

The man studied the trinket for a moment.

"It looks very much like a ring which Grant purchased for Sylvia," he declared. "Where did you get it?"

"I found it lying on the ground at the Kippenberg estate," Penny replied vaguely. She had no intention of divulging the exact locality where she had picked up the ring.

"You see," said Mr. Parker, "we have supporting facts in our possession which were not published. All in all, I think the story was handled discreetly, with due regard for the feelings of those involved."

"Then you refuse to retract the story?"

"I should like to oblige you, Mr. Atherwald, but you realize such a story as this is of great interest to our readers."

"You care only for sensationalism!"

"On the contrary, we try to avoid it," Mr. Parker corrected. "In this particular case, we deliberately played the story down. If it develops that your son actually has disappeared—"

CHAPTER 8 - PARENTAL PROTEST

"I tell you it was only a practical joke," Mr. Atherwald interrupted. "No doubt my son is at home by this time. The wedding has merely been postponed."

"You are entitled to your opinion," said Mr. Parker. "And I sincerely hope that you are right."

"At least do not use that picture which your photographer took of Mrs. Kippenberg. I'll pay you for it."

Mr. Parker smiled and shook his head.

"I might have expected such an attitude!" Mr. Atherwald exclaimed angrily. "Good afternoon."

He left the office, slamming the door behind him.

"Well, you've lost another subscriber, Dad," said Penny flippantly.

"He's not the first," returned her father.

"I intended to give Mr. Atherwald the wedding ring, but he went off in too big a hurry. Should I go after him?"

"No, don't bother, Penny. You might take it around to the picture room and have it photographed. We may use it as Exhibit A if the story develops into anything."

"How about the alligator?" Penny asked. "Would you like to have me bring that to the office, too?"

"Move out of here and let me work," her father retorted.

Penny went to the photographic department and made her requirements known.

"I'll wait for the ring," she announced. "You don't catch me trusting you boys with any jewelry."

While the picture was being taken Salt came by with several damp prints in his hand.

"Take a look at this one, Penny," he said proudly. "Mrs. Kippenberg wielding a wicked plate. Will she burn up when she sees it on the picture page?"

"She will, indeed," agreed Penny. "Nice going."

When the ring had been returned to her she slipped it into her pocket and left the newspaper office. Her next stop was at a corner hamburger shop where she fortified herself with two large sandwiches.

"That ought to hold me until the dinner bell rings," she thought. "And now to pay my honest debts."

A trolley ride and a short walk brought Penny to the home of her chum, Louise Sidell. As she came within sight of the front porch she saw her friend sitting on the steps, reading a movie magazine. Louise threw it aside and sprang to her feet.

"Oh, Penny, I'm glad you came over. I telephoned your house and Mrs. Weems said you had gone away somewhere."

"Official business for Dad," Penny laughed. She dropped two dollars into Louise's hand. "Here's what I owe you. But don't go spend it because I may need to borrow it back in a couple of days."

"Is Leaping Lena running up huge garage bills again?" Louise inquired sympathetically.

Penny's second-hand car was a joke to everyone save herself. She was a familiar figure at nearly every garage in Riverview, for the vehicle had a disconcerting way of breaking down.

"I had to buy new spark plugs this time," sighed Penny. "But then, I should get along better from now on. Dad raised my allowance."

"Doesn't that call for a celebration? Rini's have a special on today. A double chocolate sundae with pineapple and nuts, cherry and—"

"Oh, no, you don't! I'm saving my dollar for the essentials of life. I may need it for gasoline if I decide to drive over to Corbin again."

"Again?" Louise asked alertly.

"I was over there today, covering the Kippenberg wedding," Penny explained. "Only it turned out there was no ceremony. Grant Atherwald jilted his bride, or was spirited away by persons unknown. He was last seen near a lily pool in an isolated part of the estate. I picked up a wedding ring lying on the ground close by. And then as a climax Mrs. Kippenberg hurled a plate at Salt."

"Penny Parker, what are you saying?" Louise demanded. "It sounds like one of those two-reel thrillers they show over at the Rialto."

"Here is the evidence," Penny said, showing her the white gold ring.

"It's amazing how you get into so much adventure," Louise replied enviously as she studied the trinket. "Start at the beginning and tell me everything."

DANGER AT THE DRAWBRIDGE

The invitation was very much to Penny's liking. Perching herself on the highest porch step she recounted her visit to the Kippenberg estate, painting an especially romantic picture of the castle dwelling, the moat, and the drawbridge.

"Oh, I'd love to visit the place," Louise declared. "You have all the luck."

"I'll take you with me if I ever get to go again," promised Penny. "Well, I'll see you tomorrow."

And with this careless farewell, she sprang to her feet, and hastened on home.

The next morning while Mrs. Weems was preparing breakfast, Penny ran down to the corner to buy the first edition of the *Star*. As she spread it open a small headline accosted her eye.

"NO TRACE OF MISSING BRIDEGROOM."

Penny read swiftly, learning that Grant Atherwald had not been seen since his strange disappearance from the Kippenberg estate. Members of the family refused to discuss the affair and had made no report to the police.

"This story is developing into something big after all," she thought with quickening pulse. "Now if Dad will only let me work on it!"

At home she gave the newspaper to her father, remarking rather pointedly: "You see, your expert reporters haven't learned very much more than I brought in yesterday. Why wouldn't it be a good idea to send me out there again today?"

"Oh, I doubt if you could get into the estate, Penny."

"Salt and I managed yesterday."

"You did very well, but you weren't known then. It will be a different matter today since we antagonized the family by using the story. I'll suggest that Jerry Livingston be assigned to it."

"With Penny as first assistant?"

Mr. Parker smiled and shook his head. "This isn't your type of story. Now if you would like to cover a lecture at the Women's Club—"

"Or a nice peppy meeting of the Ladies Sewing Circle," Penny finished ironically. "Thank you, no."

"I am sure you wouldn't have a chance of getting into the estate," her father said lamely. "We must have good coverage."

"What does Jerry have that I haven't got?" Penny demanded in an aggrieved voice.

"Eight years of experience for one thing."

"But I really should go out there," Penny insisted. "I ought to show Miss Kippenberg the ring I found."

"The ring might provide an entry," Mr. Parker admitted thoughtfully. "I'll tell you, why don't you telephone long distance?"

"And if I'm able to make an appointment, may I help Jerry cover the story?"

"All right," agreed Mr. Parker. "If Sylvia Kippenberg talks with you we'll be able to use anything she says."

"I'm the same as on my way to the estate now, Dad."

With a triumphant laugh, Penny left the breakfast table and hastened to the telephone.

"Long distance," she said into the transmitter. "The Kippenberg estate at Corbin, please."

She hovered anxiously near the telephone while she waited for the connection to be made. Ten minutes elapsed before the bell jingled several times. Eagerly, she jerked down the receiver. She could hear a faint, far-away voice saying, "hello."

"May I speak with Sylvia Kippenberg?" Penny requested.

"Who is this, please?"

"Miss Parker at Riverview."

"Miss Kippenberg is not at home," came the stiff response.

"Then let me speak with Mrs. Kippenberg," Penny said quickly. "I have something very important to tell her. Yesterday when I was at the estate I found a ring—"

The receiver had clicked at the other end of the line. The connection was broken.

CHAPTER 9 - A SOCIETY BAZAAR

"You see, Penny," said Mr. Parker sympathetically, "wealthy people have a way of being inaccessible to the press. They surround themselves with servants who have been trained to allow no invasion of their privacy. They erect barriers which aren't easily broken down."

"If only I could have reached Miss Kippenberg I feel sure she would have wished to learn about the ring," returned Penny. "Oh, well, let Jerry cover the story. I've lost interest."

All that morning the girl went about the house in a mood of deep depression. She felt completely out of sorts and would scowl at her own reflection whenever she passed a mirror. Nothing seemed to go right.

"I declare, I wish you would forget that silly wedding," Mrs. Weems said wearily. "Why don't you try working out your resentment on a tennis ball?"

"Not a bad idea," admitted Penny. "Only I have no partner. Louise is going away somewhere today to a charity bazaar."

"Here in Riverview?" inquired Mrs. Weems with interest.

"No, it's to be held at Andover, twenty miles from Corbin. Louise is going with an aunt of hers. She invited me several days ago, but I didn't think it would be any fun."

"You might enjoy it. Why don't you go?"

"I wonder if it isn't too late?" Penny glanced at the clock.

A telephone call to the Sidell home assured her that she would have ample time to get ready for the trip. She quickly dressed and was waiting when Louise and her aunt, Miss Lucinda Frome, drove up to the door.

"What sort of an affair is it?" Penny inquired as they traveled toward the distant town.

Miss Frome explained that the bazaar was being sponsored by members of the D.A.R. organization and would be held at one of the fashionable clubs of the city. As Miss Frome belonged to the Riverview chapter she and her guests would have an entry.

"I look forward to meeting a number of prominent persons today," the woman declared. "The Andover chapter has a very exclusive membership."

Louise winked at Penny, for it was a source of amusement to her that her aunt stood in awe of society personages. Neither she nor her chum suffered from social ambition or a feeling of inferiority.

At Andover, Miss Frome drove the car to the City Club and parked it beside a long row of other automobiles, many of which were under the charge of uniformed chauffeurs.

"Oh, dear," remarked Miss Frome nervously, "I didn't realize how shabby my old coupe looks. I do hope no one notices."

"Now don't start that, Aunty," Louise said, taking her by the arm. "Your car is perfectly all right. And so are you."

They went up the steps of the stone building and mingled with the other women. So many persons were present that the three newcomers attracted no attention. Miss Frome was reassured to see that she was as well dressed as anyone in the room.

Several long tables were covered with various articles offered for sale. Penny and Louise wandered about examining objects which struck their fancy. Miss Frome bought a vase and an imitation ivory elephant, but the girls considered the prices too high for their purses.

Presently, Penny's gaze was drawn to a young woman who stood behind one of the tables at the far end of the room. She stopped short and stared.

"See someone you know?" inquired Louise.

"Why, that young woman with the dark hair and the lace dress, Louise! She is Sylvia Kippenberg!"

"Really? I must say she has courage to come here today after all that happened!"

The young woman did not realize that she was being subjected to scrutiny. However, she seemed fully aware that she was a general object of curiosity, for her lips were frozen in a set smile and her face was pale despite the rouge on the smooth cheeks.

"I suppose she must be on the bazaar committee," Louise went on. "But my, if anyone had jilted me, I would not have come here today."

"Jerry must have missed his interview after all," Penny murmured, half to herself.

"Jerry?"

"Yes, Dad assigned him to the Kippenberg story. I suppose he drove to Corbin today in the hope of seeing Miss Sylvia."

"And she may have come here just to escape reporters."

"For two cents I'd try to interview her myself," Penny said.

"Do you think she would talk with you?"

"Not if she realizes I am a reporter. But at least I can try."

"Don't create a scene whatever you do," Louise warned uneasily. "Not that I would mind. But Aunt Lucinda would die of mortification."

"I'll try to be careful," Penny promised.

She sauntered forward, gradually working toward the table where the young woman served. Selecting an article at random from the display, she inquired its price.

"Ten dollars," Miss Kippenberg answered mechanically.

Penny loitered at the table until two elderly women had moved on. She was now alone with Sylvia Kippenberg. She would have no better opportunity to speak with her.

"Miss Kippenberg," she began.

"Yes?" The young woman really gazed at the girl for the first time. Penny saw that her eyelids were red and swollen from recent tears.

"I should like to talk with you alone, please."

"Do I know your name?" Miss Kippenberg asked coldly.

"Penny Parker."

"Parker—Parker," the young woman repeated and her eyes hardened. "Oh, yes, you are the girl who came to our place yesterday with that photographer! And you telephoned again this morning."

"Yes," Penny admitted reluctantly, "but—"

The young woman did not allow her to finish.

"I'll not talk with you or any other reporter. You have no right to come here and annoy me."

"Please, I'm not really a reporter, Miss Kippenberg. I have something to show you."

Miss Kippenberg had closed her ears to Penny's words. She turned abruptly and fled in the direction of the powder room.

Penny hesitated, remembering her promise to create no scene. Still, she could not allow Miss Kippenberg to elude her so easily. Determinedly, she followed.

"Please, Miss Kippenberg, you must listen to me," she pleaded.

Observing that her words had not the slightest effect upon the girl, she suddenly opened her purse and took out the white gold ring. She thrust it in front of Miss Kippenberg.

"I only wish to show you this."

The young woman stopped short, gazing down at the ring.

"Where did you get it?" she asked in a low tone.

"Then you do recognize it?"

"Of course. Grant showed it to me the night before we were to have been married. Tell me, how did it come into your hands?"

"We can't talk here."

Miss Kippenberg glanced quickly about and observing that many eyes were focused upon them, led the girl into the deserted powder room. They sat down on a sofa in a secluded corner.

CHAPTER 9 - A SOCIETY BAZAAR

"I didn't mean to be so rude before," Miss Kippenberg apologized. "It was only because I must protect myself from reporters and photographers. You have no idea how I have been annoyed."

"I do understand," said Penny, "and I wish to help you. That was why I was so insistent upon talking with you. I think this ring may be a clue to Mr. Atherwald's disappearance."

"Then you believe as I do that he did not go away purposely?"

"My theory is that Mr. Atherwald was a victim of a plot. Did he have any known enemies?"

"Oh, no, everyone liked Grant. Tell me about the ring. Who gave it to you?"

"No one. I found it while I was exploring a path on the estate, the trail which is blocked off."

"You shouldn't have gone there, but no matter. Just where did you pick up the ring?"

"I found it near the lily pool."

Miss Kippenberg stared at Penny with expressionless, half-glazed eyes.

"Oh!" she murmured. Her head dropped low, her body sagged and she slumped down on the sofa in a faint.

CHAPTER 10 - A THROWN STONE

Penny's first thought was to call for assistance, but sober reflection made her realize that to do so would likely result in awkward questions. She felt certain Miss Kippenberg had only fainted and would soon revive.

Stretching the young woman full length upon the sofa, the girl ran to the washroom for a glass of water. She dampened a towel and folded it across Miss Kippenberg's forehead, at the same time rubbing the limp hands and trying to restore circulation. Noticing the white gold ring which had fallen to the floor, she reached down and picked it up.

"Miss Kippenberg must have fainted because of what I told her about the lily pond," thought Penny. "I should have used more tact."

She watched the young woman anxiously, fearing that what she had assumed to be an ordinary faint might really be a heart attack. A wave of relief surged over her as Miss Kippenberg stirred slightly. Her long dark eyelashes fluttered open and she stared blankly about her.

"Where am I?" she asked, moistening her dry lips.

"Here, drink this," Penny urged, offering the glass of water. "You'll feel much better in a few minutes."

"Now I remember," Miss Kippenberg murmured. "You were saying—"

"Don't think about that now. Just lie still and relax."

Miss Kippenberg did not try to speak again for some little time. Then, despite Penny's protests, she raised herself to a sitting position.

"I feel quite all right now," she insisted. "How stupid of me to faint."

"I am afraid I was very tactless."

"On the contrary, our conversation had nothing to do with it."

"I thought—"

"It was the heat," Miss Kippenberg insisted. "I had a sunstroke once and since then I can't bear even an overheated room."

"But it really isn't very warm in here," protested Penny. "I don't notice it at all."

"You might not but I am very sensitive to it."

"Well, I'm glad your faint wasn't caused by anything I said," Penny declared, although she continued to regard the young woman dubiously. "I thought you seemed shocked by what I told you about the ring."

"You were saying that you picked it up near the lily pond?" Miss Kippenberg questioned in a low tone.

"Yes," replied Penny, watching her closely.

"I wish I knew the exact place."

"If we could go to your estate together I could show you," Penny said eagerly.

Miss Kippenberg hesitated in her reply, obviously still prejudiced against the girl because of her connection with the *Riverview Star*.

"Very well," she agreed. "Will you please ask that my car be sent to the door?"

"Gladly," said Penny, trying not to show her jubilance.

Leaving Miss Kippenberg in the powder room she returned to the main hall. Louise separated from the crowd and hurried to meet her.

"Oh, Penny, I saw you go off with Miss Kippenberg," she began. "Would she talk with you?"

"She did," answered Penny, "and now I'm going with her to the estate."

"But Aunt Lucinda expects to start home in a few minutes," protested Louise. "How long will you be gone?"

CHAPTER 10 - A THROWN STONE

"I haven't the slightest idea. If I'm not back here by the time you are ready to leave don't wait for me."

"But how will you get home?"

"Oh, I'll find a way. The important thing now is to learn everything I can from Miss Kippenberg. She's in a mood to talk."

"I'd love to visit the estate," Louise said wistfully.

"I wish I could take you," Penny told her sincerely, "but I don't see how I can this time."

"Of course not, Penny. It would be very foolish of you to try. You might lose your own chance to gain an exclusive news story."

"Will you explain to your aunt about my sudden disappearance?"

"Yes, she'll understand," Louise replied. "We'll wait here for you at least an hour."

Penny left a call for Miss Kippenberg's car and then went back to the powder room. The young woman walked a bit unsteadily even with aid. However, no one paid attention to them as they crossed the main hall and made their way to the waiting automobile.

With Penny and Miss Kippenberg as passengers the big limousine rolled away from the clubhouse and sped toward Corbin. During the ride the young woman scarcely spoke. She sat with her head against the cushion, eyes half closed. As they came within view of the drawbridge she made an effort to arouse herself.

"I see you have visitors at the estate," Penny commented, noticing a number of cars parked near the river's edge.

"Reporters, always reporters," returned Miss Kippenberg impatiently. "They may try to board as we pass."

Penny wondered how the limousine would be taken across the river. The old watchman had noted their approach. Before the car reached the end of the road he had lowered the creaking drawbridge into position.

"Is the bridge really safe?" Penny inquired of her companion.

"For light traffic only," Miss Kippenberg answered briefly.

The arrival of the car had created a stir of interest among the group of men gathered near the bridge. Penny caught sight of Jerry Livingston and could not resist rolling down the side window so he would be sure to obtain a clear view of her. It gave her a very pleasant feeling to see him stare as if he could not believe his own eyes.

Several of the reporters attempted to stop the limousine but without success. The car clattered over the drawbridge which was pulled up again before anyone could follow.

Penny and Miss Kippenberg alighted at the front door of the great house.

"Now show me where you found the ring," requested the young woman.

Penny led her down the winding path into the grove.

"I hope we don't meet your head gardener," she said significantly. "He seems to be such an unpleasant individual."

Miss Kippenberg glanced at her queerly.

"Why, how do you mean?"

"Oh, yesterday he ordered me away from here in no uncertain terms."

"He only meant to do his duty."

"Then the man has been ordered to keep persons away from this part of the estate?"

"I really couldn't tell you," Miss Kippenberg answered aloofly. "Mother has charge of the servants."

"Has the man been in your employ long?"

"I can't tell you that either." Miss Kippenberg's voice warned Penny that she did not care to be questioned.

There was no sign of the old gardener as they came presently to the lily pool. Penny searched about in the grass for a few minutes.

"Here is where I found the ring," she revealed. "And see this!"

"What?" Miss Kippenberg drew in her breath sharply.

"Footprints."

"That doesn't seem so remarkable." The young woman bent to examine them. "They probably were made by Grant's own shoe."

"But it looks as if there might have been a struggle here," Penny insisted. "From those marks wouldn't you say a body had been dragged across the ground toward the pool?"

31

"No!" cried Miss Kippenberg. "The grass is trampled, but I can't believe Grant has met with violence. I refuse to think of such a thing! The pool—" she broke off and a shudder wracked her body.

"It is best to know the truth. Have you notified the police about Mr. Atherwald's disappearance?"

Miss Kippenberg shook her head. "Until today I thought he would return. Or at least I hoped so."

"It seems to me an expert should be called into the case," Penny urged. "Why don't you telephone the police station now?"

"I couldn't," returned Sylvia looking very miserable. "Not without consulting Mother."

"Then let's talk with her now."

"She isn't at home this afternoon."

"But something should be done, and at once," Penny protested. "The first rain will destroy all these footprints and perhaps other important evidence. Do you really love Grant Atherwald?"

"With all my heart," answered the young woman soberly.

"Then I should think you would have some interest in what became of him. I can't understand your attitude at all."

"I—I have others to think of besides myself."

"Your mother, you mean?"

"Yes." Sylvia avoided Penny's penetrating gaze.

"Surely your mother wouldn't wish an act of violence to go unpunished. So much time has been lost already."

"We aren't certain anything has happened to Grant," Sylvia responded, her eyes downcast. "If we should bring the police into the case, and then it turns out that he has merely gone away to some other city, I'd be held up to ridicule once more."

"It seems to me you are taking a most foolish attitude."

"There is another reason why we must be very careful," Sylvia said unwillingly.

"And what is that?"

For just an instant Penny dared hope that the young woman meant to answer the question. But Sylvia seemed to reconsider for she said quickly:

"I can't tell you. Please don't ask me any more questions."

"Are you afraid you may be blamed for Mr. Atherwald's disappearance?" Penny persisted.

"No, no, I assure you I am not thinking of myself. Please, let's return to the house."

Penny deliberately blocked the path.

"Unless you wish me to notify the police there is a little matter which I must ask you to explain."

Reaching down she picked up a small stone and hurled it into the lily pond. As the ripples died away they both observed a convulsive movement of the water, a churning which had no relation to the missile thrown.

"I think," said Penny evenly, "that you understand my meaning."

CHAPTER 11 - QUESTIONS AND ANSWERS

Miss Kippenberg watched the concentric circles race each other to the far edge of the lily pool.

"Then you know the reason why this part of the estate is kept closed off?" she murmured, very low.

"I learned about the alligator yesterday," said Penny. "Why is such an ugly brute kept here?"

"It was none of my doing, I assure you. I hate the horrid thing. Surely you don't mean to suggest—"

"I am not suggesting anything yet," said Penny quietly. "But you must realize that it is rather unusual to keep an alligator on one's estate."

"My father brought it here from Florida," Miss Kippenberg revealed reluctantly. "For some reason the creature seemed to fascinate him. He insisted upon keeping it in the pond."

"Your father is not living here now I am told."

"That is true." Miss Kippenberg quickly switched the subject back to the alligator. "Mother and I would like to get rid of the beast but we've never been able to do it."

"Any zoo should be willing to take it off your hands."

"Mother often spoke of getting in touch with one but for some reason she never did. I suppose she hesitated to give the alligator away upon Father's account."

Penny remained silent, wondering how deeply she dared probe into the private life of the Kippenberg family. After all there were certain inquiries which a person of sensibility could not make. She couldn't very well ask: "Have your parents separated? Why did your father leave home? Is it true he is wanted by the authorities for evading income tax?" although these questions were upon the tip of her tongue.

She did say carelessly, "Your father is away, isn't he?"

"Yes," Miss Kippenberg answered briefly. After a moment she went on: "Father was rather peculiar in many ways. He had a decided flare for the unusual. Take this estate for instance. He had it built at great expense to resemble a castle he once saw in Germany."

"I've never visited such an elegant place."

"It is entirely too flamboyant for my taste. But Father loved every tower and turret. If only things had turned out different—"

Her voice trailed away and she stared at the ground, lost in deep thought. Arousing herself, she went on once more.

"If you had known Father you would understand it was not strange for him to have an alligator on the estate. At one time he kept imported peacocks. The place was fairly overrun with them."

Penny offered no comment. She moved closer to the edge of the lily pool, gazing down into the now tranquil waters.

"I know what you are trying to imply," Miss Kippenberg said jerkily. "It couldn't be possible. I refuse even to consider such a ridiculous theory."

"It does seem rather far-fetched," Penny admitted. "Of course, tragedies do occur and those foot-prints—"

"Please, not another word or you'll drive me into hysterics!" Sylvia cried. "You are trying to play upon my feelings so that I will tell you things! You are only trying to get a story! I'll not talk with you any longer."

She turned and ran up the path toward the house.

"Overplayed my hand that time," thought Penny ruefully. "As Dad says, I really have too much imagination to make a good reporter. Also too lively a tongue."

Miss Kippenberg had vanished into the house by the time the girl retraced her way to the garden. The black limousine no longer stood at the front door so she knew she was expected to get back to Andover by her own efforts.

"If Jerry is still waiting at the drawbridge, I'll ride home with him," she told herself. "Otherwise, I'm out of luck completely."

The path which Penny followed brought her toward the rear of the house. As she drew near, the kitchen door suddenly opened and a stout woman in a blue uniform came outside. In her arms she carried two large paper sacks which appeared to be filled with garbage for the bottoms were moist.

Just as the woman reached Penny one of the bags gave away, allowing a collection of corn husks, watermelon rinds and egg shells to fall on the sidewalk.

"Now I've done it!" she exclaimed crossly. "Splattered my stockings too."

"Oh, that's too bad," said Penny, pausing.

"This is the only place I ever worked where the cook was expected to carry out the garbage!" the woman complained. "It makes me good and mad every time I do it."

"I should think a house of this size would have an incinerator so that the garbage could be burned," Penny remarked.

"Say, this place doesn't have any conveniences for the servants," the cook went on. "You're expected to work, work, work from morning to night."

She broke off quickly, regarding Penny with a suspicious gaze. "You're not one of Miss Sylvia's guests?" she demanded.

"Oh, no, I only came here on an errand. I wouldn't repeat anything to the family."

"That's all right then," the woman said in relief. "I liked my job here well enough until lately. All month it's been one dinner party after another. Then we spent days getting ready for the wedding feast and not one scrap of food was touched!"

"But I suppose Mrs. Kippenberg pays you well."

"Listen, she didn't give me one extra cent for all the work I did. Mrs. Kippenberg always has been real close, and she's a heap worse since her husband went away. Another week like this last one and I quit!"

"Well, I can't say I blame you," Penny said, leading the woman on. "I suppose Miss Sylvia is as overbearing as her mother?"

"Oh, Miss Sylvia is all right, as sweet a girl as you'll find anywhere. I felt mighty sorry for her when that no-account man threw her over."

Penny knew by this time that she must be talking with Mrs. Latch, for the footman had mentioned the cook's name. As the woman walked on with her bundles of garbage she fell into step with her.

"It was strange about Mr. Atherwald's disappearance," she remarked. "I hear he came to the house and then went away just before the wedding."

"I can tell you about that," replied Mrs. Latch with an important air. "Yesterday morning a boy came to the back door with a letter for Mr. Atherwald. It's my opinion he sent it to himself."

"Didn't the boy tell you where he had obtained the letter?"

"He said it was given to him by one of Mr. Atherwald's friends. A man in a boat."

"Oh, I see," said Penny, making a mental note of the information. Realizing that the cook had told everything she knew about the matter, she quickly switched the subject. "By the way, who is the head gardener here?"

"Do you mean Peter Henderson?"

"A fairly old man," described Penny. "Gray hair, stooped shoulders, and I might add, an unpleasant manner."

"I guess that's Peter. He's not much of a gardener in my opinion. And he feels too high and mighty to associate with the other servants. He doesn't even stay here nights."

"Is he a new man?"

"Mrs. Kippenberg hired him only three days before the wedding. I don't think he's done a lick of honest work since he came here."

"And Mrs. Kippenberg doesn't mind?"

CHAPTER 11 - QUESTIONS AND ANSWERS

"She's been too busy and bothered to pay any attention to him," the cook declared. "But she always has time to boss me. I tell you, if dishes aren't prepared perfectly she raves!"

"No wonder Mr. Kippenberg was forced to leave home," Penny interposed slyly. "You can't blame him for running away from a violent temper."

"Oh, the Kippenbergs never had any trouble," Mrs. Latch corrected. "Mr. Kippenberg would just laugh and not say a word when she jumped on him. They were never heard to quarrel."

"Then it seems odd that he went away."

"Yes, it does," agreed the cook, frowning. "I never did understand it. And then the way Mrs. Kippenberg changed all the servants!"

"You mean after Mr. Kippenberg went away?"

"She fired everyone except me. I guess she knew she couldn't get another cook half as good if she let me go. Right away I struck for more money and she gave it to me without a whimper. But since then she works me like a dog."

Mrs. Latch clattered the lid of the garbage can into place and turned toward the house. But as Penny once more fell into step with her, she paused and regarded the girl with sudden suspicion.

"Say, why am I telling you all this anyway? Who are you? You're not one of those sneaking reporters?"

"Do I look like a reporter?" countered Penny.

"Well, no, you don't," admitted Mrs. Latch. "But you're as inquisitive as one. You must be the girl who brought Miss Sylvia's new dress from the LaRue Shoppe."

Penny hesitated too long over her reply, and the woman gazed at her sharply.

"You *are* a reporter!" she exclaimed with conviction. "And you've been deliberately pumping me! Of all the tricks! I'll tell Miss Kippenberg!"

"Wait, I can explain."

Mrs. Latch paid no heed. With an angry toss of her head she hastened into the house.

"Overstepped myself again," Penny thought in dismay. "I'll be getting away from here while the getting is good."

Turning, she ran down the walk toward the river, only to stop short as she reached the boat dock. The drawbridge was in open position and the old watchman did not appear to be at his usual post. She had no way of reaching the mainland.

CHAPTER 12 - FISHERMAN'S LUCK

Penny looked anxiously about for a means of crossing the river. There were no small boats available and the only person who stood on the opposite shore was Jerry Livingston. The other reporters and photographers, evidently tiring of their long vigil, had gone away.

She cupped her hands and shouted to Jerry: "How am I going to get over there? Can you lower the bridge?"

"The mechanism is locked," called back the reporter. "And the watchman won't be back for an hour."

Penny walked a short distance up the shore searching for a boat. The only available craft was the large launch which she could not hope to operate. She might return to the house and appeal to Miss Kippenberg but such a course was not to her liking.

As she considered whether or not to ruin her clothing by swimming across, Jerry called her attention to a small boat some distance up the river. The boy who was fishing from it obligingly rowed ashore after Penny had signaled him.

"I'll give you fifty cents to ferry me across," she offered.

"I'll be glad to do it," he agreed.

Penny stepped into the boat and then asked: "Aren't you the same lad I saw here yesterday?"

The boy nodded as he reached for the oars. "I remember you," he answered.

"You seem to fish here nearly every day."

"Just about. I caught some nice ones today." Proudly he held up two large fish for her to see.

"Beauties," praised Penny. "I take it the motor boats haven't been bothering you as much as they were."

"It's been pretty quiet on the river today," the boy agreed. "Want to see something else I fished up?"

"Why, yes. What did you hook, a mud turtle?"

The boy opened a large wooden box which contained an assortment of rope, fishing tackle and miscellaneous articles. He lifted out a man's high silk hat, bedraggled and shapeless.

"You fished that out of the water?" Penny demanded, leaning forward to take the article from him. "Where did you find it?"

"Up there a ways." The boy motioned vaguely toward a point on the Kippenberg estate.

Penny turned the hat over in her hand, examining it closely. She found no identifying marks, yet she believed that it had belonged to Grant Atherwald for he had worn similar headdress. The point indicated by the boy was not far distant from the Kippenberg lily pool.

"How would you like to sell this hat?" she asked.

"Why, it's not worth anything."

"I'd like to have it," said Penny. "I'll give you another fifty cents."

"It's a deal."

Penny offered the boy a dollar bill, and a moment later he beached the boat. Jerry was waiting to help her ashore. His alert gaze fastened upon the hat which she hugged close, but he withheld comment. To the boy he said:

"Son, how would you like to earn five dollars?"

The boy's eyes brightened. "Say, this is my lucky day!" he exclaimed. "What doin'?"

"It's easy," Jerry told him. "All you need to do is to be here for a couple of days with your boat. You're not to allow anyone to use it except me."

"And me," added Penny. "I'll need taxi service myself if I come back here."

"That's all right," agreed the boy.

CHAPTER 12 - FISHERMAN'S LUCK

"Here's a dollar on deposit," Jerry said. "Now remember, be here tomorrow from eight o'clock on, and don't hire out to any other person."

"I won't," the boy promised.

Jerry took Penny's elbow and escorted her to the press car.

"So you found Atherwald's hat?" he asked without preliminaries.

"It resembles the one he wore. The boy fished it out of the river."

"Then that looks as if the fellow really was the victim of a plot!"

"I've thought so all along," Penny declared soberly.

"What else did you learn? You seemed to be very chummy with Miss Kippenberg."

"I'll not be from now on," Penny returned ruefully.

As Jerry backed the car around in the dusty road, she told of her meeting with Sylvia Kippenberg and the ensuing conversation.

"So Miss Kippenberg doesn't like questions?" Jerry asked. "And she refuses to notify the police? Well, after we publish our story in the *Star* it won't be necessary. The police will come to do their own investigating."

"I can't really believe she is trying to deceive the authorities," Penny said thoughtfully. "She seems to have a sincere regard for Grant Atherwald."

"It may be pretense."

"She wasn't pretending the day of the wedding. Atherwald's disappearance was a great shock to her."

"Well, even so, she may know a lot more than she's putting out."

"I think that myself. She closed up like a clam when I talked about her father."

The car came to the main road and a short time later entered the town of Corbin. As they stopped for a red light, Penny touched Jerry's arm.

"Look over there," she directed. "See those two men standing in front of the drugstore?"

"What about them?"

"They're G men who attended the Kippenberg wedding. Salt pointed them out to me."

"You don't say! Maybe we can learn a fact or two from them."

Jerry parked the car at the curb and sprang out. Penny saw him walk over to the men, introduce himself and show his press credentials. She was too far away to hear the conversation.

In a few minutes Jerry returned to the car looking none too elated.

"You didn't learn anything, did you?" Penny inquired as they drove on again.

"Not very much. Government men never will talk. But they did admit they were here trying to locate James Kippenberg."

"Then they think he is in the locality."

"They had an idea he would show up at his daughter's wedding. But it didn't turn out that way."

"Did you say anything to them about Grant Atherwald's disappearance?"

"Yes, but they wouldn't discuss it. They said they had nothing to do with the case."

Penny lapsed into reflective silence as the car went on toward Andover. Mentally she sorted over the evidence which she had gathered that day, trying to fit it into a definite pattern.

"Jerry," she said at last.

"Yes?"

"You'll probably laugh at this, but I have a theory about Grant Atherwald's disappearance."

"Go ahead, spill it."

"Yesterday when Salt and I were waiting at the drawbridge we saw a motorboat cruise down the river. It was driven by a burly looking fellow who paid no heed when we tried to hail him."

"You're not suggesting that the man may have had something to do with Atherwald's disappearance?" Jerry questioned, mildly amused.

"I knew you would laugh."

"Your theory sounds pretty far-fetched to me, I'll admit. It happens there are any number of burly, tough looking boatmen on the Kobalt. You can't arrest a man for a crime just because of his appearance."

"All the same, there is supporting evidence. Mrs. Latch told me that Atherwald's note had been handed to her by a boy who in turn received it from someone in a boat."

"Boats are rather common too. Your theory is interesting, but that's all I can say for it."

"All right," said Penny. "I was about to tell you another idea of mine. Now I won't do it."

No amount of coaxing could induce her to reveal her thought, and the remainder of the drive to Andover was made in silence. It was well after five-thirty when the car finally drew up in front of the City Club.

Penny was not surprised to find the doors locked and no sign of Louise or Miss Frome.

"I thought they would go home without me," she said to Jerry. "I only wanted to make certain."

For many miles the road led through pleasant countryside and then swung back toward the Kobalt river. The sun had dropped below the horizon by the time the automobile sped through the town of Claxton.

"Thirty miles still to go," Jerry sighed. "I'm getting hungry."

"Two souls with but a single thought," remarked Penny.

Directly ahead they noticed an electric sign which drew attention to a roadside gasoline station with an adjoining restaurant. Jerry eased on the brake.

"How about it, Penny? Shall we invest a few nickels?"

"I could do with a sandwich," Penny agreed. "Several, in fact."

Not until Jerry had parked the car did they notice the dilapidated condition of the building. It stood perhaps fifty yards back from the main road, its rear porch fronting on the Kobalt.

"Strange how one is always running into the river," Penny remarked absently. "It seems to twist itself over half the state."

Jerry had not heard her words. He was gazing at the restaurant with disapproval.

"This place doesn't look so good, Penny. If you say the word we'll drive on."

"Oh, I'd brave anything for a beef barbecue," she laughed.

Through the screen door they caught a discouraging glimpse of the cafe's interior—dingy walls, cigarette smoke, a group of rough looking men seated on stools at the counter. Upon the threshold Penny hesitated, losing courage.

"Let's not go in," Jerry grunted in an undertone. "They'll probably serve cockroaches in the sandwiches."

Penny half turned away from the door only to stop short. Her attention focused upon two men who were sitting at the far end of the cafe drinking coffee from heavy mugs. In the indistinct light she could not be absolutely sure, yet she was instantly convinced that the heavy-set fellow in shirt sleeves was the same boatman who had been seen near the Kippenberg estate.

To Jerry's surprise, Penny resisted the tug of his arm as he sought to lead her toward the car.

"This place isn't half bad," she said. "Let's try it and see what happens."

Boldly she reached for the knob of the screen door and entered the cafe.

CHAPTER 13 - TWO MEN AND A BOAT

Penny ignored several empty tables at the front of the dreary restaurant and selected one not far from where the two men sat. As they glanced at her with insolent, appraising eyes, her pulse quickened. She was almost certain that the heavy-set man was the same fellow she had noticed near the Kippenberg estate.

A waiter in a soiled white apron shuffled up to take their order.

"Hot roast beef sandwich and coffee," said Jerry. "With plenty of cream."

"Make mine the same," added Penny without looking at the menu.

All her attention centered upon the two men who were now talking together in low tones. After the first glance they had taken no interest in her and were unaware of her scrutiny. The heavy-set man bent nearer his companion and with the point of his knife drew a pattern on the tablecloth.

"What do you think of this route, Joe?" he asked.

"Too risky," the other muttered. "Once we start we got to make a quick shoot to the sea."

"Any way we take we might run into trouble. Y'know, I wish we had never agreed to do the job."

"You and me both!"

"Dietz ain't to be trusted," the heavy-set man said and his shaggy eyebrows drew together in a scowl. "He's thinking first and last of his own skin. We've got to watch him."

"And the girl, too. She's a dumb one and plenty apt to talk if the going gets rough."

Penny lost the remainder of the conversation as Jerry spoke to her.

"We couldn't have picked a worse place," he complained. "Look at all the breakfast egg on the tablecloth. I'm in favor of walking out even now."

"I'm not," replied Penny.

"Say, what's got into you anyway?" Jerry demanded. "You're acting mighty funny."

"Notice those two men at the last table," she indicated.

"What about them?"

"See that heavy-set fellow with the tattooed anchor on his arm? Well, I'm satisfied he is the same boatman who cruised near the Kippenberg estate yesterday afternoon."

"It might be," Jerry agreed, unimpressed. "The Kobalt is only a stone's throw away. And this place seems to be frequented by rivermen."

"You didn't hear what they were saying?" whispered Penny. "Listen!"

Jerry immediately fell silent, centering his attention upon the two men. But by this time they had lowered their voices so that only an occasional word could be distinguished.

"What were they saying anyway?" Jerry asked curiously.

Before Penny could answer, the proprietor came from the kitchen bearing two plates of food which he set down before them. The sandwiches were covered with a dark brown, watery gravy, potatoes bore a heavy coating of grease and the coffee looked weak.

"Anything more?" the man inquired indifferently.

"That's all," Jerry replied, with emphasis. "In fact, it's too much."

At the adjoining table the two men abruptly hauled to their feet. Paying their bill they quitted the restaurant.

"Let's leave, too," suggested Penny. "I should like to see where they go."

Jerry pushed his plate aside. "Suits me," he agreed. "Even my cast-iron stomach can't wrestle with such food as this."

He paid at the cash register and they went out into the night. Penny looked about for the two men and saw them walking toward the river.

"Hold on," said Jerry as she started to follow. "Tell me what all the excitement is about."

Tersely, Penny repeated the conversation she had overheard.

"They're tough looking hombres all right," Jerry admitted. "Likely as not mixed up in some dirty business. But to say they're involved in the Kippenberg affair—"

"Oh, Jerry," Penny broke in impatiently, "we'll never learn anything if we take that attitude. We must run down every possible clue. Please, let's see if they go down to the river."

"We ought to be getting our story back to the office," Jerry reminded her. "If we miss the last edition there will be fireworks."

"It will only take a minute," Penny insisted stubbornly. "If you won't come with me, then I'm going alone!"

She started away and the reporter had no choice but to follow. A narrow, well-trod path led down a steep slope toward the river. Long before they came within sight of it they could hear the croak of bullfrogs and feel the damp, night mists enveloping them like a cloak.

Drawing closer to the two men, Penny and Jerry slackened pace and moved with greater care. But if they hoped to learn anything from the conversation of the pair ahead they were disappointed. The talk concerned only the weather.

Reaching the banks of the river, the two men boarded a sturdy cabin cruiser which had been moored to a sagging dock.

"It's the very same boat," Penny whispered jubilantly. "I knew I wasn't mistaken."

"Even so, what does that prove?" demanded Jerry. "It's no crime to run a motorboat near the Kippenberg estate. The river is free."

"But you must admit there *is* other evidence. Oh, why can't we follow them? We might learn something really important."

"We're not going off on any wild chase tonight," stated Jerry sternly. "Come on, it's home for us before your father sends a police squad to search for his missing daughter."

"You're losing a golden opportunity, Jerry Livingston."

"Listen, by the time we located a boat those men would be ten miles from here. They're leaving now. Use your head."

"Oh, all right," Penny gave in. "We'll go home, but I'll bet a cent you'll be sorry later on."

She waited until the cruiser was lost to view in the darkness and then allowed the reporter to guide her back up the steep path.

"At least let's try to find out who the men are," Penny urged as they came near the cafe. "The restaurant owner might know."

More to please her than for any other reason, Jerry said that he would inquire. He re-entered the cafe, returning in a few minutes to report that the proprietor had never seen either of the men before.

"And now let's be traveling," he urged. "We've killed enough time here."

During the remainder of the ride back to Riverview, Penny had little to say. But long after she knew Jerry had forgotten the two boatmen she kept turning their conversation over in her mind. She only wished she might prove that her theories were not ridiculous.

Presently, the automobile drew up in front of the Parker residence.

"Won't you come in, Jerry?" Penny invited. "Dad may wish to talk with you about the case."

"I might stop a minute. I have a question or two to ask him."

The door of the house swung open as Penny and the reporter crossed the front porch. Anthony Parker stood framed in the bright electric light, a tall, imposing figure.

"That you, Penny?"

"Yes, Dad."

"I'm glad you're home safe," he said, not trying to hide his relief. "Mrs. Weems and I have both been worried. It's going on nine o'clock."

"So late? Didn't Louise telephone you?"

"Yes, she said you had gone on to the Kippenberg estate. Knowing you, I worried all the more. What mischief did you get into this time, Penny?"

CHAPTER 13 - TWO MEN AND A BOAT

"None. Jerry took care of that!"

Mr. Parker held the door open for his daughter and Jerry to pass through. "Have you had your dinners?" he asked.

"We stopped at a roadside cafe, Dad. But the food was horrible. We didn't even try to eat it."

"Mrs. Weems can find something for you, I'm sure. She's upstairs."

"Don't call her just yet," said Penny. "First, we want to tell you what we've learned."

Mr. Parker listened attentively as Penny gave a detailed account of her visit to the estate, the finding of the silk hat, and finally of her encounter with the two boatmen at the river cafe.

"I might have learned a lot more if only Jerry hadn't played grandmother," she said crossly. "He refused to follow the boat down the river—said it would only be a wild chase."

"Jerry, I'm glad you had will power enough to overrule her," declared Mr. Parker. "The possibility of those men being connected with the Atherwald case seems very vague to me."

"Dad, you should have heard what they were saying! The one man drew a design on the tablecloth and asked his companion what he thought of the route. They talked about a quick get-away to the sea."

"The men may have been fugitives," Mr. Parker commented. "But even that isn't very likely."

"They spoke of being uneasy about a certain job they had agreed to do," Penny went on earnestly. "They mentioned a girl and said that a fellow named Dietz would bear watching."

Mr. Parker leaned forward in his chair. "Dietz?" he questioned. "Are you certain that was the name?"

"Yes, I heard it clearly."

"I don't see how there could be any connection," Mr. Parker mused. "And yet—"

"Where did you hear the name before, Dad?" Penny asked, all eagerness.

"Well, DeWitt has been digging up all the facts he can about James Kippenberg. As it happens, the man once had a business associate named Aaron Dietz who was dismissed because of alleged dishonesty."

"Then there must be a relationship!" Penny cried. She whirled triumphantly to face the crestfallen reporter. "You see, Mr. Jerry Livingston, my theory wasn't so crazy after all! Now aren't you sorry?"

CHAPTER 14 - THE STONE TOWER

Louise Sidell was washing the breakfast dishes when Penny walked boldly in at the back door.

"Don't you ever answer doorbells, Lou?" she demanded. "I stood around front for half an hour, ringing and ringing."

"Why, hello, Penny. I didn't hear you at all," apologized Louise. "The radio is on too loud. I see you reached home last night."

Penny picked up a towel and began to dry dishes. "Oh, yes, and did I have a day!"

"What happened after you left Andover?"

"It's a long story, so I'll begin at the end. Last night, coming home with Jerry we stopped at a cafe along the river. Guess whom we saw!"

"Knowing your luck, I'd say Charlie Chaplin, or maybe the Queen of England."

"This particular cafe wasn't quite their speed, Lou. Jerry and I saw that same boatman I told you about!"

"The fellow you saw cruising about the Kippenberg estate? What's so remarkable about that?"

"It just happens I've dug up other evidence to show he may know something about Grant Atherwald's disappearance," Penny revealed proudly. "Jerry and I overheard a conversation. It seems this man and a companion of his are mixed up with another fellow named Aaron Dietz."

"Which doesn't make sense to me," complained Louise, scrubbing hard at a sticky plate.

"Aaron Dietz was a former associate of James Kippenberg. Dad said he probably knew more about the Kippenberg financial affairs than any other person. Oh, I tell you, Jerry feels pretty sick because we didn't follow the men last night! Dad assigned him to try to pick up the trail today. He's chartered a motor boat and will patrol the river."

"If you don't mind," said Louise patiently, "I'd like to hear the first part of the story now. Then I might know what this is all about."

Talking as fast as she could, Penny related everything which had happened since she had taken leave of her chum at Andover.

"Which brings me to the point of my visit," she ended her tale. "How about going out there with me this morning?"

"To the Kippenberg estate?" Louise asked eagerly.

"Yes, we may not be able to get across the river, but I mean to try."

"You know I'm wild to visit the place, Penny!"

"How soon can you start?"

"Just as soon as these stupid dishes are done. And I ought to change my dress."

"Wear something dark which won't attract attention in the bushes," advised Penny. "Now get to working on yourself while I finish the dishes."

Louise dropped the dishcloth and hurried upstairs. When she returned ten minutes later, her chum was swishing the last of the soapsuds down the sink drain. Another five minutes and they were in Penny's battered car, speeding toward Corbin.

The sun rode high in the sky by the time they came within view of the drawbridge. Noticing that a press car from a rival newspaper was parked at the end of the road, Penny drew up some distance away. She could see two reporters talking with the old watchman.

"Evidently, they're having no luck in getting over to the estate," she remarked.

"Then what about us?"

CHAPTER 14 - THE STONE TOWER

"Oh, we have our own private taxi service," Penny chuckled. "At least I hope so."

Taking a circuitous route so they would not be noticed by the bridgeman, the girls went down to the river's edge. Far up the stream Penny saw the familiar rowboat drifting with the current. At her signal the small boy seized his oars and rowed toward shore.

"I was here at eight o'clock just as you said," he declared. "That fellow up there by the bridge offered me a dollar to take him across the river. I turned him down."

"Good," approved Penny.

"Do you want to go across the river now?" the boy asked.

"Yes, please." Penny stepped into the boat and made room for Louise. "Keep close to the bank until we are around the bend. Then I'll show you where to land."

"I guess you're afraid someone will see you," the boy commented.

"Not exactly afraid," corrected Penny. "But this way will be best."

The boat moved quietly along the high bank, well out of sight of those who stood by the drawbridge.

"The cops were here this morning," volunteered the boy as he pulled at the oars.

"You saw them visit the estate?" Penny questioned.

"Sure, there were four of 'em. They drove up in a police car and they made old Thorndyke let the bridge down so they could go across."

"Are the policemen at the estate now?"

"No, they left again in about an hour. What do you suppose they wanted over there?"

"Well, now, I couldn't guess," replied Penny. "Like as not they only wished to ask a few questions. Are the Kippenbergs at home?"

"I saw Mrs. Kippenberg drive away right after the police left."

"And her daughter?"

"I guess she must be still there. Anyway, she wasn't in the car."

The boat rounded the bend, and Penny pointed out a place on the opposite shore where she wished to land.

"Shall I wait for you?" the boy asked as the girls stepped from the craft.

"Yes, but not here," directed Penny. "You might row back to the opposite shore and keep watch from there. We ought to be ready to leave within at least an hour."

The roof top of the Kippenberg house could be seen towering above the tall trees. But as the two girls plunged into the bushes which grew thickly along the shore they lost sight of it entirely.

"I hope," said Louise uneasily, "that you know where you are going. It would be easy to lose one's self in this jungle."

"Oh, I have my directions straight. We should come out near the lily pool at any minute."

"What do you hope to gain by coming here, Penny?" Louise inquired abruptly.

"I thought I would try to talk with Miss Kippenberg again. There's an important question I forgot to ask her yesterday. Then I wanted to show you the estate, especially the lily pond."

"Is there anything unusual about it?"

"I'll let you be the judge," Penny answered. "We're almost there now."

They came in a moment to a path which made walking much easier. Penny went in advance of her chum. Suddenly she halted.

"See what is ahead, Lou! I never saw that thing before."

She stepped to one side so that Louise might see the tall stone tower which loomed up against a background of scarlet maples.

"How curious!" murmured Louise.

"This isn't the only queer thing I've found on the estate."

"What purpose could the tower have?" speculated Louise.

"Decoration, perhaps," replied Penny, moving forward again. "Or it might have been built for a prison."

"Listen, you have too many different theories about Grant Atherwald," laughed Louise. "Why don't you get one and stick to it?"

"My mind is always open to new possibilities and impressions."

"I'll say it is," agreed Louise. "I suppose you think Mrs. Kippenberg is keeping young Atherwald a prisoner in yonder tower?"

"Well, no, but you must admit it would make a lovely one. So romantic."

"Are you trying to kid me?" Louise demanded.

Penny smiled broadly as she stared up at the tower which rose perhaps twelve feet. Like every other building on the estate it had been built to resist the ages. High above her head a circular window had been cut in the wall and there was a heavy oaken door.

Reaching for the knob, Penny turned it. Then she pressed her shoulder against the door and pushed with her entire strength.

"Locked!" she announced.

"Then we won't learn what is inside after all."

"Yes, we will," declared Penny. "You lift me up and I'll peep in the window."

"You only weigh a ton," complained Louise.

She obligingly raised Penny up as high as she could.

"Look fast," she panted. "What do you see?"

"Not much of anything."

"I can't hold you forever," Louise said, and released her hold. "Didn't you see anything at all?"

"Just a lot of machinery."

"Tools, you mean?"

"No, an electric motor and something which looked like it might be a pump. Oh, I get it now!"

"Get what?" demanded Louise.

"Why, the idea of this tower. It must be used as a pump house. I wondered how the lily pool was ever drained and this must be the answer."

"You didn't see any prisoners chained inside?" Louise teased.

"Not one. Well, let's be getting on to the lily pond. It must be somewhere close."

Louise could not understand why her chum was so determined that she should see the pool. But since Penny seldom did anything without a purpose, she speculated upon what might be in store. She knew from the girl's manner that certain facts had been withheld deliberately to make this visit the more impressive.

"Here we are," said Penny as they came to the clearing. "What do you think of it?"

Louise was aware of a deep sense of disappointment as she gazed at the lily pool.

"I really don't see anything so remarkable about it, Penny."

"This was the place where I found the wedding ring. And there were footprints indicating that a struggle probably took place."

"I read all that in the paper," Louise said. "From the hints you've been passing out, I thought you brought me here to show me something mysterious."

"Go close to the pool."

"What for, Penny? You want to push me in?"

"Oh, you're too suspicious! Go on and look."

Louise went to the edge of the pool and peered down into the water.

"I don't see anything."

"You will in just a minute. Keep looking."

Louise was more than half convinced that Penny meant to play some prank, but she dropped down on her knees so her eyes would be closer to the water.

"Why, I do see some large object on the floor of the tank!" she exclaimed after a moment. "What is it, Penny?"

"An alligator."

Louise gave a smothered scream and drew back from the pool's edge.

"I—I might have fallen in. You ought to be ashamed of yourself!"

"I only wanted you to get a nice thrill," Penny grinned. "Pretty fellow, isn't he?"

"I didn't really see him," Louise admitted.

Overcoming her fear, she again leaned over the edge of the pool but with great caution. This time she could make out the alligator's form distinctly.

"Horrible!" she shuddered. "I wish you hadn't brought me—"

Her words ended in a little wail as a tiny object splashed into the water directly beneath her.

CHAPTER 14 - THE STONE TOWER

"My cameo pin!" she cried. "Oh, Penny, it slipped from my dress and now it's gone!"

CHAPTER 15 - A CAMEO PIN

In dismay, the two girls watched the trinket settle slowly to the bottom of the pool.

"Oh, my beautiful pin," moaned Louise. "Aunt Lucinda gave it to me for my birthday. I wouldn't have lost it for anything in the world."

"I guess it was my fault," Penny said self-accusingly.

"No, it wasn't. I must have been careless about fastening the clasp. When I leaned over it slipped off. Well, it's gone, and that's that."

The cameo pin had fallen into the deepest part of the pool not far from where the alligator lay. The girls were unable to see it plainly because of the lily pads and plants which cluttered the water.

"If that old alligator would just behave himself we could wade in and get it easy," Penny said.

"Fancy trying it!"

"I'm afraid he would take special delight in snapping off an arm or a leg. And we don't dare ask anyone to help us get the pin or we'll be ejected from the grounds as trespassers."

"We may as well forget about it, Penny. Come along, I'm sick of this place."

"No, wait, Louise. We might be able to fish it out with a stick."

"I don't think we'd have a chance."

"Anyway, it will do no harm to try."

Penny searched the woods until she found a long stick with a curve at the end. Lying flat on the flagstones at the edge of the pool she prodded for the pin.

"I can touch it all right!" she cried. "I'll pull it over to the side."

"Be careful you don't tumble in," Louise warned, anxiously holding her chum by the waist. "If you should lose your balance—"

Penny hooked the cameo pin in the curve of the stick and began raising it inch by inch up the side of the pool.

"If I can get it up high enough reach down and snatch it," Penny advised her chum. "Oh, shoot, there it goes!"

The pin had slipped away from the stick and settled once more on the bottom of the pool.

"You can't get it, Penny," Louise insisted. "You're making the alligator all excited by prodding around."

"I don't care about *him*. I'll try once more if I can locate the pin. It seems to be hiding from me now."

The water was so disturbed that Penny could not see the pin or the bottom of the pool. She waited several minutes for the dirt to settle and then gazed down once more.

"There it is!" she exclaimed. "It moved over quite a ways to the right."

Louise flattened herself beside Penny. "Oh, let the pin go," she said.

"No, I think I can get it. Say, there seems to be something else on the bottom of the pool."

"Where?"

Penny pointed, and then, as her chum still could not distinguish anything, parted the lily pads with her stick.

"Yes, I do see something now," Louise declared. "What can it be?"

"Doesn't it look like a metal ring?" Penny asked. She had lost all interest in the cameo pin.

"Yes, it does. Someone probably threw it into the pool."

"But it looks to me as if it's attached to the bottom of the tank, embedded in the cement," Penny said. She bent closer to the water, trying to see.

"Be careful," Louise warned nervously. "That alligator might come up and snap off your nose."

CHAPTER 15 - A CAMEO PIN

Penny paid no heed.

"It is attached!" she announced in an excited voice. "Louise, do you know what I think?"

"What?"

"It's the ring of a trapdoor!"

"A trapdoor!" Louise echoed incredulously.

"You can see for yourself that it's an iron ring."

"It does look a little like one from here," Louise admitted. "But whoever heard of a trapdoor in a lily pool? No one but you would even think of such a thing. It doesn't make sense."

"Does anything on this estate make sense?"

"The ring might have something to do with draining the pool," Louise said without replying to her chum's question. "I suppose a section of the pool could be lifted up and removed. But I'd never call it a trapdoor."

"I wish we could tell for sure what it is." Penny tried to prod the ring with her stick but it was well beyond her reach. "Maybe the alligator has a room down under the pool where he spends his winters!"

"You're simply filled with ideas today," Louise declared. "What about my pin? Shall we let it go?"

Reminded of her original task, Penny set to work once more, trying to draw the cameo to the edge of the tank. She was so deeply engrossed, that she jumped as her chum touched her on the arm.

"Listen, Penny, I think someone is coming!"

From the path at the right they could hear approaching footsteps and the low murmur of voices.

Penny struggled to her feet, dropping the stick.

"We mustn't be caught here," she whispered.

Taking Louise's hand, she drew the girl into the dense bushes directly behind the pool. Scarcely had they secreted themselves when Sylvia Kippenberg and the head gardener came into view. They seated themselves on a rustic bench not far from where the two girls stood.

"I had to talk with you," Sylvia said to the old man. "The police came this morning and asked so many questions. Mother put them off but they'll be back again."

"They didn't learn about the alligator?" the gardener asked gruffly.

"No, they came here but only stayed a few minutes. I don't think they noticed anything wrong."

"Then that's all right."

"Their investigation is only beginning," Sylvia said nervously. "Mother and I both believe it would be wise to get rid of the alligator."

"Wise but not easy," the gardener replied.

"You'll see what you can do about it?"

"Yes. I'll try to get rid of him."

"Then I guess that's all," Sylvia said, but she made no move to leave. She sat staring moodily at the pool.

"Anything else on your mind?" asked the gardener.

"I—I wanted to ask you something, but I scarcely know how."

The gardener waited, watching the girl's face intently.

"You never liked Grant Atherwald," she began nervously.

"Say, what are you driving at?" the man asked quickly. "You're not trying to hint that I had anything to do with Grant Atherwald's disappearance?"

The two faced each other and Sylvia's gaze was the first to fall.

"No, no, of course not," she said.

"I don't know any more about his disappearance than you do," the man told her angrily. "I didn't even see him on the day of the wedding."

"But he came here. The wedding ring was found near the pool. Surely you must have heard some sound for I know you were in this part of the garden."

"Well, I didn't," the man said sullenly. "The only persons I saw were a newspaper photographer and a girl."

"Please don't take offense," Miss Kippenberg murmured, getting up from the bench. "I've been terribly upset these past few days."

She walked slowly to the edge of the pool. There she stopped short, staring down at an object which lay on the flagstones at her feet. It was the stick which Penny had dropped only a moment before.

"What have you found?" the gardener cried.

He went quickly to her side and took the damp stick from her hand.

"Someone has been here prying around," he said in a harsh voice. "This was used to investigate the water in the pool."

"And whoever it was must be close by even now. Otherwise the stick would have dried out in the sun."

"You go back to the house," the man commanded. "I'll look around."

In their hideout amid the bushes, Penny and Louise gazed at each other with chagrin. No word was spoken for even a whisper might have been heard. With a common desire for escape, they glided with cat-like tread toward the river.

CHAPTER 16 - GATHERING CLUES

The girls could hear no movement behind them as they darted down the path. They dared to hope that they had eluded the old gardener.

Then as they came within sight of the river, Louise stumbled over a vine. Although she stifled an outcry the dull thud of her body against the ground seemed actually to reverberate through the forest. A black crow on the lower limb of an oak tree cawed in protest before he flew away.

Penny pulled Louise to her feet and they went on as fast as they could, but they knew the sound had betrayed them. Now they could hear the man in pursuit, his heavy shoes pounding on the hard, dry path.

"Run!" Penny commanded.

They reached the river bank and looked about for the boat which would take them across. As they had feared it was on the opposite shore.

Penny gestured frantically, but the boy did not understand the need for haste. He picked up his oars and rowed toward them at a very deliberate pace.

"Oh, he'll never get here in time," Louise murmured fearfully. "Shall we hide?"

"That's all we can do."

They realized then that they had waited too long. Before they could dodge into the deeper thicket the gardener reached the clearing.

"So it's you again!" he cried wrathfully, glaring at Penny.

"Please, we didn't mean any harm. We can explain—"

"This stick is explanation enough for me!" the man shouted, waving it above his head. "You were trying to find out about the lily pool!"

"We were only trying to get a pin which I dropped into the water," Louise said, backing a step away.

"I don't believe you!" the man snapped. "You can't fool me! I know why you came here, and you'll pay for your folly! You'll never take the secret away with you!"

With a swift, animal-like spring which belied his age, the gardener hurled himself toward the girls. He seized Penny's arm giving it a cruel twist.

"You're coming along with me," he announced harshly.

"Let me go!" Penny cried, trying to free herself.

"You're going with me to the house. You've been altogether too prying. Now you'll take your punishment, both of you."

The gardener might have managed Penny alone, but he was no match for two athletic girls. As he tried to seize Louise, Penny twisted free.

Quick as a flash, she grasped the man's felt hat, jamming it down on his head over his eyes. While he was trying to pull it off, Louise also wriggled from his grasp.

The two girls ran to the water's edge. Their boat had drawn close to shore. Without waiting for it to beach they waded out over their shoetops and climbed aboard.

"Don't either of you ever come here again!" the gardener hurled after them. "If you do—"

The rest of the threat was carried away by the wind. However, Penny could not resist waving her hand and calling back: "Bye, bye, old timer! We'll be seeing you!"

"What's the matter with that man anyhow?" asked the boy who rowed the boat. "Didn't he want you on the estate?"

"On the contrary, he invited us to remain and we declined," grinned Penny. "Just temperament, that's all. He can't make up his mind which way he would like to have it."

Allowing the boy to puzzle over the remark, she busied herself pouring water from her sodden shoes. The visit to the estate had not turned out at all as she had planned. She had failed to talk with Miss Kippenberg, and it was almost certain that from now on servants would keep a much closer watch for intruders.

The only vital information she had gleaned resulted from overhearing the conversation between Sylvia Kippenberg and the gardener.

"She talked with him as if they were well acquainted," mused Penny. "Miss Kippenberg must have thought he knew more about Grant Atherwald's disappearance than he would tell. And she seems to be afraid the Law will ask too many questions. Otherwise, she wouldn't have suggested getting rid of the alligator."

One additional observation Penny had made, but she decided not to speak of it until she and Louise were alone.

The boat reached shore and the two girls stepped out on the muddy bank.

"Will you need me again?" inquired the boy.

"I may," said Penny, "and I can't tell you exactly when. Where do you keep your boat?"

"Up the river just beyond that crooked maple tree. I hide it in the bushes and I keep the oars inside a hollow log close by. You won't have any trouble finding it."

Penny and Louise said goodbye to the lad and scrambled up the bank.

"I'm sure I'll not be going back to *that* place," the latter declared emphatically. "I just wonder what would have happened if we hadn't broken away."

"We might have been locked up in the stone tower," Penny laughed. "Then another one of my theories would have proven itself."

"Oh, you and your theories! You can't make me believe that gardener didn't mean to harm us. He was a very sinister character."

"Sinister is a strong word, Lou. But I'll agree he's not any ordinary gardener. Either he's been hired by the Kippenberg family for a very special purpose or else he's gained their confidence and means to bend them to his own ends."

"His own ends! Why, Penny, what do you mean? Have you learned something you haven't told me?"

"Only this. I'm satisfied Old Peter is no gardener. He's wearing a disguise."

"Well, what won't you think of next! You've been reading too many detective stories, Penny Parker."

"Have I? Then there's no need to tell you—"

"Yes, there is," Louise cut in. "Your ideas are pretty imaginative, but I like to hear them anyway."

"Considerate of you, old thing," Penny drawled in her best imitation of an English accent. "You don't deserve to be told after that crack, but I'll do it anyhow. When I pulled the gardener's hat down over his eyes, I felt something slip!"

"Maybe it was his skin peeling off."

"He wore a wig," Penny said soberly. "That's why he looked so startled when I jerked the hat."

"Did you actually see a wig?"

"No, but he must have had one on his head. I felt it give, I tell you."

"I wouldn't put anything past that fellow. But if he isn't a gardener, then who or what is he?"

"I don't know, but I intend to do some intensive investigation."

"Just how, may I ask?"

Penny gazed speculatively toward the drawbridge, noting that the old watchman had been deserted by the group of reporters. He sat alone, legs crossed, his camp stool propped against the side of the gearhouse.

"Let's talk with him, Lou. He might be able to tell us something about the different employees of the estate."

They walked over to where the old man sat, greeting him with their most pleasant smiles.

"Good morning," said Penny.

The old man finished lighting his pipe before he deigned to notice them.

"Good morning," repeated Penny.

"Mornin'," said the watchman. He looked the two girls over appraisingly and added: "Ain't you children a long ways off from your Ma's?"

CHAPTER 16 - GATHERING CLUES

The remark both startled and offended Penny, but instantly she divined that the old fellow's memory was short and his eyesight poor. He had failed to recognize her in everyday clothes.

"Oh, we're just out for a hike," she answered. "You see, we get tired of all the ordinary places, so we thought we would walk by here."

"We're interested in your bridge," added Louise. "We just love bridges."

"This one ain't so good any more," the old man said disparagingly.

"Doesn't it get lonely here?" ventured Louise. "Sitting here all day long?"

"It did at first, Miss. But I got used to it. Anyway, it beats leanin' on a shovel for the gov'ment. I got a little garden over yonder a ways. You ought to see my tomatoes. Them Ponderosas is as big as a plate."

"Do you ever operate the bridge?" Louise inquired, for Penny had not told her that the structure was still in use.

"Oh, sure, Miss. That's what I'm here for. But it ain't safe for nothin' heavier than a passenger car."

"I'd love to see the bridge lowered." Louise stared curiously up at the tall cantilevers which pointed skyward. "When will you do it next time, Mr.—?"

"Davis, if you please, Miss. Thorny Davis they calls me. My real name's Thorndyke."

The old man pulled a large, silver watch from his pocket and consulted it.

"In about ten minutes now, Mrs. Kippenberg will be comin' back from town. Then we'll make the old hinge bend down agin'."

"Let's wait," said Louise.

Penny nodded and then as Thorny did not seem to object, she peeped into the gear house, the door of which stood half open. A maze of machinery met her eye—an electric motor and several long hand-levers.

Presently Thorny Davis listened intently. Penny thought he looked like an old fox who had picked up the distant baying of the pack.

"That's *her* car a-comin' now," he said. "I can tell by the sound of the engine. Well, I reckon I might as well let 'er down."

Thorny arose and knocked the ashes from his corn-cob pipe. He opened the door of the gear house and stepped inside.

"May I see how you do it?" asked Penny. "I always was interested in machinery."

"The women will be runnin' locomotives next," Thorny complained whimsically. "All right, come on in."

The old watchman pulled a lever on the starting rheostat of the motor which responded with a sudden jar and then a low purr. It increased its speed as he pushed the lever all the way over.

"Now the power's on. The next thing is to drop 'er."

Thorny grasped one of the long hand-levers and gently eased it forward. There was a grind of gears engaging and the bridge slowly crept down out of the sky.

Penny did not miss a single move. She noted just which levers the watchman pulled and in what order. When the platform of the bridge was on an even keel she saw him cut off the motor and throw all the gear back into its original position.

"Think you could do 'er by yourself now?" Thorny asked.

"Yes, I believe I could," Penny answered gravely.

The old watchman smiled as he stepped to the deck of the bridge.

"It ain't so easy as it looks," he told her. "Well, here comes the Missuz now and we're all ready for her. Last time she came along I was weedin' out my corn patch and was she mad?"

As the black limousine rolled up to the drawbridge Penny turned her face away so that Mrs. Kippenberg would not recognize her. She need have had no uneasiness, for the lady gazed neither to the right nor the left. The car crept forward at a snail's pace causing the steel structure to shiver and shake as if from an attack of ague.

"Dear me, I think this bridge is positively dangerous," Louise declared. "I shouldn't like to drive over it myself."

As the old watchman again raised the cantilevers, Penny studied his every move.

"For a girl you're sure mighty interested in machinery," he remarked.

"Oh, I may grow up to be a bridgeman some day," Penny said lightly. "I notice you keep the gear house locked part of the time."

"I have to do it or folks would tamper with the machinery."

The old man snapped a padlock on the door.

"Now I'm goin' to mosey down to my garden and do a little hoein'," he announced. "You girls better run along."

Thus dismissed, Louise started away, but Penny made no move to leave. She intended to ask a few questions.

"Thorny, are you any relation to the Kippenberg's head gardener?" she inquired with startling abruptness.

"Am I any relation to that old walrus?" Thorny fairly shouted. "Am I any relation to *him*? Say, you tryin' to insult me?"

"Not at all, but I saw the man this morning, and I fancied I noticed a resemblance. Perhaps you don't know the one I mean."

"Sure, I know him all right." Thorny spat contemptuously. "New man. He acts as know-it-all and bossy as if he owned the whole place."

"Then you don't like him?"

"There ain't no one that has anything to do with him. He's so good he can't live like the rest of the servants. Where do you think I seen him the other night?"

"I haven't the slightest idea. Where?"

"He was at the Colonial Hotel, eatin' in the main dining room!"

"The Colonial is quite an expensive hotel at Corbin, isn't it?"

"Best there is. They soak you two bucks just to park your feet under one of their tables. Yep, if you ask me, Mrs. Kippenberg better ask that gardener of hers a few questions!"

Having delivered himself of this tirade, Thorny became calm again. He shifted his weight and said pointedly: "Well, I got to tend my garden. You girls better run along. Mrs. Kippenberg don't want nobody hangin' around the bridge."

The girls obligingly took leave of him and walked away. But when they were some distance away, Penny glanced back over her shoulder. She saw Thorny down on his hands and knees in front of the gear house. He was slipping some object under the wide crack of the door.

"The key to the padlock!" she chuckled. "So that was why he wanted us to leave first. We'll remember the hiding place, Lou, just in case we ever decide to use the drawbridge."

CHAPTER 17 - A SEARCH FOR JERRY

After leaving the Kippenberg estate, Penny and Louise motored to Corbin. More from curiosity than for any other reason they dined at the Colonial Hotel, finding the establishment as luxurious as the old watchman had intimated. A full hour and a half was required to eat the fine dinner which was served.

"Our friend, the gardener, does have excellent taste in food," remarked Louise. "What puzzles me is where does he get the money to pay for all this?"

"The obvious answer is that he's not a gardener."

"Maybe he has rooms here too, Penny."

"I've been wondering about it. I mean to investigate."

Louise glanced at her wristwatch. "Do you think we should take the time?" she asked. "It will be late afternoon now before we reach home."

"Oh, it won't take a minute to inquire at the desk."

Leaving the dining room, the girls made their way to the lobby. When the desk clerk had a free moment Penny asked him if anyone by the name of Peter Henderson had taken rooms at the hotel.

"No one here by that name," the man told her. "Wait, I'll look to be sure."

He consulted a card filing system which served as a register, and confirmed his first statement.

"The man I mean would be around sixty years of age," explained Penny. "He works as a gardener at the Kippenberg estate."

"Perhaps you have come to the wrong hotel," said the clerk aloofly. "We do not cater to gardeners."

"Only to people who employ gardeners, I take it."

"Our rates start at ten dollars a day," returned the clerk coldly.

"And does that include free linen and a bath?" Penny asked with pretended awe.

"Certainly. All of our rooms have private baths."

"How wonderful," giggled Penny. "We thought this might be one of those places with a bath on every floor!"

Suddenly comprehending that he was being made an object of sport, the clerk glared at the girls and turned his back.

Penny and Louise went cheerfully to their car, very much pleased with themselves for having deflated such a conceited young man. They drove away, and late afternoon brought them to Riverview, tired and dusty from their long trip.

After dropping her chum off at the Sidell home, Penny rode directly to the newspaper office. Finding no parking place available on the street, she ran her car into the loading area at the rear of the building, nosing into a narrow space which had just been vacated by a paper-laden truck.

"Hey, you lady," shouted an employee. "You can't park that scrap iron here. Another paper truck will be along in a minute."

Penny switched off the engine.

"I guess you're new around here," she said, climbing out. "The next truck isn't due until five-twenty-three."

"Say, who do you think you are, tellin' me—?"

The employee trailed off into silence as another workman gave him a sharp nudge in the ribs.

"Pipe down," he was warned. "If the boss' daughter wants to park her jitney in the paper chute it's okay, see?"

"Sure, I get it," the other mumbled.

Penny grinned broadly as she crossed the loading area.

"After this, you might mention my automobile in a more respectful tone," she tossed over her shoulder. "It's not scrap iron or a jitney either!"

Riding up the freight elevator, Penny passed a few remarks with the smiling operator and stepped off at the editorial floor. She noticed as she went through the news room that Jerry Livingston's desk was vacant. And because the waste basket was empty, the floor beside it free from paper wads, she knew he had written no story that day.

Penny tapped lightly on the closed door of her father's private office and went in.

"Hello," he said, glancing up. "Just get back from Corbin?"

"Yes, Louise and I had plenty of excitement, but I didn't dig up any facts you'll dare print in the paper."

"Did you meet Jerry anywhere?"

"Why, no, Dad."

"The young cub is taking a vacation at my expense, running up a big motorboat bill! He should have been back here three hours ago."

"Oh, be reasonable, Dad," said Penny teasingly. "You can't expect him to trace down those men just in a minute."

"It was a wild chase anyway," the editor growled. "I let him do it more to please you than for any other reason. But that's beside the point. He was told to be back here by four o'clock at the latest, even if he had nothing to report."

"Jerry is usually punctual, Dad. But I suppose being on the river he couldn't get here just when he expected."

"He's probably gone fishing," Mr. Parker declared.

He slammed down the roll top on his desk and picked up his hat.

"Will you ride home with me?" Penny invited. "Leaping Lena would be highly honored."

"It's a mighty sight more comfortable on the bus," her father replied. "But then, I can stand a jolting."

As they went out through the main room he paused to speak with DeWitt, leaving an order that he was to be called at his home as soon as Jerry Livingston returned.

Mr. Parker raised his eyebrows as he saw where Penny had left the car.

"Haven't I told you that the trucks need this space to load and unload?" he asked patiently. "There is a ten cent parking lot across the street."

"But Dad, I haven't ten cents to spare. The truth is, I spent almost every bit of my allowance today over at Corbin."

"NO!" said Mr. Parker firmly. "NO!"

"No what?"

"Not a penny will you get ahead of time."

"You misjudge me, Dad. I had no intention of even mentioning such a painful subject."

They drove in silence for a few blocks and then Penny indicated the gasoline gauge on the dashboard.

"Why, it's nearly empty!" she exclaimed. "We won't have enough to reach home!"

"Well, get some," said Mr. Parker automatically. "We don't want to stall on the street."

A flip of the steering wheel brought the car to a standstill in front of a gasoline pump.

"Fill it up," ordered Penny.

While Mr. Parker read his newspaper, the attendant polished the windshield and checked the oil, finding it low. At a nod from Penny he added two quarts.

"That will be exactly two fifty-eight."

Penny repeated the figure in a louder tone, giving her father a nudge. "Wake up, Dad. Two fifty-eight."

Absently, Mr. Parker reached for his wallet. Not until the attendant brought the change did it dawn upon him that Penny had scored once more.

"Tricked again," he groaned.

"Why, it was your own suggestion that we stop for gasoline," Penny reminded him. "I shouldn't have minded taking a chance myself. You see, the gauge is usually at least a gallon off."

"Anyway, I would rather pay for it than have you siphon it out of my car."

"Thanks for the present," laughed Penny.

CHAPTER 17 - A SEARCH FOR JERRY

Dinner was waiting by the time they reached home. Afterwards, Penny helped Mrs. Weems with the dishes while her father mowed the lawn. Hearing the telephone ring he came to the kitchen door.

"Was that a call for me?" he asked.

"No, Dad, it was for Mrs. Weems."

"Strange DeWitt doesn't call," Mr. Parker said. "I believe I'll telephone him."

After Mrs. Weems had finished with the phone he called the newspaper office only to be told that Jerry Livingston had not put in an appearance.

"At least he might have communicated with the office," Mr. Parker said as he hung up the receiver.

He went back to lawn mowing but paused now and then to stare moodily toward the Kobalt river which wound through the valley far below the terrace. Penny finished drying the dishes and went outside to join him.

"You're worried about Jerry, aren't you?" she asked after a moment.

"Not exactly," he replied. "But he should have been back long ago."

"He never would have stayed away without good reason. We both know Jerry isn't like that."

"No, he's either run into a big story, or he's in trouble. When I sent him away this morning, I didn't look upon the assignment as a particularly dangerous one."

"And yet if he met those two seamen anything could have happened. They were tough customers, Dad."

"I could notify the police if Jerry isn't back within an hour or two," Mr. Parker said slowly. "Still, I hate to do it."

"Where did Jerry rent his boat, Dad?"

"I told him to get one at Griffith's dock at twenty-third street."

"Then why don't we go there?" suggested Penny. "If he hasn't come in we might rent a boat of our own and start a search."

Mr. Parker debated and then nodded. "Bring a heavy coat," he told her. "It may be cold on the river."

Penny ran into the house after the garments and also took a flashlight from her father's bureau drawer. When she hurried outdoors again her father had backed his own car from the garage and was waiting.

At the twenty-third street dock, Harry Griffith, owner of the boat house, answered their questions frankly. Yes, he told them, Jerry Livingston had rented a motor boat early that morning but had not returned it.

"I been worryin' about that young feller," he admitted, and then with a quick change of tone: "Say, you're not Mr. Parker, are you?"

"Yes, that's my name."

"Then I got a letter here for you. I reckon maybe it explains what became of the young feller."

The boatman took a greasy envelope from his trousers pocket and gave it to the editor.

"Where did you get this, Mr. Griffith?"

"A boy in a rowboat brought it up the river about two hours ago. He said the young feller gave him a dollar to deliver it to a Mr. Parker. But the kid was mixed up on the address, so I just held it here."

"Dad, it must be from Jerry," said Penny eagerly.

As her father opened the envelope, she held the flashlight close. In an almost illegible scrawl Jerry had written:

"Following up a hot tip. Think I've struck trail of key men. Taking off in boat. Expect to get back by nightfall unless Old Man Trouble catches up with me."

Mr. Parker looked up from the message, his gaze meeting the frightened eyes of his daughter.

"Oh, Dad," she said in a tone barely above a whisper, "it's long after dark now. What do you think has become of Jerry?"

CHAPTER 18 - OVER THE DRAWBRIDGE

Wasting no moments in useless conversation, Mr. Parker rented a fast motor boat and prevailed upon Harry Griffith to operate it for him. Guided by the stars and a half moon which was slowly rising over the treetops, the party swung down the river.

Riding with the current, they came before long to the locality where Penny and Jerry had first sighted the two seamen's cruiser. But now there was no sign of a boat, either large or small.

At a speed which enabled the occupants to scrutinize the shoreline, the searching craft swept on. The river had never seemed more deserted.

"Jerry might have stopped anywhere along here," Mr. Parker observed. "If he drew the boat into the bushes we haven't a chance of finding him."

They went on, coming presently to the Kippenberg estate. As they passed beneath the open drawbridge Penny noted how low it had been swung over the water. A boat with a high cabin could not possibly go through when the cantilevers were down.

Gazing upward, she saw a swinging red light at the entrance to the bridge. A lantern, no doubt, hung there to give warning to any motorist who might venture upon the private road.

"Thorny probably isn't on duty at this hour," Penny reflected. "But I should think an open drawbridge might prove more dangerous at night than in the daytime."

As the bridge was lost to view beyond a bend in the river, she gave all her attention to watching the coves and inlets. Her father sat hunched over in the seat beside her, slapping at mosquitoes. Now and then he would switch on the flashlight to look at his watch.

Gradually the river had widened, so that it was possible to cover only one shore.

"We'll search the other side on our return trip," Mr. Parker said. "But it looks to me as if we're not going to have any luck."

As if to add to the discouragement of the party, dark clouds began to edge across the sky. One by one the stars were inked out. Penny's light coat offered scant protection from the cold wind.

And then, Harry Griffith throttled down the motor and spun the wheel sharply to starboard. He leaned forward, trying to pierce the black void ahead of the boat's bright beam.

"Looks like something over there," he said pointing. "Might be a log. No, it's a boat."

"I can't see anyone in it!" Penny cried. "It's drifting with the current."

"That looks like one of my boats, sure as you're born," Griffith declared, idling the engine. "The same I rented the young feller this morning."

"But where is Jerry?" cried Penny.

Griffith maneuvered his own boat close to the one which drifted with the current. Mr. Parker was able to reach out and grasp the long rope dangling in the water.

"The flashlight, Penny!" he commanded.

She turned the beam on, and as it focused upon the floor of the boat, drew in her breath sharply. On the bottom, face downward, lay a man.

"It's Jerry!" Penny cried. "Oh, Dad, he's—"

"Steady," said her father. "Steady."

While Griffith held the two boats together, he stepped aboard the smaller one. He bent over the crumpled figure, feeling Jerry's pulse, gently turning him upon his back.

"Is he alive, Dad?"

CHAPTER 18 - OVER THE DRAWBRIDGE

"His pulse is weak, but I can feel it. Yes, he's breathing! Hold that light steady, Penny."

"Dad, there's blood on his head! I—I can see it trickling down."

"He's been struck with a club or some blunt object," Mr. Parker said grimly. "He may have a fractured skull."

"Oh, Dad!"

"Keep a grip on yourself," her father ordered sternly, "It may not be as bad as I think, but we'll have to rush him to the nearest doctor."

"If it was me, I wouldn't try to move him out of there," advised Harry Griffith. "Leave him where he is. I'll get aboard and we'll take this boat in tow."

Penny helped the man make their craft fast to the other boat, and then they both climbed aboard. Griffith started the engine and turned around in the river.

"I'll head for Covert," he said. "That's about the closest place. There ought to be a good doctor in a town that size."

While Griffith handled the boat, Penny and her father did what they could to make Jerry comfortable. They stripped off their coats, using one for a pillow, and the other to cover his body.

"Those two men he was sent to follow must be responsible for this!" Penny murmured. "How could they do such a brutal thing?"

"I'll notify the police as soon as we touch shore," her father said grimly. "We'll search every cove and inlet until we find the ones responsible!"

As he spoke Mr. Parker bent lower to examine the wound on Jerry's head. Blood had nearly stopped flowing and he was hopeful that it came from a flesh wound. He pressed a clean handkerchief against it and the young man stirred.

"How long do you suppose he's been like this, Dad?"

"Hard to tell. An hour, maybe two hours."

Presently, as the boat made full speed up the river, Jerry stirred once more. His lips moved but the words were indistinguishable.

"How far to Covert?" Mr. Parker asked anxiously.

"About four miles from this point," Griffith flung over his shoulder. "It's the next town above the Kippenberg estate. I'm making the best time I can."

Jerry moved restlessly, his hands plucking at the coat which covered him.

"Flaming eyes," he muttered. "Looking at me—looking at me—"

Penny and her father gazed at each other in startled dismay.

"He's completely out of his head," whispered Penny.

"He's gone back to that other accident which happened last year," nodded Mr. Parker. "The Vanishing Houseboat affair."

"Jerry's had more than his share of bad luck, Dad. Twice now on this same river, he's met with disaster. And this time he may not come through."

"I think he will if his skull hasn't been fractured," Mr. Parker told her encouragingly. "Listen!"

Jerry's lips were moving again, and this time his words were more rational.

"Got to get word to the Chief," they heard him mutter. "Got to get word—"

A long while after that Jerry remained perfectly quiet. Suddenly arousing, his eyes opened wide and he struggled to sit up. Mr. Parker gently pressed him back.

"Where am I?" Jerry muttered. "Let me out of here! Let me out!"

"Quiet, Jerry," soothed Mr. Parker. "You're with friends."

The reporter's tense grip on the editor's hand relaxed. "That you, Chief?"

"Yes, Jerry. Just lie quiet. We'll have you to a doctor in a few more minutes."

"Doctor! I don't need any doctor," he protested, trying once more to sit up. "What happened anyway?"

"That's what we would like to know."

"Can't you remember anything, Jerry?" Penny asked. "You went out on the river to try to trace those two men in the cruiser."

"Oh, it's coming back to me now. I ran into their boat down by Cranberry Cove. They tied up there."

"And then what happened?" Penny demanded, as Jerry paused.

"I saw 'em walk ashore. Thought I would follow so I tied up my boat, too. They started off through the trees. Pretty soon they met a third man, a well dressed fellow, educated too."

"Did you hear any of their conversation?" Mr. Parker questioned.

"I heard Kippenberg's name mentioned. That caught my interest so I crept closer. Must have given myself away because that's about the last I remember. A ton of dynamite seemed to explode in my head. And here I am."

"Obviously, you were struck from behind with some heavy object," Mr. Parker said. "They probably dumped you back in your own boat and set it adrift. You never saw your attacker?"

"No."

Jerry rested for a moment, and then as it dawned upon him that he was being speeded to a doctor, he began to protest.

"Say, Chief, I'll be all right. I don't need any doc. Head's clear as a bell now."

"That's fine, Jerry. But you'll see a doctor anyway and have X-rays. We're taking no chances."

"Then at least let me go back to Riverview," Jerry grumbled. "I don't want to be stuck in any hick town hospital."

"If you feel equal to the trip, I guess we can grant you that much. You seem to be all right, but I want to make sure. Can't take chances on the paper being sued later on, you know."

"Oh, I get the idea," said Jerry with a grimace. "Thinking of the old cash register, as usual."

Penny drew a deep sigh of relief. If Jerry were able to make jokes he couldn't be seriously injured. She still felt weak from the fright she had received.

"The police will find those men who attacked you," she told him. "I hope they're put in prison for life, too!"

"The police?" Jerry repeated. He stared up into Mr. Parker's face. "Say, Chief, you're not aiming to spill the story, are you?"

"I was."

"But see here, if you notify the police, we'll show our hand to the rival paper. If we keep this dark we could do our own investigating, and maybe land a big scoop."

"Justice is more important than a scoop, Jerry," returned Mr. Parker. "If those men had anything to do with Atherwald's disappearance, and it looks as if they did, then we are duty bound to hand our clues over to the police. By trying to handle it alone, we might let them escape."

"Guess maybe you're right at that," Jerry acknowledged.

As she saw that the reporter was rapidly recovering strength, Penny left him to the care of her father and went forward to speak with Harry Griffith.

"Where are we now?" she inquired.

"Just comin' to the Kippenberg estate," he told her.

"Only that far? We don't seem to be making very fast time."

"We're buckin' the current, Miss. And there's a right stiff wind blowing."

She had not noticed the wind before or how overcast the sky had become. One could not see many yards in advance of the boat.

Ahead loomed the drawbridge in open position as usual. But Penny could not see the red lantern which she had noticed upon the trip down. Had the light been blown out by the wind?

In any case, it would not greatly matter, she reflected. Few cars traveled the private road. And any person who came that way would likely know about the bridge.

And then, above the steady hum of the motor boat engine, Penny heard another roar which steadily increased in intensity. A car was coming down the road at great speed!

"The lantern must be there," Penny thought. "It's probably hidden by a tree or the high bank. Of course it's there."

She listened with a growing tension. The car was not slowing down. Even Harry Griffith turned his head to gaze toward the entrance ramp of the drawbridge.

It was all over in an instant. A scream of brakes, a loud splintering of the wooden barrier. The speeding automobile struck the side of the steel bridge, spun sideways and careened down the bank to bury itself in the water.

CHAPTER 19 - A DARING RESCUE

Those in the motor boat who had witnessed the disaster were too horrified to speak. They could see the top of the car rising above the water into which it had fallen, but there was no sign of the unfortunate driver or other possible occupants.

Penny began to kick off her shoes.

"No!" shouted her father, divining her purpose. "No! It's too dangerous!"

Penny did not heed for she knew that if the persons in the car were to be saved it must be by her efforts. Her father could not swim well and Harry Griffith was needed at the wheel of the motor boat.

Scrambling to the gunwale, the girl dived into the water. She could see nothing. Groping her way to the overturned coupe, she grasped a door handle and turned it. All her strength was required to pull the door open. Her breath was growing short now. She worked faster, with frantic haste.

A hand clutched her own. Before she could protect herself she felt the man upon her, clawing, fighting, trying to climb her shoulders, upward to the blessed air.

His grasp was loose. Penny ducked out of it but held fast to his hand. She braced her feet against the body of the car and pushed. They both shot upward to the surface.

Griffith and her father lifted the man out of the water into the motor boat.

"Have to go down again," Penny gasped. "There may be others."

She dived once more, doubling herself into a tight ball, and giving a quick, upthrust of her feet which sent her straight to the bottom. She swam into the car and groped about on the seat and floor. Finding no bodies, she quickly shot to the surface again. Her father pulled her over the side, saying curtly: "Good work, Penny."

The victim she had saved seemed little the worse for his ducking. With Griffith's help he had divested himself of his heavy coat and was wringing it out.

Penny had obtained no clear view of the man, nor did she ever, for just at that moment, Jerry raised himself to a sitting position. He stared at the bedraggled one and pointed an accusing finger.

"That's the fellow!" he cried in an excited voice. "The one I was telling you about—"

The man took one look at Jerry and gazed quickly about. By this time the motor boat had drifted close to shore. Before anyone could make a move to stop him, the man hurled himself overboard. He landed on his feet in shallow water. Splashing through to the shore, he scuttled up the steep bank and disappeared in the darkness.

"Don't let him get away!" shouted Jerry. "He's the same fellow I saw in the woods!"

"You're certain?" asked Mr. Parker doubtfully.

"Of course! If you think I'm out of my head now, you're the one who's crazy! It's the same fellow! Oh, if I could get out of this boat!"

Griffith brought the craft to shore. "I'll see if I can overtake him," he said, "but he's probably deep in the woods by this time."

The boatman was a heavy-set man, slow on his feet. Penny and her father were not surprised when he came back twenty minutes later to report he had been unable to pick up the trail.

"The overturned car may offer a clue to his identity," Mr. Parker said, as they started up the river once more. "The police will be able to check the license plates."

"I wonder what the man was doing at the estate?" Penny mused.

She groped her way toward the cabin, thinking that she would divest herself of some of her wet garments. Suddenly she stopped short.

"Dad, that fellow took off his coat!" she exclaimed. "He must have left it behind!"

"It's somewhere on the floor," Harry Griffith called to her.

Penny found the sodden garment lying almost at her feet. She straightened it out and searched the pockets. Her father moved over to her side.

"Any clues?" he asked.

Penny took out a water-soaked handkerchief, a key ring and a plain white envelope.

"That may be something!" exclaimed Mr. Parker. "Handle it carefully so it doesn't tear."

They carried the articles into the cabin. Mr. Parker turned on the light and took the envelope from his daughter's hand. They were both elated to see that another paper was contained inside.

Mr. Parker tore off the envelope and flattened the letter on the table beneath the light. The ink had blurred but nearly all of the words could still be made out. There was no heading, merely the initials: "J. J. K."

"Could that mean James Kippenberg?" Penny asked.

The message was brief. Mr. Parker read it aloud.

"Better come through or your fate will be the same as Atherwald's. We give you twenty-four hours to think it over."

"How strange!" Penny exclaimed. "That man I pulled out of the water couldn't have been James Kippenberg!"

"Not likely, Penny. My guess would be that he had been sent here to deliver this warning note. Being unfamiliar with the road, and not knowing about the dangerous drawbridge, he crashed through."

"But James Kippenberg isn't supposed to be at the estate," Penny argued. "It doesn't make sense at all."

"This much is clear, Penny. Jerry saw the man talking with the two seamen, and they all appear to be mixed up in Grant Atherwald's disappearance. We'll print what we've learned, and let the police figure out the rest."

"Dad, this story is developing into something big, isn't it?"

He nodded as he moved a swinging light bulb slowly over the paper, hastening the drying process.

"After the next issue of the *Star* is printed, every paper in the state will send their men here. But we're out ahead, and when the big break comes, we may get that first, too."

"Oh, Dad, if only we can!"

"Count yourself out of the case from now on, young lady," he said severely. "You scared the wits out of me tonight, risking your life to save that no-good. Now shed those wet clothes before you come down with pneumonia."

He tossed her an overcoat, a sweater and a crumpled pair of slacks which Griffith had found under one of the boat seats. Leaving the cabin, he closed the door behind him.

Penny did not change her clothes at once. Instead, she sat down at the table, studying the warning message.

"'Better come through,'" she read aloud. "Does that mean Kippenberg is supposed to pay money? And what fate did Atherwald meet?"

CHAPTER 20 - AN IMPORTANT INTERVIEW

Those same questions were pounding through Penny's mind the next morning when she read the first edition of her father's paper. Propped up in bed with pillows, she perused the story as she nibbled at the buttered muffins on her breakfast tray.

"Is there anything else you would like?" Mrs. Weems inquired, hovering near.

"No, I'm quite all right," smiled Penny. "Not even a head cold after my ducking. Have you heard about Jerry?"

"Your father said he was doing fine."

"Did he leave any message for me before going to the office?"

"He said he thought you should stay in bed all day."

"Dad would," Penny pouted. "Well, I feel just fine. I'm getting up right away." She heaved aside the bed clothes.

Then, because she couldn't get the Kippenberg case out of her head, she dressed quickly and went downstairs. She was going out the front door when Mrs. Weems stopped her.

"Now where are you going, Penny?"

Penny's bright eyes twinkled and she flashed the housekeeper an arch, provocative smile.

"Not sure just where I'm going," she replied, her smooth forehead creasing with thought. "But if Dad should get curious, you can tell him he shouldn't be surprised if he finds me visiting with the Kippenbergs."

"Penny! You're not going there again?"

"Why not? I'm after a story for the *Riverview Star* and I mean to get it. See you later."

With a wave of her hand Penny walked jauntily off. A few moments later Mrs. Weems heard the clatter of Penny's Leaping Lena careening down the street in the direction of Corbin. First, however, she called for her chum, Louise, who was eager to accompany her on the long ride.

"I won't be able to stay long, Penny," said Louise. "Mother wants me to go shopping with her later this afternoon."

"That's all right," responded Penny as the old car bolted along the road. "If I get delayed, you can take Leaping Lena back home, and I'll follow later on."

With both girls keeping up a steady run of conversation they soon reached their destination.

Penny wondered if she would be able to enter the Kippenberg estate without being challenged by the bridgeman or a servant. Her anxiety increased upon approaching the river, for she saw that a large group of persons had gathered by the drawbridge.

No one paid the slightest attention to the two girls as they abandoned the car and proceeded to the water's edge. Penny was pleased to find the youthful boatman at his usual haunt on the river. He rowed the girls across to the estate, promising to await their return.

Penny escorted Louise through the trees to the Kippenberg house. Boldly she rang the doorbell which was answered by a butler.

"I should like to speak with Mrs. Kippenberg," she requested.

"Madam will see no one," began the man.

Footsteps sounded behind him in the hallway and Mrs. Kippenberg stood in the door.

"So it is you?" she asked in an icy voice. "Julius, see that this person is ejected from the grounds."

"One moment please," interposed Penny. "If I leave now, I warn you that certain facts will be published in the *Star*, facts which will add to your embarrassment."

"You can print nothing which will humiliate us further."

"No? You might like to have me mention the alligator in your lily pool. And the reason why you and your daughter are so anxious to be rid of it before the police ask questions."

Mrs. Kippenberg's plump face flushed a deep red. But for once she managed to keep her temper.

"What do you wish of me?" she asked frigidly.

"First, tell me about that painting, 'The Drawbridge' which was presented to your daughter as a wedding gift. Was it not given to her by your husband?"

"I shall not answer your question."

"Then you prefer that I print my own conclusions?"

"You are an impudent, prying young woman!" Mrs. Kippenberg stormed. "What if the picture was given to Sylvia by her father! Is that any crime?"

"Certainly not," said Penny soothingly. "It merely proves that you both know the whereabouts of Mr. Kippenberg."

"Perhaps I do. But I'll tell you nothing, absolutely nothing!"

"I have a few questions to ask about your new gardener," Penny went on, unmoved. "For instance, why does he wear a wig?"

The door slammed in her face.

"That certainly was a very cold reception," remarked Louise as the girls walked away, the sound of the slamming door still ringing in their ears.

Penny shrugged her shoulders and smiled. "That's nothing. When you're a reporter you have to expect those things." She looked about the deserted estate. "Well, I think I'll do some more sleuthing in the vicinity of the pool."

Louise looked at her wristwatch. "Goodness, it's getting late," she stated. "I'd like to stay, Penny, but I think I'd better be getting home to meet Mother."

"Go ahead," said Penny. "You take Leaping Lena. The boy in the boat will row you across."

"But how will you get home, then?"

"Don't worry about me. I'll find a way. You just go on. I only hope the old bus holds up all the way home."

Louise laughed and then the two girls walked to the boat dock. In a few moments the boy in the rowboat appeared and took Louise across. Afterward, Penny turned back through the trees and went on to the forbidden part of the estate.

She spent a long time about the pool, examining the earth all about it, but she failed to learn anything new. Finally, she retraced her steps to the river. She expected to find the boy waiting for her, but he had disappeared. She walked through the trees to the boat dock and stood there until the old watchman on the other side observed her predicament.

He obligingly lowered the drawbridge and she crossed the river, pausing at the gear house to chat with him.

Penny listened without comment to his story of the automobile accident. Thorny had his own version of how it had occurred and she did not correct any of the details.

"I wish I had a way to get into Corbin," she remarked when he had finished his lengthy account.

"If you walk down to the main road you kin catch the county bus," he told her. "It runs every hour."

A long hike along a dusty highway, an equally tedious wait at a crossroad, and finally Penny arrived in Corbin. She went directly to the Colonial Hotel, placing a telephone call to her father's office.

"What are you doing in Corbin, Penny?" her father demanded as he recognized her voice.

Penny answered him eagerly. "I've made an important discovery which may blow your case higher than a kite. No, I can't tell you anything over the telephone. The reason I am calling is that I may need help. Is Jerry still in the hospital?"

"He never was there," responded her father. "I couldn't make him go. He and Salt are out on the river looking for the men who cracked him over the head. I expect they'll call in any time now."

"If you do get in touch with Jerry, ask him to meet me at the Colonial Hotel," urged Penny. "I have a hunch the big story is about to break. In any event I'll need a ride home."

There was a great deal more to the conversation, with Mr. Parker delivering a long lecture upon the proper deportment for a daughter. Penny closed her ears, murmuring at regular intervals, "Yes, Dad," and finally went back to her post in the lobby.

CHAPTER 21 - THE WHITE CRUISER

For at least an hour she waited. She watched the clock until the hands pointed to six o'clock. Tantalizing odors came to her from the dining room, but she resolutely downed her hunger. She did not wish to give up her vigil even for a few minutes.

Finally Penny's patience was rewarded. She saw a man moving across the lobby toward the desk. He wore well-cut tailored clothes and a low-brimmed felt hat, yet the girl recognized him at a glance. He was the Kippenberg gardener.

The man paused at the desk and asked for a key.

"Good evening, Mr. Hammil," said the clerk, handing it over.

Penny had noted that the key was taken from a mailbox which bore the number, 381.

"So my friend, the gardener, has an alias," she mused. "Several of them, perhaps."

Another half hour elapsed while the girl waited patiently in her chair. Each time the elevator descended she watched the people alight. At exactly six forty-five Mr. Hammil stepped out of the lift, and without glancing toward the girl, dropped his key on the desk and went into the dining room.

The clerk, busy with several newcomers at the hotel, did not notice. Thinking that she saw her chance, Penny slipped from her chair, sidled toward the desk and picked up the key. Her heart pounded as she walked toward the elevator, but no one called to her. Her action had passed unobserved.

"Third floor," said Penny, and the elevator shot upward.

She located room 381 at the far end of the hall, and with a quick glance in both directions, unlocked the door and entered.

An open suitcase lay upon the luggage rack by the dresser. In systematic fashion Penny went through it, finding an assortment of interesting articles—a revolver, and two wigs, one of gray hair, the other black. There were no letters or papers, nothing to positively identify the owner of the luggage. But in the very bottom of the case Penny came upon a photograph. It was a picture of Sylvia Kippenberg.

Penny slipped the picture into the front of her dress, hastily replaced everything as she had found it, relocked the door, and returned to the lobby. As she went toward the desk intending to rid herself of the key, she stopped short.

Jerry Livingston stood there talking earnestly with the clerk.

"But I was told to come here," she heard him protest.

"There was a girl in the lobby a few minutes ago," the clerk replied. "She went off somewhere."

"No, here I am, Jerry!" Penny cried.

The reporter turned around and his face lighted up.

"Come outside, Jerry," Penny said before he could speak. "I have a great deal to tell you."

"And I have some news of my own," returned the reporter.

They left the hotel together. Once beyond hearing, Penny made a complete report of her afternoon adventure, and showed Jerry the picture of Sylvia Kippenberg which she had taken from room 381.

"Now for my story," said Jerry. "I've located a place not far from here where those two seamen buy supplies. The owner of the store told me they tie their boat up there nearly every night."

"Where is Salt now, Jerry?"

"He's keeping watch at the place. I came into town to telephone the *Star* office. Your father said I was to stop here and take you in tow."

"You're not starting back to Riverview?" Penny asked in dismay.

"I don't want to, Penny. I have a feeling our big story is just about ready to break!"

"So have I, Jerry. Let's stay with it. I'll explain to Dad when we get home."

"Then let's be on our way," the reporter said crisply. "No telling what has developed while I've been in town."

In the press car, the couple took the river road which led east from the Kippenberg estate. As they bounced along, making all possible speed, Jerry told Penny how he and Salt had traced the two seamen. They had made inquiry all along the river, and quite by chance had encountered a fisherman who had given them a valuable tip.

"But so many rumors are false, Jerry," Penny said.

"This tip was straight. Salt and I found the white cruiser tied up at the dock not far from this store I was telling you about. We've been watching it for the past two hours, and Salt is still there."

"Why didn't you call the police?"

"Wouldn't have done any good. The men we're after haven't been there all day. The only person on board is a girl."

"A girl?"

"Well, maybe you would say a young woman. About twenty-two, I'd guess."

"Jerry, you must be watching the wrong boat."

Jerry shook his head as he drove the car into the bushes at the side of the road. "It's the right one, I'm sure of it. Well, we're here."

Penny was hard pressed to keep up as the reporter led her through the trees down to the winding Kobalt river. They found Salt in his hiding place, behind a large boulder.

"Anything happen since I left?" Jerry demanded.

Salt scarcely noticed Penny's presence save to give her a quick nod of welcome.

"You got back just in time," he replied to the question. "The girl went away a minute ago. Took a basket and started for the store."

"Then why are we waiting?" asked Jerry. "Come on, we'll take a look inside that boat."

"Someone ought to stay here and keep watch," Salt returned. "She may come back any minute."

"You're elected guard then. Penny and I will look the boat over and see what we can find. If the girl starts back, whistle."

Darting across the muddy shore, Penny and Jerry reached the dilapidated boat which had been tied up at the end of a sagging dock. They jumped aboard and after a hasty glance over the deck, dived down into the cabin.

The room was dirty and in great disorder. Boots lay on the floor, discarded garments were scattered about, and a musty odor prevailed.

"Nothing here," said Jerry.

"Let's look around carefully," insisted Penny. "We may find something."

Crossing the cabin she opened a closet door. Save for a pair of oilskins which hung from a nail, it was quite empty.

"Listen!" commanded Penny suddenly.

Jerry stood absolutely still, straining to hear. A long, low whistle reached his ears.

"The warning signal!" he exclaimed. "Come on, Penny, we're getting out of here."

CHAPTER 22 - TRAPPED IN THE CABIN

Penny opened the door of the cabin only to close it quickly. She and Jerry both had heard men's voices very close to the boat.

"It's too late," she whispered. "Those men have come back."

"Not the girl?"

"No, they're alone. But we're in a trap. What shall we do?"

"We could make a dash for it. If we have to fight our way out, Salt will be there to help."

"Let's stick and see what happens, Jerry. We're after information. We must expect to take a chance in order to get it."

Jerry had been thinking more of Penny's safety than his own. But thus urged, he turned the key in the lock, bolting the door from the inside.

A low rumble of voices reached the couple as they stood with ears pressed against the panel. But they were unable to distinguish words. Then presently, one of the seamen moved close to the companionway.

"I'll get it, Jake," he called. "It's down in the cabin."

Jerry and Penny kept quiet as the man turned the door knob. He heaved angrily against the panel with his shoulder.

"Hey, Jake," he shouted, "what's the idea of locking the door?"

"I didn't lock it."

"Then Flora did." Muttering under his breath, the seaman tramped back up on deck.

Perhaps ten minutes elapsed before Penny and Jerry heard a feminine voice speaking.

"That must be Flora," whispered Penny. "What will happen when she tells them that she didn't lock the door?"

The voices above rose louder and louder until the two prisoners were able to distinguish some of the words. Jake berated the girl as stupid while his companion showered abuse upon her until she broke down and wept.

"I never had the key," they heard her wail. "I don't know what became of it. You always blame me for everything that goes wrong, and I'm good and sick of it. If I don't get better treatment I may tell a few things to the police. How would you like that?"

Jerry and Penny did not hear the response, but they recoiled as a loud crashing sound told them the girl had been given a cruel push into a solid object. Her cry of pain was drowned out by another noise, the sudden clatter of the motor boat engine.

Penny and Jerry gazed at each other with startled eyes.

"We're moving," she whispered.

Jerry started to fit the key into the door lock, only to have Penny arrest his hand.

"Let's stay and see it through," she urged. "This is our chance to learn the hide-out and perhaps solve the mystery of Atherwald's disappearance."

"All right," the reporter agreed. "But I wish you weren't in on this."

From the tiny window of the cabin, he and Penny observed various landmarks as the boat proceeded downstream. Perhaps half an hour elapsed before the cruiser came to the mouth of a narrow river which emptied into the Kobalt. From that point on progress became slow and often the boat was so close to shore that Penny could have reached out and touched overhanging bushes.

"I didn't know this stream was deep enough for a motor boat," Jerry whispered. "We must be heading for a hide-out deep in the swamp."

"I hope Salt has sense enough to call Dad and the police," Penny said with the first show of nervousness. "We're going to be a long way from help."

The boat crept on for perhaps a mile. Then it stopped, and Penny assumed they had reached their destination. Gazing out of the window again, she saw why they were halted. A great tree with finger-like branches had fallen across the river, blocking the way.

"Look, Jerry," she whispered. "We'll not be able to go any farther."

"Guess again," the reporter muttered.

Penny saw then that one of the men had left the boat and was walking along shore. He seemed not in the least disturbed by the great tree and for the first time it dawned upon her that it served a definite purpose.

"Lift 'er up, Gus," called the man at the wheel of the boat.

His companion disappeared into the bushes. Several minutes elapsed and then Penny heard a creaking sound as if ropes were moving on a pulley.

"The tree!" whispered Jerry, his eyes flashing. "It's lifting!"

Very slowly, an inch at a time, the great tree raised from the water, its huge roots serving as a hinge. When it was high enough, the motor boat passed beneath the dripping branches and waited on the other side.

Slowly, the tree was lowered into place once more.

"Clever, mighty clever," Jerry muttered. "Anyone searching for the hide-out would never think of looking beyond this fallen tree. To all purposes nature put it here."

"Nature probably did," Penny added. "But our dishonorable friends adapted it to their own use."

Through the window Penny saw the man called Gus reboard the boat.

Once more the cruiser went on up the narrow stream, making slow but steady progress. Long shadows had settled over the water. Soon it became dark.

Then a short distance ahead, Jerry and Penny observed a light. As the boat drifted up to a wharf, a man could be seen standing there with a glowing lantern. They were unable to see his face, and quickly dodged back from the cabin window to avoid being noticed.

"Everything all right, Aaron?" the man at the wheel asked, jumping ashore. He looped a coil of rope about one of the dock posts.

"Aaron!" whispered Penny, gripping Jerry's hand.

"It must be Aaron Dietz, Kippenberg's former business associate. So he's the ringleader in this business!"

They listened, trying to hear the man's reply to the question which had been asked.

"Yeah, everything's all right," he responded gruffly.

"You don't sound any too cheerful about it."

"Atherwald still won't talk. Keeps insisting he doesn't know where the gold is hidden. What bothers me, I am beginning to think we made a mistake. He may be telling the truth."

"Say, this is a fine time to be finding it out!"

"Oh, keep your shirt on, Gus. You and Jake will get your pay anyhow. And even if Atherwald doesn't know the hiding place we'll make Kippenberg come through."

"You'll have to find him first," the other retorted. "If you ask my opinion, you've made a mess of the whole affair."

"No one asked your opinion! We'll make Atherwald tell tonight or else—"

The man with the lantern started away from the dock but paused before he had taken many steps.

"Get those supplies up to the shack," he ordered. "Then I want to talk with you both."

"All right," was the reply, "but we have to get the cabin door open first. Flora locked it and lost the key."

"I didn't," the girl protested shrilly. "Don't you try to blame me."

Jerry and Penny knew that their situation now was a precarious one. If they were found in the cabin they would be taken prisoners and the exclusive story which they hoped to write never would be theirs.

"We've trapped ourselves in this cubby-hole," the reporter muttered. "All my doing, too."

"We can hide in the closet, Jerry. The men may not think to search there."

Noiselessly, they opened the door and slipped into the tiny room. The air was hot and stuffy, the space too narrow for comfort.

Jerry and Penny did not have long to wait before there came a loud crash against the cabin door. The two seamen were trying to break through the flimsy panel.

CHAPTER 22 - TRAPPED IN THE CABIN

"Bring a light, Flora," called one of the men.

Penny and Jerry flattened themselves against the closet wall, waiting.

A panel splintered on the outside cabin door, and a heavy tramping of feet told them that the men had entered the room.

"No one in here, Gus."

"It's just as we thought. Flora locked the door and lied out of it."

"I didn't! I didn't!" cried the girl. "Someone else must have done it while I was at the store. The door was unlocked when I went away."

"There's no one here now."

"I—I thought I heard voices while we were coming down the river."

"In this cabin?"

"Yes, just a low murmur."

"You imagined it," the man told her. "But I'll take a look in the closet to be sure."

He walked across the cabin toward the hiding place. Penny and Jerry braced themselves for the moment when the door would be flung open. They had trapped themselves and now faced almost certain capture.

CHAPTER 23 - AT THE HIDE-OUT

Before the man could pull open the closet door, a booming voice called impatiently from shore:

"Say, are you coming? We have plenty of work ahead of us tonight."

Distracted from his purpose, the searcher turned aside without glancing into the closet. With his companion and the girl, he left the cabin.

Penny and Jerry waited at least five minutes. When all was silent above, they stole from their hiding place. From the window they assured themselves that the wharf was deserted.

"What do we do now, start after the police?" Penny questioned.

"Let's make certain Atherwald is here first. We can't afford to be wrong."

A path led through the timber. As they followed it, Jerry and Penny saw a moving lantern some distance ahead. They kept it in sight until the three men and Flora disappeared into a cabin.

Stealing on through the darkness, Penny and Jerry crept to the screen door. Peering in, they saw a barren room containing a table, a cook stove and double-deck bunks.

"Get supper on, Flora," one of the men ordered curtly.

"Am I to cook anything for the prisoner?" she asked in a whining voice.

"Not unless he decides to talk. I'll find out if he's changed his mind."

The man who had been called Aaron crossed the cabin to an adjoining room. He unlocked the door which had been fastened with a padlock, and went inside.

"Atherwald must be in there," whispered Penny.

With one accord, she and Jerry tiptoed across the sagging porch and posted themselves under a high window. Glancing up they saw it contained no glass, but had narrow iron bars in keeping with a prison chamber.

Jerry lifted Penny up so that she could peep into the room. By the light of the oil lantern she saw a haggard young man sitting on the bed. Despite a stubble of beard and unkempt hair, she instantly recognized him as the missing bridegroom. She made another observation, one which shocked her. The man's wrists were handcuffed.

"It's Grant Atherwald," she told Jerry as he lowered her to the ground. "They've treated him shamefully."

Jerry held up his hand as a signal for silence. In the room above the men were speaking and he wished to hear every word.

"Well, Atherwald, have you changed your mind? How about a little supper tonight?"

"How can I tell you something I don't know?" the bridegroom retorted wearily. "Kippenberg never confided any of his secrets to me."

"You know where his gold is hidden!"

"I don't think he ever had any!"

"Oh, yes, he did. When the government passed a law that it was illegal to keep gold, Kippenberg decided to defy it. He had over half his fortune converted into gold which he expected to re-convert into currency at a great profit to himself. His plans went amiss when government men listed him for investigation."

"You seem to know all about his private affairs," Grant Atherwald said sarcastically. "Strange that you haven't learned the hiding place of the gold—if there ever was any!"

"It will do you no good to pretend, Atherwald! Either you tell the hiding place, or we'll bring your bride here to keep you company!"

"You wouldn't dare touch her, you fiend!"

CHAPTER 23 - AT THE HIDE-OUT

"No? Well, unless you decide to talk, she'll share your fate, and I promise you it won't be a pretty one. Now I'll leave you to think it over."

The door closed with a bang.

"We'll have to get the police here right away," Jerry advised Penny in a whisper. "No telling what those scoundrels may try to do to Atherwald. We haven't a moment to waste."

"It would take us hours to bring help here," reasoned Penny. "And if we try to use the motorboat the gang will be warned and flee while we're on our way down the river."

"That's so, but we have to do something. Any ideas?"

"Yes, I have one," Penny answered soberly. "It may sound pretty crazy. Still, I really believe it would work!"

Hurriedly, she outlined what she had in mind. Jerry listened incredulously, but as the girl explained and elaborated certain details of her plan, his doubts began to clear away.

"It's dangerous," he protested. "And if your hunch about the pool is wrong, we will be in a fix."

"Of course, but we'll have to take a chance in order to save Atherwald."

"If everything went exactly according to plan it might work!"

"Let's try it, Jerry. Lift me up so I can attract Atherwald's attention."

The reporter did as she requested. Penny tapped lightly on the iron bars with her signet ring. She saw Grant Atherwald start and turn his head. Penny repeated the signal.

The man arose from the bed and stumbled toward the window.

"Who is it?" he whispered hoarsely.

"A friend."

"Can you get me out of here?"

"We're going to try. You are handcuffed?"

"Yes, and my captor keeps the key in his pocket. The room outside is always guarded. Did you bring an implement to saw through the bars?"

"No, we have another scheme in mind. But you must do exactly as we tell you."

"Yes, yes!" the bridegroom whispered eagerly, his pale cheeks flooding with color.

"Listen closely," Penny instructed. "When your captor comes back tell him you have decided to talk."

"I know nothing about the cache of gold," the man protested.

"Tell your captor that the hiding place is on the Kippenberg estate."

"That would only involve Sylvia and Mrs. Kippenberg. I'll do nothing to get them into trouble."

"You'll have to obey instructions or no one can help you," Penny said severely. "Would you prefer that those cruel men carry out their threat? They'll spirit Sylvia away and try to force the truth from her."

"I'll do as you say."

"Then tell your captor that the gold is hidden in a specially constructed vault lying beneath the lily pool." Penny had resolved to act upon her hunch that there was a trapdoor on the bottom of the pool. Now as she issued instructions she wished that she might have found some way of examining the pool to see if she were right. However, she had to take a chance on there being a vault beneath the pool.

Atherwald protested mildly. "He would never believe such a fantastic story."

"It is not as fantastic as it sounds," replied Penny. "You must convince him that it is true."

"I will try."

"Make the men understand that to get the gold they must drain the pool and raise a trapdoor in the cement bottom. Ask to be taken with the men when they go there tonight and demand that you be given your freedom as soon as the gold is found."

"They will never let me go alive. An identification from me would send them all to prison for life."

"Do you know the men?"

"The ringleader is Aaron Dietz. At one time he was employed by Mr. Kippenberg."

"Just as I thought."

"The other two call themselves Gus and Jake. I don't know their last names. Then there is a girl who seems to be a sister to Gus."

"How did they get you here?"

"On the day of the wedding I was handed a note just as I reached the estate. It requested me to come at once to the garden. While I waited there, two ruffians sprang upon me from behind. Before I could cry out they dragged me to their boat at the river's edge. I was handcuffed, blindfolded and brought to this cabin."

The slamming of an outside door warned Penny that she was wasting precious time in talk.

"You understand your instructions?" she whispered hurriedly.

"Yes."

"Then goodbye. With luck we'll have you free in a few hours."

"With luck is right," Jerry muttered as Penny slid to the ground.

Aaron Dietz stood on the front porch staring out into the night. Seeing him there, Penny and Jerry circled widely before attempting to return to the river. Satisfied that they had not been observed, they boarded the boat and descended to the cabin.

For possibly an hour they sat in the dark, waiting anxiously.

"Looks as if my little plan didn't work," Penny remarked. "I might have known it would be too simple."

Jerry had risen to his feet. He went to the window and listened.

"Hear anything?" Penny whispered hopefully.

"Sounds like someone coming down the path. We ought to get into our cubby-hole."

They tiptoed to the closet and closed the door.

Within a few minutes they heard a confusion of voices and the shuffle of feet as men boarded the cruiser. Penny wondered if the group included Grant Atherwald and was greatly relieved when she heard him speak.

"I don't see why you think I would double-cross you," he said distinctly. "I am considering my own welfare. You promised that if the gold is found you'll give me my freedom."

"Sure, you'll get it. But if you're lying about the hiding place—"

The words were drowned out by the roar of the motor boat engine. Penny and Jerry felt the floor beneath them quiver and then gently roll. The cruiser was under way.

"We're heading for the Kippenberg estate!" Penny whispered. "Oh, everything is starting out beautifully!"

"I only hope it ends the same way," said Jerry morosely. "I only hope it does."

CHAPTER 24 - SECRET OF THE LILY POOL

The moon rode high in the heavens as the cabin cruiser let go its anchor in a cove off the Kippenberg estate. Penny who had been dozing for the past hour in her self-imposed prison started up in alarm as Jerry nudged her in the ribs.

"Wake up," he whispered. "We're here."

"At the estate?"

"I think so."

On the deck above their heads they could hear the men talking together.

"You'll come along with us, Atherwald," Aaron Dietz said. "Flora, you stay here and guard the boat. If you see anyone watching or acting suspiciously, blow the whistle two short blasts."

"I don't want to stay here alone," the girl whimpered. "I'm afraid."

"You'll do as I say," the man ordered harshly. "Get started, Gus. It's two o'clock now. We won't have many hours before daylight."

In making her plans Penny had not once considered that the men might leave a guard on the cruiser. With the girl posted as a lookout they were still prisoners in the cabin.

"We have to get out of here now or never," she whispered. "What shall we do about Flora?"

"We'll rush her and take a chance on the whistle."

They slipped out of their hiding place and crawled noiselessly up the steep stairway. Pausing there, they watched the shadowy figure of the girl in the bow of the boat. She was quite alone, for her companions had disappeared into the woods.

"Now!" commanded Jerry in a whisper.

With a quick rush he and Penny were across the deck. They approached Flora from behind and were upon her before she could turn her head. Jerry grasped her arms while Penny clapped a hand over her mouth to prevent a scream. Although the girl fought fiercely, she was no match for two persons.

Stripping off her sash, Penny gave it to Jerry to use as a gag. They bound the girl's wrists and ankles, then carried her down into the cabin.

"I hate to leave her like that," said Penny as they went back on deck.

"Don't waste your sympathy," replied Jerry. "She doesn't deserve it. Anyway, we'll soon set her free. We must bring the police now."

"The nearest house with a telephone is about a half mile away."

"It won't take us long to cover the distance," Jerry said, helping her down from the boat.

"You go alone," urged Penny. "I'll stay here and keep watch."

"I don't like to leave you."

"Go on." Penny gave him a little push. "And hurry!"

After Jerry had reluctantly left, she plunged into the trees, carefully picking her way along the path which led to the lily pool. A short distance brought her to the clearing. Halting, she saw the three men and Grant Atherwald silhouetted in the bright moonlight. The latter was still handcuffed, guarded by Aaron Dietz who allowed his companions to do the hard labor.

Gus and Jake had broken open the door of the stone tower. The soft purr of a motor told Penny that they had started draining the pool. She wondered what the men would do when they discovered that the tank contained a very live alligator.

"It ought to put a crimp in their work," she chuckled. "Mr. Kippenberg couldn't have chosen a more effective guard for his gold."

But gradually as the pool drained lower and lower, it struck Penny as odd that the men did not notice the alligator. Belatedly, it occurred to her that the Kippenberg gardener had probably succeeded in getting rid of the monster since her visit to the garden earlier in the day.

"Something like that *would* happen," she thought. "Oh, well, even so Jerry ought to get here with the police in ample time."

Only the waning of the moon gave indication of how swiftly the night was passing. Penny became alarmed as she observed how fast the pool emptied. Jerry would not have as long as she had anticipated. But surely, he would bring help before it was too late.

Presently, one of the men shut off the motor in the stone tower, saying with quiet jubilance:

"There, she's empty!"

He jumped down into the tank, and almost at once uttered a cry of discovery.

"Here it is, just as he said! The ring to the trap! Give us some help, Gus."

With Aaron Dietz and the bewildered bridegroom watching from above, the two men raised the heavy block of cement. Penny drew closer for she did not wish to miss anything. She stood in the shadow of a tree scarcely fifteen yards from where the men worked.

"A stairway leads down into an underground vault!" Jake cried exultantly. "We've found the hiding place of the gold."

"Toss me your flashlight, Aaron," called Gus. "We'll soon have all of the treasure out of here."

The next ten minutes brought a confused whirl of impressions. Penny's thoughts were in turmoil. Why didn't Jerry come with the police? As soon as the men carried the burden of gold to the boat they would discover Flora, bound and gagged. Then they would suspect that a trap had been laid. Oh, why didn't Jerry hurry?

Gus and Jake had descended into the underground vault. As the light reappeared, Penny was dumbfounded to see that the men were empty handed.

"Nothing down there," Gus reported in disgust. "Nothing!"

"Then we've been tricked!" Aaron Dietz turned furiously upon his prisoner. "You'll pay for this!"

"I thought the gold was here," answered Grant Atherwald.

"Lock him up in the vault and start the water running," advised Jake harshly. "It's a good way to be rid of him."

The suggestion appealed to Aaron Dietz. At a nod from him, Atherwald was seized and dragged down into the pool. He was shoved into the vault, but before the two men could lower the heavy cement block into place, a signal from Dietz arrested their action.

"Wait!"

In her anxiety over Grant Atherwald, Penny had moved closer to the pool. Without realizing that she was exposing herself, she stood so that her shadow fell clearly across the open space. Before she comprehended her danger, Dietz hurled himself upon her, seizing her roughly by the arms.

Penny struggled to free herself but could not. The man's grip was like steel.

"So you were spying!" he exclaimed harshly.

"I—I was just watching," Penny stammered. "Don't you remember me? I am the girl who pulled you out of the river when your car went over the drawbridge."

The man looked closely at her, and for an instant she dared hope that he would recall her with gratitude. But his face hardened again and he said unfeelingly:

"You know entirely too much, my little girl. This is one story you will never write for your father's paper. Your curiosity has proven your undoing. You share the fate of your very good friend."

With a sinking heart Penny realized by the man's words that he knew her to be the daughter of a newspaper publisher, and that he had guessed her part in the trick played upon him.

"Down you go!" Dietz said harshly.

As he dragged her toward the pool, Penny screamed at the top of her lungs. A hand was clapped over her mouth. She bit it savagely, but her efforts to free herself were of no avail.

The men shoved her headlong down the stone stairway into the pit.

"Now scream as much as you like," Aaron Dietz hurled after her. "No one will hear you."

CHAPTER 24 - SECRET OF THE LILY POOL

The heavy stone slab dropped into place.

Penny picked herself up from the steps. Terror gripped her, and with a sob she called frantically:

"Mr. Atherwald! Mr. Atherwald!"

"Here at the bottom of the steps," he answered with a groan.

"Are you hurt?"

"Only bruised. But my hands are still in cuffs."

Penny limped down the stairway and helped the man to his feet.

"We're done for now," he said. "No one will ever look for us down in this vault. And our cries will never be heard."

"Don't give up," Penny murmured encouragingly. "We may be able to lift the stone. Come let's try."

Mounting the stairs, they applied their shoulders to the massive door, but their best efforts did not raise it an inch.

"Listen!" cried Atherwald suddenly.

They both could hear the sound of water running into the empty pool.

"In an hour's time no one will ever guess that a hidden vault lies beneath the tank!" Atherwald groaned. "We're doomed!"

"If we can hear the water splashing above us, our voices might carry!" Penny reasoned. "Let's cry out for help. Now, together!"

They shouted over and over until their voices failed them. Then, completely discouraged, they sagged down on the stairway to rest.

"Nothing went as I planned," Penny said dismally. "I really thought the gold was hidden in this vault. If the men had found it, they would have spent hours removing the loot to their boat. Jerry would have come with the police and everything would have been all right."

Grant Atherwald was not listening to the girl's words. He struggled to his feet, pressing his ear against the trapdoor.

"The water has stopped running!"

"Are you sure?" Penny sprang up and stood beside him, listening.

"Yes, and I hear voices!"

With one accord, they shouted for help. Could it be imagination or did they hear an answering cry? As they repeated their frantic call, there was a scraping on the stone above their heads.

"Stand away," ordered a muffled voice.

Before Penny and the bridegroom could obey, the great door lifted. A deluge of water poured in, its force nearly washing them from the steps. But in another moment the passage was clear and they stumbled up through the rectangular opening.

Jerry grasped Penny's hand, helping her out of the vault. One of the blue-coated policemen aided Atherwald, unfastening the handcuffs which held him a prisoner.

"You're all right, Penny?" the reporter asked anxiously.

"I—I feel like a drowned rat," she laughed, shaking water out of her hair. Then, with a quick change of mood she asked: "Did you get Aaron Dietz and his men?"

"No," Jerry answered in disgust. "When we crossed the river five minutes ago, the cruiser was still there. No sign of anyone around. I brought the police here, and now I suppose they've made their get-away."

"Oh, Jerry, we can't let them escape! Send the police—"

"Now don't get worked up," the reporter soothed. "A squad started back just as soon as we found out what had happened here."

"Dietz and his men must have seen the police crossing the river," speculated Penny. "They may have hidden in the bushes, biding their time. By now they've slipped away in their boat."

"I'm afraid of it," Jerry admitted. "I traveled as fast as I could."

As one of the policemen lifted Penny out of the pool, a noise which sounded like the back-firing of an automobile, broke the stillness of the night. It was followed by a volley of similar sounds.

"Gunfire!" exclaimed Penny.

DANGER AT THE DRAWBRIDGE

The policemen started at a run through the woods toward the place where the white cruiser had last been seen. Penny hesitated, and then took the opposite direction, coming out of the woods at a point directly opposite the drawbridge.

Gazing far up the river she could see the white cruiser, flashes of fire coming from the cabin window as the desperadoes exchanged shots with the police, who were concealed in the woods.

"That boat will try to run for it in another minute," Penny thought. "If only the drawbridge were down!"

Kicking off her shoes, she dived into the water, swimming diagonally across the river to take advantage of the swift current. Her powerful strokes brought her to shallow water and she waded ashore through ankle-deep mud. As she scrambled up the slippery bank, her wet clothing plastered to her body, she heard the roar of the cruiser's motor.

"They've started the engine!" she thought. "In another minute the boat will be at the bridge. Hurry! Hurry!"

Penny could force herself to no greater effort. Breathless, she reached the gearhouse and groped frantically under the door. Had Thorny failed to hide the key there? No, her fingers seized upon it.

Trembling with excitement, she turned it in the lock. The door of the gearhouse swung open. Now could she remember how to lower the bridge? Any mistake would be costly, for by this time she could hear the cruiser racing down the river at full speed. If only it were light enough so that she could see the gears!

She pulled a lever and her heart leaped as the motor responded with a pleasant purr. The power was on!

"Now to lower the bridge!" thought Penny. "But which lever is the right one? I'm not sure."

With a prayer in her heart she grasped the one closest at hand and eased it forward. There was a grinding of gears as the tall cantilevers began to move. They were coming down, but oh, so slowly!

"Hurry! Hurry! Hurry!" Penny whispered, as if her words could speed the bridge on its journey.

The white cruiser drove onward at full speed. Lower came the bridge. Penny held her breath, knowing it would be a matter of inches whether or not the boat would clear. The man at the wheel, aware of the danger, did not swerve from his course.

The bridge settled into place. As the crash came, Penny closed her eyes.

"*I did it! I've stopped them!*" she thought, and sagged weakly against the gear house.

CHAPTER 25 - VICTORY FOR PENNY

Minutes later Penny was still leaning limply against the building when a car drove up to the bridge. Her father, Salt, and a bevy of policemen and government representatives sprang out and ran to her side.

"Penny, what happened?" Mr. Parker clasped his daughter in his arms. "You're soaking wet! Didn't we hear gunfire as we turned in here?"

Penny waved her hand weakly toward the river below.

"There's your story, Dad. Pictures galore. Boat smashes into dangerous drawbridge. Police pursue and shoot it out with desperadoes, taking what's left of 'em into custody. I'm afraid to look."

"And what were you doing while all this was going on?" demanded her father.

"Me? I was just waiting for the drawbridge to go down."

Mr. Parker, Salt, and the policemen he had brought to the scene, rushed to the edge of the bridge. A police boat had drawn up beside the badly listing cruiser, and three men prisoners and a girl were being taken off.

"How bad is it?" Penny called anxiously.

"All captured alive," answered her father. "Salt, get that camera of yours into action! Where's Jerry? He would be missing at a time like this! What happened anyhow? Can't someone tell me?"

Penny had fully recovered the power of speech, and with a most flattering audience, she recounted her adventures.

"Excuse me just a minute," she interrupted herself.

Turning her back, she pulled a sodden photograph from the front of her dress and handed it to her father.

"This picture is in pretty bad shape," she said, "but it's clue number one. You see, it's a photograph of Miss Kippenberg, and on the back is written, 'To Father, with all my love.' I found the picture this afternoon in Room 381 at the Colonial Hotel."

"Then you've located Kippenberg?" one of the G men demanded.

"I have. He's been masquerading as the Kippenberg gardener, coming back here no doubt to witness the marriage of his daughter."

"We'll arrest him right away," said the government man, turning to leave. "Thanks for the tip."

"I am confident Miss Kippenberg and her mother had nothing to do with Grant Atherwald's disappearance," Penny went on. "Aaron Dietz plotted the whole affair himself. I guess he must have learned about Kippenberg's cache of gold while he worked for the man. He believed that Grant Atherwald shared the secret and could tell where the money was hidden."

"You've located the gold, too, I suppose," Mr. Parker remarked whimsically.

"No, Dad, I slipped up there. I thought the gold was in a secret vault under the alligator pool, but I was wrong. I don't know where it is."

"We'll let the G men solve that mystery when they take Kippenberg into custody," replied her father. "Our work is cut out for us now. We'll find Jerry, talk with young Atherwald, and rout Miss Kippenberg and her mother out of bed for an exclusive interview."

"And this time I am sure they'll answer questions," declared Penny.

During the next hour the "story" was taken entirely from her hands. Jerry, her father and Salt, knew exactly how to gather every fact of interest to the readers of the *Star*. Sylvia Kippenberg, overjoyed to find her fiancé alive, posed for pictures with him, and answered all questions save those which concerned her father.

Not until a telephone call came from the Colonial Hotel, saying that Mr. Kippenberg had been taken into custody, would either Sylvia or her mother admit that the man had posed as the gardener.

"Very well, it is true," Mrs. Kippenberg acknowledged at last. "James has been trying to avoid government men for over a year. Wishing to return for Sylvia's wedding, he disguised himself as a gardener. Then after Grant's disappearance, he remained here trying to help."

"And it was your husband who managed to get rid of the alligator?" Penny interposed.

"Yes, we were afraid police might ask embarrassing questions. James disposed of it to a zoo late yesterday afternoon."

"And the cache of gold under the lily pool," said Mr. Parker. "What became of that?"

"There is no gold."

"None at all?"

"None."

"And there never was any?" questioned Penny incredulously. "Then why was the vault ever built?"

"Tell her the truth, Mother," Sylvia urged. "She deserves to know. Anyway, it can do Father no harm now."

"At one time my husband did have a considerable supply of gold," Mrs. Kippenberg admitted. "Since he could not trust a bank he constructed his own vault under the pool and placed the alligator there as a precaution against prying persons."

"My father really did nothing so very wrong," Sylvia broke in. "The gold was bought with his own money. If he chose to sell it later at a profit it was his own affair."

"Not in the opinion of the government," Mr. Parker said with a smile. "He held the gold illegally. So your father disposed of it?"

"Yes, he shipped it out of the country months ago. And no one will ever be able to prove anything against him."

"My husband is a very clever man," added Mrs. Kippenberg proudly.

"That remains to be seen," said Mr. Parker. "I know a number of very clever government men, too."

Later, in dry clothing loaned to her by Miss Kippenberg, Penny motored back to Corbin with her father, Jerry, and Salt. There they learned that the three prisoners had been locked up in jail, while James Kippenberg was being questioned by government operatives. He readily admitted that he had disguised himself as the gardener but defied anyone to prove he ever had disposed of illegal gold.

Mr. Parker did not wait to learn the outcome of the interview. Instead he telephoned the big story to DeWitt and arranged for complete coverage on every new angle of the case. Satisfied that no more could be learned that night, the party sped back toward Riverview.

"Aaron Dietz and his confederates ought to get long prison sentences," Penny remarked as they drove through the night. "But what will happen to Mr. Kippenberg, Dad? Do you think he will escape punishment as his wife believes?"

"He'll get what is coming to him," replied Mr. Parker. "A government man told me tonight that Kippenberg's income tax reports have been falsified. And Kippenberg knew they had evidence against him or he never would have gone into hiding. No, even if it can't be proven that he held gold illegally, he'll certainly be fined and given a year or so in prison for tax evasion."

"I hope he receives a light sentence for Sylvia's sake," said Penny. After a moment she added: "Sylvia and Grant Atherwald are going to be married tomorrow. They told me so."

"There's a fact we missed," declared Jerry. "Penny always is showing us up."

"Oh, I didn't prove myself so brilliant tonight," responded Penny. "When I was down in that vault I decided I was just plain dumb. If you hadn't had sense enough to guess where Grant Atherwald and I were being held—well, Dad would have had to adopt a new daughter."

"It was easy enough to tell what had happened," said Jerry. "You had told me you thought there was a secret vault beneath the pool. Then, too, I found your handkerchief floating in the bottom. The water had only been running in a few minutes." He fished in his pocket and brought out a pin which he handed to Penny. "I also found this."

"Thanks, Jerry," said Penny. "That's Louise's cameo pin. She dropped it the day we were on the Kippenberg estate together."

"The police gave you full credit for the capture of those men, Penny," said her father with pride. "You yanked the drawbridge just in time to trap them."

CHAPTER 25 - VICTORY FOR PENNY

"Salt did his share, too," mentioned Penny generously. "He went for the police just as soon as he realized Jerry and I had been carried away on the cruiser."

"The only trouble was that the cops wasted too much time searching for you down river," the photographer drawled. "We finally went back to Corbin and ran into Mr. Parker who suggested we come to the estate."

"How did you happen to be in Corbin, Dad?" asked Penny curiously.

"You might know—I was looking for you. Isn't that my usual occupation?"

"You're not provoked at me, Dad?"

"No, of course not," the publisher answered warmly. "You've all done fine work tonight. This is the biggest story we've run into in over a year! We'll score a beat on the rival papers."

"Then don't you think Jerry and Salt have earned a raise?" suggested Penny.

"Yes," agreed her father absently, "I'll take care of it tomorrow."

"And you might tack on another dollar to my allowance, Dad. I'll also have a small bill to present. There will be several dollars for gasoline, lunches going and coming from Corbin, two ruined dresses, a pair of torn silk stockings, and—"

"That's enough," broke in Mr. Parker with a laugh. "If you keep on listing your expenses, I'll be broke. You turned out to be an expensive reporter."

"It was worth it, wasn't it?" Penny demanded, placing her hands on her hips.

Her father agreed heartily. "It certainly was, Penny. The *Riverview Star* obtained a smashing story to scoop all the other newspapers, and I've got my elusive daughter back again safe and sound."

Penny moved closer to her father. She grasped the lapels of his coat in her slender fingers and tipped her weary but still lovely face toward him.

"Dad, will you promise me one thing?"

"That depends on what you are after," Mr. Parker told her gravely.

"Whenever the *Riverview Star* has a baffling mystery to be run down to earth, will you promise to call in your ace sleuth?"

"And who would that be?" demanded Mr. Parker with a puzzled frown. Then as Penny laughed gaily, he also started to grin. "So you are the ace sleuth? I guess I was a little slow in understanding. But you seem to be right. This is the third mystery you've solved. Maybe we will use you on the next mystery."

"Thanks, Dad," said Penny. "I just hope I won't have to wait too long for the next mystery to come along."

THE END

BEHIND THE GREEN DOOR

PENNY'S TRAILING BODY, ACTING AS A BRAKE, SLOWED DOWN THE SLED.

CHAPTER 1 - TROUBLE FOR MR. PARKER

"Watch me coming down the mountain, Mrs. Weems! This one is a honey! An open christiana turn with no brakes dragging!"

Penny Parker, clad in a new black and red snowsuit, twisted her agile young body sideways, causing the small rug upon which she stood to skip across the polished floor of the living room. She wriggled her slim hips again, and it slipped in the opposite direction toward Mrs. Weems who was watching from the kitchen doorway.

"Coming down the mountain, my eye!" exclaimed the housekeeper, laughing despite herself. "You'll be coming down on your head if you don't stop those antics. I declare, you've acted like a crazy person ever since your father rashly agreed to take you to Pine Top for the skiing."

"I have to break in my new suit and limber up my muscles somehow," said Penny defensively. "One can't practice outdoors when there's no snow. Now watch this one, Mrs. Weems. It's called a telemark."

"You'll reduce that rug to shreds before you're through," sighed the housekeeper. "Can't you think of anything else to do?"

"Yes," agreed Penny cheerfully, "but it wouldn't be half as much fun. How do you like my suit?" She darted across the room to preen before the full length mirror.

A red-billed cap pulled at a jaunty angle over her blond curls, Penny made a striking figure in the well tailored suit of dark wool. Her eyes sparkled with the joy of youth and it was easy for her to smile. She was an only child, the daughter of Anthony Parker, editor and publisher of the *Riverview Star*, and her mother had died when she was very young.

"It looks like a good, practical suit," conceded the housekeeper.

Penny made a wry face. "Is that the best you can say for it? Louise Sidell and I shopped all over Riverview to get the snappiest number out, and then you call it *practical*."

"Oh, you know you look cute in it," laughed Mrs. Weems. "So what's the use of telling you?"

Before Penny could reply the telephone rang and the housekeeper went to answer it. She returned to the living room a moment later to say that Penny's father was in need of free taxi service home from the office.

"Tell him I'll be down after him in two shakes of a kitten's tail!" Penny called, making for the stairway.

She took the steps two at a time and had climbed halfway out of the snowsuit by the time she reached the bedroom. A well aimed kick landed the garment on the bed, and then because it was very new and very choice she took time to straighten it out. Seizing a dress blindly from the closet, she wriggled into it and ran downstairs again.

"Some more skiing equipment may come while I'm gone," she shouted to Mrs. Weems who was in the kitchen. "I bought a new pair of skis, a couple of poles, three different kinds of wax and a pair of red mittens."

"Why didn't you order the store sent out and be done with it?" responded the housekeeper dryly.

Penny pulled on her heavy coat and hurried to the garage where two cars stood side by side. One was a shining black sedan of the latest model, the other, a battered, unwashed vehicle whose reputation was as discouraging as its appearance. "Leaping Lena," as Penny called her car, had an annoying habit of running up repair bills, and then repaying its long suffering owner by refusing to start on cold winter days.

"Lena, you get to stay in your cozy nest this time," Penny remarked, climbing into her father's sedan. "Dad can't stand your rattle and bounce."

The powerful engine started with a blast. While Mrs. Weems watched anxiously from the kitchen window, Penny shot the car out backwards, wheeling it around the curve of the driveway with speed and ease. She liked to handle her father's automobile, and since he did not enjoy driving, she frequently called at the newspaper office to take him home.

The *Star* building occupied a block in the downtown section of Riverview. Penny parked the car beside the loading dock at the rear, and took an elevator to the editorial rooms. Nearly all of the desks were deserted at this late hour of the afternoon. But Jerry Livingston, one of the best reporters on the paper, was still pecking out copy on a noisy typewriter.

"Hi, Penny!" he observed, grinning as she brushed past his desk. "Have you caught any more witch dolls?"

"Not for the front page," she flung back at him. "My newspaper career is likely to remain in a state of *status quo* for the next two weeks. Dad and I are heading for Pine Top to dazzle the natives with our particular brand of skiing. Don't you envy us?"

"I certainly would, if you were going."

"If!" exclaimed Penny indignantly. "Of course we're going! We leave Thursday by plane. Dad needs a vacation and this time I know he won't try to wiggle out of it at the last minute."

"Well, I hope not," replied Jerry in a skeptical voice. "Your father needs a good rest, Penny. But I have a sneaking notion you're in for a disappointment again."

"What makes you say that, Jerry? Dad promised me faithfully—"

"Sure, I know," he nodded, "but there have been developments."

"An important story?"

"No, it's more serious than that. But you talk with him. I may have the wrong slant on the situation."

Not without misgiving, Penny went on to her father's private office and tapped on the door.

"Come in," he called in a gruff voice, and as she entered, waved her into a chair. "You arrived a little sooner than I expected, Penny. Mind waiting a few minutes?"

"Not at all."

Studying her father's lean, tired-looking face, Penny decided that something *was* wrong. He seemed unusually worried and nervous.

"A hard day, Dad?" she asked.

Mr. Parker finished straightening a sheaf of papers before he glanced up.

"Yes, I hadn't intended to tell you until later, but I may as well. I'm afraid our trip is off—at least as far as I'm concerned."

"Oh, Dad!"

"It's a big disappointment, Penny. The truth is, I'm in a spot of trouble."

"Isn't that the usual condition of a newspaper publisher?"

"Yes," he smiled, "but there are different degrees of trouble, and this is the worst possible. The *Star* has been sued for libel, a matter of fifty odd thousand."

"Fifty thousand!" gasped Penny. "But of course you'll win the suit!"

"I'm not at all sure of it." Anthony Parker spoke grimly. "My lawyer tells me that Harvey Maxwell has a strong case against the paper."

"Harvey Maxwell?" repeated Penny thoughtfully. "Isn't he the man who owns the Riverview Hotel?"

"Yes, and a chain of other hotels and lodges throughout the country. Harvey Maxwell is a rather well known sportsman. He lives lavishly, travels a great deal, and in general is a hard, shrewd business man."

"He's made a large amount of money from his hotels, hasn't he?"

"Maxwell acquired a fortune from some source, but I've always had a doubt that it came from the hotel business."

"Why is he suing the *Star* for libel, Dad?"

"Early this fall, while I was out of town for a day DeWitt let a story slip through which should have been killed. It was an interview with a football player named Bill Morcrum who was quoted as saying that he had been approached by Maxwell who offered him a bribe to throw an important game."

"What would be the reason behind that?"

"Maxwell is thought by those in the know to have a finger in nearly every dishonest sports scheme ever pulled off in this town. He places heavy wagers, and seldom comes out on the losing end. But the story never should have been published."

"It was true though?"

CHAPTER 1 - TROUBLE FOR MR. PARKER

"I'm satisfied it was," replied Mr. Parker. "However, it always is dangerous to make insinuations against a man."

"Can't the story be proven? I should think with the football player's testimony you would have a good case."

"That's the trouble, Penny. This boy, Bill Morcrum, now claims he never made any such accusation against Maxwell. He says the reporter misquoted him and twisted his statements."

"Who covered the story, Dad?"

"A man named Glower, a very reliable reporter. He swears he made no mistake, and I am inclined to believe him."

"Then why did the football player change his story?"

"I have no proof, but it's a fairly shrewd guess that he was approached by Maxwell a second time. Either he was threatened or offered a bribe which was large enough to sway him."

"With both Maxwell and the football player standing together, it does rather put you on the spot," Penny acknowledged. "What are you going to do?"

"We'll fight the case, of course, but unless we can prove that our story was accurate, we're almost sure to lose. I've asked Bill Morcrum to come to my office this afternoon, and he promised he would. He's overdue now."

Anthony Parker glanced at his watch and scowled. Getting up from the swivel chair he began to pace to and fro across the room.

A buzzer on his desk gave three sharp, staccato signals.

"Morcrum must be here now!" the editor exclaimed in relief. "I'll want to see him alone."

Penny arose to leave. As she went out the doorway she met the receptionist, accompanied by an awkward, oversized youth who shuffled his feet in walking. He grinned at her in a sheepish way and entered the private office.

While Penny waited, she entertained herself by reading all the comic strips she could find in the out-of-town exchange papers. In the adjoining room she could hear the rhythmical thumping, clicking sound of the *Star's* teletype machines. She wandered aimlessly into the room to read the copy just as the machines typed it out, a story from Washington, one from Chicago, another from Los Angeles. It was fascinating to watch the print appear like magic upon the long rolls of copy paper.

Presently, the teletype attendant, young Billy Stevens, came dashing into the room.

"Oh, hello, Miss Parker," he said with a bashful grin.

"Hello, Billy," Penny answered cordially. She studied the keyboard of the sending teletype machine, running her fingers over the letters. "I wish I could work this thing," she said.

"There's nothing to it if you can run a typewriter," answered Billy. "Just a minute, I'll throw it off the line on to the test position. Then you can try it."

At first Penny's copy was badly garbled, but under Billy's enthusiastic coaching she was soon doing accurate work.

"Say, this is fun!" she declared. "I'm coming in again one of these days and practice. Thanks a lot, Billy!"

As Penny went back into the editorial room she saw the Morcrum boy leaving her father's office. His head was downcast and his face was flushed to the ears. Obviously, he had not had a comfortable time with Mr. Parker.

The moment the boy had vanished, Penny hurried into her father's office to learn the outcome of the interview.

"No luck," reported Mr. Parker, reaching for his hat and overcoat.

"He wouldn't change his story?"

"No. He seemed like a fairly decent sort of boy, but he kept insisting he had been misquoted. I couldn't get anywhere with him. He'll testify for Maxwell when the case comes to trial."

Mr. Parker put on his overcoat and hat, and opened the door for Penny. As they left the building he told her more about the interview.

"I asked the boy point-blank if he hadn't been hired by Maxwell. Naturally, he denied it, but he acted rather alarmed. Oh, I'm satisfied he's either been bought off or threatened."

"When does the case come to trial?"

83

"The last of next month, unless we gain a delay."

"That gives you quite a bit of time. Don't you think you could take two weeks off anyhow, Dad? We both planned upon having such a wonderful time at Mrs. Downey's place."

Penny and her father had been invited to spend the Christmas holidays at Pine Top, a winter resort which attracted many Riverview persons. They especially had looked forward to the trip since they were to have been the house guests of Mrs. Christopher Downey, an old friend of Mr. Parker's who operated a skiing lodge on the slopes of the mountain overlooking Silver Valley.

"There's not much chance of my getting away," Mr. Parker replied regretfully. "That is, not unless important evidence falls into my hands, or I am able to make a deal with Maxwell."

"A deal?"

"If he would make reasonable demands I might be willing to settle out of court."

Penny gazed at her father in blank amazement.

"And admit you were in the wrong when you're certain you weren't?"

"Any good general will make a strategic retreat if the situation calls for it. It might be more sensible to settle out of court than to lose the case. Maxwell has me in a tight place and knows it."

"Then why don't you see him? He might be fairly reasonable."

"I suppose I could stop at the Riverview Hotel on our way home," Mr. Parker said, frowning thoughtfully. "There's an outside chance Maxwell may come to terms. Drop me off there, Penny."

While the car threaded its way in and out of dense traffic, the editor remained in a deep study. Penny had never seen him look so worried. Her own disappointment was keen, yet she realized that far more than a vacation trip was at stake. Fifty thousand dollars represented a large sum of money! If Maxwell won his suit it might even mean the loss of the *Riverview Star*.

Sensing his daughter's alarm, Mr. Parker reached out to pat her knee.

"Don't worry," he said, "we're not licked yet, Penny! And if there's any way to arrange it, you shall have your trip to Pine Top just as we planned."

CHAPTER 2 - A RIVAL REPORTER

Penny presently edged the sedan into a parking space across the street from the Riverview Hotel. As she switched off the ignition her father said:

"Better come along with me and wait in the lobby. It's cold out here."

Penny followed her father into the building. The hotel was an elegant one with many services available for guests. She noticed a florist shop, a candy store, a dry cleaning establishment, and even a small brokerage office opening off the lobby.

"Oh, yes," said Mr. Parker as Penny called his attention to the brokerage. "Maxwell hasn't overlooked anything. The hotel has a special leased wire which I've been told gives him a direct connection with his other places."

Walking over to the desk, Mr. Parker mentioned his name and asked the clerk if he might see Harvey Maxwell.

"Mr. Maxwell is not here," replied the man with an insolent air.

"When will he be at the hotel?"

"Mr. Maxwell has left the city on business. He does not expect to return until the end of next month."

Mr. Parker could not hide his annoyance.

"Let me have his address then," he said in a resigned voice. "I'll write him."

The clerk shook his head. "I have been instructed not to give you Mr. Maxwell's address. If you wish to deal with him you will have to see his lawyer, Gorman S. Railey."

"So Maxwell was expecting me to come here to make a deal with him?" demanded Mr. Parker. "Well, I've changed my mind. I'll make a deal all right, but it will be in court. Good day!"

Angrily, the newspaper man strode from the lobby. Penny hurried to keep pace with him.

"That settles it," he said tersely as they climbed into the sedan again. "This libel suit will be a fight to the finish. And maybe my finish at that!"

"Oh, Dad, I'm sure you'll win. But it's a pity all this had to come up just when you had planned a fine vacation. Mrs. Downey will be disappointed, too."

"Yes, she will, Penny. And there's Mrs. Weems to be thought about. I promised her a two weeks' trip while we were gone."

They drove in silence for a few blocks. As the car passed the Sidell residence, Penny's father said thoughtfully:

"I suppose I could send you out to Pine Top alone, Penny. Or perhaps you might be able to induce your chum, Louise, to go along. Would you like that?"

"It would be more fun if you went also."

"That's out of the picture now. If everything goes well I might be able to join you for Christmas weekend."

"I'm not sure Louise could go," said Penny doubtfully. "But I can find out right away."

After dinner that night, she lost no time in running over to the Sidell home. At first Louise was thrown into a state of ecstasy at the thought of making a trip to Pine Top and then her face became gloomy.

"I would love it, Penny! But it's practically a waste of words to ask Mother. We're going to my grandmother's farm in Vermont for the holidays, and I'll have to tag along."

Since grade school days the two girls had been inseparable friends. Between them there was perfect understanding and they made an excellent pair, for Louise exerted a subduing effect upon the more impulsive, excitable Penny.

Inactivity bored Penny, and wherever she went she usually managed to start things moving. When nothing better offered, she tried her hand at writing newspaper stories for her father's paper. Several of these reportorial experiences had satisfied even Penny's deep craving for excitement.

Three truly "big" stories had rolled from her typewriter through the thundering presses of the *Riverview Star*: Tale of the Witch Doll, The Vanishing Houseboat, and Danger at the Drawbridge. Even now, months after her last astonishing adventure, friends liked to tease her about a humorous encounter with a certain Mr. Kippenberg's alligator.

"Pine Top won't be any fun without you, Lou," Penny complained.

"Oh, yes it will," contradicted her chum. "I know you'll manage to stir up plenty of excitement. You'll probably pull a mysterious Eskimo out of a snow bank or save Santa Claus from being kidnaped! That's the way you operate."

"Pine Top is an out of the way place, close to the Canadian border. All one can do there is eat, sleep, and ski."

"You mean, that's all one is supposed to do," corrected Louise with a laugh. "But you'll run into some big story or else you're slipping!"

"There isn't a newspaper within fifty miles. No railroad either. The only way in and out of the valley is by airplane, and bob-sled, of course."

"That may cramp your style a little, but I doubt it," declared Louise. "I do wish I could go along."

The girls talked with Mrs. Sidell, but as they both had expected, it was not practical for Louise to make the trip.

"I'll come to the airport to see you off on your plane," Louise promised as Penny left the house. "You're starting Thursday, aren't you?"

"Yes, at ten-thirty unless there's bad weather. But I'll see you again before that."

All the next day Penny packed furiously. Mr. Parker was unusually busy at the office, but he bought his daughter's ticket and made all arrangements for the trip to Pine Top. Since Mrs. Weems also planned to leave Riverview the following day, the house was in a constant state of turmoil.

"I feel sorry for Dad being left here alone," remarked Penny. "He'll never make his bed, and he'll probably exist on strong coffee and those wretched raw beef sandwiches they serve at the beanery across from the *Star* office."

"I ought to give up my vacation," declared Mrs. Weems. "It seems selfish of me not to stay here."

Mr. Parker would not hear of such an arrangement, and so plans moved forward just as if his own trip had not been postponed.

"Dad, you'll honestly try to come to Pine Top for Christmas?" Penny pleaded.

"I'll do my best," he promised soberly. "I have a hunch that Harvey Maxwell may still be in town, despite what we were told at the hotel. I intend to busy myself making a complete investigation of the man."

"If I could help, I'd be tickled to stay, Dad."

"There's nothing you can do, Penny. Just go out there and have a nice vacation."

Mr. Parker had not intended to go to the office Thursday morning until after Penny's plane had departed, but at breakfast time a call came from DeWitt, the city editor, urging his presence at once. Before leaving, he gave his daughter her ticket and travelers checks.

"Now I expect to be at the airport to see you off," he promised. "Until then, good-bye."

Mr. Parker kissed Penny and hastened away. Later, Louise Sidell came to the house. Soon after ten o'clock the girls took leave of Mrs. Weems, taxiing to the airport.

"I don't see Dad anywhere," Penny remarked as the cabman unloaded her luggage. "He'll probably come dashing up just as the plane takes off."

The girls entered the waiting room and learned that the plane was "on time." Curiously, they glanced at the other passengers. Two travelers Penny immediately tagged as business men. But she was rather interested in a plump, over-painted woman whose nervous manner suggested that she might be making her first airplane trip.

While Penny's luggage was being weighed, two men entered the waiting room. One was a lean, sharp-faced individual suffering from a bad cold. The other, struck Penny as being vaguely familiar. He was a stout man, expensively dressed, and had a surly, condescending way of speaking to his companion.

"Who are those men?" Penny whispered to Louise. "Do you know them?"

CHAPTER 2 - A RIVAL REPORTER

Louise shook her head.

"That one fellow looks like someone I've seen," Penny went on thoughtfully. "Maybe I saw his picture in a newspaper, but I can't place him."

The two men went up to the desk and the portly one addressed the clerk curtly:

"You have our reservations for Pine Top?"

"Yes, sir. Just sign your name here." The clerk pushed forward paper and a pen.

Paying for the tickets from a large roll of greenbacks, the two men went over to the opposite side of the waiting room and sat down. Penny glanced anxiously at the clock. It was twenty minutes past ten.

A uniformed messenger boy entered the room, letting in a blast of cold air as he opened the door. He went over to the desk and the clerk pointed out the two girls.

"Now what?" said Penny in a low voice. "Maybe my trip is called off!"

The message was for her, from her father. But it was less serious than she had expected. Because an important story had "broken" it would be impossible for him to leave the office. He wished her a pleasant trip west and again promised he would bend every effort toward visiting Pine Top for Christmas.

Penny folded the message and slipped it into her purse.

"Dad won't be able to see me off," she explained to her chum. "I was afraid when DeWitt called him this morning he would be held up."

Before Louise could reply the outside door opened once more, and a girl of perhaps twenty-two who walked with a long, masculine gait, came in out of the cold. Penny sat up a bit straighter in her chair.

"Do you see what I see?" she whispered.

"Who is she?" inquired Louise curiously.

"The one and only Francine Sellberg."

"Which means nothing to me."

"Don't tell me you haven't seen her by-line in the *Riverview Record*! Francine would die of mortification."

"Is she a reporter?"

"She covers special assignments. And she is pretty good," Penny added honestly. "But not quite as good as she believes."

"Wonder what she's doing here?"

"I was asking myself that same question."

As the two girls watched, they saw Francine's cool gaze sweep the waiting room. She did not immediately notice Penny and Louise whose backs were partly turned to her. Her eyes rested for an instant upon the two men who previously had bought tickets to Pine Top, and a flicker of satisfaction showed upon her face.

Moving directly to the desk she spoke to the ticket agent in a low voice, yet loudly enough for Penny and Louise to hear.

"Is it still possible to make a reservation for Pine Top?"

"Yes, we have one seat left on the plane."

"I'll take it," said Francine.

Penny nudged Louise and whispered in her ear: "Did you hear that?"

"I certainly did. Why do you suppose she's going to Pine Top? For the skiing?"

"Unless I'm all tangled in a knot, she's after a big story for the *Record*. And I just wonder if those two mysterious-looking gentlemen aren't the reason for her trip!"

CHAPTER 3 - TRAVELING COMPANIONS

Francine Sellberg paid for her ticket and turned so that her gaze fell squarely upon Penny and Louise. Abruptly, she crossed over to where they sat.

"Hello, girls," she greeted them breezily. "What brings you to the airport?"

As always, the young woman reporter's manner was brusque and business-like. Without meaning to offend, she gave others an impression of regarding them with an air of condescension.

"I came to see Penny off," answered Louise before her chum could speak.

"Oh, are you taking this plane?" inquired Francine, staring at Penny with quickening interest.

"I am if it ever gets here."

"Traveling alone?"

"All by my lonesome," Penny admitted cheerfully.

"You're probably only going a short ways?"

"Oh, quite a distance," returned Penny. She did not like the way Francine was quizzing her.

"Penny is going to Pine Top for the skiing," declared Louise, never guessing that her chum preferred to withhold the information.

"Pine Top!" The smile left Francine's face and her eyes roved swiftly toward the two men who sat at the opposite side of the room.

"We are to be traveling companions, I believe," remarked Penny innocently.

Francine's attention came back to the younger girl. Her eyes narrowed with suspicion.

"So you're going out to Pine Top for the skiing," she said softly.

"And you?" countered Penny.

"Oh, certainly for the skiing," retorted Francine, mockery in her voice.

"Nice of the *Record* to give you a vacation."

By this time the silver-winged transport had wheeled into position on the apron, and passengers were beginning to leave the waiting room. The two men who had attracted Penny's attention, arose and without appearing to notice the three girls, went outside.

"You don't deceive me one bit, Penny Parker," said Francine with a quick change of attitude. "I know very well why you are going to Pine Top, and it's for the same reason I am!"

"You seem to have divined all my secrets, even when I don't know them myself," responded Penny. "Suppose you tell me why I am going to Pine Top mountain?"

"It's perfectly obvious that your father sent you, But I am afraid he over-estimates your journalistic powers if he thinks you have had enough experience to handle a difficult assignment of this sort. I'll warn you right now, Penny, don't come to me for help. On this job we're rivals. And I won't tolerate any bungling or interference upon your part!"

"Nice to know just where we stand," replied Penny evenly. "Then there will be no misunderstanding or tears later on."

"Exactly. And mind you don't give any tip-off as to who I am!"

"You mean you don't care to have those two gentlemen who were here a moment ago know that you are a reporter for the *Record*."

"Naturally."

"And who are these men of mystery?"

CHAPTER 3 - TRAVELING COMPANIONS

"As if you don't know!" Francine made an impatient gesture. "Oh, why pose, Penny? This innocent act doesn't go over worth a cent."

Louise broke indignantly into the conversation. "Penny isn't posing! It's true she is going to Pine Top for the skiing and not to get a story. Isn't it?"

"Yes," acknowledged Penny unwillingly. She was sorry that her chum had put an end to the little game with Francine.

The reporter stared at the two girls, scarcely knowing whether or not to believe them.

"Why not break down and tell me the identity of our two fellow passengers?" suggested Penny.

"So you really don't know their names?" Francine flashed a triumphant smile. "Fancy that! Well, you've proven such a clever little reporter in the past, I'll allow you to figure it out for yourself. See you in Pine Top."

Turning away, the young woman went back to the desk to speak once more with the ticket man.

"Doesn't she simply drip conceit!" Louise whispered in disgust. "Did I make a mistake in letting her know that you weren't on an assignment?"

"It doesn't matter, Lou. Shall we be going out to the plane before I miss it?"

The huge streamliner stood warming up on the ribbon of cement, long tongues of flame leaping from the exhausts. Nearly all of the passengers already had taken their seats in the warm, cozy cabin.

"Good-bye, Lou," Penny said, shaking her chum's hand.

"Good-bye. Have a nice time. And don't let that know-it-all Francine get ahead of you!"

"Not if I can help it," laughed Penny.

Francine had left the waiting room and was walking with a brisk step toward the plane. Not wishing to be the last person aboard, Penny stepped quickly into the cabin. All but two seats were taken. One was at the far end of the plane, the other directly behind the two strange men.

Penny slid into the latter chair just as Francine came into the cabin. As she went down the aisle to take the only remaining seat, the reporter shot the younger girl an irritated glance.

"She thinks I took this place just to spite her!" thought Penny. "How silly!"

The stewardess, trim in her blue-green uniform, had closed the heavy metal door. The plane began to move down the ramp, away from the station's canopied entrance. Penny leaned close to the window and waved a last good-bye to Louise.

As the speed of the engines was increased, the plane raced faster and faster over the smooth runway. A take-off was not especially thrilling to Penny who often had made flights with her father. She shook her head when the stewardess offered her cotton for her ears, but accepted a magazine.

Penny flipped carelessly through the pages. Finding no story worth reading, she turned her attention to her fellow passengers. Beside her, on the right, sat the over-painted woman, her hands gripping the arm rests so hard that her knuckles showed white.

"We—we're in the air now, aren't we?" she asked nervously, meeting Penny's gaze. "I do hope I'm not going to be sick."

"I am sure you won't be," replied Penny. "The air is very quiet today."

"They tell me flying over the mountains in winter time is dangerous."

"Not in good weather with a skilful pilot. I am sure we will be in no danger."

"Just the same I never would have taken a plane if it hadn't been the only way of reaching Pine Top."

Penny turned to regard her companion with new interest. The woman was in her early forties, though she had attempted by the lavish use of make-up to appear younger. Her hair was a bleached yellow, dry and brittle from too frequent permanent waving. Her shoes were slightly scuffed, and a tight-fitting black crepe dress, while expensive, was shiny from long use.

"Oh, are you traveling to Pine Top, too?" inquired Penny. "Half the passengers on this plane must be heading for there."

"Is that where you are going?"

"Yes," nodded Penny. "I plan to visit an old friend who has an Inn on the mountain side, and try a little skiing."

"This is strictly a business trip with me," confided the woman. She had relaxed now that the transport was flying at an even keel. "I am going there to see Mr. Balantine—David Balantine. You've heard of him, of course."

Penny shook her head.

"My dear, everyone in the East is familiar with his name. Mr. Balantine has a large chain of theatres throughout the country. He produces his own shows, too. I hope to get a leading part in a new production which will soon be cast."

"Oh, I see," murmured Penny. "You are an actress?"

"I've been on the stage since I was twelve years old," the woman answered proudly. "You must have seen my name on the billboards. I am Miss Miller. Maxine Miller."

"I should like to see one of your plays," Penny responded politely.

"The truth is I've been 'at liberty' for the past year or two," the actress admitted with an embarrassed laugh. "'At liberty' is a word we show people use when we're temporarily out of work. The movies have practically ruined the stage."

"Yes, I know."

"For several weeks I have been trying to get an interview with Mr. Balantine. His secretaries would not make an appointment for me. Then quite by luck I learned that he planned to spend two weeks at Pine Top. I thought if I could meet him out there in his more relaxed moments, he might give me a role in the new production."

"Isn't it a rather long chance to take?" questioned Penny. "To go so far just in the hope of seeing this man?"

"Yes, but I like long chances. And I've tried every other way to meet him. If I win the part I'll be well repaid for my time and money."

"And if you fail?"

Maxine Miller shrugged. "The bread line, perhaps, or burlesque which would be worse. If I stay at Pine Top more than a few days I'll never have money enough to get back here. They tell me Pine Top is high-priced."

"I don't know about that," answered Penny.

As the plane winged its way in a northwesterly direction, the actress kept the conversational ball rolling at an exhausting pace. She told Penny all about herself, her trials and triumphs on the stage. As first, it was fairly interesting, but as Miss Miller repeated herself, the girl became increasingly bored. She shrewdly guessed that the actress never had been the outstanding stage success she visioned herself.

Penny paid more than ordinary attention to the two men who sat in front of her. However, Miss Miller kept her so busy answering questions that she could not have overheard their talk, even if she had made an effort to do so.

Therefore, when the plane made a brief stop, she was astonished to have Francine sidle over to her as she sat on a high stool at the lunch stand, and say in a cutting tone:

"Well, did you find out everything you wanted to know? I saw you listening hard enough."

"Eavesdropping isn't my method," replied Penny indignantly. "It's stupid and is employed only by trash fiction writers and possibly *Record* reporters."

"Say, are you suggesting—?"

"Yes," interrupted Penny wearily. "Now please go find yourself a roost!"

Francine ignored the empty stools beside Penny and went to the far side of the lunch room. A moment later the two men, who had caused the young woman reporter such concern, entered and sat down at a counter near Penny, ordering sandwiches and coffee.

Rather ironically, the girl could not avoid hearing their conversation, and almost their first words gave her an unpleasant shock.

"Don't worry, Ralph," said the stout one. "Nothing stands in our way now."

"You're not forgetting Mrs. Downey's place?"

"We'll soon take care of *her*," the other boasted. "That's why I'm going out to Pine Top with you, Ralph. I'll show you how these little affairs are handled."

CHAPTER 4 - PINE TOP MOUNTAIN

Penny was startled by the remarks of the two men because she felt certain that the Mrs. Downey under discussion must be the woman at whose inn she would spend a two weeks' vacation. Was it possible that a plot was being hatched against her father's friend? And what did Francine know about it?

She glanced quickly toward the young woman reporter who was doing battle with a tough steak which threatened to leap off her plate whenever she tried to cut it. Apparently, Francine had not heard any part of the conversation.

Being only human, Penny decided that despite her recent comments, she could not be expected to abandon a perfectly good sandwich in the interests of theoretical honor. She remained at her post and waited for the men to reveal more.

Unobligingly, they began to talk of the weather and politics. Penny finished her sandwich, and sliding down from the stool wandered outdoors.

"I wish I knew who those men are," she thought. "Francine could tell me if she weren't so horrid."

Penny waited until the last possible minute before boarding the plane. As she stepped inside the cabin she was surprised to see that Francine had taken the chair beside Maxine Miller, very coolly moving Penny's belongings to the seat at the back of the airliner.

"Did you two decide to change places?" inquired the stewardess as Penny hesitated beside the empty chair.

"I didn't decide. It just seems to be an accomplished fact."

The stewardess went down the aisle and touched Francine's arm. "Usually the passengers keep their same seats throughout the journey," she said with a pleasant smile. "Would you mind?"

Francine did mind for she had cut her lunch short in the hope of obtaining the coveted chair, but she could not refuse to move. Frowning, she went back to her former place.

Actually, Penny was not particular where she sat. There was no practical advantage in being directly behind the two strangers, for their voices were seldom audible above the roar of the plane. On the other hand, Miss Miller talked loudly and with scarcely a halt for breath. Penny was rather relieved when an early stop for dinner enabled her to gain a slight respite.

With flying conditions still favorable, the second half of the journey was begun. Penny curled up in her clean, comfortable bed, and the gentle rocking of the plane soon lulled her to sleep. She did not awaken until morning when the stewardess came to warn her they soon would be at their destination. Penny dressed speedily, and enjoyed a delicious breakfast brought to her on a tray. She had just finished when Francine staggered down the aisle, eyes bloodshot, her straight black hair looking as if it had never been combed.

"Will I be glad to get off this plane!" she moaned. "What a night!"

"I didn't notice anything wrong with it," said Penny. "I take it you didn't sleep well."

"Sleep? I never closed my eyes all night, not with this roller-coaster sliding down one mountain and up another. I thought every minute we were going to crash."

Maxine Miller likewise seemed to have spent an uncomfortable night, for her face was haggard and worn. She looked five years older and her make-up was smeared.

"Tell me, do I look too dreadful?" she asked Penny anxiously. "I want to appear my best when I meet Mr. Balantine."

"You'll have time to rest up before you see him," the girl replied kindly.

"How long before we reach Pine Top?"

"We should be approaching there now." Penny studied the terrain below with deep interest, noting mountain ranges and beautiful snowy valleys.

At last the plane circled and swept down on a small landing field which had been cleared of snow. Passengers began to pour from the cabin, grateful that the long journey was finally at an end.

"I hope I see you again," said Penny, extending her hand to Miss Miller. "And the best of luck with Mr. Balantine."

Eagerly, she gathered together her possessions and stepped out of the plane into blinding sunlight. The air was crisp and cold, but there was a quality to it which made her take long, deep breaths. Beyond the landing field stood a tall row of pine trees, each topped with a layer of snow like the white icing of a cake. From somewhere far away she could hear the merry jingle of sleigh bells.

"So this is Pine Top!" thought Penny. "It's as pretty as a Christmas card!"

A small group of persons were at the field to meet the plane. Catching sight of a short, sober-looking little woman who was bundled in furs, Penny hastened toward her.

"Mrs. Downey!" she cried.

"Penny, my dear! How glad I am to see you!" The woman clasped her firmly, planting a kiss on either cheek. "But your father shouldn't have disappointed me. Why didn't he come along?"

"He wanted to, but he's up to his eyebrows in trouble. A man is suing him for libel."

"Oh, that *is* bad," murmured Mrs. Downey. "I know what legal trouble means because I've had an unpleasant taste of it myself lately. But come, let's get your luggage and be starting up the mountain."

"Just a minute," said Penny in a low tone. With a slight inclination of her head, she indicated the two male passengers who had made the long journey from Riverview to Pine Top. "You don't by any chance know either of those men?"

Mrs. Downey's face lost its kindliness and she said, in a grim voice: "I certainly do!"

Before Penny could urge the woman to reveal their identity, Francine walked over to where she and Mrs. Downey stood.

"Did you wish to see me?" inquired the hotel woman as Francine looked at her with an inquiring gaze.

"Are you Mrs. Downey?"

"Yes, I am."

"I am looking for a place to stay," said Francine. "I was told that you keep an inn."

"Yes, we have a very nice lodge up the mountain about a mile from here. The rooms are comfortable, and I do most of the cooking myself. We're located on the best ski slopes in the valley. But if you're looking for a place with plenty of style and corresponding prices you might prefer the Fergus place."

"Your lodge will exactly suit me, I think," declared Francine. "How do I get there?"

"In my bob-sled," offered Mrs. Downey. "I may have a few other guests."

"It won't take me a minute to get my luggage," said Francine, moving away.

Penny was none too pleased to know that the girl reporter would make her headquarters at the Downey Inn. Her face must have mirrored her misgiving, for Mrs. Downey said apologetically:

"Business hasn't been any too good this season. I have to pick up an extra tourist whenever I can."

"Of course," agreed Penny hastily. "One can't run a hotel without guests."

"I do believe Jake has snared another victim," Mrs. Downey laughed. "That woman with the bleached hair."

"And who is Jake?" inquired Penny.

Mrs. Downey nodded her head toward a spry man with leathery skin who was talking with Maxine Miller.

"He does odd jobs for me at the Inn," she explained. "When he has no other occupation he tries to entice guests into our den."

"You make it sound like a very wicked business," chuckled Penny.

"Since the Fergus hotel was built it's become a struggle, to the death," replied Mrs. Downey soberly. "I truly believe this will be my last year at Pine Top."

"Why, you've had your home here for years," said Penny in astonishment. "You were at Pine Top long before anyone thought of it as a great skiing resort. You're an institution here, Mrs. Downey. Surely you aren't serious about giving up your lodge?"

"Yes, I am, Penny. But I shouldn't start telling my troubles the moment you arrive. I never would have said a word if you hadn't asked me about those two men yonder."

CHAPTER 4 - PINE TOP MOUNTAIN

She gazed scornfully toward the strangers whose identity Penny hoped to learn.

"Who *are* they?" Penny asked quickly.

"The slim fellow with the sharp face is Ralph Fergus," answered Mrs. Downey, her voice filled with bitterness. "He manages the hotel and is supposed to be the owner. Actually, the other man is the one who provides all the money."

"And who is he?"

"Why, you should know," replied Mrs. Downey. "He has a hotel in Riverview. His name is Harvey Maxwell. He only comes here now and then."

"Harvey Maxwell!" repeated Penny. "Wait until Dad hears about this!"

"Your father has had dealings with him?"

"Has he?" murmured Penny. "Maxwell is the man who is suing Dad for libel!"

"Well, of all things!"

"I believe I understand why Francine came out here too," Penny said thoughtfully.

"Francine?"

"The girl who just engaged a room at your place. I think she went to your Inn for the sole purpose of keeping an eye on me."

"Why should she wish to do that?"

"Francine is a reporter for the *Riverview Record*. Dad's story about Maxwell bribing a football player served as a tip-off to other editors. Now the *Record* may hope to get evidence against him which they can build up into a big story."

"I should think that would help your father's case."

"It might," agreed Penny, "all depending upon how the evidence was used. But somehow, I don't trust Francine. If there's any fancy newspaper work to be done at Pine Top, I aim to look after it myself!"

CHAPTER 5 - OVER THE BARBED WIRE

Mrs. Downey laughed at Penny's remark, not taking it very seriously.

"I wish someone could uncover damaging evidence against Harvey Maxwell," she declared. "But I fear he's far too clever a man to be caught in anything dishonest. Sometime when you're in the mood to hear a tale of woe, I'll tell you how he is running things at Pine Top."

"I'd like to learn everything I can about him," responded Penny eagerly.

Mrs. Downey led the girl across the field to the road where the bob-sled and team of horses had been hitched. Jake, the handy man, appeared a moment later, loaded down with skis and luggage. Maxine Miller, Francine, and a well-dressed business man soon arrived and were helped into the sled.

"This is unique taxi service to say the least," declared Francine, none too well pleased. "It must take ages to get up the mountain."

"Not very long," replied Mrs. Downey cheerfully.

Jake drove, with the hotel woman and her guests sitting on the floor of the sled, covered by warm blankets.

"Is it always so cold here?" shivered Miss Miller.

"Always at this time of year," returned Mrs. Downey. "You'll not mind it in a day or two. And the skiing is wonderful. We had six more inches of snow last night."

Penny thoroughly enjoyed the novel experience of gliding swiftly over the hard-packed snow. The bobsled presently passed a large rustic building at the base of the mountain which Mrs. Downey pointed out as the Fergus hotel.

"I suppose all the rich people stay there," commented Miss Miller. "Do you know if they have a guest named David Balantine?"

"The producer? Yes, I believe he is staying at the Fergus hotel."

At the next bend Jake stopped the horses so that the girls might obtain a view of the valley.

"Over to the right is the village of Pine Top," indicated Mrs. Downey. "Just beyond the Fergus hotel is the site of an old silver mine, abandoned many years ago. And when we reach the next curve you'll be able to look north and see into Canada."

A short ride on up the mountain brought the party to the Downey Lodge, a small but comfortable log building amid the pines. On the summit of a slope not far away they could see the figure of a skier, poised for a swift, downward flight.

Mrs. Downey assigned the guests to their rooms, tactfully establishing Penny and Francine at opposite ends of a long hall.

"Luncheon will be served at one o'clock," she told them. "If you feel equal to it you'll have time for a bit of skiing."

"I believe I'll walk down to the village and send a wire to Dad," said Penny. "Then this afternoon I'll try my luck on the slopes."

"Just follow the road and you'll not get lost," instructed Mrs. Downey.

Penny unpacked her suitcase, and then set forth at a brisk walk for the village. She found the telegraph station without difficulty and dispatched a message to her father, telling him of Harvey Maxwell's presence in Pine Top.

The town itself, consisting of half a dozen stores and twice as many houses, was soon explored. Before starting back up the mountain Penny thought she would buy a morning newspaper. But as she made inquiry at a drug store, the owner shook his head.

CHAPTER 5 - OVER THE BARBED WIRE

"We don't carry them here. The only papers we get come in by plane. They're all sold out long before this."

"Oh, I see," said Penny in disappointment, "well, next time I'll try to come earlier."

"I beg your pardon," ventured a voice directly behind her. "Allow me to offer you my paper."

Penny turned around to see that Ralph Fergus had entered the drugstore in time to hear her remark. With a most engaging smile, he extended his own newspaper.

"Oh, I don't like to take your paper," she protested, wishing to accept no favor however small from the man.

"Please do," he urged, thrusting it into her hand. "I have finished with it."

"Thank you," said Penny.

She took the paper and started to leave the store. Mr. Fergus fell into step with her, following her outside.

"Going back up the mountain?" he inquired casually.

"Yes, I was."

"I'll walk along if you don't mind having company."

"Not at all."

Penny studied Ralph Fergus curiously, fairly certain he had a special reason for wishing to walk with her. For a time they trudged along in silence, the snow creaking beneath their boots.

"Staying at the Downey Lodge?" Fergus inquired after awhile.

"Yes, I am."

"Like it there?"

"Well, I only arrived on the morning plane."

"Yes, I noticed you aboard," he nodded. "Mrs. Downey is a very fine woman, a very fine woman, but her lodge isn't modern. You noticed that, I suppose?"

"I'm not especially critical," smiled Penny. "It seemed to suit my needs."

"You'll be more critical after you have stayed there a few days," he warned. "The service is very poor. Even this little matter of getting a morning newspaper. Now our hotel sees that every guest has one shoved under his door before breakfast."

"That would be very nice, I'm sure," remarked Penny dryly. "You're the manager of the hotel, aren't you?"

Ralph Fergus gave her a quick, appraising glance. "Right you are," he said jovially. "Naturally I think we have the finest hotel at Pine Top and I wish you would try it. I'll be glad to make you a special rate."

"You're very kind." It was a struggle for Penny to keep her voice casual. "I may drop around sometime and look the hotel over."

"Do that," he urged. "Here is my card. Just ask for me and I'll show you about."

Penny took the card and dropped it into her pocket. A few minutes later as they passed the Fergus hotel, her companion parted company with her.

"He thought I was an ordinary guest at Mrs. Downey's," Penny told herself. "Otherwise, he never would have dared to make such an open bid for my patronage."

Upon returning to the lodge she told Mrs. Downey of her meeting with Ralph Fergus.

"It doesn't surprise me one bit," the woman replied angrily. "Fergus has been using every method he can think of to get my guests away from me. He has runners out all the time, talking up his hotel and talking mine down."

Penny sat on the edge of the kitchen table, watching Mrs. Downey stir a great kettle of steaming soup.

"While I was coming here on the plane I heard Fergus and Maxwell speaking about you."

"You did, Penny? What did they have to say? Nothing good, I'll warrant."

"I couldn't understand what they meant at the time, but now I think I do. They said that nothing stood in their way except your place. Maxwell declared he would soon take care of you, and that he was on his way to Pine Top to show Fergus how such affairs were handled."

Mrs. Downey kept on stirring with the big spoon. "So the screws are to be twisted a bit harder?" she asked grimly.

"Why do they want your place?" Penny inquired.

"Because I take a few of their guests away from them. If my lodge closed up they could raise prices sky high, and they would do it, too!"

"They offered me a special rate, whatever that means."

"Fergus has been cutting his room rents lately for the sole purpose of getting my customers away from me. He makes up for it by charging three and even four dollars a meal. The guests don't learn that until after they have moved in."

"And there's nothing you can do about it?"

Mrs. Downey shook her head. "I've been fighting with my back to the wall this past season. I don't see how I possibly can make it another year. That is why I wanted you and your father to visit here before I gave up the place."

"Dad might have helped you," Penny said regretfully. "I'm sorry he wasn't able to come."

At one o'clock Mrs. Downey served a plain but substantial meal to fourteen guests who tramped in out of the snow. They called loudly for second and third helpings which were cheerfully given.

After luncheon Penny sat for a time about the crackling log fire and then she went to her room and changed into her skiing clothes.

"The nursery slopes are at the rear of the lodge," Mrs. Downey told her as she went out through the kitchen. "But you're much too experienced for them."

"I haven't been on skis for nearly two years."

"It will come back to you quickly."

"I thought I might taxi down and look over the Fergus hotel."

"The trail is well marked. Just be careful as you get about half way down. There is a sharp turn and if you miss it you may find yourself wrapped around an evergreen."

Penny went outside, and buckling on her skis, glided to the top of a long slope which fell rather sharply through lanes of pine trees to the wide valley below. As she was studying the course, reflecting that the crusted snow would be very fast, Francine came out of the lodge and stood watching her.

"What's the matter, Penny?" she called. "Can't you get up your nerve?"

Penny dug in her poles and pushed off. Crouching low, skis running parallel, she tore down the track. Pine trees crowded past on either side in a greenish blur. The wind whistled in her ears. She jabbed her poles into the snow to check her speed.

After the first steep stretch, the course flattened out slightly. From a cautious left traverse, a lifted stem turn gave her time to concentrate her full attention on the route ahead. She swerved to avoid a boulder which would have broken her ski had she crashed into it, and rode out a series of long, undulating hollows.

Gathering speed again, Penny made her decisions with lightning rapidity. There was no time to think. Confronted with a choice of turns, she chose the right hand trail, slashing through in a beautiful christiana. Too late, she realized her error.

Directly ahead loomed a barbed wire fence. There was no opportunity to turn aside. Penny knew that she must jump or take a disastrous fall.

Swinging her poles forward, she let them drop in the snow close to her ski tips. Crouching low she sprang upward with all her strength. The sticks gave her leverage so that she could lift her skis clear of the snow. Momentum carried her forward over the fence.

Penny felt the jar of the runners as they slapped on the snow. Then she lost her balance and tumbled head over heels.

Untangling herself, she sat up and gazed back at the barbed wire fence.

"I wish all my friends at Riverview could have seen that jump!" she thought proudly. "It was a beauty even if I did land wrong side up."

A large painted sign which had been fastened to the fence, drew her attention. It read: "Skiers Keep Out."

"I wonder if that means me?" remarked Penny aloud.

"Yes, it means you!" said an angry voice behind her.

Penny rolled over in the snow, waving her skis in the air. She drew in her breath sharply. An old man with a dark beard had stepped from the shadow of the pine trees, a gun grasped in his gnarled hands!

CHAPTER 6 - PENNY TRESPASSES

"Can't you understand signs?" the old man demanded, advancing with cat-like tread from the fringe of pine trees.

"Not when I'm traveling down a mountain side at two hundred miles an hour!" Penny replied. "Please, would you mind pointing that cannon in some other direction? It might go off."

The old man lowered the shotgun, but the grim lines of his wrinkled, leathery face did not relax.

"Get up!" he commanded, prodding her with the toe of his heavy boot. "Get out of here! I won't have you or any other skier on my property."

"Then allow me to make a suggestion," remarked Penny pleasantly. "Put up another strand of barbed wire and you'll have them all in the hospital!"

She sat up, gingerly felt of her left ankle and then began to brush snow from her jacket. "Did you see me make the jump?" she asked. "I took it just like a reindeer. Or do I mean a gazelle?"

"You made a very awkward jump!" he retorted. "I could have done better myself."

Penny glanced up with genuine interest. "Oh, do you ski?"

By this time she no longer was afraid of the old man, if indeed she had ever been.

"No, I don't ski!" he answered impatiently. "Now hurry up! Get those skis off and start moving! I'll not wait all day."

Penny began to unstrap the long hickory runners, but with no undue show of haste. She glanced curiously about the snowy field. An old shed stood not far away. Beside it towered a great stack of wood which reached nearly as high as the roof. Through the trees she caught a glimpse of a weather-stained log cabin with smoke curling lazily from the brick chimney.

As Penny was regarding it, she saw a flash of color at one of the windows. A girl who might have been her own age had her face pressed against the pane. Seeing Penny's gaze upon her, she began to make motions which could not be understood.

The old man also turned his head to look toward the cabin. Immediately, the girl disappeared from the window.

"Is that where you live?" inquired Penny.

Instead of answering, the old man seized her by the hand and pulled her to her feet.

"Go!" he commanded. "And don't let me catch you here again!"

Penny shouldered her skis and moved toward the fence.

"So sorry to have damaged your nice snow," she apologized. "I'll try not to trespass again."

Crawling under the barbed wire fence, Penny retraced her way up the slope to the point on the trail where she had taken the wrong turn. There she hesitated and finally decided to walk on to the Fergus hotel.

"I wonder who that girl was at the window?" Penny reflected as she trudged along. "She looked too young to be Old Whisker's daughter. And what was she trying to tell me?"

The problem was too deep for her to solve. But she made up her mind she would ask Mrs. Downey the name of the queer old man as soon as she returned to the lodge.

Reaching the Fergus hotel, Penny parked her skis upright in a snowbank near the front door, and went inside. She found herself in a long lobby at the end of which was a great stone fireplace with a half burned log on the hearth. Bellboys in green uniforms and brass buttons darted to and fro. A general stir of activity pervaded the place.

As Penny was gazing about, she saw Maxine Miller leave an elevator and come slowly across the lobby. The actress would not have seen her had she not spoken.

"How do you do, Miss Miller. I didn't expect to see you here."

"Oh, Miss Parker!" The actress' face was the picture of despair. "I've had the most wretched misfortune!"

"Why, what has happened?" inquired Penny, although she thought she knew the answer to her question.

"I've just seen Mr. Balantine." Miss Miller sagged into the depths of a luxuriously upholstered davenport and leaned her head back against the cushion.

"Your interview didn't turn out as you expected?"

"He wouldn't give me the part. Hateful old goat! He even refused to allow me to demonstrate how well I could read the lines! And he said some very insulting things to me."

"That is too bad," returned Penny sympathetically. "What will you do now? Go back home?"

"I don't know," the woman replied in despair. "I would stay if I thought I could change Mr. Balantine's opinion. Do you think I could?"

"I shouldn't advise it myself. Of course, I don't know anything about Mr. Balantine."

"He's very temperamental. Perhaps if I kept bothering him he would finally give me a chance."

"Well, it might be worth trying," Penny said doubtfully. "But I think if I were you I would return home."

"All of my friends will laugh at me. They thought it was foolish to come out here as it was. I can't go back. I am inclined to move down to this hotel so I'll be able to keep in touch with Mr. Balantine with less difficulty."

"It's a very nice looking hotel," commented Penny. "Expensive, I've been told."

"In the show business one must keep up appearances at all cost," replied Miss Miller. "I believe I'll inquire about the rates."

While Penny waited, the actress crossed over to the desk and talked with a clerk. In a small office close by, Ralph Fergus and Harvey Maxwell could be seen in consultation. They were poring over a ledger, apparently checking business accounts.

Miss Miller returned in a moment. "I've taken a room," she announced. "I can't afford it, but I am doing it anyway."

"Will you be able to manage?"

"Oh, I'll run up a bill and then let them try to collect!"

Penny gazed at the actress with frank amazement.

"You surely don't mean you would deliberately defraud the hotel?"

"Not so loud or the clerk will hear you," Miss Miller warned. "And don't use such an ugly word. If I land the part with Mr. Balantine, of course I'll pay. If not—the worst they can do is to throw me out."

Penny said no more but her opinion of Miss Miller had descended several notches.

"What are you doing here?" the actress inquired, quickly changing the subject.

"Oh, I just came down to look over the hotel. It's very swanky, but I like Mrs. Downey's place better."

Miss Miller turned to leave. "I am going back there now to check out," she declared. "Would you like to walk along?"

"No, thank you, I'll just stay here and rest for a few minutes."

Penny had no real purpose in coming to the Fergus hotel. She merely had been curious to see what it was like. Even a casual inspection made it clear that Mrs. Downey's modest little lodge never could compete with such a luxurious establishment.

She studied the faces of the persons in the lobby. There seemed to be a strange assortment of people, including a large number of men and women who certainly had never been drawn to Pine Top by the skiing. Penny thought whimsically that it would be interesting to see some of the fat, pampered-looking ones take a tumble on the slippery slopes.

"But what is the attraction of this place, if not the skiing?" she puzzled. "There is no other form of entertainment."

Presently, a well-fed lady in rustling black silk, her hand heavy with diamond rings, paused beside Penny.

"I beg your pardon," she said, "can you tell me how to find the Green Room?"

"No, I can't," replied Penny. "I would need a map to get around in this hotel. You might ask at the desk."

The woman fluttered over to the clerk and asked the same question.

"You have your card, Madam?" he inquired in a low tone.

CHAPTER 6 - PENNY TRESPASSES

"Oh, yes, to be sure. The manager presented it to me this morning."

"Take the elevator to the second floor wing," the man instructed. "Room 22. Show your card to the doorman and you will be admitted."

Penny waited until after the woman had gone away. Then she arose and sauntered across the lobby. She picked up a handful of hotel literature but there was no mention of any Green Room. Pausing by the elevator, she waited until the cage was deserted of passengers before speaking to the attendant, a red headed boy of about seventeen.

"Where is the Green Room, please?"

"Second floor, Miss."

"And what is it? A dining room?"

The attendant shot her a peculiar glance and gave an answer which was equally strange.

"It's not a dining room. I can't tell you what it is."

"A cocktail room perhaps?"

"Listen, I told you I don't know," the boy answered.

"You work here, don't you?"

"Sure I do," he said with emphasis. "And I aim to keep my job for awhile. If you want to know anything about the Green Room ask at the desk!"

CHAPTER 7 - THE GREEN DOOR

Before Penny could ask another question, the signal board flashed a summons, and the attendant slammed shut the door of the elevator. He shot the cage up to the fifth floor and did not return.

Hesitating a moment, Penny wandered over to the desk.

"How does one go about obtaining a card for the Green Room?" she inquired casually.

"You're not a guest here?" questioned the clerk.

"No."

"You'll have to talk with the manager. Oh, Mr. Fergus!"

Penny had not meant to have the matter go so far, but there was no retreating. The hotel manager came out of his office, and recognizing her, smiled ingratiatingly.

"Ah, good afternoon, Miss—" He groped for her name but Penny did not supply it. "So you decided to pay us a visit after all."

"This young lady asked about the Green Room," said the clerk significantly.

Mr. Fergus bestowed a shrewd, appraising look upon Penny.

"Oh, yes," he said to give himself more time, "Oh, yes, I see. What was it you wished to know?"

"How does one obtain a card of admission?"

"It is very simple. That is, if you have the proper recommendations and bank credit."

"Recommendations?" Penny asked blankly. "Just what is the Green Room anyway?"

Ralph Fergus and the clerk exchanged a quick glance which was not lost upon the girl.

"I see you are not familiar with the little service which is offered hotel guests," Mr. Fergus said suavely. "I shall be most happy to explain it to you at some later time when I am not quite so busy."

He bowed and went hurriedly back into the office.

"I guess I shouldn't have inquired about the Green Room," Penny observed aloud. "There seems to be a deep mystery connected with it."

"No mystery," corrected the clerk. "If you will leave your name and address I am sure everything can be arranged within a few days."

"Thank you, I don't believe I'll bother."

Penny turned and nearly ran into Francine Sellberg. Too late, she realized that the girl reporter probably had been standing by the desk for some time, listening to her conversation.

"Hello, Francine," she said carelessly.

The girl returned a haughty stare. "I don't believe I know you, Miss," she said, and walked on across the lobby.

Penny was rather stunned by the unexpected snub. She took a step as if to follow Francine and demand an explanation, but her sense of humor came to her rescue.

"Who cares?" she asked herself with a shrug. "If she doesn't care to know me, it's perfectly all right. I can manage to bear up."

After Francine had left the hotel, Penny made up her mind that she would try to learn a little more about the Green Room. Her interest was steadily mounting and she could not imagine what "service" might be offered guests in this particular part of the hotel.

Choosing a moment when no one appeared to be watching, Penny mounted the stairway to the second floor. She followed a long corridor to its end but did not locate Room 22. Returning to the elevator, she started in the opposite direction. The numbers ended at 20.

CHAPTER 7 - THE GREEN DOOR

While Penny was trying to figure it out, a group of four men and women came down the hall. They were well dressed individuals but their manner did not stamp them as persons of good breeding. One of the women who carried a jeweled handbag was talking in a loud, excited tone:

"Oh, Herbert, wait until you see it! I shall weep my eyes out if you don't agree to buy it for me at once. And the price! Ridiculously cheap! We'll never run into bargains like these in New York."

"We'll see, Sally," replied the man. "I'm not satisfied yet that this isn't a flim-flam game."

He opened a door which bore no number, and stood aside for the others to pass ahead of him. Penny caught a glimpse of a long, empty hallway.

"That must be the way to Room 22," she thought.

She waited until the men and women had gone ahead, and then cautiously opened the door which had closed behind them. No one questioned her as she moved noiselessly down the corridor. At its very end loomed a green painted door, its top edge gracefully circular. Beside it at a small table sat a man who evidently was stationed there as a guard.

Penny walked slowly, watching the men and women ahead. They paused at the table and showed slips of cardboards. The guard then opened the green door and allowed them to pass through.

It looked so very easy that Penny decided to try her luck. She drew closer.

"Your card please," requested the doorman.

"I am afraid I haven't mine with me," said Penny, flashing her most beguiling smile.

The smile was entirely lost upon the man. "Then I can't let you in," he said.

"Not even if I have lost my card?"

"Orders," he answered briefly. "You'll have no trouble getting another."

Penny started to turn away, and then asked with attempted carelessness:

"What's going on in there anyway? Are they selling something?"

"I really couldn't tell you," he responded.

"Everyone in this hotel seems to be blind, deaf and dumb," Penny muttered to herself as she retraced her way to the main hall. "And definitely, for a purpose. I wonder if maybe I haven't stumbled into something?"

She still had not the faintest idea what might lie beyond the Green Door, but the very name had an intriguing sound. It suggested mystery. It suggested, too, that Ralph Fergus and his financial backer, Harvey Maxwell, might have developed some special money-making scheme which would not bear exposure.

Into Penny's mind leaped a remark which her father had made, one to the effect that Harvey Maxwell was thought to have his finger in many dishonest affairs. The Green Room might be a perfectly legitimate place of entertainment for hotel guests, but the remarks she had overheard led Penny to think otherwise. Something was being sold in Room 22. And to a very select clientele!

"If only I could learn facts which would help Dad's case!" she told herself. "Anything showing that Maxwell is mixed up in a dishonest scheme might turn the trick!"

It occurred to Penny that the editor of the *Riverview Record* might have had some inkling of a story to be found at Pine Top. Otherwise, why had Francine been sent to the mountain resort? Certainly the rival reporter was working upon an assignment which concerned Harvey Maxwell. She inadvertently had revealed that fact at the Riverview airport.

"Francine thinks I came here for the same purpose," mused Penny. "If only she weren't so high-hat we could work together."

There was almost no real evidence to point to a conclusion that the Fergus hotel was not being operated properly. Penny realized only too well that once more she was depending upon a certain intuition. An investigation of the Green Room might reveal no mystery. But at least there was a slender hope she could learn something which would aid her father in discrediting Harvey Maxwell.

Without attracting attention, Penny descended to the main floor and left the hotel. As she retrieved her skis from the snowbank she was surprised to see Francine standing close by, obviously waiting for her.

"Hello, Penny," the girl greeted her.

"Goodness! Aren't you mistaken? I don't think you know me!"

"Oh, don't try to be funny," Francine replied, falling into step. "I'll explain."

"I wish you would."

"You should have known better than to shout out my name there in the lobby."

"I don't follow your reasoning at all, Francine. Are you traveling incognito or something?"

"Naturally I don't care to have it advertised that I am a reporter. I rather imagine you're not overly anxious to have it known that you are the daughter of Anthony Parker either!"

"It probably wouldn't be any particular help," admitted Penny.

"Exactly! Despite your play-acting at the airport, I know you came here to get the low-down on Harvey Maxwell. But the minute he learns who you are you'll not even get inside the hotel."

"And that goes double, I take it?"

"No one at Pine Top except you knows I am a reporter," went on Francine without answering. "So I warn you, don't pull another boner like you did a few minutes ago. Whenever we're around Fergus or Maxwell or persons who might report to them, just remember you never saw me before. Is that clear?"

"Moderately so," drawled Penny.

"I guess that's all I have to say." Francine hesitated and started to walk off.

"Wait a minute, Francine," spoke Penny impulsively. "Why don't we bury the hatchet and work together on this thing? After all I am more interested in gaining evidence against Maxwell than I am in getting a big story for the paper. How about it?"

Francine smiled in a superior way.

"Thank you, I prefer to lone wolf it. You see, I happen to have a very good lead, and you don't."

"Well, I've heard about the Green Room," said Penny, hazarding a shot in the dark. "That's something."

Francine stopped short.

"What do you know about it?" she demanded quickly. "Maybe we could work together after all."

Penny laughed as she bent down to strap on her skis.

"No, thanks," she declined pleasantly. "You once suggested that a clever reporter finds his own answers. You'll have to wait until you read it in the *Star*!"

CHAPTER 8 - A CODED MESSAGE

Penny sat in the kitchen of Mrs. Downey's lodge, warming her half frozen toes in the oven.

"Well, how did you like the skiing?" inquired her hostess who was busy mixing a huge meat loaf to be served for dinner.

"It was glorious," answered Penny, "only I took a bad spill. Somehow I missed the turn you told me about, and found myself heading for a barbed wire fence. I jumped it and made a one point landing in a snowbank!"

"You didn't hurt yourself, thank goodness."

"No, but an old man with a shotgun came out of the woods and said 'Scat!' to me. It seems he doesn't like skiers."

"That must have been Peter Jasko."

"And who is he, Mrs. Downey?"

"One of the oldest settlers on Pine Top Mountain," sighed Mrs. Downey. "He's a very pleasant man in some respects, but in others—oh, dear."

"Skiing must be one of his unpleasant aspects. I noticed he had a 'Keep Out' sign posted on his property."

"Peter Jasko is a great trial to me and other persons on the mountain. He has a hatred of skiing and everything pertaining to it, which amounts to fanaticism. A number of skiers have been injured by running into his barbed wire fence."

"Then he put it up on purpose?"

"Oh, yes! He has an idea it will keep folks from skiing."

"He isn't—?" Penny tapped her forehead significantly.

"No," smiled Mrs. Downey. "Old Peter is right in his mind, at least in every respect save this one. He owns our best ski slopes, too."

Penny shifted her foot to a cooler place in the oven.

"Not the slopes connected with this lodge?"

Mrs. Downey nodded as she whipped eggs to a foamy yellow.

"I leased the land from Jasko's son many years ago, and Jasko can do nothing about it except rage. However, the lease expires soon. He has given me to understand it will not be renewed."

"Can't you deal with the son?"

"He is dead, Penny."

"Oh, I see. That does make it difficult."

"Decidedly. Jasko's attitude about the lease is another reason why I think this will be my last year in the hotel business."

"You don't think Ralph Fergus or Harvey Maxwell have influenced Jasko?" Penny asked thoughtfully, a frown ridging her forehead.

"I doubt that anyone could influence the old man," replied Mrs. Downey. "Stubborn isn't the word to describe his character. Even if I lose the ski slopes, I am quite sure he will never lease them to the Fergus hotel interests."

"While I was down there I thought I saw a girl standing at the window of the cabin."

"Probably you did, Penny. Jasko has a granddaughter about your age, named Sara. A very nice girl, too, but she is kept close at home."

"I feel sorry for her if she has to live with that old man. He seemed like a regular ogre."

Removing her toasted feet from the oven, Penny pulled on her stiff boots again. Without bothering to lace them, she hobbled toward the door.

"Oh, by the way," she remarked, pausing. "Did you ever hear of a Green Room at the Fergus hotel?"

"A Green Room?" repeated Mrs. Downey. "No, I can't say I have. What is it, Penny?"

"I wonder myself. Something funny seems to be going on there."

Having aroused Mrs. Downey's curiosity, Penny gave a more complete account of her visit to the Fergus hotel.

"I've never heard anyone mention such a place," declared the woman in a puzzled voice. "But I will say this. The hotel always has attracted a peculiar group of guests."

"How would you like to have me solve the mystery for you?" joked Penny.

"It would suit me very well indeed," laughed Mrs. Downey. "And while you're about it you might put Ralph Fergus out of business, and bring me a new flock of guests."

"I'm afraid you're losing one instead. Maxine Miller told me she is moving down to the big hotel."

"I know. She checked out a half hour ago. Jake made an extra trip to haul her luggage down the mountain."

"Anyway, I shouldn't be sorry to see her go if I were you," comforted Penny. "I am quite sure she hasn't enough money to pay for a week's stay at Pine Top."

Going to her room, Penny changed into more comfortable clothing and busied herself writing a long letter to her father. From her desk by the window she could see skiers trudging up the slopes, some of them making neat herring-bone tracks, others slipping and sliding, losing almost as much distance as they gained.

As she watched, Francine swung into view, poling rhythmically, in perfect timing with her long easy strides.

"She *is* good," thought Penny, grudgingly.

Dinner was served at six. Afterwards, the guests sat before the crackling log fire and bored each other with tales of their skiing prowess. A few of the more enterprising ones waxed their skis in preparation for the next day's sport.

"Any newspapers tonight?" inquired a business man of Mrs. Downey. "Or is this another one of the blank days?"

"Jake brought New York papers from the village," replied the hotel woman. "They are on the table."

"Blank days?" questioned Francine, looking up from a magazine she had been reading.

"Mr. Glasser calls them that when he doesn't get the daily stock market report," explained Mrs. Downey, smiling at her guest.

"And don't the newspapers always arrive?" questioned Francine.

"Not always. Lately the service has been very poor."

"I'd rather be deprived of a meal than my paper," growled Mr. Glasser. "What annoys me is that the guests at the Fergus hotel always get their papers. I wish someone would explain it to me."

"And I wish someone would explain it to *me*," murmured Mrs. Downey, retreating to the kitchen.

In the morning Penny decided to ski down to the village for a jar of cold cream. The snow was crusted and fast but she felt no terror of the trail which curved sharply through the evergreens. Her balance was better, and this time she had no intention of impaling herself on Peter Jasko's barbed wire fence.

Seldom checking her speed, she hurtled along the ribbon of trail. Racing on to the sharp turn, she shifted her weight and swung her body at precisely the right instant. The slope stretched on past rows of tall trees, towering like sentinels along the snow-swept ridges. Presently it flattened out into an open valley. Penny sailed past a house, a barn, and gradually slowed up until she came to a low hillock overlooking the village.

Recapturing her breath, Penny took off her skis and walked on into Pine Top. She made a few purchases at the drug store and then impulsively entered the telegraph office. To her surprise, Francine Sellberg was there ahead of her.

"How late is your office open?" the reporter was asking the operator.

"Six-thirty," he replied.

"And if one has a rush message to send after that hour?"

"Well, you can get me at my house," the man answered. "I live over behind the Albert's Filling Station."

"Thank you," responded Francine, flashing Penny a mocking smile. "I may have an important story to send to my paper any hour. I wanted to be sure there would be no delay in getting it off."

Penny waited until the reporter had left the office and then said apologetically:

CHAPTER 8 - A CODED MESSAGE

"I don't suppose you've received any message for me?"

"We always telephone as soon as anything comes in," the man replied. "But wait! You're Penelope Parker, aren't you?"

"In my more serious moments. Otherwise, just plain Penny."

"I do have something for you, then. A message came in a few minutes ago. I've been too busy to telephone it to the lodge."

He handed Penny a sheet of paper which she read eagerly. As she anticipated, it was from her father, and with his usual disregard for economy he had not bothered to omit words.

"Glad to learn you arrived safely at Pine Top," he had wired. "Your information about H. M. is astonishing, if true. Are you sure it is the same man? Keep your eye on him, and report to me if you learn anything worth while. I am held here by important developments, but will try to come to Pine Top for Christmas."

Penny read the message twice, scowling at the sentence: "Are you sure it is the same man?" It was clear to her that her father did not have a great deal of faith in her identification. And obviously, he did not believe that anything could be gained by making a special trip to Pine Top to see the hotel man.

Thrusting the paper into the pocket of her jacket she went out into the cold.

"No one seems to rate my detective work very highly," she complained to herself. "But when Dad gets my letter telling him about the Green Door he may take a different attitude!"

Skis slung over her shoulder, she began the weary climb back to the Downey lodge. Before Penny had walked very far she saw that she was overtaking a man on the narrow trail ahead of her. Observing that it was Ralph Fergus, she immediately slowed her steps.

The hotel man did not turn his head to glance back. He kept walking slower and slower as if in deep thought, and after a time he reached absently into his pocket for a letter.

As he pulled it out, another piece of pale gray paper fluttered to the ground. Fergus did not notice that he had lost anything. The wind caught the paper and blew it down the slope toward Penny.

"Oh, Mr. Fergus!" she called. "You dropped something!"

The wind hurled her words back at her. Realizing that she could not make the man hear, Penny quickened her pace. After a short chase she rescued the paper when it caught on the thorns of a snow-caked bush.

At first glance Penny thought she had gone to trouble for no purpose. The paper seemed to be blank. But as she turned it over she saw a single line of jumbled letters:

YL GFZKY GLULFFLS

"What can this be?" Penny thought in amazement. "Nothing, I guess."

She crumpled the paper and tossed it away. But as it skittered and bounced like a tumble weed down the trail, she suddenly changed her mind and darted after it again. Carefully straightening out the page she examined it a second time.

"This looks like copy paper used in a newspaper office," she told herself. "But there is no newspaper in Pine Top, I wonder—?"

The conviction came to Penny that the jumbled letters might be in code. Her pulse leaped at the thought. If only she were able to decipher it!

"I'll take this to the lodge and work on it," she decided quickly. "Who knows? It may be just the key I need to unlock this strange affair of the Green Door!"

CHAPTER 9 - A CALL FOR HELP

All that afternoon and far into the evening Penny devoted to her assigned task, trying to make sense out of the jumbled sentence of typewriting. She used first one method and then another, but she could not decode the brief message. She had moments when she even doubted that it was a code. At last, completely disgusted, she threw down her pencil and put the paper away in a bureau drawer.

"I never was meant to be a cryptographer or whatever you call those brainy fellows who unravel ciphers and things!" she grumbled. "Maybe the trouble with me is that I'm not bright."

Switching off the lamp, Penny rolled up the shade, and stood for a moment gazing down into the dark valley. Far below she could see lights glowing in the Fergus hotel, mysterious and challenging.

"I feel as if I'm on the verge of an important discovery, yet nothing happens," she sighed. "Something unusual is going on here, but what?"

Penny did not believe that Francine knew the answer either. The girl reporter undoubtedly had been sent to Pine Top upon a definite tip from her editor, yet she could not guess the nature of such a tip. It was fairly evident that Francine was after some sort of evidence, but so far she had made no progress in acquiring it.

"We're both groping in the dark, searching for something we know is here but can't see," thought Penny. "And we watch each other like hawks for fear the other fellow will get the jump!"

The Green Door intrigued and puzzled her. While it might mean nothing at all, she could not shake off a feeling that if once she were able to get inside the room she might learn the answer to some of her questions.

Penny had turned over several plans in her mind, none of which suited her. The most obvious thing to do was to try to bribe an employee of the hotel to give her the information she sought. But if she failed, her identity would be disclosed to Ralph Fergus and Harvey Maxwell. It seemed wiser to bide her time and watch.

Penny awoke the next morning to find large flakes of snow piling on the window sills. The storm continued and after breakfast only the most rugged skiers ventured out on the slopes. Francine hugged a hot air register, complaining that there was not enough heat, Many of the other guests, soon exhausting the supply of magazines, became restless.

Luncheon was over when Penny stamped in out of the cold to find Mr. Glasser fretfully pacing to and fro before the fireplace.

"When will the papers come?" he asked Mrs. Downey.

"Jake usually goes down to the village after them about four o'clock. But with this thick weather, the plane may not get in today."

"It's in now, Mrs. Downey," spoke Penny, shaking snow from her red mittens. "I saw it nearly half an hour ago, flying low over the valley."

"Then the papers must be at Pine Top by this time." Mrs. Downey hesitated before adding: "I'll call Jake from his work and ask him to go after them."

"Let me," offered Penny quickly.

"In this storm?"

"Oh, I don't mind. I rather like it."

"All right, then," agreed Mrs. Downey in relief. "But don't get lost, whatever you do. If the trails become snowed over it might be better to stay on the main road."

"I won't get lost," laughed Penny. "If worse comes to worst I always can climb a pine tree and sight the Fergus hotel."

CHAPTER 9 - A CALL FOR HELP

She dried out her mittens, and putting on an extra sweater beneath her jacket, stepped outside the lodge. The wind had fallen and only a few snowflakes were whirling down. Hearing the faint tingle of bells, Penny turned to gaze toward the road, where a pair of white horses were pulling an empty lumber wagon up the hill.

The driver, hunched over on the seat, was slapping his hands together to keep them warm.

"Why, that looks like Old Whiskers himself," thought Penny. "It is Peter Jasko."

The observation served only to remind her of their unpleasant meeting. Since being so discourteously ejected from the Jasko property Penny had not ventured back. Knowing that the old man was away she felt sorely tempted to again visit the locality.

"I guess I ought not to take the time," she decided regretfully. "Mr. Glasser will be fretting for his paper."

Making a quick trip down the mountainside, Penny swung into the village. Mrs. Downey had told her that she would be able to get the newspapers at the Pine Top Cafe where a boy named Benny Smith had an agency.

Entering the restaurant, she glanced about but saw no one who was selling papers. Finally, she ventured to ask the proprietor if she had come to the right place.

"This is the right place," he agreed cheerfully. "Benny went home a little while ago."

"Then how do I get the papers for Mrs. Downey's lodge?"

"Guess you're out of luck," he replied. "They didn't come in today."

"But I saw the plane."

"The plane got through all right. I don't know what was wrong. Somehow the papers weren't put aboard."

Penny turned away in disappointment. She had made the long trip to the village for no purpose. While she did not mind for herself, she knew that Mr. Glasser and the other guests were likely to be annoyed. After a day of confinement indoors they looked forward to news from the outside world.

"It's strange the papers didn't come," she mused as she started back to the Downey lodge. "This isn't the first time they've failed to arrive either."

Penny climbed steadily for a time and then sat down on a log to rest a moment. She was not far from the Jasko cabin. By making her own trail through the woods she could reach it in a very few minutes.

A mischievous idea leaped into her mind, fairly teasing to be put into effect. What fun to climb the forbidden barbed wire fence and honeycomb Mr. Jasko's field with ski tracks! She could visualize his annoyance when he returned home to learn that a mysterious skier had paid him a visit.

"He oughtn't to be so mean," she said aloud to justify herself. "It will serve him right for trying to frighten folks with shotguns!"

Penny fastened on her skis and glided off through the woods. She kept her directions straight and soon emerged into a clearing to find herself in view of the Jasko cabin. Drawing near the barbed wire fence she stopped short and stared.

"Why, that old scamp! He really did it!"

A new strand of wire had been added to the fence, making it many inches higher. Penny's suggestion, offered as a joke, had been acted upon by Peter Jasko. Not even an expert ski jumper could hope to clear the improved barrier. Any person who came unwittingly down the steep slope must take a disastrous tumble at the base of the fence.

"This settles it," thought Penny grimly. "My conscience is perfectly clear now."

She rolled under the fence and surveyed the unblemished expanse of snowy field with the eye of a mechanical draftsman.

"I may as well be honest about it and sign my name," she chuckled.

Starting in at the far corner of the field she made a huge double-edged "P" with her long runners. It took a little ingenuity to figure out an "E" but two "N's" were fairly easy to execute. She finished "Y" off with a flourish and cocked her head sideways to view her handiwork.

"Not bad, not bad at all," she congratulated herself. "Only I've used up too much space. We'll have to have a big Penny and a little Parker."

She ran off a "P" and an "A" but even her limber body was not equal to the contortion required for an "R." In the process of making a neat curve she suddenly lost her balance and toppled over in an ungainly heap.

"Oh, now I've done it!" she moaned, slowly picking herself up. "All my wonderful artistry gone for nothing. 'Parker' looks like a big smudge!"

A sound, suspiciously suggesting a muffled shout of laughter, reached Penny's ears. She glanced quickly about. No one was in sight. The windows of the cabin were deserted.

"I think I'll be getting out of here," she decided. "If Old Whiskers should come back this wouldn't be a healthy place to practice handwriting."

Penny dug in her poles and glided toward the fence. In the act of rolling under the barbed wires, she suddenly froze motionless. She had heard a cry and this time there was no doubt in her mind as to the direction from which the sound had come. Her startled gaze focused upon the cabin amid the trees.

"Help! Help!" called a shrill, half muffled voice. "Come back, and let me out of my prison!"

CHAPTER 10 - LOCKED IN THE CABIN

Penny hesitated, and as the call was repeated, went slowly back toward the cabin. She could see no one.

"Up here!" shouted the voice.

Glancing toward the second story windows, Penny saw a girl standing there, her face pressed to the pane.

"Peter Jasko's granddaughter!" thought Penny. "And she must have seen me decorating the place with ski tracks."

However, the other girl was only concerned with her own predicament. She smiled and motioned for Penny to come directly under the window.

"Can you help me get out of here?" she called down.

"You're not locked in?" inquired Penny in astonishment.

"I certainly am! My grandfather did it. He fastened the door of the loft."

"How long have you been there?"

"Oh, not very long," the girl answered impatiently, "but I'm sick of it! Will you help me out of here?"

"How?"

"Grandfather always hides the key to the outside door in the woodshed. It should be hanging on a nail by the window."

Penny hardly knew what to do. It was one thing to annoy Peter Jasko by making a few ski tracks in his yard, but quite another to antagonize him in more serious ways. For all she could tell, he might have locked the girl in the cabin as a punishment for some wrongdoing.

"Does your grandfather often leave you like this?" she asked dubiously.

"Always when there's snow on the ground," came the surprising answer. "Oh, please let me out of this hateful place! Don't be such a goody-good!"

To be accused of being a "goody-good" was a novel experience for Penny. But instead of taking offense she laughed and started toward the woodshed.

"On a nail by the window!" the girl shouted after her. "If it isn't there look on the shelf by the door."

Penny found the key and came back. Taking off her cumbersome skis, she unlocked the front door and stepped inside the cabin. The room was rather cold for the fire had nearly gone out. Despite a bareness of furniture, the place had a comfortable appearance. Snowshoes decorated the walls along with a deer head and an out-dated calendar. There was a cook stove, a homemade table, chairs, and a cot.

"Do hurry up!" called the impatient voice from above. "Climb the steps."

At the far end of the room a rickety, crudely constructed ladder ascended to a rectangular trap door in the ceiling. Mounting it, Penny investigated the fastening, a stout plug of wood. She turned it and pushed up the heavy door. Instantly, it was seized from above and pulled out of the way.

Head and shoulders through the opening, Penny glanced about curiously. The room under the roof certainly did not look like a prison cell. It was snug and warm, with curtains at the windows and books lining the wall shelves. The floor was covered with a bright colored rag rug. There was a comfortable looking bed, a rocker and even a dressing table.

"Thanks for letting me out."

Penny turned to gaze at the girl who stood directly behind her. She was not very pretty, for her nose was far too blunt and her teeth a trifle uneven. One could see a faint resemblance to Peter Jasko.

"You're welcome, I guess," replied Penny, but with no conviction. "I hope your grandfather won't be too angry."

"Oh, he won't know about it," the girl answered carelessly. "I see you know who I am—Sara Jasko."

"My name is Penny Parker."

"I guessed the Penny part. I saw you trying to write it in the snow. You don't believe in signs either, do you?"

"I didn't have any right to trespass."

"Oh, don't worry about that. Grandfather is an old fuss-budget. But deep down inside he's rather nice."

"Why did he lock you up here?"

"It's a long story," sighed Sara. "I'll tell you about it later. Come on, let's get out of here."

Penny backed down the ladder. The amazing granddaughter of Peter Jasko followed, taking the steps as nimbly as a monkey.

Going to a closet, Sara pulled out a wind-breaker, woolen cap, and a stub-toed pair of high leather shoes which she began to lace up.

"You're not aiming to run away?" Penny asked uneasily.

"Only for an hour or so. This snow is too beautiful to waste. But you'll have to help me get back to my prison."

"I don't know what this is all about. Suppose you tell me, Sara."

"Oh, Grandfather is funny," replied the girl, digging in the closet again for her woolen gloves. "He doesn't trust me out of his sight when there's snow on the ground. Today he had to go up the mountain to get a load of wood so he locked me in."

"What has snow to do with it?"

"Why, everything! You must have heard about Grandfather. He hates skiing."

"Oh, and you like to ski," said Penny, "is that it?"

"I adore it! My father, Bret Jasko, was a champion." Sara's animated face suddenly became sober. "He was killed on this very mountain. Grandfather never recovered from the shock."

"Oh, I'm so sorry," murmured Penny sympathetically.

"It happened ten years ago while my father was skiing. Ever since then Grandfather has had an almost fanatical hatred of the hotel people. And he is deathly afraid I'll get hurt in some way. He forbids me to ski even on the easy slopes."

"But you do it anyway?"

"Of course. I slip away whenever I can," Sara admitted cheerfully. "Skiing is in my blood. I couldn't give it up."

"And you don't mind deceiving your grandfather?"

"You don't understand. There's no reasoning with him. Each year he gets a little more set in his ways. He knows that I slip away to ski, and that's why he locks me up. Otherwise, Grandfather is a dear. He's taken care of me since my father died."

Sara wriggled into her awkward-fitting coat, wrapped a red scarf about her throat and started for the door.

"Coming, Penny?"

"I haven't promised yet that I will help you get back into your cubby-hole."

"But you will," said Sara confidently.

"I suppose so," sighed Penny. "Nevertheless, I don't particularly like this."

They stepped out of the cabin into the blinding sunlight. The storm had stopped, but the wind blew a gust of snow from the roof into their faces.

"My skis are hidden in the woods," said Sara. "We'll walk along the fence so my footprints won't be so noticeable."

"The place is pretty well marked up now," Penny observed dryly. "Your grandfather would have to be blind not to see them."

"Yes, but they're your tracks, not mine," grinned Sara. "Besides, this strong wind is starting to drift the snow."

They followed the barbed wire fence to the woods. Sara went straight to an old log and from its hollow interior drew out a pair of hickory jumping skis.

"Let's walk up to Mrs. Downey's lodge," she proposed. "Her chute is a dandy, but most of the guests are afraid to use it."

CHAPTER 10 - LOCKED IN THE CABIN

"I haven't tried it myself," admitted Penny. "It looks higher than Pike's Peak."

"Oh, you have plenty of nerve," returned Sara carelessly. "I saw you take Grandfather's barbed wire entanglements."

"That was a matter of necessity."

"Nothing ventured, nothing gained," laughed Sara, linking arms with Penny and pulling her along at a fast pace. "I'll teach you a few tricks."

They climbed the slope steadily until forced to pause for a moment to catch their breath.

"Mrs. Downey isn't using the bob-sled run this year, is she?" Sara inquired curiously.

"I didn't know anything about it."

"She has a fine one on her property, but it's out of sight from the lodge. I guess there haven't been enough guests this season to make it worth while. Too bad. Bob-sled racing is even more fun than skiing."

Coming within view of the Downey lodge, Penny observed that a few of the more hardy guests had taken advantage of the lull in the storm, and were out on the slopes, falling, picking themselves up, falling again.

"I have to run into the house a minute," Penny excused herself. "I'll be right back."

She found Mrs. Downey in the kitchen and reported to her that she had been unable to purchase papers in the village.

"The plane came in, didn't it?"

"Yes, but for some reason the papers weren't put on."

"I wonder if the Fergus hotel managed to get any?"

"I don't see how they could."

"It's happened before," declared Mrs. Downey.

"Time after time we miss our papers, and then I learn later that the Fergus hotel guests had them. I don't understand it, Penny."

"Shall I tell Mr. Glasser?"

"I'll do it," sighed Mrs. Downey. "He's going to be more irritated than ever now."

Penny went outside to find Sara waiting impatiently for her. The girl had strapped on her skis, and was using two sharp-pointed sticks for poles.

"Ready to try the jump, Penny?"

"No, but I'll watch you."

"There's nothing to it, Penny," encouraged Sara as they climbed side by side. "Just keep relaxed and be sure to have your skis pointing upward while you're in the air."

As it became evident that the girls intended to try the chute, a little crowd of spectators gathered on the slope below to watch.

"I'll go first," said Sara, "and after I've landed, you come after me."

"I'll think it over," shivered Penny.

"Don't think too long, or you'll never try it. Just start."

Sara bent to examine her bindings. Then in a graceful crouch she shot down the hill and with a lifting of her arms soared over the take-off. She made a perfectly poised figure in mid-air and an effortless landing on the slope below, finishing off with a christiana turn.

"She's *good*!" thought Penny. "I'll try it, too, even if they carry me off on a stretcher!"

In a wave of enthusiasm she pushed off, keeping her arms behind her. As the edge of the chute loomed up, she swung them forward and sprang into the air. But something went wrong. In an instant she was off balance, her arms swinging wildly in a futile attempt to straighten her body into position.

The gully appeared to be miles below her. Panic surged over Penny and her muscles became rigid. She was going to take a hard fall.

"Relax! Relax!" screamed a shrill voice.

With a supreme effort Penny drew back one ski and bent her knees. She felt a hard jar, and in amazement realized that she had landed on her feet. Her elation was short lived, for the next instant she collapsed and went sliding on down the slope.

Sara ran to help her up.

"Hurt?"

"Not a bit," laughed Penny. "What a spectacle I must have made!"

"Your jump wasn't half bad. Next time you'll do much better."

"I'll never make one as good as yours," Penny said enviously. Seeing Francine standing near, she turned to the reporter and exclaimed: "Did you watch Sara's jump? Wasn't it magnificent?"

"You're both lucky you weren't injured." Francine walked over to the two girls. She stared at Sara's odd looking costume. "You're not a guest here?" she inquired.

"No," answered Sara.

"Nor at the Fergus hotel?"

"I live a ways down the mountain."

Francine regarded her coldly. "You're the Jasko girl, aren't you, whose grandfather will not allow skiers on his property?"

"Yes, but—"

"Since you Jaskos are so sign conscious I should think you might obey them yourself! Take a glance at that one over on the tree. Unless my eyesight is failing it reads: 'Only guests of the hotel may use these slopes.'"

CHAPTER 11 - A NEWSPAPER MYSTERY

Penny stared at Francine, for a moment not believing that she had meant the remark seriously. As she comprehended that the girl indeed was serious, she exclaimed in quick protest:

"Oh, Francine, what an attitude to take! Sara is my guest. I'm sure Mrs. Downey doesn't mind."

"I'll go," offered Sara in a quiet voice. "I never dreamed I would offend anyone by being here."

"I'm not particularly offended," replied Francine defensively. "It merely seems reasonable to me that if you won't allow others on your property you shouldn't trespass yourself."

"Sara had nothing to do with that sign on her grandfather's land," declared Penny. "Francine, you must have jumped out of the wrong side of the bed this morning."

Sara had turned to walk away. Penny caught her hand, trying to detain her.

"Wait, I'll run into the lodge and ask Mrs. Downey. But I know very well it will be all right for you to stay."

Sara hesitated, and might have consented, save at that instant the three girls heard the faint tinkle of bells. A sled loaded with wood came into view around a curve of the mountain road.

"That's grandfather on his way home!" exclaimed Sara. "I must get back there before he learns I've been away! Hurry, Penny!"

With several quick thrusts of her sticks, she started down the trail which led to the Jasko cabin. Penny followed, but she could not overtake her companion. Sara skied with a reckless skill which defied imitation. While Penny was forced to stem, she took the rough track with no perceptible slackening of speed, and had divested herself of skis by the time her companion reached the woods.

"We'll have to work fast," she warned, hiding the long runners in the hollow log. "I want you to lock me in the cabin and then get away before Grandfather sees you!"

"What about our tracks in the snow?"

"I'll blame them all on you," laughed Sara, "It's beginning to get dark now. And Grandfather is near sighted."

"I don't like this business at all," complained Penny as they kept close to the fence on their way to the cabin. "Why not tell your grandfather—"

"He would rage for days and never let me out again. No, this is the best way. And you'll come back soon, won't you, Penny?"

"I don't like to promise."

"I'll teach you how to jump." Sara offered attractive bait.

"We'll see. I'll think it over."

"No, promise!" persisted Sara. "Say you'll come back and at least talk to me through the window. You have no idea how lonesome I get."

"All right," Penny suddenly gave in. "I'll do that much."

Reaching the cabin, Sara had Penny tramp about in the snow with her skis so as to give the impression that a visitor had walked several times around the building but had not entered.

"You'll have to lock me in the loft," she instructed. "Then take the key back to the woodshed and get away as quickly as you can."

Sara pulled off her garments and hung them in the closet. With a mop she wiped up tracks which had been made on the bare floor. Then she climbed up the ladder to her room.

Penny turned the wooden peg, and retreating from the cabin, locked the door.

"Don't forget!" Sara called to her from the window. "Come again soon—tomorrow if you can."

Hiding the key in the woodshed, Penny tramped about the outside of the building several times before gliding off toward the boundary fence. As she began a tedious climb up the trail toward the Downey lodge, she saw the sled appear around a bend of the road.

Penny did not visit the Jasko cabin the following day nor the next. Along with other guests she was kept indoors by a raging snow and sleet storm which blocked the road and disrupted telephone service to the village.

Everyone at the Downey lodge suffered from the confinement, but some accepted the situation more philosophically than others. As usual Mr. Glasser complained because there were no daily papers. Penny overheard him telling another guest he was thinking very seriously of moving to the Fergus hotel where at least a certain amount of entertainment was provided.

"He'll leave," Mrs. Downey observed resignedly when the conversation was repeated to her. "I've seen it coming for days. Mr. Glasser has been talking with one of the runners for the Fergus hotel."

"It's unfair of them to try to take your guests away."

"Oh, they're determined to put me out of business at any cost. Miss Sellberg is leaving, too. She served notice this morning."

Penny glanced up with quick interest. "Francine? Is she leaving Pine Top?"

"No, she told me she had decided to move to the Fergus hotel because of its better location."

Penny nodded thoughtfully. She could understand that if Francine were trying to gain special information about either Ralph Fergus or Harvey Maxwell, it would be to her advantage to have a room at the other hotel. Had it not been for her loyalty to Mrs. Downey, she, too, would have been tempted to take up headquarters there.

"I can't really blame folks for leaving," Mrs. Downey continued after a moment. "I've not offered very much entertainment this year. Last season in addition to skiing we had the bob-sled run."

"I met Sara Jasko and she was telling me about it," replied Penny. "Can't you use the run again this year?"

"We could, but it scarcely seems worth the trouble and expense. Also, it takes experienced drivers to steer the sleds. The young man I had working for me last winter isn't available at present."

"Is there no other person at Pine Top who could do it?"

"Sara Jasko," responded Mrs. Downey, smiling. "However, it's not likely her grandfather would give his consent."

The following day dawned bright and clear and brought a revival of spirit at the Downey lodge. Nevertheless, with the roads open once more, both Francine and Mr. Glasser moved their belongings down to the Fergus hotel. As was to be expected, their departure caused a certain amount of comment by the other guests.

Late in the afternoon Penny offered to ski down to Pine Top for the newspapers. She planned to stop at the Fergus hotel upon her return, hoping to learn a little more about the mysterious Green Room which had intrigued her interest.

Reaching the village, Penny located Benny Smith, but the lad shook his head when she inquired for the daily papers.

"I don't have any today."

"But the plane came through! I saw it myself about an hour ago. This makes four days since we've had a newspaper at the lodge. What happened?"

The boy glared at Penny almost defiantly. "You can't blame me. It's not my fault if they're not put on the plane."

"No, of course not. I didn't mean to suggest that you were at fault. It's just queer that we miss our papers so often. And we never seem to get the back editions either."

"Well, I don't know anything about it," the boy muttered.

Penny stood watching him slouch off down the street. Something about the lad's manner made her wonder if he had not lied. She suddenly was convinced that Benny knew more about the missing newspapers than he cared to tell.

"But how would he profit by not receiving them?" she mused. "He would lose sales. It simply doesn't make sense."

As she trudged on down the street Penny turned the problem over in her mind. She walked with head bent low and did not notice an approaching pedestrian until she had bumped into him.

"Sorry," apologized the man politely.

CHAPTER 11 - A NEWSPAPER MYSTERY

"It was my fault," replied Penny. She glanced up to see that the stranger was no stranger at all, but the airplane pilot who had brought her to Pine Top several days before.

He would have passed on had she not halted him with a question.

"I wonder if you could tell me what seems to be the trouble with the newspaper delivery service here at Pine Top?"

"We couldn't get through yesterday on account of the weather," he returned.

"But what happened to the papers today?"

"Nothing."

"You mean they came through?" Penny asked in surprise.

"That's right. You can get them from Benny Smith."

"From Benny? But he said—"

Penny started to reveal that the boy had blamed the failure of service upon the pilot, and then changed her mind.

"Thank you," she returned, "I'll talk with him."

Penny was more puzzled than ever, but she had no reason to doubt the pilot's word. Obviously, the newspapers had arrived at Pine Top, and Benny Smith knew what had become of them.

"I'll just investigate this matter a little further," Penny decided as she left the village.

Approaching the Fergus hotel a few minutes later, she paused to catch her breath before going inside. In the gathering twilight the building looked more than ever like a great Swiss chalet. The pitched roof was burdened with a thick layer of white snow, and long icicles hung from the window ledges.

Inside the crowded, smoke-filled lobby there was an air of gaiety. A few lights had been turned on, and the orchestra could be heard tuning up in the dining room.

Penny saw no one that she knew. Crossing quickly to a counter at the far side of the lobby, she spoke to a girl who was in charge.

"Can I buy a newspaper here?"

"Yes, we have them." The girl reached around a corner of the counter, indicating a stack of papers which Penny had not seen. "New York Times?"

"That will do very nicely."

Penny paid for the paper and carrying it over to a chair, quickly looked at the dateline.

"It's today's issue, all right," she told herself grimly. "This proves what I suspected. Ralph Fergus has been buying up all the papers—a little trick to annoy Mrs. Downey and get her in bad with her guests!"

CHAPTER 12 - THE GREEN CARD

"Do you always talk to yourself?" inquired an amused voice from behind Penny.

Glancing up from the newspaper, the girl saw Maxine Miller standing beside her chair. For an instant she failed to recognize the actress, so elegant did the woman appear in a sealskin coat and matching hat. The outfit was so new that the fur had lost none of its glaze, an observation which caused Penny to wonder if Miss Miller had misled her regarding the state of her finances.

"Good evening, Miss Miller," she smiled. "I didn't know you for a moment."

"How do you like it?" inquired the actress, turning slowly about.

"Your new fur coat? It's very beautiful. And you're looking well, too. You didn't by chance get that role from David Balantine?"

Miss Miller's painted lips drew into a pout. "No, he left the hotel this morning."

"Oh, that's too bad. I suppose you'll be going soon, then?"

The actress shook her head, and laughed in a mysterious way.

"No, I've decided to stay here for awhile. I like Pine Top."

Penny was puzzled by Miss Miller's sudden change in manner and appearance. The woman acted as if she were the possessor of an important secret which she longed to reveal.

"You must have fallen heiress to a vast fortune," Penny ventured lightly.

"Better than that," beamed Miss Miller. "I've acquired a new job. Take dinner with me and I'll tell you all about it."

"Well—" Penny deliberated and said honestly, "I didn't bring very much money with me, and I'm not dressed up."

Miss Miller brushed aside both objections as if they were of no consequence.

"You'll be my guest, dearie. And your clothes don't matter."

She caught Penny's hand and pulled her to her feet. Her curiosity aroused, the girl allowed herself to be escorted to the dining room.

Miss Miller walked ahead, strutting a bit as she brushed past the crowded tables. Heads lifted and envious feminine eyes focused upon the actress' stunning fur coat. Penny felt awkward and embarrassed, clomping along behind in her big heavy ski boots.

The head waiter gave them a choice table near the orchestra. Miss Miller threw back her coat, exposing a form-fitting black satin gown with a brilliant blue stone pin at the neck line. She knew that she was creating an impression and thoroughly enjoyed herself.

A waiter brought menu cards. The actress proceeded to order for both herself and Penny. She selected the most expensive dishes offered, stumbling over their long French names.

"How nice it is to have money again," she remarked languidly when the waiter had gone. "Do you really like my new wardrobe, dearie?"

"Indeed, I do, Miss Miller. Your dress is very becoming, and the fur coat is stunning. Isn't it new?"

"Exactly two days old."

"Then you must have acquired it since coming to Pine Top. I had no idea such lovely skins could be bought anywhere near here."

"We're very close to the Canadian border, you know." Again the actress flashed her mysterious smile. "But the duty is frightful unless one is able to avoid it."

Penny gazed thoughtfully across the table at her companion.

CHAPTER 12 - THE GREEN CARD

"And do you know how to avoid it?" she asked as casually as she could manage.

Miss Miller steered skilfully away from the subject.

"Oh, this coat was given to me. It didn't cost me a cent."

"And how does one go about acquiring a free coat? You've not become a professional model?"

"No," the actress denied, "but your guess is fairly warm. I do have a nice figure for displaying clothes. No doubt that was why I was given the job."

"Who is your employer, Miss Miller? Someone connected with the hotel?"

The waiter had brought a loaded tray to the table, and the actress used his arrival as a pretext for not answering Penny's question. After the man went away she began to chat glibly about other subjects. However, with the serving of dessert, she once more switched to the topic of her wardrobe.

"You were asking me about my fur coat, dearie," she said. "Would you like to have one like it?"

"Who wouldn't? What must I do to acquire one—rob a bank?"

Miss Miller laughed in a forced way. "You will have your little joke. From what you've told me, I imagine your father has plenty of money."

"I don't remember saying anything about it," responded Penny dryly. "As a matter of fact, my father isn't wealthy."

"At least your family is comfortably fixed or you wouldn't be at this expensive winter resort," Miss Miller went on, undisturbed. "Now would you be able to pay as much as a hundred dollars for a coat?"

"I hadn't even thought of buying one," replied Penny, trying not to disclose her astonishment. "Can you really get a good fur coat for as little as a hundred dollars?"

"You could through my friend."

"Your friend?" asked Penny bluntly. "Do you mean your new employer?"

"Well, yes," the actress admitted with a self-conscious laugh. "He is a fur salesman. You've been very nice to me and I might be able to get a coat for you at cost."

"That's most kind," remarked Penny dryly. "Where could I see these coats?"

"My employer has a salesroom here at the hotel," Miss Miller declared. "I can arrange an appointment for you. Say tomorrow at two?"

"I haven't enough money with me to buy a coat even if I wanted one."

"But if you liked the furs you could wire your parents for more," the actress wheedled. "It is a wonderful opportunity. You'll never have another chance to buy a beautiful coat at cost."

"I'll have to think it over," Penny returned. "I suppose you get a commission on every garment sold?"

"A small one. In your case, I'll not take it. I truly am interested in seeing you get your coat, dearie. You have just the figure for it, you're so slim and svelte."

Penny was not deceived by the flattery. She knew very well that the actress had treated her to dinner for the purpose of making her feel under obligation and as a build-up to the suggestion that she purchase a fur coat.

Glancing at the bill she was relieved to see that she had enough money to pay for her share of the meal.

"No, no, I won't hear of it," Miss Miller protested grandly.

Summoning the waiter, she gave him a twenty dollar bill.

"Let me know if you decide you would like to see the coats," she said to Penny as they left the dining room together. "It won't cost you anything to look, you know."

"I'll think it over. Thanks for the dinner."

Penny looked about the crowded lobby for Ralph Fergus or Harvey Maxwell, but neither man was to be seen. While at the hotel she would have liked to acquire a little more information about the Green Room. With the actress hovering at her elbow it was out of the question.

She considered speaking of the matter to Miss Miller, and then abandoned the idea. However, it had occurred to her that the mysterious room of the hotel might have some connection with the actress' present employment, and so she ventured one rather direct question.

"Miss Miller, you're not by chance working for Ralph Fergus or the hotel?"

"Dear me, no!" the actress denied. "Whatever put such an idea in your head?"

"It just occurred to me. Well, good-bye."

Penny left the hotel and ventured out into the cold. After so much cigarette smoke, the pure air was a pleasant relief. She broke off a long icicle from the doorway, and stood thoughtfully chewing at it.

"Miss Miller must be working for some dishonest outfit," she mused. "Her talk about getting a fur coat at cost doesn't fool me one bit. If I were in her shoes I'd be more than a little worried lest I tangled with the law."

A remark by the actress to the effect that the Canadian border was close by had set Penny's active mind to working. It was not too fantastic to believe that Miss Miller might be employed by an unscrupulous man whose business concerned the sale of furs obtained duty free. She had even dared hope that Ralph Fergus or Harvey Maxwell might be implicated in the dishonest affair. What a break that would be for her father if only she could prove such a connection! But the actress' outright denial that either man was her employer had put an end to such pleasant speculation.

Penny bent down to pick up her skis which had been left at the side of the hotel building. As she leaned over, she noticed a small object lying on top of the snow in the square of light made from one of the windows. It appeared to be a small piece of colored cardboard.

Curiously, Penny picked it up and carried it closer to the window. The card was green. Her pulse quickened as she turned it over. On its face were six engraved words:

"Admit Bearer Through The Green Door."

CHAPTER 13 - AN UNKIND TRICK

Penny all but executed a clog dance in the snow. She knew that she had picked up an admittance ticket to the Green Room of the Fergus hotel which some person had lost. With no effort upon her part she would be able to learn the answer to many of the questions which had plagued her.

"At last I'll find out what lies behind that Green Door," she thought in high elation. "If this isn't the most wonderful piece of luck!"

Debating a moment, Penny decided that it probably was too late to gain admittance that evening. Mrs. Downey no doubt was worried over her long absence from the lodge. She would return there, and then revisit the hotel early the next day.

Pocketing the precious ticket, Penny set off up the mountain. It was dark before she had covered half the distance, but there were stars and a half moon to guide her.

Mrs. Downey showed her relief as the girl stomped into the kitchen.

"I was beginning to worry, Penny," she declared. "Whatever made it take you so long?"

"I stopped at the Fergus hotel and had dinner with Miss Miller."

"Were you able to get the newspapers?"

"Only one which I had to buy at the Fergus hotel. Mrs. Downey, it's queer about those papers. Benny Smith told me there weren't any to be had, and then a few minutes later I met the airplane pilot who told me he had brought them in the same as usual. Also, the Fergus hotel received its usual quota."

"Well, that's odd."

"It looks to me as if the Fergus outfit has made some arrangement with the paper boy. They may be buying up all the papers."

"As a means of annoying me," nodded Mrs. Downey grimly. "It would be in line with their tactics. But what can I do?"

"I don't know," admitted Penny. She pulled off her heavy boots and set them where they would dry. "We haven't any proof they're doing anything like that. It's only my idea."

The door opened and Jake came into the kitchen. He dropped an armload of wood behind the range.

"I started work on the bob-sled run this afternoon," he remarked to Mrs. Downey. "Got a crew of boys coming first thing tomorrow. We ought to have her fixed up by noon."

"And the sleds?"

"They seem to be in good condition, but I'll check everything."

After the workman had gone, Penny glanced questioningly at Mrs. Downey.

"Have you decided to use the run after all?"

"Yes, I started thinking about it after we talked together. We do need more entertainment here at the lodge. After you left I ordered Jake to start work on the track. But I still am in need of experienced drivers for the sled."

"You spoke of Sara."

"I thought I would ask her, but I doubt if her Grandfather will give his consent."

"I'll ski down there tomorrow and talk with her if you would like me to," offered Penny.

"I would appreciate it," said Mrs. Downey gratefully. "I hate to spare the time myself."

Early the next morning Penny paid a visit to the bob-sled run where a crew headed by Jake was hard at work. There was a stretch of straightaway and a series of curves which snaked down the valley between the pines. At the point of the steepest curve, the outer snow walls rose to a height of eighteen feet.

"A sled could really travel on that track," observed Penny. "Does it hurt to upset?"

"It might," grinned Jake. "We've never had an upset on Horseshoe Curve. If a sled went over there, you might wake up in the hospital."

Penny watched the men packing snow for awhile. Then buckling on her skis, she made a fast trip down the mountain to the Jasko cabin. This time, having a definite mission, she went boldly to the door and rapped.

There was no response until the window of the loft shot up.

"Hello, Penny," called down Sara. "I thought you had forgotten your promise. The key's in the same place."

"Isn't your grandfather here?"

"No, he went down to Pine Top. Isn't it glorious skiing weather? Hurry and get the key. I've been cooped up here half an hour already."

Penny went reluctantly to the woodshed and returned with the key. She unfastened the trapdoor which gave entrance to the loft and Sara quickly descended.

"Didn't your grandfather say anything about last time?" Penny inquired anxiously.

"Oh, he raved because someone had trespassed. But it never occurred to him I had gone away. Where shall we ski today?"

"I only stopped to deliver a message, Sara. I am on my way down to the Fergus hotel."

"Oh," said the girl in disappointment. "A message from whom?"

"Mrs. Downey. She is starting up her bob-sled run again and she wants you to help out."

Sara's eyes began to sparkle.

"I wish I could! If only Grandfather weren't so strict."

"Is there a chance he'll give his consent?"

"Oh, dear, no. But I might be able to slip away. Grandfather plans to chop wood every day this week."

"I doubt if Mrs. Downey would want you to do that."

"Need you tell her?" queried Sara coolly. "I'll fix myself a rope ladder and get out the window. That will save you the trouble of coming here to let me in and out."

"And what will your grandfather say if he learns about it?"

"Plenty! But anything is better than being shut up like a prisoner. You tell Mrs. Downey I'll try to get up to the lodge tomorrow morning, and we'll try out the track together, eh Penny?"

"I don't know anything about bob-sledding."

"I'll teach you to be my brake boy," Sara laughed. "How long will you stay at the Fergus hotel?"

"I haven't any idea."

"Then I suppose I'll have to crawl back into my cave," Sara sighed dismally. "Can't you even ski with me for half an hour?"

"Not this morning," Penny said firmly. "I have important work ahead."

She shooed Sara back into the loft and returned the key to the woodshed. The Jasko girl watched from the window, playfully shaking her fist as her friend skied away.

"Sara is as stimulating as a mountain avalanche," chuckled Penny, "but she's almost too headstrong. Sooner or later her stunts will involve me in trouble with Peter Jasko."

In the valley below, smoke curled lazily from the chimneys of the Fergus hotel. Making directly for it, Penny felt in her pocket to be certain she had not lost the green ticket which she had found the previous evening.

"This is going to be my lucky day," she told herself cheerfully. "I feel it in my bones."

Reaching the hotel, Penny stripped off her skis and entered the hotel lobby. Maxine Miller was not in evidence nor did she see any other person who likely would question her presence there. She did notice Harvey Maxwell sitting in the private office. His eyes were upon her as she crossed the room. However, Penny felt no uneasiness, realizing that if he noticed her at all he recognized her only as a guest at the Downey lodge.

"Second floor," she said quietly to the elevator boy.

Penny was the sole passenger, but as she stepped from the cage, she was dismayed to run directly into Francine Sellberg.

The reporter greeted her with a suspicious stare.

"Why, hello, Penny Parker. What are you doing here?"

"Oh, just moseying around."

"I can see you are!"

CHAPTER 13 - AN UNKIND TRICK

"Your room isn't on this floor, is it?" Penny inquired.

"No, on the fourth," Francine answered before she considered her words.

"Looking for someone?" remarked Penny with a grin. "Or should I say *something*?"

An elevator stopped at the landing. "Going down," the attendant called, opening the door. He gazed questioningly at the two girls.

Francine shook her head, although she had been waiting for an elevator. Turning again to Penny she said with a hard smile: "I've not only been looking for something, I've found it!"

"Still, I don't see you rushing to reach a telephone, Francine. Your discovery can't have such tremendous news value."

"It may have before long," hinted Francine. "I don't mind telling you I am on the trail of a really big story. And I am making steady progress in assembling my facts."

Penny regarded the girl reporter speculatively. Her presence on the second floor rather suggested that she, too, had been trying to investigate the Green Room, and more than likely had learned its location. But she was reasonably certain Francine had gathered no information of great value.

"Glad to hear you're doing so well," she remarked and started on down the hall.

Francine fell into step with her. "If you're looking for a particular room, Penny, maybe I can help you."

Penny knew that the reporter meant to stay with her so that she could do no investigation work of her own.

"The room I am searching for has a green door," she replied.

Francine laughed. "I'm glad you're so honest, Penny. I guessed why you were on this floor all the time. However, I greatly fear you're in the wrong part of the hotel."

Penny paused and turned to face her companion squarely. "Why not put an end to all this nonsense, Francine? We watch each other and get nowhere. Let's put our cards on the table."

"Yours might be a joker!"

"We're both interested in getting a story which will discredit Harvey Maxwell," Penny went on, ignoring the jibe. "You've had a tip as to what may be going on here, while I'm working in the dark. On the other hand, I've acquired something which should interest you. Why don't we pool our interests and work together?"

"That would be very nice—for you."

"I think I might contribute something to the case."

"I doubt it," replied Francine loftily. "You don't even know the location of the Green Room."

"You're wrong about that. It took no great detective power to learn it's on this floor. To get inside may be a different matter."

"You're quite right there," said Francine with emphasis.

"What do you say? Shall we work together and let bygones be bygones?"

"Thank you, Penny, I prefer to work alone."

"Suit yourself, Francine. I was only trying to be generous. You see, I have an admittance card to the Green Room."

"I don't believe it!"

Flashing a gay smile, Penny held up the ticket for Francine to see.

"How did you get it?" the reporter gasped. "I've tried—"

"A little bird dropped it on my window sill. Too bad you didn't decide to work with me."

Penny walked on down the corridor, and Francine made no attempt to follow. When she glanced back over her shoulder the reporter had descended the stairway to the lobby.

"It was boastful of me to show her my ticket," she thought. "But I couldn't resist doing it. Francine is so conceited."

Making her way to the unmarked door of the wing, Penny paused there a moment, listening. Hearing no sound she pushed open the door and went down the narrow hall. The guard sat at his usual post before the Green Door.

"Good morning," said Penny pleasantly. "I have my card now."

The man examined it and handed it back. "Go right in," he told her.

Before Penny could obey, the door at the end of the corridor swung open. Harvey Maxwell, his face convulsed with rage, came hurrying toward the startled girl.

"I've just learned who you are," he said angrily. "Kindly leave this hotel at once, and don't come back!"

CHAPTER 14 - A BROKEN ROD

"You must have mistaken me for some other person," Penny stammered, backing a step away from the hotel man. "Who do you think I am?"

The question was a mistake, for it only served to intensify Harvey Maxwell's anger.

"You're the daughter of Anthony Parker who runs the yellowest paper in Riverview! I know why he sent you here. Now get out and don't let me catch you in the hotel ever again."

Observing the green card in Penny's hand he reached out and jerked it from her.

"I wasn't doing any harm," she said, trying to act injured. "My father didn't send me to Pine Top. I came for the skiing."

Secretly, Penny was angry at Maxwell's reference to the *Riverview Star* as being a "yellow" sheet, which in newspaper jargon meant that it was a sensation-seeking newspaper.

"And what are you doing in this part of the hotel?"

"I only wanted to see the Green Room," Penny replied. "I thought I would have my breakfast here."

Harvey Maxwell and the doorman exchanged a quick glance which was not lost upon the girl.

"Where did you get your ticket?" the hotel man demanded but in a less harsh voice.

"I picked it up outside the hotel."

Penny spoke truthfully and her words carried conviction. Harvey Maxwell seemed satisfied that she had not been investigating the wing for any special purpose. However, he took her by an elbow and steered her down the corridor to the elevator.

"If you're the smart little girl I think you are, a hint will be sufficient," he said. "I don't want any member of the Parker family on my premises. So stay away. Get me?"

"Yes, sir," responded Penny meekly.

Inwardly, she was raging. Someone deliberately had betrayed her to Harvey Maxwell and she had a very good idea who that person might be. From now on employes of the hotel would be told to keep watch for her. Never again would she be allowed in the lobby, much less in the vicinity of the Green Room.

Harvey Maxwell walked with Penny to the front door of the hotel and closed it behind her.

"Remember," he warned, "stay away."

As Penny started down the walk she heard a silvery laugh, and glancing sideways, saw Francine leaning against the building.

"You didn't spend much time in the Green Room, did you?" she inquired.

"That was a dirty trick to play!" retorted Penny. "I wouldn't have done it to you."

"You couldn't have thought that fast, my dear Penny."

"I might tell Mr. Maxwell you're a reporter for the *Riverview Record*. How would you like that?"

Francine shrugged. "In that case we both lose the story. All I want is an exclusive. After the yarn breaks in the *Record*, your father will be welcome to make use of any information published. So if you really want him to win his libel suit, you'll gain by not interfering with me."

"You reason in a very strange way," replied Penny coldly.

Picking up her skis she shouldered them and marched stiffly away. She was angry at Francine and angry at herself for having given the rival reporter an opportunity to score against her. Probably she would never tell Harvey Maxwell or Ralph Fergus who the girl actually was, sorely as she might be tempted. As Francine had pointed out, her own chance of gleaning any worth while information had been lost.

CHAPTER 14 - A BROKEN ROD

"It's a bitter pill to choke down," thought Penny, "but I would rather have the *Record* get the story than to lose it altogether."

Sunk deep in depression, she tramped back to the Downey lodge. The mail had arrived during her absence but there was no letter from home.

"Dad might at least send me a postcard," she grumbled. "For two cents I would take the next plane back to Riverview."

However, Penny could not remain downhearted for any great length of time. Why worry about Francine and the silly old Green Room? She would forget all about it and try to have fun for a change.

It was not difficult to dismiss the matter from her mind, for the following morning Sara Jasko came to give her a lesson in bob-sled driving. With a crowd of interested guests watching from the sidelines, they made their first exciting ride over the track. Sara steered, Jake operated the brake, and Penny rode as sole passenger.

Horseshoe Curve was the most thrilling point on the course. As the sled tore around it at a tremendous rate of speed, Jake dug in the iron claw of the brake, sending up a plume of snow. They slackened speed perceptibly, but even so the sled climbed high on the sloping wall, and Penny thought for an anxious moment that they were going over the top. The remainder of the run was mild by comparison.

Upon later trips Penny was allowed to manage the brake, and soon became dexterous in applying it as Sara shouted the command.

Skiers abandoned the slopes to watch the new sport. Two at a time, Penny and Sara gave them rides and all of their passengers were enthusiastic.

By the following day the word had spread down the mountain that Mrs. Downey's bob-sled run was operating. Guests from the Fergus hotel joined the throng but they were given rides only when there were no passengers waiting.

"It's going over like a house afire!" Penny declared gaily to Mrs. Downey. "I shouldn't be surprised if you take some of the Fergus hotel's customers away from them if this enthusiasm lasts."

"You and Sara are showing folks a wonderful time."

"And we're having one ourselves. It's even more fun than skiing."

"But more dangerous," declared Mrs. Downey. "I hope we have no accidents."

"Sara is a skillful driver."

"Yes, she is," agreed Mrs. Downey. "There's no cause for worry so long as the track isn't icy."

Two days passed during which Penny did not even go near the Fergus hotel or to the village. As she remarked to Mrs. Downey, all of Pine Top came to the lodge. During the morning hours when the bob-sled run was in operation, a long line of passengers stood waiting. Guests from the Fergus hotel had few chances for rides. Several of them, wishing to be on the favored list, checked out and came to take lodging at Mrs. Downey's place.

"I can't understand it," the woman declared to Penny. "Last year the run wasn't very popular. I think it may have been because we had a little accident at the beginning of the season. Nothing serious but it served to frighten folks."

"I wonder how the Fergus-Maxwell interests are enjoying it?" chuckled Penny.

"Not very well, you may be sure. This flurry in our business will rather worry them. They may not put me out of business as quickly as they expected."

"At least you'll end your season in a blaze of glory," laughed Penny.

The weather had turned warmer. Late Thursday afternoon the snow melted a bit and the lowering night temperatures caused a film of ice to form over the entire length of the bob-sled run. Jake shook his head as he talked over the situation with Penny the next morning.

"The track will be fast and slippery this morning."

"A lot of folks will be disappointed if we don't make any trips," declared Penny. "Here comes Sara. Let's see what she has to say."

Sara studied the run, and walked down as far as Horseshoe Curve.

"It's fast all right," she conceded. "But that will only make it the more exciting. Brakes in good order, Jake?"

"I tested every sled last night after they were brought to the shop."

"Then we'll have no trouble," said Sara confidently. "Round up the passengers, Jake, and we'll start at once."

The sled was hauled to the starting line. Sara took her place behind the wheel, with Penny riding the end position to handle the brake. Their first passengers were to be a middle aged married couple. Sara gave them padded helmets to wear.

"What are these for?" the woman asked nervously. "The toboggan slide isn't dangerous, is it?"

"No, certainly not," answered Sara. "We haven't had a spill this year. Hang tight on the curves. Give me plenty of brake when I call for it, Penny."

She signaled for the push off. They started fast and gathered speed on the straightaway. Penny wondered how Sara could steer for her own eyes blurred as they shot down the icy trough. They never had traveled at such high speed before.

"Brakes!" shouted Sara.

Penny obeyed the order, and felt the sled slow down as the brake claw dug into the snow and ice. They raced on toward the first wide curve, and swung around it, high on the banked wall, too close to the outside edge for comfort.

"Brakes!" called Sara again.

Once more the iron claw dug in, sending up a spray of snow behind the racing sled. And then there came a strange, pinging sound.

For the briefest instant Penny did not comprehend its significance. Then, as the sled leaped ahead faster than ever and the geyser of snow vanished, she realized what had happened. The brakes were useless! A rod had snapped! They were roaring down the track with undiminished speed, and Horseshoe Curve, the most dangerous point on the run, lay directly ahead.

CHAPTER 15 - IN THE TOOL HOUSE

Sara, her face white and tense, turned her head for a fraction of a second and then, crouching lower, kept her eyes glued on the track. She knew what had happened, and she knew, too, that they never could hope to make the Horseshoe Curve. Even a miracle of steering would not save them from going over the wall of ice at terrific speed.

The two passengers, frozen with fright, gripped the side ropes, and kept their heads down. It did not even occur to them that they could save themselves by rolling off. For that matter, they did not realize that the brake had broken.

Penny, in end position, could have jumped easily, A fall into the soft snow beside the track would be far less apt to cause serious injury than an upset from the high wall of the curve. But it never occurred to her to try to save herself.

There was only one slim chance of preventing a bad accident, a costly one for herself, and Penny took it. As the perpendicular wall of Horseshoe Curve loomed up ahead, she wrapped her arm about the side rope of the sled and hurled herself off. Her entire body was given a violent jerk. A sharp pain shot through her right arm, but she gritted her teeth and held on.

Penny's trailing body, acting as a brake, slowed down the sled and kept it from upsetting as it swept into the curve. Sideways it climbed the wall of snow. It crept to the very edge, hovered there a breathless moment, then fell back to overturn at the flat side of the curve.

Untangling herself from a pile of arms and legs, Sara began to help her passengers to their feet.

"Penny, are you hurt?" she asked anxiously. "That was a courageous thing to do! You saved us from a bad accident."

Spectators, thrilled by the display of heroism, came running to the scene. Penny, every muscle screaming with pain, rolled over in the snow. Gripping her wrenched arm, she tried to get to her feet and could not.

"Penny, you *are* hurt!" cried Sara.

"It's my arm, more than anything else," Penny said, trying to keep her face from twisting. "I—I hope it's not broken."

Willing hands raised her to her feet and supported her. Penny was relieved to discover that she could lift her injured arm.

"It's only wrenched," she murmured. "Anyone else hurt, Sara?"

"You're the only casualty," Sara replied warmly. "But if you hadn't used yourself as a brake we might all have been badly injured. You ought to get a hot bath as quickly as you can before your muscles begin to stiffen."

"They've begun already," replied Penny ruefully.

She took a step as if to start for the lodge, only to hesitate.

"I wonder what happened to the brake? I heard something give way."

Sara overturned the sled and took one glance. "A broken rod."

"I thought Jake checked over everything last night."

"That's what he *said*," returned Sara. "We'll ask him about it."

The workman, white-faced and frightened, came running down the hill.

"What happened?" he demanded. "Couldn't you slow down or was it too icy?"

"No brakes," Sara answered laconically. "I thought you tested them."

"I did. They were in good order last night."

"Take a look at this." Sara pointed to the broken rod.

Jake bent down to examine it. When he straightened he spoke no word, but the expression of his face told the two girls that he did not hold himself responsible for the mishap.

"There's something funny about this," he muttered. "I'll take the sled to the shop and have a look at it."

"I'll go along with you," declared Sara.

"And so will I," added Penny quickly.

"You really should get a hot bath and go to bed," advised Sara. "If you don't you may not be able to walk tomorrow."

"I'll go to bed in a little while," Penny answered significantly.

Followed by the two girls, Jake pulled the sled to the tool house behind the lodge. Sara immediately closed and bolted the door from the inside so that curious persons would not enter.

"Now let's really have a look at that brake rod," she said. "Notice anything queer about it, Penny?"

"I did, and I'm thinking the same thing you are."

"See these shiny marks on the steel," Jake pointed out excitedly. "The rod had been sawed almost in two. Even a little strain on it would make it break."

"You're certain it was in good condition last night?" Sara questioned.

"Positive," Jake responded grimly. "I checked over both sleds just before supper last night."

"Let's have a look at the other sled," proposed Penny.

An inspection of the brake equipment revealed nothing out of order.

"Whoever did the trick may have been afraid to damage both sleds for fear of drawing attention to his criminal work," declared Penny. "But it's perfectly evident someone wanted us to take a bad spill."

"I can't guess who would try such a trick," said Sara in perplexity. "Did you lock the tool house last night, Jake?"

"I always do."

"How about the windows?" inquired Penny.

"I don't rightly remember," Jake confessed. "I reckon they're stuck fast."

Penny went over and tested one of the windows. While it was not locked, she could not raise it with her injured arm. Sara tried without any better luck.

However, as the girls examined the one on the opposite side of the tool house, they discovered that it raised and lowered readily. Tiny pieces of wood were chipped from the outside sill, showing where a blunt instrument had been inserted beneath the sash.

"This is where the person entered, all right," declared Penny.

"I can't understand who would wish to injure us," said Sara in a baffled voice. "You're not known here at Pine Top, and I have no enemies to my knowledge."

"Mrs. Downey has them. There are persons who would like to see her out of business. And our bob-sledding parties were growing popular."

"They were taking a few guests away from the big hotel," Sara admitted slowly. "Still, it doesn't seem possible—"

She broke off as Penny reached down to pick up a small object which lay on the floor beneath the window.

"What have you found?" she finished quickly.

Penny held out a large black button for her to see. A few strands of coarse dark thread still clung to the eyelets.

"It looks like a button from a man's overcoat!" exclaimed Sara. "Jake, does this belong to you?"

The workman glanced at it and shook his head.

"Not mine."

"It probably fell from the coat of the person who damaged our sled," Penny declared thoughtfully. "Not much of a clue, perhaps, but at least it's something to go on!"

CHAPTER 16 - A PUZZLING SOLUTION

Penny pocketed the button and then with Sara went outside the building to look for additional clues. The girls found only a multitude of footprints in the snow beneath the two windows, for the tool house stood beside a direct path to the nursery slopes.

"We've learned everything we're going to," declared Sara. "Penny, I do wish you would get into the house and take your bath. You're limping worse every minute."

"All right, I'll go. I do feel miserable."

"Perhaps you ought to have a doctor."

Penny laughed in amusement. "I'll be brake man on the bob-sled tomorrow as usual."

"You'll be lucky if you're able to crawl out of bed. Anyway, I doubt if I'll be able to come myself."

"Your grandfather?" asked Penny quickly.

"Yes, he's getting suspicious. I'll have to be more careful."

"Why don't you tell him the truth? It's really not fair to deceive him. He's bound to learn the truth sooner or later."

"I'm afraid to tell him," Sara said with a little shiver. "When grandfather is angry you can't reason with him. I'll have to run now. I'm later than usual."

Penny watched her friend go and then hobbled into the lodge. News of the accident had preceded her, and Mrs. Downey met her at the door. She was deeply troubled until she ascertained for herself that the girl had not been seriously injured.

"I was afraid something like this would happen," Mrs. Downey murmured self accusingly. "You know now why I wasn't very enthusiastic about using the bob-sled run."

Penny decided not to tell Mrs. Downey until later how the mishap had occurred. She was feeling too miserable to do much talking, and she knew the truth would only add to the woman's worries.

"I can't say I'm so thrilled about it myself at the moment," she declared with a grimace. "I feel as stiff as if I were mounted on a mummy board!"

Mrs. Downey drew a tub of hot water, but it required all of Penny's athletic prowess to get herself in and out of it. Her right arm was swollen and painful to lift. The skin on one side of her body from hip to ankle had been severely scraped and bruised. She could turn her neck only with difficulty.

"I do think I should call a doctor from the village," Mrs. Downey declared as she aided the girl into bed.

"Please, don't," pleaded Penny. "I'll be as frisky as ever by tomorrow."

Mrs. Downey lowered the shades and went away. Left alone, Penny tried to go to sleep, but she was too uncomfortable. Every time she shifted to a new position wracking pains shot through her body.

"If this isn't the worst break," she thought, sinking deep into gloom. "I'll be crippled for several days at least. No skiing, no bob-sledding. And while I'm lying here on my bed of pain, Francine will learn all about the Green Room."

After awhile the warmth of the bed overcame Penny and she slept. She awakened to find Mrs. Downey standing beside her, a tray in her hand.

"I shouldn't have disturbed you," the woman apologized, "but you've been sleeping so long. And you've had nothing to eat."

"I could do with a little luncheon," mumbled Penny drowsily. "You didn't need to bother bringing it upstairs."

"This is dinner, not luncheon," corrected Mrs. Downey.

Penny rolled over and painfully pulled herself to a sitting posture.

"Then I must have slept hours! What time is it?"

"Five-thirty. Do you feel better, Penny?"

"I think I do. From my eyebrows up anyway."

While Penny ate her dinner, Mrs. Downey sat beside her and chatted.

"At least there's nothing wrong with my appetite," the girl laughed, rapidly emptying the dishes. "At home Mrs. Weems says I eat like a wolf. Oh, by the way, any mail?"

"None for you."

Penny's face clouded. "It's funny no one writes me. Don't you think I might at least get an advertising circular?"

"Well, Christmas is coming," Mrs. Downey said reasonably. "The holiday season always is such a busy time. Folks have their shopping to do."

"Not Dad. Usually he just calls up the Personal Shopper at Hobson's store and says: 'She's five-feet three, size twelve and likes bright colors. Send out something done up in gift wrapping and charge to my account.'" Penny sighed drearily. "Then after Christmas I have to take it back and ask for an exchange."

"Have you ever tried giving your father a list?" suggested Mrs. Downey, smiling at the description.

"Often. He nearly always ignores it."

"What did you ask him for this year?"

"Only a new automobile."

"Only! My goodness, aren't your tastes rather expensive?"

"Oh, he won't give it to me," replied Penny. "I'll probably get a sweater with pink and blue stripes or some dead merchandise the store couldn't pawn off on anyone except an unsuspecting father."

Mrs. Downey laughed as she picked up the tray.

"I hope your father will be able to get to Pine Top for Christmas."

"So do I," agreed Penny, frowning. "I thought when I wired him that Harvey Maxwell was here he would come right away."

"He may have decided it would do no good to contact the man. Knowing Mr. Maxwell I doubt if your father could make any sort of deal with him."

"If only he would come here he might be able to learn something which would help his case," Penny declared earnestly. "Maxwell and Fergus are mixed up in some queer business."

Mrs. Downey smiled tolerantly. While she always listened attentively to Penny's theories and observations, she had not been greatly excited by her tale of the mysterious Green Room. She knew the two men were unscrupulous in a business way and that they were making every effort to force her to give up the lodge, but she could not bring herself to believe they were involved in more serious affairs. She thought that Penny's great eagerness to prove Harvey Maxwell's dishonesty had caused her imagination to run riot.

"Francine Sellberg wouldn't be at Pine Top if something weren't in the wind," Penny went on reflectively. "She followed Ralph Fergus and Maxwell here. And that in itself was rather strange."

"How do you mean, Penny?"

"Fergus must have been having trouble in managing the hotel or he wouldn't have gone to Riverview to see Maxwell. What he had to say evidently couldn't be trusted to a letter or a telegram."

"Mr. Fergus often absents himself on trips. Now and then he goes to Canada."

"I wonder why?" asked Penny alertly.

"He and Mr. Maxwell have a hotel there, I've heard. I doubt if his trips have any particular significance."

"Well, at any rate, Fergus brought Maxwell back from Riverview to help him solve some weighty problem. From their talk on the plane, I gathered they were plotting to put you out of business, Mrs. Downey."

"I think you are right there, Penny."

"But why should your lodge annoy them? You could never take a large number of guests away from their hotel."

"Ralph Fergus is trying to buy up the entire mountainside," Mrs. Downey declared bitterly. "He purchased the site of the old mine, and I can't see what good it will ever do the hotel."

"You don't suppose there's valuable mineral—"

"No," Mrs. Downey broke in with an amused laugh. "The mine played out years ago."

CHAPTER 16 - A PUZZLING SOLUTION

"Has Mr. Fergus tried to buy your lodge?"

"He's made me two different offers. Both were hardly worth considering. If he comes through with any reasonable proposition I may sell. My future plans depend a great deal upon whether or not Peter Jasko is willing to renew a lease on the ski slopes."

"When does the lease expire, Mrs. Downey?"

"The end of next month. I've asked Mr. Jasko to come and see me as soon as he can. However, I have almost no hope he'll sign a new lease."

Mrs. Downey carried the tray to the door. There she paused to inquire: "Anything I can bring you, Penny? A book or a magazine?"

"No, thank you. But you might give me my portable typewriter. I think I'll write a letter to Dad just to remind him he still has a daughter."

Pulling a table to the bedside, Mrs. Downey placed the typewriter and paper on it before going away. Penny propped herself up with pillows and rolled a blank sheet into the machine.

At the top of the page she pecked out: "Bulletin." After the dateline, she began in her best journalistic style, using upper case letters:

"PENNY PARKER, ATTRACTIVE AND TALENTED DAUGHTER OF ANTHONY PARKER, WHILE RIDING THE TAIL OF A RACING BOB-SLED WAS THROWN FOR A TEN YARD LOSS, SUSTAINING NUMEROUS BRUISES. THE PATIENT IS BEARING HER SUFFERING WITH FORTITUDE AND ANTICIPATES BEING IN CIRCULATION BY GLMLFFLS"

Penny stared at the last word she had written. Inadvertently, her fingers had struck the wrong letters. She had intended to write "tomorrow." With an exclamation of impatience she jerked the paper from the machine.

And then she studied the sentence she had typed with new interest. There was something strangely familiar about the jumbled word, GLMLFFLS.

"It looks a little like that coded message I found!" she thought excitedly.

Forgetting her bruises, Penny rolled out of bed. She struck the floor with a moan of anguish. Hobbling over to the dresser, she found the scrap of paper which she had saved, and brought it back to the bed.

The third word in the message was similar, although not the same as the one she had written by accident. Penny typed them one above the other.

    GLMLFFLS
    GLULFFLS

"They're identical except for the third letter," she mused. "Why, I believe I have it! You simply strike the letter directly below the true one—that is, the one in the next row of keys. And when your true letter is in the bottom row, you strike the corresponding key on the top row. That's why I wrote an M for a U!"

Penny was certain she had deciphered the third word of the code and that it was the same as she had written unintentionally. Quickly she wrote out the entire jumbled message, and under it her translation.

    YL GFZKY GLULFFLS
    NO TRAIN TOMORROW

"That's it!" she chortled, bounding up and down in bed.

And then her elation fled away. A puzzled expression settled over her face.

"I have it, only I haven't," she muttered. "What can the message mean? There are no trains at Pine Top—not even a railroad station. This leaves everything in a worse puzzle than before!"

CHAPTER 17 - STRANGE SOUNDS

Penny felt reasonably certain that she had deciphered the code correctly, but although she studied over the message for nearly an hour, she could make nothing of it.

"No train tomorrow," she repeated to herself. "How silly! Perhaps it means, no *plane* tomorrow."

She worked out the code a second time, checking her letters carefully. There was no mistake.

Later in the evening when Mrs. Downey stopped to inquire how she was feeling, Penny asked her about the train service near Pine Top.

"The nearest railroad is thirty miles away," replied the woman. "It is a very tedious journey to Pine Top unless one comes by airplane."

"Is the plane service under the control of the Fergus-Maxwell interests?"

"Not to my knowledge," returned Mrs. Downey, surprised by the question. "This same airline company sent planes here even before the Fergus hotel was built, but not on a regular schedule."

Left alone once more, Penny slipped the typewritten message under her pillow and drew a long sigh. Somehow she was making no progress in any line. From whom had Ralph Fergus received the coded note, and what was its meaning?

"I'll never learn anything lying here in bed," she murmured gloomily. "Tomorrow I'll get up even if it kills me."

True to her resolve, she was downstairs in time for breakfast the next morning.

"Oh, Penny," protested Mrs. Downey anxiously, "don't you think you should have stayed in bed? I can tell it hurts you to walk."

"I'll limber up with exercise. I may take a little hike down to the village later on."

Mrs. Downey sadly shook her head. She thought that Penny had entirely too much determination for her own good.

Until ten o'clock Penny remained at the lodge, rather hoping that Sara Jasko would put in an appearance. When it was evident that the girl was not coming, she bundled herself into warm clothing and walked painfully down the mountain road. Observing old Peter Jasko in the yard near the cabin, she did not pause but went on until she drew near the Fergus hotel.

"I wish I dared go in there," she thought, stopping to rest for a moment. "But I most certainly would be chased out."

Penny sat down on a log bench in plain view of the hostelry. Forming a snowball, she tossed it at a squirrel. The animal scurried quickly to a low-hanging tree branch and chattered his violent disapproval.

"Brother, that's the way I feel, too," declared Penny soberly. "You express my sentiments perfectly."

She was still sunk in deep gloom when she heard a light step behind her. Turning her head stiffly she saw Maxine Miller tramping through the snow toward her.

"If it isn't Miss Parker!" the actress exclaimed with affected enthusiasm. "How delighted I am to see you again, my dear. I heard about the marvelous way you stopped the bob-sled yesterday. Such courage! You deserve a medal."

"I would rather have some new skin," said Penny.

"I imagine you do feel rather bruised and battered," the actress replied with a show of sympathy. "But how proud you must be of yourself! Everyone is talking about it! As I was telling Mr. Jasko last night—"

"You were talking with Peter Jasko?" broke in Penny.

CHAPTER 17 - STRANGE SOUNDS

"Yes, he came to the hotel to see Mr. Fergus—something about a lease, I think. Imagine! He hadn't heard a word about the accident, and his granddaughter was in it!"

"You told him all about it I suppose?" Penny asked with a moan.

"Yes, he was tremendously impressed. Why, what is the matter? Do you have a pain somewhere?"

"Several of them," said Penny. "Go on. What did Mr. Jasko say?"

"Not much of anything. He just listened. Shouldn't I have told him?"

"I am sorry you did, but it can't be helped now. Mr. Jasko doesn't like to have his granddaughter ski or take any part in winter sports."

"Oh, I didn't know that. Then I did let the cat out of the bag. I thought he acted rather peculiar."

"He was bound to have found out about it sooner or later," Penny sighed. With a quick change of mood she inquired: "What's doing down at the hotel? Any excitement?"

"Everything is about as usual. I've sold two fur coats. Don't you think you might be interested in one yourself?"

"I would be interested but my pocketbook wouldn't."

"These coats are a marvelous bargain," Miss Miller declared. "Why don't you at least look at them and try one on. Come down to the hotel with me now and I'll arrange for you to meet my employer."

"Well—" Penny hesitated, "could we enter the hotel by the back way?"

"I suppose so," replied the actress in surprise. "You're sensitive about being crippled?"

"That's right. I don't care to meet anyone I know."

"We can slip into the hotel the back way, then. Very few persons use the rear corridors."

Penny and Miss Miller approached the building without being observed. They entered at the back, meeting neither Ralph Fergus or Harvey Maxwell.

"Can you climb a flight of stairs?" the actress asked doubtfully.

"Oh, yes, easily. I much prefer it to the elevator."

"You really walk with only a slight limp," declared Miss Miller. "I see no reason why you should feel so sensitive."

"It's just my nature," laughed Penny. "Lend me your arm, and up we go."

They ascended to the second floor. Miss Miller motioned for the girl to sit down on a sofa not far from the elevator.

"You wait here and I'll bring my employer," she offered. "I'll be back in a few minutes."

"Who is this man?" inquired Penny.

The actress did not hear the question. She had turned away and was descending the stairs again to the lobby floor.

For a moment or two the girl sat with her head against the back rest of the sofa, completely relaxed. The trip down the mountainside had tired her more than she had expected. She was afraid she had made a mistake in coming boldly to the hotel. If Harvey Maxwell caught her there he would not treat her kindly.

As for seeing the fur coats, she had no intention of ever making a purchase. She had agreed to look at them because she was curious to learn the identity of Miss Miller's employer, as well as the nature of the proposition which might be made her.

Presently, Penny's attention was directed to a distant sound, low and rhythmical, carrying a staccato overtone.

At first the girl paid little heed to the sound. No doubt it was just another noise incidental to a large hotel—some machine connected with the cleaning services perhaps.

But gradually, the sound impressed itself deeper on her mind. There was something strangely familiar about it, yet she could not make a positive identification.

Penny arose from the sofa and listened intently. The sound seemed to be coming from far down the left hand hall. She proceeded slowly, pausing frequently in an effort to discover whence it came. She entered a side hall and the noise increased noticeably.

Suddenly Penny heard footsteps behind her. Turning slightly she was dismayed to see Ralph Fergus coming toward her. For an instant she was certain he meant to eject her from the hotel. Then, she realized that his head was down, and that he was paying no particular attention to her.

BEHIND THE GREEN DOOR

Penny kept her back turned and walked even more slowly. The man overtook her, passed without so much as bestowing a glance upon her. He went to a door which bore the number 27 and, taking a key from his pocket, fitted it into the lock.

Penny would have thought nothing of his act, save that as he swung back the door, the strange sound which previously had drawn her attention, increased in volume. It died away again as the door closed behind Fergus.

Waiting a moment, Penny went on down the hall and paused near the room where the hotel man had entered. She looked quickly up and down the hall. No one was in sight.

Moving closer, she pressed her ear to the panel. There was no sound inside the room, but as she waited, the rhythmical chugging began again. And suddenly she knew what caused it—a teletype machine!

Often in her father's newspaper office Penny had heard that same sound and had watched the printers recording news from all parts of the country. There was no mistaking it, for she could plainly distinguish the clicking of the type against the platen, the low hum of the machine itself, the quick clang of the little bell at the end of each line of copy.

"What would the hotel be doing with a teletype?" she mused. "They print no newspapers here."

Into Penny's mind leaped a startling thought. The coded message in upper case letters which Fergus had dropped in the snow! Might it not have been printed by a teletype machine?

"But what significance *could* it have?" she asked herself. "From what office are the messages being sent and for what purpose?"

It seemed to Penny that the answer to her many questions might lie, not in the Green Room as she had supposed, but close at hand in Number 27.

Her ear pressed to the panel, the girl made out a low rumble of voices above the clatter of the teletype. Ralph Fergus was talking with another man but she could not distinguish a word they were saying. So intent was she that she failed to hear a step behind her.

A mop handle clattered to the floor, making a loud sound on the tiles. Penny whirled about in confusion. A cleaning maid stood beside her, regarding her with evident though unspoken suspicion.

CHAPTER 18 - QUESTIONS AND CLUES

"Good morning," stammered Penny, backing from the door. "Were you wanting to get into this room?"

"No, I never clean in there," answered the maid, still watching the girl with suspicion. "You're looking for someone?"

Penny knew that she had been observed listening at the door. It would be foolish to pretend otherwise.

She answered frankly: "No, I was passing through the corridor when I heard a strange sound in this room. Do you hear it?"

The maid nodded and her distrustful attitude changed to one of indifference.

"It's a machine of some sort," she answered. "I hear it running every once in a while."

Penny was afraid to loiter by the door any longer lest her own voice bring Ralph Fergus to investigate. As the cleaning woman picked up her mop and started on down the hall, she fell into step with her.

"Who occupies Room 27?" she inquired casually.

"No one," said the maid. "The hotel uses it."

"What goes on in there anyway? I thought I heard teletype machines."

The maid was unfamiliar with the technical name Penny had used. "It's just a contraption that prints letters and figures," she informed. "When I first came to work at the hotel I made a mistake and went in there to do some cleaning. Mr. Fergus, he didn't like it and said I wasn't to bother to dust up there again."

"Doesn't anyone go into the room except Mr. Fergus?"

"Just him and George Jewitt."

"And who is he? One of the owners of the hotel?"

"Oh, no. George Jewitt works for Mr. Fergus. He takes care of the machines, I guess."

"You were saying that the machine prints letters and figures," prompted Penny. "Do you mean messages one can read?"

"It was writing crazy-like when I watched it. The letters didn't make sense nohow. Mr. Fergus he told me the machines were being used in some experiment the hotel was carrying on."

"Who occupies the nearby rooms?" Penny questioned. "I should think they would be disturbed by the machines."

"Rooms on this corridor are never assigned unless everything else is full up," the maid explained.

Pausing at a door, the cleaning woman fitted a master key into the lock.

"There's one thing more I'm rather curious about," said Penny quickly. "It's this Green Room I hear folks mentioning."

The maid gazed at her suspiciously again. "I don't know anything about any Green Room," she replied.

Entering the bedroom with her cleaning paraphernalia, she closed the door behind her.

"Went a bit too far that time," thought Penny, "but at least I learned a few facts of interest."

Turning, she retraced her steps to Room 27, but she was afraid to linger there lest Ralph Fergus should discover her loitering in the hall. Miss Miller had not put in an appearance when she returned to the elevators. She decided not to wait.

Scribbling a brief note of explanation, Penny left the paper in a corner of the sofa and hobbled down the stairway to the first floor. She let herself out the back way without attracting undue attention. Safely in the open once more she retreated to her bench under the ice-coated trees.

"I need to give this whole problem a good think," she told herself. "Here I have a number of perfectly good clues but they don't fit together. I'm almost as far from getting evidence against Fergus and Maxwell as I was at the start."

Penny could not understand why the hotel would have need for teletype machine service. Such machines were used in newspaper offices, for railroad communication, brokerage service, and occasionally in very large plants with widely separated branch offices. Suddenly she recalled that her father had once told her Mr. Maxwell kept in touch with his chain of hotels by means of such a wire service. Surely it was an expensive and unnecessary means of communication.

The cleaning woman's information that messages came through in unintelligible form convinced Penny a code was being used—a code to which she had the key. But why did Maxwell and Fergus find it necessary to employ one? If their messages concerned only the routine operation of the various hotels in the chain, there would be no need for secrecy.

The one message she had interpreted—"No Train Tomorrow"—undoubtedly had been received by teletype transmission. But Penny could not hazard a guess as to its true meaning. She feared it might be in double code, and that the words did not have the significance usually attributed to them.

"If only I could get into Room 27 and get my hands on additional code messages I might be able to make something out of it," she mused. "The problem is how to do it without being caught."

Penny had not lost interest in the Green Room. She was inclined to believe that its mystery was closely associated with the communication system of the hotel. But since, for the time being at least, the problem of penetrating beyond the guarded Green Door seemed unsolvable, she thought it wiser to center her sleuthing attack elsewhere.

"All I can do for the next day or so is to keep an eye on Ralph Fergus and Harvey Maxwell," she told herself. "If I see a chance to get inside Room 27 I'll take it."

Penny arose with a sigh. She would not be likely to have such a chance unless she made it for herself. And in her present battered state, her mind somehow refused to invent clever schemes.

The walk back up the mountain road was a long and tiring one. Finally reaching the lodge after many pauses for rest, Penny stood for a time watching the skiers, and then entered the house.

Mrs. Downey was not in the kitchen. Hearing voices from the living room, Penny went to the doorway and paused there. The hotel woman was talking with a visitor, old Peter Jasko.

"Oh, I'm sorry," Penny apologized for her intrusion. She started to retreat.

Peter Jasko saw her and the muscles of his leathery face tightened. Pushing back his chair he got quickly to his feet.

"You're the one who has been trespassing on my land!" he accused, his voice unsteady from anger. "You've been helping my granddaughter disobey my orders!"

Taken by surprise, Penny could think of nothing to say in her own defense.

After his first outburst, Peter Jasko ignored the girl. Turning once more to Mrs. Downey he said in a rasping voice:

"You have my final decision, Ma'am. I shall not renew the lease."

"Please, Mr. Jasko," Mrs. Downey argued quietly. "Think what this means to me! If I lose the ski slopes I shall be compelled to give up the lodge. I've already offered you more than I can afford to pay."

"Money ain't no object," the old man retorted. "I'm against the whole proposition."

"Nothing I can say will make you reconsider?"

"Nothing, Ma'am."

Picking up his cap, a ridiculous looking affair with ear muffs, Peter Jasko brushed past Penny and went out the door.

CHAPTER 19 - PETER JASKO SERVES NOTICE

After the old man had gone, Penny spoke apologetically to Mrs. Downey.

"Oh, I'm so sorry! I ruined everything, coming in just when I did."

Mrs. Downey sat with her hands folded in her lap, staring out the window after the retreating figure of Peter Jasko.

"No, it wasn't your fault, Penny."

"He was angry at me because I've been helping Sara get in and out of the cabin. I never should have done it."

"Perhaps not," agreed Mrs. Downey, "but it would have made no difference in regard to the lease. I've been expecting Jasko's decision. Even so, it comes as a blow. This last week I had been turning ideas over in my mind, trying to think of a way I could keep on here. Now everything is settled."

Penny crossed the room and slipped an arm about the woman's shoulders.

"I'm as sorry as I can be."

With a sudden change of mood, Mrs. Downey arose and gave Penny's hand an affectionate squeeze.

"Losing the lodge won't mean the end of the world," she said lightly. "While I may not be able to sell the place for a very good price now that the ski slopes are gone, I'll at least get something from Mr. Maxwell. And I have a small income derived from my husband's insurance policy."

"Where will you go if you leave here?"

"I haven't given that part any thought," admitted Mrs. Downey. "I may do a little traveling. I have a sister in Texas I might visit."

"You'll be lonesome for Pine Top."

"Yes," admitted Mrs. Downey, "this place will always seem like home to me. And I've lived a busy, useful life for so many years it will be hard to let go."

"Possibly Peter Jasko will reconsider his decision."

Mrs. Downey smiled and shook her head. "Not Peter. I've known him for many years, although I can't say I ever became acquainted with him. Once he makes a stand nothing can sway him."

"Is he entirely right in his mind?" Penny asked dubiously.

"Oh, yes. He's peculiar, that's all. And he's getting old."

Despite Mrs. Downey's avowal that no one was responsible for Peter Jasko's decision, Penny considered herself at fault. She could not blame the old man for being provoked because she had helped his granddaughter escape from the cabin.

"If I went down there and apologized it might do some good," she thought. "At least, nothing will be lost by trying."

Penny turned the plan over in her mind, saying nothing about it to Mrs. Downey. It seemed to her that the best way would be to wait for a few hours until Peter Jasko had been given an opportunity to get over his anger.

The afternoon dragged on slowly. Toward nightfall, finding confinement intolerable, Penny ventured out-of-doors to try her skis. She was thrilled to discover that she could use them without too much discomfort.

Going to the kitchen window, she called to Mrs. Downey that she intended to do a little skiing and might be late for dinner.

"Oh, Penny, you're not able," the woman protested, raising the sash. "It's only your determination which drives you on."

"I'm feeling much better," insisted Penny. "I want to go down the mountain and see Sara."

"It will be a hard climb back," warned Mrs. Downey. "And the radio reported another bad storm coming."

"That's why I want to go now," answered Penny. "We may be snowbound by tomorrow."

"Well, if you must go, don't overtax your strength," cautioned Mrs. Downey.

Penny wrapped a woolen scarf tightly about her neck as a protection against the biting wind. Cautiously, she skied down the trail, finding its frozen surface treacherous, and scarcely familiar. In the rapidly gathering dusk nothing looked exactly the same as by daylight. Trees towered like unfriendly giants, obscuring the path.

Before Penny had covered half the distance to Jasko's cabin, snowflakes, soft and damp, began to fall. They came faster and faster, the wind whirling them directly into her face. She kept her head down and wished that she had remained by the crackling log fire at the Downey lodge.

Swinging out of the forest, Penny was hard pressed to remember the trail. As she hesitated, trying to decide which way to go, she felt her skis slipping along a downgrade where none should have been. Too late, she realized that she was heading down into a deep ravine which terminated in an ice-sheeted river below.

Throwing herself flat, Penny sought to save herself, but she kept sliding, sliding. A stubby evergreen at last stayed her fall. She clung helplessly to it for a moment, recovering her breath. Then she tried to pull herself up the steep incline. She slipped and barely caught hold of the bush to save herself from another bad fall. Sharp pains shot through her side.

"Now I've fixed myself for sure," she thought. "How will I ever get out of this hole?"

The ravine offered protection from the chill wind, but the snow was sifting down steadily. Penny could feel her clothing becoming thoroughly soaked. If she should lie still she soon would freeze.

Again Penny tried to struggle up the bank, and again she slid backwards. From sheer desperation rather than because she cherished a hope that anyone would hear, Penny shouted for help.

An answering halloo echoed to her through the trees.

Penny dared not hope that the voice was other than her own. "Help! Help!" she called once more.

Her heart leaped. The cry which came back definitely belonged to a man! And as she marveled at the miracle of a rescue, a dark figure loomed up at the rim of the ravine.

A gruff voice called to her: "Hold on! Don't try to move! I'll get a rope and be back!"

The man faded back into the darkness. Penny clung to the bush until it seemed her arms would break. Snow fell steadily, caking her hood and penetrating the woolen suit.

Then as the girl lost all awareness of time, she caught the flash of a lighted lantern. Her rescuer appeared again at the top of the ravine and lowered a rope. She grasped it, wrapping it tightly about her wrist, and climbed as best she could while the man pulled from above.

At last Penny reached the top, falling in an exhausted heap on the snow. Raising her head she stared into the face of her rescuer. The man was Peter Jasko.

He recognized her at the same instant.

"You!" he exclaimed.

For one disturbing moment Penny thought the old man meant to push her back down into the yawning ravine. In the yellow glow of the lantern, the expression of his face was terrifying.

Gaining control of himself, Peter Jasko demanded gruffly: "Hurt?"

"I've twisted my ankle." Penny pulled herself up from the ground, took a step, and recoiled with pain.

"Let me have a look at it."

Jasko bent down and examined the ankle.

"No bones broken," he said. "You're luckier than you deserve. Any fool who doesn't know enough to keep off skis ought to be crippled for life!"

"Such a cheerful philosophy," observed Penny ironically. "Well, thanks anyhow for saving me. Even if you are sorry you did it."

The old man made no immediate reply. He stood gazing down at Penny.

"Reckon I owe you something," he said grudgingly. "Sara told me how you kept the bob-sled from going off the track. Injured yourself, too, didn't you?"

"Yes."

"You had no business helping Sara go against my will," the old man said, his anger rising again. "I told you to stay away, didn't I?"

"You did. I was sorry to disobey your orders, Mr. Jasko, but I think you are unjust to your granddaughter."

CHAPTER 19 - PETER JASKO SERVES NOTICE

"You do, eh?"

"And you're not being fair to Mrs. Downey either," Penny went on courageously. "She's struggled for years to make her lodge profitable, fought against overwhelming odds while the Fergus interests have done everything they can to put her out of business. Unless you renew her lease, she'll be forced to leave Pine Top."

"So?" inquired the old man, unmoved.

"She's fighting with her back to the wall. And now you've dealt her the final blow."

"No one asked Mrs. Downey to come here in the first place," replied Peter Jasko. "Or them other hotel people either. Pine Top can get along without the lot of 'em. The sooner they all clear out the better I'll like it."

"I'm sure of that," said Penny. "You don't care how much trouble you cause other folks. Because of your own son's death you have taken an unnatural attitude toward skiing. You hate everything remotely connected with the sport. But it isn't fair. Your granddaughter has a right to a certain amount of freedom."

Peter Jasko listened to the girl's words in silence. When she had finished he said in a strangely shaken voice: "My son met his death going on ten years ago. It was on this trail—"

"I'm sorry," Penny said contritely. "I shouldn't have spoken the way I did. Actually, I was on my way down the mountain to tell you I deeply regret helping Sara to go against your will."

"My granddaughter is headstrong," the old man replied slowly. "I want what's best for her. That's why I've tried to protect her."

"I'm sure you've done what you thought was right," Penny returned. "Why don't you see Mrs. Downey again and—"

"No!" said the old man stubbornly. "You can't say anything which will make me change my mind. Take my arm and see if you can walk!"

Penny struggled forward, supported by Jasko's strong arm. Although each step sent a wracking pain through her leg she made no sound of protest.

"You can't make it that way," the old man declared, pausing. "I'll have to fix up a sled and pull you."

Going back for Penny's skis which had been left at the top of the ravine, he lashed them together. She lay full length on the runners, and he towed her until they came within view of the cabin. A light glowed in the window.

On level ground, Penny tried walking again, and managed to reach the cabin door.

"You go on inside," the old man directed. "I'll hitch up the bob-sled and take you home."

Penny pushed open the door only to hesitate on the threshold. The room was filled with tobacco smoke. Two men sat at the table, and directly behind them stood Sara Jasko.

The girl came swiftly to the door. She gave Penny a warm smile of welcome, not noticing that she had been hurt, and said anxiously to Mr. Jasko:

"Grandfather, you have visitors. Mr. Fergus and Mr. Maxwell are waiting to see you. I think it's about the lease."

"I've nothing to say to them," returned the old man grimly.

Nevertheless, he followed the two girls into the room, closing the door against the wind and snow.

The situation was an awkward one for Penny. Ralph Fergus and Harvey Maxwell both stared at her with undisguised dislike and suspicion. Then, the former arose, and ignoring her entirely, stepped forward to meet the old man, his hand extended.

"Good evening, sir," he said affably. "Mr. Maxwell and I have a little business to discuss with you, if you can spare us a moment."

Peter Jasko ignored the offered hand.

"I haven't changed my mind since the last time we talked," he said. "I'm not signing any lease!"

Penny scarcely heard the words for she was staring beyond Ralph Fergus at his overcoat which hung over the vacated chair. The garment was light brown and the top button, a large one of the same color, had been torn from the cloth.

Shifting her gaze, Penny glanced at Sara. The girl nodded her head slowly up and down. She, too, had made the important observation, and was thinking the same thought. There could be little doubt of it—Ralph Fergus was the man who had weakened the brake rod of their bob-sled!

CHAPTER 20 - VISITORS

"May we see you alone, Mr. Jasko?" requested Ralph Fergus.

"I don't reckon there's any need for being so all-fired private," the old man retorted, his hand on the doorknob. "If you want to talk with me speak your piece right out. I got to hitch up the team."

Mr. Fergus and his companion, Harvey Maxwell, glanced coldly toward Penny who had sunk down into a chair and was massaging her ankle. They were reluctant to reveal their business before her but there was no other way.

"We can't talk with you very well while you're poised for flight, Mr. Jasko," Ralph Fergus said placatingly. "My friend, Maxwell, has prepared a paper which he would like to have you look over."

"I'm not signin' anything!"

"Good for you, Grandfather!" muttered Sara under her breath.

The two men pretended not to hear. Mr. Maxwell took a folded document from his pocket and spread it out on the kitchen table.

"Will you just read this, please, Mr. Jasko? You'll find our terms are more than generous."

"I ain't interested in your terms," he snapped. "I'm aimin' to keep every acre of my land."

"We're not asking you to sell, only to lease," Mr. Fergus interposed smoothly. "Now we understand that your deal with Mrs. Downey has fallen through, so there's no reason why you shouldn't lease the ski slopes to us. We are prepared to offer you twice the amount she proposed to give you."

Mr. Jasko stubbornly shook his head.

"You're taking a very short-sighted attitude," said Ralph Fergus, beginning to lose patience. "At least read the paper."

"No."

"Think what this would mean to your granddaughter," interposed Harvey Maxwell. "Pretty clothes, school in the city perhaps—"

"Don't listen to them, Grandfather," spoke Sara quickly. "I have enough clothes. And Pine Top school suits me."

"You're wastin' your time and mine," said Peter Jasko. "I ain't leasing my land to anybody."

"We're only asking you to sign a three-year lease—" Mr. Fergus argued.

"Can't you understand plain language?" the old man cried. "You think money will buy everything, but you got another guess coming. I've seen enough skiing at Pine Top and I aim to put a stop to it!"

"It's no use," said Harvey Maxwell resignedly to his companion.

Ralph Fergus picked up the paper and thrust it into his overcoat pocket. "You're an old fool, Jasko!" he muttered.

"Don't you dare speak that way to my grandfather!" Sara cried, her eyes stormy. "You had your nerve coming here anyway, after that trick you tried!"

"Trick?"

"You deliberately weakened the brake rod of our bob-sled."

Ralph Fergus laughed in the girl's face. "You're as touched as your grandfather," he said.

"Perhaps you can explain what became of the top button of your overcoat," suggested Penny coming to Sara's support. "And don't try to tell us it's home in your sewing basket!"

Ralph Fergus' hand groped at the vacant spot on his coat.

"What does a button have to do with the bob-sled accident?" inquired Harvey Maxwell.

CHAPTER 20 - VISITORS

"It happens that we found a large brown button in the tool house at the Downey lodge," replied Penny. "Also a little additional evidence which rather suggests Mr. Fergus is the one who tampered with the bob-sled."

"Ridiculous!" protested the hotel man. "I've not even been near Mrs. Downey's lodge in weeks."

"I know that's a lie," said Peter Jasko. "I saw you goin' up that way Friday night."

"And you went there to damage the bob-sled!" Sara accused. "You didn't care how many persons might be injured in an accident!"

Ralph Fergus' face was an angry red. "What reason would I have for doing anything like that?" he demanded.

"Guests were being drawn from your hotel because bob-sledding was increasing in popularity," said Penny quietly. "Nothing would please you more than to put Mrs. Downey out of business."

"Aren't you drawing rather sweeping conclusions?" inquired Harvey Maxwell in an insolent tone. "A button isn't very certain evidence. So many persons wear buttons, you know."

"I lost this one from my coat weeks ago," added Ralph Fergus.

"It was your button we found," Sara accused.

Peter Jasko had been listening intently to the argument, taking little part in it. But now, with a quick movement which belied his age, he moved across the kitchen toward the gun rack on the wall.

"Let's be getting out of here," muttered Harvey Maxwell.

He and Ralph Fergus both bolted out of the door. Their sudden flight delighted Sara who broke into a fit of laughter.

"Why don't you shoot once or twice into the air just to give 'em a good fright?" she asked her grandfather.

The old man, shotgun in hand, had followed the two men to the door. But he did not shoot.

"Grandfather wouldn't hurt a flea really," chuckled Sara. "At least, not unless it was trying to make him sign something."

"Ralph Fergus acted guilty, all right," declared Penny, bending down to massage her injured ankle. "But it may have been a mistake for us to accuse him."

"I couldn't help it," answered Sara. "When I saw that button missing from his coat, I had to say something about it."

Peter Jasko put away his shotgun, turning once more to the door. "I'll hitch up the team," he said. "Sara, get some liniment and see what you can do for Miss Parker's ankle."

"Your ankle?" gasped Sara, staring at Penny. "Have you hurt yourself again?"

"I managed to fall into the ravine a few minutes ago. Your grandfather saved me."

Sara darted to the stove to get a pan of warm water. She stripped off Penny's woolen stockings and examined the foot as she soaked it.

"I suppose this will put me on the shelf for another day or so," Penny observed gloomily. "But I'm lucky I didn't break my neck."

"The ankle is swollen," Sara said, "I'll wrap it with a bandage and that may make it feel better."

With a practiced hand she wound strips of gauze and adhesive tape about the ankle.

"There, how does it feel now?"

"Much better," said Penny. "Thanks a lot. I—I feel rather mean to put your grandfather to so much trouble, especially after the way I've crossed him."

"Oh, don't you worry about Grandfather," laughed Sara. "He likes you, Penny."

"He *likes* me?"

"I could tell by the way he acted tonight. He respects a person who stands up to him."

"I said some rather unnecessary things," Penny declared regretfully. "I was provoked because he wouldn't sign a lease with Mrs. Downey. After hearing what he said to Fergus and Maxwell I realize nothing will sway him."

Sara sighed as she helped her friend put on her shoe again.

"I'm afraid not. I'll do what I can to influence him, but I can tell you now he'll never listen to me. Grandfather is just the way he is, and one can't budge him an inch."

Peter Jasko soon had the team hitched to the bob-sled. He and Sara helped Penny in, wrapping blankets around her so that she would be snug and warm during the ride up the mountain.

"Come down again whenever you can," invited Sara. "Only the next time don't try it after dark if you're on skis."

Penny glanced at the old man, but his face showed no displeasure. Apparently, he no longer regarded her as an interloper.

"I'll come as soon as I can," she replied.

Peter Jasko clucked to the horses, and the sled moved away from the cabin. Sara stood in the doorway until it was out of sight.

During the slow ride up the mountain side, the old man did not speak. But as they came at last to the Downey lodge, and he lifted her from the sled, he actually smiled.

"I reckon it won't do any good to lock Sara up after this," he said. "You're both too smart for an old codger like me."

"Thank you, Mr. Jasko," answered Penny, her eyes shining. "Thank you for everything."

The door of the lodge had opened, and Mrs. Downey, a coat thrown over her shoulders, hurried out into the snow. Not wishing to be drawn into a conversation, Jasko leaped back into the sled, and with a curt, "Good evening," drove away.

With Mrs. Downey's help, Penny hobbled into the house, and there related her latest misadventure.

"I declare, you'll be in the hospital yet," sighed the woman. "I feel tempted to adopt Mr. Jasko's tactics and lock you up in your room."

"I'll stay there without being locked in," declared Penny. "I've had enough skiing to last me until Christmas at least."

In the morning she felt so stiff and battered that she could barely get out of bed. However, her ankle was somewhat better and when occasion demanded, she could hobble across the room without support.

"You ought to be all right in a day or so if only you'll stay off your foot and give it a chance to get well," declared Mrs. Downey.

"It's hard to sit still," sighed Penny. "There are so many things I ought to be doing."

From the kitchen window she could see the Fergus hotel far down in the valley. She was impatient to pay another visit there, although she realized that after the previous evening's encounter with Ralph Fergus and Harvey Maxwell, it would be more difficult than ever to gain admittance.

"Somehow I must manage to get into Room 27 and learn what is going on there," she thought. "But how? That is the question!"

Ever an active, energetic person, Penny became increasingly restless as the day dragged on. During mid-afternoon, observing that Jake had hitched up the team to the sled, she inquired if he were driving down to Pine Top.

"Yes, I am sending him after supplies," explained Mrs. Downey. "And the newspapers—if there are any."

"I wish I could go along for the ride."

Mrs. Downey regarded Penny skeptically.

"Oh, I wouldn't get out of the sled," Penny said.

"Is that a promise?"

"I'll make it one. Nothing less than a fire or an earthquake will get me out."

Jake brought the sled to the door, and helped the girl into it. The day was cold. Snow fell steadily. Mrs. Downey tucked warm bricks at Penny's feet and wrapped her snugly in woolen blankets.

The ride down the mountainside was without event. Penny began to regret that she had made the trip, for the weather was more unpleasant than she had anticipated. She burrowed deeper and deeper into the blankets.

Jake pulled up at a hitching post in front of Pine Top's grocery store.

"It won't take me long," he said.

Penny climbed down in the bottom of the sled, rearranging her blankets so that only her eyes and forehead were exposed to the cold. She had been sitting there for some minutes when her attention was drawn to a man who was approaching from far down the street. Recognizing him as Ralph Fergus, she watched with interest.

At the drugstore he paused. As if by prearrangement, Benny Smith came out of the building. Penny was too far away to hear their exchange of words, but she saw the boy give all of his newspapers to Ralph Fergus. In return, he received a bill which she guessed might be of fairly high denomination.

CHAPTER 20 - VISITORS

"Probably five dollars," she thought. "The boy sells all his papers to Fergus because he can make more that way than by peddling them one by one. And he's paid to keep quiet about it."

Penny was not especially surprised to discover that the hotel man was buying up all the papers, for she had suspected he was behind the trick.

"There's no law against it," she told herself. "That's the trouble. Fergus and Maxwell are clever. So far they've done nothing which could possibly get them into legal trouble."

Presently Jake came out of the grocery store, carrying a large box of supplies which he stowed in the sled.

"I'll get the papers and then we'll be ready to start."

"Don't bother," said Penny. "There aren't any. I just saw Ralph Fergus buy them all from the boy."

"Fergus, eh? And he's been puttin' it out that the papers never caught the plane!"

"It was just another one of his little tricks to make Mrs. Downey's guests dissatisfied."

"Now we know what he's about we'll put a stop to it!"

"Yes," agreed Penny, "but he'll only think of something new to try."

As they started back toward the Downey lodge, she was quiet, turning over various matters in her mind. Since Mrs. Downey had decided to sell her business, it scarcely seemed to matter what Ralph Fergus did.

The sled drew near the Jasko cabin and passed it, turning a bend in the road. Suddenly Penny thought she heard her name called. Glancing back she was startled to see Sara Jasko running after the sled.

"Wait, Jake!" Penny commanded. "It's Sara! Something seems to be wrong!"

CHAPTER 21 - OLD PETER'S DISAPPEARANCE

"Whoa!" shouted Jake, pulling on the reins.

The horses brought the heavy sled to a halt at the side of the road. Sara, breathless from running so fast, hurried up.

"I'm worried about Grandfather," she gasped out.

"He isn't sick?" Penny asked quickly,

"No, but I haven't seen him since early this morning. He went to chop wood at Hatter's place up the mountain. He expected to be back in time for lunch but he hasn't returned."

"He'll likely be along soon," said Jake.

"Oh, you don't know Grandfather," declared Sara, her forehead wrinkling with anxiety. "He always does exactly as he says he will do. He never would have stayed away this long unless something had happened. He's getting on in years and I'm afraid—"

"Jake, couldn't we go up to Hatter's place, wherever it is?" Penny urged.

"Sure. It's not far from Mrs. Downey's."

"Let me ride with you," Sara requested. "I'm sorry to cause you any trouble, but I have a feeling something is wrong."

"Jump in," invited Jake.

Sara climbed into the back of the sled, snuggling down in the blankets beside Penny.

"Grandfather may have hurt himself with the ax," she said uneasily. "Or he could have suffered a stroke. The doctor says he has a touch of heart-trouble, but he never will take care of himself."

"We'll probably find him safe and sound," Penny declared in a comforting way.

Jake stirred the horses to greater activity. In a short while the sled passed the Downey grounds and went on to the Hatter farm. Sara sprang out to unlock the wooden gate which barred entrance to a narrow, private road.

"I see Grandfather's sled!" she exclaimed.

Without waiting for Jake to drive through the gate, she ran on down the road. Hearing her cry of alarm, the man urged his horses on.

Reaching the clearing, Penny and Jake saw Sara gazing about in bewilderment. Peter Jasko's team had been tied to a tree and the sled box was half filled with wood. An ax lay in the deep snow close by. But there was no sign of the old man.

"Where is grandfather?" Sara asked in a dazed voice.

She called his name several times. Hearing no answer, she ran deeper into the woods. Jake leaped from the sled and joined in the search. Penny could not bear to sit helplessly by. Deciding that the emergency was equal to an earthquake or a fire, she eased herself down from the sled.

Steadily falling snow had obliterated all tracks save those made by the new arrivals. There was no clue to indicate whether Peter Jasko had left the scene of his own free will or had been the possible victim of violence.

Jake and Sara searched at the edge of the woods and returned to the clearing to report no success.

"Maybe your granddad went up to Hatter's place to get warm," the man suggested.

"He never would have left his horses without blanketing them," answered Sara. "But let's go there and inquire. Someone may have seen Grandfather."

They drove the bob-sled on through the woods to an unpainted farm house. Claud Hatter himself opened the door, and in response to Sara's anxious question, he told her that he had seen Peter Jasko drive into the place early that morning.

CHAPTER 21 - OLD PETER'S DISAPPEARANCE

"You didn't see him go away?" Sara asked.

"No, but come to think of it, I noticed a car turn into the road. Must have been about ten o'clock this morning."

"What sort of car?"

The man could give no additional information, for he had not paid particular attention to the automobile. However, he pulled on his heavy coat and boots, offering to help organize a searching party.

Sara and Penny remained at the farm house, but as it became evident that the old man would not be found quickly, Jake returned and took the girls down the mountain to the Downey lodge.

"What could have happened to Grandfather?" Sara repeated over and over. "I can't believe he became dazed and wandered away."

"I wish we knew who came in the car," said Penny. "That might explain a lot."

"You—you think Grandfather met with violence?"

"I hope not," replied Penny earnestly. "But it seems very queer. Did your grandfather have enemies?"

"He antagonizes many folks without meaning to do so. However, I can't think of anyone at Pine Top who could be called an actual enemy."

By nightfall the searching party had grown in size. Nearly every male resident of Pine Top joined in the hunt for Peter Jasko. Even the Fergus hotel sent two employes to help comb the mountainside for the missing old man.

Sara, nearly in a state of collapse, was put to bed by Mrs. Downey, who kept telling the girl over and over that she must not worry. In speaking with Penny, the woman was far from optimistic. She expressed a doubt that Peter Jasko ever would be found alive.

"He may have wandered off and fallen into a crevasse."

"I am inclined to think he may have been spirited away by whoever came up the private road in that car," commented Penny.

"I can't imagine anyone bothering to kidnap Peter Jasko," returned Mrs. Downey. "He has no money."

"It does sound rather fantastic, I admit. Especially in broad daylight. You didn't notice any automobile on the main road this morning did you?"

"Only the Fergus hotel delivery truck. But I was busy. A dozen might have passed without my noticing them."

At nine o'clock Jake came to the lodge with a discouraging report. No trace of Peter Jasko had been found. The search would continue throughout the night.

"Which way are you going?" Penny inquired as the man started to leave the house again. "Up the mountain or down?"

"Down," he returned. "I'm joining a party at Jasko's own place. We aim to start combing the woods on his farm next."

"May I ride with you?" she requested. "I want to go down to the Fergus hotel."

"Penny, your ankle—" protested Mrs. Downey.

"I can get around on it," Penny said hurriedly. "See!" She hobbled across the floor to prove her words. "And this is important. I want to see someone at the hotel."

"So late at night?"

"It really is important," Penny declared. "Please say I may go."

"Very well," agreed Mrs. Downey reluctantly.

Jake took Penny all the way to the hotel. "Shall I help you inside?" he asked.

"Oh, no," she declined hurriedly. "I'll make it fine from here."

After Jake had driven back up the road, Penny limped around to the back entrance of the hotel. She stood for several minutes staring up at the dark windows of the second floor.

"I believe Ralph Fergus and Harvey Maxwell know plenty about Jasko's disappearance," she thought. "But how to prove it?"

On the parking lot only a few steps away stood the Fergus hotel delivery truck. Penny hobbled over to it, and opened the rear door. She swept the beam of her flashlight over the floor.

At first glance the car appeared to be empty save for several cardboard boxes. Then she saw a heavy, fleece-lined glove lying on the floor half hidden by the containers. She picked it up, examined it briefly and stuffed it into the pocket of her snowsuit.

"I remember Peter Jasko wore a glove very much like this!" she thought.

Softly closing the truck door, Penny went back to the rear of the hotel. The lower hall was deserted so she slipped inside, and followed the stairway to the second floor. She tried the door of Room 27 and discovered it was locked.

"I was afraid of this," Penny muttered.

Hesitating a moment she went on down the hall. Opening another door, the one which bore no number, she saw that she was to be blocked again in her investigation. The familiar guard sat at his usual post beside the door of the Green Room.

Retreating without drawing attention to herself, Penny debated her next action. Unless she found a way to enter one of those two rooms of mystery, her night would be wasted.

Moving softly down the hall, she paused to test the door to the right of Room 27. To her astonishment, it swung open when she turned the knob. The room was dark and deserted.

Penny stepped inside, closing the door behind her. Her flashlight beam disclosed only a dusty, bare bedroom, its sole furnishing a thickly padded carpet.

Going to the window, Penny raised it and gazed at the wide ledge which she had noted from below. If she had perfect balance, if the window of Room 27 were unlocked, if her lame ankle did not let her down, she *might* be able to span the distance! It would be dangerous and she must run the risk of being observed by persons on the grounds of the hotel. Penny gazed down at the frozen yard far below and shuddered.

"I've been pretty lucky in my falls so far," she thought. "But I have a feeling if I slip this time it will be my last."

Penny pulled herself through the window. As the full force of the wind struck her body, threatening to hurl her from her precarious perch, she nearly lost her courage. She clung to the sill for a moment, and then without daring to look down, inched her way along the ledge.

Reaching the other window in safety, she tried to push it up. For a dreadful instant, Penny was certain she could not. But it gave so suddenly she nearly lost her balance. Holding desperately to the sill, she recovered, and raised the window.

Penny dropped lightly through the opening into the dark room. Pains were shooting through her ankle, but so great was her excitement she scarcely was aware of any discomfort.

She flashed her light about the room. As she had suspected, there were two teletype machines, neither of which was in operation. A chair had been pulled up to a direct-keyboard machine similar to one Penny had seen in her father's newspaper office. Save for a wooden table the room contained nothing else.

Penny went over to the machines and focused her light upon the paper in the rollers. It was blank.

"This is maddening!" she thought. "I take a big risk to get in here and what do I find—nothing!"

Footsteps could be heard coming down the hallway. Penny remained perfectly still, expecting the person to pass on. Instead, the noise ceased altogether and a key grated in the door lock.

In panic, Penny glanced frantically about. She could not hope to get out the window in time to escape detection. The only available hiding place was a closet.

Switching off her light, Penny opened the door. Stepping inside, she closed it softly behind her.

CHAPTER 22 - THE SECRET STAIRS

In the darkness, Penny felt something soft and covered with fur brush against her face. She recoiled, nearly screaming in terror. Recovering her poise and realizing that she had merely touched a garment which hung in the closet, she flattened herself against the wall and waited.

The outside door opened and soft footsteps approached the wall switches. Lights flashed on. A tall, swarthy man in a gray business suit blinked at the sudden flood of illumination. After a moment he stepped over to the teletype machines, and throwing a switch, started them going.

Sitting down to the keyboard he tapped out a message. Then he lit a cigarette and waited. In a few minutes his answer came, typed out from some distant station. The man ripped the copy from the machine and read it carefully. Its contents seemed to please him for he smiled broadly as he arose from the chair, leaving the teletypes still running.

Penny froze with fear when she heard the man stride toward the closet where she had hidden herself. Instinctively, she burrowed back behind the fur garments which her groping hands encountered.

The door was flung open and light flooded into the closet. However, the teletype attendant seemed to have no suspicion that anyone might be hiding there. He pressed a button on the wall and then heaved against the partition with his shoulder. The section of wall, suspended on a pivot, slowly revolved. After the man had passed through, it swung back into its original position.

Penny waited several minutes and then came out of her hiding place. She flung open the closet door to admit more light.

"Just as I thought!" she muttered.

The closet, a long narrow room, was hung solidly with fur coats!

"So Maxine Miller was working for the hotel interests after all," Penny told herself. "I've stumbled into something big!"

Groping along the wall of the storage room, she found a switch and pressed it. Again the partition revolved, revealing a flight of stairs leading downward. She slipped through and the wall slid into place behind her.

The stairway was lighted with only one weak electric bulb. Penny's body cast a grotesque shadow as she cautiously descended. There were so many steps that she decided they must lead to a basement in the hotel.

She reached the bottom at last and followed a narrow sloping tunnel, past a large refrigerated vault which she reasoned must contain a vast supply of additional furs, and kept on until a blast of cool air struck her face. Penny drew up sharply.

Directly ahead, at a bend in the tunnel, sat an armed guard. He was reading a newspaper in the dim light, holding it very close to the glaring bulb above his chair.

Penny dared go no farther. Quietly retreating the way she had come, she stole back up the long stairway. At the top landing she found herself confronted with a blank wall. After groping about for several minutes, her hand encountered a tiny switch similar to the one on the opposite side of the partition. She pressed it, and the wall section revolved.

Letting herself out of the storage closet, Penny started toward the door, only to pause as she heard one of the teletypes thumping out a message. She crossed over to the machine and stood waiting until the line had been finished and a bell jingled. The words were unintelligible in jumbled typewriting, and Penny had no time to work out the code.

Tearing the copy paper neatly across, she thrust it in the pocket of her jacket.

Fearing that at any moment the printer attendant might return, Penny dared linger no longer. She went to the door but to her surprise it would not open.

"Probably a special trick catch which automatically locks whenever closed," she thought. "The only way to get in or out is with a key, and I haven't one. That means I'll have to risk my neck again."

Going to the window she raised it and looked down. All was clear below. Two courses lay open to her. She could return the way she had come through the hotel, or she might edge along the shelf past two other windows to the fire escape, and thence to the ground. Either way was fraught with danger.

"If I should happen to meet Ralph Fergus or Harvey Maxwell, I might not get away with my information," Penny decided. "I'll try the fire-escape."

Closing the window behind her, she flattened herself along the building wall, and moved cautiously along the ledge. She passed the first room in safety. Then, as she was about to crawl past the second, the square of window suddenly flared with light.

For a dreadful moment Penny thought that she had been seen. She huddled against the wall and waited. Nothing happened.

At last, regaining her courage, she dared to peep into the lighted room. Two men stood with their backs to the window, but she recognized them as Harvey Maxwell and Ralph Fergus.

Penny received a distinct shock as her gaze wandered to the third individual who sat in a chair by the bed. The man was old Peter Jasko.

A low rumble of voices reached the girl's ears. Harvey Maxwell was speaking:

"Well, Jasko, have you thought it over? Are you ready to sign the lease?"

"I'll have the law on you, if I ever get out of here!" the old man said spiritedly. "You're keepin' me against my will."

"You'll stay here, Jasko, until you come to your senses. We need that land, and we mean to have it. Understand?"

"You won't get me to sign, not if you keep me here all night," Mr. Jasko muttered. "Not if you keep me a year!"

"You may change your mind after you learn what we can do," said Harvey Maxwell suavely.

"You aim to starve me, I reckon."

"Oh, no, nothing so crude as that, my dear fellow. In fact, we shall treat you most kindly. Doctor Corbin will be here presently to examine you."

"Doctor Corbin! That old quack from Morgantown! What are you bringing him here for?"

Harvey Maxwell smiled and tapped his head significantly.

"To give you a mental examination. You are known to the good people of Pine Top as a very peculiar fellow, so I doubt if anyone will question Doctor Corbin's verdict."

"You mean, you're aimin' to have me adjudged insane?" Peter Jasko asked incredulously.

"Exactly. How else can one explain your fanatical hatred of skiing, your blind rages, your antagonism to the more progressive interests? While it will be a pity to bring disgrace upon your charming granddaughter, there is no other way."

"Not unless you decide to sign," added Ralph Fergus. "We're more than reasonable. We're willing to pay you a fair price for the lease, more than the land is worth. But we want it, see? And what we want we take."

"You're a couple of thievin', stealin' crooks!" Peter Jasko shouted.

"Not so loud, and be careful of your words," Harvey Maxwell warned. "Or the gag goes on again."

"Which do you prefer," Fergus went on. "A tidy little sum of money, or the asylum?"

Peter Jasko maintained a sullen silence, glaring at the two hotel men.

"The doctor will be here at ten-thirty," said Harvey Maxwell, looking at his watch. "You will have less than a half hour to decide."

"My mind's made up now! You won't get anyone to believe your cock and bull story. I'll tell 'em you brought me here and held me prisoner—"

"And no one will believe you," smiled Maxwell. "We'll give out that you came to the hotel and started running amuck. Dozens of employes will confirm the story."

"For that matter, I'm not sure you don't belong in an asylum," muttered Fergus. "Only a man who isn't in his right mind would turn down the liberal proposition we've made you."

CHAPTER 22 - THE SECRET STAIRS

"I deal with no scoundrels!" the old man defied them.

Harvey Maxwell looked at his watch again. "You have exactly twenty-five minutes in which to make up your mind, Jasko. We'll leave you alone to think it over."

Fergus trussed up the old man's hands and placed a gag in his mouth. Then the two hotel men left the room, turning out the light and locking the door behind them.

CHAPTER 23 - RESCUE

After the door had closed there was no further sound for a moment. Then in the darkness Penny heard a choked sob.

Moving closer to the window she tried to raise it. Failing, she tapped lightly on the pane. Pressing her lips close to the glass she called softly:

"Don't be afraid, Mr. Jasko! Keep up your courage! I'll find a way to get you out!"

The old man could not answer so she had no way of knowing whether or not he heard her words. Moving back along the ledge she reached another window, and upon testing it was elated to find that it could be raised up.

She climbed through, lowered it behind her and hastened to the door. Quietly letting herself out, she went down the deserted hall to the next door. Without a key she could not hope to get inside. For a fleeting instant she wondered if she were not making a mistake by delaying in starting after the authorities.

"I never could get back here in time," she told herself. "Maxwell will return in twenty-five minutes with the doctor, possibly earlier. Jasko may sign the paper before help could reach him."

Penny was at a loss to know how to aid the old man. As she stood debating, the cleaning woman whom she had seen upon another occasion, came down the hall. The girl determined upon a bold move.

"I wonder if you could help me?" she said, going to meet the woman. "I've locked myself out of my room. Do you have a master key?"

"Yes, it will unlock most of the bedrooms."

"The doors on this floor?"

"All except number 27."

Penny took a two dollar bill from her jacket pocket and thrust it into the woman's hand.

"Here, take this, and let me have the key."

"I can't give it to you," the woman protested. "Show me your room and I'll unlock it for you."

"We're standing in front of it now. Number 29."

The woman stared. "But these rooms aren't usually given out, Miss."

"I assure you number 29 is very much occupied," replied Penny. "Unlock it, please."

The woman hesitated, and finally inserted the key in the lock.

"Thank you," said Penny as she heard the latch click. "No, keep the two dollars. You are welcome to it."

She waited until the maid had gone on down the hall before letting herself into the dark room. Groping for the electric switch, she turned it on.

"Mr. Jasko, you know me," she whispered as the old man blinked and stared at her almost stupidly. "I'm going to get you out of here."

She jerked the gag from his mouth, and unfastened the cords which bound his wrists.

"We don't dare go through the hotel lest we be seen," she told him. "I think we may be able to get out by means of the fire escape. If luck is only with us—"

Making certain that the coast was clear, Penny led the old man down the hall to a room which she knew would be opposite the fire escape. She was afraid it would be locked, but to her intense relief it had not been secured.

Only a minute was required to cross the room, raise the window and help Peter Jasko through it.

CHAPTER 23 - RESCUE

"I can't come with you," she said. "I have something else to do. Now listen closely. I want you to go to Pine Top as fast as you can and bring the sheriff or the police or whoever it is that would have authority to arrest Fergus and Maxwell."

"I aim to do that on my own account," the old man muttered. "I've got a debt to square with them."

"We both have," said Penny. "Now this is what I want you to do. If I'm not in evidence when you get back, bring the police to the Green Room."

"Where's that?"

"It's on this same floor. You go down the hall to the left, enter an unmarked door into another corridor, and finally through a green door which may be guarded. If necessary, force an entrance."

"I don't know what it's all about," the old man muttered. "But I'll do as you say."

"And hurry!" Penny urged.

She watched anxiously from the window until Peter Jasko had reached the bottom of the fire escape in safety. He ran across the yard, gaining the roadway without having been observed.

Returning once more to the main corridor, Penny glanced anxiously up and down. Hearing someone moving about at the far end of the hall, she went to investigate, certain that it was the cleaning woman putting away her mops and broom.

"You ain't locked out again?" the maid asked as she saw Penny standing beside her.

"No, but I have another request. How would you like to earn some more money?"

"How?" inquired the woman with quick interest.

"Do you have an extra costume?"

"Costume?"

"Dress, I mean. Like one you're wearing."

"Not here." As the maid spoke she divested herself of an old pair of shoes, and setting them back against the closet wall, slipped on a pair of much better looking ones. "I'm changing my clothes now to go home."

"I'll give you another two dollars if you'll lend me the outfit for the evening."

"Is it for a party?" the maid asked.

"A masquerade," said Penny. "I want to play a little joke on some acquaintances of mine."

She waved another bill before the woman's eyes, and the temptation of making easy money was too great to resist.

"All right, I'll do it," the maid agreed. "Just wait outside until I get my clothes changed."

Penny waited, watching the halls anxiously lest she be observed by someone who would recognize her. Soon the maid stepped from the closet, and handed over a bundle of clothing.

"And here is your money," said Penny. "Don't mention to anyone what we've done—at least not until tomorrow."

"Don't worry, Miss, I won't," replied the woman grimly. "I might lose my job if they caught me."

After the maid had gone away, Penny slipped into the closet and quickly changed into the costume. Pulling off her cap, she rumpled her hair and rubbed a streak of dirt across her face. The shoes were a trifle too large for her, and their size, together with the painful ankle, made her walk in a dragging fashion.

Snatching up a feather duster, she went hurriedly down the hall toward the corridor which led to the Green Room. As always, the guard sat in his chair by the door. But this time Penny had high hopes of gaining entrance.

Boldly, she walked over to him and said: "Good evening. I was sent to tell you you're wanted in the office by Mr. Maxwell."

"Now?" he inquired in surprise.

"Yes, right away."

"Someone ought to stay here."

"I'll wait until you get back."

"Don't let anyone inside unless they have passes," the guard instructed.

Penny barely could hide her excitement. It had been almost too easy! At last she was to penetrate beyond the Green Door! And if she found what she expected, the entire mystery would be cleared up. She would gain evidence against Ralph Fergus and Harvey Maxwell which would make her case iron-clad.

From within the room, Penny could hear the low murmur of voices. She waited until the guard had disappeared, and then, summoning her courage, opened the green door and stepped inside.

Penny found herself in an elegantly furnished salon, its chairs, davenports, carpet and draperies decorated in soft shades of green and ivory. A little dark-haired man she had never seen before, who spoke with an artificial French accent, stood talking with three women who were trying on fur coats. A fourth woman, Maxine Miller, sat in a chair, her back turned to Penny.

"Now Henri, I want you to give my friends a good price on their coats," she was saying in a chirpy voice.

"*Oui*" he agreed, bobbing his head up and down. "We say one hundred and ninety-two dollars for zis beautiful sealskin coat. I make you a special price only because you are friends of Mademoiselle Miller."

The opening of the outside door had drawn Henri's attention briefly to Penny. As she busied herself dusting, he paid her no heed, and Maxine Miller did not give the girl a second glance.

Penny wandered slowly about the room, noting the long mirrors and the tall cases crowded with racks of sealskin coats.

"These are smuggled furs," she thought. "This Green Room is the sales salon, and Henri must be an employee of Ralph Fergus and Harvey Maxwell. I believe I know how they get the furs over the Canadian border, too, without paying duty!"

Satisfied that she could learn no more by lingering, Penny turned down the long corridor leading to the door which opened on the main hallway. She knew that the guard would soon discover he had been tricked and expose her. And while she had been inside the salon less than five minutes, already she had waited a moment too long.

As she opened the door she saw Harvey Maxwell and the guard coming down the corridor toward her. Retreat was out of the question.

"There she is now!" said the guard, accusingly. "She told me you wanted me in the office."

Harvey Maxwell walked angrily toward Penny.

"What was the big idea?" he began, only to stop short. "Oh, so it's *you*? My dear little girl, I am very much afraid, you have over-played your hand this time!"

CHAPTER 24 - HENRI'S SALON

Penny sought to push past the two men, but Harvey Maxwell caught her roughly by the arm.

"Unfortunately, my dear Miss Parker, you have observed certain things which you may not understand," he said. "Lest you misinterpret them, and are inclined to run to your father with fantastic tales, you must be detained here. Now I have a great distaste for violence. I trust it will not be necessary to use force now."

"Let me go," Penny cried, trying to jerk away.

"Take her, Frank," instructed the hotel man. "For the time being put her in the tunnel room. I'll be down as soon as I talk with Ralph."

Before Penny could scream, a hand was clapped over her mouth. The guard, Frank, held her in a firm grip from which she could not free herself.

"Get going!" he commanded.

But Penny braced her feet and stood perfectly still. From the outside corridor she had heard a low rumble of voices. Then Ralph Fergus spoke above the others, in an exasperated, harassed tone:

"This old man is crazy, I tell you! We never kept him a prisoner in our hotel. We have a Green Room, to be sure, but it is rented out to a man named Henri Croix who is in the fur business."

Penny's pulse quickened. Peter Jasko had carried out her order and had brought the police!

Harvey Maxwell and the guard well comprehended their danger. With a quick jerk of his head the hotel man indicated a closet where Penny could be secreted. As the two men tried to pull her to it, she sunk her teeth into Frank's hand. His hold over her mouth relaxed for an instant, but that instant was enough. She screamed at the top of her lungs.

The outside door swung open. Led by Peter Jasko, the sheriff and several deputies filed into the corridor. Ralph Fergus did not follow, and Penny saw him trying to slip away.

"Don't let that man escape!" she cried. "Arrest him!"

Peter Jasko himself overtook Fergus and brought him back.

"I've got a score to settle with you," he muttered. "You ain't a good enough talker to get out of this."

"Gentlemen—" It was Harvey Maxwell who spoke, and his tone was irritated. "What is the meaning of this intrusion?"

"We've had a complaint," said the sheriff. "Jasko here says you kept him a prisoner in the hotel, trying to make him sign a paper."

"The old fellow is right in a way," replied Mr. Maxwell. "Not about the paper. We did detain him here for his own good, and he managed to get away. I regret to say he went completely out of his mind, became violent, threatened our guests, and it was necessary to hold him until the doctor could arrive. We've already sent for Doctor Corbin."

"That's just what I was telling them," added Ralph Fergus.

"Now let me speak my piece," said Penny. "Peter Jasko was held a prisoner here because Fergus and Maxwell wanted him to sign a paper leasing his ski slopes to the hotel. That was only one of their many little stunts. Fergus and Maxwell are the heads of a gigantic fur smuggling business, and they use their hotels merely as a legitimate front."

"Your proof?" demanded Harvey Maxwell sarcastically. "The real truth is that I am suing this girl's father for libel. He sent her here to try to dig up something against me. She's using every excuse she can find to involve me in affairs about which I know nothing."

"If you want proof, I'll furnish it," said Penny. "Just step into the Green Room where Henri Croix, a phony Frenchman, is engaged in selling fur coats to three ladies."

"There's no crime in that," declared Ralph Fergus angrily. "Mr. Croix pays the hotel three hundred dollars a month for the use of this wing. So far as we know his business is legitimate. If for any reason we learn it is not, we will be the first to ask for an investigation."

"Not quite the first," smiled Penny, "for I've already made the request. To go on with my proof, it might be well to investigate Room 27 on this same floor."

"Room 27 is given over to our teletype service," interrupted Maxwell. "Our guests like to get the stock reports, you know, and that is why we have the machines."

"In Room 27 you will find a storage vault for furs," Penny went on, thoroughly enjoying herself. "A panel revolves, opening the way to a secret stair which leads down into the basement of the hotel. I'm not certain about the rest—"

"No?" demanded Maxwell ironically.

"There are additional storage vaults in the basement," Penny resumed. "A man is down there guarding what appears to be a tunnel. Tell me, is this hotel close to the old silver mine?"

"About a quarter of a mile from the entrance," replied the sheriff. "Some of the tunnels might come right up to the hotel grounds."

"I understand the hotel bought out the mine, and I believe they may be making use of the old tunnels. At least, the place will bear an investigation. Oh, yes, this paper came off one of the teletype machines."

Penny took the torn sheet from her pocket and gave it to the sheriff.

"I can't read it," he said, frowning.

"Code," explained Penny. "If I had a typewriter I could figure it out. Suppose we go to Room 27 now. I'm positive you'll learn that my story is not as fantastic as it seems."

Leaving Peter Jasko and two deputies to guard Fergus and Maxwell and to see that no one left the Green Room, Penny led the sheriff and four other armed men down the hall. In her excitement she failed to observe Francine Sellberg standing by the elevator, watching intently.

"Here are the teletype machines," Penny indicated, pausing beside them. "Now let me have that message. I think I can read it."

Studying the keyboard of the teletype for a moment, she wrote out her translation beneath the jumbled line of printing. It read:

"Train Arrives approximately 11:25."

"What does that mean?" the sheriff inquired. "We have no trains at Pine Top."

"We'll see," chuckled Penny.

She showed the men the vault filled with furs, and pressed the spring which opened the wall panel.

"Be careful in descending the stairway," she warned. "I know they have one guard down there and possibly others."

Sheriff Clausson and his men went ahead of Penny. The guard, taken completely by surprise, was captured without a shot being fired.

"Now what have we here?" the sheriff inquired, peering into the dimly lighted tunnel.

As far as one could see stretched a narrow, rusted track with an extra rail.

"A miniature electric railway!" exclaimed the sheriff.

"How far is it from here to the border?" inquired Penny thoughtfully.

"Not more than a mile."

"I've been told Harvey Maxwell has a hotel located in Canada."

"Yeah," nodded the sheriff, following her thought. "We've known for years that furs were being smuggled, but we never once suspected the outfit was located here at Pine Top. And no wonder. This scheme is clever, so elaborate a fellow never would think of it. The underground railroad, complete with drainage pumps, storage rooms and electric lights, crosses the border and connects with the Canadian hotel. Fergus and Maxwell buy furs cheap and send them here without paying duty."

"And teletype communication is maintained just as it is on a real railroad," added Penny. "Fergus and Maxwell must have bought up the old mine just so they could make use of the tunnels. And they wanted to get rid of

CHAPTER 24 - HENRI'S SALON

Mrs. Downey's Inn so there would be no possible danger of a leak. How large do you suppose the smuggling ring is, Mr. Clausson?"

"Large enough. Likely it will take weeks to get all of the guilty persons rounded up. But I'm satisfied we have the main persons."

"If I interpreted the code message right, a fur train should be coming in about eleven-thirty."

"My men will be waiting," the sheriff said grimly. "I'll get busy now and tip off the Canadian authorities, so they can close in on the gang from the other end of the line."

"What about Fergus and Maxwell?" asked Penny. "There's no chance they can trump up a story and get free?"

"Not a chance," returned the sheriff gruffly. "You've done your work, and now I'll do mine."

Penny started to turn away, then paused. "Oh, may I ask a favor?"

"I reckon you've earned it," the sheriff answered, a twinkle in his eye.

"There's one person involved in this mess who isn't really to blame. An actress named Maxine Miller. She's only been working for the hotel a few days, and I doubt if she knows what it's all about."

"We'll give her every benefit of the doubt," promised the sheriff. "I'll remember the name. Miller."

In a daze of excitement Penny rushed back up the stairway to the Green Room. Fergus and Maxwell, Henri Croix, and Maxine Miller were in custody, all angrily protesting their innocence. The commotion had brought many hotel guests to the scene. Questions were flying thick and fast.

Penny drew Peter Jasko aside to talk with him privately.

"I think you ought to go to Mrs. Downey's lodge as soon as you can," she urged. "Sara is there, and she's dreadfully worried about you."

"I'll go now," the old man said, offering his gnarled hand. "Much obliged for all you done tonight."

"That's quite all right," replied Penny. "I was lucky or I never would have discovered where those men were keeping you."

The old man hesitated, obviously wishing to say something more, yet unable to find the words.

"I done some thinkin' tonight," he muttered. "I reckon I been too strict with Sara. From now on maybe I'll let her have a looser rein."

"And ski all she likes," urged Penny. "I really can't see the harm in it."

"I been thinkin' about that lease, too," the old man added, not looking directly at the girl. "When I see Mrs. Downey tonight I'll tell her I'm ready to sign."

"Oh, I'm so glad!" Penny exclaimed. "With the Fergus-Maxwell hotel out of the running, she ought to have a comfortable time of it here on Pine Top mountain."

"Thanks to you," grinned Peter Jasko. He offered his hand again and Penny gave it a firm pressure.

"I must hurry now," she said. "This is a tremendous story, and I want to telegraph it to Dad before Francine Sellberg beats me to the jump."

"Sellberg?" repeated the old man. "She ain't that girl reporter that's been stayin' here at the hotel?"

Penny nodded.

"Then you better step," he advised. "She's on her way to the village now."

"But how could Francine have learned about it so soon?" Penny wailed in dismay.

"I saw her talking with one of the deputies. She was writing things down in a notebook."

"She couldn't have learned everything, but probably enough to ruin my story. When did Francine leave, Mr. Jasko?"

"All of fifteen minutes ago."

"Then I never can overtake her," Penny murmured. "This is absolutely the worst break yet! Francine will reach the telegraph office first and hold the wire so I can't use it. After all my work, her paper will get the big scoop!"

CHAPTER 25 - SCOOP!

Penny knew that she had only one chance of getting her story through to Riverview, and that was by means of long distance telephone. At best, instead of achieving a scoop as she had hoped, she would have only an even break with her rival. And if connections could not be quickly made, she would lose out altogether.

Hastily saying goodbye to Peter Jasko, Penny raced for the stairway. She did not have a word of her story written down. While she could give the facts to a rewrite man it would take him some time to get the article into shape.

"Vic Henderson writes such colorless stories, too," she moaned to herself. "He'll be afraid some fact isn't accurate and he'll jerk it out. This is the one yarn I want to write myself!"

Penny ran full tilt into Sheriff Clausson. She brought up shortly, observing that he had a prisoner in custody.

"Miss Parker, we caught this fellow down in the tunnel," he said. "Can you identify him?"

"I'm not sure of his name. He works for Fergus and Maxwell as a teletype attendant. He may be George Jewitt."

Penny started to hasten on, and then struck by a sudden idea, paused. Addressing the prisoner she demanded:

"Isn't it true that there is a direct wire connection between this hotel and the one in Riverview?"

The man did not speak.

"You may as well answer up," said the sheriff. "It's something which can be checked easily."

"Yes, there is a direct connection," answered the attendant.

"And if I know anything about leased wires," continued Penny with mounting excitement, "it would be possible to have the telephone company switch that wire right over to the *Riverview Star* office. Then I'd have a direct connection from here to the newspaper. Right?"

"Right except for one minor detail," the man retorted sarcastically. "The telephone company won't make a switch just to oblige a little girl."

Penny's face fell. "I suppose they wouldn't do it," she admitted. "But what a whale of an idea! I could send my story directly to the newspaper, and get my scoop after all. As it is, the *Record* is almost certain to beat me."

"Listen!" said the sheriff. "Maybe the telephone company couldn't make the switch on your say-so, but they'll pay attention to an order from me. You get busy writing that story, young lady, and we'll see what can be done."

Sheriff Clausson turned his prisoner over to a deputy, and returned to find Penny busily scribbling on the back of an envelope, the only writing paper available. Together they went to the long distance telephone, and in a quicker time than the girl had dared hope, arrangements were made for the wire shift to be made.

"Now get up to Room 27 and start your story going out," the sheriff urged. "Will you need the attendant to turn on the current for you?"

"No, I know how it's done!" Penny declared. "You're sure the connection has been made?"

"The telephone company reports everything is set. So go to it!"

Penny hobbled as fast as her injured ankle would permit to Room 27. She switched on the light, and turned on the current which controlled the teletype machines. Sitting down at a chair in front of the direct keyboard, she found herself trembling from excitement. She had practiced only a few times and was afraid she might make mistakes. Every word she wrote would be transmitted in exactly that form to a similar machine stationed in the *Star* office.

CHAPTER 25 - SCOOP!

She could picture her father standing there, waiting, wondering what she would send. He had been warned that a big story was coming.

Penny consulted her envelope notes and began to tap the keys. Now and then she had moments of misgiving, wondering if her work was accurate, and if it were going through. She finished at last, and sat back with a weary sigh of relief. Her story was a good one. She knew that. But had it ever reached the *Star* office?

A machine to her right began its rhythmical thumping. Startled, Penny sprang to her feet and rushed over to see the message which was slowly printing itself across the copy paper.

"STORY RECEIVED OK. WONDERFUL STUFF. CAN YOU GET AN INTERVIEW WITH SHERIFF CLAUSSON?"

Penny laughed aloud, and went back to her own machine to tap out an answer. Her line had a flippant note:

"I'LL HAUL HIM UP HERE AS SOON AS THE 11:30 TRAIN COMES IN. LET ME TALK TO DAD."

There was a little wait and then the return message came in over the other teletype.

"YOU'VE BEEN TALKING WITH HIM. AM SENDING SALT SOMMERS BY PLANE TO GET PICTURES. SORRY I DIDN'T TAKE YOU SERIOUSLY WHEN YOU WROTE MAXWELL WAS INVOLVED IN ILLEGAL BUSINESS AT PINE TOP. THIS OUGHT TO MOP UP HIS SUIT AGAINST THE PAPER. GREAT STUFF, PENNY! WHO UNCOVERED THE STORY?"

Chuckling to herself, Penny went back to her keyboard and tapped:

"DON'T ASK ME. I'M TRYING TO BE MODEST."

She waited eagerly for the response and it came in a moment.

"I WAS AFRAID OF IT. ARE YOU ALL RIGHT?"

Thoroughly enjoying the little game of questions and answers, Penny once more tapped her message.

"FINE AS SILK. WHEN ARE YOU COMING TO PINE TOP? WHAT ARE YOU GOING TO GIVE ME FOR XMAS? IT SHOULD BE SOMETHING GOOD AFTER THIS."

Soon Mr. Parker's reply appeared on the moving sheet of paper.

"SOON. PERHAPS SOMETHING WITH FOUR WHEELS AND A HORN."

Penny scarcely could control herself long enough to send back:

"OH, YOU WONDERFUL DAD! I COULD HUG YOU! PLEASE MAKE IT MAROON WITH MOHAIR UPHOLSTERY. AND HANG A WREATH ON LEAPING LENA."

Sinking back in her chair, Penny gazed dreamily at the ceiling. A new car! It was almost too good to believe. She knew that her father must have been swayed by excitement or else very grateful to offer such a magnificent Christmas present as that. What a night of thrills it had been! Within a few hours Pine Top would be crowded with reporters and photographers, but she had uncovered the story, and had saved her father from a disastrous lawsuit.

As Penny waited, her thoughts far away, one more message came through on the teletype. She tore it from the roller of the machine, and smiled as she read her father's final words:

"PRESSES ROLLING. FIRST EDITION ON THE STREET AHEAD OF THE RECORD. THE STAR SCORES AGAIN. THIS IS ANTHONY PARKER SIGNING OFF FOR A CUP OF COFFEE."

THE END

CLUE OF THE SILKEN LADDER

"It's a ladder, Lou! A ladder made of silk!"

CHAPTER 1 - DOUBLE TROUBLE

"Now I ask you, Lou, what have I done to deserve such a fate?"

Jerking a yellow card from beneath the windshield of the shiny new maroon-colored sedan, Penny Parker turned flashing blue eyes upon her companion, Louise Sidell.

"Well, Penny," responded her chum dryly, "in Riverview persons who park their cars beside fire hydrants usually expect to get parking tickets."

"But we were only inside the drugstore five minutes. Wouldn't you think a policeman could find something else to do?"

"Oh, the ticket won't cost you more than five or ten dollars," teased Louise wickedly. "Your father should pay it."

"He should but he won't," Penny answered gloomily. "Dad expects his one and only daughter to assume her own car expense. I ask you, what's the good of having a weekly allowance when you never get to use it yourself?"

"You *are* in a mood today. Why, I think you're lucky to have a grand new car."

Louise's glance caressed the highly polished chrome plate, the sleek, streamlined body which shone in the sunlight. The automobile had been presented to Penny by her father, Anthony Parker, largely in gratitude because she had saved his newspaper, *The Riverview Star*, from a disastrous law suit.

"Yes, I am lucky," Penny agreed without enthusiasm. "All the same, I'm lonesome for my old coupe, Leaping Lena. I wish I could have kept her. She was traded in on this model."

"What would you do with that old wreck now, Penny? Nearly every time we went around a corner it broke down."

"All the same, we had marvelous times with her. This car takes twice as much gasoline. Another thing, all the policemen knew Lena. They never gave her a ticket for anything."

Penny sighed deeply. Pocketing the yellow card, she squeezed behind the steering wheel.

"By the way, whatever became of Lena?" Louise asked curiously, slamming the car door. She glanced sharply at Penny.

"Oh, she's changed hands twice. Now she's at Jake Harriman's lot, advertised for fifty dollars. Want to drive past there?"

"Not particularly. But I'll do it for your sake, pet."

As the car started toward the Harriman Car Lot, Louise stole an amused glance at her chum. Penny was not unattractive, even when submerged in gloom. Upon the slightest provocation, her blue eyes sparkled; her smile when she chose to turn it on, would melt a man of stone. She dressed carelessly, brushed a mop of curly, golden hair only if it suited her fancy, yet somehow achieved an appearance envied by her friends.

The automobile drew up at the curb.

"There's Lena." Penny pointed to an ancient blue coupe with battered fenders which stood on the crowded second-hand lot. A *For Sale* sign on the windshield informed the public that the auto might be bought for forty dollars.

"Lena's value seems to have dropped ten dollars," commented Louise. "My, I had forgotten how wrecky the old thing looks!"

"Don't speak of her so disrespectfully, Lou. All she needs is a good waxing and a little paint."

The girls crossed the lot to inspect the coupe. As they were gazing at it, Jake, the lot owner, sidled toward them, beaming ingratiatingly.

"Good afternoon, young ladies. May I interest you in a car?"

"No, thank you," replied Penny. "We're just looking."

"Now here is a fine car," went on the dealer, indicating the coupe. "A 1934 model—good mechanical condition; nice rubber; a lively battery and fair paint. You can't go wrong, ladies, not at a price of forty dollars."

"But will it run?" asked Louise, smothering a giggle.

"There's thousands of miles of good service left in this little car, ladies. And the price is only fifteen dollars above the junk value."

The thought of Leaping Lena coming to an inglorious end in a junk yard was disconcerting to Penny. She walked slowly about the car, inspecting it from every angle.

"Forty dollars is too much for this old wreck," she said firmly.

"Why, Penny, such disrespect!" mocked Louise.

Penny frowned down her chum. Sentiment and business were two different matters.

"What *will* you give?" inquired the car owner alertly.

"Not a cent over twenty-five."

Louise clutched Penny's arm, trying to pull her away.

"Have you lost your mind?" she demanded. "What could you do with this old car when you already have a new one?"

Penny did not listen. She kept gazing at the coupe as one who had been hypnotized.

"I'd take it in a minute, only I don't have twenty-five dollars in cash."

"How much can you raise?" asked the dealer.

"Not more than five dollars, I'm afraid. But my father is publisher of the *Riverview Star*."

Jake Harriman's brows unknitted as if by magic.

"Anthony Parker's daughter," he said, smiling. "That's plenty good enough for me. I'll sell you the best car on the lot for nothing down. Just come inside the office and sign a note for the amount. Will that be okay?"

Disregarding Louise's whispered protests, Penny assured the dealer that the arrangement would be perfectly satisfactory. The note was signed, and five dollars in cash given to bind the bargain.

"I'll throw in a few gallons of gas," the man offered.

However, Jake Harriman's gasoline did not seem suited to Leaping Lena's dyspeptic ignition. She coughed feebly once or twice and then died for the day.

"You have acquired a bargain, I must say!" exclaimed Louise. "You can't even get the car home."

"Yes, I can," Penny insisted. "I'll tow her. A little tinkering and she'll be as good as new."

"You're optimistic, to say the least," laughed Louise.

Penny produced a steel cable from the tool kit of the maroon sedan, and Jake Harriman coupled the two cars together.

"Penny, what will your father say when he learns of this?" Louise inquired dubiously. "On top of a parking ticket, too!"

"Oh, I'll meet that problem when I come to it," Penny answered carelessly. "Louise, you steer Lena. I'll drive the sedan."

Shaking her head sadly, Louise climbed into the old car. Although Penny was her dearest friend she was forced to admit that the girl often did bewildering things. Penny's mother was dead and for many years she had been raised by a housekeeper, Mrs. Maud Weems. Secretly Louise wondered if it were not the housekeeper who had been trained. At any rate, Penny enjoyed unusual freedom for a high school girl, and her philosophy of life was summed up in one headline: ACTION.

Penny put the sedan in gear, towing the coupe slowly down the street. The two vehicles traveled several blocks before a hill loomed ahead. Penny considered turning back, and then decided that the cars could make the steep climb easily.

However, midway up the hill the sedan suddenly leaped forward as if released from a heavy burden. At the same instant Lena's horn gave a sharp warning blast.

Glancing into the mirror, Penny was horrified to see Leaping Lena careening backwards down the steep slope. The tow rope had unfastened.

CHAPTER 1 - DOUBLE TROUBLE

Bringing the sedan to the curb, she jerked on the hand brake, and sprang to the pavement. Louise, bewildered and frightened, was trying desperately to control the coupe. The car gathered speed, wobbling crazily toward the line of traffic.

"Guide it! Guide it!" shouted Penny. "Put on the brakes!"

So confused was Louise that she lost her head completely. Straight toward a long black limousine rolled the coupe. The chauffeur spun his wheel, but too late. There was a loud crash as the two cars came together.

Penny raced down the hill to help her chum from the coupe.

"Are you hurt?" she asked anxiously.

Louise shook her head, wailing: "Penny Parker, just see what has happened now! You never should have bought this stupid old wreck!"

Both the chauffeur and an elderly gentleman who carried a cane, alighted from the limousine. With grim faces they surveyed the fender which had been crushed.

"The owner is Mr. Kohl," Louise whispered nervously. "You know, president of the First National Bank."

The banker did not recognize either of the girls. Addressing them both, he made several pointed remarks to the effect that irresponsible young people were very thoughtless to endanger the property of others with their ancient "jalopies."

"It was entirely my fault, Mr. Kohl," acknowledged Penny meekly. "Of course, I'll pay for the fender."

The banker softened somewhat, gazing at the girls in a thoughtful, more friendly way.

"Haven't I seen you somewhere before?" he asked.

"Oh, yes, Mr. Kohl." Penny was quick to press for an advantage. "Why, I am one of your best customers. Ever since I was six years old I've trusted your bank with my savings!"

"I remember you now," said Mr. Kohl, smiling. "You're the Parker girl."

Adding a mental note that Anthony Parker actually was one of the bank's largest depositors, he decided it would be excellent policy to make light of the accident. A moment later as a policeman came to investigate, he insisted that the incident had been unavoidable and that it would be a mistake to arrest the girls.

"Mr. Kohl, you were noble, absolutely noble," declared Penny gratefully after the policeman had gone. "The least I can do is to pay for the damage."

"I'll stop at Sherman's Garage and have a new fender put on," the banker responded. "The bill can be sent to your father."

After Mr. Kohl had driven away, Louise helped Penny hook the coupe to the sedan once more. She remarked cuttingly:

"You've done right well today. One parking ticket, a bill for twenty-five dollars, and another one coming up. Just what *will* your father say?"

"Plenty," sighed Penny. "I wonder if it might not be a good idea to break the news by easy stages? Perhaps he'll take it more calmly if I telephone."

"Don't be too sure."

The street was a narrow, dingy one with few business houses. Noticing a Japanese store which bore a sign, "Kano's Curio Shop," she started toward it, intending to seek a public telephone.

Louise seized her arm. "Penny, you're not going in there!"

"Why not?"

"This is Dorr Street—one of the worst places in Riverview."

"Oh, don't be silly," chuckled Penny. "It's perfectly safe by daylight. I'll go alone if you're afraid."

Thus challenged, Louise indignantly denied that she was afraid, and accompanied her chum.

The door of Mr. Kano's shop stood invitingly open. Pausing on the threshold, the girls caught a pleasant aroma of sandalwood.

So quietly did Louise and Penny enter that the elderly, white-haired shop owner did not immediately see them. He sat behind a high counter, engrossed in something he was sewing.

"Good afternoon," said Penny pleasantly.

The Japanese glanced up quickly and as quickly thrust his work beneath the counter. Recovering poise, he bowed to the girls.

"May we use your telephone if you have one?" Penny requested.

"So very sorry, Miss," the Japanese responded, bowing again. "Have no telephone."

Penny nodded, absently fingering a tray of tiny ivory figures. The Japanese watched her, and mistaking curiosity for buying interest, brought additional pieces for her to inspect. The curios were all too expensive for Penny's purse, but after endless debate she bought a pair of wooden clogs. The shop owner padded away into a back room, intending to wrap the package for her.

Scarcely had he vanished when Penny turned excitedly to her chum.

"Lou, did you notice how funny he acted when we came in here?"

"Yes, he didn't want us to see what he was making evidently."

"Exactly what I thought! But we'll fool Mr. Kano!"

Giving Louise no opportunity to protest, Penny boldly peered behind the counter.

"Here it is," she whispered. "But *what* is it?"

Hidden in a pasteboard box lay coil upon coil of what appeared to be fine, black silk rope. Curiously, she lifted it up, exposing a network of crossbars.

"Well, of all things!" she exclaimed. "It's a ladder, Lou! A ladder made of silk!"

CHAPTER 2 - A ROPE OF SILK

Even as Penny spoke, she felt a hard, warning tug on her skirt. Quickly she turned around.

In the doorway stood the old Japanese. His smile was not pleasant to behold.

"We-we were just looking at this rope," Penny stammered, trying to carry off the situation with dignity. "I hope you don't mind."

The Japanese shopkeeper gazed steadily at the girl, his face an emotionless mask. Since he spoke no word, it became increasingly evident that he regarded her with anger and suspicion.

"May I ask what use is made of this silk rope?" Penny inquired. "Do you sell it for a special purpose?"

The Japanese coldly ignored the direct questions.

"So very sorry to have kept you waiting," he said softly. "Your change please."

Penny knew that she deserved the rebuke. Accepting the package and coins, she and Louise hastily left the shop. Not until they were some distance away did the latter speak.

"Penny, you would do a trick like that! One of these days your curiosity will get us into serious trouble."

"At least I learned what was hidden behind the counter," chuckled Penny. "But that Jap didn't seem very eager to answer my questions."

"Can you blame him? It certainly was none of our affair what he kept inside the box."

"Perhaps not, Lou, but you must admit he acted strangely when we first entered the shop. You know—as if we had surprised him in a questionable act."

"He naturally was startled. We came in so quietly."

"All the same, I'm not one bit sorry I looked behind the counter," Penny maintained. "I like to learn about things."

"I agree with you there!"

"Lou, what purpose do you suppose silk ladders serve? Who uses them and why?"

"Now, how should I know? Penny, you ask enough questions to be master of ceremonies on a radio quiz program."

"I can't recall ever having seen a silk ladder before," Penny resumed, undisturbed by her chum's quip. "Would acrobats use them, do you think?"

"Not to my knowledge," Louise answered. "If I were in your shoes I should worry about more serious matters than those connected with a mere silk ladder."

"The world is filled with serious things," sighed Penny. "But mystery! One doesn't run into it every day."

"You do," said Louise brutally. "If a stranger twitches his ears twice you immediately suspect him of villainy."

"Nevertheless, being of a suspicious nature won me a new car," Penny defended herself. "Don't forget Dad gave it to me for solving a mystery, for telling his newspaper readers what was going on *Behind the Green Door*."

"Oh, your curiosity has paid dividends," Louise admitted with a laugh. "Take for instance the time you trailed the *Vanishing Houseboat*, and again when you lowered the Kippenberg drawbridge to capture a boatload of crooks! Those were the days!"

"Why dwell in the past, Lou? Now take this affair of the silk ladder—"

"I'm afraid *you'll* have to take it," Louise interrupted. "Do you realize it's nearly four o'clock? In exactly ten minutes I am supposed to be at the auditorium for orchestra practice."

"Lou, you can't desert me now," Penny protested quickly. "How will I get Lena home? I need you to steer her."

"Thanks, but I don't trust your tow rope."

"At least go as far as the *Star* office with me. Once there, maybe I can get one of the reporters to help me the rest of the way."

"Oh, all right," Louise consented. "But the *Star* office is my absolute limit."

Deciding not to take time to telephone her father, Penny once more climbed into the maroon sedan, posting Louise behind the wheel of the coupe. At a cautious speed the two cars proceeded along the street, coming presently to a large corner building which housed the *Riverview Star*. No parking space being available on the street, Penny pulled into the newspaper plant's loading dock.

"Say, you!" shouted a man who was tossing stacks of freshly inked papers into a truck. "You can't park that caravan in here!"

Penny's eyes danced mischievously.

"Oh, it's quite all right," she said. "I guess you don't know who I am."

"Sure, I do," the trucker grinned. "But your dad gave orders that the next time you tried to pull that daughter-of-the-publisher stuff we were to bounce you! This dock is for *Star* trucks."

"Why, the very idea," said Penny, with pretended injury. "The night edition doesn't roll for an hour and I'll be away from here before then! Besides, this is a great emergency! When Dad hears about all the trouble I'm in, a little matter such as this won't even ruffle him."

"Okay, chase along," the trucker returned good-naturedly. "But see to it that you're out of here within an hour."

Penny bade Louise good-bye, and with plaid skirt swinging jauntily, crossed the cement runway to the rear elevator entrance. Without waiting for the cage to descend, she took the steps two at a time, arriving at the editorial floor gasping for breath.

"What's your rush?" inquired an amused voice. "Going to a fire?"

Jerry Livingston, ace reporter for the *Star*, leaned indolently against the grillwork of the elevator shaft, his finger pressed on the signal button. He and Penny were friends of long standing.

"Oh, hello, Jerry!" Penny greeted him breathlessly. "Guess what? I've just come from Dorr Street—Kano's Curio Shop—and I had the most amazing adventure!"

"I can imagine," grinned Jerry. "If you breezed through the place the way you do this building, you must have left it in ruins."

"Just for that, I won't tell you a thing, not a thing," retorted Penny. "What sort of a mood is Dad in today?"

"Well, I heard him tell DeWitt that unless the news output improves on this sheet, he aims to fire half the force."

"Sounds like Dad on one of his bad days," Penny sighed. "Maybe I should skip home without seeing him."

"Trouble with the old allowance again?" Jerry asked sympathetically.

"You don't know the half of it. I'm submerged so deeply in debt that I'll be an old lady before I get out, unless Dad comes to my rescue."

"Well, good luck," chuckled Jerry. "You'll need it!"

Walking through the newsroom, between aisles of desks where busy reporters tapped on their typewriters, Penny paused before a door marked: *Anthony Parker, Editor*.

Listening a moment and hearing no voices within, she knocked and entered. Her father, a lean, dignified man with tired lines about his eyes and mouth, sat working at his desk. He smiled as he saw his daughter, and waved her toward a chair.

Instead, Penny perched herself on a corner of the desk.

"Dad, I have a splendid surprise for you," she began brightly. "I've just accomplished a wonderful stroke of business!"

"Never mind beating about the bush," interrupted Mr. Parker. "Shoot me the facts straight. What have you done this time?"

"Dad, your tone! I've bought back my old car, Leaping Lena. And it only cost me a trifling sum."

Mr. Parker's chair squeaked as he whirled around.

"You've done *what*?"

CHAPTER 2 - A ROPE OF SILK

"It's a long story, Dad. Now don't think that I fail to appreciate the grand new car you gave me last winter. I love it. But between Lena and me there exists a deep bond of affection. Today when I saw her on Jake Harriman's lot looking so weather-beaten and unhappy—why, a little voice inside me whispered: 'Penny, why don't you buy her back?' So I did."

"Never mind the sentimental touches. When I gave you the new car I thought we were well rid of Lena. How much did you pay for it?"

"Oh, Lena was a marvelous bargain. Five dollars cash and a note for twenty more. The man said you could pay for it at your convenience."

"Very considerate of him," Mr. Parker remarked ironically. "Now that we have three cars, and a double garage, where do you propose to keep Lena?"

"Oh, anywhere. In the back yard."

"Not on the lawn, young lady. And what do you plan to do with two cars?"

"The maroon one for style, and Lena when I want a good time. Why, Dad, she bears the autographs of nearly all my school friends! I should keep her as a souvenir, if for no other reason."

"Penny, it's high time you learned a few lessons in finance." Mr. Parker spoke sternly although his mouth twitched slightly. "I regret that I cannot assume your debts."

"But Dad! I'm a minor—under legal age. Isn't it a law that a father has to support his child?"

"A child, but not two cars. If you decide to take the case to court, I think any reasonable judge will understand my viewpoint. I repeat, the debt is yours, not mine."

"How will I pay?" asked Penny gloomily. "I've already borrowed on my allowance for a month ahead."

"I know," said her father. "However, with your ingenuity I am sure you can manage."

Penny drew a deep breath. Argument, she realized, would be utterly useless. While her father might be mildly amused by her predicament, he never would change his decision.

"Since you won't pay for Lena, I suppose it's useless to mention Mr. Kohl's fender," she said despairingly.

"Does he have one?"

"Please don't try to be funny, Dad. This is tragic. While I was towing Lena, the rope broke and smash went the fender of Mr. Kohl's slinky black limousine."

"Interesting."

"I had to promise to pay for it to keep from being arrested. Oh, yes, and before that I acquired this little thing."

Penny tossed the yellow card across the desk.

"A parking ticket! Penny, how many times—" Mr. Parker checked himself, finishing in a calm voice: "This, too, is your debt. It may cost you five dollars."

"Dad, you know I can't pay. Think how your reputation will be tarnished if I am sent to jail."

Mr. Parker smiled and reached as if to take money from his pocket. Reconsidering, he shook his head.

"I know the warden well," he said. "I'll arrange for you to be assigned to one of the better cells."

"Is there nothing which will move you to generosity?" pleaded Penny.

"Nothing."

Retrieving the parking ticket, Penny jammed it into her pocket. Before she could leave there came a rap on the door. In response to Mr. Parker's "Come in," Mr. DeWitt, the city editor, entered.

"Sorry to bother you, Chief."

"What's wrong now, DeWitt?" the publisher inquired.

"Miss Hilderman was taken sick a few minutes ago. We had to send her home in a cab."

"It's nothing serious I hope," said Mr. Parker with concern.

"A mild heart attack. She'll be out a week, if not longer."

"I see. Be sure to have the treasurer give her full pay. You have someone to take her place?"

"That's the problem," moaned DeWitt. "Her assistant is on vacation. I don't know where we can get a trained society editor on short notice."

"Well, do the best you can."

DeWitt lingered, fingering a paper weight.

"The society page for the Sunday paper is only half finished," he explained. "Deadline's in less than an hour. Not a chance we can pick up anyone in time to meet it."

CLUE OF THE SILKEN LADDER

Penny spoke unexpectedly. "Mr. DeWitt, perhaps I can help you. I'm a whiz when it comes to writing society. Remember the Kippenberg wedding I covered?"

"Do I?" DeWitt's face relaxed into a broad grin. "That was a real write-up. Say, maybe you could take over Miss Hilderman's job until we can replace her."

"Service is my motto." Penny eyed her father questioningly. "It might save the *Star* from going to press minus a society page. How about it, Dad?"

"It certainly would solve our problem," contributed DeWitt. "Of course the undertaking might be too great a one for your daughter." He winked at Penny.

"She'll have no difficulty in taking over," said Mr. Parker stiffly. "None whatsoever."

"Then I'll start her in at once," DeWitt replied. "Come with me, Miss Parker."

At the door Penny paused and discreetly allowed the city editor to get beyond hearing. Then, turning to her father she remarked innocently:

"Oh, by the way, we overlooked one trifling detail. The salary!"

The editor made a grimace. "I might have expected this. Very well, I'll pay you the same as I do Miss Hilderman. Twenty-five a week."

"Why, that would just take care of my debt to Jake Harriman," protested Penny. "I simply can't do high pressure work without high pay. Shall we make it fifty a week?"

"So you're holding me up?"

"Certainly not," chuckled Penny. "Merely using my ingenuity. Am I hired?"

"Yes, you win," answered Mr. Parker grimly. "But see to it that you turn out good work. Otherwise, you soon may find yourself on the *Star's* inactive list."

CHAPTER 3 - SOCIETY ROUTINE

Penny followed City Editor DeWitt to a small, glass-enclosed office along the left hand wall of the newsroom. Miss Hilderman's desk was cluttered with sheets of copy paper which bore scribbled notations, items telephoned to the *Star* but not yet type-written.

"There should be a date book around here somewhere," DeWitt remarked.

Finally he found it in one of the desk drawers. Penny drew a deep breath as she scanned the long list of social events which must be covered for the Sunday page.

"Do the best you can," DeWitt said encouragingly. "Work fast, but be careful of names."

The telephone bell rang. As Penny reached for the receiver, DeWitt retreated to his own domain.

"Hello, Miss Hilderman?" a feminine voice cooed, "I wish to report a meeting, please."

"Miss Hilderman isn't here this afternoon," replied Penny politely. "I will take the item."

Gathering up paper and pencil, she slid into the revolving chair behind the telephone, poised for action.

"Yes," she urged, "I am ready."

There was a lengthy pause, and then the woman at the other end of the line recited as if she were reading from a paper:

"'A meeting of the Mystical Society of Celestial Thought, Order of Amar, 67, will be held Tuesday night at eight o'clock in the Temple, 426 Butternut Lane. The public is cordially invited.'"

"What sort of society is the Order of Amar?" Penny inquired curiously, taking notes. "I never heard of it before."

"Why, my dear, the society is very well known," the woman replied. "We hold our meetings regularly, communing with the spirits. I do hope that the item appears in print. So often Miss Hilderman has been careless about it."

"I'll see that the item is printed under club notices," Penny promised. "Your name, please?"

The woman had hung up the receiver, so with a shrug, Penny typed the item and speared it on a wire spindle. For the next hour she was kept busy with other telephone calls and the more important stories which had to be rushed through. Copy flowed steadily from her office by way of the pneumatic tube to the composing room.

Shortly after five o'clock, DeWitt dropped in for a moment to praise her for her speed and accuracy.

"You're doing all right," he said. "So far I've only caught you in one mistake. Mignonette is spelled with a double t."

"This job wouldn't be half bad if only brides could learn to carry flowers with easy names," laughed Penny. "When I get married I'll have violets and sweet peas!"

DeWitt reached for the copy on the spindle. "What's this?" he asked. "More to go?"

"Club notices."

The editor tore the sheet from the wire, reading it as he walked toward the door. Abruptly, he paused and turned toward her.

"Miss Parker, this can't go through."

"Why, what is wrong?" Penny asked in surprise. "Have I made another error in spelling?"

DeWitt tore off the lead item and tossed it on her desk.

"It's this meeting of the so-called Mystical Society of Celestial Thought. The *Star* never runs stuff like that, not even as a paid advertisement."

"I thought it was a regular lodge meeting, Mr. DeWitt."

"Nothing of the sort. Merely a free advertisement for a group of mediums and charlatans."

"Oh, I didn't know," murmured Penny.

"These meetings have only one purpose," Mr. DeWitt resumed. "To lure victims who later may be fleeced of their money."

"But if that is so, why don't police close up the place?" Penny demanded. "Why doesn't the *Star* run an exposé story?"

"Because evidence isn't easy to get. The meetings usually are well within the law. Whenever a police detective or a reporter attends, the services are decorous. But they provide the mediums with a list of suckers."

Penny would have asked DeWitt for additional information had not the city editor walked hurriedly away. Scrambling the item into a ball, she tossed it into the waste paper basket. Then upon second thought she retrieved it and carefully smoothed the paper.

"Perhaps, I'll drop around at the Temple sometime just to see what it is like," she decided, placing the item in her pocket. "It would be interesting to learn what is going on there."

For the next half hour Penny had no time to think of the Celestial Temple. However, at twenty minutes before six, when her father came into the office, she was well ahead of her work.

"Hello, Penny," he greeted her. "How do you like your new job?"

"Fine and dandy. Only routine items rather cramp one's style. Now if I were a regular reporter instead of a society editor, I know several stories which would be my dish!"

"For instance?" inquired Mr. Parker, smiling.

"First, there's an Oriental Shop on Dorr Street that I should investigate. The Japanese owner acted very mysteriously today when I went there. Louise and I saw him making a silk ladder, and he refused to reveal its purpose."

"A silk ladder?" repeated Mr. Parker. "Odd perhaps, but hardly worthy of a news story."

"Dad, I only wish you had *seen* that old Japanese—the sinister way he looked at me. Oh, he's guilty of some crime. I feel it."

"The *Star* requires facts, not fancy or emotion," Mr. Parker rejoined. "Better devote your talents to routine society items if you expect to remain on my payroll."

Penny took the announcement of the Celestial Thought meeting from her pocket and offered it to the publisher.

"Here's one which might be interesting," she said. "How about assigning me to it after I get this society job in hand?"

Mr. Parker read the item and his eyes blazed with anger.

"Do you know what this means, Penny?"

"Mr. DeWitt told me a little about the Celestial Temple society. He said the paper never ran such items."

"Certainly not! Why, I should like nothing better than to see the entire outfit driven out of town! Riverview is honeycombed with mediums, fortune tellers and faith healers!"

"Perhaps they mean no harm, Dad."

"I'll grant there may be a small number of persons who honestly try to communicate with the spirit world," Mr. Parker replied. "My concern is not with them, but with a group of professional mediums who lately have invaded the city. Charlatans, crooks—the entire lot!"

"Why don't you write an editorial about it?" Penny suggested.

"An editorial! I am seriously tempted to start a vigorous campaign, but the trouble is, the police cannot be depended upon to cooperate actively."

"Why, Dad?"

"Because experience has proven that such campaigns are not often successful. Evidence is hard to gain. If one place is closed up, others open in different sections of the city. The mediums and seers operate from dozens of private homes. When the police stage raids they acquire no evidence, and only succeed in making the department look ridiculous."

"Yet the mediums continue to fleece the public?"

"The more gullible strata of it. Until recent months the situation here has been no worse than in other cities of comparable size. Lately an increasing number of charlatans has moved in on us."

"Why don't you start a campaign, Dad?" Penny urged. "You would be doing the public a worthwhile service."

CHAPTER 3 - SOCIETY ROUTINE

"Well, I hesitate to start something which I may be unable to finish."

"At least the public deserves to be warned."

"Unfortunately, Penny, many persons would take the attitude that the *Star* was persecuting sincere spiritualists. A campaign must be based on absolute evidence."

"Can't it be obtained?"

"Not without great difficulty. These mediums are a clever lot, Penny. They prey upon the superstitions of their intended victims."

"I wish you would let me work on the story, Dad."

"No, Penny," responded her father. "You attend to your society and allow DeWitt to worry about the Celestial Temple crowd. Even if I should launch a campaign, I couldn't allow you to become mixed up in the affair."

The telephone bell jingled. With a tired sigh, Penny reached for the receiver.

"Society desk," she said mechanically.

"I am trying to trace Mr. Parker," informed the office exchange operator. "Is he with you, Miss Parker?"

"Telephone, Dad," said Penny, offering him the receiver.

Mr. Parker waited a moment for another connection to be made. Then Penny heard him say:

"Oh, it's you, Mrs. Weems? What's that? Repeat it, please."

From her father's tone, Penny felt certain that something had gone wrong at home. She arose, waiting anxiously.

Mr. Parker clicked the receiver several times. "Apparently, Mrs. Weems hung up," he commented.

"Is anything the matter, Dad?"

"I don't know," Mr. Parker admitted, his face troubled. "Mrs. Weems seemed very excited. She requested me to come home as soon as possible. Then the connection was broken."

"Why don't you try to reach her again?"

Mr. Parker placed an out-going call, but after ten minutes the operator reported that she was unable to contact the housekeeper.

"Mrs. Weems never would have telephoned if something unusual hadn't happened," Penny declared uneasily. "Perhaps, she's injured herself."

"You think of such unpleasant things."

"Something dreadful must have happened," Penny insisted. "Otherwise, why doesn't she answer?"

"We're only wasting time in idle speculation," Mr. Parker said crisply. "Get your things, Penny. We'll start home at once!"

CHAPTER 4 - A TURN OF FORTUNE

Penny immediately locked her desk and gathered up hat and gloves. She was hard pressed to keep pace with her father as they hastened to the elevator.

"By the way, you have your car downstairs?" the publisher inquired absently. He seldom drove his own automobile to the office.

"What a memory you have, Dad!" chuckled Penny. "Yes, I have all two of them! Parked in the loading dock for convenience."

"Penny, haven't I told you a dozen times—" Mr. Parker began, only to check himself. "Well, it will save us time now. However, we may discuss a few matters when we get home."

The elevator shot them down to the first floor. Leaping Lena and the maroon sedan remained in the loading dock with a string of *Star* paper trucks blocking a portion of the street.

"Hey, sister," a trucker called angrily to Penny. "It's time you're getting these cars out of here." He broke off as he recognized Mr. Parker and faded behind one of the trucks.

"Dad, do you mind steering Lena?" Penny asked demurely. "We can't leave her here. You can see for yourself that she seems to be blocking traffic."

"Yes, I see," Mr. Parker responded grimly.

"Of course, if you would feel more dignified driving the sedan—"

"Let me have the keys," the publisher interrupted. "The important thing is to get home without delay."

Penny became sober, and slid into her place at the wheel of Leaping Lena. Amid the smiles of the truckers, Mr. Parker drove the two cars out of the dock.

Once underway, the caravan made reckless progress through rush-hour traffic. More than once Penny whispered a prayer as Lena swayed around a corner, missing other cars by scant inches.

Presently the two automobiles drew up before a pleasant, tree-shaded home built upon a high terrace overlooking a winding river. Penny and her father alighted, walking hurriedly toward the front porch.

The door stood open and from within came the reassuring howl of a radio turned too high.

"Nothing so very serious can have happened," remarked Penny. "Otherwise, Mrs. Weems wouldn't have that thing going full blast."

At the sound of footsteps, the housekeeper herself came into the living room from the kitchen. Her plump face was unusually animated.

"I hope you didn't mind because I telephoned the office, Mr. Parker," she began apologetically. "I was so excited, I just did it before I stopped to think."

"Penny and I were nearly ready to start home in any case, Mrs. Weems. Has anything gone wrong here?"

"Oh, no, Mr. Parker. It was the telegram."

"Telegram? One for me, you mean?"

"No, my own." The housekeeper drew a yellow paper from the pocket of her apron, offering it to the publisher. "My Cousin David died out in Montana," she explained. "The funeral was last Saturday."

"That's too bad," remarked Penny sympathetically. And then she added: "Only you don't look particularly sad, Mrs. Weems. How much did he leave you?"

"Penny! You say such shocking things! I never met Cousin David but once in my life. He was a kind, good man and I only wish I had written to him more often. I never dreamed he would remember me in his will."

"Then he did leave you money!" exclaimed Penny triumphantly. "How much does the telegram say, Dad?"

CHAPTER 4 - A TURN OF FORTUNE

"You may as well tell her, Mr. Parker," sighed the housekeeper. "She'll give me no peace until she learns every detail."

"This message which is from a Montana lawyer mentions six thousand dollars," returned the publisher. "Apparently, the money is to be turned over without legal delay."

"Why, Mrs. Weems, you're an heiress!" cried Penny admiringly.

"I can't believe it's true," murmured Mrs. Weems. "You don't think there's any mistake, Mr. Parker? It would be too cruel if someone had sent the message as a joke."

Before returning the telegram to the housekeeper, Mr. Parker switched off the radio.

"This message appears to be authentic," he declared. "My congratulations upon your good fortune."

"What will you do with all your money?" inquired Penny.

"Oh, I don't know." The housekeeper sank into a chair, her eyes fastening dreamily on a far wall. "I've always wanted to travel."

Penny and her father exchanged a quick, alarmed glance. Mrs. Weems had been in charge of the household for so many years that they could not imagine living without her, should she decide to leave. During her brief, infrequent vacations, the house always degenerated into a disgrace of dust and misplaced furniture, and meals were never served at regular hours.

"The oceans are very unsafe, Mrs. Weems," discouraged Penny. "Wars and submarines and things. Surely you wouldn't dare travel now."

"Oh, I mean in the United States," replied the housekeeper. "I've always wanted to go out West. They say the Grand Canyon is so pretty it takes your breath away."

"Mrs. Weems, you have worked for us long and faithfully and deserve a rest," said Mr. Parker, trying to speak heartily. "Now if you would enjoy a trip, Penny and I will get along somehow for two or three weeks."

"Oh, if I go, I'll stay the entire summer." The housekeeper hesitated, then added: "I've enjoyed working here, Mr. Parker, but doing the same thing year after year gets tiresome. Often I've said to myself that if I had a little money I would retire and take life easy for the rest of my days."

"Why, Mrs. Weems, you're only forty-eight!" protested Penny. "You would be unhappy if you didn't have any work to do."

"At least, I wouldn't mind trying it."

"Such a change as you contemplate should be considered carefully," contributed Mr. Parker. "While six thousand seems a large sum it would not last long if one had no other income."

Before Mrs. Weems could reply, a strong odor of burning food permeated the room.

"The roast!" exclaimed the housekeeper. "I forgot it!"

Penny rushed ahead of her to the kitchen. As she jerked open the oven door, out poured a great cloud of smoke. Seizing a holder, she rescued the meat, and seeing at a glance that it was burned to a crisp, carried the pan outdoors.

"What will the neighbors say?" Mrs. Weems moaned. "I never did a thing like that before. It's just that I am so excited I can't think what I am doing."

"Don't you mind," laughed Penny. "I'll get dinner tonight. You entertain Dad."

With difficulty she persuaded the housekeeper to abandon the kitchen. Left to herself, she opened a can of cold meat, a can of corn, a can of peaches, and with a salad already prepared, speedily announced the meal.

"Mr. Parker, I truly am ashamed—" Mrs. Weems began.

"Now don't apologize for my cooking," broke in Penny. "Quantity before quality is my motto. Anyway, if you are leaving, Dad will have to accustom himself to it."

"I'll hide the can opener," said Mr. Parker.

"That's a good idea, Dad."

"Before I go, I'll try to teach Penny a little more about cooking," Mrs. Weems said uncomfortably. "Of course, you'll have no difficulty in getting someone efficient to take my place."

"No one can take your place," declared Penny. "If you leave, Dad and I will go to wrack and ruin."

"You are a pair when you're left to yourselves," Mrs. Weems sighed. "That's the one thing which makes me hesitate. Penny needs someone to keep her in check."

"An inexperienced person would be putty in my hands," declared Penny. "You may as well decide to stay, Mrs. Weems."

"I don't know what to do. I've planned on this trip for years. Now that it is possible, I feel I can't give it up."

Penny and Mr. Parker regarded each other across the table, and immediately changed the subject. Not until that moment had they actually believed that the housekeeper was serious about leaving Riverview. Somehow they had never contemplated a future without Mrs. Weems.

"I happen to have two complimentary tickets to a show at the Rialto," Mr. Parker said offhand. "I'll be tied up with a meeting tonight, but you folks might enjoy going."

"Shall we, Mrs. Weems?" inquired Penny.

"Thank you," responded the housekeeper, "but I doubt if I could sit still tonight. I thought I would run over to see Mrs. Hodges after dinner. She'll be pleased to learn about my inheritance, I know."

"A friend of yours?" asked Mr. Parker.

"Yes, Penny and I have been acquainted with her for years. She lives on Christopher Street."

"Perhaps this is none of my affair, Mrs. Weems. However, my advice to you is not to tell many persons about your inheritance."

"Oh, Mrs. Hodges is to be trusted."

"I am sure of it, Mrs. Weems. I refer to strangers."

"I'll be careful," the housekeeper promised. "No one ever will get that money away from me once I have it!"

Penny helped with the dishes, and then as her father was leaving the house, asked him if she might have the two theatre tickets.

"Since Mrs. Weems doesn't care to go, I'll invite Louise," she explained.

Mr. Parker gave her the tickets. Making certain that the housekeeper was upstairs, he spoke in a low tone.

"Penny, Mrs. Weems is serious about leaving us. You must try to dissuade her."

"What can I do, Dad?"

"Well, you usually have a few ideas in the old filing cabinet. Can't you think of something?"

"I'll do my best," Penny said with a twinkle. "We can't let an inheritance take Mrs. Weems from us, that's certain."

After her father had gone, Penny telephoned Louise, agreeing to meet her chum at the entrance of the Rialto. Arriving a few minutes early, she idly watched various cars unloading their passengers at the theatre.

Presently a long black limousine which Penny recognized drew up at the curb. The chauffeur opened the door. Mr. Kohl and his wife stepped to the pavement. Observing the girl, they paused to chat with her.

"I see you have the new fender installed on your car, Mr. Kohl," Penny remarked with a grin. "May I ask how much I owe the garageman?"

"The sum was trifling," responded the banker. "Twelve dollars and forty cents to be exact. I may as well take care of it myself."

"No, I insist," said Penny, wincing inwardly. "You see, I am one of the *Star's* highly paid executives now. I write society in Miss Hilderman's absence and Dad gives me a salary."

"Oh, really," remarked Mrs. Kohl with interest. "We are giving a dinner for eight tomorrow night. You might like to mention it."

"Indeed, yes," said Penny eagerly.

Obtaining complete details, she jotted notes on the back of an envelope. Mrs. Kohl, at Penny's request, was able to recall several important parties which had been held that week, providing material for nearly a half-column of society.

After the Kohls had entered the theatre, Penny turned to glance at the black limousine which was pulling away from the curb. A short distance away stood a young man who likewise appeared to be watching the car. He wore a gray suit and a gray felt hat pulled unnaturally low over his eyes as if to shield his face.

As Penny watched, the young man jotted something down on a piece of paper. His gaze remained fixed upon the Kohl limousine which was moving slowly down the street toward a parking lot.

"Why, that's odd!" thought Penny. "I do believe he noted down the car license number! And perhaps for no good purpose."

CHAPTER 5 - THE MAN IN GRAY

Deciding that the matter should be brought to Mr. Kohl's attention, Penny looked quickly into the crowded theatre lobby. The banker and his wife no longer were to be seen.

Turning once more, the girl saw that the young man in gray had also disappeared.

"Now where did he go?" thought Penny. "He must have slipped into the alley. I wish I knew who he was and why he wrote down that car license number."

Curious to learn what had become of the man, she walked to the entrance of the alley. At its far end she could barely distinguish a shadowy figure which soon merged into the black of the starless night.

Penny was lost in thought when someone touched her arm. Whirling, she found herself facing Louise Sidell.

"Oh, hello, Lou," she laughed. "You startled me."

"Sorry to have kept you waiting," apologized Louise. "I missed my bus. May I ask what you find of such interest in this alley?"

"I was looking for a man. He's disappeared now."

Penny told Louise what she had observed, mentioning that in her opinion the man might be a car thief.

"I've heard that crooks spot cars ahead of time and then steal them," she declared. "I think I should have Mr. Kohl paged in the theatre, and tell him about it."

"You'll make yourself appear ridiculous if you do," Louise discouraged her. "The man may not have taken down the license number at all. Even if he did, his purpose could have been a legitimate one."

"Then why did he slip down the alley?"

"It's merely a short-cut to another street, isn't it? Penny, your imagination simply works at high speed twenty-four hours of the day."

"Oh, all right," said Penny with a shrug. "But if Mr. Kohl's car is stolen, don't blame me."

"It won't be," laughed Louise, linking arms with her chum. "Not with a chauffeur at the wheel."

Entering the theatre, the girls were escorted to their seats only a few minutes before the lights were lowered. Penny glanced over the audience but failed to see either Mr. Kohl or his wife. The curtain went up, and as the entertainment began, she dismissed all else from her mind.

The show ended shortly before eleven and the girls mingled with the crowd which filed from the theatre. Penny watched for Mr. and Mrs. Kohl but did not see them. As she walked with Louise toward the bus stop she spoke of her new duties as society editor of the *Star*.

"Lou," she asked abruptly, "do you mind going home alone?"

"Why, no. Where are you taking yourself?"

"To the *Star* office, if you don't mind."

"At this time of night?"

"I have a few notes I should type. Unfinished work always makes me nervous."

"You, nervous!" Louise scoffed. "I'll bet you want to see Jerry Livingston!"

"No such thing," denied Penny indignantly. "Jerry doesn't work on the night force unless he's assigned to extra duty."

"Well, you have something besides work on your mind."

"Come along with me, Suspicious, and I'll prove it."

"No, thanks," declined Louise. "It's home and bed for me. You run along."

CLUE OF THE SILKEN LADDER

The girls separated, Penny walking three blocks to the *Star* building. The advertising office was dark, but blue-white lights glowed weirdly from the composing room. Only a skeleton night staff occupied the newsroom.

Without attracting attention, Penny entered her own office. For an hour she worked steadily, writing copy, and experimenting with various types of make-up to be used on Monday's page.

The door creaked. Glancing up, Penny momentarily was startled to see a large, grotesque shadow of a man moving across the glass panel. However, before she actually could be afraid, Jerry Livingston stepped into the room.

"Oh, it's you!" she laughed in relief. "I thought it was against your principles to work overtime."

The reporter slumped into a chair, and picking up a sheet of copy paper, began to read what Penny had composed.

"I'm not working," he replied absently. "Just killing time." With a yawn he tossed the paper on the desk again.

"Is my stuff that bad?" inquired Penny.

"Not bad at all. Better than Miss Hilderman writes. But society always gives me a pain. Not worthy of your talents, Penny."

"I wish you would tell Dad that, Jerry. I'd love to work on a big story again—one that would rock Riverview on its foundation!"

"I could bear up under a little excitement myself, Penny. Ever since you broke the Green Door yarn, this sheet has been as dead as an Egyptian tomb."

"Things may pick up soon."

"Meaning—?"

"Dad is thinking rather seriously of launching a drive against an organized group of mediums."

"So I hear," nodded Jerry. "You know, for a long while I've thought that a clever reporter might be able to dig up some evidence at the Celestial Temple."

"Then you know about the place?"

"I've been there several times."

"What are the meetings like, Jerry?" Penny asked eagerly.

"Similar to a church musical service. At least everything was dignified when I was there. But I sure had a feeling that the lid was about to blow off."

"Perhaps you were suspected of being a *Star* reporter, Jerry."

"Oh, undoubtedly. I could tell that by the way folks stared at me. The only person who would have a chance to get real evidence would be someone unknown as a reporter."

"I wish Dad would let me try it."

"I don't," said Jerry flatly. "The Celestial Temple is no place for a little girl like you."

Penny did not reply as she lowered her typewriter into the cavity of the desk. She was thinking, however, that if Louise could be persuaded to accompany her, she would investigate the Celestial Temple at the first opportunity.

"I'll take you home," Jerry offered as Penny reached for her hat.

The night was a warm, mellow one in early June, marred only by dark clouds which scudded overhead, threatening rain. Deciding to walk, Penny and Jerry crossed the park to Oakdale Drive where many of Riverview's most expensive homes had been built.

"Doesn't Mr. Kohl live on this street?" Penny presently asked her escort.

"Yes," he answered, "in a large stone apartment building. I'll point it out when we get there."

They walked for a time in silence. Then Penny found herself telling about the afternoon meeting with Mr. Kohl which had led her to Kano's Curio Shop. She spoke, too, of the silken ladder which had so aroused her speculation. Jerry listened with polite interest.

"You and Louise shouldn't have chased around Dorr Street alone," he said severely. "It's a bad district."

"Oh, it was safe enough, Jerry. I'd like to go back there. I can't help being curious about that strange ladder which the old Japanese man was sewing."

"I doubt if there's a story connected with it. The Japanese make any number of curious articles of silk, you know."

174

CHAPTER 5 - THE MAN IN GRAY

"But a ladder, Jerry! What purpose could it serve?"

"For one thing it would be more convenient to carry than the ordinary type."

"One couldn't stand it against a wall or use it in the ordinary way, Jerry. I asked the Japanese about it but he refused to answer."

"He may not have understood you."

"Oh, he understood, all right. Do you know what I think? He was afraid I might discover something which would involve him with the police!"

"Better forget the Kano Curio Shop," Jerry said tolerantly. "I repeat, Dorr Street is no place for you."

"And I'm supposed to forget the Celestial Temple, too," grumbled Penny. "Oh, I see you grinned behind your hand! Well, Mr. Livingston, let me tell you—"

She paused, and Jerry's hand tightened on her own. Unmistakably, both had heard a muffled scream. The cry seemed to have come from one of several large brick and stone buildings only a short distance ahead.

"What was that?" Penny asked in a low tone. "Someone calling for help?"

"It sure sounded like it!" exclaimed Jerry. "Come on, Penny! Let's find out what's going on here!"

CHAPTER 6 - AN APARTMENT BURGLARY

Together Penny and Jerry ran down the street, their eyes raised to the unevenly lighted windows of the separate apartment houses. They were uncertain as to the building from which the cry had come.

Suddenly the front door of the corner dwelling swung open, and a young woman in a maid's uniform ran toward them.

Jerry, ever alert for a story of interest to the *Star*, neatly blocked the sidewalk. Of necessity the girl halted.

"Get a policeman, quick!" she gasped. "Mr. Kohl's apartment has been robbed!"

"Mr. Kohl—the banker?" demanded Penny, scarcely believing her ears.

"Yes, yes," the maid said in agitation. "Jewels, silverware, everything has been taken! The telephone wire was cut, too! Oh, tell me where I'll find a policeman!"

"I'll get one for you," offered Jerry.

The information that it was Mr. Kohl's house which had been burglarized dumbfounded Penny. As the reporter darted away to summon help, she showered questions upon the distraught maid.

"I don't know yet how much has been taken," the girl told her excitedly. "The rooms look as if a cyclone had swept through them! Oh, what will the Kohls say when they learn about it?"

"Mr. and Mrs. Kohl aren't home yet?"

"No, they went to the theatre. They must have stopped at a restaurant afterwards. When they hear of this, I'll lose my job."

"Perhaps not," said Penny kindly. "Surely you weren't to blame for the burglary."

"They'll think so," the maid responded gloomily.

"I am acquainted with Mr. and Mrs. Kohl. Perhaps, if I speak a good word for you it may help."

"I doubt it," the girl responded. "I was supposed to have stayed at the apartment the entire evening."

"And you didn't?"

"No, I went to a picture show."

"That does throw a different light on the matter," commented Penny.

"I didn't think it would make any difference. I intended to get here ahead of the Kohls."

"The robbery occurred while you were away?"

"Yes. As soon as I opened the door I knew what had happened! Oh, I'll lose my job all right unless I can think up a good story."

"I wouldn't lie if I were you," advised Penny. "The police are certain to break down your story. In any case, you owe it to yourself and your employers to tell the truth."

A misty rain had started to fall. The maid, who was without a wrap, shivered, yet made no move to re-enter the building. Overhead, all along the dark expanse of apartment wall, lights were being turned on.

"I am afraid your scream aroused nearly everyone in the building," said Penny. "If I were in your place I would return to the Kohl apartment and not answer many questions until the police arrive."

"Will you stay with me?"

"Gladly."

The apartment door had slammed shut and locked with the night latch. Fortunately the maid had a key with her so it was not necessary to ring for the janitor. Ignoring the persons who had gathered in the hall, they took an automatic lift to the third floor, letting themselves into the Kohl suite.

"This is the way I found it," said the maid.

CHAPTER 6 - AN APARTMENT BURGLARY

She switched on a light, revealing a living room entirely bare of rugs. Where three small Oriental rugs had been placed, only rectangular rims of dirt remained to mark their outlines.

Beyond, in the dining room with its massive carved furniture, the contents of a buffet had been emptied on the floor. Several pieces of china lay in fragments. A corner cupboard had been stripped, save for a vase and an ebony elephant with a broken tusk.

"The wall cabinet was filled with rare antiques," disclosed the maid. "Mrs. Kohl has collected Early American silver for many years. Some of the pieces she considered priceless."

The bedrooms were in less disorder. However, bureau drawers had been overturned, and jewel cases looted of everything save the most trivial articles.

"Mrs. Kohl's pearls are gone, and her diamond bracelet," the maid informed, picking up the empty jewel box. "I am pretty sure she didn't wear them to the theatre."

"I wouldn't touch anything if I were you," advised Penny. "Fingerprints."

The maid dropped the case. "Oh!" she gasped. "I never thought of that! Do you think the police will blame me for the robbery?"

"Not if you tell them the truth. It surely will be unwise to try to hide anything."

"I won't hold anything back," the maid promised. "It happened just like I said. After Mr. and Mrs. Kohl left I went to a picture show."

"Alone?"

"With my girl friend. After the show we had a soda together, and then she went home."

"What time did you get here?"

"Only a minute or two before I called for help. I tried the telephone first."

"Why didn't you summon the janitor?"

"I never thought of that. I was so excited I ran outside hoping to find a policeman."

Penny nodded and, returning to the living room, satisfied herself that the telephone wires actually had been cut.

"You didn't notice anyone in the halls as you went downstairs."

"No one. Old Mr. Veely was on the lower floor when I came from the show, but he's lived here for seven years. I don't see how the burglar got into the apartment."

"I was wondering about that myself. You're quite sure you locked the suite door?"

"Oh, yes, I know I did," the maid said emphatically. "And it isn't possible to get into the building without a key. Otherwise, the janitor must be called."

Penny walked thoughtfully to the living room window. The apartment stood fully thirty-five feet from a neighboring building, with the space between much too wide to be spanned. Below, the alley was deserted, and no fire escape ascended from it.

"The burglar couldn't have entered that way," declared the maid. "He must have had his own key."

Before Penny could respond, a sharp knock sounded on the door. The servant girl turned to open it. However, instead of the anticipated police, the apartment janitor, George Bailey, peered into the disordered room.

"I heard someone scream a minute or so ago," he said. "Some of the tenants thought it came from this apartment. Maybe they were mistaken."

"There's no mistake," spoke Penny from across the room. "The Kohls have been robbed. Will you please come inside and close the door?"

"Robbed! You don't say!" The janitor stared with alarmed interest. "When did it happen?"

Penny allowed the maid to tell what had occurred, adding no information of her own. When there came a lull in the excited flow of words, she said quietly:

"Mr. Bailey, do you mind answering a few questions?"

"Why should I?" the janitor countered. "I'll tell you right now I know nothing about this. I've attended strictly to my duties. It's not my lookout if tenants leave their suite doors unlocked."

"No one is blaming you," Penny assured him. "I merely thought you might contribute to a solution of the burglary."

"I don't know a thing about it."

"You didn't let anyone into the apartment building tonight?"

"Not a soul. I locked the service door at six o'clock, too. Now let me ask this: Who are you, and how did you get in here?"

"That's fair enough," smiled Penny. She told her name, explained that she was an acquaintance of the Kohls, and had been summoned by the maid.

"Please don't think that I am trying to play detective," she added. "I ask these questions in the hope of gaining information for my father's paper, the *Star*."

"Well, it looks to me as if it was an inside job," the janitor replied, mollified. "Come to think of it though, I've seen a suspicious-acting fellow hanging around the building."

"You mean tonight?"

"No, several days ago. He stayed on the other side of the street and kept watching the doorway."

"What did he look like, Mr. Bailey?"

"Oh, I don't remember. He was just an average young man in a gray overcoat and hat."

"Gray?" repeated Penny alertly.

"It may have been light blue. I didn't pay much attention. At the time I sized up the fellow as a detective."

Penny had no opportunity to ask additional questions for just then voices were heard in the hallway. As she opened the door, Jerry Livingston, followed by a policeman, came toward her.

"Learn anything?" the reporter asked softly in her ear.

"A little," answered Penny. "Let's see how much the officer turns up before I go into my song and dance."

Making a routine inspection of the rooms, the police questioned both the maid and the janitor. From an elderly lady who occupied the adjoining suite he gleaned information that the Kohls' telephone had rung steadily for fifteen minutes during the early evening hours.

"What time was that?" interposed Penny.

The policeman gazed at her with sharp disapproval. "Please," he requested with exaggerated politeness.

"Sorry," apologized Penny, fading into the background.

"It rang about eight o'clock," the old lady revealed.

"The information is not significant," said the officer, glancing again at Penny.

She started to speak, then bit her lip, remaining silent.

"Well, sister, what's on your mind?" he demanded abruptly.

"Excuse me, officer, but I think the information does have importance. Couldn't it mean that the crooks, whoever they were, telephoned the apartment to make certain it was deserted before breaking in?"

"Possibly," conceded the policeman. His frown discouraged her. "Any other theories?"

"No," said Penny shortly.

The policeman began to herd the tenants into the hall. For a moment he paid no attention to Penny and Jerry, who with the maid were permitted to remain.

"Never try to show up a policeman, even if he is a stuffed shirt," remarked the reporter softly. "It gets you nowhere."

The door closed and the officer faced the pair.

"Now young lady," he said, quite pleasantly. "What do you know about this burglary? I'll be very glad to listen."

"I don't really know a thing," admitted Penny. "But here's a little clue which you may be able to interpret. I can't."

Leading the policeman to the window, she started to raise the sash. The officer stopped her, performing the act himself, his hand protected by a handkerchief.

"There is your clue," said Penny.

She indicated two freshly made gashes on the window ledge. Separated by possibly a foot of space, they clearly had been made by a hook or sharp instrument which had dug deeply into the wood.

CHAPTER 7 - MARK OF THE IRON HOOK

"What do you think of it?" Penny asked as the officer studied the marks in silence.

"I'd say they were made by something which hooked over the ledge," the policeman replied. "Possibly a ladder with curving irons."

Jerry gazed down over the window ledge into the dark alley.

"No ordinary ladder could reach this high," he commented. "Raising an extension would be quite a problem, too."

The Kohl maid timidly approached the window, gazing at the two deep gashes with interest. Asked by the policeman if she ever had noticed them before, she shook her head.

"Oh, no, sir. They must have been made tonight. I know they weren't there this afternoon when I dusted the window sills."

"Incredible as it seems, the thief came through this window," decided the policeman. "How he did it is for the detectives at Central Station to figure out."

Explaining that the rooms must not be disturbed until Identification Bureau men had made complete fingerprint records, the officer locked Penny, Jerry and the maid outside the suite. He then went to a nearby apartment to telephone his report.

"Maybe this is an ordinary burglary, but it doesn't look that way to me," remarked Jerry as he and Penny went down the stairway.

"In any case, the story should be front page copy. Anything the Kohls do is news in Riverview."

"How high would you estimate the loss?"

"Oh, I couldn't guess, Jerry. Thousands of dollars."

Passing groups of tenants who cluttered the hallway excitedly discussing the burglary, they evaded questioners and reached the street.

"Jerry," said Penny suddenly, "I didn't mention this to the policeman because he seemed to resent my opinions. But it occurred to me that I may have seen the man who robbed the Kohls—or at least had something to do with it."

"How could you have seen him, Penny? We were together when the Kohl maid yelled for help."

"Earlier than that. It was while I was at the theatre."

Half expecting that Jerry would laugh, Penny told how she had observed the man in gray note down the license number of the Kohl limousine.

"It came to me like a flash! That fellow may have telephoned the Kohl apartment after seeing the car at the theatre. Making sure no one was at home, he then looted the place at his leisure."

"Wait a minute," interrupted Jerry. "The Motor Vehicle Department closes at six o'clock. How could your man have obtained Kohl's name and address from the license number?"

"I never thought about the department being closed," confessed Penny. "How you do love to shoot shrapnel into my little ideas!"

"At least you have original theories, which is more than I do," comforted Jerry. "Before we leave, shall we take a look at the alley?"

Penny brightened instantly and accompanied the reporter to the rear of the building. The alley was deserted. Without a light they were unable to examine the ground beneath the Kohl's apartment window.

Suddenly, both straightened as they heard a sound behind them. The brilliant beam of a flashlight focused on their faces, blinding them.

"Oh, it's you again," said a gruff voice.

The beam was lowered, and behind it they saw the policeman.

"You young cubs are a pest," he said irritably.

Ignoring them, he moved his light over the ground. There were no footprints or other marks visible beneath the window.

"If a ladder had stood here it would show," remarked Jerry. "The thief must have used some other means of getting into the building."

While the policeman was inspecting the ground, the janitor stepped from a rear basement door, joining the group.

"Officer, I have some more information for you," he volunteered.

"What is it?"

"I was talking with my wife. She says that about two hours ago she noticed a man walking through the alley. He carried a suitcase, and kept looking at the upstairs windows."

"No ladder?"

"Only a suitcase."

"I'll have the detectives talk with your wife," the policeman promised. "They'll be here any minute now."

Penny and Jerry lingered until the two men arrived, bringing a photographer with them. No new evidence being made available, it seemed a waste of time to remain longer.

"Don't bother to take me home," Penny insisted. "Dash straight to the office and write your story. The other papers won't have a word about the robbery until the police report is made."

"I don't like to abandon you."

"Don't be silly, Jerry. It's only a few blocks farther."

Thus urged, the reporter bade Penny good-bye. As she hastened on alone, it began to rain and the air turned colder. To save her clothing, she ran the last block, reaching the porch quite breathless.

The house was dark, the front door locked. Penny let herself in with a key, switched on the lights, and after getting a snack from the refrigerator, started upstairs.

From her father's room issued loud snores. However, Mrs. Weems' door stood open, and as Penny glanced in she was surprised to see that the bed had not been disturbed.

"Mrs. Weems must still be at the Hodges'," she thought. "Perhaps I should go after her. She'll have a long walk in this rain."

Penny went to a window and looked out. The downpour showed no sighs of slackening. With a sigh she found her raincoat and started for the garage.

During her absence, Mr. Parker had towed Leaping Lena to a vacant lot adjoining the property. The maroon car awaited her beneath shelter, and she drove it through dark streets to the Hodges' modest home.

Lights glowed cheerily from the lower floor windows. In response to Penny's knock, a bent old man, his hands gnarled by hard labor, opened the door.

"Is it Penelope?" he asked, squinting at her through the rain. "Come in! Come in!"

"Good evening, Mr. Hodges. Is Mrs. Weems still here?"

"Yes, I am, Penny," called the housekeeper. "Goodness, what time is it anyway?"

"Nearly midnight."

Penny shook water from her coat and stepped into the spic and span living room. An unshaded electric light disclosed a rug too bright, wallpaper too glaring, furniture stiff and old fashioned. Yet one felt at once welcome, for the seamstress and her husband were simple, friendly people.

"Have a chair, Penelope," invited Mrs. Hodges. She was short like her husband, with graying hair and an untroubled countenance.

"Thank you, but I can't stay," replied Penny. "I came to drive Mrs. Weems home."

"I had no idea it was so late," the housekeeper said, getting to her feet. "Mrs. Hodges and I have been planning my traveling outfit."

"I'll try to have the dresses for you within the next two weeks," promised the seamstress. "Your good fortune makes me very happy, Maud. Isn't the news of her inheritance wonderful, Penelope?"

"Oh, yes, yes, of course," stammered Penny. "Only I hope Mrs. Weems isn't leaving us within two weeks. What's this about a traveling outfit?"

CHAPTER 7 - MARK OF THE IRON HOOK

"I've always wanted fine clothing," said Mrs. Weems dreamily. "Mrs. Hodges is making me a suit, three silk dresses, a tissue velvet evening gown—"

"An evening gown!" Penny gasped. "Where will you wear it?"

"I'll find places."

"Maybe she aims to catch a husband while she's galavantin' around out there in Californy," contributed Mr. Hodges with a sly wink.

"The very idea!" laughed Mrs. Weems, yet with no displeasure.

Penny sagged into the nearest rocking chair. The conversation was paced too fast for her.

"Evening gowns—husbands—California," she murmured weakly. "Wait until Dad hears about this."

"Mr. Hodges was only joking," declared Mrs. Weems, reaching for her hat. "I wouldn't marry the best man on earth. But I definitely am going west this summer."

"I envy you, Maud," said the seamstress, her eyes shining. "Pa and I want to go out there and buy a little orange grove someday. But with taxes what they are, we can't seem to save a penny."

Mrs. Weems squeezed her friend's hand.

"I wish I could take you along, Jenny," she said. "All these years you've sewed your poor fingers almost to the bone. You deserve an easier life."

"Oh, Pa and I don't complain," the seamstress answered brightly. "And things are going to look up."

"Sure they are," agreed Mr. Hodges. "I'll get a job any day now."

Penny, who was watching the seamstress' face was amazed to see it suddenly transformed. Losing her usual calm, Mrs. Hodges exclaimed:

"Pa! It just this minute came to me! Maud getting her inheritance is another psychic sign!"

Penny rocked violently and even Mrs. Weems looked startled.

"I don't know what you mean, Jenny," she said.

"We said we wouldn't tell anybody, Ma," protested Mr. Hodges mildly.

"Mrs. Weems is my best friend, and Penelope won't tell. Will you, Penelope?"

"Not what I don't know," replied Penny in bewilderment. "How can Mrs. Weems' inheritance have anything to do with a psychic sign?"

"You may as well tell 'em," grinned Mr. Hodges, "If you keep the news much longer you'll bust."

"The strangest thing happened three nights ago," Mrs. Hodges began, her voice quivering with excitement. "But wait! First I'll show you the letter!"

CHAPTER 8 - PSYCHIC SIGNS

As Penny and Mrs. Weems waited, the seamstress went to another room, returning with a stamped, slit envelope.

"Notice the postmark," she requested, thrusting the letter into Penny's hand.

"It was mailed from New York," the girl observed.

"I mean the hour at which the envelope was stamped by the postmaster."

"I make it 11:30 P.M. June fifteenth," Penny read aloud. "Does the time and date have special significance?"

"Indeed, it does," the seamstress replied impressively. "You tell them, Pa."

"It happened three nights ago," began Mr. Hodges. "Ma worked late stitchin' up some playsuits for Mrs. Hudson's little girl. Afterwards we had bread and milk like we always do, and then we went to bed."

"At the time, I said to Pa that something queer was going to happen," broke in the seamstress. "I could feel it in my bones. It was as if something was hovering over us."

"A feeling of impending trouble?" questioned Penny.

"Nothing like that," said Mr. Hodges.

"No, it was as if one almost could feel a foreign presence in the room," Mrs. Hodges declared, lowering her voice. "A supernatural being."

"Surely you don't believe in ghosts...?" Penny began, but the seamstress did not hear. Unheeding, she resumed:

"Pa rubbed my back to ease the pain I get from working too long at the machine. Then we went to bed. Neither of us had gone to sleep when suddenly we heard it!"

"Six sharp raps on the outside bedroom wall," supplied Mr. Hodges. "It was like this." He demonstrated on the table.

"We both heard it," added Mrs. Hodges. "It scared me nearly out of my wits."

"Possibly it was someone at the door," suggested Penny.

"No, it wasn't that. Pa got up and went to see."

"Could it have been a tree bough brushing against the wall?"

"It wasn't that," said Mr. Hodges. "The maple is too far off to strike our bedroom."

"There's only one explanation," declared the seamstress with conviction. "It was a psychic sign—the first."

"I don't believe in such things myself," announced Penny. "Surely there must be another explanation."

"That's what I told Jenny," nodded Mr. Hodges. "But since the letter came, doggoned if I don't think maybe she's right."

"What has the letter to do with it?" inquired Mrs. Weems.

The seamstress pointed to the postmark on the envelope.

"The hour at which we heard the strange tappings was eleven-thirty! Pa looked at the clock. And it was three days ago, June fifteenth."

"Corresponding to the marking on this envelope," commented Penny. "That is a coincidence."

Mrs. Hodges shook her head impatiently.

"You surely don't think it just happened by *accident*?" she asked. "It must have been intended as a sign—an omen."

"What did the letter say?" Penny inquired, without answering Mrs. Hodges' question. She knew that her true opinion would not please the woman.

CHAPTER 8 - PSYCHIC SIGNS

"It wasn't rightly a letter," the seamstress returned. "The envelope contained six silver dollars fitted into a stiff piece of cardboard."

"We figured it was another sign," contributed Mr. Hodges. "Six raps on the wall—six dollars."

"I wish some ghost would come and pound all night long on my bedroom door," remarked Penny lightly.

"Penelope, you shouldn't speak so disrespectfully," Mrs. Weems reproved in a mild voice.

"Excuse me, I didn't mean to," said Penny, composing her face. "What else has happened of a supernatural nature?"

"Why, nothing yet," Mrs. Hodges admitted. "But Pa and I have had a feeling as if something important were about to take place. And now Maud inherits six thousand dollars!"

"There was nothing psychic about that," said Mrs. Weems. "Cousin David had no close relatives so he left the money to me."

The seamstress shook her head, and an ethereal light shone in her eyes.

"Night before last when I went to bed I was thinking that I wished with all my heart something nice would happen to you, Maud. Now it's come to pass!"

Even Mrs. Weems was somewhat startled by the seamstress' calm assumption that her thoughts had been responsible for the inheritance.

"Don't you see," Mrs. Hodges resumed patiently. "It must mean that I have great psychic powers. I confess I am rather frightened."

Penny arose and began to button her raincoat.

"Excuse me for saying it," she remarked, "but if I were you, Mrs. Hodges, I'd spend the six dollars and forget the entire affair. Someone must have played a joke on you!"

"A joke!" The seamstress was offended. "People don't give away money as a joke."

"No, these days they squeeze the eagles until they holler," chuckled Mr. Hodges.

"The letter was postmarked New York City," went on his wife. "We don't know a soul there. Oh, no one ever can make me believe that it was done as a joke. The letter was mailed at exactly the hour we heard the six raps!"

"And there wasn't a sign of anyone near the house," added Mr. Hodges.

"Well, at least you're six dollars ahead," said Penny. "Shall we go, Mrs. Weems? It's after midnight."

The seamstress walked to the door with the callers.

"I'll get busy tomorrow on those new dresses," she promised Mrs. Weems. "Drop in again whenever you can. And you, too, Penelope."

Driving home through the rain, Penny stole a quick glance at the housekeeper who seemed unusually quiet.

"Do you suppose Jenny could be right?" Mrs. Weems presently ventured. "I mean about Cousin David and the inheritance?"

"Of course not!" laughed Penny. "Why, your cousin died a long while before Mrs. Hodges discovered that she was psychic. It's all the bunk!"

"I wish I really knew."

"Why, Mrs. Weems!" Penny prepared to launch into a violent argument. "I never heard of such nonsense! How could Mrs. Hodges have psychic powers? Everyone realizes that communication with the spirit world is impossible!"

"You are entitled to your opinion, Penny, but others may differ with you. Who can know about The Life Beyond? Isn't it in the realm of possibility that Mrs. Hodges may have had a message from Cousin David?"

"She didn't speak of it."

"Not in words, Penny. But those strange rappings, the arrival of the letter—it was all very strange and unexplainable."

"I'll admit it was queer, Mrs. Weems. However, I'll never agree that there's anything supernatural connected with it."

"You close your mind to things you do not wish to believe," the housekeeper reproved. "What can any of us know of the spirit world?"

Penny gazed at Mrs. Weems in alarm. She realized that the seamstress' story had deeply impressed her.

"I'll stake my knowledge against Mrs. Hodges' any old day," she declared lightly. "I met one ghost-maker—Osandra—remember him?"

"Why remind me of that man, Penny?" asked the housekeeper wearily.

"Because you once paid him good money for the privilege of attending his séances. You were convinced he was in communication with the world beyond. He proved to be an outrageous fraud."

"I was taken in by him as were many other persons," Mrs. Weems acknowledged. "Mrs. Hodges' case is different. We have been friends for ten years. She would not misrepresent the facts."

"No, Mrs. Hodges is honest. I believe that the money was sent to her. But not by a ghost!"

"Let's not discuss it," said Mrs. Weems with finality. "I never did enjoy an argument."

Penny lapsed into silence and a moment later the car swung into the Parker driveway. The housekeeper hurried into the house, leaving the girl to close the garage doors.

Penny snapped the padlock shut. Unmindful of the rain, she stood for a moment, staring into the night. Nothing had gone exactly right that day, and her disagreement with Mrs. Weems, minor though it was, bothered her.

"There's more to this psychic business than appears on the surface," she thought grimly. "A great deal more! Maybe I am stubborn and opinionated. But I know one thing! No trickster is going to take advantage of the Hodges or of Mrs. Weems either—not if I can prevent it."

CHAPTER 9 - MRS. WEEMS' INHERITANCE

The clock chimed seven-thirty the next morning as Penny came downstairs. She dropped a kiss on her father's forehead and slid into a chair at the opposite side of the breakfast table.

"Good morning, Daddykins," she greeted him cheerfully. "Any news in the old scandal sheet?"

Mr. Parker lowered the newspaper.

"Please don't call me Daddykins," he requested. "You know I hate it. Here's something which may interest you. Your friends the Kohls were robbed last night."

"You're eight hours late," grinned Penny, reaching for the front page. "I was there."

"I suppose you lifted the pearls and the diamond bracelet on your way to the theatre."

"No," said Penny, rapidly scanning the story which Jerry had written, "but I think I may have seen the man who did do it."

She then told her father of having observed a stranger note the license number of the Kohl car, and mentioned the events which had followed.

"You may have been mistaken about what the man wrote down," commented her father.

"That's possible, but he was staring straight at the car."

"I doubt if the incident had any connection with the burglary, Penny. With the Motor Vehicle Department closed, he would have had no means of quickly learning who the Kohls were or where they lived."

"Couldn't he have recognized them?"

"In that case he would have no need for the license number. You didn't see the man note down the plates of other cars?"

"No, but he may have done it before I noticed him standing by the theatre."

Turning idly through the morning paper, Penny's attention was drawn to another news story. Reading it rapidly, she thrust the page into her father's hand.

"Dad, look at this! There were two other burglaries last night! Apartment houses on Drexel Boulevard and Fenmore Street were entered."

"H-m, interesting. The Kohls occupy an apartment also. That rather suggests that the same thief ransacked the three places."

"And it says here that the families were away for the evening!" Penny resumed with increasing excitement. "I'll bet a cent they were at the theatre! Oh, Dad, that man in gray must have been the one who did it!"

"If all the persons you suspect of crime were arrested, our jails couldn't hold them," remarked Mr. Parker calmly. "Eat your breakfast, Penny, before it gets cold."

Mrs. Weems entered through the kitchen door, bearing reenforcements of hot waffles and crisp bacon. Her appearance reminded Penny to launch into a highly entertaining account of all that had transpired at the Hodges' the previous night.

"Penny!" protested the housekeeper. "You promised Mrs. Hodges to say nothing about the letter."

"Oh, no, I didn't promise," corrected Penny. "I was careful to say that I couldn't tell what I didn't know. Years ago Dad taught me that a good reporter never agrees to accept a confidence. Isn't that so, Dad?"

"A wise reporter never ties his own hands," replied Mr. Parker. "If he promises, and then obtains the same story from another source, he's morally bound not to use it. His paper may be scooped by the opposition."

"You two are a pair," sighed Mrs. Weems. "Scoops and front page stories are all either of you think about. I declare, it distresses me to realize how Penny may be trained after I leave."

"The way to solve that problem is not to leave," said Penny. "You know we can't get along without you."

Mrs. Weems shook her head.

"It cuts me almost in two to leave," she declared sadly, "but my mind's made up. Mrs. Hodges says I am doing the right thing."

"And I suppose a ghost advised her," muttered Penny.

Mr. Parker glanced sternly at his daughter and she subsided into silence. But not for long. Soon she was trying to reopen the subject of the mysterious letter received by the Hodges. For a reason she could not understand, her father was loath to discuss it.

"Come, Penny," he said. "If we're having that game of tennis this morning, it's time we start."

En route to the park, the publisher explained why he had not chosen to express an opinion in the housekeeper's presence.

"I quite agree with you that Mrs. Hodges has no psychic powers, Penny. She's been the victim of a hoax. However, Mrs. Weems is intensely loyal to her friend, and any disparaging remarks made by us will only serve to antagonize her."

"I'll try to be more careful, Dad. But it's so silly!"

Monday morning found Penny busy once more with her duties at the society desk. No new information had developed regarding the Kohl burglary, and she did not have time to accompany Mrs. Weems who went frequently to the Hodges' cottage.

Secretly Penny held an opinion that the housekeeper's inheritance might be the work of a prankster. Therefore, upon returning from the office one afternoon and learning that the money actually had been delivered, she was very glad she had kept her thoughts to herself.

"The lawyer came this morning and had me sign a paper," Mrs. Weems revealed to the Parkers. "Then he turned the money over to me—six thousand dollars."

"I hope the cheque is good," remarked Penny.

"It was. I had the lawyer accompany me to the bank. They gave me the money without asking a single question. I have it here."

"You have six thousand dollars cash in the house!"

"Yes, I had the cashier give it to me in hundred dollar bills."

"Do you consider it safe to keep such a large sum?" Mr. Parker inquired mildly. "I should advise returning it to the bank, or better still, why not invest it in sound securities?"

Mrs. Weems shook her head. "It gives me a nice rich feeling to have the cash. I've hidden it in a good place."

"Where?" demanded Penny.

"I won't tell," laughed Mrs. Weems.

Again later in the evening, Mr. Parker tried without success to convince the housekeeper that she should return the money to a bank. Never one to force his opinions upon another, he then dropped the subject.

"When will you be leaving us, Mrs. Weems?" he inquired.

"Whenever you can spare me. Now that I have the money, I should like to leave within ten days or two weeks."

"Since we can't persuade you to remain, I'll try to find someone to take your place," Mr. Parker promised.

Both he and Penny were gloomy at the prospect of replacing the housekeeper. Not only would they miss Mrs. Weems but they honestly believed that she would never be happy without two incorrigibles and a home to manage.

"Dad," Penny ventured when they were alone, "just supposing that Mrs. Weems' money should mysteriously disappear—"

"Don't allow your mind to dwell on that idea," cut in her father sternly. "We'll play fair."

"Oh, I wouldn't do it," said Penny hastily. "I was only joking. But if something *should* happen to the money, it would solve all our problems."

"Mrs. Weems has earned her vacation. Even though it will be hard to lose her, we mustn't stand in her way."

"I guess you're right," sighed Penny.

The following day Miss Hilderman resumed her duties at the *Star*, and Penny once more found herself a person of leisure. To her annoyance, Mrs. Weems insisted that she spend many hours in the kitchen, learning

CHAPTER 9 - MRS. WEEMS' INHERITANCE

how to bake pies and cakes. A particularly distasteful lesson came to an end only when Penny, with brilliant inspiration, remembered that the housekeeper had an appointment with the seamstress.

"Dear me, I had forgotten it!" exclaimed Mrs. Weems. "Yes, I must try on my new dresses!"

"I'll drive you over," offered Penny.

Not in recent days had the girl called upon the Hodges. As she and Mrs. Weems alighted from the car, they both noticed freshly ironed curtains at the windows. Mr. Hodges was pounding dust from a carpet on the line.

"Housecleaning?" inquired Penny, pausing to chat with the old man.

"Yes, Jenny's got me hard at it," he grinned. "She's been tearin' the house upside down gettin' ready for the new roomer."

"Oh, have you taken one?"

Penny was surprised, knowing that in past years the Hodges had been too proud to rent rooms.

"There's a young feller moving in today," Mr. Hodges said, picking up the carpet beater. "Go on inside. Jenny'll tell you about it."

Penny and Mrs. Weems entered the cottage where the seamstress was running a dust mop over the floors. She was somewhat dismayed to see the housekeeper.

"Oh, Maud, I've been so busy I didn't get your dresses ready to be tried on."

"It doesn't matter," replied Mrs. Weems. "What's this about a new roomer?"

"I always said I wouldn't have one cluttering up the place. But this young man is different. His coming here—well, I interpret it as another sign."

"A sign of what?" inquired Penny with her usual directness.

"Well, it seemed as if I had a direct message from the spirit world to take him into our home. He came here last night. Instead of knocking in the usual way, he rapped six times in succession!"

"Probably he was the one who sent the letter," said Penny alertly.

"Oh, no! He didn't know anything about it. I asked him."

"What is his name, Mrs. Hodges?"

"Al Gepper. He's such a nice young man and he talks so refined. I am letting him have the entire floor upstairs."

"That should bring you a nice income," remarked Mrs. Weems.

"I am asking only two dollars a week," admitted the seamstress. "He said he couldn't pay more than that."

"Why, Jenny," protested Mrs. Weems, "such a small amount hardly will cover the lights and various extras."

"I know, Maud, but I couldn't turn him away. He moved his apparatus in last night and will bring his personal belongings sometime today."

"His apparatus?" echoed Penny. "What is he, a chemist?"

"No," replied the seamstress, smiling mysteriously. "I'll show you the rooms."

Penny and Mrs. Weems followed the woman upstairs. The upper floor was divided into two small bedrooms with a wide, old-fashioned sliding door between which could be opened to make one large chamber. The larger of the rooms had been cleared of its usual furniture. Where a bed previously had stood was a circular table with six or eight chairs, and behind it a tall cabinet with a black curtain across the front.

"Mr. Gepper plans to use this room for his studio," explained Mrs. Hodges.

Penny's gaze had fastened upon the cabinet. She crossed to it and pulled aside the curtain. Inside were several unpacked boxes and a suitcase.

"Mrs. Hodges, to what purpose does your young man expect to put this studio?" she asked.

"I don't know. He didn't tell me. But I think he intends to carry on psychic experiments. He's a student, he said."

"Mr. Gepper was afraid to tell you the truth lest you refuse to rent the rooms," declared Penny. "Mrs. Hodges, your roomer is a medium."

"Why do you think so?"

"Because I've seen trappings such as these before at other séance chambers," replied Penny. "Mrs. Hodges, you must send him away before he involves you with the police."

CHAPTER 10 - OUIJA BOARD WISDOM

"Trouble with the police!" Mrs. Hodges echoed, regarding Penny with unconcealed dismay. "How can it be illegal to rent Mr. Gepper these rooms?"

"Renting the rooms isn't illegal," Penny corrected. "But if the young man conducts public séances here—filches money from people—then you may be considered a party to the scheme. This city has a local ordinance prohibiting fortune telling, mind reading and the like."

"I am sure the young man means no wrong."

"Penny," commented Mrs. Weems, "it seems to me that you are overly concerned. Why are you convinced that Mr. Gepper is a medium?"

"Doesn't this cabinet indicate it?"

"I thought it was some sort of wardrobe closet," Mrs. Hodges admitted.

"Al Gepper is a medium, or pretends to have spiritualistic powers," Penny repeated. "In my opinion you'll be very unwise to allow him to start an illegal business here."

"Oh, dear, I don't know what to do now," declared the seamstress. "I'll have to ask Pa about it."

She and Mrs. Weems started downstairs, expecting that Penny would follow. Instead, the girl lingered to inspect the cabinet.

On the lower floor a door slammed, and there were footsteps ascending the stairway. She paid no heed, assuming that it was either Mr. Hodges or his wife who approached.

The door swung open. Turning, Penny saw a young man, possibly thirty years of age, standing on the threshold. His dark eyes were sharp and appraising.

"Hello," he said, without smiling. "Aren't you afraid a monkey may jump out of that cabinet?"

Penny, who seldom blushed, felt a wave of heat creeping over her cheeks.

"Hello," she stammered. "You must be Mrs. Hodges' new roomer."

"Al Gepper, at your service. Who are you, girlie?"

"You guessed it," said Penny shortly, edging away from the cabinet.

Al Gepper remained in the doorway, blocking the exit with his arm. He did not move as the girl attempted to move past him.

"What's your hurry?" he drawled. "Stick around and let's get acquainted. I'll show you some neat card tricks."

"Thanks, but I haven't time, Mr. Gepper."

"What's your name anyhow?" he persisted. "You're not Mrs. Hodges' daughter."

"No, only a friend."

"You needn't be so icy about it," he rebuked. "Any friend of Mrs. Hodges' is a friend of mine."

"I never make friends easily," Penny replied. "For that matter, I don't mind telling you that I have advised Mrs. Hodges not to rent you these rooms."

"Oh, you have?" inquired the man, his eyes hardening. "And what business is it of yours?"

"None, perhaps. I merely am not going to allow her to be taken in if I can prevent it!"

"Oh, indeed. Do you mind explaining?"

"It's perfectly obvious that you're one of these fake spiritualists," Penny accused bluntly. "Your nickname should be Six-Raps Al!"

"A little spit-fire, aren't you?" the man retorted. "But you have style. Now I may be able to use you in my business."

CHAPTER 10 - OUIJA BOARD WISDOM

"You admit that you're a medium?"

"I am a spiritualist. Not a fake, as you so crudely accuse. And I assure you I have no intention of deceiving or taking advantage of your dear friends, the Hodges."

"You expect to use these rooms for public séances?"

"I do."

"Then you are certain to get the Hodges into trouble with the police."

"Not unless you start squawking." Al Gepper's manner changed abruptly. He grasped Penny's wrist and pushed a leering face close to hers. "I'm not looking for any trouble from you or anyone else—see! If you try to make it, you'll wake up with a headache!"

Penny jerked free and, shouldering through the door, raced downstairs.

Glancing back, she saw that Al Gepper was following, though at a more leisurely pace. Instantly she divined that he intended to make sure no report of the incident was given to the Hodges, save in his presence.

Mrs. Weems and the old couple were talking in the kitchen.

"Well, Ma, it's for you to decide," Mr. Hodges was saying. "We gave our word to the young feller, and it's kinda mean to turn him out so sudden like."

"I regret Penny said anything about the matter." apologized Mrs. Weems. "You know how out-spoken and impulsive she is. Of course, she has no information about Mr. Gepper."

"Oh, but I do have information," spoke Penny from the doorway. "Mr. Gepper has just admitted that he intends to use the room for public séances. Isn't that true?"

Defiantly, she turned to face the young man who had followed her.

"Quite true," he acknowledged loftily. "One who has a great psychic gift is duty-bound to allow the world to benefit from one's talents. The selection of this house as a Temple for Celestial Communication was not mine, but the bidding of the Spirits. In a dream I was instructed to come here and take up residence."

"What night did you have the dream?" questioned Mrs. Hodges, deeply impressed.

"It was June fifteenth."

"The very night we heard the strange rappings on our bedroom wall, Pa."

"Dogonned if it wasn't!"

"Mr. Gepper, do you truly believe it is possible to communicate with the spiritual world?" Mrs. Weems inquired politely.

"My dear madam, I can best answer by offering a demonstration. Have you a ouija board in the house?"

"Yes, we have," spoke Mrs. Hodges eagerly. "Pa and I got it from a mail order house years ago, but it never worked for us. You fetch it, Pa."

Mr. Hodges brought a large, flat board which bore letters and figures. Upon it he placed a small, triangular piece with cushioned legs.

"This do-dad is supposed to spell out messages, ain't it?" he asked. "Ma and I could never make it work right."

Al Gepper smiled in a superior way, and placing the board on his lap, motioned for Mrs. Weems to sit opposite him. However, before the housekeeper could obey, Penny slid into the vacant chair. The medium frowned.

"Place your hands lightly on the triangular piece," he instructed. "Concentrate with me as we await a message from the spiritual world."

Penny fastened her eyes on the distant wall with a blank stare.

A minute passed. The ouija board made several convulsive struggles, but seemed unable to move.

"The Spirits encounter resistance," the medium said testily. "They can send no message when one's attitude is antagonistic."

"Shall I take off the brakes?" asked Penny.

Even as she spoke the pointer of the triangle began moving, rapidly spelling a message.

"AL GEPPER IS A FRAUD," it wrote.

The medium sprang to his feet, allowing the board to fall from his lap.

"You pushed it!" he accused. "The test was unfair."

"Why, the very idea," chuckled Penny.

"Penny, please allow Mr. Gepper to conduct a true test," reproved Mrs. Weems severely. "Let me try."

Al Gepper, however, would have no more of the ouija board. Instead, he took a pad of white paper from his pocket. Seating Mrs. Weems at the kitchen table he requested her to write a message, which, without being shown to anyone in the room, was sealed in an envelope.

The medium pointedly requested Penny to examine the envelope to assure herself the writing could not be seen through the paper.

"You are satisfied that I have not read the message?" he asked.

"Yes," Penny admitted reluctantly.

The medium took the envelope, ran his fingers lightly over it, and returned it still sealed to Mrs. Weems.

"If I am not mistaken, Madam, you wrote, 'Is the spirit of my cousin in this room?'"

"Why, I did!" exclaimed Mrs. Weems. "Those were the exact words! How did you know?"

Al Gepper smiled mysteriously.

"You have seen nothing, Madam," he said. "Now if conditions are right, it may be possible for us to learn if a Spirit has joined our group. Lower the blinds, please."

Mr. Hodges hastened to obey. With the kitchen in semi-darkness, the medium motioned for his audience to move a few paces away. Taking his own position behind the kitchen table, he intoned:

"Oh, Spirit, if you are with us in the room, signal by lifting this piece of furniture."

Slowly the man moved his hands above the table. At first nothing happened, then to the astonishment of his audience, it lifted a few inches from the floor. There it hung suspended a moment before dropping into place again.

"You see?" With a triumphant ring to his voice, the medium crossed the room to raise the window shades. "Now do you doubt me?"

"No! No!" cried Mrs. Hodges tremulously. "Only a Spirit could have moved that table. Maud, perhaps it *was* your Cousin David."

The medium gazed at Mrs. Weems with sympathetic interest.

"You have lost a loved one recently?" he inquired.

"Cousin David and I never were well acquainted," replied the housekeeper. "That was why I was so surprised when he left me an inheritance."

"Mrs. Weems!" remonstrated Penny. She was dismayed by the revelation so casually offered.

"No doubt you would like to communicate with your departed cousin at some later time," the medium said smoothly. "Allow me to offer my services as an intermediary. No charge, of course."

"Why, that's very generous of you, Mr. Gepper."

"Not at all. Friends of the Hodges are my friends. Shall we set a definite date—say tomorrow at two o'clock?"

"Yes, I'll come. That is, if the Hodges are to be present."

"Assuredly. Mrs. Hodges is definitely psychic and should contribute to our séance."

It was with the greatest of difficulty that Penny finally induced the housekeeper to leave the cottage. Al Gepper accompanied them to the door.

"Tomorrow at two," he repeated, smiling slyly at Penny. "And you may come also, my little doubter. I assure you it will be well worth your time."

CHAPTER 11 - THE CELESTIAL TEMPLE

"Penny, tell me the truth," Mrs. Weems urged as they drove home together. "Didn't you push the ouija board?"

"Of course," laughed Penny. "But if I hadn't, Al Gepper would have. He was trying hard enough!"

"He said you were resisting the spirits."

"That was the worst sort of nonsense," Penny returned impatiently. "Gepper is a fraud, and I wish you hadn't told him about your inheritance."

"How can you accuse him of being a fraud after you saw his marvelous demonstration? The table actually rose from the floor."

"I know it did," Penny acknowledged unwillingly. "But it must have been trickery."

"How could it have been? The table was an ordinary one. Mrs. Hodges uses it every day of her life."

"I don't know how he did it," Penny responded. "All the same, I am sure he's a trickster. Promise me you won't tell him anything more about yourself or the inheritance."

"Very well, I'll promise if it gives you satisfaction," the housekeeper replied. "However, I do intend to keep my appointment."

Penny had no opportunity to relate to her father what had occurred at the Hodges home, for Mr. Parker was absent on a two-day business trip to a distant town. Feeling that she must tell someone, she sought Louise Sidell, and they discussed every angle of the affair.

"Will you attend the séance with Mrs. Weems?" Louise asked her curiously.

"Will I?" Penny repeated. "I'll be right there with bells! I intend to expose Mr. Al Gepper if it's the last act of my life!"

Returning home later in the afternoon, she found Mrs. Weems sitting on the living room floor, sorting a drawer of old photographs.

"You're not packing your things already?" Penny asked in alarm.

"Only these photographs," the housekeeper responded. "I wouldn't have started the task, only I got into it when the agent came."

"Agent?"

"A man from the Clamont Photograph Studio."

"Never heard of the place."

"It's opening this week. They're having a special offer—three old photographs enlarged for only twenty-five cents. I gave the man Cousin David's picture and two others."

"That is a bargain," remarked Penny. "I wish I had been here."

The evening meal was served, and afterwards Mrs. Weems devoted herself to the reading of travel books borrowed from the library. Penny could find no occupation to satisfy her. She turned the radio on, switched it off again, and wandered restlessly from room to room. Finally she went to the telephone and called Louise.

"How about a little adventure?" she proposed. "And don't ask for explanations."

"Will we be home by ten o'clock? That's the parental deadline."

"Oh, yes, we'll make it easily. Meet me at the corner of Carabel and Clinton Streets."

Mrs. Weems was so engrossed in her book that she merely nodded as Penny explained that she and Louise were going for a walk. Reaching the appointed corner the girl found her chum awaiting her.

"Tell me about this so-called adventure," she commanded. "Where are we going?"

"To the Celestial Temple, Lou. At least, we'll look at it from the outside. Meetings are held there nearly every night at eight o'clock."

"Penny, I don't think I care to go."

"Nonsense! The meetings are open to the public, aren't they? We'll have a very interesting time."

"Oh, all right," Louise consented reluctantly. "But I can't understand why you're so interested in the place."

The girls took a bus to the end of the line, then walked three blocks until they came to Butternut Lane. For long stretches there were only scattered houses and the street lamps were far between. Becoming increasingly uneasy, Louise urged her chum to turn back.

"Why, we're at our destination now," Penny protested. "I am sure that must be the building."

She pointed to an old, rectangular brick structure only a few yards ahead. Obviously it once had been a church for there was a high bell tower, and behind the building a cluster of neglected tombstones gleamed in the moonlight.

The evenly spaced windows were illuminated, and music could be heard.

"Are you sure this is the place?" Louise inquired dubiously. "It looks like a church to me, and they're holding a service."

"Oh, the building hasn't been used for such purposes in over fifteen years," Penny explained. "I investigated, so I know its history. Until three years ago it was used as a county fire station. Only recently it was reclaimed by this Omar Society of Celestial Thought."

The girls moved closer. Through an open window they were able to see fifteen or twenty people seated in the pews. A woman played a wheezing organ while a man led the off-key singing.

"Let's go inside," Penny proposed.

Louise held back. "Oh, no, we can see everything from here. It looks as if it were a very stupid sort of meeting."

"Appearances are often deceiving. I want a ringside seat."

Penny pulled her chum toward the entrance door. There they hesitated, reading a large placard which bore the invitation:

The Public Is Invited. Services at eight p.m. daily.

"We're part of the public, Lou," urged Penny. "Come along."

She boldly opened the door, and there was no retreat.

Heads turned slightly as the girls entered the rear of the Temple. As quickly they turned forward again, but not before Penny had gained an impression, of sharp, appraising faces.

A man arose, bowed, and offered the girls his bench, although many others were available. They slipped into the pew, accepting a song book which was placed in Louise's hand.

While her chum sang in a thin, squeaky voice, Penny allowed her gaze to wander over the room. At the far end she saw a door which apparently opened into the bell tower. On a slightly raised platform where the leader stood, were two black-draped cabinets somewhat similar to the one she had seen at Mrs. Hodges' cottage. Otherwise, there was nothing of unusual interest.

The services were decorous to the point of being boring. Yet as the meeting went on, Penny and Louise both felt that they were being studied. More than once they surprised persons gazing at them.

At the conclusion of the session which lasted no longer than thirty minutes, the leader asked the audience if any "brother" were present who wished to attempt a spirit communication. Immediately, Penny sat up a bit straighter, anticipating that interesting demonstrations were in store.

Nor was she mistaken. A thin, hard-faced man went to the rostrum, and in a loud voice began to call upon the spirits to make known their presence. Signs were at once forthcoming. The empty pews began to dance as if alive. The speaker's table lifted a foot from the floor and a pitcher of water fell from it, smashing into a dozen pieces.

Louise, her eyes dilated with fear, edged closer to Penny.

"Let's go," she pleaded.

Penny shook her head.

A woman dressed in blue silk glided down the aisle, stopping beside the girls. She held a tray upon which were a number of objects, an opal ring, a knife, and several pins.

CHAPTER 11 - THE CELESTIAL TEMPLE

"Dearie," she said to Penny, "if you would care to have a message from a departed soul, place a trinket in this collection. Any personal object. Our leader will then exhort the spirit to appear."

"No, thank you," replied Louise, without giving her chum a chance to speak.

"Perhaps, you would prefer a private reading," the woman murmured. "I give them at my home, and the fee is trivial. Only a dollar."

"Thank you, no," Louise repeated firmly. "I'm not interested."

The woman shrugged and moved on down the aisle, pausing beside an elderly man to whom she addressed herself.

"Lou, why did you discourage her?" Penny whispered. "We might have learned something."

"I've learned quite enough. I'm leaving."

Louise squeezed past her chum, heading for the exit. Penny had no choice but to follow.

Before they could reach the door, it suddenly opened from the outside. A young man who had not bothered to remove his hat, entered. Seeing the girls, he abruptly halted, then turned and retreated.

Penny quickened her step. Taking Louise's hand she pulled her along at a faster pace. They reached the vestibule. It was deserted. Penny peered up and down the dark street.

"Well, he's gone," she remarked.

"Who?" Louise questioned in a puzzled voice. "You mean that man who entered the Temple and then left so suddenly?"

"I do," responded Penny. "Unless my eyes tricked me, he was none other than Al Gepper!"

CHAPTER 12 - A MESSAGE FOR MRS. WEEMS

"I don't know anyone answering to that name," remarked Louise. "However, the fellow did act as if he were retreating from us."

Penny glanced up and down the dark street. No one was to be seen, and since so little time had elapsed, she reasoned that the man had taken refuge either in the high weeds or the nearby cemetery.

"It must have been Gepper," she declared. "Naturally he wouldn't care to meet me here." Quickly Penny recounted the events of the afternoon.

"Then you think he may be connected with the Temple, Penny?"

"That would be my guess. Lou, this place is nothing but a blind. The members of the society pretend to be honest spiritualists, while in reality they're charlatans. They hold services for one purpose only—to solicit persons for private readings."

"Isn't that illegal?"

"Of course it is. The police should raid the place."

"Then why don't they, Penny?"

"Dad says it's because they've been unable to obtain sufficient evidence. But they'll have it after we report what we've seen tonight!"

"How do you suppose they made things jump around as if they were alive?" Louise remarked as the girls walked slowly toward home. "It frightened me."

"Everything was done by trickery. I'm sure of that, Lou. Just as soon as Dad returns I shall make a full report to him. We'll see what he can do about it."

By the time Penny arrived home, Mrs. Weems had retired to her room. However, the light still burned and the door was open a crack. Rapping, the girl entered, for she was eager to tell the housekeeper about her visit to the Celestial Temple.

Mrs. Weems sat at the desk. Hastily she closed one of the drawers, and turned the key.

"You startled me, Penny!" she exclaimed. "I do wish you would give more warning before you descend upon one."

"Sorry," apologized Penny, glancing curiously toward the desk. "Oh, I see!"

"You see what?" demanded the housekeeper.

"Six thousand dollars reposing in a desk drawer!"

Mrs. Weems' look of consternation betrayed her. She glanced at the locked drawer, and then laughed.

"For an instant I thought you actually could see the money, Penny."

"Then my guess was right?"

"I keep the money in the drawer," Mrs. Weems admitted.

Penny sat down on the edge of the bed, drawing up her knees for a chin rest.

"Mrs. Weems, don't you think it's risky keeping so much money here?"

"It will only be for a few days, Penny. I'll have it converted into traveler's cheques as soon as I am ready to start west."

"The desk doesn't seem a safe place to me."

"You're the only person who knows where I keep the money, Penny. Oh, yes, I told Mrs. Hodges, but she is to be trusted. No one can steal it as long as I have the key."

Mrs. Weems tapped a black velvet ribbon which she wore about her neck.

"I keep this on me day and night," she declared. "No thief ever will get it way from me."

CHAPTER 12 - A MESSAGE FOR MRS. WEEMS

Penny said nothing more about the matter. Instead, she launched into a highly colored account of her visit to the Celestial Temple. The housekeeper expressed disapproval, remarking that she never would have granted permission had she known in advance where the girls were going. Nevertheless, her eager questions made it evident that she was deeply interested in the demonstration which had been witnessed.

"I don't see how you can call it trickery," she protested. "You have no proof, Penny."

"Never in the world will I believe that spirits can make tables do a dance, Mrs. Weems! Probably the furniture had special wiring or something of the sort."

"You can't say that about the table at Mrs. Hodges', Penny."

"No, it seemed to be just an ordinary piece of furniture," the girl admitted reluctantly. "All the same, Al Gepper is a fraud, and I wish you wouldn't attend his old séance tomorrow."

"But Penny, I gave my promise."

"I can run over to the house and tell him you've changed your mind."

Mrs. Weems shook her head. "No, Penny, I am curious to learn if he will be able to communicate with the spirits. Tomorrow's séance should provide a genuine test. The man knows nothing about me or my ancestors."

"Mrs. Hodges probably has provided all the information he'll require."

"I telephoned her yesterday and requested her not to tell Mr. Gepper anything about me. She'll respect my wishes. The test should prove a true one."

Penny sighed and arose from the bed. Knowing Mrs. Weems as she did, she realized that her opinion could not be changed by argument. It was her hope that Al Gepper would discredit himself by failing in the séance.

"Penny, please promise that you'll do nothing outrageous tomorrow," Mrs. Weems begged as the girl started to leave. "I am sure Mr. Gepper feels that you are antagonistic."

"I'll try to behave myself," Penny laughed. "Yes, we'll give Mr. Gepper a chance to prove what he can do."

At two the following afternoon she and Mrs. Weems presented themselves at the Hodges' cottage. Both Mr. Hodges and his wife, who were to sit in at the séance, were trembling with anticipation.

"Mr. Gepper is simply wonderful," the seamstress confided to Mrs. Weems. "He tells me that I have great healing powers as well as a psychic personality."

"Jenny, I hope you haven't told him anything about me," the housekeeper mentioned.

"Oh, no, Maud. For that matter, he's said nothing about you since you were here."

Mrs. Weems cast Penny an "I-told-you-so" glance which was not lost upon Al Gepper who entered the room at that moment.

"I am ready for you, ladies," he said. "Kindly follow me."

In the upstairs room blinds had been drawn. Al Gepper indicated that his audience was to occupy the chairs around the circular table.

"Before we attempt to communicate with the departed souls, I wish to assure you that I employ no trickery," he announced, looking hard at Penny. "You may examine the table or the cabinet if you wish."

"Oh, no, Mr. Gepper," murmured Mrs. Hodges. "We trust you."

"I'll look, if you don't mind," said Penny.

She peered beneath the table, thumped it several times, and pulled aside the curtain of the cabinet. It was empty.

"Now if you are quite satisfied, shall we begin?" purred Mr. Gepper. "It will make it much easier, if each one of you will give me a personal object."

"A la the Celestial Temple method," muttered Penny beneath her breath.

"What was that?" questioned the medium sharply.

"Nothing. I was merely thinking to myself."

"Then please think more quietly. I must warn you that this séance cannot be successful unless each person present concentrates, entering into the occasion with the deepest of sincerity."

"I assure you, I am as sincere as yourself," Penny responded gravely.

Mr. Hodges deposited his gold watch on the table. His wife offered a pin and Mrs. Weems a plain band ring. Penny parted with a handkerchief.

After everyone was seated about the table, Al Gepper played several phonograph records, all the while exhorting the Spirits to appear.

Taking Mrs. Weems' ring from the tray before him, he pressed it to his forehead. A convulsive shudder wracked his body.

"Someone comes to me—" he mumbled. "Someone comes, giving the name of David—David Swester."

"My cousin," breathed Mrs. Weems in awe.

"He is tall and dark with a scar over his left eye," resumed the medium. "I see him plainly now."

"That *is* David!" cried the housekeeper, leaning forward in her eagerness.

"David, have you a message for us?" the medium intoned.

There was a long silence, during which the man could be seen writhing and twisting in the semi-darkness. Then his voice began again:

"David has a message for a person called Maud."

"I am Maud," said Mrs. Weems tremulously. "Oh, what does he say?"

"That he is well and happy in the Spirit World, but he is worried about Maud."

"Worried about me? Why?"

The medium again seemed to undergo physical suffering, but presently the message "came through," although not in an entirely clear form.

"David's voice has faded. I am not certain, but it has something to do with six thousand dollars."

"The exact amount he left to me!" Mrs. Weems murmured.

"David is afraid that you will not have the wisdom to invest the money wisely. He warns you that the present place where you have it deposited is not safe. He will tell you what to do with it. Now the voice is fading again. David has gone."

With another convulsive shudder, Al Gepper straightened from the position into which he had slumped. Resuming his normal tone he said:

"That is all. The connection with Cousin David has been broken."

"Can't we contact him again?" Mrs. Weems asked in disappointment.

"Not today. Possibly tomorrow at this same hour."

"Couldn't you call up another Spirit by using my pin or Pa's watch?" Mrs. Hodges suggested wistfully.

Al Gepper raised one of the window blinds. "I am very, very tired," he said. "This séance was particularly exhausting due to the presence of someone antagonistic. Tomorrow if conditions are right, I hope actually to materialize Cousin David. The poor soul is trying so hard to get a message through to the one he calls Maud."

"You mean I'll be able to see him?" the housekeeper asked incredulously.

"I hope and believe so. I must rest now. After a séance I should refresh myself with sleep."

"Of course," agreed Mrs. Hodges. "We are selfish to overtax you."

Recovering their trinkets, the elderly couple and Mrs. Weems went from the room. Penny was the last to leave.

"Well, sister?" inquired the medium in a low voice. "Were you convinced, or do you still think that you can show up Al Gepper?"

"I think," said Penny softly, "that you are a very clever man. But clever as you are, one of your well-trained ghosts may yet lead you to the city jail!"

CHAPTER 13 - COUSIN DAVID'S GHOST

When Penny reached the lower floor she found Mrs. Weems and the Hodges excitedly discussing the séance. The seamstress and her husband emphatically declared that they had given the medium no information regarding either the housekeeper or the deceased Cousin David.

"Then there can be only one explanation," Mrs. Weems said. "We were truly in communication with a departed spirit."

"Don't you agree, Penny?" inquired Mrs. Hodges.

"I am afraid I can't," she replied.

"The test was a fair one," Mrs. Weems insisted. "Mr. Gepper couldn't have described Cousin David so accurately if he hadn't actually seen him as he materialized from the spirit world."

"Al Gepper could have obtained much of his information from persons in Riverview," Penny responded.

"About me, perhaps," the housekeeper conceded. "But not about Cousin David. Why, I doubt if anyone save myself knew he had a scar over his eye. He received it in an automobile accident twelve or thirteen years ago."

"Just think!" murmured Mrs. Hodges. "Tomorrow you may actually be able to see your departed cousin!"

In vain Penny argued that Al Gepper was a trickster. She was unable to offer the slightest evidence to support her contention while, on the other hand, the Hodges reminded her that the medium had never asked one penny for his services.

From the cottage Penny went directly to the *Star* office, feeling certain that her father would have returned there from his trip. Nor was she mistaken. Gaining admittance to the private office, she wasted no words in relating everything which had transpired during his absence. Her father's attention was flattering.

"Penny, you actually saw all this?" he questioned when she had finished.

"Oh, yes! At the Celestial Temple Louise was with me, too. We thought you might take up the matter with the police."

"That's exactly what I will do," decided Mr. Parker. "I've turned the matter over in my mind for several days. The *Star* will take the initiative in driving these mediums, character readers and the like out of Riverview!"

"Oh, Dad, I was hoping you'd say that!"

Mr. Parker pressed a desk buzzer. Summoning DeWitt, he told of his plan to launch an active campaign.

"Nothing will please me better, Chief," responded the city editor. "Where do we start?"

"We'll tip the police to what is going on at the Celestial Temple. Have them send detectives there for tonight's meeting. Then when the usual hocus-pocus starts, arrests can be made. Have photographers and a good reporter on hand."

"That should start the ball rolling," agreed DeWitt. "I'll assign Jerry Livingston to the story. Salt Sommers is my best photographer."

"Get busy right away," Mr. Parker ordered. "We'll play the story big tomorrow—give it a spread."

"How about Al Gepper?" Penny inquired after DeWitt had gone. "Could he be arrested without involving the Hodges?"

"Not very easily if he lives at their place. Has he accepted money for the séances he conducts there?"

"He hasn't taken any yet from Mrs. Weems. I am sure he must have other customers."

"You have no proof of it?"

"No."

"Suppose we forget Al Gepper for the time being, and concentrate on the Celestial Temple," Mr. Parker proposed. "In the meantime, learn everything you can about the man's methods."

"No assignment would please me more, Dad. I've the same as promised Mr. Gepper he'll land in jail, and I want to make good."

Mr. Parker began to pace the floor. "I'll write a scorching editorial," he said. "We'll fight ignorance with information. Our reporters must learn how these mediums do their tricks, and expose them to the gullible public."

"I'll do everything I can to help," Penny promised eagerly. "May I have Al Gepper for my particular fish bait?"

"He's your assignment. And I'm depending upon you to see that he doesn't work any of his trickery on Mrs. Weems. If she can't be persuaded to remain away from the Hodges', then we must protect her as best we can."

"I'll try to accompany her every time she goes there, Dad. I am afraid he may be after her money."

"Gepper doesn't know she inherited six thousand dollars?" Mr. Parker asked in alarm.

"Yes, she dropped the information that she had come into money. He supplied figures himself."

"I wonder how?"

"I haven't the slightest idea, Dad. Gepper is as clever a man as ever I met. Honestly, it wouldn't surprise me if he does produce Cousin David at tomorrow's séance."

Mr. Parker snorted in disgust.

"Tommyrot! The man will make an excuse about the conditions not being right, and fail."

"Perhaps, but he seems pretty confident."

"You expect to attend the séance?"

"Oh, definitely. Jungle beasts couldn't keep me away."

"Then be alert every instant—without appearing too suspicious, of course. Try to learn how the man accomplishes his tricks."

"Leave it to me," chuckled Penny. "Mr. Al Gepper is due for his first shock when he wakes up tomorrow and reads that the Celestial Temple has been raided. Unless I am much mistaken, that place is one of his favorite haunts."

Leaving the newspaper office, Penny went directly home. She longed to stop at the Sidell home, but she had promised her father to say nothing about the planned raid until it was an accomplished fact. Feeling the need of work to occupy her time, she washed the maroon car and waxed the fading paint of Leaping Lena.

At six o'clock her father came home for dinner.

"Any news?" Penny asked, running to meet him.

"Everything's set," he answered. "DeWitt laid your information before the police. Tonight three detectives will attend the meeting at the Temple. If anything out of the way happens, the raid will be staged."

Penny was so tense with expectation that she was unable to do justice to the delicious dinner which Mrs. Weems had prepared. Her father, too, seemed unusually restless. After dinner he made a pretense of reading the paper, but actually his eyes did not see the print.

The hands of the clock scarcely appeared to move, so slowly did time pass. Eight o'clock came, then nine. Suddenly the telephone rang.

Penny was away in an instant to answer it. From the next room she called to her father:

"It's for you, Dad! DeWitt, I think."

"I told him to telephone me as soon as the raid was staged." Mr. Parker arose and went quickly to take the receiver. Penny hovered at his elbow.

"Hello! DeWitt?" the publisher asked, and after a slight pause: "Oh, I see. No, I don't think Penny was mistaken. It's more likely there was a tip-off."

He hung up the receiver and turned toward Penny who anticipated the news.

"The raid was a failure?"

"Yes, Penny. Detectives spent two hours at the meeting. Nothing happened. It was impossible to make arrests."

"They must have been recognized as detectives."

"Undoubtedly."

"Others will be assigned to the case?"

CHAPTER 13 - COUSIN DAVID'S GHOST

"I doubt it, Penny. DeWitt reports that the police have become convinced that the spiritualists who use the Temple are not operating for profit."

"Louise and I know better because she was approached." Penny anxiously regarded her father. "Dad, even if the police do give up, we won't, will we?"

"No, we're in this fight and we'll stay in it," he answered grimly. "We'll put some new teeth in our trap. And the next time it's sprung, I warrant you we'll catch a crook."

CHAPTER 14 - WET PAINT

Promptly at two o'clock the following afternoon, Penny and Mrs. Weems presented themselves at the Hodges' cottage for the appointed séance. Already Mr. Gepper awaited them in the darkened apartment on the second floor.

Penny's glance about the room found everything in the same order as upon the previous visit, save that an easel with a large black sheet of artist's paper stood beside the cabinet.

She moved as if to examine it. Al Gepper intercepted her by saying:

"Sit here, if you please. Beside Mrs. Weems. I'll call the Hodges and we'll start at once."

The medium went to the door and shouted down the stairway. Penny noticed that he remained where he could watch her every move in a mirror which hung on the wall. She shrewdly guessed that he was afraid she might attempt to examine either the cabinet or the easel.

Mr. and Mrs. Hodges came in response to the call, taking chairs about the circular table. The gaze which they fastened upon Al Gepper was almost worshipful.

"Now today I hope to materialize the Spirit of Cousin David," announced the medium. "The task will be difficult, as you must realize. After the séance begins I am compelled to request absolute quiet. The slightest movement may frighten away the Spirits."

"Why are spirits so timid?" asked Penny.

"Because their beings are so sensitive that they instantly feel an unfriendly presence," the man responded glibly. "Please hold hands, and use every precaution that contact is not broken."

Mrs. Weems took one of Penny's hands and Mr. Hodges the other. Mrs. Hodges sat next to her husband.

After lowering black curtains over the window blinds to further darken the room, the medium returned to his chair. Those at the table were unable to distinguish his form, and for a time there was no sound save the scratching music of a phonograph record.

Presently the medium exhorted the Spirit of Cousin David to appear. For at least ten minutes there was no indication that communication was to be established. Then a cowbell tinkled, causing Mrs. Weems to shake and tremble.

"Are you there, David?" called the medium.

The bell jingled violently.

"We are ready, David," intoned the medium. "Have you a message for us?"

To Penny's amazement, a pair of shapely white hands slowly materialized, apparently pulling aside the curtain of the cabinet above the medium's head. In the darkness they glowed with a weird phosphorescent light.

Next appeared a white-rimmed slate, upon which luminous words were written: "I am the Spirit of Cousin David. Is Maud here?"

"Yes, yes," responded Mrs. Weems, quivering with excitement. "Have you a message for me?"

Again the hand wrote: "My happiness in this world beyond is disturbed. Maud, do not squander the money which I gave to you."

"Squander it?" the housekeeper said aloud. "Why, I've scarcely spent a penny!"

"A trip to California is ill-advised," wrote the hand. "Invest your money in good eight per cent securities. There are many excellent companies—the Brantwell Corporation, White and Edwards, the Bierkamp Company."

The slate vanished and once more the jingling of the cowbell denoted that the spirit was moving away.

The medium spoke. "Contact has been broken. Shall we try to reach Cousin David again?"

CHAPTER 14 - WET PAINT

"Oh, please!" pleaded Mrs. Weems. "I don't know what to do now. I've planned on the western trip and I can't understand why Cousin David should advise me to give it up."

"I wouldn't go agin' the Spirits if I was you," advised Mr. Hodges. "You better change your plans, Maud."

"But how can I be certain that the message came from Cousin David?" the housekeeper quavered. "Oh, dear, I am so upset! If only I could be certain."

"Madam, I hope you do not distrust me," said Al Gepper reprovingly.

"Oh, no, it's not that. I'm just upset."

"Perhaps, if you actually saw your cousin it would set your mind at rest."

"Is it possible to see him?"

"I cannot promise, but we will try. Hold hands again please, and everyone concentrate."

There followed an interval during which the medium pleaded with the Spirit of Cousin David to return and show himself. Suddenly the group was startled to see a luminous banjo move high through the air, unsupported by any hand. It began to play "Down upon the Swanee River."

Midway through the selection, the music broke off and the banjo disappeared. An instant later Mrs. Hodges uttered a choked cry.

"The easel! Look at it, Maud!"

All eyes turned toward the painter's canvas. As the medium focused a flashlight upon it, the face of an elderly man slowly materialized on the blank surface, the picture appearing in red, blue and finally black oil paint.

"It *is* Cousin David!" whispered Mrs. Weems, gripping Penny's hand so tightly that it hurt. "He looks exactly as he did when last I saw him!"

The medium extinguished his light and again the room was dark. Mrs. Weems' chair creaked as she stirred restlessly. Mr. Hodges' heavy breathing could be plainly heard. There was no other sound. Everyone waited in tense expectancy, sensing that the climax of the séance was at hand.

Suddenly, behind Al Gepper's chair a spot of ethereal light appeared. As Penny watched, it grew in size until the figure had assumed the proportions of a man. Then, to her further amazement, it slowly rose toward the ceiling, hovering above Mrs. Weems' chair.

Throughout the séance Penny had remained firm in her conviction that the medium had resorted to trickery to produce his startling effects. Although she could not be sure, she thought that several times he had slipped from his chair to enter the conveniently placed cabinet. She also believed that the only way he could have materialized the ghost was by donning luminous robes.

"I'll end his little game once and for all," she thought.

Deliberately she waited until the ghostly figure floated close to her own chair. Then with a sudden upward spring, she snatched at it.

Greatly to her chagrin, her hand encountered nothing solid. With the speed of lightning, the figure streaked toward the cabinet behind Al Gepper's chair and was seen no more.

Arising, the medium switched on the room lights. His face was white with anger.

"I warned you to make no move," he said harshly to Penny. "You deliberately disobeyed me."

"Oh, Penny, why did you do it?" wailed Mrs. Weems. "I was so eager to get another message from Cousin David."

"His Spirit has been frightened away," announced the medium. "It will be impossible ever to recall him. For that matter, I shall never again conduct a séance with this young person present. She is a disturbing element."

"Oh, Penny, you've ruined everything," said Mrs. Weems accusingly. "Why do you act so outrageously?"

Penny started to speak and then changed her mind. Mrs. Weems, the seamstress and her husband, all were gazing at her with deep reproach. She realized that there was nothing she could say which would make them understand.

She arose and walked to the easel. The painting of Cousin David remained clearly visible. She touched it and then glanced at her finger which bore a streak of red.

The paint was still wet.

Penny stared at her finger a moment. Lifting her eyes she met the triumphant gaze of Al Gepper.

"Not even a skillful artist could have painted a picture so quickly," he said with a smirk. "Only a spirit would have the ability. You are dumbfounded, my little one?"

"No, just plain dumb," answered Penny. "I salute you, Mr. Gepper."

Without waiting for Mrs. Weems, she turned and went from the house.

"Now how *did* he do it?" she muttered. "I saw everything and yet I am more in the dark than ever. But I am sure of one thing. Unless I work fast, Al Gepper is almost certain to obtain Mrs. Weems' inheritance."

CHAPTER 15 - HIDDEN MONEY

One of Penny's first acts upon arriving home was to scan the telephone directory under the heading, Investment Firms. The three companies mentioned during the séance, White and Edwards, Brantwell, and Bierkamp, were unlisted.

"Evidently there are no such firms in Riverview," she reflected. "But why was Mrs. Weems advised to invest her money with one of them? It looks very suspicious to me!"

Not until after five o'clock did Mrs. Weems return from the Hodges'. She seemed rather upset, and when Penny tried to bring up the subject of the séance, said distantly:

"Please, Penny, I prefer not to discuss it. Your conduct was disgraceful."

"I apologize for grabbing at the ghost, Mrs. Weems. I only did it to prove that Al Gepper is a fraud."

"Your motives were quite apparent. One could not blame Mr. Gepper for being angry."

"Oh, Mrs. Weems," said Penny in desperation. "How can you be taken in by his smooth line? His one purpose is to obtain your money."

"You are very unjust," the housekeeper responded. "Today I tried to pay Mr. Gepper for the séance and he would not accept one penny."

"That's because he is playing for higher stakes."

"It's no use discussing the matter with you," Mrs. Weems shrugged. "You are prejudiced and will give the man credit for nothing."

"I give him credit for being very clever. Mrs. Weems, please promise that you'll not allow him to invest your money for you."

"I have no intention of doing so, Penny. It does seem to me that I should consider Cousin David's wishes in the matter. Very likely I shall abandon my plans for the western trip."

"And stay here with us?" Penny cried eagerly.

"No, I am thinking of going to a larger city and taking an apartment. With my money invested in eight per cent securities, I should have a comfortable little income."

"Mrs. Weems, I've heard Dad say over and over that sound securities will not pay such a high rate of interest. Promise you won't invest your money until you've talked with him."

"You're always asking me to promise something or other," the housekeeper sighed. "This time I shall use my own judgment."

Realizing that further argument was only a waste of breath, Penny wandered outside to await her father. When he came, they sat together on the front porch steps, discussing the situation.

"I'll drop a word of advice to Mrs. Weems at the first opportunity," offered Mr. Parker. "If she is in the mood you describe, it would not be wise to bring up the subject tonight. She merely would resent my interference."

"What worries me is that I am afraid she may have told Al Gepper where the money is kept."

"Tomorrow I'll urge her again to deposit it in a bank. We'll do our best to protect her from these sharpers."

The publisher had been very much interested in Penny's account of the séance. However, he was unable to explain how the various tricks had been accomplished.

"Dad," Penny said thoughtfully, "you don't suppose there's any chance it wasn't trickery?"

"Certainly not! I hope you're not falling under this fellow's spell?"

"No, but it gave me a real shock when I saw Cousin David's face materialize on the canvas. It was the absolute image of him—or rather of a picture Mrs. Weems once showed me."

A startled expression came over Penny's face. Without explanation, she sprang to her feet and ran to the kitchen.

"Mrs. Weems," she cried, "did you ever get it back? Your picture!"

"What picture, Penny?" The housekeeper scarcely glanced up as she vigorously scrubbed carrots.

"I mean the one of Cousin David. You allowed a photographer to take it for enlargement."

"It hasn't been returned," Mrs. Weems admitted. "I can't imagine why the work takes so long."

"I think I can," announced Penny. "But you never would believe me if I told you, so I won't."

Racing to the porch, she revealed to her father what she thought had occurred. It was her theory that the agent who had called at the Parker home days earlier had in actuality been one of Al Gepper's assistants.

"Don't you see, Dad!" she cried. "The man obtained a picture of Cousin David, and probably turned it over to the medium." Her face fell slightly. "Of course, that still doesn't explain how the painting slowly materialized."

"Nor does it explain the ghost or the banjo. Penny, couldn't Gepper have painted the picture himself in the darkness?"

"There wasn't time, Dad. Besides, he held a flashlight on the painting. No human hand touched it."

"You say, too, that the banjo was high overhead when it played?"

"That's right, Dad. Gepper couldn't have reached the strings. The instrument floated free in the air."

"Sounds fantastic."

"Believe me, it was, Dad. It's no wonder Gepper is gaining such influence over Mrs. Weems. He's as slick as a greased fox!"

"I'll have Jerry go to the house and try to learn how the fellow operates," declared Mr. Parker. "We can't break the story until we have absolute evidence that Gepper has obtained money under false pretenses."

The next day Penny remained close at home. Mrs. Weems still treated her somewhat distantly, leaving the house immediately after lunch and declining to explain where she was going. Penny was quite certain that her destination was the Hodges' cottage.

"Guess I'll run over and see Louise," she thought restlessly. "Nothing to do here."

Before she could leave the house, the doorbell rang. A man of perhaps thirty, well dressed, with a leather briefcase tucked under his arm, stood on the front porch. He bowed politely to Penny.

"This is where Mrs. Weems resides, I believe?"

"Yes, but she isn't here now."

"When will she be home?"

"I can't say," replied Penny. "Are you an agent?"

The man's appearance displeased her although she could not have said exactly why. His smile was too ingratiating, his eyes calculating and hard.

"My name is Bierkamp," he explained. "I represent the Harold G. Bierkamp Investment Company."

Penny stiffened. She glared at the agent. "You mean you represent the Al Gepper Spookus Company," she said in a cutting voice. "Well, Mrs. Weems doesn't want any of your wonderful eight per cent stocks! She'll not see you, so don't come here again!"

"And who are you to speak for her?" the man retorted.

"If you come here again, I'll call the police," Penny threatened. "Now get out!"

Without another word, the man retreated down the street. Penny watched until he turned a corner and was lost to view. She was a trifle worried as to what she had done.

"If Mrs. Weems learns about this she'll never forgive me," she thought uneasily. "But he was a crook sent by Al Gepper. I know it."

Wandering upstairs, she entered the bathroom, intending to wash before going to Louise's home. On the tiled floor lay a velvet ribbon with a key attached. At once, Penny realized that Mrs. Weems had left it there inadvertently.

"It's the key to her desk," she reflected, picking it up. "And she insists that her money is kept in a safe place! I have a notion to play a joke on her."

The longer Penny considered the idea, the more it pleased her. Jubilantly, she set forth for the Sidell home. Taking Louise into her confidence, she visited a novelty shop and purchased a supply of fake money.

CHAPTER 15 - HIDDEN MONEY

Returning home, she then unlocked the drawer of Mrs. Weems' desk and, removing the six thousand dollars, replaced it with neat stacks of imitation bills. Louise watched her with misgiving.

"Penny, this joke of yours isn't likely to strike Mrs. Weems as very funny," she warned. "You're always doing things which get you into trouble."

"This is in a good cause, Lou. I am protecting Mrs. Weems from her own folly."

"What will you do with the money?"

"Deposit it in a bank."

"You are taking matters into your hands with a vengeance! Suppose you're robbed on the way downtown?"

"That would complicate my life. Upon second thought, I'll send for an armored truck."

To Louise's amazement, Penny actually carried through her plan. A heavily guarded express truck presently drew up before the Parker residence, and Mrs. Weems' money was turned over to the two armed men who promised that it would be delivered safely to the First National Bank.

"There, that's a load off my mind," said Penny. "Just let Al Gepper try to steal Mrs. Weems' money now!"

Louise shook her head sadly. "You may be accused of stealing yourself. I wouldn't be in your slippers when Mrs. Weems learns about this."

"Oh, I'll be able to explain," laughed Penny.

The joke she had played did not seem quite so funny an hour later. Mrs. Weems returned home and without comment recovered the key which had been replaced on the lavatory floor. She did not open her desk or mention the money.

At dinner Penny was so subdued that the housekeeper inquired if she were ill.

"Not yet," the girl answered. "I'm just thinking about the future. It's so depressing."

"Perhaps a picture show would cheer us all," proposed Mr. Parker.

Mrs. Weems displayed interest, and Penny, without enthusiasm, agreed to go. Eight o'clock found them at the Avalon, a neighborhood theatre. The show was not to Penny's liking, although her father and the housekeeper seemed to enjoy it. She squirmed restlessly, and finally whispered to her father that she was returning home.

In truth, as Penny well knew, she was suffering from an acute case of "conscience." Now that it was too late, she regretted having meddled with Mrs. Weems' money.

Gloomily she walked home alone. As she entered, she heard the telephone ringing, but before she could answer, the party hung up. With a sigh Penny locked the front door again, switched out the lights and went to bed.

For a long while she lay staring at a patch of moonlight on the bedroom carpet. Although she felt tired she could not sleep.

"It's just as Louise said," she reflected. "I'm always getting myself into hot water and for no good reason, either!"

Her morose thoughts were interrupted as a hard object thudded against a nearby wall. Penny sat up, listening. She believed that the sound had come from Mrs. Weems' room, yet she knew she was alone in the house.

Rolling from bed, she groped for a robe, and without turning on the lights, tiptoed down the hall. Mrs. Weems' door stood open. Was some intruder hidden in that room?

Peering inside, Penny at first noticed nothing amiss. Then her gaze fastened on the window sill, plainly visible in the moonlight. Two iron hooks, evenly spaced, had been clamped over the ledge!

CHAPTER 16 - OVER THE WINDOW LEDGE

As Penny flattened herself against the wall, the head and shoulders of a man slowly rose into view. Although his body was plainly silhouetted in the moonlight, she could not see his face.

The intruder raised the sash, making no sound. He hesitated, listening a moment, then dropped lightly into the bedroom.

Without turning on a flashlight which he carried, he went directly to Mrs. Weems' desk. So deliberate was the action that Penny instantly decided the fellow had come for a particular purpose and knew the lay-out of the entire house.

"He means to steal Mrs. Weems' money!" she thought.

Opening the desk, the man tried the drawer where the inheritance funds had been hidden. Failing to unlock it with a key, he took a tool from his pocket and in a moment had broken the lock.

Removing the stack of fake bills which Penny had substituted, he thrust them into his coat. Taking no interest in anything else in the room, he moved stealthily toward the window.

Penny knew there was no one within calling distance and that the man probably was armed. Wisdom dictated that she remain in hiding, but she was determined the thief should not escape. Hoping to take him by surprise, she stalked forward.

A board creaked. With a muttered exclamation the man whirled around. At the same instant Penny flung herself upon him, diving low in imitation of a football tackle.

The thief reeled, but instead of falling he recovered his balance and gave Penny a tremendous shove which sent her sprawling backwards. Before she could regain her feet, he ran to the window. Swinging himself over the ledge, he vanished from view.

By the time Penny reached the window there was no sign of the intruder. He had disappeared as if into thin air. However, she knew that the man must have descended by means of a ladder which he had hastily removed.

She ran her hand over the window ledge. The iron hooks no longer were there, only the scars which had been cut in the wood.

"This undoubtedly was the same fellow who broke into the Kohl apartment!" she thought. "But how did he escape so quickly?"

Penny started for a telephone, intending to notify the police. However, when it occurred to her that her father might not wish the matter made public, she changed her mind and ran downstairs.

Unlocking the rear door, she glanced carefully about the yard. There was no one in sight, no movement behind any of the shrubbery.

"He's gone, of course," she thought.

Penny wore no shoes. Finding a pair of old galoshes on the porch, she protected her feet with them, and hobbled into the yard.

The grass beneath Mrs. Weems' window had been trampled, but at first glance there was no clue to indicate how the burglar had gained entrance to the house.

"Obviously he used a ladder," she reasoned. "But how did he descend so quickly? And what became of the ladder? I know he never had time to carry away one of the ordinary type."

A dark object lying on the grass attracted Penny's attention. Picking it up, she carried it to the porch and switched on a light that she might see to better advantage. In her hand she held a torn strand of black silk rope.

"This may be an important clue!" she thought excitedly. "I know now how the man entered the house!"

CHAPTER 16 - OVER THE WINDOW LEDGE

As Penny examined the piece of rope, automobile headlight beams cut a path across the yard. The Parker car drew up on the driveway and both Mrs. Weems and Mr. Parker alighted.

"Dad, come here quickly!" Penny called as he started to open the garage doors.

"What's wrong, Penny?"

Both the publisher and Mrs. Weems came toward the porch.

"We've had a burglar," Penny announced. "He broke into Mrs. Weems' room, smashing the lock on the desk—"

"My money!" the housekeeper exclaimed in horror. "Oh, Penny, don't tell me that it's gone!"

"He escaped with the contents of the drawer."

Mrs. Weems gave a moan of anguish. "Haven't you called the police?" she demanded. "When did it happen? Tell me everything!"

"First, I'll set your mind at rest," Penny replied. "Your money is safe."

"Oh! I never was so relieved in all my born days." Mrs. Weems sagged weakly into a porch rocker. "Penny, how could you torture me by letting me think the money was stolen?"

"Because I have a confession to make, Mrs. Weems. You left the key to your desk lying on the bathroom floor. I thought it might be a good joke to move the money to another place."

"Oh, you darling blessed girl!" laughed Mrs. Weems. "Where did you hide it, Penny? Are you sure it's safe?"

"It should be. I had it taken to the First National Bank and deposited in your name. The thief carried off a package of fake money."

"Rather high-handed weren't you?" commented her father.

"Now don't you scold her," spoke Mrs. Weems quickly. "I am glad Penny acted as she did. Otherwise, I might have lost my entire inheritance."

Penny drew a deep breath. "I'm relieved you feel that way about it. I wish I could see the burglar's face when he discovers he stole worthless money!"

Both the housekeeper and Mr. Parker pressed her with questions. She revealed exactly what had occurred during their absence, showing them the strand of black silk rope.

"Dad, I think this may be a valuable clue," she declared. "What does it suggest to you?"

"Not much of anything, I am afraid."

"You remember that when the Kohls were robbed the police couldn't figure out how the burglar gained entrance?"

"Yes, I recall the story."

"Well, I believe the same man committed both burglaries."

"Why do you think so, Penny?"

"At the Kohl's the police found two marks on the window ledge apparently made by iron hooks. Similar marks are on the sill in Mrs. Weems' room. For that matter, I distinctly saw the iron pieces bite into the wood."

"Let's look at them," proposed Mr. Parker.

"Only the marks are there now, Dad. The man jerked the hooks loose after he descended. They must have been attached to his ladder."

"I thought you said he had none, Penny."

"There was no time for him to have carried away an ordinary, heavy ladder. I think the one he used must have been made of silk."

"And this is a piece of it!" Mr. Parker exclaimed, examining the twisted strand with new interest. "Your theory sounds plausible. It would be possible for a man to scale a wall with such a ladder."

"He could jerk loose the hooks in an instant, too, Dad. The ladder would fit into a small suitcase, or even his pocket!"

"There's one objection to your theory, Penny. How could such a ladder be raised to the window ledge? It naturally would be limp."

"That part has me puzzled, I'll admit."

"I never even heard of a silken ladder," said Mrs. Weems doubtfully.

"I once saw one being made," declared Penny with deliberate emphasis. "At a Japanese Shop on Dorr Street."

"That's right, you spoke of it!" exclaimed her father. "Penny, you may have something!"

"I think so, Dad. This strand of twisted silk may lead straight to Kano's Curio Shop."

"And from there?"

Penny hesitated, glancing at Mrs. Weems. She knew that the housekeeper might take offense, but she answered quietly:

"My guess would be to Al Gepper, Dad. Who but he or an accomplice could have known where the money was hidden?"

CHAPTER 17 - KANO'S CURIO SHOP

As Penny had anticipated, Mrs. Weems indignantly declared that she did not believe Mr. Gepper could have had any connection with the attempted robbery. Yet, even as she made the assertion, a startled expression came over her face.

"Think back, Mrs. Weems," urged Mr. Parker. "How many persons knew where you had secreted the money?"

"I told Mrs. Hodges."

"And Al Gepper?" Penny probed.

"Well—" The housekeeper looked ill at ease. "He may have heard me talking with Mrs. Hodges. I remember he passed through the hall while we were together."

"What day was that?" inquired Penny.

"Yesterday. After the séance. But I can't believe that Mr. Gepper would try to steal the money. I just can't!"

"From what Penny has told me of the man, I should judge that he is a schemer," contributed Mr. Parker. "You know the *Star* has started a vigorous campaign directed against such mediums as Al Gepper."

"But he told me such remarkable things about Cousin David," protested Mrs. Weems. "Facts which couldn't be faked."

"Oh, Gepper doesn't make many false moves," acknowledged Penny. "He's a smooth worker. All the same, he's a fake."

"How could he have faked Cousin David's message? You forget we actually saw the picture of my relative painted without the aid of a human hand."

"Did the picture closely resemble your cousin?" inquired Mr. Parker.

"Oh, yes, indeed. It looked exactly as I saw him many years ago."

"Isn't that rather odd?" demanded Penny. "One would expect Cousin David to age a little."

"Penny believes that a photographer's agent who came here a few days ago was sent by Gepper to obtain a picture of your relative," explained Mr. Parker. "Did the man ask you many questions about your cousin?"

"Well, yes, he did," Mrs. Weems admitted unwillingly. "I made a mistake giving him the photograph."

"It seems fairly evident that the picture was used by Gepper," Mr. Parker commented. "Whether he plotted to steal your money remains to be proven. Penny, you saw the man plainly?"

"No, I didn't, Dad. Not his face. He was about the same build as Gepper."

"That's not much to go on."

"From the first Gepper was determined to get Mrs. Weems' money, Dad. He sent a man here who pretended to be from the Bierkamp Investment Company."

"You didn't tell me that," said Mrs. Weems.

"Well, no I didn't. I was afraid you would invest your money with him, so I drove the man away. He must have been Gepper's accomplice. Failing to acquire the money by that means, he plotted the burglary."

"Surely you don't agree with Penny?" the housekeeper asked Mr. Parker unhappily.

"In general, I am afraid I do. Mr. Gepper is an undesirable character, and I should like nothing better than to send him to jail."

"Come upstairs, Mrs. Weems," urged Penny. "I'll show you the desk."

Both the housekeeper and Mr. Parker followed her to the second floor. An examination of the bedroom disclosed no additional clues, but after studying the marks on the window ledge, the publisher favored Penny's theory that a silk ladder had been utilized.

"It was unwise of me to keep my money here," Mrs. Weems remarked in a crestfallen tone. "I—I've been silly about everything, I guess."

Penny gave her a quick hug. "No, you haven't. Anyone might have been taken in by Al Gepper."

"I shall never attend another of his séances. I'll urge Mrs. Hodges to turn him from her house."

"Mrs. Weems, are you willing to help get evidence against him?" asked Mr. Parker abruptly.

"Why, yes, if I can."

"Then go to the Hodges' exactly as you have in the past," instructed the publisher. "Penny has been warned by Gepper not to attend any of the séances, but you'll still be welcome. Learn everything you can and report to me."

"I'll be glad to do it, Mr. Parker."

"Don't allow him to guess that you have become suspicious. Above all, never withdraw your money from the bank at his suggestion."

"You may be sure I won't. This has taught me a bitter lesson."

"Haven't you an assignment for me, Dad?" inquired Penny. "How about Kano's Curio Shop?"

"Early tomorrow I'll send Jerry there to question the old Jap."

"Will you notify the police?"

"Not for the present. If we can crack this story I'd like to get it ahead of the *Record*."

"I wish you would send me to Kano's instead of Jerry."

"Dorr Street is no place for you, Penny," Mr. Parker replied, dismissing the matter. "Shall we get to bed now? It's nearly midnight."

After the doors had been locked once more Penny went to her room, but she did not immediately fall asleep. Instead, she kept mulling over the events of the night. The more she thought about it the more firmly she became convinced that both the Kohl home and her own had been entered by the same person.

"The telephone was ringing when I came from the movie," she recalled. "Now I wonder who called? It may have been a trick of the thief to learn if anyone were in the house. When no one answered, the assumption would be that the coast was clear."

Penny felt rather well satisfied with the way matters had developed. In one bold stroke she had saved Mrs. Weems' inheritance, convinced the housekeeper that Al Gepper was not to be trusted, and had made definite progress in gaining evidence to be used in her father's campaign against the charlatan invaders of Riverview. Yet it annoyed her that the story, now that it had reached an active stage, was to be turned over to Jerry.

"I have a notion to visit the Kano Curio Shop ahead of him," she thought. "That's exactly what I'll do!"

Having made up her mind, she rolled over and promptly fell asleep.

In the morning Penny ate breakfast and wiped the dishes with a speed which astonished Mrs. Weems. Shortly after her father left for the office, she backed her own maroon car from the garage, and offering only a vague explanation, departed for Kano's Curio Shop.

Dorr Street was quite deserted at such an early hour, and the Japanese shop owner had just unlocked his doors. He was sweeping the floor as Penny boldly entered.

"Good morning, Mr. Kano," she greeted him. "You remember me, I believe?"

Mr. Kano bowed, regarding her warily. "Yes," he replied. "You are the young lady whose curiosity is very large."

Penny smiled. "You are right, Mr. Kano. It is very large, especially about a certain silken ladder."

Mr. Kano frowned as he leaned on his broom. "I am very sorry," he said. "I am a merchant, not one who answers what you call the quiz-bee."

Penny understood that the Japanese never would tell her what she wished to know save under compulsion. She decided to adopt firm tactics.

"Mr. Kano," she said, "my father is the owner of the *Riverview Star* and he intends to expose certain crooks who have been robbing wealthy persons such as the Kohls. You read in the paper that their home was entered?"

"Yes, I read," the Japanese shrugged.

"My own theory is that the thief gained entrance by means of a silk ladder," Penny declared. "*A ladder made in this shop!*"

The shopkeeper's eyes narrowed. "I know nothing," he replied. "Nothing. You go now, please."

CHAPTER 17 - KANO'S CURIO SHOP

"If I go," said Penny, "I'll return with the police. You would not like that, I take it?" Her voice was crisp and full of menace.

Mr. Kano lost some of his poise. "No!" he answered sharply. "I am an honest man and want no sad trouble with the police."

Chancing to glance toward the street, Penny observed Jerry Livingston standing on the opposite corner. He was gazing thoughtfully toward the Curio Shop, and she knew that he must have been sent by her father to interview Mr. Kano. Inspired, she turned again to the old Japanese.

"You see that young man yonder?" she asked, indicating Jerry. "I have but to summon him and he'll come here."

"Detective?" demanded Mr. Kano, peering anxiously through the window. "Do not call him! I am an honest man. I will answer your questions."

"Then tell me about the silken ladder."

"I know little," the shopkeeper insisted. "I made the rope for a man who said: 'Do this or we will burn your shop down, Mr. Kano.' So I made the ladder and he paid me well for fashioning it."

"And what was the man's name?"

"His name I do not know. But his eyes were small and evil. His skin was dark, his nose crooked."

Mr. Kano ceased speaking with an abruptness which caused Penny to glance toward the door. Her first thought was that Jerry had entered. Instead a strange young man stood there, regarding her suspiciously.

As she stared at him he quickly retreated, but not before she had caught a fleeting impression of a face which matched Mr. Kano's description with startling accuracy.

"Was he the one?" she demanded as the door slammed. "The man for whom you made the ladder?"

"No, no!" denied the Japanese.

His words failed to convince Penny. Darting to the door, she saw that the young man already was far down the street, walking rapidly.

"He is the one," she thought. "I'll follow him."

"Wait," called the Japanese as she started away, "I have more to tell you."

It was a ruse to detain her, Penny knew. Pushing past the shopkeeper who sought to bar the exit, she reached the street and ran toward Jerry Livingston.

"Why, Penny!" he exclaimed in surprise. "What are you doing in this part of town?"

"Never mind that," she answered hastily. "If you're after a story, come along with me. We're trailing the man who just left Kano's Shop."

CHAPTER 18 - THE BELL TOWER

Jerry fell into step with Penny. As they walked along, she told him of her conversation with Mr. Kano.

"I believe this man we're following is the same one who entered our house last night," she declared. "He's the same build as the fellow I grabbed. Besides, he fits Kano's description of the person who bought the silken ladder."

"Here's hoping you're right," replied Jerry. "If I muff this assignment, I may wake up looking for another job."

Fearing that the man ahead would discover he was being followed, Jerry and Penny dropped farther and farther behind. Presently they saw him enter a pawnshop.

"I know that place," commented Jerry. "It's run by Spike Weiser, a notorious *fence*. He buys stolen goods and gets rid of it at a profit. Has a swell home on Clarmont Drive."

"Why don't the police arrest him?"

"Oh, they watch the place, but Spike is too smart to be caught. He has a system for handling *hot* goods."

"I'll venture some of the Kohl loot was sold through him, Jerry."

"It wouldn't surprise me. But if the police search the place they won't find a thing."

Loitering on the opposite side of the street, Penny and the reporter kept close watch of the pawnbroker's shop. Thirty minutes elapsed. The man whom they had trailed, did not reappear.

"He must have slipped out the back door," Jerry remarked. "Probably knew he was being watched."

"I'm beginning to think so myself."

Jerry glanced at his watch. "I can't take any more time," he said. "I'll have to get back to the office."

"I'll watch a few minutes longer," answered Penny. "If anything develops I'll try to telephone."

Jerry walked hurriedly away. Scarcely had he disappeared when the door of the pawnshop opened, and the young man who had entered a half hour earlier, appeared. Penny hastily moved back into the vestibule of an office building.

Without observing her, the stranger crossed the street and walked briskly toward an intersecting boulevard. There was no opportunity for Penny to telephone the *Star* office. Following, she was hard pressed to keep the man within view.

Not until they reached the entrance of Butternut Lane did it dawn upon her that the Celestial Temple might be their destination. Then, indeed, her pulse stepped up a pace.

"It's exactly as I guessed!" she thought triumphantly. "He's connected with Al Gepper and the other mediums!"

Not wishing to attract attention in the deserted lane, Penny took a short cut through the cemetery, emerging at the rear of the Celestial Temple. There was no door on that side of the building but a window had been left raised. Placed beneath it, as if for her particular convenience, was a large rock.

Penny stood on it, peering into the Temple. The room was unoccupied. However, as she waited, the same man she had trailed, quietly let himself in through the front entrance, using a key. He glanced about and called in a low voice: "Pete! Pete! Anyone here?"

There was no answer, which seemed to please the young man. He moved quickly down the aisle, crossed the platform to a door which opened into the bell tower. Kneeling he began to fit keys into the lock, seeking one which would serve.

As Penny watched, the young man suddenly straightened. Apparently he had heard footsteps in the vestibule for he moved away from the bell tower door.

CHAPTER 18 - THE BELL TOWER

A middle-aged woman with dyed hair and a skin of unusual pallor entered the Temple. She stopped short as she saw the young man.

"You here, Slippery?" she commented, gazing at him with distrust. "Where's Pete?"

"Hello, Sade. I was wonderin' about Pete myself. Just got here a minute ago."

The woman's gaze fastened upon the key which had been left in the bell tower door.

"Say, what's coming off here?" she demanded. "You were trying to get inside!"

"Now don't ruffle your feathers, Sade," the man said soothingly. "I was only testing the door to make sure it was locked."

"I'll bet! You were aiming to break in! Slippery, they sure named you right. Why, you'd double-cross your own mother!"

"Oh, quiet down," the man retorted angrily. "I only came here to make sure Pete was on the job. The lazy loafer has skipped out and left the place unguarded."

The woman deliberately seated herself in a chair beside the bell tower door.

"I'm parking here until Pete shows up," she announced. "Maybe you're on the square, Slippery, but I don't trust you."

"Thanks for your flattering opinion," the man responded mockingly. "You give me a pain, Sade. I do all the dangerous work, and what do I get? A measly ten per cent."

"Plus what you stick in your pocket when you're on a job," the woman shot back with rising anger. "You've been doing pretty well for yourself, Slippery—you and Al. But the boys are getting wise. From now on it may not be so easy. Better play fair with the rest of us—or else."

"You always did have a wagging tongue," the man retorted. "Always trying to stir up trouble. Don't you realize we've got to work together or we'll be jailed separately? Our ranks must be united."

"Gettin' sort of jittery, ain't you?"

"Maybe you haven't been reading those editorials in the *Star*."

"Sure, I read them and get a big laugh. This guy Parker has to blow off steam. Nothing will come of it."

"The police have visited this place once already."

"And what did they find? Nothing."

"That's no guarantee they won't try again. I tell you this town is getting too hot for comfort."

"Figurin' on blowing?" the woman inquired, watching him shrewdly.

Slippery's laughter had an unpleasant edge. "You sure do get ideas, Sade. Don't start peddling that line of talk. Understand?"

"I hear."

Suddenly losing his temper, the man strode nearer, seizing her arm.

"Just start something and see where you wake up!" he said harshly. "One word to Pete or any of the boys and you won't do any more pretty fortune telling!"

The woman jerked her arm free, gazing at the man in sullen silence. Nor did she speak as he left the Temple, slamming the door behind him.

CHAPTER 19 - PENNY INVESTIGATES

Penny debated whether or not to follow Slippery. Deciding that she should try to keep him within sight, she abandoned her post beneath the window and ran to the front of the building.

Already the young man was far down the lane, walking rapidly. Before Penny could overtake him he hailed a taxi and drove away. By the time she obtained another cab, pursuit was futile.

"To the *Star* office," Penny ordered the driver.

Although Slippery had eluded her, she did not feel that her morning's work had been wasted. She believed that her father would be very much interested in a report of her findings.

"It's evident that Slippery is connected with Al Gepper and various mediums of the Celestial Temple," she reflected. "I am sure, too, that he's the one who broke into our house, but to prove it may not be so easy."

Penny had not fully understood the conversation which she had overheard between Slippery and Sade. That they distrusted each other was evident, but why had the woman feared Slippery might break into the bell tower during the guard's absence?

"Something of great value to the organization must be kept there," she reasoned. "But what can it be?"

Penny believed that her father would not delay in requesting police to search the bell tower of the Celestial Temple. However, a disappointment awaited her.

Upon arriving at the newspaper office DeWitt stopped her as she went past his desk.

"Don't go in there," he said, jerking his thumb toward Mr. Parker's private room.

"Why not?" asked Penny in surprise. "Is Dad having a conference?"

DeWitt nodded as he composed a two column headline. "With J. P. Henley."

"The *Star's* Sugar Daddy?"

"Our biggest advertiser. He's threatening to go over to the *Record*."

"Why, that's serious!"

"It is if he quits the *Star*. The old man—Mr. Parker—" DeWitt corrected hastily, "has been trying to soften him up for the past two hours. Whatever you do, don't bust in there now."

"I won't, Mr. DeWitt, but I did wish to see Dad."

"Anything I can do for you?"

Penny hesitated. "Well, I wanted to talk to him about something I learned today at the Celestial Temple."

"Oh, yes," nodded the city editor, his attention on a sheet of copy. "Mr. Parker is handling the campaign personally. Sorry I can't be of service."

Rather startled by DeWitt's unusual politeness, Penny glanced hopefully toward Jerry Livingston's desk. It was littered with papers, but quite deserted.

With a sigh she left the building and walked to Dorr Street where she had left her maroon car. Upon reaching home she found that Mrs. Weems was not there and she had forgotten her own key. For a time she sat disconsolately on the front porch. Then she decided to go to the Hudell Garage where Leaping Lena had been left for repairs three days earlier.

The car was ready, and with it a bill for eight dollars and forty-two cents.

"I'll have to give you a dollar on account and pay the remainder next week," said Penny. "Or would you rather keep the car as a deposit?"

"Give me the dollar," said the garage man hastily.

CHAPTER 19 - PENNY INVESTIGATES

Penny became even more depressed as she drove the automobile home. Not for the world would she openly admit that she had made a mistake in repurchasing Lena. Secretly she acknowledged that two cars were an unbearable financial drain upon slender resources.

Turning into her own street, Penny saw Mrs. Weems walking toward home, and stopped for her.

"I've just come from the Hodges'," the housekeeper commented, climbing into the car.

"You have?" inquired Penny eagerly. "Did you learn anything?"

"No, I didn't. Mr. Gepper seemed very unwilling to conduct another séance. He acted so different this time—almost as if he bore me a personal grudge."

"He's probably provoked because your inheritance eluded him."

"He did tell Mrs. Hodges that he doubted I had any money," Mrs. Weems responded.

"What happened at the séance?"

"Why, nothing. The table moved and we heard a few raps. That was all."

"No message from Cousin David?"

"Not a word or a sign. Mr. Gepper seemed very indifferent about it all. He said he couldn't give me another appointment unless I paid for it."

"What do you think about him now?" Penny asked curiously. "Don't you agree with Dad and me that he was after your money?"

"Yes, I was very silly," the housekeeper acknowledged. "Mrs. Hodges has begun to lose faith in him, too. She says he's been bringing all sorts of folks to her place. When she told him she didn't care to have the house over-run with strangers, he became very unpleasant."

"You mean he threatened her?"

"In a mild way. He told her that he would stay as long as he pleased and she could do nothing about it. Mrs. Hodges is afraid to go to the police for fear she'll be arrested with Mr. Gepper."

"I wonder if he ever has charged for his séances?" Penny said thoughtfully.

"I am sure he has, Penny. Of course I have no proof."

"Mrs. Weems, you must go there again this afternoon," Penny urged. "Insist upon another séance, and pay him for it! Then you'll be able to testify as a witness against him!"

"But I don't wish to go into court," the housekeeper protested. "Besides, Mr. Gepper won't be at the cottage this afternoon."

"Where is he going?" Penny questioned alertly.

"I don't know. I heard him tell Mrs. Hodges he would be gone this afternoon, but would return for an eight o'clock séance."

"Why, that's fine—wonderful!" chuckled Penny.

Mrs. Weems gazed at the girl with sudden suspicion. "Now what have you thought up?" she demanded.

"Nothing alarming," grinned Penny. "I merely plan to visit Mr. Gepper's studio during his absence. Who knows, I may yet master a few of the finer points of ghost-making!"

CHAPTER 20 - INSIDE THE CABINET

Despite Mrs. Weems' protests, Penny remained firm in her decision to investigate Mr. Gepper's studio. She ate a belatedly prepared lunch and did not reach the Hodges' cottage until nearly four o'clock, having driven there in Lena.

The doors were closed and Penny knocked several times without receiving a response.

"Everyone must have gone away," she thought. "Oh, dear, now what shall I do?"

Penny reasoned that it was of vital importance for her to inspect Al Gepper's room during his absence. She might never have another opportunity. Yet she hesitated to enter the house while the Hodges were away, even though she felt certain the seamstress would not mind.

Walking to the rear, Penny noticed that the porch screen had been left unfastened. Entering the kitchen, she called Mrs. Hodges' name but received no answer.

"If I wait for her to come home it may be too late," decided Penny. "This is an emergency."

Her mind made up, she took the stairs two at a time to Al Gepper's room. Her knock went unanswered. Satisfied that he was not there, she tried the door and found it unlocked.

Penny raised a blind to flood light into the darkened room. Save that a film of dust covered the furniture, everything was approximately the same as she had last seen it.

Her gaze fell upon two suitcases which had been pushed beneath the bed. The first contained only miscellaneous clothing. The second merited a more careful inspection.

Almost at once Penny came upon an old faded picture, the one of Cousin David which Mrs. Weems had given to the photographer's "agent."

"So that was how it was done!" she thought. "Al Gepper sent one of his confederates to see Mrs. Weems and obtain information about her cousin. The painting which appeared so miraculously during the séance was merely a copy of this! Even so, how was it painted so quickly?"

Forgetting the picture for a moment, Penny picked up several newspaper clippings which were fastened together with a rubber band. All had been taken from the obituary column and concerned the death of well-to-do Riverview persons.

"Al Gepper and his pals are ghouls!" Penny told herself. "They prey upon the relatives of persons who have died, realizing that at such a time it will be much easier to interest them in trying to communicate with the departed!"

Lifting a tray from the suitcase, her attention focused upon a small red booklet. As she turned rapidly through it, a folded sheet of paper fell to the floor.

Examining it, Penny saw a long list of names, together with pertinent information about each person. Not only was the address and financial standing of the individual given, but the deceased relatives in each family and other facts of a personal nature. The list had been mimeographed.

"This must be a 'sucker' list!" thought Penny. "No wonder it's easy for a medium to find victims and tell them astonishing facts."

Thrusting the paper into her pocket, she turned her attention to the wardrobe closet. Al Gepper's clothes hung in orderly rows from the hangers. Behind them, half hidden from view, was a small box.

Pulling it to the window, Penny examined the contents. There were many bottles filled with chemicals, the names of which were unfamiliar. She noted a bottle of varnish, another of zinc white, and some photographic paper in a sealed envelope.

CHAPTER 20 - INSIDE THE CABINET

A glance satisfying her, she replaced the box and next turned her attention to the cabinet behind the large circular table. Here she was richly rewarded as her gaze fell upon a banjo.

"The same one which played during Mrs. Weems' séance!" she thought. "We were able to see it in the dark because it's covered with luminous paint. But what made it rise into the air, and how could it play without the aid of human hands?"

Penny examined the instrument closely. She chuckled as she discovered a tiny phonograph with a record built into its back side. As she pressed a control lever, it began a stringed version of "Down Upon the Swanee River."

Quickly turning it off, she inspected other objects in the cabinet. At once she found a rod which could be extended to a height of five feet.

"That's how the banjo was raised!" she reasoned. "And by use of this rod it would be easy to make a ghost appear to float high overhead. This luminous material must have been used."

Penny picked up a filmy robe, shaking out the many folds. While it was clear to her that Al Gepper had employed the garment to materialize the so-called spirit of Cousin David, she could only guess how he had made it enlarge from a mere spot to a full sized figure.

"He must have wadded the cloth in his hand, and held it above his head," she mused. "Then he could have slowly shaken it out until it covered his entire body. Thus the figure would appear to grow in size."

In one corner of the cabinet Penny came upon a luminous slate.

"This was used for Cousin David's message," she thought. "Al probably had an assistant who wrote on it and thrust it through the curtain."

While many questions remained unanswered, Penny had obtained sufficient evidence to indicate that Al Gepper was only a clever trickster. Greatly elated, she decided to hasten to the *Star* office to report her findings.

Noticing that she had neglected to return the two suitcases to their former places, Penny pushed them under the bed again. As she straightened, a door slammed on the lower floor.

For an instant she hoped that it was Mrs. Hodges or her husband who had come home. Then she heard footsteps on the stairs, and their rapidity warned her that they could belong only to a young person.

Frantically, she gazed about the room. The cabinet seemed to offer the safest hiding place. Slipping into it, she pulled the black curtain across the opening.

CHAPTER 21 - STARTLING INFORMATION

Scarcely had Penny hidden herself when Al Gepper entered the room. With him was the hook-nosed young man known as Slippery.

"I tell you, Al," the latter was saying, "this town is getting too hot for comfort. We've got to blow."

"It was that Parker girl who queered everything," muttered Gepper. "How could I know that her father was a newspaper publisher? He's stirred up folks with his editorials."

"You never should have let her in here. We had a swell set-up, but now we can expect a raid any day."

"I tell you I thought she was just a smart-aleck kid, a friend of the Hodges'. Didn't learn until yesterday who she was."

"We've got to blow, Al. Sade's threatening to make trouble, too. She thinks we're holding out on the others."

"We have picked up a little extra coin now and then."

"Sure, Al, but we've always been the brains of the outfit. We take most of the risk, plan all the big jobs, so why shouldn't we have more?"

"It's time we cut loose from 'em, Slippery."

"Now you're talking! But we can't pull out until the Henley job comes off. I've had a tip that the house is likely to be deserted tonight. Let's make the haul and then skip."

"Okay," agreed Gepper. "I have some suckers coming for a séance at eight. I'll get rid of them in quick time, and be waiting. So long, Slippery."

A door slammed, telling Penny that the hook-nosed man had left. She was somewhat stunned by what she had overheard, believing that the Henley who had been mentioned must be her father's chief advertiser.

Nervously she waited inside the cabinet, wishing that she might take her information to the police. To her intense annoyance, Al Gepper did not leave the room even for a moment.

Instead he threw himself on the bed and read a tabloid newspaper. After an hour, he arose and began to prepare his supper on an electric grill.

Penny shifted from one position to another, growing more impatient. Every time the man came toward the cabinet her heart beat a trifle faster. She was quite sure the Hodges had not yet returned home, and should Al Gepper discover her, he would not treat her kindly.

The medium finished his supper and stacked the dishes in the closet without washing them. Then he started to get ready for the night's séance.

Peeping from between the cracks of the curtain, Penny saw him seat himself before the easel. With painstaking care he painted a picture of a woman, using a photograph as a model. After a coating of varnish had been applied, he allowed it to dry and afterwards covered the entire picture with zinc white. The original painting was entirely hidden.

Penny knew that hours had elapsed. The room gradually darkened, and Al Gepper turned on the lights.

"Oh, dear, I must get out of here soon!" the girl thought desperately. "But if I make a break for it he'll be sure to see me. That will ruin all my plans."

Eight o'clock came. Al Gepper put on his coat, combed his hair and was alertly waiting when the doorbell rang. However, instead of descending the stairs he shouted an invitation for the visitors to come up.

Two women in their early forties were ushered into the séance chamber, to be followed almost immediately by an elderly man.

CHAPTER 21 - STARTLING INFORMATION

"We will start at once if you please," said Al Gepper brusquely. "I have another engagement tonight. However, before the séance is undertaken I must ask that each of you pay the required fee, five dollars."

The money was paid, and the three persons seated themselves at the table. Gepper switched off the lights.

The séance began in much the same manner as the one Penny had attended. The medium called upon the spirit of a woman named Flora to appear.

"Now concentrate hard—everyone," he instructed. "Flora, where are you? Can you not show yourself that we may know it is truly your spirit which communicates with us?"

From the cabinet, so close to Al Gepper that she could have touched his hand, Penny was able to see his every move. Yet so swift was his next action, that she barely discerned it.

Taking a wet sponge from his pocket he wiped it across the painting previously prepared. The picture immediately became visible to the audience as Gepper focused his flashlight on the canvas.

"That wasn't the way he made Mrs. Weems' picture appear," thought Penny. "The fellow must have a great repertoire of tricks!"

The séance had become so interesting that she no longer thought of escape. Nevertheless, she came to a sudden realization of her precarious position as she heard the medium say that he would next endeavor to persuade the Spirit of Flora to take actual shape. With a shock it dawned upon her that in another moment the man would enter the cabinet to make use of the luminous gauze robe and other paraphernalia.

Knowing that she could not hide from him, Penny decided upon a bold break for freedom. Dropping the ghostly robe over her face and shoulders, she pulled aside the dark curtain and flitted into the room.

Her dramatic entrance brought gasps of astonishment from the persons who sat at the circular table. The medium, as dumbfounded as his audience muttered: "What the dickens!" and pushed back his chair, his legs rasping on the floor.

Penny did not linger, but darted past the group and groped for the door. In the darkness she could not immediately find it. Her shining robe, on the other hand, made her an easy target for Al Gepper.

Angrily the medium strode across the room, seizing her arm. She jerked away, but he grasped a fold of the robe. It tore and was left behind.

At that critical instant, Penny's hand encountered the door. She swung it open, and bounded down the stairway.

In the séance chamber a light went on, then the hallway became brilliantly illuminated. But by that time the girl was in the dining room.

She could hear Al Gepper clattering down the steps, intent upon capturing her. Penny was determined that he should never learn her identity.

Letting herself out of the house by way of the kitchen door, she decided that if she attempted to cross the yard, the medium certainly would recognize her. The woodpile offered a hiding place and she crouched behind it.

Scarcely had she secreted herself, when Al Gepper ran into the yard. He glanced about carefully and circled the house twice.

Finally, convinced that the "ghost" had escaped he came back to the porch. His customers, greatly agitated by what had occurred, were demanding explanations.

"Someone played a prank," Gepper explained briefly. "It will be impossible to resume the séance for the spirits are offended. You will leave, please."

The customers departed and the medium locked himself in the house. He did not bother to lower the upstairs hall blind, and Penny caught occasional glimpses of him as he moved to and fro.

"He's packing to leave!" she observed. "Unless I act in double-quick time, he'll skip town! I must notify Dad and the police without an instant's delay!"

CHAPTER 22 - SCALING THE WALL

The nearest drugstore with a public telephone was two blocks away. Penny ran the distance, and slipping into the booth, she dialed the *Star* office. Informed by the building switchboard operator that neither her father nor DeWitt was available, she inquired for Jerry Livingston, and to her relief was connected with him.

"Listen, Jerry, this is Penny!" she began excitedly. "I haven't time to explain, but the lid is blowing off the fake spiritualist story! Rush the police out to the Hodges' cottage and demand Al Gepper's arrest! Send another squad or some private detectives to Mr. Henley's home."

"Henley!" Jerry exclaimed. "Say, have you gone loco?"

"I'm not making any mistakes," Penny replied tersely. "If you act quickly we may prevent a robbery. I'm on my way there now to warn Mr. Henley! Oh, yes, try to find Dad or DeWitt and warn them a big story is breaking!"

"Penny, what's this all about?" the reporter demanded. "I can't go to the police unless I know what I am doing."

"You must, Jerry. I have plenty of evidence against Gepper and his crowd, but unless you take the police to the Hodges' in the next fifteen minutes it will be too late!"

Without giving Jerry opportunity to delay her with other questions, Penny hung up the receiver. Hastening to the street, she gazed frantically about for a taxi. None was to be had.

"I'll get to the Henley place quicker in Lena than by waiting for a cab to come along," she thought.

The battered old car had been parked a short distance from the Hodges' cottage. Hurrying there, Penny jumped into the ancient vehicle and started the motor. As usual it made a loud clatter, but she did not suspect that the sound carried far up the street. Nor did she guess that Al Gepper stood at the darkened window of his room, watching her.

Penny drove as fast as she could to the Henley home in the southern section of Riverview. Lights blazed from the downstairs windows.

Abandoning her car in the driveway, she rang the doorbell. After a long wait, a maid appeared.

"Is Mr. Henley here?" Penny asked breathlessly. "Or Mrs. Henley? It's most important that I talk with them at once."

"Mrs. Henley has been at the seashore for a month," the maid replied in an agitated voice. "Mr. Henley is somewhere downtown. I've been trying to get him, but the telephone wire has been cut!"

"The house hasn't been robbed?"

"Mrs. Henley's jewelry has been taken! I don't know what else."

"When did it happen?" Penny asked.

"It must have been during the last half hour. I went to the corner store for a book of stamps. When I came back five minutes ago I discovered what had occurred. I ought to call the police, but I am afraid to do it until I've talked with my employer."

"The police already have been notified," said Penny. "They'll be here any minute."

"But how did you know—?" the maid began in astonishment.

Penny had turned away. She was convinced that the burglary had been committed by Slippery. Perhaps, by this time he had fled town, but she did not believe he would leave without his pal, Al Gepper.

Climbing into the car again, Penny debated. It was reasonable to suppose that, having accomplished the burglary, Slippery would return to the Hodges' cottage to meet the medium.

CHAPTER 22 - SCALING THE WALL

"If he does, the police should be on hand to seize him," she thought. "At least, he and Al will be held for questioning. But there's one place I forgot to cover—the Celestial Temple."

Like a flash came the recollection that Slippery had been deeply interested in something which was guarded in the bell tower. Was it not possible that he might return there before leaving Riverview?

Shifting gears, Penny turned the car and headed for Butternut Lane. Anxiously, she glanced at the gasoline gauge. It registered less than a gallon of fuel and she had used her last dime in the telephone booth.

"If I coast on all the downgrades I should just make it," she estimated.

In starting for the Celestial Temple Penny was acting upon a "hunch." However, it disturbed her that the Henley burglary had been accomplished, and she was afraid she might again be wasting precious time. Now that it was too late, she wondered if it would not have been wiser to remain at the Hodges' cottage until the police arrived.

"I only hope that end of the affair isn't bungled," she thought. "I'll never get over it if Al and Slippery both escape."

Penny had reached the entrance to Butternut Lane. Parking at the side of the road, she continued afoot toward the Celestial Temple.

From a distance the building appeared dark. However, as she drew closer she could distinguish a dim light. Inside the Temple, a stout man wearing a hat sat with his chair tilted against the door of the bell tower room.

"He must be the guard," thought Penny. "Probably the one they call Pete."

Suddenly she paused, retreating into a clump of elder bushes near the walk. From the direction of the cemetery a figure emerged. At first, all that Penny could distinguish was a man carrying a suitcase. As he drew closer, her pulse quickened. Unmistakably, it was Slippery.

Without passing the bushes where the girl had taken refuge, the man walked on toward the Temple. Presently he halted. Glancing carefully about to assure himself that he was unobserved, he shoved his suitcase into the tall weeds which lined the walk. Then he moved to one of the Temple windows, peering into the gloomy interior.

"Now what?" thought Penny, watching alertly. "This should prove interesting."

Slippery remained beneath the window a minute or two. Instead of entering the Temple, he presently returned to the high weeds, stooping to remove some object from his suitcase. Hiding it under his coat, he circled the building and approached the side adjoining the cemetery.

Thoroughly mystified, Penny cautiously followed, taking care that her body cast no shadow which would attract Slippery's attention.

The man seemed deeply engrossed in the task he had set for himself. From his coat he took a collapsible rod which he extended to the approximate length of a fish pole. To its end he attached a trailing silken ladder.

Deftly the man raised the ladder until two metal hooks bit into a projection of the bell tower. He tested the ropes to make certain they would bear his weight then, with the agility of a cat, mounted the silken rungs. Penny saw him disappear into the bell tower.

"Now why did he climb up there?" she asked herself. "He must be after something hidden in the belfry."

Penny knew that she was a long distance from police aid, but it was unthinkable that Slippery should be allowed to escape. Impulsively, she moved from her hiding place to the base of the tower.

Grasping the silken ladder, she gave it a quick jerk which dislodged the two iron hooks. Down it tumbled into her arms, leaving the man trapped in the turret.

"He'll never dare call for help when he discovers what has happened," reasoned Penny. "If he does, the guard, Pete, will have something to say!"

Rolling the ladder into a small bundle, she started across the clearing, intending to seek the nearest telephone. With no thought of lurking danger, she brushed past a clump of bushes. A hand reached out and grasped her arm.

Penny screamed in terror and tried to break free. The hand help her in a grip of steel.

As she struggled, her captor emerged from the shelter of leaves. It was Al Gepper.

"I thought I might find you here, my little one," he said grimly. "You have had your fun. Now you must pay, and the entertainment shall be mine!"

CHAPTER 23 - A PRISONER IN THE BELFRY

Penny tried to scream, only to have Al Gepper clamp his hand over her mouth.

"None of that!" he said harshly. "Behave yourself or you'll get rough treatment."

Inside the Temple, lights suddenly were turned on, for the brief struggle had been heard by Pete. The squat, stupid-faced man appeared in the doorway of the building, peering down the lane.

"Who's there?" he demanded suspiciously.

Al Gepper uttered an angry word beneath his breath. It was not to his liking that Pete should be drawn into the affair. However, he could not avoid detection.

"It's Al!" he called softly. "This girl broke up my séance tonight, and I trailed her here. She was prowling around the bell tower."

As he spoke, he dragged Penny toward the Temple entrance. His words convinced her that he had not observed her remove the silken ladder from the belfry wall, nor was he aware that Slippery was a prisoner in the tower.

"Let's have a look at her," said Pete. He flashed a light directly into Penny's face.

"She's the Parker girl—daughter of the publisher," informed Al.

"Yeah," commented Pete. "I saw her at one of our meetings. Another girl was with her. How much has she learned?"

"Enough to get us all run out of town. The question is, what shall we do with her?"

"Bring her inside, and we'll talk it over," said Pete. "Maybe we ought to call a meeting."

"No," replied Al Gepper impatiently, shoving Penny through the doorway. "We can take care of this ourselves."

The door was locked from the inside. Al pushed Penny into a chair on the front platform.

"Now sit there," he ordered. "One peep out of you and we'll tie you up and tape your mouth. Understand?"

"*Oui, oui, Monsieur*," said Penny, mockingly.

The two men stepped a few paces away and began to whisper together. Pete seemed to protest at Al's proposals.

Penny watched them uneasily, speculating upon their final decision. Whatever it was, she would never be given an opportunity to report to the police until it was too late to apprehend members of the Temple.

"I was stupid not to realize that Gepper might trail me," she told herself. "If only I had used an ounce of caution, I might have brought about the capture of the entire gang. Not to mention a grand scoop for Dad's paper."

Penny slumped lower in her chair. Her own predicament concerned her far less than the knowledge that she had bungled a golden opportunity.

Speculatively, her gaze shifted toward the bell tower room. The door was closed and she believed that it must be locked. There was no sound from the belfry, adding to her conviction that the man imprisoned there was fearful of attracting attention to his plight.

Al Gepper and Pete came toward her. With no explanation, the medium seized her arm and ordered her to walk toward the exit.

"Where are you taking me?" Penny asked.

"Never mind. You'll find out in good time."

"Wait!" exclaimed Penny, bracing her legs and refusing to be pushed. "If you'll let me go, I'll tell you something very much worth your while."

CHAPTER 23 - A PRISONER IN THE BELFRY

Deliberately, she allowed the silken ladder to slip from beneath her coat. The men would not have heeded her words, but the familiar object served its purpose.

"Where did you get that ladder?" demanded Al Gepper.

"So you would like to know what became of your friend, Slippery?" responded Penny evenly. "You'll be surprised when I tell you that he has double-crossed you both!"

"You're lying," accused Gepper.

Penny shrugged and did not speak.

"What were you going to say?" Gepper prodded in a moment. "Out with it! How did you get Slippery's ladder?"

"It fell into my hands, literally and figuratively."

"Stalling for time will get you nowhere," snapped Gepper, losing patience. "If you know anything about Slippery spill it fast or you'll not have another chance."

"Your friend tried to double-cross you," declared Penny. She decided to make a shrewd guess. "Tonight, after he robbed the Henley home he came here intending to loot the bell tower."

"Why, the dirty sneak!" exclaimed Pete.

"Weren't you here on guard all evening?" Gepper demanded, turning to him.

"Sure, I was. I never set foot outside the building."

"Slippery wasn't here?"

"Haven't seen him since yesterday morning."

"Then the girl is lying!"

"Oh, no, the girl isn't," refuted Penny. "If you care for proof you'll find it in the tower."

"Proof?"

"I mean Slippery. He's hiding in the belfry now, hoping you'll not discover him there. You see, he scaled the wall by means of this silk ladder. I removed the ladder, and I assume he's still up there."

"Why, the low-down skunk!" Pete exclaimed wrathfully. "So he planned to rob us! I'll get him!"

Leaving Al to watch Penny, the guard ran to the tower room door and unlocked it. Stealthily he crept up the iron stairway which led to the belfry.

Suddenly those below heard a cry of rage, followed by the sound of scuffling. Al Gepper listened tensely, yet made no move to join the fight. He remained standing between Penny and the outside door.

"You were right," he admitted in a stunned voice. "Slippery's up there. He meant to get all the swag for himself."

The fight increased in intensity as the two men struggled on the belfry steps. Over and over they rolled, first one delivering a hard blow, and then the other. Still locked, they finally toppled to the floor, but even then Al Gepper remained a bystander.

Penny was less concerned with the fight than with thoughts of escape. She had hoped that Al, too, would join the battle. Apparently, he was taking no chance of letting her get away.

She considered attempting a sudden break for freedom, but immediately abandoned it. The outside door had been locked by Pete. Before she could turn the key, Al would be upon her. As for the windows, none were open. While they might not be locked, it was out of the question to reach one quickly enough.

Penny's gaze roved to the tower room once more, and the struggling men. High above their heads she saw something which previously had not drawn her attention. It was a loop of rope, hanging from the belfry.

"Why, that must be attached to the old church bell!" thought Penny. "If only I could reach it, I might be able to bring help here."

However, the rope dangled high overhead. Even if she were able to reach the room leading to the tower, there was nothing upon which she could stand to grasp the loop. Obviously the rope had been cut short years before to prevent anyone from ringing the bell.

Penny glanced toward Al Gepper. The medium's gaze was upon the two struggling men, not her. A golden opportunity presented itself, if only she had the wits to make use of it.

Almost at the girl's feet lay the tangle of silken ladder. As she stared at it, a sudden idea took possession of her. The iron hooks would serve her purpose, but dared she try it? If she failed—and the chances were against her—punishment would be certain.

Yet, if she did nothing and merely waited, it was likely that Al Gepper and his pals never would be brought to justice. She must take the chance, no matter how great the personal risk.

For a moment Penny remained inactive, planning what she must do. If she made a single mistake, fumbled at the critical instant, everything would be lost. Above all, her aim must be accurate. If she missed the loop—

Slippery and Pete were beginning to tire, their blows becoming futile and ineffective. Further delay in executing her plan only increased the danger. She must act now or never.

Her mind made up, Penny no longer hesitated. With a quick movement she seized the silken ladder and darted to the doorway of the bell tower.

"Hey!" shouted Al Gepper, starting after her.

Penny slammed the door in his face. Taking careful aim, she hurled the silken ladder upward. One of the iron hooks caught in the loop of the rope. She jerked on it, and to her joy, the bell began to ring.

CHAPTER 24 - THE WOODEN BOX

Penny pulled the rope again and again, causing the huge bell to sway back and forth violently. It rang many times before Al Gepper succeeded in opening the tower room door.

His face was crimson with fury when he seized the girl, hurling her away from the rope. With one quick toss he released the hooks of the silken ladder, stuffing the soft strands beneath his coat. The bell made a final clang and became silent.

Penny retreated against the wall, anticipating severe punishment for her act. However, Al and his companions were more concerned with thoughts of escape than with her.

"We've got to get out of here," muttered Al. "Come on!"

The two men on the floor had ceased their struggles. Painfully they regained their feet. In this sudden emergency they had forgotten their differences.

"What shall we do about the box in the tower?" Pete demanded, nursing a swollen eye.

"Leave it here," returned Al. "We can't save anything now. The police are apt to swoop down on us any minute."

Turning, he fled to the street. Pete and Slippery hesitated, then followed. Penny heard a key turn in the lock. Even before she tested the door she knew she had been imprisoned in the tower room.

"They've escaped after all," she thought dismally. "But I may have saved some of the loot. I'll take a look."

Quickly she climbed the iron stairs to the belfry. From the turret she obtained a perfect view of the entire Lane. Al Gepper was running down the street, while Pete and Slippery had turned toward the cemetery.

There were no other persons in the vicinity, Penny thought at first glance. Then her heart leaped as she saw three men entering the Lane at its junction with the main street. They, too, were running.

"They must have heard the bell!" she told herself. "Oh, if only I can make them understand what has happened!"

Her best means of attracting attention was by ringing the bell. She pushed against it and was rewarded by a deafening clang.

The men stopped short, staring toward the belfry. Penny cupped her hands and shouted. Her words did not carry plainly, but the newcomers seemed to gain an inkling of what was amiss, for they wheeled and began to pursue the two who had taken refuge in the cemetery.

From her high perch, Penny saw Al Gepper nearing the end of the Lane, unobserved by all save herself. Tapping the bell again, she called:

"Get him, too! At the end of the street!"

One of the pursuers halted, turning toward the tower. In the moonlight Penny saw his face and recognized Jerry Livingston. He was close enough now to hear her voice.

"It's Al Gepper!" she shouted. "Don't let him escape!"

The reporter turned, but as he started off in the new direction, both he and Penny saw the fleeing man climbing into Leaping Lena. With a grinding of gears, he drove away. Jerry stopped, thinking that he never could overtake the car.

"Keep after him, Jerry!" encouraged Penny. "The gas tank is almost empty. He can't possibly go more than three or four blocks!"

As the reporter again took up the chase, she began tolling the bell once more, determined to arouse everyone within a mile of the Temple.

CLUE OF THE SILKEN LADDER

Her energy was rewarded, for in another minute she heard the familiar wail of a siren. A police cruiser swerved alongside the tower, stopping with a lurch.

"What's the idea of ringing that bell?" demanded an officer, leaping to the ground.

Tersely Penny explained the situation. The two policemen took a short-cut through a vacant lot, circling the cemetery. Darkness swallowed them, but presently there came a muffled command to halt, followed by a revolver shot.

So excited was Penny that she nearly tumbled from the bell tower. Recovering her balance, she sat on the stone ledge, trying to remain calm. Her nerves were jumpy and on edge.

"If only Jerry captures Al Gepper—that's all I ask!" she breathed.

As the minutes elapsed, it occurred to her that she had not yet searched for the loot which she believed to be hidden in the belfry. With questing fingers she groped beneath the ledge. For a short distance she felt nothing. Then she encountered a long wooden box.

Before she could open it, she heard shouts from the direction of the cemetery. Four men, two of them police officers, were marching Slippery and Pete toward the Temple. As they came nearer she received another pleasant surprise. The two who had aided in the capture were her father and Salt Sommers, a photographer for the *Star*.

"Dad!" shouted Penny. "Can you get me down from this pigeon roost?"

Mr. Parker, separating from the others, came to the foot of the bell tower.

"So it was you who sounded the alarm!" he exclaimed. "I might have known! How did you get up there?"

"I'm locked in. Dad, send the police to help Jerry. He's after Al Gepper who rode off in my car."

The police cruiser was dispatched, leaving one officer to guard the two prisoners. Mr. Parker unlocked the door of the tower room, releasing his daughter.

"You're all right?" he asked anxiously.

"Of course. Here's a little present for you." Penny thrust the wooden box into his hands.

"What's this?"

"I don't know yet. I found it hidden in the belfry."

"Penny, if you fell into a river you would come up with a chest of gold!" exclaimed the publisher admiringly.

"Open it quick, Dad."

Mr. Parker required no urging. The box was locked but he pried off the cover hinges, exposing the contents.

"A real treasure!" exclaimed Penny.

The box contained several bracelets, one of them set with rubies and diamonds, countless rings, four watches, and several strings of matched pearls.

"Stolen loot!" ejaculated the publisher.

"And what a collection!" chuckled Penny as she examined the separate pieces. "There's enough plunder here to start a jewelry store."

"Likewise sufficient evidence to put this Celestial Temple gang out of circulation for a long, long time," added her father.

"I learned a lot tonight, Dad. Wait until I tell you!"

"A scoop for the *Star*?"

"You'll be able to use your largest, blackest headlines."

Penny began to tell her story, interrupting only when Slippery and Pete were brought into the building handcuffed together. Starting again, she made her charges, accusing Slippery not only of having committed the Henley burglary, but also of having robbed the Kohls and many prominent Riverview families.

After inspecting the jewelry found in the wooden box, one of the police officers definitely identified several of the pieces as stolen goods. He expressed an opinion that the jewelry had been hidden in the belfry because it was too "hot" to be disposed of by fences.

"The organization members had an agreement by which all shared in the loot," added Penny. "That caused trouble. Al Gepper and Slippery thought they were taking most of the risk without sufficient return. So they pulled a few extra jobs of their own."

Before she could reveal more, the police car was heard outside the Temple. From the window Penny saw that Jerry and the policeman were returning with Al Gepper who had been handcuffed.

CHAPTER 24 - THE WOODEN BOX

"They've caught him!" she cried jubilantly.

The prisoner was brought into the Temple to be identified. He had been captured when Leaping Lena had stalled for lack of gasoline.

As Gepper was searched, the silken ladder, and various small objects were removed from his coat. Penny noticed two tiny rubber suction cups no larger than dimes, and immediately made up her mind that later she would try to obtain them. She was quite certain she knew their purpose.

Penny told her story and learned, in turn, that after she had telephoned Jerry, he had traced her father, and with the police both had hastened to the Hodges' cottage. Arriving there, they discovered that Gepper had fled. Jerry, Mr. Parker, and Salt Sommers had immediately proceeded to the Celestial Temple.

"It was lucky you rang that bell, Penny," chuckled Jerry. "If you hadn't, we never would have arrived here in time."

"It was lucky, too, that Mr. Gepper tried to escape in Lena," she laughed. "I guess my old rattle-trap has redeemed itself."

One of the officers picked up the silken ladder, examining it with critical interest. He agreed that it had undoubtedly been used in many mysterious burglaries committed during the past month.

"It's obvious that Slippery approached the houses on the 'blind' side, and scaled the wall after hooking his ladder into a window ledge," Penny remarked. "I suppose he reasoned that second-story windows nearly always are left unlocked. But how did he learn the houses were deserted? By telephoning?"

"That would be my opinion," nodded the policeman. "If someone answered, he could hang up. Otherwise, he would be fairly sure the house was empty."

"One night at the theatre I saw a man who resembled Slippery noting down the license number of the Kohl car. But the house was robbed within a few hours after that. How could he have obtained the name and address?"

"Easily. There are 'information fences' who supply such data to fellow members of the underworld. It is also possible that Slippery previously had watched the Kohl house, obtained the car license number, and then watched for it later at the theatre."

Jerry already had supplied police with the name of the fence whose establishment Slippery had visited earlier in the day. Later, a raid staged there brought to light much loot taken from various Riverview homes.

However, for the moment, police were most interested in gaining complete information which could be used in rounding up all members of the Celestial Temple Society who had not fled the city.

Searching Slippery they found, not only jewelry stolen from the Henley residence, but a booklet containing many names and telephone numbers.

"Sadie Beardsell," Penny read. "She's one of the members, I am sure."

Lest Mr. and Mrs. Hodges might also be arrested, she explained that the old couple had been an innocent dupe of Al Gepper. Turning to the medium she said:

"I think I know how you accomplished most of your tricks. Of course, you were the one who sent Mrs. Hodges a letter with six dollars. Undoubtedly, you had it mailed by an accomplice from New York at exactly the hour you specified. Then at that same hour you slipped up to the Hodges' cottage, and rapped six times on the bedroom wall."

"You seem to have everything figured out," Al Gepper responded sarcastically. "Clever girl!"

"I saw how you made the spirit painting tonight at the séance," resumed Penny. "May I ask if that same method was used in regard to Mrs. Weem's picture of Cousin David?"

She did not dream that the medium would answer her question. With a shrug which implied that the entire matter was very boring, he replied:

"No, the picture was painted with a solution of sulphocyanid of potassium and other chemicals, invisible until brought out with a re-agent. During the séance, an assistant sprayed the back of the canvas with an atomizer, bringing out the colors one by one."

"And how was the paint made to appear wet?"

"Poppy oil."

"One more question, Mr. Gepper. I never could understand how you were able to raise the kitchen table at Mrs. Hodges' cottage."

"No?" Al Gepper smiled mockingly. "I assure you I had nothing to do with that demonstration. It was a true spirit manifestation."

"I'll never believe that," declared Penny.

"Then figure it out for yourself," replied the medium. "You are such a very brilliant child."

Before the prisoners were led to the police car, Salt Sommers set up his camera and took a number of flashlight pictures for the *Star*.

"How about it, Mr. Parker?" inquired Jerry eagerly. "Are we putting out an extra?"

"We are," said the publisher crisply. "This is the big break I've been hoping we would get! We should beat the *Record* on the story by at least a half hour."

The three men hurriedly left the Celestial Temple, with Penny trailing behind them. At the main street intersection they finally obtained a taxicab.

"To the *Star* office," Mr. Parker ordered. "An extra dollar if you step on it."

"How about my pictures?" Salt Sommers asked, as the cab rocked around a corner. "They ought to be dandies."

"Rush them through as soon as we get to the office," Mr. Parker instructed. "If they're any good we'll run 'em on page one. Jerry, you handle the story—play it for all it's worth."

Jerry glanced at Penny who sat very still between her father and Salt. Their eyes met.

"Chief," he said, "there's a sort of fraternity among reporters—an unwritten rule that we never chisel on each other's work."

"What's that?" Mr. Parker asked, startled. "I don't get it."

Then his glance fell upon his daughter, and he smiled.

"Oh, so it's that way! You think Penny should write the story?"

"I do, Chief. It's hers from the ground floor up."

"Please, Dad, may I?" Penny pleaded.

The cab rolled up to the *Star* office, stopping with a jerk. Mr. Parker swung open the door, helping her alight.

"The story is yours, Penny," he said. "That is, if you can crack it out fast enough to make the extra."

"I'll do it or die in the attempt."

"Keep to the facts and write terse, simple English—" Mr. Parker began, but Penny did not wait to hear his instructions.

With a triumphant laugh, she ran ahead into the *Star* office. Her entry into the newsroom was both dramatic and noisy.

"Big scoop, Mr. DeWitt," she called cheerily. "Start the old print factory running full blast!"

Dropping into a chair behind the nearest typewriter, she began to write.

CHAPTER 25 - EXTRA!

Penny stood at the window of her father's office, listening to the newsboys crying their wares on the street.

"*Extra! Extra! Read all about it! Police Capture Three in Raid on Celestial Temple! Extra! Extra!*"

Mr. Parker rocked back in his swivel chair, smiling at his daughter.

"Your story was first-class, Penny," he said. "Thanks to you we scooped the *Record*. Tired?"

"I do feel rather washed out," Penny admitted. "Writing at high speed with a deadline jabbing you in the back is worse than facing a gang of crooks. But it was exciting."

"You turned in a good story," her father praised again. "In fact, you may as well take credit for breaking up that outfit of fake spiritualists."

"So far the police have only captured Al Gepper, Slippery and Pete. There's not much evidence against the others."

"True, but rest assured those who aren't rounded up will leave Riverview. The backbone of the organization has been smashed."

Penny sank wearily into a chair, picking up a copy of the *Star* which lay on her father's desk. Two-inch, black headlines proclaimed the capture, and opening from the banner was her own story tagged with a credit line: *by Penelope Parker*. Salt Sommer's photographs had made the front page, too, and there was a brief contribution by Jerry telling of Al Gepper's attempted flight in Leaping Lena.

"Dad, you must admit that it was a stroke of genius when I bought back that old car," remarked Penny. "Why, if it hadn't been for Lena, Al Gepper surely would have escaped."

"That and the fact you always run your cars on an empty tank," responded Mr. Parker. "I suppose you foresaw the future when you made your brilliant purchase?"

"Not exactly. It was just a feeling I had—the same sort of hunch which came to me when I found the silken ladder at Kano's Curio Shop. If I depended upon a mere brain to solve mysteries, why I'd be no better than the police."

"Your modesty overwhelms me," chuckled her father. "I'm thankful my other reporters aren't guided by their instincts. Otherwise I might have a scoop a day."

"There's one thing which annoys me," Penny said, frowning.

"And what is that?"

"Two of Al Gepper's tricks haven't been explained. How was he able to raise a table and read a message in a sealed envelope?"

"I was talking to the Chief of Police about that letter trick only this morning, Penny. Magicians often employ it. Wasn't the message written on a pad of paper before it was placed in the envelope?"

"Yes, it was."

"Then very likely Gepper read the message from the pad. He could have placed carbon paper beneath the second or third sheets. Possibly he resorted to a thin covering of paraffin wax which would be less noticeable."

"Now that I recall it, he did glance at the pad! How would you guess he lifted the table?"

"Were his hands held high above it, Penny?"

"Only an inch or two. However, he never touched the table. I was able to see that."

"Could he have used sharp, steel pins held between his fingers?"

"I doubt it. But I think I know what he may have used! Did you notice two small suction cups which were taken from his pockets by the police?"

"Well, no, I didn't, Penny."

"The longer I mull over it, the more I'm convinced he used them to raise the table. They could be held between the fingers and wouldn't be observed in a darkened room. Dad, if I can get those rubber cups from the police, I'll have some fun!"

The telephone rang. It was Mrs. Weems calling to ask if Penny were safe. Mr. Parker replied in the affirmative and handed the receiver to his daughter.

"Penny, I just read your story in the paper," the housekeeper scolded. "You never should have pitted yourself against those dangerous men! I declare, you need someone to watch you every minute."

"I need you," said Penny. "And so does Dad. Why not promise to stay with us instead of going away on a trip?"

"Of course, I'll remain," came Mrs. Weems' surprising answer. "I made up my mind to that two days ago. You and your father never could take care of yourselves."

"What will you do with your inheritance, Mrs. Weems?"

"I hope your father will invest it for me," replied the housekeeper meekly. "One thing I know. No medium will tell me what to do with it."

The hour was late. Penny felt relieved when her father locked his desk in preparation for leaving the office.

They walked through the newsroom, down the stairway to the street. A middle-aged man in a brown suit and derby hat alighted from a taxi, pausing as he saw them.

"Mr. Parker!" he called. "May I speak with you?"

The publisher turned, recognizing him. "Mr. Henley!" he exclaimed.

"I have just come from the police station," the advertiser said in an agitated voice. "I was told that your daughter is responsible for the capture of the men who robbed our home tonight."

"Yes, Penny managed to have a rather busy evening," smiled Mr. Parker. "I hope you suffered no loss."

"Everything was recovered, thanks to your daughter. Miss Parker, I realize I never can properly express my appreciation."

"I was sorry I couldn't prevent the burglary," replied Penny stiffly. "As it turned out, the capture of the crooks was mostly due to luck."

"You are too modest," protested Mr. Henley. "I've talked with the police, you know. I am truly grateful."

The man hesitated, evidently wishing to say more, yet scarcely knowing how to shape his words. Penny and her father started to move away.

"Oh, about that contract we were discussing today," the advertiser said quickly.

"Yes?" Mr. Parker paused.

"I've been thinking it over. I acted too hastily in deciding to cancel."

"Mr. Henley, please do not feel that you are under obligation," said the publisher quietly. "Even though Penny accidentally did you a favor—"

"It's not that," Mr. Henley interrupted. "The *Star* is a good paper."

"The best in Riverview," said Penny softly.

"Yes, it is!" Mr. Henley declared with sudden emphasis. "I tell you, Parker, I was irritated because of a trivial mistake in my firm's copy. I've cooled off now. Suppose we talk over the matter tomorrow at lunch."

"Very well," agreed Mr. Parker. "The Commodore Hotel at one."

Bowing to Penny, Mr. Henley retreated into a waiting taxi and drove away.

"How do you like that, Dad?" Penny inquired after a moment's silence.

"I like it," answered Mr. Parker. "The *Star* could have limped along without Mr. Henley. But the going would have been tough."

"He'll renew the old contract?"

"Oh, yes, and probably give us a better one. Stealing Mr. Henley's words, I am truly grateful."

Penny gazed at her father with twinkling eyes.

"Are those idle words, Dad? Or are you willing to back them in a material way?"

"I might," grinned Mr. Parker. "Present your bill."

"Well, Dad, I've discovered to my sorrow that I can't support two cars on my present allowance. I need a generous raise."

"You could get rid of Lena."

"Why, Dad! After her noble work tonight!"

CHAPTER 25 - EXTRA!

"No, I suppose not," sighed Mr. Parker. "You've earned an increase, and I may as well grant it."

"Retroactive to the time I started working on the story," added Penny. "I figure if you pay back allowance, I'll be solvent once more!"

"You drive a hard bargain," chuckled the publisher. "But I'll agree."

Arm in arm, they started on down the street. Rounding a corner of the *Star* building they abruptly paused before the plate-glass window to watch a long, unbroken sheet of white paper feed through the thundering press. Freshly inked newspapers, cut and folded, slid out one upon the other to be borne away for distribution.

"It's modern magic, isn't it, Dad?" Penny said reflectively as the great machine pounded in steady rhythm.

"Yes, Penny," her father agreed. "And for this edition, at least, you were the master magician!"

THE END

THE SECRET PACT

SUDDENLY PENNY'S EYES FELL UPON THE UPPERMOST LINE OF THE FRONT PAGE.

CHAPTER 1 - ABOARD THE GOODTIME

A blanket of fog, thick and damp, swirled about the decks of the excursion steamer, *Goodtime*, cautiously plying its course down the river. At intervals, above the steady throb of the ship's engines, a fog horn sounded its mournful warning to small craft.

"I hope we don't collide with another boat before we make the dock," remarked Louise Sidell who stood at the railing with her chum, Penelope Parker.

"That would be a perfect ending for an imperfect day," returned Penny, fitting her coat collar more snugly about her throat.

"An imperfect day! I call it a miserable one. Rain and fog! Rain and fog! It's made my hair as straight as the shortest distance between two points."

"Mine's as kinky as wool." Impatiently Penny brushed a ringlet of golden hair from her eyes. "Well, shall we go inside again?"

"No, I'd rather freeze than be a wallflower," the dark-eyed girl responded gloomily. "We haven't been asked to dance once this evening."

"That's because we came without our own crowd, Lou. Except for that couple yonder, we're practically the only persons aboard unattached to a group."

Penny jerked her head in the direction of a young man and girl who slowly paced the deck. Earlier in the evening their peculiar actions had attracted her attention. They kept strictly to themselves, avoiding the salon, the dining room, and all contact with other excursionists.

"I wonder who they are?" mused Louise, turning to stare. "The girl wears a veil as if she were afraid someone might recognize her."

"Yes, I noticed that, and whenever anyone goes near her, she lowers her head. I wish we could see her face."

"Let's wander over that way," proposed Louise.

Arm in arm, they sauntered toward the couple. The young man saw them coming. He touched his companion's arm and, turning their backs, they walked away.

"They did that to avoid meeting us!" Louise declared in an excited undertone. "Now why, I wonder?"

The couple had reached the end of the deck. As the young woman turned to glance over her shoulder, a sudden gust of wind caught her hat. Before she could save it, the head-gear was swept dangerously close to the railing.

Not giving the young man an opportunity to act, Penny darted forward. Rescuing the hat, she carried it to the couple.

"Thank you," the girl mumbled, keeping her head lowered. "Thank you very much."

Quickly she jammed the felt hat on her head and replaced the veil, but not before Penny had seen her face clearly. The young woman was unusually pretty with large brown eyes and a long, smoothly brushed black bob.

"This is certainly a miserable night," Penny remarked, hoping to start a conversation.

"Sure is," replied the young man with discouraging brevity.

He tipped his hat and steered his companion away from the girl.

Ruefully Penny returned to Louise who had been an interested spectator.

"Did you get a good look at the pair?" she asked eagerly.

"Yes, but I've never seen either of them before."

"They wouldn't talk?"

"No, and the girl lowered her veil as soon as she could."

"Perhaps she's a movie actress traveling in disguise."

"Aboard a river excursion boat? I'm afraid not, Lou."

"Then maybe she's a criminal trying to elude the police."

"I fear the mystery of her identity must remain forever unsolved," chuckled Penny. "We'll dock in another five minutes."

Through the fog could be seen a dim glow of lights along the Riverview wharf. The *Goodtime*, its whistle tooting repeated signals, was proceeding more slowly than ever. Sailors stood ready to make the vessel fast to the dock posts when she touched.

Passengers began to pour from the salon, and Penny and Louise joined the throng. Many persons pushed and jostled each other, trying to obtain a position close to the gangplank.

Suddenly a girl who stood not far from Penny gave an alarmed cry.

"My pocketbook! It's gone!"

Those near her expressed polite concern and assisted in searching the deck. The missing purse was not found. Before the captain could be notified, the gangplank was lowered, and the passengers began to disembark from the steamer.

The girl, whose pocketbook had been lost, remained by the railing, quite forgotten. Tears streamed down her cheeks.

"Excuse me," said Penny, addressing her, "is there anything I can do to help?"

Disconsolately, the girl shook her head. She made a most unattractive picture, for her blouse was wrinkled and her skirt was spotted with an ugly coffee stain. Beneath a brown, misshapen roll-brim hat hung a tangle of brown hair.

"Someone stole my pocketbook," she said listlessly. "I had twelve dollars in it, too."

"You're sure you didn't leave it anywhere?" Louise inquired.

"No, I had it in my hand only a minute ago. I think someone lifted it in the crowd."

"A pickpocket, no doubt," Penny agreed. "I've been told they frequent these river boats."

"Nearly everyone has left the steamer now, so I suppose it would do no good to notify the captain," commented Louise.

She and Penny started to turn away, then paused as they noticed that the girl remained in the same dejected posture.

"You have friends meeting you at the boat?" Penny inquired kindly.

"I haven't any friends—not in Riverview."

"None?" Penny asked in surprise. "Don't you live here?"

"No," answered the girl. "I've been working as a waitress at Flintville, up-river. The job played out last week. Today I took this boat, thinking I might find work in Riverview. Now I've lost my purse and I don't know what to do or where to go."

"Haven't you any money?" inquired Penny.

"Not a cent. I—I guess I'll have to sleep in the park tonight."

"No, you won't," declared Penny. Impulsively, she opened her own purse and, removing a five dollar bill, thrust it into the girl's hand. "This isn't much, but it may tide you over until you can find work."

"Oh, you're kind to help me. I'll pay you back just as soon as I get a job."

"Don't worry about that," replied Penny. "However, I should like to know your name."

"Tillie Fellows."

"Mine is Penelope Parker and my friend is Louise Sidell. Well, good luck in finding that job."

Edging away from Tillie who would have detained them indefinitely, the girls crossed the gangplank to shore.

"You were generous to give a stranger five dollars, Penny," commented Louise when they were beyond hearing.

"Oh, she needed it."

"Your allowance money, wasn't it?"

"Yes, but I couldn't allow the girl to go hungry or sleep in the park."

"No, I suppose not," replied Louise.

CHAPTER 1 - ABOARD THE GOODTIME

Penny paused, scanning the crowd on the dock. Her father, Anthony Parker, had promised to meet the excursion boat, but there was no sign of him or his car.

"Dad must have been detained at the newspaper office," she remarked. "I suppose we must wait here until he comes."

Removing themselves from the stream of traffic, the girls walked a short distance along the dock, halting beside a warehouse. The throng rapidly dispersed, and still Mr. Parker did not arrive.

"I hope we haven't missed him," Penny remarked anxiously. "In this fog one can't see many yards."

They had waited only a few minutes longer when Louise suddenly touched her chum's arm.

"Penny, there she is! Alone, too!"

"Who, Louise?"

"Why, that girl whose hat you recovered on the *Goodtime*. See her coming this way?"

Penny turned to stare at the young woman who was walking hurriedly along the dock. At first glance she was inclined to agree with Louise that it was the same girl, then she was uncertain. The one who approached wore an expensive fur and carried a distinctive beaded bag.

"I don't believe I ever saw her before," she commented.

"I guess I was mistaken," admitted Louise. "She's too well dressed."

Apparently the girl did not observe Penny and her chum, for she passed them without a glance. Hurriedly she walked a short distance down the wharf. Then, with a deft movement, she took a package from beneath her smart-fitting coat, and tossed it into the water.

Turning, she retraced her steps to the gangplank of the *Goodtime*. A moment later the girls saw her meet a young man in topcoat and derby who had emerged from the crowd on the dock. Entering a gray sedan, they drove away.

"I wonder what she threw into the river?" mused Penny. "Didn't you think she acted as if she were afraid someone would see her, Lou?"

"Yes, I did. Whatever it was, it's gone to the bottom of the river."

Curiously the girls walked to the edge of the dock. Penny glanced over the side and gave an excited cry. Instead of falling into the water, the package had caught fast on a jagged dock post.

"It's hanging by the string!" she exclaimed.

Eagerly Louise peered down. "You're right!" she agreed. "But we can't get it."

"I'm going to try."

"Please don't," pleaded Louise. "It's too far down. You'll tumble into the water."

"Not if you sit on my heels."

Undisturbed by what anyone who saw her might think, Penny stretched flat on the dock. With Louise holding to her, she jack-knifed over the edge, clutching at the bundle which dangled an inch above the water.

"Got it!" she chuckled. "Haul away, Lou."

Louise pulled her friend to safety. Eagerly they examined the package which was wrapped in ordinary newspaper.

"I'll venture it contains nothing more than the remains of a lunch," declared Louise. "This is going to be a good joke on you, Penny."

"A joke?" quavered Penny.

Her gaze had focused upon a hole in the paper. Through the opening protruded a long strand of dark hair.

Louise saw it at the same instant and uttered a choked, horrified scream.

"Human hair—" she gasped. "Oh, Penny! Turn it over to the police!"

"It can't be that," said Penny in a calmer voice.

With trembling fingers she untied the string. The paper fell away and several objects dropped at Penny's feet. Stooping, she picked up a girl's long black wig. In addition, there was a dark veil, a crushed felt hat, and a cheap cloth jacket.

"A disguise!" exclaimed Louise.

"Yes, the girl who tossed this bundle into the river was the same one we saw aboard the steamer! But why did she wear these things and then try to get rid of them?"

"Why, Penny, don't you understand?" Louise demanded impressively. "She was a crook just as I thought. And she must have been the one who robbed Tillie Fellows!"

CHAPTER 2 - THE RIVER'S VICTIM

Penny stared at the curious array of objects found in the discarded bundle. Unquestionably, they had been worn by the mysterious young woman observed aboard the *Goodtime*. However, she was not certain she agreed with Louise that the girl or her escort had robbed Tillie Fellows.

"I never heard of a professional pickpocket bothering with a disguise," she said doubtfully.

"Why else would the girl wear one?"

"I haven't an idea," admitted Penny. "Everything about it is queer. For instance, what became of her escort after the steamer docked? And who was that other young man in the gray car?"

"He appeared to be fairly well-to-do."

"Yes, he did. For that matter, the girl was elegantly dressed."

Louise kicked at the bundle with her foot. "What shall we do with these things? Toss them away?"

"Indeed, not!" Penny carefully rewrapped the wig, jacket, and other articles in the crumpled newspaper. "I shall take them home with me. One never knows what may develop."

Before Louise could inquire the meaning of her chum's remark, a taxi drew up nearby. The door swung open and out leaped a lean young man in a well-tailored blue suit and snap-brim hat.

"Why, it's Jerry Livingston!" exclaimed Penny, recognizing one of her father's reporters.

The young man saw the girls and came toward them. "Hello," he greeted cheerily. "Swell night for a murder."

"I hope you're not carrying concealed weapons," laughed Penny. "Where's Dad?"

"Delayed at the *Star* office. He sent me to meet the boat in his place. The fog made traffic slow. That's why I'm late."

Taking each of the girls by an elbow, he steered them to the waiting taxi.

"*Riverview Star*," he instructed the driver, and slammed the car door.

The fog was not so dense after the cab left the docks, but the entire river valley was blanketed, making it necessary for automobiles to proceed with headlights turned on.

"Have a nice time?" Jerry inquired as the cab crept along the waterfront streets.

"Not very," answered Penny, "but we ran into a little adventure."

"Trust you for that," chuckled the reporter. "City Editor DeWitt was telling the boys at the office that he'd bet you would come home dragging a mystery by its tail!"

"Here it is," Penny laughed, thrusting the newspaper bundle into his hands. "Lou and I did a little fishing from the dock and this is what we hooked."

While Jerry examined the contents of the strange package, the girls competed with each other in relating their experiences aboard the steamer. Although the reporter was deeply interested, he could offer no theory to explain why the young woman had discarded the bundle of clothing.

"Louise's guess seems as good as any," he commented. "The girl may have been the one who robbed Tillie Fellows."

"Pickpockets usually frequent crowds," said Penny. "During the entire trip both the girl and her escort kept strictly to themselves."

Jerry retied the bundle, tossing it into her lap.

"Your mystery is too much for me," he said lightly. "Afraid you'll have to solve it yourself."

Penny lapsed into meditative silence, yet oddly her thoughts centered upon nothing in particular. For a reason she never tried to explain, the waterfront seldom failed to cast its magical spell over her. She loved the

CHAPTER 2 - THE RIVER'S VICTIM

medley of sounds, deep-throated blasts of coal boats mingling with the staccato toots of the tugboats, the rumble and clank of bridges being raised and lowered.

Always Penny had felt an intimate connection with the river, for her home overlooked the Big Bear. Not many miles away flowed the Kobalt, so closely associated with Mud-Cat Joe and the Vanishing Houseboat. It was the Kobalt which very nearly had claimed Jerry's life, yet had brought the *Star* one of its greatest news stories.

Ever since she was a little girl, Penny had loved newspaper work. Her entire life seemed bound up with printer's ink and all that it connoted. She had learned to write well and Mrs. Weems, who had served as the Parker housekeeper for many years, predicted that one day the girl would become a celebrated journalist.

The taxi came to a sudden halt and with a start Penny emerged from her reverie. Jerry leaned forward to ask the driver why they had stopped.

"I can't see the road very well," the man replied. "And there's a bridge ahead."

As the car crept forward again, Penny peered from the window. Through the swirling gray mist the indistinct lights which marked the arching steel bridge were faintly visible. A pillar gradually emerged, and beside it the shadowy, slouching figure of a man. His burning cigarette made a pin point of light as he tossed it into the river.

Suddenly Penny's blood ran cold, for a second man appeared on the bridge. Stealthily he approached the one who gazed with such absorption into the inky waters. His purpose was shockingly clear to those who watched.

Penny screamed a warning; the taxi driver halted his cab, shouting huskily. Their cries came too late.

They saw the attacker leap upon his victim. There was a brief, intense struggle, then a body went hurtling from the bridge, fifty feet to the water below.

"You saw that?" cried Penny. "That man was pushed off the bridge! He'll drown!"

"We've got to save him," said Jerry.

As the cab came to a standstill, Jerry, the driver, and the two girls, sprang to the pavement. In the murky darkness the bridge appeared deserted, but they could hear the pounding footsteps of the attacker who sought to escape.

"Leave that guy to me!" exclaimed the cab driver. "I'll get him!"

Abandoning his taxi, he darted across the bridge in pursuit.

Jerry and the girls ran to the river bank. Below they could see a man struggling in the water and hear his choked cry for help.

Jerry kicked off his shoes.

"Wait!" commanded Penny. "You may not need to jump in after him. That boat will be there in a minute."

She indicated a tugboat which had passed beneath the bridge and was swerving toward the struggling man. As the young people anxiously watched, they saw it lay to while the captain fished the victim from the water with a boat-hook.

"Thank goodness for that," murmured Penny. "I hope the poor fellow is all right."

"And I hope our driver catches the man who did the pushing," declared Louise feelingly. "I never witnessed a more vicious attack in my entire life!"

As she spoke, the cabman recrossed the bridge, scrambling down to the river bank.

"The fellow got away," he reported. "He had a car waiting."

"You didn't see the license number?" Jerry inquired.

"Not a chance."

"Too bad."

Penny was watching the tugboat which had been tied up only a short distance from the bridge.

"Jerry, let's go down there," she proposed. "I want to be certain that man is all right."

The reporter hesitated, then consented. Leaving Louise with the cab driver, he and Penny descended the steep, muddy slope.

The boat had been made fast to a piling. Face downward on the long leather seat of the pilot-house, lay the rescued man. Working over him was the captain, a short, stocky man with grease-smeared hands and clothing saturated with coal dust.

"Anything we can do?" called Jerry from shore.

"Don't know yet if he'll need a doctor," answered the tugboat captain, barely glancing up. "It was a nasty fall."

Jerry leaped on deck, leaving Penny behind, for the space was too wide to be easily spanned.

Inside the cabin Captain Dubbins was expertly applying artificial resuscitation, but he paused as the man on the seat showed signs of reviving.

"Struck the water flat on his back," he commented briefly. "Lucky I saw him fall or I never could have fished him out. Not on a night like this."

"The fellow didn't fall," corrected Jerry. "He was pushed."

Captain Dubbins glanced up, meeting the reporter's gaze steadily. He offered no comment for the man on the seat groaned and rolled over.

"Steady," said the captain. "Take it easy. You'll tumble off the seat if you don't stay quiet."

"My back," mumbled the man.

In the glare of the swinging electric light his face was ghastly white and contorted with pain. Jerry judged him to be perhaps thirty-two. He wore tight-fitting blue trousers and a coarse flannel shirt.

"My back," he moaned again, pressing his hand to it.

"You took a hard wrench when you hit the water," commented the captain. "Here, let's see."

He unbuttoned the shirt, and rolling the man over, started to strip it off.

"No!" snarled the other with surprising spirit. "Leave me alone! Get away!"

Jerry stepped forward to assist the captain. Ignoring the man's feeble struggles, they pulled off his shirt.

Immediately they understood why he had tried to prevent its removal. Across his bruised, battered back had been tattooed in blue and black, the repulsive figure of an octopus.

CHAPTER 3 - THE OCTOPUS TATTOO

Jerry bent closer to examine the strange tattoo. Between the two foremost arms of the octopus was sketched a single word: ALL.

"'All,'" he read aloud. "What does that signify?"

His question angered the man on the couch. Snatching the shirt from Captain Dubbins, he made a feeble, ineffectual effort to get his arms into it.

"I want out o' here," he muttered. "Quit starin', you two, and give me a hand!"

"Take it easy," advised the tugboat captain soothingly. "We was just tryin' to see if your back was badly hurt."

"Sorry," the man muttered. Relaxing, he leaned weakly against the leather cushions. "I ain't myself."

"You swallowed a little water," remarked the captain.

"A little?" growled the other. "Half the river went down my gullet." As an afterthought he added: "Thanks for pullin' me out."

"You're welcome," responded the captain dryly. "Ex-sailor, aren't you?"

"Yeah. How did you know?"

"I can usually tell 'em. Out of work?"

"No." The man's curt answers made it clear that he resented questions.

"You haven't told us your name."

"John Munn," the man replied after a slight hesitation.

"We tried to catch the man who pushed you off the bridge," contributed Jerry. "He got away."

The sailor gazed steadily, almost defiantly at the reporter.

"No one pushed me off the bridge," he said. "I fell."

"You fell?" echoed Jerry. "Why, I thought I saw you and another man struggling—"

"You thought wrong," the sailor interrupted. "I was leaning over, lookin' into the water an' I lost my balance. That was how it happened."

"As you please, Mr. Munn," said Jerry with exaggerated politeness. "Oh, by the way, what's the significance of that octopus thing on your back?"

"Leave me alone, will you?" the sailor muttered. "Ain't a man got any right to privacy?"

"Better not bother him while he's feeling so low," said the tugboat captain significantly. "I'll get him into some dry clothes."

"Nothing I can do?"

"No, thanks, he'll be all right."

"Well, so long," Jerry said carelessly. With another curious glance directed at the sailor, he left the pilothouse, leaping from the deck to shore. Penny stood waiting.

"Jerry, what was the matter with that fellow?" she demanded in a whisper. "What did he have on his back? And why did he lie about being pushed off the bridge?"

"You heard us talking?"

"I couldn't help it. You were fairly shouting at each other for awhile."

"Mr. John Munn wasn't very grateful to the captain for being saved. He took offense when we tried to look at his back."

"I thought I heard you say something about an octopus. Was it a tattoo, Jerry?"

"Yes, and as strange a one as I've ever seen. The picture of an octopus. Between its forearms was the word: 'All.'"

"What could that mean?"

"I tried to learn, but Mr. John Munn wasn't in a talkative mood."

"It seems rather mysterious, doesn't it?"

"Oh, I don't know." Jerry took Penny's arm to aid her in making the steep climb. "Sailors have some funny ideas regarding self-decoration. This Munn was a peculiar fellow."

"It was odd that he would lie about being pushed off the bridge. Jerry, will you write it for the paper?"

"The story isn't worth more than a few lines, Penny. We can't say that Munn was pushed off the bridge."

"Why not? It's true."

"Munn would deny it, and then the *Star* would appear ridiculous."

"If I owned a paper, I certainly would use the story," declared Penny. "Why, it has wonderful possibilities."

"I fear your father never would agree. You talk him into printing the yarn and I'll be glad to write it."

"Oh, I suppose we must forget about it," Penny grumbled. "All the same, I'd like nothing better than to work on the story myself."

Reaching the pavement, they cleaned mud from their shoes before walking on to the waiting taxi. Louise immediately plied them with questions, displaying particular interest in the octopus tattoo.

"Do you suppose the man knew who pushed him off the bridge?" she inquired thoughtfully.

"I'll venture he did," replied Penny. "Probably that was the reason he wouldn't tell."

The taxi crossed the bridge and made slow progress away from the river. As the road gradually wound toward higher ground, the fog became lighter and the driver was able to make faster time. A clock chimed the hour of eleven.

"How about stopping somewhere for a bite to eat?" Jerry suddenly proposed.

"Won't Dad be waiting at the *Star* office?" Penny asked.

"He suggested that I keep you girls entertained until around eleven-thirty if I could."

"That being the case, we'll accept your invitation with alacrity," laughed Penny. "How about the Golden Pheasant?"

"Oh, no, you don't! Phillip's Bean Pot is nearer my speed."

A block farther down the street Jerry paid the driver and escorted the girls into a clean but low-priced restaurant.

"No item on the menu over ten cents," he chuckled. "Do your worst. I can take it."

Penny and Louise ordered sandwiches, while the reporter fortified himself with a plate of scrambled eggs, two doughnuts, and a cup of coffee. Returning to the front counter for a forgotten napkin, he nodded carelessly at an elderly man who sat alone, sipping a glass of orange juice.

The man acknowledged the greeting in an embarrassed way, quickly lowering his head. Within a few minutes he left the café.

"Jerry, who was he?" Penny inquired curiously. "I am sure I've seen him before, yet I can't remember where."

"That was old man Judson. Matthew Judson."

"Not the former publisher of the *Morning Press*!"

"Yes, the old man's been going to pieces fast since he closed his newspaper plant. Looks seedy, doesn't he?"

"His clothes were a bit shiny. I thought he seemed rather embarrassed because you spoke to him."

"Old Judson feels his come-down I guess. In the flush days he wouldn't be caught dead in a beanery."

"Is he really poor, Jerry?"

"Probably down to his last hundred thousand," the reporter grinned.

"What you say is conflicting," declared Penny impatiently. "First you imply that Mr. Judson is poor, and then that he's rich. I wish you would make up your mind."

"Frankly, I don't know. Judson owns a fine home on Drexell Boulevard which he's allowed to run down. I've been told he sold the *Morning Press* building several months ago. Some say he has plenty of cash salted away, others that he's broke."

"How did he lose so much of his money, Jerry?"

CHAPTER 3 - THE OCTOPUS TATTOO

"No one seems to know for certain. According to rumor he plays the stock market heavily."

"It's strange he closed down the *Morning Press*," Penny remarked thoughtfully. "I always thought it was a profitable paper."

"So did everyone else. The *Press* had a large circulation. But one bright Monday morning Judson posted a notice, closed the plant, and threw over a thousand employes out of work."

"That was nearly a year ago, wasn't it, Jerry?"

"Thirteen months to be exact. Why this sudden interest in Judson?"

"Oh, I don't know," Penny replied vaguely. "His case seems rather pathetic. Then, too, he reminds me of someone I've seen recently. I wish I could recall—"

Jerry glanced at the wall clock, swallowing his coffee with a gulp.

"Time to move along," he announced. "We mustn't keep your father waiting, Penny."

They left the café and Jerry hailed a passing taxicab.

"It's only four blocks to the *Star* building," protested Penny. "Aren't you being too lavish with your money, Jerry?"

"Oh, I'll add this item to my expense account," he laughed. "Jump in."

The taxi turned left at Adams street, rolling slowly through the downtown business section. Jerry peered from the car window at a large, four-story stone building which occupied a corner.

"That place sure looks like a morgue these days," he commented. "*The Morning Press.*"

Penny and Louise likewise twisted sideways to stare at the dark, deserted building. Windows were plastered with disfiguring posters and the white stone blocks, once so beautiful, were streaked with city grime.

"When the *Press* closed, machinery, furniture and everything else was left exactly as it stood," remarked Jerry. "Too bad an enterprising newspaper man doesn't take over the place before it's a complete loss. The present owner doesn't even employ a watchman to protect the property."

"It does seem a shame—" Penny began, only to break off. "Why, that's funny!"

"What is?" inquired Jerry.

Penny had turned to glance back at the *Morning Press* plant.

"The building isn't deserted!" she exclaimed. "There's a light in one of the upstairs rooms!"

CHAPTER 4 - A PROSPECTIVE TENANT

Jerry rolled down the window beside him and, thrusting his head through it, glanced back at the *Morning Press* building.

"Where do you see a light?" he demanded.

"It was on the third floor," declared Penny. "I can't see it myself now."

Jerry grinned as he settled back into his place between the two girls. "You certainly get a kick out of playing jokes," he accused.

"But it wasn't a joke, Jerry. Honestly, I saw a light. Didn't you, Louise?"

"Sorry, but I didn't. I'm afraid your imagination works overtime, Pet."

"I know what I saw," insisted Penny.

As Jerry and Louise smiled, she lapsed into injured silence. However, she was certain she had not been mistaken. Distinctly she had observed a light on the third floor, a moving light which had been extinguished before her companions had noticed it.

The car presently drew up at the curb in front of the *Star* building. Anthony Parker, a newspaper tucked beneath his arm, stepped from the vestibule where he had been waiting. He was a tall, slender man, alert and courageous in following his convictions. Under his management the *Riverview Star* had grown to be one of the most influential papers in the state.

"Hope we haven't kept you waiting, Mr. Parker," Jerry greeted him, swinging open the cab door.

"Only a minute or two. Thanks, Jerry, for bringing the girls from the boat. May we offer you a ride home?"

"No, thanks, Chief. I'll walk from here. Good evening."

Jerry tipped his hat politely to Penny and Louise as the cab drove away. Mr. Parker asked the girls if they had enjoyed their trip aboard the *Goodtime*.

"The boat wasn't very well named, I'm afraid," answered Penny. "The trip proved to be rather terrible but we met some interesting people."

During the drive to the Sidell home, she and Louise talked as fast as they could, telling Mr. Parker about Tillie Fellows, the mysterious young woman who had dropped a bundle of clothing into the water, and particularly the man with the strange octopus tattoo.

"You'll have to tell the rest of it, Penny," laughed Louise as she bade her chum good-bye. "Thanks for bringing me home."

The cab rolled on, and Penny glanced questioningly at her father.

"What do you think of the tattoo story?" she asked hopefully. "Won't it make a dandy feature for the *Star*?"

"I regret to say it sounds like first-grade fiction."

"Why, Dad! Louise and Jerry will confirm everything I've said."

"Oh, I don't doubt your word, Penny. I am sure everything occurred as you report. Nevertheless, were we to use the story our readers might question its veracity."

"Don't crush me with such big words, Dad."

"Veracity means truth, Penny. Now your story is very interesting, but I think you may have placed your own interpretation upon certain facts."

"For instance?"

"Well, according to John Munn's statement, he fell from the bridge and was not pushed."

"But I saw it with my own two eyes, Dad."

CHAPTER 4 - A PROSPECTIVE TENANT

"The night is foggy. You easily could have been mistaken. As for the octopus tattoo, what is so strange about it? Sailors compete in striving for startling decorative effects."

"Dad, you could rationalize the national debt," accused Penny. "Very well, since you scorn my story I'll give it to the High School paper!"

"An excellent idea. That is, if your editor favors highly colored journalism."

Penny made a grimace, knowing that her father was deliberately teasing her. It was a constant source of irritation that a boy named Fred Clousky had been elected editor of the Riverview High School Chatter instead of Penny by the margin of one vote. She disapproved of Fred, his pimples, and particularly the way he blue-penciled the occasional stories which she submitted.

"The Riverview High Chatter is just as silly as its name," she announced. "If I had that sheet I'd make it into a real paper."

"Sour grapes?" inquired her father softly.

"Maybe," grinned Penny. "But Fred is such an egg, even more conservative than you."

The cab drew up before the Parker home. A light still burned in the living room where Mrs. Weems, the housekeeper, sat reading a magazine.

"I am glad you have come, Penny," she remarked, switching on another light. "I was beginning to worry."

Since the death of Mrs. Parker many years before Mrs. Weems had taken complete charge of the household, caring for Penny and loving her as her own daughter. There were occasions when she found the impulsive girl difficult to restrain, but certainly never dull or uninteresting.

Mrs. Weems soon went to bed, leaving Penny and her father to explore the refrigerator. As they helped themselves to cold ham, potato salad, and celery, Penny spoke of the light which she had seen in the abandoned *Morning Press* building.

"It may have been a watchman making his usual rounds," commented her father.

"Jerry tells me the building has no watchman."

"Could it have been a reflection from a car headlight?"

"I don't think so, Dad."

"Well, I shouldn't lose sleep over it," remarked Mr. Parker lightly. "Better run along to bed now."

Penny arose at six-thirty the next morning, and before breakfast had written a two-page story about John Munn for the Riverview High School Chatter. She read it twice and was very well pleased with her work.

"Editor Fred is lucky to get this," she thought. "He should make it the lead story."

Off to school at a quarter to nine, Penny deposited her literary treasure in a box provided for journalistic contributions. All that day she went from class to class, warmed by the knowledge that she had accomplished an excellent piece of writing. To Louise she confided that she thought the work might improve her grade in English Composition.

"I'm glad you've decided to contribute to the paper again," declared her chum. "It's time you and Fred buried the hatchet."

"Oh, I don't bear him any grudge," returned Penny. "Of course, everyone knows he campaigned for the editorship with free candy and soda pop."

At three-thirty, a minute before the closing bell rang, Fred Clousky sauntered down the aisle. With a flourish he dropped two pages of copy on Penny's desk, face upward. Across one of the pages in huge blue letters had been written: "Too imaginative for *Chatter*. Language too flowery. Spelling bad. Try us again sometime."

A red stain crept over Penny's cheeks. Her blue eyes began to snap.

"The poisonous little mushroom!" she muttered. "If he thinks he can do this to me—"

The closing bell rang, and immediately a group of sympathetic friends gathered about Penny. They all tried to soothe her feelings.

"Don't let it bother you," Louise advised her chum. "Of course, he did it just to make you peeved."

"'Spelling bad,'" Penny read aloud. "Look at this word he underlined! Anyone could tell I merely struck a wrong letter on my typewriter!"

Crumpling the page, she tossed it into the waste paper basket.

"'Too imaginative,'" she muttered. "'Language too flowery'!"

"Oh, forget it, Penny," laughed Louise, leading her toward the locker room. "Fred always has been jealous of you because you've had stories published in the *Star*. Don't let him know that you're annoyed."

"I guess I am acting silly," admitted Penny, relaxing. "What I must do is to give this problem a good, hard think. Editor Fred will hear from me yet!"

Declining an invitation to play tennis, she went directly home. For an hour she lay on the davenport, staring at the ceiling.

"Penny, are you ill?" inquired Mrs. Weems anxiously.

"No, I'm in conference with myself," answered Penny. "I am trying to arrive at a momentous decision."

Presently, she began to scribble figures on a sheet of paper. When her father came home at five o'clock he found her engaged in that occupation.

"Well, Penny," he remarked, hanging up his hat, "how did it go today? The editor of *Chatter* accepted your contribution I hope."

Penny grinned ruefully. "If you don't mind, let's discuss a less painful subject," she replied. "Suppose you tell me what you know about Matthew Judson and the *Morning Press*."

"Why this sudden display of interest?"

"Oh, I saw Mr. Judson last night at the Bean Pot. He looked rather depressed."

Mr. Parker sat down on the arm of the davenport. "It's too bad about Judson," he remarked. "I always admired him because he was a clever newspaper man."

"Clever? Didn't he mis-manage the paper so that it had to close?"

"Not that anyone ever learned. No, I never could figure out why Judson quit. The *Press* had a large circulation and plenty of advertisers."

"What became of the building?"

"It's still there."

"No, I mean who owns it," Penny explained. "Not Mr. Judson?"

"The building was taken over a few months ago by a man named George Veeley. Come to think of it, I once brought him home with me. You should remember him, Penny."

"I do. He was rather nice. I wonder what he plans to do with the *Press* building and its equipment."

"Hold it for speculation, I assume. In my opinion he'll have it empty for a long while."

"I rather doubt it," said Penny. "He has a prospective tenant now, only he doesn't know it."

"Indeed? Who?"

"You're looking at her."

"You!" Mr. Parker smiled broadly.

"I have it all planned," announced Penny with quiet finality. "What this town needs is a good, live newspaper, and an imaginative editor to run it."

"Oh, I see." With difficulty Mr. Parker kept his face composed. "And where do you propose to start your newspaper? In the old *Press* building?"

"You took the words out of my mouth, Dad. Everything is there, awaiting the touch of my magic wand."

"There's a little matter of rent. Several thousand a month."

"I have a solution for that problem."

"Your staff?"

"I'll gather it as I prosper."

"The necessary capital?"

"A mere detail," said Penny grandly. "I meet only one obstacle at a time. Tomorrow I shall accost Mr. Veeley with an attractive proposition. If he falls into my net, Riverview's newest paper, *The Weekly Times*, makes its bow to the public."

CHAPTER 5 - COBWEBS AND RUST

"My dear young lady, do I understand you correctly? You are asking for the use of the *Morning Press* building without the payment of rent."

Mr. Veeley, slightly bald and with a bulging waistline, regarded Penny across the polished mahogany desk. Upon arriving at his office that Saturday morning, he had found the girl awaiting him. For the past ten minutes she had stunned him with her remarkable figures and plans.

"Yes, that's about the size of it," Penny acknowledged. "What Riverview needs is a newspaper unhampered by the conservatism of over-aged minds. Now you have a fine building and equipment which is standing idle, fast falling into decay—"

"Decay?" Mr. Veeley inquired mildly.

"Expensive machinery soon rusts and becomes practically worthless unless kept in use," declared Penny with authority. "If you'll agree to my proposition, I'll publish a weekly paper there, see that your property is kept in good condition, and turn the plant back to you whenever you can find a prosperous renter."

"Your father sent you here?"

"Oh, goodness, no! Dad thinks it's all a great joke. But it isn't! I *know* I can make a success of the paper if only I have a chance to test my ideas."

Mr. Veeley could not fail to be impressed by Penny's earnest, appealing manner. The novelty of her plan both amused and intrigued him.

"I wish I could help you start your paper," he said. "However, I doubt if you comprehend the cost of such a venture. Even should I permit the use of my building rent free, how would you meet such expenses as light, water and heat?"

"Oh, I have a plan for everything," insisted Penny grandly. "All I need is a building. I'll have the windows washed for you and do a good job of house cleaning. With me in charge you'll be able to dismiss your watchman."

"I haven't one."

"No watchman?" Penny inquired innocently. "Last night when I drove past the building I saw a light on the third floor. Evidently someone is prowling about there, Mr. Veeley."

"You're certain you saw a light?" the man inquired, disturbed by the information.

"Oh, yes, indeed. Excuse me for advising you, Mr. Veeley, but you really should have someone to guard your property."

Mr. Veeley smiled broadly. "You are a very convincing young lady. While I realize it is a foolish thing to do, I am tempted to let you have the key."

"Oh, Mr. Veeley, that's wonderful! You'll never regret it!"

"I'll allow you the use of the building for a month," resumed Mr. Veeley. "At the end of that time we'll discuss the future."

Penny was thrown into such a frenzy of excitement that she scarcely could remain outwardly serene until she had left the office. Once on the street she ran the entire distance to the *Star* building, dashing into her father's suite with all the sound effects of a laboring steam engine.

"Dad!" she cried dramatically. "I have it! The key to the *Morning Press* plant! Now I'm on my way to draw my savings from the bank."

"What's that?" demanded Mr. Parker. "Don't tell me Mr. Veeley listened to your crazy scheme!"

"He's heartily in favor of it, Dad. Now I must rush off to the bank."

"Come back here," her father commanded as she started for the door. "I can't allow you to withdraw your savings."

"How can I launch the *Weekly Times* without capital?"

"You're really determined to try it?"

"Of course."

Mr. Parker reached for a cheque book. "How much will you need?"

"Oh, just sign your name at the bottom and leave the amount blank."

"Sorry, I prefer not to financially cripple myself for life. One hundred dollars is my limit. I'm throwing it down a sink-hole, but the lessons you'll learn may be worth the cost."

"I can do a lot with a hundred dollars," said Penny. "Thanks, Dad."

She picked up the cheque before the ink was dry and, dropping a kiss lightly on her father's cheek, was gone.

From the corner drugstore Penny telephoned Louise, telling her the news and asking her to come downtown at once. Fifteen minutes later her chum met her at the entrance to the *Morning Press* building.

"Just think, Lou!" she murmured, unlocking the front door. "This huge plant all mine! I'm a publisher at last!"

"You're completely insane if you ask me," retorted Louise. "This place is a dreadful mess. You'll never be able to clean it up, let alone get out an issue of the paper!"

The girls had passed through the vestibule to the lower floor room which once had served as the *Press'* circulation department. Behind the high service counter, desks and chairs remained untouched, covered by a thick layer of dust. Cobwebs hung from the ceiling light fixtures and festooned the walls.

Climbing the stairs, the girls glanced briefly into the newsroom, and then wandered on to the composing room. Penny's gaze roved over long rows of linotype machines and steel trucks which were used to hold page forms. There were bins of type, Cheltenham, Goudy, Century—more varieties than she had ever seen before.

Passing the stereotyping department, the girls entered the press room where slumbered ten giant double-decked rotary presses. Lying on the roller of one was a torn strip of newspaper, the last issue of the *Morning Press* ever printed.

"It gives one a queer feeling to see all this," said Louise. "Why do you suppose Judson closed the plant when it was prosperous?"

"No one seems to know the answer," Penny replied, stooping to peer into an empty ink pot. "But it doesn't seem possible a man would give up his business, throw so many persons out of work, without a good reason."

"His bad luck seems to be yours," Louise remarked gloomily. "Well, since you've fallen heir to all this, what will you do with it? It will take a sizeable chunk of your hundred dollars just to get the place cleaned."

"Not according to my calculations," chuckled Penny. "Let's choose our offices and then we'll discuss business."

"Our offices?" echoed Louise. "I'm not in on this brain-storm of yours."

"Oh, yes, you are. You'll be the editor."

"But I thought you were that!"

"I'll be the managing editor," said Penny gently. "You'll have your office, and oodles of authority. Of course, you'll have to work hard keeping our staff in line."

"What staff?"

"We'll recruit from Riverview High, concentrating on the journalism majors. Now I think Jack Malone will be our new advertising manager."

"Jack Malone! Why, Penny, he hasn't an ounce of push."

"I know, Lou. But his father is president of the Malone Glass Company. I figure if his son is in charge of advertising—"

"I get the idea," interrupted Louise. "Penny, with a head like yours, we should land all the important accounts in town."

"I aim to win several fat ones away from the *Star*," Penny said with quiet confidence. "If we don't, it will be bankruptcy before the first issue of the paper is off the press."

Louise glanced dubiously at the dusty machinery.

CHAPTER 5 - COBWEBS AND RUST

"There's no denying you're a genius, Penny. Even so, I don't see how you expect to get these presses running."

"We'll only need one."

"True, but you can't recruit pressmen or linotype operators from Riverview High."

"Unfortunately, no," sighed Penny. "The first issue of the *Times* will be printed at the *Star* plant. Dad doesn't know it yet. After that—well, I'll think of something."

"How do you propose to get this place cleaned?"

"Every person who works on our paper must wield a broom, Lou. After we've chosen our offices, we'll scamper forth and gather our staff together."

Returning to the second floor, the girls inspected the offices adjoining the newsroom. Penny selected for hers the one which previously had been occupied by Matthew Judson. His name remained on the frosted-glass door, and the walls bore etchings and paintings of considerable value.

In the top drawer of the flat-top desk there remained an assortment of pens, erasers, thumbtacks, and small articles. All letters and papers had been removed.

"Mr. Judson apparently left here in a great hurry," she remarked. "For some reason he never returned for the paintings and personal trifles."

Louise chose an office adjoining Penny's new quarters. They both were admiring the view from the window when her chum suddenly drew herself into an attitude of attention.

"What's wrong?" inquired Louise, mystified.

"I thought I heard someone moving about," whispered Penny. "Quiet!"

They remained motionless; listening. A board creaked.

Darting to the door, Penny flung it open. The newsroom was deserted, but she was almost certain she heard footsteps retreating swiftly down the hall.

"Lou, we're not alone in this building!"

"I thought I heard someone, too."

The girls ran through the newsroom to the hall, and down the stairway. Three steps from the bottom, Penny suddenly halted. On the service counter of the advertising department lay a man's grimy felt hat.

"Look at that," she whispered. "Someone *was* upstairs!"

"He may still be here, too. Penny, did you leave the entrance door unlocked?"

"I guess so. I don't remember."

"A loiterer may have wandered into the building, and then left when we gave chase."

"Without his hat?"

"It probably was forgotten."

"Anyhow, I intend to look carefully about," declared Penny. "After all, I am responsible for this place now."

Both girls were uneasy as they wandered from room to room. Penny even ventured into the basement where a number of rats had taken refuge. The building seemed deserted.

"We're only wasting precious time," she said at last. "Whoever the intruder was, he's gone now."

Retracing their way to the advertising department, the girls stopped short, staring at the counter. The hat, observed there only a few minutes before, had vanished.

CHAPTER 6 - HEADLINES AND HEADACHES

Penny and Louise stared at the counter, unable to believe their eyesight. They knew that they had not touched the hat. Obviously it had been removed by the man who had left it there.

"The hat's gone," whispered Louise nervously. "That means someone is still inside the building!"

"He could have slipped out the front door while we were in the basement."

Once more the girls made a complete tour of the building, entering every room. Unable to find an intruder they finally decided to give up the futile search.

"After this I'll take care to lock the door," declared Penny as they prepared to leave the building. "Now let's get busy and gather our staff."

During the next hour she and Louise motored from house to house, recruiting school friends. Early afternoon found the old *Press* building invaded by a crew of willing and enthusiastic young workers. A group of fifteen boys and girls, armed with mops, window cloths and brooms, fell to work with such vigor that by nightfall the main portion of the building had emerged from its cocoon of grime.

Weary but well satisfied with her first day as a newspaper publisher, Penny went home and to bed. At breakfast the next morning she ate with such a preoccupied air that her father commented upon her sober countenance.

"I hope you haven't encountered knotty problems so soon in your journalistic venture," he remarked teasingly.

"None which you can't solve for me," said Penny. "I've decided to run the octopus tattoo story on the front page of our first issue."

"Indeed? And when does the first issue appear?"

"I'll print one week from today."

"A Sunday paper?"

"I thought probably your presses wouldn't be busy on that day."

"*My* presses!"

"Yes, I haven't hired my pressroom force yet. I plan to make up the paper, set the type and lock it in the page forms. Then I'll haul it over to your plant for stereotyping and the press run."

"And if I object?"

"You won't, will you, Dad? I'm such a pathetic little competitor."

"I'll run off the first edition for you," Mr. Parker promised. "But mind, only the first. How many papers will you want? About five hundred?"

"Oh, roughly, six thousand. That should take care of my street sales."

Mr. Parker's fork clattered against his plate. "Your street sales?" he repeated. "Where, may I ask, did you acquire your distribution organization?"

"Oh, I have plans," Penny chuckled. "Running a paper is really very simple."

"Young lady, you're riding for a heartbreaking fall," warned her father severely. "Six thousand copies! Why, you'll be lucky to dispose of three hundred!"

"Wait and see," said Penny confidently.

During the week which followed there were no idle moments for the staff of the newly organized *Weekly Times*. Leaving Louise in charge of the news output, Penny concentrated most of her attention on the problem of winning advertisers. Starting with a page taken by the Malone Glass Company, she and Jack Malone toured the city, selling a total of forty-two full columns.

CHAPTER 6 - HEADLINES AND HEADACHES

The novelty of the enterprise intrigued many business men, while others took space because they were friends of Mr. Malone or Mr. Parker. Money continued to pour into the till of the *Weekly Times*.

Yet, when everything should have been sailing along smoothly, Louise complained that it was becoming difficult to keep her staff of writers satisfied. One by one they were falling away.

"We must expect that," declared Penny. "Always the weak drop by the wayside. If only we can get on a paying basis, we'll be able to offer small salaries. Then we'll have more workers than we can use."

"You certainly look to the future," laughed Louise. "Personally I have grave doubts we'll ever get the first issue set up."

Every moment which could be spared from school, Penny spent at the plant. Long after the other young people had left, she remained, trying to master the intricacies of the linotype machine. Although in theory it operated somewhat like a typewriter, she could not learn to set type accurately.

Friday night, alone in the building, the task suddenly overwhelmed her.

"Machines, machines, machines," she muttered. "The paper is going to be a mess and all because I can't run this hateful old thing!"

Dropping her head wearily on the keyboard, Penny wept with vexation.

Suddenly she stiffened. Unmistakably, footsteps were coming softly down the hall toward the composing room.

Twice during the week Louise had declared that she believed someone prowled about the plant when it was deserted. Penny had been too busy to worry about the matter. But now, realizing that she was alone and without protection, her pulse began to hammer.

A shadow fell across the doorway.

"Who—who is there?" Penny called, her voice unsteady.

To her relief, a young man, his bashful grin reassuringly familiar, stepped into the cavernous room. Bill Carlyle was one of her father's best linotype operators.

"You nearly startled me out of my wits," she laughed shakily, "What brought you here, Bill?"

"I noticed the light burning," the operator replied, twisting his hat in his hands. "I thought I would drop in and see how you were getting along."

"Why, that's nice of you, Bill." Penny saw that he was gazing hard at her. She was afraid he could tell that she had been crying.

"The boys say you're doing right well." Bill moved nearer the linotype machine.

"Don't look at my work," pleaded Penny. "It's simply awful. I can't get the hang of this horrid old machine. I wish I hadn't started a newspaper—I must have been crazy just as everyone says."

"You're tired, that's what's the trouble," said Bill soothingly. "Now there's nothing to running a linotype. Give me a piece of copy and I'll show you."

He slid into the vacant chair and his fingers began to move over the keyboard. As if by magic, type fell into place, and there were no mistakes.

"You do it marvelously," said Penny admiringly. "What's the trick?"

"About ten years practice. Shoot out your copy now and I'll set some of it for you."

"Bill, you're a darling! But dare you do it? What about the union?"

"This is just between you and me," he grinned. "You need a helping hand and I'm here to give it."

Until midnight Bill remained at his post, setting more type in three hours than Penny had done in three days.

"Your front page should look pretty good at any rate," he said as they left the building together. "Using rather old stories though, aren't you?"

"Old?"

"That one about the man who was pushed off the bridge."

"The story is still news," Penny said defensively. "No other paper has used it. Didn't you like it?"

"Sure, it was good," he responded.

Now that several days had elapsed since her experience at the river, even Penny's interest in John Munn and his strange tattoo, had faded. However, she was determined that the story should appear in the paper if for no other reason than to plague the editor of *Chatter*.

THE SECRET PACT

According to a report from Louise, Fred Clousky had called at the *Times* early that afternoon, and had seemed very gloomy as he inspected the plant. He had spent nearly a half hour in the composing room, a fact which Penny later was to recall with chagrin.

"Poor Fred," she thought. "After my paper comes out his *Chatter* will look more than ever like a sick cat."

Saturday was another day of toil, but by six o'clock, aided by the few faithful members of her staff, the last stick of type was set, the pages locked and transported to the *Star* ready for the Sunday morning run.

"I'll be here early tomorrow," Penny told the pressman. "Don't start the edition rolling until I arrive. I want to press the button myself."

At her urging, Mr. Parker, Jerry Livingston, Salt Sommers, and many members of the *Star's* staff, came to view the stereotyped plates waiting to be fitted on the press rollers.

"You've done well, Penny," praised her father. "I confess I never thought you would get this far. Still figuring on a street sale of six thousand?"

"I've increased the number to seven," laughed Penny.

"And how do you plan to get the papers sold?"

"Oh, that's my secret, Dad. You may be surprised."

Exhausted but happy, Penny went home and to bed. She was up at six, and after a hastily eaten breakfast, arrived at the *Star* office in time to greet the workmen who were just coming on duty.

"Everything is set," the foreman told her presently. "You can start the press now."

Penny was so nervous that her hand trembled as she pressed the electric switch. There was a low, whining noise as the wheels began to turn, slowly at first, then faster and faster. Pressmen moved back and forth, oiling the machinery and tightening screws.

Penny's gaze was upon the long stream of paper feeding into the press. In a moment the neatly folded newspapers would slide out at the rate of eight hundred a minute. Only slightly over an hour and the run would be completed.

The first printed paper dropped from the press, and the foreman reached for it.

"Here you are," he said, offering it to Penny.

Almost reverently she accepted the paper. Even though there were only eight pages, each one represented hours of labor. She had turned out a professional job, and could rightly feel proud.

And then suddenly Penny's eyes fell upon the uppermost line of the front page. She gasped and leaned against the wall.

"I'm ruined!" she moaned. "Ruined! Someone has played a cruel joke on me!"

"Why, what's wrong?" inquired the press foreman, reaching for another paper.

"Look at this," wailed Penny. "Just look!"

She pointed to the name of the paper, printed in large black letters. It read: THE WEAKLY TIMES.

"I'll be the laughing stock of Riverview," Penny moaned. "The papers can't go out that way. Stop the press!"

CHAPTER 7 - PETER FENESTRA

As the foreman turned off the rotarypress, the loud throb of machinery died away and the flowing web of paper became motionless.

"How could the mistake have been made?" Penny murmured disconsolately. "I know that originally the name-plate was set up right."

"You should have taken page proofs and checked the mat," said the foreman.

"But I did! At least I took page proofs. I'll admit I was careless about the mats."

"Well, it looks as if someone played a joke on you," replied the foreman.

Penny's face hardened. "I can guess who did it! Fred Clousky! Louise told me he spent a long while in the composing room one afternoon while I was away. He must have changed the type just to make me look ridiculous."

"Well, it's done anyway," said the foreman with a shrug. "What will you do about the run?"

"I'll never let it go through this way. I'd rather die."

The foreman reminded Penny that with paid advertisements she would be compelled to print an issue. She knew that it would not be possible to make a change in the starter plate. The entire page must be recast.

"I don't suppose the type can be matched in this plant," she said gloomily.

"We may have some like it," replied the foreman. "I'll see."

Soon he returned to report that type was available and that the work could be done by the stereotypers. However, the men would expect overtime pay.

"I'll give them anything they want," said Penny recklessly. "Anything."

After a trying wait the new plate was made ready and locked on the cylinder. Once more the great press thundered. Again papers began to pour from the machine, every fiftieth one slightly out of line.

"What do you want done with 'em?" inquired the foreman.

"Have the papers carried to the mailing room and stacked by the door," she instructed. "I'll be around in the morning to arrange for deliveries."

Monday's first issue of the *Star* was hot off the press when Penny stationed herself beside the veritable mountain of papers. The room was a bedlam, with newsboys shouting noisily for their wares. As they passed her on their way to the street, she waylaid them one by one.

"Here you are, boys," she said with an expansive smile. "Two dozen papers each. Sell them for a nickel and keep half of it for yourself. Turn in the money at the *Weekly Times* office."

"Two and a half cents!" exclaimed one of the boys. "Gee, that's more than we get for selling the *Star*!"

"Generosity is my motto," laughed Penny. "Just push those papers for all you're worth."

Leaving the *Star* plant, she went directly to the *Weekly Times* building. Permission had been granted to absent herself from school, and she planned to be busy throughout the day, checking on paper sales.

As Penny unlocked the front door, she noticed that a faint odor of tobacco lingered in the air. A perplexed frown knitted her brow.

"That's funny," she thought. "None of the boys are allowed to smoke here. I wonder if someone disobeyed rules, or if there's really a prowler in the building?"

Too busy to search the plant again, Penny gave the matter scant consideration. Tossing a package of lunch on the counter, she prepared for a hard day's work.

Now and then, to rest her mind from columns of figures, she wandered to the window. Down the street, newsboys called their wares and it pleased her that they shouted the *Weekly Times* as frequently as they did the *Star*.

By ten o'clock the boys began to straggle in with their money. Only a few had failed to sell all of their papers, and not one neglected to make a report. Penny's final check-up disclosed that six thousand eight hundred and twenty-nine Weeklies had been sold.

"I can't expect to do that well after the novelty wears off," she thought. "But one thing is assured. My *Weekly* isn't going to be *weakly*!"

With a large sum of money in her possession, Penny decided to take no chance of losing it. After making a careful count, she poured the coins into a bag which she transported by car to the bank.

It was lunch-time when she returned to the plant. She went to the counter for the package of sandwiches. To her surprise it had disappeared.

"Now who took my food?" she muttered.

Penny was annoyed. She did not believe that one of the newsboys had picked up the package. Accumulative evidence pointed to a likelihood that someone was hiding in the building. The moving light, tobacco smoke, unexplained footsteps, suggested that a tramp might be using the empty plant as a comfortable shelter.

"But how can he get in?" she asked herself. "Doors and windows are kept locked."

As Penny considered whether or not to report the matter to police, the front door opened. A man of early middle age, well dressed, but with a sharp, weather-beaten face and a mis-shapen nose, entered.

"This the office of the *Weekly Times*?" he demanded grumpily.

"Yes," said Penny. "Is there anything—"

"I want to see the editor."

"You're looking at her now."

"You! A girl!"

Penny smiled and waited. The stranger hesitated and then took the *Weekly Times* from his overcoat pocket. With his forefinger he jabbed at a story on the front page—Penny's account of the tattooed man who had been pushed from the bridge.

"You know who wrote this?" he questioned.

"I did."

Again Penny's words surprised the man although he tried not to disclose it.

"That's a right interesting yarn," he said after a long pause.

"I'm glad you like it." Penny stared at the man with interest, wondering why he had come and what he wanted.

"I was kind of curious to know where you got your information."

"Why, I saw it happen, Mr—I don't believe you told me your name."

"Fenestra. Peter Fenestra."

"I was driving near the bridge at the time the man was pushed into the water," Penny resumed.

"You didn't see the one who did it?"

"Not clearly. May I ask why you are so interested in the story?"

"I thought maybe I knew that man, Munn. What became of him?"

"I can't tell you that. He was rescued by a tugboat captain. Everything I know about the affair is in the story."

"Well, thank you kindly," Mr. Fenestra said, tipping his hat.

Penny watched him leave the office and walk to his car. She had never seen the man before to her knowledge. Although she should have felt flattered by his visit, it left her with a vague, unexplainable sensation of distrust.

"There's something queer about the way he came here," she reflected. "Perhaps he knows more than he pretended."

Penny soon dismissed the matter from her mind, turning her thoughts to the problem of the missing lunch. Resolutely she made a tour of the building, venturing everywhere save into the basement. As she had half expected, she found no one. However, returning once more to her work, she occasionally caught herself listening for footsteps.

CHAPTER 7 - PETER FENESTRA

At three-thirty Louise came from school with other members of the *Times* staff. She and Penny retired to the latter's private office there to discuss plans for the next week's paper.

"Lou," said Penny abruptly, "did you ever hear of a man named Peter Fenestra?"

"Why, yes, I have."

"He was here today to ask me about the octopus tattoo story. What can you tell me?"

"Not very much, Penny. He lives on a farm two miles from the south edge of Riverview. A place called The Willows."

"Oh, is he a farmer?" Penny was surprised. "I never would have guessed that."

"He isn't one. He merely lives there. According to the report, he has prospered by leaps and bounds."

"How does he make his money?"

"No one seems to know. When Fenestra came here a year or so ago he didn't appear to have anything. Lately he bought a fine car, and he spends money rather lavishly."

"He inquired about John Munn," Penny remarked. "Somehow I had a feeling that he was trying to pump information from me for a particular reason."

"Those who know Fenestra say he's a sly old fox."

"That's the way he impressed me, Lou. Perhaps I flatter myself, but I believe my tattoo story may cause quite a stir in Riverview."

"Was Fenestra annoyed by it?"

"I think so, Lou, although he tried to cover his feelings. He may or may not be a friend of John Munn, but he certainly was anxious to learn what became of him."

"You didn't ask him any questions?"

"No, his visit took me by surprise. But I've been thinking, Lou. I very much want a follow up story on John Munn for next week's paper. Suppose we run out to Fenestra's farm tomorrow."

"What purpose would there be in that?"

"Fenestra may be able to tell us interesting facts which will throw light on the mystery. He may understand the significance of the octopus tattoo."

"You're rather hopeful, I think."

"But you'll go with me?"

"Yes," promised Louise. "I've always had a curiosity to see The Willows. Besides, I need a vacation from my strenuous duties as editor."

CHAPTER 8 - THE STORM CAVE

"Well, Penny," remarked Mr. Parker casually at the breakfast table. "I finally bought the cottage."

Penny closed her history book with a loud snap, favoring her father with complete attention. "You bought a cottage?" she echoed. "Where? When? Why?"

"I've talked about it for the past week, but you were so busy stealing the *Star's* advertisers that you never listened."

"I'm all ears now, Dad," Penny assured him, absently reaching for a piece of toast. "Tell me all about it."

"The cottage is located on the Big Bear River. Four rooms and a boathouse. Incidentally, I've hired a man to look after the place and keep the boat in shape. He calls himself Anchor Joe."

"Are we going to live at the cottage this summer?" Penny inquired.

"No, I merely bought it for week-end trips. I plan on a bit of fishing now and then. You may enjoy going with me."

"Oh, Dad," groaned Penny, "how can I? These days I don't even have time to wash my neck. Running a newspaper is more work than I figured."

"I'll give you the address of the cottage, at least," smiled Mr. Parker. "If you have any spare time during the next three months drive out and look over the place."

"I'll get there somehow," Penny promised, pocketing the card. Her hand encountered a typed, folded sheet of paper which she immediately placed in front of her father. "Oh, by the way, sign this for me, will you?"

"No more cheques."

"This is only an order for a ton-roll of paper. I'm trying to store up a few supplies so that eventually I can publish the *Weekly* in my own plant."

Mr. Parker signed the order, inquiring teasingly: "Have you engaged your pressman yet? Their wages come rather high you know."

"It takes everything the *Weekly* makes to meet its current bills," sighed Penny. "But one of these days I'll get the paper out in my own plant. Just wait and see!"

"I'll wait," chuckled Mr. Parker. "My hope is that you don't fail in your studies before that happy day arrives."

On her way to school, Penny studied the card given her by her father, and noticed that the new cottage was situated not far from The Willows. Often she and Louise had talked of calling upon Peter Fenestra, but both had been kept busy at the *Times* office. Now that a linotype operator had been hired to set type, they had a little more free time.

"If Louise will accompany me, I'll visit both places tonight," decided Penny.

Four-thirty found the two girls walking through a dense maple and oak woods which rimmed the Big Bear River. A breeze stirred the tree leaves, but even so the day was hot and sultry.

"I wish it would rain," remarked Louise, trudging wearily beside her companion. "I never knew it to be so warm at this time of year."

"Maybe we can cool off by taking a boat ride when we get to the cottage," encouraged Penny. "I think I see the place through the trees."

Directly ahead, in a tiny clearing, stood a freshly painted white cottage. Quickening their steps, the girls soon arrived at the front door. No one seemed to be within call, so they pushed it open.

A long living room with a cobblestone fireplace met their gaze. Beyond was the kitchen, a dining alcove, and two bedrooms.

CHAPTER 8 - THE STORM CAVE

As they went outside again, they saw a short, wiry man coming toward the cottage from the river.

"You're Miss Parker?" he asked, looking at Louise.

"No, *I* am," corrected Penny. "And you must be Anchor Joe." Her eyes fastened for an instant upon the tattoo of a four-masted sailing ship imprinted on his arm.

"That's me," agreed the man. "Go ahead an' look around all you like."

Penny and Louise wandered about the grounds, then returned to find Anchor Joe giving the motor boat, which was upturned on the grass, a coat of varnish.

"We thought you might take us for a ride," remarked Penny. "It must be cool on the water."

"I sure would like to, Miss Parker," said Anchor Joe regretfully. "But I dasn't get 'er wet now. Not until this varnish dries."

Penny nodded, and then asked: "You're a sailor, aren't you? Where have you sailed?"

"The Atlantic, the Great Lakes, the Gulf o' Mexico. Oh, I been everywhere."

Penny and Louise chatted with Anchor Joe for a time but, although they asked any number of questions, they gained very little definite information. The sailor seemed unwilling to tell anything about himself, save in generalities.

"We may as well go on to Peter Fenestra's place," Penny presently remarked. "It's getting late."

Anchor Joe's varnish brush became motionless. He glanced up with sudden interest.

"I wouldn't go there if I was you gals," he said.

"Why not?" questioned Penny in astonishment.

"The weather don't look so good. She might blow up a gale before sundown."

"Oh, we're not afraid of a little wind or rain," answered Penny carelessly. "Come along, Lou."

Anchor Joe said nothing more, but his sober gaze followed the girls as they walked away.

Keeping close to the river, Penny and Louise trod a path which they knew would lead to the main road and Peter Fenestra's farm.

"Queer sort, wasn't he?" Penny remarked thoughtfully.

"Anchor Joe?"

"Yes, I wonder where Dad found him? He certainly didn't tell us much about himself."

Crossing the river by means of a swaying, suspension bridge, the girls came out from beneath the solid canopy of trees. Penny paused to stare up at the sky.

"Aren't those clouds odd?" she observed. "Just watch them boil!"

"They must be filled with wind," declared Louise uneasily. "Anchor Joe said he thought a storm would blow up."

"It's not far away either. Unless we step right along, we'll surely get caught in it."

"Perhaps we should forget The Willows and start home."

"We never could get there now," responded Penny. "If we hurry we may reach Fenestra's place before the storm breaks."

Walking even faster, the girls hastened along the winding path. The air remained sultry and very still. The sky, Penny noted, had changed to a peculiar yellowish color.

Then, as she watched with increasing alarm, a writhing, twisting, funnel-shaped arm reached down from the boiling clouds, anchoring them to earth. For a moment the entire mass seemed to settle and flatten out.

"Listen!" commanded Penny.

Plainly they both could hear a sullen, deep-throated roar as the storm moved forward.

"A tornado!" gasped Louise. "It's coming this way!"

"Run!" urged Penny, seizing her hand. "We still have a chance to make Fenestra's place."

In a clearing beyond a weed-grown field stood a white farmhouse, a red barn and a silo. One side of the property was bounded by the willow-rimmed river, the other by the road.

Crawling beneath a barbed-wire fence, the girls cut across the field. The sky was darker now, the roar of the wind ominous. They could see the tail of the funnel whipping along the ground, veering to the south, then coming toward them again.

"We'll never make the house," Louise cried fearfully.

"Yes, we will," encouraged Penny.

She raised another wire strand for Louise to roll beneath. Her own sweater caught on the sharp barbs, tearing a large hole as she jerked free.

Dust had begun to blow. Trees and bushes bowed before the first gusts of wind.

Glancing frantically about for a place of refuge, Penny saw a low, circular cement hump rising from the ground not many yards distant. Instantly she recognized it as an old fashioned storm cellar.

"We'll get in there, Lou!" she shouted. "Come on!"

Running across the yard, they reached the cave. Entrance was guarded by a door built in the side of the cement dome. A brass padlock hung unsnapped in the hasp.

"Thank goodness, we can get in," gasped Louise. "Hurry!"

Penny tugged at the heavy door. It would not raise, and then it gave so suddenly that she nearly tumbled backwards.

The door clattered back against the cement dome. Through the rectangular opening protruded the head and shoulders of Peter Fenestra. His face was convulsed with rage.

"What are you trying to do?" he demanded harshly. "Speak up!"

CHAPTER 9 - A FALLEN TREE

"Speak up!" Peter Fenestra commanded again as the girls stared at him in blank astonishment. "Why are you trying to get into my cave?"

"Listen to that wind!" cried Penny, recovering the power of speech. She pointed toward the sky.

"A tornado!" exclaimed Fenestra in a stunned voice.

"And it's coming this way," added Louise. "Let us down into the cave!"

Instead of stepping aside, the man came up the stone steps. Slamming the door of the cave, he padlocked it.

"Quick! Into the house!" he ordered.

"We'll be much safer underground," argued Penny. "That twister easily can lift a building from its foundation."

"Do as I say!" commanded Peter Fenestra harshly. "The cave is half filled with water. You can't go down there."

Deserting the girls, he ran toward the house. Mystified by the old man's actions, Penny and Louise followed, overtaking him as he reached the porch.

"Get inside!" he ordered.

The girls scurried through the door and he closed it behind them. Barely had they reached shelter when the wind struck the house in full force, fairly shaking it to its foundation. Windows rattled, a tree bough came crashing down on the porch, the air was filled with flying debris.

As a hard object shattered a pane of glass, Penny and Louise heard a terrified scream from the kitchen. A moment later a girl ran into the room. She stopped short as she saw Penny and Louise. They also stared, for it was Tillie Fellows.

"Stop that silly screeching!" Fenestra ordered sharply. "The center of the storm is passing to the south. Now get back to your work!"

"Yes, sir," Tillie mumbled.

Still gazing at Penny and Louise, she slowly retreated. However, as Peter Fenestra went to the window, turning his back, she made strange signs to the girls which they were unable to understand. Obviously she did not wish them to speak to her for she raised a finger to her lips, indicative of silence.

A gate was wrenched from its hinges and carried across the yard. From across the road came the crash of an uprooted tree. With a stifled scream Tillie fled to the kitchen.

"That stupid girl drives me crazy," Fenestra muttered. "I don't know why I ever hired her."

"You can't blame her for being frightened," declared Louise quickly. "This is a dreadful storm."

"The worst is over now," said Fenestra. "You'll be able to go in a few minutes."

Penny and Louise glanced at each other. Peter Fenestra's remark made it very clear that he did not wish them to linger after the storm had passed. Without inviting them to sit down, he nervously went from window to window, watching the clouds.

Rain began to fall. At first it came in a heavy downpour, then slackened somewhat. The wind no longer tore at the doors.

"You'll be able to go any time now," said Fenestra. "I can let you have an umbrella."

"It's still rather bad," answered Penny. "If you don't mind, I believe we'll wait a few minutes longer."

The decision displeased the man. Frowning, he turned to gaze at the girls somewhat critically.

"Who sent you here?" he demanded. "Why did you come?"

His manner was so suspicious that Penny sensed it was no time to reveal the real purpose of the visit. Instead she said:

"My father has a cottage along the river. We were returning from there when the storm broke."

Her explanation seemed to satisfy the man. He shrugged and fell to pacing the floor restlessly.

The rain presently ceased. Penny and Louise felt that they no longer could delay their departure. Saying good-bye to Fenestra, they left the house.

Rounding a corner of the building, they were startled to hear a light tap on the window. Glancing up, they saw Tillie Fellow's face pressed against the pane.

"She's signaling for us to wait," observed Penny. "I guess she wants to talk with us."

The girls stepped into the doorway of a woodshed. In a moment Tillie slipped from the house, a coat thrown over her head.

"I hope old Fenestra doesn't see me," she greeted the girls nervously. "Let's get out of sight."

Penny and Louise followed her into the woodshed, closing the door.

"How long have you worked here?" the latter inquired curiously.

"Ever since I met you girls on the boat. I answered an advertisement the next morning and got this job."

"Do you like it?" asked Penny. "I imagine farm work is hard."

"The work is easy enough. But I hate the place! That's why I wanted to talk with you. Do you know of anyone who needs a girl? I'll work for very small wages."

"I don't know of anyone at the moment," responded Penny.

"I can't stay here much longer," Tillie said, a note of desperation in her voice. "Mr. Fenestra is so overbearing and mean! He can't bear noise either. If I as much as rattle a dish he berates me."

"Does he pay you a decent wage?" inquired Louise.

"Ten dollars a week. I can't complain on that score. But there's something about him—I can't explain—it gives me the creeps."

"Fenestra is a peculiar type," admitted Penny. "He didn't act very friendly toward Louise and me. By the way, why does he keep the storm cellar padlocked?"

"That's something I wish you would tell *me*."

"He wouldn't allow us to enter it even when the storm was coming."

"Fenestra always keeps the cave padlocked," revealed Tillie. "He goes there every day, too. Sometimes he spends hours beneath ground. It rather frightens me."

"What do you think he does there?"

"I don't know. Once I asked him about the cave and he flew into a violent rage. He said if he ever caught me near it he would discharge me."

"He told us that the cave was half filled with water."

"I don't believe that," said Tillie. "He has something hidden down there."

"Haven't you any idea what it is?"

"No, and I don't care very much," returned Tillie. "All I want to do is get away from this place. If you hear of a job anywhere will you let me know?"

"Of course," promised Penny. "Mrs. Weems, our housekeeper, may know of a vacancy. If she does, I'll telephone."

"We haven't a telephone. Mr. Fenestra had it taken out because the ringing of the bell made him jumpy. He said the neighbors always listened to his conversations, too. He's very suspicious of everyone."

"Then I can run out in the car," said Penny. "I don't blame you for not liking this place. I shouldn't either."

"Thanks for everything," replied Tillie gratefully. "You've been awfully good to me. I must run back now or old Fenestra will ask me a million questions."

Hastily saying good-bye, she darted away. Walking slowly toward the road, Penny and Louise discussed Peter Fenestra's strange actions. They were inclined to agree with Tillie that he had hidden something of value beneath ground.

Across the road from the farmhouse a giant elm tree had been uprooted. They saw overturned chicken houses, fences laid flat, tangles of telephone and electric wires.

"Even more damage must have been done farther down the river," remarked Penny anxiously. "I hope our new cottage hasn't blown away."

CHAPTER 9 - A FALLEN TREE

"Shall we go there and see?"

"I wish we could."

For several hundred yards the girls followed the road, then once more they cut across the fields toward the winding river. As they approached the Parker property their misgivings increased. All along the water front, trees had been toppled and split. In sections there were wide paths cut as if by a scythe.

"The cottage is still there!" Penny cried as they presently ascended to higher ground. "I can see it."

"Several trees are down," observed Louise. "One has fallen across the porch."

"A beautiful birch, too," murmured Penny. "Anchor Joe will have a job clearing it away."

Approaching the cottage, the girls saw no glimpse of the workman. Penny called his name several times.

"I wonder where he went?" she murmured.

The girls rounded the corner of the cottage. As their eyes fell upon the giant birch which had demolished the porch railing, they were startled to see a slight movement among the leaves. A hand lay limp against the trunk.

"Anchor Joe!" gasped Penny in horror. "He's pinned beneath the tree!"

CHAPTER 10 - A WORD TO THE WISE

Penny and Louise stooped beside the groaning man who lay pinned on his side beneath the tree. As they attempted to move him he writhed in pain and pleaded with them not to touch him.

"The tree will have to be lifted," declared Penny. "I'll go for help."

Leaving Louise to encourage Anchor Joe, she ran the entire distance to the main road. The nearest house was the one owned by Peter Fenestra. However, as she hastened in that direction, she observed a truck filled with telephone linemen coming toward her. Hailing the men, she told them what had occurred.

"I am afraid Anchor Joe is badly hurt," she added. "I'll telephone for a doctor while you go on to the cottage."

One of the linemen offered to make the call, leaving her free to guide the other four men to the Parker camp. Reaching the spot, the men raised the fallen tree. Carefully they lifted Anchor Joe who had lapsed into unconsciousness.

"Bring him into the cottage," Penny directed, going ahead to open doors.

One of the rooms had been furnished as a bedroom with an old cot, a chest of drawers and odd pieces brought from the Parker home. Penny spread a blanket over the mattress and the injured man was stretched upon it.

"He's seriously hurt, isn't he?" she asked anxiously.

"Afraid he is," admitted one of the linemen. "Heat up some water and I'll do what I can until the doctor gets here."

Penny and Louise hastened to the kitchen to struggle with the wood-burning range. By the time they had the fire going well they heard voices in the yard. Glancing out the window they saw a lineman coming toward the cottage and walking beside a doctor who carried a light, black bag.

"It's Doctor Griswold," observed Louise. "He made a quick trip from town."

Penny ran to open the door for the two men. Then, at the doctor's bidding, she went to the kitchen again for the boiling water.

"You carry it in," urged Louise. "I can't bear to see poor Anchor Joe."

The linemen had left by the time Penny reentered the bedroom. The doctor was working over Anchor Joe, and she observed in relief that he had recovered consciousness.

"Where do you feel pain?" the doctor inquired as he unfastened the man's shirt.

"My back and chest, doc," the sailor mumbled. "Feels like all my insides is crushed."

"Hardly that," said the doctor cheerfully, "or you wouldn't be telling me about it. Now let's see."

He took Anchor Joe's pulse, then gently probed his chest and sponged a break in the skin. Carefully he turned the man upon his back.

Penny drew in her breath, nearly dropping the pan of water. Across Anchor Joe's back was tattooed the sprawling figure of an octopus. She bent closer. Beneath the front arms of the repulsive sea creature appeared a single word: *One*.

"John Munn's tattoo was exactly the same, save for the word!" thought Penny. "It was 'All' while this is 'One.' What can be the significance?"

Even the doctor was startled by the strange tattoo for he glanced at it curiously as he probed.

"You are a sailor?" he inquired.

"That's right," muttered Anchor Joe. "Ouch, doc! Take it easy, will you?"

Penny could not remain silent. "Joe, do you know a man named John Munn?" she asked.

CHAPTER 10 - A WORD TO THE WISE

"Sure I know him," the sailor mumbled. "We shipped together on the *Dorasky*."

"Your tattoo is very similar to his."

Anchor Joe's pain-glazed eyes turned upon Penny as if he were seeing her for the first time. He made an effort to pull the blanket over his back.

"We had 'em put on together," he muttered. "Jack an' John, and that rat, Otto—"

"Please don't talk to the patient," said the doctor significantly. "He should be kept quiet."

"I'm sorry," apologized Penny.

She did not speak again until the doctor had completed his examination and had bandaged Anchor Joe's cuts and bruises.

"What do you advise, doctor?" she asked. "Will it be necessary to remove Joe to a hospital?"

"Neither advisable nor desirable for at least twenty-four hours," he replied. "I find no indication of internal injury, but it is best to be safe. The patient should be kept quiet, in bed, for at least a day or two."

"It's something of a problem to care for him here," said Penny frowning. "Do you suggest a nurse?"

"Any woman who has had practical experience in caring for the sick would do."

"Mrs. Weems may be willing to come," said Penny. "I'll telephone home at once and learn what arrangements can be made."

When the doctor left, Penny accompanied him as far as the first house. From there she telephoned her father, who promised to get Mrs. Weems and come at once to the cottage.

Louise was uneasily waiting by the time Penny returned. Outside the bedroom they held whispered consultation.

"Has Anchor Joe talked?" Penny questioned. "You know what I mean. Has he said anything about John Munn or the tattoo?"

"Not a word. But every so often he mutters that he'll get even with someone by the name of Otto—a fellow sailor who 'ratted.'"

"He mentioned Otto when I was in the room," nodded Penny. "I wish we dared question Joe, but the doctor advised against it."

"I don't think we should annoy him now. Perhaps later on he'll tell us about the tattoo and its meaning."

"Perhaps," echoed Penny. "However, if I am any judge of character, Anchor Joe isn't the talkative type. As soon as he gets over the shock of this accident, he'll lock those lips of his. We'll learn nothing."

"Why are you so convinced there's a deep mystery connected with the tattoo?"

"I can't explain it, Lou. I just *know* there is. I'll never rest until I learn the significance of those words, *All* and *One*."

Within a half hour Mrs. Weems and Mr. Parker arrived at the cottage, bringing a supply of linen, food, and comforts for the injured man. The housekeeper agreed to assume charge until Anchor Joe could be safely removed to a hospital.

When Mr. Parker drove to Riverview the girls accompanied him. During the ride Penny questioned her father regarding Anchor Joe.

"I know almost nothing about him," he replied. "He was sent to me by the Acme Employment Agency, and I didn't bother to ask for a recommendation."

"I've learned that he's a friend of John Munn," revealed Penny. "As soon as he's able to get about again, I mean to ask him a number of things."

Mr. Parker drove Louise to her home, and at Penny's request dropped her off at the *Weekly Times* office.

"By the way, what about dinner tonight?" he inquired. "Shall we dine at the Commodore Hotel?"

"Oh, Dad, I wish I could," Penny sighed wistfully. "Work is stacked a mile high on my desk. I'll just grab a sandwich somewhere and work late."

"I am afraid you are taking the newspaper business too seriously," replied her father. "Shall I leave the car for you?"

"It would be a help."

"All right, Penny."

Mr. Parker gave her the car keys, and walked on to his own newspaper. Entering the *Times* building, Penny spoke to several high school boys who were working in the advertising office, and climbed the stairs to her own office.

THE SECRET PACT

For the next half hour she checked over galley proofs, marking corrections on the margins.

"I never imagined there could be so many things to do on a weekly," she sighed. "One never gets through."

A board creaked in the newsroom. Penny heard it and glanced up. A shadow passed slowly across the frosted glass of the office door.

"Come in," she called.

No one answered, and the shadow disappeared. Penny waited a moment, then impatiently arose and went to the door. The newsroom was deserted.

"Queer," she thought. "Someone walked past my office door."

Thinking that it might have been one of the high school boys, Penny went to the head of the stairs and called:

"Did anyone come up here a moment ago?"

"Not unless it was by way of the back entrance," was the reply.

Decidedly puzzled, Penny returned to her desk. As she sat down a sheet of paper lying on the blotter pad drew her attention. She was certain it had not been there a few minutes earlier.

Reaching for it, she gasped in astonishment. The paper bore a message scrawled in black ink and read:

"To the Editor of the *Weekly Times*:
You are hereby warned to give up your newspaper which offends public taste. We give you three days to wind up your business and close doors. A word to the wise is sufficient."

CHAPTER 11 - MR. JUDSON'S DAUGHTER

Penny read the message three times. Obviously, it had been placed on her desk during the few minutes she had been absent. Yet she reasoned that it would be useless to search for the cowardly person who undoubtedly had slipped from the building.

"So I am warned to close shop!" she muttered angrily. "And the *Weekly Times* offends public taste!"

Penny crumpled the paper into a ball, hurling it toward the wire basket. Reconsidering her action, she recovered the note and, carefully smoothing the wrinkles, placed it in her purse.

"I'll show this to Dad," she told herself. "But no one else."

When Penny's anger had cooled she was left with a vague sensation of misgiving. Resolutely she reflected that it was not unusual for editors to receive threatening notes. Often her father had shown her such communications sent to the *Star* by cranks.

"It doesn't mean a thing," she assured herself. "Not a thing. I'll keep on publishing the *Weekly* as long as I please."

One fact contributed to Penny's uneasiness. Often she worked late in the building, and a single light burning from an upper story window proclaimed to any street watcher that she was alone. In the future she must use far more caution.

Try as she would, Penny could not forget the warning. After the boys who comprised the advertising staff had gone home for dinner, she caught herself listening tensely to every unusual sound. At length she shut the desk and arose.

"I'm doing no good here," she thought in disgust. "I may as well go home."

Taking particular care to lock all doors and windows, Penny left the building. Street lights were blinking on as she climbed into the parked automobile.

Driving mechanically, she weaved through downtown traffic, now and then halting for a red light. As she was starting ahead from an intersection, an elderly man suddenly stepped from the curb. His gaze was upon the pavement, and he did not see the car.

Penny swerved the wheel and slammed on the foot brake. The edge of the fender brushed the man's overcoat. He gasped in astonishment and staggered backwards.

Penny brought the car to a standstill at the curb.

"You're not hurt?" she called anxiously.

"No—no," the man murmured in a bewildered way.

As he turned his face toward her, Penny recognized Matthew Judson, the former publisher of the *Morning Press*. Calling him by name, she invited him into the car.

"Let me take you home, or wherever you are going," she urged. "You don't look well, Mr. Judson. I am afraid I frightened you."

"It was my fault," admitted the old gentleman, staring at Penny. "I—I was thinking about something when I stepped from the curb."

"This is a dangerous intersection. Please, Mr. Judson, can't I take you home?"

"If you insist," he murmured, entering the car. "You seem to know my name, but I haven't the pleasure of your acquaintance."

"I'm Penny Parker. My father publishes the *Star*."

"Oh, yes." Mr. Judson's voice became spiritless.

"Your home is on Drexel Boulevard, I believe?" Penny inquired.

THE SECRET PACT

Matthew Judson nodded and in the same dull, lifeless voice supplied the address. He made no attempt at conversation.

As she stole occasional glimpses at the man, Penny thought that his face bore lines of mental fatigue and discouragement. He stared straight ahead with glazed, unseeing eyes.

Hoping to start a conversation, she presently remarked that she was the managing editor of the *Weekly Times*. For the first time Matthew Judson displayed interest.

"Oh, are you the girl who has taken over my building?" he asked.

"Yes, Mr. Veeley allows me the use of it rent free. I hope you don't mind?"

"Mind?" repeated Mr. Judson, laughing mirthlessly. "Why should I?"

"Well, I thought—that is—" Penny began to stammer.

"You thought that because I gave up my own paper I might not wish to see the building used by another?"

"Something like that," admitted Penny.

"I try not to think about the past," said Mr. Judson quietly. "Long ago I made my decision, and now must abide by it. I realize that I never can publish the *Press* again. I'm broken, beaten!"

The old man spoke with such bitterness that Penny glanced quickly at him. There was an expression in his dark eyes which startled her.

"Surely one can't be defeated as long as he's willing to fight," she ventured. "Why, if you chose to make a come-back, I'm certain you would succeed."

Mr. Judson shook his head impatiently. "You don't understand. I am through—finished. All I can hope to do is to hold fast to what little I have, and try to protect Pauletta."

"Pauletta is your wife?" Penny inquired kindly.

"My daughter. If it weren't for her—" Mr. Judson hesitated, then finished in a voice quite casual: "If it weren't for her, I probably would end it all."

Penny was shocked.

"Why, Mr. Judson!" she protested. "You can't mean that!"

"Don't be alarmed," he said, smiling faintly. "I have no intention of taking the easy way out."

A dozen questions flashed through Penny's mind, but she was afraid to ask any of them. From Mr. Judson's remarks it was fairly evident that he never had relinquished the *Press* voluntarily. Could financial difficulties alone account for his state of mental depression?

In the darkening twilight the car approached a white-painted brick house, set back some distance from the boulevard. Once an elegant dwelling, peeling paint had made it an unsightly residence. Roof shingles were curling, the front porch sagged, while an iron fence only partially hid a wide expanse of untended lawn.

"This is my home," said Mr. Judson. "Turn into the driveway if you wish."

Penny stopped the car just inside the iron gate.

As Mr. Judson alighted, a girl who appeared to be in her early twenties, arose from a bench. A white collie at her side, she came toward the car. Midway across the lawn, she paused, staring. Then, she half turned as if to retreat.

"Pauletta," called Mr. Judson. "Will you come here, please?"

Reluctantly the girl approached the car, her gaze meeting Penny's almost defiantly. Pauletta was a beautiful girl with auburn hair and steel-blue eyes.

"Pauletta, this is Miss Parker," said her father.

"How do you do," responded the girl coldly.

The instant Penny heard the voice she knew where she previously had seen Mr. Judson's daughter—on the steamer *Goodtime*! Pauletta was the girl who had tossed a wig and clothing into the river.

"How do you do, Miss Judson," she responded. "Haven't we met before?"

Pauletta kept her face averted from her father. She met Penny's gaze with a bold stare.

"I think not," she said evenly. "No, Miss Parker, you are mistaken."

CHAPTER 12 - OLD HORNEY

Penny made no reply to Pauletta and the silence became unbearable.

"Won't you stay for a few minutes?" Mr. Judson invited. "Pauletta, why not show Miss Parker our rose garden?"

"It's rather dark," his daughter replied. "Anyway, she wouldn't care to see it."

"Indeed, I should," contradicted Penny. Deliberately she switched off the car ignition.

Pauletta glared at her, but dared make no protest in her father's presence. With a shrug she led Penny along a gravel path to the rear of the house. Mr. Judson remained behind.

As soon as they were beyond hearing, Penny said quietly:

"Need we pretend? I am sure you recall that we met aboard the *Goodtime*."

"Yes, I remember now," admitted Pauletta coldly. "You were with another girl."

"And you were accompanied by a young man."

"A friend of mine."

"This may be something of a shock," said Penny, "but my chum and I saw you drop a bundle containing a wig into the river."

"Oh!"

"The bundle caught fast and I fished it out."

"You have no proof it was mine! You—you won't tell Father?"

"Not if you can offer a good reason why I shouldn't."

"There are any number of them. You mustn't tell my father! That's why I pretended not to know you."

"I certainly wish you would explain. Tillie Fellows was robbed that night."

"Who is Tillie Fellows?"

"One of the excursionists. Her pocketbook was taken shortly before the boat docked."

"You can't believe I had anything to do with it!"

"I don't wish to think so, but your actions were very strange."

"I can explain everything," Pauletta said hurriedly. "My reason for wearing a disguise was a simple one. I didn't care to have anyone on the boat recognize me."

"Why, may I ask?"

Before Pauletta could answer, Mr. Judson came around the corner of the house.

"Please say nothing about it to Father," the young woman pleaded in a whisper. "I'll explain everything later."

Penny nodded, and for Mr. Judson's benefit, offered a few remarks about the roses.

"We once had a beautiful garden," commented Pauletta. "Now it's in ruin, the same as the yard. Father doesn't look after the place as he should."

"The grounds are large," replied Mr. Judson mildly.

"You shouldn't try to do the work yourself," Pauletta protested. "It was foolish of you to let the gardener go."

Penny felt increasingly ill at ease. As they wandered about the grounds, Pauletta kept making disparaging remarks, thoughtless comments which wounded her father. However, he offered no rebuttal, nor did he reprove his daughter.

"I really must be going," said Penny at last. "It's getting very dark."

Mr. Judson walked with her to the car, closing the gate after she had driven from the grounds. He stood there a moment, the wind rumpling his gray hair. Then he raised his hand in friendly salute and turned toward the house.

"Poor Mr. Judson," she thought. "So discouraged and yet so gallant! How can Pauletta be completely blind to his suffering? Doesn't she realize?"

Penny did not regret having kept the young woman's secret, for she felt that the revelation of their meeting would only add to Mr. Judson's troubles. Pauletta represented his entire life, and if it developed that she had acted unbecomingly, the shock might be a severe one.

"I can't believe that Pauletta would steal," she told herself. "She must have had another reason for wearing the disguise."

Penny was satisfied that if Mr. Judson had not interrupted, the young woman would have explained her puzzling actions. Therefore, she was willing to give her the benefit of the doubt. She made up her mind that she would return as soon as she could to talk privately with Pauletta.

The Parker house was dark and deserted when Penny let herself in with a key. Her father had not expected her home so early and, disliking an empty house, had remained away. There was no telling where he had gone.

After preparing a belated dinner for herself, Penny spent an hour with her studies. However, her mind kept reverting to the events of the day. A great deal had happened. Her meeting with Peter Fenestra had been interesting. Anchor Joe's mishap worried her, and she remained disturbed by the threatening message left on her desk.

"Could it have been written by a prowler in the building?" she mused. "Ever since we started the paper I've felt that someone was hiding there. It may be a scheme to get me away."

Before dropping off to sleep Penny made up her mind that the following night she would set a trap for the intruder. Taking Louise into her confidence, she made careful plans. Preparing a tasty lunch, the girls wrapped and laid it conspicuously on the counter of the downstairs advertising room.

"Now the stage is set," declared Penny. "Louise, you go upstairs to my office and tap on the typewriter. I'll hide here and see what happens."

After Louise had gone, Penny secreted herself in a storage closet not far from the counter. By leaving the door open she could see fairly well in the dark room for street lights cast a reflection through the plate glass windows.

The minutes stretched into a half hour. Louise's typewriting, at first very energetic, began to slacken in speed. Penny moved restlessly in the cramped quarters. She had not imagined that waiting could be so tedious.

An hour elapsed. Far down the street a clock struck ten times.

With a weary sigh Penny arose from the floor. Inactivity bored her, and she no longer could sit quietly and wait.

As she started from her hiding place, intending to call Louise, a door opened at the west end of the room. Instantly Penny froze against the wall, waiting.

A flashlight beam played across the floor, missing her by a scant two feet.

Penny, her heart beating at a furious rate, remained motionless. She could see the squat, shadowy figure of a man moving toward her. Boards squeaked beneath his weight.

Midway across the room, the man paused, evidently listening to the steady clatter of Louise's typewriter. Satisfied, he went to the window where he stood for several minutes watching street traffic.

As he turned again, the beam of his flashlight swept across the front counter, focusing upon the package of food. The man gave a low exclamation of pleasure. With the swiftness of a cat he darted to it and tore off the paper wrapping.

Penny waited until he was eating greedily. Then stealing along the wall, she groped for the electric light switch. As she pressed it, the room was brilliantly illuminated. At the same instant, the girl gave a shrill whistle, a signal to Louise that the culprit had been trapped.

The man at the counter whirled around, facing Penny with startled dismay. He was a gaunt, unshaven fellow in his late fifties with shaggy hair, and soiled, unpressed clothing.

Before he could retreat, Louise came down the stairway, blocking the exit.

"What are you doing here?" Penny questioned him. "Why did you steal my lunch?"

The man's lips moved nervously but no sound issued from them.

CHAPTER 12 - OLD HORNEY

"Shall I call the police?" prodded Penny. She gave him a severe glance.

"No, don't do that," the man pleaded, finding his voice. "Don't call the police. I'll go. I won't bother you any more."

"Why have you been hiding in the building?"

"Because I have no other place to sleep, Miss. The cops chase you off the park benches."

Penny was surprised by the man's speech which belied his disreputable garments. His tone was well modulated, his manner respectful.

"You've been living in this building a long while?" she asked curiously.

"Maybe six months. I sleep down in the furnace room. I didn't do any harm."

"You're hungry, aren't you?" Penny inquired, less severely.

"Yes, I am, Miss. Lately I haven't been eating any too often."

"You may finish the lunch," said Penny. "And there's a thermos bottle of coffee under the counter."

"Thank you, Miss, thank you. I surely am obliged."

With a hand which trembled, the man poured himself a cup of the steaming beverage.

"You haven't told me your name," said Penny after a moment.

"Folks just call me Horney. Old Horney."

"What is your real name?"

"Mark Horning," the man answered reluctantly.

"I'm curious to learn how you've been getting in and out of the building."

"With a key." Old Horney devoured the last bite of sandwich, and poured himself a second cup of coffee.

"A skeleton key, you mean?" Penny asked in surprise.

"No, Miss. I have my own key. In the old days I used to work here."

"You're a former *Press* employee?"

"Sure, I know it's hard to believe," Old Horney replied, "but when a fellow's out of a job and money, it doesn't take long to go to seed. I lost my place when Judson closed down."

"And you've been unable to find other work?"

"In the past nine months I've worked exactly six days. No one hires an old fellow any more. If I could have kept on with Judson three more years I'd have been due for my pension."

"What work did you do on the paper?" asked Penny with growing interest.

"I was a pressman."

Penny shot Louise a glance which was almost triumphant. Her voice when she spoke held an undertone of excitement.

"Horney," she said, "it's barely possible I may be able to find some sort of work for you later on. Do you mind writing your name on this paper?"

The old man took the sheet she handed him, without hesitation scrawling his name, *Mark Horning*.

Penny studied the writing a moment. To her relief it bore not the slightest resemblance to the warning message left on her desk the previous night.

"Horney," she questioned, "did you ever try to frighten me away from this building?"

"Oh, no, Miss," he replied. "Once I tiptoed up to your office. When I saw you were working there, I slipped down to the basement again."

"Did you ever place a note on my desk?"

"I never did."

Penny was satisfied that Horney had told the truth. Yet if he were not the culprit she was unable to guess who had warned her to abandon the plant.

"Horney, I've decided that we need a watchman around this place," she said abruptly. "If you want the job, it's yours."

"You're not turning me out?"

"No, you may stay. I can't promise much of a salary, but at least you'll have a place to sleep and enough food."

"You're mighty kind," Horney mumbled gratefully. "Mighty kind." He hesitated and then added: "I promise you won't be sorry you did it, Miss. Maybe you'll find I can be of some real use around this plant. I'm at your service and what's more, I'm for you one hundred per cent."

CHAPTER 13 - PAPER PROBLEMS

The next afternoon Penny and Louise arrived at the *Weekly Times* to find that the entire lower floor had been cleaned and swept. Old Horney was discovered in the composing room, stirring up a great cloud of dust with a stub of a broom.

"I was just cleaning the place up a bit," he said apologetically. "Hope you don't mind."

"Mind?" laughed Penny. "I'm delighted. Our staff of janitors has lost interest here of late."

"I set a little type for you last night, too."

"Why, Horney! I didn't know you were a linotype operator."

"I'm not," answered the old man, "but I can learn most anything if I set my mind to it. If you have any jobs you want done just turn them over to me."

"Horney," said Penny soberly, "more than anything else I would like to publish the *Weekly* in my own plant. The obstacles seem almost too great to overcome; do you think it could be accomplished?"

"Why, sure," said Horney. "If I had some tools and a little to do with I could get the presses ready in a day."

"What about the stereotyping work?"

"I could master the trick of it," declared Horney confidently.

"Horney, you're a jewel!" laughed Penny. "I'll place you in charge of my production department, but I fear I can't give you a salary in proportion to your duties."

"Don't worry about that, Miss. I would rather be working than sitting around with nothing to do."

"Then look over the plant and make up a list of the things you must have," suggested Penny. "I'll go over to the *Star* this minute and arrange for printing paper."

Leaving Louise in charge of the office, she jubilantly set forth for her father's plant. Now that Old Horney had been added to the staff of the *Weekly*, problems which previously had seemed unsurmountable suddenly had become easily solved.

Entering the *Star* building, Penny went directly to the stockroom, wandering about until she found Mr. Curry, the foreman.

"Here's something for you," she grinned, offering a slip of paper.

"What's this?" Mr. Curry asked with a puzzled frown. "An order for a roll of paper?"

"Yes, Mr. Curry," explained Penny. "At last I am going to publish my own sheet over in the old *Press* building. Dad is staking me to a little paper."

"A little! Why, one of these big rolls would print more copies of your paper than you could sell in six months! And paper is expensive. How about a half-roll or even a quarter? It would be a lot easier to handle."

"Oh, all right," agreed Penny. "Just so I get enough to print my first issue."

Mr. Curry led the way to one of the presses, pointing to a roll of paper mounted on a feeding rack.

"That one is about half used up," he said. "Will it do?"

"Yes, I guess so," agreed Penny. "May I have it right away?"

Mr. Curry replied by pushing a tram along a miniature railway which ran under the press. With surprising skill, he maneuvered the roll into position on the carrier. Then he pushed the tram to the elevator, moved the portable paper lift over the roll, and up it went to the platform. The elevator grounded at the first floor where the paper was rolled to the loading dock with pry bars.

"There you are," said the foreman.

"All I need now is a truck," Penny cried exultantly. "Thanks, Mr. Curry!"

CHAPTER 13 - PAPER PROBLEMS

Standing guard beside her paper she waited until one of the *Star* drivers had finished unloading his cargo and was ready to pull from the dock.

"How's chances fer a ride, buddy?" asked Penny, jerking her thumb in the manner of a hitch-hiker. "Me and my paper to the *Weekly Times*."

"Okay," laughed the trucker.

He rolled the paper onto the truck, and Penny climbed into the cab beside him. At the *Times* building she had the roll set off at the rear entrance where Old Horney easily could get it to the press room.

Highly elated, Penny mounted the steps two at a time, bursting in upon Louise who was busy writing headlines.

"Got it!" she announced. "About six hundred pounds of paper. That should keep the *Weekly* going for awhile."

"Here's something to dampen your enthusiasm." Louise thrust a letter toward her. "Another kick on that octopus tattoo story you wrote. A Mrs. Brown says she heartily disapproves of such outlandish tales, and that she'll never buy another copy of the *Times*."

"At least it proves my story attracted attention," chuckled Penny. "Anything else while I was gone?"

"Yes, Mrs. Weems telephoned to ask that you come to the cottage as soon as possible. And that reminds me—the telephone bill. The company requires a month's advance—"

"Never mind the bills," interrupted Penny. "Did Mrs. Weems say anything about Anchor Joe?"

"He appears to be much better."

"I'm glad of that. I suppose I should drive out to the cottage before it gets dark."

"Run along. I'll look after everything here."

Penny swept her desk clear of papers and locked the drawers. "If you have any spare time you might see what you can do with my algebra assignment," she suggested. "I missed every problem but one yesterday."

"I have my own lesson troubles," responded Louise. "I'm wading up to my neck in Latin, and the next monthly quiz is certain to drown me."

"Teachers have no consideration," sighed Penny. "None at all."

Gathering up her school books, she bade Louise good-bye and left the office. On the stairway she met Old Horney.

"I've made my list," he said, offering it to her. "I figure we can't get out the paper with less than this."

Penny glanced at the paper and slipped it into her purse.

"I'll get the things somehow," she promised. "By the way, there's a roll of paper on the loading dock."

"I've already hauled 'er in," replied Old Horney. "Any other jobs for me?"

"No, you seem to be one jump ahead," laughed Penny.

They descended the stairway together, the steps creaking beneath their weight. There was a different look to Old Horney, Penny thought, stealing a glance at him. His hair had been cut and his face was clean-shaven. Work had given him a new outlook, a desire to recover his self respect.

"I suppose you knew Matthew Judson rather well?" she remarked reflectively.

"Oh, sure."

"What was he like, Horney?"

"Well—" the old man hesitated, at a loss for words. "Judson was queer, sort of cold and unfriendly except to those who knew him best, but he was a square-shooter."

"The employes liked him?"

"Everyone did except a few chronic sore-heads."

"Horney, was it true that the *Press* was making money at the time it closed?"

"That's what everyone on the paper thought. It was a shock to us all when Judson closed down. I'll never forget the day he told us he was giving up the plant. The old man looked like death had struck him, and he cried when he said good-bye to the boys."

"I wonder why he closed the plant?"

"Some say it was because he had lost a pile of money speculating on the stock market. But I never believed that. Judson wasn't the gambling type."

"Why do you think he gave up the paper, Horney?"

"I've done a lot of speculating on it," the old man admitted. "This is just my own idea, but I figure Judson may have been blackmailed."

"Blackmailed! By whom?"

"I can't tell you—it's only my guess."

"You have no evidence to support such a theory, Horney?"

"Nothing you could call that. But the day before Judson quit he was in the pressroom. He was sort of thinking out loud, I guess. Anyhow he said to me, 'Horney, the dirty blackmailer couldn't do this to me if it weren't for my daughter. If it didn't mean smearing her name, I'd fight!'"

"Did you ask him what he meant?"

"I made some reply, and then he closed up like a clam. I figure he hadn't realized what he was saying."

"You haven't any idea as to whom he meant?"

"I couldn't make a guess."

"No matter what the reason, it was a pity the *Press* had to close," declared Penny. "I feel very sorry for Mr. Judson."

Bidding Horney good-bye, she hurried home for her automobile. However, as she drove toward the river cottage she kept thinking about what the old pressman had told her.

"It's barely possible his theory is right," she mused. "But why should Mr. Judson submit to blackmail even for his daughter's sake? Somehow the pieces of the puzzle refuse to fit."

CHAPTER 14 - AN EMPTY BEDROOM

Darkness was inking the sky as Penny drew up at the end of the road. Parking her car between scraggly boxelders, she walked swiftly along the river trail, soon approaching within view of the Parker cottage.

The fallen tree had been sawed into cord wood, the yard cleaned of sticks and debris, and only the damaged porch remained to remind one of the severe storm.

As Penny opened the screen door, Mrs. Weems came from the kitchen.

"Joe is asleep," she warned in a whisper. "Perhaps we should talk outside."

Penny nodded and followed the housekeeper to the porch swing.

"How is he doing?" she inquired.

"Oh, much better," replied Mrs. Weems. "The doctor was here an hour ago. Joe is out of danger but must remain in bed for at least another day."

"I was afraid when you telephoned that something had gone wrong here."

"No," confessed the housekeeper, "I was merely lonesome for news. Is everything going well at home?"

"Oh, yes, we're getting along fine."

"I hope you remembered to bring in the milk. And you didn't neglect the dusting?"

Penny smiled ruefully.

"I might have known you would let everything go," sighed Mrs. Weems. "No doubt it's my duty to remain here, but I feel I should be at home."

"Anchor Joe needs you, Mrs. Weems. Has he talked very much?"

"Not a great deal. He ate a hearty lunch and seems in no pain."

"Did you see his back, Mrs. Weems?"

"Yes, the cut was an ugly one. The doctor changed the dressing while he was here."

"I mean the tattoo," said Penny impatiently. "Didn't you notice it?"

"I saw that he had one, if that's what you mean."

"You didn't question him about it?"

"Certainly not, Penny. Why should I?"

"Don't you read the *Weekly Times*? Anchor Joe's tattoo is a dead ringer for the one John Munn had on his back. Joe's already admitted that he knows Munn. For all we know they may be bitter enemies. Perhaps it was Anchor Joe who pushed Munn off the bridge!"

"Penny, your ideas grow wilder each day," protested Mrs. Weems. "I hope you don't talk such nonsense to other people."

"All the same, Anchor Joe bears someone a grudge," insisted Penny. "He mentioned a person who had 'ratted.' Didn't you learn a single fact about him, Mrs. Weems?"

"His last name is Landa and he came to Riverview three weeks ago. He has no family."

"I think I'll question him myself when he awakens."

"No, I can't allow that," said Mrs. Weems sternly. "The doctor would never approve."

"I promise not to excite him."

"The answer is no! Now I wish you would help me by bringing in the washing. I must start supper."

Penny obediently took the basket and unpinned sheets and pillow cases from the line. She had just finished when she observed a tall, well-built young man with military stride, approaching through the trees. He tipped his hat politely.

"I beg your pardon," he said, "I am trying to find the Parker cottage."

THE SECRET PACT

"Your search is at an end," answered Penny. "You've come to the right place."

"Do you have a man working here named Joe Landa?"

"Why, yes, we have."

"Where may I find him, please?"

"Joe is confined to his bed," explained Penny. "Unless it is very important I am afraid we can't allow you to talk with him today."

"It is important," said the stranger. "I am Clark Moyer, from the Federal Bureau of Investigation."

Penny's eyes opened wide. "A G-man?" she demanded.

"I am an investigator for the government," he replied, smiling.

"And you're after Anchor Joe?"

"I am here to question him."

"What has he done, Mr. Moyer?"

"I am not permitted to discuss a case to which I have been assigned," he returned, amused by her display of interest. "It's quite possible that Landa is not the man I seek. How long has he worked here?"

"Only a few days. He—he hasn't killed anyone, has he?"

"No," smiled the government man, "it's not that serious. The man I am after is short and wiry, sandy hair and blue eyes. He has a tattooed anchor on his right arm."

"And one on his back?" Penny asked eagerly.

"I wouldn't know about that. Does my description fit the man who has been working here?"

"Yes, it does! Almost exactly."

"Then I'd like to talk with him."

"Come into the cottage," invited Penny. "I'll call Mrs. Weems."

Summoned from the kitchen, the housekeeper listened to Mr. Moyer's request that he be permitted to see the injured man.

"If you are a government investigator I suppose it will be all right," she said reluctantly. "But the doctor's orders were that he was to be kept absolutely quiet."

"I'll only ask a question or two," promised Mr. Moyer.

"Is Joe wanted on a criminal charge?" the housekeeper asked.

"I was sent to check up on a man who calls himself Joe Landa. That's all I can tell you."

From the kitchen came the unmistakable odor of scorching potatoes. Mrs. Weems ran to jerk the pan from the stove.

"Penny, you see if Joe is awake yet," she called over her shoulder.

"I'll go with you," said Mr. Moyer quickly. "If I have made a mistake it may not be necessary to disturb the man."

"This way," directed Penny.

She led the government man down the hall to the rear bedroom. The door was closed. She twisted the knob and pushed, at first easily, and then with increasing force.

"It seems to be stuck," she said. "The recent rains must have caused the wood to swell."

"Let me try," offered Mr. Moyer.

He took Penny's place, and after testing the door, gave it a hard upward push. There was a loud crash as it suddenly swung open.

"Goodness! What was that?" exclaimed Penny.

"A barricade. Keep back."

To Penny's astonishment the government man drew his revolver before entering the room. Disregarding the order to remain behind, she followed him inside.

"I might have expected this!" he muttered.

Penny's gaze swept the room. A chair lay overturned on the floor. The bed, still bearing the imprint of a man's body, was empty.

"Why, where's Joe?" murmured Penny. "His clothing is gone, too!"

Mr. Moyer strode to the open window.

"You think he left that way?" Penny questioned. "He must have heard us talking!"

The government man nodded as he stepped through the opening to the ground.

CHAPTER 14 - AN EMPTY BEDROOM

"He heard us all right. There's no question now that he's the man I am after! And I'll get him, too!"

Briefly examining the ground beneath the window, Mr. Moyer turned and walked swiftly toward the river.

CHAPTER 15 - INFORMATION FROM TILLIE

Penny lost no time in telling Mrs. Weems that Anchor Joe had disappeared.

"Well, of all things!" exclaimed the housekeeper as she saw the deserted bedroom. "He was here a half hour ago. I know because I came in while he was sleeping."

"He must have heard Mr. Moyer inquiring about him," declared Penny. "Obviously he ran away to avoid the interview."

"Then that means he's guilty."

"I'm afraid so, Mrs. Weems. What do you suppose he did to have a government man after him?"

"He may have been a gangster."

"Anchor Joe?" asked Penny, smiling. "He hardly looked the type."

"In any event, we're fortunate to be rid of him."

"I wish we could have questioned him," Penny said gloomily. "Now I may never learn about that octopus tattoo."

"You and your tattoo!" scoffed Mrs. Weems, beginning to strip linen from the bed. "Anchor Joe certainly deceived me. He seemed such a pleasant sort and I was sorry for him."

"I still am," said Penny. "The poor fellow is in no condition to be wandering around. I rather hope Mr. Moyer overtakes him soon. Then at least he'll get the medical attention he requires."

While Mrs. Weems straightened the bedroom, she wandered to the river's edge. Only a few stars were pricking the sky, and it was impossible to see very far. There was no sign either of Mr. Moyer or the man he pursued.

Penny returned to the cottage to eat supper with Mrs. Weems.

"Now that Anchor Joe has gone, I may as well go home tonight," declared the housekeeper. "I can't leave, though, until I've cleaned the cottage and set it to rights."

"How much longer will it take?"

"Oh, an hour or two."

"While I am waiting I may walk over to Peter Fenestra's place," Penny remarked. "I shouldn't mind seeing Tillie Fellows again."

"You'll be cautious in crossing the river?"

"Of course," laughed Penny. "I won't be gone long."

She washed the dishes for Mrs. Weems and then set forth for the Fenestra farmhouse. Frogs croaked as she crossed the swaying bridge, and far upstream she heard the faint chug of a motorboat. Otherwise, the night was unusually still.

Emerging from among the trees, Penny saw a light glowing in the distance. Knowing that it came from the Fenestra house, she used it as a beacon to guide her.

Passing the barn, she climbed a fence and entered the yard. The house was dark save for a single light burning in the kitchen. She could see Tillie Fellows moving about.

Penny knocked on the side door. Through the window she observed Tillie freeze into a tense attitude of fear. To reassure the girl she called her name in a loud voice.

Immediately Tillie ran to open the door.

"Oh, it's you!" she exclaimed in relief. "I was frightened."

To Penny's surprise Tillie wore a silk dress. Pocketbook, hat and gloves lay upon the kitchen table.

"I am afraid I've come at an awkward time," she apologized. "You were going somewhere?"

CHAPTER 15 - INFORMATION FROM TILLIE

"I'm leaving here," Tillie answered grimly. She closed the door behind Penny.

"You mean for good? You've found another job?"

Tillie shook her head. "I've been discharged. He didn't give me a week's advance wages either."

"Oh, that's too bad," said Penny sympathetically. "But you'll find a better place. You said you didn't like it here anyway."

"I've hated it. Peter Fenestra is such a suspicious person. Why do you think he discharged me?"

"I can't guess, but I should like to know."

"He accused me of prying!"

"How unjust."

"Well, in a way, I was trying to learn about things I shouldn't," Tillie admitted honestly. "It was that storm cave."

"Did you get down into it?" Penny asked.

"No, but I tried. Old Peter was gone this afternoon and I decided to find out what he keeps hidden underground."

"The padlock wasn't locked?"

"Usually it is, but today he forgot. I got the door open. Just as I started down the steps he grabbed me by the shoulder. I was scared half to death."

"You mean Fenestra had hidden himself in the cave?" Penny questioned in astonishment.

"Yes, it was a trick to catch me prying. He said so himself, Penny. He only pretended to go away, then lay in wait."

"Did he threaten you?"

"No, he just told me to get out and never come back. It wouldn't surprise me if he leaves here himself soon."

"Why do you say that, Tillie?"

"Because he's afraid of his own shadow. But I don't blame him for being nervous. This house is being watched!"

As if fearing that unfriendly eyes were upon her at that very moment, Tillie went to the window and after peering into the yard, lowered the blind.

"Twice I've seen men hiding in the wheat field just back of this place," she confided. "The first time there was only one, but yesterday I saw three."

"Are you sure they were watching this house, Tillie?"

"Oh, yes, they were lying on the ground. For an hour they scarcely moved."

"Didn't you tell Fenestra?"

"I was afraid to do it, but I think he knew. All day he kept inside the house, and I saw him at the windows. He was as jumpy as a cat. Another thing—I saw him loading his revolver."

"He must fear for his life."

"I'm sure of it, Penny. Even if he's only going to the barn he carries the revolver with him."

A clock on the shelf above the stove struck eight times.

"Mercy!" exclaimed Tillie, "I must hurry or I'll never get away before Old Peter returns. Excuse me while I run upstairs for my suitcase."

"Where is Fenestra now?" Penny inquired before the girl could leave.

"In Riverview I suppose. He went away right after supper."

"Run along and get your suitcase," Penny advised. "I'll drive you into town."

"Oh, thanks," the girl answered gratefully. "It won't take me long."

After Tillie had gone, Penny walked to the window and rolled up the blind. Across the yard she could see the disfiguring mound of earth and cement. What secret did the storm cave guard? Why was it always kept padlocked?

Abruptly she went to the foot of the stairs and called:

"Oh, Tillie, I'm going outside for a minute. I'll come back."

"All right," agreed the girl. "Sorry to keep you waiting but I still have a few things to pick up."

Leaving by the side door, Penny paused on the porch for a moment. Carefully she glanced about the yard and surrounding fields. A thin quarter moon rising over the pine trees gave dim shape to the barn and silo. She could see no one, yet Tillie's revelation that strange men spied upon the house, made her attentive to danger.

Swiftly she crossed the lawn to the storm cave. As she had fully expected, the slanting door was padlocked.

"Oh, shoot!" she exclaimed impatiently. "I want to get down there!"

She jerked at the padlock several times, and then accepting the situation, turned toward the house. As she walked, Penny's eyes fastened absently upon a clump of lilac bushes some twenty yards from the cave. They were moving gently as if stirred by a wind. Yet there was no wind.

Penny did not pause, but every sense became alert. Her heart pounded. Distinctly she could see a man crawling on hands and knees behind the lilacs.

CHAPTER 16 - BEHIND THE LILACS

Without disclosing by her actions that she had observed anything amiss, Penny walked steadily on toward the house. Her first thought had been that it was Peter Fenestra who spied upon her. However, as the figure straightened she knew she had been mistaken. The man was not Fenestra.

Before she could see his face, he moved to another clump of bushes, and then was enveloped by darkness.

Entering the house, Penny blew out the kerosene lamp and stood by the window, watching. She could not see the man. He had vanished completely.

"That proves that Tillie was correct," she thought. "This house *is* being watched. I wonder why."

As she waited, Tillie came down the stairway, carrying her luggage. Observing that the kitchen was dark, she paused in alarm.

"It's all right," Penny called reassuringly. "I blew the light out so that I wouldn't be seen from outside."

"Is anyone there?" Tillie demanded, coming quickly to the window. Her pallid features were rigid with fear and her breathing quickened.

"He's gone now, I think."

"There was someone a moment ago?"

"Yes, a man, hiding behind the lilacs. I believe he must have been watching the house—or possibly the storm cellar!"

"Then you see I was right," Tillie declared. "Oh, this is a dreadful place, and I'll be glad to leave it."

"I almost wish you were staying," said Penny slowly. "You might be able to learn what's hidden in that cave."

"Not with Peter Fenestra so suspicious. Anyway, you couldn't hire me to remain even if he would allow it. I'd rather starve."

"You have no place to go, Tillie?"

"I'll find work. If not in Riverview then I can return to the country. Anything will be better than what I've had."

Penny groped in the dark for the lamp, relighting it.

"Tillie," she said, "how would you like to work at our place for a few days?"

"You don't mean it."

"I do if it can be arranged," Penny affirmed. "We have a housekeeper, but it occurred to me that she might take your place here."

"She'd be very foolish to give up a good job for this."

"It would only be temporary. I think I can induce her to make the change for a few days. The question is, can we get Peter Fenestra to accept her?"

"I doubt if he'll hire anyone now that I am leaving. Why do you want your housekeeper in such a place as this, Penny?"

"Only for one reason. To learn what's going on here. I confess you've made me very curious about the storm cave."

"Fenestra would watch her every minute, the same as he did me. It won't work."

"It will if Mrs. Weems can get the job," declared Penny confidently. "First of all, we must make Fenestra so uncomfortable he'll want someone to take care of the house. Is he a good cook?"

"Oh, wretched. And the trick of keeping a good fire going is simply beyond him. Why, if we turned the damper, it never would occur to him to change it."

THE SECRET PACT

"Thanks for the idea," laughed Penny. "Let's hide the breakfast supplies, too."

Tillie was quite certain that her friend did not know what she was doing, but she offered no objection to the plan. Before leaving the house they altered the stove damper, hid the coffee pot, and placed salt in the sugar bowl.

"If Old Peter doesn't get his coffee in the morning he'll simply rave," chuckled Tillie. "Missing it may be the one thing which will make him hire a new housekeeper."

The girls were watchful as they crossed the yard, but they observed no one lurking about the premises. Evidently the man who had hidden behind the lilacs had taken himself elsewhere.

Penny escorted Tillie to the parked automobile, leaving her there while she went to the cottage for Mrs. Weems. The housekeeper was ready and waiting by the time she arrived.

"Penny, I nearly gave you up," she sighed. "Why did it take so long?"

"I've been busy finding you a new position," chuckled Penny. "Starting tomorrow morning, you're to work for Peter Fenestra instead of us."

In the act of locking the cottage door, Mrs. Weems turned to face the girl.

"Penny," she said, "I am tired tonight and in no mood for your jokes."

"This isn't a joke, Mrs. Weems. I really do want you to change jobs with Tillie Fellows. You remember I told you about her."

Not giving the housekeeper an opportunity to speak, she rapidly outlined her plan.

"Early tomorrow morning I'll drive you to Fenestra's farm," she ended gleefully. "You're to knock on the door, and say you're looking for a job at very low wages. Fenestra will be so desperate he'll welcome you with open arms. Then as soon as he's off his guard you learn what is hidden in the storm cave."

"How lovely," said Mrs. Weems. "I've listened to your crazy schemes for years, Penny, but this one takes the prize!"

"You'll do it, won't you?"

"I certainly will not." The housekeeper spoke with biting emphasis.

"Oh, Mrs. Weems," Penny moaned. "You don't realize how much this means to me! If only you'll go there, I may be able to get a wonderful scoop for the *Weekly Times*."

"I wish you never had started that paper. I declare, ever since you took over the old *Press* plant, you've done the wildest things."

"This isn't wild," Penny argued. "It's absolutely logical. I would try for the job myself only I know Fenestra wouldn't give it to me. Besides, I am kept busy at the plant."

"I refuse to play detective for you, Penny. That's final."

Completely downcast, Penny followed Mrs. Weems along the river trail. However, she had no intention of giving up so easily.

"Then if you won't," she remarked, "I must take Tillie to a charity home. She had intended to start working at our place."

"The girl may spend the night with us, if you like. We have an extra room."

"Tillie would never accept such a favor," insisted Penny. "More than anything else she wants a job. Mrs. Weems, please reconsider—"

"It's a crazy scheme!"

"No, it isn't," Penny refuted, and noting indications of weakening, launched into another lengthy argument.

Mrs. Weems drew a deep sigh. "I don't know why I allow you to twist me around your finger the way you do."

"You'll try for the job?"

"I suppose so. But what will your father say?"

"He'll call it clever journalism," chuckled Penny. "Don't you worry about Dad. Just leave everything to me."

During the ride to Riverview Mrs. Weems was further influenced by Tillie Fellows' account of Fenestra's peculiar actions. Gradually she began to share Penny's opinion that the man might have reason to fear for his life. However, she could not agree with the girls that anything of great value was hidden in the cave.

CHAPTER 16 - BEHIND THE LILACS

"Perhaps we're wrong," Penny conceded, "but you must go there with an open mind, Mrs. Weems. Observe everything you can and report to me. Particularly I want to learn what Fenestra knows about John Munn and the octopus tattoo."

"I shan't try very hard to get the job," threatened the housekeeper.

At seven the next morning Penny awakened Mrs. Weems from a sound slumber, reminding her that it was time to start for the Fenestra farm. Protesting that the idea seemed crazier than ever, the housekeeper snuggled down beneath the covers again.

"You promised you would go," reminded Penny brutally. "Please hurry, because I must get you established before I go to school."

By the time Mrs. Weems was dressed, breakfast and the car awaited her. She drank the bitterly strong coffee and, still protesting, allowed Penny to drive her within view of the Fenestra farm.

"Is that the place?" she inquired with distaste as the automobile halted.

"Yes, I don't dare go any closer for fear Fenestra will see me. You know the story you're to tell him."

"Which one? You've suggested so many that my mind is a-whirl."

"Then make it simple. Just say you're a widow, out of work, and that you're a wonderful housekeeper. I'll wait here. If you go inside I'll know you've been given the job."

"When will you come for me?"

"I'll try to see you tomorrow. But hold the fort until I arrive even if it's a week."

A bundle of clothing under her arm, Mrs. Weems trudged on down the road. Penny watched her with misgiving. The adventure was not to the housekeeper's liking, and it was doubtful that her application for work would be an enthusiastic one.

Turning the car in the road, she pulled to one side and waited. Mrs. Weems had reached the farmhouse. Following instructions, she knocked at the side entrance. In a moment or two the door was opened by Peter Fenestra.

Anxiously, Penny watched. The interview seemed to be taking a long while, but at least Fenestra had not closed the door in the housekeeper's face.

Then, to her delight, Mrs. Weems followed the man into the house.

"The job is hers!" she thought exultantly. "If she doesn't fail me, I may yet break an important story in my paper! I feel in my bones that Peter Fenestra's cave soon will yield its secret!"

CHAPTER 17 - THE ART OF TATTOO

At school, during the afternoon assembly period, Penny received a note from Louise which read:

"The *Weekly Times* is in urgent need of feature stories for our next issue. Any ideas?"

Penny scrawled a huge zero on the paper, decorated it with angel wings, and sent it down the aisle. An answer came immediately.

"You'll have to do something about it. All of our reporters are taking a vacation until after monthly exams. Can't you write some sort of story?"

Penny considered the problem as she studied her history lesson. Just as the dismissal bell rang an inspiration seized her.

"Lou, I do have an idea!" she declared, linking arms with her chum. "How about an interview with Ellis Saal?"

"Who is he?" inquired Louise, somewhat dubiously.

"A tattoo artist who has a little shop on Dorr Street. He takes passport pictures, too. I noticed the place weeks ago."

"What makes you think the story would be worth printing?"

"Tattooing is a fascinating subject."

"It is to you. I doubt if our readers share your enthusiasm."

"They will when they read my story," countered Penny.

Early the next morning she presented herself at Mr. Saal's place of business, a den-like crack in the wall, barely wide enough to accommodate a door.

Pausing, she stared at a sign which proclaimed that for a nominal sum Mr. Saal would tattoo or photograph all comers. In a glass frame were displayed many samples of tattooing—bleeding hearts, clasped hands, sailing ships, birds in flight and other artistic conceptions.

Penny entered the shop. The front end of the long, narrow room was unoccupied, but the sound of hammering led her to the rear. A man of some sixty-odd years was engaged in making a new shelf. As he saw her the hammer dropped from his hand.

"Good morning," said Penny in her friendliest tone. "Are you Mr. Saal?"

"That's me," he replied, regarding her curiously.

"Excuse me for bothering you," apologized Penny, "but I should like to interview you for my newspaper."

Mr. Saal's intelligent but somewhat child-like eyes fixed her in a steady stare.

"A reporter," he said finally in a long suffering tone. "They wouldn't respect a man's privacy—or anything else for that matter, I reckon."

"There is one thing I am sure all reporters respect, Mr. Saal," responded Penny. "Art. From the samples of your work which I saw out front I am sure you are a great tattoo artist."

Mr. Saal melted like a lump of butter on a hot stove. Penny had struck his weakest spot.

"You flatter me," he said, a faint pattern of a smile etching his face. "I admit I'm good, although maybe not quite the best in the business. What do you want to know?"

"A story about the tattooing business in general and you in particular, Mr. Saal. How do you do it? How did you start? Who was the most famous person you ever tattooed? What is your favorite design? Do you think a tattoo looks better on the arm or the chest? What—?"

"Hold it, young lady, hold it. You seem to be a living question mark."

CHAPTER 17 - THE ART OF TATTOO

Mr. Saal motioned for Penny to follow him to the front of the shop. As he offered her a chair she took a quick glance at a row of dirty, smeary bottles of chemicals on a shelf above her head.

"Now let's take your first question," said Mr. Saal, seating himself opposite the girl. "I can't tell you how to tattoo—that's a secret of the profession."

"How much do you charge for one?"

"Depends upon how much a fellow is willing to pay. Take this town—it's a cheap place. Nobody has any money. The King of England paid fifty dollars for his tattoo and what do I get? I'm lucky if it's a dollar. And mostly hoodlums to work on. You can't give a man much of a tattoo for a dollar."

"Do you ever remove tattoos, Mr. Saal?"

"It's against the law," the man replied briefly.

"I didn't know that," said Penny in surprise. "Why?"

"Crooks can be identified by their tattoos. Oh, it's easy for a fellow to get one on, but not so easy to get it off."

"But it can be done?" Penny persisted. "Have you ever removed one?"

"I'm the only man in the state who can take off a tattoo so it doesn't show," boasted Mr. Saal. "The surgeons have tried, but you always can see where it was."

"Tell me about some of the tattoos you've removed," urged Penny.

"I've told you more than I should now," said Mr. Saal. "You'll print it in the paper and then I'll get into trouble with the police."

"This will be strictly confidential," promised Penny.

"It's this way," Mr. Saal justified himself. "I never do any work for crooks—not me. But if a law-abiding, respectable citizen comes here and says he's sick of his tattoo, then sometimes I take it off for him if he's willing to pay the price. Fact is, I'm workin' on a mighty interesting case right now. It's a design that's rare—an octopus."

Penny did not trust herself to speak for a moment. Carefully she controlled her voice as she said casually:

"How interesting, Mr. Saal, An octopus tattoo! Was the man a sailor?"

"He was an old salt all right, though he denied it."

"What is his name?"

"I couldn't tell you that," answered Mr. Saal. "I have to protect my customers."

"Tell me more about the tattoo," urged Penny.

"It's just a figure about so large—" Mr. Saal demonstrated with his hands, "on the man's back. Funny place for a tattoo, ain't it?"

"I should say so," agreed Penny. "Is it merely a figure of an octopus? No words or anything like that?"

"There are two words. I took 'em off last week."

"Two?" inquired Penny. "What are they, Mr. Saal?"

"They don't make sense. The words are *For One*."

"I once saw an octopus tattoo such as you describe," declared Penny. "But I distinctly recall that the design used only a single word. It was *One*."

"Is that so?" inquired Mr. Saal. "Maybe the tattoo isn't as uncommon as I thought. But I never saw one like it before."

"I wonder what can be the significance of the words?"

"I was asking my customer about it. He pretended he didn't know, but I figure maybe he and some buddies had a sentence tattooed on 'em."

"You mean that if one were able to read several tattoos together, the words would make sense?"

"That's right," nodded Mr. Saal. "I don't know about this octopus tattoo, but I figure it may have been that way."

"Did your customer have any other tattoos on his body?" Penny questioned. "An anchor, for instance?"

"Didn't notice 'em if he did."

"I suppose it takes a long while to remove a tattoo. Does your customer come often?"

"Every Tuesday and Thursday night. He complains because I don't do the work faster, but I tell him if he wants a good job it has to be done carefully."

Before Penny could ask another question, two young sailors swaggered into the shop. Ellis Saal, scenting business, immediately arose.

"Be careful what you write up," he warned as he left her. "There's been a lot of articles on tattooin', but not a one that's right. It just ain't possible for a reporter to write a true story unless it's about a murder or a fire!"

"I'll be careful," promised Penny.

Leaving the shop, she walked slowly to her parked car. The information obtained from the tattoo artist both excited and mystified her.

"I don't believe Mr. Saal could have been mistaken about the words which were incorporated in the design," she thought. "And I'm equally certain I wasn't mistaken about Anchor Joe's tattoo. It had only the single word, 'One.'"

Mr. Saal's declaration that his customer was not the possessor of a tattooed anchor caused Penny to wonder if the person could be Joe Landa. However, the man was wanted by government agents and it seemed reasonable to believe that he might seek to remove tell-tale markings.

"I know what I'll do," she decided. "Thursday night I'll watch Mr. Saal's shop. In that way I may be able to learn the identity of his mysterious customer!"

CHAPTER 18 - PAULETTA'S EXPLANATION

Penny compressed the facts given her by Ellis Saal into a brief, lively feature story for the *Weekly Times*. She was careful not to divulge that the man had removed a tattoo from a customer, but to Louise she confided the entire story.

"All unwittingly, Mr. Saal gave me just the clue I need," she declared enthusiastically. "It will be a gigantic step forward if I learn the identity of his mysterious customer."

"What's to be gained by it?" asked Louise as she slugged a story and speared it on a hook. "What will be proven?"

"Well, if I'm ever going to solve the mystery I must gather every fact I can," Penny said defensively. "I aim to learn the meaning of those strange tattoos and, above all, the reason why John Munn was pushed from the bridge."

"You have your work cut out for you," responded Louise dryly.

"But Mr. Saal's information helps. You remember I told you that John Munn's tattoo bore the word *All*. Anchor Joe's was exactly the same except for the word, *One*. And now Ellis Saal has a customer with two words on his back: *For One*. Why, I believe I have it!"

Penny sprang from her chair, eyes dancing with excitement.

"You have what?" asked Louise calmly.

"It came to me like a flash—the meaning of those tattooed words! If we haven't been dumb!"

"Kindly stop jumping around, and explain."

"Mr. Saal told me he thought several sailors might have had a sentence incorporated in their tattoo. That is, only a word or two was used in each design, but taken as a whole it would make sense."

"And you think you have the phrase?"

"I do, Louise! Why couldn't it be: *All for one, one for all*?"

"If the men were close friends, that would be fairly logical. But the words we have to juggle don't make such a sentence, Penny."

"Obviously there must be a fourth sailor whose tattoo includes the words, 'for all,'" argued Penny. "Then it would fit perfectly."

"Just because four men were pals, you think they would have such nonsense tattooed on their backs?"

"That's my theory."

"If you're right, then the mystery is solved."

"Far from it," corrected Penny. "I haven't learned who pushed John Munn from the bridge or why. You remember how Anchor Joe talked about someone who had 'ratted'? The four of them must have been in on a scheme, and one man betrayed his comrades."

"Better bridle that imagination before it takes you for too wild a ride," chuckled Louise.

"Then you think there's nothing to my theory?" Penny demanded in an injured tone.

"I think that if you speculate upon it much longer we'll never get any work done," Louise replied, turning once more to her typewriter. "These headlines must be composed if ever we expect to get another paper on the street."

Disappointed that her chum did not take the matter more seriously, Penny went to consult Old Horney in the composing room. The pressman had proven to be worth many times the small salary which the girls paid him. Not only had he made the rotary presses ready for service, but he had cleaned and oiled every useable piece of machinery in the building. Eagerly he awaited the day when Penny would print the *Weekly* in her own plant.

THE SECRET PACT

"Everything's all set," he told her with a worshipful grin. "Whenever you give the word, we can go to press."

"That's fine," Penny praised. "Louise and I have been having a few difficulties, financial and otherwise. But I hope it won't be long now."

She talked with Old Horney about various technical problems, then returned to her desk. Slipping a sheet of paper into her typewriter, she composed a letter to a well known steamship, the *Dorasky*.

Slipping it into her pocket, she opened the door of Louise's office.

"Do you mind staying here alone for awhile?"

"No, of course not. Where are you going?"

"To mail an important letter. Then I want to drive out to Fenestra's farm and see Mrs. Weems."

"I'll look after everything until you get back," Louise promised. She glanced curiously at the letter but did not ask to whom it was directed.

Penny dropped the stamped envelope into a convenient corner mailbox, and then drove toward the outskirts of the city. Nearing Drexel Boulevard it suddenly occurred to her that she never had found time to revisit Matthew Judson's home.

"Pauletta owes me an explanation for the way she acted the other day," she thought. "I have a notion to stop and see if she's alone."

Penny impulsively spun the wheel, and followed the boulevard to the Judson home. The iron gate stood open. She drove through, up the curve of cement to the house.

In response to her knock, an untidy colored maid admitted her to a dark, dusty living room. As she awaited Pauletta, her wandering gaze noted a number of significant details. The walls had not been decorated in many years, upholstered furniture had assumed a moth-eaten appearance, and the entire room seemed spiritless.

Pauletta came slowly down the circular stairway. She hesitated as she recognized Penny, but could not retreat.

"How do you do," she said somewhat stiffly. "Nice of you to call."

"I think you know why I came," said Penny. "We were unable to talk when I was here before."

"I've told you all there was to it," Pauletta declared, seating herself opposite the girl. "Frankly, I can't see that the affair is any of your concern. I wore the disguise because I didn't wish to be recognized on board the *Goodtime*."

"Your explanation isn't very satisfactory, I'm afraid. Tillie Fellows is staying at our home now."

"What of it?"

"She was robbed that night on the boat."

"We discussed it before," Miss Judson said in exasperation. "You insult me by suggesting that I may have snatched the girl's pocketbook! Why should I steal when my father is wealthy? I've always had everything I want."

"I should like very much to believe you," said Penny quietly. "But unless you are willing to offer a complete explanation, I am afraid I can't."

"Very well, if I must, I'll tell," Miss Judson replied angrily. "You may have read in the newspapers that I am engaged to marry Major Howard Atchley?"

"The story escaped me."

"I admire Howard very much," resumed Pauletta, still in an icy tone. "He comes from an excellent family, is well-to-do, and in Father's opinion will make me a good husband."

"Your opinion differs?" Penny inquired softly.

"I do not love Howard, and I never shall. On the night you saw me aboard the *Goodtime* I had gone with another friend of mine, Carl Feldman, intending to enjoy the excursion trip."

"Your father knew nothing about it?"

"I told him I was going with another girl."

"Oh, I see."

"There was nothing wrong about it," Pauletta said irritably. "But I'm fairly well known. I realized that if I were recognized, Father or Howard might learn about it. Then there would be trouble, for Howard is a very jealous person."

"So you resorted to the wig and glasses?"

CHAPTER 18 - PAULETTA'S EXPLANATION

"Yes, that was my sole reason. Major Atchley met me at the boat. Before joining him I threw the bundle of clothing into the river. Now are you satisfied with my explanation?"

"I am," said Penny. "In fact, I never believed that you had robbed Tillie."

"You certainly acted that way."

"Perhaps, I only wanted to learn the truth."

Miss Judson did not reply. Her cold stare made it evident that she disliked Penny and regarded her as a meddler.

"Is there anything else you wish to know?" she asked after a lengthy silence.

"Nothing, Miss Judson. I was only thinking that I would like to help you and your father."

"Thank you. We don't require assistance."

"Perhaps you don't," said Penny, "but your father needs friends. He admitted to me that if it weren't for you he would be tempted to end everything."

The words stunned Pauletta. "Father never said that!" she exclaimed.

"He did."

"I can't believe it. Why, Father's the most cheerful person in the world!"

"In your presence, possibly. The loss of the *Morning Press* must have been a heavy blow to him."

"Father wasn't forced to give up the paper," Pauletta protested. "He did it because he was tired of working so hard."

"Was that what he told you?"

"Why, yes. I know of no other reason."

"The general belief seems to be that your father speculated on the stock market, losing large sums of money."

"That can't be true," denied Pauletta. "To my knowledge Father never gambled. He may have bought a few stocks from time to time, but only for investment."

"Then you feel sure he did not dispose of the *Press* because he needed money?"

Pauletta hesitated before she answered. "It never occurred to me before, but Father has been rather close the past year. I thought it was sheer carelessness when he let this place run down. He always gave me everything I wanted."

"Why does he favor your marriage to the Major?"

"Perhaps money does enter into it," Pauletta said slowly. "Many times Father has reminded me that I would have every luxury as Howard's wife."

"Your friend Carl is poor?"

"He has a fairly good position, but not much money. Father always seemed to like Carl. That was why I couldn't understand when he asked me not to see him again."

"I am sure your father thinks only of your welfare."

"But I would rather marry Carl and be poor always than to have riches with Howard."

"You've not told your father that?"

"Why, no. It never occurred to me that money had influenced him."

"There's another rumor," said Penny. "I suppose I shouldn't mention it."

"I wish you would."

"I've heard it said that your father disposed of the *Press* because he had been blackmailed."

"By whom?"

"I haven't the slightest idea. It was only a rumor."

"There may be truth in it," Pauletta replied in a low voice. "You've opened my eyes, Miss Parker. I've been very blind."

"Then you think someone may have forced your father to pay money?"

"I don't know. But Father has acted strangely ever since he gave up the paper. Once a month, on the fourth, he receives a visit from a queer looking man. Always he tries to get me out of the house before the fellow comes."

"Don't you know his name?"

"No, Father has never told me. The man seldom stays longer than ten minutes."

"Can you describe him?"

"Not very well because I never saw him at close range. I should say he's middle-aged, dark and cruel looking. Not at all the sort Father would choose for a friend."

"Your father offers no explanation as to why the man comes?"

"None. He refuses to discuss the subject. I've noticed, though, that for days after the fellow leaves he's very nervous and uneasy."

"Excuse me for asking so many questions, Miss Judson, but do you know of any reason why your father might be blackmailed?"

"No, I don't. I am sure he's never been involved in anything dishonorable."

Penny had no more to tell, and she was convinced that Pauletta had given a truthful account of the situation. Feeling that she was not particularly welcome, she arose to leave.

"I am glad you came," Pauletta said, extending her hand. "Please excuse my rudeness. There were so many things I failed to understand."

"You must forgive me, too," replied Penny. "I didn't mean to meddle. I truly want to help your father."

"I wish I could help him, too," said Pauletta in a troubled voice. "In the past I fear I've been very selfish and inconsiderate."

"There's a way to help if you're willing to do it."

"I don't understand."

"You say that on the fourth of each month a man comes here to see your father. If you tried could you learn his name?"

"I might drop in upon them at an awkward moment, compelling Father to introduce me."

"Are you willing to do it?"

"Why, yes, but I fail to see what will be gained."

"Perhaps nothing, perhaps a great deal," replied Penny. "If the man is a blackmailer, it should help for us to know his name."

"I'll learn what I can."

"Then until the fourth, good-bye. And please, not a word to Mr. Judson. We must work secretly."

Reflecting upon the information given her by Pauletta, Penny drove on toward Peter Fenestra's home. A quarter of a mile away she parked the car, and set off afoot, hoping to attract no attention should the owner be at home.

It was well that she took the precaution. She was three hundred yards from the grounds when suddenly she saw a man emerge from behind the barn. At a glance she observed that he was too short to be Peter Fenestra.

As Penny paused to watch, the man moved stealthily across the yard to the front door of the farmhouse. His face turned slightly in her direction, and she recognized Anchor Joe.

"What can he be doing here?" she thought in amazement.

The question soon was answered. Glancing quickly about, Anchor Joe dropped a white envelope on the front porch. Then he pounded several times on the door before darting to the shelter of the lilac bushes.

CHAPTER 19 - MRS. WEEMS' REPORT

Several minutes elapsed before the door was opened by Peter Fenestra. He glanced alertly about the yard, and then his gaze fell upon the envelope. Penny heard him mutter to himself as he picked it up.

Fenestra's face became convulsed with rage as he tore open the flap and saw the message. Still muttering, he crumpled the paper and thrust it into his pocket. Entering the house, he slammed the door.

With Peter at home Penny dared not try to see Mrs. Weems. As she hesitated, debating, Anchor Joe came from his hiding place. He did not see the girl.

"Joe!" she called softly.

The sailor turned. Recognizing her, he ran in the opposite direction across the yard. Keeping low behind a hedge, he started toward the river.

"Joe! Come back!" Penny called again.

Paying no heed, the sailor fled through the fields. Soon he was hidden by tall trees and bushes.

Penny felt deeply disturbed, wondering if Anchor Joe made a practice of watching the Fenestra home. She was inclined to believe that this had not been his first visit there.

Unexpectedly the farmhouse door swung open. Penny barely had time to step behind a large maple before Peter Fenestra came down the path. He went directly to the barn, and a few minutes later backed out his automobile.

"Good!" thought Penny. "He's likely driving to Riverview. Now I can talk to Mrs. Weems without fear of interruption."

As soon as the car had disappeared down the main road, she ran to the kitchen door and knocked. When it was not opened immediately, she thrust her head inside and called the housekeeper's name.

"Here I am," answered Mrs. Weems, hurrying from the dining room. "I hope you've come to take me home, Penny Parker!"

"No, only to receive your report." Penny sank into a chair beside the stove. "You don't act very pleased with your new job."

"It's a dreadful place. I was crazy to say I would stay here."

"Haven't you learned anything?"

"I've learned that Peter Fenestra is one of the most disagreeable men I ever met in my life! There's no satisfying him. He requires a slave, not a housekeeper!"

"But what about the storm cave?" Penny asked. "Were you able to find out what Fenestra stores in it?"

"Of course not. The padlock always is locked, and he keeps the key in his pocket."

"But he does have something hidden there?" Penny questioned eagerly. "He goes down into it at night?"

"I've seen him enter the cave once since I came here."

"When was that?"

"Last night after I had gone to bed. I heard the door close, so l went to the window and watched."

"How long did he stay there, Mrs. Weems?"

"About three hours I'd judge. It was after two o'clock when he returned to his room."

"What *can* he have hidden in the cave?"

"Nothing in my opinion," declared Mrs. Weems. "I think he cooks something. At least he builds a fire."

"What makes you think that?"

"I could see smoke seeping out from the cracks of the cave door."

THE SECRET PACT

Penny frowned. "I can't guess what he could be cooking," she said. "Surely he doesn't have a still down there."

"I doubt it very much. Probably you've built up a great mystery about nothing."

Pouring hot water over the dishes, Mrs. Weems began to wash them. Penny picked up a towel and automatically wiped and stacked them away.

"I didn't imagine that this house was being watched," she replied. "Only a few minutes ago I saw Anchor Joe steal to the door and leave a letter for Mr. Fenestra."

"Anchor Joe!"

"Mr. Moyer never caught him it seems. But why should the fellow come here? What message did he leave Fenestra?"

"I heard a knock on the front door," Mrs. Weems admitted. "Fenestra answered it, and when he came back into the kitchen he was in a dreadful temper."

"The letter upset him?"

"I didn't know he had received one."

"Yes, Anchor Joe left it on the doorstep. It may have been a threatening note. I'd give a lot to know."

"Fenestra has been very nervous since I came here," Mrs. Weems contributed. "If he hears any unusual sound in the yard he immediately becomes alert."

"As if he were afraid for his life?"

"Yes, he does act that way. I doubt if he'll stay here much longer. His clothes are all packed in suitcases."

"That *is* important information," declared Penny. "Oh, dear, if only we knew why he's being threatened, and why he intends to leave! I believe I'll go upstairs and inspect his room."

"You'll learn nothing there," responded Mrs. Weems. "Fenestra is a careful man. He leaves no papers lying about."

"It will do no harm to look."

Penny climbed the creaking stairs and was followed by Mrs. Weems.

"This is his room," said the housekeeper, opening a door. "I haven't made the bed yet."

She busied herself smoothing covers while Penny wandered about. The room had no rug. It was furnished with an old fashioned dresser, a wash stand and a bed with a high headboard.

Penny opened the closet door. The hangers were dangling together, without clothing. Everything had been packed into two suitcases which stood against the wall.

"I've already inspected the luggage," said Mrs. Weems as the girl bent to open one of the bags. "You'll find nothing except clothing. I tell you, Peter Fenestra is a very cautious man."

"I can believe it," agreed Penny. "This room is as bare of evidence as Mother Hubbard's cupboard."

"Just what do you hope to find?"

"Well, I don't know. What's this?" Penny picked up a sheet of notebook paper from the dresser.

"Don't get excited over that," laughed Mrs. Weems.

"It's only a grocery list which Fenestra made up. He doesn't trust anyone to spend his money for him."

"Is this Fenestra's writing?" Penny studied the paper with intense interest.

"Yes, it is."

"Mrs. Weems, I've seen this writing before!" Penny exclaimed. "I'm almost certain of it. There's a marked resemblance!"

"A resemblance to what, Penny?"

"Why, to a threatening note I received. I guess I never told you. Someone left a message on my desk at the newspaper office, warning me to give up my paper."

"And you think Peter Fenestra left it there?" inquired the housekeeper, smiling.

"This looks like the same writing."

"Probably you are mistaken, Penny. Why should he have any interest in your paper?"

"He came to the office one day, questioning me about a story I ran concerning John Munn. I shall keep this and compare it with the note."

Carefully folding the paper, Penny slipped it into her dress pocket. Mrs. Weems had finished making the bed and was ready to leave.

"I've learned everything I can for you," she said. "Now I hope you're willing to let me return home."

CHAPTER 19 - MRS. WEEMS' REPORT

"Please stay another day," pleaded Penny. "I feel in my bones that we're about to make an important discovery."

"Those bones of yours!" complained the housekeeper. "Tell me, how is Tillie Fellows getting along?"

"Well, she tries hard, but I'll admit Dad doesn't like the arrangement."

"Then I must return. It's nonsense for me to stay here."

Penny was paying no attention to Mrs. Weems' words. She had picked up the waste paper basket and was examining the contents. There were a few advertising circulars, an unaddressed envelope and a crumpled ball of paper. The latter, Penny carefully smoothed.

"Mrs. Weems!" she exclaimed. "Look at this!"

The housekeeper hastened to her side. Curiously, she examined the paper. It bore no writing, only a crude drawing of an octopus.

"This must be the paper which Anchor Joe left on the doorstep only a few minutes ago!" cried Penny excitedly.

"You think it may have been intended as a warning to Peter Fenestra?" The housekeeper regarded the drawing rather dubiously.

"I'm sure of it, Mrs. Weems! Don't you see? The drawing is a copy of the tattoo which both Anchor Joe and John Munn had on their backs!"

"Yes, it does look the same as Joe's marking," conceded the housekeeper. "But what does it mean? Why was it sent to Fenestra?"

"I wish I knew."

"One thing is clear. That boatman your father hired is a downright scamp."

"He's wanted by the government. We know that. But Fenestra may be a rascal, too. Why should Anchor Joe threaten him unless he's done something he shouldn't?"

"Why indeed? This is a case for the police, not one for you or me," declared Mrs. Weems with finality. "I am ready to leave here whenever you are. I've decided not to bother giving Fenestra notice."

"You can't go now. You can't!" moaned Penny. "Stay until after Thursday, at least. I'm positive everything will be cleared up by then."

"Why Thursday?"

"Well, I have a little matter coming up on that day. Besides, I've sent off a letter which may help solve the mystery. Please, Mrs. Weems, do this one favor and I'll never ask another."

"Until next time, you mean. But to please you I'll stay until Friday. Not a day longer. However, I warn you, if I see Anchor Joe prowling about, I shall summon the sheriff."

"That's all right with me," grinned Penny. "I must skip now before Fenestra gets back from town. Just keep your eye on him and report to me if anything unusual happens."

CHAPTER 20 - PICNIC BY MOONLIGHT

Penny had never found it necessary to explain fully to her father what had become of Mrs. Weems. She had mentioned rather carelessly that the housekeeper was helping out at the Fenestra home for a few days, and he had accepted the substitution of Tillie Fellows without too many questions.

At breakfast on Wednesday morning, the publisher waited until Tillie had gone to the kitchen, and then asked in an undertone:

"How much longer is this to continue? When is Mrs. Weems coming home?"

"Friday morning, Dad. Don't you like Tillie's cooking?"

"It's awful," he whispered. "These eggs taste as if they had been fried in lard."

"They were," chuckled Penny. "Tillie was brought up to be frugal. She never wastes butter."

The discussion was brought to an abrupt end by the appearance of Tillie. Mr. Parker immediately switched to another subject, that of a barbecue picnic which he gave each summer to the *Star* employes. Penny had forgotten that the outing was scheduled for that night at the cottage.

"I'm glad you reminded me, Dad," she said. "I'll be there with bells to eat my share of roast beef. Mind if I bring Old Horney?"

"Invite him if you like," replied Mr. Parker. "But no others. This is a newspaper picnic, not a bread line as you made it last year."

After school that afternoon Penny worked as usual at the *Times* office. She was busy figuring advertising space when she glanced up and saw Fred Clousky standing in the doorway.

"Are—are you busy?" asked the boy diffidently.

"Yes, I am," said Penny with discouraging brevity.

"I don't want to bother you," Fred murmured, "but I was wondering—do you have a job for me around here? I'd like to work on a real paper. Being editor of *Chatter* is okay but you don't get any practical experience."

"Oh, so you want a job?" inquired Penny. Inclined to give him a short answer, she thought better of it. "Everything considered," she said, "what you need, Fred, is to learn about different kinds of type. It's so easy to get name-plates and various headlines mixed!"

Fred kept his gaze on his shoes.

"I have just the job for you," resumed Penny. "You can sort and clean the type when it's broken out of the page forms. If you do that well, perhaps you can work up later on."

"When do I start?" Fred asked in a crushed voice.

Penny was surprised for she had expected him to decline such a dirty, menial job. In a far more friendly tone she directed him to seek Old Horney who would be found in the composing room.

"Fred isn't so bad after all," she thought after he had gone. "I'll give him an office job next week."

Penny returned to her work. In need of an extra sheet of paper, she tried to open the lower drawer of her desk. It was stuck fast. She tugged at it several times, finally pulling it out entirely. A folded newspaper clipping dropped to the floor.

Wondering what it might be, she picked it up. The torn sheet, yellow with age, bore the picture of a young man. The face was vaguely familiar although the name beneath it read, Matthew Jewel.

"Matthew Jewel," she whispered. "But it's Matthew Judson! Judson as a young man. He must have changed his name!"

The two column headline drew her attention.

CHAPTER 20 - PICNIC BY MOONLIGHT

MATTHEW JEWEL BEGINS TEN YEAR SENTENCE IN NEW YORK PRISON FOR MISAPPROPRIATION OF BANK FUNDS

The clipping, she noted, had been cut from a New York paper and was dated twenty years earlier. It reported Matthew Jewel's conviction, following an admission that he had stolen two thousand dollars belonging to the Berkley Savings Bank.

Penny studied the picture again. Not the slightest doubt entered her mind that the young man of the story and Matthew Judson were the same individual. Evidently the clipping had been saved by the former publisher, and in some manner had become lodged beneath the drawer.

"I'm sure no one in Riverview ever knew that Judson served a term in prison," she thought. "He came here years ago with his daughter, and to all appearances had led an upright life."

After perusing the item again, she returned it to the drawer which she carefully locked. She knew that the information was of utmost importance. Was it not possible that she had stumbled upon a motivation for Judson's strange behavior of the past year? Could not the data contained in the clipping have provided an unscrupulous person with a basis for blackmail?

"But why should Judson ruin his career rather than face exposure?" she reflected. "Other men have made mistakes in their youth and started over again. The truth might have humiliated him, but Riverview people would have taken a charitable attitude."

Deeply troubled, Penny gathered together her belongings and went in search of Old Horney. Finding him initiating Fred Clousky in his new duties, she discreetly invited him to attend the picnic.

"Thank you mightily," responded the pressman, "but I'm not dressed for it. These pants are so shiny you could use 'em for a mirror."

"Don't you worry about your clothes, Horney. Besides, it will be so dark no one will notice. Dad gave you a special invitation."

"Did he now?" The old pressman could not hide his pleasure. "Well, if you think he really wants me, maybe I'll go."

"You wash up while I get the car," Penny urged. "We're rather late."

Within ten minutes, Old Horney met her at the front entrance. His hair was combed, he wore a frayed coat, and had contrived to polish his shoes.

"Horney," Penny said abruptly as they drove toward the river, "did you ever hear that Matthew Judson had been in trouble before he gave up his paper?"

"You mean financial?" the pressman inquired.

"No, I meant of a personal nature. I've been thinking over your theory that Judson was blackmailed."

"Maybe I oughtn't to have said what I did. It was just my own idea."

"I'm inclined to believe there may be something to it, Horney. Now supposing that Judson had stolen money or had been in prison—"

"It couldn't have been that," interrupted the pressman. "Why, Judson was so honest he bent over backwards."

Penny was tempted to tell Horney about the clipping, but refrained from doing so. However, she was satisfied that employes of the *Morning Press* had gained no inkling of Mr. Judson's prison record.

The picnic was well under way by the time Penny and the pressman arrived at the river cottage. A caterer had taken complete charge, and with his crew of helpers, prepared to serve nearly two hundred boisterous, hungry newspaper employes.

Always a favorite, Penny immediately was surrounded by a group of friends. Assured that Horney had found welcome with pressmen acquaintances, she entered wholeheartedly into the frivolity.

Jerry Livingston, frowning away all other young men, became her escort for the evening. After supper had been served, he guided her firmly away from the group.

"We don't want to hear any speeches," he said. "Let's go look at the moon."

"Can't we see it here?" countered Penny.

"A moon to be appreciated properly must be seen from a sandy beach," chuckled Jerry. "Preferably from a nice comfortable shoulder."

Breaking away, Penny raced ahead of him, along the beach to the suspension bridge. She was halfway across when he overtook her, rocking it so violently that she had to cling to him for support.

"Stop that, Jerry Livingston! You'll break the bridge!"

"Then don't try to run away from me. Will you let me show you the moon?"

"No, I know you, Jerry. You show it to all the girls."

"If I do, it's just as a rehearsal. You see, Penny, I've hoped that someday I might get a chance to show it to you."

"What a line you have," laughed Penny. "But I won't play. As a moon-shower your technique is terrible. Better practice some more."

Jerry chuckled and slipping his hand in hers, led her on across the bridge.

"If you won't look at the moon," he said, "then take a squint at Old Man River."

"I believe I prefer the moon after all," Penny returned, raising her eyes to the disc of light sailing serenely through the star-pricked sky. "It *is* beautiful."

Her reverie was broken by Jerry's voice. His hand tightened on her own.

"Penny!" he exclaimed. "Look over there!"

Farther down the river in an open space, the forms of two struggling men were silhouetted in the moonlight.

"Oh, Jerry," Penny cried, "they're fighting!"

"And to the death," added Jerry grimly. "Come on, before it's too late!"

CHAPTER 21 - ELLIS SAAL'S CUSTOMER

Penny followed the reporter, quickly overtaking him. Their pounding footsteps were heard by the two men who abruptly ceased their desperate struggles. Observing the pair, they turned and fled, one toward the river, the other toward the road.

"Well, we broke that up in a hurry!" exclaimed Jerry. "Wonder what made them run?"

"They must have been afraid we would recognize them," answered Penny. "Didn't you think that one man looked like Peter Fenestra?"

"I never have seen him to my knowledge. He was the fellow who ran along the river?"

"No, the other. Fenestra's farmhouse is across the fields." Penny pointed toward a light shining dimly from a window.

"They've both disappeared now," Jerry commented, moving to the river bank. "Wonder how the row started anyway?"

"Fenestra has been threatened," revealed Penny. "Yesterday Anchor Joe left a drawing of an octopus on his doorstep."

"What was the idea?"

"It must have been intended as a warning of some sort. Anchor Joe, and other men, too, keep watch of the house."

"How did you learn that, Penny?"

"I've made observations. Besides, Tillie Fellows, who worked there, told me what she had seen. Fenestra is afraid for his life."

"Maybe it was Anchor Joe who attacked him tonight."

"It may have been. I wish we could have seen those men at close range."

Penny walked on to the clearing where the pair had fought. Grass had been beaten down over a large area, indicating that the struggle had not been a brief one. A shiny object gleamed in the moonlight. Penny picked it up, then called softly to Jerry who had remained by the river bank.

"What is it?" he asked, coming quickly to her side.

"I've found a key, Jerry! It was lying here on the ground."

"One of the men must have lost it from his pocket."

"This may have been what they were fighting over, Jerry!"

"What makes you think that?"

"Doesn't the key look as if it belonged to a padlock?"

"Yes, it does, Penny."

"Then I am convinced this key will fit the lock on Peter Fenestra's storm cellar! His attacker was trying to get it away from him!"

"Just a minute," remonstrated Jerry. "You're traveling too fast for me. Explain the storm cellar part."

"You'll promise not to use anything I tell you for the *Star*?"

"That's fair enough."

Satisfied that Jerry would keep his promise, Penny told him everything she had learned at the Fenestra farm. The reporter asked many questions about the storm cave.

"So you believe this key may unlock the door?" he mused.

"I'd like to try it, at least."

"Now?"

"There never will be a better time. Mrs. Weems thinks that Fenestra is getting ready to leave Riverview."

Jerry hesitated only briefly. "All right, I'm with you," he said. "Lead the way."

They were leaving the river when both were startled to hear the suspension bridge creak beneath human weight. As they paused, listening, a familiar voice called:

"Jerry! Hey, Jerry!"

"Here!" responded the reporter.

A figure emerged from the trees, and they recognized Salt Sommers, the *Star* photographer.

"Say, I've been lookin' everywhere for you," he complained. "You're wanted back in Riverview."

"What is this, a gag?" Jerry asked suspiciously.

"It's no gag. The Fulton Powder Company just blew up. Joe, and Gus, and Philips are already on their way. DeWitt sent me to get you."

"The Fulton Powder Plant!" Jerry exclaimed, falling into step with Salt. "That's a big story!"

"It sure is, and we're late! Get a move on, brother."

Jerry glanced toward Penny, remembering that she too had a "story" to be covered.

"We'll go to Fenestra's place tomorrow," he promised hurriedly.

Knowing that Penny might try to investigate the cave alone, he hooked his arm through hers, pulling her along.

"Back you go to camp," he said. "This is no place for a little girl at night."

Penny's protests went unheeded. Jerry and Salt marched her between them to the cottage. Unceremoniously turning her over to her father, they leaped into a press car, and were gone.

Hours later the picnic came to an end. Riding home with her father after taking Horney to the *Times* building, Penny was startled to observe a light in an upstairs window of the Parker house.

"Why, that's in Mrs. Weems' room!" she exclaimed. "She can't be home!"

Penny was mistaken. Upon hastening upstairs to investigate, she was met at the bedroom door by the housekeeper.

"Why, Mrs. Weems! I thought you intended to stay on the farm until tomorrow!"

"I decided a few hours would make no difference. Penny, the place was unbearable."

"How did you get home?"

"By taxicab."

"Oh, I wish you had stayed one day longer," sighed Penny. "Did you learn anything since I saw you last?"

"Nothing of value. Fenestra came home a short time before I left. He was in a dreadful temper."

"Had he been in a fight?" Penny asked quickly.

"There was a black and blue mark across his cheek."

"Then I was right!" exclaimed Penny triumphantly. "I wish I knew for certain who attacked him."

Questioned by Mrs. Weems, she described the scene witnessed at the river, and proudly displayed the key.

"Why, it does resemble one I've seen Fenestra use," declared the housekeeper.

"Then it must unlock the cave! Tomorrow I'll go there and find out!"

"You'll do no such thing," replied Mrs. Weems firmly. "That is, not without your father's permission."

"But you know Dad won't be in favor of it," groaned Penny. "I simply must go there and get a scoop for the *Weekly*."

"No, Penny, you need to be protected from your own recklessness. Your father must be consulted before you visit the farm again."

"Either he'll say I can't go, or if he thinks there's anything to the story, he'll turn it over to a *Star* reporter. Whichever he does, I lose."

"Penny, I am in no mood to listen to your pleadings," Mrs. Weems said wearily. "If you'll excuse me, I'll go to bed."

Grumbling at the decision, Penny went to her own room. She did not feel equal to a spirited discussion with her father that night.

"Here, I'm on the verge of solving a great mystery," she grieved. "Perhaps the most stupendous of my life! And now I'm told I must stay away from Fenestra's farm. It's enough to turn my hair gray."

CHAPTER 21 - ELLIS SAAL'S CUSTOMER

Penny overslept the next morning, barely awakening in time to reach school by nine o'clock. A surprise oral history quiz caught her completely unprepared. She missed three questions in succession, and was told that she must remain after school for a special study session.

Released at four-thirty, Penny hastened to the *Star* office. Neither her father nor Jerry were there, nor could anyone tell her when they would return. Discouraged, she sought Louise who as usual was working at the *Times* plant.

"Such luck as I am having," Penny complained. "Mrs. Weems says I can't go to Fenestra's farm without Dad's permission, and he's hiding from me."

"I wish you would forget that storm cave and the octopus tattoo," said Louise unsympathetically. "Maybe then we could get out another issue of this old paper."

Penny gazed at her rather queerly. "You're sick of it, aren't you?" she asked.

"No," Louise denied, "it's been fun, and we've learned a lot. But there's so much work. It never ends."

"It will soon," replied Penny quietly. "Our advertisers are dropping off one by one. Sales are falling, too."

"We always can quit," said Louise cheerfully.

"No, we can't," Penny's mouth drew into a tight line. "Fred Clousky would taunt me to my dying day. I'll never close the plant except in a blaze of journalistic glory!"

"But you just said we're failing—"

"What the *Weekly* needs and must have is a tremendous story! Somehow I'm going to get it!"

"You're nothing if not persistent," said Louise admiringly. "Oh, before I forget it, Old Horney has been up here several times inquiring for you."

"More bad news I suppose."

"He didn't say why he wished to talk with you. I thought he seemed rather disturbed, though."

"I'll see what he wants."

Penny sought Horney in the composing department and pressroom, and even ventured into the basement. The old man was not to be found. Concluding that he had left the building, she gave up the search.

She helped Louise read proof until six o'clock, and then telephoned home to inquire if her father were there. Learning from Mrs. Weems that he did not expect to come until later, she decided to remain downtown for her own dinner.

"Why don't you stay with me, Lou?" she invited. "Afterwards, I'll take you on a little adventure."

"Not to Fenestra's?" her chum demanded suspiciously.

"Unfortunately, no. I shall do a bit of spade work by watching Ellis Saal's shop. This is Thursday, you know."

"It will be a long, tedious wait."

"I'll consider it well worth the time if I learn the identity of Saal's customer. You don't care to come?"

"On the contrary, I do. I'll telephone Mother."

The girls dined at a café not far from the *Weekly Times* and soon thereafter stationed themselves a half block from Ellis Saal's shop. An hour elapsed. Several times they became hopeful as persons paused to gaze at the exhibits in the show window, but no one entered. A cold wind made their vigil increasingly uncomfortable.

"If we don't get action in another fifteen minutes I am going home," chattered Louise.

A clock struck eight-thirty. Five minutes later Penny observed a familiar figure coming briskly down the street. She touched her chum's arm.

"It's Peter Fenestra," Louise murmured. "You don't think he's the one?"

"We'll soon see."

Fenestra was too far away to notice the girls. As they watched, he walked to the doorway of Ellis Saal's shop. Quickly he glanced about as if to ascertain that the street was deserted. Then he slipped into the shop, closing the door behind him.

CHAPTER 22 - GHOSTS OF THE PAST

"Peter Fenestra," murmured Louise. "Can there be any doubt that he is the customer Ellis Saal meant?"

"Not in my opinion," rejoined Penny.

"Isn't it possible that he went into the shop to have a photograph taken, or for some other reason?"

"Possible but not probable. No, Lou, we should have guessed long ago that Fenestra is an ex-sailor. It's all becoming clear now."

"Then I wish you would explain to me."

"Don't you see? Anchor Joe, John Munn, Fenestra, and perhaps a fourth man must have been good friends at one time. They had their tattoos with that phrase, *All for one, one for all*, pricked on their backs. Then Fenestra must have done something which made the others angry. They followed him here to get even with him."

"What makes you think that?" Louise asked dubiously.

"Anchor Joe gave us a good broad hint. Then we know that he and at least one other man have kept watch of the Fenestra farm."

"What can the man have done to offend them?"

"I can't guess that part," admitted Penny. "Another thing, why should Fenestra decide to have his octopus tattoo removed?"

"And who pushed John Munn off the bridge?" Louise added. "We're as much in the dark as ever."

"Not quite," amended Penny. "I feel that if only we could get into that storm cave, we might learn the answer to some of our questions."

"You're not thinking of investigating it tonight?"

Penny shook her head. "I can't without Dad's permission. It's a pity, too, because I know a big story is awaiting me, if only I could go out there and get it."

"I'm sure of one thing. We'll never dare print a word against Fenestra without absolute proof."

"No," agreed Penny, her eyebrows knitting in a frown, "it would lead to legal trouble."

Deciding that nothing more could be learned by waiting, the girls returned to the parked car. Motoring toward Louise's home, they discussed various angles of the baffling case. Confronting them always was the fact that Peter Fenestra's reputation in Riverview was excellent, while Anchor Joe and John Munn appeared to be persons of questionable character.

"You never learned why Joe was wanted by the authorities?" Louise inquired, alighting at her doorstep.

"No, I haven't seen Mr. Moyer since that day at the cottage. I'm reasonably sure Joe is still at liberty."

"He may be the one at the bottom of all the trouble," declared Louise. "We tend to suspect Fenestra of evil doing because we dislike him so heartily."

"That's so, Lou. The best way is to have no opinions and wait for facts. But waiting wears me to a frazzle!"

After parting from her chum, Penny did not drive home. Instead, she turned into Drexel Boulevard, and presently was ringing the doorbell of the Judson home.

The door was opened by Matthew Judson. Penny had not expected to meet the former publisher. Somewhat confusedly she inquired for Pauletta.

"My daughter isn't here now," replied Mr. Judson. "I expect her home within a few minutes. Won't you wait?"

"No, thank you," Penny declined. "I'll drop in some other time."

"I wish you would stay," urged Mr. Judson. "I find an empty house so depressing."

CHAPTER 22 - GHOSTS OF THE PAST

Penny hesitated, and then followed the former publisher to the living room. Mr. Judson had been reading the newspaper. He swept it from a chair so that the girl could sit opposite him.

"Tell me how you are getting on with your newspaper," he urged in a friendly tone.

Penny talked entertainingly, relating the various difficulties which beset a young publisher.

"I've even received threatening notes," she revealed. "Or rather, one. I think it was left on my desk by a man named Peter Fenestra."

"Fenestra?" Mr. Judson's face darkened.

"Yes," answered Penny, watching the publisher attentively. "Do you know him?"

"Only by reputation. He's a scoundrel!" His voice grew quite intense.

"Can you tell me anything definite against him?"

"No—no, I can't. I only advise you to have nothing whatsoever to do with him."

The telephone rang and Mr. Judson arose to answer it. During his absence, Penny thought swiftly. Dared she mention the clipping which she had found in the publisher's desk? She did not wish to antagonize him, yet there were many questions she longed to ask.

Mr. Judson presently returned. Penny decided to risk his anger.

Casually she introduced the subject by mentioning that she was using Mr. Judson's former office and desk as her own.

"Yesterday I came upon a clipping caught beneath the lower drawer," she said quietly. "It concerned a man named Matthew Jewel. He bore a striking resemblance to you."

The publisher raised his eyes to stare intently at Penny. His hands gripped the chair arms so hard that the knuckles became a bluish-white. Splotches of red appeared on his forehead.

"Matthew Jewel?" he murmured at last.

"Yes, Mr. Judson, but you have nothing to fear from me. I shall not expose you."

"Then you know?"

"The likeness was unmistakable. I read the clipping, too."

The publisher arose, nervously walking to the fireplace. His hands trembled as he fingered an ornament on the shelf.

"I searched everywhere for that clipping when I cleaned out my desk," he mumbled. "I've gone through every imaginable torture fearing it would be found. And now I am to be exposed!"

"But I assure you I have no intention of telling anyone," said Penny earnestly. "Your past is your own."

"A man's past never is his own," responded Mr. Judson bitterly.

"I shouldn't have mentioned it. I hoped I might be able to help you."

"You haven't told Pauletta?"

"No, nor any other person."

Mr. Judson's tenseness relaxed slightly. He paced across the room and back, then faced Penny.

"All my life," he said very quietly, "I have tried to spare Pauletta the knowledge that her father was—a convict. I haven't much to offer, but I'll give anything within reason to keep the story out of the paper."

"You don't understand," interrupted Penny. "I have no intention of printing the information, or of telling anyone. I want nothing from you. But I do wish you would tell me the true story. I am sure there were extenuating circumstances."

Mr. Judson sagged into an armchair. "None," he said. "None whatsoever. I used money which did not belong to me. My wife was desperately sick at the time and I wanted her to have the care of specialists. She died while I was serving my sentence."

"Why, you did have a reason for taking the money," said Penny kindly. "You should have been granted a pardon."

"A theft is a theft. When I left prison, I made a new start here, and devoted myself to Pauletta who was then a little girl."

"How old was she?" inquired Penny.

Mr. Judson gave no indication that he heard the question. He resumed:

"The truth had been kept from Pauletta. She believes that I was abroad during those years I spent in prison. Here in Riverview I prospered, people were kind to me. I made money and made it honestly. The future was very bright until a year ago."

"Then you gave up your newspaper," commented Penny. "Why?"

"Can't you guess?"

"Blackmail?"

Mr. Judson nodded. "One day a man came to me, a man I had known in prison. He threatened to expose me unless I paid him a large sum of money."

"And you agreed?"

"I did."

"Wasn't that rather foolish? People would have been charitable if you had admitted the truth."

"I considered it from every angle, particularly from Pauletta's standpoint. I gave the man what he asked, although it cost me the *Morning Press*. But that was not the end."

"He still bothers you?"

"Yes, I'll pay as long as I have a penny. I've thought of taking Pauletta and going away, but he would trace me."

"Who is the man, Mr. Judson?"

"I can't tell you."

"Is it either Anchor Joe Landa or Peter Fenestra?"

Mr. Judson's face did not alter. "I can't tell you," he repeated.

"I wish you would talk to Dad," Penny said after a moment. "He might be able to help you."

"No," returned Mr. Judson, growing agitated again, "you gave your promise that you would not tell."

"Of course, I'll keep it," responded Penny. "It does seem to me, though, that the easiest thing would be to admit the truth and be rid of the man who robs you. Pauletta would understand."

Mr. Judson shook his head. "I have made my decision," he said. "As long as I can, I shall abide by it."

There was nothing Penny could do but bid Mr. Judson good evening and leave the house. His secret troubled her. If he had told her the entire truth, it seemed very foolish of him to meet the demands of a blackmailer.

"I wonder if Mr. Judson did tell me everything?" she mused. "I had a feeling that he was keeping something back."

The car rolled into the driveway of the Parker home. As Penny jumped out to open the garage doors, a man, who had been sitting on the back doorstep, arose. His face was hidden, but she knew it was not her father.

"Who is it?" she called uneasily.

The voice was reassuring. "It's Horney, Miss Penny. I've been waitin' for you."

"What brings you here?" she asked, hurrying to meet him. "I hope nothing bad has happened at the *Times*."

"Everything's fine there. I've got a letter I thought you would want to see right away. Found it tonight when I was sweeping up. It answers a lot of questions you've been askin'."

Penny took the paper from Old Horney's gnarled hand. "Not about Matthew Judson?" she asked.

"Read it and you'll see," encouraged the pressman. "Judson was blackmailed just as I always thought. And by the man who signed this letter."

CHAPTER 23 - PENNY'S PLIGHT

It was too dark for Penny to read the letter. Stepping to the car, she switched on the headlights and held the paper in its brilliant beam.

The letter read:

> Dear Matthew:
> Sorry to bother you again, Old Pal, but I know you're always willing to give an old buddy and cellmate a helping hand. I don't want to tip off the New York cops where you are, and you can trust me to keep mum if you come through with another six thousand. This is my last request.
>
> Peter F.

"Peter Fenestra!" exclaimed Penny. "And it's no surprise either! Horney, where did you find this letter?"

"It was in a pile of rubbish down in the basement. I don't know how it got there."

"Peter Fenestra has a habit of leaving notes on Mr. Judson's desk," declared Penny. "This one may have blown off and been swept out without the publisher seeing it!"

"Don't you figure it's a blackmail attempt?"

"Of course it is, Horney. You've not shown the letter to anyone?"

"Only to you. From the threat I dope it out that Judson was sent to prison years ago, and he's still wanted."

Penny nodded as she placed the letter in her pocketbook. His guess was a shrewd one, but she could tell him nothing without breaking her promise to Mr. Judson.

"Horney," she said, "a great deal hinges upon this letter. You'll not tell anyone what you've learned?"

"Oh, I'll keep it to myself. I'm not one to get Judson into trouble. He's had enough of it already."

Penny noticed that her father's car was not in the garage. She reasoned that since he had not come home he must be working late at the *Star* office as he frequently did.

"Jump in, Horney," she invited, swinging wide the car door. "I'm going downtown to find Dad. I'll give you a ride."

She was grateful that the pressman had little to say as they sped through dimly lighted residential streets.

How much he suspected she could only guess. But the letter had made it clear to her that the former publisher never had completed his prison sentence.

"That was why he didn't answer me when I asked about Pauletta's age!" she thought. "He must have escaped from prison soon after he was sent there!"

No longer did Penny wonder why Mr. Judson had not refused Peter Fenestra's repeated demands for money. Obviously he had feared a far worse fate than exposure—return to the New York state prison.

The car turned into the deserted *Star* loading dock. Few lights were visible in the building, for the day staff had gone home and only the scrub women were at work. Penny could not see the windows of her father's office from the street. Nor did she observe a man who slouched against a wall, not far from where the car had stopped.

Old Horney stepped from the running board, thanking Penny for the ride.

"Guess I'll amble up the street and get a cup of coffee."

"You'll be sure not to mention the letter?" Penny reminded him.

"I won't tell a soul. You know, I was thinkin' about it as we rode downtown. Peter Fenestra came into the office a couple of times just before Judson closed the plant. He was a dirty blackmailer, all right! Wouldn't that letter I gave you be enough to send him up?"

"I should think so, Horney. But the problem is how to take care of him without ruining Mr. Judson."

THE SECRET PACT

"Better show the letter to your father," advised the pressman. "Maybe he'll have some ideas."

Tipping his hat, Old Horney moved briskly away.

Penny entered the rear vestibule, speaking to three scrub women who were locking up their cleaning equipment before leaving the building. Not even the elevator man was on duty, so she climbed the stairs. Switching on a light in the newsroom, she passed through it to her father's office.

The room was dark.

"Not here," thought Penny. "I was afraid of it."

Deciding to telephone home, she entered one of the glass enclosed booths at the end of the newsroom. As she lifted the receiver, a voice from behind her said distinctly:

"Put that down!"

Startled, Penny whirled around. Peter Fenestra stood in the doorway of the booth.

"Come out of there!" he ordered harshly.

Penny obeyed with alacrity as she tried to gather her wits. The building was practically deserted, and Fenestra took care to stand between her and the outside door.

"What do you want here?" she demanded coldly.

"The letter."

Penny stared at him blankly. Her astonishment was genuine.

"Don't pretend you don't know," Fenestra said harshly. "I want the letter you and that old man were talking about."

"Oh!" Light broke upon Penny. "So you heard our conversation! You were listening!"

"I happened to be standing in the loading dock. I know you have the letter. Hand it over."

Penny backed a few steps away toward her father's office. "So you admit you wrote it?" she challenged.

"I admit nothing. But I want that letter."

"You'll not get it," Penny defied him. "Peter Fenestra, you were the one who put that warning note on my desk a few days ago! And I know why, too! You were afraid I'd learn too much about the octopus tattoo. Well, I've learned plenty!"

Fenestra's face became contorted with rage. He choked, "You've been down in the cave!" and started toward Penny.

Thoroughly frightened, she eluded his grasp. Running into her father's office, she slammed the door. Bracing her body against it, she managed to turn the key before Fenestra could force it open.

"Come out of there!" he shouted furiously. "Come out, I say!"

"And I say I won't!" retorted Penny. "Just try to get in!"

She pushed her father's heavy desk across the room, placing it in front of the door.

Fenestra rattled the handle several times, and threw his body against the panel once or twice. Then she heard footsteps as he walked away.

"That's only a trick to get me to come out," thought Penny. "I won't be stupid enough to fall into his trap. I'll stay right here."

Walking to the window, she gazed down. Cars were passing along the street. If she shouted for help someone might hear her. However, to explain her predicament would be rather awkward.

Penny's gaze fell upon the telephone which had fallen from the desk to the floor. Picking it up, she dialed the number of her own house. Mrs. Weems answered.

"Hello," said Penny cheerfully, "Dad hasn't come home yet by any chance?"

"He's just now driving into the garage," the housekeeper replied. "I'll call him."

A moment later Penny heard her father's voice at the other end of the wire.

"Dad," she said, "I'm down at your office, sitting behind some barbed wire entanglements. I wish you'd get a policeman and see what you can do about rescuing me."

"Is this one of your jokes?" Mr. Parker demanded.

Fearful that her father would hang up the receiver, Penny talked fast and to the point. Mr. Parker assured her he would come without a moment's delay.

"I guess that will teach Peter Fenestra not to get funny with me!" she congratulated herself. "It pays to do a little thinking. Fenestra will be arrested, and then I'll drive out and learn what he hides in his cave."

CHAPTER 23 - PENNY'S PLIGHT

Penny sniffed the air. She could smell smoke, and she thought it must be coming from a cigarette. Evidently Fenestra had stolen to the door and was patiently waiting for her to emerge.

"He'll have a long wait," she chuckled.

Gradually her elation died. The odor of smoke had grown stronger. She saw a wisp of it filter beneath the door crack. Penny's heart caught in her throat. Tensely she listened. Was it imagination or could she hear the crackle of flames?

"Fenestra may be burning the papers of a scrap basket just to smoke me out," she thought. "Probably that's just what he's doing."

Pulling the heavy desk away from the door, she stood with her ear against the panel. Distinctly she could hear the crackle of flames. The wood felt warm to her cheek.

Suddenly Penny was afraid. Frantically she turned the key in the lock.

The door swung outward to the pressure of her shoulder. A wave of heat rushed in.

Penny staggered backward, horrified by the sight which met her eyes. At the end of the newsroom, where the exit should have been, rose a towering barrier of flames.

CHAPTER 24 - A BARRIER OF FLAMES

Escape through the newsroom was cut off. Panic seized Penny, but only for an instant. Retreating, she telephoned the fire department. Then finding a chemical extinguisher, she began fighting the flames.

Black, rolling smoke billowed into her face, choking and blinding her. The heat drove her back.

From far down the street came the wail of a siren. Penny rushed to a window. A pumper and a hook-and-ladder truck swung around the corner, lurching to a stop.

Raising the sash, she stepped out onto the ledge, waving to the men below.

"Stay where you are!" shouted a fireman. "We'll get you!"

A ladder shot up, but Penny did not wait to be carried to safety. Before a fireman could mount, she scrambled down with the agility of a monkey.

"The fire started in the newsroom," she gasped. "But it's already spread into the composing department."

"Anyone else in the building?"

"I don't think so. There were three scrub women, but they're probably out now."

Lines of hose were stretched to the hydrants, and streams of water began to play on the flames. A crowd, following in the wake of the fire engines, was ordered back by the police. One young man broke through, darting to Penny's side.

"Jerry!" she exclaimed.

"Gosh, how did it start?" he demanded. "Why, Penny, your hair is singed!"

"I was in it," she said briefly. "I can't explain now, but the fire was started by Peter Fenestra."

"On purpose?"

"I don't know about that. He was smoking a cigarette."

"Have you told the police?"

"Not yet. I'm waiting for Dad."

A car inched through the crowd, stopping a few yards away. Mr. Parker leaped out and ran toward the burning building. He was stopped at the entrance by a fireman.

"Let me in there!" the publisher shouted, trying to free himself. "My daughter's inside!"

"No, here I am, Dad!" Penny cried, grasping his hand.

Mr. Parker said no word, but he pulled her to him in a rough embrace. The next moment he was trying once more to enter the building, intending to save important papers.

"Take it easy, Parker," advised the fireman, barring the door with his hose. "The smoke's bad in there."

"Will the building go?"

"We'll save most of it," the fireman assured him confidently.

Penny plucked at her father's sleeve. "Dad, oughtn't the police be sent after Peter Fenestra? He's responsible for this, and a lot of other things, too!"

"You mean Fenestra set the fire?"

Above the roar of flames, Penny tersely disclosed how the man had compelled her to take refuge in the inner office room. Jerry also heard the story, and when she had finished, he said to Mr. Parker:

"Chief, let me take a couple of policemen and nail that fellow! Maybe we can arrest him at the farm before he makes a get-away."

"Go ahead," urged Mr. Parker.

"I'm going along," declared Penny, and darted away before her father could stop her.

CHAPTER 24 - A BARRIER OF FLAMES

Twenty minutes later, with a police cruiser dispatched to Fenestra's place, she and Jerry drove there in Mr. Parker's car. Parking some distance down the road, they walked cautiously toward the farmhouse which loomed dark against the sky. No lights burned in the windows. The grounds appeared deserted.

"Looks as if Fenestra isn't here," observed Jerry. "No use waiting for the police."

Boldly going to the front door he pounded on it, ordering in a loud voice: "Open up!"

"He's not here," said Penny after a moment. "Unless perhaps he's hiding."

"The place looks deserted to me."

Penny glanced toward the storm cave, remembering that she had the key to the padlock in her pocket. Jerry read her thought, and followed as she went quickly toward the mound.

"It's locked," he said, indicating the padlock.

"Here's the key." Eagerly Penny offered it to Jerry. "I'm sure this must be the one."

The reporter gave her a flashlight to hold while he tried to fit the key into the lock.

"It's no go, Penny."

"But I was so sure, Jerry." She stooped to examine the padlock. "Well, no wonder! It's been changed."

"Then we're out of luck until the police get here."

"Isn't there any way we can open it ourselves?"

"Maybe I can break it."

"There should be tools in the barn, Jerry."

"I'll see what I can find."

Leaving Penny, the reporter disappeared in the direction of the barn. Extinguishing the flashlight, she patiently waited.

Suddenly she was startled to hear running footsteps. Barely had she crouched behind the storm cave before a man emerged from among the pine trees adjoining the road. It was Peter Fenestra and he was breathing hard.

Straight toward the cave he ran. Pausing at the slanting door, he peered quickly about, and then fumbled with the padlock. In desperate haste he jerked it loose, swung back the hinged door, and descended the stone steps.

Penny waited a moment, then crept to the entrance.

Fenestra had not taken time to lower the door behind him. A light shone from an underground room at one side of the main passageway, and she could hear the man's heavy boots scuffing on a cement floor.

Penny considered going after Jerry and decided against it. Fenestra's frantic haste suggested that he might not linger long in the cave. What could he be doing beneath ground?

With Jerry so near, she felt that it would not be too dangerous to investigate. Warily she tiptoed down the steps.

A low, rounding doorway opened from the descending passage. Peering into the dimly lighted room, Penny did not immediately see Peter Fenestra.

Instead her gaze roved about the walls of what appeared to be a workshop. Tools were neatly arranged over a bench, while a cupboard of shelves contained miscellaneous mechanical parts.

At the far end of the cave stood an urn-like contrivance which the girl took to be an electric furnace. An armored cable ran from it to a heavy wall switch having two blades and a sizable wooden handle. Plainly it was designed to carry a very heavy current.

Peter Fenestra came from behind the furnace. Penny saw him throw the switch. Almost immediately she heard a low hissing sound from the interior of the metal oven. Slowly the furnace heated, and soon glowed weirdly.

As she pondered what the man could be intending to do, she heard a slight sound at the stairway entrance. Thinking that Jerry had returned, she started up the steps. Not one figure but three loomed in the doorway!

Penny flattened herself against the dirt wall. But she could not avoid being seen. A flashlight beam focused upon her, and the next instant a revolver muzzle bit into her side.

"Keep quiet!" she was ordered in a whisper. "You won't be hurt!"

Penny stared into the grim face of Anchor Joe. Behind him came John Munn, and a man she had never seen before. In a flash she knew why they were there—to avenge themselves upon Peter Fenestra.

Quietly as the men had moved, they had been heard in the next room.

"Who's there?" Fenestra called sharply.

THE SECRET PACT

John Munn and Anchor Joe stepped into the rectangle of light, their revolvers trained upon the man.

"Just three of your old pals, Otto," drawled Anchor Joe. "Reach!"

"Listen, Joe, you got me all wrong," Peter Fenestra whined. "I can explain why I kept the gold. I'll give it all to you if that's what you want. I'll do anything—don't shoot."

"Shootin' would be too good for you," retorted Anchor Joe. "We got other plans." His face was dark with rage.

"Sure, we know how to deal with a traitor," added John Munn, deftly whisking a revolver from Fenestra's hip pocket. "You thought you could hide from us. You thought by changing your name, and coming to this out-of-the-way town you could fool us. Why, you dirty rat, you even thought you could get by with pushing me off a bridge!"

"Your greed kept you here," taunted Anchor Joe. "You couldn't bear to leave any of those gold bars behind."

"You thought you'd melt down the last of 'em tonight and skip," added John Munn. "You're goin' on a long trip all right, but with us!"

A pair of steel cuffs were slipped over Fenestra's wrists. Speedily, the sailors searched the cave, gathering up several bags of what Penny assumed to be gold.

"How about this bar?" John Munn asked his companions. "Can we handle it?"

"Too heavy," answered Anchor Joe. "With Moyer hot on our trail, we've got to travel light. Get going and I'll follow."

Munn and his companion marched Peter Fenestra from the cave. Taking a cord from his pocket, Anchor Joe bound Penny's hands and feet.

"I'm tying 'em loose," he said. "And I'll leave the cave door open. After we're gone you can yell for help."

"Joe, where are you taking Fenestra? What has he done?"

The sailor did not answer. Seizing a bag of gold, he slung it over his shoulder and went quickly up the stairs. Penny was left in the darkness.

CHAPTER 25 - SAILORS' REVENGE

Minutes later, Jerry, returning from the barn, heard Penny's muffled scream for help. Descending into the cave he immediately freed her and learned what had happened.

"Fenestra used this furnace for melting down gold all right!" he exclaimed, peering into the dark cavern. "Wonder where he got it?"

"It must be stolen gold—government gold, perhaps," gasped Penny. "Jerry, those men have been gone only a minute or two!"

"Then maybe we can get 'em yet!"

Jerry had heard an automobile turn into the yard. Hopeful that it might be the awaited authorities, he and Penny ran up the stone steps. To their joy they saw that it was the police cruiser.

In terse sentences they told their story to the officers. Penny had no idea which direction the men had gone, but the reporter recalled having seen a group of four walking toward the river just as he had left the barn.

With Jerry and Penny standing on the running board, the police car headed in the direction of the Big Bear. Suddenly a series of explosive sounds were heard, staccato noises similar to the back-firing of an automobile exhaust.

"Shots!" exclaimed Jerry. "From the river, too!"

The car drew to a halt. The policemen leaped out and started across the fields. Disregarding orders to remain behind, Penny and Jerry followed.

Breathlessly, they reached the rim of the river. A beam of light directed their gaze to the opposite shore. A high-powered motor boat had pulled away and was fast gathering speed. Flashes of gunfire from its decks were answered by the revolvers of men on the river bank.

Shielding Penny with his body, Jerry drew her behind a tree. In a moment as the motor boat passed beyond range, firing ceased. Then they slid down the bank to learn what had occurred.

Penny saw that Peter Fenestra had been captured. He was handcuffed to Mr. Moyer, and she instantly guessed that the other four men were government operatives.

"Find a boat and start after those three sailors who got away!" Moyer ordered his men tersely. "I'll take this fellow to town."

Penny edged forward, obtaining an excellent view of Peter Fenestra's downcast face. Quietly she made her accusations, telling of the cave where she had been imprisoned.

"So that was how the gold was melted down," commented Moyer.

He then explained that for days his operatives had watched the river where they knew Anchor Joe had hidden a motorboat. Surprised in the act of taking off, the sailors had exchanged shots with the government men, but by abandoning Fenestra and the gold, they had escaped.

"This man's real name is Otto Franey," Moyer revealed, indicating Fenestra. "He and the three sailors were shipmates aboard the *Dorasky*."

"They're wanted for stealing gold?" questioned Penny.

"Yes, they got away with four gold bars taken from the *Dorasky*. You see, about a year ago a consignment of gold was shipped by a Swiss bank to the New York Federal Reserve. Because of heavy fog the bars were unloaded at the pier instead of being taken off at Quarantine. They were removed in a sling and dumped on the wharf to await the mail truck."

"And the four sailors saw a chance to steal some of the bars?" questioned Jerry.

"Yes, how they accomplished it we don't know. But hours later a mail driver refused to sign for one of the bags because it had been slit open. Four bars valued at approximately fourteen thousand dollars each were missing. Investigation disclosed that a sailor, Otto Franey, had jumped ship. A few days later Joe Landa, John Munn and Jack Guenther also disappeared."

"Each man was marked with an octopus tattoo, wasn't he?" Penny inquired eagerly.

"Yes, although I did not learn that until a day or so ago. Otto has been trying to get his tattoo removed so that it would be harder to trace him. The four sailors had their backs marked with an octopus design and words which read, *All for one, one for all*, when put together. They were feeling very friendly toward each other at that time."

"Then I was right!" exclaimed Penny. "And the four conspired to steal the gold bars?"

"Otto was entrusted by his pals to dispose of the stolen gold. Instead, he gave them the slip and tried to keep it for himself. Evidently he rigged up a furnace and melted the metal into useable form. But the three sailors trailed him here, determined to avenge themselves."

As Fenestra was hustled to a waiting car, Penny told Mr. Moyer everything she knew about the prisoner, save his connection with Matthew Judson. Deliberately she withheld information about the blackmail plot.

While the prisoner was being loaded into the government car, another automobile drew up nearby. Recognizing Mr. Parker at the wheel, Penny and Jerry ran to tell him the latest news.

"Full speed ahead, Chief!" exclaimed the reporter, sliding into the front seat. "We've got a big story by the tail!"

"A lot of good it does us," responded the publisher gloomily.

"You mean the firemen failed to save the *Star* building?" Penny asked anxiously.

"The building's saved, but considerable damage was done by fire and water. We can't use the plant for several days. It's enough to make a man ill! Scooped by the opposition when the story is ours!"

"You forget the little *Weekly Times*," reminded Penny. "Old Homey has everything ready to roll. I'm turning the plant over to you."

"To me?" Mr. Parker did not understand her meaning.

"Yes, gather your mechanical force. The plant's yours for the night."

"Penny, you're the tops!" the publisher exclaimed, starting the car with a lurch. "Together we'll get out an extra that will be an extra!"

After that Penny lost all sense of time as events transpired with rapidity and precision. As if by magic the staff of the *Star* appeared to take over the *Times* plant. The building shook off its lethargy and machinery began to turn.

Allowing Jerry to write the big story, Penny tried to be everywhere at once. She fluttered at DeWitt's elbow as he drew a dummy of the front page.

"Let's make it 96-point type," she urged. "Splashy! A double column story with a break-over to page three."

"Anything you say," was DeWitt's surprising answer.

In the composing room, printers were locking the forms, using pages previously made ready for the next issue of the *Weekly Times*. Stereotypers were testing the pneumatic steam tables. Pressmen under Old Horney's direction oiled the double-deck rotaries and tightened bolts.

At last came the moment when the starter plate was fitted into place on the cylinder. With a half turn of a T wrench Old Horney made it secure.

"She's ready," he announced, flashing the signal light. "You push the button, Penny."

Trembling with excitement, she started the press rolling. Faster and faster it went. In a moment papers dropped so swiftly from the folder that her eye could not follow. A conveyer carried them upward over the presses to the distributing room.

Mr. Parker offered Penny a paper, smiling as he saw her stare at the nameplate. Instead of the *Star* it read: *The Weekly Times*.

"Why, Dad!" she exclaimed. "They've made a mistake."

"It's no mistake," he corrected. "This is your extra. Your name appears as Managing Editor."

"So that was why DeWitt was so agreeable to all my suggestions?" she laughed. "I might have guessed."

CHAPTER 25 - SAILORS' REVENGE

Later, while newsboys cried their wares, Penny and her father sat in the private office, talking with Matthew Judson. From his own lips they learned how he had submitted to blackmail rather than disgrace Pauletta by returning to prison.

"Your case is a deserving one," Mr. Parker told him kindly. "I assure you we'll never publish the story, and I'll do everything in my power to help you obtain a pardon."

Before leaving the office, Mr. Judson promised Penny he would tell his daughter the truth, allowing her to break her engagement to Major Atchley if she chose.

"We'll go away somewhere," he said. "California, perhaps. Although I'll never try to publish a paper again, at least my life will cease to be a torment."

Alone with her father once more, Penny had two requests to make.

"Name them," he urged.

"Can you get Tillie Fellows a job?"

"Easily."

"And will you take Horney into your own plant?"

"I'll be glad to do it as soon as the *Star* operates again. Until remodeling work is completed I have no plant."

"Yes, you have, Dad. This building is yours if you can make arrangements with Mr. Veeley."

"Penny! You're willing to give up the *Weekly*?"

"Willing?" she laughed. "I'm hilariously crazy to get rid of it. Matters have reached a state where either I must abandon the paper or my education. I've only awaited a chance to end my career in a blaze of glory."

"A blaze expresses it very mildly," smiled Mr. Parker. "In all modesty, let us say a conflagration!"

"Oh, why be modest?" grinned Penny. "Let's come right out and call it a holocaust! That's the strongest word I know."

THE END

THE CLOCK STRIKES THIRTEEN

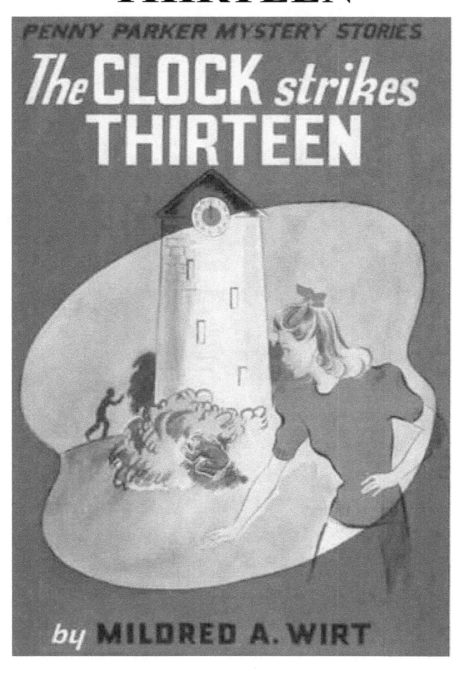

THE CLOCK STRIKES THIRTEEN

PENNY HUDDLED AGAINST THE WALL WATCHING FEARFULLY.

CHAPTER 1 - SANDWICHES FOR TWO

Jauntily, Penny Parker walked through the dimly lighted newsroom of the *Riverview Star*, her rubber heels making no sound on the bare, freshly scrubbed floor. Desks were deserted, for the final night edition of the paper had gone to press half an hour earlier, and only the cleaning women were at work. One of the women arrested a long sweep of her mop just in time to avoid splashing the girl with water.

"I sorry," she apologized in her best broken English. "I no look for someone to come so very late."

"Oh, curfew never rings for me," Penny laughed, side stepping a puddle of water. "I'm likely to be abroad at any hour."

At the far end of the long room a light glowed behind a frosted glass door marked: "Anthony Parker—Editor." There the girl paused, and seeing her father's grotesque shadow, opened the door a tiny crack, to rumble in a deep voice:

"Hands up! I have you covered!"

Taken by surprise, Mr. Parker swung quickly around, his swivel chair squeaking a loud protest.

"Penny, I wish you wouldn't do that!" he exclaimed. "You know it always makes me jump."

"Sorry, Dad," Penny grinned, slumping into a leather chair beside her father's desk. "A girl has to have some amusement, you know."

"Didn't three hours at the moving picture theatre satisfy you?"

"Oh, the show was worse than awful. By the way, here's something for you."

Removing a sealed yellow envelope from her purse, Penny flipped it carelessly across the desk.

"I met a Western Union boy downstairs," she explained. "He was looking for you. I paid for the message and saved him a trip upstairs. Two dollars and ten cents, if you don't mind."

Absently Mr. Parker took two crisp dollar bills from his pocket and reached for the telegram.

"Don't forget the dime," Penny reminded him. "It may seem a trifle to you, but not to a girl who has to live on a weekly allowance."

For lack of change, the editor tossed over a quarter, which his daughter pocketed with deep satisfaction. Ripping open the envelope, he scanned the telegram, but as he read, his face darkened.

"Why, Dad, what's wrong?" Penny asked in surprise.

Mr. Parker crumpled the sheet into a round ball and hurled it toward the waste paper basket.

"Your aim gets worse every day," Penny chuckled, stooping to retrieve the paper. Smoothing the corrugations, she read aloud:

"YOUR EDITORIAL 'FREEDOM OF THE PRESS' IN THURSDAY'S STAR THOROUGHLY DISGUSTED THIS READER. WHAT YOUR CHEAP PAPER NEEDS IS A LITTLE LESS FREEDOM AND MORE DECENCY. IF OUR FOREFATHERS COULD HAVE FORESEEN THE YELLOW PRESS OF TODAY THEY WOULD HAVE REGULATED IT, NOT MADE IT FREE. WHY DON'T YOU TAKE THAT AMERICAN FLAG OFF YOUR MASTHEAD AND SUBSTITUTE A CASH REGISTER? FLY YOUR TRUE COLORS AND SOFT-PEDAL THE PARKER BRAND OF HYPOCRISY!"

"Stop it—don't read another line!" the editor commanded before Penny had half finished.

"Why, Dad, you poor old wounded lion!" she chided, blue eyes dancing with mischief. "I thought you prided yourself that uncomplimentary opinions never disturbed you. Can't you take it any more?"

"I don't mind a few insults," Mr. Parker snapped, "but paying for them is another matter."

"That's so, this little gem of literature did set you back two dollars and ten cents. Lucky I collected before you opened the telegram."

Mr. Parker slammed his desk shut with a force which rattled the office windows.

"This same crack-pot who signs himself 'Disgusted Reader' or 'Ben Bowman,' or whatever name suits his fancy, has sent me six telegrams in the past month! I'm getting fed up!"

"All of the messages collect?"

"Every one. The nit-wit has criticised everything from the *Star*'s comic strips to the advertising columns. I've had enough of it!"

"Then why not do something about it?" Penny asked soothingly. "Refuse the telegrams."

"It's not that easy," the editor growled. "Each day the *Star* receives a large number of 'collect' messages, hot news tips from out-of-town correspondents and from reporters who try to sell free lance stories. We're glad to pay for these telegrams. This fellow who keeps bombarding us is just smart enough to use different names and send his wires from various places. Sometimes he addresses the telegrams to me, and then perhaps to City Editor DeWitt or one of the other staff members."

"In that case, I'm afraid you're out of luck," Penny said teasingly. "How about drowning your troubles in a little sleep?"

"It is late," Mr. Parker admitted, glancing at his watch. "Almost midnight. Time we're starting home."

Reaching for his hat, Mr. Parker switched off the light, locked the door, and followed Penny down the stairway to the street. At the parking lot opposite the *Star* building, he tramped about restlessly while waiting for an attendant to bring the car.

"I'll drive," Penny said, sliding behind the steering wheel. "In your present mood you might inadvertently pick off a few pedestrians!"

"It makes my blood boil," Mr. Parker muttered, his thoughts reverting to the telegram. "Call my paper yellow, eh? And that crack about the cash register!"

"Oh, everyone knows the *Star* is the best paper in the state," Penny said, trying to coax him into a better mood. "You're a good editor too, and a pretty fair father."

"Thanks," Mr. Parker responded with a mock bow. "Since we're passing out compliments, you're not so bad yourself."

Suddenly relaxing, he reached out to touch Penny's hand in a rare expression of affection. Tall and lean, a newspaper man with a reputation for courage and fight, he had only two interests in life—his paper and his daughter. Penny's mother had been dead many years, but at times he saw his wife again in the girl's sparkling blue eyes, golden hair, and especially in the way she smiled.

"Hungry, Dad?" Penny asked unexpectedly, intruding upon his thoughts. "I know a dandy new hamburger place not far from here. Wonderful coffee too."

"Well, all right," Mr. Parker consented. "It's pretty late though. The big clock's striking midnight."

As the car halted for a traffic light, they both listened to the musical chimes which preceded the regularly spaced strokes of the giant clock. Penny turned her head to gaze at the Hubell Memorial Tower, a grim stone building which rose to the height of seventy-five feet. Erected ten years before as a monument to one of Riverview's wealthy citizens, its chimes could be heard for nearly a mile on a still night. On one side, its high, narrow windows overlooked the city, while on the other, the cultivated lands of truck farmers.

"How strange!" Penny murmured as the last stroke of the clock died away.

"What is strange?" Mr. Parker asked gruffly.

"Why, that clock struck thirteen times instead of twelve!"

"Bunk and bosh!"

"Oh, but it did!" Penny earnestly insisted. "I counted each stroke distinctly."

"And one of them twice," scoffed her father. "Or are you spoofing your old Dad?"

"Oh, I'm not," Penny maintained. As the car moved ahead, she craned her neck to stare up at the stone tower. "I know I counted thirteen. Why, Dad, there's a green light burning in one of the windows! I never saw that before. What can it mean?"

"It means we'll have a wreck unless you watch the road!" Mr. Parker cried, giving the steering wheel a quick turn. "Where are you taking me anyhow?"

CHAPTER 1 - SANDWICHES FOR TWO

"Out to Toni's." Reluctantly Penny centered her full attention upon the highway. "It's only a mile into the country."

"We won't be home before one o'clock," Mr. Parker complained. "But since we're this far, I suppose we may as well keep on."

"Dad, about that light," Penny said thoughtfully. "Did you ever notice it before?"

Mr. Parker turned to gaze back toward the stone tower.

"There's no green light," he answered grimly. "Every window is dark."

"But I saw it only an instant ago! And I did hear the clock strike thirteen. Cross my heart and hope to die—"

"Never mind the dramatics," Mr. Parker cut in. "If the clock struck an extra time—which it didn't—something could have gone wrong with the mechanism. Don't try to build up a mystery out of your imagination."

The car rattled over a bridge and passed a deserted farm house that formerly had belonged to a queer old man named Peter Fenestra. Penny's gaze fastened momentarily upon an old fashioned storm cellar which marred the appearance of the front yard.

"I suppose I imagined all that too," she said, waving her hand toward the disfiguring cement hump. "Old Peter never had any hidden gold, he never had a SECRET PACT with tattooed sailors, and he never tried to burn your newspaper plant!"

"I'll admit you did a nice piece of detective work when you uncovered that story," her father acknowledged. "Likewise, you brought the *Star* one of its best scoops by outwitting slippery Al Gepper and entangling him in his own *Silken Ladder*."

"Don't forget the *Tale of the Witch Doll* either," Penny reminded him. "You laughed at me then, just as you're doing now."

"I'm not laughing," denied the editor. "I merely say that no light was burning in the tower window, and I very much doubt that the clock struck more than twelve times."

"Tomorrow I shall go to the tower and talk with the caretaker, Seth McGuire. I'll prove to you that I was right!"

"If you do, I'll treat to a dish of ice cream decorated with nuts."

"Make it five gallons of gasoline and I'll be really interested," she countered.

Due to an unusual set of circumstances, Penny had fallen heir to two automobiles, one a second-hand contraption whose battered sides bore the signature of nearly every young person in Riverview. The other, a handsome maroon sedan, had been the gift of her father, presented in gratitude because of her excellent reporting of a case known to many as *Behind the Green Door*. Always hard pressed for funds, she found it all but impossible to keep two automobiles in operation, and her financial difficulties were a constant source of amusement to everyone but herself.

Soon, an electric sign proclaiming "Toni's" in huge block letters loomed up. Penny swung into the parking area, tooting the horn for service. Immediately a white-coated waiter brought out a menu.

"Coffee and two hamburgers," Penny ordered with a flourish. "Everything on one, and everything but, on the other."

"No onions for the little lady?" the waiter grinned. "Okay. I'll have 'em right out."

While waiting, Penny noticed that another car, a gray sedan, had drawn up close to the building. Although the two men who occupied the front seat had ordered food, they were not eating it. Instead they conversed in low tones as they appeared to watch someone inside the cafe.

"Dad, notice those two men," she whispered, touching his arm.

"What about them?" he asked, but before she could reply, the waiter came with a tray of sandwiches which he hooked over the car door.

"Not bad," Mr. Parker praised as he bit into a giant-size hamburger. "First decent cup of coffee I've had in a week too."

"Dad, watch!" Penny reminded him.

The restaurant door had opened, and a man of early middle age came outside. Immediately the couple in the gray sedan stiffened to alert attention. As the man passed their car they lowered their heads, but the instant he had gone on, they turned to peer after him.

THE CLOCK STRIKES THIRTEEN

The man who was being observed so closely seemed unaware of the scrutiny. Crossing the parking lot, he chose a trail which led into a dense grove of trees.

"Now's our chance!" cried one of the men in the gray sedan. "Come on, we'll get him!" Both alighted and likewise disappeared into the woods.

"Dad, did you hear what they said?" asked Penny.

"I did," he answered grimly. "Tough looking customers too."

"I'm afraid they mean to rob that first man. Isn't there anything we can do?"

Mr. Parker barely hesitated. "I may make a chump of myself," he said, "but here goes! I'll tag along and try to be on hand if anything happens."

"Dad, don't do it!" Penny pleaded, suddenly frightened lest her father face danger. "You might get hurt!"

Mr. Parker paid no heed. Swinging open the car door, he strode across the parking lot, and entered the dark woods.

CHAPTER 2 - NIGHT RIDERS

Not to be left behind, Penny quickly followed her father, overtaking him before he had gone very far into the forest.

"Penny, you shouldn't have come," he said sternly. "There may be trouble, and I'll not have you taking unnecessary risks."

"I don't want you to do it either," she insisted. "Which way did the men go?"

"That's what I wonder," Mr. Parker responded, listening intently. "Hear anything?"

"Not a sound."

"Queer that all three of them could disappear so quickly," the editor muttered. "I'm sure there's been no attack. Listen! What was that?"

"It sounded like a car being started!" Penny exclaimed.

Hastening to the edge of the woods, she gazed toward the parking lot. The Parker car stood where it had been abandoned, but the gray sedan was missing. A moving tail light could be seen far down the road.

"There go our friends," Mr. Parker commented rather irritably. "Their sudden departure probably saved me from making a chump of myself."

"How could we tell they didn't mean to rob that other man?" Penny asked in an injured tone. "You thought yourself that they intended to harm him."

"Oh, I'm not blaming you," the editor answered, starting toward the parking lot. "I'm annoyed at myself. This is a graphic example of what we were talking about awhile ago—imagination!"

Decidedly crestfallen, Penny followed her father to the car. They finished their hamburgers, which had grown cold, and after the tray was removed, started home.

"I could do with a little sleep," Mr. Parker yawned. "After a hard day at the office, your brand of night life is a bit too strenuous for me."

Selecting a short-cut route to Riverview, Penny paid strict attention to the road, for the narrow pavement had been patched in many places. On either side of the highway stretched truck farms with row upon row of neatly staked tomatoes and other crops.

Rounding a bend, Penny was startled to see tongues of flame brightening the horizon. A large wooden barn, situated in plain view, on a slight knoll, had caught fire and was burning rapidly. As she slammed on the brake, Mr. Parker aroused from light slumber.

"Now what?" he mumbled drowsily.

"Dad, unless I'm imagining things again, that barn is on fire!"

"Let 'er burn," he mumbled, and then fully aroused, swung open the car door.

There were no fire fighters on the scene, in fact the only person visible was a woman in dark flannel night robe, who stood silhouetted in the red glare. As Penny and Mr. Parker reached her side, she stared at them almost stupidly.

"We'll lose everything," she said tonelessly. "Our entire crop of melons is inside the barn, packed for shipment. And my husband's new truck!"

"Have you called a fire company?" the editor asked.

"I've called, but it won't do any good," she answered. "The barn will be gone before they can get here."

With a high wind whipping the flames, Penny and her father knew that the woman spoke the truth. Already the fire had such a start that even had water been available, the barn could not have been saved.

"Maybe I can get out the truck for you!" Mr. Parker offered.

As he swung open the barn doors, a wave of heat rushed into his face. Coughing and choking, he forced his way into the smoke filled interior, unaware that Penny was at his side. Seeing her a moment later, he tried to send her back.

"You can't get the truck out without me to help push," she replied, refusing to retreat. "Come on, we can do it!"

The shiny red truck was a fairly light one and stood on an inclined cement floor which sloped toward the exit. Nevertheless, although Penny and her father exerted every iota of their combined strength, they could not start it moving.

"Maybe the brake is on!" Mr. Parker gasped, running around to the cab. "Yes, it is!"

Pushing once more, they were able to start the truck rolling. Once in motion its own momentum carried it down the runway into the open, a safe distance from the flames.

"How about the crated melons?" Penny asked, breathing hard from the strenuous exertion.

"Not a chance to save them," Mr. Parker answered. "We were lucky to get out the truck."

Driven back by the heat, Penny and her father went to stand beside the woman in dark flannel. Thanking them for their efforts in her behalf, she added that her name was Mrs. Preston and that her husband was absent.

"John went to Riverview and hasn't come back yet," she said brokenly. "This is going to be a great shock to him. All our work gone up in smoke!"

"Didn't you have the barn insured?" the editor questioned her.

"John has a small policy," Mrs. Preston replied. "It covers the barn, but not the melons stored inside. Those men did it on purpose, too! I saw one of 'em riding away."

"What's that?" Mr. Parker demanded, wondering if he had understood the woman correctly. "You don't mean the fire deliberately was set?"

"Yes, it was," the woman affirmed angrily. "I was sound asleep, and then I heard a horse galloping into the yard. I ran to the window and saw the rider throw a lighted torch into the old hay loft. As soon as he saw it blaze up, he rode off."

"Was the man anyone you knew?" Mr. Parker asked, amazed by the disclosure. "Were you able to see his face?"

"Hardly," Mrs. Preston returned with a short laugh. "He wore a black hood. It covered his head and shoulders."

"A black hood!" Penny exclaimed. "Why, Dad, that sounds like night riders!"

"Mrs. Preston, do you know of any reason why you and your husband might be made the target of such cowardly action?" the newspaper man inquired.

"It must have been done because John wouldn't join up with them."

"Join some organization, you mean?"

"Yes, they kept warning him something like this would happen, but John wouldn't have anything to do with 'em."

"I don't blame your husband," said the editor, seeking to gather more information. "Tell me, what is the name of this disreputable organization? What is its purpose, and the names of the men who run it?"

"I don't know any more about it than what I've told you," Mrs. Preston replied, suddenly becoming close-lipped. "John never said much about it to me."

"Are you afraid to tell what you know?" Mr. Parker asked abruptly.

"It doesn't pay to do too much talking. You act real friendly and you did me a good turn saving my truck—but I don't even know your name."

"Anthony Parker, owner of the *Riverview Star*."

The information was anything but reassuring to the woman.

"You're not aiming to write up anything I've told you for the paper?" she asked anxiously.

"Not unless I believe that by doing so I can expose these night riders who have destroyed your barn."

"Please don't print anything in the paper," Mrs. Preston pleaded. "It will only do harm. Those men will turn on John harder than ever."

Before Mr. Parker could reply, the roof of the storage barn collapsed, sending up a shower of sparks and burning brands. By this time the red glare in the sky had attracted the attention of neighbors, and several men

CHAPTER 2 - NIGHT RIDERS

came running into the yard. Realizing that he could not hope to gain additional information from the woman, Mr. Parker began to examine the ground in the vicinity of the barn.

"Looking for hoof tracks?" Penny asked, falling into step beside him.

"I thought we might find some, providing the woman told a straight story."

"Dad, did you ever hear of an organization such as Mrs. Preston mentioned?" Penny inquired, her gaze on the ground. "I mean around Riverview, of course."

Mr. Parker shook his head. "I never did, Penny. But if what she says is true, the *Star* will launch an investigation. We'll have no night riders in this community, not if it's in my power to blast them out!"

"Here's your first clue, Dad!"

Excitedly, Penny pointed to a series of hoof marks plainly visible in the soft earth. The tracks led toward the main road.

"Apparently Mrs. Preston told the truth about the barn being fired by a man on horseback," Mr. Parker declared as he followed the trail leading out of the yard. "These prints haven't been made very long."

"Dad, you look like Sherlock Holmes scooting along with his nose to the ground!" Penny giggled. "You should have a magnifying glass to make the picture perfect."

"Never mind the comedy," her father retorted gruffly. "This may mean a big story for the *Star*, not to mention a worthwhile service to the community."

"Oh, I'm heartily in favor of your welfare work," Penny chuckled. "In fact, I think it would be wonderfully exciting to capture a night rider. Is that what you have in mind?"

"We may as well follow this trail as far as we can. Apparently, the fellow rode his horse just off the main highway, heading toward Riverview."

"Be sure you don't follow the trail backwards," Penny teased. "That would absolutely ruin your reputation as a detective."

"Jump in the car and drive while I stand on the running board," Mr. Parker ordered, ignoring his daughter's attempt at wit. "Keep close to the edge of the pavement and go slowly."

Obeying instructions, Penny drove the car at an even speed. Due to a recent rain which had made the ground very soft, it was possible to follow the trail of hoof prints without difficulty.

"We turn left here," Mr. Parker called as they came to a dirt road. "Speed up a bit or the tires may stick. And watch sharp for soft places."

"Aye, aye, captain," Penny laughed, thoroughly enjoying the adventure.

Soon the car came to the entrance of a narrow, muddy lane, and there Mr. Parker called a halt.

"We've come to the end of the trail," he announced.

"Have the tracks ended?" Penny asked in disappointment as she applied brakes.

"Quite the contrary. They turn into this lane."

Both Mr. Parker and his daughter gazed thoughtfully toward a small cabin which could be seen far back among the trees. Despite the late hour, a light still glowed in one of the windows.

"The man who set the fire must live there!" Penny exclaimed. "What's our next move, Dad?"

As she spoke, the roar of a fast traveling automobile was heard far up the road, approaching from the direction whence they had just come.

"Pull over," Mr. Parker instructed. "And flash the tail light. We don't want to risk being struck."

Barely did Penny have time to obey before the head-beams of the oncoming car illuminated the roadway. But as it approached, the automobile suddenly slackened speed, finally skidding to a standstill beside the Parker sedan.

"That you, Clem Davis?" boomed a loud voice. "Stand where you are, and don't make any false moves!"

CHAPTER 3 - A BLACK HOOD

"Good Evening, Sheriff," Mr. Parker said evenly as he recognized the heavy-set man who stepped from a county automobile. "I'm afraid you've mistaken me for someone else this time."

Sheriff Daniels put away his revolver and moved into the beam of light.

"Sorry," he apologized. "Thought you might be Clem Davis, and I wasn't taking any chances. You're Parker of the *Riverview Star*?"

"That's right," agreed the editor, "Looking for Clem Davis?"

"I'm here to question him. I'm investigating a fire which was set at the Preston place."

"You're a fast worker, Sheriff," Mr. Parker remarked. "My daughter and I just left the Preston farm, and we didn't see you there. What put you on Davis' trail?"

"Our officer received an anonymous telephone call from a woman. She reported the fire and said that I'd find my man here."

"Could it have been Mrs. Preston who notified you?" Mr. Parker inquired thoughtfully.

"It wasn't Mrs. Preston," answered the sheriff. "I traced the call to the Riverview exchange. Thought it must be the trick of a crank until our office got a report that a fire actually had been set at the Preston farm. By the way, what are you doing around here, Parker?"

"Oh, just prowling," the editor replied, and explained briefly how he and Penny had chanced to be at the scene of the fire.

"If you followed a horseman to this lane there may be something to that anonymous telephone call," the sheriff declared. "I'll look around, and then have a talk with Davis."

"Mind if we accompany you?" inquired Mr. Parker.

"Come along," the sheriff invited.

Penny was hard pressed to keep step with the two men as they strode down the muddy lane. A light glowed in the window of the cabin, and a woman could be seen sitting at a table. The sheriff, however, circled the house. Following the trail of hoof marks he went directly to the stable, quietly opening the double doors.

Once inside, Sheriff Daniels switched on a flashlight. The bright beam revealed six stalls, all empty save one, in which stood a handsome black mare who tugged restlessly at her tether. Her body was covered with sweat, and she shivered.

"This horse has been ridden hard," the sheriff observed, reaching to throw a blanket over her.

"Here's something interesting," commented Mr. Parker. Stooping, he picked up a dark piece of cloth lying in plain view on the cement floor. It had been sewed in the shape of a headgear, with eye holes cut in the front side.

"A black hood!" Penny shouted in awe.

Sheriff Daniels took the cloth from the editor, examining it closely but saying very little.

"Ever hear of any night riders in this community?" Mr. Parker asked after a moment, his tone casual.

"Never did," the sheriff replied emphatically. "And I sure hope such a story doesn't get started."

Mr. Parker fingered the black mask. "All the same, Sheriff, you can't just laugh off a thing like this. Even if the November elections aren't far away—"

"I'm not worried about my job," the other broke in. "So far as I know there's no underground organization in this county. All this mask proves is that Clem Davis may be the man who set the Preston fire."

The officer turned to leave the stable. Before he could reach the exit, the double doors slowly opened. A woman, who carried a lighted lantern, peered inside.

CHAPTER 3 - A BLACK HOOD

"Who's there?" she called in a loud voice.

"Sheriff Daniels, ma'am," the officer answered. "You needn't be afraid."

"Who said anything about bein' afraid?" the woman belligerently retorted.

Coming into the stable, she gazed with undisguised suspicion from one person to another. She was noticeably thin, slightly stooped and there was a hard set to her jaw.

"You're Mrs. Davis?" the sheriff inquired, and as she nodded, he asked: "Clem around here?"

"No, he ain't," she answered defiantly. "What you wanting him for anyhow?"

"Oh, just to ask a few questions. Where is your husband, Mrs. Davis?"

"He went to town early and ain't been back. What you aimin' to lay onto him, Sheriff?"

"If your husband hasn't been here since early evening, who has ridden this horse?" the sheriff demanded, ignoring the question.

Mrs. Davis' gaze roved to the stall where the black mare noisily crunched an ear of corn.

"Why Sal *has* been rid!" she exclaimed as if genuinely surprised. "But not by Clem. He went to town in the flivver, and he ain't been back."

"Sorry, but I'll have to take a look in the house."

"Search it from cellar to attic!" the woman said angrily. "You won't find Clem! What's he wanted for anyway?"

"The Preston barn was set afire tonight, and your husband is a suspect."

"Clem never did it! Why, the Prestons are good friends of ours! Somebody's just tryin' to make a peck o' trouble for us."

"That may be," the sheriff admitted. "You say Clem hasn't been here tonight. In that case, who rode the mare?"

"I don't know anything about it," the woman maintained sullenly.

"Didn't you hear a horse come into the yard?"

"I never heard a sound until your car stopped at the entrance to the lane."

"I suppose you never saw this before either." The sheriff held up the black hood which had been found in the barn.

Mrs. Davis stared blankly at the cloth. "I tell you, I don't know nothin' about it, Sheriff. You ain't being fair if you try to hang that fire onto Clem. And you won't find him hidin' in the house."

"If your husband isn't here, I'll wait until he comes."

"You may have a long wait, Sheriff," the woman retorted, her lips parting in a twisted smile. "You can come in though and look around."

Not caring to follow the sheriff into the house, Penny and her father bade him goodbye a moment later. Tramping down the lane to their parked car, they both expressed the belief that Clem Davis would not be arrested during the night.

"Obviously, the woman knows a lot more than she's willing to tell," Mr. Parker remarked, sliding into the car seat beside Penny.

"Dad, do you think it was Clem who set fire to the Preston barn?"

"We have no reason to suspect anyone else," returned the editor. "All the evidence points to his guilt."

Penny backed the car in the narrow road, heading toward Riverview.

"That was the point I wanted to make," she said thoughtfully. "Doesn't it seem to you that the evidence was almost too plain?"

"What do you mean, Penny?"

"Well, I was just thinking, if I had been in Clem Davis' place, I never would have left a black hood lying where the first person to enter the barn would be sure to see it."

"That's so, it was a bit obvious," Mr. Parker admitted.

"The horse was left in the stable, and the hoof tracks leading to the Davis place were easy to follow."

"All true," Mr. Parker nodded.

"Isn't it possible that someone could have tried to throw the blame on Clem?" suggested Penny, anxiously awaiting her father's reply.

"There may be something to the theory," Mr. Parker responded. "Still, Mrs. Davis didn't deny that the mare belonged to her husband. She claimed that she hadn't heard the horse come into the stable, which obviously was a lie. Furthermore, I gathered the impression that Clem knew the sheriff was after him, and intends to hide out."

"It will be interesting to learn if Mr. Daniels makes an arrest. Do you expect to print anything about it in the paper?"

"Only routine news of the fire," Mr. Parker replied. "There may be much more to this little incident than appears on the surface, but until something develops, we must wait."

"If you could gain proof that night riders are operating in this community, what then?" Penny suggested eagerly.

"In that case, I should certainly launch a vigorous campaign. But why go into all the details now? I'm sure I'll not assign you to the story."

"Why not?" Penny asked in an injured tone. "I think night riders would be especially suited to my journalistic talents. I could gather information about Clem Davis and the Prestons—"

"This is Sheriff Daniel's baby, and we'll let him take care of it for the time being," Mr. Parker interrupted. "Why not devote yourself to the great mystery of the Hubell clock? That should provide a safe outlook for your energies."

The car was drawing close to Riverview. As it approached the tall stone tower, Penny raised her eyes to the dark windows. Just then the big clock struck twice.

"Two o'clock," Mr. Parker observed, taking a quick glance at his watch. "Or would you say three?"

"There's no argument about it this time, Dad. All the same, I intend to prove to you that I was right!"

"How?" her father asked, covering a wide yawn.

"I don't know," Penny admitted, favoring the grim tower with a dark scowl. "But just you wait—I'll find a way!"

CHAPTER 4 - A NEW CARETAKER

"I declare, getting folks up becomes a harder task each morning," declared Mrs. Maud Weems, who had served as the Parker housekeeper for eleven years, as she brought a platter of bacon and eggs to the breakfast table. "I call and call until I'm fairly hoarse, and all I get in response is a few sleepy mutters and mumbles. The food is stone cold."

"It's good all the same," praised Penny, pouring herself a large-size glass of orange juice. "There's not a woman in Riverview who can equal your cooking."

"I'm in no mood for blarney this morning," the housekeeper warned. "I must say quite frankly that I don't approve of the irregular hours in this house."

"Penny and I did get in a little late last night," Mr. Parker admitted, winking at his daughter.

"A little late! It must have been at least four o'clock when you came in. Oh, I heard you tiptoe up the stairs even if you did take off your shoes!"

"It was only a few minutes after two," Penny corrected. "I'm sorry though, that we awakened you."

"I hadn't been asleep," Mrs. Weems replied, somewhat mollified by the apology. "I'm sure I heard every stroke of the clock last night."

"You did!" Penny exclaimed with sudden interest. "How many times would you say it struck at midnight? I mean the Hubell Tower clock."

"Such a question!" Mrs. Weems protested, thoroughly exasperated.

"It's a very important one," Penny insisted. "My reputation and five gallons of gas are at stake, so weigh well your words before you speak."

"The clock struck twelve, of course!"

"There, you see, Penny," Mr. Parker grinned triumphantly. "Does that satisfy you?"

"Mrs. Weems," Penny persisted, "did you actually count the strokes?"

"Certainly not. Why should I? The clock always strikes twelve, therefore it must have struck that number last night."

"I regret to say, you've just disqualified yourself as a witness in this case," Penny said, helping herself to the last strip of bacon on the platter. "I must search farther afield for proof."

"What are you talking about anyhow?" the housekeeper protested. "It doesn't make sense to me."

As she finished breakfast, Penny explained to Mrs. Weems how the disagreement with her father had arisen. The housekeeper displayed slight interest in the tale of the clock, but asked many questions about the fire at the Preston farm.

"That reminds me!" Mr. Parker suddenly exclaimed before Penny had finished the story. "I want to 'phone Sheriff Daniels before I start for the office. Excuse me, please."

Pushing aside his chair, he went hurriedly to the living room. Not wishing to miss any news which might have a bearing on the affair of the previous night, Penny trailed him, hovering close to the telephone. However, her father's brief comments told her almost nothing.

"What did you learn?" she inquired eagerly as he hung up the receiver. "Was Clem Davis arrested last night?"

"No, it turned out about as we expected. Apparently, Davis knew the sheriff was looking for him. Anyway, he never returned home."

Jamming on his hat, Mr. Parker started for the front door. Penny pursued him to the garage, carrying on a running conversation.

"This rather explodes my theory about Clem not being guilty," she remarked ruefully. "If he were innocent, one would expect him to face the sheriff and prove an alibi."

"Davis can't be far away," Mr. Parker responded, getting into the maroon sedan. "The sheriff will nab him soon."

Penny held open the garage doors, watching as her father backed down the driveway, scraping the bark of a tree whose gnarled trunk already bore many scars. Before she could reenter the house, Louise Sidell, a dark-haired, slightly plump girl, who was Penny's most loyal friend, sauntered into the yard.

"Hi!" she greeted cheerily. "About ready?"

"Ready for what?" Penny asked, her face blank.

Louise regarded her indignantly. "If that isn't just like you, Penny Parker! You make promises and then forget them. Don't you remember telling Mrs. Van Cleve of the Woman's Club that we would help sell tags today, for the Orphans' Home summer camp?"

"Now that you remind me, I have a vague recollection. How many are we to sell?"

"Twenty-five at not less than a quarter each. I have the tags, but we'll have to work fast or the other girls will sell all the easy customers."

"I'll be with you in two shakes," Penny promised, heading for the house. "Wait until I tell Mrs. Weems where I am going."

Returning a moment later with the car ignition keys, she found Louise staring disconsolately at the empty space in the garage.

"What became of your new car?" asked her chum.

"Dad's auto is in the garage for repairs," Penny explained briefly. "I didn't have the heart to make him walk."

"I should think not!" laughed Louise. "Imagine having three cars in one family—if you can call this mess of junk by such a flattering name." Depreciatingly, she kicked the patched tire of a battered but brightly painted flivver which had seen its heyday in the early thirties.

"Don't speak so disrespectfully of my property," Penny chided, sliding into the high, uncomfortable seat. "Leaping Lena is a good car even if she is a bit creaky in the joints. She still takes us places."

"And leaves us stranded," Louise added with a sniff. "Oh, well, let's go—if we can."

Penny stepped on the starter and waited expectantly. The motor sputtered and coughed, but true to form, would not start. Just as the girls were convinced that they must walk, there was an explosive backfire, and then the car began to quiver with its familiar motion.

"You should sell Lena to the government for a cannon," Louise teased as they rattled down the street. "What do you burn in this smoke machine? Kerosene?"

"Never mind the slurs. Where do we start our business operations?"

"We've been assigned to the corner of Madison and Clark streets," Louise answered as she separated the yellow benefit tags into two evenly divided piles. "It shouldn't take us long to get rid of these."

Neither of the girls regretted their promise to help with the tag-day sale, for the cause was a worthy one. The campaign to raise sufficient funds with which to purchase and equip an orphans' summer camp site, had been underway many weeks, and was headed by Mrs. Van Cleve, a prominent club woman.

Parking Leaping Lena at the designated street corner, the girls went to work with a will. All their lives they had lived in Riverview, and Penny in particular, had a wide acquaintance. Accosting nearly everyone who passed, she soon disposed of all her tags, and then sold many for her chum.

"They've gone fast," Louise declared as the morning wore on. "We have only one left."

"Don't sell that tag!" Penny said impulsively. "I have it earmarked for a certain person—Old Seth McGuire."

"The caretaker at the Hubell Clock Tower?" Louise asked in astonishment.

"Yes, he always liked children and I think he would be glad to help."

"But why drive so far?" protested Louise. "I'm sure we could dispose of it right here, and much quicker."

"Oh, I have a special reason for going to see Seth," Penny answered carelessly. "I'll tell you about it on the way there."

From her chum's manner, Louise deducted that something interesting lay ahead. She had learned, frequently to her sorrow, that Penny enjoyed interviewing unusual characters and engaging in amazing activities. Only a

CHAPTER 4 - A NEW CARETAKER

few months earlier, the girls had operated their own newspaper in an abandoned downtown building with results which were still the talk of Riverview. Another time they had attended a society wedding on an island guarded by a drawbridge, and had ended by using the drawbridge as a means of capturing a boatload of crooks. In fact, Louise took delight in remarking that if ever her chum chose to write an autobiography, a suitable title would be: "Life with Penelope Parker: Never a Dull Moment."

"What's up now, Penny?" she inquired, as they rattled toward the Hubell Tower in Leaping Lena.

"Just a little argument I had with Dad last night. I maintain that the big clock struck thirteen last night at midnight. He thinks I'm a wee bit touched in the head."

"Which you must be," retorted Louise. "Who ever heard of such a thing?"

"What's so crazy about it?" Penny asked with a grimace. "Didn't you ever hear a clock strike the wrong number?"

"Of course, but not the Hubell clock. Why, the works were purchased in Europe, and it's supposed to be one of the best in the country."

"Even a good clock can make a mistake, I guess. Anyway, we'll see what Seth McGuire has to say about it."

Penny brought Leaping Lena to a quivering halt opposite the tall Hubell Tower. Glancing upward at the octagonical-shaped clock face, she saw that the hands indicated twenty minutes to twelve.

"Rather an awkward time to call," she remarked, swinging open the car door, "but Seth probably won't mind."

As the girls walked toward the tower entrance, they noticed that the grounds surrounding the building were not as neat as when last they had viewed them. The shrubs were untrimmed, the lawn choked with weeds, and old newspapers had matted against the hedge.

"I wonder if Mr. McGuire has been well?" Penny commented, knocking on the tower door. "He always took pride in looking after the yard."

"At least he seems to be up and around," Louise returned in a low tone. "I can hear someone moving about inside."

The girls waited expectantly for the door to open. When there was no response to their knock, Penny tried again.

"Who's there?" called a loud and not very friendly voice.

Penny knew that it was not Old Seth who spoke, for the caretaker's high-pitched tones were unmistakable.

"We came to see Mr. McGuire," she called through the panel.

The door swung back and the girls found themselves facing a stout, red-faced man of perhaps forty, who wore a soiled suede jacket and unpressed corduroy trousers.

"McGuire's not here any more," he informed curtly. "You'll probably find him at his farm."

Before the man could close the door, Penny quickly asked if Mr. McGuire had given up his position as caretaker because of sickness.

"Oh, he was getting too old to do his work," the man answered with a shrug. "I'm Charley Phelps, the new attendant. Visiting hours are from two to four each afternoon."

"We didn't come to see the clock," persisted Penny.

"What did bring you here then?" the man demanded gruffly. "You a personal friend of Seth's?"

"Not exactly." Penny peered beyond the caretaker into an untidy living room clouded with tobacco smoke. "We thought we might sell him one of these tags. Perhaps you would like to contribute to the orphans' camp fund?"

She extended the bit of yellow cardboard, bestowing upon the attendant one of her most dazzling smiles.

"No, thanks, Sister," he declined, refusing to take the tag. "You'll have to peddle your wares somewhere else."

"Only twenty-five cents."

"I'm not interested. Now run along and give me a chance to eat my lunch in peace."

"Sorry to have bothered you," Penny apologized woodenly. Without moving from the door, she inquired: "Oh, by the way, what happened to the clock last night?"

"Nothing happened to it," the caretaker retorted. "What d'you mean?"

"At midnight it struck thirteen times instead of twelve."

"You must have dreamed it!" the man declared. "Say, what are you trying to do anyhow—start stories so I'll lose my job?"

"Why, I never thought of such a thing!" Penny gasped. "I truly believed that the clock did strike thirteen—"

"Well, you were wrong, and I'll thank you not to go around telling folks such bunk!" the man said angrily. "The clock hasn't struck a wrong hour since the day it was installed. I take better care of the mechanism than Seth McGuire ever did!"

"I didn't mean to intimate that you were careless—" Penny began.

She did not complete the sentence, for Charley Phelps slammed the door in her face.

CHAPTER 5 - OLD SETH

"Well, Penny, you certainly drew lightning that time," Louise remarked dryly as the girls retreated to Leaping Lena. "I thought Mr. Phelps was going to throw the tower at you!"

"How could I know he was so touchy?" Penny asked in a grieved tone.

"You did talk as if you thought he had been careless in taking care of the big clock."

"I never meant it that way, Lou. Anyway, he could have been more polite."

Jerking open the car door, Penny slid behind the steering wheel and jammed her foot on the starter. Leaping Lena, apparently realizing that her young mistress was in no mood for trifling, responded with instantaneous action.

"I guess you're satisfied now that the clock never struck thirteen," Louise teased as the car fairly leaped forward.

"I should say not!" Penny retorted. "Why, I'm more convinced than ever that something went wrong with the mechanism last night. Phelps knew it too, and for that reason didn't want us asking questions!"

"You die hard, Penny," chuckled Louise. "From now on, I suppose you'll go around asking everyone you meet: 'Where were you at midnight of the thirteenth?'"

"It wouldn't do any good. Most folks just take things for granted in this world. But there's one person who would pay attention to that clock!"

"Who?"

"Why, old Seth McGuire. We'll drive out to his farm and ask him about it."

"It's lunch time and I'm hungry," Louise protested.

"Oh, you can spend the rest of your life eating," Penny overruled her. "Business before pleasure, you know."

Seth McGuire, one of Riverview's best known and well loved characters, had been caretaker at the Hubell Clock Tower from the day of its erection, and the girls could not but wonder why he had been relieved of his post. The old man had personally installed the complicated machinery, caring for it faithfully over the years. In fact, his only other interest in life was his farm, located a mile from the city limits, and it was there that Penny hoped to find him.

"Watch for a sign, 'Sleepy Hollow,'" she instructed. "Mr. McGuire has given his place a fancy name."

A moment later Louise, seeing the marker, cried: "There it is! Slow down!"

Penny slammed on the brakes and Leaping Lena responded by shivering in every one of her ancient joints. Louise was thrown forward, barely catching herself in time to prevent a collision with the windshield.

"Why don't you join a stunt circus?" she said irritably. "You drive like Demon Dan!"

"We're here," replied Penny cheerfully. "Nice looking place, isn't it?"

The car had pulled up near a small, neatly-kept cottage framed in well-trimmed greenery. An even, rich green lawn was highlighted here and there by beds of bright red and blue flowers.

After admiring the grounds, the girls rang the front bell. Receiving no response, they went around to the rear, pounding on the kitchen screen door.

"Mr. McGuire's not here," said Louise. "Just another wild goose chase."

"Let's try this out-building," Penny suggested, indicating a long, low structure made of cement building blocks which was roofed with tin. A sign dangling above the door proclaimed that it was the foundry and machine shop of one Seth McGuire, maker of bells and clocks.

THE CLOCK STRIKES THIRTEEN

As the girls peered through the open door an arresting sight met their gaze. Through clouds of smoke they saw a spry old man directing the movements of a muscular youth who pulled a large pot-shaped crucible of molten metal on an overhead pulley track.

"Are you Seth McGuire?" Penny shouted to make herself heard above the noise of running machinery.

The old man, turning his head, waved them back.

"Don't come in here now!" he warned. "It's dangerous. Wait until we pour the bell."

With deft, sure hands, the old fellow pulled control chains attached to the crucible. The container twisted and finally overturned, allowing the molten metal to pour into a bell-shaped mold. As the last drops ran out of it, a great cloud of steam arose, enveloping both the old man and his helper.

"Won't they be burned?" Louise murmured in alarm, moving hastily backwards.

"Mr. McGuire seems to know what he's doing," Penny answered, watching with interest.

In a moment the steam cleared away, and the old man motioned that the girls might come inside.

"You'll have to excuse my manners," he apologized, his mild blue eyes regarding them with a twinkle. "Pouring a bell is exacting work and you can't stop until it's done."

"Is that what you were doing?" Penny inquired, staring at the steaming mass which had been poured into the mold. "It's sort of like making a gelatin pudding, isn't it?"

"Jake and me never thought of it that way," the old man replied. "I learned from an old Swiss bell maker when I was a lad. And I apprenticed under a master, you may be sure of that."

"How do you make a bell anyway?" Louise inquired curiously.

"You can't tell in five minutes what it takes a lifetime to learn," the old man answered. "Now a bell like this one I'm making for the Methodist Church at Blairstown takes a heap o' work. Jake and me have worked a solid week getting the pattern and mold ready for that pouring job you just saw."

"Do you ever have any failures?" Penny asked, seeking to draw him out.

"Not many, but once in awhile a bell cracks," the old fellow said modestly. "That happens when the mold is damp, or not of proper temperature. If gasses collect you may get a nice healthy explosion, too!"

"Does it take a long while to finish a bell after it's been poured?" Penny pursued the subject.

"A large one may require a week to cool, but I'll have this fellow out of the mold by tomorrow night," Mr. McGuire returned. "Then we'll polish her off, put in the clapper, and attach the bell to a sturdy mounting. If the tone is right, she'll be ready to install."

"How do you tell about the tone?" Louise questioned in perplexity.

"This one should have a deep, low tone," the old man replied. "Other things being equal, a large bell gives a deeper tone than a small one. Pitch depends upon diameter, and timbre upon the shape and the alloy used."

"I never realized there was much to a bell besides its ding-dong," commented Penny. "But tell me, Mr. McGuire, do you find this work more interesting than taking care of the Clock Tower?"

"Looking after that place wasn't work. It was more like a rest cure. I took the job because, twelve years ago when the tower went up, they couldn't find a competent man to look after the clock."

"And now you've gone back to your old trade?"

"Oh, I liked it at the tower," Old Seth admitted truthfully. "I'm a bit old to do heavy work such as this. More than likely I'd have gone on putting in my time if Mr. Blake hadn't wanted the job for a friend of his."

"Mr. Blake?" Penny inquired thoughtfully. "Do you mean Clyde Blake, the real estate man?"

The old bell maker nodded as he gazed moodily out the window toward the distant tower which could be seen outlined against the blue sky.

"Yes, it was Blake that eased me out of that job. He has a lot of influence and he uses it in ways some might say isn't always proper. I can make a fair living as long as I have my health, so I'm not complaining."

"We met the new caretaker this morning," Penny said after a moment. "He wasn't very polite to us, and the grounds have gone to wrack and ruin."

"Did you notice the flower beds?" Old Seth asked, feeling creeping into his voice. "Half choked with weeds. Charley Phelps hasn't turned a hand since he took over there six weeks ago."

"I suppose he spends most of his time looking after the big clock," Penny remarked, deliberately leading the old man deeper.

CHAPTER 5 - OLD SETH

"Charley Phelps spends most of his hours smoking that vile pipe of his and entertaining his roustabout friends," Old Seth snapped. "He doesn't know as much as a child about complicated clock machinery. What he can't take care of with an oil can goes unrepaired!"

The conversation had moved in exactly the channel which Penny desired.

"No doubt that explains why the clock hasn't always been striking right of late," she said in an offhand way. "Last night I was almost sure I heard it strike thirteen instead of twelve times. In fact, I had a little argument with my father about it."

"You were correct," the old man assured her. "I was working late here in the shop and heard it myself."

"There! You see, Louise!" Penny cried triumphantly, turning to her chum.

"Mr. McGuire, what would cause the clock to strike wrong?" the other asked.

"I was wondering myself," he admitted. "In all the ten years I was at the tower, it never once struck an incorrect hour. I think that there must have been something wrong with the striking train."

"Pardon my ignorance," laughed Penny, "but what in the world is the striking train?"

"Oh, we apply that name to the center section of the mechanism which operates the clock. The going train drives the hands, while the quarter train chimes the quarter-hours, sounding four tuned bells."

"Just as clear as mud," sighed Louise who disliked all mechanical things. "Does the clock strike wrong every night?"

"Last night was the first time I ever heard it add a stroke," Mr. McGuire answered. "I'll be listening though, to see if Phelps gets it fixed."

Penny and Louise had accomplished the purpose of their trip, and so, after looking about the shop for a few minutes, left without trying to sell the old man a camp-benefit tag.

"Why didn't you ask him to take one?" Louise asked as she and her chum climbed into the parked car.

"Oh, I don't know," Penny answered uncomfortably. "It just came over me that Old Seth probably doesn't have much money now that he's out of steady work."

"He must make quite a lot from his bells."

"But how often does he get an order?" Penny speculated. "I'd guess not once in three months, if that often. It's a pity Mr. Blake had to push Mr. McGuire out of the tower job."

Louise nodded agreement, and then with a quick change of subject, reminded her chum that they had had no lunch.

"It's too late to go home," said Penny, who had other plans. "I'll treat you to one of the biggest hamburger sandwiches you ever wrapped your teeth around! How's that?"

"I'll take anything so long as you pay for it," Louise agreed with a laugh.

Driving on to Toni's, the girls lunched there without incident, and then started for Riverview by a different route.

"Say, where are you taking me anyway?" Louise demanded suspiciously. "I've never been on this road before."

"Only out to the Davis farm," Penny responded with a grin. "We have a little detective work to do."

During the bumpy ride, she gave her chum a vivid account of the adventure she had shared with her father the previous night.

"And just what do you expect to learn?" Louise inquired at the conclusion of the tale. "Are we expected to capture Clem Davis with our bare hands and turn him over to the authorities?"

"Nothing quite so startling. I thought possibly Mrs. Davis might talk with us. She seemed to know a lot more about the fire than she would tell."

"I don't mind tagging along," Louise consented reluctantly. "It doesn't seem likely, though, that the woman will break down and implicate her husband just because you want a story for the *Riverview Star*."

Undisturbed by her chum's teasing, Penny parked Leaping Lena at the entrance to the lane, and the girls walked to the cabin.

"It doesn't look as if anyone is here," Louise remarked, rapping for the second time on the oaken door.

"I'm sure there is," Penny replied in a whisper. "As we came up the lane, I saw the curtains move."

Louise knocked a third time, so hard that the door rattled.

"At any rate, no one is going to answer," she said. "We may as well go."

"All right," Penny agreed, although it was not her nature to give up so easily.

THE CLOCK STRIKES THIRTEEN

The girls walked down the lane until a clump of bushes screened them from the cabin.

"Let's wait here," Penny proposed, halting. "I have a hunch Mrs. Davis is hiding from us."

"What's to be gained by waiting?" grumbled Louise.

Nevertheless, she crouched beside her chum, watching the house. Ten minutes elapsed. Both Louise and Penny grew very weary. Then unexpectedly, the cabin door opened and Mrs. Davis peered into the yard. Seeing no one, she took a wooden water bucket and started with it to the pump which was situated midway between cabin and stable.

"Now's our chance!" Penny whispered eagerly. "Come on, Louise, we'll cut off her retreat and she can't avoid meeting us!"

CHAPTER 6 - TALL CORN

Hastening up the lane, Penny and Louise approached the pump in such a way that Mrs. Davis could not return to the house without meeting them. Not until the woman had filled the water bucket and was starting back did she see the two girls.

"Well?" she demanded defiantly.

By daylight the woman appeared much younger than Penny had taken her to be the previous night. Not more than thirty-two, she wore a shapeless, faded blue dress which had seen many washings. Rather attractive brown hair had been drawn back into a tight, unbecoming knot that made her face seem grotesquely long.

"I don't suppose you recognize me," Penny began diffidently. "My father and I were here last night with Sheriff Daniels."

"I remember you very well," the woman retorted. "What do you want?"

"Why, I should like to buy some melons," Penny replied, the idea only that instant occurring to her. "Have you any for sale?"

"Melons," the woman repeated, and the hard line of her mouth relaxed. "I thought you came to pester me with questions. Sure, we've got some good Heart o' Gold out in the patch. How many do you want?"

"About three, I guess."

"You can pick 'em out yourself if you want to," Mrs. Davis offered. Setting down the water bucket, she led the way through a gate to a melon patch behind the cabin. Her suspicions not entirely allayed, she demanded: "Sheriff Daniels didn't send you out here?"

"Indeed not," Penny assured her. "I haven't seen him since last night."

"It's all right then," Mrs. Davis said in a more friendly tone. She stooped to examine a ripe melon. "I figured maybe he sent you to find out what became of my husband."

"Oh, no! Didn't Mr. Davis return home last night?"

"Not on your life!" the woman answered grimly. "And he won't be back either—not while Sheriff Daniels is looking for him."

From Mrs. Davis' manner of speaking, Penny was convinced that she had been in communication with her husband since the sheriff's visit. Trying to keep her voice casual, she observed:

"Don't you think it would be wise for your husband to give himself up? By hiding, he makes it appear as though he actually did set fire to the Preston barn."

"Clem would be a fool to give himself up now! Why, they'd be sure to hang the fire onto him, even though he wasn't within a mile of the Preston place."

"Then couldn't he prove it?"

"Not a chance," the woman said with a short, hard laugh. "Clem was framed. He never rode the horse last night, and that black hood was planted in the stable."

"Does your husband have any enemies?"

"Sure, he's got plenty of 'em."

"Then perhaps you can name a person who might have tried to throw blame on your husband."

"I could tell plenty if I was a mind to," the woman said significantly. "I'd do it in a minute, only it would make things worse for Clem."

Penny started to reply, then remained silent as she saw that Mrs. Davis' gaze had focused upon a section of cornfield which fringed the melon patch. The tall stalks were waving in an agitated manner, suggesting that someone might be moving among them.

"Here are your melons," Mrs. Davis said nervously, thrusting three large ones into Penny's hands. "That will be a quarter."

As the girl paid her, she abruptly turned and hurried toward the house.

"Just a minute, Mrs. Davis," Penny called. "If you'll only talk to me I may be able to help your husband."

The woman heard but paid no heed. Picking up the water bucket, she entered the cabin, closing the door behind her.

"Well, we gained three melons, and that's all," Louise shrugged. "What's our next move?"

"I think Mrs. Davis was on the verge of telling us something important," Penny declared, her voice low. "Then she saw someone out there in the corn field and changed her mind."

"I don't see anyone now," Louise said, staring in the direction her chum had indicated. "The stalks aren't even moving."

"They were a moment ago. Clem Davis may be hiding out there, Lou! Or it could be some of Sheriff Davis' men watching the cabin."

"Or an Indian waiting to scalp us," teased Louise. "Let's go back to the car."

Penny shook her head and started toward the corn patch. Reluctantly, Louise followed, overtaking her at the edge of the field.

"Sheriff Daniels!" Penny called through cupped hands.

There was no answer, only a gentle rippling of the corn stalks some distance from them.

"Whoever the person is, he's sneaking away," Penny whispered. "Come on, let's stop him!"

"Don't be foolish—" Louise protested, but her chum had vanished into the forest of tall corn.

After a moment of indecision she, too, entered the field. By that time there was no sign of Penny, no sound to guide her. Wandering aimlessly first in one direction, then another, she soon became hopelessly lost.

"Penny!" she shouted frantically.

"Here!" called a voice not far away.

Tracing the sound, and making repeated calls, Louise finally came face to face with her chum.

"Such a commotion as you've been making," chided Penny. "Not a chance to catch that fellow now!"

"I don't care," Louise retorted crossly. Her hair was disarranged, stockings matted with burs. "If we can get out of this dreadful maze I want to go to the car."

"We're at the edge of the field. Follow me and I'll pilot you to safety."

Emerging a minute later at the end of the corn row, Penny saw the stable only a few yards away. Impulsively, she proposed to Louise that they investigate it for possible clues.

"I've had enough detective work for one day," her chum complained. "Anyway, what do you hope to discover in an old barn?"

"Maybe I can induce the horse to talk," Penny chuckled. "Sal must know all the answers, if only she could speak."

"You'll have to give her the third degree by yourself," Louise decided with finality. "I shall go to the car."

Taking the melons with her, she marched stiffly down the lane and climbed into Leaping Lena. Carefully she rearranged her hair, plucked burs, and then grew impatient because her chum did not come. Fully twenty minutes elapsed before Penny emerged from the stable.

"Sorry to keep you waiting so long, Lou," she apologized as she reached the car. "See what I found!"

Penny held up a bright silver object which resembled a locket, save that it was smaller.

"What is it?" Louise inquired with interest.

"A man's watch charm! It has a picture inside too!"

With her fingernail, Penny pried open the lid. Flat against the cover had been fastened the photograph of a boy who might have been ten or twelve years of age.

"Where did you get it, Penny?"

"I found it lying on the barn floor, not far from the place where we picked up the black hood last night."

"Then it must belong to Clem Davis!"

"It may," Penny admitted, sliding into the seat beside her chum. "Still, I don't believe the Davis' have any children."

"What will you do with the charm? Turn it over to the sheriff?"

CHAPTER 6 - TALL CORN

"I suppose I should, after I've shown it to Dad," Penny replied, carefully tying the trinket into the corner of a handkerchief. "You know, Lou, since finding this, I wonder if Mrs. Davis may not have told the truth."

"About what, Penny?"

"She said that her husband had been framed."

"Then you think this watch charm was left in the barn to throw suspicion upon Clem Davis!"

Penny shook her head. "No, this is my theory, Louise. Perhaps someone hid the black hood there, and rode Clem's horse to make it appear he was the guilty person. Inadvertently, that same person lost this watch charm."

"In that case, you would have a clue which might solve the case."

"Exactly," Penny grinned in triumph. "Get ready for a fast ride into town. I'm going to rush this evidence straight to the *Star* office and get Dad's opinion."

CHAPTER 7 - MR. BLAKE'S DONATION

Not wishing to ride to the *Star* building, Louise asked her chum to drop her off at the Sidell home. Accordingly, Penny left her there, and then drove on alone to her father's office. The news room hummed with activity as she sauntered through to the private office.

"Just a minute, please," her father requested, waving her into a chair.

He completed a letter he was dictating, dismissed his secretary, and then was ready to listen. Without preliminary ado, Penny laid the watch charm on the desk, explaining where she had found it.

"Dad, this may belong to Clem Davis, but I don't think so!" she announced in an excited voice. "It's my theory that the person who planted the black hood in the stable must have lost it!"

Mr. Parker examined the charm carefully, gazing at the picture of the little boy contained within it.

"Very interesting," he commented. "However, I fear you are allowing your imagination to take you for a ride. There isn't much question of Clem Davis' guilt according to the findings of the sheriff."

"Has any new evidence come to light, Dad?"

"Yes, Penny, the sheriff's office has gained possession of a document showing beyond question that Clem Davis is a member of a renegade band known as the Black Hoods."

"Where did they get their proof?"

"Sheriff Davis won't disclose the source of his information. However, our star reporter, Jerry Livingston, is working on the case, and something may develop any hour."

"Then you're intending to make it into a big story?" Penny asked thoughtfully.

"I am. An underground, subversive organization, no matter what its purpose, has no right to an existence. The *Star* will expose the leaders, if possible, and break up the group."

"Since the Hoods apparently burned the Preston storage barn, their purpose can't be a very noble one," Penny commented. "Nor are their leaders especially clever. The trail led as plain as day to Clem Davis—so straight, in fact, that I couldn't help doubting his guilt."

"Penny, I'll keep this watch charm, if you don't mind," Mr. Parker said, locking the trinket into a drawer. "I'll put Jerry to work on it and he may be able to learn the identity of the little boy in the picture."

Abruptly changing the subject, the editor inquired regarding his daughter's success in selling Camp-Benefit tags.

"I have only one left," Penny replied, presenting it with a flourish. "Twenty-five cents, please."

"The cause is a worthy one. I'll double the amount." Amiably, Mr. Parker flipped a half dollar across the desk.

"While you're in a giving mood I might mention that my allowance is due," Penny said with a grin. "Also, you owe me five gallons of gasoline. I saw old Seth McGuire this morning and he agreed with me that the Hubell clock struck thirteen last night."

Mr. Parker had no opportunity to reply, for just then his secretary re-entered the office to say that Mr. Clyde Blake wished to see him.

"I suppose that means you want me to evaporate," Penny remarked, gazing questioningly at her father.

"No, stay if you like. It's probably nothing of consequence."

Penny welcomed an invitation to remain. After her talk with Seth McGuire she was curious to see the man who had caused the old bell maker to lose his position at the Hubell Tower.

"Blake probably wants to ask me to do him a personal favor," Mr. Parker confided in a low tone. "He's a pest!"

CHAPTER 7 - MR. BLAKE'S DONATION

In a moment the door opened again to admit the real estate man. He was heavy-set, immaculately dressed, and the only defect in his appearance was caused by a right arm which was somewhat shorter than the left.

"Good afternoon, Mr. Parker," he said expansively. "And is this your charming daughter?"

The editor introduced Penny, who bowed politely and retreated to a chair by the window. Prejudiced against Mr. Blake, she had no desire to talk to him.

"What may I do for you?" Mr. Parker asked the caller.

"Ah, this time it is I who shall bestow the favor," Mr. Blake responded, taking a cheque book from his pocket. "Your paper has been campaigning for a very worthy cause, namely the Orphans' Summer Camp Fund. It wrings my heart that those unfortunate kiddies have been denied the benefit of fresh air and sunshine."

"If you wish to make a donation, you should give your money to Mrs. Van Cleve," the editor cut him short.

"I much prefer to present my cheque to you," the caller insisted. "Shall I make it out for a hundred and fifty dollars?"

"That's a very handsome donation," said Mr. Parker, unable to hide his surprise. "But why give it to me?"

Mr. Blake coughed in embarrassment. "I thought you might deem the offering worthy of a brief mention in your paper."

"Oh, I see," the editor responded dryly.

"I don't wish publicity for myself, you understand, but only for the real estate company which bears my name."

"I quite understand, Mr. Blake. If we should use your picture—"

"That will be very acceptable," the real estate man responded, smiling with satisfaction. "I'll be happy to oblige you by posing."

Helping himself to a pen, he wrote out the cheque and presented it to the editor.

"Penny, how would you like to write the story?" inquired her father. "You've been helping Miss Norton with the publicity, I believe."

"I'm rather bogged down with work," Penny demurred. "I think Mrs. Weems wants me to clean the attic when I get home."

"Never mind the attic. Please conduct Mr. Blake to the photography room and ask one of the boys to take his picture."

Penny arose obediently, but as the real estate man left the office ahead of her, she shot her father a black look. She considered a publicity story very trivial indeed, and it particularly displeased her that she must write honeyed words about a man she did not admire.

"You have a very nice building here, very nice," Mr. Blake patronizingly remarked as he was escorted toward the photographic department. Noticing a pile of freshly printed newspapers lying on one of the desks, he helped himself to a copy.

"I see the sheriff hasn't captured Clem Davis yet," he commented, scanning the front page. "I hope they get him! It's a disgrace to Riverview that such a crime could be perpetrated, and the scoundrel go unpunished."

"He'll probably be caught," Penny replied absently. "But I wonder if he's the guilty person."

"What's that?" Mr. Blake demanded, regarding her with shrewd interest. "You think Davis didn't burn the Preston barn?"

"I was only speculating upon it."

"Reflecting your father's opinion, no doubt."

"No, not anyone's thought but my own."

"Your father seems to be making quite a story of it," Mr. Blake resumed. "It will be most unfortunate for the community if he stirs up talk about underground organizations."

"Why unfortunate?" Penny asked.

"Because it will give the city a bad reputation. I doubt there is anything to this Black Hood talk, but if there should be, any publicity might lead to an investigation by state authorities."

"A very good thing, I should think."

"You do not understand," Mr. Blake said patiently. "Depredation would increase, innocent persons surely would suffer. With Riverview known unfavorably throughout the country, we would gain no new residents."

Penny did not reply, but opened the door of the photographic room. While Mr. Blake wandered about, inspecting the various equipment, she relayed her father's instructions to Salt Sommers, one of the staff photographers.

"Better get a good picture of Blake," she warned him. "He'll be irritated if you don't."

"I'll do my best," Salt promised, "but I can't make over a man's face."

Mr. Blake proved to be a trying subject. Posed on a stool in front of a screen, he immediately "froze" into a stiff position.

"Be sure to make it only a head and shoulders picture, if you please," he ordered Salt.

"Can't you relax?" the photographer asked wearily. "Unloosen your face. Think of all those little orphans you're going to make happy."

Mr. Blake responded with a smirk which was painful to behold. Nothing that Salt could say or do caused him to become natural, and at length the photographer took two shots which he knew would not be satisfactory.

"That'll be all," he announced.

Mr. Blake arose, drawing a deep sigh. "Posing is a great ordeal for me," he confessed. "I seldom consent to having my picture taken, but this is a very special occasion."

Completely at ease again, the real estate man began to converse with Penny. In sudden inspiration, Salt seized a candid camera from a glass case, and before Mr. Blake was aware of his act, snapped a picture.

"There, that's more like it," he said. "I caught you just right, Mr. Blake."

The real estate man turned swiftly, his eyes blazing anger.

"You dared to take a picture without my permission?" he demanded. "I'll not have it! Destroy the film at once or I shall protest to Mr. Parker!"

CHAPTER 8 - PUBLICITY BY PENNY

The real estate man's outburst was so unexpected that Penny and Salt could only stare at him in astonishment.

"It's a good full length picture," the photographer argued. "Much better than those other shots I took."

"I can't allow it," Blake answered in a calmer tone. He touched his right arm. "You see, I am sensitive about this deformity. Unreasonable of me, perhaps, but I must insist that you destroy the film."

"Just as you say," Salt shrugged. "We'll use one of the other pictures."

"No, I've changed my mind," Blake said shortly. "I don't care for any picture. Kindly destroy all the films—now, in my presence."

"Why, Mr. Blake!" Penny protested. "I thought you wanted a picture to accompany the story I am to write."

"You may write the article, but I'll have no picture. The films must be destroyed."

"Okay," responded Salt. Removing two plates from a holder he exposed them to the light. He started to take the film from the candid camera, but did not complete the operation. Mr. Blake, however, failed to notice.

"Thank you, young man," he said, bowing. "I am sorry to have taken so much of your valuable time, and I appreciate your efforts."

Nodding in Penny's direction, Mr. Blake left the studio, closing the door behind him.

"Queer duck," commented Salt. "His picture on the front page would be no break for our readers!"

"I can't understand why Mr. Blake became so provoked," Penny said thoughtfully. "That excuse about his arm seemed a flimsy one."

"Let's develop the film and see what it looks like," Salt suggested, starting for the darkroom. "It was just an ordinary shot though."

Penny followed the young photographer into the developing room, watching as he ran the film through the various trays. In exactly six minutes the picture was ready, and he held it beneath the ruby light for her to see.

"Nothing unusual about it," he repeated. "Blake's right arm looks a bit shorter than the left, but we could have blocked that off."

Salt tossed the damp picture into a wastepaper basket, only to have Penny promptly rescue it.

"I wish you would save this," she requested. "Put it in an envelope and file it away somewhere in the office."

"What's the big idea, Penny?"

"Oh, just a hunch, I guess. Someday the paper may want a picture of Blake in a hurry, and this one would serve very nicely."

Aware that time was fast slipping away, Penny returned to her father's office to report Mr. Blake's strange action. Mr. Parker, well versed in the peculiarities of newspaper patrons, shrugged indifferently.

"Blake always was a queer fellow," he commented, fingering the cheque which still lay on his desk. "I never trusted him, and I wish I hadn't accepted this money."

"How could you have refused, Dad?"

"I couldn't very well. All the same, I have a feeling I'll regret it."

"Why do you say that?" Penny asked curiously.

"No reason perhaps. Only Blake isn't the man to give something for nothing. He aims to profit by this affair, or I'm no judge of human nature."

"He craves publicity, that's certain."

"Yes, but there's more to it than that," Mr. Parker declared. "Oh, well"—he dismissed the subject, "I'll turn the cheque over to the camp committee and let someone else do the worrying."

"I'll tell you why I dislike Mr. Blake," Penny said with feeling. "He caused Seth McGuire to lose his job at the Hubell Tower."

"That so?" the editor asked in surprise. "I hadn't heard about it."

"Blake gave the position to a special friend of his. Can't you do something about it, Dad?"

"I don't know any of the basic facts, Penny. Why should I interfere in a matter which is none of my affair?"

"At least let's not give Mr. Blake a big build-up because of his donation."

"The story must be written," Mr. Parker said with finality. "I always keep a bargain, even a bad one."

"Then you might write the story," Penny proposed mischievously. "I can't spell such a big word as hypocrite!"

"Never mind," Mr. Parker reproved. "Just get busy and see that you handle the article in a way favorable to Blake."

With a deep sigh, Penny took herself to the adjoining newsroom. Selecting a typewriter, she pecked listlessly at the keys. Presently Jerry Livingston, one of the reporters, fired a paper ball at her.

"Your story must be a masterpiece," he teased. "It's taken you long enough to write it."

Penny jerked the sheet of copy from the typewriter roller. "It's not fair," she complained. "I have to dish out soft soap while you handle all the interesting stories. There should be a law against it."

"Learn to take the bitter along with the whipped cream," chuckled Jerry. "I've also just been handed an assignment that's not to my liking."

"Covering the Preston fire, I suppose."

"Nothing that spectacular. DeWitt's sending me out to the Riverview Orphans' Home to dig up human interest material in connection with the camp-fund campaign. Want to ride along as ballast?"

"Well, I don't know?" Penny debated. "I've had almost enough of publicity stories for one day."

"Oh, come on," Jerry coaxed, taking her by the arm. "You can talk to the orphans and maybe turn up a lot of interesting facts."

"For you to write," she added ruefully. "Just a Sister Friday—that's my fate in this office."

Actually Penny welcomed an opportunity to accompany Jerry, for she liked him better than any young man of her acquaintance. Spearing the story she had just written on the copy desk spindle, she followed the reporter to the parking lot. Jerry helped her into one of the press cars, and they expertly drove through heavy downtown traffic.

"What's the latest on the Preston case?" Penny inquired, clutching her hat to keep it from blowing out the window.

"No latest," Jerry answered briefly. "The Prestons won't talk, Mrs. Davis won't talk, the sheriff won't talk. So far it totals up to one little story about a fire."

"Dad said the sheriff had learned Clem Davis was a member of a secret organization, probably known as the Black Hoods."

"Sheriff Daniels claims he has documentary proof," Jerry admitted. "He won't produce it though, and I have a sneaking suspicion that he may be bluffing."

"Then you think he wants to convict Clem Davis whether or not he's guilty?"

"He wants to end the case just as quickly as he can, Penny. The November elections aren't far away. If this night rider story gets a start, the dear public might turn on him, demanding action or his job."

"Do you think there actually is such an organization as the Black Hoods, Jerry?"

"I do," he returned soberly. "After talking with the Prestons and Mrs. Davis, I'm convinced they could tell quite a bit about it if they were willing to furnish evidence."

It pleased Penny that Jerry's opinion so nearly coincided with her own. Eagerly she told him of her own talk with Mrs. Davis, mentioning that someone had been hiding in the cornfield near the cabin.

"What time was that?" Jerry asked, stopping the car at a traffic light.

"Shortly after twelve o'clock."

"Then it couldn't have been Sheriff Daniels or his deputies," the reporter declared. "I was at the county office talking to them about that same time."

"It might have been Clem Davis," Penny suggested. "I'm sure his wife knows where he is hiding."

CHAPTER 8 - PUBLICITY BY PENNY

As the car sped over the country road, she kept the discussion alive by mentioning the watch charm which she had picked up at the Davis stable. Jerry had not seen the picture of the little boy, but promised to inspect it just as soon as he returned to the *Star* offices.

"Clem Davis has no children," he assured Penny, "so it's unlikely the charm ever belonged to him. You may have found an important clue."

"I only wish Dad would officially assign me to the story," she grumbled. "He never will, though."

Presently the car approached the Riverview Orphans' Home, a large brick building set back some distance from the road. Children in drab blue uniforms could be seen playing in the front yard, supervised by a woman official.

"Poor kids," Jerry said with honest feeling, "you can't help feeling sorry for 'em. They deserve the best summer camp this town can provide."

"The project is certain to be possible now," Penny replied. "Mr. Blake's cheque put the campaign over the top."

Jerry gave the steering wheel an expert flip, turning the car into the private road.

"Don't tell me that old bird actually parted with any money!"

"Oh, he did, Jerry. He donated a cheque for a hundred and fifty dollars."

"And no strings attached?"

"Well, he hinted that he wanted a nice write-up about himself. I was torturing myself with the story when you interrupted."

"It's mighty queer," the reporter muttered. "Leopards don't change their spots. Blake must expect something more tangible than publicity out of the deal."

His mind centering on what Penny had just told him, Jerry gave no thought to his driving. Handling the steering wheel skillfully, but automatically, he whirled the car into the play area of the institution, drawing up with a loud screeching of brakes.

Uncertain that the reporter could stop, the children scattered in all directions. One little girl remained squarely in front of the car. Covering her face with her hands, she began to scream.

"Gosh all fish hooks!" Jerry exclaimed in dismay. "I didn't mean to frighten the kid."

Jumping from the coupe, he and Penny ran to the child.

"You're all right," Jerry said, stooping beside the little girl. "The car didn't come within a mile of you. I'm mighty sorry."

Nothing that either he nor Penny could say seemed to quiet the child. Her screams did not subside until a matron appeared and took her by the hand.

"Come Adelle," she said gently. "We'll go into the house."

"I'm as sorry as I can be," Jerry apologized, doffing his hat. "I didn't intend to drive into the yard so fast. It's all my fault."

The attendant smiled to set him at ease. "Don't mind," she said quietly. "Adelle is very easily upset. I'll explain to you later."

CHAPTER 9 - JERRY'S PARTY

Both Penny and Jerry regretted the incident, feeling that they had been at fault because they had driven into the play area at such high speed.

"Maybe I can send the kid a box of candy or make it up to her in some way," the reporter remarked.

Roving about the yard, he and Penny talked to many of the orphans. Nearly all of the children answered questions self-consciously and had little to say.

"We'll not get much of a story here," Jerry commented in an undertone. "These youngsters are as much alike as if they had been cut from one pattern."

"Adelle was different," Penny returned with a smile. "Almost too much so."

In a short while, Miss Anderson, the young woman who had taken the child away, returned to the play yard. Penny and Jerry immediately inquired about the little girl.

"Oh, she is quite herself again," the young woman responded. "The upset was only a temporary one."

"Is Adelle easily frightened?" Penny inquired curiously.

"Unfortunately, she is terrified of automobiles," responded Miss Anderson. "I am afraid it is becoming a complex. You see, about a year ago both of her parents were killed in a motor accident."

"How dreadful!" Penny gasped.

"Adelle was in the car but escaped with a broken leg," the young woman resumed. "The incident made a very deep impression upon her."

"I should think so!" exclaimed Jerry. "How did the accident occur?"

"We don't know exactly, for Adelle was the only witness. According to her story, the Hanover automobile was crowded off the road by another motorist who drove at reckless speed, without lights. The car upset, pinning the occupants beneath it."

"It seems to me I remember that story," Jerry said thoughtfully. "The hit-run driver never was caught."

"No, according to Adelle he stopped, only to drive on again when he saw that her parents were beyond help."

"The man must have been heartless!" Penny declared indignantly. "How could he run away?"

"Because he feared the consequences," Miss Anderson answered. "Had he been apprehended he would have faced charges for manslaughter, and undoubtedly would have been assessed heavy damages."

"I take it the child has no property or she wouldn't be at this institution," Jerry said soberly.

"Adelle is penniless. Her parents were her only relatives, so she was brought to us."

"It's a shame!" Penny declared feelingly. "Wasn't there any clue as to the identity of the man who caused the fatal accident?"

"No worthwhile ones. Adelle insists that she saw the driver's face plainly and could recognize him again. However, she never was able to give a very good description, nor to make an identification."

Having heard the story, Jerry was more than ever annoyed at himself because he had caused the child needless suffering.

"Miss Anderson, isn't there something I can do to make amends?" he asked earnestly. "What would the little girl like? Candy, toys?"

"It isn't necessary that you give her anything."

"I want to do it," Jerry insisted.

"In that case, why not make some small bequest to the institution, or send something which may be enjoyed by all the children."

CHAPTER 9 - JERRY'S PARTY

"Jerry, I have an idea!" cried Penny impulsively. "Why not give a party? Would that be permissible, Miss Anderson?"

"Indeed, yes. The children love them, and outings away from the institution are their special delight."

"Let's give a watermelon party!" Penny proposed, immediately considering herself Jerry's partner in the affair. "We could take the children to a nearby farm and let them gorge themselves!"

"The children would enjoy it, I'm sure," Miss Anderson smiled. "Can transportation be arranged? We have sixty boys and girls."

"I'll take care of everything," Jerry promised. "Suppose we set tomorrow afternoon as the date."

"Oh, can't we have the party at night?" Penny pleaded. "There will be a full moon. A watermelon feast wouldn't be much fun by daylight."

Miss Anderson replied that she thought the children might be allowed to attend such a party, providing it were held early in the evening. Penny and Jerry talked with her about various details of the plan, and then drove away from the institution.

"Well, you certainly got me into something," Jerry chuckled as the car turned into the main road. "Where are we going to throw this party?"

"Oh, any melon farmer will be glad to let the children invade his patch, providing we pay for the privilege," Penny answered carelessly. "You might turn in at the next farm."

Her confidence proved to be ill-founded, for Mr. Kahler, the farmer whom they accosted, would not consider the proposition.

"The children will trample the vines, and do a lot of damage," he declined. "Why don't you try the Wentover place?"

At the Wentover farm, Jerry and Penny likewise were turned down.

"No one wants sixty orphans running rampant over his place," the reporter observed in discouragement. "We may as well give up the idea."

"It's possible Mrs. Davis would allow us to hold a muskmelon party at her farm," Penny replied thoughtfully. "Now that her husband has skipped, she must be in need of money."

The chance of success seemed unlikely. However, to please Penny, Jerry drove to the Davis property. To their surprise they found the place humming with activity. Professional melon pickers were at work in the patch, and Mrs. Davis, dressed in overalls, was personally supervising the laborers.

"I have no time to answer questions!" she announced to Jerry before he could speak. "Please go away and leave me alone!"

"Oh, I'm not here in an official capacity this time," the reporter grinned. "We want to make you a business proposition."

He then explained what he had in mind. Mrs. Davis listened attentively but with suspicion.

"It's likely some trick!" she declared. "I'll have nothing to do with it!"

"Mrs. Davis, we're not trying to deceive you," Penny interposed earnestly. "We've tried several other farms before we came here. No one is willing to let the children trample the vines."

"I suppose it wouldn't hurt mine," the woman admitted. "By tomorrow night we'll have all the best melons picked and sorted. I reckon the youngsters can have what's left in the patch."

"We'll pay you well for the privilege," Jerry promised, taking out his wallet.

"I don't want your money," the woman answered shortly. "Just see to it that the youngsters don't tear up the place."

Neither Penny nor Jerry wished to accept such a favor, but Mrs. Davis firmly refused to take pay.

"You know, I think the old girl has a tender heart beneath a hard exterior," the reporter remarked after the woman had gone back to the patch. "Down under she's a pretty decent sort."

For a time Penny and Jerry watched the laborers at their work. Heaping baskets of melons were brought from the patch to the barn. There they were sorted, stamped, and packed into crates which were loaded into a truck.

"Nice looking melons," the reporter remarked. "Mrs. Davis should make a pretty fair profit."

An elderly workman, who was sorting melons, glanced sideways at Jerry, grinning in a knowing way.

"Maybe," he said.

"What do you mean by that?" Jerry questioned him.

THE CLOCK STRIKES THIRTEEN

"Sellin' melons is a speculative business," the old fellow shrugged. "You ain't sure o' anything until your harvest is sold and you get the money in your fist."

Penny and Jerry watched the sorting work for a few minutes longer and then returned to the car.

"You know, for a minute I thought that old duffer was hinting at something," the reporter remarked. "He acted as if it would give him real pleasure to see something happen to Mrs. Davis' melons."

"Oh, I didn't take it that way," Penny responded. "He was only waxing philosophical."

The hour was late. Knowing that he might be wanted at the *Star* office, Jerry drove rather fast over the bumpy road.

As the press car sped around a bend, a man who stood leaning against a fence post, quickly retreated into the woods. His act, however, had drawn Penny's attention.

"Stop the car, Jerry!" she cried. "There he is again!"

"Who?" demanded the reporter, slamming on brakes.

"I think it's the same man who hid in the cornfield!" Penny exclaimed excitedly. "It must be Clem Davis!"

CHAPTER 10 - IN THE MELON PATCH

"Which way did the fellow go?" Jerry demanded, bringing the car to a standstill.

"Into the woods," Penny answered tersely.

Leaping from the automobile, they climbed a fence, and reached the edge of the woods. Pausing there, they listened intently. No sound could be heard, not even the crackling of a stick.

"This timber land extends for miles," said Jerry. "We'd only waste time playing hide and seek in there. Our best bet is to notify Sheriff Daniels and let him throw a net around the entire section."

"I guess you're right," Penny acknowledged regretfully.

Making all haste to Riverview, they stopped briefly at the sheriff's office to make their report. Penny then said goodbye to Jerry and went to the newspaper building where she had parked Leaping Lena. The car would not start. Experienced in such matters, Penny raised the hood and posed beside it, a picture of a young lady in deep distress. Soon a taxi-cab cruised along.

"Having trouble, sister?" the driver asked.

Penny slammed down the hood, and scrambled into Leaping Lena.

"Just give me a little push," she instructed briskly.

Obligingly, the taxi driver backed into position behind Leaping Lena. After the two cars had gathered speed, Penny shifted gears. Lena responded with an ailing cough and then a steady chug.

"Thanks!" Penny shouted, waving farewell to her benefactor. "I'll return the favor someday."

"Not with that mess of junk!" the taxi man laughed.

By keeping the motor running at high speed, Penny reached home without mishap. Her father had arrived ahead of her, she noted, for the maroon car had been put away for the night.

Locking the garage doors, Penny entered the house by way of the kitchen.

"Where's Dad?" she asked the housekeeper, absently helping herself to a freshly baked cookie.

"Listen, and I think you can tell," Mrs. Weems answered.

A loud hammering noise came from the basement. Inspired by an advertisement of Waldon's Oak Paneling, Mr. Parker had decided to wall up the recreation room without the services of a carpenter. Much of his spare time was spent carrying on a personal feud with boards which refused to fit into the right places.

"Poor Dad," Penny grinned as she heard a particularly loud exclamation of wrath. "I'll go down and drip a few consoling words."

Descending the stairs, she stood watching her father from the doorway of the recreation room.

"Hello, Penny," he said, looking over his shoulder. "You may as well make yourself useful. Hold this board while I nail it in place."

"All right, but be careful where you pound. Remember, I have only two hands and I prize them both."

With Penny holding the board, Mr. Parker nailed it to the underpinning.

"Well, what do you think of the job?" he asked, standing back to admire his work.

"As a carpenter you're a very good editor," Penny answered with exaggerated politeness. "Aren't walls supposed to come together at the corners?"

"I made a little mistake in my calculations. Later on I may build a corner cupboard to cover up the slight gap."

"Slight!" Penny chuckled. "Dad, if I were you I wouldn't get tangled up in any more carpenter jobs. It's too hard on your disposition."

"I never was in a better mood in my life," Mr. Parker insisted. "Good reason, too. At last I've got the best of Mr. Ben Bowman!"

"Bowman?" Penny inquired in a puzzled tone.

"That crank who keeps sending me collect messages."

"Oh, to be sure! I'd forgotten about him."

"He sent another telegram today," Mr. Parker declared, smiling grimly. "I suspected it came from him and refused to pay for it."

"Bravo," Penny approved. "I knew you could get the best of that fellow if you just put your mind to it."

On the floor above a telephone rang, but neither of them paid any heed, knowing that Mrs. Weems would answer. In a moment the housekeeper called down the stairway, telling Mr. Parker he was wanted on the 'phone.

"It's Mr. DeWitt from the office," she informed him.

Putting aside his hammer, Mr. Parker went upstairs. Soon he returned to the basement, his manner noticeably subdued.

"What's the matter, Dad?" Penny inquired curiously. "You look as if you had just received a stunning blow."

"DeWitt telephoned to tell me the *Star* lost an important story today."

"How did that happen, Dad?"

"Well, a correspondent wired in the news, but by accident the message never reached DeWitt's desk."

Penny regarded her father shrewdly. "Ben Bowman's telegram?"

"I'm afraid it was," Mr. Parker admitted. "The message came to two dollars. I didn't know DeWitt had hired a correspondent at the town of Altona. Naturally I jumped to conclusions."

"So you lost a news story because you refused a bona fide telegram," Penny said, shaking her head. "Ben Bowman scores again."

"You see what I'm up against," the editor growled. "I'd give a hundred dollars to be rid of that pest."

"You really mean it?" Penny demanded with interest.

"My peace of mind would be well worth the price."

"In that case, I may apply my own brain to the task. I could use a hundred dollars."

The discussion was interrupted by Mrs. Weems who called that dinner was ready. As Mr. Parker went to his usual place at the dining room table, he saw a yellow envelope lying on his plate.

"What's this?" he demanded sharply.

"A telegram," explained Mrs. Weems. "It came only a moment ago. I paid the boy."

"How much was the message?" the editor asked, his face grim.

"A dollar and a half." Mrs. Weems regarded her employer anxiously. "Did I do anything I shouldn't have? I supposed of course you would want me to accept the message."

"This is just too, too good!" Penny chuckled, thoroughly enjoying the situation. "Everything so perfectly timed, almost as if it were a play!"

"I don't understand," Mrs. Weems murmured. "I've done something I shouldn't—"

"It was not your fault," Mr. Parker assured her. "In the future, however, refuse to accept any collect message."

As her father did not open the telegram, Penny seized upon it.

"This is from a man who calls himself Isaac Fulterton," she disclosed, glancing at the bottom of the typed page.

"Merely one of Ben Bowman's many names," Mr. Parker sighed.

"Ah, this is a gem!" Penny chuckled, and read aloud: "'Here is a suggestion for your rotten rag. Why not print it on yellow paper? I know you will not use it because editors think they know everything. I once knew a reader who got a little good out of your paper. He used it to clean the garbage can.'"

"How dreadful!" Mrs. Weems exclaimed, genuinely shocked.

"Penny, if you insist upon reading another line, I shall leave the table," Mr. Parker snapped. "I've had quite enough of Ben Bowman."

"I'm sorry, Dad," Penny apologized, slipping the message into her pocket. "I can appreciate that this doesn't seem very funny to you."

CHAPTER 10 - IN THE MELON PATCH

The telegram was not mentioned again. Nevertheless, Mr. Parker's good humor had given way to moody silence, contributing no cheer to the evening meal. Mrs. Weems kept glancing uneasily at her employer, wondering if she had offended him. Only Penny, whose appetite never failed, seemed thoroughly at ease.

"Dad," she said suddenly. "I have an idea how Ben Bowman might be trailed!"

"Never mind telling me," her father answered. "I prefer not to hear his name mentioned."

"As you like," she shrugged. "I'll shroud myself in mystery and silence as I work. But when the case is ended, I'll present my bill!"

Actually, Penny held slight hope that ever she would be able to turn the elusive Ben Bowman over to the police. The wily fellow was far too clever ever to file two messages from the same telegraph office, and very seldom from the same city. However, the town of Claymore, from which the last message had been sent, was only fifty-five miles away. It had occurred to her that by going there she might obtain from telegraph officials the original message filed.

"In that way I'd at least have Ben Bowman's signature," she reflected. "While it wouldn't be much, it represents a start."

Always, Penny's greatest problem was insufficient time. Greatly as she desired to drive to Claymore, she knew it would be out of the question for several days. Not only must arrangements for the orphans' melon party be completed, but other interests demanded attention.

Temporarily dismissing Ben Bowman from her mind, Penny devoted herself to plans for the outing. Cars easily were obtained, and the following night, sixty excited orphans were transported to the Davis farm. With shrieks of laughter, the boys and girls took possession of the melon patch.

"Pick all you like from the vines," Penny called, "but don't touch any of the crated ones."

In the yard not far from the storage barn stood a truck loaded with melons which were ready for the market.

"This must represent the cream of Mrs. Preston's crop," Jerry remarked, lifting the canvas which covered the load. "Maybe she'll be luckier than her neighbors, the Doolittles."

"What happened to them?" Penny asked, surprised by the remark.

"Don't you ever read the *Star*?"

"I didn't today. Too busy. Tell me about the Doolittles, Jerry."

"Mr. Doolittle was taking a load of melons to market. Another truck brushed him on the River road. The melon truck upset, and the entire shipment was lost."

"Can't he get damages?"

"Doolittle didn't learn who was responsible."

"Was it an accident or done deliberately?" Penny asked thoughtfully.

"Sheriff Daniels thinks it was an accident. I'm inclined to believe the Black Hoods may have had something to do with it."

"Why should anyone wish to make trouble for Mr. Doolittle, Jerry? All his life he has stayed on his little truck farm, and strictly attended to his own affairs."

"There's only one possible reason so far as I know," the reporter answered. "Not long ago Doolittle refused to join the Holloway County Cooperative, an organization that markets crops for the truck farmers."

"And you believe the Hoods may be connected with the Cooperative?"

"I wouldn't go so far as to say that," Jerry replied hastily. "Fact is, the Holloway Cooperative always has had a good reputation."

"There's no question the Preston barn was destroyed by the Hoods," Penny said reflectively. "Although the evidence pointed to Clem Davis, I've never felt satisfied he was guilty."

"Same here," agreed Jerry. "Another thing, I keep mulling over what that melon sorter said yesterday."

"You mean his hint that something might happen to Mrs. Davis' crop?"

"Yeah. Maybe he knew more than he let on."

"The Hoods will have to work fast if they destroy the Davis melons," Penny rejoined. "Besides, didn't the sheriff uncover proof that Clem Davis is a member of the organization?"

"That's what he says. I wonder about that too."

Not far from the truck was a small pile of discarded melons, culls which were misshapen or over-ripe. Selecting one, Jerry tossed it into the air and caught it.

"Just the right size for a hand grenade," he remarked. "Watch!"

He threw the melon hard against the barn. It burst against the siding, breaking into a dozen fragments and leaving an unsightly blotch of oozing seeds.

"Jerry, you shouldn't do that," Penny chided. "Mrs. Davis won't like it."

"Okay, I'll be good," the reporter promised. "The temptation was just too strong to resist."

By this time, the hubbub in the melon patch had slightly subsided as the youngsters gained their fill of cantaloupe. Soon institution officials began to pilot the children to the waiting cars. Several lads protested at the early termination of the party.

"Do let the boys stay awhile longer," Penny pleaded. "Jerry and I will bring them back in a few minutes."

"Very well," the matron consented. "But don't allow them to eat so many melons that they will be sick."

The responsibility of looking after six orphans weighed heavily upon Penny. After the cars had driven away, she and Jerry patrolled the patch, trying vainly to maintain order. With institution authorities no longer present, the boys proceeded to enjoy themselves. They ran races down the furrows, lassoed one another with vines, and pelted ripe melons against the fence posts.

"Hey, you little hoodlums!" Jerry shouted. "Cut it out or you'll go back to the Home pronto!"

"Says who?" mocked one saucy little fellow in a piping voice.

"Quiet everyone!" commanded Penny suddenly. "Listen!"

In the silent night could be heard the clatter of horses' hoofs. Jerry whirled around, gazing toward the entrance to the lane. Two horsemen, black hoods covering their faces, rode at a hard gallop toward the storage barn.

CHAPTER 11 - PENNY'S CLUE

"The nightshirt riders!" Jerry exclaimed. "Duck down, everyone!"

Penny and the six lads from the Riverview Home crouched low, watching the approach of the two riders.

"One of those men may be Clem Davis, but I doubt it!" muttered Jerry. "They're here to destroy the crated cantaloupes!"

"Jerry, we can't let them get away with it!" Penny exclaimed. "Why not pelt them with melons when they get closer?"

"Okay," he agreed grimly, "we'll give 'em a spoiled cantaloupe blitz. Gather your ammunition, gang, and get ready!"

Screened from the approaching horsemen by trees and bushes, the young people hastily collected a few over-ripe cantaloupes which were small enough to throw with accuracy.

Unaware of the barrage awaiting them, the two hooded men rode into the yard.

"Now!" Jerry gave the signal. "Let 'em have it!"

Taking careful aim, he hurled his own melon with all his strength. It found its mark, striking one of the men with stunning force, nearly causing him to fall from the saddle.

Penny and the boys from the orphans' home concentrated their efforts on the other horseman. While many of their shots were wild, a few went true. One struck the horse which reared suddenly on her hind legs, unseating the rider.

"Give it to him!" Jerry shouted, observing that the fallen man was unhurt.

Handicapped by lack of ammunition, there followed a brief lull in the battle, as the young people sought to replenish their stock. Seizing the opportunity, one of the night riders galloped away. The other man, who had lost his horse, scrambled into the cab of the loaded melon truck.

"He's going to drive off!" Penny cried. "Let's stop him!"

She and Jerry ran toward the truck, but they were too late. The giant motor started with a roar, and the heavy vehicle rolled out of the yard.

Just then, Mrs. Davis came running from the cabin.

"My melons!" she screamed. "They've taken my melons! Oh, I was afraid something like this would happen!"

"Maybe I can overtake that fellow," Jerry called to her. "Ride herd on these kids until I get back!"

As he ran toward his own car, Penny was close at his heels. She slid into the seat beside him and they raced down the lane.

"Which way did the truck go?" Jerry demanded. "I was so excited I forgot to notice."

"It turned right. No sign of it now, though."

"The fellow is running without lights to make it harder for us to follow him."

Jerry and Penny both were hopeful that they could overtake the truck, which carried a heavy load. However, they had been delayed several minutes in getting started, and as the miles fell behind them, they caught no glimpse of the man they pursued.

"He must have turned off on that little side road we passed a quarter of a mile back," Penny declared in discouragement. "Switch off the engine a minute."

Bringing the car to a standstill, Jerry did as instructed. Both listened intently. From far over the hills they thought they could hear the muffled roar of a powerful motor.

"You're right, Penny! He turned off at that side road!" Jerry exclaimed, backing the coupe around. "We'll get him yet!"

Retracing their route, they started down the narrow rutty highway. Five minutes later, rounding a sharp bend, they caught their first glimpse of the truck, a dark object silhouetted in the moonlight. Only for a moment did it remain visible, and then, descending a hill, was lost to view.

"We're gaining fast," Jerry said in satisfaction. "It won't be long now."

The coupe rattled over a bridge. For no reason at all it began to bump, a loud pounding noise coming from the rear of the car.

"Gracious! What now?" Penny exclaimed.

"A flat," Jerry answered tersely. "Just our luck."

Pulling up at the side of the road, he jumped out to peer at the tires. As he had feared, the left rear one was down.

"We'll probably lose that fellow now," he said irritably.

With Penny holding a flashlight, the reporter worked as fast as he could to change the tire. However, nearly fifteen minutes elapsed before the task had been accomplished.

"We may as well turn back," he said, tossing tools into the back of the car. "How about it?"

"Oh, let's keep on a little farther," Penny pleaded. "If we drive fast we might still overtake him."

Without much hope, they resumed the pursuit. Tires whined a protest as they swung around sharp corners, and the motor began to heat.

"This old bus can't take it any more," Jerry declared, slackening speed again. "No sense in ruining the car."

Penny had been watching the road carefully. They had passed no bisecting highways, so she felt certain that the truck could not have turned off. On either side of the unpaved thoroughfare were lonely stretches of swamp and woods.

"Let's not turn back yet," she pleaded. "We still have a chance."

"Okay," Jerry consented, "but don't forget we have six orphans waiting for us at the Davis place."

The car went on for another eight miles. Then came a welcome stretch of pavement.

"We must be getting near the state line," Jerry remarked. "Yeah, there it is."

Directly ahead was a tiny brick building with an official waiting to inspect cars which passed beyond that point. A series of markers warned the motorist to halt at the designated place.

As Jerry drew up, a man came from the little building.

"Carrying any shrubs, plants or fruit?" he began but the reporter cut him short.

"We're following a stolen truck!" he exclaimed. "Has a red truck loaded with cantaloupes gone through here tonight?"

"I checked one about fifteen minutes ago."

"Fifteen minutes!" Jerry groaned. "That finishes us."

"The trucker could have reached Claymore by this time," the inspector responded. "Once in the city you wouldn't have much chance to pick him up. I have the truck license number though. If you'll give me all the facts, I'll make a report to Claymore police."

There was no point in pursuing the thief farther. Accordingly, Penny and Jerry provided the requested information, and then drove to the Davis farm. Regretfully, they told Mrs. Davis of their failure to trace the melon thief.

"I've lost my crop, the truck—everything," she said in a crushed voice. "What's the use trying anyhow? A body would be smarter to go along with 'em than to try to fight."

"I take it you have a pretty fair idea who it was that came here tonight?" Jerry said shrewdly. "Who are these Hoods?"

"I don't dare tell you," the woman answered fearfully. "You saw what they did tonight. They threw the blame of the Preston fire on Clem. They'll do worse things if I don't keep mum."

"You want to help your husband, don't you?" Penny inquired.

"Of course I do! But I know better than to talk."

"You've been warned?" Jerry pursued the subject.

"Yes, I have. Now don't ask me any more questions. I've told you too much already."

CHAPTER 11 - PENNY'S CLUE

"I just want to know one thing," Jerry said relentlessly. "Did your trouble start because you and your husband refused to join the Holloway Cooperative?"

"Maybe it did," the woman answered, her voice barely above a whisper. "I ain't saying."

It was apparent to Jerry and Penny that they could expect no assistance from Mrs. Davis. Although the events of the night had convinced them that Clem Davis was innocent, others would not share their opinion. They felt that by shielding the guilty parties, Mrs. Davis was adopting a very stupid attitude.

"Come along, Penny," Jerry said with a shrug. "Let's be moving."

Six reluctant orphans were rounded up from the hay loft where a boisterous game of hide and seek was in progress.

"I can jam four into my coupe if you can handle the other two in your car," Jerry remarked to Penny. "If they make you any trouble, just toot the horn twice, and I'll come back and settle with 'em!"

"Oh, we'll get along fine," she smiled. "Come along, boys."

"Here's a souvenir to remember the night by," Jerry said. From the ground he picked up two melons which he handed to the orphans. "Just don't sock the matron with them when you get back to the Home!"

"Jerry, let me see one of those melons!" Penny exclaimed suddenly. "They fell from the truck, didn't they?"

"I guess so," Jerry responded, surprised by her display of interest. "What about 'em?"

"I'll show you."

Turning on the dash light of the car, Penny held the melon in its warm glow. Slowly, she turned it in her hands.

"There!" she said, pointing to a tiny triangle shaped marking on the cantaloupe. "This may prove a clue which will lead to the capture of the thief!"

"I don't get it," answered Jerry. "What clue?"

"Why, this stamping on the melon!" she replied excitedly. "The Hoods must intend to sell that load of cantaloupes. If they do, we may be able to trace the shipment."

CHAPTER 12 - ADELLE'S DISAPPEARANCE

Jerry took the melon from Penny's hand to examine it.

"This stamp may be helpful," he said dubiously, "but I doubt it. The Hoods never would be so stupid as to sell melons which could be traced. No, I think our investigation will have to center close at home."

"You're referring to the Holloway Cooperative, Jerry?"

"That outfit certainly merits an investigation. In the morning I'll jog out to their packing plant and talk to the manager, Hank Holloway."

"What time will you be going, Jerry?"

"About nine o'clock probably."

"Perhaps I'll meet you there," Penny said thoughtfully. "That is, if you don't mind."

"Glad to have you," the reporter responded in a hearty voice.

The two cars soon started for the Riverview Orphans' Home, arriving there without mishap. After unloading the boys entrusted to their care, Jerry and Penny then went to their respective residences.

"I'm glad you came at last," Mrs. Weems remarked as the girl entered the house. "You're to telephone Miss Anderson at the Riverview Orphans' Home."

"But I just left there," Penny protested. "When did the call come?"

"About fifteen minutes ago."

Wondering what could be amiss, Penny went to the telephone. In a moment she was in communication with Miss Anderson, who assisted the matron of the institution. The young woman's voice betrayed agitation as she disclosed that following the night's outing, an orphan had been discovered missing.

"Oh, goodness!" Penny exclaimed, aghast. "One of those six boys?"

Miss Anderson's reply slightly reassured her.

"No, the missing child is a little girl who was not permitted to attend the party because of a severe cold. You may remember her—Adelle."

"Indeed I do, Miss Anderson. Tell me how I may help."

"We've already organized searching parties," the young woman returned. "Adelle surely will be found within a few hours. However, if the story gets out it will do the institution no good—particularly at this time when our drive for funds is on."

"I see," Penny murmured, "you would like the news kept out of the *Star*?"

"Can it be arranged?" Miss Anderson asked eagerly. "If you will talk to your father about it we'll be very grateful."

"I'll ask him not to print the story," Penny promised, none too pleased by the request. "I do hope Adelle is found soon."

She could not help feeling that the institution officials seemed far more worried about the prospect of unfavorable publicity than over the missing child's welfare. Saying goodbye to Miss Anderson, she sought her father who was reading in the library.

"Penny, you know I don't like to grant such favors," Mr. Parker frowned when the conversation was repeated to him. "As a matter of principle, it never pays to withhold information unless the telling will harm innocent persons."

"In this case, it will damage the institution," Penny argued quietly. "Besides, I feel more or less responsible. What started out as a nice little party for the orphans, ended in a regular brawl. It was planned primarily for Adelle and then she ran away because she wasn't permitted to attend."

CHAPTER 12 - ADELLE'S DISAPPEARANCE

Starting at the very beginning, Penny told her father everything that had happened during the night. The tale was one of absorbing interest to Mr. Parker. When she had finished, he said:

"Don't worry about the affair, Penny. I am as interested in the Riverview Camp fund as you are. We'll give the institution no unfavorable publicity."

"Oh, thanks, Dad!" she cried gratefully, wrapping her arms about his neck. "You're just grand!"

"Weak as water, you mean," he corrected with a chuckle. "By the way, I suppose you know that your friend Blake has been named to the Camp Fund board."

"No!" Penny exclaimed. "How did that happen?"

"He hinted to Mrs. Van Cleve that he would like to serve. Naturally, after his handsome donation, she couldn't refuse."

"Why do you suppose Mr. Blake has taken such a sudden interest in the Home?"

"I wonder myself. I've thought from the first that he's up to something. So far I've not been able to figure out his little game."

"Well, you're on the board too," Penny declared, undisturbed. "If he starts any monkey business you can put a quick stop to it."

"I fear you overestimate my talents," Mr. Parker responded. "However, I do intend to see that Blake doesn't profit too much by his donation."

The hour was late and Penny soon went to bed. Disturbed by Adelle's disappearance, she did not sleep well. Arising early, she telephoned the Orphans' Home, hoping to learn that the child had been found. No such good news awaited her.

"Searchers have looked everywhere between here and the Davis farm," Miss Anderson revealed. "Unless the child is found by noon, it will be necessary to broadcast a general alarm. And that's certain to bring unfavorable attention to the Home."

"Is there any chance she could have been kidnaped?" Penny asked thoughtfully.

"Not the slightest," was the prompt reply. "Adelle took most of her clothes with her. It's a plain case of a runaway, but most annoying at this time."

Penny ate a hasty breakfast, and then remembering her appointment with Jerry, drove to the Holloway Cooperative. The buildings were of modern concrete construction, located three and a half miles from Riverview in the heart of the truck farming district.

Jerry Livingston had not yet arrived, so Penny waited in the car. Soon his coupe swung into the drive and pulled up alongside Leaping Lena.

"Sorry to be late," he apologized. "I was held up at the office."

Knowing that her father would have told Jerry about Adelle's disappearance, Penny inquired regarding the latest news.

"So far there's not a trace of the child," the reporter answered. "Your father's sore at himself for promising not to carry the story. It may develop into something big."

Penny walked beside Jerry to the entrance of the cooperative plant.

"No one seems to worry much about Adelle," she remarked. "The institution people are afraid of unfavorable publicity, Dad's alarmed about his story, while you and I are just plain indifferent."

"I'm not indifferent," Jerry denied. "In a way I feel responsible for that kid. But what can we do?"

"Nothing, I guess," acknowledged Penny unwillingly. "Miss Anderson said they had enough searchers."

Opening the door of the building, they stepped into a huge room which hummed with activity. Girls in uniforms stood at long tables inspecting melons which moved on an endless belt arrangement before them. Sorted as to quality and size, each cantaloupe was stamped and packed in a crate which was then borne away.

"Hank Holloway around here?" Jerry asked one of the workers.

"Over there," the girl responded, pointing to a burly, red-faced man who stood at the opposite end of the room.

Jerry and Penny approached the manager of the cooperative.

"Good morning," the man said gruffly, gazing at them critically. "What can I do for you?"

"We're from the *Star*," Jerry informed. "Do you mind answering a few questions?"

"I'm pretty busy," Hank Holloway responded, frowning. "What do you want to know?"

"There's a rumor going the rounds that this cooperative has been forcing farmers to market their melons through your organization."

"It's a lie!" the manager retorted. "Why they come here begging us to take their stuff! We get better prices than anyone in this section of the state, and we pass the profit right back to the farmers."

"How do you account for the depredation that's been going on around here lately? Who would you say is behind it?"

"What d'you mean, depredation?" Hank Holloway demanded.

"The destruction of the Preston barn just as their melons were ready for market. Then last night a truck of cantaloupes was stolen from the Davis place."

"That so?" the manager asked. "Hadn't heard about it. Clem Davis always was a worthless, no-good. It wouldn't surprise me that he covered his harvest with plenty of insurance, and then arranged the snatch so he could collect."

"That hardly seems reasonable," Jerry said dryly.

"You asked for my opinion and I'm giving it to you. The Davis melons were so inferior we wouldn't handle them at the cooperative."

"Why, I thought their cantaloupes were particularly fine ones!" Penny protested.

"I don't know what you two are trying to get at!" Hank Holloway said with sudden anger. "The Cooperative does business in a fair and square way. Our books are open for inspection at any time. Now you'll have to excuse me, for I've got work to do."

With a curt nod, he turned away.

Penny and Jerry wandered about the room for a few minutes, watching the packers. They did not much blame Hank Holloway for showing irritation. Their questions had been very pointed and the man had immediately guessed that their purpose was to uncover facts detrimental to the Cooperative.

"We learned about as much as I expected to," Jerry said with a shrug, as he and Penny finally left the building. "Naturally one couldn't hope he'd break down and confess all."

"What did you really think of him, Jerry?"

"Hard to say," the reporter answered. "He's a rough and ready sort, but that's not against him. There's no real reason to believe he's crooked—just a hunch of mine."

Having been assigned to cover a board meeting, Jerry hurriedly said goodbye to Penny. Left to herself, she drove slowly toward Riverview.

"Since I am so near Seth McGuire's place, I may as well stop for a minute or two," she thought impulsively.

Despite many exciting events, Penny had not lost interest in the Hubell clock. Although it seemed reasonable that a faulty mechanism had caused it to strike thirteen, such an explanation did not completely satisfy her. She was eager to learn from the former caretaker if the difficulty had been corrected.

Leaving her car by the main road, Penny went directly to the shop. The door was closed and locked. However, as she turned away, she distinctly heard a voice inside the building. Although she could not make out the words, she was certain that a child had called.

"Who is it?" she shouted.

"Help! Let me out!" came the plaintive cry from inside the shop.

Penny ran to the window and peered into the dark interior. She scarcely was able to believe what she saw. A little girl, her face streaked with tears and dirt, pounded fiercely on the heavy door, seeking release.

"It's Adelle!" she gasped. "How in the world did she get locked in Mr. McGuire's shop?"

CHAPTER 13 - AN EXTRA STROKE

With all the windows and the door of the shop locked, Penny did not know how to free the imprisoned child. However, as she considered the problem, Seth McGuire appeared on the porch of the cottage.

"Good morning," he greeted her pleasantly.

"Oh, Mr. McGuire!" Penny exclaimed. "Did you know there is a child locked inside your shop?"

"A child!" the old man exclaimed, coming quickly down the steps. "Why bless me! How can that be?"

"I don't understand how she got inside, but she's there! Officials of the Riverview Orphans' Home have been searching for Adelle Hanover since last night."

"Wait until I get my key," the old man said in an agitated voice. "I hope you don't think I locked the child into the shop!"

Knowing Mr. McGuire as she did, Penny entertained no such thought. Waving encouragingly to Adelle through the window, she waited for the old man to return.

"I locked the door about eleven o'clock last night," he explained, fumbling nervously with the key. "The little girl must have stolen in there sometime between six o'clock and that hour."

The old man's hand shook so that he could not unlock the door. Taking the key, Penny did it for him. Adelle, her hair flying wildly about her face, stumbled out of the shop.

"I'm hungry," she sobbed. "It was cold in there, and a big rat kept running around. Why did you lock me inside?"

"Why, bless you," Mr. McGuire murmured, "I never dreamed anyone was inside the shop! How did you get in there?"

"I went inside last night and hid," Adelle explained in a calmer voice. "It was cold outside and I had to have some place to sleep."

"You never should have run away from the Home," Penny reproved. "Why did you do it?"

"Because I don't like it there," the child answered defiantly. "I'll never be adopted like the other children."

"Why, how silly!" Penny answered. "Of course someone will adopt you."

Adelle shook her head. "Miss Anderson says I won't be—I heard her tell the matron. It's on account of a nervous 'fliction. I'm afraid of things, 'specially cars."

"That's very natural, everything considered," Penny replied, thinking of the story Miss Anderson had told her. "Now I'll take you to the Home."

Adelle drew away, and as if seeking protection, crowded close beside Mr. McGuire.

"I'm never going back, even if I freeze and starve!" she announced. "I'll find me a cave and live on berries. It would be more fun than being an orphan."

Penny gazed despairingly at the old bell maker. With a chuckle, he took the child by the hand and led her toward the cottage.

"We'll have lunch and talk things over," he proposed. "How will that be?"

"I'm awful hungry," Adelle admitted, smiling up at him. "But you won't give me any old boiled potatoes, will you? We have 'em every single day at the Home."

"No potatoes," he laughed. "We'll have the very nicest things I can find in the icebox, and maybe a stick of candy to top it off."

While Mr. McGuire pottered about the kitchen preparing a warm meal, Penny washed Adelle and combed her tangled hair. Afterwards, she telephoned officials of the Home, telling them that the child had been found.

"I'll bring her there within an hour," she promised. "Just as soon as she has had her lunch."

THE CLOCK STRIKES THIRTEEN

Adelle was ravenous. She was not a pretty child, but her face had an elfin quality when she smiled. Her brown eyes, roving about the spick and span little dinette, took in every detail.

"This is almost as nice as it was at our home," she remarked. "I mean my real home, when Daddy and Mother were alive."

"You'll have a nice place again when you are adopted," Penny assured her kindly.

"I'd like to stay here," Adelle said, looking thoughtfully at the old man. "Would your wife let me?"

"Why, bless you, I haven't a wife," he answered in embarrassment. "I'm a bachelor."

"Wouldn't you like a little girl?" Adelle persisted. "I could do your dishes for you and sweep the floor. I'd be real good."

"Well, now I've often thought I would like a nice little girl," he replied, smiling.

"Then you can have me!" Adelle cried, jumping up from her chair. "You can tell the Home I won't be back!"

"Not so fast, not so fast," Mr. McGuire said hastily. "I'd like a little girl, but I am afraid I can't afford one. You see, I don't make much money any more and there are other reasons—"

"Oh, I won't eat much," Adelle promised. "Please keep me, Mr. McGuire."

The old man was so distressed that Penny tried to come to his rescue. However, despite repeated explanations, Adelle refused to understand why she could not immediately become Mr. McGuire's little girl.

"If I had my old job back, I'd be tempted, sorely tempted," the old man said to Penny. "I've always wanted someone that was near and dear to me." He drew a deep sigh. "As things are, I don't see how it could be worked out."

"Won't you keep thinking about it?" Adelle pleaded. "Anytime you want me, I'll come right away."

"Yes, I'll think about it," Mr. McGuire promised soberly. "I really will."

An hour later Penny took a very depressed Adelle back to the Riverview Orphans' Home. Leaving her there, she drove on into town, chancing to see her chum, Louise Sidell on the street. Signalling her with a toot of the horn, Penny swung wide the door.

"On your way home, Lou?" she inquired.

"No, just wandering around in a daze trying to do a bit of shopping," Louise answered, sharing the seat. "The stores here never have anything I want."

"Then why not go to Claymore?" Penny proposed suddenly.

"I would if I could get there."

"I'll take you," Penny offered. "I need to go to Claymore on special business, and I'd like to have someone ride along."

"Well, I don't know," Louise replied dubiously. "I doubt Leaping Lena would stand such a long trip."

"Oh, I'll take the other car."

"In that case the answer is 'yes,'" Louise replied instantly.

Penny drove directly home to exchange cars and tell Mrs. Weems where she was going.

"Louise and I may not be back until very late," she warned. "It's barely possible we'll attend the theatre while we're at Claymore. There's a new play on, and everyone says it's grand."

"If you drive after night, be very careful," the housekeeper responded uneasily. "There are so many accidents these days."

A brief stop was made at the Sidell residence, and then the girls took to the road. Deliberately, Penny selected the same route which she and Jerry had followed the previous night.

"Is that why we're going to Claymore?" Louise inquired curiously, as she heard the story of what had happened to the Davis truck. "You intend to trace those stolen melons?"

"I haven't much hope of doing that," Penny answered. "I want to visit the telegraph office and get an original message which was sent to Dad. His life has been made miserable by a pest who keeps sending him telegrams, and I'm out to catch the rascal."

"You jump around from one thing to another so fast I can't keep track of your enterprises," Louise sighed.

"I concentrate on the ones which offer a prospect of ready cash," Penny rejoined with a laugh. "If I catch Mr. Ben Bowman it means exactly one hundred dollars to me!"

Upon reaching Claymore, the girls spent two hours shopping at the large department stores. Penny then made a tour of the telegraph offices, finally locating the one from which Mr. Bowman's message had been sent.

CHAPTER 13 - AN EXTRA STROKE

After explaining why she wished it, she was allowed to inspect and keep the original copy which bore the sender's signature.

"I'll turn this handwriting over to the police," she explained to Louise. "They may be able to trace Ben Bowman by means of it."

"Providing the man ever comes to Riverview," Louise said skeptically. "It seems like a forlorn hope to me."

Before leaving the office, Penny inquired of the clerk who had handled the message if a description of Ben Bowman could be provided.

"I really don't remember him," the young woman answered. "In general I should say he was well-dressed—probably about thirty-five years of age."

"Not much to go on," Penny said regretfully. "Thanks anyhow."

"Where now?" Louise asked in a weary voice as they finally left the telegraph office. "Shall we buy tickets to the play?"

"Not yet," said Penny. "I'd like to wander around the market district a bit."

For the next hour they did exactly that, selecting a section of the city where farmers brought their produce to sell in open stalls. Penny went from one counter to another, inspecting cantaloupes, hoping to find one which bore the Davis stamp.

"I'm getting tired of pawing vegetables!" Louise presently complained. "When do we eat?"

"All right, we may as well call it a day," Penny replied reluctantly.

In the downtown section of the city, the girls found a small cafe which advertised a deluxe dinner for one dollar. Treating themselves to the best, they enjoyed a leisurely meal, and then bought theatre tickets.

"Penny, do you realize what all this is costing us?" Louise began to worry belatedly.

"Oh, I'll soon make it up," Penny joked. "Wait until I capture Ben Bowman! With my profit from him we'll paint the town red!"

"You're nothing if not optimistic," Louise said pityingly.

The play was an excellent one and when the curtain fell at eleven, neither girl begrudged the money paid for tickets.

"It's been a grand day," Louise sighed contentedly as they left the theatre. "Let's get home now as quickly as we can."

The drive to Riverview consumed nearly an hour. As the girls approached the Hubell Tower, they noted by the illuminated clock face that the hands pointed to twelve o'clock.

"The witching hour of midnight," Louise remarked. "Do you still think that mechanical creature has supernatural powers?"

"Quiet!" Penny commanded, idling the car as the big clock began to strike. "I'm going to count the strokes."

"I'll do it too, just so you can't pull a fast one on me. That's two now."

As each slow note sounded, Louise counted it aloud. Reaching twelve, she paused, but the clock did not. There was a slight break, then another stroke.

"Why, it did strike thirteen!" she gasped. "Or perhaps I became mixed up!"

"You made no mistake," Penny declared, easing the car to a standstill by the curb. "It struck thirteen, and that last stroke wasn't like the others!"

"It did seem to have a slightly different tone. I wonder why?"

"Someone may have struck the bell an extra tap!" Penny answered with conviction. "Louise, don't you see! It must be a signal!"

CHAPTER 14 - THROUGH THE WINDOW

"You have the craziest ideas, Penny," Louise scoffed. "I'll admit the clock struck an extra time, but it must have been because something is wrong with the mechanism. A signal, my eye!"

Lowering the car window, Penny peered curiously up at the tower which was shrouded in fog and mist.

"Lou, there's someone up there in the cupola! It may be Charley Phelps!"

"You can't make a mystery out of Charley," yawned Louise. "Probably he's trying to repair the clock. Come on, let's get home."

Reluctantly, Penny raised the window glass. Before she could drive on, another car pulled up not far from the tower. The driver, a man in an overcoat, swung open the door as if to alight. However, observing Penny's car parked close by, he seemed to change his mind. Keeping his head lowered so that his face was shadowed, he drove away.

"Who was that man?" Penny demanded suspiciously.

"I'm afraid I neglected to inquire," Louise retorted. "So careless of me!"

"Whoever he was, he intended to enter the tower! When he saw us here, he became nervous and drove away!"

"Oh, Penny, you're the limit."

"Maybe I am, but I know what I think. The striking of the clock was a signal for some sort of meeting at the tower!"

"A board of directors confab perhaps?" teased Louise.

"Listen!" said Penny, ignoring the jibes. "I want to park the car on a side street, and then come back here afoot. Something is up and I mean to find out about it!"

"Oh, Penny," Louise sighed. "If I don't get home Mother never will allow me to go anywhere with you again. Don't you realize what time it is?"

"Thirteen o'clock!" Penny chuckled. "It may never be that again, so I must strike while the clock strikes, so to speak. How about it?"

"Well, it's your car," Louise replied with a shrug. "I'm powerless in your hands."

Penny drove around a block, parking on a well-lighted street. She and Louise then approached the tower afoot. Not wishing to be seen, they took care to keep close to a high hedge which edged the grounds.

"I never felt more silly in my life," Louise complained. "What are we supposed to do now?"

"Windows were made to look through," Penny responded coolly. "Let's see what Charley Phelps is doing inside the tower."

Circling the building, the girls placed a rock beneath one of the rear windows. From that unstable perch, Penny was able to peer into the living quarters of the tower.

"Well, what do you see, Sherlock?" Louise demanded impatiently.

"Nothing."

"How perfectly amazing!" Louise taunted mischievously. "What do you make of it?"

"Charley Phelps seems to be reading a newspaper."

"Baffling! It must have some deep, dark significance."

With a sigh, Penny stepped down from the rock. "Want to look?" she invited.

"I do not!"

"Then I guess we may as well go home," Penny said reluctantly.

CHAPTER 14 - THROUGH THE WINDOW

As she spoke, both girls heard an automobile pull up in front of the tower. With reviving hope, Penny placed a restraining hand on Louise's arm, forcing her to wait in the shadow of the building. A minute elapsed and then the front door of the tower slammed shut. Without the slightest hesitation, Penny once more moved to her previous position beneath the window.

"Charley has some visitors," she reported in a whisper. "Four men I never saw before. I wish I could hear what they are saying."

"Why not smash the window, or saw a hole through the wall?" Louise proposed sarcastically.

Penny stepped from the rock, offering the place to her chum.

"Do look inside," she urged. "Maybe you'll recognize those men. It's really important."

Louise unwillingly did as requested, but after a moment moved away from the window.

"I never saw any of them either," she said. "They must be friends of Charley Phelps."

"It's a special meeting," Penny insisted. "I suspect other men may come along within a few minutes."

"I know one thing," Louise announced flatly. "I'll not be here to see them. If you're not ready to go home, then I shall walk!"

"Oh, all right, I'll go," Penny grumbled. "It seems a pity though, just when we might have learned something important."

Taking care to remove the stone from beneath the tower window, she hastened after her chum. In silence they drove to the Sidell home where Louise alighted.

"Sorry to have spoiled your fun, Penny," she apologized as she said goodnight. "If you'll only arrange to conduct your explorations by daylight I'll try to cooperate."

Arriving at her own home a few minutes later, Penny found her father waiting up for her. Mr. Parker had attended a meeting of the Camp Fund board, and upon returning at eleven-thirty, had been disturbed to find his daughter absent.

"Hold it! Hold it!" Penny greeted him before he could speak. "I know it's late, but I can explain everything."

"You're always able to explain—too well," the editor responded dryly. "Mrs. Weems expected that you would be home not later than eleven o'clock."

"Well, one thing just seemed to lead to another, Dad. Louise and I saw a wonderful show, I obtained a copy of Ben Bowman's signature, and then to top it off, the Hubell clock struck thirteen again!"

"Which in your estimation explains everything?"

"I wish it did," Penny said, neatly changing the subject. "Dad, Louise and I saw a number of men going into the tower tonight. Obviously, they were summoned there by the striking of the clock."

"Tommyrot!"

"Oh, Dad, you haven't a scrap of imagination," Penny sighed. "Has it never occurred to you that Charley Phelps may be connected with the Hoods?"

"Never," replied Mr. Parker. "And if I were you I shouldn't go around making such wild suggestions. You *might* find yourself involved in serious trouble."

"You're the only one to whom I've confided my theory, Dad. In fact, it only this minute occurred to me."

"So I thought, Penny. If I were you I would forget the Hubell clock. Why not devote yourself to something worthwhile?"

"For instance?"

"I'll provide an interesting job. I've been asked to select play equipment for the new orphans' camp. I'll be happy to turn the task over to you."

"Do you think I could do it?" Penny asked dubiously.

"Why not? You can learn from the matron of the Home what is needed, and then make your selection."

"I'll be glad to do it, Dad. When is the camp to open?"

"The actual date hasn't been set, but it will be soon. That is, unless a serious disagreement arises about the camp site."

"A disagreement?" Penny inquired curiously.

"Yes, Mr. Blake is trying to influence the board to buy a track of land which he controls."

"At a very high price?"

"The price seems to be fair enough. I personally don't care for the site, however. It's located on the river, but too close to the swamp."

"Then why does the board consider it?"

"Mr. Blake gave a very generous donation, you remember. I figured at the time he would expect something in return."

"He'll profit by the sale?"

"Obviously. I don't know who owns the land, but Blake will receive a commission on the sale. The board also is considering a wooded property closer to Riverview, and I favor that site."

"Will the board listen to you, Dad?"

"I rather doubt it. My objections weren't especially vigorous. Either property will be satisfactory, and Blake's price is a trifle more attractive."

With a yawn, Mr. Parker arose and locked the front door.

"It's after one," he said. "Let's get to bed."

Penny started up the stairway, only to pause as the telephone rang. While her father answered it, she waited, curiously to learn who would be calling at such a late hour. In a moment he replaced the receiver on its hook.

"That was the night editor of the *Star*," he explained briefly.

"Has a big story broken, Dad?"

"Another storage barn was burned to the ground about ten minutes ago. The night editor called to ask how I wanted the story handled."

"Then the depredation was done by the Hoods!"

"It looks that way."

Penny came slowly down the stairway to face her father.

"Dad, if the fire was set only a few minutes ago, doesn't that support my theory?"

"Which theory? You have so many."

"I mean about the Hubell Tower," Penny said soberly. "The clock struck thirteen on the night the Preston barn was destroyed! Don't you see, Dad? The Hoods hold their meetings and then ride forth to accomplish their underhanded work!"

CHAPTER 15 - TRACING BEN BOWMAN

"Penny, let's postpone this animated discussion until morning," Mr. Parker said wearily, reaching to switch out the bridge lamp.

"Then you don't agree with me that the caretaker of the Tower may have some connection with the Hoods, Dad?" she asked in an injured tone.

"I certainly do not," he answered firmly. "Now if you'll excuse me, I'm going to bed."

Decidedly crestfallen, Penny followed her father upstairs. For several minutes she stood by the window of her room, gazing toward the Hubell Tower whose lights could be dimly seen across the city. Then, with a shrug, she too dismissed the subject from her mind and gave herself to slumber.

Mr. Parker had gone to the office by the time Penny arose the next morning. Finding a discarded newspaper by his plate, she eagerly scanned it for an account of the midnight fire. To her disappointment, only a brief item appeared on the front page. The story merely said that the barn of John Hancock, truck farmer, had been destroyed by a blaze of unknown origin. In the right hand column was another news item to the effect that Sheriff Daniels had made no progress in tracing the missing Clem Davis.

Tossing aside the paper, Penny helped with the breakfast dishes. As gently as possible she broke the news to Mrs. Weems that she might make another trip to Claymore.

"Why bother to remain home even for meals?" the housekeeper said severely. "I declare, I don't know what your father is thinking about to allow you such liberties! When I was a girl—"

"It was considered very daring to go for a buggy ride without a chaperon," Penny completed mischievously. "Now, I'm very sorry about last night. Louise and I didn't intend to remain out so late."

"It was after one o'clock when you came in," Mrs. Weems replied, her voice stern. "You know I don't approve of such hours for a girl of your age."

"I promise it won't happen again. Please let me go to Claymore though. I'm expected to buy playground equipment for the Riverview Orphans' new camp."

Exerting all her charm, Penny explained the necessity for the trip. Finally convincing Mrs. Weems that the excuse had not been "thought up" on the spur of the moment, she was granted the requested permission.

Penny's next move was to induce Louise Sidell to accompany her on the excursion. Both girls laid siege to Mrs. Sidell who somewhat dubiously said that her daughter might go, providing she would be home by nightfall.

Recalling her father's instructions, Penny called at the Riverview Orphans' Home to talk with the matron. There she obtained a list of playground equipment to be purchased, with suggested prices for each item.

As the girls were leaving the institution they met Miss Anderson and paused to inquire about Adelle.

"The child seems to be nervous and unhappy," the young woman told them. "Especially so since she ran away. We sincerely hope she will presently become adjusted."

Penny asked if there was any prospect the little girl would be adopted.

"Not very soon," Miss Anderson answered regretfully. "In fact, her name is not on the list of eligibles. We never allow a child to leave the Home until we feel that he or she is capable of adapting himself to new conditions."

The drive to Claymore was an enjoyable one, and by eleven o'clock, the girls had purchased many of the items on their list. To the amusement of the department store salesman, they insisted upon testing teeter-totters, swings, and even the slides.

"All this equipment is for the Riverview Orphans' Home—not for ourselves," Penny explained. "The committee will pay for it."

"Very well, we'll send the merchandise just as soon as a cheque is received," the salesman promised, giving her an itemized bill.

Feeling very well satisfied with their purchases, Penny and Louise wandered into another department of the store. The delightful aroma of food drew them to a lunch counter, and from there they went to the main floor.

The store was very crowded. As Penny was inspecting a pair of gloves on a counter, a man pushed past her, and ran toward the nearest exit. In surprise she turned around, unintentionally blocking the way of a store detective. Shoving past her, he pursued the first man only to lose him in the milling crowd near the front door.

"That fellow must have been a shoplifter!" Penny remarked to Louise. "I think he got away too!"

The unexpected commotion had drawn the interest of many shoppers. Mingling with the crowd, the girls heard a woman tell a companion that the man who had escaped was wanted for attempting to pass a forged cheque.

A moment later, the store detective came striding down the aisle. Pausing at the jewelry counter he spoke to the floorman, confirming the report.

"Well, the fellow escaped! He tried to pass a bum cheque for fifty dollars."

"What name did he use?" the floorman inquired.

"Ben Bowman. It will be something else next time."

Penny had heard the words. Startled by the name, she moved hastily to the detective's side.

"Excuse me," she addressed him, "did I understand you to say that a man by the name of Ben Bowman forged a cheque?"

"That's correct, Miss," the detective answered, staring at her curiously. "Know anything about the man?"

"I think I may. Would it be possible for me to see the cheque?"

The detective removed it from a vest pocket, offering the signature for inspection. One glance satisfied Penny that the cheque had been signed by the same man who had been sending her father "crank" messages.

"At home I have a telegram which I'm sure bears this identical signature!" she revealed. "I've never seen the man though—except as he ran through the store."

The store detective questioned Penny at length about her knowledge of Bowman. Realizing that a description of the man might be of great value to her, he showed her a small card which bore a mounted photograph.

"This is Ben Bowman," he assured her. "He's an expert forger, and uses any number of names. Think you can remember the face?"

"I'll try to," Penny replied. "He doesn't seem to have any distinguishing features though."

"His angular jaw is rather noticeable," the detective pointed out. "Brown eyes are set fairly close together. He's about six feet two and dresses well."

Penny was highly elated to have gained a description of Bowman, and especially pleased that the man had been traced to Claymore. The fact that he was a known forger, encouraged her to hope that police soon would apprehend him.

"That one hundred dollars Dad offered for Bowman's capture is as good as mine already," she boasted gleefully to Louise as they left the store. "All I need to do is wait."

"No doubt you'll collect," Louise admitted grudgingly. "I never met anyone with your brand of luck."

"I feel especially lucky today too," Penny said with a gay laugh. "Tell you what! Let's make another tour of the vegetable markets."

"It will make us late in getting home. The time is sure to be wasted too."

"Oh, come along," Penny urged, seizing her by the arm. "I promise to have you in Riverview no later than three o'clock."

In driving into Claymore that morning the girls had noticed a large outdoor market near the outskirts of the city. Returning to it, Penny parked the car, and with her chum wandered about the sales area.

"A nice fat chicken?" a farm woman asked persuasively, holding up an uninviting specimen. "Fresh eggs?"

"We're looking for melons," Penny replied.

"Mr. Breldway has some nice cantaloupes," the woman returned. "He got a truck load of 'em in from Riverview just the other day."

CHAPTER 15 - TRACING BEN BOWMAN

Locating Mr. Breldway's place of business, Louise and Penny began to inspect the melons offered for sale. Almost at once they came upon a basket of cantaloupes which bore a blurred stamp.

"Louise, these look like the Davis crop!" Penny cried excitedly. "Wouldn't you say someone deliberately had blocked out the old marking?"

"It does appear that way."

"Maybe we can find just one melon with the original stamp!"

Penny dug into the basket with both hands, tossing up cantaloupes for Louise to place on the ground. Their activities immediately drew the attention and displeasure of Mr. Breldway.

"If you're looking for a good melon let me help you," he said, hurrying toward them.

Penny straightened, holding up a cantaloupe for him to see.

"I don't need any help," she said distinctly. "I've found the melon I want. It bears the Davis stamp."

CHAPTER 16 - A FAMILIAR NAME

"The melon you have selected is a very good one," the market man declared, not understanding the significance of Penny's remark. "Shall I put it in a sack for you?"

"I'm not interested in the melon—only in the stamp," Penny replied. "Do you realize that you may be liable to arrest?"

"What d'you mean, liable to arrest?" the man demanded. "I'm an honest dealer and I have a license."

"Look at these melons." Penny held up one which bore the blurred stamp. "The trade name has been altered."

The dealer took the cantaloupe from her, examining it briefly. She then offered him the single melon bearing the Davis stamp.

"Well, what about it?" he asked.

"Just this. A few nights ago a truck load of melons similar to these, was stolen from the Davis farm near Riverview. The thief was trailed right to this city."

"You're trying to say that I sell stolen melons!"

"I'm not making any direct accusations," Penny replied evenly. "No doubt you can explain where you got the melons."

"Certainly I can. I bought a truck load of them from a farmer named John Toby. The melons were good, the price cheap, and I didn't pay any attention to the stamp."

"Is Mr. Toby a regular dealer?"

"I buy from him now and then, when his prices are right. I never bothered to ask any questions."

"Where does the man live?"

"I can't tell you that. He's a large, heavy-set fellow with brown hair and eyes."

The description was too meagre to be of value to Penny.

"Does Mr. Toby drive a red truck?" she inquired thoughtfully.

"He did this last time."

"It was a red truck which was stolen from the Davis farm," Penny said quietly. "I'm sure these melons came from there too."

"I paid good money for them," the dealer retorted in a defiant tone. "So far as I knew, they belonged to this fellow Toby. I can't investigate every farmer who offers me produce."

"All the same, you could get into serious trouble for selling stolen melons," Penny replied. "Of course, I have no intention of going to the police, providing you are willing to cooperate."

"What d'you mean, cooperate?" the dealer inquired suspiciously.

"Only this. Will you see John Toby again?"

"That's hard to tell. He said he might bring in another load of melons within the next few days."

"When you receive the next shipment, will you notify me?"

"Yes, I'm willing to do that," the dealer promised. "If Toby is crooked, I want to know it myself."

Penny gave the man her name, address, and telephone number. Knowing that he might not be able to reach her quickly enough, she instructed him to detain the farmer by force if necessary.

"If I can't get in touch with you, I may have the fellow questioned by police," the dealer offered. "I don't want to put myself into a hole."

CHAPTER 16 - A FAMILIAR NAME

Penny was not entirely satisfied that the market man would keep his promise. However, she hesitated to make a report to the police without first consulting her father. Everything considered, it seemed best to let the situation work out as it would.

"Well, your luck is still running true to form," Louise said jokingly, as the girls drove toward Riverview. "Do you have any idea who John Toby may be?"

"Not the slightest," Penny confessed. "The description would fit Hank Holloway, or for that matter, any one of a dozen men I know."

The girls arrived in Riverview by mid-afternoon after an uneventful trip. Penny dropped Louise at the Sidell home and then went to the *Star* office to talk with her father. Mr. Parker was absent from his desk, but his secretary who was typing letters, explained that he would return in a moment.

Penny sat down in her father's chair to wait. A bulky, unsealed envelope lay on the desk. Peering at it curiously she noted that it bore the marking: "Property Deed: Lots 456, 457, and 458."

"What's this?" she asked aloud. "Is Dad buying property?"

"Oh, no," the secretary replied, glancing up from her typewriter. "That is the deed and abstract for the Orphans' Camp site."

"I wonder which property it is?"

"The land Mr. Blake controls, I believe. At least he brought the papers into the office this morning for your father's inspection. I heard him say that if the forms are satisfactory, the deal will be completed at once."

Penny unfolded one of the lengthy documents, shaking her head as she scanned the legal terms.

"I don't see how Dad makes anything of this," she said. "Such a mess of words and names!"

"I imagine Mr. Parker intends to turn it over to his lawyer," the secretary smiled.

The editor entered the office at that moment, and Penny directed her next question to him.

"Dad, is it all settled that the camp board will purchase Mr. Blake's land?"

"Practically so," he answered. "If my lawyer, Mr. Adams, approves the abstract, the deal will be completed. Against my advice Mrs. Van Cleve already has given Blake five hundred dollars to hold an option."

"Why did she do that, Dad?"

"Well, Blake convinced her he had another buyer for the property. It's the old story. Competition stimulates interest."

"Do the papers seem to be all right?"

"Oh, I've not looked at them," Mr. Parker replied. "Blake is a good real estate man though, so there's not likely to be any flaw."

"Who actually owns the property, Dad?"

"It's there on the abstract," he answered. "Why not look it up for yourself?"

"Too much like doing home-work," Penny grinned, but she spread the document on the desk and began to read various names aloud. "'Anna and Harry Clark to Lydia Goldwein, Lydia Goldwein to Benjamin Bowman—'"

"What was that name?" Mr. Parker demanded sharply.

"Benjamin Bowman." Penny peered at the document a second time to make certain she had made no mistake. "That's the truth, Dad. Who knows, maybe it's your old pal, Ben!"

"Are you making up that name?" Mr. Parker asked skeptically.

Penny thrust the abstract into his hand. "Here, read it for yourself, Dad. Bowman seems to be the present owner of the land."

Mr. Parker rapidly scanned the document.

"The land is held by a Benjamin Bowman," he admitted, frowning. "A strange coincidence."

"I never heard of a Bowman family living near Riverview," Penny remarked, reaching for a telephone book. "Did you?"

"No, but Bowman is a fairly common name."

Turning to the "B" section Penny went through the telephone list.

"There's only one Bowman here," she said, penciling a circle around the name. "A Mrs. Maud Bowman."

"The name Maud Bowman doesn't appear on the abstract," Mr. Parker declared, as he studied the document once more. "There's something funny about this."

"Mr. Blake seemed rather eager to dispose of the land, didn't he?"

"His price was a bit low, which surprised me," Mr. Parker said, thinking aloud. "Probably everything can be explained satisfactorily."

"Then why not ask Mr. Blake to do it?" Penny proposed. "He should be able to tell you something about his client."

"That's really a first-class idea," Mr. Parker agreed and he reached for a telephone. "I'll ask Mr. Blake to come here at once."

CHAPTER 17 - FALSE RECORDS

Mr. Blake, suave, completely at ease, sat opposite Mr. Parker and Penny in the editor's private office.

"I came as soon as I could after receiving your telephone message, Mr. Parker," he said pleasantly. "Now what seems to be the trouble?"

"Perhaps I shouldn't have bothered you," the editor apologized. "However, in glancing over the abstract for the Orphans' Camp property I noticed that the land is owned by a man named Benjamin Bowman."

"Quite true. I am acting as his agent."

"It happens that I have had dealings with a man by that same name," resumed Mr. Parker. "Rather unpleasant dealings, I might add. I'm curious to learn if this property owner is the same fellow."

"Very unlikely, I think," Mr. Blake shrugged. "My client does not reside in Riverview."

"Nor does the man I have in mind."

"Can you tell us what he looks like?" Penny interposed eagerly.

"I am very sorry, but I can't," Mr. Blake returned. "I've never met Mr. Bowman."

"Yet you act as his agent?" Mr. Parker inquired in astonishment.

"All our dealings have been by mail or telephone."

"I see," the editor commented reflectively. "Well, at least you can provide me with the man's address."

"I can't do that either," Mr. Blake declined. "Benjamin Bowman is a salesman with no permanent address. He communicates with me at fairly regular intervals, but until I hear from him, I have no idea where he will be the following week."

"Your description seems to fit the man of my acquaintance," Mr. Parker said dryly. "But tell me, how do you expect to complete this deal? Will Bowman come here to sign the necessary papers?"

"Oh, that won't be required. He's already made out the sales documents, and also given me a power of attorney."

"Mr. Bowman seems to think of everything," Mr. Parker remarked grimly. "I was hoping for the pleasure of meeting him."

"I really don't see what all this has to do with the sale of the property," Mr. Blake reproved in a mild voice. "You feel that the site is a suitable one, and the price right?"

"I have no serious objections to it."

"Then why allow your personal feelings to interfere with the deal?"

"I have no intention of doing so," Mr. Parker answered.

"Then if you'll give your approval, we'll sign the final papers tomorrow at my office. The dedication of the new camp has been set for the tenth of the month, and that means no time can be lost."

"Everything seems to have been settled without my approval," Mr. Parker said, smiling. "However, if you don't mind, I'll keep this abstract a little longer."

"As you like," the real estate man shrugged. "Have your lawyer go over the records with a fine tooth comb. He'll find no flaws anywhere."

Arising, Mr. Blake bowed politely and left the office. Penny waited until she knew that he was a considerable distance from the door before seeking her father's opinion of the interview.

"Everything may be on the level," he conceded, frowning. "I've no reason to distrust Blake, and yet I can't help feeling that there's something peculiar about this land deal."

"Blake has been rushing things through at such a furious rate," Penny nodded. "Another thing, Ben Bowman is a well-known forger."

"What makes you think that?" the editor asked alertly. "Any real information?"

Penny revealed everything she had learned that day at Claymore. Mr. Parker listened attentively, making few comments until she had finished.

"I am more than ever convinced there is something phoney about Bowman's connection with this affair," he declared grimly. "We'll see what my lawyer has to say."

Having made up his mind that the transaction merited a thorough investigation, Mr. Parker personally carried the questionable abstract to a reliable law firm, Adams and McPherson. The report came back late in the afternoon, and was relayed to Penny at the dinner table.

"Mr. Adams says that the abstract seems to be drawn up correctly," the editor disclosed. "He could find no flaw in it or in any of the records at the court house."

"Then apparently we jumped too hasty to conclusions," Penny remarked in disappointment.

"I'm not so sure. Mr. Adams tells me that the ownership of the property is a very muddled affair."

"Muddled?"

"Yes, it has changed hands many times in the past year, and oddly, none of the buyers or sellers seem to be known in Riverview."

"What does Mr. Adams think about that, Dad?"

"He advises that the records be inspected very carefully. It will take weeks though, for they are quite involved."

"I suppose that will hold up the opening of the camp."

"It may," Mr. Parker acknowledged. "However, it seems wise to take every precaution even if the camp isn't opened this year. Too much money is involved to risk paying for land which may have a faulty title."

The following day, the editor conferred with members of the Camp Fund board, telling of his findings. To his chagrin, Mrs. Van Cleve did not share his views.

"I trust Mr. Blake's judgment implicitly," she insisted. "I am sure the property will be satisfactory in every way. If there should by chance be any flaw in the title, he would make it good."

"We can't possibly delay the dedication another week," added another feminine member of the board. "The summer is nearly over now."

"At least postpone making the final payment until after I have had another report from my lawyers," Mr. Parker pleaded.

"Very well, we'll do that," Mrs. Van Cleve agreed. "Mr. Blake is so obliging I am sure he will allow us to set up equipment on the land, even though we don't actually possess title."

The entire transaction seemed very unbusinesslike to Mr. Parker, but he did not attempt to force his opinion upon the board members. Accordingly, plans went forward for the grand opening of the camp. Stories appeared regularly in the *Star*, playground equipment and floored tents were set up on the camp site, and the actual dedication program was announced.

"You might know Mr. Blake would be invited to make the main speech," Penny remarked disapprovingly as she scanned the latest story of the coming affair. "Every day, in every way, he gives me a bigger and bigger pain!"

Throughout the week both she and Louise had been very active, helping out at the new camp site. The land had been cleared of underbrush, trails had been constructed, and a well dug. While supervising the setting-up of slides, merry-go-rounds and teeter-totters, Penny upon several occasions had had disagreements with Mr. Blake. The man remained at the site almost constantly, imposing his wishes upon everyone.

"A great deal of time and money has been spent getting that place ready for the dedication," Penny commented to her father. "If anything should happen that the final papers aren't signed, it would be a pity."

"I've had no report as yet," Mr. Parker answered. "My lawyers tell me they never delved into a more involved case."

"What does Mr. Blake think about the investigation?"

"He seems to be agreeable. However, I suspect he's been working on the various board members, trying to get them to conclude the deal without waiting."

"How long will it be before you'll have a final report, Dad?"

"I don't know," he admitted. "I expected to get it long before this."

CHAPTER 17 - FALSE RECORDS

In the flurry of preparing for the camp dedication, Penny had no opportunity to give much thought to other affairs. She did not see Seth McGuire, the sheriff had nothing to disclose concerning Clem Davis' disappearance, and the Black Hoods seemed to have become an extinct organization.

On the morning of the designated date, Penny was abroad early. She and Louise planned to drive to the dedication exercises together, and wished to arrive before the grounds were congested. Eating breakfast hurriedly, Penny scarcely noticed when her father was called to the telephone. He absented himself from the dining room nearly fifteen minutes. As he returned to the table, Penny pushed back her chair, ready to leave.

"Well, I'll see you at the camp grounds, Dad," she said lightly.

"I don't know what to do about the dedication," responded Mr. Parker in a sober tone. "By rights there should be none."

Penny stared at him.

"I've just heard from my lawyers," Mr. Parker explained.

"Then, there is a flaw in the title as you suspected!"

"Decidedly. It's a very mixed-up mess, and as yet we're not sure what it may mean."

"Tell me about it, Dad," Penny pleaded, sliding back into her chair.

"Benjamin Bowman—whoever he may be—doesn't own the camp property."

"Then in whose name is it?"

"The property doesn't belong to anyone."

"Why, how ridiculous!" Penny exclaimed. "Doesn't every piece of land in the world belong to someone?"

"Actually the heirs of Rosanna and Joseph Schulta own this particular property. But there are no heirs."

"What you say doesn't make sense to me, Dad."

"The whole affair is very involved," Mr. Parker explained. "In tracing back the history of the land, my lawyers found that originally it was owned by Rosanna and Joseph Schulta, an elderly couple, who had no known relatives. They sailed for Germany more than fifty years ago. The ship sank, and presumably they were lost. Their land was never claimed, and somehow the state overlooked the case."

"But I thought the property had changed hands many times in recent years!"

"Only theoretically. All those records have been falsified."

"By whom, Dad? Ben Bowman?"

"My lawyers are inclined to think Blake may be at the bottom of it. He is a very shrewd real estate man, and in examining records at the court house, he may have learned about this floating property."

"Then he deliberately tried to cheat the Camp Fund board!"

"It looks that way. Neither Ben Bowman nor anyone else owns the property. Had you not noticed his name on the abstract, it's unlikely the fraud would have been uncovered for quite a few years to come."

"What will you do, Dad?" Penny inquired, deeply distressed. "The dedication is scheduled to start within an hour."

"I don't see how it can be postponed," Mr. Parker said soberly. "It will have to go on according to schedule."

"Afterwards you'll ask for Blake's arrest?"

"There's no real evidence against him."

"No evidence!"

"He claims to be a mere agent of Ben Bowman. All of the deeds and legal papers were drawn up by some other person. If any accusation is made against him, he can escape by maintaining that he knew nothing of the back records."

"There's one person who might be able to implicate him!" Penny exclaimed. "Ben Bowman!"

"Bowman should have it in his power to clear up some of the mystery," Mr. Parker agreed. "But how are we to find him?"

"I don't know," Penny admitted. "It looks rather hopeless unless the police just present him to us wrapped in pink ribbon."

The clock struck nine. Daring not to linger any longer, Penny hastily bade her father goodbye and left the house.

Driving to the camp site with Louise Sidell, she told her chum of the latest complications.

"Mr. Blake is one of the worst hypocrites in the world," she declared feelingly. "He pretends he wants to help the orphans, and all the while he intends to trick the Board and make a nice profit for himself."

"Your father won't let him get away with it," Louise returned confidently. "So long as the money hasn't been paid over there's no need to worry."

Arriving at the camp site, the girls went at once to the official tent. To their surprise, Mr. Blake, Mrs. Van Cleve, and all members of the Board save Mr. Parker, were there. On the table lay various legal papers which bore signatures still moist with ink.

Penny gazed from one person to another, slowly comprehending the scene.

"You're not buying this property!" she exclaimed in protest.

Mrs. Van Cleve's reply stunned her.

"It seemed unreasonable to keep Mr. Blake waiting," the woman said quietly. "The transaction has just been completed."

CHAPTER 18 - ADELLE'S ACCUSATION

"Oh, Mrs. Van Cleve! You've been cheated!"

The signing of the papers had taken Penny so by surprise that she did not weigh her words before speaking. Too late, she realized that her father never would approve of revealing the facts in such blunt fashion. However, having said so much, she was determined to go on.

"My dear, what do you mean?" inquired Mrs. Van Cleve, troubled by the unexpected accusation.

"Any money paid for this land will be lost! My father has just learned—"

"I resent such loose talk!" Mr. Blake broke in irritably. "Mr. Bowman, whom I represent, has taken a substantial loss on the property."

"And who is Ben Bowman?" Penny challenged. "You can't produce him, nor prove that he owns the land. The title is faulty. Neither you nor Ben Bowman has any right to sell it!"

"This isn't true?" Mrs. Van Cleve asked the real estate man.

"Certainly not! You may be sure that if there is the slightest flaw in the title, I shall return your cheque."

"Perhaps, considering the uncertainty, it might be wise to postpone payment until I have talked again with Mr. Parker," Mrs. Van Cleve said diffidently.

The real estate man made no attempt to hide his annoyance. "My dear Mrs. Van Cleve," he said, "the deal already has been completed. I have tried to remain patient, but really this is too much."

On the table lay several typewritten papers. Clipped neatly to the uppermost one, was the cheque endorsed by Mrs. Van Cleve. Mr. Blake reached to take possession of it, but his move was deliberate. Acting impulsively, Penny darted forward and seized the bit of paper. To the horror of everyone in the tent, she tore the cheque into a dozen pieces and tossed them into the air.

"There!" she announced, a trifle stunned by her own act.

"Penelope, you shouldn't have done that," Mrs. Van Cleve reproved, but she smiled faintly.

"You are an outrageous child!" Mr. Blake exclaimed, losing his temper. "What do you expect to accomplish by such a stupid trick? Mrs. Van Cleve will merely write out another cheque."

"Well, under the circumstance, it might be better to wait," the club woman demurred. "I really shouldn't have acted without consulting Mr. Parker."

"Unless the transaction is completed now I shall have nothing to do with the dedication," Mr. Blake declared. "I shall decline to make my speech."

Penny's broad grin made it clear that she thought the loss would not be a great one.

"Furthermore, I shall ask that my recent donation be returned," Mr. Blake resumed severely. "I shall withdraw this property for sale—"

"*You* will withdraw it!" Penny caught him up. "I thought you merely were acting as the agent for Benjamin Bowman!"

"I mean I shall make such a suggestion to him," the real estate man amended.

Penny waited anxiously for Mrs. Van Cleve's decision. To her relief, the society woman seemed annoyed by the attitude Mr. Blake had taken.

"I am sorry," she said coldly. "If you don't wish to make the dedication speech, we will manage to do without your services. As for the cheque, I cannot make out another until I have discussed the situation with Mr. Parker."

The argument went on, but Penny did not remain to hear it. Louise took her forcibly by the arm, fairly pulling her outside the tent.

"Haven't you caused enough trouble?" she demanded disapprovingly. "Such a mess as everything is in now!"

"I don't care," Penny replied. "I saved the Camp Fund money. Mrs. Van Cleve was glad I tore up the cheque too! She just didn't dare say so."

"There will be no dedication. What will everyone think?"

Disconsolately, Louise gazed toward the area which had been roped off for cars. Although it was half an hour before the formal program was to start, hundreds of persons had arrived. On a platform, built especially for the occasion, an orchestra played spritely selections. There were picnic tables and a stone fireplace for outdoor cooking.

As the girls wandered slowly toward the river, a bus loaded with orphans arrived from the Riverview Home. With shrieks of laughter, the children swarmed over the grounds, taking possession of swings, sand pile, and slides.

"It seems a pity," Louise remarked again.

By ten o'clock the grounds were jammed with visitors. Penny knew that her father must have arrived for the exercises, but although she searched everywhere, she could not find him. In roving about, she did meet Mr. Blake, who pretended not to see her.

How matters had been arranged, the girls did not know. However, promptly at ten-thirty, the dedication exercises began, exactly as scheduled. Mr. Blake occupied the platform with other members of the board, and at the proper time made a brief and rather curt speech.

"Everything seems to have turned out rather well," Louise remarked in relief. "Mr. Blake may not be such a bad sort after all."

"Don't you believe it," Penny returned. "He's just clever enough never to put himself in a bad light if he can help it. I only hope Mrs. Van Cleve didn't give in to him and sign another cheque."

Following the dedication exercises, a portion of the crowd dispersed, but many persons remained to enjoy picnic lunches. Penny and Louise ate their own sandwiches, and then watched the orphans at play.

"The new camp director seems very efficient," Louise remarked, her gaze upon a young man who supervised the children.

Presently, as the girls watched, the camp supervisor announced that he would take several boys and girls for a sail on the river. The boat, a twelve-foot dinghy, had been the gift of a well-to-do Riverview department store owner.

Immediately there was a great clamor from the children, for everyone wanted to take the first ride.

"Only six may go," the director said, and called off the names.

Penny and Louise wandered down to the water's edge to watch the loading of the boat. Adelle had been one of the orphans chosen, and they waved reassuringly to her.

The camp director shoved off, and quickly raised the sail. There were squeals of delight from the children as it filled, causing the craft to heel over slightly.

"The breeze is quite uncertain today," Penny remarked anxiously. "I hope that young man knows what he is about."

The boat sailed a diagonal course across the river, turned, and came back on another tack. Then as the breeze died, it seemed to make no progress at all. Losing interest, Penny and Louise started to walk on down the shore.

Scarcely had they turned away than they were startled to hear screams from the river. Whirling around, they saw that the camp director was in serious trouble. A sudden puff of wind had caught the boat when it did not have steerage way. Unable to drive ahead, it slowly tilted sideways.

"It's going over!" Louise screamed.

Already Penny had kicked off her shoes. Without waiting for the inevitable result, she plunged into the river. When her head emerged from the water, she saw the boat on its side. Two children were clinging to it, the camp director was frantically trying to support two others, while another girl and boy struggled wildly to keep from sinking.

Swimming as rapidly as she could, Penny reached the overturned boat. Her first act was to help the camp director who was being strangled by the two children who clung to him. Drawing the trio to the craft, she then seized a struggling boy by the hair, and pulled him to safety.

CHAPTER 18 - ADELLE'S ACCUSATION

"Adelle!" the camp director gasped. "Get her!"

The little girl had been carried a considerable distance from the boat. Penny started to swim toward her, but she saw that it would not be necessary. From the forest close by had emerged an unshaven man in rough, soiled clothing. Diving into the water, he seized Adelle, and swam with her to shore.

Penny did not return to the overturned boat for several men had waded out to tow it to land. Concerned regarding Adelle, she followed the child's rescuer.

The man bore the orphan in his arms to a grassy spot on shore. Stretching her out there, he hesitated an instant, and then before the crowd could surround him, darted quickly away toward the woods.

"Wait!" Penny shouted, wading through the shallow water.

The man heard, but paid no heed. He entered the forest and was lost to view.

"That was Clem Davis!" Penny thought tensely. "I'm sure of it!"

Before she could reach Adelle, other persons had gathered around the child. Clyde Blake pushed through the crowd.

"What is this?" he inquired. "What has happened?"

As the man bent over Adelle, the little girl opened her eyes, gazing directly into his face. For a moment she stared at him in a bewildered way. Then, struggling to a sitting position, she pointed an accusing finger.

"You are the one!" she whispered shakily. "You're the man whose car killed my Mother and Daddy!"

CHAPTER 19 - TRAILING A FUGITIVE

Adelle's accusation brought a murmur of consternation and shocked surprise from the crowd. Mr. Blake, however, seemed undisturbed. Dropping on his knees, he supported Adelle and wrapped his coat about her trembling shoulders.

"There, there, my poor child," he said soothingly. "You are quite upset, and for good reason."

"Don't touch me," Adelle shivered, cringing away. "You're mean and cruel!"

By this time, Miss Anderson and other officials of the Riverview Home had reached the scene. Somewhat sternly they tried to silence the child.

"She doesn't know what she is saying," Miss Anderson apologized to Mr. Blake. "Adelle has been very nervous since she was in an automobile accident."

"I quite understand," the real estate man responded. "The child must have a change of clothing, and no doubt, medical care. May I send her to the Home in my car?"

"Why, that is very kind of you, I am sure," Miss Anderson said gratefully.

With every appearance of concern, Mr. Blake picked Adelle up in his arms and carried her away. Penny was kept busy helping bundle up the other children who had been rescued from the water. None the worse for the misadventure, they too were taken to Mr. Blake's car.

"Here, put on my coat before you freeze," Louise said anxiously to Penny after the automobile had sped away. "We must start home at once."

"I don't want to go now!" Penny protested. "Did you notice that man who pulled Adelle from the water?"

"He looked like a tramp. I wonder what made him run away?"

"Lou, I think that man was Clem Davis. By rights I should tell the sheriff, but I can't bring myself to do it—not after the way he saved Adelle."

"Never mind all that now," Louise said, forcing Penny toward the car. "You must go home and change your wet clothes."

"But I want to find Clem Davis and talk with him!"

"That will have to wait. You're going home!" Taking her chum firmly by the arm, Louise pushed her into the car.

At the Parker home, Penny changed her clothes, discussing the day's events as she dried her hair. Adelle's accusation had not escaped her, and she had taken it more seriously than did others in the crowd.

"Perhaps that child knew what she was talking about!" she declared to Louise. "Blake's car may have been the one which killed her parents!"

"Oh, Penny, you're so hopelessly prejudiced against the man," her chum replied.

"Maybe I am, but Adelle is the only person who can identify the hit-run motorist."

"Even so, you know she probably is not a reliable witness."

"I'll grant that her accident today may have upset her emotionally," Penny conceded. "After she recovers, I'm curious to learn what she'll have to say."

The hour was so late that the girls did not return to the camp site. Louise soon went to her own home and Penny was left alone. She restlessly wandered about, polished the car, and fretted because neither her father nor Mrs. Weems came home. At length, for want of another occupation, she motored to the Riverview Home on the pretext of inquiring about the condition of the children rescued from the water.

"They're doing just fine," Miss Anderson assured her. "That is, all except Adelle. The child is very upset."

"Has she said anything more about Mr. Blake?" Penny inquired.

CHAPTER 19 - TRAILING A FUGITIVE

"She doesn't know his name, but she keeps insisting he was the man whose car killed her parents. I never was so mortified in my life as when she made the accusation. Fortunately, Mr. Blake did not take offense."

Penny was eager to talk with Adelle, and Miss Anderson said that she might do so for a few minutes. The little girl had been put to bed but seemed quite content as she played with a new doll.

"Mr. McGuire sent me this," she said, holding it up for Penny to see. "I've named her Imogene."

Miss Anderson was called to the telephone. During the young woman's absence, Penny discreetly questioned Adelle about the motor accident in which her parents had lost their lives. She was worried lest the child be upset again, but to her relief Adelle answered in a matter-of-fact tone.

"No one will believe me," the little girl said. "Just the same, that man I saw today was the one who ran into my Daddy's car. He had a big, gray automobile with a horn on it that played a tune."

"A gray car?" Penny repeated thoughtfully. "I'm quite sure Mr. Blake's sedan is dark blue. Why, you were taken home in his automobile this afternoon, Adelle."

"It wasn't that car," the child answered. "He must have another one."

Miss Anderson re-entered the room, so Penny did not ask additional questions. Soon leaving the Home, she motored slowly toward the camp site by the river. Although she readily understood that Adelle might be mistaken, a conviction was growing upon her that Clyde Blake could have been the hit-run driver.

"Even if he doesn't drive a gray car, that proves nothing," she mused. "He easily could have changed it during the past year."

Penny thought that she might find her father or some of the Camp Board officials still at the river. However, as she drove into the parking area, she observed that the grounds were entirely deserted. Paper plates, napkins and newspapers had been blown helter-skelter by the wind. Picnic tables still held the unsightly remains of lunches. The speakers' platform had been torn down, even the tents were gone, for it was not planned to make practical use of the grounds until more work had been done.

As Penny was starting to drive away, she noticed a lone man near one of the picnic tables. He was dressed in rough, unpressed garments, and seemed to be scavenging food which had been left behind.

"That's the same man who pulled Adelle from the water!" she thought alertly.

Leaping from the car, Penny ran toward him.

Hearing footsteps, the man turned and saw her. Almost in panic he started for the woods.

"Wait!" Penny shouted. "I won't turn you over to the police! Please wait!"

The man hesitated, and then apparently deciding that he had nothing to fear from a girl, paused.

"I want to thank you for saving Adelle," Penny said breathlessly. "Why did you run away?"

"Well, I don't know," the man answered, avoiding her gaze. "I never liked crowds."

Penny decided to risk a direct accusation. "You are Clem Davis," she said, eyeing him steadily.

"That's a laugh," the man retorted, starting to edge away. "My name is Thomas Ryan."

"Now please don't run away again," Penny pleaded, sensing his intention. "If you are Clem Davis, and I'm sure you are, I want to help you."

"How could you help me?"

"By exposing the men who framed you. I never believed that you set fire to the Preston barn."

"I never did."

"Please tell me about it," Penny urged, seating herself at one of the picnic benches.

"Who are you anyhow?" the man asked suspiciously. "Why are you so willing to help me, as you say?"

"I'm Penelope Parker, and my father publishes the *Star*."

"Oh, I see, you're after a story!"

"No, that part is only incidental," Penny said hurriedly. "What my father really wants to do is to expose the Black Hoods and drive them out of existence. You're the one person who might be able to provide evidence which would convict the guilty parties."

"I could tell plenty if I was a mind to do it. No one would believe me though."

"I will, Mr. Davis."

"I was in the notion of going to the Grand Jury at one time," the man said slowly. "That's what brought on all my trouble. If I'd had sense enough to have kept my mouth shut, I wouldn't be a fugitive now."

"What connection did you have with the Hoods? Were you a member of the organization?"

"Yes, I was," the man admitted reluctantly. "I didn't know much about the Hoods when I joined 'em. Then I tried to drop out, and that's what turned 'em against me."

"Suppose you tell me all about it. What is the real purpose of the organization?"

"Well, right now the Hoods are trying to force every truck farmer in this district to join the County Cooperative."

"Then Hank Holloway must be the ring leader!" Penny exclaimed, startled by the information.

"No, he's not at the head of the Hoods," Clem Davis corrected.

"Who is the man?" Penny questioned eagerly.

Clem Davis started to speak, then hesitated. An automobile had driven into the parking area only a few rods away. Several workmen who had been assigned to clean up the grounds, alighted.

"They're coming this way," Clem Davis said uneasily. "I can't risk being seen."

Abruptly, he started toward the sheltering trees.

"Wait!" Penny pleaded, pursuing him. "You haven't told me half enough. Please wait!"

"I'm not going to risk arrest," the man returned over his shoulder.

"At least meet me here again!"

"Okay, I'll do that," Clem Davis agreed.

"Tomorrow night just at dusk," Penny said quickly. "And please don't fail me. I promise. I'll help you."

CHAPTER 20 - CLEM DAVIS' DISCLOSURE

After Clem Davis had disappeared into the woods, Penny wasted no more time in the vicinity. Jumping into her car, she drove home in a daze of excitement, to tell her father the amazing story.

"Meeting that man was wonderful luck!" she assured him exultantly. "Why, if only he reveals what he knows, we will get an exclusive story for the *Star*! We'll expose the Hoods and put an end to the organization!"

"As easy as that?" laughed Mr. Parker. "Seriously though, I think we are on the verge of cracking the story. In going over the books of the County Cooperative, Jerry has discovered any number of discrepancies."

"I've always thought that Hank Holloway might be connected with the Hoods, Dad! I believe he was the night rider who made off with Mrs. Davis' melons."

"Any idea who the other members of the outfit may be?"

"Not yet, but I expect to find out when I meet Clem Davis tomorrow."

"I'll go with you," Mr. Parker declared. "Maybe I should take Sheriff Daniels along too."

"Oh, Dad," Penny protested indignantly. "I promised to help Clem, not turn him over to an officer. I am afraid that unless I go alone, he'll not even show himself."

"Perhaps it would be best for you to go by yourself," the editor admitted. "Learn what you can from Davis, and make an appointment for him to see me."

Another matter weighed heavily on Penny's mind. In her encounter with Clyde Blake that morning, she had acted in a high-handed manner, and sooner or later her father must hear about the cheque episode.

"Dad, I have a confession to make," she began awkwardly. "When I reached the camp this morning I found that Mr. Blake had induced the board members to buy the property—"

"Never mind," Mr. Parker interrupted. "I've already heard the details of your disgraceful actions from Mrs. Van Cleve."

"I'm thoroughly ashamed of myself," Penny said contritely. "I tore up the cheque on the spur of the moment."

"It was a foolish, rather dramatic thing to do. However, I must acknowledge the result was highly pleasing to everyone save Clyde Blake."

"What does he have to say, Dad?"

"He claims that he acted in good faith for Benjamin Bowman. Likewise, that he had no suspicion the title was faulty."

"Naturally he would take such an attitude."

"I've asked Blake to produce Ben Bowman," Mr. Parker resumed. "Unless he can do so and prove that the property actually is owned by him, the deal is off."

"Do you think Blake will bring the man to Riverview?"

"I doubt it very much," the editor answered. "I suspect he'll bluff, and finally let the deal go by default. It will be an easy way out for him."

"Blake always seems to escape his misdeeds. I wish we could find Ben Bowman ourselves, and bring the two men together. That would be interesting!"

"Finding Ben Bowman would serve many useful purposes," Mr. Parker said grimly. "But now that I would actually welcome a communication from him, he no longer pesters me!"

Eagerly Penny awaited the hour appointed for her meeting with Clem Davis. Knowing that the man did not obtain enough to eat, she spent considerable time the next afternoon preparing a lunch basket of substantial food. Taking it with her, she waited at the camp site for nearly a half hour. Finally, just as she began to think that the man had failed her, he appeared.

"I've brought you some hot coffee," Penny said, taking the plug from a thermos bottle. "A little food too."

"Say, that's swell!" the man murmured gratefully. "My wife slips me a handout whenever she can, but lately the house has been watched so closely, she can't get away."

Seating himself at the picnic table, Clem Davis drained the cup of coffee in a few swallows, and greedily devoured a sandwich.

"Now what do you want to know?" he asked gruffly.

Mr. Parker had told Penny exactly what questions to ask. She began with the most important one.

"Mr. Davis, tell me, who is the head man of the Hoods?"

"I don't know myself," he answered promptly. "At the meetings, the Master always wore a robe and a black hood. None of the members ever were permitted to see his face."

"You have no idea who the man may be?"

Clem Davis shook his head as he bit into another sandwich. "I doubt there are more than one or two members of the order who know his identity. Hank Holloway might, or maybe Charley Phelps."

"Is Phelps a member?" Penny asked quickly.

"One of the chief ones. Most of the meetings are held at his place."

"You don't mean at the Hubell Tower?"

Penny's pulse had stepped up to a faster pace, for the information was of the greatest value. Furthermore, it thrilled her that her own theory regarding Charley Phelps was receiving support.

"Sure, the Hoods meet at the Tower about once a month," Clem Davis disclosed. "Usually they get together on the thirteenth, but sometimes they have extra sessions. When special meetings are held, a green light burns on the tower, or the clock strikes thirteen times just at midnight."

"I thought so!" Penny exclaimed, highly elated. "Tell me, why did you decide to break your connection with the Hoods?"

"I joined the organization before I knew what I was letting myself in for. When they made plans to burn the Preston barn, I wanted to quit. The Hoods threatened me, and to get even, planted evidence that made it look as if I had set the fire."

Penny was inclined to believe that Clem Davis had told a straight story for it coincided with her own theories. Always it had seemed to her that evidence pointing to his guilt had been entirely too plain. To corroborate her conclusions, she had brought from home the watch fob found at the Davis stable, hoping that he might identify it.

"That's not mine," he said promptly when she showed the article to him. "I never saw it before."

Penny opened the tiny case, displaying the child's picture. However, the man had no idea who the little boy might be.

"Mr. Davis," she said quietly, replacing the watch fob in her pocket. "I believe in your innocence, and I want to help you. I am sure I can, providing you are willing to cooperate."

"I've already told you about everything I know."

"You've given me splendid information," Penny praised. "What I want you to do is to talk with my father. He'll probably ask you to repeat your story to the Grand Jury."

"I'd be a fool to do that," Clem Davis responded. "I can't prove any of my statements. The Preston fire would be pinned on me, and the Hoods might try to harm my wife. Why, they ran off with a truck load of our melons the other night."

"I know. But unless someone has the courage to speak out against the Hoods they'll become bolder and do even more harm. Supposing you were promised absolute protection. Then would you go before the Grand Jury?"

"Nothing would give me more pleasure. But who can guarantee I'll not be made to pay?"

"I think my father can," Penny assured him. "Will you meet him here tomorrow night at this same hour?"

"Okay," the man agreed, getting up from the table. "You seem to be on the level."

"I'll bring more food tomorrow," Penny said as an extra inducement. "You must have had a hard time since you've been hiding out in the woods."

"Oh, it's not so bad once you get used to it," the man shrugged. "I've got a pretty good place to sleep now."

CHAPTER 20 - CLEM DAVIS' DISCLOSURE

"Inside a building?" Penny asked curiously.

"An automobile," the man grinned. "Someone abandoned it in the swamp and I've taken possession."

"An old one, I suppose."

"Not so old," Clem Davis answered. "Funny thing, it's a 1941 Deluxe model with good upholstery. The only thing I can see wrong with it is that the front grill and fenders have been smashed."

"The car isn't by chance a gray one?"

"Yes, it is," the man admitted. "How did you guess?"

"I didn't guess," Penny returned soberly. "I have a suspicion that car is the one which killed two people about a year ago. Mr. Davis, you must take me to it at once!"

CHAPTER 21 - A BROKEN PROMISE

"You want me to take you to the abandoned car now?" Clem Davis echoed in surprise. "It's located deep in the swamp, just off a side road."

"Would it require long to get there?" Penny asked thoughtfully.

"A half hour at least. With night coming on you wouldn't be able to see a thing."

"It is getting dark," Penny admitted regretfully. "Everything considered, I guess it would be better to wait until tomorrow. But in the meantime, I wish you would search the car carefully. Get the engine number—anything which might help to identify the owner."

"The engine number has been filed off," Clem answered. "I'll give the car a good going over though to see what I can learn. Thanks for the food."

Raising his hand in a semi salute, the man started into the woods.

"Don't forget to meet Dad and me tomorrow night," Penny called after him. "We'll be waiting here about this same time."

The interview with the fugitive had more than fulfilled Penny's expectations. Driving straight home, she made a full report of the talk to her father. Breathlessly, she revealed that the Hoods held monthly meetings at the Hubell Tower, and that both Hank Holloway and Charley Phelps were members of the order.

"You weren't able to learn the name of the head man?" Mr. Parker questioned.

"No, Clem didn't know it himself. He says the Master never shows himself to anyone, but always appears in mask."

Mr. Parker began to pace the floor, a habit of his when under mental stress. The information Penny had acquired was of utmost importance. He believed it to be authentic, but he dared not overlook the possibility that Clem Davis had deliberately lied.

"We must move cautiously on this story," he said aloud. "Should we make false accusations against innocent persons, the *Star* would face disastrous lawsuits."

"You're not going to withhold the information from the public?" Penny demanded in disappointment.

"For the present, I must. The thing for us to do is to try to learn the identity of the head man. Any news published in the *Star* would only serve as a tip-off to him."

"You're right, of course," Penny agreed after a moment of silence.

"Now that we have such a splendid start, it should be easy to gain additional information," the editor resumed. "You say the meetings usually are held on the thirteenth of the month?"

"That's what Clem Davis told me."

"Then we'll arrange to have the Tower watched on that night. In the meantime, I'll see Davis and learn what I can from him. Jerry is working on the County Cooperative angle of the story, and should have some interesting facts soon."

Penny knew that her father was adopting a wise policy, but she could not help feeling slightly disappointed. Always eager for action, she had hoped that Clem Davis' disclosures would lead to the immediate arrest of both Hank Holloway and Charley Phelps. However, she brightened at the thought that at least additional revelations might follow her father's meeting with the fugitive.

The following night, shortly after six-thirty, Penny and Mr. Parker presented themselves at the Orphans' Camp site. They had brought a basket of food, coffee, and a generous supply of cigarettes.

"What time did Davis promise to meet you?" Mr. Parker asked impatiently.

"He should be here now," Penny returned. "I can't imagine why he's late."

CHAPTER 21 - A BROKEN PROMISE

Another half hour elapsed, and still the fugitive did not appear. Mr. Parker paced restlessly beside the picnic table, becoming increasingly impatient.

"He's probably waiting until after dark," Penny declared optimistically.

Another hour elapsed. The shadows deepened and a chill wind blew from the river. Hungry mosquitoes kept Mr. Parker more than occupied as he sought to protect himself.

"Well, I've had enough of this!" he announced at last. "The man isn't coming."

"Oh, Dad, let's wait just a little longer," Penny coaxed. "I'm sure he meant to keep his promise."

"Perhaps he did, although I'm inclined to think otherwise. At any rate, I am going home!"

Penny had no choice but to follow her father to the car. She could not understand Clem Davis' failure to appear unless he had feared that he would be placed under arrest. While it was quite possible that the man might come to the picnic grounds the following night, she was afraid she would never see him again.

"I half expected this to happen," Mr. Parker remarked as he drove toward Riverview. "Unless we can get Davis to swear to his story, we haven't a scrap of real evidence against the Hoods."

"We may learn something on the night of the thirteenth," Penny said hopefully.

"Possibly, but I'm beginning to wonder if everything Davis told you may not have been for the purpose of deception."

"He seemed sincere. I can't believe he deliberately lied to me."

Submerged in gloom, Penny had little to say during the swift ride into Riverview. She could not blame her father for feeling annoyed, because the trip had cost him two hours of valuable time. Clem Davis' failure to appear undoubtedly might deprive the *Star* of a spectacular scoop.

"Never mind," Mr. Parker said to comfort her. "It wasn't your fault. We'll find another way to get our information."

The car proceeded slowly through the downtown section of Riverview. Turning her head to read an electric sign, Penny's attention was drawn to a man in a gray suit who was walking close to the curb.

"Dad, stop the car!" she cried, seizing his arm. "There he is now!"

"Clem Davis?" Mr. Parker demanded, swerving the automobile toward a vacant space near the sidewalk.

"No! No! Ben Bowman! I'm sure it is he!"

Springing from the car, Penny glanced up the street. She had alighted just in time to see the man in gray enter a telegraph office.

"What nonsense is this?" Mr. Parker inquired impatiently. "Why do you think the fellow is Bowman?"

"I'm sure he's the same man I saw at Claymore. The one who tried to pass a forged cheque! Oh, please Dad, we can't let him get away!"

Switching off the car ignition, Mr. Parker stepped to the curb.

"If it should prove to be Ben Bowman, nothing would please me better than to nab him," he announced grimly. "But if you've made a mistake—"

"Come on," Penny urged, seizing his hand. "We can talk about it later."

Through the huge plate glass window of the telegraph office, the man in gray could be seen standing at one of the counters. His back was to the street and he appeared to be writing a message.

"I'm sure it's Ben Bowman," Penny said again. "Why not go inside and ask him if that's his name?"

"I shall. But I'm warning you again, if you've made one of your little mistakes—"

"Go ahead, faint heart!" Penny chuckled, giving him a tiny push. "I'll stay here by the door ready to stop him if he gets by you."

With no appearance of haste, Mr. Parker sauntered into the telegraph office. Deliberately taking a place at the counter close beside the man in gray, he pretended to write a message. Actually, he studied his companion, and attempted to read the lengthy telegram which the other had composed. Before he could do so, the man handed the paper to a girl clerk.

"Get this off right away," he instructed. "Send it collect."

The clerk examined the message, having difficulty in reading the writing.

"This night letter is to be sent to Anthony Parker?" she inquired.

"That's right," the man agreed.

Mr. Parker waited for no more. Touching the man on the arm, he said distinctly:

"I'll save you the trouble of sending that message. I am Anthony Parker."

The man whirled around, his face plainly showing consternation.

"You are Ben Bowman I assume," Mr. Parker said coolly. "I've long looked forward to meeting you."

"You've got me mixed up with someone else," the man mumbled, edging away. "My name's Clark Edgewater. See, I signed it to this telegram."

As proof of his contention, he pointed to the lengthy communication which lay on the counter. One glance satisfied Mr. Parker that it was another "crank" message.

"I don't care how you sign your name," he retorted. "You are Ben Bowman. We have a few matters to talk over."

The man gazed uncertainly at Mr. Parker. He started to speak, then changed his mind. Turning, he made a sudden break for the exit.

"Stop him!" Mr. Parker shouted. "Don't let him get away!"

Penny stood close to the door. As the man rushed toward her, she shot a bolt into place.

"Not quite so fast, Mr. Bowman," she said, smiling. "We really must have a chat with you."

CHAPTER 22 - THE MAN IN GRAY

With the door locked, the man saw that he could not hope to escape. Accepting the situation, he regarded Mr. Parker and Penny with cold disdain.

"All right, my name is Ben Bowman," he acknowledged, shrugging. "So what?"

"You're the man who has been sending me collect messages for the past three months!" Mr. Parker accused.

"And what if I have? Is there any law against it? You run a lousy paper, and as a reader I have a right to complain!"

"But not at my expense. Another thing, I want to know what connection you've had with Clyde Blake."

"Never heard of him."

"Then you don't own property in this city?"

"Nor anywhere else. Now if you're through giving me the third degree, I'll move on."

"Not so fast," interposed Penny, refusing to unbar the door, "if I'm not mistaken you're the same man who is wanted at Claymore for forging a cheque."

"Really, this is too much!" Ben Bowman exclaimed angrily. "Unless you permit me to pass, I shall protest to the police."

"I see an officer just across the street," Mr. Parker declared. "Penny, will you call him over?"

"Just a minute," Ben Bowman interposed in an altered tone. "We can settle this ourselves. I'll admit I was hasty in sending those messages—just a way to let off steam, I guess. If you're willing to forget about it I'll repay you for every dollar you spent."

"I'm afraid I can't forget that easily," Mr. Parker retorted. "No, unless you're willing to come clean about your connection with Clyde Blake I'll have to call the police."

"What do you want to know about him?"

"Is he acting as your real estate agent?"

"Certainly not."

"You do know the man?"

"I've done a little work for him."

"Didn't he pay you to allow him to use your name on a deed?"

"He gave me twenty-five dollars to make out some papers for him. I only copied what he told me to write."

"That's all I want to know," Mr. Parker said grimly. "Penny, call the policeman!"

"See here," Bowman protested furiously, "you intimated that if I told what I knew about Blake you'd let me off. Why, you're as yellow as that paper you run!"

"I make no deals with men of your stamp!" Mr. Parker retorted.

As Penny unlocked the door, Ben Bowman made a break for freedom. However, the editor was entirely prepared. Seizing the man, he held him until Penny could summon the policeman. Still struggling, Bowman was loaded into a patrol wagon and taken to police headquarters.

"I guess that earns me a nice little one hundred dollars!" Penny remarked as she and her father went to their own car. "Thanks, Dad."

"You're entirely welcome," Mr. Parker grinned. "I never took greater pleasure in acknowledging a debt."

"What's your next move, Dad? Will you expose Clyde Blake in tomorrow's *Star*?"

"I'm tempted to do it, Penny. The evidence still is rather flimsy, but even if Ben Bowman denies his story, I think we can prove our charges."

"It's a pity you can't break the Hood yarn in the same edition," Penny said musingly. "What a front page that would make!"

"It certainly would be a good three pennies worth," Mr. Parker agreed. "Unfortunately, it will be many days before the Hoods are supposed to hold their meeting at the Tower."

"But why wait? We could call that gathering ourselves!"

"Just how?"

"Simple as pie. All we would need to do would be to have the clock strike thirteen instead of twelve." Penny glanced at her wrist watch and added persuasively: "We have several hours in which to work!"

"You're completely crazy!" accused Mr. Parker. "Just how would you arrange to have the clock strike thirteen?"

"I'll take care of that part, Dad. All I'll need is a hammer."

"To use on the caretaker, Charley Phelps, I suppose," Mr. Parker remarked ironically.

"Oh, no," Penny corrected, "I propose to turn all the strong-arm work over to you and your gang of reporters. Naturally, Phelps will have to be removed from the scene."

"What you propose is absolutely impossible," the editor declared. "Even so, I'll admit that I find your idea rather fascinating."

"This is no time for being conservative, Dad. Why, the Hoods must know you are out to break up their organization. Every day you wait lessens your chance of getting the story."

"I realize that only too well, Penny. I pinned quite a bit of hope on Clem Davis. His failure to appear puts everything in a different light."

"Why not test what he told us?" Penny argued. "It will be easy to learn if the striking of the clock is a signal to call the Hood meeting. If the men should come, we'll have them arrested, and run a big story tomorrow morning!"

"Coming from your lips it sounds so very simple," Mr. Parker smiled. "Has it occurred to you that if we fail, we'll probably breakfast at the police station?"

"Why worry about that?" grinned Penny. "You have influence."

Mr. Parker sat for several minutes lost in thought.

"You know, I've ALWAYS been lucky," Penny coaxed. "I feel a double dose of it coming on tonight!"

"I believe in hunches myself," Mr. Parker chuckled. "No doubt I'm making the biggest mistake of my life, but I'm going to try your wild scheme. Crazy as it is, it may work!"

"Then let's go!" laughed Penny.

At the *Star* office, Mr. Parker hastily summoned a special staff of newspaper men, warning them to hold themselves in readiness to get out a special edition on short notice. From the group he chose Salt Sommers, Jerry Livingston, and two reporters known for their pugilistic prowess.

"Now this is the line up, boys," he revealed. "We're going to kidnap Charley Phelps from the Tower. It's risky business unless things break right for us, so if any of you want to drop out now, this is your chance."

"We're with you, chief!" declared Salt Sommers, tossing a pack of photographic supplies over his shoulder.

"Sure, what are we waiting for?" chimed in Jerry.

It was well after eleven o'clock by the time the over-loaded press car drew up not far from the Hubell Tower. Penny parked on a dark side street, and Jerry was sent to look over the situation. Soon he returned with his report.

"Charley Phelps is alone in the Tower," he assured the editor. "We shouldn't have any trouble handling him."

"Okay, then let's do the job," Mr. Parker returned. "Remember, if we muff it, we'll do our explaining to a judge."

Separating into groups so that they would not attract attention, Penny and the five men approached the Tower. A light glowed from within, and the caretaker could be seen moving about in the tiny living room.

Tying handkerchiefs over their faces, Salt and Jerry rapped on the back door. Charley Phelps opened it to find himself gazing into the blinding light of two flashlights.

"Say, what—" he began but did not finish.

CHAPTER 22 - THE MAN IN GRAY

Jerry and Salt had seized his arms. Before he could make another sound, they shoved a gag into his mouth, and dragging him into the Tower, closed the door. Working swiftly, they trussed his hands and feet and pushed him into a machinery room.

"Nice work, boys," Mr. Parker praised.

"Listen!" whispered Penny, who had followed the men into the Tower.

The clock had begun to strike the hour of midnight.

"Get up there quickly and do your stuff!" her father commanded. "You've not much time!"

Two steps at a time, Penny raced up the steep iron stairway which led to the belfry of the Tower. Anxiously, she counted the strokes as they pealed forth loud and clearly. Eight—nine—ten. The clock had never seemed to strike so fast before. Desperately she wondered if she could reach the belfry in time.

The stairway was dark, the footing uncertain. In her nervousness, Penny stumbled. Clutching the handrail, she clung to it a moment until she had recovered balance. But in that interval the clock had kept striking, and she was no longer sure of the count.

"It must be eleven," she thought, running up the remaining steps. "The next stroke will be the last."

Penny reached the great bell just as the clapper struck against the metal. The sound was deafening.

"Now!" she thought excitedly. "This is the moment, and I dare not fail!"

Balancing herself precariously, Penny raised a hammer high above her head. With all her strength she brought it down hard against the bell.

CHAPTER 23 - A TRAP SET

To Penny's sensitive ears, the sound which resulted from the hammer blow, seemed weak and lacking in resonance. She sagged back against the iron railing, feeling that she had failed.

"That was swell!" a low voice said in her ear. "A perfect thirteenth stroke!"

Turning around, Penny saw that Jerry Livingston had followed her into the belfry.

"Did it really sound all right?" she inquired anxiously.

"It was good enough to fool anyone. But the question is, will it bring the Hoods here?"

In the room far below, Mr. Parker had lowered the blinds of the circular windows. Making certain that Charley Phelps was securely bound and gagged so that he could make no sound, he opened the front door a tiny crack and left it that way.

"How about the lights?" Salt Sommers asked.

"Leave them on. Shove that sound apparatus under the daybed. Now I guess everything's set. Upstairs, everyone."

Mr. Parker, Salt, and the two reporters, joined Penny and Jerry on the iron stairway.

"We may have a long vigil," the editor warned. "In fact, this whole scheme is likely to turn out a bust."

Few words were spoken during the next twenty minutes. Penny stirred restlessly, and finally went to join Jerry who was maintaining a watch from the belfry.

"See anyone?" she whispered, scanning the street below.

"No sign of anyone yet."

At intervals automobiles whizzed past the tower, and presently one drew up not far from the building. Immediately, Jerry and Penny focused their attention upon it. The headlights were turned to parking, then a man alighted and came toward the Hubell Tower.

"Who is he?" Jerry whispered. "Can you tell?"

"I'm not sure," Penny said uncertainly. "It may be Hank Holloway."

As the man stepped into the light, they both saw that her identification had been correct. The man rapped on the door several times. Receiving no answer, he finally entered.

"Charley!" those on the iron stairway heard him call. "Where are you?"

The brilliantly lighted living room combined with the absence of the caretaker, seemed to mystify the newcomer. Muttering to himself, he moved restlessly about for a few minutes. Finally seating himself, he picked up a newspaper and began to read.

From their post in the belfry, Penny and Jerry soon observed two other men approaching the tower. One they recognized as a workman who had sorted melons at the Davis farm, but his companion was unknown to them. Without rapping, they too entered the building.

"Where's Charley?" inquired one of the men.

"That's what I was wondering," Hank Holloway replied, tossing aside his paper. "For that matter, I can't figure out why this special meeting was called. Something important must have come up."

Within ten minutes, three other men had arrived. Jerry was able to identify two of them by name, but he dared not risk whispering the information to Mr. Parker who crouched on the stairway.

"There's something mighty queer about this meeting," Hank Holloway growled. "Where is the Master? And what's become of Charley?"

From the machinery room in which the caretaker had been imprisoned came a slight thumping sound.

"What was that?" Hank demanded suspiciously.

CHAPTER 23 - A TRAP SET

"I didn't hear anything," answered one of the other men. "Maybe it was someone at the door."

Hank tramped across the room to peer out into the night. As the door swung back, a dark figure moved swiftly along the hedge, crouching low.

"Who's there?" Hank called sharply.

"Quiet, you fool!" was the harsh response.

A man wearing a dark robe and a black hood which completely hid his face, brushed past Holloway, and entered the Tower living room.

"Close the door!" he ordered.

Holloway hastened to obey. An expectant and rather tense silence had fallen upon the men gathered in the room.

"Now what is the meaning of this?" the Master demanded, facing the group. "Who called this meeting?"

"Why, didn't you?" Holloway asked blankly.

"I did not."

"All I know is that I heard the clock strike an extra stroke," Holloway explained. "I thought it was queer to be having another meeting so soon. Then I found Charley wasn't here—"

"Charley not here!" the Master exclaimed.

"He must have stepped out somewhere. The lights were on, and the door partly open."

"I don't like this," the Master said, his voice harsh. "Charley has no right to call a meeting without a special order from me. It is becoming increasingly dangerous for us to gather here."

"Now you're talking!" Holloway nodded. "Anthony Parker of the *Star* is on the warpath again. One of his reporters has been prying into the books of the County Cooperative."

"He'll learn nothing from that source, I trust."

"Not enough to do any harm."

"You act as though you had a grievance, Holloway. Any complaints?"

"Why, no, the Cooperative has made a lot of money since you've taken over. We want to go along with you, if your flare for the dramatic doesn't get us in too deep."

"What do you mean by that, Holloway?"

"This night riding business is getting risky. Why, if Clem Davis should talk—"

"We're not through with him yet."

"Another thing, most of us never did approve of holding meetings here at the Tower," Hank Holloway went on. "It's too public a place, and sooner or later someone will start asking questions about what goes on."

"Anything else?"

"Well, we think you ought to show yourself—let us know who you are. We're all in this together, and we ought to take the same risks. I've been carrying the heavy end."

"That settles it!" the masked man said with finality. "We're through."

"How do you mean?" Holloway asked.

"We're breaking up the organization—now—tonight."

"There's no call to do that."

"Holloway, you do a lot of talking and not much thinking," the other snapped. "This will be our last meeting. We'll divide the profits, and for a time at least, remain inactive."

"That's all very well for you," Holloway complained. "You step out of it without anyone even knowing who you are. But some of us are tied up with the County Cooperative. If there's any investigation, we'll take the rap."

"There will be no investigation."

"That's easy to say," Holloway argued. "I don't like the way things have been going lately. If we're breaking up, we have a right to know who you are."

"Sure," chimed in another. "Remove your mask, and let's have a look. We think we have your number but we ain't positive."

"You never will be," the masked man returned coolly, backing toward the door. "And now, goodnight."

"Oh, no, you don't!" Holloway cried, trying to head him off.

"Stand back!" ordered the Master harshly.

From beneath his robe he whipped a revolver.

385

"All right," Holloway sneered. "I never argue when I'm looking into a muzzle."

Before the Master could retreat, there was another disturbance from inside the machinery room. Unmistakably, the door rattled.

"Someone is in there!" Holloway exclaimed.

Startled, the Master postponed his flight. Still holding the revolver, he tried to open the door, but found it locked.

For those hiding on the stairway, the situation had become a tense one. In another moment, the members of the Black Hoods unquestionably would break the door lock and find Charley Phelps.

"Let's take 'em, Chief!" whispered Jerry, who was eager for action. "Now is our only chance."

"All set!" Mr. Parker gave the signal.

With a concerted rush, the four young men leaped down the stairway, hurling themselves on Holloway and the masked man. Catching the latter unaware, Jerry knocked the revolver from his hand and it went spinning over the floor.

Penny started down the stairway, but Mr. Parker pushed her back.

"Stay where you are!" he ordered as he too joined the fray.

Penny huddled against the wall, watching fearfully. Her father and the reporters outnumbered their opponents by one man, but the Hoods were all strong, powerful fellows who fought desperately. A chair crashed against the lamp, shattering it. In the resulting darkness, she no longer could see what was happening.

Suddenly a figure broke away from the general tangle of bodies and darted toward the circular stairway. For a moment Penny believed that he must be one of the reporters, then she saw that the man wore a hood over his face.

"The Master!" she thought, chills racing down her spine. "He's trying to get away, and I've got to stop him!"

CHAPTER 24 - TIMELY HELP

As the black-robed man started up the stairway, Penny attempted to block his path. Failing to trip him, she seized his arms and held fast.

"Out of my way!" the man cried, giving her a hard push.

Penny clung tightly and struggled to reach the hood which covered his face.

Suddenly, the man jerked free and darted on up the steep, circular stairway. Pursuing him, Penny was able to seize the long flowing black robe, only to have it tear loose in her hands.

Gaining the first landing, midway to the belfry, the man did not hesitate. Swinging his legs through an open window, he leaped to the ground twenty feet below.

"He'll be killed!" Penny thought.

Reaching the window she saw the man lying in a heap at the base of the tower. For a moment he remained motionless, but as she watched, he slowly scrambled to his feet and staggered off.

Until the man ducked behind the high hedge, Penny saw him plainly silhouetted in the moonlight. Although his black hood remained in place, his body no longer was covered by the dark robe.

"I know him!" she thought. "Even with his mask on, I'm sure I can't be wrong!"

Fearing to attempt the hazardous leap, Penny ran down the iron stairway, shouting that the Master of the Hoods had escaped. By this time, Mr. Parker's crew of reporters had gained the upperhand of the remaining members of the organization.

"Which way did the fellow go?" the editor demanded, running to the door.

"Along the hedge toward the street!" Penny directed.

Leaving Jerry, Salt, and the others to guard the prisoners, Mr. Parker and his daughter hastened outdoors. There was no sign of anyone in the vicinity of the Tower.

"He can't be far away," Penny maintained. "Anyway, I know his identity!"

"You saw his face?"

"No, but as he ran across the yard I noticed that one arm was much shorter than the other."

"Clyde Blake!"

"That's what I think. Maybe we can catch him at his home!"

"If Blake is our man, we'll get him!" Mr. Parker said tersely. "We may need help though."

Reentering the Tower building, he telephoned police headquarters, asking that a patrol wagon be sent for Hank Holloway, Charley Phelps, and the other prisoners.

"Send a squad to Clyde Blake's home," he added crisply. "I'll meet your men there and provide all the evidence they'll need to make the arrests."

Jerry, Salt, and the two reporters were instructed to remain at the Tower pending the arrival of the patrol wagon. There was slight danger that any of the prisoners could escape for all the captives had been locked into the machinery room.

Delaying only long enough to obtain the case of sound equipment hidden beneath the daybed, Mr. Parker and Penny hastened to the waiting press car.

"Dad," she marveled as they passed near a street light, "you should see your eye! It's turning black. Someone must have pasted you hard."

"Never mind that now," he returned indifferently. "We're out for a big story, and we're going to get it too!"

THE CLOCK STRIKES THIRTEEN

The police cruiser which had been summoned was not in sight by the time Mr. Parker and Penny reached the Blake home. At first glance, the house seemed to be dark. However, a dim light glowed from the windows of one of the upstairs, rear bedrooms.

"We'll not wait for the police," Mr. Parker said, starting up the walk.

His knock at the door went unanswered. Even when the editor pounded with his fist, no one came to admit him.

"Someone is inside," Penny declared, peering up at the lighted window. "It must be Blake."

Mr. Parker tried the door and finding it unlocked, stepped boldly into the living room.

"Blake!" he shouted.

On the floor above Mr. Parker and Penny heard the soft pad of slippered feet. The real estate man, garbed in a black silk dressing gown, gazed down over the balustrade.

"Who is there?" he called.

"Anthony Parker from the *Star*. I want to talk with you."

Slowly Clyde Blake descended the stairway. His gait was stiff and deliberate.

"You seem to have injured your leg," Mr. Parker said significantly.

"I stumbled on the stairway not fifteen minutes ago," Blake answered. "Twisted my ankle. May I ask why I am honored with a visit at this hour?"

"You know why I am here!" Mr. Parker retorted, reaching to switch on a living room light.

"Indeed, I don't." Deliberately Blake moved away from the bridge lamp into the shadow, but not before both Penny and her father had noted a long, ugly scratch across his cheek.

"It's no use to pretend," Mr. Parker said sharply. "I have all the evidence I need to convict you of being a ringleader of the Hoods."

"You are quite mad," the real estate man sneered. "Parker, I've put up with you and your methods quite long enough. You queered my deal with the Orphans' Camp Board. Now you accuse me of being a member of a disreputable organization. You must be out of your mind."

"You've always been a good talker, Blake, but this time it will get you nowhere. My reporters were at the Hubell Tower. I have a complete sound record of what transpired there. Either give yourself up, or the police will take you by force."

"So you've notified the police?"

"I have."

"In that case—" Blake's smile was tight. With a dextrousness which caught Penny and her father completely off guard, he whipped a revolver from beneath his dressing robe. "In that case," he completed, "we'll handle it this way. Raise your hands, if you please."

"Your politeness quite overpowers me," the editor said sarcastically, as he obeyed.

"Now turn your back and walk to the telephone," Blake went on. "Call the police station and tell the chief that you made a mistake in asking for my arrest."

"This will get you nowhere, Blake."

"Do as I say!"

Mr. Parker went to the telephone, stalling for time by pretending that he did not know the police station number.

"Garfield 4508," Blake supplied. "Say exactly what I tell you or you'll taste one of my little bullets!"

The real estate man stood with his back to the darkened dining room, in such position that he could cover both Mr. Parker and Penny. As the editor began to dial the phone, he backed a step nearer the archway. Behind him, the dark velvet curtains moved slightly.

Penny noted the movement but gave no indication of it. The next instant a muscular arm reached through the velvet folds, seizing Blake from the rear. The revolver was torn from his hand.

Dropping the telephone, Mr. Parker snatched up the weapon and covered Blake.

"All right, it's your turn to reach," he said.

As Blake slowly raised his hands, another man stepped into the circle of light. He wore rough garments and had not shaved in many days.

"Clem Davis!" Penny exclaimed.

CHAPTER 24 - TIMELY HELP

"I came here to get Blake," the man said briefly. "I've thought for a long time he was the person responsible for all my trouble. Tonight when the clock struck thirteen, I watched the Hubell Tower. I saw Blake put on his hood and robe and then enter the building, so I knew he was the Master."

"You're willing to testify to that?" Mr. Parker asked.

"Yes," Clem Davis nodded, "I've been thinking things over. I'm ready to give myself up and tell what I know."

"You'll have a very difficult time of it proving your absurd charges," Blake said scathingly.

"I think not," Mr. Parker corrected. "Ben Bowman was captured tonight, and he's already confessed his part in the real estate swindle. Even if you weren't mixed up with the Hoods, you'd go to jail for that."

Blake sagged into a chair, for the first time looking shaken.

"I'll make a deal with you, Parker," he began, but the editor cut him short.

"You'll face the music! No, Blake, you can't squeeze out of it this time."

A car had drawn up in front of the house. Running to the window, Penny saw three policemen crossing the street. She hurried to the door to open it for them.

"Here's your man," Mr. Parker said as the policemen tramped into the living room.

Turning the revolver over to one of the officers, he disclosed exactly what had occurred. Blake was immediately placed under arrest. He was granted ten minutes to change into street clothing and prepare for his long sojourn in jail.

"I am being persecuted," he whined as he was led away. "This is all a trick to build up circulation for the *Star*. If there is such an organization as the Black Hoods, Clem Davis is the man who heads it!"

Penny and Mr. Parker felt very grateful to the fugitive who had come to their aid at such a timely moment. They wished to help him if they could, but they knew he could not escape arrest. Clem Davis realized it too, for he made no protest when told that Sheriff Daniels must be called.

"I'm ready to give myself up," he repeated. "I was a member of the Hoods, but I never went along with them once I learned that they meant to defraud the truck farmers. I hope I can prove my innocence."

Within a few minutes Sheriff Daniels arrived to assume charge of his prisoner. Entertaining no sympathy for the man, he told Penny and her father that in all likelihood Davis must serve a long sentence.

"He's wanted for setting fire to the Preston barn," the sheriff insisted. "Unless he can prove an alibi for himself, he hasn't a chance."

"Can't you tell where you were at the time of the fire?" Mr. Parker asked the man.

"I was at a place called Toni's."

"Why, that's right, Dad!" Penny cried. "Don't you remember? We saw Davis leave the place, and he was followed by two men—probably members of the Hood organization."

"We saw a man leave there shortly after midnight," Mr. Parker agreed.

"You wouldn't swear he was Clem Davis?" the sheriff asked.

"I'm not sure," Mr. Parker admitted truthfully. "However, it's obvious that a man scarcely could have gone from Toni's at that time and still set fire to the barn. My daughter and I drove directly there, and when we arrived the building had been burning for some time."

"All of which proves nothing unless you can show that Clem Davis actually was at Toni's after midnight."

"Could the owner of the place identify you?" Penny thoughtfully inquired.

"I doubt it," Davis answered. "It might be worth a try, though."

"Perhaps I can prove that you weren't near the Preston farm at midnight!" Penny exclaimed as a sudden idea came to her. "Clem, you heard the Hubell clock strike the hour?"

"Yes, I did."

"How many strokes were there?"

"Thirteen," Davis answered without hesitation. "I counted them and figured the Hoods were having one of their get-togethers."

"What is this?" the sheriff demanded in bewilderment.

"We can prove that the Hubell clock did strike thirteen on that particular night," Penny resumed. "It was a signal used by the Hoods, but that's not the point."

"What are you getting at?"

"Just this. The Hubell clock can't be heard at the Preston farm."

"True."

"One can still hear the clock at Toni's but not a quarter of a mile beyond it. You see, if Mr. Davis heard the thirteenth stroke, he couldn't have had time to reach the Preston farm and set the fire."

"That's an interesting argument," the sheriff said, smiling. "And you plead Clem's case very earnestly. I'll tell you what I'll do. I'll investigate all these angles you've brought up, and if the evidence supports your theory, I promise he'll go free."

"That's fair enough," declared Mr. Parker.

The sheriff did not handcuff his prisoner. As they were leaving the house, Clem Davis turned to thank Penny for her interest in his behalf.

"Oh, I almost forgot," he said, taking a rectangular metal object from beneath his baggy coat. "Here's something for you."

"A rusty automobile license plate!" Penny exclaimed, staring at it.

"Found it in the swamp not far from that abandoned car I told you about."

"Then it must have been thrown away by the driver of the hit-skip car!"

"That's how I figure," Clem Davis drawled. "If you can learn the owner of this license plate, you'll know who killed that orphan's folks!"

CHAPTER 25 - SPECIAL EDITION

Lights blazed on every floor of the *Riverview Star* building, proclaiming to all who passed that another special edition was in the process of birth. Pressmen industriously oiled the big rotaries ready for a big run of papers; linotype men, compositors, reporters, all were at their posts, having been hastily summoned from comfortable beds.

In the editor's office, Penny sat at a typewriter hammering out copy. Jerking a long sheet of paper from beneath the roller, she offered it to her father.

"My contribution on the Hubell Clock angle," she said with a flourish.

Mr. Parker rapidly scanned the story, making a number of corrections with a blue pencil.

"I should slug this 'editorial material,'" he remarked with a grin. "Quite a plug you've put in for Seth McGuire—suggesting that he be given back his old job as caretaker of the Tower."

"Well, don't you think it's a good idea?"

"The old man will get his job back—I'll see to that," Mr. Parker promised. "But the front page of the *Star* is not the place to express wishful thinking. We'll reserve it for news if you don't mind."

Crossing out several lines, Mr. Parker placed the copy in a pneumatic tube, and shot it directly to the composing room. He glanced at his watch, noting aloud that in exactly seven minutes the giant presses would start rolling.

"Everything certainly has turned out grand," Penny sighed happily. "Hank Holloway and Clyde Blake are sure to be given long prison sentences for their Black Hood activities. You've promised to see that Old Seth gets his job back, so that part will end beautifully. He'll adopt Adelle and I won't need to worry about her any more."

"What makes you think Seth will adopt the orphan?" Mr. Parker asked curiously.

"Why, he's wanted to do it from the first. He hesitated because he had no steady work, and not enough money. By the way, Dad, how long will it take to learn the owner of that automobile license plate that Clem Davis gave us?"

"Jerry is trying to get the information now, Penny. All the registry offices are closed, but if he can pull some official out of bed, there's a chance he may obtain the data tonight. I'm not counting on it, however."

The door of the office swung back and City Editor DeWitt hurried into the room.

"Everything set?" Mr. Parker inquired.

"We need a picture of Clyde Blake. There's nothing in the morgue."

"Salt Sommers has one you might use!" Penny cried. "It was taken when Blake came here the other day. He objected to it because it showed that one arm was shorter than the other."

"Just what we need!" DeWitt approved. "I'll rush it right out. Except for the picture, the front page is all made up."

The door closed behind the city editor, but before Mr. Parker could settle comfortably into his chair, it burst open again. Jerry Livingston, breathless from running up several flights of stairs, faced his chief.

"I've got all the dope!" he announced.

"You learned who drove the hit-run car?" Penny demanded eagerly.

"The license was issued in Clyde Blake's name!"

"Then Adelle's identification at the picnic was correct!" Penny exclaimed.

"Write your story, Jerry, but make it brief," Mr. Parker said tersely. "We'll make over the front page."

Calling DeWitt, he gave the new order. In the composing room, headlines were jerked and a story of minor importance was pulled from the form to make room for the new material.

"We'll roll three minutes late," Mr. Parker said, glancing at his watch again. "Even so, our papers will make all the trains, and we'll scoop every other sheet in town."

Jerry wrote his story which was sent paragraph by paragraph to the composing room. Barely had he typed "30," signifying the end, when the lights of the room dimmed for an instant.

"There go the presses!" Mr. Parker declared, ceasing his restless pacing.

Within a few minutes, the first paper, still fresh with ink, was laid upon the editor's desk. Penny peered over his shoulder to read the headlines announcing the arrest of Blake and his followers.

"There's not much here about Ben Bowman," she commented after a moment. "What do you think will happen to him, Dad?"

"That remains to be seen," answered the editor. "He's already wanted for forgery, so it should be fairly easy to prove that he worked with Blake to defraud the Camp Board."

"I'm worried about the orphans' camp. So much money has been spent clearing the land and setting up equipment."

"Probably everything can be settled satisfactorily in the end," Mr. Parker returned. "It may take time and litigation, but there's no reason why a perfect title can't be obtained to the land."

Penny felt very well pleased at the way everything had turned out. Only one small matter remained unexplained. She had been unable to learn the significance of the watch fob found in Clem Davis' stable.

"Why, I can tell you about that," Jerry Livingston assured her. "The fob belonged to Hank Holloway. He admitted it at the police station. The little boy in the picture is his nephew."

Both Penny and her father were tired for it was very late. With the *Star* ready for early morning street sales, they thought longingly of home and bed. Yet as their car sped down a dimly lighted street, Penny revived sufficiently to say:

"How about a steak at Toni's, Dad?"

"Oh, I don't feel like eating at this late hour," Mr. Parker declined.

"That's not the idea, Dad. I'm suggesting a raw steak for that left eye of yours. By morning it will be swollen shut."

"It is quite a shiner," the editor agreed, gazing at his reflection in the car mirror. "But the story was well worth the cost."

"Thanks to whom?" Penny asked mischievously.

"If I say thanks to you, Penny, you will be expecting an increase in your allowance or something of the sort."

"Maybe I'll ask for it anyhow," Penny chuckled. "And don't forget that you owe me a hundred dollars for getting that crack-pot, Ben Bowman, out of your hair!"

"So I do," Mr. Parker conceded with a laugh. The

WISHING WELL

"That also will be worth the price."

HE WHEELED AND RAN OUT THE OPEN DOOR.

CHAPTER 1 - AN OLD HOUSE

At her desk in the assembly room of Riverview High School, Penny Parker sat poised for instant flight. Her books had been stacked away, and she awaited only the closing bell to liberate her from a day of study.

"Now don't forget!" she whispered to her chum, Louise Sidell, who occupied the desk directly behind. "We start for the old Marborough place right away!"

The dismissal bell tapped. Penny bolted down the aisle and was one of the first to reach the door. However, hearing her name called, she was forced to pause.

"Penelope, will you wait a moment please?" requested the teacher in charge of assembly.

"Yes, Miss Nelson," Penny dutifully responded, but she shot her chum a glance of black despair.

"What have you done now?" Louise demanded in an accusing whisper.

"Not a thing," muttered Penny. "About ten minutes ago I clipped Fred Green with a paper ball, but I don't think she saw me."

"Get out of it as fast as you can," Louise urged. "Unless we start for the Marborough place within half an hour we'll have to postpone the trip."

While the other pupils filed slowly from the room, Penny slumped back into her seat. She was a tall, slim girl with mischievous blue eyes which hinted of an active mind. Golden hair was accented by a brown sweater caught at the throat with a conspicuous ornament, a weird looking animal made of leather.

"Penelope, I don't suppose you know why I asked you to remain," observed the teacher, slowly coming down the aisle.

"Why, no, Miss Nelson." Penny was far too wise to make damaging admissions.

"I want to talk to you about Rhoda Wiegand."

"About Rhoda?" Penny echoed, genuinely surprised. The girl was a new student at Riverview, somewhat older than the members of her class, and lived in a trailer camp at the outskirts of the city.

Miss Nelson seated herself at a desk opposite Penny, thus indicating that she meant the talk to be friendly and informal.

"Penelope," she resumed, "you are president of the Palette Club. Why has Rhoda never been taken in as a member? She is one of our most talented art students."

"Some of the girls don't seem to like Rhoda very well," Penny answered, squirming uncomfortably. "We did talk about taking her into the club, but nothing came of it."

"As president of the organization, couldn't you arrange it?"

"I suppose so," Penny admitted, frowning thoughtfully.

"Why do the girls dislike Rhoda?"

"There doesn't seem to be any special reason for it."

"Her poverty, perhaps?"

"I don't think it's that," Penny defended the club members. "Rhoda is so quiet that the girls have never become acquainted with her."

"Then I suggest that they make an immediate effort," Miss Nelson ended the interview. "The Palette Club has no right to an existence unless it welcomes members with real art talent."

A group of girls awaited Penny when she reached the locker room. They eagerly plied her with questions as to why she had been detained by the teacher.

"I'll tell you later," Penny promised.

WISHING WELL

At the other side of the room Rhoda Wiegand was removing a coat from her locker. A sober-faced girl of seventeen, she wore a faded blue dress which seemed to draw all color from her thin face. Knowing that she was not well liked, she seldom spoke or forced herself upon the other students.

"Rhoda," began Penny, paying no heed to the amazed glances of her friends, "the Palette Club is having a meeting this afternoon at the old Marborough place. Why not come with us?"

The older girl turned quickly, a smile of surprise and pleasure brightening her face.

"Oh, I should love to go, only I don't think—" Hesitating, she gazed at the other girls who were eyeing her in a none too friendly way.

Penny gave Louise Sidell a little pinch. Her chum, understanding what was expected, said with as much warmth as she could: "Yes, do come, Rhoda. We plan to sketch the old wishing well."

"I have enough drawing material for both of us," Penny added persuasively.

"If you really want me, of course I'll come!" Rhoda accepted, her voice rather tremulous. "I've heard about the Marborough homestead, and always longed to see it."

A group of subdued girls gathered their belongings from the lockers, preparing to leave the school grounds. No one understood why Penny had invited Rhoda to attend the outing, and the act had not been a popular one.

Boarding a bus, the twelve members of the Palette Club soon reached the end of the line, and from there walked a quarter of a mile into the country. Penny and Louise chose Rhoda as their companion, trying to make her feel at ease. Conversation became rather difficult and they were relieved when, at length, they approached their destination.

"There's the old house," Penny said, indicating a steep pitched roof-top which could be seen rising above a jungle of tall oaks. "It's been unoccupied for at least ten years now."

The Marborough homestead, a handsome dwelling of pre-Civil war day, long had been Riverview's most outstanding architectural curiosity. Only in a vague way was Penny familiar with its history. The property had been named Rose Acres and its mistress, Mrs. James Marborough, had moved from the city many years before, allowing the house to stand unpainted and untended. Once so beautifully kept, the grounds had become a tangle of weeds and untrimmed bushes. Even so, the old plantation home with its six graceful pillars, retained dignity and beauty.

Entering the yard through a space where a gate once had stood, the girls gazed about with interest. Framed in a clump of giant azaleas was the statue of an Indian girl with stone feathers in her hair. Beyond, they caught a glimpse of the river which curved around the south side of the grounds in a wide bend.

"Where is the old wishing well?" Rhoda inquired. "I've heard so much about it."

"We're coming to it now," Penny replied, leading the way down an avenue of oak trees.

Not far from the house stood the old-fashioned covered well. Its base was of cut stone and on a bronze plate had been engraved the words: "*If you do a good deed, you can make a wish and it will come true.*"

"Some people around Riverview really believe that this old well has the power to make wishes come true," Louise Sidell remarked, peering at her reflection mirrored in the water far below. "In the past years when Mrs. Marborough lived here, it had quite a reputation."

"The water is still good if you don't mind a few germs," Penny added with a laugh. "I see that someone has replaced the bucket. There was none here the last time I came."

By means of the long sweep, she lowered the receptacle and brought it up filled with water.

"Make a wish, Penny," one of her friends urged. "Maybe it will come true."

"Everyone knows what she'll ask for!" teased Louise. "Her desires are always the same—a bigger weekly allowance!"

Penny smiled as she drew a dipper of water from the wooden bucket.

"How about the good deed?" she inquired lightly. "I've done nothing worthy of a demand upon this old well."

"You helped your father round up a group of Night Riders," Louise reminded her. "Remember the big story you wrote for the *Riverview Star* which was titled: *The Clock Strikes Thirteen*?"

"I did prevent Clyde Blake from tricking a number of people in this community," Penny acknowledged. "Perhaps that entitles me to a wish."

Drinking deeply from the dipper, she poured the last drops into the well, watching as they made concentric circles in the still water below.

CHAPTER 1 - AN OLD HOUSE

"Old well, do your stuff and grant my wish," she entreated. "Please get busy right away."

"But what is your wish, Penny?" demanded one of the girls. "You have to tell."

"All right, I wish that this old Marborough property could be restored to its former beauty."

"You believe in making hard ones," Louise laughed. "I doubt that this place ever will be fixed up again—at least not until after the property changes hands."

"It's Rhoda's turn now," Penny said, offering the dipper to her.

The older girl stepped to the edge of the well, her face very serious.

"Do you think wishes really do come true?" she asked thoughtfully.

"Oh, it's only for the fun of it," Louise responded. "But they do say that in the old days, this well had remarkable powers. At least many persons came here to make wishes which they claimed came true. I couldn't believe in it myself."

Rhoda stood for a moment gazing down into the well. Drinking from the dipper, she allowed a few drops to spatter into the deep cavern below.

"I wish—" she said in a low, tense voice—"I wish that some day Pop and Mrs. Breen will be repaid for looking after my brother and me. I wish that they may have more money for food and clothes and a few really nice things."

An awkward, embarrassing silence descended upon the group of girls. Everyone knew that Rhoda and her younger brother, Ted, lived at a trailer camp with a family unrelated to them, but not even Penny had troubled to learn additional details. From Rhoda's wish it was apparent to all that the Breens were in dire poverty.

"It's your turn now, Louise," Penny said quickly.

Louise accepted the dipper. Without drinking, she tossed all the water into the well, saying gaily:

"I wish Penny would grow long ears and a tail! It would serve her right for solving so many mystery cases!"

The other girls made equally frivolous wishes. Thereafter, they abandoned fun for serious work, getting out their sketching materials. Penny and Louise began to draw the old well, but Rhoda, intrigued by the classical beauty of the house, decided to try to transfer it to paper.

"You do nice work," Penny praised, gazing over the older girl's shoulder. "The rest of us can't begin to match it."

"You may have the sketch when I finish," Rhoda offered.

As she spoke, the girls were startled to hear a commotion in the bushes behind the house. Chickens began to cackle, and to their ears came the sound of pounding feet.

Suddenly, from the direction of the river, a young man darted into view, pursued by an elderly man who was less agile. To the girls, it was immediately apparent why the youth was being chased, for he carried a fat hen beneath his arm, and ran with hat pulled low over his face.

"A chicken thief!" Penny exclaimed, springing to her feet. "Come on, girls, let's head him off!"

CHAPTER 2 - BY THE COVERED WELL

Seeing the group of girls by the wishing well, the youth swerved, and fled in the opposite direction. Darting into the woods, he ran so swiftly that Penny realized pursuit would be futile.

"Who was he?" she questioned the others. "Did any of you recognize him?"

"I'm sure I've seen him somewhere," Louise Sidell declared. "Were you able to see his face, Rhoda?"

The older girl did not answer, for at that moment the man who had pursued the boy ran into the yard. Breathing hard, he paused near the well.

"Did you see a boy come through here?" he asked abruptly. "The rascal stole one of my good layin' hens."

"We saw him," Penny answered, "but I'm sure you'll never overtake him now. He ran into the woods."

"Reckon you're right," the man muttered, seating himself on the stone rim of the wishing well. "I'm tuckered." Taking out a red-bandana handkerchief, he wiped perspiration from his forehead.

Penny thought that she recognized the man as a stonecutter who lived in a shack at the river's edge. He was a short, muscular individual, strong despite his age, with hands roughened by hard labor. His face had been browned by wind and sun; gray eyes squinted as if ever viewing the world with suspicion and hate.

"Aren't you Truman Crocker?" Penny inquired curiously.

"That's my tag," the stonecutter answered, drawing himself a drink of water from the well. "What are you young 'uns doing here?"

"Oh, our club came to sketch," Penny returned. "You live close by, don't you?"

"Down yonder," the man replied, draining the dipper in a thirsty gulp. "I been haulin' stone all day. It's a hard way to make a living, let me tell you. Then I come home to find that young rascal making off with my chickens!"

"Do you know who he was?" asked Louise.

"No, but this ain't the first time he's paid me a visit. Last week he stole one of my best Rhode Island Reds. I'm plumb disgusted."

Rhoda abruptly arose from the grass, gathering together her sketching materials. As if to put an end to the conversation, she remarked:

"It will soon be dark, girls. I think I should start home."

"We'll all be leaving in a few minutes," Penny replied. "Let's look around a bit more though, before we go."

"You won't see nothin' worth lookin' at around here," the stonecutter said contemptuously. "This old house ain't much any more. There's good lumber in it though, and the foundation has some first class stone."

"You speak as if you had designs on it," Penny laughed. "It would be a shame to tear down a beautiful old house such as this."

"What's it good for?" the man shrugged. "There ain't no one lived here in ten or twelve years. Not since the old lady went off."

"Did you know Mrs. Marborough?"

"Oh, we said howdy to each other when we'd meet, but that was the size of it. The old lady didn't like me none and I thought the same of her. She never wanted my chickens runnin' over her yard. Ain't it a pity she can't see 'em now?"

With a throaty sound, half chuckle, half sneer, the man arose and walked with the girls around the house.

"If you want to look inside, there's a shutter off on the east livin' room window," he informed. "Everything's just like the old lady left it."

"You don't mean the furniture is still in the house!" Rhoda exclaimed incredulously.

CHAPTER 2 - BY THE COVERED WELL

"There ain't nothing been changed. I never could figure why someone didn't come in an' haul off her stuff, but it's stood all these years."

Their curiosity aroused, the girls hastened to the window that Truman Crocker had mentioned. Flattening her face against the dirty pane, Penny peered inside.

"He's right!" she announced. "The furniture is still covered by sheets! Why, that's funny."

"What is?" inquired Louise impatiently.

"There's a lady's hat lying on the table!"

"It must be quite out of style by this time," Louise laughed.

"A *new* hat," Penny said with emphasis. "And a purse lying beside it!"

At the other side of the house, an outside door squeaked. Turning around, the group of girls stared almost as if they were gazing at a ghost. An old lady in a long blue silk dress with lace collar and cuffs, stepped out onto the veranda. She gazed beyond the girls toward Truman Crocker who leaned against a tree. Seeing the woman, he straightened to alert attention.

"If it ain't Priscilla Marborough!" he exclaimed. "You've come back!"

"I certainly have returned," the old lady retorted with no friendliness in her voice. "High time someone looked after this place! While I've been away, you seemingly have used my garden as a chicken run!"

"How did I know you was ever coming back?" Crocker demanded. "Anyhow, the place has gone to wrack and ruin. A few chickens more nor less shouldn't make no difference."

"Perhaps not to you, Truman Crocker," Mrs. Marborough returned with biting emphasis. "You know I am home now, so I warn you—keep your live stock out of my garden!"

Penny and her friends shared the old stonecutter's chagrin, for they too were trespassers. Waiting until the woman had finished lecturing Crocker, they offered an apology for the intrusion.

"We're very sorry," Penny said, speaking for the others. "Of course we never dreamed that the house was occupied or we wouldn't have peeped through the window. We came because we wanted to sketch the old wishing well and your lovely home."

Mrs. Marborough came down the steps toward the girls.

"I quite understand," she said in a far milder tone than she had used in speaking to the stonecutter. "You may look around as much as you wish. But first, tell me your names."

One by one they gave them, answering other questions which the old lady asked. She kept them so busy that they had no opportunity to interpose any of their own. But at length Penny managed to inquire:

"Mrs. Marborough, are you planning to open up your home again? Everyone would be so happy if only you should decide to live here!"

"Happy?" the old lady repeated, her eyes twinkling. "Well, maybe some people would be, and others wouldn't."

"Rose Acres could be made into one of the nicest places in Riverview," declared Louise.

"That would take considerable money," replied Mrs. Marborough. "I've not made any plans yet." Abruptly she turned to face Truman Crocker who was staring at her. "Must you stand there gawking?" she asked with asperity. "Get along to your own land, and mind, don't come here again. I'll not have trespassers."

"You ain't changed a bit, Mrs. Marborough, not a particle," the stonecutter muttered as he slowly moved off.

Truman Crocker's dismissal had been so curt that Penny and her friends likewise started to leave the grounds.

"You needn't go unless you want to," Mrs. Marborough said, her tone softening again. "I never could endure that no-good loafer, Truman Crocker! All the stepping stones are gone from my garden, and I have an idea what became of them!"

The group of girls hesitated, scarcely knowing what to do or say. As the silence became noticeable, Penny tried to make conversation by remarking that she and her friends had been especially interested in the old wishing well.

"Is it true that wishes made there have come true?" Rhoda Wiegand interposed eagerly.

"Yes and no," the old lady smiled. "Hundreds of wishes have been made at the well over the years. A surprising number of the worthwhile ones have been granted, so folks say. Tell me, did you say your name is Rhoda?"

"Why, yes," the girl responded, surprised that the old lady had remembered. "Rhoda Wiegand."

"Wiegand—odd, I don't recall the name. Have your parents lived many years in Riverview?"

"My mother and father are dead, Mrs. Marborough. My brother and I haven't any living relatives. Mr. and Mrs. Breen took us in so we wouldn't have to go to an orphans' home. They have three children of their own, and I'm afraid we're quite a burden."

"Where do the Breens live, my child?"

"We have a trailer at the Dorset Tourist Camp."

"I've always thought I should enjoy living that way," Mrs. Marborough declared. "Big houses are entirely too much work. If I decide to clean up this place, it will take me weeks."

"Can't we all help you?" suggested Louise impulsively. More than anything else she longed to see the interior of the quaint old house.

"Thank you, my dear, but I shall require no assistance," Mrs. Marborough replied somewhat stiffly. Obviously dismissing the girls, she added: "Do come again whenever you like."

During the bus ride to Riverview, the members of the Palette exchanged comments, speculating upon why the old lady had returned to the city after such a lengthy absence. One by one they alighted at various street corners until only Rhoda, Penny, and Louise remained.

"Rhoda, you'll have a long ride to the opposite side of the city," Penny remarked as she and Louise prepared to leave the bus. "Why not get off here and let me drive you home in my car? It won't take long to get it from the garage."

"Oh, that would be too much trouble," Rhoda protested.

"I want to do it," Penny insisted. Taking the girl by the elbow, she steered her to the bus exit. To Louise she added: "Why not come along with us?"

"Perhaps I will, if you'll drive your good car—not Leaping Lena."

Penny was the proud possessor of two automobiles, one a handsome maroon sedan, the other a dilapidated, ancient "flivver" which had an unpleasant habit of running only when fancy dictated. How she had obtained two cars was a story in itself—in fact, several of them. The maroon model, however, had been the gift of Penny's devoted father, Anthony Parker, publisher of Riverview's leading daily newspaper, *The Star*. He had presented the car to her in gratitude because she had achieved an exclusive story for his paper, gaining astounding evidence by probing behind a certain mysterious *Green Door*.

Delighted with the gift, Penny promptly sold Leaping Lena only to become so lonesome for her old friend that she had bought it back from a second-hand dealer. In towing the car home she was involved in an accident, and there followed a chain of amazing events which ultimately brought the solution of a mystery case known as *Clue of the Silken Ladder*. Leaping Lena and trouble always went together, according to Louise, but Penny felt that every one of her adventures had been worth while.

"I don't mind taking the maroon car," she replied to her chum. "In fact, Lena hasn't been running so well lately. I think she has pneumonia of the carburetor."

"Or maybe it's just old age sneaking up on her!" Louise added with a teasing laugh.

Reaching the Parker home, Penny ran inside to tell Mrs. Weems, the housekeeper, that she was taking Rhoda to the trailer camp. Returning a moment later, she backed the maroon car from the garage with dazzling skill and further exhibited her prowess as a driver.

"Penny always handles an automobile as if she were enroute to a three-alarm fire!" Louise assured Rhoda. "A reporter at the *Star* taught her how to drive."

Presently, the car arrived at the Dorset Tourist Camp, rolling through an archway entrance into a tree-shaded area.

"Our trailer is parked over at the north side," Rhoda said, pointing to a vehicle with faded brown paint.

Penny stopped the car beneath a large maple tree. Immediately three small children who had been playing close by, rushed up to greet Rhoda. Their hands and faces were very dirty, frocks unpressed and torn, and their hair appeared never to have made contact with comb or brush.

"Are these the Breen youngsters?" inquired Louise.

"Yes," Rhoda answered, offering no apology for the way the children looked. "This is Betty, who is seven. Bobby is five, and Jean is our baby."

CHAPTER 2 - BY THE COVERED WELL

Penny and Louise had no intention of remaining at the camp, but before they could drive away, Mrs. Breen stepped from the trailer. She came at once to the car, and Rhoda introduced her.

"I've always told Rhoda to bring her friends out here, but she never would do it," the woman declared heartily. "Come inside and see our trailer."

"We really should be going," Penny demurred. "I told our housekeeper I'd be right back."

"It will only take a minute," Mrs. Breen urged. "I want you to meet my husband—and there's Ted."

The woman had caught a glimpse of a tall young man as he moved hastily around the back side of the trailer.

"Oh, Ted!" she called shrilly. "Come here and meet Rhoda's friends!"

"Don't bother about it, Mrs. Breen," Rhoda said in embarrassment. "Please."

"Nonsense!" the woman replied, and called again. "Ted! Come here, I say!"

With obvious reluctance, the young man approached the automobile. He was tall and slim with many of Rhoda's facial features. Penny felt certain that she had seen him before, yet for a minute she could not think where.

"How are you?" the young man responded briefly as he was presented to the two girls.

"Ted found a little work to do today," Mrs. Breen resumed proudly. "Just a few minutes ago he brought home a nice plump chicken. We're having it for dinner!"

Ted gazed over the woman's head, straight at his sister. Seeing the look which passed between them, Penny suddenly knew where she had seen the young man. Mrs. Breen's remark had given her the required clue. Unquestionably, Ted Wiegand was the one who had stolen the chicken from the old stonecutter!

CHAPTER 3 - CHICKEN DINNER

The discovery that Rhoda's brother had stolen food was disconcerting to Penny. Saying good-bye to Mrs. Breen, she prepared to drive away from the trailer camp.

"Oh, you can't go so soon," the woman protested. "You must stay for dinner. We're having chicken and there's plenty for everybody!"

"Really we can't remain," Penny declined. "Louise and I both are expected at home."

"You're just afraid you'll put me to a little trouble," Mrs. Breen laughed, swinging open the car door and tugging at Penny's hand. "You have to stay."

Taking a cue from their mother, the three young children surrounded the girls, fairly forcing them toward the trailer. Ted immediately started in the opposite direction.

"You come back here, Ted Wiegand!" Mrs. Breen called in a loud voice.

"I don't want any dinner, Mom."

"I know better," Mrs. Breen contradicted cheerfully. "You're just bashful because we're having two pretty girls visit us. You stay and eat your victuals like you always do, or I'll box your ears."

"Okay," Ted agreed, glancing at Rhoda again. "It's no use arguing with you, Mom."

Neither Penny nor Louise wished to remain for dinner, yet they knew of no way to avoid it without offending Mrs. Breen. Briskly the woman herded them inside the trailer.

"It's nice, isn't it?" she asked proudly. "We have a little refrigerator and a good stove and a sink. We're a bit crowded, but that only makes it more jolly."

A man in shirt sleeves lay on one of the day beds, reading a newspaper.

"Meet my husband," Mrs. Breen said as an afterthought. "Get up, Pop!" she ordered. "Don't you have any manners?"

The man amiably swung his feet to the floor, grinning at Penny and Louise.

"I ain't been very well lately," he said, as if feeling that the situation required an explanation. "The Doc tells me to take it easy."

"That was twenty years ago," Mrs. Breen contributed, an edge to her voice. "Pop's been resting ever since. But we get along."

Rhoda and Ted, who had followed the others into the trailer, were acutely embarrassed by the remark. Penny hastily changed the subject to a less personal one by pretending to show an interest in a book which lay on the table.

"Oh, that belongs to Rhoda," Mrs. Breen responded carelessly. "She brought it from the library. Ted and Rhoda always have their noses in a book. They're my adopted children, you know."

"Mr. and Mrs. Breen have been very kind to us," Rhoda said quietly.

"Stuff and nonsense!" Mrs. Breen retorted. "You've more than earned your keep. Well, if you'll excuse me now, I'll dish up dinner."

Penny and Louise wondered how so many persons could be fed in such a small space, especially as the dinette table accommodated only six. Mrs. Breen solved the problem by giving each of the three small children a plate of food and sending them outdoors.

"Now we can eat in peace," she remarked, squeezing her ample body beneath the edge of the low, anchored table. "It's a little crowded, but we can all get in here."

"I'll take my plate outside," Ted offered.

"No, you stay right here," Mrs. Breen reproved. "I never did see such a bashful boy! Isn't he the limit?"

CHAPTER 3 - CHICKEN DINNER

Having arranged everything to her satisfaction, she began to dish up generous helpings of chicken and potato. The food had an appetizing odor and looked well cooked, but save for a pot of tea, there was nothing else.

"We're having quite a banquet tonight," Pop Breen remarked appreciatively. "I'll take a drumstick, Ma, if there ain't no one else wantin' it."

"You'll take what you get," his wife retorted, slapping the drumstick onto Penny's plate.

Louise and Penny made a pretense of eating, finding the food much better than they had expected. Neither Ted nor Rhoda seemed hungry, and Mrs. Breen immediately called attention to their lack of appetite.

"Why, Ted! What's the matter you're not eating? Are you sick?"

The boy shook his head and got to his feet.

"I'm not hungry, Mom," he mumbled. "Excuse me, please. I have a date with a fellow at Riverview, and I have to hurry."

Before Mrs. Breen could detain him, he left the trailer.

"I can't understand that boy any more," she observed with a sad shake of her head. "He hasn't been himself lately."

The younger members of the Breen family quite made up for Ted and Rhoda's lack of appetite. Time and again they came to the table to have their plates refilled, until all that remained of the chicken was a few bones.

Penny and Louise felt quite certain that Rhoda realized what her brother had done and was deeply humiliated by his thievery. To spare the girl further embarrassment, they declared that they must leave. However, as they were presenting their excuses, there was a loud rap on the door of the trailer. Peering from the curtained window, Mrs. Breen immediately lost her jovial manner.

"*He's* here again," she whispered. "What are we going to tell him, Pop?"

"Just give him the old stall," her husband suggested, undisturbed.

Reluctantly, Mrs. Breen went to open the door. Without waiting for an invitation, a well-dressed man of middle age entered the trailer. Penny immediately recognized him as Jay Franklin, who owned the Dorset Tourist Camp. "Good afternoon, Mrs. Breen," he began, his manner falsely cheerful. "I suppose you know why I am here again?"

"About the rent?"

"Precisely." Mr. Franklin consulted a small booklet. "You are behind one full month in your payments, as of course you must be aware. The amount totals eight dollars."

"Pop, pay the gentleman," Mrs. Breen commanded.

"Well, now, I ain't got that much on me," her husband rejoined, responding to his cue. "If you'll drop around in a day or two, Mr. Franklin—"

"You've been stalling for weeks! Either pay or your electric power will be cut off!"

"Oh, Mr. Franklin," pleaded Mrs. Breen, "you can't do that to us. Why, with our refrigerator on the blink, the milk will sour. And I got three little children."

The man regarded her with cold dislike.

"I am not interested in your personal problems, Mrs. Breen," he said, delivering his ultimatum. "Either settle your bill in full by tomorrow morning, or move on!"

CHAPTER 4 - A RECORD ON ROCK

"What'll we do?" Mrs. Breen murmured, gazing despairingly at her husband. "Where will we get the money?"

Penny stepped forward into Jay Franklin's range of vision. Observing her for the first time, he politely doffed his hat, a courtesy he had not bestowed upon the Breens.

"Mr. Franklin, have you a cheque book?" she inquired.

"Yes, I have," he responded with alacrity.

"Then I'll write a cheque for the eight dollars if that will be satisfactory," Penny offered. "The Breens are friends of mine."

"That will settle the bill in full, Miss Parker."

Whipping a fountain pen from his pocket, he offered it to her.

"Penny, we can't allow you to assume our debts," Rhoda protested. "Please don't—"

"Now Rhoda, it's only a loan to tide us over for a few days," Mrs. Breen interposed. "Ted will get a job and then we'll be able to pay it back."

Penny wrote out the cheque, and cutting short the profuse thanks of the Breens, declared that she and Louise must return home at once.

"Driving into Riverview?" Mr. Franklin inquired. "My car is in the garage, and I'll appreciate a lift to town."

"We'll be glad to take you, Mr. Franklin," Penny responded, but without enthusiasm.

Enroute to Riverview he endeavored to make himself an agreeable conversationalist.

"So the Breens are friends of yours?" he remarked casually.

"Well, not exactly," Penny corrected. "I met Rhoda at school and visited her for the first time today. I couldn't help feeling sorry for the family."

"They're a no-good lot. The old man never works, and the boy either can't or won't get a job."

"Do you have many such families, Mr. Franklin?"

"Oh, now and then. But I weed them out as fast as I can. One can't be soft and manage a tourist camp, you know."

Penny smiled, thinking that no person ever would accuse Mr. Franklin of being "soft." He had the reputation of ruthless devotion to his own interests. Changing the subject, she remarked that Mrs. Marborough had returned to the city to take up residence at Rose Acres.

"Is that so?" Mr. Franklin inquired, showing interest in the information. "Will she recondition the house?"

Penny replied that she had no knowledge of the widow's future plans.

"No doubt Mrs. Marborough has returned to sell the property," Mr. Franklin said musingly. "I should like to buy that place if it goes for a fair price. I could make money by remodeling it into a tourist home."

"It would be a pity to turn such a lovely place into a roadside hotel," Louise remarked disapprovingly. "Penny and I hope that someday it will be restored as it was in the old days."

"There would be no profit in it as a residence," Mr. Franklin returned. "The house is located on a main road though, and as a tourist hotel, should pay."

Conversation languished, and a few minutes later, Penny dropped the man at his own home. Although she refrained from speaking of it to Louise, she neither liked nor trusted Jay Franklin. While it had been his right to eject the Breens from the tourist camp for non-payment of rent, she felt that he could have afforded to be more

CHAPTER 4 - A RECORD ON ROCK

generous. She did not regret the impulse which had caused her to settle the debt even though it meant that she must deprive herself of a few luxuries.

After leaving Louise at the Sidell house, Penny drove on home. Entering the living room, she greeted her father who had arrived from the newspaper office only a moment before. A late edition of the Star lay on the table, and she glanced carelessly at it, inquiring: "What's new, Dad?"

"Nothing worthy of mention," Mr. Parker returned.

Sinking down on the davenport, Penny scanned the front page. Immediately her attention was drawn to a brief item which appeared in an inconspicuous bottom corner.

"Here's something!" she exclaimed. "Why, how strange!"

"What is, Penny?"

"It says in this story that a big rock has been found on the farm of Carl Gleason! The stone bears writing thought to be of Elizabethan origin!"

"Let me see that paper," Mr. Parker said, striding across the room. "I didn't know any such story was used."

With obvious displeasure, the editor read the brief item which Penny indicated. Only twenty lines in length, it stated that a stone bearing both Elizabethan and Indian carving had been found on the nearby farm.

"I don't know how this item got past City Editor DeWitt," Mr. Parker declared. "It has all the earmarks of a hoax! You didn't by chance write it, Penny?"

"I certainly did not."

"It reads a little like a Jerry Livingston story," Mr. Parker said, glancing at the item a second time.

Going to a telephone he called first the *Star* office and then the home of the reporter, Jerry Livingston. After talking with the young man several minutes, he finally hung up the receiver.

"What did he say?" Penny asked curiously.

"Jerry wrote the story, and says it came from a reliable source. He's coming over here to talk to me about it."

Within ten minutes the reporter arrived at the Parker home. Penny loitered in the living room to hear the conversation. Jerry long had been a particular friend of hers and she hoped that her father would not reprimand him for any mistake he might have made.

"Have a chair," Mr. Parker greeted the young man cordially. "Now tell me where you got hold of that story."

"Straight from the farmer, Carl Gleason," Jerry responded. "The stone was dug up on his farm early this morning."

"Did you see it yourself?"

"Not yet. It was hauled to the Museum of Natural Science. Thought I'd drop around there on my way home and look it over."

"I wish you would," requested the editor. "While the stone may be an authentic one, I have a deep suspicion someone is trying to pull a fast trick."

"I'm sorry if I've made a boner, Chief."

"Oh, I'm not blaming you," Mr. Parker assured him. "If the story is a fake, it was up to DeWitt to question it at the desk. Better look at the rock though, before you write any more about it."

As Jerry arose to leave, Penny jumped up from her own chair.

"I'd like to see that stone too!" she declared. "Jerry, do you mind if I go along with you?"

"Glad to have you," he said heartily.

Before Penny could get her hat and coat, Mrs. Maud Weems, the Parker housekeeper, appeared in the doorway to announce dinner. She was a stout, pleasant woman of middle-age and had looked after Penny since Mrs. Parker's death many years before.

"Penny, where are you going now?" she asked, her voice disclosing mild disapproval.

"Only over to the museum."

"You've not had your dinner."

"Oh, yes, I have," Penny laughed. "I dined on chicken at the Dorset Tourist Camp. I'll be home in an hour or so."

Jerking coat and hat from the hall closet, she fled from the house before Mrs. Weems could offer further objections. Jerry made a more ceremonious departure, joining Penny on the front porch.

At the curb stood the reporter's mud-splattered coupe. The interior was only slightly less dirty, and before getting in, Penny industriously brushed off the seat.

"Tell me all about this interesting stone which was found at the Gleason farm," she commanded, as the car started down the street.

"Nothing to tell except what was in the paper," Jerry shrugged. "The rock has some writing on it, supposedly similar to early Elizabethan script. And there are a few Indian characters."

"How could such a stone turn up at Riverview?"

"Carl Gleason found it while he was plowing a field. Apparently, it had been in the ground for many years."

"I should think so if it bears Elizabethan writing!" Penny laughed. "Why, that would date it practically in Shakespeare's time!"

"It's written in the style used by the earliest settlers of this country," Jerry said defensively. "You know, before we had radios and automobiles and things, this land of ours was occupied by Indians."

"Do tell!" Penny teased.

"The natives camped all along the river, and there may have been an early English settlement here. So it's perfectly possible that such a stone could be found."

"Anyway, I am curious to see it," Penny replied.

The car drew up before a large stone building with Doric columns. Climbing a long series of steps to the front door, Penny and Jerry entered the museum through a turnstile.

"I want to see the curator, Mr. Kaleman," the reporter remarked, turning toward a private office near the entrance. "I'll be with you in a minute."

While waiting, Penny wandered slowly about, inspecting the various display cases. She was admiring the huge skeleton of a dinosaur when Jerry returned, followed by an elderly man who wore spectacles. The reporter introduced the curator, who began to talk enthusiastically of the ancient stone which had been delivered to the museum that afternoon.

"I shall be very glad to show it to you," he said, leading the way down a long corridor. "For the present, pending investigation, we have it stored in the basement."

"What's the verdict?" Jerry inquired. "Do museum authorities consider the writing authentic?"

"I should not wish to be quoted," Mr. Kaleman prefaced his little speech. "However, an initial inspection has led us to believe that the stone bears ancient writings. You understand that it will take exhaustive study before the museum would venture to state this as a fact."

"The stone couldn't have been faked?" Penny asked thoughtfully.

"Always that is a possibility," Mr. Kaleman acknowledged as he unlocked the door of a basement room. "However, the stone has weathered evenly, it appears to have been buried many years, and there are other signs which point to the authenticity of the writing."

The curator switched on an electric light which disclosed a room cluttered with miscellaneous objects. There were empty mummy cases, boxes of excelsior, and various stuffed animals. At the rear of the room was a large rust colored stone which might have weighed a quarter of a ton.

"Here it is," Mr. Kaleman declared, giving the rock an affectionate pat. "Notice the uniform coloring throughout. And note the lettering chiseled on the surface. You will see that the grooves do not differ appreciably from the remainder of the stone as would be the case if the lettering were of recent date. It is my belief—don't quote me, of course—that this writing may open a new and fascinating page of history."

Penny bent to inspect the crude writing. "'Here laeth Ananias'" she read slowly aloud. "Why, that might be a joke! Wasn't Ananias a dreadful prevaricator?"

"Ananias was a common name in the early days," Mr. Kaleman said, displeased by the remark. "Now on the underside of this stone which you cannot see, there appears part of a quaint message which begins: 'Soon after you goe for Englande we came hither.'"

"What does it mean?" questioned Jerry.

"This is only my theory, you understand. I believe the message may have been written by an early settler and left for someone who had gone to England but expected to return. The writing breaks off, suggesting that it may have been continued on another stone."

"In that case, similar rocks may be found near here," Jerry said thoughtfully.

CHAPTER 4 - A RECORD ON ROCK

"It is an interesting possibility. On the underside, this stone also contains a number of Indian characters, no doubt added at a later date. So far we have not been able to decipher them."

"Just why does the stone have historical value?" Penny interposed.

"Because there never was any proof that English colonists settled in this part of the state," Mr. Kaleman explained. "If we could prove such were the case, our contribution to history would be a vital one."

Penny and Jerry asked many other questions, and finally left the museum. Both had been impressed not only with the huge stone but by the curator's sincere manner.

"Mr. Kaleman certainly believes the writing is genuine," Penny declared thoughtfully. "All the same, anyone knows a carved rock can be made to look very ancient. And that name Ananias makes me wonder."

"The Chief may be right about it being a fake," Jerry returned. "But if it is, who planted the stone on Gleason's farm? And who would go to so much unnecessary work just to play a joke?"

Frowning, the reporter started to cross the street just as an automobile bearing Texas license plates went past, close to the curb. As Jerry leaped backwards to safety, the automobile halted. Two men occupied the front seat, and the driver, a well-dressed man of fifty, leaned from the window.

"Excuse me, sir," he said, addressing Jerry, "we're trying to locate a boy named Ted Wiegand. He and his sister may be living with a family by the name of Breen. Could you tell me how to find them?"

"Sorry, but I can't," Jerry answered. "I never heard either of the names."

"Why, I know both Ted and Rhoda Wiegand," Penny interposed quickly. "They're living at the Dorset Tourist Camp."

"How do we get there?" the driver of the Texas car inquired.

Jerry provided the requested information. Thanking him, the stranger and his companion drove on down the street.

"I wonder who they can be?" Penny speculated, staring after the car. "And why did they come all the way from Texas to see Rhoda and Ted?"

"Friends of yours?" Jerry asked carelessly.

"I like Rhoda very much. Ted seems to be a rather questionable character. I wonder—"

"You wonder what?" the reporter prompted, helping Penny into the parked automobile.

"It just came to me, Jerry!" she answered gravely. "Those men may be officers from Texas sent here to arrest Ted for something he's done! I never meant to set them on his trail, but I may be responsible for his arrest!"

CHAPTER 5 - STRANGERS FROM TEXAS

Jerry smiled broadly as he edged the car from its parking space by the curb.

"You certainly have a vivid imagination, Penny," he accused. "Those two men didn't look like plain-clothes men to me. Anyway, if Ted Wiegand had committed an illegal act, wouldn't it be your duty to turn him over to the authorities?"

"I suppose so," Penny admitted unwillingly. "Ted stole one of Truman Crocker's chickens today. It was a dreadful thing to do, but in a way you couldn't blame him too much. I'm sure the Breens needed food."

"Stealing is stealing. I don't know the lad, but if a fellow is crooked in small things, he's usually dishonest otherwise as well. Speaking of Truman Crocker, he was the man who hauled the big rock to the museum."

"Was he?" Penny inquired, not particularly interested in the information. "I understand he does a great deal of rock hauling around Riverview. A queer fellow."

Becoming absorbed in her own thoughts, Penny had little to say until the car drew up in front of the Parker home.

"Won't you come in?" she invited Jerry as she alighted.

"Can't tonight," he declined regretfully. "I have a date at a bowling alley."

Mr. Parker had been called downtown to attend a meeting, Penny discovered upon entering the house. Unable to tell him of her trip to the museum, she tried to interest Mrs. Weems in the story. However, the housekeeper, who was eager to start for a moving-picture theatre, soon cut her short.

"Excuse me, Penny, but I really must be leaving or I'll be late," she apologized, putting on her hat.

"I thought you were interested in mystery, Mrs. Weems."

"Mystery, yes," smiled the housekeeper. "To tell you the truth, though, I can't become very excited over an old stone, no matter what's written on it."

After Mrs. Weems had gone, Penny was left alone in the big house. She sat down to read a book but soon laid it aside. To pass the time, she thought she would make a batch of fudge. But, no sooner had she mixed the sugar and chocolate together than it seemed like a useless occupation, so she set aside the pan for Mrs. Weems to finish upon her return from the movie.

"I know what I'll do!" she thought suddenly. "I wonder why I didn't think of it sooner?"

Hastening to the telephone she called her chum, Louise, asking her to come over at once.

"What's up?" the other inquired curiously.

"We're going to carry out a philanthropic enterprise, Lou! I'll tell you about it when you get here!"

"One of these days you'll choke on some of those big words," Louise grumbled. "All right, I'll come."

Fifteen minutes later she arrived at the Parker home to find Penny, garbed in an apron, working industriously in the kitchen.

"Say, what is this?" Louise demanded suspiciously. "If you tricked me into helping you with the dishes, I'm going straight home!"

"Oh, relax," Penny laughed. "The dishes were done hours ago. We're going to help out the Old Wishing Well."

"I wish you would explain what you mean."

"It's this way, Lou. The Breens are as poor as church mice, and they need food. At the Marborough place this afternoon Rhoda made a wish—that her family would have more to eat. Well, it's up to us to make that wish come true."

"You're preparing a basket of food to take out to the camp?"

CHAPTER 5 - STRANGERS FROM TEXAS

"That's the general idea. We can leave it on the doorstep of the trailer and slip away without revealing our identity."

"Why, your idea is a splendid one!" Louise suddenly approved. "Of course Mrs. Weems said it would be all right to fix the basket of food?"

"Oh, she won't mind. I know she would want me to do it if she were here."

Swinging open the porcelain door of the ice box, Penny peered into the illuminated shelves. The refrigerator was unusually well stocked, for Mrs. Weems had baked that day in anticipation of week-end appetites. Without hesitation, Penny handed out a meat loaf, a plum pudding, bunches of radishes, scrubbed carrots, celery, and a dozen fresh eggs.

"Dash down to the basement and get some canned goods from the supply shelf," she instructed Louise briskly. "We ought to have jelly too, and a sample of Mrs. Weems' strawberry preserves."

"You do the dashing, if you don't mind," her chum demurred. "I prefer not to become too deeply involved in this affair."

"Oh, Mrs. Weems won't care—not a bit," Penny returned as she started for the basement. "She's the most charitable person in the world."

In a minute she was back, her arms laden with heavy canned goods. Finding a market basket in the garage, the girls packed the food, wrapping perishables carefully in waxed paper.

"There! We can't crowd another thing into the basket," Penny declared at last.

"The ice-box is as bare as Mother Hubbard's cupboard," Louise rejoined. "What will the Parker family eat tomorrow?"

"Oh, Mrs. Weems can buy more. She'll be a good sport about it, I know."

With no misgivings, Penny carried the heavy basket to the garage and loaded it into the car. Discovering that the gasoline gauge registered low, she skillfully siphoned an extra two gallons from her father's car, and then announced that she was ready to go.

"Don't you ever patronize a filling station?" Louise inquired as her chum headed the automobile down the street.

"Oh, now and then," Penny grinned. "After that cheque I wrote for the Breens' rent, I'm feeling rather poor. Dad is much better able to buy gasoline than I, and he won't begrudge me a couple of gallons."

"You certainly have your family well trained," Louise sighed. "I wish I knew how you get by with it."

The car toured through Riverview and presently arrived at the entrance of the Dorset Tourist Camp. An attendant stopped the girls, but allowed them to drive on when he learned that they did not wish to make reservations for a cabin. Penny drew up not far from where the Breen trailer was parked.

"A light is still burning there," Louise observed. "We'll have to be careful if we don't want to be seen."

As Penny lifted the heavy basket from the rear compartment of the automobile, she noticed another car standing not far away. It looked somewhat familiar and in studying it more intently she noted the license plate.

"Why, it's that same Texas car!" she exclaimed. "Those men must still be here."

"What car? What men?"

"Oh, this evening two strangers inquired the way to this tourist camp," Penny explained briefly. "They said they were looking for Ted Wiegand."

"Friends of his?"

"I don't know who they were or what they wanted. It struck me as odd though, that they would come from such a long distance."

"Whoever they are, they must be at the trailer now," Louise said after a moment. "Should we leave the basket on the doorstep or wait until they've gone?"

"We can't very well wait, Lou. They might decide to stay half the night."

Carrying the basket between them, the girls moved noiselessly toward the trailer. Blinds had not been drawn and they could see Mr. and Mrs. Breen, Rhoda, and the two men seated at the table carrying on an animated discussion.

"I wish I knew why those Texas fellows came here," Penny remarked thoughtfully. "If we wanted to find out—"

"I'll not listen at any window!" Louise cut her short.

"I was merely thinking we *could*. Of course, I never would do such an ill-bred thing."

"I'm sure you won't," Louise replied with emphasis. "For a very good reason too! I shall take you away before temptation sways you."

Depositing the basket of food on the trailer doorstep, she forcibly pulled Penny to the waiting car.

CHAPTER 6 - A WISH FULFILLED

At school the next morning, both Penny and Louise eagerly awaited some indication from Rhoda Wiegand that the basket of food had been discovered by the Breen family. The girl had failed to appear at five minutes to nine, and they began to wonder if she intended to absent herself from classes.

"Oh, by the way, what did Mrs. Weems say about last night's little episode?" Louise asked her chum curiously.

"Entirely too much," Penny sighed. "She sent me three thousand words on the budget problems of a housekeeper! If you don't mind, let's allow the subject to rest in peace."

It was time for the final school bell, and the two girls started toward the assembly room. Just then Rhoda, breathless from hurrying, came into the hallway. Her eyes sparkled and obviously, she was rather excited.

"Girls, something strange happened last night!" she greeted Penny and Louise. "You'll never guess!"

"We couldn't possibly," Louise said soberly.

"Two baskets of food were left at the door of our trailer! It's silly to say it, I know, but it seems as if my wish at the old well must have had something to do with it."

"Did you say *two* baskets of food were left?" Louise questioned, gazing sideways at Penny.

"Yes, one came early in the evening. Then this morning when Mrs. Breen opened the door, she found still another. You don't suppose any of the members of the Palette Club did it, do you? We shouldn't like to accept charity—"

"I'll ask the girls if you want me to," Penny offered hastily. "If any of them did, nothing was said about it to me."

"Maybe the old well granted your wish, Rhoda," Louise added. "You know, folks say it has a reputation for doing good deeds."

The ringing of the school bell brought the conversation to an abrupt end. However, as Louise and Penny went to their seats, the latter whispered:

"Who do you suppose left that second basket on the Breen doorstep?"

"Probably one of the other club members had the same idea you did," Louise responded. "Anyway, the Breens will be well fed for a few days at least."

At recess Penny made a point of questioning every member of the Palette Club. Not one of the girls would admit having carried the basket to the trailer park, but all were agreed that Rhoda should be invited to join the art organization. Without exception, they liked the girl after becoming acquainted with her.

"The mystery deepens," Penny commented to Louise as they wandered, arm in arm, about the school yard. "If no one in the Palette Club prepared the basket, then who did do it?"

"I guess we'll have to attribute it to the old wishing well after all," Louise chuckled. "Let me see your ears, my pet."

"What for? Don't you think I ever wash them?"

"I merely want to see if they've grown since we were at the Marborough place. Why, goodness me, I believe they are larger!"

Before Penny could think of a suitable retort, Rhoda joined the girls. Curious to learn more of the two Texas men who had arrived in Riverview, they gave the newcomer every opportunity to speak of it. As she remained uncommunicative, Penny brought up the subject by mentioning that two strangers had asked her how they might locate the trailer family.

"Yes, they found us all right," Rhoda replied briefly. "Mr. Coaten came to see Ted."

"An old friend, I suppose," Louise remarked.

"Not exactly. I can't figure out just why he did come here."

Rhoda frowned and lapsed into silence. Penny and Louise did not question her further, and a few minutes later recess ended.

The affairs of the Breen family concerned Penny only slightly. Although she kept wondering why Mr. Coaten and his companion were in Riverview, she gave far more thought to the stone which had been dug up on the Gleason farm. Directly after school she proposed to Louise that they drive into the country and interview the farmer.

"I don't mind the trip," her chum said, "but why are you so interested in an old rock?"

"Oh, Dad thinks the whole story may be a hoax. I'd like to learn the truth, if I can."

Mindful that in the past Penny had brought the *Riverview Star* many an important "scoop," Louise was very willing to accompany her on the trip. Four-thirty found the two girls at the Gleason farm in conversation with the old farmer.

"I've been pestered to death ever since that rock was found here," he told them somewhat crossly. "There's nothing new to tell. I was plowing in the south field back of the barn, when I turned it up. I didn't pay much attention until Jay Franklin come along and said the writing on it might interest the museum folks. He gave me a couple of dollars, and paid to have old man Crocker haul it to town."

"I didn't know Jay Franklin had an interest in the stone," Penny remarked. "You say he gave you two dollars for it?"

"That's right," the farmer nodded. "I was glad to have the rock hauled off the place."

Satisfied that they could learn no more, Penny and Louise inspected the hole from which the stone had been removed, and then drove toward Riverview.

"Mr. Gleason seemed honest enough," Penny commented thoughtfully. "If the rock was deliberately planted on his farm I don't believe he had anything to do with it."

"He isn't sufficiently clever to plan and carry out an idea like that," Louise added. "Maybe the writing on the rock is genuine."

"The curator of the museum thinks it may be. All the same, I'll stack Dad's opinion against them all."

The car approached the old Marborough place, and Penny deliberately slowed down. To the surprise of the girls, they observed two automobiles parked in front of the property.

"It looks as if Mrs. Marborough has guests today," Penny commented. "Shall we stop and say hello?"

"Well, I don't know," Louise replied doubtfully as the car drew up at the edge of the road. "We're not really acquainted with her, and with others there—"

"They're leaving now," Penny said, jerking her head to draw attention to a group of ladies coming down the walk toward the street.

The visitors all were known to the two girls as women prominent in Riverview club circles. Mrs. Buckmyer, a stout, pompous lady who led the procession, was speaking to the others in an agitated voice.

"In all my life I never was treated with less courtesy! Mrs. Marborough at least might have invited us into her house!"

"I always understood that she was a queer person," contributed another, "but one naturally would expect better manners from a Marborough."

"I shouldn't object to her manners if only she would allow the Pilgrimage Committee the use of her house," added a third member of the group. "What a pity that she refuses to consider opening it during the Festival Week."

Still chattering indignantly, the women entered their separate cars and drove away.

"What did you make of that?" Louise asked in perplexity.

"Apparently Mrs. Marborough gave them the brush off," Penny chuckled. "I know Mrs. Buckmyer heads the Pilgrimage Committee."

"What's that?"

"Haven't you heard about it, Louise? A group of club women decided to raise money by conducting a tour of old houses. In this community there are a number of places which date back over a hundred years."

"And people will pay money to see them?"

CHAPTER 6 - A WISH FULFILLED

"That's the general idea. Festival Week has been set for the twenty-sixth of this month. During a five-day period the various homes are open, gardens will be on display, and costume parties may be held at them."

"There's only one colonial house that I'd care about getting inside," Louise said. "I should like to see the interior of Rose Acres."

"Maybe we can do it now. Mrs. Marborough invited us to visit her again."

"Yes, but did she really mean it?"

"Why not find out?" Penny laughed, swinging open the car door.

Entering the grounds, the girls saw that very little had been done to the property since their last visit. A half-hearted attempt had been made to rake one side of the lawn and an overgrown lilac bush had been mercilessly mutilated. Shutters on the house remained closed and the entire place had a gloomy, deserted appearance.

Penny rapped on the door. Evidently Mrs. Marborough had noted the approach of the two girls for she responded to their knock immediately.

"Good afternoon," Penny began, "we were driving by and thought we would drop in to see you again."

"How nice of you," Mrs. Marborough smiled. "Look over the garden as much as you please."

"The garden—" Louise faltered, gazing quickly at Penny.

"Or make wishes at the well," Mrs. Marborough went on hastily. "Go anywhere you like, and I'll join you as soon as I get a wrap."

The door closed gently in their faces.

"Who wants to see a tangle of weeds?" Louise demanded in a whisper. "Why didn't Mrs. Marborough invite us into the house?"

"Why indeed?" echoed Penny, frowning thoughtfully. "There can be but one reason! She has a dark secret which she is trying to hide from the world!"

CHAPTER 7 - PENNY'S DISCOVERY

"Hiding a secret, my eye!" laughed Louise. "Penny Parker, sometimes I think that every person in Riverview suggests mystery and intrigue to you!"

"Then you explain why Mrs. Marborough doesn't invite us into her house!" Penny challenged her chum. "And why did she turn the members of the Pilgrimage Committee away?"

"Oh, probably the place isn't fixed up the way she wants it yet."

"That's no reason. No, she has a different one than that, Lou, and I'm curious to learn what it is."

"You're always curious," Louise teased, taking Penny by the arm. "Come along. Let's get a drink at the well."

While the girls were lowering the bucket into the bricked cavern, Mrs. Marborough joined them, a woolen shawl thrown over her head and shoulders.

"I've not had time to get much work done yet," she apologized. "I really must hire a man to clean up the grounds."

"Then you have decided to make your home here?" Louise inquired eagerly.

"For the present, I may. Much depends upon how a certain project turns out."

Penny and Louise waited hopefully, but Mrs. Marborough said no more. Changing the subject, she inquired about Rhoda Wiegand and the other members of the Palette Club.

"I like young people," she declared brightly. "Do tell your friends to come to Rose Acres whenever they wish."

"A rather strange thing occurred yesterday," Penny said suddenly. "Rhoda made a wish here at the well, and it came true."

"What was the wish?" the old lady inquired with curiosity.

"That the people with whom she lives might have more food. Two baskets were left at the trailer camp. Louise and I were responsible for one of them, but we can't account for the other."

"Very interesting," Mrs. Marborough commented. "In years past, a great many wishes which were made here, apparently came true. So I can't say that I am surprised."

"To what do you attribute it?" Louise asked quickly.

"Chance perhaps," Mrs. Marborough smiled. "One cannot explain such things."

A chill, penetrating wind blew from the direction of the river. Shivering, Louise drew her jacket collar closer about her neck, remarking rather pointedly that the weather was turning colder. Even then, Mrs. Marborough did not suggest that the girls enter the house. A moment later, however, she excused herself and went inside, leaving them alone in the garden.

"It does seem odd that she acts so secretive," Louise commented. "I'm inclined to agree with members of the Pilgrimage Committee that her manners aren't the best."

"Perhaps you'll finally decide that I am right!" Penny said triumphantly. "Take my word for it, there's something inside the house she doesn't want anyone to see!"

Louise started slowly toward the road, only to pause as her chum proposed that they walk to the river and call upon Truman Crocker, the stonecutter.

"You intend to tell him who stole his chicken?" Louise asked in surprise.

Penny shook her head. "No, I'll let him discover it for himself. I want to talk to him about that big rock he hauled to the museum."

CHAPTER 7 - PENNY'S DISCOVERY

Louise could not imagine what useful information her chum might expect to gain, but she obediently trailed Penny through the rear yard of Rose Acres, down a sloping path which led to the river.

"I hope you know the way," she remarked dubiously as the going became more difficult, and they were forced to move slowly.

"Oh, we can't miss the cabin. Crocker's place is the only one near here," Penny responded.

The trail was a narrow one, so infrequently used that bushes and vines had overgrown it in many places. Finally emerging on an open hillside, the girls were able to gaze down upon the winding river. Recent rains had swollen it to the very edges of the banks, and from a distance Truman Crocker's shack appeared to be situated dangerously close to the water.

"Wouldn't you think he would soon be flooded out?" Louise commented, pausing to catch her breath. "I shouldn't care to live so near the river."

"Oh, the water never comes much higher," Penny rejoined. "A few years ago the city built some sort of river control system which takes care of the spill should there be any. Anyway, Crocker's place wouldn't represent much of a loss if it did wash away."

The girls regained their breath, and then started down the slope. Penny, who was leading the way, did not pay particular attention to the rutty path. Suddenly catching her shoe in a small hole, she tripped and fell sideways.

"Ooh, my arm!" she squealed. "I struck it on a big rock!"

Louise helped Penny to her feet, brushing dirt from the girl's skirt.

"You've ripped your stocking," she said sympathetically.

"I guess I'm lucky it wasn't my head," Penny returned gazing ruefully at the tear. "Let's sit down and rest a minute."

Seating herself on the large smooth rock, she gingerly examined a bruised place on her elbow. Louise stood beside her, plucking burs from her chum's sweater.

"I'm all right now," Penny said a moment later, getting up. "Why, Lou! Do you see what I've been sitting on?"

"A rock, my pet."

"A stone that looks exactly like the one at the museum!" Penny cried excitedly.

"All rocks are pretty much alike, aren't they?"

"Certainly not," Penny corrected. "There are any number of varieties. This one is quartz unless I'm mistaken and it *does* resemble the one at the museum."

"Maybe you can find some writing on it," Louise teased. "The rock only weighs two or three hundred pounds. Shall I lift it for you so you can see the under side?"

"Don't bother," Penny retorted, eagerly examining the stone. "I've already found it."

"Found what?"

"The writing! I *knew* this stone looked like the one at the museum!"

Louise was certain that her chum merely pretended to have made such an important discovery. However, as Penny continued to examine the rock in an intent, absorbed way, she decided to see for herself.

"Why, it's true!" she exclaimed incredulously. "There *is* writing on the stone!"

Carved letters, so dimmed by age and weathering processes that they scarcely remained legible, had been cut unevenly in the hard surface.

"'Went hence vnto heaven 1599,'" Louise deciphered slowly. "Why, 1599 would date this stone almost before there were known settlers in the country!"

"Almost—but not quite," replied Penny. "Historians believe there were other settlements before that date. Obviously, this is a burial stone similar to the one found on the Gleason farm."

"If it's such an old rock why was it never discovered before?"

"The stone may be a fake, but that's not for us to try to figure out. We've made an important discovery and the museum is sure to be interested!"

"Don't forget that this is on Mrs. Marborough's property," Louise reminded her chum. "We'll have to tell her about it."

Retracing their way to Rose Acres, the girls knocked on the door. Mrs. Marborough soon appeared, looking none too pleased by their unexpected return.

"What is it?" she asked, blocking the doorway so that the girls could not see beyond her into the living room.

Breathlessly, Penny told of finding the dated stone on the hillside.

"Did you know such a rock was there?" she asked eagerly.

"I've never seen any stone with writing on it," Mrs. Marborough replied. "Goodness knows there are plenty of boulders on my property though."

"Another stone similar to it was found yesterday on the Gleason farm," Louise revealed. "Do come and see it, Mrs. Marborough."

Before the widow could reply, the three were startled by heavy footsteps on the veranda. Turning, the girls saw that Jay Franklin had approached without being observed. Politely, he doffed his hat.

"Excuse me, I couldn't help overhearing your conversation," he said, bowing again to Mrs. Marborough. "You were saying something about a rock which bears writing?"

"We found it on the hillside near here," Penny explained. "It has a date—1599."

"Then it must be a mate to the stone discovered by Mr. Gleason!"

"I'm sure it is."

"Will you take me to the spot where you found it?" Mr. Franklin requested. "I am tremendously interested."

"Of course," Penny agreed, but her voice lacked enthusiasm.

She glanced toward Louise, noticing that her chum did not look particularly elated either. Neither could have explained the feeling, but Jay Franklin's arrival detracted from the pleasure of their discovery. Although ashamed of their suspicions, they were afraid that the man might try to take credit for finding the stone.

CHAPTER 8 - A MOVING LIGHT

As if to confirm the thought of the two girls, Jay Franklin remarked that should the newly discovered stone prove similar to the one found at the Gleason farm, he would immediately have it hauled to the Riverview museum.

"Isn't that for Mrs. Marborough to decide?" Penny asked dryly. "The rock is on her land, you know."

"To be sure, to be sure," Mr. Franklin nodded, brushing aside the matter of ownership as if it were of slight consequence.

Mrs. Marborough had gone into the house for a coat. Reappearing, she followed Mr. Franklin and the two girls down the trail where the huge stone lay.

"Did you ever notice this rock?" Penny questioned the mistress of Rose Acres.

"Never," she replied, "but then I doubt that I ever walked in this particular locality before."

Jay Franklin stooped to examine the carving, excitedly declaring that it was similar to the marking of the Gleason stone.

"And here are other characters!" he exclaimed, fingering well-weathered grooves which had escaped Penny's attention. "Indian picture writing!"

"How do you account for two types of carving on the same stone?" Louise inquired skeptically.

"The Indian characters may have been added at a later date," Mr. Franklin answered. "For all we know, this rock may be one of the most valuable relics ever found in our state! From the historical standpoint, of course. The stone has no commercial value."

"I imagine the museum will want it," Penny said thoughtfully.

"Exactly what I was thinking." Mr. Franklin turned toward Mrs. Marborough to ask: "You would not object to the museum having this stone?"

"Why, no," she replied. "It has no value to me."

"Then with your permission, I'll arrange to have it hauled to Riverview without delay. I'll buy the stone from you."

"The museum is entirely welcome to it."

"There is a possibility that the museum will refuse the stone. In that event you would have the expense of hauling it away again. By purchasing it outright, I can relieve you of all responsibility."

Giving Mrs. Marborough no opportunity to protest, the real estate man forced a crisp two dollar bill into her unwilling hand.

"There," he said jovially, "now I am the owner of the stone. I'll just run down to Truman Crocker's place and ask him to do the hauling for me."

The wind was cold, and after Mr. Franklin had gone, Mrs. Marborough went quickly to the house, leaving the girls to await his return.

"I knew something like this would happen," Penny declared in annoyance. "Now it's Mr. Franklin's stone, and the next thing we know, he'll claim that he discovered it too!"

Louise nodded gloomily, replying that only bad luck had brought the real estate agent to Rose Acres that particular afternoon.

"I have a sneaking notion he came here to buy Mrs. Marborough's house," Penny said musingly. "He thinks it would make a good tourist place!"

For half an hour the girls waited patiently. Neither Jay Franklin nor Truman Crocker appeared, so at last they decided it was a waste of time to remain longer. Arriving at home, shortly before the dinner hour, Penny found her father there ahead of her. To her surprise she learned that he already knew of the stone which had been discovered at Rose Acres.

"Information certainly travels fast," she commented. "I suppose Jay Franklin must have peddled the story the minute he reached town."

"Yes, he called at the *Star* office to report he had found a stone similar to the one unearthed at the Gleason farm," Mr. Parker nodded.

"*He* found it!" Penny cried indignantly. "Oh, I knew that old publicity seeker would steal all the credit! Louise and I discovered that rock, and I hope you say so in the *Star*."

"Franklin let it drop that he will offer the stone to the museum for five hundred dollars."

"Well, of all the cheap tricks!" Penny exclaimed, her indignation mounting. "He bought that rock for two dollars, pretending he meant to give it to the museum. Just wait until Mrs. Marborough hears about it!"

"Suppose you tell me the facts," Mr. Parker invited.

Penny obligingly revealed how she had found the rock by stumbling against it in descending a steep path to the river. Upon learning of the transaction which Jay Franklin had concluded with Mrs. Marborough, Mr. Parker smiled ruefully.

"Franklin always did have a special talent for making money the easy way," he declared. "I'll be sorry to see him cheat the museum."

"Dad, you don't think Mr. Kaleman will be foolish enough to pay money for that rock?" Penny asked in dismay.

"I am afraid he may. He seems convinced that the Gleason stone is a genuine specimen."

"You still believe the writing to be faked?"

"I do," Mr. Parker responded. "I'll stake my reputation upon it! I said as much to Jay Franklin today and he rather pointedly hinted that he would appreciate having me keep my theories entirely to myself."

"I guess he doesn't understand you very well," Penny smiled. "Now you'll be more determined than ever to expose the hoax—if hoax it is."

Mr. Franklin's action thoroughly annoyed her for she felt that he had deliberately deceived Mrs. Marborough. Wishing to tell Louise Sidell what he had done, she immediately telephoned her chum.

"I've learned something you'll want to hear," she disclosed. "No, I can't tell you over the 'phone. Meet me directly after dinner. We might go for a sail on the river."

The previous summer Mr. Parker had purchased a small sailboat which he kept at a summer camp on the river. Occasionally he enjoyed an outing, but work occupied so much of his time that his daughter and her friends derived far more enjoyment from the craft than he did.

Louise accepted the invitation with alacrity, and later that evening, driving to the river with Penny, listened indignantly to a colored account of how Jay Franklin would profit at the widow's expense. She agreed with her chum that he had acted dishonestly in trying to sell the stone.

"Perhaps Mrs. Marborough can claim ownership even now," she suggested thoughtfully.

"Not without a lawsuit," Penny offered as her opinion. "She sold the rock to Mr. Franklin for two dollars. Remember his final words: 'Now I am the owner of the stone.' Oh, he intended to trick her even then!"

The car turned into a private dirt road and soon halted beside a cabin of logs. A cool breeze came from the river, but the girls were prepared for it, having worn warm slack suits.

"It's a grand night to sail," Penny declared, leading the way to the boathouse. "We should get as far as the Marborough place if the breeze holds."

Launching the dinghy, Louise raised the sail while her chum took charge of the tiller. As the canvas filled, the boat heeled slightly and began to pick up speed.

"Now use discretion," Louise warned as the dinghy tilted farther and farther sideways. "It's all very well to sail on the bias, but I prefer not to get a ducking!"

During the trip up the river the girls were kept too busy to enjoy the beauty of the night. However, as the boat approached Truman Crocker's shack, the breeze suddenly died, barely providing steerage way. Holding the tiller by the pressure of her knee, Penny slumped into a half-reclining position.

"Want me to steer for awhile?" Louise inquired.

"Not until we turn and start for home. We'll have the current with us then, which will help, even if the breeze has died."

CHAPTER 8 - A MOVING LIGHT

Curiously, Penny gazed toward Truman Crocker's cabin which was entirely dark. High on the hillside stood the old Marborough mansion and there, too, no lights showed.

"Everyone seems to have gone to bed," she remarked. "It must be late."

Louise held her watch so that she could read the figures in the bright moonlight and observed that it was only a quarter past ten.

"Anyway, we should be starting for home," Penny said. "Coming about!"

Louise prepared to lower her head as the boom swung over, but to her surprise the maneuver was not carried through. Instead of turning, the dinghy kept steadily on its course.

"What's the idea?" she demanded. "Isn't there enough breeze to carry us around?"

"I was watching that light up on the hill," Penny explained.

Louise twisted in the seat to look over her shoulder.

"What light, Penny?"

"It's gone now, but I saw it an instant ago. There it is again!"

Unmistakably, both girls saw the moving light far up the hill. As they watched, it seemed to approach the dark Marborough house, and then receded.

"Probably someone with a lantern," Louise remarked indifferently.

"But why should anyone be prowling about Mrs. Marborough's place at this hour?"

"It does seem strange."

Deliberately, Penny steered the sailboat toward the beach.

"I think we should investigate," she declared firmly. "Everyone knows Mrs. Marborough lives alone. Someone may be attempting to break into the house!"

CHAPTER 9 - MYSTERIOUS PROWLERS

"Oh, Penny, there must be a perfectly good reason for that moving light," Louise protested as the boat grated on the sand. "You only want an excuse for going to the Marborough place!"

"Perhaps," her chum acknowledged with a grin. "Jump out and pull us in, will you please?"

"My ankles are nice and dry and I like them that way," Louise retorted. "If it's all the same, you do the jumping."

"All right, I don't mind—much." With a laugh, Penny gingerly stepped from the dinghy into shallow water. She pulled the boat farther up onto the shore so that her chum was able to climb out without wetting her feet. Together they furled the sail and removed the steering apparatus which they hid in the nearby bushes.

"I don't see a light now," Louise protested after their various tasks had been completed. "Must we climb that steep hill?"

"We must," Penny declared firmly, taking her by the hand. "Something may be wrong at Mrs. Marborough's and we ought to find out about it."

"You just love to investigate things," Louise accused. "You know as well as I do that there's not likely to be anything amiss."

"Someone may be prowling about the grounds! At any rate, my feet are cramped from sitting so long in the boat. We need exercise."

Finding a trail, the girls climbed it until they were within a hundred yards of the Marborough mansion. Emerging from behind a clump of lilac bushes they suddenly obtained an unobstructed view of the yard.

"There's the light!" Penny whispered. "See! By the wishing well!"

To their knowledge the girls had made no unusual sound. Yet, apparently the person who prowled in the yard was aware of their approach. As they watched, the lantern was extinguished. Simultaneously, the moon, which had been so bright, moved under a dark cloud.

For several seconds the girls could not see the shadowy figure by the well. When the moon again emerged from behind its shield no one was visible in the yard.

"Whoever was there has hidden!" Penny whispered excitedly. "Louise, after we leave he may attempt to break into the house!"

"What ought we to do?"

"I think we should warn Mrs. Marborough."

"The house is dark," Louise said dubiously. "She's probably in bed."

"Wouldn't you want to know about it if someone were prowling about your premises?"

"Yes, of course—but—"

"Then come on," Penny urged, starting through the tangle of tall grass. "Mrs. Marborough should be very grateful for the warning. It may prevent a burglary."

In crossing the yard, the girls kept an alert watch of the bushes but could see no one hiding behind them. Nevertheless, they felt certain that the prowler could not have left the grounds.

Penny pounded on the rear door of the Marborough house.

"Not so loud," Louise warned nervously.

"Mrs. Marborough probably is asleep. I want to awaken her."

"You will, don't worry!"

Penny repeated the knock many times, and then was rewarded by the approach of footsteps. The door opened, and Mrs. Marborough, in lace night cap and flannel robe, peered suspiciously at the girls.

CHAPTER 9 - MYSTERIOUS PROWLERS

"What do you want?" she asked crossly. "Why do you awaken me at such an hour?"

"Don't you remember us?" Penny said, stepping into the light. "We didn't mean to startle you."

"Startle me, fiddlesticks! I am merely annoyed at being awakened from a sound slumber."

"I'm terribly sorry," Penny apologized. "We wouldn't bother you, but we saw someone with a lantern moving about in the yard. We were afraid a burglar might try to break into the house."

Mrs. Marborough gazed carefully about the yard. "I see no light," she said stiffly.

"It's gone now," Louise admitted. "As we came up from the river, we distinctly saw it near the old wishing well. Penny and I thought that whoever it was hid behind the bushes!"

"You both imagined you saw a light," the old lady said with biting emphasis. "In any case, I am not afraid of prowlers. My doors have good bolts and I'll be more than a match for anyone who tries to get inside. Thank you for your interest in my behalf, but really, I am able to look after myself."

"I'm sorry," Penny apologized meekly.

"There, your intentions were good," Mrs. Marborough said in a more kindly tone. "Better go home now and forget it. Young girls shouldn't be abroad at such a late hour."

After the door had closed, Penny and Louise slowly retraced their way to the river's edge.

"Someday I'll learn never to pay attention to your crazy ideas, Penny Parker," Louise said, breaking a lengthy silence.

"You saw the light, didn't you?"

"I thought so, but I'm not sure of anything now. It may have come from the main road."

"Sorry, but I disagree," replied Penny. "Oh, well, if Mrs. Marborough wishes to be robbed, I suppose it's her own affair."

Launching the dinghy, the girls spread their canvas, and sailing before what wind there was, presently reached the Parker camp. Penny's father awaited them by the boathouse and helped to haul in the craft.

The girls did not tell Mr. Parker of their little adventure, but the next day at school they discussed it at considerable length. During the night no attempt had been made by anyone to break into the Marborough house. Nevertheless, Penny was unwilling to dismiss the affair as one of her many "mistakes."

She was still thinking about the affair as she wandered into the library a few minutes before class time. Rhoda Wiegand sat at one of the tables and appeared troubled.

"Hello, Rhoda," Penny greeted as she searched for a book on the shelf. "You must have an examination coming up from the way you are frowning!"

"Am I?" the older girl asked, smiling. "I was thinking hard. The truth is, I am rather puzzled."

"I like puzzles, Rhoda. If you have a knotty problem, why not test it on me?"

"I doubt if you can help me with this one, Penny. Do you remember those two Texas men I told you about?"

"Yes, of course."

"I don't trust them," Rhoda said briefly. "Mr. Coaten has offered to adopt Ted and me."

"Adopt you!" Penny exclaimed. "Is that why they came here?"

"Seemingly, it is. Mr. Coaten wants to become our legal guardian. I can't understand why he should show such interest in us."

"I thought the Breens were looking after you and Ted."

"They took us in because we had no one else. We never were adopted, and the truth is, we're a financial burden."

"Is Mr. Coaten an old friend?"

"I never met him until he came to Riverview. He and his friend, Carl Addison, claim they were closely associated with my father. Neither Ted nor I ever heard Papa speak of them when he was alive."

"It does seem strange they should show such sudden interest in you," Penny commented thoughtfully. "You have no property they might wish to control?"

"Ted and I haven't a penny to our names. Papa never owned land, and what cash he had was absorbed by his last sickness."

"Then perhaps Mr. Coaten really is a friend."

"I wish I could think so, but I can't. Penny, I just feel that he has a selfish purpose behind his apparent kindness. It worries me because I can't figure it out."

"Then of course you'll not agree to the adoption?"

"I don't want to, Penny. Ted favors it, and so does Mrs. Breen. You see, Mr. Coaten has been very generous with his money." Rhoda indicated a new dress which she wore. "He gave me this. He made Mrs. Breen accept money, and he's giving Ted things too."

"If he's really a friend of the family—"

"I'll never believe that he is," Rhoda interrupted. "Never!"

The ringing of the school bell brought the conversation to an end, but all during the morning Penny thought of what the trailer-camp girl had told her. Knowing nothing concerning the characters of the two strangers, she could not judge their motives.

Another matter caused Penny considerable annoyance. The morning paper had carried a brief item about the record stone found at the Marborough mansion. From her father she had learned that instead of delivering the rock to the museum, Jay Franklin had hauled it to his own home, offering it for sale to the highest bidder. Penny felt that Mrs. Marborough should be told what had occurred, yet neither she nor Louise were eager to visit Rose Acres again.

"After last night I've had enough of that place," Louise declared as they discussed the matter. "Mrs. Marborough was very rude to us."

"Even so, we should tell her what Jay Franklin has done," Penny insisted. "Let's go right after school."

"I can't," Louise declined. "I've planned a shopping tour."

"Then, immediately after dinner," Penny persisted. "I'll stop by for you in the car."

As it developed, various duties kept both girls so busy that it was dusk before they actually drove toward Rose Acres. Louise protested that, considering what had occurred the previous night, it was much too late to call on the widow.

"Mrs. Marborough surely won't be abed before eight o'clock," Penny answered carelessly. "If the house should be dark, we can drive away without disturbing her." Louise made another protest, but knew that as usual Penny would get her way.

A few minutes later the automobile swung around a bend. Directly ahead loomed the old colonial mansion, its windows without lights.

"We may as well turn back," Louise observed.

Penny slackened speed, gazing toward the unkempt grounds.

"Louise!" she exclaimed tensely. "There it is again! The light!"

"Where?" Louise demanded in disbelief. "I don't see it."

As she spoke, the car passed beyond a tall clump of azalea bushes bordering the property. Through its branches both girls saw a light which appeared to be motionless.

"It's a lantern covered with a cloth to prevent a bright glow!" Louise discerned.

"And it's close to the wishing well!" Penny added in a thrilled voice. "Lou, there's something queer going on at this place. Let's find out about it!"

"How?" Louise asked, forgetting that she had decided to have nothing more to do with her chum's "ideas."

"Let's drive past the house and park up the road," Penny proposed with a delighted chuckle. "Then we'll steal back afoot and see what we can see!"

CHAPTER 10 - BENEATH THE FLAGSTONES

Louise offered no serious objection to Penny's proposal, for she too was curious to learn who might be prowling about the Marborough yard. Driving on down the road for a considerable distance, they parked the car just off the pavement and walked back to the estate. A high hedge bounded the front side of the Marborough property, but they were able to peer through the scanty foliage into the yard.

"It will be just our luck that the light has disappeared," Penny muttered. "I don't see it anywhere."

"I do!" Louise whispered excitedly. "Look over there by the wishing well."

In the darkness, both girls could see the faint glow of a covered lantern which had been deposited on the ground. A shadowy figure was bending over, examining some object on the ground.

"Can you tell who it is?" Penny murmured.

"Not from here. Dare we move closer?"

"Let's risk it," Penny said, and led the way through the open gateway.

Taking the precaution to keep tall bushes between themselves and the wishing well, the girls quietly stole closer. Soon they were near enough to distinguish that someone in dark clothing was kneeling on the ground, face turned away from them. Apparently the person was trying to lift one of the flagstones which formed a circular base about the covered well.

"Who can he be?" Penny whispered, pausing. "And what is he doing?"

At that moment the figure straightened, and the lantern was lifted from the ground.

"It's a *she*, not a he!" Louise observed in an undertone.

"Mrs. Marborough!"

"It looks like her from here," Louise nodded. "But what can she be doing at the well?"

Completely mystified, the girls remained motionless, watching. Mrs. Marborough raised one of the flagstones and peered beneath it.

"She's searching for something," Penny whispered. "Probably she works after dark so she won't be observed."

It was evident to both girls that the moving light which had attracted their attention the previous night had, undoubtedly, been Mrs. Marborough's lantern.

Although they now could understand the old lady's irritation at their intrusion, her actions mystified them. As they continued to watch, she pried up one stone after another, frequently resting from her labors.

"We might offer to help her," Louise proposed half-seriously.

"If we show ourselves now she'll order us never to return," Penny replied. "We want to find out what this is all about."

During the next ten minutes the girls huddled behind the friendly bush. At the end of that period, Mrs. Marborough gathered together her tools, and went wearily into the house.

"Obviously she didn't find what she was after," Penny said, coming from behind the shelter. "What do you suppose it can be?"

"Buried treasure, perhaps."

"Or possibly the family silverware hidden during the Civil War," Penny chuckled. "I'm afraid not. Mrs. Marborough lived at Rose Acres all her early years. If there had been anything valuable buried, wouldn't she have done her searching long ago?"

"If that's a question, I can't answer it," sighed Louise. "What's our next move? Home?"

"I should say not! Let's inspect the wishing well."

Penny started forward, taking pains to avoid a patch of light which came from the lower windows of the Marborough house. Even in the semi-darkness the girls were able to see that many flagstones about the well had been removed and fitted again into place.

"Just for luck I shall make a wish!" Penny announced unexpectedly, lowering the bucket into the pit.

"What will it be this time?" Louise inquired, slightly amused.

Penny drank deeply of the cool, sweet water, and tossed a token into the well.

"I wish that Rose Acres would give us a whopping big mystery!" she said gaily. "Lou, why did Mrs. Marborough return to Riverview after being away so many years?"

"This is her ancestral home."

"True, but didn't she tell us that whether or not she remains here depends upon certain conditions? Lou, she must have had a very special reason for coming, and it may be connected with this wishing well! We ought to find out about it!"

"Why?"

"Why?" Penny fairly wailed. "Oh, Lou, at times you're the most exasperating person. Here we are face to face with something baffling, and you wonder why we should interest ourselves in it!"

"I like mystery as well as you, but you know Mrs. Marborough won't care to have us interfere in her private affairs."

"Probably not," Penny conceded. "Oh, well, we can forget all about it if that's the way you feel."

"How could we learn anything without provoking Mrs. Marborough?"

"I know of no way," Penny admitted. "In fact, she'll probably be irritated when I rap on her door again."

Louise followed her chum down the path toward the house.

"Ought we bother Mrs. Marborough now?" she asked in mild protest. "She may think we have been spying on her."

"Which of course we never would consider doing," Penny chuckled.

Paying no heed to Louise, she boldly clomped across the veranda and knocked on the door. The girls did not have long to wait. In a moment Mrs. Marborough appeared, looking decidedly flustered and nervous.

"Who is it?" she asked sharply, and then recognized the girls. "Oh, I see!"

"Mrs. Marborough, do excuse us," Penny began hastily. "I've learned something which I feel sure you'll wish to hear."

"You've seen another light in the yard perhaps?" the old lady inquired, her voice slightly mocking.

Penny glanced at Louise, uncertain what to say in reply.

"There has been no one in my yard either last night or this evening," Mrs. Marborough resumed tartly. "I appreciate your interest in my welfare, but I can only repeat that I am quite capable of looking after myself."

"We came to tell you about that big rock which we discovered on the hillside," Penny interposed. "Do you care to hear what Jay Franklin did?"

Despite herself, Mrs. Marborough was interested. She hesitated, and then came outside, carefully closing the door behind her. The peculiar action was not lost upon the girls.

"It's quite chilly out tonight," Penny said significantly. "Perhaps it would be better to step inside."

"I don't mind a little fresh air," Mrs. Marborough replied. "Now what is it that you wish to tell me?"

Feeling far from comfortable, Penny explained how Jay Franklin had kept the big rock as his own property and was endeavoring to sell it to the museum at a handsome profit.

"But he told me he would give the stone to the institution!" Mrs. Marborough exclaimed indignantly. "Will you see Mr. Franklin tomorrow?"

"I can," Penny nodded.

"Then if you do, ask him to come here and see me."

As if the matter were completely settled, Mrs. Marborough started to reënter the house. She did not invite the girls to accompany her. However, sensing that they were puzzled by her lack of hospitality she said apologetically:

"I would invite you in only the house isn't fixed up yet. After everything is cleaned and straightened, you both must come to tea."

Without giving the girls an opportunity to say that they shouldn't mind a disorderly house, she gently closed the door.

CHAPTER 10 - BENEATH THE FLAGSTONES

"Well, at least Mrs. Marborough didn't slam it in our faces this time," Penny remarked cheerfully. "Lou, we're making progress!"

"Progress toward what?" Louise demanded.

"I'm not sure yet," Penny laughed as they started for their car. "All the same, I have a feeling that we're on our way!"

CHAPTER 11 - JAY FRANKLIN'S TRICKERY

"Morning, Dad," Penny greeted her father as she slid into a vacant chair at the breakfast table. "What's news and why?"

"No news." Mr. Parker lowered his paper, and folding it, devoted himself to a plate of bacon and eggs.

"Just fourteen pages of well-set type, I suppose. Isn't there anything about that big stone Lou and I found at the Marborough place?"

"Not a line. I told you the *Star* would play that yarn down."

"Why are you so convinced it's all a hoax?" Penny demanded, reaching across the table for the coffee percolator.

"Must I give you a diagram?" the publisher asked wearily. "After you've been in the newspaper business as long as I have, you don't need reasons. You sense things."

"Just like a bloodhound!" Penny teased. "How about the other papers? Aren't they carrying the story either?"

"They are," Mr. Parker admitted a bit grimly. "The *News* used a half page of pictures today and went for the story in a big way."

"I may subscribe to a rival paper just to keep posted on the latest developments," Penny teased.

"Nothing really new has come out. Jay Franklin is trying to sell the Marborough stone to the museum at a fancy price, and the institution officials are seriously considering his proposition."

"Then, in their opinion the stone is an authentic one?"

"Experts have been known to be wrong," Mr. Parker insisted. "I claim no knowledge of ancient writing, but I do have common sense. For the time being, at least, I shall continue to play down the story."

Penny finished breakfast, and before starting to school, telephoned Jay Franklin. Relaying Mrs. Marborough's message, she requested him to visit the old lady as soon as it was convenient. Somewhat to her surprise he promised that he would call at Rose Acres that afternoon.

During school, Penny kept thinking about the Marborough stone and her father's theory that the writing and symbols it bore were fakes. It occurred to her that Truman Crocker's opinion might be interesting for the old man had worked with rocks his entire life.

"Let's hike out to his shack this afternoon," she impulsively proposed to Louise Sidell.

"All right," her chum agreed. "Why not invite Rhoda too? She might enjoy accompanying us."

Upon being approached, the trailer camp girl immediately accepted the invitation. Since the last meeting of the Palette Club nearly all of the students had been very kind to her, but she seemed rather indifferent to everyone save Louise and Penny.

As the three girls trudged along the dusty road en-route to the river shack, Rhoda spoke of Mr. Coaten and his friend who still remained in Riverview.

"They've taken a room at the Riverview Hotel," she told Penny and Louise. "Perhaps I am too suspicious, but I don't trust them. Mr. Coaten never would seem like a father to me."

"Is he married?" Louise questioned curiously.

"His wife remained in Dallas. The Coatens have two children of their own. I can't understand why they should be so eager to adopt two more—penniless at that."

"What will you do?" Louise inquired.

"I don't know. Ted and I are deadlocked. He favors the adoption, but I am against it."

CHAPTER 11 - JAY FRANKLIN'S TRICKERY

"I think you are wise to be cautious—and my advice is 'stand firm,'" Penny declared promptly. "The Breens were kind enough to take you in when you had no friends, so why not stay on with them?"

"That's the trouble," Rhoda confessed. "They haven't much money, you know, and Mr. Coaten has offered to give them a hundred dollars if they make no objection to the adoption."

"Buying them off?" Penny commented.

"In a way, yes. But why should Mr. Coaten be so interested in adopting Ted and me? We'll certainly be a financial liability."

The problem was such a perplexing one that neither Penny nor Louise could offer any convincing answer. Considering everything Rhoda had told them it appeared that Mr. Coaten must be motivated entirely by generosity. Yet, it seemed odd that if he were an old family friend he had not interested himself in their case at the time of Mr. Wiegand's death.

Choosing a trail which led along the river, the girls soon came to Truman Crocker's shack. It was a long, one-story frame building which served the dual purpose of dwelling and shop. The door of the workroom stood ajar, and the stonecutter could be seen grinding a granite block.

"Good afternoon," Penny said in a loud voice to make herself heard.

The stonecutter jumped from surprise and switched off a running motor.

"You scared me out of a year's growth," he grinned. "Well, what can I do for you?"

"Not much of anything," Penny responded, glancing with interest about the cluttered workshop. "We were just out for a walk and thought we would stop in for a few minutes."

Her attention drawn to a large rock which had been covered with wet sacking, she crossed the room to examine it. Iron filings had been sprinkled on the covering, and she knew that they must have a special purpose.

"What is this for?" she inquired curiously.

"Oh, I'm removing discoloration from a stone," Mr. Crocker answered. "Don't touch the sacking. Leave it alone."

"What do you do with the rock after you finish working on it?" Louise asked, crossing the room to stand beside Penny.

"I sell it," Mr. Crocker returned briefly. "I have work to do, and I'm waiting to get at it."

"Oh, we didn't mean to interrupt you," Penny apologized. "The truth is, we came here to ask you about that stone you hauled for Jay Franklin. Do you think the writing on it is genuine?"

"Sure it is. Anyone who knows anything about stones could tell it had been lying in the ground for years."

"The aging couldn't have been faked?"

"Say, what is this?" Crocker demanded, scowling. "What are you trying to get at?"

"My father, who publishes the *Star*, believes that someone may be perpetrating a hoax."

"A what?" Crocker asked, puzzled by the word.

"A joke. He thinks that some *clever* person may have faked the writing on the two stones."

"Well, I didn't have nothing to do with it," Truman Crocker declared, his tone unpleasant. "I hauled the rock for Jay Franklin and that's all I know about it. Now go away and don't pester me."

"We're the same as absent right now," Penny laughed, retreating to the doorway. "Thanks for your splendid cooperation."

"What's that?"

"Never mind, you wouldn't understand," Penny replied. "Goodbye."

A safe distance from the shack, the three girls expressed their opinion of the old stonecutter's manners.

"He acted as if we were suspicious of him," Louise declared. "Such a simple fellow!"

"It never once entered my head that Crocker could have any connection with the hoax, assuming that the writing isn't genuine," Penny said. "But now that I think of it, why wouldn't he be a logical person to do such a trick?"

"He's far too stupid," Louise maintained. "Why, I doubt that he ever went through eighth grade in school. Likely he never even heard of Elizabethan writing."

"All true," Penny conceded, "but couldn't someone have employed him? If he were told to carve a rock in such and such a manner, I'm sure he could carry out instructions perfectly. He knows more about such work than anyone in this community."

"Oh, Penny, you're quite hopeless!" Louise laughed. "Just let anyone rebuff you, and immediately you try to pin a crime on him!"

"I'm not accusing Truman Crocker of anything—at least not yet. All the same, those two stones were found quite close to his shack. The Gleason farm isn't more than three-quarters of a mile away."

"Why should Mr. Crocker be interested in playing such a joke?" Rhoda inquired dubiously. "Or for that matter, any other person?"

"I can't figure it out," Penny acknowledged. "If the stones are fakes, one would judge them to be the creation of a rather brilliant practical joker."

"Are you sure you didn't do it yourself?" Louise asked teasingly. "After all, you were the one who found the second stone, so that throws suspicion on you!"

Penny allowed the subject to die. With a quick change of interest, she suggested to her companions that they return to Riverview by way of the Marborough place.

"Don't you think we're showing ourselves there too frequently," Louise protested mildly. "There's such a thing as wearing out one's welcome."

"Oh, we needn't try to break into the house." Penny grinned. "But if we don't go there, we'll never learn any more about the mystery."

Louise and Rhoda were not particularly eager to climb the hill. However, to oblige Penny they offered no objection to her proposal.

Approaching the Marborough property five minutes later, the girls were startled to hear loud, angry voices. The sound came from the direction of the old wishing well.

"Someone is having a fearful argument!" Penny declared, quickening her step.

As the three friends emerged into the clearing they saw Mrs. Marborough and Jay Franklin sitting together on a garden bench. The widow was speaking in a high-pitched voice, reprimanding the caller for having misled her regarding the record stone found on her land.

"She's giving it to him right, and I'm glad!" Penny chuckled.

"Let's not go any closer," Louise murmured, holding back.

Penny stared at her chum in blank amazement. "Not go closer?" she demanded. "Why, this is why we came! I thought Mr. Franklin might be here, and I want to hear what he has to say for himself."

CHAPTER 12 - NO ADMITTANCE

Neither Louise nor Rhoda approved of interfering in the argument between Mrs. Marborough and Mr. Franklin, but as usual they could not stand firm against Penny. Making considerable noise to give warning of their approach, the girls drew near the garden bench.

"Your conduct has amazed and disappointed me," they heard the old lady say in clipped words. "When I allowed you to remove the stone from my yard you promised that you would deliver it to the museum."

"I may have mentioned such a possibility, but I made no promise," Mr. Franklin replied. "You sold the rock to me. It is now mine to do with as I see fit."

"You deliberately tricked me! I am less concerned with the money than with the fact that you are trying to force the museum to pay for something which I meant them to have free."

"Mrs. Marborough, you sold the rock for two dollars. Unless I am very much mistaken, that money meant more to you than you would have the townspeople believe!"

Mrs. Marborough arose from the bench, glaring at the visitor.

"Mr. Franklin, you are insulting! Leave my premises this minute and never return!"

"I'll be very happy to depart," the man retorted, smiling coldly. "I came here only because you sent for me. However, if you were inclined to take a sensible viewpoint, I might make you a business proposition."

"What do you mean by that, Mr. Franklin?"

"I refer to this house here. If you're disposed to sell it I might make you an offer."

Mrs. Marborough had started toward the house, but then she paused and regarded him speculatively.

"What is your offer, Mr. Franklin?"

"I'll give you fifteen hundred for the house and grounds."

"Fifteen hundred!" the old lady exclaimed shrilly. "For a house which cost at least forty thousand to build! Aren't you being outrageously reckless?"

"Old houses are a drug on the market these days, Madam. You'll find no other buyer in Riverview, I am quite sure. In fact; I wouldn't make you such a generous offer except that I think this place might be fixed up as a tourist home."

"A tourist home!" Mrs. Marborough cried furiously. "You would make this beautiful, colonial mansion into a cheap hotel! Oh, go away, and never, never show your face here again!"

"Very well, Madam," Mr. Franklin responded, still smiling. "However, I warn you that my next offer for the property will not be as generous a one."

"Generous!" Mrs. Marborough fairly screamed for she was determined to have the final word. "Your price would be robbery! You're just like your father, who was one of the worst skinflints I ever knew!"

Mr. Franklin had nothing more to say. With a shrug, he turned and strode from the yard. Mrs. Marborough gazed after him for a moment, and then sinking down on the stone bench, began to cry. Hearing footsteps behind her, she turned her head and saw the three girls. Hastily, she dabbed at her eyes with a lace handkerchief.

"Oh, Mrs. Marborough, don't feel badly," Penny said quickly. "We heard what he said to you. Mr. Franklin should be ashamed of himself."

"That man doesn't affect me one way or the other," the old lady announced with a toss of the head. The girls accepted the explanation with tranquil faces although they knew very well why Mrs. Marborough had wept. Rhoda wandered to the wishing well, peering down into the crystal-clear water.

"Do you know, I'm tempted to make another wish," she remarked. "Would it be very selfish of me?"

"Selfish?" Louise inquired, puzzled.

"The last one came true. I shouldn't expect too much."

"Do make your wish, Rhoda," urged Penny, "but don't anticipate quick action. I'm still waiting for mine to come true."

Rhoda drew a bucket of water from the well, and filling the dipper which always hung on a nail of the wooden roof, drank deeply.

"I wish," she said soberly, "I wish that Ted might find a job. If he could get work, maybe it wouldn't be necessary to accept charity from Mr. Coaten or anyone!"

Rhoda's wish, so earnestly spoken, slightly embarrassed the others, for it served to remind them of the girl's poverty.

"Now you make one, Penny," Louise urged to cover an awkward silence.

"I can't think of anything I want," Penny answered.

"Well, I can!" Mrs. Marborough announced unexpectedly. "In all the years of my life I've never made a wish at this well, but now I shall!"

To the delight of the girls, she reached for the bucket of water. With a grim face she slammed the entire contents back into the well.

"Just a little token, O wishing well," she muttered. "My desire is a most worthy one. All I ask is that Jay Franklin be given his come-uppance!"

"We'll all second that wish!" Penny added gaily.

"There!" Mrs. Marborough declared, rather pleased with herself. "That makes me feel better. Now I'll forget that man and go about my business."

"I think it was selfish of him to take the attitude he did about the stone," Penny said, wishing to keep an entertaining topic alive.

Mrs. Marborough seemed to have lost all interest in the subject. Gathering her long skirts about her, she started for the house. Midway up the flagstone path she paused to say:

"There's a tree of nice summer apples out yonder by the back fence. Pick all you like and take some home if you care for them."

"Thank you, Mrs. Marborough," Louise responded politely.

After the door had closed behind the old lady, the girls did not immediately leave the vicinity of the wishing well.

"She means to be kind," Louise commented, drawing figures in the dirt with her shoe. "But isn't it funny she never invites us into the house?"

"It's downright mysterious," Penny added. "You notice Jay Franklin didn't get in there either!"

"Why does she act that way?" Rhoda asked in perplexity.

"Penny thinks she's trying to keep folks from discovering something," explained Louise. "The old lady is queer in other ways, too."

Thoroughly enjoying the tale, the girls told Rhoda how they had observed Mrs. Marborough removing the flagstones surrounding the base of the wishing well.

"There's been more digging!" Penny suddenly cried, springing up from the bench. "See!"

Excitedly she pointed to a place where additional flagstones had been lifted and carelessly replaced.

"Mrs. Marborough must have been at work again!" Louise agreed. "What does she expect to find?"

"Fishing worms, perhaps," Rhoda suggested with a smile. "Under the flagstones would be a good place."

"Mrs. Marborough never would go fishing," Louise answered. "Sometimes I wonder if she's entirely right in her mind. It just isn't normal to go around digging on your own property after night."

"Don't you worry, Mrs. Marborough knows what she is about," Penny declared. "She's looking for something which is hidden!"

"But what can it be?" Louise speculated. "Nothing she does seems to make sense."

"She's one of the most interesting characters I've met in many a day," Penny said warmly. "I like her better all the time."

"How about those apples?" Rhoda suggested, changing the subject. "I'm sure Mrs. Breen could use some of them."

As the girls started toward the gnarled old tree, a battered automobile drew up in front of the house. A man who was dressed in coat and trousers taken from two separate suits alighted and came briskly up the walk.

CHAPTER 12 - NO ADMITTANCE

"Who is he?" Louise whispered curiously.

"Never saw him before," Penny admitted. "He looks almost like a tramp."

"Or an old clothes man," Rhoda added with a laugh.

Observing the girls, the man doffed his battered derby.

"Is this where Mrs. Marborough lives?" he asked.

"Yes, she is inside," Louise replied.

Bowing again, the man presented himself at the front door, hammering it loudly with the brass knocker.

"Mrs. Marborough will make short work of him," Penny laughed. "She's so friendly to visitors!"

Before the girls could walk on to the apple tree, Mrs. Marborough opened the door.

"Mr. Butterworth?" she asked, without waiting for the man to speak.

"Yes, ma'am."

"Come in," invited Mrs. Marborough, her voice impersonal.

The caller stepped across the threshold and the door swung shut.

"Did you see that?" Louise whispered, stunned by the ease with which the man had gained admittance.

"I certainly did!" Penny murmured. "That fellow—whoever he is—has accomplished something that even Riverview's society ladies couldn't achieve! Maybe I was puzzled before, but now, let me tell you, I'm completely tied in a knot!"

CHAPTER 13 - A SILKEN LADDER

As Penny approached the school grounds the following morning, she heard her name called. A moment later, Rhoda Wiegand, breathless from running, caught up with her.

"Penny, the most wonderful thing has happened!" she exclaimed.

"Your Texas friends have left town?" the other guessed.

Rhoda shook her head. "Unfortunately, it's not quite that wonderful. They're still here. This news is about my brother, Ted. He has a job!"

"Why, that's splendid. Exactly what you wished for yesterday afternoon at the well."

"Penny, doesn't it seem strange?" Rhoda asked soberly. "This makes twice my wish has come true. How do you account for it?"

"I suppose your brother could have obtained the job through accident," Penny answered. "That would be the logical explanation."

"But it all came about in such an unusual way. Judge Harlan saw Ted on the street and liked his appearance. So he sent a note to the Camp asking if he would work as a typist in his office."

"Ted is accepting?"

"Oh, yes. The pay is splendid for that sort of work. Besides, it will give him a chance to study law, which is his life ambition. Oh, Penny, you can't know how happy I am about it!"

At the mid-morning recess, Penny reported the conversation to Louise. Both girls were pleased that Ted Wiegand had obtained employment, but it did seem peculiar to them that the judge would go to such lengths to gain the services of a young man of questionable character.

"Perhaps he wants to help him," Louise speculated. "Ted is at the critical point of his life now. He could develop into a very fine person or just the opposite."

"It's charity, of course. But who put the judge up to it?"

"Mrs. Marborough heard Rhoda express her wish."

"Yes, she did," Penny agreed, "but I don't think she paid much attention. She was too angry at Jay Franklin. Besides, Mrs. Marborough doesn't have a reputation for doing kind deeds."

"If you rule her out, there's nothing left but the old wishing well," Louise laughed.

"I might be tempted to believe it has unusual powers if ever it would do anything for me," grumbled Penny. "Not a single one of my wishes has been granted."

"A mystery seems to be developing at Rose Acres," Louise reminded her.

"I've not learned anything new since I made my wish. Mrs. Marborough hasn't decided to cooperate with the Pilgrimage Committee either."

The Festival Week program which so interested Penny had been set for the twentieth of the month and the days immediately following. Gardens were expected to be at their height at that time, and the owners of seven fairly old houses had agreed to open their doors to the public. Both Penny and Louise had helped sell tickets for the motor pilgrimage, but sales resistance was becoming increasingly difficult to overcome.

"The affair may be a big flop," Penny remarked to her chum. "No one wants to pay a dollar to see a house which isn't particularly interesting. Now Rose Acres would draw customers. The women of Riverview are simply torn with curiosity to get in there."

"I don't believe Mrs. Marborough ever will change her mind."

"Neither do I," Penny agreed gloomily.

CHAPTER 13 - A SILKEN LADDER

Two days elapsed during which nothing happened, according to the viewpoint of the girls. From Rhoda they learned that Ted was well established in his new job, and that Mr. Coaten seemed displeased about it. Mr. Parker reported that Jay Franklin had made progress in his efforts to sell the Marborough stone to the Riverview Museum. Other than that, there was no news, no developments of interest.

"Louise, let's visit Truman Crocker again," Penny proposed on Saturday afternoon when time hung heavily.

"What good would it do?" Louise demurred. "You know very well he doesn't like to have us around."

"He acted suspicious of us, which made me suspicious of him. I've been thinking, Lou—if the writing on those two stones were faked, it must have been done with a chisel—one which would leave a characteristic mark. Every tool is slightly different, you know."

"All of which leads you to conclude—?"

"That if Truman Crocker did the faking he would have a tool in his workshop that would make grooves similar to those on the stones. An expert might compare them and tell."

"Do we consider ourselves experts?"

"Of course not," Penny said impatiently. "But if I could get the right tool, I could turn it over to someone who knows about such things."

"So you propose to go out to the shack today and appropriate a tool?"

"I'll buy it from Mr. Crocker. Perhaps I can convince him I want to chisel a tombstone for myself or something of the sort!"

"I used to think you were just plain crazy, Penny Parker," Louise declared sadly. "Lately you've reached the stage where adjectives are too weak to describe you!"

A half hour later found the two girls at the Crocker shack. The door of the workshop stood open, but as Penny and Louise peered inside, they saw no sign of the old stonecutter. A number of tools lay on a bench where Crocker had been working, and with no hesitation Penny examined them.

"Here is a chisel," she said in satisfaction. "It seems to be the only one around too. Just what I need!"

"Penny, you wouldn't dare take it!"

"In my official capacity as a detective—yes. I'll leave more than enough money to pay for it. Then after I've had it examined by an expert, I'll return it to Mr. Crocker."

"O Mystery, what crimes are committed in thy name," Louise warbled. "If you land in jail, my dear Penny, don't expect me to share your cell cot."

"I'll take all the responsibility."

Selecting a bill from her purse, Penny laid it in a conspicuous place on the workbench.

"There, that should buy three or four chisels," she declared. "Now let's leave here before Truman Crocker arrives."

Emerging from the shop, Penny and Louise were surprised to see dark storm clouds scudding overhead. The sun had been completely blotted out and occasional flashes of lightning brightened a gray sky.

"It's going to rain before we can get to Riverview," Louise declared uneasily. "We'll be drenched."

"Why not go by way of Mrs. Marborough's place?" Penny proposed. "Then if the rain does overtake us, we can dodge into the summer house until the shower passes over."

Hastening toward the hillside trail, the girls observed that the river level was higher than when last they had seen it. Muddy water lapped almost at the doorstep of Truman Crocker's shack. A rowboat tied to a half submerged dock nearby swung restlessly on its long rope.

"I should be afraid to live so close to the river," Louise remarked. "If the water comes only a few feet higher, Crocker's place will sail South."

"The river control system is supposed to take care of everything," Penny answered carelessly. "Dad says he doesn't place much faith in it himself—not if it's ever put to a severe test."

Before the girls had gone far, a few drops of rain splattered down. Anticipating a deluge, they ran for the dilapidated summer house which stood at the rear edge of Mrs. Marborough's property. Completely winded, they sank down on a dusty wooden bench to recapture their breath.

"The clouds are rolling eastward," Louise remarked, scanning the sky. "It may not rain much after all."

"Lou!" Penny said in a startled voice.

She was gazing toward the old wishing well at a dark figure which could be seen bending far over the yawning hole.

"What is it?" Louise inquired, turning in surprise.

"Look over there!" Penny directed. "Mrs. Marborough is doing something at the well. Is she trying to repair it or what?"

"She's examining the inside!" Louise exclaimed. "Why, if she's not careful, she may fall. We ought to warn her—"

"Mrs. Marborough knows what she is about, Lou. Let's just watch."

From a distance it was not possible to tell exactly what the old lady was doing. So far as the girls could discern she was tapping the inside stones of the well with a hammer.

"She's trying to discover if any of them are loose!" Penny whispered excitedly. "Louise, I'm sure of it now! Something of great value is hidden in or near the wishing well, and Mrs. Marborough came back to Riverview to find it!"

"What could it be?"

"I haven't an idea."

"If there's something hidden in or around the well, why doesn't she have a workman make a thorough search?"

"Probably because she doesn't want folks to suspect what she is about, Lou. That may explain why she works at night and on very dark, gloomy days such as today. She doesn't wish to be seen."

"Mrs. Marborough searches in such obvious places," Louise said after a moment. "If anything really is hidden it might be deep down in the well. She never will find it in that case."

"We might help her," Penny suggested impulsively.

"You know she would resent our interference."

"She probably would if we tell her what we intend to do."

Louise gazed speculatively at her chum, realizing that Penny had some plan in mind. She waited expectantly, and then as the other did not speak, inquired:

"Just what scheme are you hatching now?"

"You gave me the idea yourself," Penny chuckled. "The logical place to search is deep down inside the well. I'm sure the water can't be more than a few feet deep."

"So you want me to dive in and drown myself?" Louise joked. "Thank you, but I prefer to restrict my aquatic exercise to swimming pools!"

"Remember that silk ladder I acquired when I helped police capture Al Gepper and his slippery pals?" Penny demanded, paying no heed to the teasing.

"I do," Louise nodded. "It was made of braided silk strands by a Chinese curio man, and had two iron hooks to claw into the wood of window ledges."

"Those same hooks will fit very nicely over the side of the wishing well. I've been waiting for a chance to use that ladder, and here it is!"

"Penny! You actually have the courage to climb down into a well?"

"Why not?" Penny laughed. "But it must be tonight while my enthusiasm is bubbling. Meet me at nine o'clock and bring a good flashlight."

Louise could only stare. "You're actually serious!"

"Indeed I am," Penny replied gaily. "Everything is settled. Now let's slip away from here before Mrs. Marborough sees us."

CHAPTER 14 - NIGHT ADVENTURE

The night, dark and misty, was entirely suitable for the purpose to which the two girls had dedicated it. Dinner over, Penny obtained the unique silken ladder from an attic trunk. Compressing it into a small brief-case, she sauntered through the living room.

"Aren't you becoming quite studious of late?" Mr. Parker inquired, noting the brief-case tucked under her arm. "Off to the library again?"

"Over to Louise's house," Penny corrected vaguely. "From that point on there's no guarantee."

"You'll be home early?"

"I hope so," Penny answered earnestly. "If for any reason I fail to appear, don't search in any of the obvious places."

Leaving her father to ponder over the remark, she hastily quitted the house. A clock chimed nine o'clock as she reached the Sidell house, and a moment later her chum joined her in the yard.

"I had trouble getting away," Louise reported. "Mother asked a thousand questions."

"Did you bring the flashlight?"

"Yes, here it is. My, but it's a dark night!"

"All the better for our purpose," Penny said cheerfully.

A single light burned in the kitchen window of the Marborough house as the girls presently approached it. The garden was shrouded in damp, wispy mist and the unkempt grounds never had appeared more desolate.

"Penny, must we go through with this?" Louise asked, rapidly losing enthusiasm for the venture.

"I'll admit the idea doesn't look quite as attractive as it did this afternoon," her chum replied. "All the same, I'm going through with it!"

"What can you hope to find down in that well?"

Penny did not answer. Walking ahead of Louise, she noiselessly crossed the yard to the old wishing well. Flashing her light into the circular interior, her courage nearly failed her. However, she gave no indication of it to her companion.

"Better be careful of that light," Louise warned. "That is, unless you want Mrs. Marborough to come out and catch us."

Penny switched off the flashlight and thereafter worked in darkness. Taking the silken ladder from its case, she fastened the two iron hooks over the stone ledge. Next, she lowered the ladder into the well, listening until she heard a faint splash in the water below.

"Now you stay here and keep watch," she instructed briskly. "I'll be down and back again before you know it!"

"The ladder may break," Louise said pessimistically, seating herself on the stone ledge of the well. "Silk deteriorates with age, and those braided strands never did look strong."

"They once held one of Riverview's most notorious apartment-house burglars," Penny returned with forced cheerfulness. She climbed over the ledge, gazing down into the dark well. "It's safe enough—I hope."

"In case you slip and fall, just what am I to do?"

"That's your problem," Penny chuckled. "Now hand me the flashlight. I'm on my way."

Despite their banter, both girls were tense and worried. By daylight, a descent into the well had seemed to Penny an amusing stunt; but now as she cautiously descended into the damp, circular pit, she felt that for once in her life she had ventured too far.

"What do you see?" Louise called softly from above. "Anything?"

WISHING WELL

Reminded of the work before her, Penny clung with one hand to the swaying ladder, while with the other she directed the flashlight beam about the circular walls. The sides were cracked in many places and covered with a slimy green moss.

"What do you see, Penny?" Louise called again. "Are any of the bricks loose?"

"Not that I can discover," Penny answered, and her voice echoed weirdly. Intrigued by the sound she tried an experimental yodel. "Why, it's just like a cave scene on the radio!"

"In case you've forgotten, you're in a well," Louise said severely. "Furthermore, if you don't work fast, Mrs. Marborough will come out here!"

"I have to have a little relaxation," Penny grumbled.

Descending deeper into the well, she resumed her task of examining the walls. There were no loose bricks, nothing to indicate that anything ever had been hidden in the cavern. Reaching the last rung without realizing it, she stepped not into space, but water.

Surprisingly her foot struck a solid foundation.

Hastily pulling herself back on the ladder, Penny shouted the information to her chum.

"Lou, the water isn't more than a foot and a half deep! There's an old boot or something of the sort floating around. You don't catch me drinking any more of this water. No sir!"

There was no reply from above.

"Louise!" Penny called, flashing her light upward.

"Quiet!" came the whispered response. "I think someone is coming!"

"Mrs. Marborough?" Penny gasped, thoroughly alarmed.

"No! Two men! They're turning in at the gate!"

Penny began to climb the silken ladder with frantic haste.

"You never can get out without them seeing you!" Louise hissed. "I'm ducking out!"

"Don't you dare!"

"They'll see me if I don't. Stay where you are Penny, and I'll come back after they go. Oh, the ladder! It's sure to give you away!"

In the emergency, Penny's mind worked with rapidity. Lowering herself into the well several rungs, she deliberately stepped into the water. To her relief it came just below her knees.

"Quick! Pull up the ladder!" she instructed.

The two men were so close that Louise dared not obey. Instead she loosed the iron hooks and dropped the ladder into the well. Penny barely was able to catch it and prevent a loud splash.

"Of all the tricks—" she muttered, but Louise did not hear. She had fled into a clump of bushes.

Penny huddled against the slimy wall, listening intently. Thinking that she heard footsteps, she switched out the flashlight.

"This is the place all right," a masculine voice said. "Wonder if the old lady is at home?"

"There's a light showing."

The voices faded away, and Penny drew a deep sigh of relief. Impatiently she waited for Louise to come to her aid. After several minutes she realized why her chum delayed, for she again heard voices.

"The old lady must be inside the house. Funny she wouldn't come to the door. They say she's a queer one though."

To Penny's discomfort, the two men paused by the wishing well.

"Want a drink?" she heard one ask.

The voices seemed faintly familiar to Penny and suddenly it dawned upon her that the two men were Mr. Coaten and his Texas friend. However, she could think of no reason why they should call upon Mrs. Marborough. Her reflection came to an abrupt end, as the well bucket splashed into the water beside her.

Suppressing a giggle, she groped for the old boot which floated nearby. Dropping it into the bucket, she watched as it was raised to the surface. A moment later she heard an exclamation of wrath from above.

"See what I've drawn up!" one of the men muttered. "These old wells must be filled with filth!"

Penny hoped that the strangers would immediately depart, but instead they loitered by the well, talking.

"We've been wasting entirely too much time in this," remarked the man whom she took to be Mr. Coaten. "Suppose we were to offer Ted a hundred dollars to sign the paper. Would he do it?"

"I think he might, but the girl is the one who'll make trouble. She's shrewd."

CHAPTER 14 - NIGHT ADVENTURE

"We'll get around her somehow," the other said gruffly. "This thing can't drag on forever. I have work waiting for me in Texas."

The voices gradually died away and Penny heard no more. However, from the snatch of conversation, she was convinced that Rhoda's suspicions regarding the Texas strangers had been well founded. But what had brought the two men to Riverview?

"If Rhoda or Ted own property, I could understand why it would be desirable to adopt them," she thought. "As it is, the thing doesn't make sense."

To keep from freezing, Penny gingerly waded around and around in the well. It seemed ages before Louise thrust her head over the ledge and called softly:

"Are you still there, pet?"

"I'm frozen into one big icicle!" Penny retorted. "Get me out of here."

Instructing her chum to lower the bucket, Penny fastened the silken ladder to the handle. Louise hauled it up, and again hooked the irons to the ledge of the well.

Stiffly, Penny climbed toward the surface. She had nearly reached the top when the beam of light chanced to play across a section of brick which hitherto had escaped her notice. Halting, she traced with her finger a rectangular pattern on the wall.

"That's not an ordinary crack!" she thought. "It might be an old opening which has been bricked up!"

"Are you coming?" Louise called impatiently.

"I am," said Penny, emerging from the well. "And don't you dare say that this night has been a failure. I've just made a most astounding discovery!"

CHAPTER 15 - OLD BOTTLES

Penny's startling appearance rather than her words made the deepest impression upon Louise. The girl's shoes and stockings were wet, her clothing was smeared with green slime, and strings of moss clung to her hair.

"You look like Father Neptune emerging from the briny deep," she chuckled.

"I'm freezing to death," Penny chattered. "Come on, we're going home!"

Louise hauled up the silken ladder from the well. Squeezing out the water, she compressed it into the carrying case.

"What were you saying about a discovery?" she inquired belatedly.

"Oh, nothing of consequence," Penny answered, pounding her hands together to restore circulation. "Merely an opening in the side of the well. It probably leads into a tunnel."

"Penny! Are you sure?"

"I'm not sure of anything except that I'm going home!" Penny replied crossly.

She started across the lawn with her chum hurrying after her.

"Oh, Penny, I'm terribly sorry," Louise said contritely. "I know you had an awful time down in the well. But it wasn't my fault those two men arrived just when they did."

"Who were they?" Penny asked, mollified by the apology. "From their voices I took them to be Mr. Coaten and his friend."

"That's who they were. But, I can't imagine why they came to see Mrs. Marborough. Anyway, they didn't get into the house."

"Lou, I heard those men talking while I was down in the well," Penny revealed. "I'm sure they're dishonest. They want Ted and Rhoda to sign something over to them."

"But Rhoda said she and her brother have no property."

"I know," Penny frowned. "I can't make head nor tail of the situation. I'm too miserable to think about anything now."

Pausing beside a tree, she removed one of her shoes. After pouring a little water from it, she replaced it and went through a similar procedure with the other shoe.

"Please tell me what else you learned while in the well," Louise pleaded. "Haven't I been punished enough?"

Her good humor restored, Penny grinned amiably. "To tell you the truth, Lou, I'm not sure whether I found anything or not."

"But you said—"

"I know. Just as I reached the top of the well I noticed a section of brick wall which seemed to be cracked in the exact shape of a rectangle."

"Was that all?" Louise asked in disappointment.

"I didn't even take time to examine the place. I felt so disgusted," Penny resumed. "However, I believe that if one were able to remove those loose bricks, an opening might be found behind them."

"Where something may be hidden?"

"It's possible."

"How could one remove the bricks without hiring a workman?" Louise asked after a moment.

"If they are as loose as I think they are, I might be able to get them out myself. Not tonight though."

Penny felt in no mood to discuss future possibilities or even to consider them. Already cold, the misty air added to her physical discomfort.

CHAPTER 15 - OLD BOTTLES

"Better get a hot shower and go to bed," Louise advised as they finally reached the Parker home. "We'll talk things over in the morning."

Not desiring to attract attention to herself, Penny entered the house by a side door. To her discomfiture, Mrs. Weems, who chanced to be getting a drink in the kitchen, saw the disheveled clothing.

"Why, Penny Parker!" she exclaimed. "What have you done to yourself?"

"Nothing," Penny mumbled. "I'm just a little wet. I've been down in a well."

"There are times when your jokes don't seem at all funny," the housekeeper said sternly. "How did you ruin your clothes?"

"That's the truth, Mrs. Weems. I was down in a well and I stepped off into the water—"

"Penny, you can't expect me to believe such a tall story. Now tell me exactly what *did* happen."

"Would it seem more reasonable if I said that I stumbled and fell into a ditch?"

"I rather thought something of the sort happened," Mrs. Weems declared. "How did the accident occur?"

"It didn't," Penny maintained plaintively.

Escaping upstairs before the housekeeper could question her further, she took a hot shower and went to bed. She could hear a murmur of voices in the living room below, and knew that Mrs. Weems was discussing her "behavior" with her father.

"Sometimes grownups are so unreasonable," she sighed, snuggling into the covers. "You tell them the truth and what they really want is a nice logical whopper!"

Penny slept soundly and did not awaken until the Sunday morning sun was high in the heavens. Sitting up in bed, she moved her arms experimentally. They were very sore and stiff. She swung her feet to the floor and groaned with pain.

"Guess I can't take it any more," she muttered. "I must be getting soft, or else it's old age sneaking up on me!"

Torturing herself with a limbering exercise, Penny dressed and went downstairs. Mrs. Weems had gone to church while Mr. Parker had submerged himself in fifty-eight pages of Sunday paper. Detouring around the living room, Penny went to the kitchen to prepare herself a belated breakfast. She was picking at the nuts of a fruit salad found in the ice box when her father appeared in the doorway.

"Penny—" he began sternly.

"Where was I last night?" she interrupted. "I've said before, and now repeat—in a well! A nice deep one with water in it."

"When you're ready to tell me the real story, I shall listen," Mr. Parker said quietly. "Until that time, I must deprive you of your weekly allowance."

"Oh, Dad!" Penny wailed. "You know I'm stony broke! I won't be able to drive my car or even buy a hot dog!"

"That is your misfortune. Mrs. Weems says I have been entirely too indulgent with you, and I am inclined to agree with her. I've seldom checked your comings or goings, but in the future I shall expect you to tell me your plans when you leave the house at night."

Having delivered his ultimatum, Mr. Parker quietly withdrew.

Penny had lost her appetite for breakfast. Feeling much abused she banged out the kitchen door into the yard. Her first act was to inspect the gasoline tanks of both Leaping Lena and the maroon car. As she had feared, the combined fuel supply did not equal three gallons.

"There's just about fifty-five miles between me and misery," she reflected grimly. "I wouldn't dare siphon gas out of Dad's car or ask for credit at a filling station either!"

Wandering around to the front porch, she sat down on the steps. One of her high school boy friends pedaled past on his bicycle, calling a cheery greeting. Penny barely responded.

Presently a milk wagon clattered to a stop in front of the house. The driver came up the walk with his rack of milk bottles. Penny eyed him speculatively.

"We have a lot of old bottles in the basement," she greeted him. "Does your company pay for them?"

"Sorry," he declined. "We use only our own stamped bottles. There's no deposit charge. Customers are expected to return them without rebate."

The driver left a quart of milk on the back doorstep of the Parker home. In walking to his wagon, he paused beside Penny, remarking:

"Maybe you could sell your old bottles to a second-hand dealer. I saw one on the next street about five minutes ago."

"Where?" Penny demanded, jumping to her feet.

"He was on Fulton Avenue when I drove past."

Thanking the driver, Penny ran as fast as her stiff limbs would permit to the next street corner. Far up the avenue she saw a battered old car of the second-hand man. Hurrying on, she reached the automobile just as its owner came from a house carrying an armful of corded newspapers.

"Excuse me," she called eagerly, "do you buy old bottles?"

The man turned toward her, doffing his derby hat.

"Good morning, Miss," he said. "I buy newspapers, old furniture, rubber tires, copper, brass, or gold, but not bottles."

Penny scarcely heard the discouraging information for she was staring at the man as if his appearance fascinated her. For a moment she could not think where she had seen him before. And then suddenly she remembered.

"Why, I saw you at Mrs. Marborough's place!" she exclaimed. "You're the one person who has been inside the house! I want you to tell me all about it."

CHAPTER 16 - INSIDE THE MANSION

Mr. Butterworth, the second-hand dealer, scarcely knew what to make of Penny's abrupt request.

"Tell me how the house looks inside," she requested as he remained mute. "Is it as handsome as folks say?"

"You are a friend of Mrs. Marborough?" the man inquired, cocking his head sideways as he regarded the girl.

"Of course."

"Then why do you not ask Mrs. Marborough that question?"

"Because she never invites anyone into her house," Penny explained patiently. "You're the only person to get in so far as I know. I'll venture she sold you something. Am I right?"

"Maybe so," Mr. Butterworth grinned. "My lips, they are sealed."

"Sealed?"

"I promise Mrs. Marborough I tell nothing of what I see in the house."

"Then there is something mysterious going on there!" Penny exclaimed. "Tell me, why did you go to the house?"

"Mrs. Marborough sent for me."

"But why?" Penny demanded, exasperated because she could learn nothing of importance. "Did Mrs. Marborough sell you something?"

"Maybe so, maybe not," the second-hand man answered, climbing into his overloaded car. "You ask her."

Penny watched him drive away, and then returned to her own doorstep. She was listlessly throwing acorns at a squirrel when Louise Sidell came down the street, dressed in her Sunday best.

"What's the matter, Penny?" she inquired, roving over to the porch. "How do you feel this morning?"

"Lower than the center of the earth. I've lost my reputation with Dad, my allowance, and my initiative. If I had a nickel I'd go drown myself in a coke!"

"What you need is a nice adventure," Louise said mischievously. "How about a trip out to Mrs. Marborough's tomorrow night?"

"I've had enough of wells!"

"Penny, you don't mean it!" Louise grinned. "After discovering those loose bricks, you'll just forget about them?"

"Why not?" Penny demanded wildly. "Dad won't let me leave the house at night any more without a six thousand page report on where I am going. If I so much as mention Mrs. Marborough's well, he'll clap on a double punishment."

"You can manage it somehow," Louise declared with confidence. "I'll meet you tomorrow night about eight-thirty."

"Maybe," Penny said gloomily.

Throughout the day she tried to win favor with both Mrs. Weems and her father by doing small things to please them. When the housekeeper came home from church, dinner awaited her. Penny insisted upon doing the dishes. She straightened the kitchen, she brought her father his bedroom slippers, and refrained from turning on the radio while he was reading. The schedule was a trying one for her, but she kept it up faithfully all day Sunday and until after dinner on Monday. Then came the denouement upon which she pinned her hopes.

"Dad," she said demurely, leaning on the chair arm and stroking his hair, "with your kind permission I should like to absent myself from the house for a few minutes."

"Where do you plan to go?" he asked, trying to act stern.

Penny was prepared for the question. From her pocket she whisked a lengthy typewritten paper, handsomely decorated with a diagram.

"What's this?" Mr. Parker asked, his lips twitching slightly.

"Merely a report on my proposed movements for the next hour. At eight-thirty I hope to be at Louise's house. Eight thirty-four should find me on Adams Street, moving southward. At eight thirty-eight I pass Gulbert Park—"

"Never mind," Mr. Parker interrupted. "I see by this lengthy document that your ultimate destination is Mrs. Marborough's estate. Isn't it rather late to pay a social call?"

"Eight-thirty?"

"What does this X on the map represent?" the publisher asked, his interest shifting.

"Oh that?" smiled Penny. "Merely one of the fixtures in Mrs. Marborough's yard. Louise and I think treasure may be hidden there."

Amused by what he took to be his daughter's whimsy, Mr. Parker returned the diagram to her.

"Do I have your permission to leave the house?" she asked anxiously.

"Yes, you may go," he agreed. "But mind, no late hours. And no more tall tales about falling into wells!"

Louise was waiting for Penny in the Sidell yard and the girls went as quickly as they could to the Marborough estate. The house was completely dark, leading them to believe that the widow might have absented herself for the evening.

"We'll have to be especially careful," Louise warned as they approached the old wishing well. "She might return at any moment and find us."

Penny had brought the silken ladder, extra rope, a flashlight and a suit of warm coveralls which her father used when he worked on the car. Donning the bulky garment, she prepared to descend a few feet into the well.

"Do be careful," Louise said anxiously. "If you should fall you might kill yourself."

"You think of the most cheerful things," Penny muttered, climbing nimbly down the swaying ladder. "I'm not taking any chances though. I'll tie myself to the ladder with this extra piece of rope."

After she had gained the position she desired, Louise handed down the flashlight. Penny carefully inspected the brick wall.

"I believe it is an opening!" she reported jubilantly. "I really do. Here, take this flash. I can't work and hold it."

While Louise directed the beam from above, Penny tugged at the bricks. Unable to move them, she called for a tool which she had brought with her. By means of it, she easily pried one of the bricks loose. Pushing her arm through the opening, she encountered only empty space.

"It's a little tunnel I think!" she shouted to Louise. "Take this brick, and I'll try to pry out others!"

Within ten minutes Penny had handed up enough of them to make a large pile beside the flagstones.

"Do you realize you're practically destroying Mrs. Marborough's well!" Louise said uneasily. "How will we ever explain this?"

"I can put the bricks back again," Penny assured her. "They were meant to come out. Now, the flashlight again."

Balancing herself precariously on the ladder, she directed the light through the opening she had created. A long narrow tunnel which she judged to be about five feet below the ground, extended as far as she could see.

"I'm going to try to get in there!" she called to Louise. "Toss me a life preserver if I fail!"

Calculating the space, Penny swung her feet from the ladder to the ledge. Retaining an arm hold on the ropes, she edged herself backwards into the hole.

"It's much easier than it looks," she called encouragingly to her chum. "Come on, if you want to explore."

Louise hesitated, and then daringly climbed down into the well. Penny helped her from the ladder into the tunnel.

"Where do you suppose this leads?" Louise gasped.

"Maybe to the house," Penny speculated. "I know lots of these old places had escapes made so that in time of war or Indian attacks, the householders could get away. Never heard of a tunnel opening into a well though!"

The bricked passageway was so low that for the first twelve feet the girls were forced to crawl on hands and knees. Gradually, the tunnel deepened until they were able to walk in a stooped position.

"We're coming to the end of it," Penny presently announced.

CHAPTER 16 - INSIDE THE MANSION

Directly in front of her was a heavy door which showed the effects of age. It did not move easily, but together, the girls were able to swing it open.

"Where in the world are we?" Louise murmured in perplexity.

Penny flashed her light directly ahead. A series of four steps led down from the tunnel into an empty room which barely was six feet across. So far as she could see it had no exit.

"It looks as if we're at the end of the trail," Louise remarked in disappointment.

"This must be part of the Marborough house," Penny declared, descending the steps into the tiny room.

"But there's no way out of it except through the tunnel!"

"There must be if we can find it," Penny insisted.

Wandering about the room she began to explore the walls, and Louise followed her example. Their search was rewarded, for presently they discovered a small brass knob embedded in the rough board paneling. Penny pulled on it and a section of wall slid back.

"Now we're really in the Marborough house!" she whispered excitedly. "The basement, I think."

Stepping through the opening, the girls made no sound as they tiptoed around in the dark, damp room. Penny's flashlight revealed that the walls had been boarded over, but there was no solid foundation beneath their feet, only a hard dirt floor. A steep stairway led up from the basement.

"Do you suppose Mrs. Marborough is here?" Penny whispered, listening.

There was no sound from above.

"Shall we go upstairs, or back the way we came?" she asked her chum.

"Let's risk being caught," Louise decided after a moment's hesitation. "I'd rather be sent to jail for house breaking than to climb into that well again."

Huddling together, the girls crept up the stairway. The landing was blocked by another door. Penny tested it, and finding it unlocked, pushed it gently open. Again they listened.

"The coast is clear," Louise whispered. "I'm sure Mrs. Marborough isn't here."

Penny stepped across the threshold, tense with anticipation. Ever since Mrs. Marborough's arrival in Riverview she had longed to see the interior of the grand old mansion. And now, through a strange quirk of adventure, her ambition was to be gratified.

Slowly she allowed the flashlight beam to play over the walls of the room. There were several pictures in massive gold frames, leading her to think that she had entered a library or living room. Systematically, she continued to move the light about in search of furniture. So far as she could see there was none.

"The room is empty!" Louise whispered at her elbow.

A board squeaked beneath their weight as the girls tiptoed to a doorway opening into a still larger room.

"This must be the living room," Penny decided, observing a beautiful, circular stairway which rose to the second floor.

"But where is the furniture?" demanded Louise in bewilderment.

Penny's light cut squares across the room, but the only objects revealed were a chair and a table drawn close to the fireplace.

"What can this mean?" Louise gasped. "The house always has been furnished. Now everything is gone."

Penny did not answer. The sound of shuffling feet on the front porch caused both girls to freeze against the wall. Before they could retreat to the basement stairs, the living room door opened. Light from a street lamp cut a path across the bare floor.

Mrs. Marborough stood framed in the doorway. The girls had made no sound, yet the mistress of Rose Acres seemed to sense that she was not alone.

"Who is it?" she called sharply. "Speak up! Who is hiding here?"

CHAPTER 17 - THE MARBOROUGH PEARLS

In frightened voices Penny and Louise acknowledged their presence in the dark room. Greatly relieved that the intruders were girls, Mrs. Marborough struck a match and lighted three half-burned candles which were set in a huge glass candelabra.

"Oh, so it's you!" she exclaimed as the flickering light fell upon their faces. "May I ask why you have broken into my house?"

"We're thoroughly ashamed of ourselves, Mrs. Marborough," Penny said apologetically.

"Indeed we are," added Louise. "When we started to investigate the wishing well we didn't intend to enter the house."

"Suppose you explain," suggested the mistress of Rose Acres.

"It's a long story," sighed Penny. "May we sit down somewhere?"

The request embarrassed Mrs. Marborough. She hesitated, and then indicated that the girls were to follow her. To their surprise she led them through another empty room to the kitchen, there lighting a candle. Its soft illumination revealed an old oil stove, several chairs, a porcelain table and a cot which obviously served both as a day couch and bed.

Mrs. Marborough offered no explanation or apology. Taking wood from a box, she piled it into the fireplace, and soon had a cheerful blaze on the hearth.

Drawing their chairs to the fire, Penny and Louise explained how they had entered the old mansion. Mrs. Marborough listened attentively to their story but did not appear especially surprised.

"I've always known about that old tunnel," she said when they had finished. "It was built by the first owner of this house, many, many years ago, and I doubt if it ever was used. I tried to find the entrance from the basement a few days ago, but was unable to locate it."

"We saw you with your lantern at the wishing well," Louise confessed. "That was what aroused our curiosity."

"I was looking for the other tunnel entrance. I found it without much trouble, but it was so deep down in the well that I dared not risk trying to get into it. Although I considered hiring a man, I hesitated, because I knew it would cause talk."

Penny and Louise were feeling much more at ease, sensing that the mistress of Rose Acres no longer was irritated by their actions. Eagerly they waited for her to reveal more.

"I suppose you think me a queer old lady," Mrs. Marborough resumed. "Perhaps I am, but I have a very good reason for some of the things I do. I came to Riverview to search for something which has been lost many years."

"Something hidden during the Civil War?" inquired Louise breathlessly.

"No, my dear, an object secreted by my sister, Virginia. Since you girls already have learned so much I will tell you all. Perhaps you have heard of the Marborough pearls?"

Penny and Louise shook their heads.

"I forget that you are so very young," Mrs. Marborough said. "Your mothers would remember. At any rate, the necklace was handed down in our family for many generations, always to the daughter who was the first to marry. Virginia, my younger sister, dreamed and hoped that the pearls would go to her. Naturally, I shared a similar desire. As it came about, I was the first of the family to marry."

"Then you received the necklace?" Louise commented.

CHAPTER 17 - THE MARBOROUGH PEARLS

"It should have gone to me, but my sister was determined I never should win such a victory over her. In a fit of anger she hid the pearls. Father tried to force her to tell what she had done with them, but she was very headstrong. She ran away from home, married a scamp, and sailed with him to South America. She died there less than two years after my own marriage."

"What became of the pearls?" Penny asked eagerly.

"Our family believed that she took the necklace with her. For many years we assumed that Virginia's worthless husband had obtained possession of it. He denied any knowledge of the pearls, but we never accepted his story as true. Then, a few weeks ago, a letter came from South America. It had been written by Virginia's husband shortly before his death."

"He confessed to the theft of the necklace?" Louise asked, trying to speed the story.

"No, indeed. He merely enclosed a letter written by Virginia years before. It was addressed to me, and had never been sent, because her husband deliberately withheld it. Just selfish and cantankerous, that man was! The letter told where the pearls had been hidden. I imagine that Virginia's husband had planned to gain possession of them someday, but fate defeated him. So on his death bed he sent me the original letter which I should have received forty years earlier."

"Where were the pearls hidden?" Penny questioned, her eyes sparkling with anticipation. "You haven't found them yet?"

"No, and I doubt that I ever shall," Mrs. Marborough sighed. "Virginia's letter was not very definite. She begged my forgiveness for having caused so much trouble, and said that she had hidden the necklace near the old wishing well."

"Didn't she tell you where?" Louise asked in disappointment.

"There were several words which had been blotted with ink. I suspect Virginia's husband did it to prevent anyone but himself from learning the hiding place. Then when he finally sent the letter to me, he may have forgotten what he had done. That's only my guess, of course. As the letter reads, my only clue is that the pearls were hidden near the wishing well."

"That explains why you were removing the flagstones the other night," Louise remarked.

"Yes, I've searched everywhere I can think of except in the old tunnel. When you girls went through it tonight, did you notice anything unusual?"

"No hiding place," Penny replied. "Of course we weren't looking for anything of the sort. If we could explore the passageway by daylight—"

"Can't we help you find the pearls, Mrs. Marborough?" Louise interrupted. "It would be such fun searching for them."

"I'll be very happy to have your help," the old lady said, smiling. "Upon one condition. You must tell no one. Already I am the laughing stock of Riverview and if this latest story should get around everyone would talk."

Penny and Louise promptly assured her that they would tell no one about the pearls.

"Another thing—" Mrs. Marborough hesitated and then went on. "I suppose you understand now why I never invited you into the house. It wasn't that I meant to be inhospitable."

"Because the place isn't fixed up?" Louise came to her aid. "Why, Penny and I would have thought nothing of it. This is a cozy kitchen with a cheerful fire. I think it's nice."

"I probably shan't be here long. My purpose in returning to Riverview was to find the pearls. I've nearly made up my mind that they are lost forever."

"Oh, don't say that!" Penny cried. "Tomorrow, with your permission, Louise and I will explore the tunnel. We may have luck."

"I shall be very glad to have your help, my dear." Again Mrs. Marborough groped for words and finished awkwardly: "Please, I beg of you, don't tell anyone what you have seen tonight, particularly the barren state of this house."

"We understand," Penny said gravely.

The fire had burned low. Mindful that they must be home early, the girls bade Mrs. Marborough goodbye, promising to return the following day. Once outside the mansion, they paused beside a tree so that Penny might remove the heavy coveralls which she still wore over her frock.

"What a night!" she murmured happily.

"For once, Penny, one of your crazy adventures turned out beautifully," Louise praised. "We'll have a wonderful time searching for that necklace! She's certainly queer though."

"Mrs. Marborough?"

"Yes, imagine being so sensitive about how the interior of her house looks. Who would expect it to be fixed up nicely after standing empty so many years?"

"Aren't you forgetting something?" Penny asked. She hopped grotesquely on one foot as she extricated the other from the coveralls.

"Forgetting what?" Louise demanded, puzzled.

"Remember that first day we peeped into the house through the window?"

"Why, yes, what about it?"

"Your memory isn't very good, Louise. Don't you remember the sheet-draped furniture we saw?"

"That's right! I had forgotten. What became of it?"

"If I had just one guess, I'd say—Mr. Butterworth."

"Who is he, Penny?"

"A second-hand dealer who buys old furniture, newspapers, rubber tires—everything except bottles."

"Not that funny looking man we saw enter this house the other day!"

"The same. Louise, it's my guess that Mrs. Marborough sold all of her valuable antiques—probably for a fraction of their true worth."

"How foolish of her. Why would she do that?"

"Don't you understand?" Penny asked patiently. "There can be but one explanation. Mrs. Marborough isn't wealthy any more. She's living in dire poverty and trying to keep people from learning the truth."

CHAPTER 18 - SIGNBOARD INDIANS

The realization that in all likelihood Mrs. Marborough had sold her valuable antiques to the second-hand dealer was disconcerting to Louise as well as Penny. They did not believe that Mr. Butterworth would pay a fractional part of the furniture's true value, and apparently the widow's only reason for parting with her treasures was an urgent need for money.

"Of course, I may have guessed wrong about it," Penny admitted as she and Louise started toward home. "Just to check up, I'll call at Mr. Butterworth's shop tomorrow and see what I can learn."

"I wish we dared tell someone about the condition of the house," Louise said thoughtfully. "Why, if Mrs. Marborough is in need, Mother would help."

"So would Mrs. Weems," added Penny. "But we gave our promise not to reveal anything we saw. For the time-being, our hands are tied."

The events of the night had made the girls eager to return again to Rose Acres to search for the missing pearl necklace. They agreed that immediately after school the next afternoon they would call upon Mr. Butterworth and then keep their appointment with the widow.

"Remember, we mustn't tell anyone what we have learned," Penny warned as she parted company with her chum. "Not even Rhoda."

Throughout the following day, both girls were so excited that they found it all but impossible to study. When the closing bell finally brought release, they bolted from the school building before any of their classmates could detain them.

"I have the address of Mr. Butterworth's shop," Penny said, consulting a paper. "It's not far from here."

The building proved to be a typical second-hand store with old tables and chairs piled in the windows along with cut glass and bric-a-brac. Entering, the girls wandered about until a woman asked them if they were searching for anything in particular.

"We're interested in furniture," Penny explained. "Old pieces—antiques if we can find them."

"Come into the back room," the woman invited. "Mr. Butterworth bought a number of pieces just a few days ago. From one of Riverview's best homes too."

"Where was that?" inquired Louise.

"I didn't hear him mention the name. It was from a house that has been closed many years. The owner returned only a short time ago and is closing out everything."

The girls did not doubt that the furniture under discussion had been obtained from Rose Acres. They were certain of it as they viewed rosewood and mahogany chairs, imported mirrors, porcelain ornaments, massive four-poster beds, sofas with damaged coverings, and handsome chests and bureaus. Penny ventured to price a few of the items. The amount asked was so low that she knew Mr. Butterworth had paid an extremely small sum to the widow. Making an excuse for not purchasing, she and Louise escaped to the street.

"There's no question about it," Penny declared as they set off for Rose Acres. "Mrs. Marborough sold her beautiful things to Mr. Butterworth."

"He can't appreciate their value or he never would offer them at such low prices," Louise added. "Anyone who buys those things will obtain wonderful bargains."

Penny nodded soberly. Lost in thought, she had little to say until the girls drew near Rose Acres.

"Don't let on to Mrs. Marborough that we've learned about the furniture," she warned. "It's really none of our affair if she sells her belongings."

WISHING WELL

The widow had been expecting the girls and had everything in readiness to explore the tunnel. While they searched it from end to end, she waited hopefully at the wishing well.

"Have you found anything?" she called several times.

"Not yet," Penny would reply patiently.

She and Louise laboriously examined every inch of the bricked passageway but with fading hope. The walls were firm, giving no indication that anything ever had been hidden behind or within them. To have excavated the hard-packed dirt flooring was a task not to be considered at the moment.

"There's nothing here," Penny whispered to her chum. "I doubt that the pearls ever were hidden in this tunnel."

"Mrs. Marborough will be terribly disappointed," Louise replied in an undertone. "What shall we tell her?"

"We can pretend to keep on searching. Maybe if we prowl about this place for a few days, we'll have luck."

"The pearls were hidden near the wishing well. We have that much to go on."

"They may have disappeared years ago," Penny contributed pessimistically. "To tell you the truth, I don't feel very hopeful about ever finding them."

Leaving the tunnel by means of the easier exit, the girls emerged into the basement. They were preparing to climb the stairs to the first floor when Mrs. Marborough's voice reached their ears almost as plainly as if she were in the cellar.

"Louise! Penny! Are you all right?"

Startled by the clearness of the call, the girls paused on the stairway.

"Why, her voice came through as plainly as if she were in this room!" Louise exclaimed. "You don't suppose Mrs. Marborough has ventured into the passageway?"

Thoroughly alarmed, the girls raced up the stairway and out of the house into the yard. To their relief they saw Mrs. Marborough standing by the wishing well, peering anxiously down.

"Oh, here you are!" she murmured as they ran up. "I was beginning to get worried. The last time I called you did not answer."

"We were down in the basement," Penny explained. "Mrs. Marborough, your voice came through to us as plainly as if you were in the passage."

The disclosure did not seem to surprise the widow, for she smiled and said:

"I've always known that sound carried from the well to the house. In fact, in past years I found it amusing to listen to conversations carried on by persons who never dreamed that their words were overheard."

"Then that explains why so many wishes which were made here at the well came true!" Penny cried. "You were the Good Fairy behind it all."

"Oh, now and then, if it pleased my fancy, I arranged to have a wish granted," Mrs. Marborough acknowledged, smiling grimly. "That was in the days when I had money—" she broke off and ended—"more than I have now, I mean."

"Mrs. Marborough, you must have heard those wishes we made the day of your return to Riverview," Penny said after a moment. "Were you responsible for sending a basket of food to Rhoda's people?"

"I am afraid I was."

"And did you grant Rhoda's second wish?" Louise asked quickly. "Did you have anything to do with getting her brother, Ted, a job?"

"Judge Harlan is an old friend of mine," Mrs. Marborough explained. "I merely wrote him a note suggesting that he would do me a favor by helping the boy if he found him worthy."

Although the widow's admission cleared up much of the mystery which had surrounded the old wishing well, Louise and Penny were dumbfounded, nevertheless. Never once had anyone in Riverview connected Mrs. Marborough with a particularly charitable deed.

As if guessing their thoughts, the woman said sharply:

"Now mind, I'll not have you telling this around the town! I'm through with all such silly business, and I don't propose to have busybodies discuss whether or not I am addle-brained!"

"Why, Mrs. Marborough!" protested Louise. "It was a kind, generous thing to do."

"Generous, fiddlesticks! I did it because it pleased me and for no other reason. Let's not talk about it any more."

CHAPTER 18 - SIGNBOARD INDIANS

Mrs. Marborough questioned the girls concerning their exploration of the tunnel. Her disappointment over the failure to find the pearls was keen but she tried not to show it.

"I knew it was a fool's errand coming to Riverview to look for that stupid necklace!" she declared. "Like as not, it never was hidden at Rose Acres, my sister's letter to the contrary. I intend to forget about the whole affair."

"Oh, Mrs. Marborough, don't give up so soon," Penny pleaded. "Louise and I have only started to search. We may find it yet."

"You've been very nice," the widow said, smiling almost in a friendly way. "I'll remember it always when I am far away."

"Then you intend to leave Riverview?" Louise asked in disappointment.

"I must sell Rose Acres. I have no other course open."

"Not to Jay Franklin, I hope!" Penny exclaimed.

"I have no intention of dealing with him if anyone else will make an offer. So far I have found no other person who is interested in the property."

Drawing a deep sigh, Mrs. Marborough arose. Without much enthusiasm she invited the girls to come with her into the house, but they tactfully declined.

"We'll come again tomorrow, if you don't mind," Penny said as she and Louise turned to leave.

"Do," replied Mrs. Marborough. "We might make a final search for the pearls."

Enroute to Riverview, the girls talked over the situation and agreed that the prospect of finding the necklace was a slim one. They had grown to like the eccentric widow and were sorry that she had decided to move away from the city of her birth.

"I am sure if she had money she would remain here," Louise declared. "And it will nearly kill her if she is forced to deal with Jay Franklin. How she does dislike him!"

Parting with her chum in the business section of Riverview, Penny went directly to the *Star* office. Her father was ready to start home.

"Anything new about Jay Franklin and those record stones he hopes to sell to the museum?" Penny inquired absently as the automobile sped along the congested streets.

"Nothing you haven't heard," Mr. Parker replied. "Franklin expects to make the sale and probably will. The museum people have put themselves on record as saying that the stones bear authentic writing."

"Then it appears that your original hunch was incorrect," Penny observed. "Too bad you played down the story in the *Star*."

"I may have made a mistake. All the same, I am pinning my hopes on the expert from Brimwell College."

"What expert, Dad?"

"I guess I neglected to tell you. The *Star* hired Professor Anjus from Brimwell to inspect the stones. His opinion doesn't coincide with that of the museum experts. He has pronounced them fakes."

"If the experts can't agree, then how can one prove anything?"

"It is something of a tangle," Mr. Parker smiled. "I turned that tool you obtained from Crocker over to Professor Anjus. He expects to make exhaustive tests and to report to me within a few days."

The car had reached the outskirts of Riverview. As it passed along streets which were sparsely dotted with houses, Penny called attention to several large billboards which disfigured the landscape.

"Look, Dad!" she directed, pointing to a particularly colorful poster. "An Indian show is coming to town next week!"

Mr. Parker turned his head to gaze at the billboard. To Penny's amazement, he suddenly slammed on the brake, bringing the car to a lurching halt at the side of the road.

"That's it!" he cried, his eyes on the huge sign. "The motive! I couldn't figure it out, but now I have the clue I need! Penny, we'll put a crimp in Jay Franklin's little game, or my name isn't Anthony Parker!"

CHAPTER 19 - PUBLICITY PLUS

Completely mystified by her father's remarks, Penny waited for him to explain.

"Don't you get it?" he asked, waving his hand toward the big signboard. "The finding of those stones bearing Elizabethan and Indian writing was perfectly timed! It's all a publicity stunt for the coming show!"

"How could it be?" Penny questioned, scarcely able to accept her father's theory. "I found one of the rocks myself. I know I wasn't hired by any Indian show!"

"It was pure luck that you stumbled into the stone, Penny. If you hadn't, someone hired by the Indian show would have brought it to light."

"But where does Jay Franklin figure in, Dad? You don't think he's connected with the publicity scheme as you call it!"

"Franklin wouldn't have sufficient imagination to pull off a stunt like that," Mr. Parker declared. "No, he may actually believe in the authenticity of the stones. At any rate, he saw an opportunity to make a little money for himself and seized it."

"Why should an Indian show go to the trouble of having stones carved and planted in various fields? It doesn't make sense."

"The resulting publicity should draw state-wide attention to the show, Penny. It's just the sort of idea which would appeal to a clever publicity agent. Every newspaper in Riverview except the *Star* has fallen for it, giving columns of space to the story."

"I still don't see how the show will gain. Its name never has been mentioned in connection with the finding of the stones."

"Of course not, Penny. That would be too crude. But at the proper time, the publicity agent will twist all of the stories to his own purpose."

"Dad," said Penny sadly, "in the past you have accused me of having wild ideas. I think the score is even now."

"I'll have that show traced," Mr. Parker declared, paying no heed to his daughter. "Since it is coming to Riverview next week it can't be far away now. I may find it worth while to call on the publicity agent and have a little chat with him."

Penny was gazing at the billboard again, reading the dates.

"Dad, the show will play here during Pilgrimage Week," she declared. "What a shame! It's certain to take away customers from a much more worthwhile event."

"There may not be an Indian show," responded Mr. Parker grimly. "Not when I get through with the outfit!"

Immediately upon arriving at home, the publisher called the newspaper office, delegating City Editor DeWitt to obtain complete information about the Indian Show and to report to him. All evening he talked of his theory until both Penny and Mrs. Weems confessed that they were a bit weary of redskins.

"I shall write an editorial for tomorrow's *Star*," Mr. Parker announced. "Even if I haven't absolute facts, I'll drop a few broad hints about those fake stones!"

The editorial, cleverly worded but with very definite implications, was composed that night, and telephoned to the newspaper office. Penny had the pleasure of reading it at breakfast the next morning.

"You certainly did yourself proud, Dad," she praised. "However, I imagine the museum people aren't going to be too pleased. Nor certain other folks in this town."

"Let me take a look at it," Mr. Parker requested, reaching for the paper.

CHAPTER 19 - PUBLICITY PLUS

As Penny offered it to him, the doorbell rang. Mrs. Weems was busy in the kitchen so the girl arose and went to answer it. Jay Franklin stood on the porch.

"Good morning," he said in a hard voice. "Is your father here?"

"Yes, he is eating breakfast," Penny responded. "Won't you come in, please?"

Mr. Franklin walked ahead of her into the living room.

"Good morning, Jay," called the editor, who was able to see the caller from his chair at the breakfast table. "Will you have a cup of coffee with us?"

Ignoring the invitation, Mr. Franklin entered the dinette, blocking the doorway. From his pocket he took a copy of the morning *Star*.

"Parker," he said curtly, "I've just read your editorial and I demand an explanation! Do you realize what you've done?"

"Written a pretty fair stickful—or so my daughter tells me," Mr. Parker smiled undisturbed.

"You've deliberately tried to smear me," the real estate man accused.

"I don't recall that your name was mentioned in the editorial."

"No, but you know I expect to sell those two stones to the museum. This editorial of yours may queer the sale!"

"Then it will have fulfilled its purpose. The stones are fakes. If you aren't aware of it, I suggest that you acquaint yourself with the true facts."

"Those stones bear genuine Elizabethan writing. There's no connection with any cheap Indian show, and I defy you to prove it!"

"Consider your challenge accepted," replied Mr. Parker evenly. "I expect to publish the true facts very shortly in the *Star*."

"If you prevent me from making a sale to the museum, I'll sue you!" Jay Franklin threatened. "That's all I have to say. Good morning!"

In his anger he turned so quickly that he ran into Penny who stood directly behind him. Without bothering to apologize, he brushed past her, out the front door.

"What a dreadful man!" remarked Mrs. Weems who had heard the conversation from the kitchen.

"I rather expected him to call, although not so early in the morning," the publisher remarked, reaching for a slice of toast. "His attitude doesn't bother me in the least."

"He may actually sue you if you don't make good on producing facts," Penny commented. "How are you going to do it?"

"DeWitt informs me that the Indian Show is playing at Bryan this week. I'll drive over there today and see what I can learn."

Bryan was a small city located sixty-nine miles from Riverview. Although Penny ordinarily would have spent the day in school, she immediately decided that her father would need her assistance. Accordingly, she begged so hard to accompany him that he finally gave his consent.

Early afternoon saw Mr. Parker and his daughter at the outskirts of Bryan where two large blue and red show tents had been set up. A band played, and townspeople were pouring past the ticket-taker, an Indian who wore the headdress of a chieftain.

"It looks rather interesting," Penny remarked wistfully.

Mr. Parker stripped a bill from his wallet and gave it to her.

"Go buy yourself a ticket," he said, smiling. "I'll meet you here by the entrance in an hour."

"Don't you want to see the show, Dad?"

"I've outgrown such foolishness," he rejoined. "I'll find the publicity agent and have my little talk with him."

The enticing sound of tom-toms and Indian war whoops caused Penny to forget her desire to meet the show's publicity man. Saying goodbye to her father, she bought a ticket and hastened into the big top. For an hour she sat through a very mediocre performance, consisting in the main part of cowboy and Indian horseback riding. The concluding event, a tableau, depicted an attack by redskins upon an early English colony settlement. It was all very boring, and Penny left in the middle of the performance.

Mr. Parker was not waiting at the entrance way. Loitering about for a time, she inquired of a workman and learned that her father was in one of the small tents close by. The flap had been rolled back, permitting her to see a sharp-faced man of thirty who sat at a desk piled with papers.

"Is that the show's publicity agent?" she asked the workman.

"Yep, Bill McJavins," he answered. "He's sure put new life into this outfit. We've been packin' them in ever since he took over."

Within a few minutes Mr. Parker joined Penny and from the expression of his face, she immediately guessed that his interview had not been very successful.

"I take it that Bill McJavins didn't break down and confess all?" she inquired lightly.

"He denied any connection with those stones found in Riverview," Mr. Parker replied. "But in the next breath he admitted he knew all about them and intends to capitalize on the story."

"Just how will it help the show?"

"From what McJavins told me, I gather the program includes an historical pageant."

"That would be a flattering name for it."

"In the pageant, Indians attack a white settlement. A beautiful maiden escapes, and chisels on a stone tablet an account of the massacre—then she, too, succumbs to the tomahawk."

"You seem to know more about the show than I," Penny laughed. "Anyway, I'm glad to learn how it came out!"

"It's my guess that McJavins hopes to profit by a tie-up between the stone writing of the pageant and the finding of similar rocks near Riverview. It's a cheap trick, and the hoax would have been exposed a long time ago if museum authorities were awake!"

Neither discouraged nor too much elated by the results of the trip, Mr. Parker and Penny returned to Riverview. It was exactly noon when they reached the newspaper office.

"I trust you plan to attend school this afternoon," the editor reminded his daughter. "By lunching downtown you'll have plenty of time to get there."

Loitering about the newsroom as long as she dared, Penny crossed the street to have a sandwich at a quick-lunch cafe. As she reached the restaurant she observed a familiar figure coming toward her.

"Rhoda Wiegand!" she exclaimed. "Aren't you going in the wrong direction?"

"I'm cutting classes for the afternoon," the trailer camp girl replied, pausing. "Mr. Coaten expects me to meet him at the Fischer Building. Can you tell me where it is?"

"Three blocks straight down the street," Penny directed. She hesitated and then said: "Rhoda, it's none of my affair, but I do hope you're not agreeing to Mr. Coaten's proposal."

"The adoption? Yes, I am, Penny. I've tried to hold out against them all, but I can't do it. Ted signed the papers two days ago. Since then I've had no peace. Ted keeps after me, the Breens want me to do it, and Mr. Coaten says I am selfish."

"We both know Mr. Coaten intends to profit in some way at your expense."

"I do feel that way about it. If only I dared stand firm—"

"You must," Penny said earnestly. Deliberately taking Rhoda's arm she turned her about. "You're to break that appointment and have luncheon with me. I'll assume all the responsibility."

CHAPTER 20 - RHODA'S PROBLEM

Rhoda allowed herself to be dissuaded, but not without misgiving. As she lunched with Penny at the Dolman Cafe, she painted a gloomy picture of what lay before her.

"You don't understand how it is," she said, slowly stirring a cup of hot chocolate. "I really haven't a good reason for refusing to consent to the adoption. If I had one scrap of evidence against Mr. Coaten it would be different."

"Can't you write to Texas and inquire about him and his friend?"

"I did," Rhoda admitted. "The answer came back that Mr. Coaten was unknown at the address he gave the Breens."

"I should think that would be sufficient reason for distrusting him."

"Oh, Mr. Coaten explained it by saying that his family just moved to a new house, and that he inadvertently had given me the wrong address."

"Did you ask for the second one, Rhoda?"

"Yes, he gave it to me. So far I've not had time for a reply."

"My advice is to stall for time," Penny said. "If we have even a few days more we may dig up some information. However, I'll confess I haven't an idea at the moment."

"Mr. Coaten will be furious because I didn't keep the appointment," Rhoda sighed. "He's certain to come to the trailer camp tonight and demand an explanation."

"Just tell him you changed your mind and refuse to say anything more. I wish I could talk to him."

"So do I," declared Rhoda with emphasis. "Why not take dinner with us tonight—if you can stand our brand of hospitality."

"Well, I don't know," Penny hesitated. "Louise and I plan to go to Mrs. Marborough's place directly after school—"

"Oh, I wish I could go with you!" Rhoda declared impulsively. "I never have had an opportunity to finish my sketch. Mrs. Marborough is such an interesting character, too."

"You don't know the half of it," laughed Penny. "You're welcome to come along. I think Mrs. Marborough will be willing to share our secret with you."

"Secret?"

"No questions now, please," Penny requested, capturing both luncheon checks. "We must hurry or we'll be late for school."

Having assured Mrs. Marborough that she would disclose nothing about the lost pearl necklace, she could not honorably share the adventure with her friend. However, it was her hope and belief that the widow would be willing to allow Rhoda to aid in the exciting search of the premises.

Penny's surmise proved entirely correct. Later that afternoon when the three girls called at Rose Acres, Mrs. Marborough scarcely noticed that Rhoda was an uninvited member of the party. At once she began talking of the missing pearls, which to the satisfaction of Louise and Penny, necessitated a complete explanation.

"Imagine finding a tunnel leading from the old wishing well to the house!" Rhoda cried in delight. "Take me through it! Show me everything!"

"Perhaps you can find the pearls," Penny laughed. "So far Louise and I have failed."

"They're supposed to be hidden somewhere near the old wishing well," Louise contributed. "That's the only real clue we have."

"I suppose you looked under the flagstones?"

"I did that many days ago," answered Mrs. Marborough. "In fact, I don't think there's a single place I haven't searched."

"The roof of the well?" Rhoda suggested.

"We never once thought of that place!" Louise exclaimed. "But how could the necklace be secreted there?" She frowned as she stared at the steep-pitched, shingled covering which formed a protection over the well.

"It's worth looking at anyhow!" Penny declared. "I'll get a ladder if I can find one."

"In the woodshed," directed Mrs. Marborough.

Penny soon returned carrying a dust-laden step-ladder which had not seen service in many years. Bracing it against the well, she mounted and began to inspect the roof.

"Find anything?" inquired Rhoda impatiently.

"Two birds' nests. There seems to be a hole under the edge of the roofing—"

Penny broke off as she ran her hand into the narrow opening.

"Yes, there is something here!" she exclaimed a moment later. "It feels like a tiny box!"

Mrs. Marborough and the two girls waited tensely, hardly daring to hope. Penny withdrew her hand from the hole, triumphantly holding up a small leather case.

"This isn't it?" she asked.

"Oh, yes, yes!" Mrs. Marborough cried. "It is the old jewel case. The pearls must be inside!"

In her haste to climb down from the ladder, Penny missed one of the steps. Rhoda seized her arm saving her from a hard fall. Recovering her breath, Penny politely offered the jewel case to Mrs. Marborough.

With the three girls clustered about her, the mistress of Rose Acres ceremoniously opened the lid. In a nest of yellowed silk lay a string of matched pearls, so beautiful and lustrous that no one could find words to admire it.

"The famous Marborough pearls," the widow murmured at last. "This necklace brought only unhappiness to our family. Now, however, they shall serve a useful purpose!"

The girls gazed at Mrs. Marborough expectantly, waiting for her to continue:

"I shall sell the pearls," she said quietly. "They represent a small fortune, and by disposing of them I'll be well-provided for in my old age. It won't be necessary for me to pinch and skrimp. I'll be able to hold my head up in society—live like a human being again instead of a recluse."

Realizing that she was revealing a great deal, Mrs. Marborough snapped shut the jewel case and smiled at the girls.

"I never should have found the pearls by myself. To tell you that I am grateful scarcely expresses my feelings. You've saved me from poverty."

"Rhoda did it," Penny declared, giving full credit to the trailer-camp girl. "Louise and I never would have thought of searching the roof of the well."

"Do come inside," Mrs. Marborough invited gaily. "We'll have tea in my kitchen. It's not much to offer, but I did bake a little sponge cake this morning."

No longer ashamed of the barren condition of the old mansion, the widow led the girls through the great empty rooms. By daylight, notwithstanding the stained condition of the walls, the house seemed more elegant than ever. There was a large fan-shaped window of stained glass which Penny had not noticed before, and dozens of candle holders attached to the walls.

"How gorgeous this place would look if all the candles could be lighted at one time," she remarked admiringly.

"And if the house had a little furniture in it," added Mrs. Marborough. "You know, a few days ago I did a very foolish thing."

Louise glanced quickly at Penny but said nothing.

"I was a bit hard pressed for money," the widow resumed. "On an impulse I sold all my furniture to Mr. Butterworth. Do you suppose he will sell it back to me?"

"He should," declared Penny.

"I like Riverview for I was born here," Mrs. Marborough went on, talking as if to herself. "By selling the pearls I can refurnish the house, have the grounds restored to their original beauty, and live as I formerly did!"

"Oh, I do hope you decide to stay here," Penny said eagerly.

CHAPTER 20 - RHODA'S PROBLEM

Mrs. Marborough started a fire in the kitchen stove and put a kettle of water on to boil. Soon the tea was ready, and was served with generous slices of yellow sponge cake.

"I suppose everyone in Riverview considers me a crotchety old woman," Mrs. Marborough remarked presently. "I haven't been very friendly because I didn't want folks to know I had sold my furniture. Some days ago a group of women came to see me about opening the house for some sort of Festival—"

"Pilgrimage Week," Penny supplied.

"I turned them down, not because I wasn't eager to help, but because I couldn't let folks know all my furniture was gone. I wonder if they would still care to include Rose Acres in the tour of houses?"

"Oh, Mrs. Marborough, it would practically save the Festival!" Penny cried. "A cheap Indian show is coming to town the same week. I know for a fact that the Festival tickets aren't selling very well."

"Everyone wants to see Rose Acres," Louise added enthusiastically.

"If I can re-purchase my furniture, I'll be glad to open the house to the public," Mrs. Marborough said, her eyes twinkling as she gazed directly at Penny. "That was the wish you made at the well, I believe?"

"Oh, it was! And you'll make it come true!"

"It's little enough to do in return for the favor you have bestowed upon me."

"Nothing will please me more than to see this old house in all its glory!" Penny declared enthusiastically. "May we light all the candles at one time?"

"If you like."

"And wouldn't it be fun to hold a grand ball here with everyone dressed in colonial costume!" Penny went on. "Can't you just see the place with beaux and their ladies dancing a quadrille?"

"I'll talk to the members of the Festival Committee tomorrow," Mrs. Marborough promised. "My first call, however, will be upon Mr. Butterworth."

Long shadows were falling, and the girls soon arose to depart. During the walk into Riverview, Rhoda became rather sober and Penny shrewdly guessed that she had forgotten about the Marborough pearls and was thinking of the dreaded interview with Mr. Coaten.

"You're really afraid to meet that man aren't you?" she asked curiously.

"Not exactly afraid," Rhoda responded. "He'll be waiting though, I'm sure. I just don't know what to tell him."

"Will it be easier for you if I go with you to the camp?"

"Oh, I wish you would, Penny!" Rhoda said gratefully.

Louise soon parted with her friends, and the two girls went on to the trailer camp. Mrs. Breen immediately informed them that Mr. Coaten had called earlier in the afternoon and expected to return again.

"I hope you didn't make trouble about signing the papers," she said severely. "He acted quite upset."

"I broke our appointment," Rhoda responded briefly. "So far I've not made up my mind what to do."

There followed a lengthy argument in which Mrs. Breen assured the girl that she was making a serious mistake by antagonizing such a kind, generous man as Mr. Coaten. Penny took no part in the conversation, although she readily could see how difficult had become Rhoda's position.

"You'll have to stay to dinner now," Rhoda whispered to her. "Mr. Coaten is certain to come, and I can't stand against them all."

Penny had no desire to remain for a meal, but feeling that she should support her friend, accepted the invitation. Ted soon came home from working at Judge Harlan's office, and he too expressed displeasure because his sister had broken the appointment with Mr. Coaten.

During dinner the subject was studiously avoided. Somewhat to Penny's disapproval, Rhoda began to tell the Breens about everything that had occurred at Rose Acres. At mention of the pearl necklace, Ted's fork clattered against his plate and he forgot to eat.

"You actually found a string of pearls?" he asked incredulously. "Real ones?"

"They must be worth many thousand dollars," Rhoda assured him. "Mrs. Marborough intends to sell them and use the money to remodel her place."

Ted was about to ask another question, then seemed to reconsider.

"More stew?" Mrs. Breen asked as an awkward silence fell.

"No thanks, Mom," he answered. "If you'll excuse me, I'll skip out. I have a date uptown with a fellow."

WISHING WELL

Mrs. Breen made no reply and the boy left the trailer. Penny thought that she too should be leaving, but before she could speak, there came a light tap on the door. Mr. Breen thrust his head out the open window.

"It's Mr. Coaten," he announced in a hoarse whisper. "What are you going to tell him Rhoda?"

"I don't know," she answered, gazing helplessly at Penny.

CHAPTER 21 - MRS. MARBOROUGH'S LOSS

Mrs. Breen hastily removed her apron and opened the door to admit the caller.

"Good evening," said Mr. Coaten. His gaze roved from one person to another in the crowded little room, coming to rest upon Rhoda.

"I'm sorry I couldn't keep our appointment this afternoon," she said stiffly. "The truth is, I've changed my mind about signing that paper."

"I've tried to talk sense into her," Mrs. Breen broke in. "I don't know what's come over the girl lately."

Mr. Coaten seated himself on the day bed, smiling at Rhoda in a friendly way.

"I understand how you feel," he said. "You are afraid you don't know me well enough to agree to the adoption."

"I never heard of you until you came to Riverview."

"Rhoda, that's no way to talk!" Mrs. Breen reprimanded. "What would we have done without Mr. Coaten? He's given us money, bought groceries, and made everything much easier."

"I appreciate everything. It's just that—well, I don't care to be adopted. I like things as they are."

Mrs. Breen's kindly face tightened into hard lines.

"Rhoda," she said firmly, "this is an opportunity for you, and you ought to be smart enough to realize it. Mr. Coaten will give you good clothes and schooling. Pop and I can't do it."

"You've given me too much now," Rhoda murmured, her gaze on the linoleum rug.

"I've been patient with you, but now I'm going to have my say. We can't keep you any more."

"You're telling me to go?" Rhoda gasped, scarcely believing that she had heard correctly.

"I'm asking you to sign whatever it is that Mr. Coaten wants you to."

Rhoda gazed at Penny, her lips trembling. There seemed but one course open to her, for she had no money and no relatives. Fully aware of her predicament, Mr. Coaten smiled triumphantly. From his pocket he whipped out a fountain pen and a folded, neatly-typed paper.

"Rhoda, don't sign unless you really wish to," Penny said quietly.

"But I'll have no home—"

"You may stay with me. I'll find a place for you."

Directing her gaze upon Mr. Coaten, Penny resumed:

"May I ask why you are so eager to obtain a guardianship over Ted and Rhoda? What do you expect to gain by it?"

"My dear young lady—" Mr. Coaten's voice was soft but his eyes glinted angrily. "I expect to gain nothing."

"I gathered a different impression when I heard you and your friend talking a night or so ago at the Marborough place."

At first Mr. Coaten did not appear to understand, then as Penny's meaning dawned upon him, he arose from the couch.

"I have no wish to discuss this matter with you—a stranger," he said coldly. "For some reason you are prejudiced against me, and have deliberately influenced Rhoda to go against Mrs. Breen's desires."

"It's a question for our own family to settle," Mrs. Breen added.

"I'll go at once," said Penny. She gazed questioningly at Rhoda.

"Do you really think you could take me in at your place?" the girl asked.

"Of course. My offer holds."

"Then I'll come with you!" Darting to a wardrobe closet, Rhoda began to toss garments into a suitcase.

"Rhoda, you can't go like this!" Mrs. Breen cried in protest. "Why won't you listen to reason?"

"Let her go!" Mr. Coaten said harshly. "She'll come back in a day or two glad to accept my offer."

Rhoda paid no heed to the conversation which flowed about her. Swiftly she packed her suitcase and told Penny that she was ready to leave.

"Mrs. Breen," she said, squeezing the woman's hand in parting, "you and Pop have been wonderful to Ted and me. I'll never forget it—never. Someday I'll repay you, too."

"This is the way you do it," Mrs. Breen retorted bitterly. "By defying my wishes."

There was nothing more to be said. Penny and Rhoda quickly left the trailer, carrying the suitcase between them.

"I shouldn't have done it," the girl murmured contritely. "I don't know how I'll ever manage to make a living. Ted likely will side against me, too."

"Don't think of anything tonight," Penny advised, although she too was worried. "We'll find something for you. Dad may have an opening on the *Star*."

Mrs. Weems long ago had ceased to be surprised by anything that Penny did, and so, when the two girls arrived at the Parker home, she did not ask many questions. Rhoda was comfortably established in the guest room and made to feel that she was welcome. However, ultimately learning what had occurred, the housekeeper was not at all certain that Penny had done right by helping the girl to leave home. Nor was Mr. Parker encouraging about the prospects of finding employment.

"Can she type or take shorthand?" he asked bluntly.

"I don't think so," Penny admitted.

"The *Star* can't be made a catch-all for your unemployed friends," Mr. Parker resumed severely. "My advice is to send her back to the Breens."

"I can't do that, Dad. You don't understand."

"Well, let it ride for a few days," her father replied, frowning. "I'll see what I can do."

Penny tried to keep Rhoda from realizing that her presence in the household had created a problem. In the morning the girls went to school together, returned for lunch, and then attended the afternoon session. Rhoda became increasingly gloomy.

"Penny, this can't go on indefinitely," she protested. "I'll have to get a job somehow."

"Let me worry about that."

"Ted hasn't come to see me either," Rhoda went on nervously. "I—I'm beginning to think I should go back and sign that paper."

"Don't even consider it," Penny said firmly. "You need diversion to keep your mind off the problem. Let's hike out to the Marborough place!"

Carrying their books, the girls set off for Rose Acres. Several windows on the lower floor of the house had been opened to admit fresh air and the blinds no longer were drawn. For the first time since Mrs. Marborough's return, the old mansion actually had a "lived in" appearance. However, although Penny knocked many times, the widow did not come to the door.

"She can't be here," Rhoda remarked at last.

"The windows are open," Penny said thoughtfully. "I doubt that Mrs. Marborough would go very far away without closing them."

The girls wandered to the wishing well, and then made a complete tour of the grounds. Mrs. Marborough was nowhere in the yard.

"Shall we go?" Rhoda asked.

"I'll knock on the door just once more," Penny said. "I can't help feeling that she is here."

Circling the house to the side entrance, the girls again rapped and waited.

"Listen!" commanded Penny suddenly.

"I don't hear anything," declared Rhoda, startled by the manner in which her companion had given the command.

"I thought someone called or groaned—the sound came from inside the house."

"You must have imagined it."

"Maybe I did," Penny acknowledged, "but I don't think so."

CHAPTER 21 - MRS. MARBOROUGH'S LOSS

Testing the door, she found it unlocked. As it swung back a tiny crack, she called loudly: "Oh, Mrs. Marborough, are you at home?"

Distinctly, both girls heard an answering cry, but the words were unintelligible. The sound had come from the direction of the kitchen.

"Mrs. Marborough must be ill!" Penny gasped, for the voice had been very weak.

Hesitating no longer, she entered the house, and with Rhoda trailing close behind, ran to the kitchen. Mrs. Marborough, still garbed in night clothing, lay on the daybed, her face ashen. The woman breathed with the greatest of difficulty, and both girls knew at once that she was seriously ill.

"My heart—" Mrs. Marborough whispered. "An attack—last night."

"Rhoda, run as fast as you can and get Doctor Hamilton," Penny said tersely. "I'll stay here."

As soon as her friend had gone, she busied herself trying to make Mrs. Marborough comfortable. She rearranged the disordered blankets, and fanned air toward the woman, making it easier for her to breathe.

"My pearls," Mrs. Marborough whispered after a moment. "They're gone."

Penny thought little of the remark, deciding that the widow was not entirely rational.

"Oh, you have the necklace," she said soothingly. "Don't you remember? We found it yesterday."

"Gone—" Mrs. Marborough repeated. "It gave me such a shock—I had hidden the pearls in the teapot. This morning—"

Penny bent closer, suddenly realizing that the old lady was in possession of her faculties and was trying to disclose something of great importance.

"I went there this morning," Mrs. Marborough completed with difficulty. "The pearls were gone. They've been stolen. Now I have nothing."

CHAPTER 22 - THE MISSING NECKLACE

Penny tried to quiet the old lady by assuring her that the pearl necklace must be somewhere in the house.

"No—no, it is gone," Mrs. Marborough insisted. "A thief entered the house during the night. The shock of it brought on this attack."

Spent by the effort required to speak, the widow closed her eyes, and relaxed. Thinking that she had gone to sleep, Penny left the bedside for a moment. A quick glance assured her that the kitchen window was open, and far more alarming, the screen had been neatly cut from its frame. An empty China teapot stood on the kitchen table.

"It must be true!" Penny thought with a sinking heart. "The pearls have been stolen, and the shock of it nearly killed Mrs. Marborough! But who could have known that she had the necklace here in the house?"

Louise and Rhoda were beyond suspicion, and for a moment she could think of no others who had knowledge of the pearls. Then, with a start, it came to her that the story had been told the previous night at the Breens.

"Ted knew about it and he was interested!" she thought. "But I can't believe he would do such a contemptible thing—even if he did once steal a chicken."

Penny's unhappy reflections were broken by the arrival of Rhoda with Doctor Hamilton. For the next half hour the girls were kept more than busy carrying out his instructions.

"Mrs. Marborough, in a way you have been very fortunate," the doctor said as he finally prepared to leave the house. "Your attack has been a light one and with proper care you should be on your feet again within a week or two. I'll arrange to have you taken to the hospital at once."

The widow tried to raise up in bed. "I won't go!" she announced. "Hospitals cost money—more than I have to spend."

"It won't cost you anything, Mrs. Marborough. I'll arrange everything."

"I refuse to be a charity patient," the widow declared defiantly. "I'll die first! Go away and take your pills with you!"

"Then if you refuse hospital care, I must arrange for a nurse."

"I can't afford that either," the old lady snapped. "Just go away and I'll get along by myself. I'm feeling better. If I could only have a cup of tea—"

"I'll make it for you," Rhoda offered eagerly.

Penny signaled to the doctor, indicating that she wished him to follow her into another room. Once beyond the hearing of the old lady, she outlined a plan.

"Mrs. Marborough likes Rhoda very much," she said to the doctor. "I think she might be perfectly satisfied to be looked after by her."

"The girl seems sensible and efficient," Doctor Hamilton replied. "But would she be willing to stay?"

"I think she might for she has no home of her own."

Relieved to have the problem solved so easily, the doctor declared that the plan could be tried for a few days at least.

"I'll drop in again late tonight," he promised, picking up his bag.

Consulted by Penny, Rhoda said at once that she would be happy indeed to remain with Mrs. Marborough as long as her services were required. The widow too seemed pleased by the arrangement.

"It's very good of you," she murmured to Rhoda. "I can't pay you though. Not unless my pearls are recovered."

CHAPTER 22 - THE MISSING NECKLACE

"Your pearls?" the girl echoed in astonishment.

Penny drew her friend aside, explaining what had occurred. Rhoda was shocked to learn that the necklace had been stolen.

"How dreadful!" she gasped. "Who could have taken the pearls?"

Apparently it did not occur to her that her own brother Ted might be regarded with suspicion. Penny was much too kind to drop such a hint, and kept her thoughts strictly to herself.

However, later in the day, with Mrs. Marborough's permission, she made a full report of the theft to local police. An officer visited Rose Acres, but aside from establishing exactly how the house had been entered, obtained few useful clues. Questioned at considerable length, Penny disclosed that so far as she knew only Louise Sidell, the trailer camp family, Ted, Rhoda and herself had known that the pearls were in the mansion.

"We'll keep that Breen family under surveillance," the officer promised. "I'll let you know if anything develops."

Another problem immediately confronted Penny. An inspection of the cupboards of the Marborough home had revealed that there was barely enough food to last a day.

"Buy whatever you need," the widow instructed. "You'll find money in the top bureau drawer."

By diligent search, the girls found four dollars and twenty-four cents which they felt certain was all the money the old lady possessed.

"Why, the medicines Doctor Hamilton ordered will take almost this much!" Penny said in dismay. "Something must be done."

Both girls respected Mrs. Marborough's desire for secrecy, but they knew it would not be possible to help her and, at the same time, prevent the townspeople from learning of her dire poverty. Deeply troubled, Penny placed the problem in Mrs. Weems' hands.

"Why, that poor woman!" the housekeeper explained. "To think that she is sick and hasn't the things that she needs. I'll send a basket of food at once. I am sure many people will be eager to help."

Mrs. Weems busied herself at the telephone, and within a few hours, all manner of useful gifts began to arrive at Rose Acres. Neighbors came to help Rhoda with the housework and to care for the widow.

As was inevitable, the entire story of Mrs. Marborough's poverty, including the loss of the pearl necklace, circulated throughout Riverview. Since there no longer was any excuse for secrecy, Penny disclosed to members of the Pilgrimage Committee what had become of the old lady's furniture and why she had refused to open her house during Festival Week. To her delight, a fund immediately was raised for the purpose of re-purchasing the valuable antiques. Mr. Butterworth, pleased to cooperate, agreed to sell the furniture for exactly the price he had paid.

The days drifted slowly along. Under Rhoda's faithful care, Mrs. Marborough soon was able to sit up in a wheel chair. Much subdued since the heart attack, she had little to say even when a moving van arrived with her household furnishings. But one afternoon while Penny was inserting new candles in the glass candelabrum she so much admired, the old lady watched her from her chair by the window.

"You and Rhoda have fixed the house up so nicely," she said. "You've been very kind to me, and so have all the folks in Riverview."

"You have a great many friends, Mrs. Marborough," Penny replied, smiling. "You never gave them a chance to show it before."

"Perhaps I have been unfriendly," the widow acknowledged. "I didn't mean to be. Now that I'd like to show my appreciation, there's no way to do it. If only the police would get busy and find the rascal who stole my necklace—"

Penny did not reply immediately, for she could think of nothing encouraging to say. She and Rhoda both believed that the thief who had taken the pearls never would be apprehended.

"Mrs. Marborough," she said at length, "there is a way you could show the people of Riverview how you feel—but I'm sure you wouldn't care to do it."

"By opening my home for the Pilgrimage?" the widow asked, smiling.

"That's what I had in mind, but of course—"

"When is the Festival?" Mrs. Marborough broke in. "I've lost track of time since I've been sick."

"It starts day after tomorrow." Penny drew a deep sigh. "I'm afraid the Festival may be a failure, for not half enough tickets have been sold."

"Would it help to include this house in the Pilgrimage?"

"It would save the Festival!" cried Penny. "You're not well enough to go through with it, though!"

"Fiddlesticks!" Mrs. Marborough snapped, her spirits reviving. "I'd like nothing better than a big party. What pleasure is it sitting in a wheel chair staring at a cracked wall? Now you go ahead and plan it just the way you like."

With time so short, Penny flew into action. She contacted members of the Festival Committee and immediately a new publicity campaign was launched. It was announced that Rose Acres would be included in the Pilgrimage and that a grand costume ball at the mansion would be open to the public.

"The affair is certain to be a success," Penny told her father enthusiastically. "I wish though that the Indian Show wasn't playing Riverview at the same time. By the way, have you made any further progress in proving that Jay Franklin's record stones are fakes?"

"Not very much," Mr. Parker ruefully admitted. "A report came back on that tool you picked up at Truman Crocker's shack."

"What was the verdict, Dad?"

"Professor Anjus, the expert who examined the chisel, says he believes the stones could have been marked with it."

"Then Truman Crocker may be the guilty person!"

"It's not at all certain. In all events, I still hold to my original theory that the hoax was planned by Bill McJavins of the Indian Show."

"I certainly hope Mr. Franklin fails in trying to sell the stones to the museum."

"So do I," agreed the editor. "Unfortunately, unless I dig up evidence very quickly, the transaction will take place."

Penny did not give a great deal of thought to the affair of the record stones for Mrs. Marborough's illness had centered her interest at Rose Acres. In truth, she was far more concerned about the missing pearls. The police had made no progress in tracing the necklace and held scant hope the thief would be captured.

As for Ted Wiegand, Penny was unable to make up her mind whether or not he was the guilty person. Although he still worked for Judge Harlan, she seldom saw him. Occasionally, reports of his progress were given to her by Rhoda.

"Ted isn't provoked at me any more," she assured Penny. "He's beginning to think as I do that Mr. Coaten has been up to something crooked. I know for a fact that he gave Mrs. Breen money to force me out of the family."

"Are those two men still in town?" Penny asked thoughtfully.

Rhoda nodded. "They've been here to see me twice. Mrs. Marborough sent them away the last time. She dislikes them both because they once came here to ask if they could rent rooms."

"That must have been the night I overheard them talking at the wishing well," Penny returned.

She remained silent a moment, thinking. Suddenly, she glanced up, her eyes dancing. "Rhoda, I have an idea!"

"What is it, Penny?"

"It might not work, but if it should, we'd learn why Mr. Coaten is so eager to adopt you and Ted."

"Tell me what you have in mind."

"It's like this, Rhoda! If we could induce Mr. Coaten and his friend to come to Rose Acres on the night of the costume ball, I know how they might be made to talk!"

"Strong arm methods?" Rhoda asked, slightly amused.

"Indeed not! The old wishing well will turn the trick."

"You certainly have me puzzled, Penny."

"Getting those men here will be the most difficult," Penny went on, thinking aloud. "But I can sell them a ticket to the ball. Failing that, I'll give them one free."

"There's still no guarantee they would come."

"I know how we can make sure of it! Rhoda, you can write Mr. Coaten a note, asking him to meet you here at ten o'clock. The ball will be in full sway by that time. If you hint you've decided to sign the adoption papers, he's certain to come."

"And then how will I get out of it?"

CHAPTER 22 - THE MISSING NECKLACE

"Leave that part to me," Penny chuckled. "We'll get Mr. Coaten here, and you're to talk with him beside the wishing well."

"Why in that particular place?"

"I can't tell you now," Penny said, smiling mysteriously. "Just accept my word for it that it's of utmost importance. As soon as you get the men at the wishing well, make an excuse and run into the house, leaving them together."

"And then what?" Rhoda asked, completely bewildered.

"From that point the old well and I will take over!" Penny laughed. "I can't tell you another thing. But if my scheme works—and I think it will—Mr. Coaten's little game will be exposed in a most dramatic way!"

CHAPTER 23 - GRAND BALL

"Everything will be ruined—everything!" wailed Penny. She stood in the living room at Rose Acres, her face pressed almost against the window pane. "It's been raining for an hour straight! No one will come to the party."

"Oh, don't take it so hard," Rhoda said cheerfully. "You know over three hundred tickets were sold. Even if the rain does cut down the crowd we'll still have as many people as this house can accommodate."

Admiringly, her gaze wandered about the room which glowed brilliantly with the light of dozens of candles. Every chair was in place, flowers decorated the vases, and at the square, old-fashioned piano, sat Mrs. Marborough, in rustling black silk, playing a few tinkling chords.

"You mustn't tire yourself," Rhoda said to her. "Not until the guests come, at least."

"I never felt better in my life," Mrs. Marborough insisted. "Why, I'm as excited as a school girl! Is Judge Harlan really coming to the ball?"

"Everyone of consequence in Riverview will be here," Rhoda assured her. "Even two of Penny's special guests."

"That's what worries me," Penny confessed, beginning to pace the floor. "I have my trap all ready to spring, but if this horrid rain keeps up, how can you meet Mr. Coaten by the well?"

"Why can't I talk to him in the library?"

"Because it won't do," Penny said patiently. "The entire scheme will fail unless you carry out your part exactly as we planned it."

"The rain is letting up," Mrs. Marborough declared, carefully moving from the piano to her wheel chair. "Mark my words, it will all be over within fifteen minutes."

"Oh, I hope so!" Penny breathed. "I hope so!"

To her gratification, the rain did cease within a short while, and members of the Festival Committee and hired musicians began to arrive. For the occasion, Penny, Rhoda, and Louise, had rented colonial costumes with fancy powdered wigs. They hovered near the front door, ready to greet the first guests.

"It's going to be a wonderful party," Louise remarked happily.

Soon visitors began to arrive in groups. The orchestra struck up and the ballroom became thronged with dancers.

"Mrs. Marborough is having a marvelous time," Rhoda told Louise. "In fact, so is everyone except Penny. She's worried because Mr. Coaten hasn't come."

Two men alighted from a taxi and walked up the path to the house.

"Here they come now!" Penny whispered excitedly. "Quick, Rhoda. Keep out of sight until I give the word!"

Barely had the girl vanished than Mr. Coaten and his companion reached the reception line. Penny greeted them with unusual warmth.

"Is Rhoda Wiegand here?" Mr. Coaten asked curtly. "We came to see her, not to attend the party."

"She was around a moment ago," Penny answered. "Why don't you look for her in the garden—perhaps by the wishing well."

The instant the two men had gone, Penny quickly ran to find Rhoda.

"Now remember, don't talk to Mr. Coaten except at the wishing well," she issued final instructions. "Then when he asks you to sign the paper, make an excuse and leave."

"I won't forget," Rhoda nodded. "But I still don't understand what you're up to."

CHAPTER 23 - GRAND BALL

Anxiously Penny watched from the porch until she saw that her friend actually was talking to the two men beside the wishing well. Then, running into the crowded ballroom, she signaled the musicians to stop the music. Clapping her hands for attention, she announced:

"Ladies and gentlemen—a little surprise! The Old Wishing Well speaks! Listen and you may hear the conversation of unwary guests who reveal their secrets beside it!"

Reaching for a box secreted in a clump of artificial palms, Penny turned a switch. The startled dancers heard a crackling sound, and then Rhoda's voice came in on the loudspeaker, clear and distinct.

"I've thought it over, Mr. Coaten," were her words. "Even though I can't understand why you wish to adopt Ted and me I'll agree to the guardianship."

"Ah, I knew you would come to your senses," Mr. Coaten answered. "Just sign this paper and we'll be able to go into court and settle everything."

There was a slight pause and then Rhoda said: "Will you excuse me a moment, Mr. Coaten? I want to run into the house, but I'll be back."

Those in the ballroom had gathered close to Penny, listening with interest to the conversation, but curious to learn its significance.

"Listen!" she commanded, as many persons began to comment.

The two men who stood alone at the wishing well were talking again, and Penny did not intend to miss a single word.

"Now what possessed Rhoda?" she heard Mr. Coaten mutter. "Is she going to back out again?"

"No, we have her nailed this time," the other answered. "That land is as good as ours! As soon as the adoption is legal, we'll put in our claim. The Texano Oil Company will pay handsomely. What those youngsters don't know won't hurt them."

The words, blaring out into the ballroom, were exactly what Penny wished to hear. Believing themselves to be alone, the two men were making damaging admissions. However, although it was evident that they meant to profit at Rhoda's expense, she could not understand exactly what they meant to do.

Judge Harlan stepped forward to inspect the radio equipment. "What is this?" he inquired. "A special joke of yours, Penelope?"

"It's no joke," she assured him earnestly. "Mr. Coaten has been trying to force Rhoda and Ted to agree to an adoption. We were suspicious of him, and so we arranged this little affair."

"How is the sound brought into the house?"

"I had a microphone installed inside the wishing well," Penny revealed. "The wires run through an underground tunnel."

"Very clever, very clever indeed," murmured the judge. "And the meaning of the conversation?"

"I don't know," Penny confessed. "Mr. Coaten is trying to cheat Rhoda and Ted, but how I can't guess. They own no property."

"Mr. Coaten spoke of the Texano Oil Company," the judge said thoughtfully. "That gives me a faint inkling—"

He did not finish, for at that instant Rhoda came hurriedly into the room. Penny motioned for her to join the group by the loudspeaker.

"Rhoda," said the judge, turning to her, "did your father own land in Texas?"

"Never," she replied promptly. "The only person in our family who owned property was grandfather. He had a large farm but sold it long before his death."

"Do you know the location of the property?" inquired the judge.

"I believe it was near the town of Elkland."

"Elkland! Then perhaps we have the explanation. Less than a month ago oil was discovered in that locality!"

"But the Wiegand land was sold years ago," Penny murmured.

"Much litigation has resulted from the fact that in the past many Texas properties were sold with oil rights reserved," explained the judge. "Now, this is only a guess. However, if Rhoda's grandfather kept such oil rights—as he may well have done—his heirs would have indisputable claim to any income derived from such source."

The loudspeaker had come to life again. As the two men at the wishing well resumed their conversation, everyone in the ballroom strained to hear the words.

WISHING WELL

"We'll get out of Riverview just as soon as the girl signs the paper," Mr. Coaten said to his companion. "We've wasted enough time in this one-horse town."

"Oh, I shouldn't say wasted," drawled Carl Addison. "We'll get the oil money. And that's not all. Take a look at this little trinket!"

There was a brief pause, followed by Mr. Coaten's angry exclamation: "The Marborough pearls! So you stole them!"

"Careful of your words," the other warned. "Your own record isn't so pure."

"I've never descended to stealing!"

"No?" Mr. Addison mocked. "The only difference is that you tie your packages up with legal red tape so that no one can pin anything on you."

"I use my head! Stealing the Marborough pearls was a stupid thing to do. You may go to prison for it."

"There's no risk," the other retorted. "The police didn't find a single clue."

The voices died away, indicating that the two men had moved some distance from the wishing well. Nevertheless, everyone in the ballroom had heard enough to realize that Mrs. Marborough's priceless pearls were in the possession of Mr. Coaten's companion, Carl Addison.

"I understand it all now!" Penny exclaimed. "Mr. Coaten and his friend must have been standing outside the window of the trailer that night when Rhoda told the Breen family about finding the pearls! They probably heard the conversation."

"I want those two men arrested!" Mrs. Marborough announced in a shrill voice, propelling her wheel chair toward the door. "Why doesn't someone do something?"

Spurred to action, Judge Harlan instructed several men from the group to guard the estate exits. Accompanied by Penny, Rhoda, Louise, in fact, nearly every person who had attended the party, he strode into the yard to confront the two conspirators. Taken completely by surprise, Mr. Coaten and his friend did not immediately understand the meaning of the encircling delegation.

"Your little game is up," said Penny, thoroughly savoring the moment. "We know now that your real reason for wanting to adopt Rhoda and Ted was to gain control of valuable oil lands!"

"And you stole my pearl necklace!" accused Mrs. Marborough. "I want it returned!" Thoroughly incensed, she wheeled her chair directly into Carl Addison, seizing him by the coat.

"Madam, I know nothing about your pearls," the man blustered, shaking loose from her grasp. "We came to this party only because we were given free tickets."

"Let's get out of here," Mr. Coaten said gruffly, starting away.

"It's no use," Penny interposed, blocking the path. "We have learned everything. You see, a microphone was installed at the wishing well and it carried your entire conversation into the ballroom for everyone to hear."

Mr. Coaten and his companion, gazing at the unfriendly faces encircling them, realized that they could not hope to explain the situation away.

In a sudden break for freedom, Carl Addison ran to the hedge and attempted to leap over it. One of the guards at a nearby exit seized the man and brought him back.

"Search his pockets!" Mrs. Marborough cried.

Judge Harlan did as the widow demanded, but the missing pearls were not found on either of the men.

"There, you see!" Mr. Coaten declared triumphantly. "You have falsely accused my friend."

Penny suspected that Mr. Addison had disposed of the jewel case somewhere near the hedge. Crossing to it, she groped about on the ground. After a brief search her hand encountered a tiny box which she knew must contain the stolen necklace. Returning with it, she displayed the pearls and presented them to Mrs. Marborough.

"Do we need additional evidence to hold these men?" she asked Judge Harlan anxiously.

"You have produced more than enough," he replied. Turning to the two culprits, he said sternly: "I place you both under arrest! Stand where you are until the police arrive, and remember, anything you say may be used against you."

CHAPTER 24 - RIVER RISING

The exposure of Mr. Coaten and Carl Addison had been even more dramatic than Penny had dared hope it might be. She felt very grateful to Judge Harlan for the vital information he had provided regarding oil lands, and especially for the "break" of luck which had made it possible to regain Mrs. Marborough's necklace.

"How glad I am that I never told Rhoda I suspected Ted of the theft," she thought. "I was very unjust."

After the two Texas men had been removed to jail by Riverview police, the party went on with more gaiety than before. Penny, the center of attention, was forced to tell over and over how a high-school boy friend had assisted her in installing the microphone-loudspeaker arrangement in the old wishing well.

"I wasn't at all certain it would work," she modestly declared. "I did hope that under the proper conditions, those two men would talk, and they did!"

"You are a very clever young lady," praised Judge Harlan, patting her arm. "This will make a nice story for your father's paper too."

Mrs. Marborough did not try to express in words her appreciation for the recovery of the heirloom pearls. However, throughout the evening, her worshipful gaze followed Penny wherever she went. Not until refreshments were being served did she have an opportunity to say:

"Penelope, you have brought me more happiness than I deserve—you and Rhoda together. Now that I have the pearls again, I'll be able to carry out a few of my plans."

"You'll remain in Riverview?" Penny asked eagerly.

"Yes, I shall, and I've been wondering—do you suppose Rhoda and Ted would be willing to live with me? I'm getting old. While I'll have money enough I'll need someone."

"Why not talk to Rhoda about it?"

"I think I shall," Mrs. Marborough nodded. "I'll do it tonight."

Penny was pleased a few minutes later when Rhoda relayed the widow's request to her.

"Will you agree to it?" she asked the girl, her eyes twinkling.

"Will I?" Rhoda laughed. "I love Rose Acres, and Ted and I will be together again! Mrs. Breen was kind to us, but she has her own family. Mrs. Marborough needs someone to care for her."

"I think the arrangement will be an ideal one," Penny declared. "Oh, yes, I meant to tell you. Judge Harlan has promised to look after your legal interests. With him working on the case those oil rights are the same as yours right now!"

As the night wore on, additional guests arrived at Rose Acres, crowding the spacious rooms. Nevertheless, shortly before midnight, Penny was surprised to see her father's car drive up to the door, for she had not expected him to attend the party. Mr. Parker was accompanied by a reporter, Jerry Livingston.

"What brings you two news hawks here?" Penny asked, running outside to greet the newcomers. "You must have heard about Mr. Coaten and the pearl necklace!"

"Yes, but that's not why we came," Mr. Parker tersely replied. "There's been a break in the dam above Cedarville and the river is rising fast!"

"Rose Acres isn't in danger?" gasped Penny.

"The water shouldn't come this high, but the flats will be inundated within a few minutes. Everyone is being warned to get out fast!"

"We've not been able to telephone Truman Crocker," Jerry added. "His shack has no 'phone."

"Can we drive down there?" Mr. Parker asked anxiously.

Penny shook her head. "Not without going miles around. The quickest way is to take the trail at the rear of this property. Wait, I'll show you!"

Darting into the house for a coat, she led her father and Jerry to the hillside. Then, deciding to accompany them, she went on ahead down the steep incline.

"There's a light burning in the shack," Mr. Parker observed a few minutes later. "Crocker must be up."

Reaching the building, the editor thumped once on the door of the workshop and then pushed it open. Truman Crocker was busy at his bench. Startled by the unexpected intrusion of the three visitors, he backed a few steps away from them.

"You can't do nothin' to me," he mumbled. "All I did was what I was told to do."

"I don't know what you're talking about," Mr. Parker cut him short. "We're here to warn you! The dam at Cedarville has let go, and the river is rising fast."

"The river—" the stonecutter faltered.

For a fleeting instant the man's gaze had roved toward a large object covered with a piece of canvas. As Crocker's words came back to Penny, she suddenly knew why he had been so startled to see her father. Impulsively, she darted across the room and jerked the canvas from the object it covered. Revealed for all to see was a large rounded rock, bearing a carving which had not been completed.

"A record stone!" she cried. "Truman Crocker, you are the one who planted those fakes! You've been hired by someone!"

"No, no," the man denied, cringing away.

Mr. Parker strode across the room, and one glance at the rock Penny had uncovered convinced him that his daughter's accusation was a sound one. Obviously, the stone had been treated with acid and chemicals to give it an appearance of great age. Several Indian figures remained uncompleted.

"Who hired you?" he demanded of Truman Crocker. "Tell the truth!"

"I ain't tellin' nothing," the stonecutter returned sullenly.

"Then you'll go to jail," Mr. Parker retorted. "You've been a party to a fraud. It was the publicity agent of the Indian Show who hired you. He probably gave you a hundred dollars for the job."

"Not that much," Crocker muttered. "An' you can't send me to jail because all I did was fix the stones and put 'em where he told me."

"You won't go to jail if you testify to the truth," Mr. Parker assured him. "All you'll have to do is tell what you know—"

"I ain't going to tell nothing," Crocker said sullenly.

Moving so quickly that both Jerry and Mr. Parker were caught off guard, he wheeled and ran out the open door.

"Get him!" the editor barked. "Unless he'll testify against Bill McJavins we may lose a big story!"

Penny waited anxiously at the shack while her father and Jerry pursued the fleeing man. Ten minutes later they stumbled back, completely winded, to report their failure. The laborer had hidden somewhere among the bushes dotting the hillside, and they could not hope to find him.

"Without Crocker's story we have no more evidence than we ever had," Mr. Parker declared in disgust.

Penny tapped the big rock with the half-completed carving. "You have this stone, Dad. If you could photograph it in this unfinished state, wouldn't it tell its own story?"

"We have no camera here, and the river is rising fast. How long would it take you to get to town and back, Jerry?"

"I might make it in thirty minutes."

"Before that time, this shack will be under water."

Anxiously, Mr. Parker gazed at the dark, angry flood which swept so close to the door of the cabin. Inch by inch it was eating away a board walk which led to a pier and a boat tied to it.

"Dad!" Penny suddenly cried. "If only we could get this stone into the boat we could float it to Riverview!"

"Not a chance," Mr. Parker returned briefly. "Both would sink."

"We're completely out of luck," added Jerry. "At the rate the water is coming up, this shack will be awash in another fifteen minutes."

"Dad," Penny went on determinedly, "if we could make a heavy raft, couldn't the stone be floated? It might be towed behind the boat."

CHAPTER 24 - RIVER RISING

"A raft? There's nothing from which to make one."

"Yes, there is!" Penny pointed to several barrels, up-ended in a dark corner of the shop.

"It's an idea!" cried Jerry. "We have Crocker's tools! This story means a lot to you, Chief. Isn't it worth a try?"

"Maybe it is," Mr. Parker conceded, and then with sudden enthusiasm: "Let's get to work. By moving fast we may yet outwit Old Man River!"

CHAPTER 25 - PRECIOUS CARGO

Working with feverish haste, Mr. Parker and Jerry constructed a raft of eight empty barrels, wiring them together into one solid unit. Penny aided the two men as best she could, holding tools and offering suggestions which were not especially appreciated.

"Run outside and see that the boat is all right," Mr. Parker instructed her. "We mustn't let it float away."

Obeying, Penny discovered that already the river was flowing in a shallow, muddy stream over the pier. The swift current tugged at the underpinning, threatening to carry it away. Wading through the water, she reached the boat and drew it close to the shack where she retied it.

By the time she finished, her father and Jerry had completed the raft.

"How will you ever get the stone on it?" Penny asked anxiously. "It must weigh several hundred pounds."

"Just watch," grinned Jerry.

During Penny's absence, he and Mr. Parker had constructed a small square platform of rough boards, equipped with four tiny rollers. Getting the stone on it, they were able to trundle it outside to the raft with a minimum of exertion.

"Now dump her on easy," Mr. Parker ordered Jerry. "If she sinks, our story sinks too."

Together they rolled the heavy stone from the platform to the raft which immediately began to settle beneath the great weight.

"It's going under!" Penny screamed.

As the three watched anxiously, the raft steadied and rode just beneath the surface of the water.

"She floats!" Jerry cried jubilantly. "Now unless we have an upset or strike an object in the river, we should make it to the Adams Street pier."

"We'll have a *Star* paper truck meet us there, and haul the rock to the newspaper plant," Mr. Parker added with satisfaction. "Let's shove off!"

Penny had untied the rowboat. However, as she prepared to step into it, her father pulled her back.

"This little trip isn't for you, Penny. We might upset."

"Don't be ridiculous, Dad," she argued. "You know very well I can swim circles around you. If the boat does go under, you'll be glad to have me along."

"Maybe you're right," the editor conceded. "Jump in."

Water was flowing over the floor of the Crocker shack as the boat and the cumbersome raft started downstream. Jerry, who had elected to steer, found himself hard pressed to keep the prow nosing into the waves. Mr. Parker pulled without much enthusiasm at an extra oar supplied him, content to allow the swift current to do most of the work.

"Isn't it fun?" Penny demanded, snuggling close to her father. "Just look at the beautiful stars!"

"Look at the river," Mr. Parker retorted. "Do you realize that if we should strike a floating object—if that big rock should shift—"

"And see the lovely moon," Penny went on dreamily. "I think it's laughing at the joke we're going to play on Jay Franklin in the morning."

"That old coot will get a shock when he reads the *Star*," Mr. Parker admitted, relaxing. "So will the publicity agent of the Indian Show. When I get through, the outfit won't dare put on a performance in Riverview."

"Do you suppose Franklin had any part in hiring Truman Crocker to fake those record stones?" Jerry asked, steering to avoid a floating box.

CHAPTER 25 - PRECIOUS CARGO

"Not in my opinion," the editor replied. "He merely thought he would profit by selling them to the museum at a fancy price. It was immaterial to him whether or not he sold fake stones or real."

"You'll certainly ruin his little business transaction," chuckled Penny. "What will be done about Truman Crocker?"

"We'll find him tomorrow and force him to tell the truth—that he was hired by Bill McJavins. With this stone as evidence, he can't deny his part in the hoax."

"Can't you just see that special edition of the *Star*?" Penny asked gaily. "A big splashy picture of this Pilgrim Rock we're towing, with a story telling how Truman Crocker faked the writing. Then, in the next column, a yarn about Mr. Addison's arrest, and the recovery of the Marborough pearls."

"It will be a real paper," Mr. Parker agreed heartily. "By the way, how were Mr. Coaten and Carl Addison trapped? Our reporter got the story from the police, but he was a bit vague on that point."

"I'm far too modest to tell you," Penny laughed. "If you're willing to pay me at regular space rates, I might be induced to write the story."

"Trust Penny to drive a hard bargain," grinned Jerry. "We might have guessed who was responsible, for she never fails to be on hand for the final round-up."

Penny smiled as she gazed down the dark, turbulent river. Close by she heard the deep-throated whistle of a tug boat. Along the bank, tall buildings began to appear, and far ahead, she could see the twinkling lights on the Adams Street pier.

"We've worked on some dandy stories together," she murmured, "but this one tops them all for a thrilling finish. Mrs. Marborough regained her pearls, Rhoda won a home, the two men from Texas are behind bars, and the wishing well is equipped with a brand new microphone! You know, I'd like to make one more wish down its moist old throat!"

"What would you ask for this time?" Jerry asked banteringly. "A safe arrival in port?"

Penny shook her head. "We're almost at the pier now. I'd wish that Dad's hunk of granite would turn into a lump of pure gold. Then I'd truly feel as if I were the captain of a treasure ship sailing home with precious cargo."

"Oh, I wouldn't ask for a better cargo than we have right here," Mr. Parker responded heartily. "At this moment I would rather have our old rock than all the gold in the world!"

SABOTEURS ON THE RIVER

"I'M GOING TO PUT MY CAMEO PIN INSIDE THIS ONE," PENNY SAID.

CHAPTER 1 - TROUBLE AFLOAT

A girl in blue slacks, woolen sweater and tennis shoes strode jauntily along the creaking boards of the dark river dock. A large white cotton bag slung carelessly over one shoulder added to the grace of the lithe young figure.

"Hi, Penny!" called a young man who tinkered with the engine of a motorboat. "Out to bury the body?"

Penny Parker chuckled and shifted the bag to the opposite shoulder. "Just thought it would be a good night for a sail, Bill. Have you seen Louise Sidell sneaking around anywhere?"

Before the young sailor could answer, a voice shouted from the darkness, "Here I am!"

Turning her head, Penny glimpsed her chum, a chubby silhouette in the moonlight. Louise, warmly dressed, already was comfortably established in one of the small sailing boats tied up at the wharf.

"Time you're arriving," she said accusingly as Penny tossed the sail bag into her hands. "You promised to meet me here at eight o'clock. It's at least eight-thirty now."

"Sorry, old dear." Penny leaped nimbly aboard and with practiced fingers began to put up the mainsail. "After I 'phoned you, I got hung up at home. Dishes and all that sort of thing. Then Dad delayed me ten minutes while he lectured on the undesirability of daughter taking a moonlight sail."

"I gather you gained the better of the argument," Louise grinned. "Mother made me agree to wear a life-preserver. Imagine! And there's barely enough wind stirring to whiff us across the river."

For many years Penny and Louise had been chums. Students at Riverview High School, they enjoyed the same sports, particularly swimming and sailing. The little mahogany dinghy, appropriately named "Pop's Worry," was owned by Penny's father, Anthony Parker, editor of Riverview's most enterprising newspaper, the *Star*.

Together with Mrs. Maud Weems, a housekeeper who had cared for Penny since her mother's death, he never felt entirely easy when the girls were on the river at night. Nevertheless, Penny was an excellent sailor and rather gloried in the record that her boat had overturned only once during the past season.

"All set?" she asked Louise, casting off the ropes one by one.

As Penny shoved the boat away from the dock, the flapping sail stiffened to the breeze. Louise ducked her head to avoid the swinging boom.

Bill Evans, watching from shore, called a friendly warning: "If you're planning to sail down river, better not get too close to Thompson's bridge! The new regulations say seventy-five feet."

"We'll give it a wide berth," responded Penny. She sailed the boat out through the slip into the main channel of the Big Bear river. When well beyond the dock she commented sadly: "Poor old Bill. Always giving advice. Guess he can't help it."

"His boat's just a leaky tub," replied Louise. "I hear it sunk twice while tied up to the dock. One has to feel sorry for him and treat him with kindness."

Penny steered "Pop's Worry" in a diagonal course down stream. On either side of the shore, from houses, factories, and a nearby amusement park, lights twinkled and were reflected on the unruffled surface of the water. The breeze was soft and warm; the stars seemed very close. Overhead a disc of orange moon rode lazily, now and then dodging behind a fleecy cloud.

"It's a perfect night to sail," Louise said, snuggling amid the cushions. "Wish we'd brought the phonograph along."

"Uh-huh," Penny agreed, her gaze on an approaching motorboat.

SABOTEURS ON THE RIVER

The oncoming craft showed no lights. Uncertain that the pilot would see Pop's Worry, she focused the beam of her flashlight high on the mainsail. The motorboat altered its course instantly and completely. Instead of turning only enough to avoid the sailing craft, it circled in a sharp arc and sped toward the opposite shore. There it was lost to view amid a dark fringe of trees.

"It's against the regulations to cruise without lights," Penny commented. "Wonder who piloted that boat?"

"Whoever he was, you seemed to frighten him away."

"He did turn tail when he saw my light," Penny agreed, scanning the distant shore. "I imagine the boat came from Ottman's. At least it looked like one of theirs."

Ottman's—a nautical supply shop and boat rental dock—was well known, not only to the girls, but to all sailors who plied nearby waters. Owned and operated by a brother and sister, Sara and Burt Ottman, the establishment provided canoes, sea skiffs and rowboats to all who were able to pay the hourly rate. Because many of the would-be boatmen were more venturesome than experienced, seasoned sailors were inclined to eye such pilots with distrust.

"Careful, Penny!" Louise called as she saw the mainsail begin to flap in the wind. "You're luffing!"

Reminded of her duties as steersman, Penny headed the little boat on its course once more. As the sail again became taut, she noticed a small object floating in the water directly ahead. At first she could not be certain what it was, and then she decided that it must be a corked bottle.

Deliberately Penny steered close to the object. Remarking that a bottle would create a hazard for the propellers of a motorboat, she reached to snatch it from the water. The current, however, swung it just beyond her reach.

"Bother!" she exclaimed in annoyance. "I want that bottle!"

"Oh, what do you care?" Louise demanded with a shrug. "Someone else will fish it out."

"It could do a great deal of damage. Besides, as it floated past, I thought I saw a piece of paper inside."

"If you aren't the same old Penny!" teased Louise. "Always looking for a mystery. I suppose you think yonder bottle bears a note telling where pirates buried their treasure?"

"Probably just a paper requesting: 'Please write to your lonely pen pal.' All the same, I must find out." Keeping her eye on the floating bottle, Penny skillfully brought the boat about.

"Take the tiller a minute, please," she requested her chum.

Not without misgivings, Louise reached for the long steering stick. Although she occasionally handled "Pop's Worry," she never felt confident of her ability as a sailor. An unexpected puff of wind or a sudden tilt of the boat could send her into a state of panic.

"Grab that old bottle and don't take twenty years," she urged nervously.

Penny leaned far out over the boat in an attempt to reach the bottle. Her weight tilted the light craft low into the water. Louise hastily shifted to the opposite side as a counter-balance, and in so doing, released the mainsheet. The boom promptly swung out.

Penny made a wild lunge for the running sheet, but could not prevent disaster. The end of the boom dipped into the water. As the sail became wet and heavy it slowly pulled the boat after it.

"We're going over!" Louise shrieked, scrambling for the high side.

"We are over," corrected Penny sadly.

Both girls had been tossed into the water. Louise, protected by a life preserver, immediately grasped the overturned boat and even saved her hair from getting wet. Penny, however, swam after the bobbing bottle. A moment later she came back, triumphantly hugging it against her chest.

"It's a blue pop bottle, Louise," she announced, grasping her chum's extended hand. "And there *is* a piece of paper inside!"

"You and that stupid old bottle!" Louise retorted. "I guess it was my fault we upset, but you never should have turned the tiller over to me."

"Oh, who minds a little upset?"

"I do," Louise said crossly. "The water's cold, and we're at least a quarter of a mile from shore. No boats close by, either."

"Oh, we can get out of this by ourselves," Penny returned, undismayed. "Hold my bottle while I try to haul in the sail."

"I'd like to uncork your precious bottle and drop it to the bottom of the river!"

CHAPTER 1 - TROUBLE AFLOAT

Nevertheless, while her chum worked with the halyard, Louise held tightly to the little object which had caused all the trouble. Neither in shape nor size was the bottle unusual, but the paper it contained did arouse her curiosity. Though she never would have admitted it, she too wondered if it might bear an interesting message.

After pulling in the heavy, water-soaked sail, the girls climbed to the high side of the boat, trying by their combined weight to right it. Time and again they failed. At last, breathless, cold, discouraged, they admitted that the task was beyond their strength.

"Let's shout for help," Louise proposed, anxiously watching the distant shore lights.

"All right," agreed Penny, "but I doubt anyone will hear us. My, we're drifting down river fast!"

Decidedly worried, the girls shouted many times. There were no boats near, not even the motor craft they had observed a few minutes earlier. The swift current seemed to be swinging them directly toward Thompson's bridge.

"A watchman always is on guard there night and day," Penny commented, scanning the arching structure of steel. "If the old fellow isn't asleep he should see us as we drift by."

Louise was too cold and miserable to answer. However, she rather unwillingly held the blue bottle while Penny swam and tried to guide the overturned boat toward shore.

When the girls were fairly close to the bridge, they began to shout once more. Although they could see automobiles moving to and fro across the great archway, no one became aware of their plight.

Then as they despaired, there came an answering shout from above. A powerful beam of light played over the water, cutting a bright path.

"Help! Help!" screamed Louise, waving an arm.

"Halt or I'll fire!" rang out the terse command from the bridge.

"Halt?" cried Penny, too exasperated to consider the significance of the order. "That's what we'd like to do, but we can't!"

The searchlight came to rest on the overturned sailboat. The girls were so blinded that for a moment they could see nothing. Then the searchlight shifted slightly to the left, and they were able to distinguish a short, stoop-shouldered man who peered over the railing of the bridge. Apparently satisfied that their plight was genuine, he called reassuringly:

"Okay, take it easy. I'll heave you a line."

The watchman disappeared into the little bridge house. Soon he reappeared, and with excellent aim, tossed a weighted rope so that it fell squarely across the overturned boat. Penny seized an end and made it fast.

"I'll try to pull you in," the watchman shouted. "Just hang on."

Leaving his post on the bridge, the old fellow climbed down a steep incline to the muddy shore. By means of the long rope, he slowly and laboriously pulled the water-logged boat with the clinging girls toward a quiet cove.

Once within wading depth, the chums aided the watchman by leading the craft in. Together the three of them beached "Pop's Worry" on a narrow strip of sand.

"Thanks," Penny gasped, flipping a wet curl from off her freckled nose. "On second thought, many, many thanks."

"You've no business to get so close to the bridge," the watchman retorted. "It's agin' the regulations. I could have you arrested."

"But it wasn't our fault this old sailboat upset," Penny returned reasonably. "We were reaching for a floating bottle—oh, my Aunt! Where is that bottle, Louise? Don't tell me we've lost it!"

Her chum was given no opportunity to reply, for at that moment a motorboat roared down the river at high speed. Its throttle was wide open, and it appeared to be racing straight toward the bridge.

"Halt!" shouted the watchman, jerking a weapon from a leather holster. "Halt!"

The pilot did not obey the command. Instead, to the amazement of the watchers, he leaped from the cockpit and swam for the opposite shore. Twice the watchman fired at him, but the bullets were well above the swimmer's head.

The unpiloted boat, its helm securely lashed, drove straight on its course.

"It's going to strike the bridge!" shouted Louise.

SABOTEURS ON THE RIVER

As the boat raced head on into one of the massive concrete piers, there came a deafening explosion. The entire steel structure of the bridge seemed to recoil from the impact. Girders shivered and shook, cables rattled. On the eastern approach, brakes screamed as automobiles were brought to a sudden halt.

"Saboteurs!" the watchman cried hoarsely. "They've done it—dynamited the bridge!"

CHAPTER 2 - FRONT PAGE NEWS

Although one of the main concrete piers had been damaged by the explosion, the approaches to the bridge remained intact. Several automobiles drew up at the curbing, but others, their drivers unaware of what had caused the blast, sped on across.

From their position beneath the bridge, Louise, Penny, and the watchman could see the entire steel structure quiver. The underpinning had been weakened, but whether or not it was safe for traffic to proceed, only an engineer could determine.

"Oughtn't we stop the cars?" Penny demanded, for the watchman seemed stunned by what had happened. His eyes were fixed on the opposite shore, at a point amid the trees where the pilot of the motorboat had crawled from the water.

"Yes, yes," he muttered, bringing his attention once more to the bridge. "No chance to catch that saboteur now. We must stop the autos."

Shouting as he ran, the watchman scrambled up the steep slope to the western approach of the bridge. Realizing that he would be unable to cope with traffic moving from two directions, the girls hesitated, and then decided to help him. Their wet shoes provided poor traction on the hill. Slipping, sliding, clothing plastered to their bodies, they reached the bridge level.

"You hold the cars at this end!" ordered the watchman as he glimpsed them. "I'll lower the gate at the other side!"

Stationing themselves at the entrance to the bridge, Louise and Penny forced motorists to halt at the curb. Within a minute or two, a long line had formed.

"What's wrong?" demanded one irate driver. "An accident?"

"Bridge damaged," Penny replied tersely.

All along the line horns began to toot. A few of the more curious motorists alighted and came to bombard the girls with questions. In the midst of the excitement, one of the cars broke out of line and crept to the very end of the pavement.

"Listen, Mister," Penny began indignantly to the driver. "You'll have to back up. You can't cross—" she broke off as she recognized the man at the wheel. "Dad! Well, for Pete's sake!"

"Penny!" the newspaper man exclaimed, no less dumbfonded. "What are you and Louise doing here? And in those wet clothes?"

"Policing the bridge. Dad, there's a big story for you here! A saboteur just blew up one of the piers by ramming it with a motorboat!"

"I thought I heard an explosion as I was driving down Clark Street!" exclaimed Mr. Parker. Opening the car door, he leaped out and wrapped his overcoat about Penny's shivering shoulders. "Now tell me exactly what happened."

As calmly as they could, the girls reported how the saboteur had dynamited the bridge.

"This is a front page story!" the newspaper owner cried jubilantly. "Penny, you and Louise take my car and scoot for home. When you get there call the *Star* office. Have Editor DeWitt send a reporter to help me—Jerry Livingston, if he's around. We'll need a crack photographer too—Salt Sommers."

"I can get the call through much quicker by running to the drugstore." Penny jerked her head toward a cluster of buildings not far from the bridge entrance. "As for going home at a moment like this, never!"

"So you want a case of pneumonia?" Mr. Parker barked. "How'd you get wet anyhow?"

"Sailboat," Penny answered briefly. She took the car keys from her father, and pressed them upon Louise.

"But I don't want to go if you don't," her chum argued.

"You're more susceptible to pneumonia than I am," Penny said, giving her a little push. "Dash on home, and get into warm, dry clothing. And don't forget to take off that life preserver before you hop into bed!"

Thus urged, Louise reluctantly backed Mr. Parker's car to the main street, and drove away.

"Now I'll slosh over to the drugstore and call the *Star* office," Penny offered briskly. "Lend me a nickel, Dad."

"I'm crazy as an eel to let you stay," Mr. Parker muttered, fumbling in his pocket for a coin. "You should have gone with Louise."

"Let's argue about that tomorrow, Dad. Right now we must work fast unless we want other newspapers to scoop us on this story."

While her father remained behind to direct bridge traffic, Penny ran to the nearest drugstore. Darting into the one telephone booth ahead of an astonished woman customer, she called Editor DeWitt of the *Star*. Tersely she relayed her father's orders.

"Jerry and Salt will be out there in five minutes," DeWitt promised. "Now what can you give us on the explosion? Did you witness it?"

"Did I?" echoed Penny. "Why, I practically caused it!"

With no further encouragement, she launched into a vivid, eye-witness account of the bridge dynamiting. As she talked, a re-write man on another telephone, took down everything she reported.

"Now about the saboteur's motorboat," he said as she finished. "Can you give us a description of it?"

"Not a very good one," Penny admitted. "It looked like one of Ottman's rented boats with an outboard attached. In fact, Louise and I saw a similar craft earlier in the evening which was cruising not far from the bridge."

"Then you think the saboteur may have rented his boat from Ottman's?"

"Well, it's a possibility."

"You've given us some good stuff!" the rewrite man praised. "DeWitt's getting out an extra. Shoot us any new facts as soon as you can."

"Dad's on the job full blast," Penny answered. "He'll soon have all the details for you."

Slamming out of the telephone booth, she ran back to the bridge. Her father no longer directed traffic, but had turned the task over to a pompous motorist who thoroughly enjoyed his authority.

"You can't cross, young lady," he said as she sought to pass him. "Bridge's unsafe."

"I'm a reporter for the *Star*," Penny replied confidently.

The man stared at her bedraggled clothing. "A reporter?" he inquired dubiously.

Just then a police car, its siren shrilling, sped up to the bridge. Close behind came another car which bore a printed card "*Star*" on its windshield. It braked to a standstill nearby and out leaped two young men, Jerry Livingston and Salt Sommers.

"Hello, Penny!" Jerry greeted her. "Might have known you'd be here. Where's the Chief?"

"Somewhere, sleuthing around," Penny answered. "I lost him a minute ago when I telephoned the *Star* office."

Salt Sommers, a felt hat cocked low over his eyes, began unloading photographic equipment from the coupe.

"Where'll I get the best shots?" he asked Penny. "Other side or this?"

"Under the bridge," she directed crisply. "None of the damage shows from above."

Salt slung the heavy camera over his shoulder, and disappeared down the incline which led to the river bed.

Before Jerry and Penny could move away, Mr. Parker hurried up with the watchman in tow.

"This is Carl Oaks, bridge guard," he announced without preliminary. "Take him over to the drugstore, Jerry, and put him on the wire. We want his complete story for the *Star*."

"Not so fast," drawled a voice from behind. "We want to talk to Carl Oaks."

One of the policemen, a detective, moved over to the group and began to question the watchman.

"It wasn't my fault the bridge was dynamited," the old fellow whined. "I shouted at the boatman and fired twice."

"He got away?"

CHAPTER 2 - FRONT PAGE NEWS

"Yeah. Jumped overboard before the boat struck the pier. Last I saw of him, he was climbing out of the river on the other shore."

"At what point?"

"Right over there." The watchman indicated a clump of maples beyond the far side of the bridge. "I could see him plainly from the beach."

"And what were *you* doing on the beach?" questioned the detective sharply.

"Ask her," Carl Oaks muttered, eyeing Penny.

"Mr. Oaks helped my friend and me when our sailboat upset," she supported his story. "It really wasn't his fault that he was away from his post at the time of the explosion."

Both Penny and the watchman were questioned at considerable length by the detective. Meanwhile, other officers were searching for the escaped saboteur. Several members of the squad went beneath the bridge to inspect the damage and collect shattered sections of the wrecked boat.

Dismissed at last by the detective, Penny, her father and Jerry crossed the bridge to join in the search. Carl Oaks, whose answers did not entirely satisfy police, was detained for further questioning.

"Penny, tell me more about this fellow Oaks," Mr. Parker urged his daughter. "I suppose he did his best to stop the saboteur?"

"It seemed so to me," Penny replied slowly. "He was a miserable marksman, though. I guess he must have been excited when he fired."

Following a trail of moving lights, the trio soon came to a group of policemen who were examining footprints in the mud of the river bank.

"This is where the saboteur got away," Penny whispered to her father. "Do you suppose the fellow is still hiding in the woods?"

"Not likely," Mr. Parker answered. "A job of this sort would be planned in every detail."

The newspaper owner's words were borne out a few minutes later when a policeman came upon a clump of bushes where an automobile had stood. Grass was crushed, a small patch of oil was visible, and the soft earth showed tire imprints.

Penny, her father and Jerry, did not remain long in the vicinity. Satisfied that the saboteur had made his getaway by car, they were eager to report their findings to the *Star* office.

Mr. Parker telephoned DeWitt and then joined the others at the press car. As Salt Sommers climbed aboard with his camera, an automobile bearing a *News* windshield sticker, skidded to a stop nearby.

"Too bad, boys," Salt taunted the rival photographers. "Better late than never!"

Already news vendors were crying the *Star's* first extra. Once well away from the bridge, Mr. Parker stopped the car to buy a paper.

"Nice going," he declared in satisfaction as he scanned the big black headlines. "We beat every other Riverview paper by a good margin. A colorful story, too."

"Thanks to whom?" demanded Penny, giving him a pinch.

"I suppose I should say, to you," he admitted with a grin. "However, I see you've already received ample credit. DeWitt gave you a by-line."

"Did he really?" Penny took the paper from her father's hand and gazed affectionately at her own name in print. "Nice of him. Especially when I didn't even suggest the idea."

To a newspaper reporter, a story tagged with his own name means high honor. Many times Penny, ever alert for news, had enjoyed the satisfaction of seeing her stories appear with a by-line. Early in her career as a self-made newspaper girl, her contributions had been regarded as something of an annoyance to her father and the staff of the *Star*. But of late she had turned in many of the paper's best scoops and incidentally, had solved a few mysteries.

"This is the way I like a story written," Mr. Parker declared, reading aloud from the account which bore his daughter's name. "No flowery phrases. Just a straight version of how your sailboat upset and what you saw as it floated down toward the bridge."

"It's a pretty drab account if you ask me," sniffed Penny. "I could have written it up much better myself. Why, the re-write man didn't even tell how Louise and I happened to upset!"

"A detail of no importance," Mr. Parker returned. "I mean, in connection with the story," he corrected hastily as Penny flashed him an injured look. "What did cause you to capsize?"

"A blue bottle, Dad. It had a piece of paper inside. I was reaching for it and—oh, my aunt!"

"Now what?" demanded her father.

"Turn the car around and drive back to the bridge!"

"Drive back? Why?"

"I've lost that blue bottle," Penny fairly wailed. "Louise had it, but I know she didn't take it home with her. It must be lying somewhere on the beach near our stranded sailboat. Oh, please Dad, turn back!"

CHAPTER 3 - STRAIGHT FROM THE SHOULDER

Mr. Parker did not slacken the speed of the car. Relaxing somewhat, he edged farther away from Penny, whose sodden garments were oozing water.

"A bottle!" he exclaimed. "Penny, for a minute you had me worried. I thought you meant something important."

"But Dad, the bottle is important," she argued earnestly. "You see, it contains a folded piece of paper, and I'm sure it must be a message."

"Of all the idiotic things! At a time like this when you should be worried about your health, you plague me about a silly bottle. We're going straight home."

"Oh, all right," Penny accepted the decision with a shrug. "Nevertheless, I'm curious about that bottle, and I mean to find it tomorrow!"

Mr. Parker dropped Jerry and Salt off at the newspaper plant and then drove on to his home. The house, a modern two-story dwelling, was situated on a terrace overlooking the river. Lights glowed from the living room windows and Mrs. Weems, the stout housekeeper, could be seen hovering over the radio.

"I was just listening to the news about the dynamiting," she remarked as Mr. Parker and his daughter came in from the kitchen. Turning her head, she stared at the girl's bedraggled hair and wet clothing. "Why, Penny Parker!"

"I guess I *am* a little bit moist," Penny admitted with a grin. Sitting down on the davenport, she began to strip off her shoes and stockings.

"Not here!" Mrs. Weems protested. "Take a hot shower while I fix you a warm drink. Oh, I knew you shouldn't have gone sailing at night."

"But Mrs. Weems—"

"Scoot right up to the bathroom and get out of those wet clothes!" the housekeeper interrupted. "You'll be lucky if you don't come down with your death o' cold."

Carrying a shoe in either hand, Penny wearily climbed the stairs. By the time she had finished under the shower, Mrs. Weems appeared with a glass of hot lemonade.

"Drink this," she commanded sternly. "Then get into bed and I'll fix you up with the hot water bag."

"But I'm not sick," Penny grumbled.

"You will be tomorrow," the housekeeper predicted. "Your father told me how he allowed you to stay at the bridge while police searched for the saboteur. I declare, I don't know what he was thinking of!"

"Dad and I are a couple of tough old news hawks," Penny chuckled. "Well, I suppose I'll have to compromise with you."

"Compromise?" Mrs. Weems asked suspiciously.

"I'll drink the lemonade if you'll let me skip the hot water bottle."

"Indeed not," Mrs. Weems returned firmly. "Now jump into bed, and no more arguments."

Although Penny considered the housekeeper entirely too thorough in her methods, she enjoyed the pleasant warmth of the bed. She drank the lemonade, submitted to the hot water bottle, and then snuggling down, slept soundly. When she awakened, sunlight streamed in through the Venetian blinds. Cocking an eye at the dresser clock, she saw to her dismay that it was ten o'clock.

"My Aunt!" she exclaimed, leaping out of bed. "All this good time wasted!"

With the speed of a trained fireman, Penny wriggled into her clothes. She gave her auburn hair a quick brush but took time to slap a little polish on her saddle shoes before bounding down the stairs to the kitchen.

"Is that you or a gazelle escaped from the zoo?" inquired Mrs. Weems who was washing dishes at the sink.

"Why didn't you bounce me out of bed two hours ago?" asked Penny. "I have an important business engagement for this morning."

"You're not going to the river again, I hope!"

"Oh, but I must, Mrs. Weems." Penny opened the refrigerator and helped herself to a bowl of strawberries and a Martha Washington pie.

"You're not breakfasting on that," said the housekeeper, taking the dishes away from her. "Oatmeal is what you need. Now why must you go to the river?"

"Someone has to salvage the sailboat. Besides, I lost a valuable object last night—"

The telephone jingled, and Penny darted off to answer it. As she had anticipated, the call was from Louise Sidell, who in a very husky voice asked her how she was feeling.

"Fit as a fiddle and ready to go bottle hunting!" Penny replied promptly. "And you?"

"I hurt in all the wrong places," Louise complained. "What a night!"

"Why, I enjoyed every minute of it," Penny said with sincerity. "If you're such a wreck I suppose you won't care to go with me to the river this morning. By the way, what did you do with that blue bottle?"

"I haven't the slightest idea. I'm sure I had it in my hand when we reached shore, but that's the last I remember."

"Well, never mind, if it's anywhere on the beach I'll find it," Penny said. "Sure you don't want to tag along?"

"Maybe I will."

"Then meet me in twenty minutes at Ottman's dock. Signing off now to gobble a bowl of oatmeal."

Without giving Louise a chance to change her mind, Penny hung up the receiver and returned to the kitchen. After fortifying herself with oatmeal, a glass of orange juice, bacon, two rolls and sundry odds and ends, she started off to meet Louise. Her chum, looking none too cheerful, awaited her near Ottman's dock.

"Why did you ask me to meet you at this particular place, Penny?" she inquired. "It was a block out of my way."

"I thought we might rent one of Ottman's boats and row down to the bridge. It will be easier than walking along the mud flats."

"You think of everything," Louise said admiringly. "But where's the proprietor of this place?"

Boats of all description were fastened along the dock, but neither Burt Ottman nor his sister were visible. Not far from a long shed which served as ticket office and canoe-storage house, an empty double-deck motor launch had been tied to a pier. An aged black and white dog drowsed on its sunny deck.

"Guess the place is deserted," Penny commented. After wandering about, she sat down on an overturned row boat which had been pulled out near the water's edge.

The boat moved beneath her, and an irate voice rumbled: "Would you mind getting off?"

Decidedly startled, Penny sprang to her feet.

As the boat was pushed over on its side, a girl in grimy slacks, rolled from beneath it. Barely twenty years of age, her skin was rough and brown from constant exposure to wind and sun. A smear of varnish decorated one cheek and she held a can of caulking material in her hand.

"I'm sorry," said Penny, smiling. "Do you live under that boat?"

Sara Ottman's dark eyes flashed. Getting to her feet, she regarded the girl with undisguised hostility.

"Very clever, aren't you!" she said scathingly. "In fact, quite the little joker!"

"Why, I didn't mean anything," Penny apologized. "I had no idea you were working under that thing."

"So clever, and such a marvelous detective," Sara went on, paying no heed. "Why, it was Penny Parker who not so long ago astonished Riverview by solving the Mystery of the Witch Doll! And who but Penny aided the police in trailing The Vanishing Houseboat? It was our own Penny who learned why the tower Clock Struck Thirteen. And now we are favored with her most valuable opinion in connection with the bridge dynamiting case!"

Penny and Louise were dumbfounded by the sudden, unwarranted attack. By no stretch of the imagination could they think that Sara Ottman meant her words as a joke. But what had her so aroused? While it was true that Penny had solved many local mysteries, she never had been boastful of her accomplishments. In fact, she was one of the most popular girls in Riverview.

CHAPTER 3 - STRAIGHT FROM THE SHOULDER

"Are you sure you haven't a fever, Miss Ottman?" Penny demanded, her own eyes blazing. "I certainly fail to understand such an outburst."

"Of course you do," the other mocked. "You're not used to talk coming straight from the shoulder. Why are you here anyhow?"

"To rent a boat."

"Well, you can't have one," Sara Ottman said shortly. "And if you never come around here again, it will be soon enough."

Glaring once more at Penny, she turned and strode into the boathouse.

CHAPTER 4 - AN UNWARRANTED ATTACK

"Now will you tell me what I did to deserve a crack like that?" Penny muttered as the door of the boathouse slammed behind Sara Ottman.

"Not a single thing," Louise answered loyally. "She just rolled out from beneath that boat with a dagger between her teeth!"

"I guess I am a little prig, Lou."

"You're no such thing!" Louise grasped her arm and gave her an affectionate squeeze. "Come along and forget it. I never did like Sara Ottman anyhow."

Penny allowed herself to be led away from the dock, but the older girl's unkind remarks kept pricking her mind. Although occasionally in the past she had stopped for a few minutes at the Ottman place, she never before had spoken a dozen words to Sara. Nearly all of her business dealings had been with Burt Ottman, a pleasant young man who had painted her father's sailboat that spring.

"I simply can't understand it," Penny mumbled, trudging along the shore with Louise. "The last time I saw Sara she spoke to me politely enough. I must have offended her, but how?"

"Oh, why waste any thought on her?" Louise scoffed.

"Because it bothers me. She mentioned the bridge dynamiting affair. Maybe it was my by-line story in the *Star* that offended her."

"What did it say?" Louise inquired curiously. "I didn't see the morning paper."

"Neither did I. I gave my story to a rewrite man over the telephone. I meant to read the entire account, but was in a hurry to get over here, so I skipped it."

"Well, I shouldn't worry about the matter if I were you."

"I'm sure the boat used in the dynamiting came from Ottman's," Penny declared, thinking aloud. "Perhaps Sara is just out of sorts because she and her brother lost their property."

Making their way along the mud flats, the girls came at last to the tiny stretch of sand where the sailboat had been beached the previous night. It lay exactly as they had left it, cockpit half filled with water, the tall mast nosed into the loose sand.

"What a mess," sighed Penny. "Well, the first thing to do is to get the wet sail off. We should have taken care of it last night."

Before beginning the task, the girls wandered toward the nearby bridge to inspect the damage caused by dynamiting. An armed soldier refused to allow them to approach closer than twenty yards. All traffic had been halted, and a group of engineers could be seen examining the shattered pier.

"Is Mr. Oaks around here?" Penny asked the soldier.

"Oaks? Oh, you mean the bridge watchman. He's been charged with neglect of duty, and relieved of his job."

Penny and Louise were sorry to hear the news, feeling that in a way they were responsible for the old fellow having left his post. Unable to learn whether or not the watchman was being detained by police, they returned to the beach to salvage their sailboat.

Without a pump, it was a difficult task to remove the water from the cockpit of "Pop's Worry." By rocking the boat back and forth and scooping with an old tin can, the girls finally got most of it out.

"We'll have to dry the sail somehow or it will mildew," Penny decided. "The best thing, I think, is to put it on again and sail home."

CHAPTER 4 - AN UNWARRANTED ATTACK

Together they righted the boat. As the tall mast flipped out of the sand, Penny caught glimpse of a shiny, blue object.

"Our bottle!" she cried triumphantly, making a dive for it.

"Your bottle," corrected Louise. "I'm not a bit interested in that silly old thing."

Nevertheless, as Penny sat down on the deck of "Pop's Worry" and removed the cork, she edged nearer. By means of a hairpin, the folded sheet of paper contained within was pulled from the narrow neck. Highly elated, Penny spread out the message to read.

"Well, what does it say?" Louise inquired impatiently.

"Oh, so you are interested," teased Penny.

"Now don't try to be funny! Read the message."

Penny stared at the paper in her hand. "It's rather queer," she acknowledged. "Listen:

"'*The day of the Great Deluge approaches. If you would be saved from destruction, seek without delay, the shelter of my ark.*'"

"If that isn't nonsense!" Louise exclaimed, peering over her chum's shoulder. "And the note is signed, '*Noah*.'"

"Someone's idea of a joke, I suppose," Penny replied. She tossed the paper away, then reconsidering, retrieved the message and with the bottle, placed it in the cockpit of the boat. "Well, it's rained a lot this Spring, but I don't think we'll have to worry about the Great Deluge."

"Noah was a Biblical character," Louise commented thoughtfully. "I remember that when God told him it would rain forty days and forty nights, he built an ark to resist the flood waters. And he took his family in with him and all the animals, two by two."

"Noah was a bit before our time," laughed Penny. "Suppose we shove off for home."

By dint of much physical exertion, the girls pushed "Pop's Worry" out into the shallow water. Penny, who had removed shoes and stockings, gave a final thrust and leaped lightly aboard. Raising the wet sail, she allowed it to flap loosely in the wind.

"We'll have everything snug and dry by the time we reach home," she declared confidently. "Tired, Lou?"

"A little," admitted her chum, stretching out full length on the deck. "I like to sail but I don't like to bail! And just think, if you hadn't been so crazy to get that blue bottle, we'd have spared ourselves a lot of hard work."

"Well, a fellow never knows. The bottle might have provided the first clue in an absorbing mystery! Who do you suppose wrote such an odd message?"

"How should I know?" yawned Louise. "Probably some prankster."

Taking a zigzag course, "Pop's Worry" tacked slowly upstream. Whipped by a brisk wind, the wet sail gradually dried and regained its former shape.

As the boat presently approached Ottman's dock, both girls turned to gaze in that direction. Sara could be seen moving about on one of the floating platforms, retying several boats which banged at their moorings.

"Better tack," Louise advised in a low tone. "We don't want to get too close."

Penny acted as if she had not heard. She made no move to bring the boat about.

"We'll end up right at Ottman's unless you're careful," Louise warned. "Or is that what you want to do?"

"I'm thinking about it." Penny watched Sara with thoughtful eyes.

"Well, if you'll deliberately go there again, I must say you enjoy being insulted!"

"I'd like to find out why Sara is angry at me. If it's only a misunderstanding I want to clear it up."

Louise shook her head sadly but offered no further protest as the boat held to its course. Not until the craft grated gently against one of the floats at Ottman's did Sara seem to note the girls' approach. Glancing up from her work, she stared at them, and then deliberately looked away.

"The air's still chilly," Penny remarked in an undertone. "Well, we'll see."

Making "Pop's Worry" fast to a spar, she walked across the float to confront Sara.

"Miss Ottman," she began quietly, "if I've done anything to offend you, I wish to apologize."

Sara turned slowly to face Penny. "You owe me no apology," she said in a cold voice.

"Then why do you dislike me? I always thought I was welcome around here until today. My father has given you considerable business."

"I'm sorry I spoke to you the way I did," Sara replied stiffly and with no warmth. "It was rude of me."

"But why am I such poison?" Penny persisted. "What have I done?"

"You *honestly* don't know?"

"Why, of course not. I shouldn't be asking if I did."

Sara stared at Penny as if wondering whether or not to accept her remarks as sincere.

"Do you only write for the papers?" she asked, a slight edge to her voice. "You never read them?"

"I don't know what you mean." Penny was truly bewildered. "Has this misunderstanding something to do with the bridge dynamiting?"

Sara nodded her head grimly. "It has," she agreed. "Didn't you see the morning paper?"

"Why, no."

"Then wait a minute." Sara turned and vanished into the boat shed. A moment later she reappeared, carrying a copy of the *Star*.

"Read that," she directed, thrusting the black headlines in front of Penny's eyes. "Now do you understand why I feel that you're no friend of mine?"

CHAPTER 5 - HELD ON SUSPICION

Penny gazed at the *Riverview Star's* front page headline which proclaimed:
"BURT OTTMAN ARRESTED AS SUSPECT IN BRIDGE DYNAMITING."
The opening paragraph of the news story, was even more dismaying. It began:
"Acting upon information provided by Miss Penelope Parker, police today arrested Burt Ottman, owner of the Ottman Boat Dock, charging him with participation in the Friday night dynamiting of Thompson's bridge."
Penny hastily scanned the remainder of the story and then protested: "But I never even mentioned your brother's name to police, Miss Ottman! Why, I certainly didn't think that he had any connection with the dynamiting."
"You certainly didn't think, period," Sara replied, though in a less severe tone. "You told police that the motorboat used in the dynamiting was one of our boats."
"Well, it looked like it to me. Perhaps I was mistaken."
"You weren't mistaken. The boat definitely was one of ours. It was stolen from here about a month ago."
Penny drew a deep breath. "Then in that case, I don't see why suspicion should fall upon your brother."
"Didn't you tell police that a young man corresponding to his description was handling the boat?"
"Indeed I didn't."
"Then it must have been the watchman who provided the description," Sara corrected. "At any rate, police identified the boat as ours, and arrested Burt. They have him at the station now."
"It never occurred to me that anyone would suspect your brother," Penny said soberly. "Why, everyone along the river knows him well. It should be easy for him to prove his innocence."
"True, it should be," Sara replied bitterly. "The arrest angered Burt, and he made matters worse by refusing to answer questions the police asked him."
"Oh, that was a mistake."
"Yes, but Burt has a great deal of pride. The police never should have arrested him."
"I certainly agree with you," declared Penny, for she could not envision young Ottman as a saboteur. "Can't your brother prove where he was last night at the time of the explosion?"
"That's just it." Sara looked troubled as she reached to take the newspaper. "He refuses to offer any alibi."
"But you must know yourself where your brother spent his time."
"I wish I did. He left here about seven o'clock and didn't return home until early this morning—just a half hour before the police came to arrest him."
"Oh!"
"All the same, Burt had no connection with the dynamiting," Sara said quickly. "He frequently stays out late at night. I've never questioned him, for it was none of my affair."
Penny scarcely knew what to reply. "I can understand now why you're provoked at me," she said after a moment. "But I assure you I had no intention of involving your brother with the police. I certainly never gave them his description."
Sara smiled and in a charming gesture extended her hand.
"I'm sorry I talked as I did to you," she apologized. "Forget it, will you?"
"Of course," Penny agreed generously. "And if there's anything I can do to help—"
The float creaked and both girls turned to see Bill Evans coming toward them.
"Hi!" he greeted the girls impartially. "Miss Ottman, wonder if I can get you to help me?"
"I suppose you're having trouble with that motor of yours again," sighed Sara. "Or should I say yet?"

"I've lost it in the river," Bill confessed sheepishly. "Blamed thing cost me sixty dollars second-hand too!"

"In the river!" gasped Penny. "What did you do, get peeved and toss it overboard?"

The saddened young man shook his head. "Guess I didn't have it fastened on very well. Anyhow, just as I was leaving the dock, off she fell into about ten feet of water."

"I hope you buoyed the spot," said Sara.

"Yes, I marked it with a floating can. Some of the boys have been trying to get 'er up for me, but no luck. If you can do it, I'll pay five dollars."

"Well, I'm pretty busy," Miss Ottman said in a harassed voice. "Burt's not here and it keeps me jumping to run the launch and rent the canoes. But I'll see what I can do this afternoon."

"Thanks," Bill replied gratefully, turning away. "Thanks a lot."

When the young man was beyond hearing distance, Penny spoke again of Burt Ottman's unfortunate arrest.

"I'm sorry about everything, Miss Ottman," she said earnestly. "If you wish, I'll talk to the police and assure them that so far as I know, the saboteur did not resemble your brother. It was too dark for me to really see him."

"I'll feel very grateful if you will speak a good word for Burt," Sara responded. She sank down on an overturned bucket and pressed a hand to her temple. "Oh, my head's splitting! Everything's been coming at me so fast. The police were here questioning me and they twisted my remarks all around. I'll have to raise bail for Burt, but where the money is coming from I don't know."

The last of Penny's resentment toward the girl faded away. From the jerky way Sara spoke, she knew that her thoughts were darting from one perplexing problem to another.

"I don't know what I'm doing or saying today," Sara said miserably. "If you can forgive me—"

"Of course! I don't blame you a bit for speaking to me the way you did. May I borrow a sponge for a minute?"

Sara smiled and nodded. Eager to make amends, she ran into the shed and returned with the desired article.

"There's still a little water in my boat," Penny explained. "Thought I'd sop it up."

"Let me do it," Sara offered. Without waiting for permission she went to the sailboat, and with a friendly nod at the astonished Louise, began to sponge out the cockpit.

"I see you've collected one of Old Noah's souvenirs," she remarked a moment later, noticing the blue bottle which Penny had tossed into the bottom of the boat.

"We found it floating in the water," Louise volunteered. "The message was such a queer one—an invitation to take refuge in the ark during the Great Deluge. Someone's idea of a joke, I suppose."

"It's no joke," Sara corrected. "Noah is a very real person. He actually lives in an ark too—a weird looking boat he built himself."

"You mean the old fellow actually believes there's going to be another great flood?" Penny asked incredulously.

"Oh, yes! Noah is so sure of it that he's collected a regular menagerie of animals to live with him on the ark. He keeps dropping bottles into the water warning folks that the Great Deluge is coming. I fish out dozens of them here at the dock."

"Where is the ark?" Penny inquired curiously.

Sara squeezed the last drop of water from the sponge and pointed diagonally upstream toward a gap in the trees.

"That's where Bug Run empties into the river," she explained. "Noah has his ark grounded not far from its mouth. The currents are such that whenever he dumps his bottles in the water most of them come this way."

"Rather a nuisance I should think," commented Penny.

"Noah's a pest!" Sara complained, straightening from her task. "I suppose he's harmless, but those bottles of his create a hazard for our boats. Burt has asked him several times not to throw them in the water. He just keeps right on doing it."

The sun now was directly overhead and Penny and Louise knew that they were expected at their homes for luncheon. Thanking Sara for her services, they sailed on to their own dock. As they hastened through the park to a bus line, Penny remarked that it would be fun sometime to visit Noah and his ark.

"Well, perhaps," Louise rejoined without a great deal of enthusiasm.

The buses were off schedule and for a long while the girls waited impatiently at the street corner. Penny was gazing absently toward a cafe nearby when a short, untidy man with shaggy gray hair, came out of the building.

CHAPTER 5 - HELD ON SUSPICION

"Why, isn't that Mr. Oaks, the bridge watchman?" she asked her chum.

"It looks like him."

From far up the street an approaching bus could be seen, but Penny had lost all interest in boarding it.

"Louise, let's talk to Mr. Oaks," she urged, starting toward him.

"But we'll miss our bus."

"Who cares about that?" Penny took Louise firmly by an elbow, pulling her along. "We may not have another chance to see Mr. Oaks. I want to ask him why he identified the saboteur as Sara Ottman's brother."

CHAPTER 6 - OLD NOAH

Carl Oaks saw the girls approaching, and recognized them with a curt nod of his head. He responded to their cheerful greeting, but with no warmth.

"I was hoping to see you, Mr. Oaks," Penny began the conversation. "Last night Louise and I had no opportunity to express our appreciation for the way you helped us."

"Well, I didn't help myself any," the old watchman broke in. "It was sure bad luck for me when your sailboat came floatin' down the river. Now I've lost my job."

"Oh, I'm sorry to hear it."

"I don't know what I'm going to do," Mr. Oaks resumed in a whining tone. "I've never been strong and I can't do hard work."

"Perhaps you can find another job as a watchman."

"No one will take me on after what happened last night."

"But it wasn't your fault the bridge was dynamited."

"Folks always are ready to push a man down if they get the chance," Mr. Oaks said bitterly. "No, I'm finished in this seedy town! I'd pull out if I had the price of a ticket."

Penny was decidedly troubled. "You mustn't take that attitude, Mr. Oaks," she replied. "Maybe I can help you."

The watchman looked interested, but amused. "How can you help me?" he demanded.

"My father owns the *Riverview Star*. Perhaps he can use an extra watchman at the newspaper building. If not, he may know someone who will employ you."

"I've always worked around the waterfront," Mr. Oaks returned, brightening a bit. "You know I ain't able to do much walkin' or any heavy lifting. Maybe your father can get me another job on a bridge."

"Well, I don't know," Penny responded. "I'll talk to him. Just give me your address so I can notify you later."

Mr. Oaks scribbled a few lines on the back of an old envelope and handed it to her. He did not express appreciation for the offer Penny had made, accepting it as his just due.

"I suppose the police questioned you about the bridge dynamiting," she remarked, pocketing the address.

"Sure, they gave me the works," he acknowledged, shrugging. "Kept me at the station half the night. Then this morning they had me identify one of the suspects."

"*Not* Burt Ottman?"

"Yeah."

"You didn't identify him as the saboteur?" Penny inquired in dismay.

"I told the police he looked like the fellow. And he did."

"But how could you see his face?" Penny protested. "The motorboat traveled so fast! Even when the man crawled out of the water and ran, one could only tell that he was tall and thin."

"He looked like young Ottman to me," the watchman insisted stubbornly. "Well, guess I'll shove on. You talk to your father and let me know about that job. I can use 'er."

Without giving the girls a chance to ask another question, Mr. Oaks moved off down the street.

"Now if things aren't in a nice mess," Penny remarked as she and Louise retraced their way to the bus stop. "No wonder the police held Burt Ottman! I don't see how Mr. Oaks could have thought he resembled the saboteur."

CHAPTER 6 - OLD NOAH

"I'm sure I didn't get a good look at the fellow," Louise returned. "Mr. Oaks must have wonderful eyes, to say the least."

After a ten minute wait, a bus came along, and the girls rode to their separate homes. Penny ate luncheon, helped Mrs. Weems with the dishes and then slipped away to her father's newspaper office.

An early afternoon edition of the *Star* had just rolled from the press. Entering the editorial room, Penny noted that it appeared to have been swept by a whirlwind. Discarded copy lay on the floor, and there were more wads of paper around the scrap baskets than in them.

Jerry Livingston's battered typewriter served as a comfortable foot rest for his unpolished shoes. Seeing Penny, he removed them to the floor, and grinned at her.

"Hello, Miss Pop-Eye!" he said affectionately. "How's our little sailor?"

"Never mind," returned Penny. "What's this I hear about Burt Ottman being arrested by the police?"

"That's how it is." The grin faded from the reporter's face. "Tough on DeWitt too."

"DeWitt?" Penny inquired. She could not guess what connection the editor might have with the dynamiting case.

Jerry glanced about the news room to make certain that DeWitt was not within hearing. In a low tone he confided:

"Didn't you know? Burt Ottman is DeWitt's first cousin. It rather puts him in a spot, being kin to a saboteur."

"Nothing has been proved against Ottman yet."

"All the same, it looks bad for the kid. When the story came in it gave DeWitt a nasty jolt."

"I should think so," nodded Penny. "Why, I never dreamed that he was related to the Ottmans."

"Neither did anyone else in the office. But you have to hand it to DeWitt. He took it squarely between the eyes. Didn't even play the story down nor ask your father to soft pedal it."

"Mr. DeWitt is a real newspaper man."

"Bet your life!" Jerry agreed with emphasis. "He's gone young Ottman's bail to the tune of ten thousand dollars."

"Why, that must represent a good portion of his life time savings."

"Sure, but DeWitt says the kid has been framed, and he's going to stand by him."

"I think myself that Burt Ottman was too far away to be properly identified. I mean to tell the police so, too."

"Well, we all hope for DeWitt's sake that it is a mistake," Jerry said soberly. "But the evidence is stacking up fast. The motorboat came from Ottman's. Carl Oaks said he recognized the saboteur as young Ottman. Then this morning police found a handkerchief with an initial 'O' lying along the shore not far from where the fellow crawled out of the water."

"Circumstantial evidence."

"Maybe so," Jerry agreed with a shrug, "but unless young Ottman gets a good lawyer, he's likely to find himself doing a long stretch."

Deeply troubled by the information, Penny went on toward her father's private office. As she passed the main copy desk where Editor DeWitt worked, she noticed that his face was white and tense. Although he usually had a smile for her, he barely glanced up and did not speak.

Penny tapped twice and entered her father's office. Mr. Parker had just finished dictating a letter to his secretary who quietly gathered up her notebook and departed. The newspaper owner pretended to glance at the calendar on his desk.

"Unless I'm all muddled, this is Saturday, not Thursday," he greeted his daughter teasingly. "Aren't you a bit mixed up?"

"Maybe so," Penny admitted, seating herself on a corner of the desk.

"You seldom honor me with a call except to collect your Thursday allowance."

"Oh, I'm not concerned with money these days," Penny said, trying to balance a paper weight on her father's head. "It's this dynamiting case that has me all tied in a knot."

"Stop it, Penny!" Irritably, Mr. Parker squirmed in his chair. "This is an office, not a child's play room!"

"Try to give me your undivided attention, Dad. I want you to do me a favor."

"How about granting me one first? Please stop playing with the gadgets on my desk!"

"Why, of course," grinned Penny, backing away. "Now about this job for Carl Oaks—"

"Job?"

"Yes, he was relieved of duty at the Thompson bridge, you know. It was partly my fault. So I want you to square matters by finding other work for him."

"Penny, I am *not* an employment agency! Anyway, what do I know about the man?"

"I owe him a job, Dad. He says he likes to work around the waterfront. Can't you get him something to do? Oh, yes, it has to be an easy job because he can't walk and he can't lift anything."

"How about a nice pension?" Mr. Parker demanded. He sighed and added, "Well, I'll see what I can do for him. Now run along, because I have work to get out."

Feeling certain that her father would find a suitable position for the old watchman, Penny went directly from the newspaper office to Louise Sidell's home. After relating all the latest news, she asked her chum if she would not enjoy another excursion to the river.

"But we were just there a few hours ago!" Louise protested. "I've had enough sailing for one day."

"Oh, I don't care to sail either," Penny corrected hastily. "I thought it might be interesting to call on Old Noah."

"That queer old man who has the ark?"

"What do you say?"

"Oh, all right," Louise agreed, rather intrigued by the prospect. "But if we get into trouble, just remember it was your idea."

By bus the girls rode to a point near the river. Without approaching Ottman's Dock, they crossed the Big Bear over Thompson's bridge which had just been opened to pedestrian traffic only. Making their way along the eastern shore, they came at last to the mouth of Bug Run.

"It looks like rain to me," Louise declared, scanning the fast-moving clouds. "Just our luck to be caught in a downpour."

"Maybe we can take refuge in the ark," Penny laughed, leading the way up the meandering stream. "That is, if we can find it."

Trees and bushes grew thick and green along either bank of the run. Several times the girls were forced to muddy their shoes in order to proceed. In one shady glade, a bullfrog blinked at them before making a hasty dive into the lilypads.

There was no sign of a boat or any structure remotely resembling an ark. And then, rounding a bend, they suddenly saw it silhouetted against a darkening sky.

"Why, it looks just as if it had rolled out of The Old Testament!" Louise cried in astonishment.

The ark, painted red and blue, rose three stories from the muddy water. A large, circular window had been built in the uppermost part, and there were tiny, square openings beneath. From within could be heard a strange medley of animal sounds—the cackling of hens, the squeal of a pig, the squawking of a saucy parrot who kept calling: "Noah! Oh, Noah!"

Louise gripped Penny's hand. "Let's not go any nearer," she said uneasily. "It's starting to rain, and we ought to make a double dash for home."

A few drops of rain splashed into the stream. Dropping on the tin roof of the ark like tiny pellets of metal, they made a loud drumming sound. The disturbed hens began to cluck on their roosts. The parrot screeched loudly, "Oh, Noah! Come Noah!"

"Where is Noah?" Penny asked with a nervous giggle. "I certainly must see him before we leave."

As if in answer to her question, they heard a strange series of sounds from deep within the woods. A cow mooed, and a man spoke soothing words. Soon there emerged from among the trees a bewildering assortment of animals and fowl—a cow, a goat, a pig, and two fat turkeys. An old man with a long white beard which fell to his chest, drove the creatures toward the gangplank of the ark.

"Get along, Bessie," he urged the cow, tapping her with his crooked stick. "The Lord maketh the rain to fall for forty days and forty nights, but you shall be saved. Into the ark!"

Penny fairly hugged herself with delight.

"Oh, Louise, we can't go now," she whispered. "That must be Old Noah. And isn't he a darling?"

CHAPTER 7 - ARK OF THE MUD FLATS

Unaware that he was being observed, Old Noah again rapped the cow smartly on her flanks.

"Get along, Bessie," he urged impatiently. "The Heavens will open any minute now, and all the creatures of the earth shall perish. But this calamity shall not befall you, Bessie. You are one of God's chosen."

None too willing to be saved from impending doom, Bessie bellowed a loud protest as she was driven into the over-crowded ark. Next went the goat and the squealing pig. The turkeys made more trouble, gobbling excitedly as the old man shooed them into the confines of the three-storied boat.

His task accomplished, Old Noah wiped his perspiring brow with a big red handkerchief. He stood for a moment, gazing anxiously up at the boiling storm clouds.

"This is it—the second great flood," he murmured. "For the Lord sayeth, 'I will cause it to rain forty days and forty nights and every living substance that I have made will I destroy from off the face of the earth.'"

As he stood thus, gazing at the sky, Noah made a striking figure. In his prime, the old man evidently had been a stalwart physical specimen, and advancing years had not enfeebled him. His face was that of a Prophet of old. A certain child-like simplicity shone from a pair of trusting blue eyes whose direct gaze bespoke implicit belief.

"Let's speak to him," Penny urged. Although Louise tried to hold back, she pulled her along toward the ark.

Old Noah heard the girls coming and turned quickly around. After the first moment of startled surprise, he leaned on his crooked stick and inquired with a kind smile:

"Why have you come, my daughters?"

"Well, we were curious to see this fine ark," Penny replied. "We picked up one of your floating blue bottles with a message in it."

"Blessed are they that heed the warnings of the Lord," murmured Old Noah. "I, his servant, have prepared a place of refuge for all who come."

By this time rain was falling steadily, and Louise huddled against a tree trunk for protection. "Penny, for Pete's Sake—" she protested.

"Follow me, my daughters," bade Old Noah, motioning for them to cross the gangplank into the ark. "Inside you will find food and shelter."

"We could use a little shelter," said Penny, glancing questioningly at her chum. "How about it, Lou? Shall we go inside and meet the animals?"

Louise hesitated, for in truth she was a bit afraid of the queer old man.

"Come, my daughters," Noah bade again. "Have no fear. The Lord sayeth, 'Noah, with thee will I establish my covenant, and thou shalt enter into the ark.'"

"We'll drown if we stay outside," laughed Penny, following boldly after the old man. "Come on, Louise."

Unmindful of the falling rain, Noah stooped to pick up a bedraggled kitten from underfoot.

"It's a very nice boat," Penny remarked, dodging under the shelter of the roof. Louise huddled close beside her.

"A sturdy ark," agreed Old Noah proudly. "Many, many months did I labor building it. The Lord said, 'make thee an ark of gopher wood.' But of gopher wood there was none to be had. Then the Lord came to me in a dream and said, 'Noah, use anything you can find.' So I gathered timbers from the beaches, and I wrecked an abandoned cottage I found in the woods. I felled trees. And I pitched the seams within and without as the Lord bade me."

"What animals do you keep inside?" Penny inquired curiously.

"Well, mostly creatures that aren't too exacting in their needs," said Noah, perching the wet kitten on his shoulder. "The Lord sayeth two of every kind, male and female. But it wasn't practical. Some of the animals were too big to keep aboard the ark."

A disturbance from within the boat interrupted the old man's explanation. "Excuse me, daughters, I've got to fasten Bessie in her stall," he apologized. "If I keep her waitin' she's apt to kick the ark to pieces!"

Old Noah disappeared into the lower story of the boat. Peering in the open door, the girls saw row upon row of stalls and cages. There was a sty for the pigs, a pen for the goat, a little kennel for the dog, low roosts for the fowls. The walls of the room had been whitewashed and the floor was clean.

"What a life Old Noah must lead!" Louise whispered to Penny. "Why, it must be worse than being a zoo keeper!"

In a moment the old fellow reappeared. Beckoning to the girls, he led them up a little flight of stairs to the second floor of the ark.

"This is my bird room," he said, opening a door.

"Hello, Noah!" croaked a brilliantly colored parrot, fluttering on her perch. "You old rascal! Polly wants a slug o' rum!"

Noah glanced quickly at the girls. "I am humble and ashamed," he apologized. "But the bird means no evil. I bought her of a sailor, who, I fear had wandered from the ways of righteousness."

Placing a drink of water near the parrot, the old man directed attention to a cage containing a pair of doves.

"When the flood waters recede, I shall send these birds forth from a window of the ark," he explained. "If they return with a branch of a bush or any green thing, then I shall know that the Lord no longer is angry."

"How long do you imagine it will rain?" Louise asked absently, staring out the little round window.

"Forty days and forty nights," answered Old Noah. Taking a bag of seed, he began to feed the chirping birds. "While your stay here may be somewhat confining, you will find my ark sturdy and snug."

"Our stay here," Louise echoed hollowly.

Penny gave her a little pinch and said to Old Noah, "We appreciate your hospitality and will be happy to remain until the rain slackens. But where are your living quarters?"

"On the third floor. First, before I conduct you there, I will throw out a few bottles. Although the fatal hour is near at hand, a number of persons may yet read my message and seek refuge in time to be saved."

While the girls watched with deep interest, Old Noah moved to the porthole. Opening it, he tossed into the muddy waters a half dozen corked bottles which he selected from a basket beneath the window.

"Now," he bade, turning again to Penny and Louise, "follow me and I will show you my humble quarters."

By this time the girls scarcely knew what to expect, but the third floor of the ark proved rather a pleasant surprise. Old Noah had fitted it out with compartments, a tiny kitchen, living quarters, and a bedroom. The main room had a rug on the floor, there were several homemade chairs and a radio. Evidently, the master of the ark was musically inclined, for a shelf contained an accordion, a banjo and a mouth organ.

"Just sit down and make yourselves comfortable, daughters," Old Noah invited, waving them toward chairs. "I'll stir up a bite to eat."

Entering the tiny kitchen, he poked about among the shelves. Watching rather anxiously, the girls next saw him open one of the portholes to test his fishing lines. Finding one taut, he pulled in a large catfish which he immediately began to dress.

"He intends to cook that for us," Louise whispered. "I'll not even taste it! Oh, let's get away from here!"

Penny wandered to the window. The sky had grown much lighter, and trees which had been blotted out by the heavy rain, now were visible.

"The storm is almost over," she said encouragingly. "Let's step outside and see how things look."

Noah, occupied with his culinary affairs, did not glance up as the girls quietly slipped away. Descending the steps to the main deck, they huddled close against a wall to keep dry. Rain still fell, but even as they watched it slackened.

"Let's say goodbye to Noah and streak for home," Louise suggested, eager to be off.

Before Penny could reply, both girls were startled to see a stranger emerge from among the bushes along the shore. He wore a raincoat, a broad-brimmed hat which dripped water, and a bright badge gleamed on his chest.

"I'm Sheriff Anderson," he announced, coming close to the ark. "Is Dan Grebe aboard?"

"Do you mean Old Noah?" Penny asked doubtfully.

CHAPTER 7 - ARK OF THE MUD FLATS

"Most folks call him that. An old man who's lost his buttons, but harmless. He's been maintaining a public nuisance here with his ark."

As the sheriff started to come aboard, Old Noah himself stepped out on deck.

"So here you be again!" he shouted angrily, grasping the narrow railing of the gangplank. "Didn't I warn you not to trespass on the property of the Lord?"

"Noah, we've been patient with you," the sheriff replied wearily. "The last time I was here, you promised to clean up this dump and move your ark down stream. Now you're going with me to talk to the judge."

"Stand back! Stand back!" Old Noah shouted as the officer started across the gangplank. "Beware, or I'll call the wrath of the Lord down on your head!"

The sheriff laughed and came on. With surprising strength and agility, Old Noah jerked the gangplank loose from the ark and hurled it into the water. Sheriff Anderson made a desperate lunge for an overhanging tree branch. Failing to seize it, he fell with a loud splash into the muddy river.

CHAPTER 8 - THE GREEN PARROT

Old Noah slapped his thigh and cackled with glee as he watched Sheriff Anderson splash about in the muddy water.

"That'll teach you!" he shouted jubilantly. "You meddlin' son of evil! Next time maybe you will know enough to mind your own business and leave my ark alone!"

Penny and Louise stood ready to toss the sheriff a rope, but he did not need it. Clinging to the floating gangplank, the man awkwardly propelled himself to shore. As he tried to climb up the steep bank, his boots slipped and he fell flat on his face in the mud. Old Noah went off into another fit of laughter which fairly shook the ark at its mooring.

"Laugh, you old coot!" the sheriff muttered, picking himself up. "I've been mighty patient with you, but there's a limit. Tomorrow I'm coming back here with a detail of deputies. I'll run you and your ark out o' here if it's the last thing I do!"

"Be off with you!" ordered Noah arrogantly. "Before *my* patience is gone!"

"Okay, Noah, you win this round," the sheriff muttered furiously. "I'm going, but I'll be back. And if this ark isn't cleaned up or out o' here, we'll put you away!"

A sorry figure with his clothing wet and muddy, the official stomped angrily off into the woods.

"I'm afraid you antagonized the wrong man that time, Noah," Penny remarked as the footsteps died away. "What will you do when he returns?"

"That time will never come," Old Noah replied, undisturbed. "Before the Lord will allow the ark to be taken from me, he will smite my enemies with lightning from the Heavens."

Penny and Louise had their own opinion of what would happen to the ark and its animals, but wisely said nothing to further disturb the old fellow. By this time the rain had entirely ceased and a ray of sunshine straggled through the ragged clouds.

"Well, guess this isn't to be the Great Flood after all," Penny remarked, studying the sky. "We're most grateful for the shelter of your ark, Noah. Now if we can just reach shore, we'll be on our way."

"Aren't you staying for dinner?" the old man asked in disappointment. "I'm fryin' up a nice catfish."

"I'm afraid we can't remain today," Penny answered. "Another time perhaps." Using a long, hooked pole, Old Noah retrieved the drifting gangplank and refastened it to the ark.

"Farewell, my daughters," he said regretfully as he bade them goodbye. "You and your friends always will be welcome to take refuge in my ark. The Great Flood is coming soon, but you are among the chosen."

Feeling decidedly exhilarated by their meeting with such a strange character, Louise and Penny followed the twisting stream to the main river channel. Water was rising rapidly along the banks and at many places, bushes and tree branches dipped low in the swirling eddies.

"You know, if these spring rains keep up, Noah may get his big flood after all," Penny remarked. "Poor old fellow! He certainly sealed the fate of his ark when he pushed Sheriff Anderson into Bug Run."

Turning homeward toward the Thompson Bridge, the girls soon approached the river bank where police had searched for the escaped saboteur. Curious to see the locality by daylight, they detoured slightly in order to pass it.

"This is the place," Penny said, indicating ground which had been trampled by many feet. "At the rate the river rises, the shore here will be under by tomorrow."

"I suppose police learned everything they could last night."

CHAPTER 8 - THE GREEN PARROT

"Yes, they went over the area rather thoroughly," Penny nodded. "I know they took photographs and made measurements of the saboteur's footprints. Lucky they did, because the water has washed them all away."

"You still can see where the automobile was parked," Louise declared, pointing to tire tracks in the soft earth. "Were any real clues found, Penny?"

"Jerry told me police picked up a handkerchief bearing the initial 'O.'"

"That could stand for Ottman!"

"Likewise Oscar or Oliver or Oxenstiern," Penny added, frowning. "I'll admit though, it doesn't look too bright for Sara's brother."

Having satisfied their curiosity regarding the locality, the girls started on toward the bridge. Before they had gone a dozen feet, Penny's eye was caught by an object lying half-buried in the mud. She picked it up gingerly and dangling it in front of Louise was amazed to discover that it was a man's leather billfold.

"Anything inside?" inquired Louise with interest.

Penny opened the flap and explored the various divisions of the money container. To her disappointment it held nothing save one small card upon which had been scribbled a few words.

"'The Green Parrot—'" she read aloud. "'Tuesday at 9:15.' Now what does that mean?"

Beneath the notation appeared another: "The American Protective Society."

"I guess it doesn't mean much of anything," commented Louise, digging at the mud which had collected on her shoes. "Probably an appointment card."

"You don't suppose this billfold was dropped by the saboteur?" Penny asked thoughtfully. "It's very near the place where he crawled out of the river."

"Wouldn't the police have picked it up if they had considered it of any importance?"

"I doubt they ever saw it, Lou. The billfold was half buried in mud. I'd never have seen it myself if I hadn't almost stepped on it."

"Why not turn it over to the police?"

"Guess I will," Penny decided, replacing the card in the billfold and wrapping them both in her handkerchief. "Did you ever hear of the American Protective Society, Lou?"

"Never did. Nor 'The Green Parrot' either—whatever that is."

"I think The Green Parrot is a cafe or a night club with none too good a reputation," Penny said thoughtfully. "I'm sure I've heard Dad say it's a gambling place."

Without further adventure, the girls resumed their trek and soon reached a bus line. Upon arriving home, Penny's first act was to consult the telephone directory. She could find neither The Green Parrot nor the American Protective Society listed.

"Mrs. Weems, did you ever hear of a place called The Green Parrot?" she questioned the housekeeper.

"Isn't that a restaurant the police closed down a few months ago?" replied Mrs. Weems. "Now why should you be bothering your head about The Green Parrot?"

Penny showed her the billfold and explained where she had found it.

"Dear me," sighed the housekeeper. "How you can get into so many affairs of this kind is a wonder to me. I'm sure it worries your father too."

"Not Dad," laughed Penny. "Since I dug up that big story for him about the old *Wishing Well*, he's been reconciled to my career of news gathering."

"Wishing wells and saboteurs are two entirely different matters," the housekeeper returned firmly. "I do hope you turn this billfold over to police and forget about suspicious characters."

"I'm only worried about one," rejoined Penny. "It bothers me because I involved Burt Ottman in such a mess. I'm not so sure he's guilty."

"And again, the police probably know exactly what they are about," replied Mrs. Weems. "Now please take that billfold to the authorities and let them do the worrying."

Thus urged, Penny carried the money container to the local police station. Unable to talk to any of the detectives connected with the dynamiting case, she left the billfold with a desk sergeant. As she turned to leave, after answering his many questions, she posed one of her own.

"Oh, by the way, did you ever hear of a place called The Green Parrot?"

"Sure," the sergeant responded. "It's a night club. Used to be located on Granger Street, but our boys made it too hot for 'em, so they moved to another place."

"Where is it now?"

"Couldn't tell you," answered the sergeant. "You'll have to talk to one of the detectives, Jim Adams or Bill Benson."

Having no real excuse for seeking the information, Penny decided to abandon the quest. For want of an occupation, she sauntered on toward the *Star* office. Pausing in front of the big plate glass window, she idly watched a workman who was oiling one of the great rotary presses.

"Oh, here you are!" exclaimed a voice from behind her.

Whirling around, Penny saw that her father had just come through the revolving doors at the main entrance to the building.

"Hello, Dad," she greeted him eagerly. "What's new in the dynamiting case?"

"Nothing so far as I know," he replied, rather indifferently. "Burt Ottman's been released on bail."

"Mr. DeWitt put up the money?"

"Yes, he did," Mr. Parker said, frowning. "I advised him against it, but DeWitt feels a duty to the boy. Were you looking for me, Penny?"

"Well, not in particular."

"I'm on my way to a bank meeting," Mr. Parker said, turning away. "Oh, yes, I arranged a job for that watchman complication of yours, Carl Oaks."

"You did? Oh, grand! What sort of work is it?"

"Can't take time to tell you now," Mr. Parker said hurriedly, hailing a passing taxi cab. "If you want all the details, ask Jerry Livingston. He took care of the matter for me, and can give you the information."

CHAPTER 9 - A JOB FOR MR. OAKS

Eager to learn what had been done to help Carl Oaks, Penny took an elevator to the news room of the *Star*. Jerry Livingston's desk was deserted, so she paused at the slot of the big circular copy desk to ask Editor DeWitt if the reporter were anywhere in the building.

"I just sent him to cover a fire," Mr. DeWitt replied, glancing up from copy he was correcting. "He ought to be back any minute. You know how Jerry covers a fire."

"I certainly do. He rides the big engine to the scene, just whiffs at the smoke, and races back with a column report!"

Penny hesitated. She very much wished to say something to the editor about the dynamiting case, yet was reluctant to bring up the subject.

"Mr. DeWitt, I'm sorry about Burt Ottman," she began awkwardly. "I hope you don't think that I tried to throw suspicion on him by telling police——"

"Of course not," he cut in. "It's just a case of circumstantial evidence. Burt has a good lawyer now. I'm not a bit worried."

The harassed expression of DeWitt's face belied his words. He had always been known to fellow workers as a hard yet just man, but now it seemed to Penny that the veteran newspaperman was losing his grip. Though he fancied he disguised his feelings, it was plain to all that Burt Ottman's arrest had shaken him.

"Guess I won't wait for Jerry," Penny said, turning away.

Leaving the newspaper office, she dropped in at Foster's Drugstore to perch herself on a counter stool.

"I'll take a deluxe dose of Hawaiian Delight with whipped cream," she told the soda fountain clerk.

"No pineapple," he said sadly. "And no whipped cream."

"Then make it a double chocolate malted."

"We're out of chocolate. Sorry."

"Just bring me an empty dish and let me look at it for awhile," Penny grinned.

"How about a nice vanilla sundae with crushed walnuts?" the clerk coaxed.

"Oh, all right," Penny gave in. "And don't spare the walnuts!"

She ate the ice cream leisurely and had finished the last spoonful when a young man breezed into the drugstore. Recognizing Jerry Livingston, Penny signaled frantically. Without seeing her, he dodged into a telephone booth. He slammed out again in a moment and sat down at the counter.

"Cup o' Java and make it strong," he ordered carelessly.

"Sorry, sir, no coffee served without meals," teased Penny from another stool. "How about a nice vanilla sundae with crushed walnuts?"

Jerry grinned as he saw her and moved over to an adjoining stool.

"Where was the fire?" she inquired curiously.

"At the Fulton Warehouse along the dock. It was deliberately set."

"By saboteurs?"

"Looks that way. Workmen discovered the blaze in time to prevent the whole plant going up in smoke. Just got through telephoning the story to DeWitt."

"Isn't the *Star* building across the street?"

"Sure, but that's a long walk. Besides, I'm due at the airport for my flying lesson."

"Your which?" inquired Penny alertly.

"I'm training to be an angel," Jerry laughed. "I figure it like this. I can't get along without my six cups o' Java a day, so the only place for me is in Uncle Sam's Air Corps."

"How soon will you be leaving, Jerry?"

"Not until I've completed my local training. Oh, I'll probably be grinding out news stories for quite some time yet."

Penny drew a quick breath and changed the subject. One by one familiar faces were disappearing from the *Star* office, but somehow it gave her a special twinge to think that Jerry soon must go. In the pursuit of news they had shared many an adventure.

"Jerry," she said abruptly, "Dad told me you were able to get Carl Oaks a job."

"One of sorts. It doesn't pay much, but it's soft. Oaks is hired by the Riverview Coal Company to guard their barge that's tied up at Dock 10."

"Thanks a lot, Jerry, for going to so much trouble. Mr. Oaks ought to be quite grateful."

"Not that fellow! He held out for more pay."

"Are the duties hard?"

"Hard? All he has to do is stay aboard the barge and see that no one tries to make off with it."

"I can't imagine anyone trying to steal a coal barge," laughed Penny.

"Oh, it's done now and then," Jerry rejoined carelessly. "These days they'll even steal the hawsers off a boat."

"What value would the rope have to a thief?"

"Hawsers are expensive," the reporter explained. "Right now it's almost impossible to get good grade hemp. A hawser of any size commands a big price second hand."

"How do the thieves get the ropes, Jerry?"

"Oh, they wait for a dark or foggy night and then slip up to an unguarded boat and cut her loose."

"Why, that's a form of sabotage!" Penny cried indignantly.

"Sure, it is. The boats float free and unless they're spotted, they're likely to collide with other incoming vessels. Only last week an empty coal barge was cut loose. She crashed into an oil tanker and rammed a hole in her."

"Then Carl Oaks really has an important job," Penny said thoughtfully.

"Important in the sense that he's got to keep his eyes open. But he's not required to do any hard work. All he has to do is sit."

"Then he should like the job," Penny smiled, sliding down from the stool. "When does he start work?"

"He took over this morning."

"Maybe I'll ankle down to Dock 10 and talk to him."

"Better wrap yourself in cellophane first," Jerry advised. "That is, if you value your peaches and cream complexion."

Penny was not certain what the reporter meant, but a little later, approaching the coal docks, she understood. Nearby was a private railroad yard and cars were being loaded from the many mountains of coal heaped on the ground. With the wind blowing toward the river, the dust laden air blackened her hands and clothing.

Penny stood for a moment watching a coal car race down from a steep switch-back, and then wandered along the docks in search of Mr. Oaks.

She came presently to the barge for which she searched. There was no sign of anyone aboard. A long ladder ascended from the dock to the vessel's deck. Penny hesitated and then decided to climb it. When she was midway up, a man, his face blackened with coal, stepped from a shed.

"Hey, where you think you're going?" he shouted sternly.

"I'm looking for Mr. Oaks," Penny explained, hugging the ladder.

"Oaks? The new watchman?"

"Yes. He's aboard, isn't he?"

"He should be. Well, go on up, I guess, but it's against regulations."

Penny climbed the remaining rungs of the ladder and stepped out on the deck of the barge. She was chagrined to see that she had wiped up a great deal of coal dust.

"Oh, Mr. Oaks!" she called. "Are you here?"

CHAPTER 9 - A JOB FOR MR. OAKS

From the tiny deck house the old man emerged. No smile brightened his smudged face as he recognized Penny.

"This is a swell job your father got me!" he greeted her.

"Why, Mr. Oaks, you don't act as if you like it," Penny replied, walking toward him. "What seems to be wrong?"

"The pay's poor," he said crossly. "I'm expected to stay on this rotten old tub twenty-four hours a day with only time off for my meals. It's so dirty around here that if a fellow'd take a deep breath he'd get a hunk o' coal stuck in his nose!"

"It *is* rather unpleasant," Penny admitted. "But then, the wind can't always blow in this direction."

"I want you to ask your father to find me another job," the watchman went on. "I'd like one on a bridge again."

"Well, I don't know. After what happened—"

"And whose fault was it?" Mr. Oaks interrupted angrily. "I helped you and that girl friend of yours, didn't I? Well, now it's your turn to do me a little favor, 'specially since it wasn't my fault I lost the bridge job."

"I'll talk to Dad," Penny said. Annoyed by the watchman's attitude, she did not prolong the interview, but quickly climbed down from the barge.

From the coal yards she followed the river for a distance, coming presently to more pleasant surroundings. She was still thinking about Carl Oaks as she approached the Ottman boathouse. Sara and a young man were deeply engrossed in examining a large metal object which appeared to be a homemade diving hood.

For a moment Penny assumed that Sara's companion was Bill Evans. However, as the young man turned slightly, she saw his face.

"Why, it's Burt Ottman!" she thought. "He's back on his old job after being released from jail. I'm going to talk to him and see what he'll say!"

CHAPTER 10 - SALVAGE AND SABOTEURS

Sara Ottman and her brother glanced up from their work as Penny approached the dock. Burt was a tall young man of twenty-six, brown of face, with muscles hardened by heavy, outdoor work. He nodded to Penny, but his expression did not disclose whether or not he bore resentment.

"Anything we can do for you?" he asked, his manner impersonal.

"No, I just happened to be over this way and thought I'd stop for a minute. What's this strange contraption?" Penny indicated the queer looking metal hood.

"A diving apparatus Burt made," Sara explained briefly. "We're using it to get Bill Evans' motor out of the river."

"How does it work?"

"Watch and see," invited Sara. "Burt's going to make the first dive."

Though Penny felt that she was none too welcome at the dock, she nevertheless decided to remain. Burt disappeared into the shed, reappearing a minute later in bathing trunks. He and Sara loaded the diving hood into a boat and rowed to the nearby area which had been marked with a can buoy.

Burt adjusted the metal helmet over his head and lowered himself into the water. Once her brother was beneath the surface, Sara worked tirelessly at the pump, feeding him air. Soon Bill Evans drifted by in another boat, watching the salvage operation like a worried mother.

"Think you'll get 'er?" he asked Sara. "Doggone if I know how an engine could be so hard to find."

Sara did not bother to answer, but kept pumping steadily.

After many minutes, the metal hood appeared on the surface. Burt Ottman lifted it from his head and took a deep breath.

"Any luck?" Bill asked anxiously.

"I'll have the engine up in a little bit," Burt replied. Breasting himself into the boat, he pulled on a rope tied around his waist. With Sara helping, he gradually hauled the lost motor from its muddy bed.

"Oh, say, that's swell!" Bill cried jubilantly. "How can I thank you?"

"Don't forget the five dollars," Sara reminded him. "Burt and I can use it."

"Oh, sure," Bill replied, though the light faded from his eyes. "I haven't got it on me right now. Can you wait a few days?"

"Waiting is the best thing we do," Sara assured him. "Better get this mess of junk cleaned and oiled up right away or it won't be worth a dime."

"I will," promised Bill. "Just dump 'er on the dock for me, will you?"

Sara and her brother delivered the motor to the designated place, and then rowed to their own platform where Penny waited. From the look of their faces it was evident that they never expected to be paid for their work.

Alighting from the boat, Sara noticed one of Old Noah's floating bottles which had snagged against the edge of the platform. Rather irritably she fished it from the water. Without bothering to read the message inside, she hurled it high on the shore.

"Sara, you're in an ugly mood today," her brother observed, smiling.

"I get tired of seeing those bottles!" she replied. "I get tired of doing so much charity work too! How are we to meet our expenses, pay for a lawyer, and—"

"Never mind," Burt interrupted quietly.

CHAPTER 10 - SALVAGE AND SABOTEURS

Sara subsided into silence. They moored the boat and Burt, carrying the diving bell with him, went into the shed.

"Guess you think I'm a regular old crab," Sara remarked, turning toward Penny.

"Oh, I don't know," Penny answered. "I'm sure you have plenty to worry you."

"I do! Since the papers published the bridge dynamiting story, our business has shrunk to almost nothing. Burt's case is coming up for trial in about ten days. I don't know how we'll pay the lawyer. If Mr. DeWitt hadn't put up bail, my brother still would be in jail."

"Oh, you shouldn't feel so discouraged," Penny said cheerfully. "Burt will be cleared."

"I wish I could think so. He's innocent, but to prove it is another matter."

"Can't your brother provide an alibi? Where was he at the time of the dynamiting?"

"I don't know," Sara admitted, frowning. "Burt's peculiar. I tried to talk things over with him, but he says it's a disagreeable subject. He hasn't told me where he was Friday night."

Burt's appearance in the doorway of the shed brought the conversation to an abrupt end. Before Penny could speak to him, a group of small boys ran along the bank some distance away.

"*Saboteur! Saboteur!*" they shouted jeeringly, pointing at Burt. One of the lads threw a clod of dirt which struck a moored rowboat.

"You see how it is!" Sara cried wrathfully.

"Don't take things so seriously," Burt advised, though his own eyes burned with an angry light. "They're only youngsters."

"I can't stand much more," Sara cried, running into the shed, and closing the door.

Burt busied himself cleaning the clod of dirt from the rowboat. "Don't mind Sara," he said. "She's always inclined to be high strung."

"I'm sorry about everything," said Penny quietly. "Mr. DeWitt believes you will be cleared."

Burt straightened, staring at the far shore. "Wish I felt the same way. Unless the real saboteur is caught, the police intend to tag me with the job."

"They can't convict you without evidence. Oh, by the way, did you ever lose a leather billfold?"

The question surprised Burt. He hesitated before he answered: "What made you ask me that?"

"I found an old one along the river. No money or any identification in it. Just a card which said: 'The Green Parrot. Tuesday at 9:15.'"

"The Green Parrot!"

"You've heard of the place?"

"Oh, I've heard of it," Burt answered carelessly. "That's all. I never was there. Sorry I can't claim the billfold."

As if uneasy lest he be questioned further, the young man picked up a coil of rope and walked away. Penny waited a moment and then left the dock.

"I'm just a nuisance around there," she thought unhappily. "I'd like to help, but Sara and Burt won't let me."

The following two days passed without event so far as Penny was concerned. There were no developments regarding the bridge dynamiting case and the story was relegated to an inside page of the Star. However, recalling her promise to Carl Oaks, she did speak to her father about finding him a new job.

"What does that fellow expect?" Mr. Parker rumbled irritably. "Jerry tells me he's a ne'er-do-well. Why doesn't he like his job as watchman on the coal barge?"

"Well, it's too dirty."

"Carl Oaks is lucky to get any job in this town," Mr. Parker answered. "Jerry had a hard time inducing anyone to take him on. Along the waterfront he has a reputation for shiftlessness."

"In that case, just forget it, Dad. I don't like the man too well myself."

Penny promptly forgot about Carl Oaks, but many times she caught herself wondering what had happened to Old Noah and his ark. Since she and Louise had visited the place, it had rained every day. The water was slowly rising in the river and there was talk that a serious flood might result.

On Tuesday night, as Penny and Louise paid their weekly visit to the Rialto Theatre, it was still raining. The gutters were deep with water and to cross the street it was necessary to walk stiffly on their heels.

"We've had enough H_2O for one week," Penny declared, gazing at her splashed stockings. "Well, for screaming out loud!"

505

SABOTEURS ON THE RIVER

A green taxicab, turning in the street to pick up a fare, shot a fountain of muddy water from its spinning wheels. Penny, who stood close to the curb, was sprayed from head to foot.

"Just look at me!" she wailed. "That driver ought to be sent to prison for life!"

The taxi drew up in front of the Rialto Theatre. A well-dressed man in brown overcoat and felt hat who waited at the curb, opened the cab door.

"To the Green Parrot," he ordered the driver.

"Where's that, sir?"

The passenger mumbled an address the girls could not understand. He then slammed shut the cab door and the vehicle drove away.

"Lou, did you hear what I heard?" Penny cried excitedly.

"I certainly did!"

Penny glanced quickly about. Seeing another taxicab across the street, she hailed it.

"Come on, Louise," she urged, tugging at her chum's hand.

Louise held back. "What do you intend to do?"

"Why, we're going to follow that taxi!" Penny splashed through the flooded gutter toward the waiting cab. "This is a real break for us! With luck we'll learn the location of The Green Parrot!"

CHAPTER 11 - PURSUIT BY TAXI

"Keep that green taxi in sight!" Penny instructed her own cab driver as she and Louise leaped into the rear seat.

"Sure," agreed the taxi man, showing no surprise at the request.

Thrilled, and feeling rather theatrical, Penny and Louise sat on the edge of their seats. Anxiously they watched the green cab ahead. Weaving in and out of downtown traffic, it cruised at a slow speed and so, was not hard to follow.

Louise gazed at the running tape of the taxi meter. "Do you see that ticker?" she whispered. "I hope you're well fortified with spare change."

"I haven't much money with me. Let's trust that The Green Parrot is somewhere close."

"More than likely it's miles out in the country," Louise returned pessimistically.

The green cab presently turned down a narrow, little-traveled street not many blocks from the river front. As it halted at the curb, Penny's driver glanced at her for instructions.

"Don't stop," she directed. "Drive on past and pull up around the corner."

The taxi man did as requested, presenting a bill for one dollar and eighty cents. To pay the sum, Penny used all of her own money and borrowed a quarter from her chum.

"That leaves me with just thirty-eight cents," Louise said ruefully. "No picture show tonight. And how are we to get home?"

"We're not far from a bus line. Come on, we're wasting valuable time."

"Those two words, 'Come on' have involved me in more trouble than all the rest of the English language," Louise giggled nervously. "What are we to do now we're here?"

Penny did not answer. Rounding the corner, she saw that the green cab and its passenger had disappeared. For an instant she was bitterly disappointed. Then she noticed a creaking sign which swung above a basement entrance. Although inconspicuous, it bore the picture of a green parrot.

"That's the place, Lou!" she exclaimed.

"Well, we've learned the address, so let's go home."

"Wonder what it's like inside?"

"Don't you dare start that old curiosity of yours to percolating!" Louise chided severely. "We're *not* going in there!"

"Who ever thought of such a thing?" grinned Penny. "Now I wonder what time it is?"

"About eight-thirty or perhaps a little later. Why?"

"Do you remember that card we found in the leather billfold? The notation read, 'The Green Parrot, Tuesday at 9:15.'"

"So it did, but the appointment may have been for nine fifteen in the morning."

"You dope!" laughed Penny. "Louise, we're in wonderful luck finding this place at just this hour! Why, the man we followed here may be the one who lost the billfold."

"All of which makes him a saboteur, I suppose?"

"Not necessarily, but don't you think we ought to try to learn more?"

"I knew you'd try to get me into that place," Louise complained. "Well, I have more sense than to do it. It might not be safe."

"I shouldn't think of venturing in unescorted," Penny assured her. "Why not telephone my father and ask him to come here right away?"

"Well, that might not be such a bad idea," Louise acknowledged reluctantly. "But where can we find a phone?"

Passing The Green Parrot, the girls walked on a few doors until they came to a corner drugstore. Going inside, they closed themselves into a telephone booth. Borrowing a nickel from Louise, Penny called her home, but there was no response.

"Mrs. Weems went to a meeting tonight, and I suppose Dad must be away," she commented anxiously.

"Then let's give it up."

"I'll try the newspaper office," Penny decided. "If Dad isn't there, I'll talk to one of the reporters."

Mr. Parker was not to be contacted at the *Star* plant, nor was Editor DeWitt available. Penny asked to speak to Jerry Livingston and presently heard his voice at the other end of the wire. Without wasting words she told him where she was and what she wanted him to do.

"*The Green Parrot!*" Jerry exclaimed, copying down the address she gave him. "Say, that's worthwhile information. I'll be with you girls as soon as I can get there."

"We'll be outside the corner drugstore," Penny told him. "You'll know us by the way we pace back and forth!"

Within twelve minutes a cab pulled up and Jerry leaped out to greet the two girls.

"Where is this Parrot place?" he demanded, gazing curiously at the dingy buildings.

Louise and Penny led him down the street to the basement entrance. Music could be heard from within, but blinds covered all the windows.

"It must be a cafe," commented Jerry. He turned toward Penny and stared. "Say, what's the matter with your face?"

"My face?"

"You look as if you're coming down with the black measles!"

"Oh, a taxi splashed me with mud," Penny laughed, sponging at her cheeks with a handkerchief. "How do I look now?"

"Better. Let's go."

Taking the girls each by an elbow, Jerry guided them down the stone steps. Confronted with a curving door, he boldly thrust it open.

"Now act as if you belonged here," he warned the girls.

The trio found themselves in a carpeted, luxuriously furnished foyer. From a large dining room nearby came laughter and music.

As the outside door closed behind the young people, a bell tinkled to announce their arrival. Almost at once a head waiter appeared in the archway to the left. He was tall and dark, with a noticeable scar across one cheek. His shrewd eyes scrutinized them, but he bowed politely enough.

"A party of three, sir?"

"Right," agreed Jerry.

They followed the waiter into a dimly lighted dining room with more tables than customers. A four-piece orchestra provided rather dreary music for dancing. Jerry reluctantly allowed a checkroom girl to capture his hat.

The head waiter turned the party over to another waiter.

"Table thirteen," he instructed, and spoke rapidly in French.

"Table thirteen," complained Jerry. "Can't you give us something besides that?"

"Monsieur is superstitious?" The head waiter smiled in a superior way.

"Not superstitious, just cautious."

"As you wish, Monsieur. Table two."

Jerry and the girls were guided to the far end of the room, somewhat apart from the other diners. A large potted palm obstructed their view.

"I think they've hung the Indian sign on us," Jerry muttered after the waiter had gone. "See anyone you know, Penny?"

"That man over by the door—the one sitting alone," she indicated in a whisper. "Louise and I followed him here."

"The one that's wrestling with the lobster?"

CHAPTER 11 - PURSUIT BY TAXI

"Yes, don't stare at him, Jerry. He's watching us."

The waiter arrived with glasses of water and menu cards. Jerry and the girls scanned the list in secret consternation. Scarcely an item was priced at less than a dollar, and even a modest meal would cost a large sum.

"I'm not very hungry," Louise said helpfully. "I'll take a ham sandwich."

"So will I," added Penny.

"Three hams with plenty of mustard," ordered Jerry breezily.

The waiter gave him a long glance. "And your drink, sir?"

"Water," said Jerry. "Cool, refreshing water, preferably with a small piece of ice."

The waiter favored the trio with another unflattering look and went to the kitchen.

"This is a gyp place," Penny declared indignantly. "I can't understand why anyone would come here. The waiters all seem to be French."

"Oh, all head waiters speak French," Jerry replied. "You can't tell by that. I'd say they were German myself."

Penny studied the cafe employees with new interest. She noted that the head waiter kept an alert eye upon the entire room, but particularly he watched their table.

Soon the three orders of ham sandwiches were brought by the waiter. The young people ate as slowly as they could so they would have an excuse for remaining as long as they desired.

"What time is it, Jerry?" Penny asked anxiously.

"Ten after nine," he answered, looking at his watch.

A bell jingled, and the young people knew that another customer had arrived. Craning their necks to see around the palm tree, they watched the dining room entranceway. In a moment a young man entered and was greeted by the head waiter. Jerry and the girls stared, scarcely believing their eyes.

"Why, it's Burt Ottman!" Penny whispered.

"And exactly on the dot of nine-fifteen," added Louise significantly. "He *must* be the person who lost that billfold!"

CHAPTER 12 - JERRY'S DISAPPEARANCE

Without noticing Jerry and the girls, Burt Ottman walked directly to a table at the other side of the dining room. He spoke to the stranger whom Penny and Louise had followed, and sat down opposite him.

"Ha! The plot thickens!" commented Jerry in an undertone. "Obviously our friend and Burt Ottman had an appointment together."

"This is certainly a shock to me," declared Penny. "I'd made up my mind that Burt had nothing whatsoever to do with the dynamiting. Now I don't know what to think."

"He must be the saboteur," Louise said, speaking louder than she realized. "We picked up the billfold along the river and it undoubtedly was his."

"He denied it," replied Penny. "However, when I spoke of The Green Parrot I noticed that he seemed to recognize the name. Oh, dear!"

"Now don't take it so hard," Jerry comforted her. "The best thing to do is to report what we've seen to police and let them draw their own conclusions."

"I suppose so," Penny admitted gloomily. "I had hoped to help Sara and her brother."

"You wouldn't want to protect a saboteur?"

"Of course not, Jerry. Oh, dear, it's all so mixed up."

So intent had the young people been upon their conversation that they failed to observe a waiter hovering near. Nor did it occur to them that he might be listening. As Jerry chanced to glance toward him, he bowed, and moving forward, presented the bill.

"Howling cats!" the reporter muttered after the waiter had discreetly withdrawn. "Will you look at this!"

"How much is it?" Penny asked anxiously. "We only had three ham sandwiches."

"Two dollars cover charge. Three sandwiches, one dollar and a half. Tip, fifty cents. Grand total, four dollars, plus sales tax."

"Why, that's robbery!" Penny exclaimed. "I wouldn't pay it, Jerry."

"I can't," he admitted, slightly abashed. "I only have three dollars in my pocket. Then I'll have to buy my hat back from the checkroom girl."

"Louise and I haven't any money either," Penny said. "Thirty-eight cents to be exact."

"Thirty-three," corrected her chum.

"Tell you what," said Jerry after a moment of thought. "You girls stay here and hold down the chairs. I'll go outside and telephone one of the boys at the office. I'll have someone bring me some cash."

Left to themselves, the girls tried to act as if nothing were wrong. However, they were very conscious of the waiter's scrutiny. Every time the man entered the dining room with a tray of food, he gazed suggestively at the unpaid bill.

"I'd feel more comfortable under the table," Penny commented. "Why doesn't Jerry hurry?"

"Perhaps he can't find a telephone."

"Something is keeping him. We're going to become conspicuous if we stay here much longer."

The girls fumbled with their purses and sipped at their water glasses until the tumblers were empty. Minutes passed and still Jerry did not return.

After a while, Burt Ottman's companion left the dining room. The young owner of the boat dock waited until the older man had vanished, and then called for his check. If the bill were unusually large he did not appear to notice, for he paid it without protest and likewise left the dining room.

CHAPTER 12 - JERRY'S DISAPPEARANCE

"Louise, I don't want to stay here any longer," Penny said nervously. "I can't understand what's keeping Jerry."

"Why not go out to the foyer and look for him."

"A good idea if we can get away with it," Penny approved. "I judge though, that if we start off, the waiter will pursue us with the bill."

"Couldn't we just explain?"

"We can try. Anyway, it will be interesting to see what will happen."

Before leaving the table, Penny scribbled a hasty note which she left for Jerry on his plate. It merely said that the girls would wait for him in the foyer. Choosing a moment when their own waiter was occupied at another table, they sauntered across the room and out into the hall.

"That wasn't half as hard as I thought it would be," chuckled Penny. "But where's Jerry?"

The foyer was deserted. Noticing a stairway which led to a lower level, the girls decided that the telephones must be located below. They started down, but soon realized their mistake for no light was burning in the lower hall.

"We're not supposed to be down here," Louise murmured, holding back.

"Wait!" whispered Penny.

At the far end of the dingy hall she had glimpsed a moving figure. For just a second she thought that the young man might be Jerry. Then she saw that it was Burt Ottman.

"What do you suppose he's doing down here?" she speculated. "He seems to be familiar with all the nooks and crannies of this place."

Burt Ottman had not seen or heard the girls. They saw him pause at the end of the hall and knock four times on a closed door. A circular peep-hole shot open and a voice muttered: "Who is it?"

The girls heard no more. Someone touched Penny on the shoulder from behind. With a startled exclamation, she whirled around to face the head waiter.

"So sorry, Mademoiselle, to have frightened you," he said blandly. "You have taken the wrong stairway."

"Why, yes," stammered Penny, trying to collect her wits. "We were looking for the public telephones."

"This way please. You will find them in the foyer. Just follow me."

Penny and Louise had no choice but to obey. They wondered if the head waiter knew how much they had seen. His expressionless face gave them no clue.

"We were waiting for our friend," Louise remarked to cover her embarrassment.

"The young man who escorted you here?"

"Yes," nodded Louise. "He went to telephone and we haven't seen him since."

The waiter had reached the top of the stairs. He turned and looked directly at the girls as he said: "The young man left here some minutes ago."

"He left!" Penny exclaimed incredulously. "But the bill wasn't paid."

"Oh, yes, the young gentleman took care of it."

"Why, Jerry didn't have enough money," Penny protested, unable to grasp the situation. "You're sure he left the cafe?"

"Yes, Mademoiselle."

"And didn't he leave any message for us?"

"I regret that he did not," the waiter replied. "As young ladies without escorts are not permitted at The Green Parrot, I suggest that you leave at once."

"You may be sure we will," said Penny. "I simply can't understand why Jerry would go off without saying a word to us."

The head waiter conducted the girls to the exit, bowing as he closed the door in their faces. Rather bewildered, they huddled together on the stone steps. Rain had started to fall once more and the air was unpleasantly cold.

"We certainly got out of that place in a hurry," Louise commented. "If you ask me, it was a shabby trick for Jerry to go off and leave us. Especially when he knew we didn't have the price of a taxi."

"Lou," said Penny soberly, "I don't believe that Jerry did desert us."

"But he disappeared! And the head waiter told us that he left."

"Something happened to Jerry when he went to telephone—that's certain," replied Penny, thinking aloud.

"Then you believe he was forcibly ejected?"

"No one could have tossed Jerry out of The Green Parrot without a little opposition."

"Jerry's quite a scrapper when he's aroused," Louise agreed. "We didn't hear any sound of scuffling. What do you think became of him?"

"I don't know and I'm worried," confessed Penny. Taking Louise's arm, she guided her up the stone steps to the street. "The thing for us to do is to get home and tell Dad everything! Jerry may be in serious trouble."

CHAPTER 13 - A VACANT BUILDING

Hastening to a main street, Penny and Louise waited many minutes for a bus. Finally as a taxi cruised past they hailed it, knowing they could obtain cab fare when they reached home.

"Let's go straight to my house," Penny said, giving the driver her address. "Dad should be there by this time. I know he'll be as worried about Jerry as we are."

A few minutes later the taxi drew up in front of the Parker home. Lights burned in the living room and the girls were greatly relieved to glimpse the editor reading in a comfortable chair by the fireplace.

"Dad, I need a dollar sixty for cab fare!" Penny announced, bursting in upon him.

"A dollar sixty," he protested, reaching for his wallet. "I thought you and Louise went to a picture show. What have you been doing in a taxicab?"

"I'll explain just as soon as I pay the driver. Please, this is an emergency."

Mr. Parker gave her two dollars and she ran outside with it. In a moment she came back with Louise.

"Now, Penny, suppose you explain," suggested Mr. Parker. "Has walking become an outmoded sport or are you trying to save wear and tear on rayon stockings?"

"Dad, Louise and I never went to the Rialto Theatre," Penny said breathlessly. "We've been at The Green Parrot!"

"*The Green Parrot!*"

"Oh, we didn't go alone," Penny explained hastily as she saw disapproval written on her father's face. "We telephoned Jerry and had him accompany us."

"How did you learn the location of the place?"

"We heard a man give the address to a taxi driver, and followed in another cab. Dad, we saw Burt Ottman there!"

"Interesting, but it hardly proves that he is a saboteur."

"He arrived at exactly nine-fifteen," Penny resumed excitedly. "After talking with that man we followed, they both left the dining room, though not together. We saw Burt go downstairs and knock on a door which had a peephole."

"Did he enter?"

"I don't know," Penny admitted. "Louise and I weren't able to see. Just as things were getting interesting the head waiter came and politely escorted us out of the building."

"Why didn't Jerry bring you home?"

"That's what I'm getting at, Dad. Jerry just disappeared."

"What do you mean, Penny?"

Together the girls told him exactly what had happened at The Green Parrot. Mr. Parker promptly agreed that it would not be like Jerry to leave the cafe without an explanation.

"Something has happened to him!" Penny insisted soberly. "Dad, why don't you call the police right away? It wouldn't surprise me one bit if The Green Parrot is a meeting place for saboteurs! There's no telling what they may have done to Jerry!"

By this time Mr. Parker had begun to share the alarm of the girls. Getting abruptly to his feet, he started toward the telephone. Before he could take down the receiver, the bell jingled. Answering the incoming call, a peculiar expression came over the newspaper owner's face. After talking for a moment, he hung up the receiver and turned toward Penny.

"That was Jerry," he announced dryly.

"Jerry!" Penny became confused. "But I don't understand, Dad. Is he being held at The Green Parrot?"

"Jerry is at home. He called to ask if you and Louise arrived safely."

"Well, of all the nerve!" Penny cried indignantly. "Just wait until I see him again!"

"Not so fast," advised her father. "There seems to have been a little mix-up. After Jerry left the dining room to telephone, the head waiter told him that you girls had decided not to wait."

"And he told us that Jerry had gone!" Louise cried. "I wonder why?"

"Because he wanted to get rid of our entire party!" Penny declared. "All the time we were in the cafe that head waiter seemed to keep his eye on us. Dad, what did Jerry do about paying the bill?"

"He was told that he need not settle it—that he could pay later."

"Well, it's all very peculiar," Penny said with a sigh. "I'm glad Jerry is safe, but I still maintain we were hustled out of that place."

"No doubt you were," agreed her father. "I'm curious to see the cafe—especially that door with the peep hole."

"I'll take you there," Penny offered eagerly.

"Not tonight," Mr. Parker declined, yawning. "Tomorrow morning perhaps."

Penny had to be satisfied with the decision, though she yearned for immediate action. After Louise had gone to her own home, she mulled over the situation, discussing every angle of it with her father.

"Why do you think Burt Ottman was at the Parrot?" she tried to pin him down. "Would you say he's one of the plotters?"

"I have no opinion whatsoever," Mr. Parker responded somewhat wearily.

Penny did not allow her father to forget his promise to visit The Green Parrot. The following morning she awoke early and at the breakfast table reminded him that they had an important appointment together.

"I should be at the office," Mr. Parker said, glancing at his watch. "Besides, the cafe won't be open at this hour."

"The manager should be there, Dad. You'll be able to talk to him and really look over the place."

"We can ask a few questions—that's all," Mr. Parker corrected. "One can't walk into an establishment and start searching."

"Let's go anyway," pleaded Penny.

More to please her than because he hoped to uncover vital evidence, Mr. Parker agreed to make the trip. With Penny at the wheel of the family car, they drove to the street where The Green Parrot was situated. Parking not far from the entrance to an alley, they walked the remaining distance.

"This is the place," said Penny, pausing before the familiar building. "Why, what's become of the cafe?"

Bewildered, she stared at the doorway where the painted parrot sign had swung. It was no longer there and the Venetian blinds had been removed from the window.

"This place doesn't have the appearance of a cafe," said Mr. Parker. "Are you sure you have the correct address, Penny?"

"Why, yes, I know we came here last night. But the sign has been removed."

Descending the stone steps, Penny pressed her face against the uncovered windows. Only a large, empty room confronted her astonished gaze. All of the tables and chairs had been removed, even the palm trees and decorations.

"It's deserted, Dad!" she exclaimed.

Mr. Parker came down the steps to peer through a window. Bits of colored paper and menu cards still littered the floor. Testing the door, he found it locked.

"This certainly is strange," he remarked thoughtfully. "Let's inquire next door."

Penny and her father chose to enter a bakery which adjoined the building. A stout woman in a white apron, who was arranging frosted cakes in a showcase, favored them with a professional smile.

"Good morning," Mr. Parker greeted her, removing his hat. "Can you tell me what has become of the cafe next door?"

"Are you from the police?" the woman asked quickly.

"No, I'm connected with the *Star*."

CHAPTER 13 - A VACANT BUILDING

"Oh, a reporter!" assumed the woman, and Mr. Parker did not correct her. "I thought maybe you were from the police. Yesterday I saw a man watching The Green Parrot and I said to my husband, Gus, 'The cops are going to raid that place.'"

"And did they?" interposed Mr. Parker.

"Not that I know of. The outfit just moved out. And a queer time to be doing it too, if you ask me!"

"When did they leave?"

"The van pulled up there about two o'clock last night. They were loading stuff in until almost dawn."

"Can you tell me where they went or why they moved out?"

"No, I can't," the woman replied with a shrug. "Like as not they were afraid the police were going to raid 'em. I'm telling you that place deserved to be closed up."

"Just what went on there?"

"I never was inside the place, but some mighty queer acting people seemed to be running it. Why, I've seen men go in and out of there at four o'clock of a morning, hours after the cafe closed up."

"Foreigners?"

"I couldn't rightly say as to that. My husband, Gus, thinks a lot of gambling went on. Anyway, I'm glad the outfit's gone."

Unable to learn more, Penny and her father left the bakery and walked toward their parked car. The information they had gained was not likely to prove very helpful. Obviously, The Green Parrot had closed its doors, fearing an investigation. Whether it had moved elsewhere or gone out of existence, they could not know.

"The call that Jerry, Louise and I paid there last night may have had something to do with it," Penny remarked. "I know the head waiter was eager to be rid of us."

As Mr. Parker and his daughter walked slowly along, several persons ran past them toward an alley. Approaching its entranceway, they saw that a throng of people had gathered not far from the rear exit of The Green Parrot.

"Wonder what's wrong back there?" speculated Mr. Parker, pausing. "Probably an accident of some sort."

"Let's find out," proposed Penny.

She and her father joined the group of excited men and women in the alley. They were startled to see a young man sprawled face downward on the brick pavement. A garbage collector jabbered excitedly that he had found the victim lying thus only a moment before.

Mr. Parker pushed through the circle of people. "Has anyone called an ambulance?" he asked.

"I'll send for one, Mister," offered a boy, hastening away.

Mr. Parker bent over the prone figure.

"He ain't dead is he?" the garbage man asked anxiously.

"Unconscious," replied the newspaper man, his fingers on the victim's wrist. "A nasty head wound. I'd say he either fell or was struck from behind."

Carefully Mr. Parker rolled over the limp figure. As he beheld the face, he stared and glanced quickly at Penny.

"Who is he, Dad?" she asked, and then she saw for herself.

The young man was Burt Ottman.

CHAPTER 14 - TEST BLACKOUT

As Mr. Parker covered Burt Ottman with his overcoat, the young man stirred and opened his eyes. He gazed at the newspaper owner with a dazed expression and for a moment did not attempt to speak.

"Take it easy," Mr. Parker advised.

"What happened to me?" the young man whispered.

"That's what we'd like to know. Were you struck?"

"Don't remember," Ottman mumbled. He closed his eyes again, but aroused as he heard the shrill siren of an approaching ambulance. "Don't let 'em take me to a hospital," he pleaded. "Take me home."

The ambulance drew up in the alley. Stretcher bearers carefully lifted the young man.

"I'm all right," he insisted, trying to sit up. "Just take me home."

"Where's that?" asked one of the attendants.

Burt Ottman mumbled an address which was on a street not far from the boat dock he operated.

"We'll take you to the hospital for a check up," the young man was told. "Then if you're okay, you'll be released."

Deeply interested in the case, Mr. Parker and Penny followed the ambulance to City Hospital. There, after an hour's wait in the lobby they were told that Burt Ottman had suffered no severe injury. A minor head wound had been dressed, and he was to be released within a short while.

"What caused the accident?" Mr. Parker asked one of the nurses. "Did the young man say?"

"He couldn't seem to remember what happened," she replied. "At least he wouldn't talk to the doctor about it."

Overdue at the *Star* office, Mr. Parker could remain no longer. However, Penny, whose time was her own, loitered about the lobby for an hour and a half until Burt Ottman came down in the elevator. The young man's head was bandaged and he walked with an unsteady step as he leaned on the arm of a nurse.

"I'll call a taxi for you," the young woman said. "You're really in no condition to walk far, Mr. Ottman."

Penny stepped forward to offer her services. Her father, knowing that she might have use for the car, had left it parked outside the hospital.

"I'll be glad to take Mr. Ottman home," she volunteered.

The young man protested that he did not wish to cause anyone inconvenience, but allowed himself to be guided to the waiting automobile.

As the car sped along toward the riverfront, Penny stole quick glances at Burt. He sat very still, his gaze on the pavement ahead. She half expected that he would offer an explanation of the accident, or at least ask a few questions, but he remained silent.

"You took rather a hard blow on the head," she remarked, seeking to lead him into conversation.

Burt merely nodded.

"Dad and I were astonished to find you lying in the alley at the rear of The Green Parrot," Penny went on. "Don't you remember how you came to be there?"

"Mind's a blank."

"You must have been struck by someone," Penny said, refusing to be discouraged. "Can't you recall whom you were with just before the accident?"

"What is this, a third degree?" Burt asked, and only a faint, amused smile took the edge from his question.

"I'm sorry," Penny apologized.

"It doesn't matter what happened to me," Burt said quietly. "I just don't feel like talking about it—see?"

CHAPTER 14 - TEST BLACKOUT

"Yes."

"I don't mean to seem unappreciative," the young man resumed. "Thanks for taking me home."

"You're very welcome, I'm sure," Penny responded dryly.

The car drew up in front of the home where Burt and his sister lived. A pleasant, one-story cottage rather in need of paint, it was situated high on a bluff overlooking the river.

As Burt stiffly alighted from the car, the cottage door opened, and Sara came running to meet him.

"You're hurt!" she cried anxiously. "Oh, Burt, what happened to you?"

"Nothing," he answered, moving away from her encircling arms.

"But your head!"

"Your brother was hurt sometime last night," Penny explained to Sara. "Just how, we don't know. My father and I found him lying in an alley at the rear of The Green Parrot."

"The Green Parrot—that night club!" Sara gazed at her brother in dismay. "Oh, Burt, I was afraid something like this would happen. Those dreadful men—"

"Now Sara," he interrupted brusquely. "No theatricals, please. Everything's all right." Giving her cheek a playful pinch, he wobbled past her into the cottage.

Sara turned frightened eyes upon Penny. "Tell me exactly what happened," she pleaded.

"I honestly don't know, Sara. My father thought someone must have struck your brother from behind, but he's not told us a thing."

"I just knew something of the sort would happen," Sara repeated nervously.

"What do you mean?" inquired Penny. "Does your brother have enemies who would harm him?"

"Burt's been trying to find out who framed him in the bridge dynamiting. He won't tell me much about it, but I know he's been trailing down a few leads."

"Isn't that work for the police?"

"The police!" Sara retorted bitterly. "Their only interest is in piling up more evidence against Burt!"

"Your brother knows the identity of the saboteur?"

"He won't tell me, but I think he does have an idea who blew up the bridge."

Penny scarcely knew whether or not to accept Sara's explanation of her brother's activities. Unquestionably, the girl believed that he was innocent of all charges against him. For one not prejudiced in his favor, there were many factors to be considered. Why had Burt denied losing the leather billfold? And with whom had he kept the Tuesday night appointment at The Green Parrot?

"If your brother has any clue regarding the real saboteur, he should present his evidence to the police," Penny advised Sara.

"He'll never do that until he's ready to appear in court. Not after the way the police treated him."

Penny realized that nothing was to be gained by discussing the matter further with Sara. Offering a few polite remarks to the effect that she hoped Burt would soon recover completely from his injury, she drove away.

Later, in repeating the conversation to her father, she declared that she could not make up her mind regarding Burt Ottman's guilt.

"The case does have interesting angles," Mr. Parker acknowledged. "I talked to the Police Commissioner this morning about The Green Parrot. The place long has had a reputation for cheating customers, and lately it's been under suspicion as a rendezvous for anti-American groups."

"That would fit in with what the bakery woman told us. What became of The Green Parrot, Dad? Have the police been able to trace it to a new location?"

"Not yet. The cafe may not open up again, or if it does, under a new name."

For two days Penny divided her time between school and the river. As the water remained too rough for safe sailing, she and Louise spent their spare hours painting and cleaning their boat. Upon several occasions they called at the Ottman Boat Dock. Burt never was there, but Sara assured them that her brother had completely recovered from his recent mishap.

"Did he never tell you how he was struck?" Penny inquired once.

"Never," Sara returned. "I've given up talking to him about it."

With the river high, the girls had no opportunity to visit Old Noah at his ark. However, Sara told them that she was quite certain Sheriff Anderson had not succeeded in getting rid of the old fellow and his animals.

"The ark is still anchored up Bug Run," she laughed ruefully. "I know because a steady flow of blue bottles has been floating down here!"

"Do you always read the message?" Louise inquired.

"Not always," Sara replied. "Frequently I do because they're so crazy."

Since his arrest and subsequent release from jail, Burt Ottman had seldom been seen at the boat dock. Harassed and overburdened, Sara endeavored to do the work of two people. She ran the motor launch, taking passengers up and down the river. She rented canoes and row boats, and looked after repair work which came to the shop. If she felt that her brother was shirking his duties, she gave no inkling of it to the girls.

"When does Burt's trial come up?" Louise remarked to Penny late Thursday night as they walked home from the Public Library. "Next week, isn't it?"

"Yes, the twenty-first," her chum nodded. "From all I can gather, he'll be convicted, too."

"I feel sorry for Sara."

"So do I," agreed Penny. "At first I didn't like her very well. Now I know her brusque manner doesn't mean anything."

The girls were passing a drugstore. In the window appeared a colored advertisement, a picture of a giant chocolate soda, topped with frothy whipped cream. Penny paused to gaze longingly at it.

"That's a personal invitation addressed to me," she remarked. "How about it, Lou?"

"Oh, that same picture has been in the window for months," her chum said discouragingly. "You can't get whipped cream unless you steal it from a cow."

"Well, how about a dish of ice cream then? I'm horribly hungry."

"That's your natural state," teased Louise, pulling her on. "If we stop now, we'll be caught in the test blackout."

"Is there one tonight?"

"Don't you read the papers? It's to be held between nine and ten o'clock. And it's ten after nine now."

"I think it might be fun to be caught out in one—just so long as it's not the real thing."

"I want to get home before the street lights are turned out," Louise insisted. "In fact, I promised Mother I'd come straight home when the library closed."

"Oh, all right," Penny gave in reluctantly.

The girls began to walk faster for they were many blocks from their own street. Now and then they met an air raid warden and so knew that the time for the test blackout was close at hand.

"Louise!" Penny suddenly exclaimed, stopping short.

"Now what?" the other demanded. "Don't you dare tell me you've left something at the library!"

Penny was staring at a man who only a moment before had come through the revolving doors of the Hotel Claymore.

"See that fellow!" she said impressively.

"Yes, what about him?"

"He's the head waiter at The Green Parrot."

"Why, you're right!" Louise agreed. "For a minute I didn't recognize him in street clothes."

"Let's follow him," Penny proposed as the man started down a side street. "Maybe we can learn the new location of The Green Parrot."

"Oh, Penny, I told Mother I'd come straight home."

"Then I'll follow him alone. I can't let this opportunity slip."

Louise hesitated, and then, unwilling to have Penny undertake an adventure alone, quickly caught up with her.

"There's no telling where this chase will end," she complained. "That man may not be going to The Green Parrot."

"Then perhaps we'll learn where he lives and police can question him."

As Penny spoke, a siren began to sound. A car which was cruising past, pulled up at the curb and its headlights went off. All along the street, lights blinked out one by one.

"The blackout!" Louise, gasped. "I was afraid we'd be caught in it. Now we'll lose that man, and what's worse, I'll be late in getting home!"

CHAPTER 15 - A DRIFTING BARGE

Upon hearing the shrill notes of the air raid siren, the man whom Penny and Louise followed, quickened his step. Hastening after him, the girls turned a corner and came face to face with an air raid warden.

"Take shelter!" he ordered sternly. "The closest one is across the street—the basement of the Congregational Church."

Penny started to explain, but the warden had no time to listen. Waving the girls across the street, he watched to see that they actually entered the shelter.

"I guess he thought we weren't very cooperative," Louise remarked as they followed a throng of persons downstairs to the basement. "These blackout tests really are very important."

"Of course," agreed Penny. "It's a pity though that our friend, the waiter, couldn't have been sent into this same shelter. Now we'll lose him."

For nearly twenty minutes the girls remained in the basement until the All Clear sounded. As they returned to the street level, lights were going on again, one by one. Pedestrians began to pour out of the shelters, but the girls saw no one who resembled the waiter.

"We've lost him," sighed Penny. "I guess we may as well go home."

"Let's hurry," urged Louise who was glad to abandon the pursuit. "Mother will be worried about me."

At the Sidell home, Penny turned down an invitation to come in for a few minutes. As she started on alone, she paused and called to her chum who was on the porch: "Oh, Lou, how about a sail early tomorrow morning?"

"Isn't the river too high?"

"It was dropping fast this morning. The current's not so strong now either. Let's get up bright and early."

"How early?" Louise asked dubiously.

"Oh, about seven o'clock."

"That's practically the middle of the night," Louise complained.

"I'll come by for you at a quarter to seven," Penny said, as if the matter were settled. "Wear warm clothes and don't you dare keep me waiting."

The next morning heavy mists shrouded Riverview's valleys and waterfront. Undaunted by the dismal prospect, Penny proceeded in darkness to the Sidell home. There, huddling against the gate post, she whistled several times, and finally tossed a pebble against the window of Louise's room. A moment later the sash went up.

"Oh, is it you, Penny?" her chum mumbled in a sleepy voice. "You surely don't expect to go sailing on a morning like this!"

"The fog will clear away just as soon as the sun gets up. Hurry and climb into your clothes, lazy bones!"

With a groan, Louise slammed down the window. Ten minutes later she appeared, walking awkwardly because she wore two pair of slack suits and three sweaters.

"Think we'll freeze?" she inquired anxiously.

"You won't," laughed Penny, giving her a thermos bottle to carry.

By the time the girls reached the dock, the rising sun had begun to scatter the mist. Patches of fog still hung over portions of the river however, and it was impossible to see the far shore.

"Shouldn't we wait another hour?" Louise suggested as Penny leaped aboard the dinghy.

"Oh, by the time we get the sail up the river will be clear," she responded carelessly. "Toss me the life preserver cushions."

While Penny put up the mainsail, Louise wiped the seats dry of dew. Her fingers stiff with cold, she cast off the mooring ropes, and the boat drifted away from the dock.

"Well, the river is all ours this morning," Penny remarked, watching the limp sail. "That's the way I like it."

"Where's the breeze?" demanded Louise suspiciously.

"We'll get one in a minute. The headland is cutting it off."

"You're a chronic optimist!" accused Louise. Wetting a finger, she held it up. "I don't believe there is any breeze! We'll just drift down stream and then have to row back!"

"We're getting a little now," said Penny as the sail became taut. "Hold your fire, dear chum."

The boat gradually picked up speed, but the breeze was so unsteady that the girls did not attempt to cross the river. Instead, they sailed in midstream, proceeding toward the commercial docks. The mists did not entirely clear away and Penny began to shiver.

"Don't you wish you had one of my sweaters?" asked Louise, grinning.

Penny shook her head as she reached to pour herself a cup of steaming coffee from the thermos bottle. Before she could drink it, a large, flat vessel loomed up through the mist ahead.

"Now don't try to argue the right of way with that boat," Louise advised uneasily.

"Why, it's a barge!" Penny exclaimed, bringing the dinghy about. "I do believe it's adrift!"

"What makes you think so?" Louise asked, staring at the dark hulk.

Penny maneuvered the dinghy closer before she replied. "You can see it's out of control. There's no tow boat anywhere near."

"It does seem to be drifting," Louise acknowledged. "No one appears to be aboard either."

Realizing that the large vessel would block off all the wind if she approached too close to it, Penny kept the dinghy away. The barge, almost crosswise to the current, was floating slowly downstream.

"How do you suppose it got loose?" Louise speculated.

"Saboteurs may have cut the hawser."

"The big mooring rope *has* been severed!" Louise exclaimed a moment later. "I can see the frayed end!"

Penny came about again, tacking in closer to the drifting vessel.

"That certainly looks like the barge Carl Oaks was hired to guard," she declared with a worried frown. "Can you read the numbers, Lou?"

"519-9870."

"Then it is his barge!"

"He must have deserted his post again."

"In any case that barge is a great hazard to other vessels," Penny declared, deeply troubled. "Not even a signal light on the bow or stern!"

"Oughtn't we to notify the Coast Guards?"

"We should, but while we're reaching a telephone, the barge may ram another boat. Why not board her and put up signal lights first? In this fog one can't see a vessel many yards ahead."

"It doesn't look possible to climb aboard."

"I think I can do it," Penny said, offering the tiller to her chum. "Here, take the stick."

"You know what happens when I try to steer," Louise replied, shrinking back. "I'll be sure to upset. The wind always is tricky around a big boat."

"Then I'll take down the sail," Penny decided, moving forward to release the halyard.

The billowing canvas came sliding down. Penny broke out the oars, and maneuvered the dinghy until it grated against the hull of the barge.

"Even a trained monkey couldn't get up there," Louise declared, staring at the high deck.

Penny rowed around to the other side of the barge. Discovering a rope which did not give to her weight, she announced that she intended to climb it.

"You'll fall," Louise predicted.

"Why, I'm the champion rope climber of Riverview High!" Penny chuckled, thrusting the oars into her chum's unwilling hands. "Just hold the dinghy here until I get back."

"Which shouldn't be long," Louise said gloomily. "I expect to hear your splash any minute now."

Penny grasped the dangling rope. With far more ease than she had anticipated, she climbed hand over hand to the deck of the barge. Once there she lost not a moment in lighting signal lamps at bow and stern. The task

CHAPTER 15 - A DRIFTING BARGE

accomplished, she was moving amidships when she thought she heard a slight sound from within the deck house. Pausing to listen, she called:

"Is anyone here?"

There was no answer, but distinctly she heard a scraping noise, as if someone were pushing a chair against a wall.

"Someone *is* in there!" Penny thought.

Darting across the deck, she tried the door of the cabin. It had been fastened from the outside. Fumbling with the bolt, she finally was able to push it back. The door swung outward.

For a moment Penny could discern no one in the dark, little room. Then she saw a man lying on the floor. A gag covered his mouth and his hands and feet were tied with cord.

The prisoner was Carl Oaks.

CHAPTER 16 - DANGER ON THE RIVER

Throwing the door open wide to admit more light, Penny darted into the cabin. Bending over the prisoner, she began to untie the cords which bound his wrists.

"I'll have you free in a minute, Mr. Oaks," she encouraged him.

The cords had been loosely tied. Undoing the knots, she next pulled away the gag which covered his mouth.

"What happened, Mr. Oaks?" she demanded. "Who did this to you?"

The old watchman sat up, stretching his cramped arms. He did not reply, but watched Penny intently as she loosened the thongs which bound his legs. Getting up, he walked a step or two across the cabin.

"Tell me what happened," Penny urged impatiently. "Don't you feel able to explain?"

"I'm disgusted," Mr. Oaks returned. "Plumb disgusted."

"I don't doubt you feel that way," agreed Penny. "This barge is floating in mid-channel, a hazard to incoming and outgoing vessels. We'll have to do something about it."

"I'm through with this job! I didn't want it in the first place!"

"That's neither here nor there," Penny replied, losing patience. "Suppose you stop grieving over your bad luck for a minute, and explain what occurred."

"Well, it was about midnight when they sneaked aboard."

"The men who attacked you?"

"Yes, there were three of 'em. I was in the cabin at the time, reading my newspaper. Before I knew what was happening, they were on top of me."

"Did you recognize any of the men, Mr. Oaks?"

"No."

"What did they look like?"

"It was dark and I didn't see their faces."

"How were they dressed?"

"Didn't notice that either," Mr. Oaks returned grumpily. "I was too busy tryin' to fight 'em off. They trussed me up and then cut the barge loose."

"Saboteurs!"

"Reckon so," the old watchman nodded.

"Well, what will we do?" Penny asked, scarcely able to hide her growing irritation. "It's still foggy on the river. I've put up signal lights, but an approaching freighter might not see them in time to change her course."

"There's nothing more to be done," Carl Oaks responded with a shrug. "The Coast Guard boat will come along after awhile. I'm not going to worry about it—not me! I'm done with this lousy job, and you can tell your father so."

"My father can bear the shock, I think," Penny answered coldly.

Thoroughly disgusted at the indifferent attitude of the watchman, she ran out on deck. Looking down over the side, she saw Louise waiting anxiously in the dinghy.

"Oh, there you are!" her chum cried. "I thought you never were coming!"

Penny explained that she had found Carl Oaks lying bound and gagged inside the deck house. As the old watchman himself came up behind her, she could say nothing about his indifferent attitude.

"I wondered how you got out to this barge," Oaks commented, gazing down at the dinghy. "You can take me to shore with you."

"Isn't it your duty to remain here until relieved?" Penny asked.

CHAPTER 16 - DANGER ON THE RIVER

"I resigned, takin' effect last night at midnight," Oaks grinned. "I've had enough of Riverview. I'm getting out of this town."

Penny faced the watchman with flashing eyes.

"My father obtained this job for you, Mr. Oaks. You'll show very little gratitude if you run off just because you're in trouble again."

"A man's got a right to do as he pleases!"

"Not always," Penny corrected. "Saboteurs are at work along this waterfront, and it's your duty to tell police what you know."

"I didn't see the men, I tell you! They came at me from behind."

"Even so, you may be able to contribute information to the police. In any case, you'll have to stay here until relieved—"

"Penny!" interrupted Louise from below. "There's a boat coming!"

The steady chug of a motor could be heard, but for a moment the swirling mists hid the approaching vessel. Then a pleasure yacht, with pennants flying, came into view.

"It's the *Eloise III!*" Penny cried, recognizing the craft as one belonging to Commodore Phillips of the Riverview Marine Club.

Waving their arms and shouting, the girls tried to attract the pilot's attention. To their relief, the yacht veered slightly from her course, and the engines slackened speed.

"Yacht ahoy!" called Penny, cupping hands to her lips.

"Ahoy!" came the answering shout from Commodore Phillips. "What's wrong there? Barge adrift?"

Penny confirmed the observation and requested to be taken aboard. Although she was not certain of it, she believed that the *Eloise III* was equipped with a radio telephone which could be used to notify Coast Guards of the floating barge.

Leaving Carl Oaks behind, the girls rowed to the yacht and were helped aboard. Commodore Phillips immediately confirmed that his vessel did have radio-telephone apparatus.

"Come with me," he directed, leading the girls to the radio room.

The Commodore sat down beside the transmitting apparatus, quickly adjusting a pair of earphones. Snapping on the power switch, he tuned to the wave length of the Coast Guard station. While the girls hovered at his elbow, he talked into the radio telephone, informing the Coast Guard of the floating barge and its position. The message, he explained to Penny and Louise, would be received in "scrambled speech" and automatically transformed into understandable English by means of an electrical device.

"How do you mean?" inquired Louise, deeply puzzled.

"Nearly all ship-to-shore radio telephone conversations are carried on in scrambled speech," the Commodore replied. "Otherwise, eavesdroppers could tune in on them and learn important facts not intended to be made public."

"But you spoke ordinary English into the 'phone," Louise said, still perplexed.

"The speech scrambler is an electric circuit which automatically transposes voice frequencies," the Commodore resumed. "The words are made unintelligible until unscrambled by a similar device at the receiving station. For instance, if I were to say 'Mary had a little lamb,' into this phone, anyone listening in would hear: 'Noyil hob e ylippey ylond.' Yet at the receiving post, the message would be unscrambled to its original form."

"I wish our telephone at home was fixed that way!" Penny declared with a laugh. "Wouldn't some of the neighbors develop a headache!"

Having been informed that a Coast Guard cutter would proceed at once to the locality, the girls felt relieved of further responsibility. As Commodore Phillips said that he would stand by with his yacht until the cutter reached the scene, they finally decided to return to shore. Once well away from the yacht they raised sail and tacked toward their own dock.

"I hope the Coast Guard gives Carl Oaks a good lecture," Penny remarked, turning to gaze back at the slowly drifting barge. "Why, he wasn't one bit concerned what might happen to other vessels!"

"I never did like him," said Louise with feeling. "He complains too much. Was it his fault that the barge was cut adrift?"

"Not according to his story. Three men attacked him while he was in the deck house. Of course, he couldn't have been too alert."

"Carl Oaks wouldn't be!"

"There was one rather peculiar thing," Penny said slowly. "It never occurred to me until now."

"What's that?"

"Why, Mr. Oaks' bonds were very loose. If he had tried, I believe he could have freed himself."

"That does seem strange," agreed Louise. "You don't think he allowed those saboteurs to board the barge?"

Penny brought the dinghy around, steering to avoid a floating log.

"I wouldn't know," she replied soberly. "But I'm glad we forced Mr. Oaks to wait for the Coast Guard. I hope they question him until they get to the bottom of this affair."

CHAPTER 17 - A STOLEN BOAT

The mists were lifting as Penny and Louise sailed slowly past the Ottman Dock toward their own snug berth. Sara, in blue slacks, a red bandana handkerchief over her head, was trying to start a stubborn outboard motor. Glancing up, she called a greeting, and then asked abruptly:

"Say, what's that barge doing out on the river? It looks to me as if it's adrift, but I can't see well enough to tell."

Penny and Louise, eager to impart information, brought the dinghy to a mooring at the floating platform. Sara listened with interest as they revealed how they had boarded the barge, released Carl Oaks, and then notified the Coast Guard.

"Neat work!" she praised. "That Carl Oaks! He's one of the most shiftless men I ever knew. He doesn't deserve to hold a job."

Penny glanced about the dock, searching for Burt Ottman.

"Your brother isn't here?" she remarked absently.

"No, he isn't," Sara replied, rather defiantly. "If you think he had anything to do with that barge—"

"Why, it never entered my mind!" Penny exclaimed.

"I'm sorry," the older girl apologized. "I shouldn't have said that. I don't know why I'm so jumpy lately."

"You have a great deal to worry you," said Louise sympathetically. "And you work too hard."

"I'll be all right as soon as Burt's trial is over. He's not here this morning—" Sara's voice broke. "In fact, I don't know where he is."

Louise and Penny said nothing, though the remark astonished them.

"Burt was out all last night," Sara spoke and then seemed to realize that her words easily could be misinterpreted. She added hastily: "He's been trying to gain evidence which will prove his innocence."

"You mean your brother went away yesterday and failed to return?" Penny asked after a moment.

Sara nodded. "He's on the trail of the real saboteurs, and it's dangerous business. That's why I'm so worried. I'm afraid he's in trouble."

"Have you talked to the police?" Penny inquired.

"Indeed, I haven't."

"Didn't your brother tell you where he was going when he left home?"

"No, he didn't. He keeps things from me because he says I worry too much now."

"I suppose he never explained what happened at The Green Parrot?"

"He said he couldn't remember. Oh, everything's so mixed up. I try not to think about it, because when I do my head simply buzzes."

Once more Sara tried to start the balky engine, and this time her efforts brought success.

"Thank goodness for small favors!" she muttered. "Now I've got to go out on the river and look for our stolen boat. Hope no one runs off with this place while I'm gone."

"You've not had another boat stolen?" Louise asked in surprise.

"I figure that's what happened to it. Late yesterday afternoon a man came here and rented our fastest motorboat. That's the last I've seen of him or it."

"Didn't you report your loss to the Coast Guards?" inquired Penny.

Sara answered with a trace of impatience. "Of course, I did. They searched the river last night. No accident reported, and no trace of the boat."

"The man might have drowned," Louise offered anxiously.

"It's not likely. If he had gone overboard, the boat would have been found by this time. No, it's been pulled up somewhere in the bushes and hidden. Last year one of our canoes was taken. Burt found it a month later, painted a different color!"

"Didn't you know the man who rented the boat?" questioned Penny.

"Never saw him before. He was tall and thin and dark. Wore a brown felt hat and overcoat. I noticed his hands in particular. They were soft and well manicured. I said to myself, 'This fellow doesn't know a thing about boats,' but I was wrong. He handled that motor like a veteran."

"The man didn't look like a waiter, did he?" Penny asked quickly.

"You couldn't prove it by me."

Penny groped in her mind to recall a characteristic which definitely would describe the head waiter of The Green Parrot. To her chagrin, she could think of only one unusual facial characteristic, a tiny scar on his cheek. She did remember that the man had worn a large, old fashioned gold watch which might have been of foreign make.

"Why, the fellow who rented the boat did have such a watch!" Sara cried when Penny mentioned the timepiece. "I didn't notice the scar. What is his name?"

"Louise and I never were able to learn," Penny replied with regret. "The Green Parrot has closed its doors, so I don't know how you can get in touch with him."

Sara sighed. Placing an oar, a bailer, and a can of gasoline in the boat, she prepared to leave the dock.

"I'll be lucky if I ever see the fellow again," she commented. Hesitating a moment, she asked diffidently: "Don't suppose you girls would like to go along?"

Penny and Louise wondered if their ears had betrayed them. It seemed beyond belief that Sara actually would invite them to accompany her.

"Why, of course, we'd like to go," Penny accepted, before her chum could find her voice.

Scrambling out of the dinghy, the girls made it fast to the dock and transferred to the other boat. Sara opened the throttle, and they shot away, leaving behind a trail of churning foam. Out through the slip they raced, rounding a channel buoy at breakneck speed.

"You can certainly handle a boat," Penny said admiringly.

"Been at it since I was a kid," Sara grinned. "I could cruise this river blindfolded."

They passed the floating barge, observing that a Coast Guard cutter was proceeding up river to take it in tow. Turning upstream, Sara swung the boat toward shore.

"Keep close watch of the bushes," she directed the girls. "If you see anything that looks like a hidden boat, sing out."

At low speed they crept along the river, watching for marks in the sand which might reveal where a craft had been pulled out of water. Once, venturing too close in, Sara went aground and had to push off with the oars.

"It doesn't look as if we'll have any luck," she remarked gloomily. "The boat's probably so well hidden, it would take a ferret to find it."

They kept on upstream toward the Seventh Street Bridge, a structure much in use since the more modern Thompson's Bridge had been closed to auto traffic. Penny, watching the stream of vehicles passing above, remarked that Riverview commerce would be paralyzed should anything occur to damage it.

"The Seventh Street Bridge now is the only artery open to the Riverview Munitions Plant," Sara added. "I understand it's being guarded day and night. By a better watchman than Carl Oaks, I hope."

Without passing the bridge, the girls turned downstream, searching the opposite shore. Before they had gone far, Sara beached the boat on a stretch of sand.

"It was along here that Burt found our canoe last year," she explained. "If you don't mind waiting, I'll get out and prowl around a bit."

"Aren't we near Bug Run?" Penny inquired.

Sara pointed out the mouth of the stream which was hidden from view by a clump of willows.

"If you expect to be here a few minutes, Louise and I might pay Old Noah a flying visit," Penny said eagerly. "We're curious to learn what has happened to him."

"I'll be around for at least half an hour," Sara replied. "Take your time."

CHAPTER 17 - A STOLEN BOAT

Penny and Louise set off along the twisting bank of Bug Run. Approaching the vicinity of the ark, they noticed many corked blue bottles caught amid the debris of the sluggish stream.

"I'll bet a cent and a half that Old Noah still is on the old stamping grounds!" Penny remarked. "Sheriff Anderson probably hasn't found a way to get rid of him. Why, unless a regular deluge floods this stream, the ark never could be floated out to the main river."

"The sheriff could put Old Noah in jail."

"True, but a great many people would criticize him if he did."

A moment later the girls rounded a bend and saw the ark in its usual setting. A long clothes line had been stretched from bow to stern, and wet garments fresh from the wash tub, flapped in the breeze.

"Well, Noah is still here," chuckled Penny. "He's run up the white flag though! Or should we say the white flags!"

On the deck of the ark, Old Noah was so busy that he failed to note the approach of the two girls. He stood in the center of a ring of soiled clothes, laboring diligently over a tub of steaming suds.

As the girls reached the gangplank, a dog from inside the ark began an excited barking. Startled, Old Noah glanced up. Unnoticed by him, his long white beard slipped into the soapy water and he rubbed it vigorously on the washboard.

Scarcely able to control a giggle, Penny followed her chum aboard the ark. As Old Noah kept on scrubbing his beard she could not resist asking: "Excuse me, but aren't you washing your whiskers by mistake?"

Surprised, the old man straightened to his full height. Squeezing the dripping beard, he carefully wrung it out. Next he produced a comb from his loose fitting brown pantaloons, and painstakingly unsnarled the tangles. Then turning to the girls, he greeted them with his usual dignity.

"Good morning, my daughters. I am glad you kept your promise to visit me again."

"Good morning, Noah," responded Penny, trying not to laugh. "We thought we would drop by and see if you were still here. I remember Sheriff Anderson said he was going to call on you again."

The old man's weather beaten face crinkled into deep wrinkles. "Ho, ho! So he did, but he reckoned without the Might of the Righteous. I was watching for him when he came."

"I hope you didn't mistreat him," Penny said uneasily.

"When I observed his approach I untied my two hounds, Nip and Tuck, and hid myself in the forest. He was gone when I returned to the ark."

"Likewise, part of his anatomy, I suppose," commented Penny.

"Nip and Tuck did cause a commotion," Old Noah acknowledged, "but they did him no harm. When he went away the sheriff left a cowardly note tacked to a tree. It said he would return to dispossess me. Before that happens, I will blow this ark to Kingdom Come!"

"How will you do that?" inquired Penny, rather amused.

"With dynamite."

"Do you have any aboard the ark?"

Old Noah smiled mysteriously. "I know where I can lay my hands on all I'll need. When I was hiding in the woods yesterday, I saw where they keep it."

Penny and Louise glanced quickly at each other. While it was possible that Old Noah was talking wildly, the mention of dynamite made them uneasy. If it were true that he had come into possession of such a cache, then obviously it was their duty to report to the authorities.

"Who hid the dynamite?" Penny asked.

"I do not rightly know," replied Old Noah. "It may have been those strangers who were pestering me last night. They came to my ark and were very nosey, asking me about this and that."

"Not officers?"

"They had no connection with the Law, speaking of it with great contempt."

"How many men were there, Noah?"

"Two."

"And they came by car?"

"Bless you, no," replied Noah wearily. "They arrived in a motorboat. Of all the pop-poppin' you ever heard! It almost drove my animals crazy."

"After they talked to you, the men went away again in their boat?"

"They started off, but as soon as they had turned the bend they switched out the motor. I wondered what they were up to, so I sneaked through the bushes and watched."

"Yes, go on!" Penny urged eagerly as Old Noah interrupted the narrative to wash another shirt. "What did the men do?"

"Why, nothing," answered the old man. "They just pulled the boat up into the bushes and went off and left it."

"The boat is still there?" Penny demanded.

"So far as I know, my daughter."

"Will you show us where the boat is hidden?" pleaded Penny. "And the dynamite cache too!"

"I am very busy now," Old Noah said, shaking his flowing locks. "I have this pesky washing to do, and then, there's all the animals to feed."

"Can't we help you?" offered Louise.

"I thank you kindly, but it would not be fit work for young ladies. If you will return tomorrow, I gladly will guide you to the place."

Penny and Louise tried their powers of persuasion, but the old man was not to be moved. In the end they had to be satisfied with a description of the site where the motorboat had been hidden. Old Noah stubbornly refused to tell them more about the cache of dynamite.

Finally, the girls said goodbye to the master of the ark, and hastened toward the river to join Sara. They were greatly excited by the information they had obtained.

"Old Noah may have talked for the fun of it," Penny declared as they struggled through the underbrush. "If not, I think we've stumbled into an important clue—one which may have a bearing on the bridge dynamiting case!"

CHAPTER 18 - PENNY'S PLAN

Sara was waiting beside her boat when Penny and Louise came running along the muddy shore. Without apologizing for being so late, they excitedly related their conversation with Old Noah.

"Say, maybe that hidden motorboat is mine!" the girl exclaimed. "What did it look like?"

"We didn't take time to search for it," Penny replied. "We knew you would be waiting so we came straight here."

"Let's see if we can find it," Sara said, starting up the engine.

"Noah's animals don't like motorboats," Louise chuckled. "I suggest we do our searching afoot."

"All right," Sara agreed readily, switching the motor off again. "Lead and I'll follow."

Penny and Louise guided their companion to the mouth of Bug Run and thence along its slippery banks to a clump of overhanging willows.

"According to Old Noah's description, this should be the place," Penny declared, looking about. "No sign of a boat though."

Sara took off shoes and stockings and waded through the shallow, muddy water. Whenever she came to a clump of bushes, she would pull the branches aside to peer behind them.

"Old Noah may have been spoofing us," Penny began, but just then Sara gave a little cry.

"Here it is! I've found it!"

Penny and Louise slid down the bank to the water's edge. Behind a dense thicket, a motorboat had been pulled out on the sand. The engine remained attached, covered by a piece of canvas.

"Is it your boat, Sara?" Penny asked eagerly.

"It certainly is!" She spoke with emphasis. "The hull has been repainted, but it takes more than that to fool me."

"Any positive way to identify it?"

"By the engine number. Ours was 985-877 unless I'm mistaken. I have it written down at home."

"What's the number of this engine?"

"The same!" Sara cried triumphantly after she had removed the canvas covering and examined it. "This is my property all right, and I shall take it back with me."

"Old Noah spoke of two strangers who came here last night by boat," Penny said thoughtfully.

"The fellow who stopped at the dock probably picked up a pal later on," Sara commented, trying to shove the boat into the water. "My, this old tub is heavy! Want to help?"

"Wait, Sara!" Penny exclaimed. "Let's leave the boat here."

"Leave it here! Now that would be an idea! This little piece of floating wood represents nine hundred and fifty dollars."

"I don't mean that you're to lose the boat," Penny hastened to explain. "But if we take it now, we never will catch the fellow who stole it."

"That's true."

"If we leave the boat here we can keep watch of the place and catch those scamps when they come back."

"They may not come back," Sara said, without warming to the plan. "Besides, I've no time to do a Sherlock Holmes in the bushes. I have my dock to look after."

"Louise and I could do most of the watching."

"Well, I don't know," Sara said dubiously. "Something might go wrong. I never would get over it if I lost the boat."

"You won't lose the boat," promised Penny. "It's really important that we catch those two men, Sara. From what Old Noah said, they may be connected with the bridge dynamiting."

"What makes you think that?"

"Because Old Noah found a cache of dynamite somewhere near here."

"He won't tell us its location," added Louise.

"If it should develop that the men are saboteurs, we might learn something which would help your brother's case," Penny said persuasively. "How about it, Sara?"

"I'd be glad to risk the boat if I thought it would help Burt."

"Then let's leave it here. We can watch the spot night and day."

"And what will your parents have to say?"

Penny's face fell. "Well, I suppose when it comes right to it, Dad will set his foot down. But at least we can watch during the day time. Then if necessary, we might report to the police."

"Let's leave them out of it," Sara said feelingly. "If you girls will remain throughout the day, I'll stand the night watch."

"Not alone!" Louise protested.

"Why not?" Sara asked, amused. "I've frequently camped out along the river at night. Once I made a canoe trip the full length of the river just for the fun of it."

"Louise and I will stay here now while you return to the dock," Penny declared. "Better call our parents when you get there and break the news as gently as possible."

"What will you do for lunch?"

"Maybe we can beg a sandwich or a fried egg from Old Noah," Penny chuckled. "We'll manage somehow."

"Well, whatever you do, don't leave the boat unguarded," Sara advised, starting away. "As soon as it gets dark I'll come back."

Left to themselves, Penny and Louise explored the locality thoroughly. Not far away they found a log which offered a comfortable seat, and they screened it with brush.

"Now we're all ready for Mr. Saboteur," Penny said. "He can't come too soon to suit me."

"And just what are we going to do when he does arrive?"

"I forgot to figure that angle," Penny confessed. "We may have to call on Old Noah for help."

"Noah will be busy doing a washing or giving the goat a beauty treatment," Louise laughed.

The sun lifted higher, and steam rising from the damp earth made the girls increasingly uncomfortable. As the hours dragged by they rapidly lost zest for their adventure. Long before noon they were assailed by the pangs of hunger.

"If I could catch a bullfrog I'd be tempted to eat him raw," Penny remarked sadly. "How about chasing up to the ark? Noah might give us a nibble of something."

"Dare we go away and leave the boat?"

"Oh, it's safe enough for a few minutes," Penny returned. "The idea of staying here wasn't such a good one anyhow. What if those men should never come back?"

"This is a fine time to be thinking of that possibility!"

Moving quietly through the woods, the girls came to the ark. They could hear the hens cackling, and as they called Old Noah's name, the parrot answered, squawking: "Polly wants a cracker."

"You've got nothing on me, Polly," said Penny. "Where's your master?"

The old ark keeper was nowhere in evidence. Nor were the girls able to board the boat, for the gangplank had been removed.

"Now if this isn't a situation!" Penny exclaimed, exasperated. "It looks as if we're going to starve to death."

After lingering about the ark for a few minutes, they returned to their former hiding place. By this time they were so sorry for themselves that they could think of nothing but their discomfort. Belatedly, they recalled that Sara had smiled as she went away.

"She knew what we were up against staying here!" Penny declared. "Figured us for a couple of softies, I bet!"

"While everyone knows we're regular Commandos," Louise retorted sarcastically. "Why, if necessary we could go an entire day without eating."

CHAPTER 18 - PENNY'S PLAN

"That's exactly what we will do," announced Penny with renewed determination. "I'll stay here until Sara comes if it kills me. But I hope you slug me if ever I get another idea like this."

"Don't worry, I will," promised Louise. "In fact, I may not wait that long!"

The hours dragged slowly on. All amusements failing them, the girls took turns sleeping. Twice they went to the ark, but Old Noah had not returned.

At last, as shadows lengthened, Louise and Penny were confronted with a new worry. It occurred to them that Sara might not expect to take over her duties until long after dark. The air had grown chilly, and hungry mosquitoes were swarming from their breeding places.

"Even my Mother doesn't seem concerned about me any more," Louise moaned, slapping at a foraging insect.

Penny glared at the motorboat snugly hidden in the underbrush. "If that thing weren't worth so much money, I'd certainly chuck this job. Even so, I'm just about desperate."

Louise, huddled against a tree trunk, suddenly straightened alertly. Placing a warning finger on her lips, she listened.

"Someone's coming, Penny!"

"Maybe it's Sara with a basket of food. I'd rather see her than a dozen saboteurs!"

"Keep quiet, you egg," Louise warned nervously.

Crouching low behind their shelter, the girls waited. They could hear a steady tramp, tramp of feet coming up the stream on their side of the bank.

"That's not Sara," murmured Penny. "She doesn't walk like an elephant. What'll we do if it should be a saboteur?"

"I'm scared," Louise chattered, hugging her chum's arm.

The footsteps came closer. Peering out through the screen of underbrush, the girls saw a young man coming straight toward their hiding place. In his hand he carried a safety-cap gasoline can.

"Who is he?" whispered Louise.

"Can't tell yet," Penny responded, straining her eyes to see. "He looks a little like—oh, my aunt! That's who it is—Bill Evans! Now what's he doing here?"

CHAPTER 19 - STANDING GUARD

Keeping low amid the underbrush, Penny and Louise waited and watched. Bill Evans did not see them although he approached within a few feet of their hiding place. With no hesitation, he went to the motorboat and began filling the tank with gasoline.

"Bill Evans, a thief and a saboteur!" Louise whispered. "I'll never get over it!"

"Bill hasn't the pep to be a saboteur," Penny muttered. "There's something wrong with this melodrama, and I'm going to find out about it right now!"

Before Louise could stop her, she arose from the underbrush to confront the dumbfounded young man.

"Bill Evans, what do you think you're doing?" she demanded sternly.

Bill nearly dropped the gasoline can. "Why, I'm filling this tank," he replied. "Why are you girls hiding behind that log?"

"Because we've been waiting to catch a motorboat thief! And you're it!"

"Now listen here!" said Bill, setting down the gasoline can. "You can't insult me, Miss Penny Parker! Just what do you mean by that crack?"

"This motorboat was stolen from Sara Ottman. You're filling the tank with gasoline, so you must expect to make a get-away to parts unknown."

"This boat belongs to Sara Ottman?" Bill demanded in amazement.

"It certainly does."

"You're kidding. It belongs to a Mr. Wessler."

"Who's he?" asked Penny. "I never heard of him."

"Well, neither did I until this afternoon," Bill admitted. "He gave me a dollar to come over here and fill the tank of this boat with gas. I'm only carrying out orders."

"Now we're getting somewhere," Penny declared with satisfaction. "How did you meet Mr. Wessler?"

"I was working on the dock, tinkering with my engine, when a man came up and started talking to me. He said he was a friend of Mr. Wessler who was planning a fishing trip. Then he told me where the boat was, and said he'd give me a dollar if I'd run over and fill the tank with gasoline."

"Didn't you think it a rather peculiar request?"

"Not the way the fellow explained it. Mr. Wessler is a busy man and doesn't have time to look after such details."

"Mr. Wessler is afraid this locality is being watched, and he isn't taking any chances," Penny said soberly. "Bill, you've been assisting a thief!"

"Gee Whiskers!" Bill exclaimed, aghast. "I never thought about him not owning the boat. What should I do?"

"First of all, don't fill that tank with gasoline," Penny advised.

"It's about half full now."

"Can't you siphon it out?"

"Not without a tube, and I didn't bring one."

"You'll never in the world make a G-man," sighed Penny. "Well, at least you can describe the fellow who hired you."

Bill's brow puckered. "I didn't pay much attention," he admitted. "I'd say the fellow was about thirty-eight, with a little trick moustache."

"That can't be the man who originally rented the boat from Sara," Penny remarked, frowning.

CHAPTER 19 - STANDING GUARD

"Say, are you really sure this boat belongs to the Ottmans?" Bill asked. "You know they're pretty badly tangled with the police. It said in the papers—"

"I know," interrupted Penny wearily. "Or do I know? I'm so mixed I feel like a perpetual motion machine running backwards."

"We've been watching here all day," Louise added, her voice quavering. "We've had nothing to eat. No wonder our minds are failing."

"Why don't you go home?"

"And let a saboteur run off with this boat?" Penny demanded. "We promised to stay here until Sara comes."

"Maybe she and her brother are pulling a fast one on you."

"I might think so, only this was my own idea," Penny answered. "Bill, did that man mention when his friend Wessler intended to go fishing?"

"No, he didn't."

"He might intend to use the boat tonight, and then again, perhaps not for several days. Say, Bill, how would you like to do your country a great service?"

"I'm aiming to enlist when I get through High School."

"This would be immediate service. Why not stay here and watch until Sara comes? It shouldn't be long."

"And what if those men should show up?"

"Just keep watch and see what they do. Of course, if they try to get away in the motorboat, you'll have to capture them."

"Oh, sure," Bill said sarcastically. "With my bare hands?"

"We won't leave you here long," Penny promised. "Louise and I haven't had a bite of food all day—"

"Okay, I'll do it," Bill gave in. "But see to it you're back here in an hour. Better bring the police too."

Learning that the young man had crossed the river in his own motorboat, the girls obtained permission to borrow it for the return trip. They found the craft at the mouth of Bug Run, and made a quick trip to the Ottman Dock.

"No one here," Penny observed as they alighted at the platform.

The boat shed was closed and locked. A small boy, loitering nearby, told the girls that he had not seen Sara Ottman for several hours.

"Now this is a nice dish of stew!" Penny exclaimed. "Where could she have gone? And why?"

"I know where I am going," announced Louise grimly. "Home! Be it ever so humble, there's no place like it when you're tired and hungry."

"But what about poor Bill? We can't expect him to stay in the woods all night."

"Well, there's a hamburger stand at the amusement park," Louise suggested after a moment. "We could go there for a sandwich. Then we might telephone home and request advice."

"Not a bad idea," Penny praised.

At the hamburger stand they ate three sandwiches each and topped off the meal with ice cream and pie. Seeking a public telephone, Penny then used a precious nickel to call her home. No one answered. Deciding that her father might be at the *Star* office, she phoned there. Informed that Mr. Parker was not in the building, she asked for Mr. DeWitt.

"DeWitt left the office a half hour ago," came the discouraging response.

"I wonder where I can reach him?"

"Can't tell you," was the answer. "Burt Ottman has skipped his bail, and DeWitt's upset about it. He may have gone to talk to his lawyer."

"What was that about Burt Ottman?" Penny asked quickly.

"He's disappeared—skipped town. Due for trial day after tomorrow, too. Looks like DeWitt is holding the bag."

Penny hung up the receiver, more bewildered than ever. Without taking time to repeat the conversation to her chum, she called Sara's home.

For a long while she waited, but there was no reply. At last, hanging up, she eyed the coin box, expecting her nickel to be returned. Though she jiggled the receiver many times and dialed to attract the operator's attention, the coin was not forthcoming.

"You've had no luck," said Louise, taking Penny's place at the telephone. "Now it's my turn. I'll call home. Mother's always there."

She held out her hand, expecting a coin. Penny had nothing for her, and was forced to admit that she had used the last nickel on the preceding call.

"Then we have no bus money either!" gasped Louise.

"Stony broke—that's us."

"How can you be so cheerful about it?" Louise asked crossly. "We can't walk home—it would take us all night!"

"There's only one thing to do, Louise. We'll have to go back and talk to Bill. At least he should be able to loan us bus fare."

By this time the girls had lost all enthusiasm for saboteurs and sleuthing. As they recrossed the river in Bill's boat, they vowed that never again would they involve themselves in such a ridiculous situation.

"And just wait until I see Sara!" Penny added feelingly. "If I don't tear into her for playing a shabby trick on us!"

"She probably skipped town along with her brother," Louise replied. "I'm beginning to wonder if that motorboat we guarded so faithfully ever belonged to the Ottmans."

Landing not far from the mouth of Bug Run, the girls proceeded afoot to the site where Bill Evans last had been seen. To their relief, he had not deserted his post. Cold, his face swollen by mosquito bites, he hailed them joyously.

"Thought you were never coming back! I'm getting out of here, and how!"

"What happened while we were gone?" Penny asked sympathetically. "Didn't Sara come?"

"No one has been here."

As Bill started away, the girls tried to dissuade him.

"I wouldn't stay here another hour if you'd give me the boat!" he retorted. "I'm going home!"

Jerking free from Louise who sought to hold him by main force, he moved off.

"At least telephone our folks when you get to Riverview!" Penny shouted indignantly. "Tell our parents that if they're still interested in their daughters to come and lift us out of this sink hole!"

"Okay, I'll do that," Bill promised. "So long."

After the sound of footsteps had died away, Louise and Penny sat down on the log and took stock of the situation.

"Any way you look at it, we're just a couple of goats," Penny said dismally. "It wouldn't be so bad if Old Noah would take us into his ark with the rest of the animals, but he's not at home."

"Sara played a trick on us, our parents went off and hid, and I don't think we can trust Bill too far," Louise sighed. "Why do we stay here anyway?"

"Well, something could have happened to detain Sara."

"I wish I could think so, but I can't. It would serve her right to lose this boat—if it actually is hers."

"Sara always seemed sincere and honest to me," Penny said, slapping furiously at a buzzing mosquito. "Until we have definite proof otherwise, I want to trust her."

"Even if it means staying here all night?"

"Well, my trusting nature has a limit," Penny admitted. "But surely our parents will come to rescue us before long."

"I wouldn't count on it," Louise returned gloomily. "Bill was in a bad mood when he left here."

The girls fell into a deep silence. They huddled together to keep warm, and slapped constantly at the insects. For a time it grew steadily darker, then a few stars brightened the patches of sky which could be seen through the treetops.

"Imagine explaining all this to Mother," Louise murmured once. "Why, it doesn't even make sense to me."

The noises of the forest began to annoy the girls. Overhead an owl hooted. Crickets chirped, and at frequent intervals a frog or a small animal would plop into the water.

"Listen, Lou!" Penny presently whispered. "I hear something coming!"

"Maybe it's a bear," Louise shivered.

"Silly! There aren't any bears in this part of the country."

CHAPTER 19 - STANDING GUARD

"How do you know what sort of animals are around here?" Louise countered. "Maybe one escaped from Noah's zoo."

As the sound grew louder, the girls crouched low amid the brush. Through the trees they saw the gleam of a flashlight and distinguished the figure of an approaching man.

"It's probably my father!" Louise whispered, and started forward.

Penny jerked her back. "Bill hasn't had time to get to Riverview yet! This may be the big pay off!"

"A saboteur?"

Penny nodded, her gaze on the approaching figure. The man was tall and muscular and walked with a cat-like tread. He came directly to the motorboat, muttering under his breath as he examined the half empty fuel tank.

Straightening, he turned so that he faced the girls. For a fleeting instant Penny thought that he was Burt Ottman, and then she recognized her mistake. The man was the one who had rented Sara Ottman's boat—the head waiter of The Green Parrot.

CHAPTER 20 - A SHACK IN THE WOODS

Fearing detection, Louise and Penny remained motionless as the man stared in their direction. He did not see them, and after puttering about the boat for a few minutes, started off through the woods.

"Now what shall we do?" Louise whispered anxiously.

"Let's follow and find out where he goes," proposed Penny, stealing from her hiding place.

None too eager for the adventure, Louise nevertheless kept close beside her chum as they followed the stranger. Instead of returning to the main river, he chose a trail which led deeper into the woods. Coming soon to the ark which loomed dark and mysterious against a background of trees, he paused for a moment to gaze at it. Then he veered away from the well-trampled path, keeping on through the dense thickets.

"Don't you think we should turn back?" Louise whispered anxiously. "There's no guessing where we'll end up. We easily could get lost."

Penny was plagued by the same worry, but she bantered: "Why, Lou, your Scout leader would blush with shame to hear you say that! The woods stretch for only a few miles. We always can find our way out."

"What if our folks come searching for us while we're wandering around?"

"I try not to think of such unpleasant situations," Penny responded cheerfully. "You may be sure we'll have to do some tall explaining. But if this fellow we're tailing should prove to be a saboteur, everything will be lovely."

"That's not the word I'd use," Louise muttered.

The girls had fallen many yards behind the head waiter. Failing to see the flash of his light, they quickened their pace and for a minute or two feared they had lost him. But as they paused in perplexity, they again saw a gleam of light off to the right.

"Let's do less talking and more watching," Penny said, hastening on. "If we're not careful we'll lose that fellow."

Taking care to make no noise in the underbrush, the girls soon approached fairly close to the waiter. Apparently he knew his way through the woods, for not once did he hesitate. Occasionally he glanced overhead at dark clouds which were scudding across the sky. Reaching a small clearing, he paused to look at a watch which he held close to his flashlight beam.

"What time do you suppose it is?" Louise whispered to her chum.

"Not very late. Probably about nine o'clock."

Because the waiter had paused, the girls remained motionless behind a giant oak. They saw the stranger switch off his light and gaze carefully about the clearing. In particular his attention centered upon a little shack, though no light showed there.

"Whose cabin is it?" whispered Louise. "Do you know?"

"I'm not sure," returned Penny. "I think it was built several years ago by an artist who lived there while he painted the ravine and river. But he moved out last winter."

The cabin was a curious structure, picturesquely situated beneath the low-spreading branches of an ancient tree. No windows were visible at the front, but a raised structure on the flat roof gave evidence of a large skylight.

After gazing at the shack for several minutes, the waiter raised fingers to his lips and whistled twice. To the surprise of the girls, an answering signal came from within the dark cabin.

A moment later, the front door opened, and an old man stepped outside.

"That you, Jard?" he called softly.

CHAPTER 20 - A SHACK IN THE WOODS

Without replying, the waiter left the shelter of trees to cross the clearing.

"Had any trouble?" he asked the old man.

"Everything's been going okay. I'll be glad to pull out o' here though."

The waiter made a reply which the girls could not hear. Entering the cabin, the men closed the door behind them.

"Who was that old man the waiter met?" Louise asked curiously. "Did you know him, Penny?"

"I couldn't see his face. He stood in the shadow of the door. His voice sounded familiar though."

"I thought so, too. What do you suppose those men are up to anyway?"

"Nothing good," Penny responded grimly.

The girls huddled together at the edge of the clearing, uncertain what to do. If a light had been put on inside the shack it did not show from where they stood.

"Why not go for the police?" Louise proposed hopefully.

"I have a hunch those men may not stay here long. By the time we could bring help, the place might be deserted. Besides, we haven't a scrap of real evidence against them."

"How about the stolen motorboat?"

"We're not even sure about that, Lou. Sara and her brother both have disappeared. Accusing a man falsely is a very serious offense."

"Then what are we to do?" Louise asked despairingly. "Just stand here and wait until they come outside?"

"That's all we can do—unless—"

"Unless what?" Louise demanded uneasily as Penny interrupted herself.

"Lou, I have a corking idea! See how those tree limbs arch over the roof of the shack? Why, that old maple is built to our order!"

"I don't follow you."

"You will in a minute if you're a good climber!" chuckled Penny. "We can get up that tree and onto the roof. Even if it shouldn't have a skylight we can see through, at least we can hear what's being said."

"Let's just wait here."

"And learn nothing," Penny said impatiently. "How do you expect ever to be a G woman if you don't start practicing now?"

"I'm going to be a nurse when I grow up. Climbing trees won't help me at that."

"Then wait here until I get back," Penny said, starting across the clearing.

As she had known, her chum could not bear to be left alone in the dark woods. Louise hastened after her and together they crept to the base of the scraggly old maple.

The branches were so low that Penny pulled herself into them without difficulty. She then helped Louise scramble up beside her. They clung together a moment, listening to make certain that no sound had betrayed them.

"So far, so good," Penny whispered jubilantly. "Now to get onto the roof. And it does have a skylight!"

"We'll probably tumble through it," Louise muttered.

A dim light, which came from a candle, burned inside the shack. Nevertheless, from their perch on the overhanging limb, the girls were unable to see what was happening below. Penny decided to lower herself to the roof.

"Put on your velvet shoes," she warned as she swung lightly down from the lower branch. "The slightest noise and we're finished."

Dropping on the flat roof, she waited a moment, listening. Satisfied that the men inside the shack had not heard her, she motioned for Louise to follow. Her chum however, held back, shaking her head vigorously.

Abandoning the attempt to get Louise onto the roof, Penny crept toward the skylight. Lying full length, she pressed her face against the thick glass.

In the barren room below a candle burned on a table. The head waiter whom Penny first had seen at The Green Parrot sat with his legs resting on the fender of a pot-bellied stove. Opposite him was the older man whose face she could not immediately see.

"I tell you, I'm getting worried," she heard the old fellow say. "When the Coast Guards took me off that coal barge they gave me the third degree. I can't risk having anything hung on me."

Penny pressed her face closer to the glass. Her pulse pounded. She was certain she knew the identity of the old man.

"I wish he'd turn his head," she thought. "Then I'd be sure."

As if in response to the unspoken desire, the old man shifted in his chair. The light of the candle flickered on his face, and Penny saw it clearly for the first time.

"Carl Oaks!" she whispered. "And to think that I ever helped him!"

Her feet went out from under her and she was dragged over the ice.

GHOST BEYOND THE GATE

CHAPTER 25 - A BOW IN THE CLOUD

"Yes, yes," whispered the old man. "This is the hour for which I long have waited! Behold the rainbow which rolleth back the scroll of destiny! Never again will the flood come. Never again will destruction envelop the earth and all its creatures."

"How about it Noah?" Mr. Parker asked impatiently. "If I make all arrangements will you leave the ark?"

The old man did not hesitate. "Yes, I will go," he said. "My mission here is finished. I am content."

Penny and her father did not annoy the old man with material details, but slipped quietly away from the ark. Glancing back, they saw that Noah still stood at the railing, his face turned raptly toward the fading rainbow. As the last trace of color disappeared from the sky, he bowed his head in worshipful reverence. A moment he stood thus, and then, turning, walked with dignity into the ark.

"Poor old fellow," said Penny.

"I suppose you mean Noah," chuckled Mr. Parker. "But I deserve sympathy too. Haven't I just been knicked to the tune of an expensive truck?"

"You don't really mind, do you, Dad?"

"No, it's worth it to have the old fellow satisfied," Mr. Parker responded. "And then, the ark brought me a big story for the *Star*."

Penny walked silently beside her father. With the saboteurs in jail, Burt Ottman free, and Old Noah's future settled, she had not a worry in the world. Rounding a bend of the stream, she glimpsed a shining blue bottle caught in the backwash of a fallen log. Eagerly she started to rescue it.

"Don't tell me you expect to collect every one of those messages!" protested Mr. Parker.

"Every single one," laughed Penny, raking in the bottle. "You see, last night I lost a very pretty cameo pin. Until I find it, I'll never admit that the case of the saboteurs is closed!"

SABOTEURS ON THE RIVER

From Burt Ottman, Mr. Parker and his daughter heard a story much like the one previously told them by the police. The young man rapidly had gained in strength and was much cheered because he had been cleared in connection with the bridge dynamitings.

"How did you learn that Jard Wessler was a saboteur?" Mr. Parker asked him.

"Accident," admitted Burt. "Even before the bridge was blasted, I had seen the fellow around the docks. One day I overheard him talking to Breneham, and what they said made me suspicious. After getting involved in the mess myself, I made it my business to investigate. I managed to meet one of the saboteurs at the Parrot, but he proved too shrewd for me."

"You woke up in the alley," Penny recalled.

"Yes, after that I watched a place I'd learned about on Fourteenth Street. Figured I had all the dope. But as I started for the police, someone hit me with a blackjack. That's the last I remember until I came to at the woods shack."

Penny and her father were pleased to know that the young man was recovering from his injuries.

After chatting with him for a time, they left the hospital and proceeded toward the ark in the mud flats.

"I confess I don't know what to say to Noah," Mr. Parker declared as they approached the gangplank. "Sheriff Anderson insists the ark is a nuisance and must go."

Penny paused at the edge of the stream. It had started to rain once more, and drops splattered down through the trees, rippling the quiet water.

"Poor Noah!" she sighed. "He'll be unwilling to leave his home or his animals. This ark never can be floated either."

"I'll be glad to pay for his lodging elsewhere," Mr. Parker offered. "Naturally, he'll have to forsake his pets."

Crossing the gangplank, Penny called Old Noah's name. There was no answer. Not until she had shouted many times did the old fellow come up from the ark's hold. His arms were grimy, his clothing wet from the waist down.

"Why, Noah!" Penny exclaimed, astonished by his appearance.

"All morning I have labored," the old fellow said wearily. "The commotion last night excited Bess, my cow. The critter kicked a hole in the ark. Water has poured in faster than I can pump it out."

"Well, why not abandon this old boat?" Mr. Parker proposed, quick to seize an opportunity. "Wouldn't you like to live in a steam-heated apartment?"

"With my animals?"

"No, you would have to leave them behind."

Old Noah shook his head. "I could not desert my animals. At least not my dogs and cats, or my birds or fowls. As for cows and goats, they are a burden almost beyond my strength."

"A little place in the country might suit you," suggested Penny brightly. As Noah showed no interest, she added: "Or how would you like a big bus? You could take your smaller pets and tour the United States!"

Old Noah's dull blue eyes began to gleam. "I had a truck once," he said. "They took it away from me after I had made a payment. I've always hankered to see the country. But it's not to be."

"Oh, a truck might be arranged," declared Penny, grinning at her father.

"It's not that." Old Noah leaned heavily on the railing of the ark. "You might say I made a covenant to keep this place of refuge. The Great Flood soon will be upon us—"

"There will be no flood," interrupted Mr. Parker impatiently.

"I'd be happy to leave this ark if only I could believe that," sighed Noah. "I'm getting older, and it's a great burden to care for so many animals. But I must not shirk my duty because I am tired."

Penny knew that the old man could not be influenced by mere words. Glancing at the sky, she saw that although rain still fell, the sun had straggled through the clouds. Above the trees arched a beautiful rainbow.

"Noah!" she cried, directing his attention to it. "Don't you remember the Bible quotation: 'And I do set my bow in the cloud and it shall be for a token of a covenant between me and the earth.'"

"'And the waters shall no more become a flood to destroy all flesh,'" Noah whispered, his fascinated gaze upon the rainbow.

"There, you have your sign, your token," Mr. Parker said briskly.

CHAPTER 25 - A BOW IN THE CLOUD

"Sure, he was able to spill the whole story," one of the men told them. "Seems he set out to prove that he was innocent of any association with the saboteurs. Instead of cooperating with police, he went to work on his own. He investigated an organization known as the American Protective Society. That put him on the trail of a head waiter at The Green Parrot, a foreigner by the name of Jard Wessler."

"I understand now why Burt acted so queer about that billfold he lost along the river," Penny commented. "He didn't want me to know that he was meeting one of the saboteurs at the Parrot."

"How many were involved in the dynamiting plot?" Mr. Parker asked.

"Twelve or thirteen. According to Ottman, Jard Wessler is the brains of the group. By pretending to go along with them, the kid gathered a lot of evidence."

"But at first the saboteurs tried to throw the guilt on Burt," Penny protested.

"True," nodded the policeman. "They used a boat stolen from the Ottman dock, and they planted evidence to make it appear that Burt was the guilty one."

"Then why would they take up with him later?" Penny asked in perplexity.

"They never did. One of the saboteurs met him at The Green Parrot to try to learn how much the kid knew. Young Ottman was slugged over the head when he tried to get into a basement room where the gang held their meetings."

"I guess that explains why we found Burt lying outside in the alley," Mr. Parker remarked. "It's a pity he couldn't have told us what he was attempting to do."

"The kid did get a lot of evidence," resumed the officer. "With the information he's given us, we expect to mop up the entire gang."

"Louise and I found him a prisoner here at the shack," Penny remarked slowly. "I suppose in seeking evidence, he tangled with the saboteurs again."

"Yes, young Ottman was foolhardy. He was caught spying a second time and they slugged him. Lucky for him his injuries aren't likely to prove serious."

Mr. Parker and Jerry asked many more questions, knowing the story would rate important play in the *Riverview Star*. Turning Penny and Louise over to Mr. Sidell who belatedly joined the party, the two newspaper men rushed off to scoop rival papers.

"Dad didn't even take time to say he was glad we escaped from those saboteurs!" Penny complained to Louise. "Isn't that a newspaper man for you!"

Before another hour had elapsed, reporters and photographers from other papers swarmed the woods. Louise and Penny were quizzed regarding the capture of the three saboteurs. Determined that the *Star* should print an exclusive story, they had very little to say.

Hours later, at home, Penny learned that police had lost no time in acting upon information provided by Burt Ottman. The entire group of men known to be associated with Jard Wessler had been arrested at a Fourteenth Street club. A complete confession had been signed by Carl Oaks who claimed that he was not a member of the gang, but had been hired to do as instructed.

"Well, the *Star* scooped every paper in town," Mr. Parker remarked, as he put aside the front page. "That's not important, however, compared to saving the Seventh Street Bridge."

"How about your daughter?" Penny asked, rumpling his hair. "Aren't you one speck glad about saving me?"

"I've been reserving a special lecture for you," he said, pretending to be stern. "Young ladies who go running about at night—"

"Never mind," laughed Penny, "If Lou and I hadn't done our prowling, I guess you wouldn't have any old Seventh Street Bridge!"

Actually Mr. Parker was very proud of his daughter and showed it in many ways. He would not allow Mrs. Weems to scold her for the night's escapade. Learning that she was worried about Old Noah, he promised to talk to Sheriff Anderson and do what he could for the old fellow. The next morning, he and Penny started off to see Noah, stopping enroute at the hospital.

"Oh, I'm so glad you came!" Sara Ottman greeted them at her brother's bedside. "Burt and I owe you so much. I've been very unpleasant—"

"Not at all," corrected Penny. "Anyway, I like folks who aren't afraid to speak their minds."

CHAPTER 25 - A BOW IN THE CLOUD

In the radio room of the *Eloise III*, Mr. Parker, Jerry, and the three girls hovered at the elbow of Commodore Phillips who sat at the radio-telephone.

"I've done all I can," the Commodore said, putting aside the instrument. "The Coast Guard station has acknowledged our message. Now we must wait."

The *Eloise* which had picked up Mr. Parker's party, was heading at full steam toward the Seventh Street Bridge. Unmindful of the rain, the young people went out on deck. Huddling in the lee of the cabin, they anxiously watched and listened.

"It's one fifteen," said Mr. Parker, glancing at his watch. "Any minute now—"

A loud report sounded over the water.

"The bridge!" gasped Louise. "It's been dynamited!"

"No, no!" exclaimed the Commodore impatiently. "That was gunfire! The Coast Guard boat has gone into action!"

A moment later those aboard the *Eloise* saw a flash of fire and heard another loud report.

"You may rest easy now," said the Commodore, relaxing. "With the Coast Guard on the job, that saboteur hasn't a chance. If he escapes with his life he'll be lucky."

Penny sagged weakly against the railing of the *Eloise*. Now that she knew the bridge would be saved, she felt completely exhausted from the long period of suspense.

"Wessler can't be the only one involved in this plot," she heard her father say. "There must be others."

"Oh, there are!" Penny cried, recovering her strength. "Carl Oaks is a member of the outfit! He's waiting at a shack not far from the ark. And Burt Ottman is held a prisoner there!"

"Burt!" Sara exclaimed in horror. "Oh, why didn't you tell me!"

"In the excitement it just passed out of my mind," Penny confessed. "I forgot about everything except saving the bridge!"

Once more Commodore Phillips busied himself on the radio telephone, this time contacting Riverview police. Before he left his desk he learned that a squad had been dispatched to the shack in the woods. Likewise, a message soon came from the Coast Guard station, informing him that Jard Wessler had been captured.

"Oh, I can't wait to see Burt," Sara declared, anxiously pacing the deck. "He may be seriously hurt."

To ease the girl's mind, Commodore Phillips put the entire party ashore not far from the entrance to Bug Run. Hastening through the woods, Mr. Parker and the young people reached the shack only a few minutes after the arrival of police.

"What became of Carl Oaks?" the newspaper owner asked a sergeant. "Did you get him?"

The policeman indicated a downcast figure who sat handcuffed inside the patrol car. Oaks, he explained, had been captured without a struggle.

"And Burt Ottman?" Mr. Parker inquired.

"They're taking him to the ambulance now."

Four men came out of the shack bearing the injured young man on a stretcher. Pale but conscious, he grinned as Sara tearfully bent over him.

"I'm okay, Sis," he mumbled. "Feelin' swell."

Sara was allowed to ride with her brother to the hospital. Remaining behind, Mr. Parker, Jerry and the girls, tried to learn from police officers if Burt had made any statement.

CHAPTER 24 - A MESSAGE IN THE BOTTLE

Leaving others to guard the prisoner, Mr. Parker and Jerry ran toward the mouth of Bug Run. Not to be left behind, Penny, Sara, and Louise, followed as fast as they could. By the time they reached the river, Wessler's boat had disappeared. However, the popping of its engine could be heard far out on the water.

"We'll never overtake him now," Sara said despairingly. "That boat is a fast one."

A slower craft, one the girl had used earlier in the evening to cross the river, was beached nearby. Even though pursuit seemed useless, the men launched it. Overloaded with five passengers, the boat made slow progress against the current.

"We haven't a chance to overtake that fellow," Sara repeated again.

"If only we could notify Coast Guards!" Penny murmured hopelessly. "Their station is up river. They still might be able to intercept Wessler before he reaches the bridge."

"No way to contact them," Mr. Parker responded, his voice grim. "If there were any houses along shore, we could telephone. As it is, the situation is pretty hopeless."

"Shall we give up the chase?" asked Sara who handled the tiller.

As Mr. Parker hesitated, Penny suddenly grasped his arm. To the starboard she had glimpsed an approaching yacht. Its contour was so well known along the waterfront that she had no doubt as to its identity—the *Eloise III*.

"Dad, we still have a chance!" she cried. "By radio telephone!"

"How d'you mean?" he demanded.

"The *Eloise* has a radio telephone!" Penny explained. Excitedly, she began to signal with Sara's flashlight. "Dad, if only they see us in time, we still may save the bridge!"

Breneham began to pace the floor nervously. Suddenly he halted by a porthole, listening. The girls too strained to hear.

"Someone's out there in the trees!" Breneham muttered. "This ark is being watched! Noah, stick your head out the window and ask who it is! And no tricks!"

Old Noah did as ordered.

"Hello, the ark!" shouted a voice which Penny thought belonged to Jerry Livingston. "Are you alone there, Noah?"

"Tell him yes," prodded the saboteur. "Say that you are just going to bed."

"But my son, that would be a base falsehood," Noah argued. "I have no intention of retiring—"

Penny, quick to divine that Breneham's attention was diverted, rushed to another window. In a shrill voice she screamed for help.

Breneham sprang toward Penny, intending to fell her with a blow. Louise began to shout. Realizing that he had been betrayed, Breneham jerked open the door and leaped from the high deck into the stream.

"Get him! Get him!" shouted Penny to the group of men on shore.

Breneham swam a few feet and then waded toward the far side of the stream.

"Oh, he's going to get away!" Louise murmured, watching anxiously from a porthole.

As the saboteur scrambled up the bank, two men rose from their hiding places in the tall bushes and grasped him by the arms.

"It's Dad!" cried Penny gleefully. "And your father too, Louise!"

Thrilled by the manner in which their release had been accomplished, the girls ran out of the cabin. Crossing the gangplank, they saw that the rescue party was comprised of Mr. Parker, Mr. Sidell, Jerry Livingston, several men who were strangers, and Sara Ottman.

"I found your message in the bottle!" she greeted the girls excitedly.

"Not really?" demanded Penny.

"I was in the little cove just below here, guarding my boat," explained Sara. "I intended to get back earlier to relieve you girls, but I was detained at the police station. Anyway, while I waited at the bend, wondering what to do, a swarm of corked bottles came floating downstream."

"Old Noah threw out a box full of them," chuckled Louise. "So you read our message, asking for help, Sara?"

The older girl nodded. "Yes, one of the bottles drifted ashore. Usually I don't bother to read the message, but this time I did."

"How were you able to bring help here so quickly?" asked Penny.

"Actually I didn't. Although I didn't realize it until a few minutes ago, your parents have been dreadfully worried about you girls. When Bill Evans telephoned them, they came here to search."

"I know," nodded Penny. "Dad was here earlier in the evening. The saboteurs tricked him into leaving."

"I didn't see him at the time," Sara resumed her explanation. "Penny, your father returned home, but when he learned you were not there, he organized a searching party. Just as the men reached Bug Run once more, I found your message. I gave it to Mr. Parker and—well, you know the rest."

"Did you capture Jard Wessler?" Penny demanded tensely. "That's the important thing!"

"Wessler? You mean the man who stole my motorboat?"

"Yes, he went away from the ark about five minutes ago. I'm sure he intended to use the hidden boat, Sara! You left it well guarded, I hope."

"There's no one watching it now."

"Then we've got to move fast!" Penny cried, looking anxiously about for her father. "Jard Wessler plans to destroy the Seventh Street Bridge! He's probably close by now, waiting for a chance to make his get-away!"

The three girls ran to meet Mr. Parker who at that moment had crossed the stream with the prisoner. Just then the engine of a motorboat was heard to sputter. Sara stopped short, listening. Unmistakably, the sound came from around the bend.

"That's my boat!" Sara cried.

"Jard Wessler is getting away!" Penny added. "We must stop him!"

CHAPTER 24 - A MESSAGE IN THE BOTTLE

Failing easily to retrieve the message in the bottle, Jard Wessler smashed it against a wall of the ark. Picking up the folded paper, he flashed his light across the writing.

"'The hour of the Great Deluge approaches,'" he read aloud. "'Come to my ark and I will provide shelter and comfort.'"

Penny and Louise relaxed. The message was one that Old Noah had written. Unless Wessler opened another bottle he would not suspect that they were the authors of other messages pleading for help.

"Stand back and allow me to throw my bottles into the stream!" Old Noah cried angrily. "Even though you are a guest aboard my ark, your actions are not pleasing."

"Go ahead, Grandpa," Wessler said with a shrug. "Heave out your bottles if it will keep you happy."

As Old Noah began to toss the bottles out of the porthole, Wessler again ordered Penny and Louise from the cabin.

"Upstairs!" he said, giving them a shove toward the stairway.

Penny glanced quickly toward shore. The gangplank had been raised, but the distance was not great.

As if reading her mind, Wessler said: "I wouldn't try to make a leap for it if I were you, little lady. Behave yourself, and you'll be set free before morning."

Penny and Louise were forced to go upstairs to the third floor of the ark. Although Old Noah's living quarters were more comfortable than the bird room, they provided less privacy. Wessler and his companion remained on the floor, and not a word could the girls speak without being overheard.

Old Noah soon appeared. In a much better mood, he chatted with the two men. Finding them uncommunicative, he picked up his banjo and began to sing spirituals to its accompaniment. His voice, as cracked as the fingers which strummed the strings, drove Breneham into a near frenzy.

"There's a limit to what a guy can stand," he said meaningly to Wessler.

"It won't be much longer now," the other encouraged, glancing at his watch.

"Why can't we pull the job now and get out?"

"Because the car won't be waiting for us. Everything's got to move on schedule."

As the night wore on, a light rain began to fall. Wessler and his companion went frequently to the windows, seemingly well pleased by the change of weather.

The ordeal of waiting was a cruel one for Louise and Penny. Although they knew that Old Noah had tossed their messages into the water, they held scant hope that any of the bottles would be found that night. While searching parties might continue to seek them, it was unlikely that they would be released in time to prevent the destruction of the Seventh Street Bridge.

Another hour elapsed. Wessler looked at his watch and spoke to his companion.

"Well, I'm shoving off! When you hear the explosion, lock 'em up in the bird room, and make for the shack. The car will pick you up."

"Good luck, Jard," Breneham responded.

Wessler went out the door, closing it behind him. The girls heard him lower the gangplank into place, and then his footsteps died away.

Penny gazed at Louise in despair. They both knew that Jard Wessler had gone to dynamite the Seventh Street Bridge. Although they were not certain of the plan, they believed that he intended to use Sara Ottman's boat which doubtlessly would be loaded with explosives.

Completely aroused, the old man backed away as if to make a running attack. Wessler drew his revolver, but Noah paid not the slightest heed.

"Let me get at my birds!" he cried. "Stand back!"

"Better humor him," Breneham said uneasily. "Unless you do, he'll arouse the countryside."

Wessler returned the revolver to its holster beneath his coat. "Calm down, Grandpa, calm down," he tried to soothe the old man. "No one is going to hurt your precious birds."

"Then open that door!"

"Go ahead," Wessler directed his companion. "If he makes any more trouble we'll lock him in with the girls."

"There are no doors on this ark strong enough to hold me," said Noah. "Open it I say!"

The command was obeyed. The old man stumbled across the threshold and began to murmur soothing words to the birds. At first he did not see Penny and Louise. Finally observing them, he spoke rather absently:

"Good evening, my daughters. I am happy that you have come again to my ark, but I am afraid you have disturbed my birds."

Penny chose her words carefully for Wessler and his pal stood in the cabin doorway.

"The birds do seem excited for some reason. No doubt they're alarmed by the approaching storm."

"Yes, yes, that may be it," Old Noah murmured. "And the porthole is covered. That should not be. I will fix it."

Pushing past the two men, Old Noah went outside the cabin to jerk away the canvas covering. He came back in a moment, bearing a sack of bird seed.

"Upstairs!" Wessler tersely ordered the girls.

In crossing the room, Penny deliberately stumbled against the box of blue corked bottles.

"With another storm coming up, I suppose you'll be throwing out more of your messages," she said jokingly to Noah.

Penny had hoped that the suggestion might presently cause the old man to dump the contents of the box into the water. She neither expected nor desired that he would attempt the task in the presence of the two saboteurs. However, Old Noah immediately dropped the sack of bird seed and strode over to the box of bottles.

"Yes, yes, I have been neglectful of my duty," he murmured. "With the Great Flood coming, I must warn the good people of Riverview. I shall bid them seek refuge here before their doom is sealed."

Old Noah selected a half dozen bottles and started to heave them through the porthole. Before he could do so, Wessler blocked the opening.

"Just a minute, Grandpa," he said. "What's in those bottles?"

"Messages which I wrote with my own hand," Old Noah replied earnestly. "Would you like to read them, my son?"

"That's exactly what I intend to do," said Wessler.

With a suspicious glance directed at Penny and Louise, he reached into the box and selected one of the corked bottles.

CHAPTER 23 - HELP FROM NOAH

"I wish he'd come here," said Penny. "Maybe we could get the idea over to him that we're being held prisoners."

"Not a chance of it."

"Those men evidently intend to allow him the run of the ark so long as he suspects nothing," Penny mused. "Say, I know how we might bring him here!"

"How?"

"By stirring up the birds. Then Old Noah would get excited and try to break in."

"And what would that accomplish?"

"Probably nothing," Penny admitted, sighing. "Wessler is armed. Noah couldn't overpower two men, even if he were inclined to do it."

"All Noah thinks about is the coming flood. With another rain in the offing, he'll confine his worries to how he can attract more people to his ark."

"Lou! Maybe that's an idea!"

"What is?" Louise inquired blankly.

"Why, perhaps we can bring help by means of Old Noah and his message bottles!"

"Perhaps you know what you mean, but I am sure I don't!"

"Do you have a pen or a pencil with you, Lou?"

"I might have a pencil." Louise searched in the pockets of her jacket, and finally brought forth a stub with a broken lead.

"We can fix that so it will write," Penny declared, chewing away the wood.

"I still don't understand what you have in mind."

"This is my idea," Penny explained. "You know that whenever it rains Old Noah starts tossing message bottles into the river."

"True."

Penny groped her way across the room to the box which stood by the porthole. "Well, here are the bottles," she said triumphantly. "What's to prevent us from writing our own messages? We'll explain that we are held prisoners here and appeal for help."

"How do you propose to get the bottles overboard?"

"I'll think of a scheme."

"Even if the bottles did reach the water, one never would be picked up in time to do any good," Louise argued. "It's a bum idea, Penny."

"I guess it isn't so hot," Penny acknowledged ruefully. "Anyway, why not try it just to keep occupied? It's deadly sitting here and brooding."

"All right," Louise agreed.

The girls removed corks from several bottles and by means of a bent hairpin, removed the papers already inside them. Although they had no light, Penny and Louise scribbled at least a dozen messages. Carefully they recorked every bottle, replacing it in the box.

"I'm going to put my cameo pin inside this one," Penny said, unfastening a cherished ornament from her dress. "Someone might see it and open the bottle."

"We'll likely hear from it about next Christmas," her chum responded.

Becoming weary of writing messages, Penny decided to stir up a bit of action. Moving from box to box, she aroused the sleeping birds. Her final act was to jerk the covering from Polly's cage and playfully pluck the tail feathers of the startled creature.

"Noah! Noah!" the parrot croaked. "Heave out the anchor! Help! Help!"

"Keep it up, Polly," Penny encouraged, rocking the cage.

The parrot squawked in righteous rage and the other birds chirped excitedly. In the midst of the commotion, a heavy step was heard on deck. Noah, finding the door to the bird room locked, shook it violently.

"Unbolt this door!" he shouted. "Unlock it, I say, or I will break it down!" And he banged with his fists against the flimsy panel.

"What's coming off here?" demanded another voice, that of Wessler. "Have you gone completely crazy?"

"I want to know why this door is locked!" Noah said wrathfully. "Unlock it or I will break it down!"

CHAPTER 23 - HELP FROM NOAH

A long while later, Jard Wessler and his companion reentered the cabin where Penny and Louise were imprisoned. After removing the tape from the girls' lips, and freeing them of their uncomfortable bonds, they went outside again.

"At least they're not trying to torture us," Louise said, close to tears. "Oh, Penny, your father believes we've gone home! Now we'll never be found."

"Not in time to save the bridge, that's certain," her chum agreed gloomily.

Getting up from the floor, Penny groped her way to the covered porthole. She stumbled against a box and there was a loud tinkle of glass.

"Noah's bottles!" she exclaimed, exasperated. "Where do you suppose the old fellow has taken himself?"

"Maybe the sheriff got him."

"I doubt it," returned Penny. "He probably just went off somewhere."

After testing the cabin door, she sat down again beside Louise. The girls did not sleep but they fell into a drowsy, half-stupefied state. Then suddenly they were aroused by the sound of low voices just outside the porthole.

"It's an old man coming," they heard Wessler mutter. "Must be Noah."

"What'll we do with him?" the other demanded.

"Wait and see how he acts," Wessler advised. "He's such a simple old coot he may not suspect anything. If he makes trouble we'll have to lock him up."

A silence ensued and then the girls heard heavy footsteps on the gangplank.

"Ho, and who has visited my ark while I've been away?" muttered Old Noah.

Wessler and his companion, Breneham, stepped from the shadows.

"Good evening, Noah," the waiter greeted him politely. "Looks like rain, doesn't it?"

The remark concerning the weather was all that was needed to dull the old man's perceptions. Forgetting that the ark had been invaded by strangers during his absence, he lowered an armload of groceries to the railing, and peered intently up at the sky.

"No man knoweth the hour, but when the thunder of the Lord strikes, the rain will descend. All creatures of the earth shall perish—yes, all except those who seek refuge here. Therefore, my sons, you do well to seek the shelter of my ark."

"The old fellow's sure raving," Wessler remarked to his companion.

"A raven?" inquired Noah, misunderstanding. "Ah, yes! For one hundred and fifty days the waters will prevail upon the earth. Then will I send forth a raven or a dove to search for a sprig of green. And if the bird returns with such a token, then shall I know that the waters are receding, no more to destroy all flesh."

"Toddle on, old man," Wessler said, growing irritated. "Where've you been anyway?"

"My burdens are heavy," Noah replied with a deep sigh. "All day I have labored, seeking food for my animals. Greens I cut for Bessie, my cow, and at the grocery store I bought seed for the birds, crackers—"

"Never mind," Wessler interrupted. "Go into your quarters and stay there."

"Bessie, the cow, must be fed."

"Then go feed her," Wessler snapped. "Just get out of my sight."

The girls could not hear what Old Noah said in reply. However, a medley of animal sounds beneath the deck, led them to believe that the master of the ark had gone into the lower part of the ship to care for his animals.

CHAPTER 22 - A SEARCHING PARTY

Mr. Parker called a cheery good night to Wessler. For a few minutes the girls heard the sound of retreating footsteps in the underbrush. Then all was still save for the restless stirring of the birds.

"The Seventh Street Bridge will be blasted at one o'clock," Penny said anxiously. "If it goes up, Riverview traffic will be paralyzed. Work at the munition plant will stop cold."

"The saboteurs intend to blame Burt Ottman for the job too! Well, at least we can tell police who the real plotters are."

"We can if we ever get out of here," Penny said, pacing the floor. "Oh, I'm as mad as a hornet!"

"Quiet down, and maybe we can hear something," Louise suggested calmly. "I think those men are talking."

A murmur of voices could be heard from the third floor of the ark. The partitions were thin. By standing on one of the pigeon boxes, the girls discovered they could understand nearly everything that was being said.

"Carl, you go back to the shack and keep an eye on Ottman," the waiter ordered the watchman. "As soon as Breneham comes, send him here. We'll pull the job at one o'clock just as we planned."

"Okay, Jard," the other answered.

Getting down from the pigeon box, Penny watched Carl Oaks leave the ark.

"How about taking a chance and shouting for help?" Louise suggested in a whisper.

Penny shook her head. "Not now at least. I doubt anyone is within a mile of this place—that is, anyone friendly to us."

The girls were not to enjoy their porthole for long. Within a few minutes the waiter tacked a strip of canvas over the opening. He then sat down on deck directly beneath it, and the odor of his cigar drifted into the room.

"That man must be Jard Wessler," Penny whispered to her chum. "You remember Bill said he was hired to work for a fellow by the name of Wessler."

"I don't care who he is," muttered Louise. "All *I* think about is getting out of here."

The girls sat side by side, their backs to the wall. About them in boxes and cages, Noah's birds stirred restlessly. Polly, the parrot, kept up such a chatter that at length Penny covered the cage with a sack.

Time passed slowly. It seemed hours later that Penny and Louise heard the sound of a man's voice. The cry, though low, came from shore.

"Ark ahoy! Are you there, Wessler?"

"Come aboard," invited the one in command of the boat. "Oaks told you what happened?"

"Yeah, and I have more bad news." The newcomer had reached the ark and his voice could be heard plainly by Louise and Penny. "A searching party is out looking for those two girls. Heading this way too."

"In that case—"

The door of the bird room suddenly was thrust open and a flashbeam focused upon the girls. They found themselves confronted by Jard Wessler and a stranger. At least Penny's first thought was that she had never seen him before. Then it came to her that he closely resembled the man with whom Burt Ottman had dined at The Green Parrot.

Before either of the girls realized what was in store, they were seized by the arms. Tape was plastered over their lips, and their limbs were bound.

"A precautionary measure," Wessler assured them. "You'll be released soon."

Penny and Louise understood perfectly why they had been bound and gagged. Scarcely fifteen minutes elapsed before they heard the sound of men's voices along shore. Soon thereafter someone hailed the ark. Penny's heart leaped for she recognized her father's voice.

"Hello, the ark!" he shouted.

Wessler responded, his voice casual and friendly.

"We're looking for two girls lost in the woods. Have you seen them?"

"Why, yes," Wessler answered. "A couple of girls went past here about an hour ago. They were on their way to the river."

"Then they must have started home," Mr. Parker replied, greatly relieved. "By the way, you're not the one they call Noah, are you?"

"Just a friend of his."

"I see," responded Mr. Parker, apparently satisfied with the answer. "Well, thanks. We've been worried about my daughter and her friend. It's a relief to know they're on their way home."

In the dark bird room of the ark, Penny and Louise squirmed and twisted. Though they thumped their feet on the floor, the sound conveyed no hint of their plight to those on shore.

CHAPTER 22 - A SEARCHING PARTY

"Now we'll have no more nonsense," said the man who held the revolver. "Stand over there against the tree."

Penny and Louise were so frightened that they trembled violently.

"You'll not be harmed if you do exactly as you're told," the waiter assured them.

"Why not let us go home?" Penny ventured, recovering her courage.

"Not tonight, my dear." The man smiled grimly. "Unfortunately, you have learned too much regarding my affairs."

"Then what are you going to do with us?" Penny demanded.

Apparently, the waiter did not himself know. While he guarded the girls, he cast a quick glance toward the ark. Just then running footsteps were heard in the woods, and someone whistled twice. The waiter answered the signal. A moment later, Carl Oaks, quite winded, came into view.

"So you got 'em, eh?" he demanded with pleasure.

"The question is what to do with them."

"I don't want 'em at the shack," the old watchman complained. "When young Ottman comes around I may have my hands full with him."

"This ark should serve my purpose," the waiter muttered. "The old coot that lives here has gone off somewhere. Oaks, get aboard and look around."

"There's no way to cross to it," the watchman said helplessly.

"Find the gangplank!" his companion ordered irritably. "It must be hidden somewhere in the bushes."

Thus urged, Oaks searched along the river bank and soon came upon the missing plank. Fitting it into place, he quickly crossed to the ark. A dog started to bark, but the sound was choked off.

"Well?" called the waiter impatiently.

"No one here except the animals," Oaks reported, reappearing on deck. "The only room that can be locked off is the cabin where the dope keeps his birds."

"That ought to do," decided the waiter. "We won't have to keep 'em here long."

Penny and Louise were compelled to march across the gangplank, up the steps to the bird room of the ark. The parrot, arousing from a doze, squawked a raucous welcome.

"Get in there and don't make any noise!" the waiter ordered. "If you shout for help or make any disturbance, you'll be bound and gagged. And that's not pleasant. Get me?"

"You seem to have got us," Penny retorted.

The door slammed and a bolt slid into place. Penny tiptoed at once to the porthole. It was much too small to permit an escape, but at least it provided fresh air and a view of the shore.

"Well, well, well," cackled the parrot, tramping up and down on his wide perch. "Polly wants a slug o' rum."

"You'll get a slug, period, if you don't keep quiet," Penny said crossly. "Give me a chance to think, will you?"

"Thinking won't get us out of this mess," murmured Louise, sitting down with her back to a wall. "It must be after nine o'clock now. If Bill had notified our folks, they would be looking for us long before this."

In whispers the girls discussed their unfortunate situation. They were hopeful that eventually they would be released, but they could not expect freedom until long after midnight.

Penny waited to hear no more. Creeping cautiously away from the skylight, she returned to her chum who remained perched precariously on the overhanging tree branch.

"Learn anything?" Louise demanded in a whisper.

"Did I? Lou, that old man is Carl Oaks! He and our waiter friend have a prisoner inside the cabin."

"A prisoner! My gracious! Then they must be saboteurs!"

"They're planning to blow up the Seventh Street Bridge at one o'clock," Penny went on tersely. "And they aim to blame it all on Burt Ottman!"

"He's not one of the outfit then?"

"Seemingly not. They have him trussed up inside a closet. Lou, you've got to hot-foot it to town and bring the police!"

"Come with me," Louise pleaded, frightened at the mere thought of going through the dark woods alone.

"One of us ought to stay and keep watch. I'll go if you're willing to remain."

"No, I'll go," Louise decided.

With nervous haste she started to descend the tree. Midway down, her hand loosened its hold, and she slipped several feet. Although she uttered no cry, she did make considerable noise. Penny, still on the roof of the shack, heard Carl Oaks exclaim:

"What was that? I hear someone outside!"

Realizing that her chum was certain to be seen, Penny called to her: "Run, Lou! As fast as you can!"

Her own position now had become untenable. It was too late to regain the tree branch. Darting to the roof edge, she swung herself down with her hands and dropped six feet to the ground.

The door of the cabin swung open. Penny had leaped from the rear side of the building, and so was not immediately seen. The two men started after Louise who in panic had run toward the woods.

To divert attention from her hard pressed chum, Penny gave a wild Indian whoop. Startled, the men stopped, and turned around. Carl Oaks at once took after her, while the waiter resumed pursuit of Louise.

Penny did not find it hard to keep well ahead of the watchman. Darting into the woods, she circled, hoping to rejoin her chum. She knew that Louise was not very fleet of foot, and once confused, might never find her way out of the forest.

By frequently pausing to listen to the crackle of underbrush, Penny was able to follow the flight of her chum. Instead of running toward the river, Louise seemed to be circling back in the direction of the shack.

"She'll get us both into trouble now," thought Penny anxiously.

A moment later, Louise, puffing and gasping, came running past. Penny joined her, grasping her hand to help her over the rough places.

"That man's right behind!" Louise panted. "Are we almost to the river?"

Penny did not discourage her by revealing that she had been running in the wrong direction. The chance of escape now was a slim one. Louise was nearly out of breath, while the man who pursued them, steadily gained.

"The ark!" Penny cried, guiding her chum. "We'll be safe there!"

Unmindful of thorns which tore at their clothing, the girls raced on. Although Carl Oaks had been left far behind, the other man was not to be outdistanced. He kept so close that Louise and Penny had no opportunity to hide or attempt to throw him off the trail.

"Go on, Penny," Louise gasped, slackening speed. "I can't make it."

"Yes, you can!" Penny fairly pulled her along. "We're almost there. See!"

The ark loomed up ahead. Encouraged by the sight, Louise gathered her strength and kept doggedly on. They reached the bank of the stream and gave way to despair. The ark was dark and the gangplank which usually connected it with shore, was nowhere in evidence.

"Noah! Noah!" called Louise wildly.

Only the parrot answered, crackling saucily from a porthole: "Hello, Noah, you old soak! Where are you, Noah?"

Breathless and bewildered, the girls did not know what to do. Before they could turn and run on, the man who so ruthlessly pursued them, dashed out from among the trees.

"Oh, here you are," he said, and moonlight gleamed on the revolver he held in his hand. "A very pretty race, my dears, but shall we call this the finish line?"

CHAPTER 21 - THROUGH THE SKYLIGHT

Greatly excited to learn that the old watchman and the waiter of The Green Parrot were fellow conspirators, Penny strained to catch their words. She heard the waiter reply:

"You've done good work, Oaks. All you have to do now is sit tight for a few more hours. We'll give you a five hundred dollar bonus if the job comes off right."

"That won't do me any good if I end up in jail."

"Nothing will go wrong. Everything has been planned to the last detail."

"I'm already in bad with the police," the old watchman whined. "I wouldn't have gone in with you if I'd known just what I was doing."

"You got your money for the Thompson bridge job, didn't you?"

"A hundred dollars."

"It was more than you earned," the other replied irritably. "All you had to do was let me get away after I dynamited the bridge. You blamed near shot off my head!"

"I had to make it look as if I was doin' my duty. Those girls were watching me."

"That Parker pest came snooping around at The Parrot," the waiter said, letting the tilted chair legs thud on the floor. "Brought a reporter with her too. I got rid of 'em in short order."

"She didn't act very friendly when she found me bound and gagged aboard the coal barge," Carl Oaks resumed. "I think she may have suspected that it was a put up job. That's why I want to get out o' town while the getting is good."

"You can leave after tonight. We blast the Seventh Street bridge at one o'clock."

"And what about this prisoner I've been nursemaiding?"

"We'll plant enough evidence around the bridge to cinch his guilt with the police. Then we'll dump him in Chicago where he'll be picked up."

"He's apt to remember what happened and spill the whole story."

"Even if he does, the police won't believe him," the waiter said. "They'll figure he's only trying to get out from under. Anyway, we'll be in another part of the country by then."

"What time will you pick me up here?" the watchman asked.

"Ten minutes till one. The automobile will arrive right on the tick, so synchronize your watch."

The two men compared timepieces, and then the waiter arose.

"Let's look at the prisoner," he said. "Is he still out cold?"

"He was the last time I looked at him. Hasn't moved since he was brought here, except once to ask for water."

The watchman went across the room to a closet and opened the door. A man lay on the floor, his hands and feet loosely bound. No cloth covered his face. Peering down from above, Penny was able to discern his features, and it gave her a distinct shock as she recognized him.

The waiter prodded the prisoner with his foot. The man who was bound, groaned and muttered, but made no other sign of consciousness.

"He'll not bother you tonight, Oaks," he said. "One of the boys can help you lift him into the car."

"I don't like this business," the watchman complained again. "What if his skull should be fractured?"

"He'll be okay by tomorrow," the waiter answered indifferently. "Heflanz gave him a little too much with the blackjack."

CHAPTER 1 - LOST ON A HILLTOP

The little iceboat, with two laughing, shouting girls clinging to it, sped over the frozen surface of Big Bear River.

"Penny, we're going too fast!" screamed Louise Sidell, ducking to protect her face from the biting wind.

"Only about forty an hour!" shrieked her companion gleefully.

At the tiller of the *Icicle*, Penelope Parker, in fur-lined parka, sheepskin coat and goggles, looked for all the world like a jolly Eskimo. Always delighting in a new sport, she had built the iceboat herself—spars from a wood lot, the sail from an old tent.

"Slow down, Penny!" pleaded her chum.

"Can't," shouted Penny cheerfully. "Oh, we're going into a hike!"

As one runner raised off the ice, the boat tilted far over on its side. Louise shrieked with terror, and held tight to prevent being thrown out. Penny, hard pressed, sought to avert disaster by a snappy starting of the main sheet.

For a space the boat rushed on, runners roaring. Then as a sudden puff of wind struck the sail, the steering runner leaped off the ice. Instantly the *Icicle* went into a spin from which Penny could not straighten it.

"We're going over!" screamed Louise, scrambling to free her feet.

The next moment the boat capsized. Both girls went sliding on their backs across the ice. Penny landed in a snowdrift at the river bank, her parka awry, goggles hanging on one ear.

"Are you hurt, Lou?" she called, jumping to her feet.

Louise sprawled on the ice some distance away. Slowly she pulled herself to a sitting position and rubbed the back of her head.

"Maybe this is your idea of fun!" she complained. "As for me, give me bronco busting! It would be a mild sport in comparison."

Penny chuckled, dusting snow from her clothing. "Why, this is fun, Lou. We have to expect these little upsets while we're learning."

The sail of the overturned iceboat was billowing like a parachute. Slipping and sliding, Penny ran to pull it in.

"Take the old thing down!" urged Louise, hobbling after her. "I've had enough ice-boating for this afternoon!"

"Oh, just one more turn down the river and back," coaxed Penny.

"No! We're close to the club house now. If we sail off again, there's no telling where we'll land. Anyway, it's late and it's starting to snow."

Penny reluctantly acknowledged that Louise spoke pearls of wisdom. Large, damp snowflakes were drifting down, dotting her red mittens. The wind steadily was stiffening, and cold penetrated her sheepskin coat.

"It will be dark within an hour," added Louise. Uneasily she scanned the leaden sky. "We've been out here all afternoon."

"Guess it is time to go home," admitted Penny. "Oh, well, it won't take us long to get the *Icicle* loaded onto the car trailer. Lucky we upset so close to the club house."

Setting to work with a will, the girls took down the flapping sail. After much tugging and pushing, they righted the boat and pulled it toward the Riverview Yacht Club. Closed for the winter, the building looked cold and forlorn. Penny, however, had left her car in the snowy parking lot, which was convenient to the river.

"Wish we could get warm somewhere," Louise said, shivering. "It must be ten below zero."

Pulling the *Icicle* behind them, the girls climbed the slippery river bank. Snow now swirled in clouds, half-curtaining the club house.

"I'll get the car and drive it down here," Penny offered, starting toward the parking lot. "No use dragging the boat any farther."

Abandoning the *Icicle*, Louise went with her chum. A dozen steps took the girls to a wind-swept corner of the deserted building. Rounding it, they both stopped short, staring.

On the snow-banked parking lot where the car had been left, there now stood only one vehicle, an unpainted, two-wheel trailer.

"Great fishes!" exclaimed Penny. "Where's the coupe?"

"Maybe you forgot to set the brake and it rolled into a ditch!"

"In that case, the trailer would have gone with it." Her face grim, Penny ran on toward the parking lot.

Reaching the trailer, the girls saw by tire tracks in the snow that the car had been detached and driven away.

"I knew it! I knew it!" Penny wailed, pounding her mittens together. "The coupe's been stolen!"

"What's that across the road?" Louise demanded. "It looks like an automobile to me. In the ditch, too!"

Taking new hope, Penny went to investigate the little ravine. Through a screen of bare tree branches and bushes, she glimpsed a blur of metal.

"It's the car!" she cried jubilantly. "But how did it get across the road?"

Penny's elation quickly died. Drawing nearer, she was dismayed to see that the coupe appeared to be lying on its stomach in the ditch. Four wheels and a spare had been removed.

"Stripped of every tire!" she exclaimed. "The thief ran the car out here on the road so we couldn't see him at work from the river!"

"What are we going to do?" Louise asked weakly. "We're miles from Riverview. No houses close by. We're half frozen and night is coming on."

Penny, her face very long, had no answer. She measured the gasoline tank with a stick. All of the fuel had been siphoned. She lifted the hood, expecting to find vital parts of the engine missing. However, everything appeared to be in place.

Seeking protection from the penetrating wind, the girls climbed into the car to discuss their situation.

"Can't we just wait here until someone comes along and gives us a lift to town?" suggested Louise.

"Yes, but we're on a side road and few cars travel this way during winter."

"Then why not go somewhere and telephone?"

"The nearest stores are at Kamm's corner, about two miles away."

Louise gazed thoughtfully at the soft snow which was banking deeper on the windshield of the car.

"Two miles in this, facing the wind, will be a hard hike. Think we ought to try it, Penny?"

"I'm sure I don't want to. And we needn't either! Do you remember Salt Sommers?"

"The photographer who works on your father's newspaper?"

"Yes, he spends his spare time as an airplane spotter. His station is over in the hills not more than a half mile from here! Why not tramp over there and ask him to telephone our folks?"

"Are you sure you know the way?"

"I was there once last summer," Penny said confidently. "One follows a side road through the woods. I'm sure I can find it."

"All right," Louise consented, sliding from behind the steering wheel. "If we're going, let's move right along."

Stiff with cold, the girls trudged past the club house and on down the road. Snow was falling faster and faster. Several times they paused to wipe their frosted goggles.

"This promises to be a man-sized blizzard," Louise observed uneasily. "It's getting dark early, too."

Penny nodded, her thoughts on what she would say to her father when she reached home. The car had been fully insured, but even so it would not be easy to replace five stolen tires. Ruefully she reflected that Mrs. Weems, the kindly housekeeper who had looked after her since her mother's death, had not favored the river trip.

"Oh, don't take it so hard," Louise tried to cheer her. "Maybe the thief will be caught."

"Not a chance of it," Penny responded gloomily.

CHAPTER 1 - LOST ON A HILLTOP

A hundred yards farther on the girls came to another side road which wound upward through the wooded hills. Already there was an ominous dusk settling over the valley. Penny paused to take bearings.

"I think this is the way," she said doubtfully.

"You think!"

"Well, I'm pretty sure," Penny amended. "Salt's station is up there on top of one of those hills. If this snow would stop we should be able to see the tower from here."

Slightly reassured, Louise followed her chum across a wooden bridge and up a narrow, winding road. On either side of the frozen ditches, tall frosted evergreens provided friendly protection from the stabbing, icy wind. Nevertheless, walking was not easy for the roadbed bore a shell of treacherous ice.

Confident that they soon would come to the airplane listening post, the girls trudged on. Penny, anxious to make the most of the remaining daylight, set a stiff pace.

"Shouldn't we be coming to the station?" Louise presently asked. "Surely we've gone more than a half mile."

"The post is a little ways off from the road," Penny confessed, peering anxiously at the unbroken line of evergreens. "We should be able to see it."

"In this blinding snow? Why, we may have passed the station without knowing it."

"Well, I don't think so."

"You're not one bit sure, Penny Parker!" Louise accused. "We were crazy to start off without being certain of the post's location."

"We always can go back to the car."

"I'm nearly frozen now," Louise complained, slapping her mittens together. "There's no feeling in one of my hands."

Penny paused to wipe the moisture from her goggles. From far down the road came the sound of a laboring motor. She listened hopefully.

"A car, Lou!" she cried. "Everything will be all right now! We'll hail it and ask the driver for a lift."

Greatly encouraged, the girls waited for the approaching vehicle. They could hear it climbing a steep knoll, then descending. From the sound of the engine they decided that it must be a truck and that it might round the curve at a fast speed.

Worried lest the driver fail to see them, the girls stepped out into the middle of the road. As the truck swerved around the bend, they shouted and waved their arms.

The startled driver slammed on brakes, causing the big black truck to slide like a sled. Penny and Louise leaped aside, barely avoiding being struck.

As they watched anxiously, the driver recovered control of the machine. He straightened out and brought the truck to a standstill farther up the road.

Penny seized her chum's hand. "Come on, Lou! He's going to give us a ride!"

Before they could reach the truck, the driver lowered the cab window. Thrusting his head through the opening he bellowed angrily:

"What you tryin' to do? Wreck my truck?"

Giving the girls no opportunity to reply, he closed the cab window.

Penny saw that the man was intending to drive on. "Wait!" she called frantically. "Please give us a ride! We're lost and half frozen!"

The man heard for he flashed an ugly smile. Shifting gears, he drove away.

"Of all the shabby tricks, that's the worst!" Penny said furiously. "It wasn't our fault his old truck skidded."

"But it is our fault we're lost on this road," Louise added. "How are we ever to find the listening post?"

Penny leaned against the leeward side of a giant pine. Already it was so dark that she could see only a few feet down the road. There were no houses, no lights, nothing to guide her.

"Penny, are we really lost?" Louise demanded, suddenly afraid.

"We really, truly are," her chum answered in a quavering voice. "The post must be somewhere near here, but we'll never find it. All we can do is try to get back to the car."

CHAPTER 2 - AT THE LISTENING POST

Penny's courage did not long forsake her. She had suggested to Louise that they return to the stripped car, but she knew that would not solve their problem. Staring up the dark road, she remarked that they must be close to the summit of the hill.

"Then why not keep on?" urged Louise. "We set out to find the listening post, so let's do it!"

They trudged on up the winding road. At intervals, in an attempt to restore circulation to numbed feet, they ran a few steps. Snow fell steadily, whipping and stinging their faces.

Gasping, half-winded, they kept doggedly on. Finally they struggled into a clearing at the top of the hill. Penny wiped her eyes and gazed down through a gap in the white-coated evergreens. A quarter of the way down the slope on the other side appeared a glowing dot of light.

"I'm afraid it's only a cabin," she said dubiously. "It can't be the airplane listening post."

"Let's go there anyway," advised Louise. "We can warm ourselves and ask how to get back to civilization."

They pushed on, still following the road. Downhill walking was much easier and at intervals they were encouraged by a glimpse of the light.

Then, rounding a bend of the road, the girls came to an artistic, newly constructed iron fence, banked heavily with snow. The fence led to a high gate, and behind the gate loomed a dark, sprawling house with double chimneys.

"The place is deserted!" Louise observed in disappointment. "What became of the light we've been following?"

"It must be farther on. This house looks as if it had been closed for the winter."

Penny went to the gate and rattled a heavy chain which held it in place. Peering through the palings, she could see an unshoveled driveway which curved gracefully to a pillared porch. The spacious grounds were dotted with evergreens and shrubs, so layered with snow that they resembled scraggly ghosts.

"Wonder who owns this place?" speculated Louise.

"Don't know," Penny answered, turning away. "In fact, I don't recall ever having seen it before."

Her words carried special significance to Louise.

"If you've never seen this house before, then we're on a strange road! Penny, we never will find the listening post!"

"I'm beginning to suspect it myself," Penny admitted grimly. "But we must keep plodding on. That light can't be far ahead."

Turning their backs upon the gloomy estate, they again braved the penetrating wind. Soon Louise lost her footing and fell. She remained in a dispirited little heap until Penny pulled her off the ice.

"Let's keep going, Lou," she urged. "It won't be long now."

Louise allowed Penny to pull her along. They rounded a curve in the road, and there, miraculously, the lighted cabin rose before them.

"At last!" exulted Louise. "The Promised Land!"

Staggering up a shoveled path, they pounded on the cabin door. An old man, who held a kerosene lamp, responded promptly.

"Come in, come in!" he invited heartily. "Why, you look half frozen."

"Looks aren't deceitful either," Penny laughed shakily.

As the girls went into the warm room a little whirlpool of wind and snow danced ahead of them. Quickly the old man closed the door. He made places for Penny and Louise at the stove and tossed in a heavy stick of wood.

CHAPTER 2 - AT THE LISTENING POST

"Bad night to be out," he commented cheerfully.

Penny agreed that it was. "We're lost," she volunteered, stripping off her wet mittens. "At least we can't find the airplane listening post."

"Why, it's just a piece farther on," the old man replied. "The tower's right hard to see in this storm."

While they thawed out, the girls explained that they had been forced to abandon their car at the Riverview Yacht Club. The old man, whose name was Henry Hammill, listened with deep sympathy to their tale of woe.

"I'll hitch up my horses and take you to Riverview in the sled," he offered. "That is, unless you'd rather stop at the listening tower."

"It would save you a long trip," Penny returned politely. "If Salt Sommers is on duty, I'm sure he'll take us to our homes."

In the end it was decided that Old Henry should drive the girls as far as the post. Then, if arrangements could not be made with the photographer, he would keep on to Riverview.

Warm at last, Penny and Louise declared that they were ready to start. Old Henry brought the sled to the door and the team soon was racing down the icy road. Above the jingle of bells arose occasional squeals of laughter, for the young passengers enjoyed every minute of the unexpected ride.

Presently Old Henry pulled up at the side of the road.

"There's the tower," he said, pointing to a two-story wooden observatory rising above the evergreens. "I'll wait until you find out if your friend's here."

The girls thanked the old man for his kindly help and scrambled from the sled. They were sure their troubles were over, for they could see Salt Sommers seated at a table in the lighted tower.

A flight of steps led to a narrow catwalk which ran around three sides of the glass-enclosed house. Before Penny and Louise could hammer on the door Salt opened it.

"Well, see what the storm blew in!" the young man exclaimed. "I didn't expect you girls to pop in on a night like this."

"Salt, how soon will you be driving to Riverview?" Penny asked breathlessly.

"About twenty minutes. As soon as my relief shows up."

"May we ride with you?"

"Why, sure."

Penny called down from the catwalk to tell Old Henry he need not wait. With a friendly wave of his hand, the cabin owner drove away. The girls then followed Salt into the drafty tower room.

Curiously they gazed at their surroundings. In the center of the room stood a small coal stove. Above it a tacked sign admonished: "Keep this fire going!" There was a table, two chairs and a telephone. Also a round clock which indicated seven-forty.

Before Penny and Louise could explain why they had come, Salt held up a warning finger.

"Listen!" he exclaimed. "Wasn't that a plane?"

He ran out on the catwalk, letting in an icy blast of wind. In a moment he came back, grinning sheepishly.

"A passenger airplane is due through here about this time. Sometimes I listen for it so hard I imagine the sound of the engine."

"The job must get tiresome at times," Penny ventured, making herself comfortable by the glowing stove.

"Oh, it does, but I'm glad to serve my trick. What brings you girls here on such a wild night?"

The story was quickly told. Nevertheless, by the time Penny had telephoned to Mrs. Weems, it was after eight o'clock. Footsteps pounded on the stairway. An elderly man, his hat and overcoat encrusted with snow, swept into the room.

"My relief," said Salt, presenting Nate Adams to the girls. "I'm free to shove off now."

"Hope you can start your car," commented the newcomer. "It's mighty cold, and the temperature is still dropping."

Salt's battered coupe was parked not far from the tower. Snow blanketed the windshield. He wiped it away and after several attempts started the engine.

"Think I'd better stop at the first garage and have more alcohol put in the radiator. No use in taking a chance."

Salt followed the same road over which the girls had trudged an hour earlier. In passing the estate not far from Old Henry's cabin, Penny peered with renewed interest at the big house. In the blinding snow storm she could not be sure, but she thought a light gleamed from an upstairs window.

"Salt," she inquired, "who lives in that place?"

"Can't tell you," he replied, without turning his head.

"Does anyone live there now?"

"Haven't seen anyone since I took over as observer at the tower. Nate Adams tells me the estate has a private air field. No planes have taken off or landed while I've been on duty."

"I thought I saw a light just now in an upstairs window."

"Probably a reflection from the car headlights," Salt answered carelessly.

The car passed Old Henry's cabin and crept on until it came to a crossroad. Several buildings were clustered on either side of the main highway.

"Guess I'll stop at Mattie's garage," Salt said.

As he pulled up on a gravel runway, a masculine looking woman came to the door of the car. She was in her mid-thirties and wore a man's coat much too large for her. The girls guessed, and correctly, that she was Mattie Williams, owner of the garage and filling station.

"How many will you have?" she asked Salt, briskly clearing the windshield of snow.

The photographer replied that he did not require gasoline, but wanted at least a quart of alcohol.

"Drive into the garage," the woman instructed, opening a pair of double doors. "I'll have Sam take care of it."

As the car rolled into the building, Mattie shouted loudly to a stoop-shouldered man who was busy in the rear office: "Hey, Sam! Look after this customer, will you?"

Sam Burkholder slouched over to the car and began to unscrew the radiator cap. Penny and Louise assumed that the man must be Mattie's husband, but a remark to that effect was corrected by Salt.

"Sam is Mattie's partner," he explained in an undertone. "It's hard to tell which one of them is boss of the place."

Losing interest in the pair, Penny and Louise climbed out of the coupe. They had noticed a cafe next door and thought they might go there for a cup of hot coffee.

"Go ahead," Salt encouraged. "I'll stay here until this job is finished, and join you."

As the girls let themselves out the garage door, a truck pulled up in front of the cafe. They would have given it no more than a casual glance had not the driver alighted. He was a short, ruddy-faced man with a missing front tooth which made his facial expression rather grotesque. Without glancing at the girls, he entered the restaurant.

"That man!" exclaimed Louise. "Haven't we seen him somewhere?"

"We have indeed," agreed Penny grimly. "He's the same driver who refused us a ride. Let's march in there and give him a piece of our minds!"

CHAPTER 3 - AN UNPLEASANT DRIVER

From outside the lighted cafe, the girls could see the truck driver slouched at one of the counter stools.

"I'm willing to go inside," said Louise, "but why start a fuss? After all, I suppose he had a right to refuse us a ride."

"We might have frozen to death!"

"Well, he probably didn't realize we were lost."

"I wish I had your charitable disposition," Penny said with a sniff. "He heard me shout, and he drove away just to be mean."

"Anyway, let's forget it."

Louise took Penny's elbow, steering her toward the cafe. The girls had been friends since grade school days. They made an excellent pair, for Louise exerted a subduing effect upon her impulsive chum.

The only daughter of Anthony Parker, publisher of the *Star*, Penny had a talent for innocently getting into trouble. Inactivity bored her. When nothing more exciting offered, she frequently tried her hand at writing stories for her father's newspaper. Such truly important yarns as *The Vanishing Houseboat*, *The Wishing Well*, *Behind the Green Door*, and *The Clock Strikes Thirteen* had rolled from her typewriter. Penny thoroughly enjoyed reportorial work, but best of all she loved to take an active part in the adventures she recounted.

"Now remember," Louise warned her, "not a word to that truck driver. We'll just snub him."

"Oh, all right. I'll try to behave myself."

Grinning, Penny allowed herself to be guided toward the restaurant. Near the doorway they came to the parked truck, and noticed that it was loaded with large wooden boxes.

"War equipment," commented Penny.

"How do you know?"

"Why, the boxes are unmarked except by numerals. Haven't you noticed, Lou, that's the way machines and materials are transported to and from factories. It's done so no one can tell what's inside."

Penny opened the door and they went into the warm, smoky cafe. As they seated themselves at a table the driver glanced toward them, but seemingly without recognition.

"How about a date tonight, Baby?" he asked the waitress.

Without replying, the girl slapped a menu card on the counter in front of him.

"High toned, ain't you?" he chuckled.

"What will it be?" the waitress demanded impatiently.

"How about a nice smile, Baby?"

Turning away, the waitress started to serve another customer.

"Gimme a cup o' coffee and two sinkers," the driver hurled after her. "And make it snappy too! I'm in a hurry."

Once the coffee and doughnuts had been set before him, the man was in no haste to consume them. He read a newspaper and fed a dollar and a half into a pin-ball machine.

Penny and Louise ordered coffee. Knowing that Salt might be waiting for them, they swallowed the brew scalding hot and arose to leave.

At the cashier's desk Penny paid the bill. Upon impulse she quietly asked the man behind the cash register if he knew the driver.

"Fellow by the name of Hank Biglow," he answered.

GHOST BEYOND THE GATE

Before Penny could ask another question, a police patrol car screeched to a standstill just outside the restaurant. The cafe owner turned to stare as did the driver.

"What are those cops comin' here for?" Hank Biglow demanded.

"How should I know?" retorted the cafe owner. "Maybe they want to ask you a few questions about that cargo you carry!"

"What do you mean by that crack?" the driver asked harshly.

As the cashier shrugged and did not reply, Hank allowed the matter to pass. Although he remained at the counter, he kept watching the police car through the window.

The brief interchange between cafe owner and driver had interested Penny. To delay her departure, she bought a candy bar and began to unwrap it.

Only one policeman had alighted from the car. Tramping into the cafe, he pounded his hands together and sought the warmth of a radiator.

"Mind if I have a little of your heat?" he asked the cafe owner.

"Help yourself."

Penny had been watching Hank Biglow. A moment before the man had sat tense and nervous at the counter. Now he seemed completely relaxed and at ease as he sipped his coffee.

"Hello, Hank," the policeman greeted him. "Didn't see you at first. How's the trucking business?"

"Okay," the trucker growled. "Workin' me night and day."

The casual conversation disappointed Penny. Her first thought had been that Hank Biglow feared a police investigation. Seemingly, she had indulged in wishful thinking.

Having no further reason for remaining in the cafe, the girls stepped out into the storm.

"A pity that policeman wasn't looking for Hank Biglow," Penny muttered.

"I thought for a minute he was," responded Louise, stooping to fasten the buckle of her heavy overshoe. "At least Hank acted peculiar."

"You heard what the cashier said to him?"

"About the cargo he carried?"

"Yes," nodded Penny, "what do you suppose he meant?"

"Don't you think it was intended as a joke?"

"It didn't seem that way to me, Lou. Hank took offense at the remark. He was as nervous as a cat, too."

Penny stared curiously at the big truck which was parked not far from the police car.

"I wonder what can be in those big boxes, Lou?"

"A few minutes ago you said they contained tools or defense plant products."

"That was only my guess. I assumed it from the lack of marking on the boxes."

Penny paused beside the big truck. Pressing her face close to an opening between the slats, she counted ten large crates, all the same size and shape.

"Lou, maybe this isn't defense plant merchandise," she speculated. "Maybe it's some sort of contraband...."

Penny's words trailed off. Someone had touched her on the shoulder.

Whirling around, she faced the same policeman who a moment before had entered the cafe.

"What do you think you're doing?" he inquired.

"Why, just looking," stammered Penny. "We were wondering what's inside these boxes."

"Machinery," replied the policeman. "Now skidoo! Behave yourselves or I'll have to speak to your parents."

CHAPTER 4 - STOLEN TIRES

"We're very sorry," Louise apologized to the policeman. "We didn't suppose it would do any harm to look at the outside of the boxes."

"Run along, run along," the officer said impatiently.

Penny was tempted to make a rather pointed remark, but Louise pulled her away.

"Never argue with a policeman," she whispered. "You always lose."

"We weren't doing any harm," Penny scowled. "What does he think we are, a couple of female spies?"

Entering the garage, the girls saw that the car had been serviced. Salt could be seen inside the little glass-enclosed office.

"I'm waiting for Sam Burkholder," he explained as they joined him. "He took care of the radiator and then disappeared."

Penny and Louise loitered about the office, reading the evening newspaper. After a little delay, Mattie Williams appeared.

"Can you give me my bill?" Salt requested. "We're in a hurry to get to Riverview."

"I thought Sam was looking after you," Mattie replied, making out the slip.

The bill settled, Salt backed the car from the garage. Penny noticed that Hank Biglow's truck no longer stood in front of the cafe. The police car also had gone. She would have thought no more of it, had not Louise at that moment exclaimed:

"Penny, that truck is parked at the rear of the garage now! And they're unloading the boxes!"

Penny twisted around to see for herself. It was true that the big truck had been backed up close to the rear entrance of the garage. Through the blinding snow, she could just see Hank Biglow and Sam Burkholder carrying one of the boxes into the building.

"Well, that's funny!" she exclaimed. "Those crates can't contain defense machinery or materials. Otherwise Hank wouldn't be delivering them here."

"What crates?" inquired Salt, shifting gears.

Penny told him what had transpired in the cafe, and revealed that she and Louise had been rebuked by the policeman. Salt, occupied with driving, did not consider the incident in any way significant.

"Oh, you know how some cops are," he commented carelessly.

The car went into a wild skid and Salt thereafter devoted his attention strictly to driving.

Without further mishap, the party arrived safely at Riverview. Louise alighted at her own home, and then Salt took Penny to the Parker residence.

"Won't you come in for a cup of chocolate?" she invited.

"Thanks, not tonight," Salt replied. "I'm dead tired. Think I'll hit the hay early."

Only one light burned in the living-room as Penny stomped in out of the cold. Mrs. Weems, the plump housekeeper who had served the Parkers for many years, sat beside the hearth, sewing.

"I'm glad you're home at last!" she exclaimed, getting up quickly. "You've no idea how worried I've been."

"But Louise and I telephoned."

"I couldn't hear you very well. I barely was able to make out that something had happened to your car."

"A major catastrophe, Mrs. Weems. Every tire was stolen!"

While the housekeeper bombarded her with questions, Penny stripped off overshoes and heavy outer clothing. Pools of water began to form on the rug.

"Take everything out to the kitchen," Mrs. Weems said hastily. "Have you had your supper?"

"Not even a nibble. And I'm starving!"

As Mrs. Weems began to prepare a hot meal, Penny perched herself on the kitchen table, alternately talking, and chewing on a sugared bun.

"If you ever were lost in an Arctic blizzard you have a good picture of what Louise and I endured," she narrated grandly. "Oh, it was awful!"

"Losing five practically new tires is a mere detail in comparison?"

"It's nothing less than a tragedy! I was thinking—maybe you ought to break the sad news to Dad."

"Indeed not. You'll have to tell him yourself. However, he's attending a meeting and won't be home until eleven."

"That's much too late for me," Penny said quickly. "I'll see him in the morning. And I do hope you cooperate by giving him a dandy breakfast."

"Just see to it that you don't oversleep," suggested the housekeeper dryly.

Penny consumed an enormous supper and then slipped off to bed. She did not hear her father come home a few hours later. In the morning when Mrs. Weems called her, it seemed advisable to take a long time in dressing. Her father had gone by the time she strolled downstairs.

"Did you tell Dad?" she asked the housekeeper hopefully.

"You knew I would," chided Mrs. Weems. "Your father expects to see you at his office at nine o'clock."

"How'd he take the blow?"

"Naturally one couldn't expect him to be pleased."

With a deep sigh, Penny sat down to breakfast. Worry over the coming interview did not interfere with her usual excellent appetite. She had orange juice, two slices of toast, four pancakes, and then, somewhat concerned lest she lose her slim figure, debated whether to ask for another helping.

"The batter's all gone," Mrs. Weems settled the matter. "Do stop dawdling and get on to the office. Your father shouldn't be kept waiting."

With anything but enthusiasm, Penny took herself to the plant of the Riverview *Star*. Passing through the busy newsroom where reporters pounded at their typewriters, she entered her father's private office.

"Hello, Dad," she greeted him with forced cheerfulness. "Mrs. Weems said you wanted to see me."

"So you lost five tires last night?" the editor barked. Mr. Parker was a lean, keen-eyed man of early middle age, known throughout the state as a fearless newspaper man. At the moment, Penny decided that "fearful" would prove a more descriptive term.

"Well, Dad, it was this way—" she began meekly.

"Never mind a long-winded explanation," he interrupted, smiling. "It wasn't your fault—the car was stripped."

Penny wondered if she had heard correctly.

"Your tires weren't the only ones stolen yesterday," Mr. Parker resumed. "A half dozen other thefts were reported. In fact, I've known for several weeks that a professional gang of tire thieves has been operating in Riverview."

"Oh, Dad, you're a peach!" Penny cried, making a dive for him. "I'm going to give you a great big kiss!"

"You are not," Mr. Parker grinned, pushing her away. "Try to remember, this is an office."

Penny resigned herself to a chair. Questioned by her father, she gave a straightforward account of how the car had been stripped at the Yacht Club grounds.

"The tire gang is getting bolder every day!" Mr. Parker exclaimed wrathfully. "But we'll soon put a stop to their little game!"

"How, Dad?"

Mr. Parker hesitated and then said: "I can trust you, can't I, Penny?"

"Of course."

"Then I'll tell you this in confidence. For weeks Jerry Livingston, our star reporter, has been working on the case. He's rounded up a lot of evidence against the outfit."

"Then we have a chance to get those tires back!"

"I'm not thinking about that," Mr. Parker said impatiently. "Jerry's gathered enough evidence to smash the entire gang. It will be as big a story as the *Star* ever published."

"When are you breaking it, Dad?"

CHAPTER 4 - STOLEN TIRES

"Perhaps tomorrow. Depends on the state prosecutor."

"John Gilmore? What does he have to do with it?"

"This story is loaded with dynamite, Penny. If we spread it over our front page before police have a chance to act, the guilty parties are apt to make a getaway."

"That's so," nodded Penny.

"There's another reason I want to consult the Prosecutor before I use the story," Mr. Parker resumed. "Some of the men involved—"

A tap sounded on the door. Without completing what he had started to say, the editor called, "Come in."

Jerry Livingston entered the office. He was a good-looking young man, alert and clean-cut. Smiling at Penny, he slapped a folded paper on Mr. Parker's desk.

"Here's my story on the tire thefts, Chief," he said. "As far as I'm concerned, this winds up the case."

"You've done fine work, Jerry," Mr. Parker praised. "Thanks to your work, we ought to clean out the gang."

"I hope so, Chief. Guess you have all the proofs needed to back up the story."

"All the evidence is locked in my safe. I have an appointment scheduled with the Prosecutor. If he Okays the story, we'll publish it tomorrow. By the way, Jerry, what are your plans?"

"Well, I have a couple of weeks before I go into the Army Air Corps."

"Then treat yourself to a vacation, starting right now," said Mr. Parker. "Can you use it?"

"Can I?" grinned Jerry. "Know what I'll do? I'll hop the noon train and head for the Canadian wilds on a hunting trip."

Mr. Parker wrote out a check which he presented to the young man.

"We'll be sorry to lose you, Jerry," he said regretfully. "But remember, a job always will be waiting when you return."

The reporter shook hands with Mr. Parker and Penny, then left the office.

"We'll miss Jerry around here," the editor remarked.

Penny nodded. She and Jerry had shared many an adventure together, and he was one of her truest friends. The office would not seem the same without him.

"My appointment with the Prosecutor is at ten-thirty," said Mr. Parker briskly. "I'll gather my papers and be on my way."

The editor placed Jerry's signed story in a leather portfolio. Next he went to the safe and fumbled with the dial.

"Want me to open it for you?" Penny asked, after he had tried several times.

Without waiting for a reply, she stooped down, twisted the dial a few times, and opened the heavy door.

"Young lady, how did you learn the combination?" Mr. Parker demanded in chagrin.

"Oh, the numbers are written on the under side of your desk," Penny grinned. "Not a very good place either! You must trust your office help."

"Fortunately my reporters aren't quite as observing as a certain daughter," Mr. Parker retorted grimly.

The editor removed a fat brown envelope from one of the drawers of the safe. Glancing at the papers it contained, he added them to the contents of the portfolio. He then locked the safe.

"How about letting me see that story?" Penny asked.

Mr. Parker smiled but shook his head. "Only two persons know the facts of the case—Jerry and myself."

"Let's make it a trio."

"It will be after I've talked to the Prosecutor. I've got to step right along, too, or I'll be late."

"But Dad—"

"You'll read the story in tomorrow's *Star*—I hope," her father laughed. Picking up the portfolio, he started for the door. "Just contain your impatience until I get back. And please keep those slippery little fingers away from my safe!"

CHAPTER 5 - AN IMPORTANT INTERVIEW

After her father had gone, Penny remained in the private office. Eager to be off, Mr. Parker had neglected to make any arrangements concerning the stripped car at the Riverview Yacht Club.

"Oh, bother!" she thought impatiently. "Now I must wait here until he comes back to learn what I'm to do. The car should be hauled home."

Penny wrote a letter on the typewriter. As she searched for a stamp, the door swung open. A slightly bald, angular man with hard brown eyes, paused on the threshold. The man was Harley Schirr, an assistant editor, next in authority to Mr. DeWitt. Of the entire *Star* staff, he was the only person Penny actively disliked.

"Oh, good morning, Miss Parker," he said with elaborate courtesy. "Your father isn't here?"

"No, he went away a few minutes ago."

"And you are taking care of the office in his absence?" Mr. Schirr smiled. Even so, to Penny's sensitive ears, the words had an insolent ring.

"I'm merely waiting for him to return," she answered briefly. "I came to find out what to do about the car."

"Oh, yes, I heard that all of your tires were stolen last night." Mr. Schirr's lips twitched. "Too bad."

"I may get them back again. Dad says—" Penny checked herself, remembering that the information given her by her father was to be kept secret.

"Yes?" encouraged the assistant editor.

"Perhaps police will catch the thieves," she completed.

"I shouldn't count on it if I were you, Miss Parker. Black Markets have flourished in this city for months. Nothing's been done to stop it."

"Just what do you mean by a Black Market, Mr. Schirr?"

"Illegal trading in various scarce commodities. Tires either stolen or hijacked, are sold by the crooks to so-called honest dealers who serve the public. It's now a big-time business."

"What does Dad think about it?"

"Well, now, I really couldn't tell you. Your father doesn't discuss his editorial policy with me. If he did, I'd warn him to lay off all those tire-theft stories."

Penny gazed quickly at the assistant editor, wondering how much he knew of her father's plan.

"Dad usually prints all the news," she said. "Why should he soft-pedal the tire stories?"

"For his health's sake."

"I'm sure I don't know what you mean, Mr. Schirr."

The assistant editor had closed the door behind him. Warming to his subject, he replied: "The men who have muscled into the tire theft racket are ugly lads without scruples. If your father stupidly insists upon trying to smash the outfit, he may not wake up some morning."

The suggestion that her father might ruthlessly be done away with shocked Penny. And a canny corner of her mind demanded to know how Mr. Schirr could be so well informed. She was quite certain her father had not taken him into his confidence.

"Dad is no coward," she said proudly.

"Oh, no one ever questioned his bravery, Miss Parker. Your father is courageous to the point of rashness. But if he prints an exposé story about the tire theft gang, it's apt to prove the most foolish act of his life."

"How do you know he intends to do such a thing?"

The question, sharply put, surprised Mr. Schirr.

"Oh, I don't," he denied hastily. "I merely heard the rumor around the office."

CHAPTER 5 - AN IMPORTANT INTERVIEW

Penny made no reply. As the silence became noticeable, the assistant editor murmured that he would return to see Mr. Parker later and left the office.

Penny glared at the man's retreating back. Even more intensely than before, she disliked Harley Schirr.

"The old sneak cat!" she thought. "I'll bet a cent he's been listening at the door or prying in Dad's papers! I'm sure no rumors have been circulating around the office."

The telephone rang. Automatically Penny took down the receiver.

"Mr. Parker?" inquired a masculine voice.

"He's not here now. This is his daughter speaking. May I take a message?"

"No message," said the purring voice. "Mr. Parker may hear from me later."

"Who is this, please?" asked Penny quickly.

There was no answer, only the click of a receiver being hung on its hook.

The incident, although trifling, annoyed Penny. Getting up from the desk, she walked to the window. Mr. Schirr's intimation had alarmed her, and now the telephone call added to her uneasiness.

"Probably the man who telephoned is well known to Dad," she tried to assure herself. "I'm just imagining that his voice sounded sinister."

Feeling the need of an occupation, Penny wandered out into the editorial room. She chatted with the society editor and for a time watched the world news reports coming in on the noisy teletype machines.

"Need a job?" inquired Editor DeWitt at the slot of the circular copy desk. "How about writing a few headlines for me?"

"No, thanks," Penny declined. "I'm just waiting for Dad. He should be back any minute now."

It was eleven-forty by the office clock. Never had time seemed to pass so slowly. As Penny debated whether or not to wait any longer, there was a sudden stir in the room. Glancing toward the outside door, she saw that Jerry Livingston, suitcase in hand, had entered.

Immediately reporters and editors left their desks to shake his hand.

"Jerry, you're the best reporter this paper ever had," Mr. DeWitt told him warmly. "We surely hate to see you go."

"Oh, I'll be back," the reporter answered. "You can bet on that!"

Penny crossed the room to say goodbye. Jerry surprisingly tucked her arm through his.

"Come along and see me off on the train," he invited, pulling her along. "Not doing anything special, are you?"

"Just waiting for Dad."

"Then come on," Jerry grinned. "I've got a lot to say to you."

However, once in the taxi, speeding toward the railroad station, the reporter scarcely spoke. He reached out and captured her hand.

"I'm going to miss you, little twirp," he sighed. "No telling when I'll get back to the *Star*. Maybe—"

"Now don't try to work on my sympathies," laughed Penny, though a lump came in her throat. "Oh, Jerry—"

"At your command. Just break down and confess how desolate you'll be without me."

The railroad station was close by and Penny had only a moment to talk.

"Riverview will be a blank without you," she admitted. "But it's that tire-theft story I want to ask you about. Did you ever tell anyone that Dad is planning to expose the gang?"

"Of course not!"

"I knew you wouldn't give out any information," Penny said in relief. "But somehow Harley Schirr has learned about it."

"Schirr! That egg? How could he have found out?"

"I'd like to know myself. He hinted that something dreadful might happen to Dad if the story is printed."

Jerry patted Penny's hand. "Don't give it a thought, kid," he said. "Schirr does a lot of wild talking. Probably whatever he said to you was pure bluff. He doesn't know a thing."

The arrival of the cab at the station put an end to the conversation. Jerry paid the driver and hustled Penny inside. He barely had time to purchase a ticket before the train was called.

"Well, goodbye," Jerry said, squeezing her hand.

"Have a good time in Canada," Penny replied. "And bring me a nice bear rug!"

"Sure, I'll catch him with my bare hands," Jerry rejoined, making a feeble attempt at a joke.

The train began to move. The reporter swung himself aboard the last Pullman. As he waved from the steps, Penny realized that she had forgotten to ask for his Canadian address.

Soon the train was only a blur down the frosty tracks. Penny climbed a steep ramp to the street. She felt lonesome, and for some reason, discouraged.

"First I lose my car wheels, and now it's Jerry," she reflected sadly. "What a week!"

Penny scarcely knew whether to go home or to the *Star* office. As she debated the matter, her ears were assaulted by the shrill scream of a siren.

"A fire," thought Penny.

An ambulance rushed past. It raced to the end of the short street and pulled up.

"Probably an accident," amended Penny.

Curious to learn what had happened, she began to run. At the end of the street a large crowd had gathered. A car with a smashed fender and damaged front grillwork, had piled against a street lamp.

"What happened?" Penny asked a man who stood beside her.

"Two cars in a smash-up," he answered. "Didn't see the accident myself."

"But what became of the other automobile?" asked Penny.

She pushed through the gathering crowd to the curb. Broken glass was scattered over the pavement. Ambulance men were searching the wreckage of the car which had struck the lamp post. The other automobile, apparently, had driven away.

Suddenly, Penny's gaze riveted on the rear license plate of the smashed car. In horror she read the number—P-619-10.

"Dad's car!" she whispered. "He's been hurt!"

CHAPTER 6 - FRONT PAGE NEWS

Never in her life had Penny been more frightened. Breaking away from the group of people at the curb, she ran to the parked ambulance. A glance into the interior assured her that Mr. Parker had not been placed inside on a stretcher.

"Where is he?" she asked wildly. "Where's my father?"

A white-garbed ambulance attendant turned to stare at her.

"That's my father's car!" Penny cried, pointing to the battered sedan. "Tell me, was he badly hurt?"

The attendant tried to be kind. "We don't know, Miss. Someone put in a call for us. Said we were to pick up an injured man. Evidently he was taken to a hospital before we could get here."

"That's what happened," contributed a small boy who stood close by. "A woman drove by in an auto. She offered to take the man to the hospital and he went with her."

"A tall, lean man in a gray suit?" Penny asked quickly.

"Yes. He had a leather case in his hand."

"Then it was my father!" Penny cried. "How badly was he hurt?"

"Oh, he could walk all right," the boy replied. "He seemed kinda dazed though."

Greatly relieved to learn that her father had escaped serious injury, Penny sought more information. The boy who had witnessed the accident, told her that the car which had caused the smash-up, was a blue sedan.

"Two men were in it," he revealed. "They started to go around your father's car and crowded him toward the curb. Next thing I saw, he'd plowed into the lamp post."

"The other car didn't stop?"

"I'll say it didn't! You should have seen 'em go!"

"Didn't you notice the license number?" Penny asked hopefully.

The boy shook his head.

Having learned all she could from him, Penny questioned other persons. Only one woman in the crowd was able to provide additional information. Her eye-witness account differed slightly from the boy's, but she confirmed that a middle-aged woman in a black coupe had taken the accident victim to a hospital.

"Which hospital?" asked Penny.

The woman could not tell her. She did say, however, that the accident victim seemingly had suffered only minor scratches.

A police car drove up. Penny, frantic to find her father, did not wish to be delayed by questions. Without revealing who she was to members of the investigation squad, she hailed a taxi. Mercy Hospital was only a few blocks away. It seemed reasonable that her father would be taken there for treatment.

A few minutes later, standing anxiously at the information desk of that institution, she learned that Mr. Parker had not been admitted as a patient. The nurse in charge, noting the girl's agitation, kindly offered to telephone other hospitals. After six calls, she reported that she was unable to trace the accident victim.

"Are you sure that your father sought hospital treatment?" she asked Penny.

"Perhaps not. Dad wasn't badly hurt according to witnesses. He may have gone elsewhere."

Thanking the nurse for her help, Penny taxied swiftly home. Mrs. Weems, in an old coat and a turban, was pouring salt on the icy sidewalk in front of the house. From the look on her face it was evident she had not heard the news.

"Mrs. Weems, Dad's been hurt!" Penny cried, leaping from the cab. "In an auto accident!"

"My land!" the housekeeper gasped and allowed the bag of salt to fall from her gloved hand. "How bad is it?"

"I think he was more stunned than anything else. But I've not been able to learn where he was taken. He didn't telephone here?"

"Not unless it was since I've been outdoors."

Picking up the bag of salt, Mrs. Weems followed Penny into the house. Without removing coat or hat, the girl dialed the *Star* office. Editor DeWitt answered.

"Has Dad arrived there?" Penny asked abruptly.

"No, he hasn't returned. Anything wrong?"

Tersely Penny revealed what had occurred. The news shocked the editor for he bore Mr. Parker a genuine affection.

"Now don't you worry," he tried to cheer her. "Your father can't be badly hurt or he never would have walked away from that accident. Just sit tight and our reporters will locate him for you."

During the next hour Penny and Mrs. Weems remained near the telephone. Each moment they waited, their anxiety increased. Mr. DeWitt did not phone. There was no word from the police station. They refused to believe that Mr. Parker had been seriously injured, yet it seemed strange he could not be found.

"It's not like him to allow anyone to worry," declared the housekeeper. "I simply can't understand why he doesn't call to relieve our minds."

Just then the telephone bell jingled. Penny snatched the receiver from its hook.

"DeWitt speaking," said the familiar voice of the editor.

"Any news?" Penny asked quickly. "Did you find Dad?"

"So far we haven't," the editor confessed. "I've personally called the police station, every hospital and private nursing home in Riverview."

"Dad may have gone to a doctor's office for treatment."

"I thought of that," replied DeWitt. "We've checked all the likely ones."

"What could have become of him?" Penny asked desperately. "Mrs. Weems and I are dreadfully worried."

"Oh, he'll show up any minute," comforted Mr. DeWitt. "Probably he doesn't realize anyone is looking for him."

Penny asked the editor if he had learned the identity of the hit-skip driver.

"No one took down the license number of the car," Mr. DeWitt returned regretfully. "Our reporters are still working on the story though."

"The story," murmured Penny faintly. For the first time it occurred to her that her father's accident and subsequent disappearance would be regarded as front page news.

"I don't expect to run an account of the accident until I've talked to your father," DeWitt said hastily. "Now don't worry about anything. I'll let you know the minute I have any news."

Penny hung up the receiver and reported the conversation to Mrs. Weems. A clock on the mantel chimed one-thirty, reminding the housekeeper that lunch had not been prepared.

"No food for me," pleaded Penny. "I don't feel like eating."

"I've rather lost my own appetite," confessed the housekeeper. "However, it's foolish of us to worry. Your father must be safe. No doubt he had an appointment."

Penny's face brightened. "Why, of course!" she exclaimed. "Don't know why I've been so dumb! Dad may still be in conference with Prosecutor Gilmore! I'll call there."

Darting to the telephone, she waited patiently until she was connected with the State prosecutor's office. The lawyer himself talked to her.

"Why, no, Mr. Parker hasn't been here," he replied to her eager inquiry. "I expected him at ten-thirty. Then he telephoned that he had been delayed and would see me at eleven-thirty. He failed to keep that appointment also."

The information sent Penny's hopes glimmering. She explained about the accident and listened to the Prosecutor's expression of sympathy. Replacing the receiver, she turned once more to Mrs. Weems.

"I'm more worried than ever now," she quavered. "Dad didn't keep his appointment with Prosecutor Gilmore, and it was a vitally important one."

"We'll hear from him soon—"

CHAPTER 6 - FRONT PAGE NEWS

"Perhaps we won't." Penny took a quick turn across the room.

"Why, such a thing to say! What do you mean, Penny?"

"Dad has enemies. Harley Schirr told me today that if any attempt was made to expose a certain gang of thieves, it would mean real trouble."

"But your father has had no connection with such persons."

"He and Jerry worked on a case together," Penny explained. "Today at the time of the accident, Dad carried a brief case with all the evidence in it!"

"Even so, I fail to see—"

"According to the report, Dad's car was practically forced off the road," Penny added excitedly. "I think that auto crash was deliberately engineered! Don't you understand, Mrs. Weems? He's fallen into the clutches of his enemies!"

"Now, Penny," soothed the housekeeper. "I'm sure we're making far too much of the accident. We'll soon hear from your father."

"You're saying that to comfort me, Mrs. Weems. Something dreadful has happened! I can *feel* it."

Penny ceased pacing the floor and went to the hall closet for her hat and coat.

"Where are you going?" asked the housekeeper, her eyes troubled.

"To the newspaper office. If word comes, I want to be there to get it the very first minute."

Mrs. Weems started to protest, then changed her mind. She merely said: "Telephone me the moment you have any news."

A brisk walk to the *Star* office did much to restore Penny's sagging courage. As she entered the newsroom, brushing snow from her coat, she saw a group of reporters gathered about Mr. DeWitt's desk.

"News of Dad!" she thought, her pulse pounding.

Glimpsing Penny, the men at the desk began to scatter. They gazed at her in such a kind, sympathetic manner that she became frightened again.

"What is it, Mr. DeWitt?" she asked the editor. "Has Dad been found?"

He shook his head.

"But you must have had some news," she insisted, her gaze on a folded paper which he held. "Please don't hide anything from me."

"Very well," DeWitt responded quietly. "We found this letter in your father's waste-basket."

Penny took the paper. Silently she read the message which had been typed in capital letters.

"MR. PARKER," it warned, "THIS IS TO ADVISE YOU TO LAY OFF ON TIRE THEFT STORIES IN YOUR PAPER. UNLESS YOU CHANGE YOUR POLICY YOU MAY WAKE UP IN A DITCH."

CHAPTER 7 - QUESTIONS WITHOUT ANSWERS

"I'd rather not have shown that note to you," Mr. DeWitt said quietly. "We found it only a moment ago."

"How did it get in Dad's waste-basket?" Penny asked. "Do you suppose he threw it there himself?"

"That's my guess. Your father never paid any attention to unsigned letters."

Penny reread the threatening note, trying not to show how much it disturbed her. "I wonder if this came by mail?" she remarked.

"We don't know," DeWitt replied. "There was no envelope in the basket."

"Dad never mentioned such a note to me," Penny resumed, frowning. "Probably thought I'd worry about it. This makes the situation look bad, doesn't it, Mr. DeWitt?"

The editor weighed his words carefully before he spoke. "It doesn't prove that your father was waylaid by enemies, Penny. Not at all. According to reports, Mr. Parker was involved in an ordinary automobile accident, and left the scene of his own free will."

"With a woman who drove a black car."

"Yes, according to eye-witnesses she offered to take him to a hospital for treatment."

"What became of that woman?" demanded Penny. "Can't the police find her?"

"Not so far."

Before Penny could say more, Harley Schirr came to the desk, spreading a dummy sheet for the editor to inspect.

"Here's the front-page layout," he explained. "For the banner we'll give 'em, 'Anthony Parker Mysteriously Disappears,' and beneath it, a double column story. I dug a good picture out of the morgue—the one with Parker dedicating the Riverview Orphans' Home."

DeWitt frowned as he studied the layout. "Parker wouldn't like this, Schirr. It's too sensational. Bust that banner and cut the story down to the bare facts."

"But this is a big story—"

"I'm expecting Mr. Parker to walk in here any minute," retorted DeWitt. "A 'disappearance' spread would make the *Star* look silly."

"Mr. Parker's not going to show up!" Schirr refuted, his eyes blazing. "I say we should play the story for all it's worth."

"I'm sure Dad would hate sensationalism," Penny said, siding with Mr. DeWitt.

The assistant editor turned to glare at her. Although he made no reply, she read anger and dislike in his flashing eyes.

"Cut the story down," DeWitt ordered curtly. "And try to find a more suitable picture of Mr. Parker."

Schirr swept the dummy sheet from the desk, crumpling it in his hand. As he started for the morgue where pictures were filed, he muttered to himself.

"Don't know what's got into that fellow lately," DeWitt sighed.

The editor sat down rather heavily and Penny noticed that he looked tired and pale. For fifteen years he had been closely associated with Mr. Parker, regarding his chief with deep affection.

"Do you feel well, Mr. DeWitt?" she inquired.

"Not so hot," he admitted, reaching for a pencil. "Lately I've been having a little pain in my side—it's nothing though. Just getting old, that's all."

"Why not take the day off, Mr. DeWitt? You've been working too hard."

"Now wouldn't this be a fine time to go home?" the editor barked. "Hard work agrees with me."

CHAPTER 7 - QUESTIONS WITHOUT ANSWERS

Reminded that she was keeping Mr. DeWitt from his duties, Penny soon left the *Star* office. Debating a moment, she walked to the nearby police station. There she was courteously received by Chief Jalman, a personal friend of her father's.

"We'll find Mr. Parker," he assured her confidently. "His description has been broadcast over the radio. We've instructed all our men to be on the watch for him."

Penny broached the possibility that her father had been waylaid by enemies.

"Facts fail to support such a theory," replied Chief Jalman. "It's my opinion your father will show up any hour, wondering what the fuss is all about."

Penny left the police station rather cheered. Almost without thinking, she chose a route which led toward the scene of the accident. Reaching the familiar street, she noted that her father's battered car had been towed away. All broken glass had been swept from the pavement.

"When I was here before I should have questioned more people," she thought. "It never occurred to me then that Dad would fail to show up."

Noticing a candy store which fronted the street close to the bent lamp post, Penny went inside. A friendly looking woman with gray hair came to serve her.

"I'm not a customer," Penny explained. She added that her father had been injured in the car accident, and that she was seeking information.

"I've already been questioned by police detectives," replied the owner of the candy shop. "I'm afraid I can't tell you very much."

"Did you witness the accident?"

"Oh, yes, I saw it, but it happened so fast I wasn't sure whose fault it was."

"You didn't take down the license number of the blue hit-skip car?"

"Was it blue?" the woman inquired. "Now I told the police, maroon."

"My information came from a small boy, so he may have been mistaken. Did you notice the woman who offered my father a ride?"

"Oh, yes, she was about my age—around forty."

"Well dressed?"

"Rather plainly, I would say. But she drove a fine, late-model car."

"Would you consider her a woman of means?"

"Judging from the car—yes."

Penny asked many more questions, trying to gain an accurate picture of the woman who had aided her father. She was somewhat reassured when the candy shop owner insisted that Mr. Parker had entered the car of his own free will.

"Did he seem dazed by the accident?" she asked thoughtfully.

"Well, yes, he did. I saw your father get into the car sort of holding his head. Then he asked the woman to stop at the curb."

"Why was that?"

"He'd forgotten something—a leather carrying case. At any rate, he returned to his own auto for it. Then he drove away with the woman."

As puzzled as ever, Penny went out on the street once more. The weather had turned colder, but she scarcely felt the icy blast which whipped her face.

It was silly to worry, she told herself sternly. Why, all the facts supported Police Chief Jalman's belief that her father soon would return home. Mrs. Weems was confident he would be found safe—so was Mr. DeWitt. After all, only five hours had elapsed since the accident. A disappearance couldn't be considered serious in such a short period.

But try as she might, Penny could not free her mind of grave misgivings. She could not forget the mysterious telephone call, the threatening letter, and Harley Schirr's cocksure opinion that her father would not be found.

She stood disconsolate, gazing into the whirling snow storm. At the end of the street the railroad station loomed as a dark blur, reminding her of Jerry. If only he hadn't gone away! Jerry was the one person who might help her, and she knew of no way to reach him.

CHAPTER 8 - A FEW CHANGES

Next morning, Penny, red-eyed because she had slept little, walked slowly toward the *Star* office. Throughout the long night there had been no word from Mr. Parker.

At every street corner newsboys shouted the latest headlines—that the publisher had been missing nearly twenty-four hours. Even the *Star* carried a black, ugly banner across its front page.

Penny bought a copy, reading with displeasure the story of Mr. Parker's disappearance.

"I can't understand why Mr. DeWitt let this go through," she thought. "If Dad were here, he'd certainly hate it."

Entering the lobby of the *Star* building, Penny pressed the elevator button. A long time elapsed before the cage descended. To her surprise she saw that it was operated, not by Mose Johnson, the colored man, but by the janitor.

"Sorry to keep you waiting, Miss Penny," the man apologized. "I'm not much good at operating this contraption."

"Where is Mose this morning, Charley?"

"Fired."

Penny could not hide her amazement. The old colored man had been employed ten years at the *Star* plant. Although not strictly efficient, Mose's habits were good, and Mr. Parker had taken an affectionate interest in him.

"It's a shame, if you ask me," the janitor added.

"What happened, Charley? Who discharged him?"

"That guy Schirr."

"Harley Schirr? But he has no authority."

"An editor can fire and hire. I think he was just tryin' out his stuff on poor old Mose."

"During my father's absence, Mr. DeWitt is in full charge here," Penny said emphatically.

"DeWitt *was* in charge. But they hauled him off to the hospital last night with a bad pain in his tummy. Seems he had an appendicitis attack. The doctor rushed him off and didn't even wait until morning to operate."

The news stunned Penny. She murmured that she hoped Mr. DeWitt was doing well.

"Reckon he is," agreed the janitor. "We all chipped in and sent him some flowers—roses. Mose gave fifty cents, too."

Penny's mind came back to the problem of the colored man.

"So Mr. Schirr discharged him," she commented. "I wonder why?"

The janitor pressed a button and the cage moved slowly upward.

"Mose was due on at midnight," he explained. "He didn't get here until after two o'clock."

"Didn't he have a reason for being so late?"

The cage stopped with a jerk. "Sure, Mose had a pip this time! Something about being detained by a ghost! Schirr didn't go for it at all. Swelled up like a poisoned pup and fired Mose on the spot."

"I'm sorry," Penny replied. "Dad liked Mose a lot."

"Any news from your father?"

Penny shook her head. As far as possible she was determined to keep her troubles to herself. Turning to leave the cage, she inquired:

"Where is Mose now? At home?"

CHAPTER 8 - A FEW CHANGES

"He's down in the boiler room, sittin' by the furnace. Says he's afraid to go home for fear his old lady will give him the works."

"Will you please ask Mose to wait there for me?" Penny requested. "I want to talk to him before he leaves the building."

"I'll be glad to tell him," the janitor said. Hesitating, he added: "If you've got any influence with Schirr, you might speak a good word for me."

"Why for you?" smiled Penny. "Surely your job is safe."

"I don't know about that," the janitor responded gloomily. "This morning when Schirr was comin' up in the elevator he said to me: 'Charley, there's going to be a few changes made around here. I'm going to cut out all the old, useless timber.' He looked at me kinda funny-like too. You know, I passed my sixty-eighth birthday last August."

"Now don't start worrying, Charley," Penny cheered him. "We couldn't run this building without you."

Deeply troubled, she tramped down the hall to the newsroom. Reporters were in a fever of activity, pounding out their stories. Copy boys had a nervous, tense expression as they ran to and fro on their errands. Harley Schirr, however, was not in evidence.

"The Big Shot has sealed himself in your father's office!" informed one of the copy desk men in a muted voice. "Guess you heard about DeWitt?"

Penny nodded.

"The Great Genius has taken over, and how! This place is operating on an efficiency-plus basis now. Why, he's got me so cockeyed, I compose poetry."

Penny crossed to her father's office, tapping on the frosted glass door.

"Who is it?" demanded Schirr, his voice loud and unpleasant.

Penny spoke her name. In a moment the door opened, and the editor bowed and smiled. As if she were a guest of honor, he motioned her to a seat.

"We're doing everything we can to trace your father," he said. "So far, we've had no luck and the police admit they are baffled. I can't express to you how sorry I am."

To Penny's ears the words were words only, lacking sincerity. Determining to waste no time, she spoke of DeWitt's sudden illness.

"Oh yes, he'll be off duty for at least a month," replied Mr. Schirr. "Naturally in his absence I have assumed charge. We put out a real paper this morning."

"I saw the front page."

Penny longed to say that the story about her father had displeased her. However, she knew it would do no good. The account, once printed, could not be recalled. Far better, she reasoned, to let the matter pass.

"I hear Mose Johnson has been discharged," she remarked.

"Yes, we had to let him go." Mr. Schirr opened a desk drawer, helping himself to one of Mr. Parker's cigars. "Mose is indolent, irresponsible—a drag on the payroll."

"My father always liked him."

"Yes, he did seem to favor the old coot," agreed Schirr with a shrug. "Well, thank you for dropping in, Miss Parker. If we have any encouraging news, I'll see that you are notified at once."

Well aware that she had been dismissed, Penny left the office. Schirr's attitude angered her. He had made her feel unwelcome in her own father's newspaper plant.

As she closed the door behind her, she realized that nearly every eye in the apparently-busy newsroom, had focused upon her. Deliberately, she composed herself. Acting undisturbed, she swept past the rows of desks to a rear stairway leading to the basement.

The janitor had delivered her message to Mose Johnson. She found the old colored man curled up fast asleep on a crate by the warm stove.

Penny touched Mose on the arm. He straightened up as suddenly as if someone had set off a fire-cracker.

"Oh, Miss Penny!" he beamed. "I'se suah su'prised at seein' you down heah in dis dumpy fu'nace room. But I thanks you just the same fo' wakin' me up out o' dat ghost dream."

"Were you having a ghost dream?" echoed Penny.

"Yes, Miss. Yo' see I was dreamin' about dat same ghost I saw last night on de way to work."

Penny, fully aware that Mose was directing the conversation where he wished it to go, hid a smile.

"I heard about that, Mose," she commented. "It must have been quite a lively ghost to make you two hours late."

"It suah was a lively ghost," Mose confirmed, bobbing his woolly head. "Why, it walked around jest like a live pu'son."

"Aren't you being a bit superstitious, Mose?"

"Deedy not, Miss. You is supe'stitious when you sees a ghost dat ain't dar. But when you sees one dat is dar you ain't supe'stitious. You is jest plain scared!"

"Suppose you tell me about it," Penny invited.

"Well, Miss Penny, it was like dis," began the old colored man. "At half past eleven I starts off fo' work same as always. I picks up mah lunch box de ole lady packed fo' me, an' scoots off toward de bus stop to get de 11:45. But I nevah get dar. When I was goin' down dat road runnin' past de old Harrison place, I seen de ghost."

"The Harrison place?" interrupted Penny. "Where is that?"

"You know de road that winds up Craig Hill? It's out towa'd de boat club."

"You don't mean that big estate house with the fence surrounding it?"

"Dat's de place! Well, I seed dis heah ghost a cavortin' around behind de big iron gate dat goes in to de old Harrison place. De ghost nevah sees me, but I gets a good close-up of him. He was dressed in white and he was carryin' his own tombstone around in his arms jes' like it doan weigh nothin'."

"Oh, Mose!" protested Penny. "And then what happened? Did the ghost disappear?"

"No, Miss," grinned the colored man, "but I did! I turns tail an' runs as fast as a man half mah age could go, an' I nevah stops fo' nuthin' till I gits back to mah own place.

"When I tells mah ole lady what was goin' on she says, 'Mose, you sees white ghosts 'cause you been a drinkin' some mo' o' dat white-eye. It's twelve o'clock dis minute and you'se missed de last bus. Now you start walkin'! And if you is fired, don't nevah da'ken dat do' no mo'.'"

Old Mose drew a deep sigh. "And dat's jest what happened, Miss Penny. I ain't got no job an' no mo' home than a rabbit. I'se suah bubblin' oveh with trouble. It all come from seein' dat ghost you says I didn't see."

"I'm sure you thought you saw one," replied Penny. "If you'll promise to attend strictly to your duties hereafter, I'll ask Mr. Schirr to reinstate you on the payroll."

Old Mose brightened. "I suah nuff will!" he said jubilantly. "I won't have no mo' truck with dat ghost. No sir!"

To face Mr. Schirr once more, was a most unpleasant ordeal for Penny. Nevertheless, she sought his office, apologizing for the intrusion.

"I *am* busy," the editor said pointedly. "What is it you want?"

Penny explained that she had talked with Mose Johnson and was convinced that his offense would not be repeated.

"I want you to put him back on his old job," she requested.

"Impossible!"

"Why do you take that attitude?" inquired Penny, stiffening for an argument. "Dad always liked Mose."

"One can't mix sentiment with business. I have a job to do here and I intend to do it efficiently."

"Dad probably will show up before another day."

"I don't like to dash your hopes," said Mr. Schirr. "We've tried to spare your feelings. Perhaps your father will be found, but you know I tried to warn him he was inviting trouble when he mixed with the tire-theft gang."

"So you believe Dad has fallen into the clutches of those men?"

"I do."

"What makes you think so? Have you any evidence?"

"Not a scrap."

"And how did you learn Dad intended to expose the higher-ups?"

"I don't mind telling you I heard him talking to Jerry Livingston about it."

"Oh, I see."

"We're getting nowhere with this discussion," Mr. Schirr said impatiently. "I really am busy—"

"Will you reinstate Mose?" Penny asked, reverting to the original subject.

CHAPTER 8 - A FEW CHANGES

"I've already given my answer."

"After all, this is my father's paper," Penny said, trying to control her voice. "It's not a corporation. Only Dad's money is invested here."

"So what?"

"As a personal favor I ask you to reinstate Mose."

"You're making an issue of it?"

"Call it that if you like."

Mr. Schirr's dark eyes blazed. He slammed a paper weight across the desk and it dropped to the floor with a hard thud.

"Very well," he said stiffly, "we'll restore your pet to the payroll."

"Thank you, Mr. Schirr."

"But get this, Miss Parker," the editor completed. "We may as well have an understanding. While your father is absent, I'm in full charge here. In the future I'll have no interference from you or any other person."

CHAPTER 9 - AN OPEN SAFE

Rather flattened by the interview with Mr. Schirr, Penny was glad to leave the *Star* plant. Going down in the elevator, she requested Charley to tell Mose Johnson that he had been restored to his old job.

"That's fine!" the janitor beamed. "Mighty glad to hear it." Opening the cage door, he inquired: "Will you be going to see Mr. DeWitt?"

"I thought I would."

"He's at City Hospital. You might tell him that we all miss him around here."

"I'll certainly deliver the message," promised Penny.

City Hospital was only six blocks away. Penny bought flowers and then presented herself at the institution. After a brief wait in the lobby, she was allowed to see Mr. DeWitt for a few minutes.

"Good morning," she said cheerfully, handing the box of flowers to a nurse.

Mr. DeWitt, pale and weak, stirred and turned his head so that he could see her.

"What's good about it?" he muttered with a trace of his old spirit. "They won't even let me sit up!"

"I should think not," smiled Penny. She sat down in a chair beside the bed.

"Of all times to get laid up!" the editor went on. "Heard from your father?"

Penny shook her head. A long silence followed, and then she said brightly:

"But he'll be found—probably today."

Mr. DeWitt lay with his eyes closed. "I've been thinking—" he mumbled drowsily.

"Yes?" Penny waited.

"Mind's still fogged with that blamed ether," DeWitt muttered. "About your father—" His voice trailed off.

"Do you think he could have been waylaid by enemies?" Penny asked after a moment. "Mr. Schirr believes his disappearance has a connection with the tire-theft gang."

Mr. DeWitt's eyes opened again. "I don't know," he mumbled. "Your father was planning to break a big story—didn't tell me much about it."

"You don't know what evidence he carried in the portfolio when he went to see the State Prosecutor?"

DeWitt shook his head. "Jerry'll know."

"But how can I reach him?"

"Didn't he leave an address at the office?"

"I don't think so."

"Then there's no way to reach him." Exhausted from so much talking, DeWitt fell silent. At length however, he aroused himself and asked: "Have you tried your father's safe?"

"For Jerry's address?"

"No, the names of the tire-theft gang. If the police had something to work on—"

"Dad took a lot of papers out just before he started for the Prosecutor's office," Penny replied thoughtfully. "But some of the evidence may have been left. It's worth investigating."

The nurse returned to the room with a vase for the flowers.

"I'm afraid I can't allow you to remain much longer," she said regretfully.

As she arose to go, Penny remembered to deliver Old Charley's message.

"How's everything at the office?" Mr. DeWitt asked. "Who's in charge?"

"Harley Schirr."

Mr. DeWitt's forehead wrinkled. "Now I know I've got to roll out of here!" he declared. "Things will be in a nice state by the time I get back."

CHAPTER 9 - AN OPEN SAFE

Penny did not wish to worry him. "Oh, everything will go along," she soothed. "Mr. Schirr is very efficient in his methods."

"And opinionated," muttered DeWitt. "Oh, well, I'll be back on the job in ten days."

Penny did not disillusion him. Saying goodbye, she returned to the newspaper office. Pausing at the downstairs advertising department, she talked to Bud Corbin, a close friend of Jerry's.

"This is the only address Jerry gave me," Mr. Corbin said, taking a card from his billfold. "A wire might reach him. But there's a good chance it won't. When he left here, he wasn't sure he'd stop at Elk Horn Lodge."

Grateful for the address, Penny composed a telegram which the advertising man offered to send for her. In the message she not only told of her father's strange disappearance, but asked for a complete duplication of material lost in the portfolio.

"At least I've started the ball rolling," she thought, with renewed hope in her efforts. "I believe Jerry can help if only he gets the wire."

Penny had not forgotten Mr. DeWitt's suggestion that some evidence against the tire-theft gang might be found in Mr. Parker's safe.

"I hate to open it while Dad is away," she reflected. "Still, I know the combination, and I'm sure he would want me to do it."

To brave Harley Schirr a second time was a duty not to Penny's liking. She debated waiting until after four o'clock when the editor doubtless would leave the building. But time was precious and she could not afford to wait.

"What am I, a coward?" she prodded herself. "Why should I be afraid of Harley Schirr? When Dad gets back on the job, he'll bounce him back where he belongs."

Penny's reappearance in the newsroom created a slight stir. However, no one spoke to her as she walked straight to her father's office. The door was closed.

"Mr. Schirr isn't in conference?" she asked one of the copy readers.

"No, just go right on in," the man returned carelessly.

Without knocking, Penny opened the door. On the threshold, she paused, startled. Harley Schirr was down on his knees in front of the open safe. Evidently he had been going through Mr. Parker's private papers in systematic fashion for he was circled by little piles of manila envelopes.

Mr. Schirr was even more startled than Penny. He sprang to his feet, the picture of guilt. Then, recovering his poise, he scowled and demanded: "Here again?"

Penny carefully closed the office door before she spoke. Then her words were terse.

"Mr. Schirr, kindly explain what you are doing in my father's safe."

"Looking for information about the tire-theft gang."

"A story you say the *Star* never should print."

"That's neither here nor there." A deep flush had crept over Schirr's cheeks but his manner remained confident. "As editor I have to know what's going on."

"Who gave you permission to open the safe?"

"You forget that I am editor here, Miss Parker."

"At least I've been reminded of it enough times," Penny retorted. "How did you learn the combination?"

"I've known it."

"You saw the numbers written on Dad's desk," Penny accused.

Mr. Schirr did not deny the charge. Turning his back, he started to remove a rubber band from a small stack of yellowed letters. The act infuriated Penny, for she recognized the packet. Years before, the letters had been written by her own mother, and Mr. Parker always had treasured them.

"Don't you touch those!" she cried, darting forward. "They're personal."

Snatching the packet from Mr. Schirr, she gathered up the other papers and envelopes from the floor. Thrusting everything into the safe, she closed and locked the door.

"Well!" commented the editor scathingly.

"You're through here!" said Penny, facing him with blazing eyes. "Do you understand? I'm discharging you."

Mr. Schirr looked stunned. Then he laughed unpleasantly.

"So *you're* discharging me," he mocked. "By what right may I ask?"

"This is my father's plant."

"Which doesn't necessarily make you the editor or the owner, Miss Penelope Parker. You're a minor as well as a nuisance. If your father proves to be dead, the court will step in—"

"Get out!" cried Penny, fighting to keep back the tears. "You don't care about Dad, or anything but your own selfish interests!"

"Now you're hysterical."

Penny's anger subsided, to be replaced by a cool determination that Harley Schirr should not remain in charge of the *Star* another hour.

"I meant just what I said," she told him quietly. "Please go."

Schirr smiled grimly. Seating himself at the desk, his eyes challenged hers.

"I remain as editor here," he announced. "If you wish to contest my right, take your case to court. In the meantime, keep out of my private office."

CHAPTER 10 - TALE OF A GHOST

Beaten and close to tears, Penny stumbled out of Harley Schirr's office. As she paused just beyond the closed door, every eye in the newsroom focused upon her. Salt Sommers, camera box slung over his shoulder, went over and spoke to her.

"Penny, we all heard that row. If you say the word, we'll walk out of here in a body."

Penny smiled, touched by the expression of loyalty. "That would do no good," she replied. "Thanks just the same."

"We're through taking orders from Schirr!" Salt went on. "He always has been a pain in the neck, and now that he has authority, there's no holding him down. How about it, boys?"

A chorus of approval greeted his words. One of the reporters picked up a paper weight and would have hurled it against the closed door, had not another restrained him.

"I'm sure Dad would want everyone to carry on," Penny said quietly. "The paper must be published the same as always."

"We could do our work and do it well, if Schirr would just leave us alone," growled one of the copy readers.

"That's right!" added another. "Why don't you take over, Penny?"

"Mr. Schirr just reminded me that I'm not the editor. I know nothing about running a newspaper."

"How about the time you ran the High School weekly?" Salt reminded her. "Why, you did a bang up job of it, and uncovered *The Secret Pact* story to boot! Don't try to tell us you don't know how to run a newspaper!"

"A weekly high school sheet and the *Star* are two different propositions."

"But your father has a fine organization here," Salt argued. "If Schirr can be kept from breaking it up, everything will go along. The boys all know their jobs."

Penny's eyes began to sparkle. But she said: "I don't see how I could take over, much as I would like to do it. Schirr has staked out rights in Dad's office and nothing will move him short of a court order."

"You don't need a fancy office to run a paper," Salt grinned. "We'll just take our orders from you. Schirr can sit until he's had enough of it."

Penny gazed at the eager, loyal faces about her. Nearly all of the men were old employees, personally trained by her father and Mr. DeWitt. She knew she could depend on them.

"We'll do it!" she exclaimed suddenly. "As your new editor, I wish to issue my first order. Please, let's not publish any more sensational stories about Dad's disappearance."

"Okay Chief," grinned one of the desk men. "That suits us all fine."

Penny was given a seat of honor at the slot of the circular copy desk. There she was able to read and pass upon every story which flowed from the typewriters of the various reporters. With the courteous help of one of the deskmen, she remade the front page of the noon edition. A particularly sensational story about Mr. Parker, prepared earlier in the day, was promptly "busted."

Penny found her new duties exacting, but surprisingly easy. Over the years it was astonishing how much she had learned about the workings of a newspaper plant. At different times she had served as reporter, society editor and special feature writer. As for the editorial policy of the *Star*, she was thoroughly familiar with it, for her father frequently aired his views at home.

Shortly after the noon edition rolled from the press, the buzzer in Mr. Schirr's office sounded. Mr. Parker's private secretary did not answer. The buzzer kept on for nearly five minutes. Then the door was flung open.

"What the blazes is the matter with everyone?" Schirr shouted.

His gaze fastened upon Penny at the copy desk.

"Meet our new editor, Mr. Schirr," said Salt, who had that moment come out of the camera room.

Schirr ignored Penny. Snatching up one of the noon editions, still fresh with wet ink, he glanced at the front page. His eyes flashed.

"Eckert," he said to the head copy man, "come into my office. I want to talk to you."

"Oh, sure," said Eckert, but he did not follow Schirr into the adjoining room.

Soon the ex-editor came storming out to learn what was wrong. This time his expression was baffled.

"Mr. Eckert," he said with exaggerated politeness. "Will you please step into my office?"

"Sorry," replied the copy reader. "You may as well know right now that you're not giving the orders around here!"

"We'll see about that!" cried Schirr.

Darting to one of the speaking tubes, he called the foreman of the press room.

"Schirr talking!" he said curtly. "Stop the presses! Kill that noon edition! We're making over the front page!"

"Can't hear you," was the reply, for word had been passed to the men in the pressroom. "Louder!"

Schirr shouted until he was nearly hoarse. Then suddenly conscious that he was making a spectacle of himself, he slammed into his office. A minute later he reappeared, hat jammed low over his eyes.

"This is a very clever scheme, Miss Parker," he said, facing her. "Well, it won't work. I'm leaving, but I'll be back. With a lawyer!"

He strode from the newsroom, banging the door so hard the glass rattled.

"Don't worry about that egg," Salt advised Penny. "He's mostly bluff."

"I think he does mean to get a court order," she returned soberly.

"He may try," Salt shrugged. "We can handle him."

Following Schirr's departure, everything moved smoothly at the *Star* plant. One edition after another rolled from the presses. Penny was kept busy, and frequently she was worried and in doubt. Nevertheless, everyone made the way easy for her, and as the day wore on she gained confidence.

Throughout the afternoon, news stories kept pouring into the *Star* office, but no encouraging information came in regard to Mr. Parker. Several times Penny called the police station and also talked with Mrs. Weems. The housekeeper, fearful that the girl would become ill, insisted upon bringing a hot evening meal to the office.

"Penny, you've been here all day," she chided anxiously. "You must come home with me."

"I can't just yet," Penny replied. "There's too much to do. By tomorrow, if Schirr doesn't make trouble, things will smooth out."

"You're working so hard you'll be sick abed!"

"I want to work," Penny said grimly. "It keeps me from thinking. Anyway, Dad would want me to do it."

Mrs. Weems sighed as she gathered up the lunch basket and thermos bottle. Penny barely had tasted the food.

"When will you be home?" the housekeeper asked.

"I can't say exactly. After the night editions are out. Don't sit up for me."

"You know I couldn't go to bed until you are home," Mrs. Weems responded. "You'll take a taxi?"

"Of course," promised Penny.

After the housekeeper had gone, she plunged into her duties once more. With the force short of two men, DeWitt and Schirr, there really was too much work for the desk men to do unassisted. Penny wrote headlines, copy-read stories, and passed on all matters of policy. So busy did she keep, that when at length she glanced at her watch, it was eleven-thirty.

"Gracious!" she thought. "And Mrs. Weems will be waiting up for me!"

Saying goodnight to the men who would carry on in her absence, she went down the back stairs to the street. As she glanced about for a taxicab, she saw Old Mose Johnson shuffling toward the loading dock.

"Good evening," she greeted him. "I'm glad to see you're ahead of time tonight."

"Good evenin', Miss Penny," the colored man said, doffing his tattered hat. "Yas'm. I'se heah, but I seed dat same ghost a-lurkin' behind de gate!"

"I hope that ghost isn't becoming a habit with you, Mose."

CHAPTER 10 - TALE OF A GHOST

"Deed Miss Penny, he's mo' dan a habit," the colored man sighed. "He's a suah-nuff live ghost. De fust time I seed him I thought he wasn't no imagination ghost. But when I saw him agin' tonight I was dead suah of it."

"What happened this time, Mose?"

"Well, Miss Penny, I was a walking along dat same road, down by de ole Harrison place when I seed him again. He was a-cavortin' behind dat same iron gate. And he was dressed de same too, in a long white robe."

"And you ran the same too, I suppose?" smiled Penny.

"Ah made myself scarce around dat gate, but I didn't run home dis time. I was a-skeered of mah ole woman. I beats it to de restaurant on de co'ner and waits dere 'till a bus comes. Oh, I'se gettin' good, Miss Penny! I can see a ghost and git to work on time, all de same evenin'!"

"Well, keep up the good work," Penny said jokingly as she turned away.

The meeting with Old Mose had served to divert the girl's mind from her own difficulties. Riding home by taxi, she caught herself reviewing the details of the colored man's outlandish tale.

"Mose couldn't have seen a ghost," she thought, "but he's honest about being frightened. If I didn't have so many serious troubles, I'd be tempted to investigate the old Harrison estate myself."

Penny alighted at her home and walked wearily up the shoveled path. Snow was falling once more. Already the exposed porch was covered with a half-inch coating of feathery flakes.

Inside the house a light flashed on. The bright beam shining through the window drew Penny's attention to a series of freshly-made footprints criss-crossing the porch.

"Mrs. Weems must have had a visitor," she thought, observing that the heel marks were made by a woman's shoe.

As Penny reached for the door knob, her glance fell upon a long, narrow envelope which protruded from the tin mailbox. She removed it, wondering why the housekeeper had neglected to do so.

Mrs. Weems opened the door.

"Thank goodness, you're home at last, Penny. I fell asleep on the davenport. There isn't any word—"

"Not a scrap of news," Penny completed.

Dropping the letter on the center table, she removed her wraps and flung herself full length on the davenport.

"You poor child!" Mrs. Weems murmured. "You're practically exhausted. Please go straight to bed. I'll fix some warm milk and perhaps you can sleep."

"I don't feel as if I'd ever sleep again," Penny declared. "I'm tired, but I feel so excited and tense."

Mrs. Weems picked up the girl's coat and cap. Shaking them free of snow, she hung the garments in the closet.

"Did you have a bad time of it today?" Penny asked after a moment.

"It wasn't exactly pleasant," Mrs. Weems replied. "Reporters and photographers came from every paper in Riverview. The police too—although I was glad to have them. And the telephone! I counted twelve calls in an hour."

"You must be dead. You shouldn't have waited up for me."

"I wanted to, Penny. About an hour ago I thought I heard your step on the porch, but I was mistaken."

Penny sat up. "Haven't you had a caller during the last hour, Mrs. Weems?"

"No, I've been alone."

"But I saw footprints on the porch! And I found this in the mailbox!"

Penny snatched the long envelope from the table. Holding it beneath the bridge lamp, she noticed for the first time that it bore no stamp. Strangely, it was addressed to her.

"Why, where did you get that letter?" cried Mrs. Weems.

"Found it in the mailbox." Penny's hand trembled as she ripped open the flap.

A sheet of writing paper, high quality and slightly perfumed, slid from the envelope. The message was terse and bore no signature at the end. It read:

> "Offer a suitable reward and information will be provided as to the whereabouts of your father. Make your offer known in the *Star*."

CHAPTER 11 - BY A CEMETERY WALL

Penny and Mrs. Weems reread the anonymous message many times, analyzing every word.

"Plainly this note was written by a woman of some means for the paper is fine quality," Penny commented. "She must have sneaked up on the porch about an hour ago."

"Call the police at once," urged Mrs. Weems. "They'll tell us what we should do."

"Whoever left the note may be watching the house."

"We must risk that, Penny. I'll call the station myself."

While Mrs. Weems busied herself at the telephone, Penny switched off the living-room light. She could see no one loitering anywhere near the house. Slipping on her coat, she went outside to inspect the footprints left on the porch. Only a few remained uncovered by snow. There was no way to tell in which direction the writer of the anonymous message had gone.

Mrs. Weems had completed her telephone call by the time Penny reentered the house.

"Two detectives will be here in a few minutes," she revealed. "You keep watch for them while I run upstairs and get into something more suitable than a lounging robe."

Within ten minutes a car drew up in front of the house. Penny already was acquainted with Detectives Dick Brandon and George Fuller, and had great confidence in their judgment. Anxiously she and Mrs. Weems waited while the men scanned the anonymous message.

"This might be only a crank note," commented Brandon. "Someone who's read of Mr. Parker's disappearance, and hopes to pick up a little cash."

"Then you don't think it came from the tire-theft gang?" Penny asked.

"Not likely. A professional kidnaper never would have sent a note like this. The handwriting hasn't even been disguised."

"Will it be possible to trace the person?"

"It should be if we have a little luck." Detective Brandon pocketed the letter. "Now this is what you must do, Miss Parker. Offer a reward—say five thousand dollars—for information about your father."

"I'll get the story in every edition of the *Star* tomorrow. And then what am I to do?"

"You'll likely hear from the writer of this anonymous message, either by letter or telephone. If you contact the woman, arrange a meeting. Then notify us immediately."

The discussion went on. When at length the two detectives left, Penny and Mrs. Weems were hopeful that within another twenty-four hours they might know Mr. Parker's fate.

In the morning, after only five hours of sleep, Penny was back at her desk. Her first act was to dictate the story offering a five-thousand-dollar reward for information about her father. Not even to Salt Sommers did she confide that she had received an anonymous message.

"Everything's going well here at the plant," he assured her. "Harley Schirr hasn't so much as stuck his nose through the door."

"I hope we're through with him," replied Penny soberly. "However, I don't feel that we are. By the way, no telegram has come from Jerry?"

"No message yet. Guess he didn't get your wire."

Throughout the morning, Penny worked tirelessly at her desk. Although her father's office now was vacant, she did not take possession. Even when she occasionally entered to get papers from the file, it gave her a queer, tight feeling. Her father's old neck-scarf still hung on the clothes tree. The rubbers he hated to wear stood heel to heel against the wall.

CHAPTER 11 - BY A CEMETERY WALL

"Dad is alive and well," she told herself whenever her courage faltered. "By tomorrow he'll be back. I know he will."

At noon Salt brought Penny a sandwich which she ate without leaving her desk. As she struggled with the last mouthful, the telephone rang.

"Is this Miss Parker?" inquired a woman's voice.

Penny gripped the receiver tightly. Her pulse began to pound. Although she had no real reason for thinking so, she suddenly knew that she was in contact with the mysterious writer of the anonymous message.

"Yes," she replied, keeping her voice calm.

"You offered a reward in your paper today. Five thousand dollars for information about Mr. Parker."

"True. Can you tell me anything about his disappearance?"

"I can if you're willing to pay the money."

"I'll be glad to do it."

"And no questions asked?"

"No questions," Penny promised. "If you actually can provide information that will help me find my father, I'll be happy to give you the money."

There was a long silence. Fearful lest the woman had lost her nerve and was about to hang up, Penny said anxiously:

"Where shall I meet you? Will you come to my home?"

"That's too risky."

"Then where shall I meet you?"

"Tonight at eight. You know the cemetery out on Baldiff Road?"

"Baldiff Road?" Penny repeated doubtfully.

"You'll find it on a county map," the woman instructed. "Meet me at the cemetery wall promptly at eight. And don't bring anyone with you. Just the money. I'll guarantee to tell you where you can find your father."

The receiver clicked.

Greatly excited, Penny made a futile attempt to trace the telephone call. Failing, she set off for the police station to talk to Detectives Fuller and Brandon.

"The woman must be a rank amateur or she wouldn't have arranged a meeting in the way she did!" Detective Brandon assured Penny. "Now let's find out where Baldiff Road is located."

Using a large map, he circled an area several miles south of Riverview. Penny was surprised to note that Baldiff Road branched off from the same deserted thoroughfare which she and Louise had followed on the night of the blizzard. The cemetery, Oakland Hills, was situated perhaps a mile from the old Harrison place where Mose Johnson had claimed to have seen a ghost.

"It shouldn't be hard to nab the woman when she shows up," Detective Fuller declared. "Dick and I will get there early and keep watch."

"Just what am I to do?" Penny inquired. "Shall I take the reward money with me?"

"We'll give you a package of fake money," the detective answered. "Drive to the cemetery alone at the appointed hour. If the woman shows up, talk to her, try to learn what she knows. We'll attend to the rest."

Penny returned home to consult with Mrs. Weems. How to reach the cemetery was something of a problem. Her own car, minus its wheels, remained at the Yacht Club, and Mr. Parker's automobile had been hauled to a garage for extensive repairs.

"Can't you borrow a car from someone at the *Star* office?" suggested the housekeeper. "And do take a man with you when you drive to the cemetery."

"No, I must go alone," insisted Penny. "That part is very important."

In the end she was able to borrow Salt Sommer's coupe. A little after seven o'clock she set off for Baldiff Road with the package of fake money in her possession. The night was not cold, but a stiff wind blew through the evergreens; whirlwinds of snow chased one another across the untraveled road.

"What a dreary place for a meeting," Penny shivered as she glimpsed the bleak cemetery on a hilltop.

The area, a full half-mile from any house, was bounded by a high snow-covered brick wall. Beyond the barrier, starlight revealed a cluster of rounding tombstones layered with white. No one was visible, neither the woman nor members of the police force.

Penny glanced at her watch. It lacked ten minutes of eight o'clock. She parked not far from the cemetery entrance and switched off the engine.

Twenty minutes elapsed. Nervous and cold, Penny climbed from the car and tramped back and forth to restore circulation. She had begun to doubt that the woman would keep the appointment.

Then, coming swiftly down the road, she saw a strange looking figure. The one who approached wore a long, tight-fitting coat. A hat with a dark veil covered the woman's face.

"There she is!" thought Penny, every nerve tense.

The woman came closer. While still some distance from the cemetery entrance, she suddenly paused. Her head jerked sideways. Then to Penny's dismay, she turned and fled toward the woods.

"Wait!" Penny shouted. "Don't be afraid! Wait!"

The woman paid no heed. Lifting her coat the better to run, she disappeared among the trees.

CHAPTER 12 - FLIGHT

As Penny wondered what to do, Detectives Brandon and Fuller leaped from their hiding place behind the cemetery wall. Their car had been secreted in a clump of bushes farther down the road. By pure mischance, the woman in the black veil had seen it as she approached, and fearing treachery, had fled.

"Quick, Dick, or she'll get away!" Fuller shouted.

Penny did not join in the pursuit. Reentering her car, she waited anxiously. From the crashing of underbrush, she knew the detectives were having difficulty in following the woman. In the dark forest it would be very easy for her to elude the officers.

Three quarters of an hour elapsed before the men returned.

"We lost her," Detective Brandon reported. "No use searching any longer."

Sick at heart, Penny drove slowly toward home. Her hopes had been completely dashed. Not only had she failed to contact the mysterious woman, but there now seemed little likelihood of doing so.

"I may receive another telephone message," she thought, "but I doubt it. That woman probably will be too badly frightened to try to contact me again."

At the exit of Baldiff Road, Penny headed down the winding hillside highway which she and Louise had followed on the night of the blizzard. The route, although slightly longer, would take her close to the Riverview Yacht Club.

"I'll go that way and see if my car is still there," she decided. "Then tomorrow I can have it hauled home and jacked up. I should have looked after the matter long ago."

The coupe rounded a curve and the road dipped between an avenue of swaying, whispering pines. To the left, shrouded in snow, loomed the old Harrison house. The estate was picturesque in itself, and Mose Johnson's tale about a ghost had intensified the girl's interest.

"Wonder who owns the place now?" she speculated. "Probably not any member of the Harrison family, as I believe they were old-timers in Riverview."

Penny slowed the car to idling speed. Deliberately keeping to the left hand side of the road, she studied with deep interest the long, snow-frosted fence which bounded the grounds. The barrier was an unfriendly one, high and spiked at the top.

Suddenly her attention focused upon a well-beaten path in the snow just inside the fence. The footprints, plainly visible in the bright moonlight, extended the full width of the grounds.

Into Penny's mind flashed the wild yarn told by Mose Johnson.

"Ghost tracks!" she thought. "At least those prints must have been made by whatever he saw beyond the gate."

So interested was Penny in the path that for an instant she completely forgot her driving. The front left wheel of the car struck a tiny mound of ice and snow at the road's edge.

Barely in time to avoid an accident, the girl twisted the steering wheel and brought the car back on the highway.

"Another second and I'd have been in the ditch!" she thought shakily. "If I must look for a ghost, guess I'll do the job right."

Penny pulled up, this time at the opposite side of the road. Getting out, she crossed to the iron fence and peered through it. The path which had attracted her attention had been pounded hard by someone who had walked just inside the enclosure.

"Odd!" she reflected. "Maybe Old Mose's ghost has more substance than I thought."

Penny glanced toward the big house, dark and majestic in its setting of evergreens. Obviously the place had been closed for the winter. Walks were not shoveled, blinds had been drawn, and no tire tracks led to and from the three-car garage.

"Wonder who or what could have made that path?" she mused. "Certainly not an animal."

Unable to solve the mystery, Penny turned to re-enter the parked coupe. Before she could cross the road, a light went on in a third floor room of the estate house. Startled, she stared at it. As she watched, it was extinguished.

"Someone must live here!" thought Penny. "Or am I seeing spooks myself?"

For a long while she watched the upper floor of the house. The light did not reappear. At length, wearying of the vigil, she returned to the car.

Penny started the engine and bent down to open the fins of the heater. Straightening, she cast a last, careless glance toward the old estate. Her heart did a flip-flop.

Beyond the iron gate, in the garden area, a white-robed figure slowly paced back and forth!

"My Aunt!" whispered Penny. "Am I seeing things or am I seeing things?"

For a moment she sat very straight, watching. The ghostly figure, white from head to toe, moved with measured steps toward the high gate.

"There aren't any ghosts," she encouraged herself. "But if that's not a spook, it must be someone dressed up like one! And who would play Hallowe'en games on a cold night like this?"

Alone, frankly nervous, Penny had no overpowering desire to investigate the white-robed figure at close range. A large, spreading evergreen half-blocked her view of the gate. She could not see the ghost plainly, but she distinctly heard the rattle of a chain as the apparition tested the lock.

"Real or imaginary, that spook is trying to get out!" Penny thought with a shiver. "If Mose were here now I'd challenge him to a race!"

The white-gowned figure shook the gate chain a second time, then slowly retreated. Penny watched for a moment, before abruptly swinging open the car door. She had decided to investigate.

As she crossed the road, the white figure moved away from her. By the time she reached the gate, it had disappeared around a corner of the house.

"At least Mr. Spook wasn't carrying his own tombstone!" Penny observed to herself. "Mose exaggerated that part."

She waited, leaning against the gate post. Within three minutes a light went on in the upper part of the house. For a fleeting instant before the blind was pulled, she saw someone standing in front of an old-fashioned dresser.

"Mr. Ghost seemingly has turned in for the night," thought Penny. "But is it a he, she, or it?"

Soon the bedroom light was extinguished. Cold and tired, Penny decided that the mystery must remain unsolved. However, as she drove on, she kept thinking about what she had seen. Of one thing she now was certain. The estate was not deserted!

Without stopping at the Yacht Club grounds, Penny made certain that her stripped car and ice boat remained as she last had seen them. Driving on to Riverview, she left Salt's car at the *Star* plant, then taxied home to tell Mrs. Weems of her failure at the cemetery.

"Don't feel badly about it," the housekeeper comforted. "Surely the woman who telephoned will make another attempt to reach you."

"I doubt it," Penny replied gloomily. "She'll know now that the police are watching for her."

"This entire affair is so bewildering," sighed Mrs. Weems. "How could your father have been kidnaped? If what we've learned is true, he left the scene of the accident of his own free will."

"I never was so baffled in my life," Penny returned, throwing herself on the davenport. "I used to think I was good at solving puzzles. Now I know I'm just plain dumb."

"Have you thought about employing a private detective?"

"It might be a good idea!" Penny agreed, encouraged. "I'll see what I can do tomorrow."

As she started wearily up the stairs to bed, Mrs. Weems called after her to say that Louise Sidell had telephoned earlier in the evening. Penny nodded absently, assuming that her chum had phoned to express sympathy. She did not think of the matter again until the next morning at breakfast. As she was leaving the table, Mrs. Weems came in to report that Louise once more was on the telephone.

CHAPTER 12 - FLIGHT

"Penny, I can't tell you how shocked I was to learn about your father," her chum began breathlessly. "Is there anything I can do to help?"

"I'm afraid not, Lou."

"What are you using for a car? You must need one badly."

"Salt Sommers let me have his last night. I'll get along."

"Penny, I know how you can buy tires!" Louise went on. "In fact, that's what I wanted to talk to you about."

"How can I buy tires? Rubber is supposed to be scarce."

"When I was having my hair fixed at the beauty parlor yesterday I heard two women talking!" Louise declared excitedly. "It seems there's a garage where you can get them if you pull the right strings!"

"Oh! A Black Market place?"

"I suppose that's what you would call it."

"I don't want to get tires illegally," Penny said. "I'm not interested, Lou."

"You don't even care to know the name of the garage?"

"What good would it do?"

"None perhaps, but it might give you a surprise."

"A surprise?" Penny repeated. She glanced at the clock, impatient because the conversation was being prolonged. A great deal of important work awaited her.

"You don't want to know the name of the place?" Louise persisted.

"Yes, I do. On second thought, it might be well worth while to find out what I can about Black Market operations in tires."

The conviction had come suddenly to Penny that all the evidence contained in her father's lost portfolio must be gathered anew. No word had been received from Jerry Livingston. In the quest for information, she must depend upon her own efforts.

"It's going to give you a real shock to learn the name of the place," Louise went on.

"I'm shock proof by this time," answered Penny. "Let 'er fly."

But Louise was unwilling to divulge the information over the telephone.

"I don't dare tell you now," she replied. "Just sit tight for ten minutes and I'll deliver my bombshell in person."

CHAPTER 13 - A BLACK MARKET

Ten minutes later Louise was at the front door with the Sidell family car. She tooted the horn until Penny put on her coat and went outside.

"Jump in and I'll take you to the place of mystery," Louise greeted her. "On second thought, you'd better drive. I hate icy roads."

Penny slid behind the steering wheel. "But where are we going?" she protested. "Honestly, Lou, I haven't much time—"

"Mattie Williams' garage is the place that sells the tires! Now, are you interested?"

"Am I? Why, we stopped there with Salt Sommers!"

"We did indeed. Remember the big truck?"

"Lou, you may have stumbled into something really important!"

"Glad you think so, chum. But you're not interested in Black Markets."

"I've changed my mind! I want to talk to Mattie Williams right away!"

Penny started the car. Driving with a mechanical, unthinking efficiency born of many years' practice, she questioned Louise as to the source of her information. The girls were deep in a discussion when they heard someone shout. Salt Sommers had hailed them from the curb.

"Why, hello," Penny greeted him, stopping the car with a jerk. "Any trouble at the *Star*?"

"Not from Schirr," grinned Salt. "I'm hot-footing it to the Ladies Club to mug some dames pouring tea! For the society page."

"Poor Salt!" smiled Penny, knowing how he hated trivial assignments.

"On your way to the office?" the photographer questioned.

Penny hesitated, then decided to confide in Salt. She repeated what Louise had told her about the Mattie Williams' garage.

"Well, can you beat that!" the photographer exclaimed. "I don't know Mattie and her partner well, but I always supposed they were honest. So they're dealing in stolen tires!"

"We don't know for sure," Penny said hastily. "Our information is mostly founded on rumor."

"And the tires may not be stolen ones," contributed Louise. "I only heard they can be bought there."

Penny added that she would not take time to run down the Black Market story save that her father's disappearance might have a connection with the tire-thief gang.

"I aim to learn the names of those men Dad intended to expose," she said earnestly.

Somewhat startled by the grim note of Penny's voice, Salt warned her that she might be venturing on dangerous ground.

"We all admire your courage," he said, "but you mustn't take foolish risks. Your father would turn thumbs down on that idea."

"It's because of Dad that I must investigate every angle of the tire-theft racket."

"Quite an ambitious assignment," Salt said dryly. "Now as soon as Jerry gets back from Canada—"

"We can't wait! Something has to be done right away!"

"I know how you feel," responded Salt, "but there's such a thing as being too courageous."

"I'm not courageous," Penny denied. "Last night at the cemetery I was scared half to death. And then when I saw the ghost—"

"What ghost?" interrupted Louise.

CHAPTER 13 - A BLACK MARKET

Penny had not intended to speak of what she had seen at the Harrison estate. The slip of tongue made it necessary to tell of the path by the gate, the retreating figure, and the mysterious light.

"That's funny," commented the photographer, regarding her with a peculiar expression. "Since I've been on duty at the observation tower I've never seen any activity at the estate."

"I don't believe in ghosts, but I saw one all that same!" Penny insisted. "Just watch some night and see for yourself!"

Annoyed by Salt's smile, she shifted gears and drove on down the street. Turning to Louise, she asked earnestly: "You believe I saw something wandering about the estate last night, don't you?"

"Well," Louise hesitated, unwilling to offend her chum. "You must have been quite upset after failing to meet that woman at the cemetery. Under the circumstances...."

"I was as calm as I am now," Penny cried indignantly. "I saw it, I tell you!"

"Of course you did, dear," Louise soothed. "Do please watch your driving more carefully, or I'll have to take over."

Penny suddenly relaxed. "Okay, have it your own way," she shrugged. "I wouldn't believe Mose Johnson, so why should you believe me? It's just one of those things."

For a long while they rode in silence. Few cars were on the road and there was little business activity at Kamm's Corner. Penny parked in front of the Mattie Williams' garage.

"What excuse will we have for questioning her?" Louise asked dubiously.

"I'm not going to make an excuse," said Penny. "I'll just come right out and ask her if she sells tires without a special order."

The girls entered the warm little office, stamping snow from their galoshes.

"Just a minute," called a voice which belonged to Mattie Williams.

The garage owner was busy with a customer. Soon however, she came in from the main part of the building, wiping her oily hands on a piece of waste.

"What can I do for you?" she inquired briskly.

"You remember us, don't you?" asked Penny, leading into the subject of tires as gradually as possible. "We're friends of Salt Sommers."

"Oh, sure!" the woman's face lighted. "You came in with him the night of the bad storm."

"My car had been stripped of its tires. Ever since, I've been wondering how to get new ones."

A slightly guarded expression came over Mattie Williams' face. She said nothing.

"I was told I might obtain some here," Penny plunged on.

"You can," said Mattie. "Provided you have an order from your Ration Board."

"Not without it?"

Mattie gazed at Penny with undisguised scorn. "What sort of a place do you think we run here?" she demanded. "Of course we don't sell tires without an order."

"But we were told—"

"Well, you were told wrong," snapped Mattie. "Sorry. I can't help you."

Picking up a wrench from the desk top, the woman left the office.

"I guess I didn't approach her the right way," remarked Penny sadly. "Either that, or our information was incorrect. Louise, are you sure—"

"Oh, I am!" her chum insisted. "The two women I overheard, distinctly said Mattie Williams' garage. Of course, they might have been wrong about it."

Before Penny and Louise could leave the office, a middle-aged man with glasses came in through the street door.

"Sam Burkholder here?" he demanded, warming himself by the stove.

Penny started to say that she did not know. Just then Mattie Williams' partner came in the other door.

"Hi, Sam!" the stranger greeted him. "I've got the car parked around back. Are you ready to put on that tire?"

Sam frowned, darting a quick glance at the two girls.

"Oh, the one I patched for you!" he returned. "Sure, it's fixed. Drive your car in the back entrance and I'll take care of it."

Both men went out into the main part of the garage. Just beyond the door they paused for a whispered conference, then separated.

"Shall we go?" inquired Louise, glancing at her chum.

"Not just yet," replied Penny. "I'm curious to see that patched tire. Let's kill a little more time here."

Pretending to warm themselves by the stove, they waited ten minutes. Then, without attracting attention, they sauntered out onto the main garage floor. Mattie Williams was busy washing a car and did not see them.

The garage workroom was divided into sections, separated by a double door which was closed. Penny strolled over and pushed it open just enough to see through the crack.

Sam Burkholder was working on the stranger's car. He had removed an old tire and wheel, and was replacing it with one whose tread appeared new.

"A patched tire, my left eye!" Penny whispered to Louise. "It's just as we thought! This garage must be a Black Market place!"

CHAPTER 14 - A FAMILIAR FIGURE

Only for a moment did the girls dare remain at the door watching Sam Burkholder mount the tire. Then, their curiosity satisfied, they moved quietly away. Without speaking to Mattie Williams, they returned to the parked automobile.

"Well, wasn't I right?" Louise demanded triumphantly. "What do you think we should do?"

The question plagued Penny. "I don't know," she confessed. "If only we were absolutely sure the tire was new—"

"It certainly looked new."

"Yes, but it could have had some wear. It's possible, too, that the customer had a legal right to buy a new tire."

"Then you don't intend to report to the police, Penny?"

"I want to talk to Salt about it first. We must move carefully, Lou. You see, my main objective is to learn the names of the higher-ups involved in the tire-theft racket."

"And where does this garage fit into the picture?"

"If it fits at all, my guess is that Sam and Mattie are buying illegal tires—perhaps from the same men who stripped my car and threatened Dad."

Driving slowly toward Riverview, Penny reviewed what she had seen. She was convinced the information was valuable, yet she scarcely knew how to use it.

"If Salt suggests that I report to the police, that's what I'll do," she decided.

Enroute home, Penny stopped at another garage to make arrangements to have her stripped coupe hauled into the city.

"How about the *Icicle*?" Louise asked, thinking her chum had forgotten the iceboat.

"It will have to stay where it is for the time being," Penny replied. "If it's stolen, I won't much care."

At the Sidell home, the girls separated. Thanking Louise for the use of the car, Penny returned afoot to the *Star* office. Salt Sommers was absent on assignment, so she did not linger long. As she rounded a street corner on her way home, a newsboy for a rival paper blocked her path.

"Read all about it!" he shouted. "Anthony Parker Believed Kidnaped! Paper, Miss?"

Penny dropped a coin into the lad's hand and hastily scanned the front page. The story of her father's disappearance was a highly colored account, but contained not a useful item of information. Tossing the sheet into a street paper-container, she moved on.

She was passing the Gillman Department Store when her attention was drawn to a woman who waited for a bus.

"I've seen her somewhere before," thought Penny, pausing. "Last night—"

The woman wore a small black hat and a long, old-fashioned dark coat which came nearly to her ankles. It was the shape of the garment and its unusual length which struck Penny as familiar. Why, the woman resembled the one who had fled from the cemetery!

Penny pretended to gaze into the store window. Actually she studied the woman from every angle. She might have been forty-seven years of age and was large-boned. Her face was heavily lined, and her long hands were covered by a pair of cheap, black cotton gloves.

"Can it be the same woman?" thought Penny in perplexity.

A bus bearing a county placard glided up to the curb. The woman in black was the only passenger to board it.

"That bus goes out toward Baldiff Road and the cemetery!" Penny told herself. "And that's where I'm going too!"

An instant before the folding doors slammed shut, she sprang aboard. Paying her fare, she sought a seat at the rear of the bus.

No sooner was the coach in motion than Penny regretted her hasty action. What could she hope to gain by pursuing the strange woman? She was not certain enough of her identification to make a direct accusation. County buses ran infrequently. In all likelihood, she would find herself stranded in the country.

Penny arose to leave the bus. Then changing her mind a second time, she sat down. Try as she would, she could not rid herself of a conviction that the woman she followed was the same one who had visited the cemetery.

The bus made few stops in the city. Once beyond the city limits, it sped along at a brisk speed. To Penny's satisfaction, the woman in black soon began to gather up her packages. She pressed a button and the bus skidded to a stop at a crossroads.

With no show of haste, Penny followed the woman from the bus. Pretending to enter a grocery store at the corner, she waited and watched.

Apparently the woman lived nearby, for she started off down a narrow, winding road which ran at right angles to the main highway.

"Why that's the road that runs past the Harrison place," Penny thought. "Wonder if she can be going there?"

Waiting until the woman was nearly out of sight, she trudged after her. Walking was difficult for the road had not been cleared by a snow plow. Fortunately for Penny, the woman did not once glance behind her. She kept steadily on until she came within view of the big estate house on the hill. Just before she reached the boundary fence, she cut across a field, approaching the dwelling from the rear.

Penny remained at the road, watching. The woman took a key from her pocket, unlocking a small, padlocked gate at the rear of the grounds. She snapped the lock shut again, and disappeared into the house.

Penny perched herself on top of an old-fashioned rail fence to think over what she had seen. The woman, whoever she was, obviously lived at the estate. Yet the cheap quality of her clothing suggested that she could not be the owner of such an expensive establishment.

"Probably a servant or caretaker," Penny reasoned. "But is she the one who ran away last night?"

Far over the hills in a lonely grove of pines stood Oakland Cemetery. On either side of Baldiff Road stretched dense woods, a growth that crept to the very boundaries of the Harrison estate. Penny instantly noted that it would be possible for a person to flee from the cemetery to the very door of the estate without once leaving the shelter of trees.

"Perhaps it was the same woman!" she thought. "If she lives here, it would be logical for her to specify Oakland Cemetery as a meeting place! And escape would be easy for her, too!"

Penny slid down from the fence. It would do no good to question the woman. Rather, if she were guilty, questions might serve to place her on the alert. Far better, she reasoned, to bide her time.

"I'll learn everything I can about that woman," she thought. "Tonight I'll watch the house."

In making her plans, Penny did not take into account Mrs. Weems' attitude. Upon reaching home late in the afternoon, she found the housekeeper in a most discouraged mood. No favorable news had been received from any source.

"I've been worried about you too, Penny," Mrs. Weems confessed. "Where did you go after you left the *Star* office?"

Penny told of her trip to Mattie Williams' garage and later to the Harrison estate. In particular she described the mysterious woman she had followed by bus.

"I plan to go back there tonight," she concluded. "For the first time since Dad disappeared, I feel I may have stumbled into a valuable clue!"

Mrs. Weems looked troubled. "But Penny," she protested, "you can't go to the estate alone!"

"I thought perhaps Louise would accompany me."

"Two girls alone at night! I can't give my consent, Penny. It's not safe."

"But I don't wish to call the police just yet, Mrs. Weems. I've no real evidence. Will you come with me?"

The housekeeper hesitated. Naturally a timid woman, she had no desire to stir from her own fireside that night. But she knew where her duty lay.

CHAPTER 14 - A FAMILIAR FIGURE

"Yes, I'll go with you, Penny," she consented. "Shall we start soon?"

"Not until after dark. One can't expect a ghost to show up in broad daylight."

"A ghost!" Mrs. Weems quavered. "Penny, what are you letting me in for?"

"Frankly, I don't know. Some strange things have been going on at the Harrison estate. Tonight I hope to solve part of the mystery at least."

Pressed for an explanation, Penny repeated Mose Johnson's story and told of seeing the strange white-robed figure with her own eyes. The tale did not add to Mrs. Weems' comfort of mind.

"We're crazy to go out there," the housekeeper protested. "Must we do it?"

"I think it may be our one hope of gaining a clue which will lead to Dad."

"Then I'm willing to risk it," agreed Mrs. Weems. "However, we'll drive out in a taxi. And I shall personally select the driver—a man to be depended on in an emergency."

So excited was the housekeeper that she had difficulty in preparing the evening meal. In the end Penny took over, shooing her out of the kitchen.

"I declare I don't know why I am so nervous," Mrs. Weems shivered. "I haven't felt so shaky since the time I attended a seance at Osandra's."

"You saw ghosts a-plenty on that occasion," smiled Penny. "I only hope we have as much luck tonight."

By eight o'clock everything was in readiness for the journey into the country. Dressing warmly and carrying an extra blanket, Penny and Mrs. Weems walked to a nearby cab station. There the housekeeper selected a driver, a burly man who looked as if he might have been an ex-prizefighter.

"Sure, Ma'am," he said as Mrs. Weems questioned him, "you can depend on me to look after you."

"How are you at capturing ghosts?" inquired Penny, climbing into the cab.

The driver looked a trifle startled. "Swell!" he rejoined. "Bring on your spook, and if he don't weigh no more than two hundred pounds, I'll nail him!"

Penny and Mrs. Weems were satisfied that they were in good hands. They instructed the man, Joe Henkell, to drive directly to the old Harrison estate.

"By the way, do you know who owns the property?" Penny asked as the cab rolled toward the country.

"Fellow from the East," Joe flung over his shoulder. "I'm not sure. Think his name is Deming—George Allan Deming. Wealthy sportsman. Has his own plane an' everything."

"Married?"

"Couldn't tell you. The estate has been closed up this winter."

The cab soon approached the familiar grounds. Penny directed the driver to pull up some distance from the dark house.

"Switch off the headlights," she instructed. "We'll wait here. It may be a long time too, so make yourself comfortable."

Joe, taking Penny at her word, began to smoke a vile-smelling cigar which nearly drove Mrs. Weems to distraction. After an hour had elapsed, the housekeeper scarcely could endure the stuffy air of the cab.

"Penny, must we wait any longer?" she asked plaintively.

"Why, it's early, Mrs. Weems. I expect to stay until midnight at least."

"Midnight!" The housekeeper quietly collapsed.

Just then the cab driver turned around, touching Penny's arm. He directed her attention to the house by saying briefly: "A light just went on."

Penny and Mrs. Weems focused their attention on the upper floor of the estate. A single light could be seen burning there, but as they watched it blinked off.

"Now if a ghost is to appear this is the time!" announced Penny. "Why don't we get closer?"

She sprang from the cab. Mrs. Weems and the taxi driver followed with less enthusiasm. The housekeeper, quivering and shaking, clutched the man's arm as she struggled against the wind.

"Joe, you stay right beside me!" she ordered.

"Sure, Ma'am," he said soothingly. "I couldn't get away if I had a mind to."

Penny, a step ahead, held up her hand as a warning for silence. She had seen the familiar white figure rounding a corner of the house.

"There's the ghost!" she whispered. "See! Beyond the gate!"

Joe whistled softly.

"A spook, sure's I'm alive!" he muttered.

"And you promised to nail him," reminded Penny, starting forward along the fence. "We'll creep a little closer. Then Joe, I shall expect you to do your stuff!"

CHAPTER 15 - GHOST IN THE GARDEN

The three investigators moved stealthily along the high fence. Through the iron palings they could see a white-garbed figure walking with measured tread amid the shrubs of the frozen garden. Back and forth the apparition strolled, following a well-trod path between the shrunken snowdrifts.

Penny, Mrs. Weems, and the taxi driver crept closer. The ghostly one did not note their approach. Hooded head bent low, he glided to the gate, testing chain and padlock.

"Poor restless soul!" whispered Mrs. Weems.

Penny gave the housekeeper a tiny pinch to break the spell which had fallen upon her. "That's no ghost," she whispered. "Don't you see! It's a man wearing a heavy white bathrobe over his clothing. He's pulled the wide collar up over his head like a hood!"

"It's a man all right," added the taxi driver. "You can tell by the way he walks. Ghosts kinda slither, don't they?"

"I believe it's someone imprisoned on the grounds!" Penny whispered tensely. "Watch!"

The ghost, his face shadowed, rattled the chain again. Then with a distinct, audible sigh, he turned and tramped back along the fence away from the gate.

"Aw, that spook could get out if he wanted to," muttered the taxi driver. "Why don't he climb over the fence?"

"Perhaps the man is a sleep walker," suggested Mrs. Weems nervously. "Whoever he is, the poor fellow should be in his bed."

Penny was determined to learn the identity of the man. Moving to the gate, she called softly. The figure in white whirled around, looking straight toward her.

Penny caught a fleeting impression of a lean, startled face. Then the man turned and fled toward the house. No longer could there be any doubt that he was a man, for as he ran the legs of his woolen pajamas showed beneath the white robe.

"Wait!" Penny called. "Please wait!"

The ghostly one hesitated, and glanced over his shoulder. But the next moment he was gone, having vanished through a side door into the house.

Penny, weak from excitement, clung to the gate. "Mrs. Weems!" she cried. "Did you see him?"

"Yes, you frightened him away when you shouted."

"But didn't you notice his face? As he turned toward me, I caught a glimpse of it. Mrs. Weems, the man looked like Dad!"

"Oh, Penny," the housekeeper murmured, taking her arm, "you can't be right. How could it be your father?"

"It looked like him."

"Not to me," said Mrs. Weems firmly. "Why, if it had been Mr. Parker, he would have answered when you called. He wouldn't have run away."

Penny was compelled to acknowledge the logic of the housekeeper's reasoning. "I guess that's true," she said reluctantly. "I'll admit I didn't see his face plainly. I wanted it to be Dad so badly I may have imagined the resemblance."

A light was switched on in an upstairs room of the estate house. However, blinds were lowered, and those on the ground did not obtain another glimpse of the mysterious man who haunted the snowy garden. Finally Mrs. Weems induced Penny to return to the taxi.

Speeding toward Riverview, neither of them had much to say. Penny could not blot from her mind the vision of a startled, bewildered face. Reason told her that Mrs. Weems was right—the man could not be her father. Who then, was he? Why had he refused to talk to her at the gate?

"The man may have been a sleep walker," she thought. "Possibly the owner of the estate, Mr. Deming."

The cab had reached the business section of Riverview. Upon impulse Penny decided to stop at the *Star* plant to make sure that everything was going well.

"It won't take me long," she assured Mrs. Weems. "Why don't you wait in the cab?"

Only a skeleton night force was on duty at the *Star* office. The advertising department had been closed, and on the floor above, scrub women were busy mopping up. A sleepy-eyed desk man greeted Penny as she entered the deserted newsroom.

"Everything's Okay," he assured her. "The final edition's out, and most of the boys have gone home. I was just taking a little cat nap."

"Any news?"

"Not about your father. The police have been kept busy chasing down false rumors. About four hours ago a report came in your father had been seen in Chicago."

"Chicago!"

"Just a fake report."

"Oh, I see," said Penny weakly. "No word from Jerry, I suppose?"

The deskman shook his head. "Plenty of mail for you though."

"Anything important?"

"Mostly replies to that reward offer you made. A lot of 'em are screwball letters. Your father's been seen in every section of the city from the river to the Heights."

"Where is the mail?"

"I dumped it on your father's desk."

"I'll take it home to read," Penny said. "By going through every letter carefully I may stumble upon a clue."

She crossed the newsroom and opened the door of her father's office.

The light was not on. Groping for the wall switch, her keen ears detected stealthy steps moving away from her. Sensing the presence of someone in the room she called sharply: "Who's here?"

There was no reply. Across the room, a door softly opened and clicked shut. Penny was startled. Although the private office had two entrances, one leading directly into the hall, the latter had not been used in years. Usually the door was locked and a clothes tree stood in front of it.

Her groping fingers found the switch and she flooded the room with light. A glance revealed that mail lying on the desk had been disturbed. One of the top drawers remained open. The clothes tree had been moved from in front of the hall door. Plainly, someone had just fled from the room!

Darting to the corridor door, Penny jerked it open. No one was in sight. However, at the end of the deserted hall, she saw the elevator cage moving slowly downward.

"I'll get that fellow yet!" she thought grimly.

Taking the hall at a run, she plunged down the stairway two steps at a time. Breathless but triumphant, she reached the lower corridor just as the cage stopped with a jerk.

Harley Schirr stepped out, closing the grilled door behind him.

"Fancy meeting you here!" said Penny, her eyes flashing. "What were you doing in my father's office?"

Schirr regarded her coolly. Without answering, he tried to brush past her.

"You were looking for something in Dad's desk!" Penny accused, blocking the way. "I know how you got in too! Through the hall entrance. You're such a professional snooper you probably have a skeleton key that unlocks half the doors in the building!"

"I've had about enough of your insolence!" Schirr retorted. "There's no law which says I can't come to this plant. And speaking of law, I may sue you for libel."

"What a laugh."

"You'll not be laughing in a few days, Miss Parker! Oh, no! I've hired a lawyer, and we're preparing our case. You've insulted me, humiliated me in the eyes of my fellow newspapermen, but you'll have to pay. And pay handsomely!"

The threat failed to disturb Penny. Schirr, determined to wound her deeply, went on with grim satisfaction.

CHAPTER 15 - GHOST IN THE GARDEN

"You kid yourself you'll see your father again," he jeered. "Well, you won't! Mr. Parker is dead and you may as well get used to the idea."

Penny's eyes burned. "You say that only to torture me!"

"It's the truth. If you weren't so blind you'd acknowledge it. Your father tried to run a gang of professional tire-thieves out of this town, and they did for him."

"You seem very certain of your facts, Mr. Schirr. Perhaps you know some of the higher-ups personally."

"How would I?"

"Your knowledge is so complete," Penny said scathingly.

"I'm only telling you my opinion," Schirr growled, now on the defensive. "If you want to ride along in a sweet dream that's Okay with me."

"I want to get at the truth," said Penny shortly. "Do you have one scrap of evidence that Dad has fallen into the hands of enemies?"

Schirr hesitated, knowing well that an affirmative answer might lead to questioning from the police.

"I don't have any knowledge of the case," he said. "At least not for publication!"

Flashing a superior smile, he pushed past Penny, and went out of the building.

CHAPTER 16 - A DOOR IN A BOX

Penny scarcely knew what to think of Harley Schirr's actions. All her accusations were true, of that she was sure. But she was unable to decide whether or not he had any information about her father's strange disappearance.

"The old snooper may be hand in glove with the tire thieves!" she thought bitterly. "I wouldn't put it past him. If I could prove anything, wouldn't I like to turn him over to the police!"

Climbing the stairs, Penny explained briefly to the *Star* deskman what had occurred.

"Shirr here again!" he exclaimed. "Why, I'm sure he never came through the newsroom."

"No, he got into Dad's office by means of that old hall door. Tomorrow I want a new lock put on."

"I'll have it taken care of myself," promised the deskman.

Reentering her father's office, Penny gathered up the mail and carefully locked both doors. She then returned to the waiting taxicab. During the ride home she made no mention of Mr. Schirr, preferring not to worry the housekeeper.

Later in Mr. Parker's study, she and Mrs. Weems examined every letter written in response to the reward offer. Not even one of them offered the slightest promise.

"I'll turn everything over to the police," Penny said with a sigh. "Maybe they'll find a clue I've not considered important."

Both she and Mrs. Weems were feeling the effects of such a long period of strain. Meals had been irregular, appetites poor. Penny in particular had lost so much weight that she looked thin and sallow. Yet somehow she managed to keep up her strength and to face each day with hope.

"Mrs. Weems," she said the next morning at breakfast, "if you'll advance me some money, I'm going on another taxi jaunt today."

"Not to the Harrison place."

"No, out to Mattie Williams' garage. I'm convinced that place is dealing in stolen tires. If only I can reconstruct the evidence which disappeared in Dad's portfolio, I may get a clue that will lead to him."

Without protest, Mrs. Weems gave Penny the money. Secretly she thought that the girl would do much better to turn all of her information over to the police. However, she realized that Penny needed activity to keep her from brooding, so she wisely did not discourage her.

"Don't get into any trouble," she warned anxiously.

"No danger of that, Mrs. Weems. I've not enough pep for it these days."

Engaging the same cabman who had served her so well the previous night, Penny motored to the Williams' garage. She had made no plans and scarcely knew what she would say when she entered the place. As she debated, the big doors of the building opened, and a tow car drove away with Mattie at the wheel.

"There she goes!" thought Penny, disappointed. "I'm afraid my interview will have to wait."

Getting out, she sauntered into the garage office. Mattie's partner, Sam, was nowhere to be seen. Nor did he appear to be working in the main part of the building.

Penny waited a few minutes, then wandered about the floor where a number of cars had been stored. No workmen were in evidence.

"This might be a good time to do a bit of looking around!" she thought suddenly. "I'll never have a better chance."

CHAPTER 16 - A DOOR IN A BOX

Penny opened the doors into the room where she had observed Sam Burkholder mount a new tire on the car of a customer. One wall was stacked high with large wooden boxes, not unlike those she and Louise had seen delivered by the truck driver, Hank Biglow, on the night of the blizzard.

She thumped one of the boxes with her knuckles. It gave off a hollow, empty sound. She tried another box with no better luck. Some of the big crates had been opened. They contained nothing except a little brown wrapping paper.

Disappointed, Penny turned away. But as she moved toward the exit, her eyes flashed upon one of the boxes which had escaped her attention. Boards were loose at one end, and could be hinged back on their nails like a door.

Intrigued, Penny crossed to the crate. As she pulled on one of the boards, all swung back as a unit.

"Why, it's like a door!" she thought. "A door in a box!"

Penny gazed into the box and was further amazed. It had no back wall. Instead, she saw a long, empty tunnel formed by several crates piled one in front of the other. And at the very end stood a real door!

"Maybe this is the pay-off!" thought Penny excitedly.

Pulling the boards into place behind her, she stooped and made her way through the tunnel to the door. It was locked.

"I'll bet a cent stolen tires are stored in that room!" reasoned Penny. "If only I could get in there!"

Her mind did not dwell long on the problem. A moment later she was alarmed to hear a low murmur of voices. Someone was approaching the storage room from the main part of the garage. Unless she wished to be trapped in the tunnel of boxes, she must abandon the investigation!

Penny started hurriedly toward the opening. Before she could get through the tunnel, the big double doors squeaked open and she heard heavy footsteps in the room. Peering out through a knothole in one of the boxes, she saw Mattie Williams and her partner, Sam. They were arguing and their voices came to her plainly:

"Guess you didn't look for me back quite so soon, Sam," Mattie reprimanded her partner. "When I went off in the tow car you figured I'd be gone a long time. Thought it would give you a good chance to tamper with the books!"

"That's not so, Mattie. I was marking up some expenses like I always do."

"I've been aiming to have a straight talk with you for a long time, Sam," the woman resumed. "That's why I asked you to step back here in the storage room. No use having the customers know about our differences."

"I don't see what you've got to squawk about," Sam retorted. "Ain't you made more money since I teamed up with you than you ever did before?"

"Yes."

"But you're always afraid I'll cheat you out of a penny."

"I've caught you in some dishonest tricks. About those tires—"

A loud, insistent tooting of an automobile horn broke up the conversation. Abandoning the argument, Mattie and Sam went to serve the impatient customer.

Penny did not tarry. Crawling from the tunnel, she glanced about for a means of escape. Fortunately, the room had an outside exit. Making use of it, she returned to the waiting taxi, without seeing either Sam or Mattie again.

"Police station, Joe," she instructed.

"How do you want to go?" the cab driver inquired. "This road or No. 32?"

"Let's drive past the old Harrison place."

"Sure," grinned Joe. "Maybe we'll see that spook again!"

The cab bumped along the frozen road, soon coming within view of the hillside estate. Joe slowed down without being requested to do so.

"I was tellin' the boys about that place last night," he flung over his shoulder. "They tell me the owner is this guy Deming. He's gone East for the winter. A big, fat, bald-headed man."

"Our ghost was a thin person."

"Yeah, I was thinking that," agreed Joe. "Maybe Deming's got a sick relative or something."

The explanation did not satisfy Penny. With troubled eyes she gazed toward the rambling old house which by daylight looked so deserted. No smoke curled from the chimneys. Had it not been for a trail of footprints along the fence, she easily could have convinced herself that she had imagined the events of the previous night.

"Say, who's that trackin' through the fields?" Joe suddenly demanded.

Penny turned to glance in the direction that the cabman pointed. Her heart did a little flip-flop. A woman in a long black coat, market basket on her arm, was hastening toward the rear door of the estate house.

"Stop the cab, Joe!" she cried.

The car came to a halt with a little sideways skid. Leaping out, Penny plunged through the drifts and was able to confront the woman at the rear gate of the premises.

"How do you do," she greeted her breathlessly.

The woman was so startled that she nearly dropped her market basket. Confused, she stammered a reply and started to unlock the gate.

"Just a moment, please," requested Penny. "May I come inside and talk to you?"

"About what?"

"My father's disappearance. You made an appointment to meet me at the cemetery. Why did you run away?"

The bold attack was not without an effect. The woman gasped, and fumbled nervously with the key to the padlock.

"I don't know what you're talking about!" she muttered.

"Unless you tell me everything you know regarding my father's disappearance, I'll call the police!"

"The police—" the woman repeated, plainly frightened.

"Yes," Penny went on relentlessly, "this is a serious matter. It will do you no good to bluff."

The woman gave up trying to unlock the gate. Setting her basket down in the snow she said weakly: "You advertised a reward—"

"I'll still be glad to pay it for worthwhile information. What do you know about my father?"

The woman drew a deep breath. "Well, I picked him up in my car after the accident."

"You did?" Penny became jubilant. "Where is he now?"

"I can't tell you that. Mr. Parker asked me to take him to Mercy Hospital. I let him off at the entrance to the grounds. That's the last I saw of him."

"My father entered the hospital?"

"I don't know. I didn't remain to watch."

The story was disappointing. If true, Mr. Parker's disappearance remained as mysterious as ever. Penny was silent a moment and then she asked the woman why she had fled from the cemetery.

"Because I saw a police car parked behind the bushes," the other answered defiantly. "And those detectives chased me, too! I only intended to be helpful and maybe win a reward. Now I want nothing to do with the case. I've told you everything I know."

The woman unlocked the gate and started to enter the grounds.

"You're not Mrs. Deming?" Penny asked quickly.

"Who I am is my own business."

"I suppose the ghost is your own affair too!"

"Ghost? What ghost?"

"You live here, yet you haven't learned that the grounds are haunted?" Penny inquired significantly. "Nearly every night a man in white wanders back and forth in the garden."

"I don't know anything about it!" the woman said nervously. "I'll not answer any more questions either!"

Plainly frightened, she snapped shut the padlock of the gate and fled into the house.

CHAPTER 17 - ADVENTURE BY MOONLIGHT

A moment Penny stood gazing at the estate house. She considered climbing the iron fence and trying to gain entrance to the dwelling. Then, deciding that nothing would be achieved by again accosting the strange woman, she returned to the waiting taxi.

"Where to?" asked the cabman.

"It's still the police station," directed Penny, repeating an earlier order. "I have twice as much to report now."

As the cab pulled away, she noticed a movement of curtains at the front of the estate house. Evidently the woman who had fled, was watching.

Joe made a quick trip to Riverview, depositing Penny at the doorstep of Central Station.

"Will you need me any more?" he asked hopefully.

"I may."

"Okay," said Joe, slamming the cab door. "I'll stick around. You know, I kinda like this job."

Once inside the police station, Penny inquired for Chief Jalman. Unable to see him, she asked to speak to the two detectives who had been assigned to her father's case. Both men were away from the building.

"Why not talk to Carl Burns?" suggested the desk sergeant. "He's familiar with the case."

Penny was sent to see a heavy-set man who warmed himself by a steaming radiator. Evidently he had spent several hours in an unheated police car for he stamped his feet to restore circulation.

"Mr. Burns?" inquired Penny.

The man turned, staring at her. Penny returned the stare. She had seen the officer before and the recollection was not entirely pleasant. He was the same officer she had met near Mattie's garage on the night of the blizzard.

"What may I do for you?" he asked.

Uncomfortably aware of the officer's scrutiny, Penny began to tell of her visit to the Williams' garage. She stammered a bit and lost confidence.

"You say you saw some big boxes at the garage," he demanded. "What's so suspicious about that?"

Penny tried to explain about the tunnel of boxes which led to a hidden storage room. Even to her own ears the story had a fantastic sound.

"What you *think* or *surmise* doesn't go in this business!" the officer said rather rudely. "Did you actually see any stolen tires?"

"Well, no, I didn't," Penny admitted. "The door was locked."

"Are you willing to swear out a warrant charging Mattie and her partner with dealing in stolen merchandise?"

"I don't suppose I'd dare do that. I thought if police would investigate—"

"We can't go on suspicions, Miss Parker. We act only on sound evidence."

"Well, it doesn't matter so much about the stolen tires," Penny said desperately. "I have another clue—a really important one. I've found the woman who eluded Detectives Brandon and Fuller at the cemetery!"

"Now we may get somewhere," replied the officer. "Who is the woman? Where did you see her?"

Penny told everything she knew about the woman who had taken her father to Mercy Hospital. Word for word she repeated their recent conversation together.

"I'll turn this evidence over to Detective Fuller," the policeman promised. "He'll probably want to question the woman himself."

GHOST BEYOND THE GATE

"I hope he does it right away," replied Penny. "She may take it into her head to skip out of town."

Officer Burns smiled wearily. "Just trust us to handle the case," he said. "We know our business."

Penny left the station feeling none too satisfied. Although she had nothing against Mr. Burns, she sensed that he did not like her. She wondered if she could depend on him to repeat her story as she had told it.

"If that estate house isn't investigated immediately, I'll do something myself!" she thought.

Joe, the cabman, still waited. Signaling him, Penny regretfully explained that she would have no further use for his services.

"Well, if you change your mind and want to do some more ghost huntin' tonight, just give me a ring," Joe grinned. "My number's 20476."

Penny carefully wrote it down. She then walked to the nearby *Star* building where many matters awaited her attention. There she worked without interruption until late afternoon, taking only enough time to call the police station. Detective Fuller was not available. So far as she could learn, no investigation had been made of the Harrison estate.

Thoroughly annoyed, Penny tramped home to dinner. Only a cold meal awaited her. Mrs. Weems, ill with a headache, had set out a few dishes on the kitchen table, and gone to bed.

"It's nothing," the housekeeper insisted as Penny questioned her anxiously. "I've just worried too much the past few days."

"Let me call Doctor Barnell."

"Indeed not," Mrs. Weems remonstrated. "I'll be all right tomorrow."

Penny brewed a cup of tea and made the housekeeper as comfortable as she could. By the time she had eaten a snack and washed the dishes it was eight o'clock. Debating a long while, she went to the telephone and summoned a cab.

"Number 20476," she requested.

Penny was zipping on her galoshes when the doorbell rang. Without giving her time to answer it, Louise Sidell marched into the kitchen bearing a freshly baked lemon pie.

"Mother sent this over," she explained. "I slipped on the ice coming over and nearly had a catastrophe!"

Carefully Louise deposited the pie on the kitchen table. Cutting short Penny's praise of it, she inquired alertly: "Going somewhere?"

Penny explained that she intended to motor to the Harrison estate.

"Not alone?" Louise demanded.

"I'll have to, I guess. Mrs. Weems is sick, so I can't take her along."

"You could invite me," Louise said eagerly. "I'll telephone mother to come over and stay with Mrs. Weems while we're gone!"

The arrangement proved satisfactory to everyone. Mrs. Sidell came immediately to the house, and very shortly thereafter the girls sped away in Joe's taxicab.

The night was a pleasant one, mildly cold, but with a bright moon.

"Park before you get to the estate," Penny directed the driver. "We don't want to be seen. It might defeat our purpose."

Joe drew up in a clump of trees some distance from the Harrison grounds. He then walked with the girls to the spiked fence. There was no sign of activity.

Two hours elapsed. During that time nothing unusual occurred. No lights were visible inside the house. Even Penny began to lose heart.

"This is getting pretty boring," she sighed. "I don't believe the ghost is going to show up tonight."

"We may have been observed," suggested Louise. "One can see very plainly tonight."

After another half hour had elapsed Penny was willing to return to the cab. The three started away from the fence. Just then they heard a door slam inside the house. Instantly they froze against the screen of bushes, waiting.

"There's the ghost!" whispered Louise.

A figure had appeared in the garden beyond the gate. But the one who walked alone was not a ghost. Plainly he was garbed in street clothes rather than white. Over his suit he wore a heavy overcoat. A snap-brimmed hat was pulled low on his forehead.

Penny could not see the man's face, but the silhouette seemed strangely familiar.

CHAPTER 17 - ADVENTURE BY MOONLIGHT

"That looks like Dad!" she whispered, clutching Louise's hand. "It is he! I'm sure!"

"Oh, it can't be—"

Penny paid no heed to her chum's protest. Breaking away, she ran toward the gate.

The man in the garden became suddenly alert. As he heard the approaching footsteps he gazed toward the road. Upon seeing Penny he started to retreat.

"Wait!" she called frantically. "Don't you know me, Dad? It's Penny!"

The words seemed to convey nothing to the man. He shook his head in a baffled sort of way, and walked swiftly toward the house.

Penny ran on to the gate. It was locked, but she vaulted over, landing in a heap on the other side. By the time she had picked herself up, the man had vanished into the house.

"Are you hurt?" Louise cried, hurrying to the gate.

Penny brushed snow from her coat and did not answer.

"That man couldn't have been your father," Louise said kindly. "Do come back, Penny."

"But it was Dad! I'm sure of it!"

"You called to him," Louise argued. "If it had been Mr. Parker he couldn't have failed to recognize your voice."

"It was Dad," Penny insisted stubbornly. "He's being held a prisoner here!"

"But that's ridiculous! Whoever that man is, he could escape from the grounds just as easily as you climbed the gate."

Penny did not wish to believe, yet she knew her chum was right.

"Anyway, I'm going to talk to him," she declared. "Now that I am inside the grounds, I'll ring the doorbell."

Leaving Louise and Joe on the other side of the fence, Penny went boldly to the front door. She knocked several times and rang the bell. There was no response.

"Why doesn't someone answer?" she thought impatiently.

At the rear of the house a door slammed. Suddenly Louise called from the gate: "Penny! A woman is leaving the estate by the back way!"

Penny darted to the corner of the house. The same woman she had met earlier that day had let herself out the rear gate. Holding the skirts of her long black coat, she fairly ran across the snowy fields.

"Shall I nab her?" called Joe, eager for action.

Penny's reply was surprisingly calm.

"No, let her go," she decided. "While that woman is away, I'll get into the house. I think Dad is in there alone, and I'm going to find him!"

CHAPTER 18 - THROUGH THE CELLAR WINDOW

Penny returned to the front porch and rang the doorbell many times. No one came to admit her. She tested the door, finding it locked. Windows above the porch level could not be raised.

"I'll try the back door," she said, refusing to accept defeat.

Louise and Joe followed her to the rear of the dwelling, but remained on the outside of the fence.

As Penny had feared, the back door also was locked. She tested eight windows. Finally she found one which opened into the cellar. To her delight the sash swung inward as she pushed on it.

"Here I go!" she called to Louise. "You and Joe stay where you are and keep watch."

Penny crawled through the narrow opening and swung herself down to the cellar floor. She landed with a thud beside a laundry tub. The room was dark. Groping her way toward a stairway, she tripped over a box and made a fearful clatter.

"I've certainly advertised my arrival!" she thought ruefully.

At the top of the stairway Penny found a light switch and boldly turned it on. The kitchen door was not locked. She opened it and stepped out into another semi-dark room.

A doorbell at the front of the house began to ring. Penny was dumbfounded. Then she became annoyed, thinking that Louise and the cab driver were trying to get in.

Groping her way through the house, she unlocked the door and flung it open.

"For Pity Sakes!" she exclaimed, and then her voice trailed off.

A uniformed messenger boy stood on the porch.

"Mrs. Botts live here?" he asked, taking a telegram from his jacket pocket.

Penny did not know what to answer. Thinking quickly, she replied: "This is the Deming estate."

The messenger boy turned the beam of his flashlight on the telegram. "Mrs. Lennie Botts, Stop 4, Care of G. A. Deming," he read aloud. "This is the place all right."

"But Mrs. Botts isn't at home now."

"I've had a lot of trouble getting here," the boy complained. "Even had to climb over the gate. How about signing for the telegram?"

"Oh, all right," agreed Penny, accepting the pencil. "I don't know why I didn't think of that idea myself!"

In return for the telegram she gave the boy a small tip. The moment he had gone, she closed the front door and switched on a table lamp.

Penny found herself in a luxuriously furnished living room. The rug underfoot was Chinese, the furniture solid mahogany, hand carved. However, she had no interest in her surroundings. Rather tensely, she examined the telegram. Dared she open it?

"What's ten years or so of jail in my young life?" she cajoled herself. "I'm willing to spend it in Sing Sing if only I can find Dad!"

Penny ripped open the envelope. The message, addressed to Mrs. Lennie Botts was terse and none too revealing:

"HAVE CHANGED PLANS. WILL RETURN THE TWENTY-SEVENTH BY PLANE. PLEASE HAVE EVERYTHING IN READINESS."

The telegram was signed by the owner of the estate, G. A. Deming.

"Today is the twenty-seventh of the month," thought Penny. "This message must have been several hours delayed."

CHAPTER 18 - THROUGH THE CELLAR WINDOW

The telegram had provided little information. Evidently the woman who had refused to tell her name was Mrs. Lennie Botts. Regretting that she had opened the message, Penny tossed it carelessly on the table.

Footsteps sounded on the floor directly above. Penny had taken no pains to be quiet. Nevertheless, her pulse quickened as she heard someone pad to the head of the stairway. A muffled voice called: "Who's there?"

Penny's heart leaped for she was sure she recognized the tones. Fairly trembling with excitement, she darted to the foot of the circular staircase. On the top landing in the heavy shadows stood a man whose face she could not see.

"Dad!" she cried. "I'm Penny."

"Penny?" the man demanded impatiently as if the name meant nothing to him. "Where is Mrs. Botts?"

"Why, she went away."

"And how did you get into the house?"

"Through a cellar window."

"I thought so! Young lady, I don't know what you're doing here in Mrs. Bott's absence. Unless you leave at once I'll summon the police."

Penny was not to be discouraged so easily. She started slowly up the stairway.

"Stand where you are!" the man ordered sharply. "I've been sick, but I'm still a match for any housebreaker. I have a revolver—"

So dark was the stairway that Penny could not know whether or not the man was bluffing. His voice, startlingly similar to her father's, sounded grim and determined. Knowing that a stranger would have good reason to treat her as a burglar, she was afraid to venture further.

"Dad—" she began.

"Don't keep calling me Dad!" he snapped.

"Who are you?" asked Penny, completely baffled.

"Who am I?" the man repeated. "Why, I'm Lester Jones, a salesman. I room here."

The answer dumbfounded Penny. "Then you're not being held a prisoner by Mrs. Botts?" she faltered.

"On the contrary, Mrs. Botts has been very kind to me. Especially since I've been sick."

Penny's perplexity increased. "But I've seen you wandering in the garden at night," she murmured. "Why do you do it?"

"Because—oh, hang it! Do I have to explain everything to you? My head's aching again. Unless you go away and stop bothering me, I'll call the police."

Penny was completely crushed. She had been so sure that the man was her father! Seemingly she had made a very stupid mistake.

"I'll go," she said quietly.

Retreating down the stairway, she left the opened telegram on the living-room table and switched off the light. Then unlocking the kitchen door, she rejoined Louise and Joe.

"I guess you didn't have any luck," her chum commented, observing her downcast face.

Penny ruefully admitted that the man who had been seen in the garden was Lester Jones.

"I knew he wasn't your father," Louise replied. "You wouldn't listen to reason—"

"All the same, his voice was similar," Penny cut in. "Why, the man even used one of Dad's pet expressions."

"What was it?" Louise inquired curiously.

"'Oh, hang it!' That's the expression Dad uses when he's irritated."

Louise helped her chum over the back fence and guided her toward the parked taxi. Midway there Penny paused to stare up at the dark windows of the second floor.

"Lou!" she exclaimed. "That man must have been Dad even if he didn't know me!"

"Oh, Penny, don't start that all over again," Louise pleaded. "You're only torturing yourself."

"I'm going back!"

"No, we can't let you, Penny."

Louise held her chum's arm firmly. Joe opened the door of the taxi and they pushed her in. Penny protested for a moment, then submitted.

"All right, but we're going straight to the police station!" she announced. "I'll not be satisfied until that man positively is identified as Lester Jones."

A few minutes later, at the police station, Detective Fuller heard the entire story. It was the first he had learned about Mrs. Botts, for Penny's earlier message had not been delivered by Policeman Burns.

"For that matter, I've not seen Burns today," the detective explained. "I'll go to the estate at once and question the woman."

Again Penny and Louise taxied to the estate, this time trailed by a police car. Detective Fuller broke the padlock on the gate and led the party to the front door.

A light now burned in the living room. To Penny's astonishment, the door was opened by Mrs. Botts.

"Good evening," she greeted the visitors pleasantly.

Detective Fuller flashed his badge. "We want to ask you a few questions," he said. "May we come in?"

With obvious reluctance the woman stepped aside, allowing the party to enter the living room. Penny's gaze roved to the center table. The telegram which she had opened no longer was there.

Mrs. Botts did not offer chairs to the callers. Glaring at Penny with undisguised dislike, she said coldly: "I suppose I am indebted to you for this visit. What is it you want?"

"I understand you have a roomer here," began Detective Fuller.

"A roomer?" Mrs. Botts echoed blankly.

"Yes, a man by the name of Lester Jones."

"Ridiculous! You don't seem to realize that this is the Deming estate."

"Are you an employee here?"

"I am the housekeeper. During Mr. Deming's absence I look after the property. I assure you no one but myself lives in the house at present."

"No roomer ever has stayed here?"

Mrs. Botts drew herself up proudly. "Would Mr. Deming be likely to annoy himself with roomers? He has a very substantial fortune."

"You might try to pick up a few dollars yourself."

"Mr. Deming would not hear of such a thing! He pays me well."

Detective Fuller asked additional questions, trying to learn whether or not the woman was the one who had fled from the cemetery. Mrs. Botts frankly admitted that she had taken Mr. Parker to the hospital, but she denied ever trying to collect a ransom.

"What you say now doesn't agree with your original story," Penny protested. "You admitted to me—"

"I admitted nothing," Mrs. Botts broke in indignantly. "I have no secrets to hide!"

"But I'm sure Mr. Jones is living in this house," Penny said stubbornly. "He's upstairs."

"Indeed?" mocked Mrs. Botts. "Perhaps you'd like to search the house."

"Yes, we would," said Detective Fuller.

Mrs. Botts remained undisturbed. Bestowing upon Penny a look of deep contempt, she motioned toward the stairway.

"Very well, search the house," she invited with cool assurance. "I've told you the truth. You'll find no one here but myself."

CHAPTER 19 - A BAFFLING SEARCH

In systematic, unhurried fashion, Detective Fuller went through every room in the Deming house. The bed chambers, nine in number, were in perfect order. Only Mrs. Botts' suite over the kitchen appeared to have been used recently.

As the search progressed, Penny's bewilderment increased. She knew that Lester Jones had been in the house an hour earlier, yet there was no sign of him. Personally she inspected clothes closets and bureau drawers. Not an article could she find that ever had belonged to her father. She did come upon a white woolen bathrobe. Believing it to be the garment worn by the "ghost" she called it to Detective Fuller's attention.

"Oh, that robe belongs to my employer, Mr. Deming," explained Mrs. Botts.

Penny indicated water stains along the hem which suggested that the garment had been allowed to trail in the snow.

"Sometimes I wear the robe when I go outside to bring in the washing," replied Mrs. Botts. "It is warmer than my coat."

Try as she would, Penny could not trip the woman into making any damaging admissions. Mrs. Botts had changed her original story and would not acknowledge that she had fled from the cemetery. Stubbornly, she maintained that she had told everything she knew about Mr. Parker's disappearance.

"I took him to Mercy Hospital in my employer's car," she repeated to Detective Fuller. "That's the last I saw of him."

"In what condition was Mr. Parker when you left him?" questioned the detective.

"He seemed all right. Perhaps he was a bit dazed."

"Why didn't you report to the police?"

"Because I didn't see the newspapers for a day," Mrs. Botts replied sullenly. "Later I read Miss Parker's offer of a reward."

"Then you did write, requesting me to run the ad in the *Star*!" Penny cried triumphantly.

"No, of course not," Mrs. Botts retorted, "I merely read the item."

Penny knew Mrs. Botts was not telling the entire truth, but to prove it seemed an impossible matter. Neither could she establish that a man who claimed to be Lester Jones had been living in the house. True, Louise and the taxi driver would support her story, but it would only be their word against Mrs. Botts'. The situation had become hopelessly confusing.

Detective Fuller was not entirely satisfied with the housekeeper's story. "Guess we'll have to take you along to the station for questioning," he concluded.

Only then did Mrs. Botts lose her composure.

"No, don't take me away!" she pleaded anxiously. "My employer is coming home tonight. I just received the telegram. If I'm not here when he arrives, I may lose my job!"

Actually Detective Fuller had little evidence against Mrs. Botts and doubted that he could hold her many hours in jail. Far more might be gained by allowing the woman her freedom and keeping watch of the house.

"We'll let you stay here," he decided after a moment's thought. "However, you'll be wanted for questioning a little later. Make no attempt to leave the premises."

"I won't try to go away," Mrs. Botts promised. "I want to cooperate with the police. All I ask is that my employer, Mr. Deming, doesn't hear of this. I'm innocent and it's not right for me to lose a good job."

Very shortly the party bade the woman goodbye and left the estate. Detective Fuller assigned a policeman to keep watch of the property and then returned to Riverview. Louise and Penny, completely bewildered, left with their driver, Joe, debated their next action.

"Where to?" the cabman inquired. "Home?"

"I suppose so," sighed Penny. "I never was in such a muddle in all my life. What became of that man I thought was Dad?"

"He must have left the house while we were at the police station," Louise declared. "It was a surprise finding Mrs. Botts there too! She must have returned in a hurry after we went away."

"Mrs. Botts got rid of Lester Jones somehow," Penny said with conviction. "Oh, she's a slick one!"

As Joe shifted gears, the girls observed a dark figure approaching the estate from down the road.

"Wait!" Penny instructed the cabman. "Let's see who it is."

A moment later the figure emerged from the shadow cast by a giant tree. Penny was surprised to recognize Mose Johnson. The old colored man carried a basket on his arm and evidently had been doing a little late marketing at the crossroads store.

"Good evening, Mose," Penny greeted him as he approached the cab.

"Evenin', Miss Penny," he beamed, pausing. "I'se suah astonished to see yo' all out dis way. Has yo' been lookin' for dat ghost?"

"I'm afraid I have," Penny admitted ruefully. "I've certainly had no luck."

Mose shifted the market basket to his other hand. "Dat ole ghost ain't been around so much lately," he explained. "I comes by dis spot half an hour ago on my way to de sto' to get some victuals. Dere wasn't no ghost around den either. If dere had a been I'd have seen him, you kin be suah o' dat. I was mighty skittish and ready to make mahself absent in about two shakes."

"And you didn't see a thing?" inquired Penny.

"Well now, I can't rightly say dat," Old Mose corrected. "I didn't see no ghost but I did see a taxicab."

"Ours, I suppose."

"Not dis one, Miss. De cab I see was a yelleh one."

The information interested Penny. "Which way was it going, Mose?" she asked quickly.

"It wasn't goin', Miss Penny. It was standin' right at de gate. Den I sees two dark lookin' white men git out and go into de big house."

"You did?" Penny demanded eagerly. "Then what happened? Did the cab drive away?"

"It waited 'till de two men came back, 'cept when dey comes back dere is three of 'em!"

"Three men?" Penny cried, her excitement mounting. "What did the third man look like, Mose? Think hard! It's very important."

"Well," said Mose, "he was tall and he had something in his hand. A funny lookin' little satchel. I guess you calls it a quick-case."

"You don't mean a brief case?"

"Yes, dat's it," Mose grinned. "Anyways, dey all gits in de taxicab and off dey snorts. And dat's all I sees. Dere wasn't no ghost."

The colored man's rambling information served to confirm Penny's own suspicions. Mrs. Botts had lied. A roomer known as Lester Jones had been held at the house and later hustled away. Perhaps the man *was* her father!

"Mose," she cried, "the person you saw may have been Dad! Did it look like him?"

"Why, now yo' speaks of it, dere was somethin' about dat man dat look like Mr. Parker," the colored man agreed. "Kinda de way he walked. I couldn't see his face cause he kept it sort o' tucked down in his collar."

"All the same, it must have been Dad!" Penny exclaimed. "The brief case practically proves it! Tell me, which way did the cab go?"

"Straight down de road," said Mose, pointing. "But de car's been gone a long time now. If you figures on catchin' dose men, you all bettah be travelin'."

CHAPTER 20 - ACCUSATIONS

Alarmed and excited by Mose Johnson's revelation, Penny glanced about for the policeman who had been assigned to watch the Deming mansion. The officer had taken cover somewhere and was not to be seen.

"Joe, drive as fast as you can to the airplane spotting station!" she ordered the cabman. "I'll telephone the police station from there."

As the taxi bounced along over the frozen road, the girls kept close watch for the yellow cab Mose Johnson had mentioned. They did not expect to overtake it. If the old colored man's story was accurate, the taxi bearing Mr. Parker had left the mansion at least a half hour earlier.

"Dad must have been spirited away immediately after I talked to him!" Penny said. "He's been drugged or something! Otherwise he would have known me."

"But according to Mose, your father must have gone willingly with those men," Louise returned.

"That's the queer part."

"Of course, you're not certain the man is your father."

"Yes, I am!" Penny insisted. "I was almost sure of it earlier this evening. Now I know! Oh, Lou, something terrible has happened to Dad!"

Louise drew her chum into the hollow of her arm. "Brace up!" she said sternly. "You're not going to cave in now, are you?"

Penny's slumping shoulders stiffened. She brushed away a tear. "Of course I'm not going to cave in!" she replied indignantly. "I'll find Dad—tonight, too!"

Enroute to the airplane spotting station, the cab neither met nor passed any vehicle. Leaving Louise in the taxi, Penny clattered up the tower steps and burst into the overheated room where Salt Sommers was making out a report. Her words fairly tumbled over one another as she told him what had happened.

"Will you notify police for me?" she pleaded.

"Of course," Salt assured her, reaching for a telephone. "My relief's due in five minutes now, so I'll be free to join in the search."

While the photographer waited impatiently for a connection, Penny asked him if he had seen a yellow taxi pass the tower.

"Not since I've been on duty. The cab must have taken another road."

Salt completed the call to the Riverview Police Station and was told that every radio-equipped cruiser in the city would be ordered to watch for the yellow cab. As he hung up the receiver, a low humming sound was heard outside the tower.

"Listen!" commanded Salt. "A plane!"

Distinctly they both could hear the roar of a motor to the eastward.

"That's an unidentified ship," Salt declared, reaching for another telephone. Taking down the receiver he said tersely: "Army Flash," and went on to report the position of the passing airplane.

Penny had gone to the doorway. She could see the wing lights of the passing ship. As she watched, the lights descended in a steep glide.

"Salt!" she called. "The plane is landing!"

The photographer darted to the platform to see for himself. "You're right!" he exclaimed. "It's coming down at the Deming estate!"

"Mr. Deming is due home tonight from the East," Penny added. "That must be his plane."

Salt went inside to complete his report to headquarters. As he rejoined Penny, they saw a man trudging along the road toward the tower.

"My relief," said the photographer. "I'm free to go."

Gathering up his belongings, he followed Penny to the waiting taxicab. There a brief conference was held. The girls were in favor of searching for the yellow taxi, but Salt pointed out that the chance of finding it was a slim one. He proposed that they return to the mansion and try to force information from Mrs. Botts.

"Detective Fuller had no luck," replied Penny. "She has one story and she sticks to it. Her one fear is that she'll lose her job."

"Then this is the time to make things merry for her!" urged the photographer. "If Mr. Deming just arrived home, we'll toss a few firebrands around and find out what he has to say!"

The suggestion appealed to Penny. From the first she had distrusted Mrs. Botts and felt that police had been entirely too lenient with her.

"All right, let's go!" she agreed. "If Mrs. Botts loses her job, I'm sure it's no more than she deserves."

Joe drove the party once more to the Deming mansion. No policeman was in evidence near the premises. Actually he had gone to the crossroads store to report to his superiors the arrival of Mr. Deming's airplane, but at the moment Penny assumed the man was neglecting his duties.

"If this case ever is solved, we must do it ourselves!" she declared, thumping on the front door. "I'm in no mood to take any slippery answers from Mrs. Botts!"

After a long delay the door was opened by the caretaker. Recognizing Penny and her friends, the woman sought to lock them out.

"Oh, no you don't!" said Salt, pushing her firmly aside. "We want to see Mr. Deming."

"He's not here," Mrs. Botts replied nervously. "Please leave me alone. Go away!"

Ignoring the plea, Penny, Louise, and the photographer walked boldly into the living room. A fire burned in the grate and there were fresh flowers on the table.

"Where is Mr. Deming?" asked Salt in a loud voice.

Footsteps sounded on the circular stairway. A portly, bald-headed man with a pleasant face came heavily down the steps.

"Did someone ask for me?" he inquired.

"You're Mr. Deming?" asked Salt.

"I am. Flew in from New York about ten minutes ago and was just changing my clothes. What may I do for you?"

"I've been trying to tell these folks you can't see them tonight, Mr. Deming," broke in Mrs. Botts. "You're too tired."

"Nonsense," replied the mansion owner impatiently. "Sit down by the fire, everyone. Tell me what brought you here."

Mrs. Botts began to edge toward the kitchen door. Observing the action, Salt called sharply:

"Don't go, Mrs. Botts. We want to talk to you in particular."

"I've nothing to say," the caretaker retorted tartly.

"Sit down, Mrs. Botts," ordered her employer. "For some reason you have seemed very nervous since I arrived home tonight."

"It was upsetting to get your telegram so late," Mrs. Botts mumbled, sinking down on the sofa.

"Mr. Deming," began Penny, "a great deal has happened here tonight."

"I intended to tell you about it myself," interrupted Mrs. Botts, addressing her employer. "I've not had a chance."

"Be quiet, please," commanded Mr. Deming. "Do continue, Miss—"

"Parker," supplied Penny. She introduced Salt and Louise, then resumed her story.

As the tale unfolded, Mr. Deming listened with increasing amazement. Now and then he focused his gaze upon the crestfallen Mrs. Botts, but he did not speak until Penny had finished.

"This is a very serious charge you have made against my housekeeper," he said then. "Mrs. Botts, what have you to say?"

"There's not a word of truth in it!" the woman cried. "Why, I've worked for you ten years, Mr. Deming. I've been a loyal, faithful servant. Why should I deceive you by taking a stranger into the house?"

CHAPTER 20 - ACCUSATIONS

"It does seem fantastic," replied the perplexed Mr. Deming. "Miss Parker, what proof have you that your accusations are true?"

"The proof of my own eyesight," Penny said quietly. "For that matter, a number of persons saw the ghost wandering about the grounds."

Mrs. Botts tossed her head. "I've already explained that part. Frequently when I go outdoors, I put on your old white bathrobe, Mr. Deming. It's warmer than my coat."

"The ghost happened to be a man," Penny said. "And here is something you don't know, Mrs. Botts. I was in this house earlier this evening while you were away. I talked with your mysterious roomer, and I'm satisfied it was my father."

"So *you* were here!" Mrs. Botts cried angrily. "Mr. Deming, this girl opened the telegram you addressed to me!"

"I did indeed," admitted Penny, unabashed.

Mr. Deming arose and walking over to the fire, stood with his back to it. "I confess I don't know what to say," he said. "I've never had reason to distrust Mrs. Botts."

"Thank you, sir." The housekeeper smiled triumphantly.

Penny realized that Mr. Deming was on the verge of swinging to Mrs. Botts' side. So far the interview had gained nothing. She had told the entire story. There was no further information she could add.

"I suppose we may as well go," she said, looking miserably at Salt.

Penny arose. Suddenly her eyes lighted upon a small object lying half hidden between the cushions of the sofa. Before Mrs. Botts realized what she was about, she had pounced upon it.

"Dad's spectacle case!" she cried triumphantly.

Opening the lid, she held up a pair of dark horn-rimmed glasses.

"I'm sure I don't know where the case came from," Mrs. Botts stammered.

"When Dad reads on the sofa at home, he often loses his case between the cushions!" Penny went on excitedly. "Mrs. Botts, you thought you were very clever getting him away from here and removing all the evidence!"

"A salesman who wore glasses was here last week—" the housekeeper began weakly.

"You can't talk yourself out of this," Penny cut her short, "Mr. Deming, let me show you something."

She reopened the lid of the case and pointed to the initials "A. P." engraved in gold letters.

"Anthony Parker," she said impressively. "Dad had them stamped there because he lost the case so many times. Does this prove my story?"

"It does," said Mr. Deming. Sternly he faced the housekeeper. "Mrs. Botts, you have deeply humiliated me. I shall turn you over to the police."

Mrs. Botts began to weep. Stumbling across the room, she clutched her employer's arm.

"Please don't turn me away from here," she pleaded. "Just give me a chance and I'll explain everything. Please, Mr. Deming! This time I promise to tell the truth!"

CHAPTER 21 - MRS. BOTTS' REVELATION

"Very well, tell your story," Mr. Deming bade the housekeeper. "What do you know about Mr. Parker's disappearance?"

"It was just like I said," Mrs. Botts began in an aggrieved voice. "I was driving not far from the railroad station when I saw the auto accident."

"You say you were driving?" Mr. Deming interposed. "In whose car, may I ask?"

"I used yours, Mr. Deming. I didn't think you would care."

"We'll skip that. Go on with your story."

"Well, I saw the accident. A coupe driven by a young man, crowded Mr. Parker's car off the road."

"Purposely?" asked Penny.

"I don't know. Two men were in the car and they were speeding. I read part of the license number too. It was F-215 something."

"Why didn't you give this information to the police immediately?" demanded Mr. Deming.

"I'm trying to explain. I stopped my car—your car, I mean. Mr. Parker seemed stunned so I offered to take him to the hospital. Of course at that time I didn't know who he was."

"Dad didn't seem much hurt?" Penny inquired quickly.

"He had a few scratches, but nothing serious. We started for the hospital. Before we got there Mr. Parker changed his mind and decided he didn't want to go. He asked me to take him to a hotel or a rooming house."

"How strange!" exclaimed Penny. "Why didn't he ask to go home?"

"Because he didn't remember he had a home," Mrs. Botts replied. "I guess the accident must have stunned him. Anyway, he said his name was Lester Jones. Since he wanted a room and was willing to pay, I figured I could bring him here."

"So you turned my home into a hotel," Mr. Deming remarked rather grimly.

"I—I didn't think you would be back this winter. I wouldn't have done it, Mr. Deming, only I needed extra money. My sister in Kansas has been sick and I've had to send her funds."

"Mrs. Botts, I've always paid you well," her employer responded. "Had you told me you needed more money, I would have assisted you. But go on."

"Well, I brought Mr. Parker here and gave him a room. Right off I noticed how queer he acted. He didn't seem to be sure who he was, and he kept going through some papers he carried in a portfolio, trying to puzzle things out."

"All this while you made no attempt to contact police?" Mr. Deming questioned severely.

"I was wondering what to do when I saw a picture of Mr. Parker in the paper."

"And then you dropped an unsigned letter in my mailbox?" Penny probed.

Mrs. Botts knew that the net was closing tightly about her. Although she tried to slant her story in such a way that she would not appear too much at fault, the facts remained bald and ugly.

"Yes, I left a note at your house," she acknowledged reluctantly. "Later I telephoned and made an appointment to meet you at the cemetery."

"Why didn't you go through with it?" asked Penny. "Were you afraid?"

"I began to realize I might be held for something I never intended to do. Folks started to watch this house. I tried to keep my roomer out of sight, but he'd do such queer things."

"Such as stroll in the garden at night," supplied Penny.

"Yes, I felt sorry for the poor man. He had such dreadful headaches and was so bewildered."

CHAPTER 21 - MRS. BOTTS' REVELATION

"Evidently you weren't sorry enough to tell him who he was," reprimanded Mr. Deming. "Really Mrs. Botts, I can't understand why you acted as you did."

"I just kept getting in deeper and deeper," the housekeeper whined. "Mr. Parker paid me three dollars a day for his room and board. It didn't seem wrong to take the money as long as he was satisfied."

"Where is my father now?" Penny broke in. "That's the important thing."

Mrs. Botts regarded the girl with a trace of her former arrogance. "I don't know what became of Mr. Parker after he left here," she said coldly.

"You sent him away when you knew Mr. Deming was coming home!" Penny accused. "You thought you could keep the truth from your employer!"

"And I would have too, if it hadn't been for you!" Mrs. Botts flared. "I've not done any harm, but you've made a lot out of it, and now I'll be discharged."

"You are quite right about that," agreed Mr. Deming in a quiet voice. "However, there's far more at stake than a job, Mrs. Botts. Even now you don't seem to realize the seriousness of your offense."

"You won't turn me over to the police, will you, Mr. Deming?"

"It will not be in my hands to decide your fate. I strongly advise you to tell everything you know. Where did Mr. Parker go when he left here?"

"I've no idea." Mrs. Botts covered her face. "Oh, leave me alone—don't ask me any more questions. My head buzzes."

"A taxicab with two men in it was seen at the door earlier this evening," Penny went on relentlessly. "What have you to say about that?"

"They were friends who came for Mr. Parker."

"Your friends?"

"Well, no, I found the names and addresses in Mr. Parker's brief case. They were men in the tire business."

This latest scrap of information fairly stunned Penny. As she well knew, her father's portfolio contained only evidence pertaining to the tire-theft case.

"Who were the men?" she demanded.

"One was named Kurt Mollinberg—Ropes Mollinberg his friend called him. I forget the other."

"Ropes Mollinberg!" exclaimed Salt Sommers who had listened quietly to the story. "Why, he's one of the lowest rats in this town! Connected with the numbers racket and I don't know what else!"

"Why did you summon those men, of all persons?" Mr. Deming questioned.

"Well, I found their addresses in the portfolio. I had to get rid of Mr. Parker before you came and I was afraid to call his house."

"You're a cruel, heartless woman!" accused Penny. "You sent my father away with two of the most notorious rascals in Riverview. Why, those men have been waiting for a chance to waylay him! They wanted to get possession of vital evidence Dad had in his portfolio."

"I didn't know," murmured Mrs. Botts. "When they came in the taxi, they offered me money."

"And you took it?"

"I tried not to, but they forced it on me."

Penny sprang to her feet. Only by the greatest effort of will could she keep from telling the housekeeper what she thought of her contemptible actions.

"You sent Dad away with those men," she repeated mechanically. "Didn't he realize who they were?"

"I told him they were his friends. I really thought so. He went willingly enough."

Penny was sick with despair. From the first, the situation had been grave, but now there seemed little hope. From Mrs. Botts' story she could only conclude that her father suffered from a brain injury. Even if she were fortunate enough to find him, he would not be likely to recognize her as his daughter.

"Oh, Salt," she pleaded, turning to the photographer. "What are we to do? What can we do?"

His reply though prompt, was not completely reassuring.

"We've already put every policeman in Riverview on the trail of those men!" he answered soberly. "And we'll scour every nook and cranny of this town ourselves! Chin up, Penny! Why, we've only started to fight!"

CHAPTER 22 - A PARK BENCH

Penny and her friends were heartsick with the knowledge that Mr. Parker had fallen into the hands of ruthless members of the tire-theft gang. The taxi which had borne him away had left the mansion fully an hour earlier. There seemed little likelihood that the trail could be picked up quickly.

"I'll telephone the boys at the newspaper office," Salt offered. "The police too! We'll put a description on the radio. We'll have everybody in Riverview watching for that yellow taxi."

"Call the cab companies too," urged Penny. "We may be able to trace it through the driver."

Salt made good use of the Deming telephone which had not been disconnected during the winter months. While he phoned, Penny ran outside to find the policeman assigned to guard the mansion. She soon returned with him and placed Mrs. Botts in his custody.

"Oh, Mr. Deming, don't let them take me to jail," the housekeeper pleaded. "I didn't mean to do anything wrong."

"Mrs. Botts, I can't help you," her employer returned coldly. "Your offense is a very serious one. The court must decide your fate."

The housekeeper broke into tears again and for several minutes was quite hysterical. When her act moved no one, she resigned herself to the inevitable. Packing a few articles in a bag, she prepared to leave the house in the custody of the policeman.

"I'm sorry about everything," she said as she bade the girls goodbye. "I hope Mr. Parker is found. I really do."

After Mrs. Botts had gone, Penny was too upset to remain quietly in a chair. She longed to join in an active search for the yellow taxi. Common sense told her that the cab undoubtedly had reached its destination, yet she hoped she might pick up a clue.

"By questioning filling station attendants, we may be able to learn which way it went from the crossroads," she urged.

"Come on, then," said Salt.

Joe, faithful as ever, waited in his cab outside the mansion. Penny chose to ride beside him, as the front seat offered an unobstructed view of the road.

The cab turned away from the mansion and swept down the familiar twisting highway. At the first bend, the bright headlights illuminated a patch of snow along the ditch. Penny thought she saw a small, dark object lying on the ground.

"Stop the car!" she cried.

Joe brought the cab to a standstill a little farther down the road.

Penny leaped out and ran back to the ditch. Lying just at its edge was a leather portfolio. A glance satisfied her that it had belonged to her father.

"Salt! Louise!" she shouted. "I've found Dad's satchel!"

The others came running. By that time Penny had examined the portfolio. It was empty.

"Just as I thought," she muttered. "Those men were after the evidence Dad carried! And they got it, too!"

Salt and Joe examined the snowy ditches for a long distance. There were no footprints. They could only conclude that the portfolio had been thrown from a window of the moving cab. Evidently Mr. Parker remained a prisoner.

"Now that those men have what they want, maybe they'll release Dad," Penny said hopefully. "Don't you think so, Salt?"

CHAPTER 22 - A PARK BENCH

The photographer glanced at Joe. Neither spoke.

"You believe they'll harm Dad!" Penny cried, reading their faces. "Maybe I'll never see him again—"

"Now Penny," Salt soothed, guiding her toward the taxi.

The cab rolled on, its tires crunching the hard-packed snow. At the crossroads, they met a police car and hailed it. Penny turned the empty portfolio over to one of the officers, explaining where it had been found.

"Every road is being watched," she was told in return. "The alarm has been broadcast throughout the State, too. If that yellow cab still is on the road, we'll get it."

For an hour longer, Penny and her party scoured roads in the vicinity of Riverview. Many times they stopped at filling stations and houses to inquire if a yellow cab had been seen to pass. Always the answer was in the negative.

"Don't you think we ought to go home?" Salt suggested at length. "For all we know, police may have found Mr. Parker by this time. We'd never learn about it while we're touring around."

"All right, let's go home," agreed Penny.

The taxi turned toward Riverview. Arriving at the outskirts, Joe chose a boulevard which wound through the park. The trees, each limb and twig glistening with ice, were very beautiful.

Penny gazed absently toward the frozen lake where a few boys were skating. Suddenly her gaze fastened upon a man who sat on a park bench beneath a street lamp. He wore no hat. His overcoat was unbuttoned.

"That man!" she cried. "Salt, it looks like Dad! And it is he! It is!"

The man on the bench had turned slightly so that she was able to see his face.

Joe brought the cab to a halt with a jerk. Penny leaped out, followed by the others. The first to reach the bench, she fairly flung herself headlong at the disheveled man who sat so dejectedly alone.

"Oh, Dad, I've found you at last! How thankful I am you're safe!"

The man on the bench stared blankly at her.

"Who are you?" he asked in a dazed voice.

"Why, I'm Penny—your daughter."

"I have no daughter," the man answered bitterly. "No home. Nothing. Not even a name."

Salt, Louise and Joe reached the bench.

"Who are these people?" the man asked. "Why do they stare at me?"

"Why, Mr. Parker," said Salt, taking his arm. "You remember me, don't you?"

"Never saw you before in my life."

"You're my father—Anthony Parker," Penny said desperately. "You were in a bad accident. Don't you remember?"

"I remember that I was taken by two men in a taxicab. They pretended to be my friends. As soon as we were well away from Mrs. Botts' home, they robbed me of my money and portfolio. Then they pushed me out of the cab. I started walking. I kept on until I came here."

"You're cold and tired," said Salt, trying to guide him toward the taxi.

"Who are you?" Mr. Parker demanded suspiciously. "Why should I let you take me away? You'll only try to rob me—"

"Oh, Dad, you don't understand," Penny murmured. "You're sick."

"Come along, sir," urged Salt. "We're your friends. We'll take you to the doctor."

Mr. Parker planted his feet firmly on the ground.

"I'm not going a step!" he announced. "Not a step!"

"Sorry, sir, but if you're so set about it, we'll have to do it this way."

Salt nodded to Joe. Before Mr. Parker knew what was coming, they caught him firmly by the arms and legs. Although he resisted, they carried him to the cab.

"Take us home as fast as you can!" Penny directed Joe. "Then I'll want you to go for Doctor Greer, the brain specialist. Dad's in very serious condition."

"Serious, my eye!" snorted the publisher. He struggled to free himself from Salt's grip. "Let me out of here!"

"Dad, everything will be all right now," Penny tried to soothe him. "You're with friends. You're going home."

"I'm being kidnaped!" Mr. Parker complained. "Twice in one night! If I were strong enough to get out of here—"

Again he tried to free himself. Failing, he edged into a corner of the seat and averted his face.

CHAPTER 23 - FORGOTTEN EVENTS

In the upstairs bedroom, Penny moved with velvet tread. Noiselessly she rearranged a vase of flowers and closed the slat of a Venetian blind.

"You needn't be so quiet," said Mr. Parker from the bed. "I've been awake a long time now."

Penny went swiftly to his side. "How are you feeling this afternoon, Dad?"

"Afternoon?" Mr. Parker demanded, sitting up. "How long have I been sleeping?"

"Roughly, about two days."

Mr. Parker threw off the covers.

"Oh, no, you don't," said Penny, pressing him back against the pillow. "Doctor Greer says you are to have absolute bed rest for several days. It's part of the treatment."

"Treatment for what?" grumbled Mr. Parker. "I feel fine!"

"That's wonderful," declared Penny, with a deep sigh of relief. "I'll have Mrs. Weems bring up something for you to eat."

She called down the stairway to the housekeeper, and then returned to the bedside. Her father looked more like his former self than at any time since the strange motor accident which had caused him to lose his memory. His voice too, was more natural.

"Guess I must have had a bad dream," Mr. Parker murmured, his gaze roving slowly about the room. "I seem to recall riding around in a taxi, and being pushed out into the snow."

"You know where you are now, don't you?" asked Penny.

"Certainly. I'm at home."

Mrs. Weems came into the room bearing a tray of food. Hearing Mr. Parker's words, she looked at Penny and tears sprang to her eyes.

"Doctor Greer was right," she whispered. "His memory is slowly coming back. How thankful I am!"

"What's all this?" Mr. Parker inquired alertly. "Will someone kindly tell me why I am being imprisoned in this bed?"

"Because you've been very, very sick," Penny said, arranging the food in front of him. "You know who I am now, don't you?"

"Why, certainly," replied Mr. Parker indignantly. "You're my daughter. Your name is—now let me think—"

"Penny."

"To be sure," agreed Mr. Parker, in confusion. "Fancy forgetting my own daughter's name!"

"You've forgotten a number of other things too, Dad. But events gradually are coming back to you. Suppose you tell me your name."

"My name?" Mr. Parker looked bewildered. "Why, I don't remember. It's not Jones. I took that name because I couldn't think of my own. What's wrong with me?"

Penny tucked a napkin beneath her father's chin and offered him a spoonful of beef broth.

"What's wrong with me?" Mr. Parker demanded again. "Am I a lunatic? Can't either of you tell me the truth?"

"You're recovering from a severe case of amnesia," revealed Penny. "The doctor says it was brought on by overwork in combination with the shock of being in an auto accident. Since you were hurt you've not remembered what happened before that time."

"I do recall the auto mishap," Mr. Parker said slowly. "Another car crowded me off the road. The crash stunned me, and my mind was a sort of blank. Then a pleasant woman took me to her home."

"A pleasant woman, Dad?"

"Why, yes, Mrs. Botts gave me a nice room and good food. I liked it there. But one night a girl broke in—could that have been you, Penny?"

"Indeed, it was."

"When Mrs. Botts came home she was very excited," Mr. Parker resumed meditatively. "She said I had to leave. She hustled me out of the house with two strangers."

"One of the men was Ropes Mollinberg, a member of the tire-theft gang."

"Yes, that was his name!" Mr. Parker agreed. "Speaking of tire thieves, I've been intending to write an editorial for the paper. Penny, please have my secretary come in. I'll dictate the material while it is fresh in my mind."

Mrs. Weems looked slightly distressed. Penny, however, whisked away the tray of food. Getting pencil and paper she again sat down beside her father.

"Your secretary isn't available just now, but I'll take down what you want to say."

Penny could not write shorthand so she only pretended to jot down notes. Mr. Parker led off with a few crisp sentences, then wandered vaguely from one idea to another.

"I can't seem to think straight any more," he complained. "Type that up please and let me see it before it goes to the compositors."

"How shall I sign the editorial?" Penny inquired.

"Why, with my name—Anthony Parker."

Penny jumped up and fairly laughed with joy.

"Dad, events are coming back to you! You've just recalled your name and that's a big step forward."

"Anthony Parker," the publisher murmured. "Yes, that's it! Now there's another matter that troubles me. I had a brief case—"

"It was stolen by those men who took you away," Penny supplied eagerly. "Dad, if only you could remember what those lost papers contained, we'd expose the entire tire-theft gang!"

Mr. Parker thought for a long while, then shook his head.

"Mind's a blank, Penny. What does the doctor say? Is there a chance my memory ever will return?"

"Of course," returned Penny heartily. "You've already recalled a number of important things. Me, for instance! Doctor Greer thinks that with rest, events will gradually return to mind. Or another shock, perhaps a blow somewhat similar to the one you had, might bring everything back."

"Well, what are we waiting for?" Mr. Parker joked. "Go get the sledge hammer!"

"It's not that easy, I'm afraid."

"I'm afraid not, either," sighed Mr. Parker wearily. "Guess I'll sleep some more now. I feel pretty tired."

During the days that followed, the publisher made a slow but steady recovery. At first Penny did not worry him by mentioning how matters had gone at the *Star* office. Only after Mr. Parker was well enough to spend several hours a day at the plant, did she reveal how Harley Schirr had sought to establish himself as editor of the paper.

"That fellow!" exclaimed Mr. Parker in annoyance. "Why, I meant to discharge him and he knew it. I have evidence in my safe showing that Schirr accepted money from a local politician."

"You did have evidence," Penny corrected. "While you were away, Mr. Schirr went through your safe."

Amazed by the boldness of his former employee, Mr. Parker immediately examined the contents of both his desk and strongbox. To his chagrin he found that Penny was right. Every document pertaining to Schirr was missing.

"Well, it doesn't matter," the publisher said philosophically. "He'll never set foot in this office again, nor in any other Riverview newspaper!"

"Dad," said Penny, "I've wondered if Schirr may not be hooked up with the tire-theft gang. What do you think?"

"My poor thinker isn't much good these days. However, I very much doubt it, Penny. Schirr always was a snoop and not above taking money for writing biased stories. My judgment would be that he has no connection with the Mollinberg outfit."

CHAPTER 23 - FORGOTTEN EVENTS

"If only you could remember what was in your stolen portfolio!" Penny sighed.

"If only I could!" agreed Mr. Parker. "Sometimes I doubt I'll ever fully recover my memory."

"Oh, you will, Dad. You're doing better every day."

Penny seldom spoke of the automobile accident which had caused her father's trouble for the subject was a painful one to them both. Although the publisher had been absolved of all blame, police had not succeeded in tracing the hit-skip driver.

Mr. Parker seemed well and strong. Each day he went to the office for longer and longer periods. Gradually his memory was returning, yet he had been unable to recall data which might bring about the capture of the tire-theft gang. Strangely, he could remember nothing of his intention to call at the State Prosecutor's office. Nor could he disclose a scrap of evidence which had been carried in the stolen portfolio.

"If only Jerry would wire or return from his vacation!" Penny commented anxiously. "I can't understand why he doesn't reply to my message."

The reporter's long absence had caused considerable worry at the *Star* office. Jerry was the one person who could divulge the contents of the stolen portfolio documents, but repeated wires failed to bring any response.

"Jerry will show up one of these days," Mr. Parker said confidently. "The only trouble is, by that time the higher-ups of the tire-theft gang may have skipped town."

"Dad, can't you remember the men who took you away in the taxi?"

"Only vaguely. I've described them to police as best I can. So far, no action."

Penny was silent for a moment. In her mind she had been turning over a way to bring the crooks to justice. It seemed to her that the men might be identified through Black Market operators with whom they must have dealings.

"Now what are you keeping from me?" inquired Mr. Parker lightly.

"I was thinking about a place known as Mattie Williams' garage," replied Penny. "I've good reason to suspect it deals in stolen tires."

She went on to tell of her recent adventure in the storage room of the garage. The information did not excite Mr. Parker as she had feared it might. Instead, it fired him with a determination to get at the truth of the matter.

"Penny, we'll break our story yet!" he exclaimed, reaching for his hat. "Let's go to Mattie's place now!"

"Unless we actually see the inside of the storage room we'll learn nothing. You may be sure Mattie and her partner won't cooperate."

"We'll get into that room somehow," returned Mr. Parker grimly. "I'll take along a few pet skeleton keys just for luck."

At the Williams' garage an hour later, they found Mattie and Sam busy with repair work.

"Be with you in a minute," the woman called to Mr. Parker.

"No hurry," replied the publisher. "No hurry whatsoever."

He and Penny wandered aimlessly about. Choosing a moment when both Sam and Mattie were inside the office, they slipped unnoticed into the room where the empty boxes had been stored.

"Now show me the tunnel," urged the publisher. "We'll have to work fast!"

Penny swung back the hinged boards of the big box. She led her father between a high aisle of crates to the locked door of the inner room.

"Now if only I have a key that will unlock it!" muttered Mr. Parker.

He tried several. At length one did fit the keyhole, the lock clicked, and he was able to push open the door.

In the little storage room close to the outside building wall were tires of all sizes and description. Some were new, still wrapped in clean paper. Others appeared slightly used.

"See, Dad!" Penny cried triumphantly. "I was right!"

"We still have no proof this rubber was illegally obtained."

Penny darted forward to inspect a stack of tires which rose half way to the ceiling.

"Here's one that might have come off my car!" she cried. "See! Mine had a tiny cut place where I rammed the maple tree backing out of our garage!"

"All tires look alike, Penny. Without the serial number—"

"I do remember part of it. One was 8910 something."

"Then this isn't your tire," replied Mr. Parker, reading the number. "However, I shouldn't be surprised that these are stolen tires."

Penny held up her hand as a signal for silence.

"Quiet, Dad!" she whispered.

Footsteps had sounded in the tunnel between the boxes. The next instant the door was flung open. Penny and her father stood face to face with Sam Burkholder.

CHAPTER 24 - TRICKERY

"What d'you think you're doing in here?" demanded Sam Burkholder harshly. "Snoopers, eh?"

"Call us that if you like," retorted Mr. Parker. "How long have you been dealing in stolen tires?"

The shot hit its target. Sam started to speak but no words came. He looked badly frightened. Convinced that his suspicion was correct, Mr. Parker added sternly:

"Naturally, I'll report this to the police. You and your partner will have to face charges."

"Keep Mattie out of this," growled Sam. "She had nothing to do with the tire business."

"So you carried on crooked operations all by your lonesome?"

"I've bought and sold a few tires," Sam said sullenly. "All these government regulations give me a pain. A guy can't make any money these days."

"So you admit you've been doing an illegal business?"

"Maybe," said Sam, watching Mr. Parker craftily. "But what's it to you? I take it you're not a government agent?"

"I'm interested in breaking up a gang of leeches—the men who've been cleaning this town of tires for the past three months."

"Those guys are crooks all right," agreed Sam. "Why the last time they sold me a bunch of tires they charged double. When I wasn't going to take 'em they said, 'Either you do, or else!'"

"Did you deal with Ropes Mollinberg?"

"He's just one of the little fry. What will you give me to spill?"

"Nothing."

"Will you keep Mattie out of this?"

"If she's innocent."

"She is," insisted Sam. "Supposin' I tell you how to get the whole gang, will you forget what you've seen here?"

"I make no bargains with Black Market dealers," retorted Mr. Parker. "Either you tell what you know, or I'll have you and Mattie hauled into court."

Sam Burkholder was silent a moment.

"Okay," he said abruptly. "I've had enough of this business anyhow. I'll tell you what I know, and it won't take me long. I've never seen nor dealt direct with the big shots."

"Then how do you get your tires?"

"A trucker by the name of Hank Biglow delivers them to me."

"Louise and I know that man!" cried Penny. "For whom does he work?"

"I've never asked. But from something Hank dropped I kinda suspect the boys are having a meeting tonight."

"Where?" Mr. Parker demanded eagerly.

"I'll tell you on one condition. You've got to keep Mattie out of this. So far as she knows this garage has been run pretty much on the square."

Mr. Parker was unwilling to make any sort of agreement with the man. Nevertheless, he realized that Sam had it within his power to withhold vital information.

"Very well," he said, "I'll take your word for it that Mattie is innocent. Now where is the meeting to be held?"

"At Johnson's warehouse."

"Isn't that along the river?"

"Yeah, about eight miles from here. The boys will be loading some tires there. If you're willing to take the risk, you may learn something. Meeting's at seven."

Penny glanced at her wrist watch.

"It's after six now!" she exclaimed in dismay. "Dad, if we are to get there in time, we've got to step!"

"Right you are," he agreed.

Before leaving the garage, Mr. Parker telephoned Central Police Station. Without mentioning Sam's name, he revealed a little of what he had learned and requested an immediate investigation of the Johnson Warehouse. Then, intending to meet officers there, he and Penny taxied along the winding river road.

Although not yet seven o'clock, it was darkening fast. The driver switched on headlights, illuminating a long stretch of icy pavement.

"Can't you go faster?" Mr. Parker urged impatiently.

"Don't dare, sir," replied the driver.

Even as he spoke, a crossroads traffic light flashed red. Though the driver applied the foot brake with quick stabs, the car went into a disastrous skid. Out of control, it slid crosswise in the narrow road. The front wheels rolled into a deep, slippery ditch.

"Just our luck!" muttered Mr. Parker.

Several times the driver tried to back the car from the ditch. Failing, he and Mr. Parker pushed while Penny handled the steering wheel. The tires kept spinning and would not grip the ice.

"No use," the publisher acknowledged at last. "We're only wasting time. We need a tow car."

"The nearest house or filling station is at least a mile up the road," volunteered Penny. "I'm afraid we're stalled here until the police car comes along."

They climbed into the taxi and waited. No vehicle of any description came by. With increasing impatience, Mr. Parker looked at his watch.

"It's nearly seven o'clock now!" he exclaimed. "Either the police are waiting farther down the road, or they've taken a different route!"

"What are we going to do?" Penny asked helplessly. "If we sit here much longer we'll miss catching those men at their meeting."

"I don't see what we can do. Maybe our best bet is to walk to the nearest filling station."

Penny suddenly was struck with an idea. "The Riverview Yacht Club is closer!" she cried.

"True, but it's closed for the winter."

"My iceboat is still there," said Penny. "If you're not afraid to ride with me, I could get you to Johnson's Warehouse in nothing flat."

"What are we waiting for?" demanded Mr. Parker.

Leaving the cab driver behind, Penny and her father ran most of the way to the club. The *Icicle*, covered with snow, runners frozen to the ice, remained where it had been abandoned.

"The sail's here too!" Penny declared, burrowing in a box hidden deep in the cockpit. "In this wind, we'll go places!"

"Are you sure you can handle the boat?" Mr. Parker asked anxiously. He had never ridden in the *Icicle* and from his daughter's vivid descriptions, had no great desire to do so.

"I know I can start it going," Penny replied with a quick laugh. "I'll worry about stopping it when the time comes!"

They cleared the little boat of snow and pushed it out on the smooth ice of the river. Penny made certain that all the ropes were free running.

"Now you get in, Dad," she advised as she hoisted the flapping sail. "I want to be sure where you are when the fireworks begin."

The wind filled the big sail like a balloon. Nothing happened. The iceboat did not move an inch.

"Why don't we go?" growled Mr. Parker. "Runners dull?"

Penny gave the boat a hard push.

"Want me to help?" offered her father.

"No, thanks," puffed Penny. "When this baby makes up its mind, it will go so fast you'd be left behind."

Once more she pushed. The sail filled again and the runners stirred.

CHAPTER 24 - TRICKERY

"It's moving!" shouted Penny.

The *Icicle* was pulling away from her. She clung fast, trying to scramble aboard. Her feet went out from under her and she was dragged over the ice.

"Hang on!" shouted Mr. Parker. "I can't sail this thing alone!"

Penny clung desperately. Away flew a mitten. Her scarf flapped in her face. With a supreme effort, she pulled herself aboard, and took command of the tiller.

"Are you hurt?" Mr. Parker shouted anxiously in her ear.

Penny shook her head and laughed. "Getting started always is quite a trick," she replied. "Sit tight! We have a stiff breeze tonight."

Penny and her father wore no protective goggles. The sharp wind stung their eyes even though they kept their heads low.

"How'll we know when we get to the warehouse?" Mr. Parker shouted. "I can't see anything!"

"Just trust me," laughed Penny. "All I worry about is stopping this bronco when we get there!"

The boat was moving with the speed of an express train. Penny made her decisions with lightning-like rapidity, twice steering to avoid open stretches of water. She was worried, but had no intention of letting her father know.

The boat raced on. Then far ahead loomed the dark outline of a building.

"That's the warehouse!" shouted Mr. Parker. "Don't go past it!"

Penny gradually slowed the *Icicle*. Approaching shore, she slacked the main sheet and shot up into the wind. By using her overshoes for brakes, she finally brought the boat to a standstill not far from the warehouse.

"Well done, skipper," praised Mr. Parker.

Scrambling from the boat, they glanced anxiously about. A dim light shone from inside the warehouse. Not far from its side entrance stood a truck. There were no other vehicles, no sign of the expected police car.

"Is this the place?" Penny asked doubtfully.

"Yes, it's the only warehouse within a mile. Queer the police aren't here to meet us."

The publisher waded through a shrunken snowdrift to a side door of the building. It was not locked and he pushed it open a crack. Far down a deserted corridor shone a dim lantern light.

"Oughtn't we to wait for the police?" Penny whispered uneasily.

Without answering, Mr. Parker started down the corridor. Penny quickly overtook him, padding along close at his side.

The corridor opened into a large storage room used in years past to house river merchandise. Now the walls were stacked high with tires.

On the ground floor stood a truck which several men were loading. Two others watched the work from a balcony overhead.

"Dad, do you recognize any of those men?" Penny whispered.

"No, but we've evidently come to the right place," he replied.

The men did not talk as they loaded the tires into the truck. For many minutes Penny and her father watched the work.

"That truck soon will be pulling out," Penny observed. "Why don't the police come?"

"I'm going to talk to those men," Mr. Parker decided. "You stay here."

Before Penny could protest, her father stepped boldly into the lighted room. Immediately work ceased. Every eye focused upon him.

"Good evening," said Mr. Parker casually.

The remark was greeted by a suspicious silence. Then one of the men, a red-faced fellow with a twisted lower lip, asked: "You lookin' fer somebody?"

"Just passing through and noticed the light," replied Mr. Parker. "Wondered what's going on."

"You can see, can't you?" growled one of the workmen. "We're trying to load tires. Now get out of here or I'll bounce one on your head! We got work to do."

Mr. Parker did not lack courage. However, the grim faces warned him that the men would not hesitate to make their promise good. With Penny unprotected in the corridor he could afford to take no chances.

"Sorry to have bothered you," he apologized, and retreated.

Penny waited nervously in the dark hallway. "Now what are we to do?" she whispered as her father rejoined her.

"We'll telephone again for the police. Let's get out of here."

Noiselessly they stole from the building. As they huddled in the lee of a brick wall, a car came down the road.

"That may be the police now!" Penny murmured hopefully.

The car turned in at the warehouse. A lone policeman alighted. As he came over to the building, Penny recognized him as Carl Burns.

"Where's the rest of your men?" Mr. Parker demanded. "Surely you don't expect to handle this tire gang single handed?"

"Aren't you a bit mixed up?" the policeman drawled.

"Mixed up?"

"I'm here on a routine inspection. This is a defense plant, or didn't you know?"

"A defense plant!" Mr. Parker echoed.

"A warehouse for one, I should say," corrected the policeman. "Tires intended for the Wilson war plant are earmarked and shipped out from here. A couple of trucks are going out tonight. I'm on the job to see they're not hijacked."

Penny gazed blankly at her father. If the policeman's information was correct, then they had nearly made a serious blunder.

"Guess we've been tricked," Mr. Parker muttered. "We were told this place operates in the Black Market."

"That's a laugh," responded the policeman. "Who told you that yarn?"

"I can't divulge my source."

"Well, you sure were taken for a ride!" the policeman taunted. "Mr. Parker, why not let the police handle the crooks while you look after your newspaper business? You've not been yourself since you were in that auto accident."

Penny and her father resented the implication, but wisely allowed the remark to pass without comment. Decidedly crestfallen, they bade the policeman goodbye and returned to the iceboat.

"We've made ourselves ridiculous!" Mr. Parker commented bitterly as they shoved off down river. "Taken in by Sam Burkholder!"

"He probably lied to get rid of us," agreed Penny. "By this time he's likely removed every tire from Mattie's garage!"

Mr. Parker nodded and did not speak again. His failure to learn the identity of the key men associated with Ropes Mollinberg, had been a bitter disappointment.

Penny handled the *Icicle* effortlessly and without much thought. Faster and faster the little boat traveled, its runners throwing up a powdery dust.

Then without warning the *Icicle* struck something frozen in the ice. Before Penny could make a move, the runners leaped from the surface. The boat tilted to a sharp angle, and went over.

Penny felt herself sliding. Snow filled her mouth, the sleeves of her coat. Her cap hung over one ear. Laughing shakily, she scrambled to her feet.

"Are you all right, Dad?" she called anxiously.

Then she saw him. Mr. Parker was sprawled flat on the ice a few yards away. He did not move. Terrified, she ran to him and grasped his arm.

"Dad! Speak to me!"

Mr. Parker stirred slightly. He raised a hand and rubbed his head. Slowly he pulled himself to a sitting position.

"Penny—" he mumbled, staring at her.

"Yes, Dad."

"It's come to me—in a flash!"

"What has, Dad?" Penny asked, wondering how badly her father had been stunned.

"Why, all the evidence I had in my portfolio! Names! Pictures! I know every man who was mixed up in the tire deal. Jerry gave it all to me."

CHAPTER 24 - TRICKERY

"You remember everything?" cried Penny. "Dad, that's wonderful! It's just like Doctor Greer said. You've regained your memory as the result of a sudden blow."

"Things did seem to rush back to me after I hit my head on the ice."

Gripping Penny's hand, Mr. Parker pulled himself to his feet. Still giddy, he staggered and caught the ice-boat for support. Then recovering, he exclaimed:

"We've got to go back there right away!"

"Where, Dad?"

"To the warehouse. We were tricked, but not by Sam Burkholder! Policeman Burns is one of the men I aim to expose!"

CHAPTER 25 - FINAL EDITION

Penny and her father had no definite plan as they raced toward Johnson's warehouse in the iceboat. Their only thought was to return and somehow prevent the escape of the tire thieves.

"Dad, is Harley Schirr one of the gang?" Penny shouted in Mr. Parker's ear.

"Schirr?" he repeated impatiently. "Of course not!"

"Then why didn't he want you to publish the tire stories in the *Star*?"

"Oh, Schirr's a natural-born coward," Mr. Parker answered. "He likes to snoop and give unasked advice. Let's forget him."

The *Icicle* slowed to a standstill near the warehouse. Penny and her father leaped out and climbed the slippery bank. Nearby they saw a loaded truck about to pull away from the building.

"We never can stop those men now!" gasped Penny.

"Yes, we can!" cried her father. "A police car is coming, and this time it's no fake!"

As he spoke, an automobile bearing the notation, "Police Department" in bold letters, skidded into the driveway. Detective Fuller was at the wheel and at least four policemen were with him.

"Stop that truck!" Mr. Parker shouted. "Don't let it get away!"

Detective Fuller and four companions leaped from the police car. As the loaded truck started off with a roar, they blocked the road.

"Halt!" shouted Detective Fuller.

When the order was ignored, he fired twice. The bullets pierced the rear tires of the truck. Air whistled out and the rubber slowly flattened.

For a few yards the truck wobbled on, then stopped. Two detectives leaped for the cab.

"All right, get out!" ordered Detective Fuller, covering the men.

The truck driver and two others slouched sullenly out of the cab. As flashlights swept their faces, Penny recognized one of the men.

"Hank Biglow!" she identified the driver.

"And this man is Ham Mollinberg, a brother of Ropes," said Mr. Parker, indicating a red-faced fellow in a leather jacket. "The man beside him is Al Brancomb, wanted for skipping parole in California."

"Any others in the warehouse?" demanded Detective Fuller.

"There should be," said Penny excitedly. "Where's Mr. Burns?"

"What Burns do you mean?" questioned one of the detectives.

"Connected with your police force, unfortunately," informed Mr. Parker. "That's why I planned to consult the Prosecutor before I spread the story on the *Star's* front page. You boys have done good work in Riverview and I didn't want to make the department look bad."

"Burns, eh?" Detective Fuller repeated. "We'll find out what he has to say!"

The policeman, however, was not to be apprehended so easily. Four men, including Ropes Mollinberg, were captured inside the warehouse. Burns had left the building some minutes earlier and had returned to Riverview.

"Don't worry, we'll get him!" Detective Fuller promised Mr. Parker. "How about these other eggs? Can you identify them?"

"They're all members of the outfit," the publisher said without hesitation. "One of my reporters, Jerry Livingston, spent weeks watching these men and getting wise to their methods."

"Then he can testify against them."

CHAPTER 25 - FINAL EDITION

"He can if he gets back," agreed Mr. Parker. "Jerry's in Canada and for some reason we've been unable to locate him."

Penny and her father remained at the warehouse until the handcuffed prisoners had been taken away. They were jubilant over the capture. Not only would the tire-theft gang be broken up, but the *Star* had achieved another exclusive front-page story.

"The best part of all is that you've recovered your memory!" Penny declared to her father. "After this, you won't dare fuss when I tell you I'm going ice-boating!"

"You're right," agreed Mr. Parker. "The *Icicle* is the best pal I ever had!"

Within an hour after Penny and her father left the warehouse they were notified that Mr. Burns had been taken into custody. Evidence piled up rapidly against the policeman. As it definitely was established that he had accepted money from Ropes Mollinberg, he was stripped of his badge and put behind bars.

Police were not compelled to search the Williams' garage. Before they could act, Sam Burkholder came voluntarily to Central Station, offering to make a clean breast of his part in the Black Market dealings. Both he and Mattie were held as witnesses against the tire thieves.

"Will Mattie be kept in jail long?" Penny asked her father.

"I doubt it," he replied. "Apparently, Sam acted alone in selling illegal tires. Since he's showing a disposition to cooperate with police, he'll probably escape with a heavy fine."

With the tire theft case soon to come up for trial, Penny was disturbed lest Jerry Livingston fail to return from Canada in time to testify. For many days she tormented herself with wild speculations. Then one afternoon her worries were brought to an end by the arrival of a telegram. Nothing had happened to the young reporter. He had failed to reply to messages only because he had been out of touch with civilization.

In his wire, Jerry stated that he would return to Riverview at once to aid in the search for the publisher.

"Jerry doesn't know yet that you've been found!" Penny said to her father. "We must wire him right away to set his mind at rest."

The message was sent, and within a few hours a reply arrived, addressed to Penny.

"COMING ANYWAY," it read. "AM BRINGING YOU A BEAR RUG TOGETHER WITH A NICE BEAR HUG."

As if pleasant surprises never would end, still another came Penny's way. Police notified her that among the tires seized at the Johnson Warehouse was a set of five belonging to her stripped car.

"You're much better off than I," Mr. Parker teased her. "Your car now is in running order again. Mine will be in the garage for many a day. I'll have to pay my own repair bill, too."

"Unless the hit-skip driver is found."

"I'm afraid he never will be," sighed Mr. Parker. "I'll always believe the men who crowded me off the road were hired by the tire-theft gang. No way to prove it though."

"The car license number Mrs. Botts gave police didn't seem to be accurate," Penny replied. "By the way, have you decided what you'll do about her?"

"Mrs. Botts?"

"Yes, so far you've placed no formal charge against her."

Mr. Parker smiled as he reached for a final edition of the *Star*. The paper carried not only an account of the round-up at Johnson's Warehouse, but a full confession from Mrs. Botts.

"I bear the woman no ill will," he said. "She's already lost her position as caretaker at the Deming estate. That's punishment enough as far as I'm concerned."

Presently Mrs. Weems entered the living-room with a glass of milk. When she tried to make the publisher take it he complained that he no longer was an invalid.

"Now drink your milk like a good lad," Penny scolded. "Why, you're still as thin as a ghost."

With a wry face Mr. Parker gulped down the drink.

"Let's not speak of ghosts," he pleaded. "I'm well now, and I don't like to be reminded of those disgraceful night-shirt parades."

"Are you sure you're perfectly well?" teased Penny.

"Of course I am. My memory is as good as it ever was!"

"Haven't you forgotten a rather important financial item?"

Mr. Parker looked puzzled. Then light broke over his face.

"Your allowance! I've not paid it for a long while, have I?"

"You certainly haven't," grinned Penny. "The old till is painfully empty. I can use a little folding money to good advantage."

Her father smiled and opened his pocketbook. "Here you are," he said. "Go out and paint the town red!"

When Penny thumbed over the little stack of "folding money" she drew in her breath. Then she leaped to her feet in youthful exuberance.

"Oh, Dad, you're a darling!" she cried. "Why, this will buy a brush and a whole barrel of red paint! Look out, Riverview, here I come!"

HOOFBEATS ON THE TURNPIKE

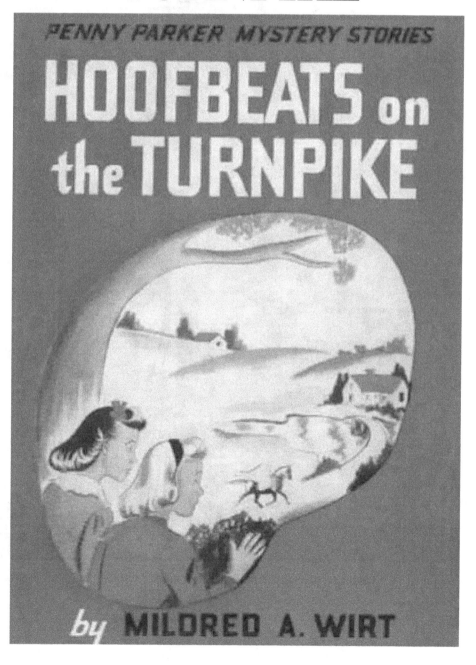

"I've been robbed!" Mrs. Lear proclaimed wildly.

CHAPTER 1 - OLD MAN OF THE HILLS

A girl in crumpled linen slacks skidded to a fast stop on the polished floor of the *Star* business office. With a flourish, she pushed a slip of paper through the bars of the treasurer's cage. She grinned beguilingly at the man who was totaling a long column of figures.

"Top o' the morning, Mr. Peters," she chirped. "How about cashing a little check for me?"

The bald-headed, tired looking man peered carefully at the crisp rectangle of paper. Regretfully he shook his head.

"Sorry, Miss Parker. I'd like to do it, but orders are orders. Your father said I wasn't to pass out a penny without his okay."

"But I'm stony broke! I'm destitute!" The blue eyes became eloquent, pleading. "My allowance doesn't come due for another ten days."

"Why not talk it over with your father?"

Penny retrieved the check and tore it to bits. "I've already worked on Dad until I'm blue in the face," she grumbled. "Talking to a mountain gives one a lot more satisfaction."

"Now you know your father gives you almost everything you want," the treasurer teased. "You have a car of your own—"

"And no gas to run it," Penny cut in. "Why, I work like a galley slave helping Dad build up the circulation of this newspaper!"

"You have brought the *Star* many new subscribers," Mr. Peters agreed warmly. "I'll always remember that fine story you wrote about the Vanishing Houseboat Mystery. It was one of the best this paper ever published."

"What's the use of being the talented, only daughter of a prosperous newspaper owner if you can't cash in on it now and then?" Penny went on. "Why, the coffers of this old paper fairly drip gold, but do I ever get any of it?"

"I'll let you have a few dollars," Mr. Peters offered unexpectedly. "Enough to tide you over until the day your allowance falls due. You see, I know how it is because I have a daughter of my own."

Penny's chubby, freckled face brightened. Then the light faded. She asked doubtfully:

"You don't intend to give me the money out of your own pocket, Mr. Peters?"

"Why, yes. I wouldn't dare go against your father's orders, Penny. He said no more of your checks were to be cashed without his approval."

Unfolding several crisp new bills from his wallet, the treasurer offered them to Penny. She gazed at the money with deep longing, then firmly pushed it back.

"Thanks, Mr. Peters, but it has to be Dad's money or none. You see, I have a strict code of honor."

"Sorry," replied the treasurer. "I'd like to help you."

"Oh, I'll struggle on somehow."

With a deep sigh, Penny turned away from the cage. She was a slim, blue-eyed girl whose enthusiasms often carried her into trouble. Her mother was dead, but though she had been raised by Mrs. Weems, a faithful housekeeper, she was not in the least spoiled. Nevertheless, because her father, Anthony Parker, publisher of the *Riverview Star* was indulgent, she usually had her way about most matters. From him she had learned many details of the newspaper business. In fact, having a flare for reporting, she had written many of the paper's finest stories.

Penny was a friendly, loveable little person. Not for long could she remain downhearted. As she walked down the long hallway, its great expanse of polished floor suddenly looked as inviting as an ice pond. With a quick little run she slid its length. And at the elevator corner she collided full-tilt with a bent old man who hobbled along on a crooked hickory cane.

"Oh, I'm terribly sorry!" Penny apologized. "I didn't know anyone was coming. I shouldn't have taken this hall on high."

The unexpected collision had winded the old man. He staggered a step backwards and Penny grasped his arm to offer support. She could not fail to stare. Never before in the *Star* office had she seen such a queer looking old fellow. He wore loose-fitting, coarse garments with heavy boots. His hair, snow white, had not been cut in many weeks. The grotesque effect was heightened by a straw hat several sizes too small which was perched atop his head.

"I'm sorry," Penny repeated. "I guess I didn't know where I was going."

"'Pears like we is in the same boat, Miss," replied the old man in a cracked voice. "'Lows as how I don't know where I'm goin' my own self."

"Then perhaps I can help you. Are you looking for someone in this building?"

The old man took a grimy sheet of paper from a tattered coat pocket.

"I want to find the feller who will print this advertisement for me," he explained carefully. "I want everybody who takes the newspaper to read it. I got cash money to pay for it too." He drew a greasy bill from an ancient wallet and waved it proudly before Penny. "Ye see, Miss, I got cash money. I ain't no moocher."

Penny hid a smile. Not only did the old man look queer but his conversation was equally quaint. She thought that he must come from an isolated hill community many miles distant.

"I'll show you the way to the ad department," she offered, guiding him down the hall. "I see you have your advertisement written out."

"Yes, Miss." The old man hobbled along beside her. "My old woman wrote it all down. She was well edijikated before we got hitched."

Proudly he offered Penny the paper which bore several lines of neatly inscribed script. The advertisement, long and awkwardly worded, offered for sale an old spinning wheel, an ancient loom and a set of wool carders.

"My old woman used to be one o' the best weavers in Hobostein county," the old man explained with pride. "She could make a man a pair o' jeans that'd wear like they had growed to his hide. But they ain't no call for real weavin' no more. Everything is cheapened down machine stuff these days."

"Where is your home?" Penny questioned curiously.

"Me and my old woman was born and raised in the Red River Valley. Ever been there?"

"No, I can't say I have."

"It's one of the purtiest spots God ever made," the old man said proudly. "You never seen such green pastures, an' the hills kinda take your breath away. Only at night there's strange creatures trackin' through the woods, and some says there's haunts—"

Penny glanced quickly at her companion. "Haunts?" she inquired.

Before the old man could answer they had reached the want-ad counter. An employee of the paper immediately appeared to accept the advertisement. His rapid-fire questions as he counted words and assessed charges, bewildered the old hillman. Penny supplied the answers as best she could. However, in her haste to be finished with the task, she forgot to have the old fellow leave name and address.

"You were saying something about haunts," she reminded him eagerly as they walked away from the desk. "You don't really believe in ghosts do you, Mister—"

"Silas Malcom," the old man supplied. "That's my name and there ain't a better one in Hobostein County. So you be interested in haunts?"

"Well, yes, I am," Penny admitted, her eyes dancing. "I like all types of mystery. Just lead me to it!"

"Well, here's something that will make your pretty eyes pop." Chuckling, the old man fumbled in his pocket and produced a worn newspaper clipping. Penny saw that it had been clipped from the Hobostein County Weekly. It read:

"Five hundred dollars reward offered for any information leading to the capture of the Headless Horseman. For particulars see J. Burmaster, Sleepy Hollow."

"This *is* a strange advertisement," Penny commented aloud. "The only Headless Horseman to my knowledge was the famous Galloping Hessian in the story, 'Legend of Sleepy Hollow.' But in reality such things can't exist."

CHAPTER 1 - OLD MAN OF THE HILLS

"Maybe not," said the old man, "but we got one in the valley just the same. An' if what folks says is so, that Headless Horseman's likely to make a heap o' trouble fer someone before he's through his hauntin'."

Penny stared soberly into the twinkling blue eyes of her aged companion. As a character he completely baffled her. Did he mean what he said or was he merely trying to lead her on with hints of mystery? At any rate, the bait was too tempting to resist.

"Tell me more," she urged. "Exactly what do you know about this advertisement?"

"Nothin'. Nary a thing, Miss. But there's haunts at Sleepy Hollow and don't you think there ain't. I've seen 'em myself from Witching Rock."

"And where is Witching Rock?" Even the words intrigued Penny.

"Jest a place on Humpy Hill lookin' down over the Valley."

Finding her companion none too willing to impart additional information, Penny reread the advertisement. The item had appeared in the Hobostein County paper only the previous week. The words themselves rather than the offer of a reward enchanted her.

"Headless Horseman—Witching Rock!" she thought excitedly. "Why, even the names scream of mystery!"

Aloud she urged: "Mr. Malcom, do tell me more about the matter. Who is Mr. Burmaster?"

There was no answer. Penny glanced up from the advertisement and stared in astonishment. The elderly man no longer stood beside her. Not a soul was in the long empty hall. The old man of the hills had vanished as quietly as if spirited away by an unseen hand.

CHAPTER 2 - PLANS

"Now what became of that old man?" Penny asked herself in perplexity. "I didn't hear him steal away. He couldn't have vanished into thin air! Or did he?"

Thinking that Mr. Malcom might have gone back to the want-ad department, she hastily returned there. To her anxious inquiry, the clerk responded with a grin:

"No, Old Whiskers hasn't been here. If you find him, ask for his address. He forgot to leave it."

Decidedly disturbed, Penny ran down the hall which gave exit to the street. Breathlessly she asked the elevator attendant if he had seen an old man leave the building.

"A fellow with a long white beard?"

"Yes, and a cane. Which way did he go?"

"Can't tell you that."

"But you did see him?" Penny demanded impatiently.

"Sure, he went out the door a minute or two ago. He was talking to himself like he was a bit cracked in the head. He was chuckling as if he knew a great joke."

"And I'm it," Penny muttered.

She darted through the revolving doors to the street. With the noon hour close at hand throngs of persons poured from the various offices. Amid the bustling, hurrying crowd she saw no one who remotely resembled the old man of the hills.

"He slipped away on purpose!" she thought half-resentfully. "He gave me the newspaper clipping just to stir my interest, and then left without explaining a thing!"

Abandoning the search as hopeless, Penny again reread the clipping. Five hundred dollars offered for information leading to the capture of a Headless Horseman! Why, it sounded fantastic. But the advertisement actually had appeared in a country newspaper. Therefore, it must have some basis of fact.

Still mulling the matter over in her mind, Penny climbed a long flight of stairs to the *Star* news room. Near the door stood an empty desk. For many years that desk had been occupied by Jerry Livingston, crack reporter, now absent on military leave. It gave Penny a tight feeling to see the covered typewriter, for she and Jerry had shared many grand times together.

She went quickly on, past a long row of desks where other reporters tapped out their stories. She nodded to Mr. DeWitt, the city editor, waved at Salt Sommers, photographer, and entered her father's private office.

"Hello, Dad," she greeted him cheerfully. "Busy?"

"I was."

Anthony Parker put aside the mouthpiece of a dictaphone machine to smile fondly at his one and only child. He was a tall, lean man and a recent illness had left him even thinner than before.

Penny sank into an upholstered chair in front of her father's desk.

"If it's money you want," began Mr. Parker, "the answer is no! Not one cent until your allowance is due. And no sob story please."

"Why, Dad." Penny shot him an injured look. "I wasn't even thinking of money—at least not such a trivial amount as exchanges hands on my allowance day. Nothing less than five hundred dollars interests me."

"Five hundred dollars!"

"Oh, I aim to earn it myself," Penny assured him hastily.

"How may I ask?"

CHAPTER 2 - PLANS

"Maybe by catching a Headless Horseman," Penny grinned mischievously. "It seems that one is galloping wild out Red Valley way."

"Red Valley? Never heard of the place." Mr. Parker began to show irritation. "Penny, what are you talking about anyway?"

"This," explained Penny, spreading the clipping on the desk. "An old fellow who looked like Rip Van Winkle gave it to me. Then he disappeared before I could ask any questions. What do you think, Dad?"

Mr. Parker read the advertisement at a glance. "Bunk!" he exploded. "Pure bunk!"

"But Dad," protested Penny hotly. "It was printed in the Hobostein Weekly."

"I don't care who published it or where. I still say 'bunk!'"

"Wasn't that the same word you used not so long ago when I tried to tell you about a certain Witch Doll?" teased Penny. "I started off on what looked like a foolish chase, but I came back dragging one of the best news stories the *Star* ever published. Remember?"

"No chance you'll ever let me forget!"

"Dad, I have a hunch," Penny went on, ignoring the jibe. "There's a big story in this Headless Horseman business! I just feel it."

"I suppose you'd like to have me assign you the task of tracking down your Front Page gem?"

"Now you're talking my language!"

"Penny, can't you see it's only a joke?" Mr. Parker asked in exasperation. "The Headless Horseman of Sleepy Hollow! That story was written years ago by a man named Washington Irving. Or didn't you know?"

"Oh, I've read the 'Legend of Sleepy Hollow,'" Penny retorted loftily. "I remember one of the characters was Ichabod Crane. He was chased by the Headless Horseman and nearly died of fright."

"A nice bit of fiction," commented Mr. Parker. He tapped the newspaper clipping. "And so is this. The best place for it is in the scrap basket."

"Oh, no, it isn't!" Penny leaped forward to rescue the precious clipping. Carefully she folded it into her purse. "Dad, I'm convinced Sleepy Hollow must be a real place. Why can't I go there to interview Mr. Burmaster?"

"Did you say Burmaster?"

"Yes, the person who offers the reward. He signed himself J. Burmaster."

"That name is rather familiar," Mr. Parker said thoughtfully. "Wonder if it could be John Burmaster, the millionaire? Probably not. But I recall that a man by that name built an estate called Sleepy Hollow somewhere in the hill country."

"There!" cried Penny triumphantly. "You see the story does have substance after all! May I make the trip?"

"How would you find Burmaster?"

"A big estate shouldn't be hard to locate. I can trace him through the Hobostein Weekly. What do you say, Dad?"

"The matter is for Mrs. Weems to decide. Now scram out of here! I have work to do."

"Thanks for letting me go," laughed Penny, giving him a big hug. "Now about finances—but we'll discuss that angle later."

Blowing her father an airy kiss, she pranced out of the office.

Penny fairly trod on clouds as she raced toward the home of her chum, Louise Sidell. Her dark-haired chum sat listlessly on the porch reading a book, but she jumped to her feet as she saw her friend. From the way Penny took the steps at one leap she knew there was important news to divulge.

"What's up?" she demanded alertly.

"Hop, skip and count three!" laughed Penny. "We're about to launch forth into a grand and glorious adventure. How would you like to go in search of a Headless Horseman?"

"Any kind of a creature suits me," chuckled Louise. "When do we start and where?"

"Lead me to a map and I'll try to answer your questions. Our first problem is to find a place called Red Valley."

For a half hour the two girls poured over a state map. Hobostein County was an area close by, while Red Valley proved to be an isolated little locality less than a day's journey from Riverview. Penny was further encouraged to learn that the valley she proposed to visit had been settled by Dutch pioneers and that many of the original families still had descendants living there.

"It will be an interesting trip even if we don't run into any mystery," Louise said philosophically. "Are you sure you can go, Penny?"

"Well, pretty sure. Dad said it was up to Mrs. Weems to decide."

Louise gave her chum a sideways glance. "That seems like a mighty big 'if' to me."

"Oh, I'll bring her around somehow. Pack your suitcase, Lou. We'll start tomorrow morning bright and early."

Though Penny spoke with confidence, she was less certain of her powers as she entered her own home a few minutes later. She found Mrs. Weems, the stout, middle-aged housekeeper in the kitchen making cookies.

"Now please don't gobble any of that raw dough!" Mrs. Weems remonstrated as the girl reached for one of the freshly cut circles. "Can't you wait until they're baked?"

Penny perched herself on the sink counter. Reminded that her heels were making marks on the cabinet door, she drew them up beneath her and balanced like an acrobat. Forthwith she launched into a glowing tale of her morning's activities. The story failed to bring a responsive warmth from the housekeeper.

"I declare, I can't make sense out of what you're saying!" she protested. "Headless Horsemen, my word! I'm afraid you're the one who's lost your head. The ideas you do get!"

Mrs. Weems sadly heaved a deep sigh. Since the death of Mrs. Parker many years before, she had assumed complete charge of the household. However, the task of raising Penny had been almost too much for the patient woman. Though she loved the girl as her own, there were times when she felt that running a three-ring circus would be much easier.

"Louise and I plan to start for Red Valley by train early tomorrow," said Penny briskly. "We'll probably catch the 9:25 if I can get up in time."

"And has your father said you may go?"

"He said it was up to you."

Mrs. Weems smiled grimly. "Then the matter is settled. I shall put my foot down."

"Oh, Mrs. Weems," Penny wailed. "Please don't ruin all our plans. The trip means so much to me!"

"I've heard that argument before," replied Mrs. Weems, unmoved. "I see no reason why I should allow you to start off on such a wild chase."

"But I expect to get a dandy story for Dad's paper!"

"That's only an excuse," sighed the housekeeper. "The truth is that you crave adventure and excitement. It's a trait which unfortunately you inherited from your father."

Penny decided to play her trump card.

"Mrs. Weems, Red Valley is one of those picturesque hidden localities where families have gone on for generation after generation. The place must fairly swim with antiques. Wouldn't you like to have me buy a few for you while I'm there?"

Despite her intentions, Mrs. Weems displayed interest. As Penny very well knew, collecting antiques had become an absorbing hobby with her.

"Silas Malcom has a spinning wheel for sale," Penny went on, pressing home the advantage she had gained. "I'll find him if I can and buy it for you."

"Your schemes are as transparent as glass."

"But you will let me go?"

"I probably will," sighed Mrs. Weems. "I've learned to my sorrow that in any event you usually get your way."

Penny danced out of the kitchen to a telephone.

"It's all set," she gleefully told Louise. "We leave early tomorrow morning for Red Valley. And if I don't earn that five hundred dollar reward then my name isn't Penny Gumshoe Parker!"

CHAPTER 3 - INTO THE VALLEY

The slow train crept around a bend and puffed to a standstill at the drowsing little station of Hobostein. Louise and Penny, their linen suits mussed from many weary hours of sitting, were the only passengers to alight.

"Yesterday it seemed like a good idea," sighed Louise. "But now, I'm not so sure."

Penny stepped aside to avoid a dolly-truck which was being pushed down the deserted platform by a station attendant. She too felt ill at ease in this strange town and the task she had set for herself suddenly seemed a silly one. But not for anything in the world would she make such an admission.

"First we'll find the newspaper office," she said briskly. "This town is so small it can't be far away."

They carried their over-night bags into the stuffy little station. The agent, in shirt sleeves and green eye shade, speared a train order on the spindle and then glanced curiously at the girls.

"Anything I can do for you?"

"Yes," replied Penny. "Please tell us how to find the offices of the Hobostein Weekly."

"It's just a piece down the street," directed the agent. "Go past the old town pump, and the livery stable. A red brick building. Best one in town. You can't miss it."

Penny and Louise took their bags and crossed to the shady side of the street. A horse and carriage had been tied to a hitching post and by contrast an expensive, new automobile was parked beside it. The unpaved road was thick with dust; the broken sidewalk was coated with it, as were the little plots of struggling grass.

In the entire town few persons were abroad. An old lady in a sunbonnet busily loaded boxes of groceries into a farm wagon. The only other sign of activity was at the livery stable where a group of men slouched on the street benches.

"Must we pass there?" Louise murmured. "Those men are staring as if they never saw a girl before."

"Let them," said Penny, undisturbed.

Two doors beyond the livery stable stood a newly built red brick building. In gold paint on the expanse of unwashed plate glass window were the words: "Hobostein Weekly."

With heads high the girls ran the gantlet of loungers and reached the newspaper office. Through the plate glass they glimpsed a large, cluttered room where desks, bins of type, table forms and a massive flat-bed press all seemed jammed together. A rotund man they took to be the editor was talking to a customer in a loud voice. Neither took the slightest notice of the girls as they pushed open the door.

"I don't care who you are or how much money you have," the editor was saying heatedly. "I run my paper as I please—see! If you don't like my editorials you don't have to read them."

"You're a pin-headed, stubborn Dutchman!" the other man retorted. "It makes no difference to me what you run in your stupid old weekly, providing you don't deliberately try to stir up the people of this valley."

"Worrying about your pocketbook?"

"I'm the largest tax payer in the valley. If there's an assessment for repairs on the Huntley Lake Dam it will cost me thousands of dollars."

"And if you had an ounce of sense, you'd see that without the repairs your property may not be worth a nickel! If these rains keep up, the dam's apt to give way, and your property would go in the twinkling of an eye. Not that I'm worried about your property. But I am concerned about the folks who are still living in the valley."

"Schultz, you're a calamity-howler!" the other accused. "There's no danger of the dam giving way and you know it. By writing these hot editorials you're just trying to stir up public feeling—you're hoping to shake me down so I'll underwrite a costly and unnecessary repair bill."

The editor pushed back his chair and arose. His voice remained controlled but his eyes snapped like fire brands.

"Get out of this office!" he ordered. "The Hobostein Weekly can do without your subscription. You've been a pain to this community ever since you came. Good afternoon!"

"You can't talk like that to me, Byron Schultz!" the other man began hotly. Then his gaze fell upon Louise and Penny who stood just inside the door. Jamming on his hat, he went angrily from the building.

The editor crumpled a sheet of paper and hurled it into a waste basket. The act seemed to restore his good humor, for with a wry grin he then turned toward the girls.

"Yes?" he inquired.

Penny scarcely knew how to begin. Sliding into a chair beside the editor's desk, she fumbled in her purse for the advertisement clipped from the Hobostein Weekly. To her confusion she could not find it.

"Lose something?" the editor inquired kindly. "That's my trouble too. Last week we misplaced the copy for Gregg's Grocery Store and was Jake hoppin' mad! Found it again just before the Weekly went to press."

"Here it is!" said Penny triumphantly. She placed the clipping on Mr. Schultz' desk.

"Haven't I had enough of that man in one day!" the editor snorted. "The old skinflint never paid me for the ad either!"

"Who is J. Burmaster?" Penny inquired eagerly.

"Who is he?" The editor's gray-blue eyes sent out little flashes of fire. "He's the most egotistical, thick-headed, muddle-brained property owner in this community."

"Not the man who was just here?"

"Yes, that was John Burmaster."

"Then he lives in Hobostein?"

"He does not," said the editor with emphasis. "It's bad enough having him seven miles away. You don't mean to tell me you haven't seen Sleepy Hollow estate?"

Penny shook her head. She explained that as strangers to the town, she and Louise had made no trips or inquiries.

"Sleepy Hollow is quite a show place," the editor went on grudgingly. "Old Burmaster built it about a year ago. Imported an architect and workmen from the city. The house has a long bridge leading up to it, and is supposed to be like the Sleepy Hollow of legend. Only the legend kinda backfired."

"You're speaking about the Headless Horseman?" Penny leaned forward in her chair.

"When Burmaster built his house, the old skinflint didn't calculate on getting a haunt to go with it," the editor chuckled. "Served him right for being so muleish."

"But what is the story of the Headless Horseman?" Penny asked. "Has Mr. Burmaster actually offered a five hundred dollar reward for its capture?"

"He'd give double the amount to get that Horseman off his neck!" chuckled the editor. "But folks up Delta way aren't so dumb. The reward never will be collected."

"Is Delta the name of a town?"

"Yes, it's up the valley a piece," explained Mr. Schultz. "You don't seem very familiar with our layout here."

"No, my friend and I come from Riverview."

"Well, you see, it's like this." The editor drew a crude map for the girls. "Sleepy Hollow estate is situated in a sort of 'V' shaped valley. Just below it is the little town of Delta, and on below that, a hamlet called Raven. We're at the foot of the valley, so to speak. Huntley Lake and the dam are just above Sleepy Hollow estate."

"And is there really danger that the dam will give way?"

"If you want my opinion, read the Hobostein Weekly," answered the editor. "The dam won't wash out tomorrow or the next day, but if these rains keep on, the whole valley's in danger. But try to pound any sense into Burmaster's thick head!"

"You started to tell me about the Headless Horseman," Penny reminded him.

"Did I now?" smiled the editor. "Don't recollect it myself. Fact is, Burmaster's ghost troubles don't interest me one whit."

"But we've come all the way from Riverview just to find out about the Headless Horseman."

"Calculate on earning that reward?" The editor's eyes twinkled.

CHAPTER 3 - INTO THE VALLEY

"Perhaps."

"Then you don't want to waste time trying to get second-hand information. Burmaster's the man for you to see. Talk to him."

"Well—"

"No, you talk to Burmaster," the editor said with finality. "Only don't tell him I sent you."

"But how will we find the man?" Penny was rather dismayed to have the interview end before it was well launched.

"Oh, his car is parked down the street," the editor answered carelessly. "Everyone in town knows Burmaster. I'd talk to you longer only I'm so busy this afternoon. Burmaster is the one to tell you his own troubles."

Thus dismissed, the girls could do nothing but thank the editor and leave the newspaper building. Dubiously they looked up and down the street. The fine new car they had noticed a little while earlier no longer was parked at the curb. Nor was there any sign of the man who had just left the newspaper office.

"All we can do is inquire for him," said Penny.

At a grocery store farther down the street they paused to ask if Mr. Burmaster had been seen. The store keeper finished grinding a pound of coffee for a customer and then answered Penny's question.

"Mr. Burmaster?" he repeated. "Why, yes, he was in town, but he pulled out about five minutes ago."

"Then we've just missed him!" Penny exclaimed.

"Burmaster's on his way to Sleepy Hollow by this time," the store keeper agreed. "You might catch him there."

"But how can we get to Sleepy Hollow?"

"Well, there's a train. Only runs once a day though. And it went through about half an hour ago."

"That was the train we came in on. Isn't there a car one can hire?"

"Don't know of any. Clem Williams has some good horses though. He keeps the livery stable down the street."

Their faces very long, the girls picked up their overnight bags and went outside again.

"I knew this trip would be a wash-out," said Louise disconsolately. "Here we are, stuck high and dry until our train comes in tomorrow."

"But why give up so easily?"

"We're licked, that's why. We've missed Mr. Burmaster and we can't go to Sleepy Hollow after him."

Penny gazed thoughtfully down the street at Clem Williams' livery stable.

"Why can't we go to Sleepy Hollow?" she demanded. "Let's rent horses."

Louise waxed sarcastic. "To be sure. We can canter along balancing these overnight bags on the pommel of our saddles!"

"We'll have to leave our luggage behind," Penny planned briskly. "The most essential things we can wrap up in knapsacks."

"But I'm not a good rider," Louise complained. "The last time we rode a mile I couldn't walk for a week."

"Seven miles isn't so far."

"Seven miles!" Louise gasped. "Why, it's slaughter."

"Oh, you'll last," chuckled Penny confidently. "I'll see to that."

"I am curious to see Sleepy Hollow estate," Louise admitted with reluctance. "All that talk about the Huntley Dam interested me too."

"And the Headless Horseman?"

"That part rather worries me. Penny, do you realize that if we go to Sleepy Hollow we may run into more than we bargain for?"

Penny laughed and grasping her chums arm, pulled her down the street.

"That's what I hope," she confessed. "Unless Sleepy Hollow lets us down shamefully, our adventure is just starting!"

CHAPTER 4 - A STRANGER OF THE ROAD

Even for late September it was a warm day. The horses plodded slowly up a steep, winding trail heavily canopied with yellowing maple leaves. Louise and Penny swished angrily at the buzzing mosquitoes and tried to urge their tired mounts to a faster pace.

"I warned you this trip would be slaughter," Louise complained, ducking to avoid a tree limb. "Furthermore, I suspect we're lost."

"How could we be, when we haven't turned off the trail?" Penny called over her shoulder.

She rode ahead on a sorry looking nag appropriately named Bones. The animal was more easily managed than the skittish mare Louise had chosen at Williams' Livery Stable, but had an annoying appetite for foliage.

"Mr. Williams' directions were clear enough," Penny resumed. "He said to follow this trail until we reach a little town named Delta."

"Providing we survive that long," Louise interposed crossly. "How far from Delta to Sleepy Hollow?"

"Not more than two or three miles. And once we get down out of these hills into the valley, the going should be much easier."

Penny spoke with forced cheerfulness. In truth, she too had wearied of the trip which in the last hour had become sheer torture instead of adventure. Her freckled face was blotched with mosquito bites. Every hairpin had been jolted from her head and muscles fairly screamed a protest. Louise, on an unruly horse, had taken even more punishment.

Penny gave Bones a dig in the ribs. The horse quickened his step, weaving a corkscrew path around the trunks of the giant trees.

Gradually the tangle of brush and trees began to thin out. They came at last to a clearing at the brow of the hill. Penny drew rein beside a huge, moss-covered rock. Below stretched a beautiful rich, green valley through which wound a flood-swollen river. From the chimney-tops of a cluster of houses smoke curled lazily, blending into the blue rim of the distant hills.

"Did you ever see a prettier little valley?" Penny asked, her interest reviving. "That must be Delta down there."

Louise was too weary to look or answer. She slid out of the saddle and tossed the reins over a tree limb. Near by a spring gushed from between the rocks. She walked stiffly to it and drank deeply of the cool water.

"Lou, the valley looks exactly as I hoped it would!" Penny went on eagerly. "It has a dreamy, drowsy atmosphere, just as Irving described the Sleepy Hollow of legend!"

Louise bent to drink of the spring again. She sponged her hot face with a dampened handkerchief. Pulling off shoes and stockings, she let the cool water trickle over her bare feet.

"According to legend, the valley and its inhabitants were bewitched," Penny rambled on. "Why, the Indians considered these hills as the abode of Spirits. Sometimes the Spirits took mischievous delight in wreaking trouble upon the villagers—"

Penny's voice trailed off. From far down the hillside came the faint thud of hoofbeats. The girl's attention became fixed upon a moving horseman on the road below.

"Now what?" inquired Louise impatiently. "Don't try to tell me you've seen the Headless Horseman already?"

"I've certainly seen a horseman! My, can that fellow ride!"

Louise picked up her shoes and hobbled over the stones to the trail's end. Through a gap in the trees she gazed down upon a winding turnpike fringed on either side with an old-fashioned rail fence. A horseman,

CHAPTER 4 - A STRANGER OF THE ROAD

mounted on a roan mare, rode bareback at a full run. As the girls watched in admiration, the mare took the low fence in one magnificent leap and crashed out of sight through the trees.

"You're right, Penny," Louise acknowledged. "What wouldn't I give to be able to ride like that! One of the villagers, I suppose."

The hoofbeats rapidly died away. Louise turned wearily around, intending to remount her horse. She stared in astonishment. Where the mare had grazed, there now was only trampled grass.

"Where's my horse?" she demanded. "Where's White Foot?"

"Spirited away by the witches maybe."

"This is no time for any of your feeble jokes, Penny Parker! That stupid horse must have wandered off while I was admiring your old valley and that rider!"

Penny remained undisturbed. "Oh, we'll find the mare all right," she said confidently. "She can't be far away."

The girls thought that they heard a crashing of underbrush to the left of the trail. Investigation did not disclose that the horse had gone that way. They could hear no hoofbeats, nor was any of the grass trampled.

"I'll bet White Foot's on her way back to Williams' Stable by this time," Louise declared crossly. "Such luck!" She sat down on a stone and put on her shoes and stockings.

"We didn't hear the horse run off, Lou. She can't be far."

"Then you find her. I've had all I can stand. I'm tired and I'm hungry and I wish I'd never come on this wild, silly chase." Tears began to trickle down Louise's heat-mottled face.

Penny slid down from Bones and patted her chum's arm awkwardly. Louise pulled away from her.

"Now don't give me any pep talk or I'll simply bawl," she warned. "What am I going to do without a horse?"

"Why, that's easy, Lou. We'll ride double."

"Back to Williams' Stable?"

"Well, not tonight. It's getting late and after coming this far it would be foolish to turn around and start right back."

"It would be the most sensible act of our lives," Louise retorted. "But then I might know you'd insist on pushing on. You and Christopher Columbus have a lot in common!"

"We came to find out about that Headless Horseman, didn't we?"

"You did, I guess," Louise sighed, getting up from the rock. "I just came along because I'm weak minded! Well, what's the plan?"

"Let's ride down to Delta and try to get a room for the night."

Louise's silence gave consent. She climbed up behind Penny on Bones and they jogged down the trail toward the turnpike.

"It's queer how White Foot sneaked away without making a sound," Penny presently commented. "According to the old legend strange things did happen in the Sleepy Hollow valley. The Spirit was supposed to wreak all sorts of vexations upon the inhabitants. Sometimes he would take the shape of a bear or a deer and lead bewildered hunters a merry chase through the woods."

"You're the one who is bewitched," Louise broke in. "And if you ask me, you've been that way ever since you were born. There's a little spark—something deep within you that keeps saying: 'Go on, Penny. Sic 'em, Penny! Maybe you'll find a mystery!'"

"Perhaps I shall too!"

"Oh, I don't doubt that. You've turned up some dandy news stories for your father's paper. But this is different."

"How so?"

"In the first place we both know there's no such thing as a Headless Horseman. It must all be a joke."

"Would you call that advertisement in the Hobostein paper a joke?"

"It could have been. We don't know many of the facts."

"That's why we're here." Penny guided Bones onto the wide turnpike. Before she could add more, Louise's grasp about her waist suddenly tightened.

"Listen, Penny! Someone's coming!"

Penny drew rein. Distinctly, both girls could hear the clop-clop of approaching hoofbeats. Their hope that it might be White Foot was quickly dashed. A moment later the same horseman they had observed a few minutes earlier, swung around the bend.

The young man rapidly overtook the girls. From the way he grinned, they suspected that they presented a ridiculous sight as they rocked along on Bones' swaying back. He sat his own horse, a handsome roan, with easy grace.

Louise tugged at her skirt which kept creeping above her knees. "He's laughing at us!" she muttered under her breath.

The rider cantered up, then deliberately slowed his horse to a walk. Louise stole a quick sideways glance. The young man was dark-haired, about twenty-six and very good looking. His flashing brown eyes were friendly and so was his voice as he spoke a cheery, "'Lo, girls."

"Hello," Penny responded briefly. Louise immediately nudged her in the ribs, a silent warning that she considered the stranger "fresh."

Nevertheless, Penny twisted sideways in the saddle the better to look at their road companion. He wore whipcord riding breeches and highly polished boots. From the well-tailored cut of his clothes she decided that he too was a comparative stranger to the hill country.

"Not looking for a horse by any chance, are you?" the young man inquired.

Louise's snub nose came down out of the sky. "Oh, we are!" she cried. "Where did you see her?"

"A mare with a white foot? Her left hind one?"

"Yes, that's White Foot!" Louise exclaimed joyfully. "The stupid creature wandered off."

"Saw her making for the valley about five minutes ago. Like enough she turned in at Silas Malcom's place."

The name took Penny by surprise. Although she had hoped to find the old man who had visited the *Star* office, she had not thought it possible without a long search.

"Does Mr. Malcom live near here?" she inquired.

"Yes, his farm's on down the pike. Want me to ride along and show you the way?"

Under the circumstance, Penny and Louise had no choice but to accept the offer. However, they both thought that the young man merely was making an excuse to accompany them. He seemed to read their minds for he said:

"I didn't actually see your missing horse turn in at the Malcom place. Know why I think she'll be there?"

"Perhaps you have supernatural powers," Penny said lightly. "From what we hear, this valley is quite a place for witches and Headless Horsemen."

The young man gave her an amused glance.

"The explanation is quite simple," he laughed. "Silas used to own that horse. All horses have a strong homing instinct, you know."

"I've noticed that," Louise contributed a bit grimly.

"Guess I should introduce myself," the young man resumed. "Name's Joe Quigley. I'm the station agent at Delta."

"We're glad to meet you," Penny responded. Though Louise scowled at her, she gave their own names. She added that they had come to the valley seeking information about the mysterious Headless Horseman.

"Friends of Mr. Burmaster?" Quigley inquired casually.

"Oh, no," Penny assured him. "We just came for the fun of it. Is it true that some prankster has been causing trouble in the valley?"

"Prankster?"

"Yes, someone fixed up to resemble the Headless Horseman of fable."

Quigley grinned broadly. "Well, now, you couldn't prove it by me. Some folks say that on certain foggy nights the old Galloping Hessian does ride down out of the hills. But then there are folks who claim their butter won't churn because it's been bewitched. I never put much stock in such talk myself."

"Then you've never actually seen such a rider?"

Joe Quigley remained silent. After a thoughtful interval he admitted: "Well, one night over a month ago, I did see something strange."

"What was it?" Louise asked quickly.

Quigley pointed far up the hillside. "See that big boulder? Witching Rock it's called."

CHAPTER 4 - A STRANGER OF THE ROAD

Penny nodded. "We were there only a few minutes ago."

"At night fog rises up from the valley and gives the place a spooky look. Years ago a tramp was killed there. No one ever did learn the how or why of it."

"What was it you saw?" Penny inquired.

"Can't rightly say," Quigley returned soberly. "I was on this same turnpike when I chanced to glance up toward that big rock. I saw something there in the mist and then the next minute it was gone."

"Not the Headless Horseman?" Penny asked.

"Maybe it was, maybe it wasn't. I'd have thought I imagined it only I heard clattering hoofbeats. But I can tell you one thing about this valley."

"What's that?" asked Louise.

"All the inhabitants are said to be bewitched! That's why I act so crazy myself."

Penny tossed her head. "Oh, you're just laughing at us," she accused. "I suppose it does sound silly to say we came here searching for a Headless Horseman."

"No, it's not in the least silly," Quigley corrected. "I might pay you a compliment by saying you impress me as very courageous young ladies. May I offer a word of advice?"

"Thank you, I don't think we care for it."

"Nevertheless, I aim to give it anyway." Quigley grinned down at Penny. "You see, I know who you are. You're Anthony Parker's daughter, and you've built up a reputation for solving mysteries."

Penny was astonished for she had not mentioned her father's name.

"Never mind how I knew," said Quigley, forestalling questions. "Here's my tip. No one ever will collect Burmaster's reward offer. So don't waste time and energy trailing a phantom."

"Why do you say the reward never will be collected?"

Quigley would not answer. With a provoking shake of his head, he pointed down the pike to an unpainted cabin and a huge new barn.

"That's the Malcom place," he said. "If I'm not mistaken your missing horse is grazing by the gate. Goodbye and good luck."

With a friendly, half-mocking salute, he wheeled his mount. The next instant horse and rider had crashed through a gap in the roadside brush and were lost to view.

CHAPTER 5 - SLEEPY HOLLOW ESTATE

"I'm afraid that young man was having fun at our expense," Penny remarked after horse and rider had gone. "How do you suppose he knew about my father?"

"Read it in a newspaper probably. You've both made the headlines often enough." Louise sighed wearily and shifted positions. "I certainly wish we never had come here."

"Well, I don't," Penny said with emphasis. She clucked to Bones and when he failed to move smartly along, gave him a quick jab with her heels. "If Joe Quigley won't tell us about that galloping ghost, perhaps Mr. Malcom will."

"I'll settle for my missing horse," Louise responded.

The girls jogged on down the road toward the Malcom cabin. Already the hills were casting long blue shadows over the valley floor. With night fast approaching Penny began to wonder where they could seek lodging.

"You don't catch me staying at the Malcom place," Louise said, reading her chum's thought. "It's too ramshackle."

Drawing nearer the cabin, both girls were elated to see White Foot grazing contentedly in a stony field adjoining the Malcom barn yard. At the gate Penny alighted nimbly and threw it open so that Louise could ride through.

The creaking of the rusty hinges brought Silas Malcom from the tumble-down house. He stared blankly for a moment and then recognized Penny.

"Well, bless my heart," he said. "If it ain't the young lady that helped me at the newspaper office!"

"And now it's your turn to help us," laughed Penny. "We've lost our horse."

"I knowed somebody would be along for her purty soon," the old man chuckled. "She run into the barn yard 'bout ten minutes ago an' I turned her out to graze. I'll git her for you."

If Mr. Malcom was surprised to see Penny so far from Riverview he did not disclose it. He asked no questions. Hobbling to the fence, he whistled a shrill blast. White Foot pricked up her ears and then came trotting over to nuzzle the old man's hand.

"You certainly have that horse under control," said Penny admiringly. "I guess it's all in the way you handle 'em."

"It's also all in the way you handle a Flying Fortress or a stick of dynamite," Louise cut in. "You may have my share of horses!"

"White Foot didn't throw you off?" Mr. Malcom inquired.

"Oh, no," Louise assured him, and explained how the horse had run away.

Old Silas chuckled appreciatively. "White Foot always did have a habit o' sneakin' off like that. Raised her from a colt, but sold her to Williams down in Hobostein when I got short o' cash."

Wrapping the reins about a hitching post, the old man allowed his gaze to wander toward the valley. With a gesture that was hard to interpret, he indicated the long stretch of fertile pasture land, golden grain fields and orderly rows of young orchard trees.

"See that!" he commanded.

"It's a beautiful valley," Louise murmured politely.

"It's mor'n that," corrected the old man. "You're lookin' at one o' the richest parcels o' land in this here state. Me and the old woman lived down there fer goin' on twenty years. Then we was put out o' our cabin. Now that penny-pinchin' Burmaster owns every acre fer as you can see—not countin' the village o' Delta an' three acres held fer spite by the Widder Lear."

CHAPTER 5 - SLEEPY HOLLOW ESTATE

Old Silas took a chew of tobacco and pointed to a trim little log cabin visible through a gap in the trees.

"Stands out like a sore thumb, don't it? Burmaster's done everything he can to git rid o' that place, but the Widder Lear jes' sits tight an' won't have no dealings with him. Says that if the old skinflint comes round her place again she's goin' to drive him off with a shotgun."

Penny and Louise waited, hoping that the old man would tell more. After a little silence, he resumed meditatively:

"The Widder was the smartest o' the lot of us. From the first she said Burmaster was out to gobble up all the best land for hisself. Nobody could get her to sign no papers. That's why she's got her little place today and the rest of us is tryin' to make a livin' out o' these stone patches."

"Burmaster forced all of the valley folk off their land?" Penny inquired, perplexed. "How could he do that?"

"Some of 'em sold out to him," Old Silas admitted. "But mostly the land was owned by a rich feller in Boston. He never paid no attention to his holdings 'cept to collect a bit o' rent now and then. But last spring he up and sold out to Burmaster, and we was all told to git off the land."

Penny nodded thoughtfully. "I suppose that was entirely legal. If Mr. Burmaster bought and paid for the land one couldn't accuse him of dishonest dealings."

"I ain't accusin' nobody o' nothin'," Old Silas replied. "I'm jes' tellin' you how things are in this here valley. Ye came to find out about that Headless Horseman, didn't ye?"

"Well, yes, we did," Penny acknowledged.

"Figured you would. You'll never win that reward Burmaster's offerin', but you could do a heap o' good in this here valley."

"How?" asked Penny, even more puzzled.

"You got a pa that runs a big city newspaper. When he prints an editorial piece in that paper o' his, folks read it and pay attention."

"I'm afraid I don't understand."

"You will after you been here awhile," the old man chuckled. "Where you gals calculatin' to spend the night?"

"I wish we knew."

"Me and the ole woman'd be glad to take you in, only we ain't got no room fitten for city-raised gals. The Widder Lear'll be glad to give you bed and fodder."

The girls thanked Mr. Malcom, though secretly they were sure they would keep on until they reached Delta. A suspicion was growing in Penny's mind that she had not come to the valley of her own free will. Rather she had been lured there by Old Silas' Headless Horseman tale. She had assumed the old fellow to be a simple, trusting hillman, while in truth he meant to make use of her.

"Calculate you're anxious-like to git down to the valley 'fore night sets on," the old man resumed. "The turnpike's no fitten place for a gal after dark."

"You think we might meet the Headless Horseman?" Penny asked, smiling.

Old Silas deliberately allowed the question to pass.

"Jes' follow the turnpike," he instructed. "You'll come fust to the Burmaster place. Then on beyond is the Widder Lear's cabin. She'll treat you right."

Penny had intended to ask Old Silas if he still had a spinning wheel for sale. However, a glimpse of the darkening sky warned her there was no time to waste. She and Louise must hasten on unless they expected to be overtaken by night.

"Goodbye," Penny said, vaulting into the saddle. "We'll probably see you again before we leave the valley."

"Calculate you will," agreed Old Silas. As he opened the gate for the girls he smiled in a way they could not fathom.

Once more on the curving turnpike, Penny and Louise discussed the old man's strange words. Both were agreed that Silas had not been in the least surprised to see them.

"But why did he say I could do good in the valley?" Penny speculated. "Evidently he thinks I'll influence my father to write something in the *Star*."

"Against Burmaster perhaps," nodded Louise. "Everyone we've met seems to dislike that man."

HOOFBEATS ON THE TURNPIKE

The girls clattered over a little log bridge and rounded a bend. Giant trees arched their limbs over the pike, creating a dark, cool tunnel. Penny and Louise urged their tired horses to a faster pace. Though neither would have admitted it, they had no desire to be on the turnpike after nightfall.

"Listen!" Louise commanded suddenly. "What was that sound?"

Penny drew rein to listen. Only a chirp of a cricket disturbed the eerie stillness.

"Just for a minute I thought I heard hoofbeats," Louise said apologetically. "Guess I must have imagined it."

Emerging from the long avenue of trees, the girls were slightly dismayed to see how swiftly darkness had spread its cloak on the valley. Beyond the next turn of the corkscrew road stood a giant tulip tree. Riding beneath it, Penny stared up at the gnarled limbs which were twisted in fantastic shapes.

"There was an old tulip tree in the Legend of Sleepy Hollow," she murmured in awe. "And it was close by that the Headless Horseman appeared—"

"Will you please hush?" Louise interrupted. "I'm jittery enough without any build-up from you!"

Some distance ahead stretched a long, narrow bridge with a high wooden railing. By straining their eyes the girls could see that it crossed a mill pond and led in a graceful curve to a rambling manor house of clapboard and stone.

"Mr. Burmaster's estate!" Louise exclaimed.

"And it looks exactly as I imagined it would!" Penny added in delight. "A perfect setting for the Galloping Hessian!"

"Too spooky if you ask me," said Louise with a shiver. "Why would anyone build an expensive home in such a lonely place?"

The girls rode on. A group of oaks, heavily matted with wild grapevines, threw a deeper gloom over the road. For a short distance the dense growth of trees hid the estate from view.

Suddenly the girls were startled to hear the sharp, ringing clop-clop of steel-shod hoofs. Unmistakably, the sound came from the direction of the long, narrow bridge.

"There! I knew I heard hoofbeats a moment ago!" Louise whispered nervously. "Maybe it *is* the Headless Horseman!"

"Be your age!" chided Penny. "We both know there's no such thing—"

The words died on her lips. From somewhere in the darkness ahead came a woman's terrified scream. Frightened by the sound, Bones gave a startled snort. With a jerk which nearly flung Penny from the saddle, he plunged on toward the bridge.

CHAPTER 6 - GHOSTS AND WITCHES

His ears laid back, Bones plunged headlong toward the gloom-shrouded bridge. Pins shook from Penny's head, and her hair became a stream of gold in the wind. She hunched low in the saddle, but could not stop the horse though she pulled hard on the reins.

As she reached a dense growth of elder bushes, a man leaped out to grasp the bridle. Bones snorted angrily and pounded the earth with his hoofs.

"Oh, thank you!" Penny gasped, and then she realized that the man had not meant to help her.

"So you're the one who's been causing so much trouble here!" he exclaimed wrathfully. "Get down out of that saddle!"

"I'll do no such thing!" Penny retorted. She tried to push him away.

Louise came trotting up on White Foot. Her unexpected arrival seemed to disconcert the man for he released Bones' bridle.

"What's he trying to do?" Louise demanded sharply, pulling up beside her chum.

Before Penny could find tongue, another man, heavily built, came running across the narrow bridge. His bald head bore no covering and the long tails of his well-cut coat flapped wildly in the wind.

"You let that rider get away, Jennings!" he cried accusingly to the workman. "Did you see him ride across the bridge and then take a trail along the creek bed?"

"No, I didn't, Mr. Burmaster," the workman mumbled. "I heard hoof beats and came as fast as I could from the grist mill. The only rider I saw was this girl. There's two of 'em."

"We have a perfect right to be here," Penny declared. "We were riding along the pike when we heard hoof-beats, then a scream. My horse became frightened and plunged down this way toward the bridge."

"I'm sorry I grabbed the bridle, Miss," the workman apologized. "You see, I thought—"

"Your trouble, Jennings, is that you never think!" cut in the owner of Sleepy Hollow curtly. "You never even saw the rider who got away?"

"No, sir. But I'll get the other workmen and go after him."

"Don't waste your efforts. He was only a boy—not the man we're after."

"Only a boy, sir?"

"The scamp clattered a stick against the railing of the bridge just to frighten my wife. Mrs. Burmaster is a very nervous woman."

"Yes, sir," replied the workman rather emphatically. "I know, sir."

"Oh, you do?" Mr. Burmaster asked, his tone unfriendly. "Well, get to the house and tell her there's no cause to scream to high heaven. The boy, whoever he was, is gone."

"I'll tell her," the workman mumbled, starting away.

"And mind, next time I order you to watch this road, I mean watch it!" the estate owner called after him. "If you don't, I'll find another man to take your place."

As Mr. Burmaster turned toward the girls, they obtained a better view of his face. He wore glasses and his cheeks were pouchy; a hooked nose curved down toward a mouth that was hard and firm. Yet when he spoke it was with a surprisingly pleasant tone of voice.

"I must apologize for the stupid actions of my workman," he said to Penny. "He should have known that you were not the one we are after."

"Not the Headless Horseman?" Penny asked, half jokingly.

Mr. Burmaster stepped closer so that he could gaze up into the girl's face. He scrutinized it for a moment, and then without answering her question said: "You are a stranger to the valley."

"Yes, we are."

"Then may I ask how you knew about our difficulties here at Sleepy Hollow?"

Penny explained that she had seen the estate owner's advertisement in the *Hobostein Weekly*. She did not add that it was the real reason why she and Louise had made the long trip from Riverview.

"I'll be willing to pay any amount to be rid of that so-called ghost who annoys us here at Sleepy Hollow," Mr. Burmaster said bitterly. "Night after night my wife has had no rest. The slightest sound terrifies her."

"Tell us more about the mysterious rider," Penny urged. "What time does he appear?"

"Oh, there's no predicting that. Often he rides over the bridge on stormy or foggy nights. Then again it's apt to be just after dusk. Tonight we thought we had the scamp, but it proved to be only a mischievous boy."

"Your workmen stand guard?"

"They have orders to watch this bridge day and night. But the men are a lazy lot. They wander off or they go to sleep."

"Isn't it possible that the disturbance always has been caused by a boy—perhaps this lad who clattered over the bridge tonight?"

"Impossible!" Mr. Burmaster snapped impatiently. "I've seen the Headless Horseman at least five times myself."

"You mean the rider actually has no head?" Louise interposed in awe.

"The appearance is that. Of course there's no question but someone from the village or the hills has been impersonating Irving's celebrated character of fiction. The point is, the joke's gone too far!"

"I should think so," Louise murmured sympathetically.

"My wife and I came to this little valley with only one thought. We wanted to build a fine home for ourselves amid peaceful surroundings. We brought in city workmen, a clever architect. No expense was spared to make this house and estate perfect. But when we tried to recreate the atmosphere of Sleepy Hollow, we didn't anticipate getting a ghost with it."

"When did the trouble first start?" Penny asked.

"Almost from the hour of our arrival. The country folks didn't like it because we imported city labor. They hindered our efforts. The women were abusive to my wife. Then last Halloween, the Headless Horseman clattered over this bridge."

"Couldn't it have been a holiday prank?"

"We thought so at first, but a month later, the same thing happened again. This time the scamp tossed a pebble against our bedroom window. Since then the rider has been coming at fairly frequent intervals."

"If you know it's a prank why should it worry you?" Penny inquired.

"A thing like that wears one down after awhile," the owner of the estate said wearily. "For myself I shouldn't mind, but my wife's going to pieces."

"Was it your wife we heard scream?" Louise asked, seeking to keep the conversational ball rolling.

"Yes, she's apt to go off the deep end whenever anyone rides fast over the bridge. My wife—"

Mr. Burmaster did not complete what he had intended to say. At that moment a soft padding of footsteps was heard, a creaking of boards on the bridge. From the direction of the house came a tall, shadowy figure.

"What were you saying about me, John?" The voice was that of a woman, shrill and strident.

"My wife," murmured the estate owner. He turned toward her. "Matilda," he said gently, "these girls are strangers to the Valley—"

"You were complaining about me to them!" the woman accused. "Oh, you needn't deny it! I distinctly heard you! You're always saying things to hurt my feelings. You don't care how I suffer. Isn't it enough that I have to live in this horrible community, among such cruel hateful people without you turning against me too?"

"Please, Matilda—"

"Don't 'Matilda' me! Apologize at once."

"Why, certainly I apologize," Mr. Burmaster said soothingly. "I was only telling the girls how nervous it makes you when anyone rides at a fast pace over the bridge."

"And why shouldn't I be nervous?" the woman demanded. "Since we've come to this community, I've been subjected to every possible insult! I suppose you let that rider get away again?"

CHAPTER 6 - GHOSTS AND WITCHES

"He was only a mischievous boy."

"I don't care who he was!" the woman cried. "I want him caught and turned over to the authorities. I want everyone who rides over this bridge arrested!"

"This is a public highway, Matilda. When we built this footbridge over the brook we had to grant permission for pedestrians and horseback riders to pass."

"Then make them change the ruling! Aren't you the richest man in the Valley? Or doesn't that mean anything?"

Mr. Burmaster glanced apologetically at Penny and Louise. The girls, quite taken aback by the woman's tirade, felt rather sorry for him. It was plain to see that Mrs. Burmaster was not a well woman. Her sharp, angular face was drawn as if from constant worry, and she kept patting nervously at the stiff rolls of her hair.

"Well, I guess we'd better be moving on," Penny said significantly to Louise.

"Yes, we must," her companion agreed with alacrity. "Mr. Burmaster, is Mrs. Lear's place on down this road?"

The owner of Sleepy Hollow was given no opportunity to answer. Before he could speak, his wife stepped closer, glaring up at Louise in the saddle.

"So you're friends of Mrs. Lear?" she demanded mockingly. "I suppose that old hag sent you here to snoop and pry and annoy me!"

"Goodness, no!" gasped Louise.

"We've never even seen the woman," Penny added. "Silas Malcom told us that Mrs. Lear might give us a room for the night."

"Silas Malcom!" Mrs. Burmaster seized upon the name. "He's another who tries to make trouble for us!"

"If you're in need of a place to stay, we'll be glad to have you remain with us," Mr. Burmaster invited. "We have plenty of room."

Mrs. Burmaster remained silent, but in the semi-darkness, the girls saw her give her husband a quick nudge. No need to be told that they were unwelcome by the eccentric mistress of Sleepy Hollow.

"Thank you, we couldn't possibly stay," Penny said, gathering up the reins.

She and Louise walked their horses single file over the creaking bridge. Just as they reached the far end Mr. Burmaster called to them. Pulling up, they waited for him.

"Please don't mind my wife," he said in an undertone. "She doesn't mean half what she says."

"We understand," Penny assured him kindly.

"You said you were interested in the Headless Horseman," the estate owner went on hurriedly. "Well, my offer holds. I'll pay a liberal reward to anyone who can learn the identity of the prankster. It's no boy. I'm sure of that."

Penny replied that she and Louise would like to help if they knew how.

"We'll talk about that part later on," Mr. Burmaster said. He glanced quickly over his shoulder, observing that his wife was coming. "No chance now. You'll stay with Mrs. Lear tonight?"

"If she'll take us in."

"Oh, she will, though her place is an eye-sore. Now this is what you might do. Get the old lady to talking. If she should give you the slightest hint who the prankster is, seize upon it."

"Then you think Mrs. Lear knows?"

"I suspect half the community does!" Mr. Burmaster answered bitterly. "Everyone except ourselves. We're hated here. No one will cooperate with us."

Penny thought over the request. She did not like the idea of going to Mrs. Lear's home to spy.

"Well, we'll see," she answered, without making a definite promise.

Mrs. Burmaster was coming across the bridge. Not wishing to talk to her, the girls bade the owner of Sleepy Hollow a hasty farewell and rode away. Once on the turnpike, they discussed the queer mistress of the estate.

"If you ask me, everyone in this community is queer," Louise grumbled. "Mrs. Burmaster just seems a bit more so than the others."

Intent upon reaching the Lear homestead, the saddle-weary girls kept on along the winding highway. It was impossible to make good time for White Foot kept giving Louise trouble. Presently the mare stopped dead in her tracks, then wheeled and started back toward the Burmaster estate. Louise, bouncing helplessly, shrieked to her chum for help.

"Rein her in!" Penny shouted.

When Louise seemed unable to obey, Penny rode Bones alongside and seized the reins. White Foot then stopped willingly enough.

"All I ask of life is to get off this creature!" Louise half sobbed. "I'm tired enough to die! And we've had nothing to eat since noon."

"Oh, brace up," Penny encouraged her. "It can't be much farther to Mrs. Lear's place. I'll lead your horse for awhile."

Seizing the reins again, she led White Foot down the road at a walk. They met no one on the lonely, twisting highway. The only sound other than the steady clop of hoofbeats was an occasional guttural twang from a bullfrog.

The night grew darker. Louise began to shiver, though not so much from cold as nervousness. Her gaze constantly roved along the deep woods to the left of the road. Seeing something white and ghostly amid the trees, she called Penny's attention to it.

"Why, it's nothing," Penny scoffed. "Just an old tree trunk split by lightning. That streak of white is the inner wood showing."

A bend in the road lay just ahead. Rounding it, the girls saw what appeared to be a camp fire glowing in the distance. The wind carried a strong odor of wood smoke.

"Now what's that?" Louise asked uneasily. "Someone camping along the road?"

"I can see a house on ahead," Penny replied. "The bonfire seems to have been built in the yard."

Both girls were convinced that they were approaching the Lear place. The fire, however, puzzled them. And their wonderment grew as they rode closer.

In the glare of the leaping flames they saw a huge, hanging iron kettle. A dark figure hovered over it, stirring the contents with a stick.

Involuntarily, Penny's hand tightened on the reins and Bones stopped. Louise pulled up so short that White Foot nearly reared back on her hind legs.

"A witch!" Penny exclaimed, half jubilantly. "I've always wanted to meet one, and this is our chance!"

CHAPTER 7 - BED AND BOARD

For a moment the two girls watched in awe the dark, grotesque figure silhouetted against the leaping flames of the fire. A woman in a long, flowing gown kept stirring the contents of the iron kettle.

"Doesn't she look exactly like a witch!" Penny exclaimed again. "Maybe it's Mrs. Lear."

"If that's the Lear place I know one thing!" Louise announced dramatically. "I'm going straight on to Delta."

Penny knew better than to argue with her chum. Softly she quoted from "Macbeth":

"'Double, double, toil and trouble
Fire burn and cauldron bubble.'"

"Trouble is all we've had since we started this wild trip," Louise broke in. "And now you ask me to spend the night with a witch!"

"Not so loud, or the witch may hear you," Penny cautioned. "Don't be silly, Lou. It's only a woman out in her back yard cooking supper."

"At this time of night?"

"Well, it is a bit late, but so are we. Any port in a storm. Come along, Louise. I'll venture that whatever is cooking in that kettle will be good."

Penny rode on and Louise had no choice but to follow. A hundred yards farther on they came to an ancient farmhouse set back from the road. Dismounting, the girls tied their horses to an old-fashioned hitching rack near the sagging gate. A mailbox bore the name: Mrs. M. J. Lear.

"This is the place all right," said Penny.

Just inside the gate stood an ancient domicile that by daylight was shaded by a giant sycamore. Built of small bricks, it had latticed windows, and a gabled front. An iron weathercock perched on the curling shingle roof seemed to gaze saucily down at the girls.

Going around the house to the back yard, Penny and Louise again came within view of the blazing fire. An old woman in a long black dress bent over the smoke-blackened kettle which hung from the iron crane. Hearing footsteps, she glanced up alertly.

"Who is it?" she called, and the crackled voice was sharp rather than friendly.

"Silas Malcom sent us here," Penny said, moving into the arc of flickering light.

"And who be you? Friends o' his?" The hatchet-faced woman peered intently, almost suspiciously at the two girls.

Penny gave her name and Louise's, adding that they were seeking lodging for the night.

"We'll pay, of course," she added.

The old woman scrutinized the girls for so long that they were certain she would send them away. But when she spoke, her voice was friendly.

"Well, well," she cackled, "anybody that's a friend of Silas is a friend of mine. You're welcome to bed and board fer as long as you want to stay."

Penny thanked her and stepped closer to the kettle. "We've not had anything to eat since noon," she said suggestively. "My, whatever you're cooking looks good!" She sniffed at the steam arising from the iron pot and backed hastily away.

Old Mrs. Lear broke into cackling laughter. "You gals don't want none o' that! This here is soap and I'm head over heels in it. That's why I'm workin' so late."

"Soap," repeated Penny with deep respect. "Why, I thought soap was made in a factory."

Mrs. Lear was pleased at the girl's interest. "Most of it is," she said, "but not my soap. This here is homemade soap and I wouldn't trade a cake of it for all the store soap ye can lug home—not for heavy cleanin', I wouldn't."

Moving near enough to the fire to see the greasy mixture bubbling in the kettle, Penny asked Mrs. Lear if she would explain how soap was made.

"Bless you, yes," the old lady replied with enthusiasm. "You are the first gal I ever ran across that was interested in anything as old fashioned as soap makin'. Why, when I was young every girl knew how to make soap and was proud of it. But nowdays! All the girls think about is gaddin' and dancin' and having dates with some worthless good-for-nothin'. Come right up to the fire and I'll show you something about soap makin'."

Mrs. Lear poked the glowing logs beneath the kettle.

"First thing," she explained, "is to get your fire good and hot. Then you add your scrap grease."

"What is scrap grease?" Louise asked, greatly intrigued.

"Why, bless you, child, that's the odds and ends of cookin' that most folks throw away. Not me though. I make soap of it. Even if it ain't so good smellin' it's better soap than you can buy."

The girls looked over the rim of the steaming kettle and saw a quantity of bubbling fats. With surprising dexterity for one of her age, Mrs. Lear inserted a long-handled hoe-shaped paddle and stirred the mixture vigorously.

"Next thing ye do is to cook in the lye," she instructed. "Then you let it cool off and slice it to any size you want. This mess'll soon be ready."

"And that's all there is to making soap," Penny said, a bit amazed in spite of herself.

"All but a little elbow grease and some git up and git!" the old lady chuckled. "Them two commodities are mighty scarce these days."

While the girls watched, Mrs. Lear poured off the soap mixture. She would not allow them to help lest they burn themselves.

"I kin tell that you girls are all tuckered out," she said when the task was finished. "Just put your horses in the barn and toss 'em some corn and hay. While you're gone I'll clean up these soap makin' things and start a mess o' victuals cookin'."

Mrs. Lear waved a bony hand toward a large, unpainted outbuilding. Louise and Penny led their horses to it, opening the creaking old barn door somewhat cautiously. A sound they could not instantly identify greeted their ears.

"What was that?" Louise whispered, holding back.

"Only a horse gnawing corn!" Penny chuckled. "Mrs. Lear must keep a steed of her own."

It was dark in the barn even with the doors left wide open. Groping their way to empty stalls, the girls unsaddled and tied the horses up for the night. Mrs. Lear's animal, they noted, was a high-spirited animal, evidently a thoroughbred.

"A riding horse too," Penny remarked. "Wonder how she can afford to keep it?"

Finding corn in the bin, the girls fed Bones and White Foot, and forked them an ample supply of hay.

"Now to feed ourselves," Penny sighed as they left the barn. "My stomach feels as empty as the Grand Canyon!"

The girls had visions of a bountiful supper cooked over the camp fire. However, Mrs. Lear was putting out the glowing coals with a bucket of water.

"Come into the house," she urged. "It won't take me long to git a meal knocked up. That is, if you ain't too particular."

"Anything suits us," Louise assured her.

"And the more of it, the better," Penny muttered, though under her breath.

Mrs. Lear led the way to the house, advising the girls to wait at the door until she could light a kerosene lamp. By its ruddy glow they saw a kitchen, very meagerly furnished with old-fashioned cook stove, a homemade table and a few chairs.

CHAPTER 7 - BED AND BOARD

"While you're washin' up I'll put on some victuals to cook," Mrs. Lear said, showing the girls a wash basin and pitcher. "It won't take me a minute."

With a speed that was amazing, the old lady lighted the cook stove and soon had a bed of glowing coals. She warmed up a pan of potatoes, fried salt pork and hominy. From a pantry shelf she brought wild grape jelly and a loaf of homemade bread. To complete the meal she set before the girls a pitcher of milk and a great glass dish brimming with canned peaches.

"It ain't much," she apologized.

"Food never looked better," Penny declared, drawing a chair to the kitchen table.

"It's a marvelous supper!" Louise added, her eyes fairly caressing the food.

Mrs. Lear sat down at the table with the girls and seemed to take keen delight in watching them eat. Whenever their appetites lagged for an instant she would pass them another dish.

"Now that you've et, tell me who you are and why you came," Mrs. Lear urged after the girls had finished. "You say Silas sent you?"

Good food had stimulated Penny and Louise and made them in a talkative mood. They told of their long trip from Riverview and almost before they realized it, had spoken of the Headless Horseman. Mrs. Lear listened attentively, her watery blue eyes dancing with interest. Suddenly Penny cut her story short, conscious that the old lady deliberately was pumping her of information.

"So you'd like to collect Mr. Burmaster's reward?" Mrs. Lear chuckled.

"We shouldn't mind," Penny admitted. "Besides, we'd be doing the Burmasters a good turn to help them get rid of their ghost rider."

"That you would," agreed the old lady exactly as if the Burmasters were her best friends. "Yes, indeed, you've come in a good cause."

"Then perhaps you can help us," Louise said eagerly. "You must have heard about the Headless Horseman."

Mrs. Lear nodded brightly.

"Perhaps you know who the person is," Penny added.

"Maybe, maybe not." Mrs. Lear shrugged, and getting quickly up, began to carry the dishes to the sink. The firm tilt of her thin chin warned the girls that so far as she was concerned, the topic was closed.

Rather baffled, Penny and Louise made a feeble attempt to reopen the conversation. Failing, they offered to wipe the dishes for their hostess.

"Oh, it ain't no bother to do 'em myself," Mrs. Lear said, shooing them away. "You both look tired enough to drop. Just go up to the spare bedroom and slip beneath the covers."

Louise and Penny needed no further urging. Carrying their knapsacks and a lamp Mrs. Lear gave them, they stumbled up the stairs. The spare bedroom was a huge, rather cold chamber, furnished with a giant fourposter bed and a chest of drawers. The only floor covering was a homemade rag rug.

Louise quickly undressed and left Penny to blow out the light. The latter, moving to the latticed window, stood for a moment gazing out across the moonlit fields toward the Burmaster estate.

"Nothing makes sense about this trip," she remarked.

From the bed came a muffled: "Now you're talking!"

Ignoring the jibe, Penny resumed: "Did you notice how Mrs. Lear acted just as if the Burmasters were her friends."

"Perhaps she did that to throw us off the track. She asked us plenty of questions but she didn't tell us one thing!"

"Yet she knows plenty. I'm convinced of that."

"Oh, come on to bed," Louise pleaded, yawning. "Can't you do your speculating in the morning?"

With a laugh, Penny leaped into the very center of the feather bed, missing her chum's anatomy by inches.

Soon Mrs. Lear came upstairs. She tapped softly on the door and inquired if the girls had plenty of covers. Assured that they were comfortable, she went on down the hall to her own room.

Worn from the long horseback ride, Louise fell asleep almost at once. Penny felt too excited to be drowsy. She lay staring up at the ceiling, reflecting upon the day's events. So far, the journey to the Valley had netted little more than sore muscles.

"Yet there's mystery and intrigue here—I know it!" Penny thought. "If only I could get a little tangible information!"

An hour elapsed and still the girl could not sleep. As she stirred restlessly, she heard Mrs. Lear's bedroom door softly creak. In the hallway boards began to tremble. Penny stiffened, listening. Distinctly, she could hear someone tiptoeing past her door to the stairway.

"That must be Mrs. Lear," she thought. "But what can she be doing up at this time of night?"

The question did not long remain unanswered. Boards squeaked steadily as the old lady descended the stairs. A little silence. Then Penny heard two long rings and a short one.

"Mrs. Lear is calling someone on the old-fashioned party-line telephone!" she identified the sound.

Mrs. Lear's squeaky voice carried clearly up the stairway through the half open bedroom door.

"That you, Silas?" Penny heard her say. "Well, those gals got here, just as you said they would! First off they asked me about the Headless Horseman."

A slight pause followed before Mrs. Lear added: "Don't you worry none, Silas. Just count on me! They'll handle soft as kittens!"

And as she ended the telephone conversation, the old lady broke into cackling laughter.

CHAPTER 8 - A RICH MAN'S TROUBLES

Rain was drumming on the roof when Penny awakened the next morning. Yawning sleepily, she sat up in bed. Beside her, Louise, curled into a tight ball, slumbered undisturbed. But not for long. Penny tickled an exposed foot until she opened her eyes.

"Get up, Lou!" she ordered pleasantly. "We've overslept."

"Oh, it's still night," Louise grumbled, trying to snuggle beneath the covers again.

Penny stripped off all the blankets and pulled her chum from the bed. "It's only so dark because it's raining," she explained. "Anyway, I have something important to tell you."

As the girls dressed in the cold bedroom, Penny told Louise of the telephone conversation she had heard the previous night.

"Mrs. Lear was talking to Silas Malcom I'm sure," she concluded. "And about us too! She said we'd handle very easily."

Louise's eyes opened a trifle wider. "Then you figure Silas Malcom intended to get us here on purpose!"

"I'm beginning to think so."

"But why?"

"Don't ask me," Penny said with a shrug. "These Valley folk aren't simple by any means! Unless we watch our step they may take us for a merry ride."

"Not with the Headless Horseman, I hope," Louise chuckled. "Why don't we go home this morning and forget the whole silly affair?"

Penny shook her head. "I'm sticking until I find out what's going on here," she announced. "It might mean a story for Dad's paper!"

"Oh, that's only your excuse," Louise teased. "You know you never could resist a mystery, and this one certainly has baffling angles."

The girls washed in a basin of cold water and then went downstairs. Mrs. Lear was baking pancakes in the warm kitchen. She flipped one neatly as she reached with the other hand to remove the coffee pot from the stove.

"Good morning," she chirped. "Did you sleep right last night?"

Penny and Louise agreed that they had and edged close to the stove for warmth. An old-fashioned clock on the mantel showed that it was only eight o'clock. But eight o'clock for Mrs. Lear was a late hour, judging by the amount of work she had done. A row of glass jars stood on the table, filled with canned plums and peaches.

"You haven't put up all that fruit this morning?" gasped Louise.

Mrs. Lear admitted that she had. "But that ain't much," she added modestly. "Only a bushel and a half. Won't hardly last no time at all."

Mrs. Lear cleared off the kitchen table, set it in a twinkling, and placed before the girls a huge mound of stacked cakes.

"Now eat hearty," she advised. "I had mine hours ago."

As Penny ate, she sought to draw a little information from the eccentric old woman. Deliberately, she brought up the subject of the Burmaster family.

"What is it you want to know?" Mrs. Lear asked, smiling wisely.

"Why is Mrs. Burmaster so disliked in the community?"

"Because she's a scheming, trouble maker if there ever was one!" the old lady replied promptly. "Mr. Burmaster ain't so bad, only he's pulled around by the nose by that weepin', whinin' wife of his."

"Mrs. Burmaster seems to think that the valley folk treat her cruelly."

"She should talk about being cruel!" Mrs. Lear's dark eyes flashed. "You know what them Burmasters done?"

"Only in a general way."

"Well, they come here, and forced folks to git off the land."

"Didn't Mr. Burmaster pay for what he bought?"

"Oh, it was done legal," Mrs. Lear admitted grudgingly. "You see, most o' this valley was owned by a man in the East. He rented it out in parcels, an' never bothered anyone even if they was behind in their payments."

"Then Mr. Burmaster bought the entire track of land from the Eastern owner?" inquired Penny.

"That's right. All except these here four acres where my house sets. They ain't nothin' in this world that will git me in a mood to sell to that old skinflint. He's tried every trick in the bag already."

Penny thoughtfully reached for another pancake. As an impartial judge she could see that there was something to be said on both sides of the question. Mr. Burmaster had purchased his land legally, and so could not be blamed for asking the former renters to move. Yet she sympathized with the farmers who for so many years had considered the valley their own.

"This house o' mine ain't much to look at," Mrs. Lear commented reflectively, "but it's been home fer a long time. Ain't nobody going to get me out o' here."

"You own your own land?" inquired Louise.

"That I do," nodded Mrs. Lear proudly. "I got the deed hid under my bed mattress."

"Won't you tell us about Mr. Burmaster's difficulty with the Headless Horseman," Penny urged, feeling that the old lady was in a talkative mood.

"What do you want to know?" Mrs. Lear asked cautiously.

"Is there really such a thing or is it just a story?"

"If you girls stay in this valley long enough you'll learn fer yourselves," Mrs. Lear chuckled. "I'll warrant you'll see that Horseman."

"And you know who the prankster is!" Penny ventured daringly.

"Maybe I do," Mrs. Lear admitted with a chuckle. "But a ten-mule team couldn't pry it out o' me, and neither can you!"

Before Penny could resume the subject, chickens began to squawk and scatter in the barn yard. A large, expensive looking car pulled up near the side door. Mrs. Lear peeped out of a window and her jaw set in a firm, hard line.

"That's Mr. Burmaster now," she announced in a stage whisper. "Well, he ain't goin' to pressure me. No sir! I'll give him as good as he sends!"

After Mr. Burmaster pounded on the kitchen door, the old lady took her time before she let him in.

"Good morning," he said brightly.

"Humph! What's good about it?" Mrs. Lear shot back. "It's rainin', ain't it? And if we git much more o' it this fall, the dam up Huntley way's goin' to let go shore as I'm a standin' here."

"Nonsense!" replied the estate owner impatiently. He stepped into the kitchen. Seeing Penny and Louise, he looked rather surprised and a trifle embarrassed.

"Go on and say what you come to say," Mrs. Lear encouraged. "Don't stand on no ceremony jus' cause I got city visitors."

Obviously Mr. Burmaster did not like to speak before strangers, but there was no other way.

"You know why I am here, Mrs. Lear," he began. "I've already made several offers for your property—"

"And I've turned 'em all down."

"Yes, but this time I hope you'll listen to reason. Last night my wife had a near collapse after a boy rode a horse across the bridge by our house. All this stupid talk about Headless Horsemen has inspired the community to do mischief. Now every boy in the Valley is trying pranks."

"Then why not ketch the Horseman and put an end to it?" Mrs. Lear asked impudently.

"Nothing would please me better. But we've had no success. My wife can't endure the strain much longer. It's driving her to a frenzy."

"I'm sorry about that," replied Mrs. Lear stonily. "There ain't nothin' I can do."

CHAPTER 8 - A RICH MAN'S TROUBLES

"I want you to sell this property," Mr. Burmaster pleaded. "At least that will remove one irritation. You see, my wife considers the place an eyesore. She can see your house from our living room window. It ruins an otherwise perfect view of the valley."

"Now ain't that too bad!" Mrs. Lear's tone was sarcastic. "Well, let me tell you somethin'. That place o' yorn spoils my view too!"

"I'm afraid I haven't made myself clear," Mr. Burmaster said hastily. "It's a matter of my wife's health."

"Your wife ain't no more ailin' than I be," Mrs. Lear retorted. "If she didn't have my house to bother her it would be somethin' else. I ain't goin' to sell and that's all there is to it!"

"You've not heard my offer. I'll give you two thousand dollars for this place—cash."

Mrs. Lear looked a trifle stunned.

"At best the place isn't worth five hundred," Mr. Burmaster resumed. "But I aim to be generous."

"I won't sell," Mrs. Lear said firmly. "Not at any price. Them's my final words."

Mr. Burmaster had kept his voice carefully controlled but the old lady's decision angered him.

"You'll regret this!" he said in a harsh tone. "I've been very patient but I warn you! From now on I shall act in my own interests."

"Have you ever acted in any other?" drawled a voice from behind the estate owner.

Everyone turned quickly. Joe Quigley, the young station agent, stood framed in the open doorway. Smiling at Burmaster in a grim way, he came slowly into the kitchen.

CHAPTER 9 - STRAIGHT FROM THE SHOULDER

A silence had fallen upon those in the room. Joe Quigley shook rain drops from his overcoat. Deliberately he took his time hanging the coat over a chair in front of the cook stove. Then, still smiling in an ironic way, he faced Burmaster.

"I repeat," he challenged, "did you ever act in any manner except for your own interest?"

"You are insulting! Insolent!" Mr. Burmaster snapped. "But I'll not be drawn into an argument with you. Good morning!"

Quigley blocked the door. "Not so fast," he drawled. "Matter of fact, I was on my way to your house. Saw your car standing in Mrs. Lear's yard, so I figured you were here."

"If you have a telegram for me I'll take it."

"The only message I have is a verbal one," answered Quigley. "Our mayor from Delta, Bradley Mason, asked me to talk to you about the Huntley Dam."

"The subject doesn't interest me."

"It should interest every man, woman and child in this valley!" Quigley retorted. "If the dam gives way flood waters will sweep straight down the valley. Your house would be destroyed before you knew there was any danger!"

"Really?" Mr. Burmaster's smile was a sneer. "Let me worry about my own property."

"As a matter of record, I don't lose any sleep over you," Quigley responded heatedly. "But I am thinking about Mrs. Lear and the people living in Delta. Not to mention the towns on down the line which would be in the direct path of the flood."

"If the good people of Delta are endangered why don't they repair the dam themselves?"

"For the reason that we can't raise the money. We've tried."

"Then the State should act in the matter. I'm willing to write my senator—"

"Repairs are needed now, not three months later. Mr. Burmaster, you have the money and you'd be doing the community a great service to lend help. We're not asking for a donation. It's as much to your interest as ours to protect the valley."

"There's no danger," Burmaster said angrily. "Not a particle. It's only a scheme to shake me down for money."

Brushing past the station agent, the man went out into the rain. In driving out of the yard he turned the car so sharply that it skidded on its wheels.

"Well, that's that," Quigley remarked with a shrug. "I should have saved my breath."

"I'm glad *he's* gone," Mrs. Lear announced tartly. "Will you have a bite o' breakfast, Joe?"

"No, thanks," the young station agent replied. "I'm due for my trick at the Depot in twenty minutes. Have to run along."

The girls were sorry to see Joe Quigley go so soon for they had hoped to have a long talk with him. After he had disappeared into the rain they tried without much success to draw more information from Mrs. Lear. The old lady was in no mood to discuss the Burmasters, but she did have a great deal to say about flood danger to the valley.

"'Tain't usual that we have so much rain," she declared. "Not at this time o' year. Old Red River's floodin' to the brim, an keeps pourin' more and more into the Huntley Lake basin. The dam there was built years ago and it wasn't much to brag on from the start."

"Haven't authorities inspected the dam recently?" Penny inquired thoughtfully.

CHAPTER 9 - STRAIGHT FROM THE SHOULDER

"Oh, some young whippersnapper come here a month ago and took a quick look and said the dam would hold," Mrs. Lear replied, tossing her head.

"But he ain't livin' in the Valley. We want repairs made and we want 'em quick—not next year."

"Since Mr. Burmaster refuses to help is there nothing that can be done?"

"There's some as thinks a little piece in the city papers might help," Mrs. Lear said, giving Penny a quick, shrewd glance. "Your pa's a newspaper owner, ain't he?"

"Yes, he owns the *Riverview Star*."

Penny gazed across the table at Louise. It struck both girls that Mrs. Lear was very well informed about their affairs. How had the old lady learned that Mr. Parker was a newspaper man if not from Silas Malcom? More than ever Penny was convinced that she had been lured to Red Valley, perhaps for the purpose of interesting her famous father in the Huntley Dam project.

"You've been very kind, Mrs. Lear," she said, abruptly arising from the table. "Louise and I appreciate your hospitality. However, we want to pay for our room and meals before we go."

"You don't owe me a penny," the old lady laughed. "Furthermore, you ain't leavin' yet."

"We must. There's an afternoon train—"

"And there'll be another along tomorrow. Why, you'd catch your death o' cold ridin' hoss back all the way to Hobostein."

"The rain should let up soon."

"It should, but it won't," Mrs. Lear declared. "Why don't you stay until tomorrow anyhow? Then you could go to the barn dance tonight at Silas' place."

At the moment, the girls were not greatly intrigued at the prospect of attending a barn dance. The steady rain had depressed them. Though the long journey to Red Valley had proven interesting, it scarcely seemed worth the exhausting effort. They had learned very little about the so-called Headless Horseman and doubted that any truly valuable information would come their way.

"If you stay over maybe you'll git a chance to see that hoss-ridin' ghost," Mrs. Lear said slyly. "Seems like it's mostly on bad nights that he does his prowlin'."

The girls helped with the dishes. They made the bed and watched Mrs. Lear sew on a rag rug. At intervals they wandered to the windows. Rain fell steadily, showing not the slightest sign of a let up.

"Didn't I tell you," Mrs. Lear said gleefully. "It's settlin' for a good healthy pour. You might jest as well calculate on stayin' another night."

"But our parents will be expecting us home," Louise protested.

"Send 'em a wire from Delta," Mrs. Lear urged. "Reckon this rain'll maybe slacken a bit come afternoon."

Throughout the long morning Louise and Penny wandered restlessly about the house. Now and then they sought without success to draw information from Mrs. Lear about the mysterious prankster. From the merry twinkle in her eyes they were convinced she knew a great deal. Pry it from her they could not.

"Maybe that Headless Horseman ain't nobody human," she chuckled. "Maybe it's a real haunt. I mind the time somebody witched my cow. The stubborn critter didn't give no milk for eight days steady."

Penny and Louise weren't sure whether the old lady was serious or trying to tease them. After awhile they gave up attempting to solve such an enigma. By noon they had reconciled themselves to staying another night at Red Valley. However, scarcely had they made their decision to remain, than the sky cleared.

"We're stuck here anyway," Penny sighed. "We couldn't possibly ride our horses back to Hobostein in time to catch the afternoon train."

After luncheon the girls hiked across-fields to the picturesque little town of Delta. There they dropped in at the depot to chat with Joe Quigley and send a telegram to their parents.

"If time's heavy on your hands why not take a little jaunt to the Huntley Dam?" the station agent suggested. "It should be well worth your time."

Penny and Louise decided to do just that. At Mrs. Lear's once more, they saddled their horses and took the pike road to a well-marked trail which led up into the hills. Ditches were brimming with fast running water, yet there was no other evidence of flood.

"Do you suppose all this talk about the dam being weak is just talk?" Penny speculated as they rode along. "In case of real danger one would think State authorities would step into the picture."

Soon the girls came to the winding Red River. Swollen by the fall rains, the current raced madly over rocks and stones. The roar of rushing water warned them that they were close to the dam. In another moment they glimpsed a mighty torrent of water pouring in a silvery white ribbon over the high barrier.

Men could be seen working doggedly as they piled sandbag upon sandbag to strengthen the weakened structure.

Suddenly Penny noticed a man and woman who wore raincoats, watching the workmen.

"Lou, there's Mr. and Mrs. Burmaster!" she exclaimed.

They drove closer to the dam. Mr. and Mrs. Burmaster were talking so earnestly together that they did not observe the newcomers. The roar of water drowned the sound of hoofbeats. But the wind blew directly toward the girls. Mrs. Burmaster's voice, shrill and angrily, came to them clearly:

"You can't do it, John! I won't allow it!" she admonished her husband. "You're not to give the people of this valley one penny! The dam is perfectly safe."

"I'm not so sure," he said, pointing to the far side of the structure.

As he spoke a tiny portion of the dam seemed to melt away. The girls, watching tensely, saw several sandbags swept over the brink. Workmen raced to repair the damage. Mrs. Burmaster seemed stunned by the sight, but only for an instant.

"I don't care!" she cried. "Not a penny of our money goes into this dam! It will hold. Anyway, I'd rather drown than be bested by that hateful old lady Lear!"

"But Matilda—"

"Don't speak to me of it again! Get her out of this Valley—tear down her shack! If you don't, I warn you, I'll take matters into my own hands!"

Turning abruptly, Mrs. Burmaster walked angrily down the trail.

CHAPTER 10 - BARN DANCE

Mr. Burmaster was too distracted to pay heed to Penny and Louise. Brushing past them, he hastened after his wife.

Neither of the girls commented upon the conversation they had overheard. For a long while they sat on their horses, gazing in awe at the tumbling water.

"If ever that dam should let go—" Penny shuddered, "why, the valley would be flooded in just a few minutes. I doubt folks could be warned in time."

"It looks as if it could give way any second too," Louise added uneasily. "Why don't we get out of this valley and stay away?"

"And forget the mystery?"

"A lot of good a mystery would do us if that dam lets go! Penny, we were crazy to come here in the first place!"

"But I want to get a big story for Dad's paper. There's one here."

"I know not what course others may take," Louise quoted grandly. "As for myself, I'm going home on tomorrow's train—rain or shine."

"We'll both have to go," Penny agreed in a discouraged tone. "I had my chance here, but somehow I've muffed it."

For a half hour longer the girls remained at the dam watching the workmen. Presently returning to the Lear cottage they found Mrs. Lear in the warm kitchen, cooking supper.

"I'm settin' the victuals on early tonight," she announced. "We ain't got any too much time to git to the frolic at Silas' place."

Penny and Louise were not sure that they cared to attend the barn dance. Mrs. Lear, however, was deaf to all excuses. She whisked supper onto the table and the instant dishes were done, said that she would hitch Trinidad to the buggy.

"It won't take us long to git there," she encouraged the girls as they reluctantly followed her to the barn. "Trinidad's a fast steppin' critter. Best horse in the county fer that matter."

Soon the ancient buggy was rattling at a brisk clip along the winding woodland road. Mrs. Lear allowed Trinidad to slacken pace as they neared the Burmaster estate.

"Look at that house!" she chortled, waving her buggy whip. "Every light in the place lit up! Know why? Mrs. Burmaster's afeared o' her shadder. Come dark and she's skeared to stick her nose out the door."

"You don't seem to be afraid of anything," Penny remarked in admiration.

"Me afeared?" the old lady laughed gleefully. "What's there to be skeared of?"

"Well—perhaps a certain Headless Horseman."

Mrs. Lear hooted. "If I was to see that critter a-comin' right now and he had twenty heads, I wouldn't even bat an eye!"

Horse and buggy approached the giant tulip tree whose gnarled branches were twisted into fantastic shapes. "See that tree?" Mrs. Lear demanded. "In Revolutionary days a traitor was hanged from that lower limb. Sometimes you kin still hear his spirit sighin' and moanin'."

"You mean the wind whistling through the tree limbs," Penny supplied.

"Didn't sound like wind to me," Mrs. Lear corrected with a grin. "There's some that's afeared to pass under this tree come night—but not me!"

The buggy rattled on, its top brushing against the overhanging branches of the giant tulip. It had grown very dark and the shadows of the woods had a depressing effect upon the girls. They were glad to see the lights of the Malcom place on the hill and even more pleased to drive into the yard.

"You gals go right on in," Mrs. Lear advised, leaping lightly from the buggy. "I'll look after Trinidad."

The barn dance already was in progress. Crossing the yard, the girls could hear gay laughter above the lively squeak of fiddles. Through the open barn door they glimpsed a throng of young people whirling in the intricate steps of a square dance.

"We're certain to be wall flowers at a party such as this," Louise remarked sadly.

The girls found themselves a quiet corner from which to watch the merrymakers. However, they were not permitted to remain there. At the end of the first dance, Joe Quigley came to ask Penny for a dance. To Louise's secret joy he brought along a young man who promptly invited her to be his partner.

"But we don't know how to square dance," Penny protested.

"Won't take you long to learn," Joe chuckled, pulling her to her feet.

The fiddler broke into a lively tune. Silas Malcom, acting as caller, shouted boisterous directions to the dancers: "Balance all, balance eight, swing 'em like a-swingin' on a gate."

Joe Quigley, expert dancer that he was, fairly swept Penny through the intricate formations. Before she hardly was aware of it, the dance was over and Silas called out: "Meet your partner and promenade home."

After that the girls did not lack for partners. The night sped on magic wings. Penny danced many times with Joe and ate supper with him. Then, noticing that the party was starting to break up, she looked about for Mrs. Lear. The old lady was nowhere to be seen. Nor could Louise recall having seen her for the past half hour. Somewhat disturbed, they crossed the room to talk to old Silas Malcom.

"Mrs. Lear went home a good hour ago," he told them. "She said she had to git some sleep, but you gals was havin' so much fun she didn't have the heart to take you away."

Penny and Louise could not hide their consternation. With Mrs. Lear gone they would have no way of getting back to the cottage.

"Don't you worry none," Old Silas chuckled. "Joe Quigley will take you home. An' if he don't there's plenty o' young bucks waitin' fer the chanst."

The arrangement was not in the least to the girls' liking. The party, they could see, rapidly was breaking up. Joe Quigley seemed to have disappeared. Nearly all of the girls except themselves were supplied with escorts.

"I don't like this—not by a little bit!" Penny muttered. "Let's get out of here, Lou."

"How will we get back to Mrs. Lear's place?"

"Walk."

"Without an escort?"

"It's not far."

"We'll have to pass the Burmaster place and that horrid tulip tree."

"Who's afraid of a tulip tree?" Penny laughed. "Come on, if we don't get away quickly Old Silas will ask some young man to take us home. That would be humiliating."

Louise reluctantly followed her chum. The girls obtained their wraps and without attracting attention, slipped out a side door.

"Why do you suppose Mrs. Lear slipped off without saying a word?" Louise complained as she and Penny walked rapidly along the dark, muddy road. "Our shoes will be ruined!"

"So is my ego!" Penny added irritably. "Joe Quigley certainly let us down too. He was attentive enough until after supper. Then he simply vanished."

The night was very dark for driving clouds had blotted out the stars. Overhanging trees cast a cavernous gloom upon the twisting hillside road. Louise caught herself shivering. Sternly she told herself that it came from the cold air rather than nervousness.

Presently the girls approached the Burmaster estate. No lights were burning, but the rambling building loomed up white and ghost-like through the trees.

"I'll breathe natural when we're across the bridge," Penny admitted with a laugh. "If Mr. Burmaster keeps a guard hidden in the bushes, the fellow might heave a rock at us on general principles."

There was no sign of anyone near the estate. Yet both Penny and Louise sensed that they were being watched. The unpleasant sensation of uneasiness increased as they drew nearer the foot bridge.

CHAPTER 10 - BARN DANCE

"Penny, I'm scared," Louise suddenly admitted.

"Of what?" Penny asked with forced cheerfulness.

"It's too quiet."

The half-whispered words died on Louise's lips. Unexpectedly, the stillness of the night was broken by the clatter of hoofbeats.

Startled, the girls whirled around. A horse with a rider had plunged through the dense bushes only a short distance behind them. At a hard run he came straight toward the foot bridge.

"The ghost rider!" Louise whispered in terror.

She and Penny stood frozen in their tracks. Plainly they could see the white-robed figure. His lumpy, misshapen hulk, seemed rigidly fastened to the horse. Where his head should have been there was only a stub.

CHAPTER 11 - THE HEADLESS HORSEMAN

Swift as the wind, the headless horseman approached the narrow bridge. Penny seized Louise's hand, jerking her off the road. The ghost rider thundered past them onto the bridge planks which resounded beneath the steel-shod hoofs.

"Jeepers creepers!" Penny whispered. "That's no boy prankster this time! It's the real thing!"

The thunder of hoofbeats had not gone unheard by those within the walls of Sleepy Hollow. Lights flashed on in the house. Two men with lanterns came running from the mill shack.

"Get him! Get him!" screamed a woman's voice from an upstairs window of the house.

The clamor did not seem to disturb the goblin rider. At unchanged pace he clattered across the bridge to its far side. As the two men ran toward him, he suddenly swerved, plunging his horse across a ditch and up a steep bank. There he drew rein for an instant. Rising in his stirrups, he hurled a small, hard object at the two guards. It missed them by inches and fell with a thud on the bridge. Then with a laugh that resembled no earthly sound, the Headless Horseman rode through a gap in the bushes and was gone.

Louise and Penny ran to the bridge. Half way across they found the object that had been hurled. It was a small, round stone to which had been fastened a piece of paper.

Penny picked up the missile. Before she could examine it, Mr. Burmaster came running from the house. He had not taken time to dress, but had thrown a bathrobe over his pajamas.

"You let that fellow get away again!" he shouted angrily to the two workmen. "Can't you ever stay on the job?"

"See here, Mr. Burmaster," one of the men replied. "We work eight hours a day and then do guard duty at night. You can't expect us to stay awake twenty-four hours a day!"

"All right, all right," Mr. Burmaster retorted irritably. Turning toward the bridge he saw Louise and Penny. "Well, so you're here again?" he observed, though not in an unfriendly tone.

Penny explained that she and Louise had attended the barn dance and were on their way to the Lear cabin.

"What's that you have in your hand?" he interrupted.

"A stone that the Headless Horseman threw at your workmen. There's a paper tied to it."

"Let's have it," Mr. Burmaster commanded.

Penny handed over the stone though she would have preferred to have examined it herself. Mr. Burmaster cut the string which kept the paper in place. He held it beneath one of the lanterns.

Large capital letters cut from newspaper headlines had been pasted in an uneven row across the page. The words spelled a message which read:

"KICK IN HANDSOMELY ON THE HUNTLEY DAM FUND. IF YOU OBLIGE, THE GALLOPING GHOST WILL BOTHER YOU NO MORE."

Mr. Burmaster read the message aloud and crumpling the paper, stuffed it into the pocket of his robe.

"There, you see!" he cried angrily. "It's all a plot to force me to put up money for the Huntley Dam!"

"Who do you think the prankster is?" Penny asked.

"How should I know!" Mr. Burmaster stormed. "The townspeople of Delta may be behind the scheme. Or those hill rats like Silas Malcom! Then it could be Old Lady Lear."

"Can she ride a horse?" Louise interposed.

"Can that old witch ride?" Mr. Burmaster snorted. "She was born in a saddle. Has one of the best horses in the valley too. A jumper."

CHAPTER 11 - THE HEADLESS HORSEMAN

Penny and Louise thought of Trinidad with new respect. Not without misgiving they recalled that Mrs. Lear had slipped away from the barn dance ahead of them. Wisely they kept the knowledge to themselves.

"I'll give a thousand dollars for the capture of that rascal!" Mr. Burmaster went on. "And if it proves to be Mrs. Lear I'll add another five hundred."

"Why, not be rid of the Ghost in an easier way?" Penny suggested. "Give the money to the Huntley Dam Fund."

"Never! I'll not be blackmailed! Besides, the rains are letting up. There's no danger."

Penny and Louise did not attempt to argue the matter. The Huntley Dam feud was none of their concern. By the following day they expected to be far from the valley.

"There's another person who might be behind this," Mr. Burmaster continued. "A newspaper editor at Hobostein. He always hated me and he's been using his paper to write ugly editorials. I ought to sue him for slander."

Though the Headless Horseman episode had excited the girls, they were tired and eager to get to Mrs. Lear's. Accordingly, they cut the conversation short and started on down the road. Mr. Burmaster fell into step walking with them as far as the house.

"Come to see us sometime," he invited with a cordiality that astonished the girls. "Mrs. Burmaster gets very lonesome. She's nervous but she means well."

"I'm sure she does," Penny responded kindly. She hesitated, then added: "I do hope you catch the prankster. Have you considered putting a barricade at the end of the bridge?"

"Can't do it. When we built this place we had to agree to keep the footbridge open to pedestrians."

"Suppose one had a moveable barrier," Penny suggested. "Couldn't your workmen keep watch and swing it into place after the Horseman started across the bridge? With one at each end he'd be trapped."

"It's an idea to be considered," Mr. Burmaster admitted. "The only trouble is that my workmen aren't worth their salt as guards. But we'll see."

Penny and Louise soon bade the estate owner goodnight and went on down the road. Once beyond hearing they discussed the possibility that Mrs. Lear might have masqueraded as the Headless Horseman.

"It was queer the way she disappeared from the dance," Penny speculated. "Granting that she's a spry old lady, I doubt she'd have it in her to pull off the trick."

"I'm not so sure," Louise argued. "Mr. Burmaster said she was a wonderful rider. Didn't you think that horse tonight looked like Trinidad?"

"Goodness, it was too dark to see! In any case, what about the buggy?"

"Mrs. Lear could have unhitched it somewhere in the woods."

Penny shook her head. "It doesn't add up somehow. For that matter, nothing about this affair does."

Rounding a curve, the girls came within view of the Lear cabin. No light burned, but they took it for granted Mrs. Lear had gone to bed.

"Let's give a look-see in the barn," Penny proposed. "I want to make sure that our horses are all right."

"And to see that the buggy is there too," laughed Louise.

They went past the dripping water trough to the barn and opened the doors. White Foot nickered. Bones kicked at the stall boards. Penny tossed both horses a few ears of corn and then walked on to Trinidad's stall. It was empty. Nor was there any evidence of a buggy.

"Well, what do you think of that!" Penny commented. "Mrs. Lear's not been home!"

"Then maybe Mr. Burmaster's theory is right!" Louise exclaimed, staring at the empty stall. "Mrs. Lear could have been the one!"

"Listen!" commanded Penny.

Plainly the girls could hear a horse and vehicle coming down the road. It was Mrs. Lear, and a moment later she turned into the yard. Penny swung open the barn doors. Trinidad rattled in and pulled up short. His sleek body was covered with sweat as if he had been driven hard.

Mrs. Lear leaped lightly to the barn floor and began to unhitch the horse.

"Well, I'm mighty glad to find you here," she chirped. "Joe brought you home, didn't he?"

Penny replied that she and Louise had walked.

"You don't say!" the old woman exclaimed. "I went down the road a piece to see a friend o' mine. By the time I got back the frolic was over. I calculated Joe must have brought you home."

Penny and Louise offered little comment as they helped Mrs. Lear unhitch Trinidad. However, they could see that the old lady was fairly brimming-over with suppressed excitement.

"It's late, but I ain't one bit tired," Mrs. Lear declared as they all entered the house. "There's somethin' mighty stimulatin' about a barn dance."

Penny was tempted to remark that her hostess had spent very little time at Silas Malcom's place. Instead she remained silent.

The girls went at once to bed. Mrs. Lear did not follow them upstairs immediately, but puttered about the kitchen preparing herself a midnight snack. Finally her step was heard on the stairs.

"Good night, girls," she called cheerfully as she passed their door. "Sleep tight."

Mrs. Lear entered her own bedroom. Her door squeaked shut. A shoe was heard to thud on the floor, then another.

"I wish I knew what to think," Penny confided to Louise in a whisper. "She's the queerest old lady—"

Louise had no opportunity to reply. For both girls were startled to hear a shrill cry from the far end of the hall.

The next instant their bedroom door burst open. Mrs. Lear, grotesque in old fashioned flannel nightgown, staggered into the room.

"Why, what's wrong?" Penny asked in astonishment.

"I've been robbed!" Mrs. Lear proclaimed wildly. "I've been robbed!"

CHAPTER 12 - PREMONITIONS

Penny leaped out of bed and touched a match to the wick of an oil lamp. In its flickering yellow glow Mrs. Lear looked as pale as a ghost.

"While we were at the barn dance someone broke into the house," the old lady explained in an agitated voice. "The deed's gone! Now I'll be put off my land like the others. Oh, lawseeme, I wisht I was dead!"

"What deed do you mean?" Penny asked, perplexed.

"Why, the deed to this house and my land! I've always kept it under the mattress o' my bed. Now it's gone!"

"Isn't the deed recorded?"

"No, it ain't. I always calculated on havin' it done, but I wanted to save the fee long as I could. Figured to have the property put in my son's name jes' before I up and died. He's married and livin' in Omaha. Now see what a mess I'm in."

"If the deed is lost and not recorded, you are in difficulties," Penny agreed.

"Perhaps it isn't lost," said Louise, encouragingly. "Did you search everywhere, Mrs. Lear?"

"I pulled the bed half to pieces."

"We'll help you look for it," Penny offered. "It must be here somewhere."

"This is the fust time in twenty years that anyone ever stole anything off me," the old lady wailed as she led the way down the dark hall. "But I kinda knowed somethin' like this was goin' to happen."

Mrs. Lear's bedroom was in great disorder. Blankets had been strewn over the floor and the limp mattress lay doubled up on the springs.

"You see!" the old lady cried. "The deed's gone! I've looked everywhere."

Penny and Louise carefully folded all the blankets. They straightened the mattress and searched carefully along the springs. They looked beneath the bed. The missing paper was not to be found.

"Are you sure you didn't hide it somewhere else?" Penny asked.

"Fer ten years I've kept that deed under the bed mattress!" the old lady snapped. "Oh, it's been stole all right. An' there's the tracks o' the thievin' rascal that did it too!"

Mrs. Lear lowered the oil lamp closer to the floor. Plainly visible were the muddy heelprints of a woman's shoe. The marks had left smudges on the rag rugs which dotted the room; they crisscrossed the bare floor to the door, the window and the bed. Penny and Louise followed the trail down the hallway to the stairs. They picked it up again in the kitchen and there lost it.

"You don't need to follow them tracks no further," Mrs. Lear advised grimly. "I know who it was that stole the deed. There ain't nobody could o' done it but Mrs. Burmaster!"

"Mrs. Burmaster!" Louise echoed, rather stunned by the accusation.

"She'd move Heaven and Earth to git me off this here bit o' land. She hates me, and I hate her."

"But how could Mrs. Burmaster know you had the deed?" Penny asked. "You never told her, did you?"

"Seems to me like onest in an argument I did say somethin' about having it here in the house," Mrs. Lear admitted. "We was goin' it hot and heavy one day, an' I don't remember jest what I did tell her. Too much, I reckon."

The old lady sat down heavily in a chair by the stove. She looked sick and beaten.

"Don't take it so hard," Penny advised kindly. "You can't be sure that Mrs. Burmaster stole the deed."

"Who else would want it?"

"Some other person might have done it for spite."

Mrs. Lear shook her head. "So far's I know, I ain't got another enemy in the whole world. Oh, Mrs. Burmaster done it all right."

"But what can she hope to gain?" asked Penny.

"She aims to put me off this land."

"Mr. Burmaster seems like a fairly reasonable man. I doubt he'd make any use of the deed even if his wife turned it over to him."

"Maybe not," Mrs. Lear agreed, "but Mrs. Burmaster ain't likely to give it to her husband. She'll find some other way to git at me. You see!"

Nothing Penny or Louise could say cheered the old lady.

"Don't you worry none about me," she told them. "I'll brew a cup o' tea and take some aspirin. Then maybe I kin think up a way to git that deed back. I ain't through yet—not by a long shot!"

Long after Penny and Louise had gone back to bed the old lady remained in the kitchen. It was nearly three o'clock before they heard her tiptoe upstairs to her room. But at seven the next morning she was abroad as usual and had breakfast waiting for them.

"I've thought things through," she told Penny as she poured coffee from a blackened pot. "It won't do no good to go to Mrs. Burmaster and try to make her give up that deed. I'll jes wait and see what she does fust."

"And in the meantime, the deed may show up," Penny replied. "Even though you think Mrs. Burmaster took it, there's always a chance that it was only misplaced."

"Foot tracks don't lie," the old lady retorted. "I was out lookin' around early this morning. Them prints lead from my door straight toward the Burmasters!"

Deeply as were the girls interested in Mrs. Lear's problem, they knew that they could be of no help to her. Already they had lingered in Red Valley far longer than their original plan. They shuddered to think what their parents would say if and when they returned to Riverview.

"Lou, we have to start for Hobostein right away!" Penny announced. "We'll be lucky if we get there in time to catch a train home."

Mrs. Lear urged her young guests to remain another day, but to her kind invitation they turned deaf ears. In vain they pressed money upon her. She refused to accept anything so Penny was compelled to hide a bill in the teapot where it would be found later.

"You'll come again?" the old lady asked almost plaintively as she bade them goodbye.

"We'll try to," Penny promised, mounting Bones. "But if we do it will be by train."

"I got a feeling I ain't goin' to be here much longer," Mrs. Lear said sadly.

"Don't worry about the deed," Penny tried to cheer her. "Even if Mrs. Burmaster should have it, she may be afraid to try to make trouble for you."

"It ain't just that biddy I'm worried about. It's somethin' deeper." Mrs. Lear's clear gaze swept toward the blue-rimmed hills.

Penny and Louise waited for her to go on. After a moment she did.

"Seen a rain crow a settin' on the fence this morning. There'll be rain an' a lot of it. Maybe the dam will hold, an' again, maybe it won't."

"Shouldn't you move to the hills?" Penny asked anxiously.

Mrs. Lear's answer was a tight smile, hard as granite.

"Nothin' on Earth kin move me off this land. Nothin'. If the flood takes my house it'll take me with it!"

The old lady extended a bony hand and gravely bade each of the girls goodbye.

Penny and Louise rode their horses to the curve of the road and then looked back. Mrs. Lear stood by the gate for all the world like a statue of bronze. They waved a fast farewell but she did not appear to see. Her eyes were raised to the misty hills and she stood thus until the trees blotted her from view.

CHAPTER 13 - RAIN

"Somehow I can't get Old Mrs. Lear out of my mind, Lou. I keep wondering what happened at Red Valley after we left."

Penny sprawled on the davenport of the Parker home, one blue wedge draped over its rolling upholstered arm. Her chum, Louise, had curled herself kitten fashion in a chair across the room.

A full week now had elapsed since the two girls had returned to Riverview from Red Valley. During that time it had rained nearly every day. Even now, a misty drizzle kept the girls indoors.

"Wonder if it's raining at Red Valley?" Penny mused.

"Why don't you tear that place out of your mind?" Louise demanded a bit impatiently. "We tried to solve the mystery and we couldn't, so let's forget it."

"I do try, but I can't," Penny sighed. "I keep telling myself Mrs. Lear must be the person who masquerades as the Headless Horseman. Yet I can't completely accept such a theory."

"You'll go batty if you keep on!"

"The worst of it is that everyone laughs at me," Penny complained. "If I so much as mention the Headless Horseman Dad starts to crack jokes."

A step sounded on the porch. "Speaking of your father, here he comes now," Louise observed, and straightened in her chair.

Penny did not bother to undrape herself from the davenport. "'Lo, Dad," she greeted her father as he came in. "Aren't you home early for lunch?"

"I am about half an hour ahead of schedule," Mr. Parker agreed. He spoke to Louise as he casually dropped an edition of the *Riverview Star* into his daughter's hands. "That town of yours has smashed into print, Penny."

"What town?" Penny's feet came down from the arm of the davenport and she seized the paper. "Not Red Valley?"

"Red Valley is very much in the news," Mr. Parker replied. "These rains are weakening the dam and some of the experts are becoming alarmed. They are sending someone up to look it over."

"Oh, Dad! I tried to tell you!" Penny cried excitedly. With Louise peering over her shoulder, she spread out the front page of the paper and read the story.

"Oh, it hardly tells a thing!" she complained after she had scanned it.

"So far there's not been much to report," Mr. Parker replied. "But if the dam should let go—wow! Would that be a story! I'm sending my best staff photographer there to get pictures."

Penny pricked up her ears. "Salt Sommers?" she demanded.

"Yes, the *Star* can't take a chance on being scooped by another paper."

"Speaking of chances, Lou, this is ours!" Penny cried. "Why don't we go to Red Valley with Salt?"

"Now just a minute," interrupted Mr. Parker. "Salt's going there on business and he'll have no time for any hocus-pocus. You'll be a bother to him!"

"A bother to Salt!" Penny protested indignantly. "Why, the very idea!"

"Another thing," Mr. Parker resumed, "Red Valley isn't considered the safest place in the world just now. While it's unlikely the dam will give way, still the possibility exists. If it should, the break will come without warning and there's apt to be a heavy loss of life."

"But not mine," said Penny with great confidence. "Don't forget that I won three ribbons and a medal this year. Not for being a poor swimmer either."

"All the same, I shouldn't be too boastful," her father advised dryly.

"When is Salt leaving?" Penny demanded.

"Any time now. But I'm sure he won't let you tag along."

"We'll see if we can change his mind," Penny grinned, reaching for the telephone. Disregarding her father's frown, she called the photographer at the *Star* office. Salt was leaving for Red Valley in twenty minutes, and he willingly agreed to take two passengers.

"There, you see!" Penny cried triumphantly, slamming the receiver into its hook.

"I don't like the idea," Mr. Parker grumbled. "Let's hear what Mrs. Weems has to say."

The housekeeper, it developed, had a great deal to say. Penny, however, was equal to all arguments. So eloquently did she plead her case that Mrs. Weems weakened.

"You've wanted an old spinning wheel for months," Penny reminded her. "While I'm at Red Valley I'll get one for you."

"It seems to me I've heard that argument before," Mrs. Weems said dryly.

"I didn't get a chance to see about it when I was there last time," Penny hastened on. "This time I'll make it a point, I promise. I'm pretty sure I can get the one Silas Malcom has."

"If you must go, please don't distract Salt with spinning wheels," Mr. Parker said crossly. "Or Headless Horseman rot. Remember, he has a job to do."

"Lou and I will help him," Penny laughed. "Just wait and see!"

In the end, Mr. Parker and Mrs. Weems reluctantly said that Penny might go. Louise obtained permission from her mother to make the trip, and fifteen minutes later the girls were at the *Star* office. As they entered the wire photo room, a loudspeaker blared forth: "All right, Riverview, go ahead with your fire picture!"

"Goodness, what was that?" Louise exclaimed, startled.

"Only the wire photo dispatcher talking over the loudspeaker from New York," Penny, chuckled. "We're about to send a picture out over the network."

"But how?"

"Watch and see," Penny advised.

In the center of the room stood two machines with cylinders, one for transmitting pictures to distant stations, the other for receiving them. On the sending cylinder was wrapped a glossy 8 by 10 photograph of a fire. As Penny spoke, an attendant pressed a starter switch on the sending machine. There was a high pitched rasp as the clutch threw in, and the cylinder bearing the picture began to turn at a steady measured pace.

"It's a complicated process," Penny said glibly. "A photo electric cell scans the picture and transmits it to all the points on the network. Salt here could tell you more about it."

"Too busy just now," grinned the young photographer. He stood beside a cabinet stuffing flashbulbs into his coat pocket. "It's time we're traveling."

Salt grinned in a harassed but friendly way at the girls. He was tall and freckled and not very good looking. Nevertheless, he was the best photographer on the *Star*.

"I'm afraid we took advantage of you in asking for a ride to Red Valley," Penny apologized.

"Tickled to have you ride along," Salt cut in. He picked up his Speed Graphic camera and slung a supply case over his shoulder. "Well, let's shove off for the wet country."

The ride by press car to Delta was far from pleasant. Salt drove too fast. The road was slippery once the auto left the pavement and ditches brimmed with brown muddy water.

At one point they were forced to detour five miles to avoid a bridge that had washed out. Instead of reaching Delta early in the day as they had planned, it was well into the afternoon before they arrived.

"Where shall I drop you girls?" Salt inquired wearily. "I'll have to work fast if I get any pictures this afternoon."

"Drop us anywhere," Penny said. "We'll spend the night with Mrs. Lear and go home by train tomorrow."

"Wonder which way it is to the Huntley Dam?"

"We'll show you the road," Penny offered. "It's directly on your way to let us off at the Malcom place. I want to stop there to see about a spinning wheel."

Guided by the two girls, Salt drove up the winding hillside road to Silas Malcom's little farm. There Penny and Louise said goodbye to him and sought to renew acquaintances with the elderly hillman. The old man got up from a porch rocker to greet them cordially.

CHAPTER 13 - RAIN

"Well! Well! I knowed you'd come back one o' these days," he chuckled. "Thank ye mightily fer puttin' them write-ups about Red Valley in the paper."

"I'm afraid I didn't have much to do with it," Penny said modestly. "Red Valley really is a news center these days."

"We're sittin' on a stick o' dynamite here," the old man agreed. "I'm worried about Mrs. Lear. Me and the wife want her to move up here on the hill where she'd be safe, but not that ole gal. She's as stubborn as a mule."

"And what of the Burmasters?"

"I ain't worryin' none about them. They kin look after themselves. They're so cock sure there ain't no danger."

"Then you feel the situation really is serious?"

Old Silas spat into the grass. "When that dam lets go," he said, "there ain't goin' to be no written notice sent ahead. The Burmaster place will be taken, and then Mrs. Lear's. After that the water'll sweep down on Delta faster'n an express train. From there it'll spread out over the whole valley."

"But why don't people move to safety?"

"Down at Delta plenty of 'em are pullin' up stakes," Old Silas admitted. "The Burmasters are sittin' tight though and so is Mrs. Lear."

"We were planning on staying with her tonight," Louise contributed uneasily.

"Reckon you'll be safe enough," Old Silas assured her. "Water level ain't been risin' none in the last ten hours. But if we have another rain above us—look out."

After chatting a bit longer, Penny broached the matter of the spinning wheel. To her delight, Mr. Malcom not only offered to sell it for a small sum, but he volunteered to haul it to the railroad station for shipment.

The slow, tedious wagon ride down to Delta gave the girls added opportunity to seek information from the old man. Penny deliberately spoke of the Headless Horseman. Had the mysterious rider been seen or heard of in the Valley in recent days?

"You can't prove it by me," the old man chuckled. "I been so busy gettin' in my crops I ain't had no time fer such goins on."

Arriving at Delta, Mr. Malcom drove directly to the railroad station.

"Joe Quigley ought to be around here somewhere," he remarked. "See if you can run him down while I unload this spinnin' wheel."

Penny and Louise entered the deserted waiting room of the depot. The door of the little station office was closed and at first glance they thought no one was there. Then they saw Joe Quigley standing with his back toward them. He was engrossed in examining something on the floor, an object that was below their field of vision.

"Hello, Mr. Quigley!" Penny sang out.

The station agent straightened so suddenly that he bumped his head against the ticket counter. He stared at the girls. Then as they moved toward the little window, he hastily gathered up whatever he had been examining. As if fearful that they would see the object, he crammed it into an open office closet and slammed the door.

CHAPTER 14 - A MOVING LIGHT

"Well, well," Joe Quigley greeted the girls cordially. "It's good to see you again. When did you blow into town?"

Louise and Penny came close to the ticket window. They were curious as to what the young station agent had hidden in the closet. However, they did not disclose by look or action that they suspected anything was wrong.

"We drove in about an hour ago," Penny replied carelessly. "We want to ship a spinning wheel by freight to Riverview."

"I'd advise you to send it by express," Quigley said briskly. "That way you'll have it delivered to your door and the difference will be trifling."

"Any way you say," Penny agreed.

Joe went outside with the girls. Silas already had unloaded the spinning wheel. He turned it over to the station agent and after a bit of goodnatured joshing, drove away.

"I can get this out for you on No. 73," Joe promised the girls. "Come on back to the office while I bill it out."

Penny and Louise followed the station agent into the little ticket room. Their ears were assailed by the chatter of several telegraph instruments mounted around the edge of a circular work desk.

"How many wires come in here?" Penny asked curiously.

"Three. The Dispatcher's wire, Western Union and the Message wire."

Penny listened attentively to the staccato chatter of one of the wires. "D-A, D-A," she said aloud. "Would that be the Delta station call?"

"It is," Quigley agreed, giving her a quick look of surprise.

He sat down at the circular desk and reached for the telegraph key. After tapping out a swift, brief message, he closed the circuit.

"Get that?" he grinned at Penny.

She shook her head ruefully. "I learned the Morse code and that's about all," she confessed. "I used to practice on a homemade outfit Dad fixed up for me."

"Quite a gal!" Quigley said admiringly. "What can't you do?"

This was Penny's opportunity and she seized it. "Quite a number of things," she answered. "For one, I can't solve a certain mystery that plagues me."

Joe Quigley finished making out the way bill. His eyes danced as he handed Penny her receipt.

"So you admit that you've met your Waterloo in our Galloping Ghost?"

"I admit nothing," Penny retorted. "You could help me if you would!"

"How?"

"I'm sure you know the person who has been causing the Burmasters so much trouble."

"Trouble?" Quigley's eyebrows jerked. "The way I look at it, that Headless Horseman may do 'em a good turn. He may actually save their worthless necks by driving them out of the valley."

"Meaning?"

"Meaning that Burmaster can't keep on in his bull headed fashion without bringing tragedy upon himself as well as the valley. Even now it's probably too late to reinforce the dam."

"Then what does your prankster hope to gain?"

CHAPTER 14 - A MOVING LIGHT

"You'll have to ask him," Joe Quigley shrugged. "This is the way I look at it. Mrs. Lear and the Burmasters are deep in a feud. The old lady lost the deed to her place and she figures if she moves off, the Burmasters somehow will take advantage of her."

"They've made no attempt to do so?"

"Not yet. But old Mrs. Lear is convinced Mrs. Burmaster is biding her time."

"It all sounds rather silly."

"Maybe it does to an outsider. But this is the serious part. If the dam should let go there'd be no chance to warn either the Burmasters or Mrs. Lear. Both places should be evacuated."

"Then why isn't it done?"

"Because two stubborn women refuse to listen to reason. Mrs. Burmaster won't budge because she says there's no danger—that it's a scheme to get her out of the valley. Mrs. Lear won't leave her home while the Burmasters stay."

"What's to be done?"

"Ask me something easy." The telegraph instrument was chattering the Delta station call again so Quigley turned to answer it. "If you see Mrs. Lear before you leave here, try to reason with her," he tossed over his shoulder. "I've given up."

The girls nodded goodbye and went outside. Silas Malcom's wagon was nowhere to be seen, and after a brief debate they decided to walk to Mrs. Lear's place.

"Maybe we still can catch a ride home with Salt," Louise remarked dubiously. "With all this talk about the dam, I certainly don't relish spending a night in the valley."

"Oh, Silas said there was no immediate danger unless it rains again," Penny reminded her chum. "What Joe Quigley said about Mrs. Lear worries me. We must try to get her to leave the valley."

"Why not move a mountain?" Louise countered. "It would be a lot easier."

When the girls reached Mrs. Lear's cabin they discovered that word of their arrival in Delta had traveled ahead of them.

"Your room's all ready fer you," the old lady beamed as she greeted them at the door. "This time I hope you're stayin' fer a week."

Nothing seemed changed at the Lear cabin. Mrs. Lear had spent the morning canning fruit, and the kitchen table was loaded with containers. A washing flapped lazily on the line. While waiting for the clothes to dry, the old lady filled in her time by sewing on a rag rug of elaborate pattern.

"I'm a mite behind in my work," she confessed to her young visitors. "These infernal rains set a body back. Fer three days I couldn't get my washin' hung, an' I never will git my corn dried less I do it in the oven."

"Speaking of rain," Penny began hesitantly, "Don't you think it's dangerous to remain here much longer?"

"Maybe it is, maybe it ain't," the old lady retorted. "Either way I'm not worryin'. There ain't nothin' going to put me off my place—not even a flood."

"Joe Quigley thinks that you and the Burmasters both should move to a safer place."

"Then let 'em go fust," Mrs. Lear declared. "Didn't Mrs. Burmaster steal the deed to my land jest fer meanness and spite? If I was dumb enough to leave this place fer an hour she'd find some way to git it away from me."

"That couldn't be done so easily," smiled Penny. "After all, Mr. Burmaster has more sense than his wife. Did you never talk to him about the missing deed?"

"We had words," Mrs. Lear said with emphasis. "'Course he stood up fer his wife—said she'd never do such a thing. But I know better!"

"Yet since the deed disappeared no one has tried to put you off your land."

"That's cause the Burmasters are waitin' their chance. Oh, they're sly and cunning. But I'm jest as smart as they are, and they'll never git me off this place!"

The discussion, Penny felt, was traveling in the same familiar circle. One could not influence Mrs. Lear. Her mind had been made up. Nothing would move her.

Thinking that they might at least talk matters over with Mr. Burmaster, the girls presently walked down the road to Sleepy Hollow estate. A workman who was busy with hammer and saw told them that Mr. and Mrs. Burmaster had motored to Delta for the afternoon.

"What are you building?" Penny inquired curiously. "A gate?"

"You might call it that," he grinned. "Mr. Burmaster ordered me to knock together a couple of 'em, one for each end of the bridge."

"Oh! I see!" Light dawned upon Penny. "Moveable barriers to trap the Headless Horseman prankster!"

"It's a lot o' nonsense if you ask me," the workman grumbled. "That fellow ain't been around here in a week. Reckon he may never show up again."

"Yet Mr. Burmaster keeps watch of the bridge?"

"Every night. That wife of his wouldn't give him no peace if he didn't." The workman hammered a nail into place and added: "The Burmasters have got something to worry about if they only had sense enough to realize it."

"You mean the Huntley Dam?"

The workman nodded. "I'm quittin' here tonight," he confessed. "Maybe that dam will hold, but I'm takin' no chances!"

Penny and Louise were even more troubled as they walked back to Mrs. Lear's home. A fine supper awaited them. They scarcely did justice to it and found it difficult to respond to the old lady's cheerful conversation.

"She just doesn't seem to realize that she's in any danger," Louise whispered despairingly to her chum as they did the dishes together.

"Oh, she knows," Penny replied. "But Mrs. Lear is set in her ways. I doubt anyone can induce her to take to the hills."

After the dishes had been put away, the girls played card games with the old lady. Promptly at nine o'clock Mrs. Lear announced that it was bed time. As she locked up the doors for the night she stood for a time on the back porch, staring thoughtfully at the clouds.

"It looks like rain again," Penny remarked.

Mrs. Lear said nothing. She closed the door firmly and turned the key.

Once in their bedroom, the girls undressed quickly and blew out the light. For awhile they could hear Mrs. Lear moving about on the bare floor of her own room. Then the house became quiet.

"I'll be glad when we're home again," Louise whispered, snuggling down under the quilts. "Think how wet we'd get if that dam should break tonight!"

"Stop talking about it or you'll give me nightmares!" Penny chided. "Let's go to sleep."

Try as they would, the girls could not settle down. First Penny would twist and turn and then Louise would do her share of squirming. Finally just as they were beginning to feel drowsy, they were startled to hear a drumming sound on the tin roof above their heads.

"What was that?" Louise muttered, sitting up.

The sounds were coming faster and faster now.

"Rain!" Penny exclaimed.

Jumping out of bed, she went to the window. Already the panes were splashed and rivulets were chasing one another to the sill.

"If this isn't the worst luck yet!" she muttered. "It looks like a hard rain too."

Louise joined her chum at the window. Disheartened, they gazed toward the woods and the hills. Ominous warnings arose in their minds to plague them. With an added burden of water could the dam hold? Sleep seemed out of the question. Wrapping blankets about them, the girls drew chairs to the window and watched.

Then as suddenly as the rain had started, it ceased. A moon struggled through a jagged gap of the clouds. The woods and the barn became discernible once more.

"Rain's over," Louise said, covering a yawn. "Let's go to bed, Penny."

Penny gathered up the quilts from the floor. But as she turned away from the window, an object outside the house captured her attention. For an instant she thought that she was mistaken. Then she gripped Louise's hand, pulling her back to the sill.

"What is it?" Louise asked in bewilderment.

"Look over there!" Penny commanded.

From the woods across the road the girls could see a moving light.

"Someone with a lantern," Louise said indifferently.

"Watch!" Penny commanded again.

CHAPTER 14 - A MOVING LIGHT

Even as she spoke, the lantern was waved in a half circle from side to side. The strange movement was repeated several times.

"What do you make of it?" Louise whispered in awe.

"I suspect someone is trying to signal this house," Penny replied soberly. "Let's keep quiet and see what we can learn."

CHAPTER 15 - INTO THE WOODS

For several minutes nothing very spectacular happened. At intervals the strange lantern signals were repeated.

"It looks to me as if that person over in the woods is trying to signal someone here!" Penny said, peering from behind the window curtain.

"Mrs. Lear?" asked Louise.

"Who else? Certainly no one would have reason to try to attract our attention."

"But why should anyone come here tonight?"

As the girls speculated upon the meaning of the mysterious signals, they heard a door at the end of the hall softly open. Footsteps padded noiselessly past their door.

"Are you asleep, girls?" Mrs. Lear's voice chirped.

Louise would have answered had not Penny clapped a hand firmly over her mouth.

After a moment the footsteps pattered on down the stairway.

"Where can Mrs. Lear be going?" Penny speculated in a whisper. "She wanted to make certain that we were asleep."

The girls did not have long to wait. Soon they heard an outside door close. A moment later they saw the spry old lady crossing the yard to the barn. She was fully dressed and wore a grotesque tight-waisted jacket as protection against the biting night wind.

Penny turned her gaze toward the woods once more. The lantern signals had ceased.

"What do you think is going on?" Louise asked in bewilderment.

Penny reached for her clothing which had been left in an untidy heap on the floor. "I don't know," she replied grimly. "With luck we'll find out."

They dressed as quickly as they could. As Penny was pulling on her shoes she heard the barn door close. She rushed to the window. Old Lady Lear, riding with an easy grace that belied her years, was walking Trinidad toward the road.

"Now where's she going?" Penny demanded, seizing Louise by the hand. "Come on, or we'll never learn!"

Clattering down the stairs, they reached the yard in time to see Mrs. Lear riding into the woods.

"Know what I think?" Louise asked breathlessly. "She's the one who's been pulling off these Headless Horseman stunts!"

"Someone signaled to her from the woods," Penny reminded her chum. "She's starting off to meet whoever flashed the lantern!"

To attempt to follow the old lady afoot seemed a foolish thing to do. Nevertheless, Penny was convinced that Mrs. Lear would not ride far into the woods. She argued that a golden opportunity would be lost forever if they did not try to learn where she went.

"Then come on if we must do it!" Louise consented. "It won't be easy to keep her in sight though."

In their haste the girls had provided themselves with no light. Nor had they imagined that a night could be so dark. Once among the trees they had difficulty in keeping to the trail that old Mrs. Lear had chosen.

"Let's turn back," Louise pleaded. "We're apt to get lost."

Penny, however, was stubbornly determined to learn the old lady's destination. Though she could not see Trinidad she could hear the crashing of underbrush only a short distance ahead.

"Penny, I can't keep on!" Louise gasped a moment later. "I'm winded."

"You're scared," Penny amended. "Well, so am I. But it's just as easy to go on now as it is to turn back."

CHAPTER 15 - INTO THE WOODS

The trail Mrs. Lear had taken led at a steep angle uphill. The old lady allowed her horse to take his time. Even so, the girls were hard pressed to keep fairly close.

"Listen!" Penny presently commanded in a whisper.

No longer could they hear the sound of Trinidad's hoofbeats.

"We've lost her," Louise said anxiously.

"I think Mrs. Lear has stopped," Penny replied, keeping her voice low. "Perhaps she heard us and suspects that we followed her."

More cautiously than before, the girls moved forward. It was well that they did, for unexpectedly they came to a brook and a clearing. Mrs. Lear had dismounted and tied Trinidad to an elm tree close to the water's edge.

Huddling behind a clump of bushes, the girls waited and watched. Mrs. Lear did not appear to be expecting anyone. She gave Trinidad a friendly pat. Then making certain that he was securely fastened to the tree, walked briskly toward the girls.

Penny and Louise cringed closer to the ground. The old lady passed them and went on down the trail.

"You stay here and keep watch of Trinidad!" Penny instructed. "I'll follow Mrs. Lear."

Louise did not want to remain alone. She started to say so, but Penny was gone.

The moment her chum had vanished from sight, sheer panic took possession of Louise. An owl hooted. The cry sent icy chills racing down the girl's spine.

Tensely she listened. She was certain she could hear footsteps approaching the brook. Suddenly she lost all interest in solving the mystery. Her one desire was to get safely out of the woods. Shamelessly, she turned and fled.

Penny, doggedly following Mrs. Lear, was startled to hear a crashing of the bushes behind her. As she paused, Louise came running up.

"What is it?" Penny demanded. "Did someone come for Trinidad?"

"I don't know, and I don't care!" Louise answered grimly. "Call me a coward if you like—I'll not stay by myself!"

Penny did not chide her chum, though she was disappointed. A moment's thought convinced her that since Louise was unwilling to remain by the brook, it now would be better for them both to trail Mrs. Lear. If they were not to lose her, they must hasten along.

"Where do you think the old lady is going?" Louise presently asked as they stumbled over a vine-clogged trail. "Not back home."

"No," Penny agreed in a whisper, "we're going in the wrong direction for that."

Unexpectedly, the girls emerged into a clearing, Not daring to cross the open space lest Mrs. Lear see them, they huddled at the fringe of trees. Overhead, dark clouds scudded and boiled; a strengthening wind whipped their clothing about them.

Mrs. Lear moved spryly across the open space. Pausing near the edge of a cliff, she crouched beside a huge boulder. Grasping a bush for support, she peered down into the valley.

"We may be directly above Sleepy Hollow estate!" Penny whispered excitedly. "Let's try to get closer and see!"

Treading cautiously over the sodden leaves, the girls made a wide circle along the edge of trees. Keeping a safe distance from Mrs. Lear, they peered down over the rim of the valley. As Penny had guessed, Sleepy Hollow was to be seen below. A light, dimly visible, burned on the lower floor of the dwelling. They barely were able to discern the long, narrow bridge spanning the mill pond.

"Now why do you suppose Mrs. Lear came here at this time of night?" Louise speculated. "Do you think—"

Penny gave her chum a quick little jab. From far away she had caught the sound of approaching hoofbeats.

"The Headless Horseman!" Louise whispered in awe.

"We'll soon see. Mrs. Lear is waiting for something!"

Minutes elapsed. Penny began to doubt that she had heard an approaching horseman. Then suddenly he emerged from a thicket that edged the valley road. The rider was garbed in white which plainly silhouetted his huge, misshapen body. Where his head should have been there was nothing.

The sight of such an apparition did not seem to dismay old Mrs. Lear. The old lady leaned farther over the cliff, fairly hugging herself with delight.

Having gained the road leading to Sleepy Hollow, the horseman came on at a swift pace. Sparks flew from the steel shod hoofs as they clipped smartly on the stones.

Penny's gaze swept ahead of the ghost rider to the bridge. Her heart leaped. Even as the horseman rode onto the structure, workmen sprang from the thickets at either side of the road. High wooden barriers were jerked into place at both ends of the bridge. The Headless Horseman's retreat was cut off.

"They've got him!" Penny whispered tensely. "He's trapped on the bridge!"

The horse faltered for an instant and slackened speed. Then as the mysterious rider apparently urged him on, he bore down on the barrier blocking the bridge's exit.

"He's going to try to jump!" Louise murmured. "But no one could take such a high barrier!"

Nervously the girls watched. By this time they were certain that the horse was Trinidad. Magnificent though he was, age had crept upon him, and the wooden gate could prove a difficult test for a trained jumper.

If Penny and Louise were tense, Mrs. Lear was even more so. "Take it, Trinidad!" they heard her mutter. "Over!"

Trinidad did not falter. Approaching the barrier at full tilt, he gathered his strength, and cleared the structure in a beautiful, clean leap. The startled workmen, amazed at the feat, fell back out of the way. Only one made any attempt to stop the rider. The Headless Horseman plunged his gallant steed through a gap in the trees and was gone.

"You did it Trinidad!" cackled Mrs. Lear. "You showed 'em!"

Stooping to pick up a pebble, the old lady hurled it contemptuously toward the bridge. Her aim though carelessly taken was surprisingly good. The stone fell with a loud, resounding thud on the bridge planks.

"Let 'em wonder where that came from!" the old lady chuckled gleefully. "Let 'em wonder."

Wrapping her black coat about her, she quickly retreated into the woods.

CHAPTER 16 - A FRUITLESS SEARCH

"We'll give Mrs. Lear a little start and then follow," Penny instructed. "Undoubtedly she'll return to the brook to meet the Headless Horseman."

"Then you believe she's been behind the scheme from the first?" Louise asked, backing away from the cliff's crumbling edge. Below, on the grounds of Sleepy Hollow, men roved about with lighted lanterns. Apparently no very vigorous effort was being made to pursue the mysterious rider into the woods.

"Who else?" Penny countered. "At least she's been a party to it."

"But she's not actually the rider. We know that."

"She certainly knows the identity of the man," Penny said with conviction. "And we should too before the night's over. Come on!"

Fearful lest Mrs. Lear get too much of a start, the girls set off in pursuit. However, they had not gone far before they realized that the old lady was not returning to the brook. Instead she seemed to be heading for home.

"We didn't figure this so well after all!" Penny observed in deep disgust. "Now it's too late to go back to the brook, so we've lost our chance to learn who the fellow is."

"Maybe not," Louise said cheerfully. "Someone will have to bring Trinidad home."

They had now reached the main road with Mrs. Lear's cabin visible over the hill. Not once glancing over her shoulder, the old lady trod a muddy path to her own gate. Once inside the grounds, she peered up at the windows of the bedroom Penny and Louise had occupied. Satisfied that no light was burning, she quietly entered the house.

The two girls waited for awhile in the woods. They thought it wise to give the old lady ample time to go to bed and fall asleep.

"Come on, we've waited long enough," Penny said at last.

They crossed the road and stole to the front door. To their astonishment it was locked. The back door also was fastened from the inside.

"We'll have to try a window," Penny proposed.

The windows also were locked or so stuck by dampness that they could not be budged.

"If this isn't a pretty mess!" Penny exclaimed impatiently. "Mrs. Lear never used to lock anything. She must have started doing it since the deed to her property disappeared."

"What are we going to do? Sleep in the barn?"

"That might not be such a bad idea. Then if Trinidad ever comes home we'd be able to see who rode him!"

"You'll have to get another idea!" Louise retorted. "That old barn has rats and mice. I wouldn't sleep there for a million dollars."

Penny circled the house, searching for a way out of the difficulty. She could find no ladder. A rose trellis rising along the front wall suggested that if they could use it to reach the second story, they might creep along the porch roof to their own room. There at least, the window had been left unlocked.

"It looks flimsy," Penny said, testing the structure. "I'll try it first."

Gingerly she climbed the trellis, trying to avoid the thorns of a withered rose plant. She reached the porch roof and skillfully rolled onto it. From there she motioned for her chum to follow.

Louise was heavier than Penny and less adept at climbing. The rose bush tore at her clothing and wounded her arms. Just as she was reaching for Penny's outstretched hand one of the cross pieces gave way. Startled, Louise let out a scream of terror.

"Now you've done it!" Penny muttered, pulling her by brute force onto the porch. "Mrs. Lear's deaf if she didn't hear that!"

Tiptoeing with frantic haste across the porch roof, they tested the window of their bedroom. It raised easily. But as they scrambled over the sill, the girls were dismayed to hear Mrs. Lear's door open farther down the hall.

"She heard us!" Louise whispered tensely. "Now what'll we do?"

"Into bed and cover up!" Penny ordered.

Not even taking time to remove their shoes, they made a dive for the big four-poster bed. Scarcely had they pulled the coverlet up to their ears than they heard Mrs. Lear just outside the door.

"Are you all right?" she called anxiously. "I thought I heard a scream."

The girls did not answer. They closed their eyes and pretended to be asleep. Mrs. Lear opened the door and peeped inside. Not entirely satisfied she crossed the room and stood for a moment at the open window. Closing it half way, she then tiptoed out the door.

"Was that a close call!" Penny whispered, sitting up in bed. "Lucky for us she didn't notice anything wrong."

Waiting a few minutes longer, the girls slid from beneath the covers and quickly undressed.

"At least we learned one important thing tonight," Penny observed, quietly lowering a shoe to the floor. "Mrs. Lear is behind this Headless Horseman escapade. But who is the fellow?"

"Silas Malcom perhaps. Only he's a bit too old for pranks."

Penny did not reply. Moving to the window, she gazed thoughtfully toward the barn.

"Someone may bring Trinidad back," she commented. "By watching—"

"Not for me," Louise cut in. She rolled back into bed. "I'm going to get myself a little shut-eye before dawn."

Penny drew a chair up to the window. The room was cold. Her chair was straight-backed and hard. Minutes dragged by and still Trinidad did not put in an appearance.

"The horse may not come back tonight," Penny thought, covering a yawn. "Guess I'll jump into bed. I can hear just as well from there."

She snuggled in beside Louise and enjoyed the warmth of the covers. A delightful drowsiness took possession of her. Though she struggled to stay awake, her eyelids became heavier and heavier.

Presently Penny slept. She slept soundly. When she awakened, the first rays of morning light were seeping in through the window. But it was not the sun that had aroused her from slumber. As she stirred drowsily, she became aware of an unusual sound. At first she could not place it. Then she realized that someone was pounding on the downstairs screen door.

Penny nudged Louise. When that did not arouse her, she gave her a vigorous shake.

"What now?" Louise mumbled crossly.

"Wake up! Someone's downstairs pounding on the screen door."

"Let 'em pound." Louise rolled away from her chum's grasp and tried to go back to sleep.

The thumping noise was repeated, louder and more insistent. Penny was sure she heard the rumble of many voices. Thoroughly puzzled, she swung out of bed and reached for a robe.

"Open up!" called a man's voice from below.

Penny ran to the window. The porch roof half obstructed her view, but in the yard she could see at least half a dozen men. Others were at the door, hammering to be let in.

By this time the thumpings had thoroughly awakened Louise. She too deserted the bed and went to the window.

"Something's wrong!" she exclaimed. "Just see that mob of men! I'll warrant they're here to make trouble for Mrs. Lear—perhaps because of what happened last night!"

CHAPTER 17 - ACCUSATIONS

Penny and Louise scrambled into their clothes. As they pulled on their shoes, they heard Mrs. Lear going down the hall. Fearful lest she encounter trouble, they hastened to overtake her before she reached the front door.

"Do you think it's safe to let those men in?" Penny ventured dubiously.

"Why shouldn't I open the door?" Mrs. Lear demanded. "I've nothing to hide."

She gazed sharply at Penny, who suddenly was at a loss for words.

Mrs. Lear swung wide the door to face the group of men on the porch. Joe Quigley was there and so was Silas Malcom. Seeing friends, Penny and Louise felt reassured.

"Well?" demanded Mrs. Lear, though not in an unfriendly tone. "What's the meaning of waking a body up in the middle o' the night?"

"Word just came in by radio," Joe Quigley spoke up. "There's been a big rain over Goshen way."

"I could have told you that last night," Mrs. Lear replied, undisturbed. "Knew it when I seen them big clouds bilin' up."

"You oughter get out o' here right away," added Silas Malcom. "That dam at Huntley Lake ain't safe no more, and when all that water comes down from Goshen it ain't too likely she'll hold."

"Are the people of Delta leaving for the hills?" Mrs. Lear asked coldly.

"Some are," Quigley assured her. "We're urging everyone who can to take the morning train. A few stubborn ones like yourself refuse to budge."

"Oh, so I'm stubborn! I suppose you're leaving, Joe Quigley?"

"That's different. I have a job to do and I can't desert my post at the depot."

"And the Burmasters? Are they leaving?"

"We're on our way up to the estate now to warn them."

"I'll make you a bargain," Mrs. Lear agreed, a hard glint in her eye. "If Mrs. Burmaster goes, then I'll go too. But so long as she stays in this valley I'm not stirrin' one inch!"

"You're both as stubborn as one of Silas' mules!" Joe Quigley said impatiently. "Don't you realize that your life is in danger?"

"When you've lived as long as I have, young man, life ain't so precious as some other things."

"If you won't listen to reason yourself, what about these girls?" Quigley turned toward Penny and Louise.

Mrs. Lear's face became troubled. "They'll have to go at once," she decided. "What time's that train out o' Delta?"

"Eleven-forty," Joe Quigley replied. "Or they can catch it at Witch Falls at eleven. Getting on at that station they might find seats."

"We'll pack our things right away," Louise promised, starting for the stairs.

Penny followed reluctantly. Though she realized that it would be foolhardy to remain, she did not want to leave Red Valley. Particularly she disliked to desert old Mrs. Lear.

"If Mrs. Lear is determined to stay here, what can we do about it?" Louise argued reasonably. "You know our folks wouldn't want us to remain."

The girls quickly gathered their belongings together and went downstairs again. To their surprise Mrs. Lear had put on her coat and was preparing to accompany the men to Sleepy Hollow.

"I ain't leavin' fer good," she announced, observing Penny's astonished gaze. "Leastwise, not unless the Burmasters do. I'm going there now to see what they've got to say."

"Come along if you like," one of the men invited the girls. "Maybe you can help persuade them to leave the valley."

Penny and Louise doubted that they would be of any assistance whatsoever. However, it was several hours before train time, so they were very glad indeed to ride in one of the cars to Sleepy Hollow estate. At the crossroad Joe Quigley turned back to Delta for he was scheduled to go on duty at the railroad station. The others kept on until they reached the estate.

Silas Malcom rapped sharply on the front door. In a moment a light went on in an upstairs room. A few minutes later a window opened and Mr. Burmaster, clad in pajamas, peered down.

"What's wanted?" he demanded angrily.

"There's been a big rain above us," he was told. "Everyone's being advised to get out while there's time."

Mr. Burmaster was silent a moment. Then he said: "Wait a minute until I dress. We'll talk about it."

Ten minutes elapsed before the estate owner opened the front door and bade the group enter. He led the party into a luxuriously furnished living room.

"Now what is all this?" Mr. Burmaster asked. "We had one disturbance here last night and it seems to me that's about enough."

Silas Malcom explained the situation, speaking quietly but with force.

"And who says that the dam won't hold?" Mr. Burmaster interrupted.

"Well, it's the opinion of them that's been workin' on it for the past two weeks. If we'd had money and enough help—"

"So that's why you rooted me out of bed!"

"We came here to do you a favor!" one of the men retorted angrily. "It's too late to save the dam unless nature sees fit to spare her. But it ain't too late for you and your household to get out of here."

"I have two hundred thousand dollars sunk in this place."

"That's a heap o' money," Silas said thoughtfully. "But it ain't going to mean anything to you if that dam lets go. You ought to leave here without waitin'."

"Perhaps you're right," Mr. Burmaster said, pacing back and forth in front of the fireplace. "It was my judgment that the dam would hold. Naturally no one could predict these heavy, unseasonable rains."

A door opened. Everyone turned to see Mrs. Burmaster on the threshold. Her hair was uncombed and she wore a brilliant red housecoat.

"Who are these people?" she asked her husband in a cold voice.

"Villagers. They've come to warn us that we ought to leave here."

"Warn us, indeed!" Mrs. Burmaster retorted bitterly. "I don't know what they've said to you, but it's just another scheme to get us away from here! Haven't they tried everything?"

"This ain't no Headless Horseman scare, Ma'am," spoke Silas Malcom. "The Huntley dam is likely to give way at any minute."

"I've heard that for weeks!" Mrs. Burmaster's gaze was scornful. "Oh, I know you've hated us ever since we built this house! You've tried every imaginable trick to make us leave."

"That ain't true, ma'am," Silas replied soberly.

Mrs. Burmaster's angry gaze swept the group and came to rest on Mrs. Lear.

"That old witch who lives down the road has set you all against me!" she fairly screamed. "She's lied and fought me at every turn!"

Mrs. Lear detached herself from the group. She spoke quietly but with suppressed fury.

"I've stood a lot from you in the past, Mrs. Burmaster," she retorted. "But there ain't no one alive can call me a witch!"

"Oh, I can't?" Mrs. Burmaster mocked. "Well, you're worse than an old witch!"

"At least I ain't a sneak thief! I don't go breakin' into folks' houses to steal the deed to their property!"

"How dare you accuse me of such a thing!"

"Because I know you got the deed to my cabin right here in the house!" Mrs. Lear accused. "You've got it hid away!"

"That's a lie!"

"Ladies! Ladies!" remonstrated one of the men from the village.

Mrs. Lear paid not the slightest heed. Advancing toward Mrs. Burmaster, she waved a bony finger at her.

CHAPTER 17 - ACCUSATIONS

"So it's a lie, is it?" she cackled. "Well, let me tell you this! Mary Gibson that worked out here as maid until last Wednesday saw that deed o' mine in your bureau drawer. She told me herself!"

"How dare you say such a thing!" gasped Mrs. Burmaster.

Mr. Burmaster stepped between his wife and Mrs. Lear.

"Enough of this!" he said firmly, "We know nothing about the deed to your property, Mrs. Lear."

"Then prove that it ain't here!" the old lady challenged. "Look in your wife's bureau drawer and see!"

"Certainly. Since you have made such an accusation we shall by all means disprove it."

As Mr. Burmaster started toward the circular stairway, his wife caught nervously at his arm.

"No, John! Don't be so weak as to give in to her!"

"Mrs. Lear has made a very serious accusation against you. We must prove to all these people that she misjudged you."

"You can't search—you mustn't! It's insulting to me!"

"But my dear—"

"I'll never speak to you again if you do! Never!"

Mr. Burmaster hesitated, not knowing what to do. "So you're afraid to look?" Mrs. Lear needled him.

"No, I'm not afraid," the estate owner said with sudden decision. "Furthermore, I want someone to accompany me as witness." His gaze swept the little group and singled out Penny. "Will you come?"

Penny did not wish to be drawn into the feud, but as the others urged her to accompany Mr. Burmaster, she reluctantly agreed.

Mrs. Burmaster's bedroom was a luxurious chamber directly above the living room. There was a canopied bed with beautiful hangings and a dressing table that fairly took Penny's breath away.

"There's the bureau," said Mr. Burmaster, pointing to another massive piece of furniture. "Suppose you search."

Rather reluctantly, Penny opened the top drawer. It was filled with lace handkerchiefs, and neat boxes of stockings. The second drawer contained silk lingerie while the third was filled with odds and ends.

"So it's not there!" Mr. Burmaster exclaimed in relief as Penny straightened from her task. "I was sure it wouldn't be!"

From the tone of his voice it was evident that he had been very much afraid the deed would be found. Penny's eyes wandered toward the dressing table.

"You may as well search there too," Mr. Burmaster said. "Then there can be no further accusations."

One by one Penny opened the drawers of the dressing table. Mrs. Burmaster's jewel box caught her eye. It was filled to overflowing with bracelets, pins, and valuable necklaces. Just behind the big silver box, another object drew her attention. At a glance she knew that it was a legal document. As she picked it up she saw that it was the deed to Mrs. Lear's property.

"What's that?" Mr. Burmaster demanded sharply when Penny did not speak.

Without answering, she gave him the document.

"It is the deed!" he exclaimed, dumbfounded. "Then my wife did steal it from Mrs. Lear! But why—why would she do such a thing?"

"I'm sure she didn't realize—"

"Mrs. Burmaster is a sick woman, a very sick woman," the estate owner said unhappily. "But what must I do?"

"What can you do except go downstairs and tell the truth?"

"Face them all? Admit that my wife is a thief?"

"It seems to me that the only honorable thing is to return the deed to Mrs. Lear."

"The deed must be returned," Mr. Burmaster acknowledged. "But not tonight—later."

"I realize that you wish to protect your wife," Penny said quietly. "It's natural. But Mrs. Lear has to be considered."

"I'll pay you handsomely to keep quiet about this," Mr. Burmaster said. "Furthermore, I'll promise to return the deed to Mrs. Lear tomorrow."

Penny shook her head.

"Very well then," Mr. Burmaster sighed. "I suppose I must face them. I don't mind for myself. It's my wife I'm worried about. She's apt to go into hysterics."

Tramping down the stairs, the estate owner confronted the little group of villagers. In a few words he acknowledged that the deed had been found, apologized to Mrs. Lear, and placed the document in her hands. Throughout the speech Mrs. Burmaster stood as one stricken. Her face flushed as red as the robe she wore, then became deathly white.

"I thank you, Mr. Burmaster, you're an honorable man," Mrs. Lear said stiffly. "I feel mighty sorry fer the way things turned out. Maybe—"

"Oh, yes, everyone can see that you're sorry!" Mrs. Burmaster broke in shrilly. "You're a hateful, scheming old hag. Now get out of my house! Get out all of you and never come back!"

"About the dam—" Silas Malcom started to say.

"The dam!" Mrs. Burmaster screamed. "Let it break! I wish it would! Then I'd never see any of you again! Go on—get out! Do you hear me? Get out!"

The little group retreated toward the door. Mrs. Burmaster did not wait to see the villagers leave. Weeping hysterically, she ran from the room.

CHAPTER 18 - FLOOD WATERS

Rain splattered steadily against the car windows as the noon passenger train pulled from the Witch Falls station. Penny and Louise watched the plump drops join into fat rivulets which raced one another to the sill. Since saying goodbye to Mrs. Lear, Silas Malcom, and their other valley friends, they had not done much talking. They felt too discouraged.

"I wish we'd decided to catch the train at Delta," Penny remarked, settling herself for the long ride home. "Then we could have said goodbye to Joe Quigley. We'll be passing through the station soon."

Louise nodded morosely.

"Things certainly ended in one grand mess," she commented. "Mrs. Lear got the deed to her property back, but the feud will be worse than ever now. Furthermore, we never did solve the Headless Horseman mystery—not that it matters."

Reaching for a discarded newspaper which lay on the coach seat, Penny shot her chum a quick, knowing look.

"Just what does that mean?" Louise demanded alertly.

Penny pretended not to understand.

"You gave me one of those wise-owl looks!" Louise accused. "Just as if you *had* solved the mystery."

"I assure you I haven't, and never will now that we're leaving the valley."

"But you do have an idea who was back of the scheme?"

"Mrs. Lear, of course. We saw that much with our own eyes."

"But we didn't learn who actually rode the horse. Or did you?"

"Not exactly."

"You do know then!"

"No," Penny denied soberly. "I noticed something about the rider that made me think—but then I'd better not say it."

"Please go on."

"No, I have no proof. It would only be a guess."

"I think you're mean to keep me in the dark," Louise pouted.

"Maybe I'll tell you my theory later," Penny replied, opening the newspaper. "Just now, I'm not in the mood."

Both girls had been strangely depressed by their last few hours in the valley. Mrs. Lear had refused to come with them or to seek refuge in the hills. Gleeful at her victory over Mrs. Burmaster, she had seemed insensible to danger.

"Look at this headline," Penny said, indicating the black type of the newspaper. "FLOOD MENACES RED VALLEY!"

Quickly the girls scanned the story. The account mentioned no facts new to them. It merely repeated that residents of the valley were alarmed by heavy up-state rains which had raised Lake Huntley to a dangerous height behind the dam.

"Wonder if Salt got any good pictures when he was here yesterday?" Penny mused. "Probably not. This is the sort of news story that doesn't amount to much unless the big calamity falls."

"You don't think the dam actually will give way?" Louise asked anxiously.

"How should I know? Even the experts can't agree."

"At any rate we're leaving here, and I'm glad. Somehow, I've had an uneasy feeling ever since last night."

HOOFBEATS ON THE TURNPIKE

Penny nodded and glanced from the car window again. Rain kept splashing fiercely against the thick pane, half obscuring the distant hills. Along the right of way, muddy water ran in deep torrents, washing fence and hedgerow.

As the train snailed along toward Delta, there was increasing evidence of flood damage. A row of shacks near the railroad tracks was half submerged. Along the creek beds, giant trees bowed their branches to the swirling water. Many landmarks were completely blotted out.

"We're coming into Delta now," Penny presently observed. "Perhaps if we watch sharp we'll see Joe Quigley and can say goodbye."

The train stopped with a jerk while still some distance from the station. Then it pulled to a siding and there it waited. After ten minutes Penny sauntered through the train, thinking that if she could find an open door, she might get out and walk to the depot. Stopping a porter who was passing through the car, she asked him the cause of the delay.

"We'se waitin' fo' ordehs," the colored man answered. "Anyhow, dat's what de cap'n says."

"The captain?"

"The conducteh o' dis heah train."

"Oh! And what does he say about the high water?"

"He says de track between heah and Hobostein's a foot undeh."

"Then that means the river must be coming up fast. Any danger we'll be stranded at Delta?"

"You betteh talk to de conductor," the porter said, jerking his head toward a fat, bespectacled trainman who had just swung aboard the coach. "Dat's Mr. Johnson."

Penny stopped the conductor to ask him what the chances were of getting through the flooded area.

"Doesn't look so good," he rumbled. "The rails are under at Mile Posts 792 and 825."

"Then we're tied up here?"

"No, we're going as far as we can," the conductor answered. "The dispatcher's sending a work train on ahead to feel out the track. But we'll be lucky to make ten miles an hour."

Penny chatted with the conductor for a few minutes, then ambled back to the coach where she had left Louise. The prospects were most discouraging. At best it would be late afternoon before they could hope to reach Riverview.

"I'm starving too," Louise said. "I suppose there's no diner on this train."

As a stop gap the girls hailed a passing vendor and bought candy bars. Having thus satisfied their hunger, they tried to read magazines.

Presently the car started with a jerk. However, instead of proceeding toward the station it backed into the railroad yard.

"Now what?" Penny demanded impatiently. "Aren't we ever going to start?"

The porter hastened through the car, his manner noticeably nervous and tense. He paid no heed to a woman passenger who sought to detain him.

"Something's wrong!" Penny said with conviction.

"A wash-out, do you think?"

"Might be. Let's see what we can learn."

With a vague feeling of foreboding they could not have explained, the girls arose and followed the porter. Something was amiss. They were certain of it.

Losing sight of the colored man, they kept on until they reached the rear platform. Penny started to open the screen door. Just then the train whistle sounded a shrill, unending blast.

Startled, Louise gripped her chum's hand, listening tensely.

In the car behind, they heard the conductor's husky voice. He was shouting: "Run! Run, for your lives! Take to the hills!"

Penny was stunned for an instant. Then seizing Louise's arm, she pulled her out on the train platform. At first glance nothing appeared wrong. The tracks were well above the river level. Between the road bed and a high hill on the left, flood water was running like a mill race, but the ditch was narrow and represented no immediate danger.

"Listen!" Penny cried.

From far away there came a deep, rumbling roar not unlike the sound of distant thunder.

CHAPTER 18 - FLOOD WATERS

Leaning far over the train platform railing, Penny gazed up the tracks. The sight which met her eyes left her momentarily paralyzed.

Down the valley charged a great wall of water, taking everything before it. Trees had been mowed down. Crushed houses were being carried along like children's blocks. Far up the track a switch engine was lifted bodily from the rails and hurled backwards.

Penny waited to see no more.

"The dam's given away!" she shouted. "Quick, Louise! Climb over the railing and run for your life!"

CHAPTER 19 - TRAGEDY

Leaping over the platform railing, Penny held up her arms to assist Louise. Now awakened to danger, her chum scrambled wildly after her only to stop aghast as she beheld the gigantic wall of water rushing toward them.

"Jump the ditch and make for the hill!" Penny ordered tersely. "Be quick!"

Passengers were pouring from the other cars, their terrified cries drowned by the grinding roar of the onrushing torrent. The wall of water moved with incredible speed. It tore into the railroad yard, shattering a tool house and a coal dock. It roared on, sweeping a row of empty box cars into its maw.

Spurred by the sight, Penny and Louise tried to leap the ditch. They fell far short and both plunged into the boiling water up to their arm pits.

Penny's feet anchored solidly. With a gigantic shove, she helped Louise to safety. By swimming with the current she then reached shore a few yards farther down the railroad right of way.

"Run!" she shouted to the bewildered, bedraggled Louise. "Up the hill!"

Scrambling over the muddy edge of the ditch, she raced after her chum for higher ground. Just then the wall of water swept into the siding. As the train was struck it seemed to shudder from the terrific impact, then slowly settled on its side.

"Horrible!" Louise shuddered. "Some of the passengers may have been trapped in there!"

"Most of them escaped," Penny gasped. "There goes the water tower!"

A building borne by the flood, rammed into the ironwork of the big dripping tower. It crumpled, falling with a great, shuddering splash.

With the back-wash of the flood sloshing against their knees, the girls raced for high ground. Reaching a point midway up the hill where other passengers had paused, they turned to glance below. Yellow, angry water, rising easily ten feet, flowed over the railroad right of way.

With unbelievable speed the flood rolled on. In one angry gulp it reached a long freight train farther down the track. The caboose and a string of coal cars were lifted and hurled. Strangely, the coal tender and engine which had been detached, remained on the rails.

"Oh, look!" Louise gasped in horror. "The engineer's trapped in the cab!"

The trainman, plainly visible, valiantly kept the engine whistle blowing. Higher and higher rose the water. Penny and Louise were certain the courageous man must meet his doom. But the crest of the flood already had swept on down the valley, and in a moment the waters about the engine remained at a standstill.

So quickly had disaster struck that the girls could not immediately comprehend the extent of the tragedy. From their own train nearly all of the passengers had escaped. But the town of Delta had not fared so well. Apparently the flood had roared through the low section, taking all before it. Farther up the valley, directly below Huntley Lake where the gorge was narrow, damage to life and property might be even greater.

"What chance could poor Mrs. Lear have had," Louise said brokenly. "Or the Burmasters."

"There's a possibility they took to the hills in time."

"I doubt it," Louise said grimly. "The flood came so quickly."

Already the yellow, muddy waters were carrying evidence of their work. Houses, many with men and women clinging desperately to rooftops, floated past. Other helpless victims clung to logs, orange crates and chicken coops. At terrific speed they sailed past the base of the hillside. Several shouted piteously for help.

"We must do something to save those people!" Penny cried desperately.

"What?" Louise asked.

CHAPTER 19 - TRAGEDY

By this time the hillside was dotted with people who had saved themselves. Several of the women were weeping hysterically. Another had fainted. For the most part, everyone stared almost stupidly at the endless stream of debris which was swept down the valley. No one knew how to aid the agonized victims who clung to whatever their fingers could clutch.

On one rooftop, Penny counted six persons. The sight drove her to action.

"If only we had a rope—" she cried, and broke off as her eyes roved up the hillside.

Two hundred yards away stood a farmhouse.

"I'll see if I can get one there!" she cried, darting away.

The hill was steep, the ground soft. Penny's wet clothing impeded her. She tripped over a stone and fell, but scrambling up, ran on. Finally, quite out of breath, she reached the farmhouse. A woman with two small children clinging to her dress, met the girl in the yard.

"Ain't it awful?" she murmured brokenly. "My husband's workin' down at the Brandale Works. Did the flood strike there?"

"It must have spread through all of Delta," Penny answered. "This disaster's going to be frightful unless we can get help quickly. Do you have a telephone?"

"Yes, but it's dead. The wire runs into Delta."

Penny had been afraid of that. She doubted that a single telephone pole had been left standing in the town. Nor was it likely that the other valley cities had 'phone service.

"Do you have a rope?" she asked. "A long one?"

"In the barn. I'll get it."

The woman came back in a moment, a coil of rope over her arm.

"Send some of those poor folks up here," she urged as Penny started away with the rope. "I'll put on a wash boiler of coffee and take care of as many as I can."

Half sliding, Penny descended the steep hillside. During her absence two persons had been rescued from the water by means of an improvised lasso made from torn strips of clothing. Others were drifting past, too far away to be reached.

A woman and a child floated past, clinging to a log. Penny stood ready, the rope coiled neatly at her feet. She took careful aim, knowing that if she missed she would have no second chance.

Penny hurled the rope and it ran free, falling just ahead of the helpless pair. The half-drowned mother reached with one hand and seized it before it sank beneath the surface.

"Hold on!" Penny shouted. "Don't let go!"

Several men ran to help her. By working together, they were able to pull the woman and her child to safety.

Abandoning the rope to skilled hands, Penny rounded the hill to a point providing a clear view of the flooded railroad yard. The roundhouse, the coal chutes and the signal tower were gone. But her heart leaped to see that the station was still standing. Built on high ground it was surrounded with water which did not appear to be deep.

Penny turned to Louise who had followed her. Just then they both heard someone shout that the railroad bridge was being swept away. They saw the massive steel structure swing slowly from its stone foundation. One side held firm which immediately set up great swirling currents. Any persons carried that way would be faced with destruction in the whirling pools of water.

"It's too late to warn the towns directly below Delta!" Penny gasped. "But there still may be time to get a message through to Hobostein. In any case, we must get help here!"

"But how?" Louise asked hopelessly. "Any wires that were left standing must have been torn away when the bridge went."

Penny gazed again toward the Delta depot. Between it and the hillside ran a fast-moving stretch of water, yet separated from the main body of the racing flood.

"If only I could get over to the station, I might somehow send a message!"

"Don't be crazy!" Louise remonstrated. "You haven't a chance to cross that stretch of water!"

"I think I could. I'm a pretty fair swimmer."

"But the current is so swift."

"There's a certain amount of risk," Penny admitted soberly. "But we can't stand here and wait. Someone must do something to bring help."

"Don't do it, Penny!" Louise pleaded. "Please!"

Penny hesitated, but only for an instant. She understood perfectly that if she misjudged the strength of the current it would sweep her down—perhaps carry her along into the main body of water. Once in the grip of that angry torrent, no one could hope to battle against it.

The risk, however, was one she felt she must take. Struggling free from Louise's clinging hands, she kicked off her shoes and tucked up her skirt. Then she plunged into the swirling water.

CHAPTER 20 - EMERGENCY CALL

The current was much swifter than Penny had anticipated. It tugged viciously at her feet, giving her no opportunity to inch her way along the ditch. A dozen steps and she was beyond her depth, fighting desperately to keep from being swept with the current.

Although a strong swimmer, Penny found herself no match for the wild torrent. Only by going with it could she keep her head above water. To attempt to swim against it was impossible. Despairingly, she saw that she would miss the railroad station by many yards.

"I'll be swept into the main body of the flood!" she thought in panic. "I shouldn't have attempted it!"

Too late she tried to turn back toward the hillside. The swift current held her relentlessly. Struggling against it, her head went under. She choked as she breathed water, then fought her way to the surface again. The current carried her on.

After that first moment of panic, Penny did not waste her strength uselessly. Allowing the flood to carry her along, she took only a few slow strokes, swimming just enough to keep from being pulled beneath the surface. As calmly as she could she appraised the situation.

The station now was very close. Scarcely fifty yards separated her from it, but she knew her physical powers. Her strength was no match for that racing, swirling, debris-studded current. She could not hope to span the distance, short though it was.

Penny despaired. And then her heart leaped with new hope. Directly ahead, a foot and a half above the water's murky surface, rose a steel rod with red and green signal targets. She recognized the object as a switch stand, used by trainmen to open and close the passing track switch.

"If I could reach that steel rod I could hold on!" she thought. "But do I have the strength?"

The swift current swept Penny on toward the upright rod. She took three, four powerful strokes and reached frantically for the standard. Her fingers closed around the metal. The swift flowing water whipped her violently, but she held fast. Drawing herself close to the rod, she shoved her feet downward. Still she could find no bottom.

Hopefully, Penny glanced toward the station, now less than twenty-five yards away. Although water completely surrounded the squat little building, it had not risen to the window level. Yet there was no sign of anyone near the place—no one to help her.

Still clinging to the rod, she groped again with her bare feet. This time she located a steel rail. By standing on it, she raised herself a few inches and found firm footing. Suddenly an idea came to her.

"If I shove off hard from this rail, maybe I can get enough momentum to carry me through the current! If I fail—"

Penny decided not to think about that. Releasing her hold on the rod, she pushed off with all her strength and began to swim. Digging her face into the water, she held her breath and put everything she had into each stroke. Pull, pull, pull—she had to keep on. Her breath was nearly gone, strength fast was deserting her. Yet to turn her head and gulp air might spell defeat when victory was near. She could feel the torrent swinging her downstream. She made a final, desperate spurt.

"I can't make it!" she thought. "I can't!"

Yet she struggled on. Then suddenly her churning feet struck a solid object. It was the brick platform of the station!

Raising her head, she saw the building loom up in front of her. The current no longer tugged at her body. She had reached quiet water.

Penny stood still a moment, regaining her breath.

Then she waded to the front door of the station. It could not be opened. Penny pounded and shouted. Her cries went unanswered.

"The place is deserted!" she thought with a sinking heart. "Joe Quigley must have taken to the hills when the flood came."

Slowly Penny waded around the building, unwilling to acknowledge failure. Somehow she had to get word of the disaster through to the outside world. Yet even if she did get inside the station, she was far from certain it would do any good. Telephone wires undoubtedly were down.

Penny made a complete circuit of the depot without seeing anyone. Sick with disappointment, she paused beside the glass-enclosed bay of the ticket office and peered inside. She could see no one. But as she pressed her face against the pane of glass she thought she heard the chatter of a telegraph instrument.

"That means there still must be a wire connection!" she thought hopefully.

Nearby, the flood had lodged a small board against the depot wall. Seizing it, Penny smashed the lower pane of glass with one well-aimed blow.

She scrambled through the opening, crawled over the operator's table and dropped to the floor. The little ticket office was deserted though Joe Quigley's hat still lay on the counter.

"If only I knew how to telegraph!" Penny despaired, hearing again the chatter of the instrument. "Just knowing Morse code won't help me much."

The telegraph sounder was signaling the station call for Delta: "D-A, D-A, D-A." Over and over it was repeated.

Penny hesitated and then went to the instrument. She opened the key and answered with the station call, "D-A."

"Where have you been for the past twenty minutes?" the train dispatcher sent angrily at top speed. "What's happened to No. 17?"

Penny got only part of the message and guessed at the rest. Nervously, at very slow speed, she tapped out in Morse code that the train had been washed off the track.

The dispatcher's next message came very slowly, disclosing that he knew from Penny's style of sending that he was talking to an amateur telegrapher.

"Where's Joe Quigley?" he asked in code.

"Don't know," Penny tapped again. "Station's half under water. Can you send help?"

"Shoot me the facts straight," came the terse order.

Penny described what had happened at Huntley Dam and told how the railroad bridge had washed out. In return the dispatcher assured her that a relief crew would be sent without delay.

"Stay on the job until relieved," was his final order.

Weak with excitement, Penny leaned back in her chair. Help actually was on the way! The dispatcher would notify the proper authorities and set in motion the wheels of various relief organizations. For the moment she had done all she could.

She listened tensely as the dispatcher's crisp call flashed over the wire. He was notifying stations farther up the line to hold all trains running into the valley. Repeatedly Penny heard the call "W-F" which she took to be Witch Falls. It went unanswered.

Half sick with dread, she waited, hoping for a response. It was likely, almost a certainty that the station had been swept away, for the town would have been squarely in the path of the flood. What had happened to old Mrs. Lear and the Burmasters? Penny tried not to think about it.

Unexpectedly, the outside office door opened. Joe Quigley, bedraggled and haggard, one arm hanging limp at his side, splashed toward the desk. Seeing Penny, he stopped short, yet seemed too dazed to question the girl's presence in the inner office.

"It's awful," he mumbled. "I was on the station platform when I saw that wall of water coming. Tried to warn the men in the roundhouse. Before I could cross the tracks, it was too late. One terrific crash and the roundhouse disappeared—"

"You're hurt," Penny cried as the agent reeled against the wall. "Your arm is crushed. How did it happen?"

CHAPTER 20 - EMERGENCY CALL

"Don't know," Joe admitted, sinking into a chair the girl offered. "I was knocked off my feet. Came to lying in a pile of boards that had snagged against a tree trunk." He stared at Penny as if really seeing her for the first time. "Say," he demanded, "how did you get in here?"

"Smashed the window. It was the only way."

The agent got to his feet, staggering toward the telegraph desk.

"I've got to send a message," he said jerkily. "No. 30's due at Rodney in twenty minutes."

"All the trains have been stopped by the dispatcher," Penny reassured him, and explained how she had sent out the call for help.

Joe Quigley slumped back in the chair. "If you can telegraph, let the dispatcher know I'm on the job again. This hand of mine's not so hot for sending."

Penny obediently sent the stumbling message, but as she completed it the telegraph sounder became lifeless. Although she still could manipulate the key, the signals had faded completely.

"Now what?" she cried, bewildered.

"The wire's dead!" Quigley exclaimed. Anxiously he glanced toward the storage batteries, fearing that water had damped them out. However, the boxes were high above the floor and still dry.

"What can be wrong?" Penny asked the operator.

"Anything can happen in a mess like this."

Reaching across the table with his good hand, Quigley tested the wire by opening and closing the lifeless telegraph key.

"It's completely out," he declared with finality.

"Isn't there anything we can do?"

Quigley got to his feet. "There's just one chance. The wire may have grounded when the bridge was swept away. Then if it tore loose again we'd be out of service."

"In that case we're up against it."

"Maybe not," Quigley replied. He splashed across the room to the switchboard. "If that should happen to be the trouble, we can ground it here."

He inserted a plug in the groundplate of the switchboard. Immediately the sounder came to life, closing with a sharp click.

"I call that luck!" grinned Quigley. "Now let's try that dispatcher. Want to get him on the wire for me?"

Penny nodded and sat down at the desk again. Insistently she sent out the call, "D-S, D-S, D-S." All the while as she kept the key moving, her thoughts raced ahead. She was afraid that persons had lost their lives in the flood. Property damage was beyond estimate. But catastrophe spelled Big News and she was certain her father would want every detail of the story for the *Riverview Star*. If only she could send word to him!

"What's the matter?" Quigley asked, his voice impatient. "Can't you get an answer?"

Just then it came—a crisp "I—DS" which told the two listeners that the train dispatcher again was on the wire.

Quigley took over, explaining the break in service and giving the dispatcher such facts as he desired. Hovering at the agent's elbow, Penny asked him if the dispatcher would take an important personal message.

"For the *Riverview Star*," she added quickly. "My father's newspaper."

"I doubt he'll do it," Quigley discouraged her. "This one wire is needed for vital railroad messages. But we'll see."

He tapped out a message and the reply came. It was sent so fast that Penny could not understand the code. Quigley translated it as "Okay, but make it brief."

With no time to compose a carefully worded message, Penny reported the bare facts of the disaster. She addressed the message to her father and signed her own name.

"There, that's off," Quigley said, sagging back in his chair.

Penny saw that the station agent was in no condition to carry on his work.

"You're in bad shape," she said anxiously. "Let me bandage that smashed hand."

"It's nothing. I'll be okay."

"I'll find something to tie it up with," Penny insisted.

In search of bandage material, she crossed the room to a wall closet. As she reached for the door handle, Quigley turned swiftly in his chair.

"No, not there!" he exclaimed.

Penny already had opened the door. Her gaze fastened upon a white roll of cloth on the top shelf. She reached for it and it came fluttering down into her hands—a loose garment fashioned somewhat like a cape with tiny slits cut for eyes. In an instant she knew what it was. Slowly she turned to face Joe Quigley.

"So it was you!" she whispered accusingly. "The Headless Horseman of Sleepy Hollow!"

CHAPTER 21 - A MYSTERY EXPLAINED

Joe Quigley did not deny the accusation. He slumped at the telegraph desk, staring straight before him.

"Why did you do it?" Penny asked. "How could you?"

"I don't know—now," Quigley answered heavily. "It seemed like a good idea at the time."

Penny shook out the garment. The whole, when worn over one's head, would give an appearance of a sheeted goblin with body cut off at the shoulders. She tore off a long strip of the material and began to wrap Quigley's injured hand.

"You've known for a long time, haven't you?" he asked diffidently.

"I suspected it, but I wasn't sure," Penny replied. "Your style of riding is rather spectacular. Last night when I saw Trinidad leap the barrier at Sleepy Hollow I thought I knew."

"Nothing matters now," Quigley said, self accusingly. "Sleepy Hollow's gone."

"Don't you think Mrs. Lear and the Burmasters had any chance to reach the hills?"

"I doubt it. When the dam broke, the water raced down the valley with the speed of an express train. Probably they were caught like rats in a trap."

"It seems too horrible."

"I knew this would happen," Quigley went on. "It was what I fought against. We tried through the Delta Citizens' Committee to get Burmaster to help repair the dam before it was too late. You know what luck we had."

"So failing in ordinary methods, you tried to bring him around with your Headless Horseman stunt?"

"It was a foolish idea," Quigley acknowledged. "Mrs. Lear really put me up to it—not that I'm trying to throw any blame on her. She never liked Mrs. Burmaster, and for good reasons. The Headless Horseman affair started out as a prank, and then I thought I saw a chance to influence Burmaster that way."

"At that he might have come around if it hadn't been for his wife."

"Yes, she was against the town from the first. She hated everyone. Why, she believed that our only thought was to get her away from the valley just to trick her."

"I guess it doesn't matter now," Penny said. "The estate's gone and everyone with it. Somehow I can't realize it—things happened so fast."

"This is a horrible disaster, and it will be worse if help doesn't get here fast," Quigley replied. "Fortunately, the water doesn't seem to be coming higher."

Penny had completed a rough bandaging job on the station agent's hand. Thanking her, he got up to test the two office telephones. Both were out of service.

Presently a message came in over the telegraph wire. It was addressed to Penny and was from her father. Quigley copied it on a pad and handed it to her.

"Thank God you are safe," the message read. "A special circuit will be cut through to the Delta station as soon as possible. Can you give us a complete, running story of the flood?"

"What's a running story?" Quigley asked curiously.

"I think Dad wants me to gather every fact I can," Penny explained. "He wants a continuous story—enough material to fill a wire for several hours."

"You'll do it?"

"I don't know," Penny said doubtfully. "I've never handled a story as big as this—I've had no experience on anything so important."

"There's no other person to do it."

"I want to find Louise," Penny went on, rereading the message. "I ought to try to learn what happened to poor Mrs. Lear and the Burmasters."

"Listen," Quigley argued quietly. "You can't do anything for your friends now. Don't you see it's your duty to get news out to the country? Your father expects it of you."

Penny remained silent.

"Don't you realize there's no one else to send the news?" Quigley demanded. "You're probably the only reporter within miles of here."

"But I'm not really a reporter. I've written stories for Dad's paper, it's true. But not big stories such as this."

"Red Valley needs help. The only way to get it is by arousing the public. Do I wire your father 'yes' or 'no'?"

"Make it 'yes,'" Penny decided. "Tell Dad I'll try to have something for him in an hour."

"You'll need longer than that," Quigley advised. "Anyhow, it's apt to be several hours before we get a special wire through."

While the agent sent the message, Penny searched the office for pencil and paper.

"You won't get far without shoes," Quigley said over his shoulder. "What became of yours?"

"Left them over on the hillside."

"Well, you can't go back for them now," Quigley replied, gazing ruefully through the window at the racing torrent which separated the station from the high hill. "Let's see what we can find for you."

He rummaged through the closet and came upon a pair of boots which looked nearly small enough for Penny.

"We had a boy who wore those when he worked here," he explained. "See if they'll do. And here's my coat."

"Oh, I can't take it," Penny protested. "You'll need it yourself."

"No, I'm sticking here at my post," Quigley answered. "I'll be warm enough."

He insisted that Penny wear the coat. She left the station and waded toward higher ground. The coat over her drenched clothing offered only slight protection from the chill wind. With the sun dropping low, she knew that soon she would actually suffer from cold.

Penny wondered where to start in gathering vital facts for her father. The flood had followed the narrow V-shaped valley, cutting a swath of destruction above Delta, and there spreading out to the lowlands. She decided to tour the outlying section of Delta first, view the wreckage and question survivors.

"If only Salt were here!" she thought. "Dad would want pictures, but there's no way for me to take them."

Keeping to the hillside, Penny reached a high point of land overlooking what had been the town of Delta. Two or three streets remained as before. One of the few business places still standing was the big white stone building that housed the local telephone company. Elsewhere there was only water and scattered debris.

Penny headed up the valley, passing and meeting groups of bedraggled refugees who had taken to the hills at the first alarm. She questioned everyone. Nevertheless, definite information eluded her. How many lives had been lost? How great was the property damage? What fate had befallen Mrs. Lear and the Burmasters? No one seemed to know.

Half sick with despair, she kept on. She jotted down names and facts. Mr. Bibbs, an old man who ran a weekly newspaper at Delta, was able to help her more than anyone else. Not only did he give her a partial list of the known missing, but he recited many other facts that had escaped Penny.

"A million thanks—" she began gratefully, but he waved her into silence.

"Just get back to the railroad station and send your story," he urged.

Penny lost all count of time as she retraced her way along the muddy hillside. Everywhere she saw suffering and destruction. Her mind was so numbed to the sight that she recorded impressions automatically.

It was long after nightfall before Penny reached the station. Every muscle protested as she dragged herself wearily to the doorstep. During her absence the flood had lowered by nearly a foot. However, the current remained swift, and she steadied herself for a moment against the building wall.

"Who's there?" called Quigley sharply.

"Penny Parker."

"Okay, come on in," the agent invited. "Thought you might be a looter."

CHAPTER 21 - A MYSTERY EXPLAINED

Penny pushed open the door. The waiting room was filled with men, women and children who slumped in cold misery on the uncomfortable row of seats. Few were provided with any warm clothing.

Penny splashed through the dark, musty room to the inner office. Quigley had lighted a smoky oil lamp which revealed that he had made himself a bed on top of the telegraph desk.

"I'm turning in for the night," he explained. "There's nothing more we can do until morning."

"How about my story to the *Star*?" Penny asked wearily. "Is the special wire set up yet?"

"Don't make me laugh," Quigley replied. "The Dispatcher's wire went out for good over an hour ago. Too bad you killed yourself to get that story, because it will have to wait."

"But it mustn't wait," Penny protested. "Dad's counting on me. I gave my promise. How about the telephone company?"

"Their lines are all down."

"Western Union?"

"It's the same with them. Repair crews are on their way here but it will take time. The valley's completely cut off from communication."

"For how long?"

"Listen, Penny, you know as much about it as I do. The airfields are under water."

"How about the roads?"

"Open only part of the way."

Completely discouraged, Penny sagged into a chair by the ticket counter. She was wet through, plastered with mud, hungry, and tired enough to collapse. After all of her work and suffering, her efforts had been in vain. By morning experienced city reporters and photographers would swarm into the valley. Her scoop would be no scoop at all.

"Oh, brace up," Quigley encouraged carelessly.

"But I've failed Dad. It would mean a lot to him to get an exclusive story of this disaster. I gave him my promise I'd send the facts—now I've failed."

"It's not your fault the wire couldn't be set up," Quigley tried to encourage her. "Here, I managed to get ahold of a blanket for you. Wrap up in it and grab some sleep. You'll need your strength tomorrow."

"I guess you're right," Penny acknowledged gloomily.

Taking off the muddy boots, she rolled herself into the warm blanket. Curling up into the chair she pillowed her head on the desk and slept the untroubled sleep of complete exhaustion.

CHAPTER 22 - WANTED—A WIRE

Toward morning Penny awoke to find her limbs stiff and cramped. Murky, fetid water still flowed over the floor of the station. However, it had lowered during the night, leaving a rim of oozy mud to mark the office walls. The first ray of light streamed through the broken window.

Penny yawned and stretched her cramped feet. She felt wretched and dirty. Her clothing was stiff and caked with mud. She scraped off what she could and washed face and hands in a basin of water she found at the back end of the room.

When she returned, Joe Quigley was awake.

"My neck! My arm! My whole anatomy!" he complained, rubbing a hand over his stubbly beard. "I'm a cripple for life."

"I feel the same way," Penny grinned. "I'm hungry too. Anything to eat around here?"

"Not a crumb. The folks out in the waiting room broke into all the vending machines last night. There's not so much as a piece of candy left."

"And there's no place in Delta where food can be bought."

"Not that I know of. Only a few relief kitchens were set up last night. They can't begin to take care of the mob."

Penny peered out into the crowded waiting room. Mothers with babies in their arms had sat there all night. Some of the refugees were weeping; others accepted their lot with stoical calm. Seeing such misery, Penny forgot her own hunger and discomfort.

"Don't you think help will come soon?" she asked Quigley.

"Hard to tell," he replied. "It should."

Penny went out into the waiting room but there was very little she could do to help the unfortunate sufferers. She gave one of the women her blanket.

"That was foolish of you," Quigley told her a moment later. "You'll likely need it yourself."

"I'd rather go without," Penny replied. "Anyway, I can't bear to stay here any longer. I'm going to the telephone office."

"Why there?"

"The building stands high and should be one of the first places to reopen," Penny declared hopefully. "Maybe I can get a long distance call through to Dad."

"Better leave some of your story with me," advised Quigley. "If we get a wire before the telephone company does, I'll try to send it for you."

Penny scribbled a hundred word message, packing it solidly with facts. If ever it reached Riverview a *Star* rewrite man could enlarge it to at least a column.

Saying goodbye to Joe, Penny made her way toward all that remained of Delta's business section. She had not seen Louise since the previous afternoon and was greatly worried about her.

"I know she's safe," she told herself. "But I must find her."

Penny was not alone on the devastated streets. Refugees wandered aimlessly about, seeking loved ones or treasured possessions. Long lines of shivering people waited in front of a church that had been converted into a soup kitchen.

Penny joined the line. Just as a woman handed her a steaming cup of hot broth, she heard her name spoken. Turning quickly, she saw Louise running toward her from across the street.

"Penny! Penny!" her chum cried joyfully.

CHAPTER 22 - WANTED—A WIRE

"Careful," Penny cautioned, balancing the cup of soup. "This broth is as precious as gold."

"Oh, you poor thing!" cried Louise, hugging her convulsively. "You look dreadful."

"That's because I'm so hungry," Penny laughed. "Have you had anything to eat?"

"Oh, yes, I stayed at that farmhouse on the hill last night. I actually had a bed to sleep in and a good hot breakfast this morning. But I've been dreadfully worried about you."

"And that goes double," answered Penny. "Wait until I gobble this soup, and we'll compare notes."

She drank the broth greedily and the girls walked away from the church. Penny then told of her experiences since leaving her chum on the hillside. Louise was much relieved to learn that word had been sent to Riverview of their safety.

"But what of Mrs. Lear and the Burmasters?" she asked anxiously. "Have you heard what happened to them?"

Penny shook her head. "Joe Quigley thinks they didn't have a chance."

"I can't comprehend it somehow," Louise said with a shudder. "It just doesn't seem possible. Why, we were guests in Mrs. Lear's home less than twenty-four hours ago."

"I know," agreed Penny soberly. "I keep hoping that somehow they escaped."

"If only we could learn the truth."

"There's not a chance to get through now," Penny said slowly. "The water's gone down a little, but not enough."

"If we had a boat—"

"The current is still so swift we couldn't handle it."

"I suppose not," Louise admitted hopelessly. "When do you suppose the Relief folks will get here?"

"They should be moving in at any time. And when they come they'll probably be trailed by a flock of reporters and photographers."

"This flood will be a big story," Louise acknowledged.

"Big? It's one of the greatest news stories of the year! And here I am, helpless to send out a single word of copy."

"You mean that folks outside of the valley don't know about the flood?" Louise gasped.

"The news went out, but only as a flash. Before we could give any details, our only wire connection was lost."

"Then the first reporter to get his news out of the valley will have a big story?"

"That's the size of it," Penny nodded. "The worst of it is that Dad's depending upon me."

"But he can't expect you to do the impossible. If there are no wire connections it's not your fault. Anyhow, as soon as one is set up you'll be able to send your story."

"Other reporters will be here by that time. Experienced men. Maybe they'll get the jump on me."

"I'll venture they won't!" Louise said with emphasis. "You've never failed yet on a story."

"This is more than a story, Lou. It's a great human tragedy. Somehow I don't feel a bit like a reporter—I just feel bewildered and rather stunned."

"You're tired and half sick," Louise said. She linked arms with Penny and guided her away from the long line of refugees.

"Where to?" she asked after they had wandered for some distance.

"I was starting for the telephone company office when I met you."

"Why the telephone office?" Louise asked.

"Well, it's high and dry. I thought that by some chance they might have a wire connection."

"Then let's go there by all means," urged Louise.

Farther down the debris-clogged street the girls came to the telephone company offices. The building, one of the newest and tallest in Delta, had been gutted by the flood. However, the upper floors remained dry and emergency quarters had been established there. Nearly all employees were at their posts.

Penny and Louise pushed their way through the throng of refugees that had taken possession of the lower floor. Climbing the stairs to the telephone offices they asked to see the manager.

"Mr. Nordwall isn't seeing anyone," they were informed. "He's very busy."

Penny persisted. She explained that her business was urgent and concerned getting a news story through to Riverview. After a long delay she was allowed to talk to the manager, a harassed, over-worked man named Nordwall.

"Please state your case briefly," he said wearily.

Penny explained again that she wished to get a story of the flood through to her father's paper, and asked what hope there was.

"Not much, I'm afraid," the man replied. "We haven't a single toll line at present."

"How soon do you expect to get one?"

The manager hesitated, unwilling to commit himself. "By noon we may have one wire west," he said reluctantly.

Penny asked if she could have first chance at it. Nordwall regretfully shook his head.

"Relief work must come before news."

"Then there's no way to get my story out?"

"I suggest that you place your call in the usual way," Mr. Nordwall instructed. "I'll tell our Long Distance Chief Operator to put it ahead of everything except relief work messages."

Penny obeyed the manager's suggestion. However, she and Louise both knew that there was slight chance the call would go through in time to do any good.

"No use waiting around here," Penny said gloomily. "The wire won't even be set up before noon."

Leaving the telephone building, the girls sloshed back toward the railroad. Suddenly Louise drew Penny's attention to an airplane flying low overhead. It flew so close to the ground that they could read "United Press," on the wings.

"Well, it looks as if the news boys are moving in," Penny observed. "Probably taking photographs of the flood."

The airplane circled Delta and then vanished eastward. Walking on, the girls met an armed soldier who passed them without a glance.

"The National Guard," Penny commented. "That means a road is open."

"And it means that help is here at last!" Louise cried. "Property will be protected now and some order will be established!"

Penny remained silent.

"Aren't you glad?" Louise demanded, staring at her companion.

"Yes, I'm glad," Penny said slowly. "I truly am. But the opening of the road means that within a very little while every news service in the country will have men here."

"And you've lost your chance to send an exclusive story to the *Star*."

"I've let Dad down," Penny admitted. "He depended upon me and I failed him dismally."

CHAPTER 23 - TOLL LINE TO RIVERVIEW

Penny and Louise trudged slowly on toward the railroad tracks. They were too discouraged for much conversation, and avoided speaking of Mrs. Lear or the Burmasters. Sleepy Hollow had been washed away, but no one could tell them what had happened to the unfortunate ones caught in the valley.

"It doesn't matter now," Penny said dispiritedly, "but I know who masqueraded as the Headless Horseman. Joe Quigley."

"The station agent!"

"Yes, he told me about it last night. Of course Mrs. Lear let him use her horse, and no doubt she encouraged him in the idea."

"They did it to plague the Burmasters?"

"Joe thought he could bring Mr. Burmaster around to his way of thinking about the Huntley Dam."

"How stupid everyone was," Louise sighed. "If it hadn't been for Mrs. Burmaster's stubbornness, her husband might have given the money to save the dam. Then this dreadful disaster would have been prevented."

Penny nodded absently. Her gaze was fixed upon a stout man just ahead who wore climbing irons on his heavy shoes. She nudged Louise.

"See that fellow?"

"Why, yes. What about him?"

"I'm sure he's a telephone lineman. Probably he's working on the line by the railroad."

"Probably," Louise agreed, without much interest.

"Come on," Penny urged, quickening pace. "Let's talk to him."

The girls overtook the workman and fell into step. Penny questioned him and readily learned that he was working close by at the washed-out railroad bridge.

"We're aiming to shoot a wire across the river," the man volunteered. "It's going to be one tough little job."

"Mind if we go along?" Penny asked eagerly.

"It's okay with me," the telephone man consented. "Hard walking though."

Flood waters had receded from the railroad right-of-way leaving a long stretch of twisted rails and slimey road-bed. They waded through the mud, soon coming to the break where the bridge had swung aside. Debris of every variety had piled high against the wrecked steel structure. Flood water boiled through the gap at a furious rate.

"I don't see how they'll ever get a cable across there," Penny commented dubiously.

"Coast Guardsmen are helping us," the lineman explained. "They'll shoot it over with a Lyle gun—we hope."

Penny and Louise wandered toward the gap in the roadbed. On both shores, linemen and cable splicers were hard at work. Coast Guardsmen already had set up their equipment and all was in readiness to shoot a cable across the river.

"Okay, let 'er go!" rang out the terse order. "Stand clear!"

A Coast Guardsman raised the Lyle gun. Making certain that the steel wire would run free, he released the trigger. The weighted cable flashed through the air in a beautiful arch only to fall short of its goal.

"Not enough allowance for the wind," the guardsman said in disgust. "We'll need a heavier charge."

The gun was reloaded, and again the wire spun from its spool. Again it fell short of the far shore by three feet. Undaunted by failure, the men tried once more. This time the aim was true, and the heavy powder charge carried rod and cable to its mark.

"They've done it!" Penny cried jubilantly. "Now it shouldn't be long before we get a wire connection with the outside world!"

Immediately telephone company men seized the flexible cable, anchoring it solidly. Heavy cables then were drawn across and made fast, permitting a courageous lineman in a bosun's chair to work high above the turbulent river.

"If that cable should break, he'd be lost!" Louise said with a shudder. "It makes me jumpy to watch him."

Fearlessly the man accomplished his task, suspending a temporary emergency telephone line. Cable splicers promptly carried the ends of the new cable to terminal boxes.

So absorbed was Penny in watching the task that for a time she forgot her own urgent need of a message wire. But as she observed the men talking over a test phone, the realization suddenly came to her that a through wire had been established west from Red Valley.

"Lou, they've done it!" she exclaimed. "The wire connection is made!"

"It does look that way."

"If only I could use that test set to get my news story through to Dad!"

"Fat chance!"

"I'd still be the first to send out the story!" Penny went on excitedly. "It will do no harm to ask anyhow."

Breaking away from Louise, she sought the lineman of her acquaintance. Eagerly she broached her request.

"Not a chance to use that line, Sister," he answered impatiently. "Our 'phones are for testing purposes only."

"But this is a very great emergency—"

"Sorry," the lineman brought her up short. "You'll have to put your call through the regular channels. Regulations."

Baffled by the cold refusal, Penny turned away. Even though she knew the telephone man had no authority to grant her request, she was none the less annoyed.

"This is enough to drive one mad!" she complained to Louise. "It may be hours before the downtown telephone office will offer toll service."

"Well, it does no good to fret about it," her chum shrugged. "There's nothing you can do."

"I'm not so sure about that," Penny muttered.

Her attention had been drawn to a man in a gray business suit who was talking earnestly to the fireman of the line gang.

"That's Mr. Nordwall!" she announced.

Again abandoning Louise, she pushed through the throng of spectators. Touching the man's arm to attract his attention, she said breathlessly:

"Mr. Nordwall, do you remember me?"

He gazed at her without recognition.

"I'm Penny Parker. I want to get a message through to my father."

"Oh, yes, now I remember!" the telephone company manager exclaimed. "You're trying to send a call through to Riverview."

"Is there any reason why I can't use the phone now—the test instrument?"

"Such a procedure would be very irregular."

"But it would save hours in getting my story through," Penny went on quickly. "Hundreds of persons are desperately in need of food and shelter. If the public can be aroused by newspaper publicity, funds will be subscribed generously. Mr. Nordwall, you must let me send my story!"

"This is a very great emergency," the manager agreed. "I'll see what can be done."

Penny waited, scarcely daring to hope. However, Mr. Nordwall kept his word. To the delight of the girls, the call was put through. Within ten minutes Penny was summoned to the test box.

"You have your connection with Riverview," she was told. "Go ahead."

Penny raised the receiver to her ear. Her hand trembled she was so nervous and excited. She spoke tensely into the transmitter: "Hello, is this the *Star* office?"

"Anthony Parker speaking," said the voice of her father.

"Dad, this is Penny! I have the story for you!"

She heard her father's voice at the other end of the line but it became so weak she could not distinguish a word. Nor could he understand her. The connection had failed.

CHAPTER 24 - A BIG STORY

Penny despaired, fearing that she never could make her father understand what she had to tell him. Then unexpectedly the wire trouble cleared and Mr. Parker's voice fairly boomed in her ear.

"Is that you, Penny? Are you all right?"

"Oh, yes, Dad!" she answered eagerly. "And so is Louise! We have the story for you—couldn't get it out before."

"Thought we never would hear from you again," Mr. Parker said, his voice vibrant. "Your flash on the flood scooped the country. We're still ahead of the other newspapers. Shoot me all the facts."

Penny talked rapidly but distinctly. Facts had been imprinted indelibly on her memory. She had no need to refer to notes except to verify names. Now and then Mr. Parker interrupted to ask a question. When the story had been told he said crisply:

"You've done marvelously, Penny! But we'll need more names. Get as complete a list of the missing as you can."

"I'll try, Dad."

"And pictures. So far all we have are a few airplane shots of the flooded valley. Can you get ahold of a camera?"

"I doubt it," Penny said dubiously.

"Try anyhow," her father urged. "And keep on the lookout for Salt Sommers. He's on his way there now with two reporters. They're bringing in a portable wire photo set."

"Then you plan to send flood pictures direct from here to Riverview?"

"That's the set up," Mr. Parker replied. "If you can get the pictures and have them waiting, we'll beat every other paper in the country!"

"I'll do my best," Penny promised. "But it's a hard assignment."

She talked a moment longer before abandoning the test 'phone to one of the linemen. Seeking Louise, she repeated the conversation.

"But how can we get a camera?" her chum asked hopelessly. "Delta's stores are under water—most of them at least."

Though the situation seemed impossible, the girls tramped from one debris-clogged street to another. After an hour's search they came upon a man who was snapping pictures with a box camera. Questioned by Penny, he agreed to part with it for twenty dollars.

"I haven't that many cents," Penny admitted. "But my father is owner of the *Riverview Star*. I'll guarantee that you'll receive your money later."

"How do I know I'll ever see you again?"

"You don't," said Penny. "You'll just have to trust me."

"You look honest," the man agreed after a pause. "I'll take a chance."

He gave Penny the camera, together with three rolls of film. The girls carefully wrote down his name and address.

"Now to get our pictures," Penny said, as she and Louise started on once more. "We'll take a few of the streets. Then I want to get some human-interest shots."

"How about the railroad station?" Louise suggested. "A great many of the refugees are being cared for there."

Penny nodded assent. Hastening toward the depot, they paused several times to snap pictures they thought were especially suitable for newspaper reproduction.

Along the railroad right-of-way crews of men were hard at work, but it was evident that it would be days before train service could be resumed.

Penny and Louise went into the crowded waiting room of the depot. Joe Quigley had locked himself into the inner office, but even there he was surrounded by a group of argumentative young men.

"Reporters!" Penny observed alertly. "I knew it wouldn't take them long to get here!"

The newspaper men were bombarding Quigley with questions, demanding to know when and how they could send out their newspaper copy.

"I can't help you, boys," he said regretfully. "It will be two hours at least before we have wire service. Better try the telephone company."

Just then one of the newsmen spied Penny and her camera. Immediately he hailed her. The other reporters flocked about the two girls, offering to buy any of the films at fancy prices.

"Sorry," Penny declined. "My pictures are earmarked for the *Riverview Star*."

"What? Didn't you hear?" one of the men bantered. "Their wire photo car broke down just this side of Hobostein. The *Star* won't move in here before night. By then your pictures will be old stuff."

"Better sell to us," urged another.

Penny shook her head. She wasn't sure whether or not the men were joking. In any case she meant to hold her pictures until her father released them.

Between Hobostein and Delta there was only one highway over which a car could pass. The arrival of newspaper men led Penny to believe that this road now was open.

"Dad told me to keep a sharp watch for Salt Sommers," she said to Louise. "Let's post ourselves by the road where we can see incoming cars."

"What about the pictures we planned to take here?"

"I do want to snap one or two," Penny admitted. "It's embarrassing though, just to walk up to a group and ask to take a picture."

As the girls debated, the door swung open. Into the already over-crowded room stumbled a new group of refugees.

Suddenly Penny's gaze fastened upon a haggard woman who looked grotesque in a man's overcoat many sizes too large for her. The face was half-buried in the high collar, and she could not see it plainly. Then the woman turned, and Penny recognized her.

"Mrs. Burmaster!" she cried.

The woman stared at the two girls with leaden eyes. She did not seem to recognize them.

"Oh, we're so glad you're safe!" Penny cried, rushing to her. "Your husband?"

Mrs. Burmaster's lips moved, but no sound came. She seemed stunned by what she had gone through.

"Do you know what happened to Mrs. Lear?" Penny asked anxiously. "Have you heard?"

Even then Mrs. Burmaster did not speak. But a strange light came into her eyes.

"Tell me," Penny urged. "Please."

Her words seemed to penetrate the befogged mind of the dazed woman. Mrs. Burmaster's lips moved slightly. Penny bent closer to hear.

"Mrs. Lear is dead," the woman whispered. "She was drowned when she saved me."

CHAPTER 25 - MISSION ACCOMPLISHED

The information shocked Penny.

"Mrs. Lear—dead," she repeated. "Oh, I was hoping that somehow she escaped."

"She would have if it hadn't been for me," Mrs. Burmaster said dully. "Ten minutes before the dam gave way, a telephone warning was sent out. Mrs. Lear thought my husband and I might not have heard it. She rode her horse to Sleepy Hollow, intending to warn us."

"And then what happened?"

"Just as Mrs. Lear reached our place, the wall of water came roaring down the valley. We all ran out of the house, hoping to reach the hills. We did get to higher ground but we saw we couldn't make it. Mrs. Lear made my husband and me climb into a tree. Before she could follow us, the water came."

"Mrs. Lear was swept away?"

"Yes, we saw her struggling and then the water carried her beyond sight." Mrs. Burmaster covered her face. "Oh, it was horrible! And to think that it was all my fault!"

"Where is your husband now?" Penny inquired kindly.

"Outside, I think," Mrs. Burmaster murmured. "We were brought here together in a boat."

Penny and Louise went outdoors and after a brief search found Mr. Burmaster. His clothing was caked with mud, his face was unshaven and he looked years older.

To his wife's story he could add little. "This has been a dreadful shock," he told Penny. "Now that it's too late I realize what a stubborn fool I was. My wife and I are responsible for Mrs. Lear's death."

"No, no, you mustn't say that," Penny tried to comfort him. "It was impossible for anyone to predict what would happen."

"Sleepy Hollow is gone—completely washed away," Mr. Burmaster went on bitterly. "The estate cost me a fortune."

"But you can rebuild."

"I never shall. My wife never could be happy in Red Valley. Now that this terrible thing has occurred, it would be intolerable to remain. I've been thinking matters over. I've decided to deed all the land I bought back to the valley folk. It's the least I can do to right a great wrong."

"It would be very generous of you," said Penny, her eyes shining.

The girls talked with Mr. Burmaster for a little while and then started toward US highway 20, intending to watch incoming cars. Ambulances, army and supply trucks now were flowing into Delta in a steady stream. However, midway there, they spied a car coming toward them which bore *"Riverview Star"* on its windshield.

"There's Salt now!" Penny cried, signaling frantically.

The car stopped with a jerk. The *Star* photographer sat behind the wheel, while beside him were two men from the paper's news department.

"Well, well," Salt greeted the girls jovially. He swung open the car door. "If it isn't Penny, the child wonder! Meet Roy Daniels and Joe Wiley."

Acknowledging the introduction, Penny and Louise squeezed into the front seat of the sedan. Driving on, Salt plied them with questions. Penny told him how rival newsmen had tried to buy her camera pictures.

"Good for you, hanging onto them!" Salt approved warmly. "Our car never did break down. By the way, where can we set up our portable wire photo equipment?"

"There's only one possibility. The telephone company. Right now they have the only wire service in Delta."

Penny directed Salt through the few streets that were clear of debris to the telephone building. There the portable wire photo equipment quickly was set up. Penny's camera pictures were developed, and though some of the shots were over-exposed there were four good enough to send over the network.

"Mr. Nordwall has six toll lines out of Delta now," Salt told the girls jubilantly. "He's letting us have one of them."

Carefully the photographer tested the controls of the wire photo machine. He listened briefly to the hum of the motor. Satisfied that everything was running properly, he attached one of the freshly printed pictures to the transmitting cylinder.

"Okay," he signaled to Mr. Nordwall. "Give us a toll to the *Riverview Star*."

Within a few minutes the order came: "Network clear. Go ahead, Delta."

Salt turned on a switch and the sending cylinder began to revolve. One by one Penny's pictures were transmitted over the wire.

"Your shots are the first to get out of Red Valley!" Salt told her triumphantly. "Your work's done now. Better crawl off somewhere and sleep."

Penny nodded wearily. She was glad to know that the *Star* would scoop every other paper in the country on the flood story and pictures. Still, for some reason she couldn't feel very happy about it. As she turned away, Salt called: "Hey, wait! Your father's on the wire photo phone. He wants to talk to you."

Penny caught up the receiver eagerly.

"That you, Penny?" a blurred voice asked in her ear. "Congratulations! You came through with flying colors!"

"Guess I was lucky to come through at all," Penny said slowly. "Some weren't so fortunate."

"Just now the important thing is when are you coming home?" Mr. Parker asked. "Can you get here today?"

To Penny, the thought of home and a soft bed was more alluring than any other earthly bliss.

"I'll certainly try, Dad," she promised. "Yes, somehow I'll get there."

After Penny ended the conversation with her father, she and Louise talked to Salt about the prospects of a trip home. Regretfully he explained that with a big story to cover, he probably would not be leaving that day.

"But there are plenty of cars going out of here," he encouraged them. "Why not go down to the depot and make inquiries."

The idea seemed an excellent one. At the station the girls talked again with Joe Quigley who assured them he knew of a car that was leaving very shortly.

"Hurry out to Highway 20 and I think you can catch the fellow," he urged.

Hastily saying goodbye not only to Joe but to Mr. and Mrs. Burmaster who remained in the crowded station, the girls went outside. As they rounded a corner of the building a voice fairly boomed at them: "Hello, folks!"

Penny and Louise whirled around to see Silas Malcom coming toward them. Clinging to his arm was a spry little woman in a borrowed coat and hat.

"Mrs. Lear!" gasped the girls in one voice.

"It takes more than a flood to wash me away!" chirped the old lady, bright as a cricket.

Penny and Louise rushed to embrace her. Eagerly they plied her with questions.

"I'm jest like a cat with nine lives," old Mrs. Lear chuckled. "When the flood carried me off, I didn't give up—not me. I was a purty good swimmer as a gal and I ain't so bad even now. I kinda went with the current until I got ahold of a log. There I clung until a Red Cross boat picked me up."

Mrs. Lear's safe arrival at Delta thrilled Penny and Louise. They rushed into the station to bring Mr. and Mrs. Burmaster who shared their great relief over the rescue. And Penny was delighted when Mr. Burmaster repeated to the old lady what he had told her—that he intended to allow his property to revert to the former tenants.

"That's mighty good of you, Mr. Burmaster," the old lady thanked him. "What we've been through has taught us all a bitter lesson. I'm ashamed of the way I acted."

"You were justified in your attitude," the estate owner acknowledged.

"No, I wasn't. It was childish o' me tryin' to take my spite out on your wife. I'm especially sorry about the way I egged Joe Quigley onto that Headless Horseman trick."

"I was afraid you were behind it," smiled Mr. Burmaster. "Oh, well, it all seems trivial now. We'll forget everything."

CHAPTER 25 - MISSION ACCOMPLISHED

"There are some things," said Penny quietly, "that I doubt we'll ever erase from our minds." She turned to the old lady and asked: "Won't you come to Riverview with Louise and me? You'll need a place to stay—"

Mrs. Lear's gaze met hers, challengingly but with a twinkle of humor.

"And what better place could I have than this?" she demanded with quiet finality. "Red Valley is my home, and my home it will be till the end o' time!"

VOICE FROM THE CAVE

"Where are you taking our car?" Penny demanded.

CHAPTER 1 - AN UNINVITED GUEST

"Mrs. Weems, what can be delaying Dad? He promised faithfully to be home by three o'clock and it's nearly five now. Unless we start soon we'll never get to Sunset Beach tonight."

Penny Parker, in blue slacks and a slightly mussed polo shirt, gazed disconsolately at the over-loaded automobile standing on the gravel driveway of the Parker home. Aided by Mrs. Weems, the family housekeeper, she had spent hours packing the sedan with luggage and camping equipment. Though the task long had been finished, Mr. Parker failed to arrive.

"Your father is a very busy man," Mrs. Weems responded to the girl's question. "No doubt he's been held up at the office."

"Then why doesn't he telephone? It's driving me crazy to wait and wonder."

Penny's freckled little face twisted into a grimace of worry. For weeks she and her father, editor-owner of the *Riverview Star*, had planned a vacation camping trip to the nearby seashore resort, Sunset Beach. Twice the excursion had been postponed. Penny, who knew well her father's habit of changing his mind, was fearful that even now something would cause another vexing delay.

"I'm going to call the *Star* office this minute!" she declared, starting for the house.

Mrs. Weems busied herself gathering up loose odds and ends that had blown about the yard. She was cramming waste paper into a box when Penny banged out the door, her eyes tragic.

"I couldn't reach Dad!" she announced. "He left the office more than an hour ago."

"Then he should have been home before this," Mrs. Weems agreed.

"Something's happened. Maybe he's been run down by a car—"

"Now Penny, stop such wild talk," the housekeeper interrupted sternly. "You know better."

"But Dad was struck by an automobile last winter. What else could delay him?"

"A dozen things," Mrs. Weems replied. "Probably a business engagement."

"In that case, wouldn't he have telephoned me?"

"Perhaps not. Now do stop fretting, Penny. Your father will be here before long."

"He'd better be," Penny said darkly.

Sitting down on the stone step by the door, she scuffed the toe of her tennis shoe back and forth in the gravel. Mrs. Weems who had cared for the girl ever since the death of Mrs. Parker, gazed at her sternly.

"Now do stop grieving!" she chided. "That's no way to act just because you're impatient and disappointed."

"But I've been disappointed three times now," Penny complained. "We planned on starting early and having a picnic lunch on the road. Dad promised faithfully—"

A car drove up to the curb at the front of the house. Penny sprang hopefully to her feet. However, it was not her father who had arrived. Instead, her chum, Louise Sidell, alighted and came running across the yard.

"Oh, I'm glad I'm not too late to say goodbye to you, Penny!" she cried. "How soon are you starting?"

"I'd like to know the answer to that one myself. Dad hasn't put in an appearance. He was due here at three o'clock."

"Why, I saw him about twenty minutes ago," Louise replied, turning to inspect the over-loaded sedan. "My, how did you accumulate so much luggage?"

Penny ignored the question to ask one of her own. "Where did you see Dad, Lou?"

"Why, riding in a car." Louise's dark eyes sparkled mischievously as she added: "With a beautiful brunette too."

"You're joking."

"I am not. Your father was riding with Mrs. Deline. She's a widow, you know, and has lived in Riverview less than a month."

Mrs. Weems, who had overheard the conversation, came over to the steps.

"Mrs. Deline, did you say?" she inquired, slightly disturbed. "I've heard of her."

"And so have I!" declared Penny with biting emphasis. "Why, that woman would make the Merry Widow look like a dead number! She'd better not try to sink her hooks into Dad!"

"Penelope!" the housekeeper reproved sternly.

"Well, you know what everyone says—"

"Please don't repeat idle gossip," Mrs. Weems requested. "I'm sure Mrs. Deline is a very fine woman."

"She's the slickest serpent that ever free-wheeled into Riverview!" Penny said heatedly. "I saw her in action last week-end at the Country Club. Why, she simply went out of her way to cultivate any man who had an income of more than twenty-five thousand a year."

"Penny, your father is a sensible man," the housekeeper reproved. "Unfortunately, it's a quality I'm afraid you didn't inherit."

Louise, unhappy to have stirred up such a hornet's nest, said hastily: "Maybe it wasn't Mrs. Deline I saw. The car went by so fast."

"Oh, I'm not worried. Dad can handle a bigger package of dynamite than Mrs. Deline. It just makes me irritated because he doesn't get here."

Tossing her head, Penny crossed to the loaded automobile where she switched on the radio. She tuned it carelessly. After a moment a blurred voice blared forth:

"Attention Comrades!"

Penny turned quickly to glance at the dial, for she realized that she did not have the local station WZAM.

"Attention Comrades!" the announcer commanded again. "This is the Voice from the Cave."

There followed a strange jibberish of words which were in no language that Penny ever before had heard.

"Mrs. Weems! Louise!" she called excitedly. "I think I've tuned in an outlaw short wave station! Just listen!"

Louise and the housekeeper hastened over to the car. Penny tried desperately to tune the station in more clearly. Instead she lost it completely.

"Did you hear what that announcer said?" she asked eagerly. "Most of it I couldn't understand. I'm sure it was in code!"

"Code!" Mrs. Weems exclaimed in amazement.

"I'm sure I didn't have one of the regular stations! It must have been a short wave broadcast beamed at a particular group of persons. The announcer began: 'Attention Comrades!'"

"Can't you tune in again?" Louise demanded.

Penny twisted the dial without success. She was still trying when a taxi cab drew up at the front door.

"There's your father now!" Louise declared.

"And see who's with him!" Penny added, craning her neck. "It *is* Mrs. Deline."

Mrs. Weems, decidedly flustered, hurriedly removed her apron. In an undertone she warned Penny to be polite to the unexpected visitor.

Mr. Parker, a tall, lean man with hair only touched by gray, stepped from the taxi. The woman he assisted was attractively slender, and dressed in an expensive tailored suit. Her face was cold and serene, but so striking that it commanded instant interest. Penny's spirits sagged as she observed that the widow came equipped with luggage.

"Now what?" she muttered.

Mr. Parker escorted Mrs. Deline across the yard, introducing her first to Mrs. Weems and then to the girls.

"Mrs. Deline is riding with us to Sunset Beach," he explained to Penny. "She intended to go by train but failed to get a reservation."

"Coaches are so unbearable," Mrs. Deline said in an affected drawl. "It was so nice of Mr. Parker to invite me to share your car."

"I'm afraid it may not be so pleasant for you," Penny replied. She tried to speak cordially but the words came in stiff little jerks. "There's not much room."

CHAPTER 1 - AN UNINVITED GUEST

"Nonsense!" said Mr. Parker. "Mrs. Deline will ride up front. Penny, you'll have to battle it out with the luggage."

By the time Mrs. Deline's suitcase and hat boxes were stowed away, there was indeed little room left in the rear seat for a passenger. Penny's face was very long. For weeks she had planned on a vacation trip with her father, and now all her plans had been shattered.

"Will you be staying long at Sunset Beach?" she asked the widow politely.

"Probably a week," Mrs. Deline replied. "I've engaged a suite at the Crystal Inn. I'm sure I couldn't endure a camping trip. Mosquitoes—hard beds—cooking over a camp fire—it all seems rather difficult to me."

"Oh, it will be fun to camp!"

"I'm not so certain of it myself." Mr. Parker assisted the widow into the front seat. "Penny, why don't we ditch this camp stuff and try a hotel ourselves?"

"No!" answered Penny fiercely.

"It would be a far more sensible arrangement."

"But I don't want to be sensible," Penny argued. "We've planned on this trip for weeks, Dad."

"Oh, all right, if that's the way you feel about it," he gave in willingly enough. "Only I never did care much for the rough and tumble life myself. Are we ready to start?"

"Just a minute," Penny requested. "I have to get my pocketbook from the house."

She went indoors, her face as dark as a summer rain cloud. Mrs. Weems and Louise followed her in, corraling her in the kitchen.

"Now Penny, just a word of advice," the housekeeper cautioned. "Mrs. Deline seems like a very nice woman. I trust that you'll be pleasant to her."

"I don't see why Dad had to invite her! It's ruined everything!"

"Aren't you being selfish?"

"Maybe I am," said Penny. "But why should I be crammed back with the pots and pans and luggage while she sits up front with Dad?"

"Mrs. Deline is your guest."

"She's Dad's guest," Penny corrected. "Furthermore, I suspect she invited herself."

"Whatever you think, I hope you'll keep your thoughts to yourself," Mrs. Weems said severely. "I'm really ashamed of you."

The deep scowl disappeared from Penny's face and she laughed. Wrapping her arms about the housekeeper's ample waist she squeezed until it hurt.

"I know I'm a spoiled brat," she admitted. "But don't worry. I'll pretend to like Mrs. Deline if it kills me."

"That's much better, Penny. At any rate, you'll not be troubled with her company long. You'll reach Sunset Beach by nightfall."

Penny made no reply. She turned to say goodbye to Louise.

"Wish you were going along," she said wistfully. "A vacation won't seem fun without you."

A staccato toot of the auto horn reminded Penny that her father and Mrs. Deline were waiting. Hurriedly she gathered up her purse.

"Have a nice time," Louise said, kissing her goodbye. "And don't let Mrs. Deline get in your hair."

Penny turned to make certain that Mrs. Weems was beyond hearing.

"Don't worry about that, Lou," she whispered. "Mrs. Deline's already in my hair. What I'm really worried about is keeping her from building a nest in it!"

CHAPTER 2 - STORMY WEATHER

For an hour the Parker car had rolled smoothly along the paved road enroute to Sunset Beach. In the back seat, firmly wedged between boxes and suitcases, Penny squirmed and suffered.

"How much farther, Dad?" she inquired, interrupting an animated conversation he was having with Mrs. Deline.

"Oh, about fifty miles," Mr. Parker tossed over his shoulder. "We can't make much time at thirty-five an hour."

"How about lunch somewhere along the road?"

"Well, should we take the time?" the publisher asked. He turned toward his companion. "What do you think, Mrs. Deline?"

"Picnics always seemed stupid to me," she replied in a bored manner. "Perhaps we'll find a nice tea house along the way."

"But Mrs. Weems prepared such a good lunch," Penny argued. "I thought—"

"We can use the food after we make camp," Mr. Parker decided briskly. "A warm meal will be much better."

Penny subsided into hurt silence. Since the party had left Riverview she felt that she had been pushed far into the background. Mrs. Deline had made no attempt to talk to her. On the other hand, the widow fairly hypnotized Mr. Parker with her dazzling smile and conversation.

"Dad," Penny began, determined to get in a word, "just before you came home this afternoon, something queer happened."

"That so?" he inquired carelessly.

"Yes, I turned on the radio, and a station I'd never heard before came in. The announcer said: 'Attention Comrades, this is the Voice from the Cave.'"

"Sounds like a juvenile radio serial."

"Oh, but it wasn't, Dad! I'm sure it was an outlaw station. Then the announcer spoke very rapidly in a language I'd never heard before. It really sounded like code."

"Sure you didn't imagine it? You know you do get ideas, Penny. Especially when you're on the prowl for a mystery to solve."

"Aren't children quaint?" Mrs. Deline laughed.

Penny's lips tightened, but by great effort of will she kept silent. A child indeed! She knew now that Mrs. Deline disliked her and that they had launched an undeclared war.

"I heard the broadcast all right," she said. "For that matter, so did Mrs. Weems and Louise. But probably it's of no consequence."

The subject was dropped. It was stuffy in the closed car and Penny presently rolled down a window. Immediately Mrs. Deline protested that the wind was blowing her hair helter-skelter. At a stern glance from her father, Penny closed the window again, leaving only a tiny crack for air.

"All the way, please," requested Mrs. Deline.

"Penny, you're being very, very difficult," Mr. Parker added.

Penny rolled the window shut, but her blue eyes cast off little sparks of fire. As a rule, she was a very pleasant person, not in the least spoiled. In Riverview where she had lived for fifteen happy, eventful years, her friends were beyond count. Penny liked people and nearly everyone liked her. But for some reason, she and Mrs. Deline had taken an instant dislike to each other.

CHAPTER 2 - STORMY WEATHER

"Maybe I'm jealous," Penny thought ruefully. "I shouldn't be, but Dad's all I have."

Between Mr. Parker and his daughter there existed a deep bond of affection. Penny's mother was dead and the noted publisher had devoted himself to filling the great void in the girl's life. He had given her companionship and taught her to think straight. Knowing that she was dependable, he allowed her more freedom than most girls her age were permitted.

Penny adored her father and seemingly had inherited his love of newspaper work. Upon various occasions she had helped him at the *Riverview Star*, writing and obtaining some of the paper's most spectacular front page stories. Only the past winter, following her father's severe illness, she had acted as editor of the *Star*, managing the paper entirely herself.

"And now Dad and Mrs. Deline treat me as if I were a child!" she reflected resentfully.

Though very much upset, Penny kept her thoughts to herself. Curling up with her head on a pile of blankets, she pretended to sleep.

The car went over a hard bump. Penny bounced and opened her eyes. She was surprised to see that it had grown quite dark. The automobile was moving in a wide curve between long rows of pine trees.

"What time is it?" she asked, pressing her face to the window.

"Not so late," replied her father. "We're running into a rain storm. Just our luck."

Dark clouds had entirely blotted out the late afternoon sun. Even as Mr. Parker spoke, several big raindrops splashed against the windshield.

Soon the rain came down in such a thick sheet that the road ahead was obscured. Stopping suddenly for a crossroads traffic light, the car went into a slight skid. Mrs. Deline screamed in terror, and clutched Mr. Parker's arm.

"Oh, can't we stop somewhere?" she pleaded. "I'm so afraid we'll have an accident."

"Yes, we'll stop," Mr. Parker agreed. "The storm is certainly getting worse."

A short distance ahead the party glimpsed a group of buildings. One was a filling station and beside it stood a small three-story hotel and tea room.

"Doesn't look too bad," Mr. Parker commented, pulling up close to the door. "We'll have dinner and by that time the storm may be over."

While Penny and Mrs. Deline went into the tea room, the publisher took the car next door to the filling station to have the tank refueled. He rejoined them soon, shaking the raindrops from his coat.

"It's coming down harder than ever," he reported. "And we still have a long drive ahead of us."

"Do you think we'll reach our camp site tonight, Dad?" Penny inquired anxiously.

"We'll be lucky to get to Sunset Beach. As for making camp, that's out of the question."

"Maybe it will stop raining soon," Penny ventured hopefully.

Mr. Parker ordered dinner for the party and an hour was consumed in dining. The rain, however, showed no signs of slackening.

"We could go on—" Mr. Parker said thoughtfully. "Of course, the roads are slippery."

"Oh, please let's not venture out in this," Mrs. Deline pleaded before Penny could speak. "I know I am being silly, but I'm so afraid of an accident. Once I was in a car that overturned and I've never forgotten it."

"There's no great hurry," Mr. Parker replied. "If we can't reach Sunset Beach tonight, I suppose we could stay here."

Mrs. Deline did not comment upon the suggestion, but from the way she smiled, Penny was sure that the idea appealed to her. Taking her father aside, the girl urged him to try to drive on to Sunset Beach that night.

"Our vacation is so short, Dad. Even now we'll lose almost a day in setting up camp."

"We'll certainly push on if we can," he promised. "This storm complicates everything."

For two hours the rain fell steadily. With the prospects anything but improved, Mr. Parker made inquiry as to lodging for the night. From the hotel keeper he learned that rooms already were at a premium.

"We'll have to make up our minds soon," he reported to Penny and Mrs. Deline. "If we wait much longer we'll probably find ourselves sleeping in the lobby."

"Then let's stay," the widow urged. "Please engage a room and a bath for me. Preferably one at the rear of the building away from the highway."

"I'm afraid you'll have no choice," Mr. Parker told her regretfully. "We'll have to take what we can get."

The publisher consulted with the hotel clerk, and returned to report that only two rooms remained available.

"You and Penny will have to share one together," he explained. "I hope you won't mind."

It was evident by the expression of Mrs. Deline's face that she minded a great deal. However, she consented to the arrangement and the luggage was taken upstairs. The door closed behind the bellboy. For the first time Penny and Mrs. Deline were left alone.

"Such a cheap, dirty hotel!" the widow exclaimed petulantly. "And I do hate to share a room with anyone."

Penny busied herself unpacking her over-night bag. Crossing to the window, she raised it half way.

"Do put that down!" Mrs. Deline ordered. "I detest air blowing directly on me."

Penny lowered the window.

Mrs. Deline smoked a cigarette, carelessly allowing the ashes to fall on the bed. Getting up, she moved nervously about the room.

"This place is so small it seems like a prison," she complained. "Why do you sit there and stare at me?"

"I didn't realize I was staring," Penny apologized. "If you'll excuse me, I'll go to bed."

Undressing quickly, she crawled beneath the covers. Mrs. Deline smoked still another cigarette and then began to prepare for bed. As she removed the jacket of her suit, Penny noticed that the woman wore a beautiful jade elephant pin.

"Why, what an attractive ornament!" she exclaimed. "Is it a locket or just a pin?"

"I bought it in China," the widow answered without replying to the question.

"In China! Have you been there?"

"Of course!" Mrs. Deline gave Penny an amused glance. Without removing the pin or offering to show it to the girl, she completed her preparations for bed.

Just at that moment there came a light tap on the door.

"Oh, Penny!" Mr. Parker called.

"Yes, Dad, what is it?" Penny leaped out of bed.

"I'm worried about the car keys," he called through the transom. "You didn't by chance see them after we left the dining room?"

"Why, yes," Penny reassured him. "You left them lying on the table. I picked them up and forgot to tell you. They're here on the dresser. I'll hand them out."

"No, never mind. Keep them. I was just afraid they were lost. Goodnight."

Mrs. Deline glanced curiously at the key ring on the dresser. She remarked that she had not seen Penny pick it up.

"You were talking to Dad at the time," the girl replied.

Leaving the keys on the dresser, she leaped into bed again and settled herself for a comfortable sleep. Mrs. Deline presently turned out the light and took the other bed. For a time Penny was annoyed by voices from the hallway, then all became quiet. She slept.

Much later Penny awoke. She stirred and rolled over. The rain had ceased and moonlight was flooding into the room. A beam fell directly across Mrs. Deline's bed, revealing a mass of crumpled sheets and covers.

Penny stared, scarcely believing her eyes. The bed was empty.

CHAPTER 3 - A JADE GREEN CHARM

Sitting up in bed, Penny gazed about the room. Mrs. Deline was not there and her clothes were gone from the chair where they had been placed earlier that night.

"Queer," mused the girl.

Jumping out of bed, she darted to the door. Though it had been carefully locked a few hours before, the latch now was off.

Thoroughly puzzled, Penny switched on a light and glanced carefully about. Mrs. Deline's suitcase remained in the closet, but coat and hat were missing. And then Penny made an even more disturbing discovery. The car keys were gone from the dresser!

"Why, I know I put those keys on the bureau just before I went to bed!" she told herself in dismay. "Now I wonder if that woman—" Ashamed of her thoughts, she muttered: "Guess I *am* a suspicious brat!"

Deeply mystified, she moved quickly to the window overlooking the parking lot and filling station. It was reassuring to see the Parker automobile standing where her father had left it earlier that night. But as she stood staring down into the dark, deserted yard, she was startled to observe a shadowy figure rounding a corner of the hotel.

"Mrs. Deline!" she recognized the woman.

Penny waited only long enough to see that the widow was walking straight toward the Parker sedan.

"She intends to steal it!" thought the girl. "Why else would she take the keys?"

Snatching dress and coat from a chair, Penny scrambled into them without taking time to remove her pajamas. She tucked up the unsightly legs of the garment and put on her shoes. Thus clad she ran downstairs through the semi-dark lobby to the side exit of the hotel.

As she reached the outside door, she heard the blast of an automobile engine.

"That's our car!" Penny thought, recognizing the sound of the running motor. "She'll get away before I can stop her!"

The engine, evidently cold, sputtered a moment, then died.

Hopeful that she might still get there in time, Penny raced across the parking lot. Reaching the car just as it started to move backwards, she jerked open the door.

"Mrs. Deline!" she cried.

Startled, the woman released the clutch so suddenly that the motor died again.

"Where are you taking our car?" Penny demanded, sliding into the seat beside the widow.

The girl's unexpected arrival seemed to completely unnerve Mrs. Deline. She lost composure, but only for an instant. Lighting a cigarette, she gazed at Penny with cold disdain.

"I had intended to go for a little ride," she replied. "Any objections?"

The question placed Penny on the defensive. "You shouldn't have taken the car without asking Dad," she said stiffly. "We barely have enough gasoline to reach Sunset Beach."

"Oh, I had no thought of going far. I'll just drive a few miles and come back."

"At this time of night? It must be nearly two o'clock."

"I always enjoy night driving. Particularly if I am nervous and unable to sleep. Now run back to bed like a good child."

Penny did not like the widow's tone of voice. She liked it less that Mrs. Deline ignored her hint that the car was not to be used. More than ever she was convinced that the woman had intended to steal the automobile.

"I'm sorry," she said firmly. "I must ask you not to take the car without Dad's permission."

"Well!" Mrs. Deline exclaimed indignantly. "You expect me to rap on your father's door at this time of night to ask if I may use the car!"

"I don't see why you need to use the car at all."

"Oh, you don't?" Mrs. Deline's tone was scornful. "Well, let me tell you this! I've already given you as much of an explanation as I intend to! I need the car."

"I thought you said you only intended to go for a little drive—to quiet your nerves," Penny reminded her.

"That's what I meant." Mrs. Deline tossed her cigarette through the open window and stepped on the car starter. "I intend to go too."

Penny, equally determined, switched off the ignition.

"Why, how dare you!" Mrs. Deline turned furiously upon the girl. "In all my life I never met such a spoiled child."

"I don't mean to be rude, but I can't allow you to take the car."

Mrs. Deline swung open the door on Penny's side of the seat. She reached as if to push the girl out of the car.

Just then a man stepped from one of the hotel garages. Obviously he had been listening to the conversation, for he deliberately approached the car.

"Anything wrong here?" he inquired.

Penny recognized one of the night hotel clerks. She began to tell him of the disagreement between herself and Mrs. Deline.

"This child doesn't know what she's talking about!" the widow declared irritably. "Mr. Parker doesn't mind if I use the car."

"Then please ask him!" Penny challenged.

"Why not allow me to do it for you," the hotel clerk offered. "Wait here and I'll call Mr. Parker. He can settle the entire matter."

"No, don't bother him," Mrs. Deline decided suddenly. "I've changed my mind anyhow. After such a commotion I wouldn't enjoy a ride."

"In any case, I'd prefer to call Mr. Parker," said the hotel man.

"Do," urged Penny in deep satisfaction. "We'll wait here."

"I'm going back to bed," Mrs. Deline announced, getting out of the car.

She followed the hotel clerk into the building. Left in possession of the car, Penny reparked it and locked the doors. Then, feeling a trifle uneasy, she sauntered into the hotel.

The lobby was deserted. Penny climbed the stairs, and in the hallway leading to her room, met her father and the hotel clerk. Summoned from bed, Mr. Parker garbed in dressing gown and slippers, looked more annoyed than alarmed.

"Penny, what is this I hear?" he inquired. "I can't get the straight of the story."

Penny drew a deep breath. "Well, it was this way, Dad. I awakened and discovered that Mrs. Deline had disappeared with the car keys."

"Mrs. Deline!"

"Yes, I think she meant to steal the car. But she explained that she only intended to borrow it for a night ride."

"Anything wrong about that?"

Penny regarded her father in blank amazement.

"Why, Dad, would you borrow another person's car without asking?"

"No, but Mrs. Deline probably didn't stop to consider the matter. No doubt she was too thoughtful to awaken you."

"Thoughtful, my left eye! Dad, I'm sure Mrs. Deline meant to steal the car. Either that or she had a very important appointment—a meeting with someone she wasn't willing to tell us about."

"Nonsense!" Mr. Parker exclaimed impatiently. "Penny, you made a serious mistake in refusing to allow Mrs. Deline to use the car. She is our guest and I'm afraid you were rude."

"But Dad—"

"You must apologize to her at once."

CHAPTER 3 - A JADE GREEN CHARM

Penny did not answer for a moment. She bent to tie her flapping shoe strings and took her time at the task. When she straightened, she said quietly:

"All right, Dad. If you say so, I'll apologize. But I don't think I was wrong."

"We'll not discuss it now, Penny. Suppose you turn the car keys over to me and go to your room."

Penny gave up the keys and without another word went down the hall. Tears stung her eyes, but she brushed them away. She knew she had been unpleasant to Mrs. Deline. Nevertheless, she felt that her father had not been entirely just in his attitude.

Entering the bedroom, she hesitated before turning on the light. Mrs. Deline had undressed and was in bed. She ignored the girl.

"I—I guess I made a bad mistake," Penny began awkwardly. "I shouldn't have been so rude."

Mrs. Deline rolled over in bed. Her dark eyes flashed and she made no effort to hide her dislike.

"So you admit it?" she asked. "Well, we will forget the matter. Do not speak of it to me again."

In silence Penny undressed and hung up her coat and dress. As she prepared to snap out the light, she noticed that Mrs. Deline still wore the jade elephant charm about her neck.

"Aren't you afraid you'll break the chain?" she asked before she thought. "You forgot to take it off."

Mrs. Deline raised herself on an elbow, fairly glaring at Penny.

"Will you kindly worry about your own affairs?" she asked insolently. "I've had about all I can take from you in one night."

"But I didn't mean anything personal."

"Good night!" said Mrs. Deline with emphasis.

Penny turned out the light and crept into her own bed. She felt beaten and hurt. It was easy to understand why Mrs. Deline disliked her, but her own attitude was bewildering.

"I distrusted the woman the instant I met her," she reflected. "Perhaps I had no reason for it at first. Now I'm not so sure."

Penny rolled over to face the window. Moonlight was flooding into the room. In the diffused light the girl could see Mrs. Deline plainly. The woman had propped herself up in bed and was fingering the jade green elephant charm which hung on its slender chain. Though Penny could not be certain, she thought the lid of the figure lay open and that Mrs. Deline quickly snapped it shut.

"Good night, Mrs. Deline," she ventured, still trying to make amends.

The widow did not answer. Instead she turned her back and pretended to sleep.

CHAPTER 4 - NO CAMPING ALLOWED

Breakfast the next morning was a trying ordeal for Penny. Over the coffee cups Mr. Parker apologized to Mrs. Deline for what he termed his daughter's "inexcusable behavior."

The widow responded graciously, quite in contrast to her attitude of the previous night. Without saying much, she conveyed the impression that Penny had been completely in the wrong, and was in fact, a spoiled child who must be humored.

The journey on to Sunset Beach was equally unpleasant. Mr. Parker and Mrs. Deline seemed so absorbed in animated conversation, that they scarcely spoke or noticed Penny. Wedged between the luggage and the camping equipment, she indulged in self pity.

"At least we'll get rid of Mrs. Deline when we reach Sunset Beach," she cheered herself.

Presently the car rounded a wide curve in the road, and Penny caught her first glimpse of the seashore. Big waves were rolling in, washing an endless stretch of white sand.

"Oh, isn't it beautiful!" she exclaimed, brightening. "I wish we were camping right on the beach instead of in the State Forest."

"I fear the authorities wouldn't permit that," Mr. Parker laughed. "By the way, Penny, is your heart really set on this camping trip?"

Penny gave him a quick look. "Yes, it is, Dad," she said briefly. "Why do you ask?"

"Well, I was thinking that we'd be a lot more comfortable at one of the big hotels. We'd be right on the beach and—"

"Oh, I was just talking when I said I'd like to camp on the beach," Penny cut in. "I'd like the State Forest much better."

"Then we'll go there just as we planned," Mr. Parker said, sighing. "But you know I never was cut out for a rough and tumble life, Penny. I'm far from sure I'll make a good camper."

The car rolled on along the ocean road, presently entering the little village of Sunset Beach. Normally a tourist center, the town now was practically deserted, and the Parkers had chosen it because it was within easy driving distance of Riverview. Nearly all of the fine hotels along the water front were closed. However, the Crystal Inn remained in operation, and it was there that Mrs. Deline had engaged a suite.

The car swung into the driveway and halted in front of the hotel. An attendant did not come immediately so Mr. Parker himself unloaded the widow's luggage. Mrs. Deline gave him a dazzling smile as she bade him goodbye.

"Oh, we'll not say goodbye just yet," Mr. Parker corrected. "Penny and I will camp only a short distance away. We'll run down to the beach often."

"Do," urged Mrs. Deline. "I have no friends here and I'll be happy to see you."

Mr. Parker carried the widow's luggage into the hotel. While he was absent, Penny moved up to the front seat. She tuned in a radio program, listening to it with growing impatience. Finally her father sauntered out of the hotel.

"I nearly gave you up," Penny remarked pointedly.

Mr. Parker slid behind the steering wheel and started the car. When they were driving along the ocean front road he said quietly:

"Penny, I can't imagine what has come over you lately. You're not in the least like the little girl who was my pal and companion. Why have you been so unkind to Mrs. Deline?"

"I just don't like her," Penny said flatly. "Furthermore, I distrust her."

CHAPTER 4 - NO CAMPING ALLOWED

"You've acted very stupid and silly."

"I'm sorry if you're ashamed of me," Penny replied glaring at her own reflection in the car mirror. "At any rate, I saved the car for you."

"That accusation was ridiculous, Penny. Mrs. Deline is a wealthy woman who could buy herself a dozen cars in ordinary times. She merely gave in to a sudden whim."

"Just what do you know about Mrs. Deline, Dad?"

"Not a great deal," Mr. Parker admitted. "I met her at the club. She served as a special War correspondent in China, I believe. She has traveled all over the world and speaks a half dozen languages."

"I never heard of her until she came to Riverview," Penny said with a sniff. "Nor did I ever see any of her writing in print. If you ask me, she's a phony."

"Let's not discuss the subject further," Mr. Parker replied, losing patience. "When you're older, I hope you'll learn to be more gracious and charitable."

Penny subsided into hurt silence. In all her life she could recall only a few occasions when her father had spoken so sternly to her. Close to tears, she studied the tumbling surface of the ocean with concentrated interest.

In silence the Parkers drove through the village, stopping at a filling station to inquire the way to Rhett State Forest. Supplies were purchased at one of the stores, and by that time it was noon. At Mr. Parker's suggestion they stopped at a roadside inn for lunch. After that they drove on a half mile beyond the outskirts of Sunset Beach, past a tall lighthouse to the end of the pavement.

"We follow a dirt road for a quarter of a mile to Bradley Knoll," Mr. Parker said, consulting directions he had jotted down on an envelope.

"A mud road, you mean," Penny corrected, peering ahead at the narrow, twisting highway. "It really rained here last night."

The car had no chains. Not without misgiving, Mr. Parker drove off the pavement onto the slippery road. The car wallowed about and at times skidded dangerously.

"Once we reach the State park we'll have gravel roads," Penny said, studying a map.

"*If* we get there," Mr. Parker corrected.

Barely had he spoken than the car went out of control. It took a long skid, turned crosswise in the road, and then the rear wheels slipped into a deep ditch. Opening the car door, Penny saw that the car was bogged down to the hub caps.

Mr. Parker tried without success to pull out of the ditch. Alighting, he inspected the rear wheels which had spun deeper and deeper into the mud.

"Not a chance to get out of here without help," he said crossly. "I'll have to find someone to give us a hand."

Farther down the road stood a weatherbeaten farmhouse. Penny offered to go there to summon help, but her father insisted upon doing it himself. He presently returned with a farmer and a small tractor. After considerable difficulty the car was pulled out of the ditch.

"How much do I owe you?" Mr. Parker asked the man.

"Ten dollars."

The amount seemed far too high for the service rendered, but Mr. Parker paid it without comment. His shoes were caked with mud, and so were the trouser legs of his suit. Only by an effort of will did he keep his temper under control.

"Figurin' on camping in the Rhett Forest?" the farmer asked Mr. Parker.

"That's right. Is it much farther?"

"Only a little piece down the road. You'll strike gravel at the next corner. You can make it if you're careful. I don't calculate you'll have much fun camping in the Park though."

"Why not?" asked Penny.

"We've had a lot o' rain lately. The mosquitoes are bitin' something fierce. And the ground's mighty damp."

"We have a floor to our tent," Penny said optimistically. "I think camping will be fun. I've always wanted to try it."

The farmer started the tractor. "Then don't let me discourage you," he shrugged. "So long."

Mr. Parker rejoined Penny in the car. "Why not call this whole thing off?" he suggested. "We could go to the hotel and—"

"No, Dad! You promised me!"

"All right, Penny, if that's the way you feel, but I know we're asking for punishment."

By careful driving the Parkers reached the gravel road without mishap. At the entrance to the Rhett Park area they were stopped by a pleasant, middle-aged forest ranger who took down the license number of the car.

"Be careful about your camp fire," he instructed. "Only last week several acres of timber were destroyed at Alton. We're not certain whether it was started by a camper or was a case of sabotage. In any case, one can't be too careful."

"We will be," promised Mr. Parker.

"Camp only in the designated sites," the ranger added. "I'll be around later on to see how you're getting along."

Once beyond the gateway arch, Penny's sagging spirits began to revive. The road curled lazily between dense masses of timber fringed by artistic old-fashioned rail fences. Numerous signs pointed to trails that invited exploration.

"Oh, Dad, it's really nice here!" she cried. "We'll have a wonderful time!"

Presently the car came to an open space with picnic tables. There was a picturesque spot beside a rocky brook which looked just right for a camp site.

"Let's pitch our tent here!" pleaded Penny. "You set it up while I cook supper."

Mr. Parker unloaded the car and went to work with a will hammering the metal stakes of the umbrella tent. Penny busied herself sorting pots and pans and trying to get the gasoline stove started. Despite her best efforts she could not induce it to burn.

In the meantime, Mr. Parker was having his own set of troubles. Three of the tent stakes were missing. Twice he put up the umbrella framework, only to have the entire structure collapse upon his head.

"Penny, come here and help me!" he called. "I've had about enough of this!"

Penny ran to her father's rescue, pulling the canvas from his head and shoulders. By working together they finally got the tent set up. Another half hour was required to put up the cots and make them.

"Well, that job is done," Mr. Parker sighed, collapsing on one of the beds. "Such a life!"

"Dad, I hate to bother you," Penny apologized, "but I can't start the stove. Do you mind looking at it?"

Grumbling a bit, Mr. Parker went to tinker with the stove. Three-quarters of an hour slipped away before he succeeded in coaxing a bright flame.

"All this work has given me a big appetite for supper," he announced. "What are we having, Penny?"

"Steaks."

"Sounds fine."

"I forgot the salt though," Penny confessed, slapping the meat into a frying pan.

The burner was too hot. While Penny had her back turned and was opening a can of beans, the steaks began to scorch. Mr. Parker tried to rescue them. In his haste he seized the hot skillet handle and burned his hands.

"Oh, Dad, I'm so sorry!" Penny sympathized. "I guess the steaks are practically ruined too."

"Anything else to eat?" the publisher asked, nursing his blistered hand.

"Beans."

"Beans!" Mr. Parker repeated with bitter emphasis. "Oh, well—dish them up."

Penny was serving the food on tin plates when a car drove up and stopped. A ranger climbed out and walked over to the tent.

"What's the idea, camping here?" he demanded. "Can't you read signs?"

"We didn't see any sign," said Penny.

The ranger pointed to one in plain sight tacked on the trunk of a tree. It read:

"Restricted Area. No Camping Permitted."

"You can't stay here," the ranger added. "You'll have to move on."

Penny and her father gazed at each other in despair. After all the work they had done, it didn't seem as though they could break camp.

"Any objections if we stay here until morning?" Mr. Parker requested. "We've had a pretty hard time of it getting established."

CHAPTER 4 - NO CAMPING ALLOWED

The ranger looked sympathetic but unmoved.

"Sorry," he said curtly. "Regulations are regulations. You may finish your supper if you like, then you must move on. The regular camp site is a quarter of a mile farther up the road."

CHAPTER 5 - OVER THE AIR

The ranger's order so discouraged Penny and her father that they lost all zest for supper. Too weary for conversation, they tore up the beds, repacked the dishes, and pulled the tent stakes.

"I've not worked so hard in years," Mr. Parker sighed. "What a mistake to call this a vacation!"

"Perhaps it won't be so hard once we get settled," Penny said hopefully. "After all, we've had more than our share of bad luck."

Bad luck, however, continued to follow the campers. In the gathering darkness, Penny and her father had trouble finding the specified camp ground. It was impossible to drive a car into the cleared space, so they were forced to carry all of the heavy luggage and equipment from the automobile to the camp site.

By that time it was quite dark. Mr. Parker misplaced one of the tent stakes and could not find it without a lengthy search. As he finally drove it in, he hammered his thumb instead of the metal pin.

"Drat it all! I've had enough of this!" he muttered irritably. "Penny, why not give it up—"

"Oh, no, Dad!" Penny cut in quickly. "Once we get the tent up again, we'll be all right. Here, I'll hold the flashlight so you can see better."

Finally the tent was successfully staked down, though Mr. Parker temporarily abandoned the idea of putting up the front porch. Penny set up the cots again and made the beds.

"Hope you packed plenty of woolen blankets," Mr. Parker commented, shivering. "It will be cold tonight."

Penny admitted that she had brought only two thin ones for each bed. "I didn't suppose it could get so cold on a summer night," she confessed ruefully.

Worn by his strenuous labors, Mr. Parker climbed into the closed car to smoke a cigar. Penny, finding the dark tent lonesome, soon joined him there. She switched on the car radio, tuning in an orchestra. Presently it went off the air so she dialed another station. A strange jargon of words which could not be understood, accosted her ears.

"Hold that, Penny!" exclaimed Mr. Parker.

"What station can it be?" Penny speculated, peering at the luminous dial. "It sounds like a short wave broadcast. Must be a station off its wave band."

She and her father listened intently to the speaker who had a resonant, baritone voice. Not a word of the broadcast could they understand. Obviously a message was being sent in code.

"Dad, that sounds like the same station I heard yesterday!" Penny broke in. "Where can it be located?"

"I'd like to know myself."

Penny glanced quickly at her father. His remark, she thought, had definite significance. Before she could question him, the strange jargon ceased. The deep baritone voice concluded in plain, slightly accented English: "This is the Voice from the Cave, signing off until tomorrow night. Stand by, Comrades!"

"That was no regular station," Penny declared, puzzled. "But what was it?"

Mr. Parker reached over to turn off the panel switch. "It was an outlaw station," he said quietly. "The authorities have been after it for weeks."

"How did you learn about it?"

"Through various channels. Most outlaw radio stations can be traced quite easily by the use of modern radio-detecting devices. The enemy agent who operates this station is a particularly elusive fellow. Just when the police are sure they have him, he moves to another locality."

Penny was silent a moment and then she said:

"You seem to know quite a bit about this mysterious Voice, Dad."

CHAPTER 5 - OVER THE AIR

"Naturally I've been interested in the case. If the police catch the fellow it will make a good story for the *Star*."

"Where is the station thought to be located, Dad?"

"Oh, it moves nightly. The fellow obviously has a portable broadcasting outfit."

"But isn't the general locality known?"

Mr. Parker smiled as he knocked ashes from his cigar.

"Authorities seem to think that it may be somewhere near here. Sunset Beach has countless caves, you know."

"Really?" The information excited Penny. "You never told me that before, Dad. And I suspect that you're keeping a lot of other secrets from me too!"

"Sunset Beach's caves are no secret. They're part of the tourist attraction."

"All the same you never mentioned them, Dad. I thought it was odd that you chose this place for a vacation. Now I'm beginning to catch on."

Mr. Parker pretended not to understand.

"Isn't it true that you came here to do a bit of investigation work?" Penny pursued the subject relentlessly.

"Now don't try to pin me down," Mr. Parker laughed. "Suppose we just say we came here for a vacation."

Penny eyed her father quizzically. From the way he sidestepped her questions she was certain that he had more than a casual interest in the outlaw radio station.

"Dad, will you let me help you?" she pleaded eagerly.

"Help me?" Mr. Parker joked. "Why, you seem to think that I'm a Government investigator in disguise!"

"You don't deny that you came here largely because of your interest in that station?"

"Well, I may be a tiny bit interested. But don't jump to conclusions, young lady! It doesn't necessarily follow that I have set out to track down any enemy agent single handed." Mr. Parker brought the discussion to an end by opening the car door. "I'm dead tired, Penny. If you'll excuse me, I'll turn in."

After her father had gone to the tent, Penny remained for a while in the car. Soberly she stared at the stars and thought over what she had learned.

"I don't care what Dad says," she reflected, "he came here to find that radio station! But maybe, just maybe, I'll beat him to it!"

CHAPTER 6 - BREAKFAST BLUES

Penny awoke next morning to find the tent cold and damp. She rolled over on the hard cot and moaned with pain. Every muscle in her battered body felt as if it had been twisted into a knot.

Swinging her feet to the canvas floor, she pulled away the curtain to peer at her father's cot. It was empty.

"Guess I've overslept," she thought. "Hope Dad's started breakfast."

Penny dressed quickly, cringing as she pulled on damp shirt and shorts. Dew lay heavy upon the tent and the grass outside was saturated. She walked gingerly as she picked her way toward the parked car.

Mr. Parker had set up a portable table nearby and was tinkering with the gasoline stove. He was unshaven and looked very much out of sorts.

"Hi, Dad!" Penny greeted him with as much cheer as she could muster. "What are we having for breakfast?"

"Nothing, so far as I can see! This stove is on strike again. I've tried for half an hour to get it started."

Penny climbed into the car to use the mirror. The sight of her face horrified her. One cheek was blotched with ugly red mosquito bites, there were dark circles under her eyes, and her hair hung in strings.

"If anyone ever gets me on another camping trip I'll be surprised!" Mr. Parker exclaimed. He slammed the stove down on the table. "I'm through monkeying with this contrary beast!"

"Oh, Dad, such a temper," Penny chided, giggling despite her own discouragement.

"Suppose you suggest how we're to eat."

"Well, there's cold breakfast food with canned milk." Penny burrowed deep in a box of supplies stored in the car. "Two soft bananas. No coffee, I'm afraid."

"Wonderful!" Mr. Parker said grimly. "Well, bring on the bird food."

Penny set the table and dished up the dry breakfast cereal.

"At least we have beautiful scenery," she remarked as she sat down to the dismal repast with her father. "Just look at those grand old trees."

"The place is all right. It's camping that has me tied in a knot. Now at the Crystal Inn we could be comfortable—right on the beach too."

"No," Penny said, though not very firmly. "We'll like it here after we get adjusted."

"Need any supplies today?" Mr. Parker asked abruptly.

"Yes, we'll have to have fresh meat and milk. I forgot salt too and bread."

"I'll drive down to Sunset Beach and get the things. May as well take the stove along too and try to have it repaired."

"That might be a good idea," Penny admitted, though with reluctance. "Don't be gone long, will you? I thought we might explore some of the trails."

"Oh, there's plenty of time for that."

Mr. Parker was noticeably cheerful as he stowed the portable stove in the car and drove away. Not without misgiving Penny watched him go. She remained somewhat troubled as she washed the breakfast dishes at the brook and struggled with the beds. The camping trip hadn't worked out as she had hoped and expected. So far it had been all work and no fun.

"Dad was up to something when he skipped out of here so fast," she mused. "Wonder why he doesn't come back?"

The sun rose high above the trees, drying the grass and tent. Penny went for a short hike in the woods. She returned to find that her father still had not returned.

CHAPTER 6 - BREAKFAST BLUES

Just then a car rattled up the twisting road. Recognizing the same ranger who had caused so much trouble the previous night, Penny prepared herself for further blows. However, the government man was all smiles as he pulled up not far from the umbrella tent.

"Just dropped by to see if you're getting along all right," he greeted her in a friendly way. "Everything Okay?"

"I wouldn't venture such a rash statement as that," Penny answered, her face downcast.

Because the ranger, whose name was Bill Atkins, seemed to have a genuine interest, she found herself telling him all about her troubles.

"Why, you've not had a decent meal since you came here!" he exclaimed, climbing out of the car. "Maybe I can help you."

"Can you wave a magic wand and produce hot food?"

"We'll see," laughed the ranger. "Gasoline stoves are more bother than they're worth in my opinion."

As Penny watched in amazed admiration he built a good fire which soon made a bed of glowing cherry red coals.

"How about a nice pan of fish fried to a crisp brown?" the ranger tempted her. "I caught a string of them this morning. Beauties!"

From the car he brought a basket of fat trout, already dressed and ready for cooking. Without asking Penny for anything, he wrapped them in corn meal, salted each fish and let it sizzle in hot butter.

"Do you always travel with your car equipped like a kitchen cabinet?" Penny joked. Crouching beside the fire, she barely could take her eyes from the food.

"Not always," the ranger laughed. "I've been on an overnight trip. Usually have the fixings of a meal with me though."

While the fish slowly sizzled, Bill put on a pot of coffee and fried potatoes. He accomplished everything with such ease that Penny could only watch dumbfounded.

"Guess you and your father considered me an old crab last night," he remarked. "Sometimes we hate to enforce the rules, but we have to treat everyone alike. If we allowed folks to camp wherever they pleased the danger of forest fire would be greatly increased."

"You're right, of course. Have you had any fires this season?"

"Not here." Deftly the ranger dished up the potatoes and crisply browned fish. "Plenty of them farther South. Not all caused by carelessness of campers either."

Penny was quick to seize upon the remark. "Sabotage?" she questioned.

"That's what we think," the ranger nodded. He poured two cups of steaming, black coffee. "Fact is, enemy agents have made quite a few attempts to set fire to our forests. Nearly always they're caught, but that doesn't mean we dare let up our vigilance."

Penny ate every morsel of the food, praising the ranger highly for his cooking ability.

"I wish Dad could have had some of this fish," she added. "He went down to Sunset Beach for supplies and for some reason hasn't returned."

"I'll have to be on the road myself," the ranger declared, getting up from the ground. "I'm due in town at twelve o'clock and it's nearly that now."

"You're driving to Sunset Beach?"

"Yes, want to ride along?"

Penny debated briefly. "Wait until I get my coat," she requested. "It's lonesome here alone. Anyway, I want to learn what's keeping Dad."

The park road had dried considerably, but even so the car skidded from side to side until it reached the paved highway. At Sunset Beach, the ranger dropped Penny off at the postoffice. Rather at a loss to know what to do with herself, she wandered about the half-deserted streets in search of her father. He was not at any of the stores, nor did inquiry reveal his whereabouts.

"Perhaps he's sunning himself on the beach," she thought.

A boardwalk led over the dunes to the water front. The tide was at ebb, revealing a long, wide stretch of white sand strewn with shells and seaweed. Penny paused to gaze meditatively upon the wind-swept sea. For a time she watched the waves break and spill their foam on the sandy shore. Then she walked slowly on toward the imposing Crystal Inn.

VOICE FROM THE CAVE

Approaching the private beach area, Penny met only a few persons, mostly soldiers on furlough with their girls. There were no bathers for a sharp, cool wind blew off the water.

"Sunset Beach is nice," thought Penny, "but it's lonesome."

At the Crystal Inn there was more activity. Tennis courts were in use and so was the swimming pool. Penny circled the well-kept grounds, not intending to enter the building. However, as she drew near, her attention was drawn to the flagstone terrace overlooking the formal garden. Though it was set with tables there were not many diners.

Suddenly Penny stopped short, scarcely believing her eyes. At one of the tables near the stone railing sat her father with Mrs. Deline.

CHAPTER 7 - THE BEARDED STRANGER

Penny's first thought upon seeing her father and Mrs. Deline was to steal quietly away. Then amazement and injury gave way to a feeling of indignation. Perhaps her father had a perfect right to lunch with Mrs. Deline, but it was inconsiderate of him to so completely forget his own daughter.

"I might just as well be an orphan!" Penny sighed. "Well, we'll see!"

Stiffly she marched across the lawn to the railed-in hotel veranda. Her father saw her coming. His look of surprise changed to one of guarded welcome.

"Come up and have lunch with us," he invited. "The food here is quite an improvement on what we've been having at camp."

Penny could find no outside entranceway to the terrace. To Mrs. Deline's horror and her father's amusement, she climbed over the stone railing.

"Dad," Penny began, ignoring the widow except for a curt nod, "I was just about ready to get out a search warrant for you."

Mr. Parker drew another chair to the table for his daughter. Her hair was none too well combed, she wore no stockings, and the coat did not entirely cover her camp costume. By contrast Mrs. Deline was perfectly turned out in tailored tweed suit with a smart little hat of feathers. Though the woman said nothing, her gaze was scornful as she appraised Penny.

"What shall I order for you?" Mr. Parker asked, signaling a waiter.

"Nothing, thank you." Penny was coldly polite. "I had a very fine lunch at camp, thanks to one of the rangers."

"I'm sorry I didn't get back," Mr. Parker apologized. "It took a long while to have the stove repaired. Then I met Mrs. Deline and—"

"Oh, I understand," Penny broke in. "The point is, when, if ever, are you coming back to camp?"

"Why, right now I suppose. We've finished our luncheon."

The waiter had come to the table. Mr. Parker asked for the bill, paid it, and arose. As he bade Mrs. Deline goodbye, he remarked that he probably would see her again soon.

Walking to the hotel parking lot where Mr. Parker had left the car, neither he nor Penny had much to say. Not until they were driving through the village was the subject of Mrs. Deline mentioned.

"I don't see why you can't be a bit nicer to her," Mr. Parker commented. "You scarcely spoke a word to her."

"Did she say anything to me?"

"Well, I don't recall."

"I've treated Mrs. Deline just as well as she treats me!" Penny defended herself. "I'll admit I don't like her."

"And you show it too."

"Maybe I do, but she has no business taking so much of your time."

"So that's where the shoe pinches," chuckled Mr. Parker. "My little girl is jealous."

"The very idea!"

"Mrs. Deline is brilliant—a highly educated woman and I enjoy talking to her," Mr. Parker said thoughtfully. "I assure you it's no more serious than that."

Penny moved close to her father and squeezed his arm.

"We've been pals for such a long while," she said wistfully. "If anything ever should come between us—"

"Penny, you're positively morbid!" her father interrupted. "Of course nothing ever will come between us! Now let's talk of more cheerful subjects."

"Such as?"

"I've been thinking, Penny. You need a friend, someone to pal around with."

"You're the only friend I need, Dad."

"I mean someone your own age, Penny. Why not send for Louise Sidell? I'll gladly pay her train fare."

"It would be fun having Lou here."

"Then it's settled. We'll send a wire now." Mr. Parker turned the car around and drove to the local telegraph office.

Before Penny could change her mind, the message was sent. Not until long after she and her father had returned to the park did it occur to her that unwittingly she might have fashioned her own undoing. Though camping would be far more interesting with Louise to share her experiences, it also would give her father added opportunity to see Mrs. Deline.

"Maybe he didn't think of that angle," Penny reflected uneasily. "I'll keep it to myself."

The following day Mr. Parker spent the entire day in camp. With the gasoline stove in working order, hot meals were prepared though not without endless effort. There were dishes to wash, beds to make, and by the time the tasks were done, neither Penny nor her father had any energy left for hiking.

The second day was much easier. However, with more free time, Mr. Parker became increasingly restless. He missed his morning paper and was dissatisfied with the skimpy news reports that came in over the radio. Penny was not surprised when he mentioned that he would walk down to Sunset Beach.

"Mind if I go with you?" Penny asked quickly.

"Of course not," her father answered. "Why should I?"

At Sunset Beach a call at the local telegraph office disclosed a message for Penny which had been held for lack of an address. The wire was from Louise and read:

"ARRIVING AT SUNSET BEACH THURSDAY ON THE 12:30 PLANE. HOLD EVERYTHING."

"Thursday!" Penny cried, offering the telegram to her father. "That's tomorrow! My, will I be glad to see Lou! This place has been like a morgue without her."

"I imagine the town will brighten up quite a bit within the next few days," Mr. Parker said, a twinkle in his eye. "In fact, Louise may not be the only new arrival."

"Is someone else coming to see us?"

Mr. Parker would not answer her many questions. "Wait and see," he teased.

Since arriving at Sunset Beach Penny had been eager to visit the lighthouse located on Crag Point. Noticing that the tide was low, she suggested to her father that they go there together.

"Too long a walk," he complained. "You run along by yourself. I'll sun myself on the beach."

Leaving her father, Penny started off alone. The sun was warm and there were a number of bathers splashing about in the surf. A long row of picturesque cottages lined the water front. They thinned out as she went farther up the beach, and presently there were no habitations, only desolate, wind-blown sand.

Midway to the lighthouse, Penny met a man of early middle age who carried fishing rod and creel. He stared at her, hesitated, then paused to speak.

"I notice you're going toward Crag Point," he remarked pleasantly. "Are you a stranger to this locality?"

Penny admitted that she was.

"Then perhaps you haven't been told that the Point is a dangerous place to be at high tide."

"No, I hadn't heard."

"The Point is very nearly covered at that time," the stranger explained. "There's no danger at the present moment, of course."

"How long will I have here?"

"Oh, several hours," the stranger replied. "There's no cause for alarm if you just keep watch of the tide."

Penny thanked the stranger and walked on toward the lighthouse. The structure rose to a height of seventy-five feet above the beach and was reached by means of a narrow little iron stairway.

No one was about the premises as Penny approached. However, as she started up the iron steps, a door far above her head opened. A burly, stout man whose face was browned by wind and sun, peered down at her.

"You can't come up here!" he shouted. "No visitors are allowed!"

CHAPTER 7 - THE BEARDED STRANGER

"Oh," Penny murmured, retreating a step. "I didn't know. I only wanted to see the tower."

"No visitors," the keeper of the light repeated. "War regulations."

The rule seemed a reasonable one, but after such a long hike, Penny was disappointed. Walking back to the main section of the beach, she looked about for her father. He had disappeared.

"I'll bet a cookie he's at the Crystal Inn!" she thought indignantly.

But Penny could not find her father there nor at any other place along the water front. After an hour's search she decided that he must have returned to camp. Returning there, she approached the tent, noticing that the flap was closed, though not buttoned as she had left it.

"Dad must be here," she thought.

Drawing nearer she could see movement within the tent as someone brushed against the canvas walls.

"Oh, Dad!" she called.

There was no answer. But the next instant a man in rough garments and straw hat rushed out of the tent. Penny never before had set eyes upon him. She was so astonished that she gained only a fleeting impression of the bearded stranger. Seeing her, he thrust some object beneath his coat and fled into the woods.

CHAPTER 8 - KEEPER OF THE LIGHT

Recovering from astonishment, Penny darted to the tent and jerked open the flap. The beds had been torn apart. Her purse, hidden beneath the pillow, was gone. Suitcases lay open on the canvas floor.

"That man was a thief!" she thought angrily.

Too late, she tried to determine which direction he had taken. She could hear no sound of crackling leaves or running feet.

"He's lying low," she told herself. "No use chasing him. I never could find him among the trees."

Thoroughly incensed, she went back to the disordered tent. A preliminary check revealed that besides the pocketbook, a pair of her father's shoes and a sweater had been taken.

"Lucky I didn't have much money in my purse," Penny congratulated herself. "It was a good leather pocketbook though, and I hate to lose it."

Going outside, she discovered other losses. The supply of groceries had been ransacked. Bread was gone, several oranges and a tin of cold meat.

"That fellow was hungry," Penny reflected. "Probably some shiftless person who isn't willing to work for a living."

Entering the tent again, she busied herself making the beds and repacking the suitcases. As she finished the task, she heard footsteps outside. Fearful that the thief had returned, she jerked open the canvas flap. It was her father who had arrived.

"Oh, Dad, I'm glad you're back!" she exclaimed, rushing out to meet him. "We've been robbed!"

"What?"

Penny told him how she had frightened away the bearded stranger.

"That's bad," Mr. Parker said, frowning. "I didn't suppose there was another camper within miles of us."

"This man didn't look like a camper, Dad. He wore dirty, mussed clothing and a beard of at least a week's growth."

"How old a fellow?"

"Why, he looked young to me. And he ran like a young person."

"We'll report it to the ranger," Mr. Parker said, entering the tent to check over his belongings. "Probably never will get any of our things back though."

"The ranger may know who the fellow is, Dad."

"That's possible," Mr. Parker admitted. "Penny, I'm glad Louise is coming tomorrow. I certainly don't like the idea of your remaining here in camp alone."

"Then why don't you stay with me?" Penny countered instantly.

"Well, I'm planning on being rather busy."

"With Mrs. Deline."

"Penny, you're impossible!"

"Weren't you with her today? I looked everywhere for you."

"Mrs. Deline and I did go for a little walk. No harm in that, is there?"

"It all depends upon your viewpoint," Penny said loftily. "Personally, I consider her about as harmless as a Grade A rattler!"

"Penny, enough of such talk!"

"Okay," she returned grimly, "but never say I didn't warn you."

CHAPTER 8 - KEEPER OF THE LIGHT

"I was about to tell you," Mr. Parker resumed, "that I expect to be busy the next few days helping local authorities trace that outlaw radio station we heard on the air."

"Oh!"

"In fact, Army experts are being sent here to aid in the work. My days will be pretty well tied up."

"I'm sorry, Dad," Penny said contritely. "Naturally I thought—"

"I'm afraid your trouble is that you don't stop to think," Mr. Parker lectured. "Please, will you forget Mrs. Deline?"

"I promise not to bother you about her again, Dad."

"Good!" Mr. Parker awkwardly patted his daughter's hand. "I realize you've had an unpleasant time of it so far, Penny. But things should pick up after Louise arrives."

"And that other surprise you hinted about?"

"Oh, you'll have to wait and see," Mr. Parker smiled. "However, I promise you that what's coming really will prove a pleasant surprise."

Though Penny kept up a running fire of questions, her father would tell her no more. From a few hints he dropped, she gathered that he was expecting a visitor within a day or so. That rather disappointed her, for with the exception of Louise, she could think of no one she particularly wanted to see at Sunset Beach.

Later that day when a forest ranger stopped at camp for a few minutes, Mr. Parker reported the theft of food and clothing to him.

"So the thief was a young man with a beard?" the ranger pondered. "Don't know of anyone in the area answering such a description. We'll certainly be on the watch for him."

Penny and her father expected to hear no more from the matter. Toward sundown, however, the same ranger returned to camp, bringing the missing pocketbook. It was stripped of money but still contained a compact and various toilet articles.

"Where did you find the purse?" Penny inquired eagerly.

"On the Beech Trail not far from here."

"Then it was dropped on purpose?"

"Apparently it was. I followed the trail for a quarter of mile, then lost the fellow when he took to the brook."

"Rather a smart fellow to think of that," commented Mr. Parker thoughtfully. "Perhaps he wasn't an ordinary snatch-thief after all."

The ranger offered no comment. As he turned to go, he did assure Penny again that every effort would be made to capture the culprit.

"If the fellow still is in the park we'll get him," he declared. "Don't you worry about that."

With the coming of dusk a penetrating chill settled over the camp. Even the hot supper of steak and potatoes that Penny prepared failed to sufficiently warm the two tenters. They did the dishes and then, not wishing to go to bed, sought the enclosed car for heat.

"It's starting to rain," Mr. Parker observed as a few drops splashed against the windshield. "Looks as if we're in for another siege of it."

"And Louise is due tomorrow," Penny sighed. "Unless the weather improves I'd not blame her one bit if she turns right around and starts back to Riverview."

The rain came down steadily with a promise of continuing throughout the night. Mr. Parker read a day-old newspaper by the light in the car, grumbling because the news was so old. Presently he switched on the radio, trying without success to tune in the outlaw station which had been heard previously at the same hour.

"No luck," he commented. "Reception must be poor tonight, or the station has changed to another time. Probably it's shifted to a different locality too."

"Dad, isn't it true that the operator of that secret station is an enemy agent?" Penny asked curiously.

"It's a possibility."

"Why not tell me all about it?"

"Nothing to tell yet, Penny. Confidentially I'll admit I came here hoping to help State authorities find the station. So far I've accomplished nothing."

"What clues have you gained?"

"Now Penny, don't quiz me," Mr. Parker laughed. "I'll tell you everything as soon as I'm free to do so."

"In the meantime, maybe I'll find out for myself!" Penny hinted. Abruptly swinging open the car door, she bolted through the rain to the tent.

Breakfast the next morning was a more cheerful meal than had been expected. During the night the rain had ceased and a hot morning sun soon dried out the drenched canvas. Mr. Parker prepared coffee, eggs and bacon, an unbelievable example of perfect cooking.

"Dad, I didn't think you had it in you!" Penny praised as she sat down on a camp stool beside him. "Maybe you'll develop into a real camper after all."

"Not if I have anything to say about it." Grinning, Mr. Parker dropped two plump fried eggs on his daughter's plate and took the remaining four for himself. "This life could be worse though."

"Dad, what time shall we start for the airport?"

Mr. Parker poured himself a cup of coffee and then answered: "Afraid I won't be able to go with you, Penny."

"But Dad! Louise will be expecting you."

"It's not me she wants to see," Mr. Parker corrected. "I have an important engagement I can't break."

Penny glanced quickly up. She was tempted to ask her father if he intended to see Mrs. Deline. Recalling that she had made her father a promise, she wisely withheld comment. Instead she asked if she might use the car.

"By all means," he consented. "Just go easy on the gasoline."

Breakfast over, dishes were dispatched and the camp put in order. By eleven o'clock Penny and her father were in Sunset Beach.

"Drop me anywhere," Mr. Parker instructed vaguely.

Leaving her father on a street corner, Penny drove slowly toward the airport a mile and a quarter away. There was little travel on the winding highway which curled along the beach. A government jeep whizzed past and two soldiers shouted and waved. Penny waved back.

There was no need to hurry for Louise's plane was not yet due. Penny took her time and enjoyed the ocean scenery. The tide was coming in and gulls free-wheeled over the waves, dipping down at intervals in search of food.

Gazing along the deserted beach, Penny was startled to see a familiar feminine figure hastening toward the lighthouse on Crag Point. The woman wore a white scarf that half obscured her face, yet the girl easily recognized her.

"Mrs. Deline!" she thought, idling the car. "She's certainly going to the lighthouse! I wonder if that gruff old keeper will drive her away as he did me?"

Curious to learn what would happen, the girl drew up at the side of the road. Mrs. Deline was too far away to observe the automobile. Intent only upon her own affairs, she walked swiftly along the beach until she reached the base of the lighthouse.

"Now to see the fun!" chuckled Penny.

The keeper had appeared on the platform and was gazing down upon the visitor. He called something to the woman that Penny could not hear. But to her amazement, Mrs. Deline started up the iron stairway.

Penny waited expectantly. She was certain that the keeper of the light would order Mrs. Deline away. Instead, he greeted her with a hearty handshake as if they were old friends. They entered the lighthouse tower room together, and the heavy door closed behind them.

CHAPTER 9 - A SURPRISE FROM THE SKY

"Well, if that isn't strange!" Penny muttered. "I wasn't permitted to set foot inside the lighthouse, but in goes Mrs. Deline without a single question asked!"

Her curiosity aroused, the girl decided to wait and watch. Twenty minutes elapsed. During that time Mrs. Deline did not reappear. Penny grew tired of her vigil.

"Mrs. Deline evidently intends to stay there a long while," she thought as she drove on. "For all I know, she and the lighthouse keeper may be old friends. They did greet each other as if they were acquainted."

At the airport Penny parked on the crowded lot. She dropped into the lunch room for a sandwich and then wandered out on the cement runway. The noon passenger plane presently was announced through the loudspeaker system. A moment later Penny glimpsed the big silver twin-motor transport gliding down over the tree tops. As it taxied up to unload passengers, she held her breath. Knowing that there had been several last-minute cancellation of tickets, she was afraid that Louise might not be aboard.

But as the door of the big transport swung back, her chum was the second passenger to alight. Fresh and trim in a yellow wool suit, she flung herself into Penny's arms.

"Have a nice trip, Lou?"

"Oh, heavenly! Only it didn't last long enough. We were here almost before I knew we'd started. I nearly lost my ticket to an Army Major too!"

"I was afraid you might not get here," Penny laughed, picking up Louise's light over-night case. "What happened to the Major?"

"Oh, at the last minute he changed his mind, so the company decided I could have my ticket back. And here I am! How's camping?"

"Not much fun so far," Penny confessed truthfully. "But I can feel things starting to pick up."

"We'll have a wonderful time together."

"You just bet we will!" Penny declared with emphasis. "Had anything to eat?"

"Oh, yes, lunch was served on the plane."

"Then we may as well start for camp. I have oodles to tell you, Lou."

Midway to the parking lot, Louise paused, calling attention to a Flying Fortress that was coming in against the wind.

"Let's watch it land," she pleaded. "Did you ever see such a beautiful ship?"

The huge Fortress came in fast for a perfect landing. Crew members began to tumble out through the door. One of the young men in captain's uniform evidently was a passenger for he carried a suitcase.

"Lou!" Penny grasped her chum's arm. "That flier looks like Jerry Livingston!"

"Oh, it couldn't be!"

"All the same, I think it is!"

Penny was so excited that she barely could control her voice. Jerry Livingston was one of her very best friends, a former reporter on the *Riverview Star*. In the days before he had joined the Army Air Force, she and Jerry had shared many an exciting adventure. However, since he had gone away there had been only a few letters and those brief communications had contained no real news.

"It *is* Jerry!" Penny cried an instant later. "Oh, Lou, this must have been the surprise that Dad knew about! How could he keep it from me?"

VOICE FROM THE CAVE

Breaking away from her chum, Penny darted across the runway. As she called Jerry's name, the young man turned toward her. His handsome, wind-tanned face became a brilliant smile. A dozen long strides carried him to her side.

"Penny!" he cried. He didn't hesitate. He just swept her into his arms and kissed her.

"Sorry, Penny," Jerry apologized, his eyes twinkling. "Guess I shouldn't have done that. But when you've not seen your one and only girl for going on a year—"

"Your which?" Penny stammered, too confused to blush.

"You are my one and only, you know," Jerry grinned. "Always were for that matter. Even in the days when we tracked down news stories together."

Louise came hurrying up. Jerry turned to greet her and the conversation became less personal. But from the way Louise smiled, Penny knew she had seen the kiss and would demand lengthy explanations later on.

"Jerry!" she cried, noticing the decorations on his trim uniform. "They've given you the Distinguished Flying Cross! And the Purple Heart! You didn't write a word about that."

"Nothing to write."

Indignantly, the girls pried the story from Jerry. He had piloted a Flying Fortress in a highly successful raid over the Romanian oil fields. To reach its target, the Fortress had flown through flaming refineries, so low to the ground that fire actually had leaped up through the bomb bay of the plane. Swarms of enemy fighter ships had been fought off. Jerry's plane was one of the few to get back to its base safely.

"I was luckier than some of the other fellows," Jerry said modestly. "That was all. Now they've sent me home to rest up for a while."

"Oh, that's marvelous!" Penny said, guiding him toward the waiting car. "You can spend all of your spare time with us!"

Jerry grinned down at her. "I'd like nothing better. But I'm not exactly on furlough."

"I thought you just said—"

"I'm doing a special mission here at Sunset Beach for the Army."

"Anything you dare tell about?"

Jerry helped the girls into the car, stowed the suitcases away, and then slid in beside Penny.

"I can't tell you very much," he replied quietly. "But I can give you a general idea of why I'm here. There's a certain outlaw radio station that has been causing the government considerable annoyance. I've been sent here to try to trace its location."

"And that's why Dad's here too!" Penny cried. "So you two schemers intended to join forces all along! A pity no one could let me know!"

"I didn't want your father to tell you, because until the last minute I wasn't sure I was coming," Jerry explained. "The radio station assignment is only part of the reason why I'm here."

"What's the other?" Penny asked as she started the car.

"I'm on the lookout for an escaped German flier. The fellow escaped from a Canadian prison camp and was traced to this locality."

"And you're supposed to be taking a rest from flying!"

"This assignment will be a vacation."

"I'd call it anything but one," Penny said indignantly. Her face suddenly became grave. "Jerry!"

"Yes?"

"What does that escaped prisoner look like?"

"Oh, I can't describe him. I have a photograph in my brief case. Why do you ask?"

"Maybe I've seen him."

"Where?" Jerry could not hide a smile.

"Why at our camp in the woods!" Excitedly Penny told of the bearded stranger who had robbed the Parker stores of food and clothing. Her description of the man was so vague that Jerry could make little of it.

"I'm afraid your thief isn't the man we're after," he said kindly. "After I get to a hotel and open my luggage, I'll show you his picture."

"And will you let me help you trail him?"

"Oh, sure," Jerry answered, only half meaning it. "By the way, drive me to the Crystal Inn. I have a reservation there."

CHAPTER 9 - A SURPRISE FROM THE SKY

Penny's face fell.

"Anything wrong with the place?" Jerry inquired, observing her change of expression.

Penny shook her head. "The place is all right. It's the people who stay there. Jerry—"

"Yes?"

"Are you susceptible to brunettes?"

"Never noticed it."

"You'll likely meet a Mrs. Deline at the hotel," Penny warned. "Don't have a thing to do with her."

"Why should I?" Jerry was amused.

"She's already made a jelly fish of Dad," Penny went on. "Jerry, stop grinning! This is serious."

"Sorry, I didn't know I was smiling."

"I need your help, Jerry. The truth is, I'm terribly worried about Dad."

"If I know your father, there's no need to worry about him."

"But you don't understand this Mrs. Deline," Penny said desperately. "She's a very clever, scheming woman. Jerry, will you promise to help me try to save Dad from her clutches?"

Jerry managed to keep his face straight. "I'll do my best," he promised.

Penny drew a deep sigh. "Oh, I'm so glad you're here," she murmured gratefully. "With you fighting on my side, the war's as good as won!"

CHAPTER 10 - HELP FROM MR. EMORY

With Jerry at Sunset Beach, the vacation already promised to take on a rosy hue. Penny was so thrilled to be with her friends again that she paid scant heed to her driving. Several times, enroute to the Crystal Inn, Louise had to warn her to steer more carefully.

"Oh, Jerry, now that you're here the fun will start!" Penny declared happily. "You've no idea how dull things have been without you."

"And that goes double," Jerry said with emphasis. "How's your father?"

"Oh, fine!" Penny laughed. "Camping has made him cross though. By the way, did he know you were coming?"

"Yes, I sent him a wire."

"I thought so! Dad's been keeping it from me. Why all the secrecy, I wonder?"

"Well, my trip here isn't exactly a pleasure jaunt. And if I have luck, I'll be gone again in a few days."

"I certainly hope you have no luck then," Penny said with a laugh.

The car drew up at the Crystal Inn and Jerry unloaded his suitcase. He was taller, Penny thought, or at least more filled out. The trim uniform set off his broad shoulders. As he bent to pick up his luggage, a group of women on the hotel veranda turned to stare at him.

"I'll check in and clean up a bit," Jerry said. "Then where can I meet you girls?"

"Oh, we'll be somewhere on the beach," Penny replied carelessly. "Do hurry, Jerry. We have a million things to talk over."

The girls parked the car not far from the hotel. As they walked along, scuffing their shoes in the loose sand, they saw Mrs. Deline coming toward them from the direction of Crag Point.

"She's evidently been at the lighthouse all this time!" Penny commented in an undertone. "Now how did she get in there for a visit when I couldn't?"

Mrs. Deline saw that she would meet the girls. Frowning, she glanced quickly toward the boardwalk as if seeking an avenue of escape. However, she could not avoid meeting them without appearing to do so deliberately.

"How do you do," she greeted Penny coldly.

Penny paused to introduce Louise. Mrs. Deline acknowledged the girl with an indifferent nod. Somewhat confused, Louise nervously twisted a silver ring she wore. It slipped from her finger and fell into the loose sand.

"Oh, how awkward of me!" she exclaimed, and stooped to retrieve it.

The ring buried itself deeper in the sand.

"You'll lose it entirely if you're not careful!" Penny warned. "Here, let me help you."

Getting down on their knees, the girls sifted the sand with their hands. Mrs. Deline seemed amused by their difficulties and did not offer to help.

"Well, I must be getting on to the hotel," she said casually. "I took a long walk this afternoon and I'm tired."

"To the lighthouse?" Penny commented, before she stopped to think.

Mrs. Deline glanced at her sharply. "No, not to the lighthouse," she replied in a tone meant to put the girl in her place. "I shouldn't think of walking that far."

"But I thought I saw you there."

"You saw me?" Mrs. Deline laughed. "Well, my dear, you certainly were mistaken. I walked to the 12th Street bridge. No farther."

CHAPTER 10 - HELP FROM MR. EMORY

Penny started to reply, then thought better of it. There was no point in arguing with Mrs. Deline. However, she was certain she had seen the widow at the lighthouse. Why the woman should deny it she could not imagine.

After Mrs. Deline had gone, Penny and Louise searched in vain for the missing ring. They knew it could not be many inches away, yet it kept eluding them.

"Oh, I can't afford to lose the ring!" Louise wailed.

"How valuable is it?"

"It's not worth much from a money standpoint. I drew it as a prize in a piece of wedding cake and I've always kept it as a good luck piece."

"We'll find it," Penny said confidently. "That is, if the tide doesn't catch us first."

Just as she spoke, a wave came rippling up the beach. It broke only a few feet away, showering the girls with spray and wetting their shoes.

"If the tide flows over this spot, I never will find the ring," Louise cried in vexation. "Such wretched luck!"

"Having trouble?" inquired a deep masculine voice.

Penny and Louise raised their heads. Unnoticed by them, a stranger had approached. The man wore a wet bathing suit plastered with sand. He had on glasses and a moment elapsed before Penny recognized him as the same fisherman who had warned her about the tide at Crag Point.

"I'm George Emory," he introduced himself. "Have you lost something?"

"My ring," Louise explained.

The man helped the girls search for the missing trinket. By now waves were creeping higher and higher on the beach. A particularly big one sent Penny and Louise scurrying for safety.

"It's no use looking any longer for the ring," Louise gave up. "Perhaps I can find it after the tide turns."

"By then it will be washed away," replied Mr. Emory. "Ah! What's this?"

He stooped to pick a shiny object from the sand.

"It's my ring!" Louise cried in delight. "Oh, thank you for finding it!"

The three retreated to higher ground. As Penny and Louise were about to start for the hotel, Mr. Emory suggested that they might like to share a picnic lunch with him. Neither of the girls was hungry, but to offend the man after he had found Louise's ring was unthinkable. Accordingly, they accompanied him to one of the gaily painted wooden umbrellas along the beach. Beneath its shade Mr. Emory spread a paper tablecloth and produced ample supplies of sandwiches, fruit and lemonade.

"Were you expecting to eat all this food yourself?" Penny asked in amazement.

"No, I was hoping to find a companion who would share it," replied Mr. Emory. "The truth is, I'm a pretty lonely old fellow."

Penny and Louise stole a quick look at the stranger. By no stretch of the imagination could they call him old. Judging from appearances, he was not yet forty years old.

"My wife died a few years ago," Mr. Emory explained sadly. "Since then I've been like a ship without a rudder. I have plenty of money, but I don't get much enjoyment out of life. I go wherever it suits my fancy, stay until I weary of it, then move on."

"Oh, I see," Penny murmured with a show of sympathy.

She felt ashamed of herself that the story did not move her more deeply. Mr. Emory evidently was a lonely fellow, deserving of companionship. Yet for some reason, he failed to interest her.

"Have you been at Sunset Beach long?" she inquired politely.

"Oh, about a month. I know every nook and cranny along the shore."

"You do?" Penny asked, and her interest revived. "Are there many caves near Sunset Beach?"

"Plenty of them, though none very close. There are several near the lighthouse, back among the rocks. Crystal Cave probably is the most interesting. Then there are half a dozen scattered on up the shore. Interested in caves?"

"Oh, in a general way," Penny replied carelessly.

"Penny is interested in anything that suggests mystery," Louise volunteered with a grin.

"Mystery?"

"Lou's joking," Penny said quickly. She gave her chum a hard look which was not lost upon Mr. Emory.

"Why, Penny!" Louise refused to be silenced. "Only a few minutes ago you were telling me about a radio broadcast said to come from a cave!"

"That was just my idea," Penny said, confused. She jumped hastily to her feet. "We really should be going, Lou."

"Oh, don't hurry away." Mr. Emory offered Louise another sandwich. "Speaking of mysterious radio stations, I've heard of one that is said to be located in a cave somewhere along these shores. Fact is, I've searched for it."

"You have?" Penny asked, sinking back into the sand. "Any luck?"

"None. But I did manage to kill quite a few afternoons. I take it that your father came to Sunset Beach to help the authorities search for the station. Right?"

"Why, whatever made you think that?" Penny asked, instantly on guard. "Do you know my father?"

"I regret I haven't the honor. I chanced to overhear a conversation at the hotel."

"Oh," Penny murmured. She was certain that the information could have leaked out in only one way. Her father had told Mrs. Deline, who in turn had spread the news about the hotel.

"I trust I'm not inquiring into secrets," Mr. Emory went on cheerfully. "Fact of the matter is, I might be able to help your father."

"I'm sure Dad will want to talk with you."

"I'll look forward to meeting your father. Think you can arrange it?"

"Why, I suppose so," Penny said, though with no great enthusiasm. Again she experienced a queer, uneasy feeling. She did not entirely trust Mr. Emory.

The man smiled and seemed to relax. As the girls arose to leave he tried once more to detain them.

"See that old fellow down the beach?" he inquired, pointing to an aged man who was picking up objects from the sand with a sharp-pointed stick.

"Yes, what about him?" Penny asked, turning to stare. "Just an ordinary beachcomber, isn't he?"

"I'd not call Old Jake Skagway ordinary," Mr. Emory corrected. "If you're really interested in solving the radio station mystery, I'd advise you to keep watch of that rascal."

"But why him?" Penny asked.

"I can't explain," Mr. Emory said with finality. "It's just a tip. Take it or leave it."

Yawning, he stretched himself full length on the sand and turned his back to the girls.

CHAPTER 11 - A MAN OF MYSTERY

The following day when Penny told her father of Mr. Emory's desire to meet him, Mr. Parker showed little interest.

"I've no time to waste getting acquainted with strangers," he said. "Why is the man so eager to know me?"

"He thinks he may be able to help you locate that hidden radio station."

Mr. Parker's annoyance visibly increased. "Penny," he said severely, "you've evidently been talking out of turn."

"I didn't mean to let him know why you're at Sunset Beach, Dad. It sort of slipped out."

Louise, who was washing the breakfast dishes, spoke quickly.

"It was my fault," she insisted. "Penny tried to stop me, but I gave the information before I thought."

"Well, it doesn't matter," Mr. Parker assured her kindly. "I came here mostly for a vacation. If I should be lucky enough to dig up a few facts about the radio station, well and good. If not, no harm will have been done."

"You sent for Jerry to help you?" Penny inquired curiously.

Mr. Parker shook his head. "No, I knew he was coming, but I didn't send for him. If I had, I'm afraid the Army wouldn't have been obliging enough to have filled my order."

Penny helped Louise put away the camp dishes and pick up loose papers. It was only eight-thirty but already most of the work had been done. With Louise to help, camping no longer was a burden. Even Mr. Parker seemed to have moments of enjoying the outdoor life.

"Anyone riding to Sunset Beach with me?" he inquired cheerfully. "I have a date with Jerry this morning."

Penny and Louise both wanted to go. They washed at the brook, changed into becoming "town" dresses, and soon were ready.

At the Crystal Inn, Jerry was not to be found. A clerk explained that the young man had left the hotel a half hour earlier but was expected to return soon.

"He probably went somewhere for breakfast or a walk," Mr. Parker remarked, sinking into a comfortable chair. "I'll wait for him."

Penny and Louise loitered in the lobby. Presently Mrs. Deline came from the dining room and Mr. Parker politely arose to greet her. The widow took a chair beside him and they began to chat in an animated way.

"Let's get away from here!" Penny muttered to Louise. "I don't like the scenery."

The girls went outside into the warm sunshine. Because the Parker automobile was at the curb they climbed into it and sat watching the sea.

"Why do you dislike Mrs. Deline so intensely?" Louise presently asked her chum.

"Because she's aiming to be my stepmother, that's why!"

"Oh, Penny!" Louise laughed outright. "I'm sure you have a mistaken idea about the entire situation. Your father isn't serious in liking her."

"Then he's certainly developed remarkable talents for acting," Penny retorted with a sniff. "I wish we'd never come to Sunset Beach."

"You'd be willing to forego the mystery?"

"Who cares about a radio station?" Penny asked crossly. "Dad won't tell me anything about the case, and probably Jerry won't either. It seems to be one of those affairs for the experts only."

"If I know you, Penny, you'll manage to get in on the affair," Louise said, her eyes twinkling.

Penny turned on the ignition and started the car. "I'm just not interested," she announced flatly. "Mrs. Deline has taken all the fun out of me. Want to go for a ride?"

VOICE FROM THE CAVE

"Where?"

"Oh, just up the beach."

"Isn't it dangerous to drive on the sand?"

"Everyone does it at low tide. The sand is hard and firm along this stretch of beach."

Louise offered no further objection, so Penny drove slowly away from the hotel. The car rode on silken tires, making only a soft swishing sound as it rolled smoothly over the sand.

"Oh, this is fun!" Louise cried in delight.

"We might drive to the lighthouse," Penny proposed, steering to avoid two bathers who crossed in front of the car.

Following the curve of the beach, the girls kept on until the sand became so soft that they were afraid to drive farther. The lighthouse was close by. Penny, curious to learn what sort of reception the keeper would accord her on the second visit, proposed to Louise that they call there.

"If he let Mrs. Deline visit the tower why can't we?" she argued. "Come along, let's try to get in!"

Abandoning the car on the beach, they waded through the dunes, climbed a fence, and ultimately reached the base of the tower. No one seemed to be in evidence. Penny started boldly up the iron steps. However, before she had gone very far, the keeper, Jim McCoy, came out on the platform.

"Didn't I tell you no visitors are allowed here?" he called down angrily.

"I saw a lady come here yesterday!" Penny returned.

"You must have dreamed it," retorted the lighthouse keeper. "No visitors allowed. Don't make me tell you again!"

Penny retreated, decidedly crushed.

"You asked for it, kitten," Louise teased as they walked toward the car. "I don't blame the keeper for not wanting visitors."

"Mrs. Deline was there," Penny insisted stubbornly. "Why should he deny it?"

Half way to the car, the girls paused to pick up a few large shells lying in the deep sand. The task became an absorbing one. Before they realized it, the sun was high overhead and their faces were being burned by the direct rays.

"Let's go," Louise urged. "The tide turned a long while ago. We should be returning to the hotel."

"Okay," Penny agreed. She stooped to pick up another shell. As she straightened, she observed an old man in ragged clothing coming down the beach.

"Lou," she said in a low tone, "there's that same man Mr. Emory was telling us about!"

"The beachcomber?" Louise turned to stare.

"Yes, and he's coming this way. Perhaps it might be worth while to watch him."

"He's not seen us yet."

Penny glanced about for a hiding place. The only one that offered was a huge sand dune. Pulling Louise along with her, she crouched down out of sight.

In a moment the old beachcomber came along. He was whistling and seemed to have not a care in the world. His face, viewed at close range, was weather-beaten, his hair uncombed, and his clothing had not been washed in many a day.

"What's so mysterious about him?" Louise whispered. "Why did Mr. Emory say he'd bear watching?"

"Maybe he's not really a beachcomber," Penny returned, low. "He may be an Enemy Agent in disguise."

"You have Enemy Agents on the brain!" Louise chuckled. "Likewise, man-snatching widows."

The beachcomber passed within a few feet of the girls. He crossed the courtyard of the lighthouse and was seen to take a trail which led amid the rocks.

"Lou, perhaps he's going to one of the caves!" Penny cried. "You know Mr. Emory said this locality is honeycombed with them."

"Let him go," Louise answered indifferently. "It's lunch time and I'm hungry."

"Your appetite will have to wait. I'm going to follow that man!"

"Oh, Penny."

"But this may be important."

"And it may be just another of your so-called bright ideas," Louise retorted. "Well, lead on, and let's get it over with."

CHAPTER 11 - A MAN OF MYSTERY

The beachcomber already had disappeared amid the mass of piled-up rock farther back from shore. Penny had marked the locality well with her eye. She was able to lead Louise to the place where he had vanished.

"See, there's a well-worn trail," she indicated triumphantly. "He must have taken it."

They followed the path, and a moment later caught a fleeting glimpse of the beachcomber. At times the trail was so narrow that the girls barely could squeeze between the rocks. Wind whistled around the cliffs, whipping hair and blowing skirts.

Unexpectedly, Penny, who was in the lead, came to the low entranceway of a cave.

"He must have gone in there!" she declared excitedly. "Listen!"

From deep within the cave the girls could hear a strange sound.

"Rushing water!" Louise said in awe. "The Cave must have a waterfall or an underground river."

"We'll soon know." Penny started into the cave only to have Louise clutch at her hand.

"Don't be silly, Penny. We have no flashlight."

"But we can't let that beachcomber get away. We want to learn what he does."

"I can bear up without knowing."

"Well, I can't," Penny announced with equal firmness.

"But it may be dangerous. Let's go back to the hotel and get Jerry or your father."

Penny hesitated, then shook her head. "You stay here if you like, Lou," she replied. "I'm going inside."

Before her chum could detain her, she stooped low and crawled into the narrow, dark tunnel.

CHAPTER 12 - CAUGHT BY THE TIDE

Unwilling to be left behind, Louise followed her chum into the dark cavern. Once she and Penny were well beyond the yawning mouth of the cave, they could not see a foot ahead of them. Guided by the sound of rushing water, they groped their way along a damp wall.

"This is awful!" Louise whispered nervously. "Let's turn back."

Penny might have yielded to her chum's coaxing but at that moment the tunnel broadened out and became lighter. Directly ahead a series of steps led down to a lower room of the cave.

"This place must be safe enough or steps wouldn't have been built here," she whispered. "Don't be nervous, Lou. We may discover something important."

Louise muttered that they were more likely to break their necks. However, she cautiously followed Penny down the rock-hewn steps. Half way down, they both paused. From below came a weird sound.

"What was that?" Louise whispered.

"It sounded for all the world like the note of a pipe organ!" Penny observed. "There it is again—a different tone this time."

Noiselessly the girls moved on down the steps. Ahead of them they now could see a moving light which undoubtedly was a flash lantern carried by the beachcomber. Drawing closer, they saw the man himself. In the great cavern his shadow appeared grotesque and huge.

"What is he doing?" Louise whispered in awe.

The man was unaware that he had been followed. He stood in the center of the great chamber, gazing with wrapt expression at the stalagmites which rose in strange formations from the cave floor. The girls could hear him muttering to himself. At the risk of being seen they moved closer.

"Music! Music!" the old man mumbled. "Talk about your pipe organs! They ain't in it with *this*!"

He held a long stick in his hand and with it began to explore the row of stalagmites, striking them one by one, at first with a slow tempo and then faster and faster. The weird sounds echoed and reached through the galleries of the cavern.

"Pretty!" the old man prattled. "It's the music o' Heaven. There ain't no music to equal it."

Again the beachcomber struck the stalagmites, listening raptly while the sounds died slowly away.

"Come on, Penny," Louise urged, tugging at her hand. "Let's get out of here. That old goof has lost his buttons."

Decidedly crestfallen, Penny permitted herself to be pulled along the passage and up the steps. As the girls groped their way to the cave's mouth, they still could hear the weird echoing tones.

"That was a good joke on you!" Louise teased. "You thought you were going to find a hidden radio station!"

"Well, we did find a cave," Penny said defensively.

"We didn't exactly discover it," Louise amended. "This must be Crystal Cave. Seemingly that old beachcomber regards it as his own personal property."

"Mr. Emory certainly gave us a wrong steer. A mysterious character, my eye!"

"You'll admit that the old fellow is interesting," Louise laughed. "However, I doubt he'll warrant much attention from the FBI."

"All right, laugh," Penny retorted grimly. "You think my detective efforts are a joke anyway."

"No, I don't, Penny. But I will say I doubt you'll have success tracing a hidden radio station. After all, it's a problem that has the State authorities baffled. Not to mention Uncle Sam's Army."

CHAPTER 12 - CAUGHT BY THE TIDE

The girls stepped from the cave out into the brilliant sunshine. Gazing toward the sea, they were amazed to see how high the tide had risen. Giant waves were washing very close to the Parker automobile left on the beach.

"Ye fishes!" Penny exclaimed in horror. "I forgot all about the car!"

"And the tide's coming in fast!"

"The Point will be cut off in a few more minutes!" Penny added, recalling Mr. Emory's warning. "We'll have to travel, and travel fast!"

Scrambling down from the rocks, the girls plunged through the dunes to the beach. A wind was blowing and the sea had an angry look.

"If just one wave strikes the car, the wheels will sink in the sand, and then we'll be in it!" Penny cried.

With increasing alarm she noted that sand was damp within a foot of the rear wheels. And as she jerked open the car door, a greedy wave nipped again at the rubber.

"We'll soon be out of here," Louise said encouragingly.

Penny stepped on the starter and to her relief the motor caught instantly. In great haste she turned the car around, circling away from the inrushing sea.

"Careful!" Louise warned. "The sand is dreadfully soft this far up shore."

Too late Penny realized the same thing. She could feel the car starting to bog down. The motor began to labor. Then the car stalled completely.

"We're stuck!" she gasped.

Both girls sprang out to look at the wheels. Their spirits sank. On one side, front and rear tires were bogged deep in sand.

"Start the engine again!" Louise urged desperately. "I'll try to push."

Penny obeyed, but her chum's puny strength made not the slightest impression upon the car. It could not be moved a foot. The spinning wheels only drove deeper and deeper into the sand.

"What shall we do?" Louise asked helplessly. She turned to stare at the incoming sea. Each wave was breaking a little closer to the car.

"This place will be under in another twenty minutes," Penny calculated. "Even if the car isn't washed away, the salt water will ruin it. How did we ever get into such a mess?"

"Just by being careless. If only we weren't so far from the hotel!"

"I'll run to the lighthouse," Penny decided desperately. "Maybe the keeper will help us."

Both girls were badly frightened, not for their own safety, but because they feared that the car would be damaged beyond repair. Once the waves began to strike it, it would sink deeper and deeper into the sand. Salt water would corrode all of the bright chromium.

"We've no time to waste!" Penny cried, darting away.

The girls plunged through the sand drifts to the lighthouse. Evidently the keeper already had observed their plight, for he was standing on the upper platform peering down into the courtyard.

"Our car is stuck in the sand!" Penny shouted. "Can you help us get it out?"

"No, I can't," the keeper answered gruffly. "You should have watched the tide."

"There's no one else to help us," Penny pleaded. "Just a little push—"

"I'm forbidden to leave my post."

"Then will you telephone to the Inn? Or to a garage?"

"I could 'phone but it wouldn't do any good," the keeper said reluctantly. "Your car will be under water before a tow-car could get here."

Exasperated by the man's unwillingness to help, Louise and Penny ran back to the car. Already waves were lapping against the rear wheels. The situation seemed hopeless.

"Shall I try to push again?" Louise asked.

"It wouldn't do any good. We're not strong enough." In desperation, Penny's gaze wandered down the deserted shore. Suddenly she saw a lone fisherman who was wading through the surf. She recognized him as George Emory.

"He'll help us!" she cried confidently.

VOICE FROM THE CAVE

The girls shouted Mr. Emory's name. Apparently he heard, for he turned his head quickly. Their plight, they thought, must be instantly evident, but Mr. Emory did not seem to comprehend. He waved his hand as if in friendly greeting, and then, reeling in his fish line, turned and walked away from them.

CHAPTER 13 - A HIDDEN PACKAGE

"Why, Mr. Emory doesn't understand!" Penny cried, aghast. "Can't he see that we're stuck here with the tide rolling in?"

The girls shouted again and again. If the man heard, he gave no sign.

"I don't believe he wanted to help us!" Penny declared furiously. "Probably he's afraid he'll over-strain himself pushing!"

Unwilling to give up without a last try, she sprang into the car and once more started the engine. It roared and labored but could not pull the vehicle. Sick with despair, Penny allowed the motor to idle. She slumped behind the steering wheel, only to straighten suddenly as she thought she heard her name called.

Louise too heard the cry for she turned quickly toward the main road some yards back from the beach. A young man in uniform was running across the dunes toward the girls.

"It's Jerry!" Penny cried jubilantly. "He'll help us!"

"He will if he can," Louise corrected. "The tide's coming in so fast now. I doubt anyone can get us out of here now."

Jerry did not waste time asking questions. Taking in the situation at a glance, he instructed Penny to remain at the wheel. With the motor racing, he and Louise pushed with all their strength. At first the rear wheels kept spinning in the sand. A great wave slapped the rear end of the car, spraying Louise from head to foot.

"It's no use!" she gasped. "We can't do it."

"Yes, we can!" Jerry insisted. "Try once more, Louise."

Again they pushed and this time the car actually moved a few feet before it bogged down. Encouraged, Jerry and Louise tried harder than before. The wheels suddenly struck firm sand, dug in, and the car began to creep forward. Penny kept it moving until she was sure the footing beneath the tires was solid. Then she pulled up so that Jerry and Louise might leap aboard.

"Drive as fast as you can for the hotel!" Jerry instructed crisply. "We'll be lucky to make it."

Where an hour before the roadway along the beach had been wide and ample, there now was only a fringe of white sand. To avoid the incoming waves, Penny had to drive dangerously close to the dunes. And midway to the hotel, they came to a flooded stretch of beach.

"We'll have to risk it," Jerry advised as Penny hesitated to drive on.

The water was not deep but the sand was wet and treacherous. Choosing a moment between breakers, Penny braved it, and to her intense relief the car rolled through without sinking down.

"It's clear sailing now," Jerry said as a wider strip of beach opened before them. "We're well beyond the Point."

Mr. Emory was walking along the shore and as the car went past, he waved his hand in a friendly way. Penny did not bother to return the salute, pretending she did not see him.

"I'm sure he knew we were in trouble and didn't want to help," she told Jerry. "The more I see of that man the less I like him."

"Who is he anyhow?"

"Just a vacationer. He got Lou and me all excited yesterday with his talk about that hidden radio station."

"How do you mean?" Jerry asked with interest.

Penny repeated the conversation, and mentioned how Mr. Emory had suggested that the old beachcomber was a mysterious character that would bear watching.

"Not old Jake Skagway?" Jerry asked, amused.

"I believe that was his name."

"Jake's the only beachcomber I know hereabouts. He makes his living picking up things on the beach and selling them. Folks say he buries some of his loot in the caves."

"How do you know so much about him, Jerry?"

"Oh, I used to run down to Sunset Beach real often years ago. I know this locality like a book. Guess that's why the Army sent me here to do a little scouting around."

Penny waited expectantly, but Jerry offered no more information as to the reason for his visit to Sunset Beach.

"Probably Lou and I were taken in by Jake Skagway," she admitted after a moment. "If we hadn't followed him into the cave, we certainly wouldn't have involved ourselves in such difficulties."

Upon reaching the Crystal Inn a few minutes later, the girls searched for Mr. Parker. He was nowhere to be found. After waiting for a time, they left the car with Jerry and hiked to the forest camp. There the early afternoon was devoted to camp tasks. When Mr. Parker still did not come, Penny proposed that they return to Sunset Beach for a plunge in the surf.

"Too cold," Louise shivered.

"Well, let's go down to Sunset Beach anyhow," Penny urged. "I get restless just sitting here in camp."

"You know you want to see Jerry again," Louise teased. "'Fess up."

"All right, I do want to see him," Penny admitted unabashed. "Jerry's my very best friend. I've not been with him in months and I suppose in a few days he'll be shot off to goodness-knows-where."

"He's not told you very much about why he came here."

"No," Penny said briefly. The subject was a sore one with her. She felt that both her father and Jerry were keeping secrets.

The tide was still high when the girls reached the beach, but the flow was outward. Sprawling in the warm sand, they watched the gulls.

"Wonder what became of Jerry and Dad?" Penny speculated. "They're probably together somewhere."

"Or with Mrs. Deline," Louise suggested wickedly.

She was sorry that she had spoken for Penny's face immediately became as black as a thundercloud.

"Sorry," Louise apologized. "I was only joking."

Penny continued to scowl for at that moment she glimpsed Mrs. Deline walking rapidly down the beach. The widow came from the direction of the lighthouse and was alone. To avoid the incoming waves she waded ankle deep through the great sand ridges along the drift fence.

"That's queer," Penny muttered, sitting up.

"What is?"

"Why, Mrs. Deline apparently has been at the lighthouse again. What's she doing now?"

The widow had paused. Carefully she gazed up and down the deserted shore, but she did not see Penny and Louise who were hidden from view by a sand dune. However, by raising up slightly, they could see her plainly.

Mrs. Deline carried a package of considerable size under her arm. Seemingly satisfied that no one was at hand to observe her actions, she moved swiftly to one of the sand dunes near the drift fence. As the girls watched in amazement, she dug a deep hole and buried the package. Her work completed, she carefully brushed sand over the spot and obliterated her own footprints one by one.

"What was the idea of that?" Louise asked in bewilderment.

"That's what I want to know!" Penny muttered. "We'll wait until she leaves and then find out the contents of that package!"

But Mrs. Deline did not immediately go away. Instead she sat down in the sand close by. The girls could not see very well but they thought she was writing something on the skirt of her white suit.

"Why is she doing that?" Louise asked in bewilderment.

"I'll bet a cookie she's writing down the location of what she hid in the sand dune!" Penny speculated. "That's so she can find it again!"

"But why write it on her skirt? And why should she hide anything here on the beach?"

"Because she's a spy!" Penny declared triumphantly. "I've been suspicious of her from the first!"

CHAPTER 13 - A HIDDEN PACKAGE

"Yes, you have, darling," agreed Louise. "But would a spy necessarily hide a package? If Mrs. Deline had information to communicate wouldn't she send it to her superiors? Besides, Sunset Beach isn't even an important manufacturing town."

"That's true. But I've heard Dad say that the Coast Guards watch this place closely. Because of its isolation and jagged coastline it's considered a likely spot for surprise night landings by the Enemy."

"Only this morning you thought old Jake Skagway was a rascal," Louise chuckled. "You don't catch me falling for your theories this time."

"Then you have no interest in that hidden package?"

"Of course I have! I merely don't agree that Mrs. Deline is a spy."

"Quiet!" Penny warned. "Here she comes!"

Mrs. Deline had arisen from the sand and came rapidly down the beach. She did not see the girls until she was very close to them. Involuntarily, she paused, and looked somewhat disconcerted. Recovering, she spoke coldly.

"Hello," Penny responded, her gaze on the woman's white flannel skirt. It bore not a single tell-tale mark.

Mrs. Deline went on down the beach.

"You see," Louise whispered when the woman was beyond hearing, "she didn't write anything on her dress."

"But we saw her do it!"

"We only thought we did."

"Maybe she wrote it in invisible ink."

"Oh, Penny, you certainly have an imagination," Louise sighed.

"I suppose I imagined about the package too?"

"No, she really did bury something in the sand."

"Then what are we waiting for?" Penny demanded, leaping to her feet. "Let's dig it up, and then maybe we'll have the answer to a few of our questions."

CHAPTER 14 - VOICE FROM THE CAVE

From a distance Penny and Louise had marked well the spot where Mrs. Deline had buried the package. But as they approached the drift fence all of the dunes seemed strikingly similar in appearance. They could not agree as to the exact mound which contained the hidden package.

"It was buried in this one, I think," Penny said, starting to dig. "Mrs. Deline certainly did a good job of covering her tracks."

"You're wasting time working on that dune," Louise insisted. "I'll get busy over here and turn up the package in nothing flat."

Selecting a mound of sand several feet from Penny, she began to dig with a will. The mysterious package proved elusive. Scarcely had the girls started work than a few raindrops splattered down.

"Oh, it's going to storm!" Louise exclaimed, turning startled eyes toward the dark sea.

The rain came down faster and faster. Faced with a choice of abandoning the search or being drenched, the girls decided to make a dash for the hotel.

As they darted up the steps at the Crystal Inn, they were surprised to see Mrs. Deline sitting on the veranda. A spyglass lay in her lap. Whether she had been watching the sea or their own antics they had no way of knowing.

"Have you seen my father, Mrs. Deline?" Penny asked, shaking the raindrops from her flying hair.

"Indeed, I don't keep track of his whereabouts," Mrs. Deline replied coldly. "By the way, did you find what you were searching for in the sand?"

The question caught Penny off guard. She stammered a few words which only caused the widow to smile in a knowing, amused way.

"I don't mind telling you what I buried in the sand," she resumed. "It may save you a little trouble. The package contained nothing but fish bones."

"Fish bones!"

"Yes, I had just visited my friend, Jim McCoy, at the lighthouse. It's most difficult to bury anything there because of so many rocks. He asked me to dispose of the scraps for him."

"Oh," Penny murmured, completely deflated.

"I've been watching you girls through the spyglass," Mrs. Deline went on. "It really was amusing."

"I can imagine," Penny agreed grimly. "Oh, well, I'm glad to provide a little amusement for this dead place."

She and Louise retreated until they were screened from the widow by a potted palm.

"I guess she scored on you that time, Penny," Louise commented. "So we wasted our strength digging for garbage!"

"You needn't rub it in."

"But it's all so silly. Why don't we try to like Mrs. Deline, Penny?"

"I'll leave that job up to you. Furthermore, how do I know she was telling the truth? Maybe she just handed us that story so we wouldn't go on digging in the dunes!"

"That's so!" Louise acknowledged. "Mrs. Deline isn't the type to be doing gracious little jobs for anyone."

"If Jim McCoy asked her to bury a package of garbage, she would have disposed of it long before she did," Penny reasoned. "Instead, she walked quite a distance down shore. Then she seemed to select a particular dune, as if by pre-arrangement."

"You think she may have hidden something there expecting another person to pick it up?"

CHAPTER 14 - VOICE FROM THE CAVE

"That's my theory, Lou. Oh, I wish this rain would let up."

Restlessly Penny walked to a window. The rain showed signs of slackening. And as she watched, a taxi drew up in front of the hotel. Jerry Livingston leaped out.

"Wait for me!" he instructed the driver. "I'll be right back."

Penny and Louise managed to block Jerry's path as he came hurrying into the hotel.

"Hello, girls," he greeted them offhanded. "Want to go for a drive into the country?"

"We certainly do," Penny accepted for both. "What's our destination?"

"Tell you on the way," Jerry answered.

He disappeared into an elevator, but was back in the lobby within a few minutes. Taking Penny and Louise each by an elbow, he escorted them to the waiting cab.

"In a way, this is a secret trip," he said after he had given directions to the driver. "Ever see a radio monitoring truck?"

"Never even heard of one," Penny replied. "What is it?"

"Well, we have a truck equipped so that our instruments pick up the direction from which any short wave broadcast is sent. It's not generally known that the Army's at work here, so whatever you girls see you must keep under your sunbonnets."

The taxi sped along the country road, following a route that was unfamiliar to the girls. By the time it drew up several miles from Sunset Beach the rain had ceased.

"Tumble out," Jerry said, opening the cab door. "This is the end of the line."

He went ahead, breaking a hole in the tall hedge at one side of the road. Eagerly the girls followed him through the gap. In a clearing just beyond a clump of saplings stood what appeared to be an ordinary covered Army truck.

An enlisted man came toward Jerry and the girls, saluting smartly.

"Are you picking up any signals?" Jerry asked him.

"Nothing yet, sir. The weather hasn't been very favorable."

"You've had your equipment set up here two days now?"

"Right, sir."

"It's not likely we'll get anything today or tonight," Jerry replied. "Oh, well, we'll have to have patience. Sooner or later the station will go on the air again, and then we'll learn its location."

Louise and Penny were curious to learn more about the monitoring truck. Jerry took them inside, introduced them to the officers, and showed them the radio apparatus.

"Our truck is equipped with rotating antennae," he explained. "Whenever the unknown station starts to broadcast we'll be able to swing our loops toward the signals. Then we chart the signals and where the lines intercept, the station is located."

"As you explain it, Jerry, finding any radio station is a simple matter."

"It is, providing the station doesn't move in the meantime. Unfortunately, Mr. Voice from the Cave is an elusive fellow."

"You have no idea who the man may be?"

"No, he's known to FBI agents only as B4 which is a code number."

"What is the purpose behind the broadcasts?" Louise inquired. "Enemy propaganda?"

"We know that the station is enemy owned and operated," Jerry replied. "So far that's about all we do know, for we've been unable to break the code. We suspect that persons connected with the station may be aiding German prisoners to escape from the country."

"Prisoners originally held in Canada?" Penny inquired.

"Yes, they've been aided by a ring of very clever spies."

Penny was silent as she thought over the information. There were many questions she longed to ask.

"Jerry—" she began, but just then there came an interruption.

In the Army truck an officer had adjusted his earphones. His attitude as he listened was one of tense expectancy.

"Picking up any signals?" Jerry demanded.

The other man nodded. "Something's coming in! Yes, it's our friend, the Voice. In just a minute we should know exactly where the station is located."

Jerry and the girls remained in the truck, eagerly awaiting a report from the efficient men who manned the radio direction finders.

"Okay, we've got it charted!" came the terse announcement a moment later.

"Where's the station located?" Jerry demanded eagerly. "Let's see the chart."

It was thrust into his hand. Jerry stared at the intercepting lines and then at a map of the district.

"Why, the station seems to be located along the shore!" he exclaimed. "Apparently in one of the caves—Crystal Cave I'd judge."

"That's the cave where Louise and I were!" Penny exclaimed. "But we saw no shortwave radio apparatus. Only crazy old Skagway who was playing a tune on the stalagmites."

"All the same, direction finders don't lie. The broadcast came from Crystal Cave! But that doesn't mean the station will be there fifteen minutes from now."

"What's to be done?" Penny asked. "Can't the Voice be caught before he has a chance to move his portable outfit?"

"A message already has been sent to Headquarters. Army men should be on their way to the cave now."

"Jerry, we're not far from Crystal Cave ourselves!" Penny exclaimed, her eyes dancing with excitement. "Can't we go there too?"

"We can and will!" Jerry laughed. "But if we expect to catch our friend, the Voice, there's no time to lose. Come along, girls, if you're traveling with me."

CHAPTER 15 - AFTERGLOW

Penny sprawled on the grass beside the dying embers of the camp fire. Listlessly, and with very bad aim, she hurled acorns at a brown squirrel chattering overhead.

"You've been in a bad mood ever since we got back from Crystal Cave," Louise observed, coming out of the tent. "But why take it out on that poor creature?"

Penny raised herself on an elbow. She scowled and did not reply.

Louise moved over to the fire, seating herself on a log beside her chum.

"Oh, brace up," she said, slipping an arm about Penny's shoulders. "In all my life I've never seen you act so discouraged."

"I feel lower than the worms. Nothing's gone right since we came to Sunset Beach."

"On the contrary, I can't see that anything has gone so very wrong."

"Wasn't our trip to the Crystal Cave a bust?" Penny demanded.

"Well, it wasn't a success."

Louise smiled wryly at the recollection. With Jerry and the Army men, she and Penny had spent the afternoon searching various caves along the water front. Not a trace had been found of the mysterious radio station which so plagued local authorities. The search had been a long and exhausting one. In the end, though the others kept on, she and Penny had been compelled to give up.

"My feet hurt yet from scrambling over the rocks," Penny declared. "I suppose Jerry and those Army officers will keep searching half the night."

"And I'll warrant they never do find the station," Louise contributed. "This is one mystery I wish you had never stumbled into, Penny."

"I'm beginning to feel the same way, Lou. This is supposed to be a vacation. I'd like to see Dad and Jerry once in awhile."

"So that's what's bothering you!"

"Well, you know Jerry will be here only a few days at most," Penny said defensively. "I've barely had a chance to say 'hello' to him. Dad's always down at the hotel too."

"What you crave seems to be male companionship."

Penny tossed a stick of wood on the fire, making the sparks fly. "I could do with a little," she admitted. "Life is too dull here."

"Dull?" Louise gazed at her chum suspiciously.

"It's no use being surrounded by mystery if one can't get into the thick of it. So far all the adventure has by-passed us."

"We might stir up a little excitement by looking for that package Mrs. Deline buried in the sand."

"Not today," Penny said with a sigh. "Too tired. Besides, I told Jerry about it and he wasn't much impressed."

"So that's the reason for your gloom," Louise remarked wisely. "As a detective you don't rate."

"Something like that. Jerry met Mrs. Deline at the hotel today and he thought her a very charming lady."

"Oh!" Louise laughed. "No wonder you're all smashed to bits!"

Penny got up from the grass and began preparations for supper. She peeled a pan of potatoes and opened a can of corn.

"We need a bucket of water from the spring," she said suggestively. "Want to help me carry it?"

"I will," Louise agreed without enthusiasm.

The trail led up a steep path to a rocky ledge from which cool spring water gushed out of a steel pipe. Penny drank deeply and then hung her tin bucket over the outlet to fill.

"It's starting to get dark," she observed, noticing how shadowy the woods had grown. "I hope Dad returns to camp soon."

"Someone's coming now," Louise remarked as her keen ears detected the sound of footsteps on the trail below.

"Probably one of the rangers."

Penny unhooked the water bucket from the pipe, and the girls started down the trail, carrying it between them. Emerging from among the trees, they glimpsed a figure below them. A woman in a dark cloak who carried a picnic hamper, was walking rapidly up the winding trail.

Penny stopped so suddenly that she spilled water on her sandals.

"Lou, that's Mrs. Deline!" she whispered.

"What of it, pet? She's evidently going on a picnic."

"At this time of day? And alone?"

"Well, that part of it does seem a bit odd."

Penny pulled her chum into the bushes beside the path. Crouching low beside their water bucket, they allowed the woman to pass. Looking neither to the right nor left, she hastened on up the trail.

"She seems to be in a big hurry," Penny commented, coming out of hiding. "Now where do you suppose she's going?"

"Probably to the cabin. One of your ranger friends told me about a rustic place farther up the trail. It was built especially for the enjoyment of the public."

"But why would Mrs. Deline go there alone?"

"Maybe she intends to meet someone."

"Lou, that's probably what she is going to do!" Penny exclaimed. "Let's follow her and find out."

"What about supper?"

"Who cares for food?" Penny demanded. "If Dad comes home he can rustle a little for himself. It's more important that we follow Mrs. Deline."

"Okay," Louise agreed, "only I'm in no mood to walk very far. Remember, we've had one wild chase today."

Leaving the water bucket behind the bushes, the girls set out in pursuit of Mrs. Deline. Not without admiration they acknowledged that the widow was a better trail climber than they. Though the hamper she carried evidently was heavy, she fairly skimmed up the rough trail. Penny and Louise fell farther and farther behind.

"She's heading for the cabin all right," Penny puffed. "Of course she intends to meet someone. Otherwise, she'd have had her picnic on the beach or some place closer to the hotel."

A clearing opened up through a gap in the trees. Mrs. Deline paused as she came within view of the rustic log cabin and gazed carefully about. The girls saw her look at her wrist watch.

"She has an appointment with someone," Penny declared.

Mrs. Deline walked to the door of the cabin and tested it to make certain that it was unlocked. She did not go inside. Instead, she set down the hamper and gazed slowly about the clearing. Louise and Penny, at the fringe of woods, saw her start as she looked directly toward them.

"She's seen us!" Louise gasped.

"We'll have to go out and meet her," Penny decided instantly. "Let's pretend we just happened to be coming this way. But we'll stick around and see who she's meeting."

Mrs. Deline stiffened visibly as the girls sauntered out of the woods toward her.

"Well, this is a surprise meeting you," she said in a tone none too friendly. "Is your camp located near here?"

"Down the trail a short distance," Penny replied, thoroughly enjoying the widow's discomfiture. "Having a picnic?"

"Why, yes. I love the outdoors and thought I'd take a hike this afternoon."

"It's rather late for a picnic," Penny said pointedly.

"It took me longer to get here than I expected."

CHAPTER 15 - AFTERGLOW

In an effort to discourage her young annoyers, Mrs. Deline pushed open the door of the cabin. Before she could pick up the hamper, Penny seized it.

"Let me," she said quickly. "My how heavy! All this food for one person?"

"Certainly," Mrs. Deline answered. "Who else?"

Penny set the hamper on the table. Deliberately she raised the lid. The basket was filled with food, enough for a dozen persons, and in the bottom she saw a folded wool blanket. Beneath the blanket were several bulky garments which she took to be men's clothing. Before she could see plainly, Mrs. Deline jerked the lid of the hamper into place.

"Please!" she said with emphasis.

"I was only trying to be helpful," Penny said, pretending to look injured. "Don't you want Lou and me to dust off the table and spread out the picnic things?"

"I do not. If you'll excuse me for saying so, I came on this picnic to be alone. I enjoy solitude."

"But it's getting dark," Penny argued. "We wouldn't think of deserting you. The cabin has no light."

"I don't mind the dark. Anyway, I brought candles. I really prefer to be alone."

Thus dismissed, Louise started to leave. Penny lingered, trying to think of some excuse. Just then, from somewhere in the woods, she heard a shrill whistle unlike any bird call.

"What was that?" she asked alertly.

"I heard nothing," said Mrs. Deline.

Nevertheless, a moment later the woman sauntered to an open cabin window. Deliberately she turned her back to the girls, trying to block their view. Quickly she raised and lowered her handkerchief.

The movement was deftly executed, but swift though it was, Penny saw and understood. Mrs. Deline had signaled to an unseen person beyond the fringe of trees!

CHAPTER 16 - SUSPICION

Penny moved swiftly to the open cabin door, gazing toward the darkening woods. No one was visible amid the shadows. Yet she was certain that Mrs. Deline had signaled to someone lurking among the trees.

The widow had turned from the window to unfasten the lid of the picnic hamper.

"Since you girls are here you may as well stay and share my supper," she said without warmth. "There's enough food for all."

Louise's chin tilted proudly. The invitation was grudgingly given, and she meant to decline. Penny forestalled her by saying:

"How nice of you, Mrs. Deline! Of course we'll be delighted to remain."

Mrs. Deline made no reply, though obviously she had not expected an acceptance. Irritably she laid out the picnic dishes—sandwiches, a salad, cake, cookies, and fruit—all carefully prepared and cooked at the hotel kitchen.

"You certainly did bring plenty of food for one person," Penny commented, helping herself to a chicken sandwich. "Isn't that clothing in the bottom of the basket?"

"Only a blanket." Mrs. Deline closed the lid firmly. "I thought I might need it if I should sit on the damp ground."

Hungry as bears, Penny and Louise did not try to curb their healthy, young appetites. Mrs. Deline, on the other hand, scarcely nibbled at the food. Several times she arose and paced nervously to the window.

"It's growing dark and I should return to the hotel," she said the instant the girls had finished eating. "I'll not bother to repack the lunch basket."

"Oh, we'll help you pick up everything," Penny offered.

"Please don't bother. I'll merely pay the hotel for the basket."

Penny was convinced that Mrs. Deline deliberately intended to leave the hamper behind. Despite the deep inroads she and Louise had made, considerable food remained. It occurred to her that the widow hoped to leave what remained so that the person hiding in the woods might come to the cabin for it after the party had gone.

"I can't be bothered with a heavy basket," Mrs. Deline said impatiently. "We'll just leave it on the table."

"Oh, the rangers wouldn't like to have us leave food here," Penny protested. "It will only take a minute to clean up everything."

Disregarding Mrs. Deline's order, she began to repack the remains of the lunch.

"But I don't wish to carry the basket all the way to the hotel!"

"Louise and I will help you."

Tossing her head, Mrs. Deline walked out of the cabin, allowing the door to slam behind her. Louise and Penny finished packing the lunch and hastened down the trail in pursuit.

"Maybe we shouldn't cross her so," Louise whispered uneasily. "I think she intended to meet someone here!"

"I'm sure of it," agreed Penny. "We spiked her little plan. I have an idea who she intended to meet too!"

"Who?"

Penny could not answer, for by this time she and Louise were practically at Mrs. Deline's heels. The widow was walking as fast as she could.

"You'll have to keep the basket," she told the girls irritably. "I'm sure I'll never carry it back to the hotel."

All the way to the Parker camp Mrs. Deline ignored Penny and Louise. And as they bade her goodbye, she barely responded.

CHAPTER 16 - SUSPICION

"Can't we drive you down to the hotel in the car?" Penny offered, feeling slightly ashamed of her actions.

"Thank you, no," the widow answered icily. "You've done quite enough for one day." She vanished down the darkening road.

After Mrs. Deline was beyond view, the girls retraced their way to the spring for the water bucket. As they approached, they thought for a moment that they heard retreating footsteps. The realization that they were alone in the woods, made them a bit nervous. Hurriedly they recovered the bucket and carried it to camp.

"Now tell me what you think, Penny!" Louise commanded when they were inside the tent.

"Why, it's clear as crystal." Penny struck a match to the wick of the gasoline lantern and hung it on a hook of the tent pole. "Mrs. Deline went to the cabin intending to meet someone. She carried extra food, a blanket, and if I'm not mistaken, clothing for a man."

"You thought she signaled from the window?"

"I'm sure she did, Lou. She warned the person, whoever he was, not to approach. She hoped by leaving the basket behind to get it into his hands after we'd gone."

"You thwarted her in that."

"We did together," Penny chuckled. Her face suddenly became sober. "Lou—"

"Yes?"

"It just occurred to me! Maybe the man she intended to meet was the same fellow who stole food from our camp."

"That's possible. But why should Mrs. Deline be interested in a common tramp?"

"How do we know that fellow was a tramp?" Penny speculated. "Jerry told us about a young soldier that had escaped from a Canadian prison camp. Mrs. Deline may be trying to help him by supplying food and heavy clothing!"

"As usual, Penny, aren't you leaping to hasty conclusions?"

"Maybe I am, but everything fits in beautifully. I've thought from the first that Mrs. Deline was nothing less than a spy or an international crook."

"You've aired that theory before," Louise said, stretching out on the cot. "Wonder when your father will get here?"

"I wish he would come," Penny replied, glancing anxiously toward the road. "At least I have one consolation."

"What's that?"

"I know he's not with Mrs. Deline. Oh, Lou, think how horrible it would be to have a spy for a stepmother!"

"It would be something different anyhow," Louise chuckled. "Want to listen to the radio awhile?"

"Okay," Penny agreed, "maybe we can tune in that outlaw station. It's about time for the regular nightly broadcast."

Closing themselves into the car, the girls tried without success to get the outlaw shortwave station. Tuning instead to a dance orchestra, they discussed the day's happenings and made elaborate plans for the morrow.

"I'm really going to work," Penny announced grimly. "No Mrs. Deline ever will outwit me! Our first job must be to find that package she buried in the sand."

"And what of the person hiding in the woods?"

"The rangers ought to take over that part." Penny peered out through the car window at the dark woods which hemmed in the camp. "Somehow," she admitted, "I don't like the idea of being here at night. I'm not exactly afraid, but—"

"Listen!" Louise ordered sharply, "Someone's coming!"

Penny snapped off the radio. Tensely, the girls watched the road. The next instant they relaxed, for it was Mr. Parker who trudged wearily up the slope. Seeing Penny and Louise in the car, he came over to apologize for being so late.

"I've been with Jerry for the past two hours," he explained. "Time went faster than I realized."

"Any news?" Penny asked eagerly.

"Not about the radio station if that's what you mean. The fellow got away with his portable outfit slick as a whistle."

"The authorities have no idea who the man is, Dad?"

"Not the slightest. So far they've not been able to break the code he uses either. But in time they'll get him."

Having gleaned what information they could from Mr. Parker, the girls related their own adventure. As they fully expected, he made light of the episode at the cabin.

"Why should Mrs. Deline expect to meet anyone there?" he argued. "Penny, I'm afraid you don't understand her and misinterpret her actions."

"I don't understand her, that's certain."

"As to a man loitering about the camp," Mr. Parker resumed, "I've been worried about that ever since food was stolen. As I must be gone so much of the time, why wouldn't it be better for us to move to the hotel?"

Penny stiffened for an argument, and then suddenly changed her mind.

"All right, Dad," she astonished him by saying, "as far as I'm concerned, we can move tomorrow. I've had enough of the lonesome life."

"Why, that's fine!" Mr. Parker said heartily. "Splendid!"

After he had moved on, to sit for awhile by the dying embers of the fire, Louise remarked to Penny that explanations were in order.

"How come you're ready to desert the rough and rugged life?" she demanded. "At first you were dead set against moving into the hotel."

Penny carefully raised the car window so that her father would not overhear.

"I believe in fighting the Enemy on his own territory," she explained elaborately. "Mrs. Deline will bear watching. I intend to devote all my waking hours to the cause."

"So Jerry has nothing to do with it?"

"Jerry?"

"You wouldn't want to move to the hotel so you'd see more of him?"

"What an idea!" Penny scoffed. "Whoever thought of such a thing!"

"You did or I'm no mind reader."

"Well, it may have crossed my mind," Penny acknowledged with a giggle. "In fact, I can see quite a few advantages to hotel life. With luck we'll yet make something of this vacation!"

CHAPTER 17 - VISITORS NOT PERMITTED

Penny stood before the mirror in the hotel room and struggled to coax a little curl into her damp hair. She and Louise had spent two hours splashing in the surf that morning. The salt water had tightened their skins and produced discouraging results with their tresses.

"This place does have it over a forest camp," Penny said, gazing about the comfortably furnished room she shared with Louise. Her father's room was three doors down the hall. "A shower bath, no meals to cook, no dishes to wash, and the sea at one's elbow."

"I like it better," replied Louise. She had curled up kitten fashion on the bed and was making deep inroads into a box of chocolates. "So far though, we've not done much fancy sleuthing."

"We've only been here a few hours. Where do you suppose Mrs. Deline keeps herself?"

"In her room no doubt. Why do you worry about her so much, Penny?"

Penny twisted a few ringlets over her finger and abandoned the project as hopeless. "Lou, you know all the prize answers without asking me," she said. "I've told you a dozen times why I distrust that woman."

"Doesn't it all simmer down to one thing? You're jealous as a green-eyed cat!"

"Maybe I do dislike her," Penny grinned. "On second thought, I'm sure of it! But facts are facts and have nothing to do with my personal feelings. In the first place, didn't she get Dad to bring her with us to Sunset Beach?"

"But what does that prove? She has no car of her own and the trains are so crowded."

"I think she knew that Dad was coming here to try to dig up a story about the outlaw radio station," Penny went on, unruffled. "She's probably pumped him of information."

"Your father knows how to look after himself."

"That's what *he* thinks!" Penny muttered. "I wouldn't place any wagers on it myself. Why, he's been as blind as a bat."

"I'm afraid you see enough for two or three people," Louise chuckled.

"I told you, didn't I, how that vampire tried to steal our car while we were on our way here?"

"Two or three times, darling."

"Well, it would bear repeating. I think she intended to meet someone that night—perhaps the same person who was hiding in the woods!"

Louise, methodically eating chocolates, mulled over the possibility.

"Jerry told us that an escaped flier from a Canadian prison camp may be hiding somewhere near here," Penny resumed, wandering to the window. "Perhaps Mrs. Deline is trying to help him!"

"You have a new theory every minute," Louise yawned. "Why not think up one and stick to it?"

Penny did not answer for at that moment she observed Jerry Livingston leaving the veranda of the hotel.

"Come on, Lou!" she cried, jerking her chum off the bed. "I want to see Jerry before he escapes!"

"Talk about Mrs. Deline pursuing your defenseless father!" Louise protested as she was pulled down the hall to the elevator. "Her tactics at least are more subtle than yours!"

"This is different," Penny retorted shamelessly. "Jerry and I are old friends."

Swinging through the revolving doors of the hotel, the girls raced after Jerry. Breathless from running, they finally overtook him far down the boardwalk.

"Why, hello," he greeted them with a broad smile. "I hear you've moved into the hotel."

"Lock, stock and barrel," Penny laughed. "We want to be in the thick of things. Any news about the radio station?"

"Nothing I can report, I'm on my way now to Intercept Headquarters."

"Did you see Dad this morning?"

"Only for a few minutes. He's doing a little special work for me."

"At least I'm glad it's for you and not Mrs. Deline," Penny said stiffly. "Jerry, there are some things you should know about that woman."

"Suppose you unburden your heart," Jerry invited, seating himself on a sand dune. "I have about ten minutes to listen."

"Don't encourage her," sighed Louise. "She's slightly cracked on the subject, you know."

"Nevertheless, Penny has ideas at times," Jerry paid her tribute. "Shoot!"

Talking like a whirlwind, Penny delved deeply into the subject of Mrs. Deline. She repeated how the widow had buried a package in the sand, but it was not until the episode of the cabin was described that Jerry really seemed interested.

"Penny, at first I didn't take your Mrs. Deline talk very seriously," he admitted. "Perhaps you have something after all!"

"I'm sure of it, Jerry!"

"Have you reported to the park rangers?"

"Dad may have seen them, I'm not sure. We left camp in a big rush."

"Then I'll take care of that, Penny. We'll have the park searched again and try to find that fellow!"

"Then you do believe he's the escaped flier!" Penny exclaimed.

"Probably not," was Jerry's discouraging reply. "Nevertheless, we can't afford to overlook any possibility."

"What about the package in the sand?"

"You remember where it was buried?"

"Approximately."

"I'll not have time to go with you now," Jerry said, looking at his wrist watch.

"Louise and I haven't much to do this morning. We'll be glad to search."

"Go ahead," Jerry urged. "If you fail then I can take over. The important thing is not to tip off your hand. Don't let anyone suspect what you're about."

Penny and Louise nodded soberly. They felt rather important to have been assigned a definite task.

"Report to me as soon as you find that package," Jerry urged as he started on. "It may contain something of vital importance. It may not. We'll withhold judgment until we have the facts."

Left to themselves, the girls lost not a moment in hastening to the section of beach where Mrs. Deline had been seen to bury the package.

"Now just where was it?" Penny asked, gazing about the deserted dunes. "What became of our marker?"

"We left a stick to show the exact spot."

"Not a sign of it now. What wretched luck!"

Though the girls knew the general locality where the package had been buried, all of the dunes looked discouragingly alike. Not a footprint remained to guide them.

"I'll bet a cent Mrs. Deline came back here and removed that stick!" Penny declared. "Maybe she dug up the package too!"

"Anyone could have taken the stick. Why do you think she did it?"

"Because she watched us digging for the package. Well, let's look for it anyhow."

With none too much enthusiasm, the girls set to work. The tide was much lower than upon their last visit and the shoreline did not look the same. Nor could they agree within forty feet of the right place to dig.

"You try one dune, and I'll work on another," Penny offered as a compromise.

An hour of unavailing work found the pair too discouraged to keep on digging.

"If this is the right place, Mrs. Deline or someone has removed the package," Penny declared, sinking back on her heels.

"We may as well give up," Louise added wearily.

Penny slid down the dune and emptied sand from her shoes.

"There should be an easy way to beat Mrs. Deline at her own little game," she remarked thoughtfully. "For instance, why does she always wear that jade green charm?"

"Because she likes it I'd imagine."

CHAPTER 17 - VISITORS NOT PERMITTED

"But wouldn't you think she'd take it off at night?"

"Perhaps she does, Penny."

"Not the night I was with her. I distinctly gained the impression that there was something about it she was afraid I'd see."

"A message contained inside?"

"That's been my theory from the first, Lou. Now if only we could lay our hands on the charm—"

"Finding the package would be a lot easier. We can't waylay the woman and take the jade elephant by force. Or can we?"

"No," Penny agreed reluctantly, "I don't think Dad would like that. And there's always the possibility I might be wrong."

"The probability, you mean," corrected Louise.

Penny retied her shoes and glanced toward the hotel. Far up the beach she saw Mrs. Deline, and the widow was walking slowly toward the sand dunes.

"Duck!" Penny ordered, rolling over one of the high ridges. "We don't want her to see us here. She'll suspect what we've been up to."

Louise crouched behind the dune with her chum, though she complained that she felt silly doing it. Apparently, Mrs. Deline had not seen the girls. She came steadily on.

Drawing close, she peered directly at the dune where the girls had taken refuge. For a second they feared that she had seen them. But she passed on without another glance.

"It looks to me as though she's on her way to the lighthouse again," Penny remarked after Mrs. Deline was far down the beach. "Wonder why she goes there so often?"

"I thought visitors weren't allowed."

"According to the rules they're not."

From behind the dune, the girls kept watch of the widow. Presently they saw her climb the steps of the lighthouse and disappear into the interior.

"Well, that settles it!" Penny exclaimed indignantly.

"Settles what?" Louise straightened up, brushing sand from her skirt.

"If Mrs. Deline can get into that lighthouse, so can I. We'll make an issue of it!"

"Not today," said Louise dubiously.

"Right now!" Penny corrected, starting down the beach. "That lighthouse is government property, and as citizens we have certain rights. Let's assert them and see what happens!"

CHAPTER 18 - INSIDE THE LIGHTHOUSE

Unchallenged, Penny and Louise reached the base of the lighthouse. But as they slowly climbed the iron stairs, their courage fast slipped away.

"What will we say to the keeper?" Louise faltered. "I've even forgotten his name."

"I haven't," said Penny. "It's Jim McCoy. If Mrs. Deline is allowed inside the tower, shouldn't we have the same privileges?"

"She's a personal friend."

"That should make no difference," Penny argued. "This is government property."

"Let's not do it," Louise pleaded, holding back.

Having proceeded so far. Penny was in no mood to retreat. Quickly, lest she too lose her courage, she rapped hard on the tower door.

Minutes elapsed. Then the heavy oak door swung back and Jim McCoy, the burly keeper, peered out at the girls. His bushy brows drew together in an angry scowl.

"You here again!" he exclaimed.

"Yes," said Penny, making the word crisp and firm.

"I'll have to report you if you keep pestering me," the keeper scolded. "How many times have I told you no visitors are allowed?"

"But you don't treat everyone the same!" Penny remonstrated. "Mrs. Deline just came here."

"Mrs. Deline? Who's she?"

"Why, a woman who stays at the hotel. She came through this door not five minutes ago!"

"You must have imagined it. I've had no visitors."

Penny's silence said more plainly than words that she did not believe the keeper.

"So you think I'm lying, eh?" he demanded unpleasantly. "Okay, come in and see for yourselves. I'm breaking a rule to invite you into the tower, but maybe then you'll be satisfied and quite bothering me. We have work to do here, you know."

The keeper stepped aside so that the girls might enter.

"My living quarters," he said curtly. "You see, I have no visitors."

Decidedly ill at ease, the girls gazed about the little circular room. The walls were lined with built-in cupboards. Nearly all of the furniture had been made with a view to conserving space. As Mr. McCoy had said, there were no visitors—no evidence that Mrs. Deline ever had been there.

"Are you satisfied?" the keeper demanded unpleasantly.

"But we were sure Mrs. Deline came here," Penny stammered.

"There's been no one today except early this morning when a government inspector paid me a visit."

Penny did not believe the man but she deemed it wise to appear to do so.

"I'm sorry," she apologized. "I guess we have made nuisances of ourselves."

"That's all right," the keeper said in a less unfriendly tone. "Kids are kids. Now that you're here, look around a bit."

"Oh, thank you," Louise replied gratefully. "I've always wanted to see the inside of a lighthouse."

"I have some work to do," Mr. McCoy announced. "The light's not been operating right and I'm trying to get the mechanism adjusted. I'll be back."

He went out, allowing the door to slam hard.

CHAPTER 18 - INSIDE THE LIGHTHOUSE

The girls surveyed their surroundings with keen interest. On a table near the window there was a shortwave radio. A circular couch occupied another curving corner of the room.

"What became of Mrs. Deline?" Penny whispered. "She certainly came here."

"Of course she did! We saw her plain as day!"

"She must be somewhere in the tower. Probably there's a room above this one."

Penny tiptoed to the door and tried to open it. To her surprise and chagrin, it would not budge.

"My Great Aunt!" she whispered. "We're locked in!"

"Maybe the door's just stuck." Louise strode across the room to help Penny. Both of them tried without success to open it.

"Let's shout and pound!" Louise suggested.

"No, wait! I think we've been locked in here on purpose."

"Oh, Penny!"

"Now don't get nervous. The keeper's no fool. He'll have to let us out."

"But why would he lock us in?"

"Because he's provoked at us for one reason, Lou. Another, something's going on here that he doesn't want us to know about. He and Mrs. Deline may be having a tête-à-tête in the room above."

"Then let's listen. Maybe we can overhear their conversation."

Penny nodded and fell silent. Though the girls listened for a long while, no sound reached their ears.

"This is a nice situation!" Louise fumed. "I think the door locked itself. We ought to shout for help."

"Goose, a door doesn't lock itself."

"This one might have a trick catch."

"It was Mr. Jim McCoy who accomplished the trick," Penny said. "Listen! Someone's coming now."

Plainly the girls could hear footsteps on the iron balcony outside the door. A moment later they were able to distinguish a murmur of men's voices. The footsteps moved on and a moment later they heard a door close overhead.

"Another visitor!" Penny announced. "Did you hear what was said, Lou?"

"Couldn't make out a word."

"Nor could I. But that voice sounded familiar. I'm sure I've heard it somewhere."

"I had the same feeling, Penny."

The girls listened intently, hoping to overhear conversation on the floor above. However, the walls of the lighthouse were so thick that not a word reached them. Now and then they thought they heard Mrs. Deline's high pitched voice.

"Louise, it's just come to me!" Penny whispered a moment later. "I believe Mr. McCoy's visitor may be George Emory!"

"The voice did sound a little like his. But why would he come here?"

"Maybe we've under-rated George Emory. Why, all this time he may have been trying to get information from us."

"He did ask us quite a few questions, particularly about your father."

"And he seemed to know a lot about that outlaw radio station, Lou. Maybe he tried to throw us off the track by suggesting that we watch old Jake Skagway."

"We certainly fell for it, Penny."

"We did, if you assume that George Emory is upstairs having a conference with Mrs. Deline and the lighthouse keeper. But we're not sure."

"No, we're not, Penny. One easily can be mistaken in voices."

Determined to hear more, Penny cautiously climbed up on the radio table, so that her head and ear were close to the ceiling.

"Can you make out anything?" Louise whispered.

Penny shook her head in disgust. After a few minutes she dropped lightly down from the table.

"Walls are too thick," she announced. "I could hear three voices though. Two were men and the other, a woman."

"Then Mrs. Deline must be here. The keeper lied about that part."

VOICE FROM THE CAVE

Presently the girls heard footsteps again on the iron stairway. They moved to the window, hoping to see whomever was descending from the room above. However, the little round aperture was so situated that it gave a view of only one side of the Point. They could not see the stairway nor the stretch of beach leading to the hotel.

"We're certainly learning a lot!" Louise said crossly. "I've had enough of this. Let's shout for help."

"All right," Penny agreed. "We may as well find out whether or not we're prisoners."

Crossing to the heavy oak door, she pounded hard on the panels. Almost at once the girls heard someone coming.

"Don't let on what we suspect," Penny warned her companion.

The next moment the door swung open to admit the keeper of the light.

CHAPTER 19 - A LOCKED DOOR

"I was gone a little longer than I meant to be," Jim McCoy apologized as he came into the room. "Did I keep you waiting?"

"We probably wouldn't have waited if you hadn't locked the door!" Louise said sharply.

The keeper's eyebrows lifted and he looked slightly amused. "Locked in?" he echoed.

"Yes, we couldn't get the door open."

"Oh, it sticks sometimes. Been intending to fix it for several days. If you had pushed hard it would have opened."

"We certainly pushed hard enough," Penny said dryly. She was more than ever certain that the lighthouse keeper had unlocked the door only a moment before entering. Clearly, he had meant to prevent Louise and her from seeing and hearing what went on in the room above.

"Come along," the keeper invited. "I'll show you the tower."

"No thank you," Penny replied coldly. "We've spent so much time here that we'll have to be getting back to the hotel."

"As you like." The keeper shrugged, and looked relieved by the decision.

Jim McCoy stepped away from the door, and the girls hastened down the iron stairway. No one was in sight on the beach. Whoever had visited the lighthouse during the time they were imprisoned, had disappeared.

When they were well down the beach, Louise and Penny slackened their pace. Glancing back they saw that the keeper of the light still stood on the tiny iron balcony watching them.

"That man gives me the creeps," Louise remarked. "Did you believe what he said about the door sticking?"

"I did not," Penny returned with emphasis. "I think he locked us in on purpose, probably because he was expecting visitors and didn't want us to see too much."

"As it turned out we didn't learn a thing."

"We have no proof of anything," Penny admitted slowly. "Nevertheless, we're pretty sure Mrs. Deline visited the tower."

"George Emory too."

"That part is pure guess," Penny said, "so we don't dare consider it too seriously. Did you ever see Mrs. Deline with George Emory?"

"Why, no. But then, we've not been at the hotel long."

"Let's find Jerry or Dad," Penny said abruptly. "We ought to report to them."

Returning to the hotel, the girls looked in vain for Mr. Parker. The publisher was not in his room nor anywhere in the lobby. Jerry apparently had not returned from Intercept Headquarters.

"There's Mrs. Deline," Louise whispered, jerking her head toward a high-backed chair not far from the elevator.

The widow was reading a newspaper. If she saw the girls she paid no attention to them.

"Let's talk to her and see what we can learn," Louise suggested.

Penny had another thought. "No," she vetoed the suggestion. "Mrs. Deline would be more likely to learn things from us. That woman is clever."

Just then Mrs. Deline arose, picked up her purse, and went out the front door of the hotel. On their way to the elevator. Penny and Louise noticed that the woman carelessly had left a handkerchief and her room key lying on the chair.

"I'll turn them in at the desk," Louise said, picking up the articles.

VOICE FROM THE CAVE

"Wait, Lou!"

Louise glanced at her chum in surprise.

"I have an idea!" Penny revealed, lowering her voice. "Are you game to try something risky?"

"Well, I don't know."

"This chance is tailor-made for us!" Penny went on. "Mrs. Deline simply handed her room key over to us. Let's use our opportunity."

"Enter her room?" Louise asked, shocked.

"Why not? FBI agents think nothing of examining the belongings of a suspected person."

"But we're not FBI agents, Penny. I don't want to do it without asking Jerry."

"By that time it will be too late. It's now or never."

"Mrs. Deline might catch us in the act."

"That's a chance we'll have to take." Penny, in possession of the room key, walked to the front door of the hotel. She was reassured to see that Mrs. Deline had seated herself on a bench some distance from the veranda.

"The coast's clear," Penny reported, coming back to Louise. "What do you say?"

"Well, I suppose so," Louise consented nervously.

An elevator shot the girls up to the fourth floor. To locate Mrs. Deline's room required but a moment, and the halls fortunately were deserted. Penny fitted the key into the lock and pushed open the door.

"We'll have to work fast," she said, closing it behind them again.

The room was in perfect order. Only a few toilet articles had been set out on the dresser. Mrs. Deline's suitcase was only half unpacked.

"It looks to me as if the widow is holding herself ready to fly at a moment's notice," Penny commented. "Otherwise, why didn't she unpack everything?"

"What do you expect to find here?" Louise asked nervously. "Let's get it over with fast, Penny."

"Start with the bureau drawers," Penny instructed. "Search for any papers, letters or the sort. I'll go through the suitcase."

Carefully the girls began examining Mrs. Deline's personal belongings. Almost at once Louise reported that the bureau contained nothing of interest. Penny, however, had more luck. She came upon a pearl-handled revolver buried beneath a pile of silk underclothing.

"Jeepers!" she whispered, touching the weapon gingerly. "Now will you believe me when I say that the widow isn't the sweet little girl she'd have us believe!"

Louise's eyes had opened wide at sight of the revolver.

"And here's that white suit she wore!" Penny cried, lifting out a folded garment from the suitcase. "Look, Lou!"

From the skirt of the suit had been cut a neat, square hole.

"Well, of all things!" Louise exclaimed. "What's the meaning of that?"

"Mrs. Deline wrote something on the skirt—don't you remember? Probably she used a pen with invisible ink."

"But why on her skirt, Penny?"

"She'd just been to the lighthouse. Perhaps she learned something there and she wanted to write it down before she forgot. Possibly she didn't have any paper. Then when she got back here, she either destroyed the message, or sent it to someone."

"Well, I don't know," Louise said doubtfully. "It's all so fantastic. I wouldn't believe a bit of it except for this revolver. Having it doesn't look so good."

"And don't forget the green elephant charm," Penny reminded her. "I wish we could find it here."

"Not a chance. Mrs. Deline always wears it around her neck. She had it on today. I noticed."

Time fast was elapsing and the girls were worried lest someone discover them in the room. Hastily they replaced everything as they had found it, and relocking the door, stepped out into the hall.

"What's our next move?" Louise asked as they buzzed for a down-going elevator.

"To tell Jerry and Dad, of course. But before that, there's one thing I wish we could do, Lou. It would give everything we have to report a more substantial basis."

"What's that, Penny?"

CHAPTER 19 - A LOCKED DOOR

"Why don't we get our hands on the jade green elephant? I've a hunch that it contains something important—perhaps evidence that would crack the case wide open."

"And just how do you propose that we acquire the charm?" Louise asked sarcastically. "Are we to waylay Mrs. Deline and take it by force?"

"Afraid that wouldn't do."

"There's no other way to get it. Mrs. Deline wears that charm as if it were her skin. I've never seen her without it."

The elevator was coming down so Penny spoke hurriedly.

"There is a way," she said softly, "if only it will work. Think we could get Mrs. Deline to go bathing in the surf with us?"

"And ruin that lovely hair-do? Don't be silly."

"All the same, it's worth trying," Penny urged. "Let's go to our room now and get our bathing suits."

"I don't see any point in it."

"You will," Penny laughed, entering the elevator. "If my little plan works we'll have keen sport and maybe do our country a good turn!"

CHAPTER 20 - NYMPHS OF THE SEA

"How you expect to get Mrs. Deline to go swimming with us is beyond me!" Louise opined as she and Penny left the hotel, their bathing suits swinging over their arms. "It's none too warm today. She dislikes us both intensely. Furthermore, she never swims."

"Any other reasons?" Penny asked cheerfully.

"That should be enough."

"Just wait and watch," Penny chuckled. "I just hope she doesn't suspect we've been prowling in her room. If she got wise to that she'd report us to the hotel management."

Before leaving the hotel the girls had taken care to drop the room key in the chair where Mrs. Deline had left it. They were confident that no one had seen them take the key or enter the room.

The widow remained as the girls last had seen her. She was sitting on a bench facing the sea, her gaze fixed on the deep blue line of the horizon. As the girls passed beside her, she looked up, frowning slightly.

"We're on our way to the bath house," said Penny, her tone implying that the matter was one of great importance.

"Really?" Mrs. Deline's voice barely was polite.

"Wouldn't you like to come with us?" Louise invited cordially.

The invitation took Mrs. Deline by surprise. "No, thank you," she declined. "I can't swim."

"We'll teach you," offered Penny.

"You're too kind. I don't care for the water. I particularly detest cold water."

"The air is warming up," Penny tried to encourage her. "Why not try it with us?"

"Nothing could induce me."

Louise nodded grimly, as much as to say that she had known how it would be. Penny would not give up. She decided to adopt drastic measures.

"No, I didn't suppose you would go into the water," she said. "You're probably afraid you'll get salt water on that lovely skin of yours, or muss up your hair."

"Oh!" gasped Mrs. Deline. "The very idea!"

"Isn't that the reason?" Penny pursued ruthlessly. "You have to protect your beauty?"

"No, it's not the reason!" Mrs. Deline snapped. "If I had a bathing suit, I'd show you!"

"You can use mine," Penny said promptly. "Louise has an extra one she'll let me have."

Mrs. Deline looked trapped and angry. She sprang to her feet.

"All right, I'll go swimming!" she announced. "If I catch pneumonia I suppose you'll be satisfied!"

"Oh, you'll love the water once you're in," Penny said sweetly. "The bath house is this way."

Mrs. Deline spent so long getting into the borrowed suit that the girls began to fear she had outwitted them. But just as they were ready to give up, the woman came out of the dressing room. Penny's suit was a size too small for her so that she looked as if she had been poured into it. Her legs were skinny, her hips bulged. She still wore the elephant charm.

"Don't I wish Dad could see her now!" Penny muttered. "What a disillusionment!"

Ignoring the girls, Mrs. Deline walked stiffly toward the surf. A wave rolled in, wetting her to the knees. Mrs. Deline shrieked and backed away.

"It's freezing!" she complained.

"You have to get wet all at once," Penny instructed kindly. "This way."

She seized Mrs. Deline's hand and pulled her toward the deeper water.

CHAPTER 20 - NYMPHS OF THE SEA

"Let me go!" Mrs. Deline protested, trying to shake free. "Stop it!"

Penny held fast to her hand. A big roller broke over their heads. Mrs. Deline sputtered and choked and struggled.

"Oh, this is dreadful!" she whimpered.

"You have to watch for the waves and jump just as they strike you," Penny laughed. "Now!"

She leaped, but the widow mistimed the roller. It struck her a resounding whack on her shoulders and head.

"Oh! Oh!" she moaned.

"Here comes another!" warned Louise. "A big one too!"

Mrs. Deline broke away from Penny. She started to run for shore. The big roller overtook her, sweeping her from her feet.

This was the opportunity that Penny awaited. Pretending that she too had lost her balance, she allowed the tide to carry her straight into Mrs. Deline. For an instant they both were beneath the surface of the water.

Penny worked fast. Clutching Mrs. Deline as if in terror, she yanked hard at the slender chain that held the green elephant charm. It snapped and the jade piece came off into her hands. Deftly she thrust the charm into the front of her bathing suit. Then she popped up above the water, winking at Louise.

Mrs. Deline scrambled to her feet, clutching at the broken chain.

"See what you've done!" she accused Penny. "You pulled it apart. My beautiful charm has fallen into the water!"

"Let me help you look for it," Louise offered, darting forward.

As the pair were groping about on the sandy floor, another wave rolled in. Penny neglected to warn Mrs. Deline. It struck her from behind, toppling her over on her face. Her cap slipped awry and she swallowed salt water.

"Oh, I can't stand any more of this!" she spluttered. "It was cruel of you to get me to come into the surf! Now I've lost my charm, and it was all your fault, Penny Parker."

"I'll buy you another ornament," the girl offered. Seeing Mrs. Deline's distress she felt a bit ashamed of herself.

"Another ornament!" the widow mocked. "I don't want another! I want the one I've lost. It's of vital importance to me to keep it."

Mrs. Deline made another futile search for the charm.

"It's been washed away," she cried. "I'll never find it now!"

Glaring furiously at Penny, she turned and fled to the bath house.

"Did she really lose the charm?" Louise demanded the moment the girls were alone. "Or did you get it, Penny?"

Penny answered by producing the green elephant charm from the front of her bathing suit where she had hidden it.

"Easy as taking candy from a babe," she chuckled. "My, but was she hopping mad!"

"You may not be laughing if your father hears about this," Louise warned. "He's apt to look at matters from a different angle than we do."

Penny skipped through the shallow water and sat down on the beach well beyond the reach of the waves. Louise flopped beside her. Eagerly they examined the jade green trinket.

"Looks like any ordinary charm to me," Louise remarked. "No special carving."

"It should open," Penny said. "The first night when Mrs. Deline and I shared a room, I was sure I saw her close it."

Louise turned the charm over and pried at it with a hairpin.

"It does have a back lid!" she exclaimed excitedly. "Penny, I think it's going to open!"

"I'll say magic words while you work," Penny laughed. "Furthermore, I'll keep watch of the bath house. We don't want Mrs. Deline to pop out here and see us."

Louise pried again at the lid of the charm. It gave suddenly.

Inside the tiny cavity was a folded piece of paper. While Louise stared in delighted awe, Penny gained possession. With nervous haste she unfolded the paper. She gazed at it a moment and her face fell.

"Why, I can't make anything of the writing!" she declared in disappointment. "The words don't make sense."

VOICE FROM THE CAVE

"Just a mess of letters," Louise agreed, peering over her shoulder.

The girls were decidedly let-down for they had gone to much trouble and risk to obtain the jade ornament. But Penny's disappointment did not last long. As she stared at the paper, its significance dawned upon her.

"Why, this is important, Lou!" she cried. "Maybe we've stumbled into something big!"

"How do you mean?"

"Don't you see?" Penny demanded triumphantly. "The letters, of this message must comprise a secret code! If only we can break it down we may learn all we need to know about Mrs. Deline and her strange friends!"

CHAPTER 21 - THE CARDBOARD BOX

While Penny and Louise were puzzling over the strange writing found inside the jade charm, Mrs. Deline appeared in the doorway of the bath house. Barely in time to escape detection, the girls hid the tiny elephant and the paper in the sand.

Mrs. Deline crossed the beach to speak to the girls. Her hair was damp and stringy, her face pinched and blue from cold.

"Here's your suit!" she snapped, slapping the wet garment into the sand at Penny's feet. "I hope you enjoyed the swim! I'm sure I didn't."

Turning her back, the widow marched to the hotel.

The moment Mrs. Deline had disappeared into the white brick building, Penny dug the jade elephant and paper from the sand.

"Let's get dressed," she urged Louise. "We've no time to waste."

So thrilled were the girls over what they had accomplished that they could talk of nothing else. Penny felt that by obtaining the jade elephant she had proven her case.

"You thought I was only jealous of Mrs. Deline," she told Louise triumphantly as they dressed in adjoining booths. "Now what do you say?"

"That you're a genius!" Louise praised. "Mrs. Deline certainly is mixed up in some shady business."

Once dressed, the girls wrapped the jade elephant in a handkerchief and carried it to the hotel. Jerry was nowhere to be found, and a bellboy told Penny that her father had gone for a walk.

"Perhaps we can work the message out ourselves," Penny suggested hopefully. "Let's try."

In their hotel room, the girls spent an hour attempting to decipher the strange jargon of letters appearing on the paper. At the end of that time. Penny tossed aside her pencil in disgust.

"This is a job for an expert," she declared. "I certainly don't classify as one."

The telephone jingled. Penny answered it and was delighted to hear Jerry's familiar voice. He was down in the lobby and had been told that the girls wished to see him.

"We certainly do!" Penny answered gaily. "Hold everything! We'll be with you in a jiffy."

The elevator being entirely too slow, the girls raced down the stairs. Breathlessly they started to tell Jerry what they had learned.

"Not here!" he said quickly. "Let's go outside where we won't be overheard."

Once out in the open with no one close by, Jerry lent an attentive ear to Penny's tale of their afternoon adventure. He did not have much to say in return, but he studied the jade green elephant and the paper with deep interest.

"You don't think it's anything?" Penny asked in disappointment.

"On the contrary, it may be something of very great importance," he returned soberly. "I'll take this to Headquarters. We have an expert on codes who should be able to break it in a short while."

The girls hoped that Jerry would invite them to accompany him, but he did not do so. Instead he said:

"Penny, you were telling me that Mrs. Deline had buried a package in the sand. Any luck in finding it?"

"Not a bit."

"You don't think that she went back there and dug it up herself?"

"We didn't see any footprints."

"How did you mark the place?"

"By a stick that someone removed."

"Not a very reliable way to take observations," Jerry remarked. "Ever try the clock system?"

The girls looked blank.

"For example," Jerry illustrated, "imagine that the landscape is like the face of a clock. Now what do you see on the hour of two?"

"I don't get it," Louise complained.

"Oh, I do!" laughed Penny. "A big tree!"

"That's right," agreed Jerry. "And at the hour of six?"

"Why, a signboard!" chuckled Penny. "At the hour of seven there's a big sand dune!"

"If you picture things in your mind as if they're on the face of a clock it's much easier to remember and keep them in proper proportion. Now, using that same system can you recall anything more about the place where Mrs. Deline buried the package?"

"Not very much," Penny admitted. "I didn't take notations at the time."

"Speaking of signboards, I remember one," Louise said thoughtfully. "It was a long distance back from the beach, slightly to the right. A cigarette advertisement."

"That's right!" agreed Penny.

"Perhaps that will help some," Jerry said. "We'll have to find the package."

"Then you believe Mrs. Deline is an Enemy Agent?" Penny asked eagerly.

"I've thought so for quite a while now," Jerry admitted. "I didn't say it for fear of building up your hopes. Anyhow, we've got to work quietly in this business."

"Poor Dad," Penny murmured, "I'm afraid it will break him up to learn the truth. Do you say I should tell him right away, Jerry?"

"Why not?" Jerry demanded, his eyes amused. "Your father may have a few things to break to you too, Penny."

"Meaning what?"

"I'll let your father do his own talking," Jerry said, getting up from the hotel bench. "Have to go now."

"Wait!" Penny pleaded. "You've not told us anything. Do you think Mrs. Deline has been aiding that flier who escaped from a Canadian prison camp?"

Jerry deliberately let the question pass. "Listen!" he said urgently. "I may not see you girls again until after dinner. Want to help me tonight?"

"Doing what?" Penny asked.

"I want you to lead me to the place where Mrs. Deline buried that package."

"We'll do our best."

"Then if I don't see you earlier, meet me here at nine o'clock. It should be dark by that time."

"We'll be here," Penny promised, her eyes glowing.

At dinner that night the girls told Mr. Parker of their appointment to meet Jerry. Penny would have explained about the package, but before she could do so, Mrs. Deline joined the group. Mr. Parker immediately invited her to dine with them. To the annoyance of Penny and Louise she accepted with alacrity.

The girls fully expected that Mrs. Deline would make some reference to the incident of the afternoon. Instead she avoided the subject, talking of her experiences in China and the Orient. Despite their prejudice, Penny and Louise were compelled in all honesty to acknowledge to themselves that the widow was a brilliant, entertaining conversationalist.

Over the coffee cups Mrs. Deline spoke casually of a play which was showing at the local theatre. Before Penny could say a word, Mr. Parker had suggested that he buy tickets for the night's performance.

"I'd love to go," Mrs. Deline accepted instantly.

"Good!" Mr. Parker, approved. "I'll get four tickets."

"Two," Penny corrected grimly. "Louise and I already have an appointment."

"That's so," Mr. Parker recalled belatedly.

Mrs. Deline looked so pleased that Penny was sorely tempted to abandon the meeting with Jerry. Only the realization that the task ahead was vitally important, kept her silent.

At eight o'clock Mr. Parker and Mrs. Deline left the hotel for the theatre. With an hour to kill, Penny and Louise were very restless. They read the evening paper and watched the clock.

CHAPTER 21 - THE CARDBOARD BOX

"Here's an interesting news item," Penny remarked, indicating a brief story on an inner page of the paper. "It says an enemy submarine was sighted not many miles from here—just off the coast."

"Did they get it?" Louise inquired absently.

"I guess not. The story doesn't say, except that the air patrol dropped bombs."

"Wonder what a single sub was doing so close here?" Louise speculated. "Oh, well, we've nothing to fear."

A clock chimed the hour of nine. On the first stroke, the girls arose and hastened to keep their appointment with Jerry. The night was closing in dark. Along the shore no lights were showing for the dim-out was rigidly enforced at Sunset Beach.

"Where's Jerry?" Penny asked as they reached the bench where they had promised to meet him. "Hope he didn't forget."

Ten minutes elapsed. Penny was examining the luminous dial of her wrist watch when someone came striding down the gravel path.

"Hello," Jerry greeted the girls. "Sorry to have kept you waiting. All set for adventure?"

"Lead on!" Penny laughed.

Taking each of them by an elbow, Jerry guided the girls down the deserted beach. Twice they passed guards who merely stared and allowed them to pass unchallenged.

"Any news about that code?" Penny questioned as they walked along.

"It's a tough one to break," Jerry replied briefly. "Experts have been trying to take it apart ever since I left you girls this afternoon."

"Then it really is something?" Penny asked, scarcely daring to hope.

"It certainly is," Jerry replied heartily. "We're pretty sure now that Mrs. Deline is mixed up in a bad business. But we can't act until we know absolutely."

"This will be a horrible shock to Dad," Penny remarked. "He's at the theatre with Mrs. Deline now."

"At least she's out of the way, so there's no chance she'll see us at work," Jerry commented. "Think you can find the place to dig?"

Penny had marked it well in her mind, but at night everything looked different. After some uncertainty, the girls agreed upon the dune where the package had been buried.

"With the tide low we'll have plenty of time," Jerry said. "Well, let's go! Was the package buried deep?"

"Not more than a foot," Penny supplied.

"Then if it's here, we'll find it. Let's block this area off and cover it systematically."

For an hour the trio toiled. Twice one of the beach guards passed by and Penny was surprised that he paid no heed to what they were doing.

"Orders!" Jerry chuckled. "You didn't think we could come out here and prowl around without questions being asked? The guard was tipped off. He'll help us by whistling if anyone comes this way."

Louise, who had been industriously digging, gave a low cry.

"Find something?" Jerry demanded.

"I'm not sure. I think so."

The next instant Louise lifted a small package from its sand tomb. Before Jerry could warn her, she had torn apart the pasteboard cover.

"Why, it contains pencils!" she exclaimed in disgust. "Pencils!"

Jerry leaped to her side. One glance and he took the box from her.

"Those objects may look like pencils," he drawled. "But take it from me, they're a bit more deadly."

Penny had moved close. She and Louise stared in awe at the collection.

"Bombs," Jerry explained briefly. "One of these little pencils contains enough explosive to blow us all to Kingdom Come!"

CHAPTER 22 - UNFINISHED BUSINESS

The cardboard box contained in addition to the pencil bombs a shiny knife and several grooved, pear-shaped objects.

"What are those?" Louise asked curiously. "They look like hand grenades."

"That's what they are," said Jerry, lifting one from the box. "It's a mighty useful weapon for close fighting. A strong man can throw a grenade twenty-five to thirty-five yards and it does damage over a large area."

Penny gingerly inspected one of the grenades.

"It won't bite you," Jerry laughed. "Nor will it explode in your hand. When you're ready to throw a grenade you hold it with the lever under your fingers. Just before you toss it, pull the pin."

"Isn't it apt to explode while you're holding it?" Penny asked dubiously.

"Not while the lever is held. When the grenade leaves the hand, the lever flies off. Then the fuse ignites and in about seven seconds you have your explosion."

"Nice little gadgets," Penny said. She replaced the grenade in its box and ran a finger over the sharp edge of the steel-bladed knife.

"Mrs. Deline evidently planted these weapons here for someone else to use," Jerry remarked. "We'll put them back just as they were."

"Put them back!" Penny echoed. "Why, Jerry, wouldn't that be playing right into their hands? Shouldn't we destroy these things?"

"No, it's much wiser to have the place watched."

Light dawned upon Penny. "Oh, I see!" she exclaimed. "In that way you hope to learn Mrs. Deline's accomplices!"

"Exactly."

Jerry replaced everything in the box which he carefully buried in the sand. Then he obliterated all freshly made footmarks.

"It may be necessary to watch this place for days," he said thoughtfully.

"And what of Mrs. Deline?" Penny asked. "Will she be allowed complete freedom?"

"That's for my superiors to decide. It seems to me, though, that more is to be gained by allowing her to remain at liberty than by arresting her."

"I'm all for jail myself," said Penny.

"Just be patient," Jerry smiled. "And whatever you do, don't drop a hint to Mrs. Deline of what we suspect."

"She knows I dislike her."

"That's all right, but don't let her guess that you consider her guilty of anything more serious than making a play for your father."

"What about Dad? Shouldn't I warn him?"

"Let me take care of that part," Jerry smiled.

"All right," Penny agreed reluctantly. "Just be sure that you don't muff it. Remember, you're playing with my future!"

Jerry finished smoothing out the footprints in the sand and then escorted the girls to the hotel.

"I must report to Headquarters without delay," he said, pausing at the hotel entrance. "Don't worry about the package. We'll have the place watched every minute."

After Jerry had gone, Penny and Louise entered the hotel.

"Is my father here yet?" Penny asked the desk clerk.

CHAPTER 22 - UNFINISHED BUSINESS

"No, Miss. And there's a message for him. As soon as he comes in he's to call Major Gregg."

Penny repeated the name thoughtfully. "That's a new one on me," she remarked. "Dad seems to have friends I know nothing about."

"Oh, the Major comes to the hotel frequently," the clerk returned, smiling. "He and your father are well acquainted."

As the girls crossed the lobby to a drinking fountain, Louise said teasingly:

"I'm afraid you've lost track of your father lately, Penny. You've been so upset about Mrs. Deline that you've scarcely noticed anything or anyone else."

"Dad's been holding out on me, that's evident. Wonder what he's to call Major Gregg about?"

"Why not wait up and see?"

"Not a bad idea," Penny approved instantly. "He and Mrs. Deline should be getting in anytime now."

"I'm not waiting up," announced Louise with a sleepy yawn. "In fact, I'm on my way to bed this minute."

To prove her words she started for the elevator. Penny debated whether or not to follow and finally decided to remain in the lobby.

An hour elapsed. Penny was half asleep by the time Mrs. Deline and Mr. Parker entered the hotel together. They were chatting animatedly and would not have seen her had she not scrambled from the wing chair.

Seeing Penny, Mrs. Deline quickly bade Mr. Parker good night and vanished into an elevator.

"You shouldn't have waited up," Mr. Parker chided his daughter. "Why, it's nearly midnight."

"There's an important message for you, Dad. You're to call Major Gregg."

Mr. Parker looked disconcerted. "How long ago did that call come, Penny?"

"About an hour ago. Or that's when I learned of it."

Mr. Parker went quickly to a telephone booth and was gone for some time. When he returned his face was animated.

"Good news?" Penny asked eagerly.

"Not exactly," Mr. Parker replied, sliding into a chair beside her and dropping his voice. "A message from Interceptor Headquarters. Monitoring machines have traced the outlaw radio station again. The broadcast finished about an hour ago."

"And where was the station located this time, Dad?"

"Seemingly at or near the lighthouse."

"The lighthouse!" Penny exclaimed. She was so startled that her voice rose to a high pitch, attracting the attention of a passing bellboy.

"Not so loud, Penny," her father warned. "The strange thing was that the broadcast seemed to come from a cave, the same as before, although the monitoring machines charted it as being close to the lighthouse."

"The only one I know about near the Point is Crystal Cave," Penny said thoughtfully. "Dad, maybe the broadcast did come from the lighthouse!"

"That's government property. Penny, and the man in charge is beyond suspicion. Furthermore, the deep, echo effect couldn't come from anywhere except a cave."

"Unless it were a sound effect, Dad."

"What's that?" Mr. Parker asked, startled. "I don't get you, Penny."

"I mean, maybe the cave set-up is just a sound effect and nothing more. Only the other night I heard one in a radio play and it sounded as if the actors really were in a cave. Isn't it done by an echo chamber or something of the sort?"

"That would be possible," Mr. Parker agreed. "At Interceptor Headquarters it was assumed that a mistake had been made in charting the location of the station."

"Then the lighthouse hasn't been investigated?"

"Not to my knowledge."

"Well, it should be!" Penny exclaimed. "Louise and I were there today and we saw—"

"Yes?" Mr. Parker questioned as she suddenly broke off.

"We saw a lot that didn't look right," Penny finished, deciding not to bring Mrs. Deline's name into the discussion. "Mr. McCoy had visitors and while they were there he kept us locked up."

"My word! Why didn't you report to the police?"

"Well, we weren't entirely sure," Penny said lamely. "The door just closed and locked, and Mr. McCoy let on that it had a trick latch. Then he released us, but not until after the visitors had gone."

"Did you see the persons?"

"No, we only heard their voices. We weren't able to overhear any of the conversation."

Without explaining what he intended to do, Mr. Parker again closed himself into a telephone booth. Not until he returned did he tell Penny that he had called Interceptor Headquarters and that Army men had been sent to the lighthouse to make a thorough check-up.

"Now it's late," he said briskly, "and you're overdue for bed, Penny. Better fly up."

"Aren't you coming?"

"Not just now. I have a little unfinished business."

Penny hesitated, unwilling to go to bed when she sensed adventure in the offing. As she groped in her mind for an excuse to remain, the doors at the front entrance to the hotel began to spin. Jerry came hurrying into the lobby. Seeing Penny and her father he made a straight line for them.

"The code's been broken!" he announced, addressing Penny.

"What did they learn, Jerry?" she asked eagerly.

"It's just as you thought, Penny." Jerry dropped his bombshell. "Mrs. Deline definitely is an Enemy Agent. Apparently she was sent to Sunset Beach to aid that escaped prisoner I told you about!"

CHAPTER 23 - NIGHT ADVENTURE

As Jerry made the startling announcement, Penny glanced anxiously at her father. In the excitement of the moment she had not thought how much of a shock it might be to him to learn that Mrs. Deline was an agent employed by a foreign country. To her astonishment, he looked neither surprised nor dismayed.

"So you have the proof, Jerry!" Mr. Parker exclaimed. "That's fine! But what's all this about a code? How did you stumble onto it?"

"No time for details now," Jerry answered tersely. "Penny turned the trick—she and Louise saw Mrs. Deline bury a package in the sand."

"And Mrs. Deline brought that package from the lighthouse," Penny interposed eagerly. "Mr. McCoy must have given it to her."

"What's the plan of action?" Mr. Parker demanded. "Army men already have gone to the lighthouse to search that place thoroughly."

"Our job is to keep watch of the dune where the package was buried. Naturally we have no way of knowing what time anyone will show up there. It may be an all night wait."

"I'll be with you in a minute," Mr. Parker declared. "Just as soon as I get an overcoat."

He started toward the elevator, then came back to the group.

"What about Mrs. Deline?" he asked. "She's here in the hotel. Went to her room only a few minutes ago."

"She'll be placed under arrest," Jerry said. "Better call her on the telephone and get her down here. Don't let her suspect that you think anything is wrong."

Mr. Parker vanished into the nearest telephone booth.

"I can't understand it," Penny murmured to Jerry. "I was sure Dad was head over heels in love with Mrs. Deline. Why, it didn't even seem to ruffle him when he learned the truth about her."

Jerry grinned. "Maybe," he drawled, "that was because he knew all the time."

Penny was dumbfounded. "You mean—" she stammered, "You mean that Dad's been acting a part? Pretending to admire Mrs. Deline while actually he didn't?"

"Something like that. You see, your Dad became interested in the outlaw radio station and the men who operate it. By making inquiries before he left Riverview, he obtained information that made him think Mrs. Deline might be involved in some way. He knew she never had been in China but spent many years in Japan. He learned also that instead of being a newspaper correspondent, she had carried on secret work for various governments."

"Dad knew all that! And he never let on to me!"

"He couldn't very well, Penny. If you had guessed the truth, you'd have given it away by your manner—no matter how much you tried to act natural."

"What a little nit-wit I've been!"

"You have not," Jerry denied warmly. "Anyone else would have acted the same. Without knowing it, you helped your father a lot. You turned up evidence he never could have obtained alone."

"Where do you fit into the picture, Jerry? Did Dad send for you?"

"You don't send for anyone in the Army," Jerry explained, grinning. "By pure luck I was assigned here on a special mission. Your father learned I was coming, so we united forces."

"Then you've both known from the first about Mrs. Deline?"

"We've had a dark brown suspicion, Penny. But no proof until tonight."

Penny drew a deep breath. Before she could ask another question, her father came hurrying down the hotel corridor.

"Mrs. Deline's not in her room!" he reported. "She doesn't answer."

"She went upstairs only a few minutes ago," Penny recalled.

"Yes, she did, but she's not there now."

"Maybe she's asleep," Jerry said, "and failed to hear the 'phone. We'll have to check."

Without explaining why the matter was urgent, Mr. Parker arranged with the desk clerk to have one of the hotel maids go to Mrs. Deline's room. While the trio waited in the upstairs corridor, the woman rapped several times on the bedroom door, and failing to get a response, unlocked it with her master key.

"Mrs. Deline!" she called, softly at first, then in a louder voice.

There was no answer.

The maid then snapped on the light. "Why, there's no one here!" she cried. "The bed's not been slept in!"

"That's what I was afraid of," muttered Mr. Parker.

With Jerry and Penny, he entered the bedroom. Everything was in perfect order. However, Mrs. Deline's suitcase was gone and all her belongings had been removed from the closet.

"She's skipped without paying her room rent!" the maid exclaimed. "I'll call the manager!"

Penny was peering into the waste paper basket beside the desk.

"Look!" she drew the attention of her father and Jerry. "Burned letters and papers!"

Digging into the basket, she brought up several charred sheets of paper. They were unreadable and crumpled in her hand.

"This was a bad break for us—Mrs. Deline getting away!" Jerry exclaimed in disgust. "Evidently her work at Sunset Beach is finished. She's moving on to another pasture."

"But she can't be far away," Penny reasoned. "After all, we know when she came to her room."

"There still may be a chance to nab her," Mr. Parker said. "We'll notify the police to guard all the roads and the airport. I'll report to Major Gregg too."

Without awaiting the arrival of the hotel manager, the trio hastened to the lobby. There Jerry and Mr. Parker made several telephone calls.

"Now let's be on our way up the beach," Jerry urged anxiously. "We've killed too much time as it is."

Penny half expected that her father would refuse permission for her to go along. To her delight he merely said:

"I suppose there's no keeping you here, Penny. Well, come with us. I guess you've earned the right by your good work."

It was a dark night, warm but misty. No lights were showing outside the hotel, though far up the beach the powerful lighthouse beacon cut swathes across the black sea.

"What's the plan?" Mr. Parker asked Jerry.

"The entire coast for fifty miles is being watched. I thought just on a chance we might keep vigil at the place where Mrs. Deline buried the package of explosives. Someone may show up there. On the other hand, Penny tipped off the fact that she knew where the bundle was buried."

"Mrs. Deline watched Louise and me through a spy glass," Penny recalled ruefully. "She knew we didn't find the package though."

"That's our assignment anyhow," Jerry said. "To keep watch of that particular place until relieved by Army men."

The Parker car was on the hotel lot close by. Getting it, the trio took the beach road but stopped some distance from the lighthouse. Not wishing the car to attract the attention of any passer-by, it was left parked on a private driveway. Jerry, Penny and her father then crossed the dunes afoot and proceeded up the beach until they came to their station.

"Think this is the place?" Penny asked skeptically.

"I know it is," Jerry replied. "Remember what I told you about taking observations? Let's see if the package is still here?"

He began digging in one of the dunes. Almost at once he came upon the box of explosives.

"Exactly as we left it," he reported, replacing the sand. "No one's been here."

"I doubt anyone will come," Mr. Parker commented. "Probably afraid."

CHAPTER 23 - NIGHT ADVENTURE

High overhead and out of sight, Penny heard the drone of planes on coastal patrol. She stared up into the dark sky and then toward the sea. The tide was coming in and long rolling waves washed the beach, dashed themselves on the shoreline and retreated.

"We'll have to get down out of sight," Jerry warned. "Mustn't be seen from the road or the ocean either one."

"How about this spot?" Mr. Parker suggested, pointing to a hollow between two giant dunes.

The place seemed exactly right, so the trio flattened themselves on the sand. Jerry looked at the luminous dial of his watch.

"One fifteen," he announced. "No sign of activity."

"And no sign of any soldiers," Mr. Parker added. "I hope that whoever is to take over here shows up before long."

"I don't," Penny said, snuggling close between her father and Jerry. "I'm having fun!"

"If anything should develop, it's apt to be serious business," Jerry warned. "I'm inclined to think that we tipped our hand and nothing will happen."

An hour elapsed. During that time there was no sound save the roar of the restless sea. The warm sand made a comfortable couch, and despite her best intentions, Penny caught herself dozing. She had all she could do to keep awake.

"What time is it now?" she presently asked.

"Two thirty-five," Jerry answered. "It doesn't look as if there's to be any activity, but then the night's young."

"The night may be, but I'm not," Mr. Parker grumbled, shifting into a more comfortable position. "Wonder when our relief is to show up?"

"Must be some mix up on orders. We're probably stuck here for the night."

"In that case, Penny should return to the hotel."

"Oh, no. Dad! Anyway, if I left now I might attract the attention of anyone watching this place."

"You thought that one up!" her father chuckled. "Except for ourselves, there's no person within a quarter of a mile of this place."

"You're wrong about that," murmured Jerry, stiffening to alert attention.

"What's up, Jerry?" Mr. Parker said quickly. "You act as if you were seeing things!"

"I am, Chief! Look to the right—between us and the lighthouse!"

Mr. Parker and Penny gazed intently in the direction indicated.

"Can't see a thing," Mr. Parker whispered. "Your eyes must be tricking you, Jerry."

"Wait just a minute."

Even as Jerry spoke, a shadowy figure emerged from the mists. The man came swiftly down the beach, making no sound as he walked. When he was very close, the revolving beacon of the lighthouse singled him out for a fleeting instant. Brief as was the moment of illumination, Penny recognized the man.

"George Emory!" she whispered tensely. "What's he doing here?"

CHAPTER 24 - OUT OF THE SEA

The answer to Penny's whispered question soon became obvious. George Emory looked carefully about the windswept beach. The three tense watchers thought that he might approach the dune where they lay hidden, but he did not.

Instead, the man paused while several yards away and gazed toward the sea. A moment he stood thus, silhouetted against the sky. Then using a glowing flashlight, he began making wide sweeps with his arm.

"A signal!" Jerry whispered. "He's trying to attract the attention of a boat out at sea!"

"Shall we go for him?" asked Mr. Parker.

"Wait!" Jerry advised. "He's not the only one we're after. We're stalking bigger game."

At intervals for the next fifteen minutes, George Emory repeated the flashlight signals. Then he turned off the light and waited.

Anxiously, Jerry, Penny and Mr. Parker kept their faces turned to the sea. They sensed that the hour of action was at hand, and it worried them that Army men had failed to arrive.

"Look, Dad!" Penny suddenly whispered. She had glimpsed far from shore a long shadowy object which easily could be a boat. No lights were showing nor had she heard any sound.

"I don't see a thing," Mr. Parker whispered back. "Yes! Now I do! Jove! It looks like a submarine that's surfaced. I can make out the conning tower!"

"But why would it dare come here?" Penny speculated. "Won't it be detected by the patrol planes?"

"Tonight's a bad night," Jerry pointed out. "Besides, the shore is so indented at this point of coast that perfect protection is almost impossible. They're sending a boat, that's sure!"

A small craft had been launched from the wave-washed deck of the submarine. Manned by two men who rowed with muffled oars, it slowly approached the shore. When it was very close the watchers behind the sand dune saw by its grotesque sausage shape that it was a large, rubber boat. Like a gray ghost it slid over the water.

Mr. Parker gripped Penny's hand in an encouraging squeeze.

"Wish you were safe at the hotel," he whispered. "I was a fool to let you come."

Penny's heart pounded but she shook her head vigorously. Not for anything would she have missed the adventure. However, she was cool headed enough to realize that the situation was not shaping up well for her father and Jerry.

There were two men visible in the rubber boat, unquestionably armed. Then George Emory must be reckoned with and the arrival of others might be expected at any moment. Jerry carried a revolver but her father had no weapon. Already it was too late for any member of the trio to safely go for help.

"That sub may intend to land Secret Agents here," Jerry speculated. "But from the code message we deciphered, it's more likely they plan to take aboard one or more passengers."

"Perhaps that escaped flier," Penny supplied.

"He's a valuable man to them. Well worth the risk they're taking to try to rescue him."

"If passengers are to go aboard, where are they?" Penny whispered. "There's no one here but George Emory."

"We must wait and watch. We'll soon see enough or I miss my guess."

The rubber boat had reached the surf and was being churned by the waves. Two men in full military uniform, leaped out and guided the boat to the beach. George Emory waded out to meet them. Shaking the hand of each, he spoke rapidly in German. Though Mr. Parker understood the language, he was unable to catch a word.

CHAPTER 24 - OUT OF THE SEA

Tensely, the trio waited and watched. At any moment they feared that the men from the submarine might seek the cache of explosives hidden not far away. Soberly Jerry and Mr. Parker considered trying to reach the box in the sand. To do so they must cross an open, unprotected span of beach with every likelihood of being seen.

"Let's wait and see what happens," Mr. Parker advised. "We shouldn't risk calling attention to ourselves."

George Emory and his two companions obviously were awaiting someone. Nervously they paced the beach. Several times Mr. Emory looked at his watch. Then from far down the road came the sound of a car traveling at high speed. Tires screamed in protest as the auto came to a sudden halt on the paved road back from the beach.

"That's why they've waited!" Jerry whispered.

Barely a minute elapsed before two figures were seen coming swiftly from the direction of the road. A man and a woman crawled through the bushes, under the fence, and walked hurriedly across deep sand to the beach.

"Mrs. Deline!" Penny identified the woman. "The man with her is the same fellow who stole food from our camp!"

"I'd know his face from photographs I've seen," contributed Jerry. "He's Oscar Kleinbrock, escaped German prisoner. The man I was sent here to trace!"

Mrs. Deline and her companion reached the group of men who awaited them.

"You are five minutes late," George Emory reproved.

"Can we help it?" Mrs. Deline snapped. "We're lucky to be here at all. Do you know that the road is being watched?"

"By whom?"

"Army men. We were nearly stopped but were able to turn off into the thicket and wait."

"Then there's no time to waste in talk," George Emory said curtly. Turning, he spoke to the German flier in his own language.

"He's telling him to get aboard the rubber boat," Mr. Parker interpreted tensely. "Now they're saying goodbye to Emory and Mrs. Deline."

"Somehow we must hold them all here!" Jerry whispered grimly.

"It's two against five. And they're armed."

Mr. Parker and Jerry looked at each other, fully realizing how slim was their chance of success. They were not thinking of themselves but of Penny and what could happen to her if they failed. Mr. Parker touched her arm.

"Penny," he whispered. "Slip away in the darkness and make a dash for the hotel. Jerry and I will try to hold them until help comes. Just keep low as you run or those fiends may take a pot-shot at you." Penny would not desert her father and Jerry. Stubbornly, she shook her head.

"We want to know that you are safe," Jerry urged. "Please go while you still have a chance. You can help us most by bringing help."

Penny's determination to remain, weakened. Yet reason told her she never could reach the hotel and return with help in time to do any good. It dawned upon her that Jerry was only saying what he did to get her safely away.

"If only we had the box of explosives!" she whispered. "With it we might have a chance against those men!"

"It's too late to dig up the box now," said Jerry. "We probably couldn't find it without a light. And the noise we'd make—"

"Let me try," Penny interrupted.

"All right, see if you can get your hands on the box," her father agreed suddenly. "Slip back of the dune, and then circle. Don't try to cross the beach. Be careful! Remember the least sound will bring a hail of bullets."

Penny nodded and slipped away into the darkness, crawling on hands and knees. Barely had she left the shelter of the big sand dune than she heard two shots fired in quick succession.

"Those came from Jerry's revolver!" she thought. "Oh, it was a trick to get me safely away! Now he and Dad are in for fireworks!"

Raising her head above the protecting sand dune, Penny saw why Jerry had fired. The rubber boat was being launched. To delay the attack would mean that the entire party might escape.

"They'll all get away!" Penny thought in dismay. "How can Jerry and Dad hold them single handed?"

George Emory returned Jerry's fire with deadly aim. The bullets bit into the dune, throwing up little geysers of sand.

"Launch the boat!" he shouted savagely to the men from the submarine. "Get away while you can! Be quick!"

Jerry and Mr. Parker were determined that the party should not escape. As the men sought to launch the rubber boat, they made a concerted rush for the German flier who was to be taken aboard the waiting submarine. Caught by surprise, he went down beneath their blows.

Fearful of hitting his own man, George Emory dared not fire again. Instead, he and the crewmen of the submarine fell upon Jerry and Mr. Parker. In the melee, one person could not be distinguished from another.

"Fools! Fools!" cried Mrs. Deline as she watched the fierce, uneven struggle. "There is no time to be lost!"

Jerry and Mr. Parker were putting up the fight of their lives, but they were no match for four able bodied, trained men. Penny, desperate with anxiety, saw that the struggle could end only in one way—disaster for Jerry and her father.

"If I had that box of explosives maybe I could help them!" flashed through her mind.

Rolling over a dune, she ran to the place near the fence where she thought the cache was buried. Frantically she clawed and dug at the sand. She could not find the box.

"It must be here!" she told herself desperately. "Or was it hidden in the next dune?"

She tried another place slightly to the right. As she dug, she heard a sound behind her. Turning swiftly, she saw Mrs. Deline starting across the beach toward her.

"Oh, no, you don't!" the woman shouted.

Penny's hand encountered something hard and firm. The box of explosives! Digging wildly, she lifted it from the bed of sand and sprang to her feet. Her fingers closed upon one of the hand grenades.

"Get back!" she ordered Mrs. Deline, balancing herself as if to throw.

The woman stopped short, then retreated a few steps. But only for a moment was she frightened.

"Why, you infant, you couldn't throw a grenade!" she jeered. "You don't know how. Besides, you haven't the nerve!"

"Get back!" Penny ordered again. "I warn you."

Mrs. Deline laughed scornfully and came on.

Even the thought of throwing a hand grenade terrified Penny. She knew that she could not deliberately harm Mrs. Deline or even the men who were mercilessly beating her father and Jerry. Yet she had to do something.

"Maybe I can destroy the rubber boat!" she thought. "It's far enough away so that no one should be hurt by the explosion."

Whirling away from Mrs. Deline, Penny faced the sea. Fixing her eyes on her target, the rubber boat at the water's edge, she hurled the grenade.

"Idiot!" cried Mrs. Deline, flinging herself flat on the sand to protect her face from flying fragments.

Penny did likewise. The grenade dropped with a thud on the sand beside the rubber boat. Her aim had been perfect. But there was no explosion. Belatedly, Penny realized that she had forgotten to pull the safety pin.

Mrs. Deline kept her face buried beneath her arms and did not yet know what had happened. Sick with the knowledge that she had failed, Penny was desperate. Her father and Jerry were being cruelly beaten by their opponents. In another minute they would be overpowered and the Germans would escape to the waiting submarine.

"I can't let them get away!" Penny whispered. "I must do something!"

Remembering the pencil bombs, she groped in the cardboard box for them. They were not there. Instead, her fingers closed upon the sharp bladed knife.

"I'll slash the rubber boat!" she thought. "I'll try to make a hole in it!"

Before Mrs. Deline realized what the girl was about, Penny darted down the beach. The men from the submarine did not see her. Reaching the rubber boat, she leaped into it. Working with desperate haste, she jabbed the knife through the bottom. The material was tough and it took all of her strength to make a long jagged gash. Water seeped in, slowly at first, then faster.

"I've done it!" Penny thought jubilantly. "I've done it!"

CHAPTER 24 - OUT OF THE SEA

Her triumph was fleeting. The next instant the girl was struck a hard stunning blow from behind. As she collapsed in a limp little heap on the sand, she dimly saw the cruel, angry face of Mrs. Deline. Then all went black and she knew no more.

CHAPTER 25 - A SCOOP FOR UNCLE SAM

Penny opened her eyes and wondered where she was. For a moment she could remember nothing of what had transpired. Gradually, she realized that she was lying down, her head pillowed in someone's lap. She seemed to be in a fast-moving motor boat for she could hear the wash of waves against the craft. In panic she decided that she must be a prisoner enroute to the German submarine. She struggled to sit up.

"Easy there, partner," said a soothing voice.

Penny twisted sideways to look at the speaker. "Jerry!" she whispered.

"You're all right," he said, pressing her gently back. "We'll get you to a doctor in a few minutes."

"A doctor, my eye!" Penny protested with spirit.

"That was a nasty blow Mrs. Deline gave you on the head," contributed another voice.

Penny turned again and saw her father. His shirt was half torn off and there was a long gash on his cheek.

"Dad, you're hurt!"

"Nothing but a few scratches, Penny. Jerry took worse punishment than I did. But you should see the other fellows!"

"What happened?" Penny asked. "Where am I anyhow?"

"In a patrol boat bound for the hotel."

"But what happened on the beach? The last I remember was when I tried to slash the rubber boat."

"You not only tried, you did!" chuckled Jerry. "Mrs. Deline struck you on the head with something—maybe a rock—and you went down for the count. About that time, some of the Army boys arrived. Mrs. Deline and her crowd tried to make a get-away, but the boat couldn't be launched."

"Then what happened?" Penny demanded as Jerry paused for breath.

"The two members of the sub crew tried to swim. They were picked up by a patrol boat that had been drawn to the locality by the gun fire."

"And Mrs. Deline?"

"She and her pal Emory, together with the escaped flier, struck off across the sand dunes."

"They didn't get away?"

"Not on your life. They reached the road and there found a nice reception awaiting them! Right now the three are lodged at Headquarters."

Penny took a deep breath. Her head was throbbing but she scarcely felt the pain.

"What about Jim McCoy at the lighthouse?" she inquired.

"He was taken into custody earlier in the evening. A portable broadcasting outfit was found on the premises."

"Then Mr. McCoy really was the man responsible for those mysterious broadcasts—the Voice from the Cave?"

"No doubt he had helpers," Mr. Parker contributed. "We expect to track down most of the ring now that the leaders have been captured. At any rate, we've put an end to the broadcasts. Your other theory was right too, Penny."

"What theory, Dad?"

"That the cave effect was produced by an echo chamber."

"Then no broadcast ever originated in a cave?"

"Probably not. We know McCoy shifted locations frequently. Tonight was the first time he ever dared broadcast from the lighthouse."

CHAPTER 25 - A SCOOP FOR UNCLE SAM

"And what of the old beachcomber, Jake Skagway?"

"Just a beachcomber," Jerry answered. "He had no connection with Emory or Mrs. Deline."

Penny lay perfectly still for a few minutes, gazing up at the dark sky. A few stars pricked the black canopy above her, and now and then a quarter moon peeped from behind a cloud screen.

"How did I get aboard this boat?" she presently inquired.

"Another patrol boat came by," Jerry explained. "In fact, after all the fireworks, just about everyone in Sunset Beach arrived on the scene. We wanted to get you to a doctor so we took the first transportation that offered."

"Almost there now too," added Mr. Parker.

Penny sat up. The shore was dark but she could dimly see the dark Crystal Inn hotel.

"I don't need a doctor," she laughed. "I'm feeling better every minute. My, won't Louise be green with envy when she learns what she missed!"

"I'd say she was lucky," Mr. Parker corrected. "Penny, you don't seem to realize what a narrow escape we all had."

"That's right," added Jerry, "those men were desperate, and they'd have stopped at nothing. I guess we owe our lives to you, Penny."

Penny loved the praise. Nevertheless, she replied with a show of modesty:

"Oh, I didn't do a thing, Jerry. As a matter of record, I nearly messed up the show. When I threw that hand grenade I forgot to pull the safety pin."

"I'm glad you did," chuckled Jerry. "If it had exploded, we might not be here now."

Penny sat very still, thinking over what had happened. Events were a bit hazy in her mind and many questions remained unanswered.

"The submarine?" she asked after a moment.

"Sunk," Jerry replied. "One of our patrol planes scored a direct hit."

"I guess that brings me up to date," Penny sighed, "There's only one thing that bothers me."

"What's that?" inquired her father.

"Did you know who Mrs. Deline was when you invited her to come with us to Sunset Beach?"

"No, but I had a healthy suspicion that she might be working against our country, Penny. I first met Mrs. Deline at the Club. However, she was rather transparent in making a play for my attention. In checking up I discovered that she never had been in China and never had written a newspaper story in her life. When she practically invited herself to ride with us to Sunset Beach, I thought I'd try to find out more about her little game."

"I acted so silly about everything," Penny acknowledged, deeply ashamed. "I'm sorry, Dad."

"You needn't be, Penny. At times you were rude to Mrs. Deline which was wrong. But your actions served a good purpose by keeping the woman so diverted that she never was on her guard."

Shore was very close. As the powerful engines of the motor boat became muted, Penny said wistfully:

"Now that your work is done here, Jerry, I suppose you'll be winging off to some far corner of the country."

"Not for a few days at least," he reassured her. "I'm expecting a furlough and I'll spend it right here at Sunset Beach. We'll cram those days full of fun, Penny. We'll swim and golf and dance. We'll make every minute count."

The boat grated gently against the dock and a sailor leaped out to make the craft fast. Mr. Parker and Jerry helped Penny ashore. Though she tried to stand steady upon her feet, the boards rocked beneath her.

"Hook on," invited Jerry, offering an arm.

Mr. Parker supported her on the other side, and thus they walked slowly toward the hotel.

"The Three Musketeers!" chuckled the editor. "'One for all, and all for one.'"

"We do make a trio," agreed Penny. "Tonight it seems just as it did when we were together in Riverview working on a big news story. There's one difference though."

"What's that?" asked Jerry.

"Tonight we were actors in a little drama that should be page one on any newspaper. Yet neither of you news hawks so much as spoke of trying to get a scoop for the *Riverview Star*."

"Good reason," rumbled Mr. Parker. "The story of what happened tonight may never be published."

"I understand, Dad. If the news were printed now it might give valuable information to the enemy."

VOICE FROM THE CAVE

Penny paused to catch her breath. With Jerry and her father still supporting her, she turned to face the restless sea. The patrol boat had slipped away into the darkness. Far up shore, unmindful that her faithless master had gone, the bright beacon from the lighthouse swept the water at regular intervals. Nothing seemed changed.

"Curtain going down on one of the best adventures of my life," Penny said softly. "Who cares that the *Riverview Star* missed the story? Why, this was an A-1 scoop for Uncle Sam!"

GUILT OF THE BRASS THIEVES

Dedicated to ASA WIRT

TREADING WATER, THE GIRL SHOUTED FOR HELP.

CHAPTER 1 - ADRIFT

"This is the limit! The very limit!" Giving his leather suitcase an impatient kick, Anthony Parker began to pace up and down the creaking old dock.

His daughter Penny, who stood in the shadow of a shed out of the hot afternoon sun, grinned at him with good humor and understanding.

"Oh, take it easy, Dad," she advised. "After all, this is a vacation and we have two weeks before us. Isn't the river beautiful?"

"What's beautiful about it?" her father growled.

However, he turned to gaze at a zigzag group of sailboats tacking gracefully along the far rippled shore. Not a quarter of a mile away, a ferryboat churned the blue water to whip cream foam as it steamed upstream.

"Are you certain this is the dock where we were to meet Mr. Gandiss?" Penny asked after a moment. "It seems queer he would fail us, for it's nearly five o'clock now. We've waited almost an hour."

Ceasing the restless pacing, Mr. Parker, publisher of the *Riverview Star*, a daily newspaper, searched his pockets and found a crumpled letter.

Reviewing it at a glance, he said: "Four o'clock was the hour Mr. Gandiss promised to meet us at dock fourteen."

"This is number fourteen," Penny confirmed, pointing to the numbers plainly visible on the shed. "Obviously something happened to Mr. Gandiss. Perhaps he forgot."

"A nice thing!" muttered the publisher. "Here he invites us to spend two weeks at his island home and then fails to meet us! Does he expect us to swim to the island?"

Penny, a slim, blue-eyed girl with shoulder length bob which the wind tossed about at will, wandered to the edge of the dock.

"That must be Shadow Island over there," she observed, indicating a dot of green land which arched from the water like the curving back of a turtle. "It must be nearly a mile away."

"The question is, how much longer are we to wait?" Mr. Parker glanced again at his watch. "It's starting to cloud up, and may rain in another half hour. Why not taxi into town? What's the name of this one-horse dump, anyhow?"

"Our tickets read 'Tate's Beach.'"

"Well, Tate's Beach must do without us this summer," Mr. Parker snapped, picking up his suitcase. "I've had my fill of this! We'll spend the night in a hotel, then start for Riverview on the early morning train."

"Do you know Mr. Gandiss well?" Penny inquired, stalling for time.

"He advertises in the *Star*, and we played golf together occasionally when he came to Riverview. I must have been crazy to accept an invitation to come here!"

"Oh, we'll have a good time if only we can get to the island, Dad."

"I can't figure out exactly why Gandiss invited us," Mr. Parker added thoughtfully. "He has something in mind besides entertainment, but what it is, I haven't been able to guess."

"How about hiring a boat?" Penny suggested.

Her father debated, then shook his head. "No, if Gandiss doesn't think enough of his guests to meet them, then he can do without us. Come on, we're leaving!"

Never noted for an even temper or patience, the publisher strode down the dock.

"Wait, Dad!" Penny called excitedly. "I think someone may be coming for us now!"

GUILT OF THE BRASS THIEVES

A mahogany motorboat with glittering brasswork, approached at high speed from the direction of Shadow Island. As Penny and her father hopefully watched, it swerved toward their dock, and the motor was throttled.

"That's not Mr. Gandiss," the publisher said, observing a sandy-haired, freckled youth at the steering wheel.

Nevertheless, suitcase in hand, he waited for the boat.

The craft came in smoothly, and the young man at the wheel leaped out and made fast to a dock post.

"You're Anthony Parker!" he exclaimed, greeting Penny's father, and bestowing an apologetic smile upon them both. "I'm Jack—Jack Gandiss."

"Harvey Gandiss' son?" Mr. Parker inquired, his annoyance melting.

"A chip off the old block," the boy grinned. "Hope I haven't kept you waiting long."

"Well, we had just about given up," Mr. Parker admitted truthfully.

"I'm sure sorry, sir. I promised my father I would meet you sharp at four. Fact is, I was out on the river with some friends, and didn't realize how late it was. We were practicing for the trophy sailboat race."

Penny's blue eyes sparkled with interest. An excellent swimmer, she too enjoyed sailing and all water sports. However, she had never competed in a race.

"Suppose we get along to the island," Mr. Parker interposed, glancing at the sky. "I don't like the look of those clouds."

"Oh, it won't rain for hours," Jack said carelessly. "Those clouds are moving slowly and we'll reach the island within ten minutes."

Helping Penny and Mr. Parker into the motorboat, he stowed the luggage under the seat and then cast off. In a sweeping circle, the craft sped past a canbuoy which marked a shoal, and out into the swift current.

Penny held tightly to her straw hat to keep it from being blown downstream. A stiff breeze churned the waves which spanked hard against the bow of the boat.

"My father was sorry he couldn't meet you himself!" Jack hurled at them above the whistle of the wind. "He was held up at the airplane factory—labor trouble or something of the sort."

Mr. Parker nodded, his good humor entirely restored. Settling comfortably in the leather seat, he focused his gaze on distant Shadow Island.

"Good fishing around here?" he inquired.

"The best ever. You'll like it, sir."

Jack was nearly seventeen, with light hair and steel blue eyes. His white trousers were none too well pressed and the sleeves of an old sweater bore smears of grease. Steering the boat with finger-tip control, he deliberately cut through the highest of the waves, treating his passengers to a series of jolts.

Some distance away, a ferryboat, the *River Queen*, glided smoothly along, its railings thronged with people. In the pilot house, a girl who might have been sixteen, stood at the wheel.

"Look, Dad!" Penny exclaimed. "A girl is handling that big boat!"

"Sally Barker," Jack informed disparagingly. "She's the daughter of Captain Barker who owns the *River Queen*. A brat if ever there was one!"

"She certainly has that ferryboat eating out of her hand," Mr. Parker commented admiringly.

"Oh, she handles a boat well enough. Why shouldn't she? The captain started teaching her about the river when she was only three years old. He taught her all she knows about sailboat racing, too."

Jack's tone of voice left no doubt that he considered Sally Barker completely beneath his notice. As the two boats drew fairly close together, the girl in the pilot house waved, but he pretended not to see.

"You said something about a sailboat race when we were at the dock," Penny reminded him eagerly. "Is it an annual affair?"

Jack nodded, swerving to avoid a floating log. "Sally won the trophy last year. Before that I held it. This year I am planning on winning it back."

"Oh, I see," Penny commented dryly.

"That's not why I dislike Sally," Jack said to correct any misapprehension she might have gained. "It's just—well, she's so sure of herself—so blamed stubborn. And it's an insult to Tate's Beach the way she flaunts the trophy aboard that cheap old ferryboat!"

"How do you mean?" Mr. Parker inquired, his curiosity aroused.

Jack did not reply, for just then the engine coughed. The boat plowed on a few feet, and the motor cut off again.

CHAPTER 1 - ADRIFT

"Now what?" Jack exclaimed, alarmed.

Even as he spoke, the engine died completely.

"Sounds to me as if we're out of gas," observed Mr. Parker. "How is your supply?"

A stricken look came upon Jack's wind-tanned face. "I forgot to fill the tank before I left the island," he confessed ruefully. "My father told me to be sure to do it, but I started off in such a hurry."

"Haven't you an extra can of fuel aboard?" Mr. Parker asked, trying to hide his annoyance.

Jack shook his head, gazing gloomily toward the distant island. The current had caught the boat and was carrying it downstream, away from the Gandiss estate.

"Nothing to do then, but get out the oars. And it will be a long, hard row."

"Oars?" Jack echoed weakly. "We haven't any aboard and no anchor either."

Mr. Parker was too disgusted to speak. A man who demanded efficiency and responsibility in his own newspaper plant, he had no patience with those negligent of their duties. Because he and Penny were to be guests of the Gandiss family, he made an effort not to blame Jack for the mishap.

"I—I'm terribly sorry," the boy stammered. "But we shouldn't be stranded here long. We'll soon be picked up."

Hopefully, Jack gazed toward the nearest shore. No small boats were visible. The ferry, plying her regular passenger route, now was far upstream.

Although the sun still shone brightly, clouds frequently blocked it from view. Waves slapped higher against the drifting boat and the river took on a dark cast.

Neither Penny nor her father spoke of the increasing certainty of rain. However, they watched the shifting clouds uneasily. Soon there was no more sun, and the river waters became inky black.

Presently the wind died completely and a dead calm held the boat. But not for many minutes. Soon a ripple of breeze ruffled the water, and far upstream a haze of rain blotted out the shoreline.

"Here it comes!" Mr. Parker said tersely, buttoning up his coat.

The next instant, wind and rain struck the little boat in full force. Penny's hat was swept from her head and went sailing gaily down river. Waves which broke higher and higher, spanked the boat, threatening to overturn it when they struck broadside.

"If we just had an anchor—" Jack murmured but did not finish.

Above the fury of the storm could be heard the faint clatter of a motorboat engine. Straining their eyes, they pierced the wall of rain to see a small speedboat fighting its way upstream.

"A boat!" Penny cried. "Now we'll be picked up!"

Jack sprang to his feet, waving and shouting. Closer and closer approached the boat, but there was no answering shout from those aboard.

Mr. Parker, Penny and Jack yelled in unison. They thought for a moment that the occupants must have heard their cries and would come to the rescue. But the craft did not change course.

Keeping steadily on, it passed the drifting motorboat well to starboard, and disappeared into the curtain of rain.

CHAPTER 2 - THE BRASS LANTERN

The rain dashed into Penny's face and ran in rivulets down her neck. With a change in the wind direction, the air had become suddenly cold. Shivering, she huddled close to her father for warmth.

Veiled by rain, the shore no longer was visible. Far to the right, the chug of a laboring motorboat was heard for an instant, then died away. It was apparent to Penny that they were drifting downstream quite rapidly.

"Listen!" she cried a moment later.

From upriver had come three sharp blasts of a whistle.

"That's the *River Queen*," muttered Jack, tossing a lock of wet hair out of his eyes. "We must be right in her path."

"Then maybe we'll be picked up!" Penny exclaimed hopefully.

Jack gave a snort of disgust. "I'd rather drown than accept help from Sally Barker! Wouldn't she gloat!"

"Young man," interposed Mr. Parker with emphasis, "this is no time for false pride. We're in a predicament and will welcome help from any source."

"Yes, sir, I guess you're right," murmured Jack, completely squelched. "I sure am sorry about getting you into this mess."

Gazing through the curtain of driving rain, Penny tried to glimpse the *River Queen*. Suddenly she distinguished its high decks and was dismayed to see that the ferry was bearing at full speed directly toward the drifting motorboat.

Jack leaped to his feet, frantically waving his arms. Realizing the danger of being run down, Mr. Parker likewise sprang up, shouting.

Straight on came the *River Queen*, her pilot seemingly unaware of the little boat low in the water and directly in the path.

"They don't see us!" Jack shouted hoarsely. "We'll be run down!"

The ferryboat now was very close. Its dark hull loomed up. Expecting a splintering crash, Penny struggled to her feet, preparing to jump overboard. But instead, she heard a series of sharp whistle toots, and the ferryboat swerved, missing them by a scant three yards.

"Wow! Was that close!" Jack muttered, collapsing weakly on the seat. Then he straightened up again into alert attention, for the ferry had reduced speed.

"Maybe we're going to be picked up!" he exclaimed.

The ferryboat indeed had maneuvered so that the current would swing the drifting craft directly toward it.

Five minutes later, wet and bedraggled, the three stranded sailors scrambled up a lowered ladder onto the *River Queen's* slippery deck. A few curious passengers who braved the rain, stared curiously at them as they sought shelter.

"Well, if it isn't Jack Gandiss, and in trouble again!" boomed Captain Barker, owner of the ferry. He was a short, stubby, red-faced man, with twinkling blue eyes. "What happened this time? Engine conk out?"

"We ran out of gas," the boy admitted briefly. "Thanks for picking us up."

"Better thank Sally here," replied the captain, giving orders for the motorboat to be taken in tow. "It was her sharp eyes that picked you up out o' the storm."

Penny turned to see a dark-haired girl of her own age standing in the doorway of the pilot house. In oilskin hat and coat, one easily might have mistaken her for a boy. Impatiently she brushed aside a strand of wet hair which straggled from beneath the ugly headgear, and came out on the rain-swept deck.

CHAPTER 2 - THE BRASS LANTERN

"Well, well, if it isn't Jack!" she chortled, enjoying the boy's discomfiture. "Imagine an old tar like you running out of gas!"

"Never mind the cracks!" he retorted grimly. "Just go back to your knitting!"

Turning her back upon Jack, Sally studied Penny with curious interest.

"Do I know you?" she inquired.

"My father and I are to be guests at the Gandiss home," Penny explained, volunteering their names. "We were on our way to Shadow Island when we ran out of gas."

"Let's not go into all the gory details here," Jack broke in. "We're getting wet."

"You mean you *are* all wet," corrected Sally, grinning.

"Sally, take our guests to the cabin," Captain Barker instructed with high good humor. "I'll handle the wheel. We're late on our run now."

"How about dropping us off at the island?" Jack inquired. "If we had some gasoline—"

"We'll take care of you on the return trip," the captain promised. "No time now. We have a hundred passengers to unload at Osage."

Penny followed Sally along the wet deck to a companionway and down the stairs to the private quarters of the captain and his daughter.

"Osage is a town across the river," Sally explained briefly. "Pop and I make the run every hour. This is our last trip today, thank Jupiter!"

The cabin was warm and cozy, though cramped in space. Sally gave Mr. Parker one of her father's warm sweaters to put on over his sodden garments, offered Penny a complete change of outer clothing, and deliberately ignored Jack's needs.

"You may return the duds later," she said, leading Penny to an adjoining cabin where she could change her clothes. "How long do you folks expect to stay at Shadow Island?"

"Two weeks probably." Penny wriggled out of the limp dress.

"Then we'll have time to get better acquainted. You'll be here for the trophy race too!" Sally's dark eyes danced and she added in a very loud voice: "You'll be around to see Jack get licked!"

"In a pig's eye!" called Jack through the thin partition of the cabin. "Why, that old sailboat of yours is just a mess of wormwood!"

"It was fast enough to win the brass lantern trophy!" Sally challenged, winking at Penny. In a whisper she explained: "I always get a kick out of tormenting Jack! He's so cocky and sure of himself! It does him good to be taken down a peg."

"Tell me about the race," urged Penny. "It sounds interesting—especially your feud with Jack."

"Later," promised Sally carelessly. "Right now I want to get you something warm to drink before we dock at Osage. Here, give me those wet clothes. I'll dry them for you, and send them to Shadow Island tomorrow."

Rejoining Jack and Mr. Parker, the captain's daughter conducted the party to a food bar in the passenger lounge.

"Hot Java," she instructed the counter man. "And what will you have to go with it? Hamburgers or dogs? This is on the house."

"Make mine a dog with plenty of mustard," laughed Penny, enjoying the girl's breezy slang.

"Nothing for me except coffee," said Jack stiffly. "I'll pay for it too."

Mr. Parker decided upon a hamburger. Food, especially the steaming hot coffee, revived the drooping spirits of the trio. Even Jack thawed slightly in his attitude toward Sally.

Sipping the brew from a thick China mug, Penny's gaze roved curiously about the lounge. The room was poorly furnished, with an ancient red carpet and wicker chairs. Passengers were absorbed with newspapers, their fretful children, or the *River Queen's* supply of ancient magazines.

The lounge however, was scrupulously clean, and every fixture had been polished until it shone like gold. Sam Barker, whose father before him had sailed a river boat, was an able, efficient captain, one of the best and most respected on the waterfront.

Attached to an overhead beam near the food bar, swung an ancient brass lantern. The body was hexagonal in shape, its panes of glass protected by bars of metal. A two-part ornamental turret was covered with a hood from which was attached the suspending ring.

"That lantern came from an old whaling boat nearly a century ago," Sally explained. "For many years it was kept in the Country Club as a curio. Then two seasons ago, it was offered as a trophy in the annual Hat Island sailboat race held here."

"I won the lantern the first year," Jack contributed. He pointed to his name and the date engraved on the trophy's base.

"The second year, I upset the apple cart by winning," Sally added with a grin. "The race next week will decide who keeps the lantern permanently."

"Providing it isn't stolen first!" Jack cut in pointedly. "Sally, why must you be so stubborn about hanging it here on the *River Queen?* Every Tom, Dick, and Harry rides this old tub."

"Don't call the *River Queen* a tub," drawled Sally, her tone warning him he had gone far enough. "And as for our passengers—"

"What I mean," Jack corrected hastily, "is that you can't vouch for the honesty of every person who rides this ferry."

"I'm not in the least worried about the lantern being stolen," Sally retorted. "I won it fairly enough, didn't I?"

"Yes."

"Then it's mine to display as I choose. The racing committee agreed to that. The lantern is chained to a beam and is safe enough."

"I hope so," Jack said grimly. "I aim to win it back, and I don't want to see it do a disappearing act before the day of the race."

"You won't," Sally returned shortly. "I accept full responsibility, so let me do the worrying."

A signal bell tapped several times, a warning to the passengers that the ferry was approaching shore. As those aboard began to gather up their belongings, Sally buttoned her oilskin coat tightly about her.

"Excuse me for a minute," she said to Penny and Mr. Parker. "I've got to help Pop. See you later."

CHAPTER 3 - A "PROBLEM" BOY

Penny, Jack and Mr. Parker reached the deck of the *River Queen* in time to see Sally leap nimbly across a wide space to the dock. There she looped a great coil of rope expertly over the post and helped get the gangplank down.

"Step lively!" she urged the passengers pleasantly, but in a voice crisp with authority.

In a space of five minutes, she had helped an old man on crutches, found a child who had become separated from his mother, and refused passage to three young men who sought to make a return trip on the ferry.

"Sorry, this is the end of the line," she told them firmly. "Our last trip today."

"Then how about a date?" one of the men teased.

Sally paid not the slightest heed. Raising the gangplank, she signalled for the ferry to pull away.

"Sally always likes to put on a show!" Jack muttered disapprovingly. "To watch her perform, one would think she were the captain!"

"Well, she impresses me as a most capable young lady," commented Mr. Parker. "After all, we owe our rescue to her and Captain Barker."

Taking the hint, Jack offered no further disparaging remarks. Rain had ceased to fall, but deep shadows blotted out the river shores. Watching from the railing, Penny saw the island loom up, a dark, compact mass of black.

"The ferry can't land there?" she inquired in surprise.

Jack shook his head. "Shoals," he explained briefly. "In the spring during the flood season, the channel is fairly safe. Now—"

He broke off, and turned to stare toward the pilot house. The engines had been stilled and the ferry was drifting in toward the island. Captain Barker stood by his wheel, silent, watchful as a cat.

"By George!" Jack exclaimed admiringly. "The old boy intends to take her in through the shoals. But it's a risky thing to do."

"It is necessary?" asked Mr. Parker, deeply concerned. "After all, we've already caused the Barkers great inconvenience. Surely there is no need for them to risk going aground just to put us off at the Island."

"Captain Barker could give us a little gasoline, but he gets a big kick out of doing it this way," Jack muttered. "He and Sally both like to show off. It wouldn't surprise me if the old boy oversteps himself this time. We're running into shoal water."

Sally, evidently worried, stationed herself at the bow of the *River Queen*, dropping a leadline over the side.

"Eight and a half feet!" she called. "Seven and three-quarters—"

"We'll never make it," Jack murmured. "We're going aground now!"

Even as he spoke, the ferryboat grated on the sandy river bottom.

Captain Barker seemed not in the least disturbed. "Let 'er have it!" he shouted through the speaking tube. "Every ounce we've got!"

Rasping and groaning in its timbers, the stout little ferryboat ground her way through the sand. For one terrifying moment it seemed that she had wedged herself fast. But she shuddered and went over the bar into deeper water.

Sally drew a long sigh of relief, and grinned at Jack. "I knew Pop could make it," she chuckled, "but he sure had me scared for a minute."

"That was a remarkable demonstration of piloting," Mr. Parker declared. "Are we in safe waters now?"

"Yes, the channel is deep all the way to our dock," Jack replied. "I guess Captain Barker aims to dump us off at our front door."

Bells jingled again, the engines were cut, and the ferry drifted up to Shadow Island wharf. While Mr. Parker and Penny were thanking Captain Barker, Sally helped Jack and one of the sailors set loose the towed motorboat. Their loud, argumentative voices could be heard from the stern.

"Those kids scrap like a dog and a cat when they're together," chuckled Captain Barker. "But I calculate they'll outgrow it when they're a little older. At least, I hope so."

Saying a reluctant goodbye, Mr. Parker and Penny tramped ashore, and with Jack, watched until the *River Queen* had safely passed the shoal and was well out in the main channel again.

Before they could pick up the luggage, an elderly, gray-haired man came hurriedly down a flagstone walk from the brightly lighted house on the knoll.

"Mr. Gandiss!" exclaimed Anthony Parker, grasping his outstretched hand. "This is my daughter, Penelope. Or Penny, everyone calls her."

The owner of Shadow Island greeted the girl with more than casual interest. But as he spoke, his puzzled gaze followed the *River Queen* whose lights now could be seen far upstream.

"I may as well make a clean breast of it, Dad," Jack said before his father could request an explanation. "We ran out of gas, and the *Queen* picked us up."

"You ran out of gas? I distinctly recall warning you this afternoon that the tank would need to be refilled."

"I forgot," Jack said, edging away. Before his father could reprimand him further, he disappeared in the direction of the boathouse.

Mr. Gandiss, a stout, pleasant man, was distressed by his son's behavior. As he led the way to the house, he apologized so profusely that Penny and her father began to feel uncomfortable.

"Oh, boys will be boys," Mr. Parker declared, trying to put an end to the discussion. "No harm was done."

"We enjoyed the adventure," added Penny sincerely. "It was a pleasure to meet Captain Barker and his daughter."

Mr. Gandiss refused to abandon the subject.

"Jack worries me," he confessed ruefully. "He's sixteen now—almost seventeen, but in some respects he has no responsibility. He's an only child, and I am afraid my wife and I have spoiled him."

"Jack doesn't seem to get along with Sally Barker very well," Penny remarked, smiling at the recollection.

"That's another thing," nodded the island owner. "Sally is a fine girl and smart as a whip. Jack has the idea that because she isn't the product of a finishing school, she is beneath notice. Sally likes to prick holes in Jack's inflated ego, and then the war is on!"

"You have a fine son," Mr. Parker said warmly. "He'll outgrow all these ideas."

"I hope so," sighed Mr. Gandiss. "I certainly do." His expression conveyed the impression that he was not too confident.

The Gandiss home, surrounded by shrubs, was large and pretentious. At the front there was a long, narrow terrace which caught the breeze and commanded a view of the river for half a mile in either direction. There were tennis courts at the rear, and a garden.

"I'm glad you folks will be here for the annual sailboat race," Mr. Gandiss remarked, pausing to indicate the twinkling shore lights across the water. "If it were daytime, you could see the entire course from here. Jack is to race a new boat built especially for him."

"Sally Barker is his chief competitor?" inquired Penny.

"Yes, in skill they are about equally matched, I should say. They take their feud very seriously."

In the open doorway stood Mrs. Gandiss, a silver-haired woman not yet in her fifties. Cordially, she bade the newcomers welcome.

"What a dreadful time you must have had out on the river!" she said sympathetically. "The storm came up so quickly. My husband would have met you himself, but he was delayed at the factory."

A servant was sent for the luggage, and Effie, a maid, conducted Penny to her room. The chamber was luxuriously furnished with a green tiled bath adjoining. Pulling a silken cord to open the Venetian blinds, Penny saw that the window overlooked the river. She breathed deeply of the damp, rain-freshened air.

"Where do the Barkers live?" she asked Effie who was laying out embroidered towels.

CHAPTER 3 - A "PROBLEM" BOY

"Wherever it suits their fancy to drop anchor, Miss. Since I came here to work, the only home they ever have had was aboard their ferryboat."

The luggage soon was brought up, and Effie unpacked, carefully hanging up each garment. Penny inquired if she would have time for a hot bath.

"Oh, yes, Miss. The Gandiss' never dine until eight. I will draw your tub. Pine scent or violet?"

Penny swallowed hard and nearly lost her composure. "Make it pine," she managed, "and omit the needles!"

Exposure to rain and cold had stiffened her muscles and made her feel thoroughly miserable. However, after fifteen minutes in a steaming bath, she felt as fresh as ever. Her golden hair curled in ringlets tight to her head, and when she came from the bathroom, she found a blue dinner dress neatly pressed and laid on the bed.

"Two weeks of this life and I won't even be able to brush my own teeth," she thought. "No wonder Jack is such a spoiled darling."

Penny wondered what Mrs. Maud Weems would say if she were there. The Parkers lived nearly a hundred miles away in a city called Riverview, and Mrs. Weems, the housekeeper, had looked after Penny since the death of her mother many years before.

Mr. Parker, known throughout the state, published a daily newspaper, the *Star*, and his daughter frequently helped him by writing news or offering unrequested advice.

In truth, neither she nor her father had been eager to spend a vacation with members of the Gandiss family, feeling that they were practically strangers. Jack, Penny feared, might prove a particular trial.

In the living room, a cheerful fire had been started in the grate. Mr. and Mrs. Gandiss were chatting with Mr. Parker, trying their best to make him feel at home.

An awkward break in the conversation was covered by announcement that dinner was served. Jack's chair at the end of the table remained conspicuously empty.

"Where is the boy?" Mr. Gandiss asked his wife in a disapproving tone.

"I'm sure I don't know," she sighed. "The last I saw him, he was down at the dock."

A servant was sent to find Jack. After a long absence, he returned to say that the boy was nowhere on the island, and that the motorboat was missing.

"He's off somewhere again, and without permission," Mr. Gandiss said irritably. "Probably to the Harpers'. You see what I mean, Mr. Parker? A growing boy is a fearful problem."

Penny and her father avoided a discussion of such a personal subject. An excellent dinner of six courses was served in perfect style, but while the food was well cooked, no one really enjoyed the meal.

Coffee in tiny China cups was offered in Mr. Gandiss' study. His wife excused herself to go to the kitchen for a moment and the two men were left alone with Penny.

Unexpectedly, Mr. Gandiss said:

"Anthony, I suppose you wonder why I really invited you here."

"I am curious," Mr. Parker admitted, lighting a cigar. "Does your son Jack have anything to do with it?"

"I need advice in dealing with the boy," Mr. Gandiss acknowledged. "It occurred to me that association with a sensible girl like your daughter might help to straighten him out."

"I wouldn't count on that," Penny interposed hastily. "As Dad can tell you, I have a lot of most unsensible ideas of my own."

"Jack is a problem," Mr. Gandiss resumed, "but I have even more serious ones. How are you two at solving a mystery?"

Mr. Parker winked at his daughter and paid her tribute. "Penny has built up quite a reputation for herself as an amateur Sherlock Holmes. Running down gangsters is her specialty."

"Dad, you egg!" Penny said indignantly.

Both men laughed. But Mr. Gandiss immediately became serious again.

"My problem is difficult," he declared, "and I believe you may be able to help me, because I've heard a great deal about the manner in which you have solved other mysteries."

"Only in the interests of gaining good stories for our newspaper, *The Star*," Mr. Parker supplied.

"This probably would not net a story for your paper," the island owner said. "In fact, we are particularly anxious to keep the facts from getting into print. The truth is, strange things have occurred at my airplane factory in Osage—"

Mr. Gandiss did not finish, for at that moment someone rapped loudly on an outside screen door.

CHAPTER 4 - THROUGH THE WINDOW

"Now who can that be?" Mr. Gandiss remarked, startled by the knock on the door. "I heard no motorboat approach the island."

He waited, and a moment later a servant entered to say that two detectives, Jason Fellows and Stanley Williams, had arrived from the factory and wished to report to him.

Penny and her father politely arose to withdraw, but Mr. Gandiss waved them back into chairs.

"No, don't go," he said. "I want you to meet these men."

The two detectives, who had reached the island in a rented motorboat, appeared in the doorway. Mr. Gandiss introduced them to Penny and her father, and then inquired what had brought them to the house at so late an hour.

"It's the same old story only more of it," Detective Williams said tersely. "Another large supply of brass disappeared from the factory yesterday."

"Any clues?"

"Not a one. Obviously the brass is being stolen by employes, but so far the guilty persons have eluded all our traps."

"Have you calculated how much I am losing a year?" Mr. Gandiss asked bitterly.

"At the present resale value of brass and copper, not less than $60,000 a year," Mr. Fellows reported. "However, the thieves are becoming bolder day by day, so your loss may run much higher."

"See here," Mr. Gandiss said, showing irritation. "I'm paying you fellows a salary to catch those thieves, and I expect action! You say you have no clues?"

"Several employes are under suspicion," Mr. Williams disclosed. "But we haven't enough evidence to make any accusations or arrests."

"Then get some evidence!" Mr. Gandiss snapped. "This ring of petty thieves must be broken up! If you can't produce results, I'll turn the case over to another agency."

After the two detectives had gone, the island owner began to pace the floor nervously.

"Now you know why I wanted you to come here, Mr. Parker," he said, slumping down into a chair again. "My plant, which is making war materials, is being systematically looted of valuable copper and brass. The pieces smuggled out are small in size, but they count up to a staggering total."

"Sabotage?" Mr. Parker inquired.

"I doubt it," the island owner replied, frowning. "While the thefts slow up our war work, the delay is not serious. Materials disappear from the stock rooms and from the floors where the girls work. I hold a theory that the metal is being taken by employes who resell it for personal gain."

"It looks like a simple case of theft," Mr. Parker declared. "I should think your detectives would have no trouble running down the guilty persons."

"That's what I thought at first," Mr. Gandiss answered grimly. "It appeared as easy as A B C. But all ordinary methods of catching the thieves have failed. Obviously, the thefts are well organized by someone thoroughly familiar with the plant. It's getting on my nerves."

"Have you called in the police?"

"No, and I don't intend to. The matter must be handled quietly. That's why I need your advice."

"But I'm no detective," Mr. Parker protested. "Why call on me?"

"Because you and your daughter have solved some pretty tangled cases."

"Only for the newspaper," Mr. Parker replied. "How many employes do you have at the plant?"

CHAPTER 4 - THROUGH THE WINDOW

"About 5000. And not a scrap of real evidence against any individual. There seems to be a perfect system in accounting for all the stock, yet somehow it gets away from the factory."

"Have you had employes searched as they leave the building?"

"No, we haven't dared resort to that," Mr. Gandiss answered. "You can't search such a large number of workers. If we tried it, half the force would quit."

"I'd be glad to help you, if I could," Mr. Parker offered. "Unfortunately, I don't see how I can if professional detectives have failed."

"Let me be the judge of that," said the island owner quickly. "Will you and your daughter visit the factory with me in the morning?"

"We'd welcome the opportunity."

"Then we'll go into the records and all the details tomorrow," Mr. Gandiss declared, well satisfied. "I know you'll be able to help me."

Penny and her father were tired, and shortly after ten o'clock went to their rooms. Mr. Gandiss' problem interested them, though they felt that he had greatly overrated their ability in believing they could contribute to a solution of the mystery.

"I'm not certain I care to become involved," Mr. Parker confessed to Penny, who in robe and slippers had tiptoed into his room to say goodnight.

"But Dad, we can't decently refuse," Penny returned eagerly. "I think it would be fun to try to catch those thieves!"

"Well, we'll see," yawned Mr. Parker. "Skip back to bed now."

Penny read a magazine for an hour, and then switched off the light on the night table. Snuggling down under the silk coverlet, she slept soundly.

Sometime later, she found herself suddenly awake, though what had aroused her she could not guess. The room remained dark, but the first glimmer of dawn slanted through the Venetian blinds.

Penny rolled over and settled down for another snooze. Then she heard a disturbing sound. The wooden blinds were rattling ever so slightly, yet there was no breeze. Next her startled gaze focused upon a hand which had been thrust through the window to stealthily push the blinds aside.

A leg appeared over the sill, and a dark figure stepped boldly into the bedroom.

Terrified, Penny sat up so quickly that the bed springs creaked a loud protest. Instantly the intruder turned his face toward her.

"Keep quiet!" he hissed.

With mingled relief and indignation, Penny recognized Jack. He tiptoed to the bed.

"Now don't let out a yip," he cautioned. "I don't want Mom or my father to hear."

"Well, of all the nerve!" Penny exclaimed indignantly. "Is this my room or is it your private runway?"

"Don't go off the deep end. All the doors are locked and the servants have orders not to let me in if I am late."

"It's nearly morning," said Penny, hiding a yawn. "Where in the world did you go?"

"Town," Jack answered briefly.

Penny began to understand the cause of Mr. Gandiss' worry about his son.

"Now don't give me that 'holier than Thou' line," Jack said, anticipating a lecture. "I'm not going to the dogs nearly as fast as the old man believes. He's an old fossil."

"You shouldn't speak of your father that way," Penny replied. "After all, hasn't he given you everything?"

"He tries to keep me tied to his apron strings." Jack sat down on the bed, stretching luxuriously. "Mom isn't quite so unreasonable."

"Both of your parents seem like wonderful people to me."

"Maybe I know 'em better than you do," Jack grinned. "Oh, they're okay, in their way. Don't get me wrong. But my father always is trying to shove me around. If it hadn't been for your open window, I'd have had to sleep out in the cold."

"And it would have served you right too! You went off without saying a word to your parents, and worried them half to death. Now kindly remove your carcass from this bed!"

"Oh, cut the lecture," Jack pleaded, getting up and yawning again. "Gosh, I'm hungry. Let's find something to eat in the kitchen."

"Let's not," retorted Penny, giving him a shove. "Clear out of here, or I'll heave the lamp at you!"

"Oh, all right, kitten," he said soothingly. "I'm going. Remember your promise not to go wagging your tongue about what time I got in."

"I didn't promise a thing!"

"But you will," chuckled Jack confidently. "See you in the morning."

He tiptoed from the room, and Penny heard him stirring about in the kitchen. The refrigerator door opened and closed several times. Then at last all became quiet again.

"The conceited egg!" she thought irritably. "Now I'm so thoroughly awakened, I can't possibly go back to sleep."

Tossing about for a few minutes, she finally arose and dressed. Deciding to take an early morning walk about the island, she moved noiselessly through the house to the kitchen.

There she paused to note the wreckage Jack had left in his wake. The refrigerator door was wide open. As she closed it, she saw dishes of salad, chicken, pickles and tomatoes in a depleted state. Jack had topped off his feast with a quart of milk, and the bottle, together with, a pile of chicken bones, cluttered the sink.

A step was heard in the dining room. Startled, Penny turned quickly around, but it was too late to retreat.

The Gandiss' cook stood in the kitchen doorway, eyeing her with obvious disapproval.

CHAPTER 5 - UNWANTED ADVICE

"Just having an early morning snack?" Mrs. Bevens, the cook, inquired.

"Why, no," stammered Penny. "That is—." Confronted with the empty milk bottle, a chicken skeleton, and two empty food dishes, it seemed futile to deny such incriminating evidence. Though tempted to speak of Jack, she decided it would not be sporting of her.

"Young people have such healthy appetites," the cook sighed. "I had counted on that chicken for luncheon. But never mind. I can send to the mainland for something else."

Feeling like a criminal, Penny fled to her room.

"I could tar and feather Jack!" she thought furiously. "If he ever gets up, I'll make him explain to the cook."

The breakfast bell rang at eight o'clock. When Penny joined the group downstairs, she was surprised to see Jack in a fresh suit, looking little the worse for having been out all night.

"What time did you get in, Jack?" his father inquired pointedly.

"Well, now I just don't remember," the boy answered, winking at Penny.

"*How* did you get in, might be a better question. If I recollect correctly, all of the doors were locked last night at midnight."

Penny, decidedly uncomfortable, would have confessed her part, had not Jack sent her a warning glance. As everyone went in to breakfast, the matter was allowed to rest.

Ravenously hungry, Penny ate two waffles and several pieces of bacon. Observing the butler's amazed gaze upon her, she guessed that the cook had told him of the chicken episode.

Breakfast over, she managed to get Jack into a corner.

"Listen," she said indignantly, "why don't you tell your parents exactly what happened. Mrs. Bevens thinks I ate up all the chicken."

"Does she?" Jack chuckled. "That's rich! Don't you dare give me away!"

"You give me a pain!" Penny retorted, losing all patience. "If I weren't a guest in your house, I think I might slug you!"

"Go ahead," Jack invited, unruffled. "You're a little spitfire just like Sally! Oh, by the way, how about a trial run in the *Spindrift*?"

"Not the new sailboat?"

Jack nodded, his face animated. "She was delivered yesterday and is smooth as silk. The mast may need to be stepped back a notch or so, but otherwise she's perfect for the race. Want to sail with me?"

"I'd love to," Penny said, forgetting her resentment.

Hand in hand they ran down the path to the docks. *The Spindrift*, built to Mr. Gandiss' specifications, at a cost of nearly two thousand dollars, was a magnificent boat. Sixteen feet from bow to stern, its new coat of white was satin smooth, and its metalwork gleamed in the morning sun.

"She's fast," Jack declared proudly. "Sally Barker hasn't a chance to win that race!"

"Will she have a new boat?"

"No, the captain can't afford it. She'll have to sail *Cat's Paw* again." In all honesty, Jack added: "It's a good boat though. Captain Barker built it himself."

Together they put up the snowy white mainsail, and Jack shoved off from the dock. Heading upstream, the boy demonstrated how close to the wind the *Spindrift* would sail.

"She's good in a light breeze too," he declared. "No matter what sort of weather we get for the race, I figure I'll win."

"There's an old saying that pride goeth before a fall," Penny reminded him. "Also one about not counting your chickens."

"Poultry never interested me," Jack grinned, his eyes on the peak of the mainsail. "I'll win that brass lantern trophy from Sally if it's the last act of my life."

Penny, who had sailed a boat for several seasons in Riverview, hoped that Jack would offer her the tiller. Oblivious to her hints, he kept the *Spindrift* heeling along so fast that water fairly boiled behind the rudder. Jack was a good sailor and knew it.

Observing the *River Queen* plying her usual course, the boy deliberately steered to cross her path. As Penny well knew, by rules of navigation the ferryboat was compelled to watch out for the smaller boat. With apparent unconcern, Jack forced the *Queen* to change courses.

As the boats passed fairly close to each other, Sally appeared at the railing. A bandana handkerchief covered her hair and she wore slacks and a white sweater. Watching the *Spindrift* with concentration, she cupped her hands and shouted:

"If you sail near Hat Island, better be careful, Jack! The river level is dropping fast this morning. There's a shoal—"

"When I need advice from you, I'll ask for it!" Jack replied furiously, turning his back to the ferry.

Sally waved derisively and disappeared into the pilot house.

"Why aren't you two nicer to each other?" Penny demanded suddenly. "It seems to me you deliberately try to wave a red flag at her. For instance, sailing across the *River Queen's* bow—"

"Oh, I just intend to show Sally she can't push me around! Let's go home."

Suddenly tiring of the sport, Jack let out the mainsail, and the boat glided swiftly before the wind. Approaching a small island tangled with bushes and vines, Penny noted that the water was growing shallow. She called Jack's attention to the muddy bottom beneath them.

"Oh, it's deep enough through here," the boy responded carelessly. "I make the passage every day."

"What island are we passing?"

"Hat. The water always is shoal here. Just sit tight and quit scowling at me."

"I didn't know I was," Penny said, sinking back into the cushions.

The *Spindrift* gently grazed bottom. Dismayed, Penny straightened up, peering over the side. The boat was running hard into a mud bank.

"About! Bring her about, Jack!" she cried before she considered how he might take the uninvited advice.

"The water is deep enough here," Jack answered stubbornly. "It's only a tiny shoal. We'll sail through it easily."

Penny said nothing more, though her lips drew into a tight line.

Jack held to his course. For a moment it appeared that the boat would glide over the shoal into deeper water. Then the next instant they were hard aground. The sail began to flap.

"We're stuck like a turtle in a puddle," commented Penny, not without satisfaction.

"We'll get off!" Jack cried, seizing a paddle from the bottom of the boat.

He tried to shove away from the shoal, but the wind against the big sail resisted his strength.

"You'll never get off that way," Penny said calmly. "Why not take down the sail? We're hard aground now."

Jack glared, and looked as if he would like to heave the paddle at her.

"Okay," he growled.

Winds which came from the head of Hat Island were tricky. Before Jack could lower the sail, the breeze, shifting slightly, struck the expanse of canvas from directly aft.

"Look out, Jack!" Penny screamed a warning. "We're going to jibe!"

Jack ducked but not quickly enough. With great violence, the wind swung the sail over to the opposite side of the boat, the boom striking him a stunning blow on the back of the head.

Moaning with pain, he slumped into the bottom of the *Spindrift*.

CHAPTER 6 - SWEEPER JOE INFORMS

Alarmed for Jack, Penny scrambled over a seat to his side. He had been struck a hard blow by the swinging boom and there was a tiny jagged cut just behind his ear. A glance satisfied the girl that he was not seriously injured and that she could do nothing for him at the moment.

Turning her attention to the sail which was showing an inclination to slam over again, she quickly pulled it in and lowered it to the deck.

By then Jack had opened his eyes. His bewildered gaze rested upon her, and he rubbed his head.

"You—" he mumbled, raising on an elbow.

Penny firmly pushed him back. "Lie still!" she commanded.

Seizing the paddle, she tried to shove the boat backwards off the mud bank. Her best efforts would not move it an inch.

Slowly Jack raised himself to a sitting position. He rubbed his head. Bewilderment changed to a look of comprehension.

"I'm okay now," he said huskily. "We're hard aground, aren't we?"

"Solid as a rock," agreed Penny, wiping perspiration from her forehead. "Any ideas?"

"I'll get out and push."

"You're not strong enough. You took a nasty blow on the head."

Had not Jack looked so thoroughly miserable, Penny might have been tempted to adopt an "I told you so" attitude. There had been no excuse for running aground. Sally Barker had warned them about the shoal, and Jack deliberately had disregarded her advice.

"I guess it was my fault," Jack mumbled, the words coming with difficulty. "The water was deep enough here yesterday. I was so sure—"

His eyes, like those of an abused puppy, appealed to her for sympathy. Suddenly, Penny's resentment vanished and she felt sorry for Jack.

"Never mind," she said kindly. "We'll get off somehow. If necessary, I can swim to Shadow Island for help."

"It won't be necessary." Jack pulled off shoes and socks, and rolled up his slacks above his knees. "I got us into this, and I'll get us out. Just sit tight."

Despite Penny's protests, he swung over the side, into the shallow water. Applying his shoulder to the *Spindrift's* bow, he pushed with all his strength. Penny dug into the mud with the paddle.

The boat groaned and clung fast to the shoal. Then inch by inch it began to move backwards.

"We're off!" Penny cried jubilantly.

Jack pushed until the *Spindrift* was safely away from the shoal. Wet and plastered with mud, he scrambled aboard.

"No use putting up the sail," he said gloomily. "The centerboard is damaged. When we went aground I should have pulled it up, but things happened so fast I didn't think of it."

"Can't it be repaired?"

"Oh, sure, but it means hauling the boat out of water for several days. And the race will be held in a week. I'll have no chance to practice."

"It's a bad break," Penny said sympathetically. "Perhaps the centerboard isn't much damaged."

They paddled to the Shadow Island dock. There with the help of the Gandiss chauffeur, Jack tied ropes under the bottom of the *Spindrift* and by means of a hoist and crane, lifted the boat a few feet out of water. A piece had been broken from the centerboard and the bottom was so badly scratched that it would have to be repainted before the race.

"I call this wretched luck!" Jack fumed. "It will take days to repair and repaint the *Spindrift*."

The accident had a subduing effect upon the boy, and the remainder of the day he tried to make amends to Penny. They swam together and played three sets of tennis. In each contest Penny won with ease.

"You're about the first girl who ever beat me at anything," Jack said ruefully. "Guess that rap on the head did me no good."

"How about the sailboat race?" Penny tripped him. "Didn't Sally win the lantern trophy?"

Grudgingly, Jack admitted that she had. "But the race was a fluke," he added. "The wind was tricky and favored Sally's old tub. It won't happen twice."

Annoyed by the youth's alibis, Penny turned and walked away.

At dinner that night, Mr. Gandiss suggested that Mr. Parker and his daughter might like to visit his steel plant and airplane factory on the mainland. Despite vigorous protests, Jack was taken along.

The buildings owned by Mr. Gandiss were situated across the river in the town of Osage. Occupying many city blocks, the property included an airplane testing ground, and was protected by a high guard fence electrically charged.

"Every employee must pass inspection at the gate," Mr. Gandiss explained as the taxi cab approached the entrance to the main factory. "We operate on a twenty-four hour basis now, and even so can't keep abreast of orders."

Lights blazed in the low rows of windows, and from the chimneys of the steel plant, fire leaped high into the dark sky.

"Will we be able to see steel poured from the furnaces?" Penny asked eagerly. "I've always wanted to watch it done."

"You may tour every building if your feet hold out," Mr. Gandiss chuckled.

A squat, red-faced man with pouchy eyes, halted the taxi cab at the gate.

"No visitors allowed here at night," he began in a surly voice, and then recognized the plant owner. His manner changed instantly. "Oh, it's you, Mr. Gandiss! How are you this evening?"

"Very well, thank you, Clayton. I have some friends with me who wish to see the plant."

"Drive right in," the gateman invited, swinging open the barrier.

The taxi rolled through the gate, and drew up in front of one of the buildings. Inside, fluorescent lights gave the effect of daylight. Overhead carriers were lifting newly blanked and formed airplane parts from power presses, carrying them to sub-assembly lines.

"Raw materials, brought up-river by boats, enter one end of the building," Mr. Gandiss explained proudly. "Miraculously they come out the other end as finished airplanes ready for testing."

The plant had four main assembly lines along which the wings, fuselages, engines, tail surfaces, pilot and bombardier floors were assembled, he explained. In one room the party paused to watch row upon row of fuselages being put together ready for transfer to the main assembly line.

"You have a wonderful factory here, Mr. Gandiss," Penny's father praised, much impressed. "It must be a job to keep tab on the personnel."

"Oh, everything has been reduced to a system. One department meshes into another. But if production falls down in any one department, results could be serious." Mr. Gandiss frowned and added: "Now take those petty brass thefts. In a way it is a trivial matter, but the practice is spreading."

"The disappearance of parts hasn't curtailed production to any extent?"

"Not as yet, but it has caused our stockrooms serious annoyance. Then the loss on a yearly basis will become considerable. The guilty persons must be caught, and the organizers broken up before it gets more serious."

Mr. Gandiss escorted the visitors into another large room where hundreds of girls in slacks, their hair bound by nets, worked over machines with concentrated attention.

"Our beginners start here," he explained. "Strangely, we lose more brass and copper from this shift than anywhere else in the plant."

"How do you explain it?" Penny asked.

CHAPTER 6 - SWEEPER JOE INFORMS

"The girls are new and we are convinced they are being misled by someone. The entire situation has us baffled."

Few of the workers paid the visitors heed as they wandered along the rows of machines. However, a slovenly, sharp-eyed man with a push broom, watched them with deep interest. Known as Joe the Sweeper, though his real name was Joseph Jakaboloski, he once had been a skilled mechanic. Two of his fingers were missing, and he no longer did any useful work.

"See that man?" Mr. Gandiss said in an undertone. "Shortly after he started working for us, two years ago, he had an accident that was entirely his own fault. We immediately put him in an easy job and still pay him his former salary. But he doesn't even sweep a room properly."

"Why not let him go?" Mr. Parker questioned.

Mr. Gandiss smiled and shook his head. "He was injured while working for us, so we are responsible for looking after him. We would like to pension him off. You see, he constantly stirs up trouble among the new employes."

Joe the Sweeper had been watching Mr. Gandiss with concentrated attention, though too far away to hear what was said. With amusing haste, he swept his way closer to the group. Finally he smirked and sidled up to the factory owner.

"Can I see you alone fer a minute, Mr. Gandiss?" he asked, his voice a whine.

"I am very busy," the factory owner discouraged him. "What is it you want?"

Joe edged even closer, dropping his voice so that it was barely audible above the clatter of the machinery.

"You been losin' copper and brass from your factory, ain't you?"

The direct approach startled Mr. Gandiss. He gazed at Joe keenly, then nodded.

"Well, maybe I kin help you. What's it worth?"

Mr. Gandiss was careful not to show his dislike for the man. "If you are able to provide information which will lead to the apprehension of the thieves, I'll see that you get a substantial salary increase."

Joe blinked and grinned. "Last night I seen a girl in this room stick a piece of brass into her shirt front. She carried it off with her."

"Who was the girl?"

"Dunno her name. A blond piece in blue slacks."

"I'm afraid your information is of no value," Mr. Gandiss said impatiently. "Unless you know who she is—"

"She's a new gal that's only been workin' here a few nights," Joe supplied hastily. "You'll give me that salary raise if I turn her in?"

"If your information proves correct."

Joe's eyes brightened with a crafty light and he jerked his head toward the left.

"You can't see her from here," he muttered, "but you can get her name easy enough. She's the gal that operates machine No. 567."

CHAPTER 7 - NIGHT SHIFT WORKER

"I detest a stool pigeon," said Mr. Gandiss after Joe the Sweeper had slouched away. "However, his information may be valuable. I can't afford not to investigate it."

Not wishing to attract comment from the other employes, the factory owner made no attempt to see the girl under suspicion. Instead, he escorted the party to his private office. Ringing a buzzer, he asked one of the foremen to bring the operator of Machine 567 to him.

Presently she came in, a thin, wiry girl in ill-fitting blue slacks and sweater. Her hair was bound beneath a dark net and she wore goggles. As she faced Mr. Gandiss, she removed the latter. Everyone stared.

For the girl was Sally Barker.

"You sent for me, Mr. Gandiss?" Subdued and embarrassed, her eyes roved from one person to another.

"Why, Sally," said the factory owner in astonishment. "I had no idea you were working here on the night shift. When were you employed?"

"A week ago."

Perplexed, Mr. Gandiss stared at the girl's factory badge. There could be no mistake. Plainly it bore the number 567.

"You like the work?" he asked after an awkward silence.

"Not very well," she confessed truthfully. "However, I can use the pay I receive."

"During the daytime I believe you help your father aboard the *River Queen*," Mr. Gandiss resumed, trying to be friendly. "Rather a strenuous program. When do you sleep?"

"Oh, I get enough rest." Sally spoke indifferently, though her eyes were red and she looked tired. "Pop didn't want me to take the job, but I have a special use for the money."

"Pretty clothes, I suppose—or perhaps a new sailboat?"

"A college education."

Mr. Gandiss nodded approvingly, and then, recalling the serious charge against the girl, became formal again. "You wonder why I sent for you?"

"I know my work hasn't been very good. I've tried, but I keep ruining materials."

This gave Mr. Gandiss the opening he sought. "What do you do with the discarded pieces?" he inquired.

"Why, I just throw them aside." The question plainly puzzled Sally.

"You may have heard that we are having a little trouble here at the factory."

"What sort of trouble, Mr. Gandiss?"

"Small but valuable pieces of copper and brass seem to disappear with alarming regularity. Most of the thefts have been attributed to workers on the night shift."

Sally's blue eyes opened wide, but she returned Mr. Gandiss' steady gaze. Her chin raised. "I've heard talk about it among the girls," she replied briefly. "That's all I know."

"You have no idea who may be taking the materials?"

"Not the slightest, sir."

An awkward silence fell. Mr. Gandiss started to speak again, then changed his mind.

"Was there anything else?" Sally asked stiffly.

"Nothing."

"Then may I return to my work?"

CHAPTER 7 - NIGHT SHIFT WORKER

"Why, yes." It was Mr. Gandiss' turn to appear awkward and ill at ease. "We hope you will enjoy your work here, Sally," he said, feeling that a friendly word was necessary to end the interview. "If you should learn anything that will lead to the arrest of the thieves, I hope you will give us the information."

Sally inclined her head slightly in assent. With dignity, she walked from the office.

No one spoke for several minutes after the girl had gone. Then Mr. Gandiss drew a deep sigh.

"I had no idea Sally was working here," he said, frowning.

"Father, you shouldn't have accused her of stealing!" Jack burst out.

"My dear boy, I accused her of nothing."

"Well, Sally is proud. She took it that way. You don't really believe she would stoop to such a thing?"

"I confess I don't know what to think. Joe the Sweeper may not be a reliable informer."

"If he saw her hide brass in her clothing as he claims, why didn't he report her last night?" Jack demanded. "Sally is no thief. I've known her since she was a kid. I get mighty sore at her sometimes, she's so cocky. But she never did a dishonest act in her life."

"I'm glad to hear you defend her, Jack," Mr. Gandiss said quietly. "Certainly no action will be taken without far more conclusive evidence. Now suppose you and Penny amuse yourselves for a few minutes. Mr. Parker and I have a few business matters to discuss."

Thus dismissed, Penny and Jack wandered outside.

"Want to see the steel plant?" Jack asked indifferently. "They should be pouring about this time."

At Penny's eager assent, he led her to another building, up a steep flight of iron stairs to an inner balcony which overlooked the huge blast furnaces. In the noisy, hot room, conversation was practically impossible.

Gazing below, Penny saw a crew of men in front of one of the furnaces, cleaning the tapping hole with a long rod.

In a moment a signal was given and the molten steel was poured into a ladle capable of holding a hundred and fifty tons. An overhead crane, operated by a skilled worker, lifted the huge container to the pouring platform.

Next the molten mass was turned into rectangular ingots or molds.

"The steel will cool for about an hour before it is ready to be taken from the mold," Jack shouted in Penny's ear.

Moving on, they saw other ingots already cooled, and in a stripping shed observed cranes with huge tongs engage the lugs of the molds and lift them from the ingots.

"Each one of those ingots weighs twenty thousand pounds," Jack said, surprising Penny with his knowledge. "After stripping, they are placed in gas-heated pit furnaces and brought to rolling temperature."

To see fiery ribbons of steel rolled from cherry red ingots was to Penny the most fascinating process of all. She could have watched for hours, but Jack, bored by the familiar sight, kept urging her on.

Leaving the steel plant, they returned to the main factory buildings, and without thinking, sauntered toward the room where Sally worked. A portable lunch cart had just supplied hot soup and sandwiches to the employees. Sally sat eating at her machine. Seeing Jack, she quickly looked away.

"Now she's really sore at me, and I can't blame her," Jack commented. "Who is Joe the Sweeper anyhow? Riff-raff, I'll warrant."

Though somewhat amused by the boy's staunch defense of Sally, Penny was inclined to agree in his second observation. Although she knew nothing of the man who had turned informer, she had not liked the sly look of his face.

Before the pair could approach Sally, the brief lunch period came to an end. A whistle blew, sending the girls back to their machines.

"You'll have to step on it," a foreman told Sally. "You're behind in your quota."

Her reply was inaudible, but as she adjusted her machine and started it up, she began to work with nervous haste.

"This is no place for Sally," Jack said, obviously bothered. "She never was cut out for factory work. And that foreman, Rogers, who is over her! He's a regular slave driver!"

"I thought you didn't like Sally," Penny teased.

"I want to see her get a square deal, that's all," Jack replied, his face flushing.

Joe the Sweeper sidled over to the couple. "What's the verdict?" he asked in a confidential tone.

Jack pretended not to understand.

"Is the gal going to get fired?"

"I'm sure I don't know," Jack answered coldly. "Why does it mean so much to you?"

"Why, it don't," the sweeper muttered. "She ain't no skin off my elbow."

Penny and Jack walked on through the workroom, aware that many pairs of eyes followed them. Sally, bending over a grinding machine, looked up self-consciously. She was grinding pieces of metal, measuring each with a micrometer. There was a streak of grease across her cheek and she looked very tired.

Suddenly as Sally threw the wheel in, there was a loud clattering noise. The foreman came running. He threw the wheel back.

"What did I do?" Sally gasped, shaking from nervousness.

"You forgot to pull this lever." The foreman said curtly. "Ruined a piece of work too! Now try to think what you're doing and get down to business."

Penny and Jack moved away, not wishing to add to the girl's embarrassment. But a few minutes later, in leaving the workroom, they again passed close to Sally's machine. This time she did not see them until they were almost beside her.

"How is it going, Sally?" Jack asked in a friendly way.

Sally raised her eyes, and in so doing forgot her work. As she automatically placed the metal in line with the wheel, she held her fingers there without thinking. Another instant and they would have been mangled.

Horrified, Penny saw what was about to happen.

"Sally!" she cried. Acting instinctively, she reached and jerked the girl's hand away from the swift turning machinery. The wheel had missed Sally's fingers by a mere fraction of an inch.

The foreman came running again, obviously annoyed. Shutting off the machine, he demanded to know what was wrong.

Sally leaned her head weakly on the table, trying to regain composure. Her face was drained of color and she trembled as from a chill. "Thanks," she said brokenly to Penny. "I—I don't know what's the matter with me tonight. I'm not coordinated right."

"Go take a walk," the foreman advised, not unkindly. "A nice long walk. Get a drink or something. You'll be okay."

"I'll never learn," Sally said in a choked voice.

"Sure, you will. Everyone has to go through a beginner's stage. Get yourself a drink. Then you'll feel better."

"Let me go with you," Penny said, taking Sally by the arm.

Without conversation, they made their way between the long rows of machines to the locker room. There Sally sank down on a bench, burying her face in her hands.

"I'm nervous and upset tonight," she excused herself. "I can't seem to get the hang of machine work."

"Why not give it up? Do you really need the money so badly?"

"No," Sally admitted truthfully. "I've set my heart on a college education, but Pop could raise the money somehow. It's just that he's had financial troubles the past year, and I wanted to help out."

"Some persons aren't cut out to be factory workers," Penny resumed. "Do you realize that you nearly lost several of your fingers tonight?"

"Yes," Sally agreed, her freckled face becoming deadly sober. "I'll always be grateful to you. What Mr. Gandiss said in his office upset me. I wasn't thinking of my work."

"I thought that might be it. Well, forget the entire matter if you can."

Sally nodded and getting up, drank at the fountain. "I'll have to go back to work now," she said with an effort. "First, I'll get myself a clean hanky."

With a key which she wore on a string about her neck, the girl opened her locker. On the floor lay a leather jacket that had fallen from its hook.

As Sally picked it up, a heavy object slipped from one of the pockets, thudding against the tin of the locker floor.

She stooped quickly to retrieve it, and then, embarrassed, tried to shield the article from view. But she could not hide it from Penny who stood directly behind. The object that had fallen from the jacket was a small coupling of brass!

CHAPTER 8 - OVERHEARD IN THE GATEHOUSE

"Why, where did that come from?" Sally murmured as she fingered the piece of metal. "I never put it in my locker."

Confused, she raised bewildered eyes to Penny. Just then the locker room door opened and a forelady came in. Miss Grimley's keen gaze fastened upon the brass coupling in Sally's hand. Awkwardly, the girl tried to hide it in a fold of her slacks.

"What do you have?" the forelady asked, moving like a hawk toward the girls.

"Why, nothing," Sally stammered.

"Isn't that a piece of brass?" Miss Grimley demanded. "Where did you get it?"

"I found it in my locker."

"In your locker!"

"I don't know how it got there," Sally said quickly, reading suspicion in the other's face. "I'm sure I never put it there."

Miss Grimley took the brass from her, inspecting it briefly.

"This looks very much like one of the parts that has been disappearing from the stockroom," she said, her voice icy.

"But I've never been near the stockroom!" Sally cried. "In the few days that I've been employed here, I've barely left my machine."

Penny tried to intercede in the girl's behalf.

"I'm sure Sally knew nothing about the article being in her locker," she assured the forelady. "When she opened it a moment ago and lifted her jacket, the piece of brass fell from a pocket."

"Someone must have put it there!" Sally added indignantly. "I'm certain I never did."

"Have you given your locker key to anyone?"

"No."

"And have you always kept it locked?"

"Why, I think so."

"I am sorry," said Miss Grimley in a tone which implied exactly the opposite, "but I will have to report this. You understand my position."

"Please—"

"I have no choice," Miss Grimley cut her short. "Come with me, please."

Penny started to accompany Sally, but the forelady by a gesture indicated that she was not to come. The door closed behind them.

For ten minutes Penny waited, hoping that Sally would return. Finally she wandered outside. Sally was not on the floor and another girl had taken her place at the machine.

Seeing Joe the Sweeper cleaning a corridor, Penny asked him about Sally.

"No. 567?" the man inquired with a grin which showed a gap between his front upper teeth. "You won't see her no more! She's in the employment office now, and they're giving her the can!"

"You mean she's being discharged?"

"Sure. We don't want no thieves around here!"

"Sally Barker isn't a thief," Penny retorted loyally. "By the way, how did you know why the girl was taken to the office?"

The question momentarily confused Joe. But his reply was glib enough.

"Oh, I have a way o' knowin' what goes on around here," he smirked. "I figured that gal was light-fingered the day they hired her. It didn't surprise me none that they found the stuff in her locker."

"And who told you that?" Penny pursued the subject.

"Why, you said so yourself—"

"Oh, no I didn't."

"It was the forelady," Joe corrected himself. "I seen the brass in her hand when she came out of the locker room with that gal."

Disgusted, Penny turned her back and walked away in search of Jack. It was none of her affair, she knew, but it seemed to her that Joe the Sweeper had taken more than ordinary interest in Sally's downfall. His statements, too, had been confused.

"I don't trust that fellow," she thought. "He's sly and mean."

Penny could not find Jack, and when she returned to Mr. Gandiss' office, a secretary told her that the factory owner and her father expected to meet her at the main gate.

Hastening there, Penny saw no sign of them. Nor was the gateman on duty. However, hearing low voices inside the gatehouse, she stepped to the doorway. No one was in view, but two men were talking in the inner office.

"It worked slick as a whistle," she heard one of them say. "The girl was caught with the stuff on her, and they fired her."

"Who was she?"

"A new employee named Sally Barker."

"Good enough, Joe. That ought to take the heat off the others for awhile at least."

The name startled Penny who instantly wondered if one of the speakers might be Sweeper Joe. Confirming her suspicion, the man came out of the inner room a moment later. Seeing her, he stopped short and his jaw dropped.

"What you doin' here?" he demanded gruffly.

"Waiting for Mr. Gandiss," Penny replied. "And you?"

Joe did not answer. Mumbling something, he pushed past her and went off toward the main factory building.

"He's certainly acting as if he deliberately planned to get Sally into trouble," she thought resentfully.

Clayton, the gateman, showed his face a moment later, and he too acted self-conscious. As he checked a car through into the factory grounds, he glanced sideways at Penny, obviously uneasy as to how much she might have overheard.

"Been here long?" he inquired carelessly.

"No, I just came," Penny answered with pretended unconcern. "I'm waiting for my father."

The men did not come immediately. However, as Penny loitered near the gatehouse, she saw Sally Barker hurriedly leaving the factory building.

"Ain't you off early tonight?" the gateman asked as she approached.

"I'm off for good," Sally answered shortly. Her face was tear-stained and she did not try to hide the fact that she had been crying.

"Fired?"

"That's right," Sally replied. "Unjustly too!"

"Shoo, you don't say!" the gateman exclaimed, sympathetically. "What did they give you the can for?"

Sally, in no mood to provide details, went on without answering. Penny ran to overtake her.

"I'll walk with you to the boundaries of the grounds," she said quickly. "Tell me what happened."

"Just what you would expect," Sally shrugged. "They asked me a lot of questions in the personnel office. I told the truth—that I knew nothing about that putrid piece of brass that turned up in my locker! Then they gave me a nice little lecture, and said they were sorry but my services no longer were required. Branded as a thief!"

"Don't take it so hard, Sally," Penny said kindly. "Someone probably planted the brass in your locker."

"Of course! But I can't prove it."

"Why not appeal to Mr. Gandiss? He likes you and—"

"No," Sally said firmly, kicking at a piece of gravel on the driveway, "I'll ask no favors of Mr. Gandiss. He would have me reinstated, no doubt, but it would be too humiliating."

"Do you know of anyone in the factory who dislikes you?"

CHAPTER 8 - OVERHEARD IN THE GATEHOUSE

Sally shook her head. "That's the funny part of it. I'm not acquainted with anyone. I just started in."

"How about Joe the Sweeper?"

"Oh, him!" Sally was scornful. "He caught me in the hall the other day and tried to get fresh. I slapped his face!"

"Then perhaps he was the one that got you into trouble."

"He's too stupid," Sally dismissed the subject.

"I'm not so sure of that," returned Penny thoughtfully.

The girls had reached the street and Sally's bus was in sight.

"What will you do now?" Penny asked hurriedly. "Get a job at another factory?"

"I doubt it," Sally replied, fishing in her pocketbook for a bus token. "I'll help Pop on the *River Queen*. If I do take another job it won't be until after the sailboat races."

"I'd forgotten about that. When is the race?"

"The preliminary is in a few days—next Friday. The finals are a week later."

"I hope you win," said Penny sincerely. "I'll certainly be on hand to watch."

The bus pulled up at the curb. Swing-shift employes, arriving at the factory for work, crowded past the two girls. Impulsively Sally turned and squeezed Penny's hand.

"I like you," she said with deep feeling. "You've been kind. Will you come to see me sometime while you're here?"

"Of course! I've not brought back those clothes I borrowed yet!"

"I'll look for you," Sally declared warmly. "I feel that you're a real friend."

Squeezing Penny's hand again, she sprang aboard the bus and was lost in the throng of passengers.

CHAPTER 9 - SALLY'S HELPER

Several days of inactivity followed for Penny at Shadow Island. For the most part, Jack was friendly and tried to provide entertainment. However, he was away much of the time, supervising the work of repairing and getting the *Spindrift* into condition for the coming trophy race.

Sally Barker's name seldom was mentioned in the Gandiss household, though it was known that the girl intended to enter the competition regardless of her disgrace at the factory. Once Penny asked Jack point-blank what he thought of the entire matter.

"Just what I always did," he answered briefly. "Sally never took anything from the factory. It wouldn't be in keeping with her character."

"Then why isn't she cleared?"

"Father did take the matter up with the personnel department, but he doesn't want to go over the manager's head. The brass was found in her locker and quite a few employes learned about it."

"The brass was planted!"

"Probably," agreed Jack. "But it's none of my affair. Sally wasn't a very good factory worker and the personnel director thought he had to make an example of someone—"

"So Sally became the goat! I call it unfair. Did the thefts cease after she left?"

"They're worse than ever."

"Then obviously Sally had nothing to do with it!"

"Not just one person is involved. The brass is being taken by an organized ring of employes."

"I suppose it's none of my affair, but in justice I think Sally should be cleared. I don't know the girl well, but I like her."

"You may as well hear the whole story," Jack said uncomfortably. "Father wrote her a letter, inviting her to come in for an interview. She paid no attention."

"Perhaps she didn't get the letter."

"She got it all right. I met her on the street yesterday, and when I tried to talk to her, she threatened to heave a can of varnish in my face! Furthermore, she gave me to understand she intends to defeat me soundly in the race tomorrow."

"I'll be there to watch," grinned Penny. "The contest should be interesting."

While Jack was out on the river practicing for the approaching competition, Penny accompanied her father to the mainland to mail letters and make a few purchases Mrs. Gandiss had requested. In returning to the waterfront, they wandered down a street within view of the Gandiss factory.

Penny's attention was drawn to a man who came out of an alley at the rear of the plant and stood staring at a tiny junk shop which was situated directly opposite the Gandiss factory.

"There's Joe the Sweeper," she observed aloud. And then an instant later added: "That's queer!"

"What is?" inquired her father.

"Why, that junk shop! I've been down this street several times, but I never noticed it there before. I would have sworn that the building was empty."

Mr. Parker gave her a quick, amused look. "It was until yesterday," he informed.

"You seem to know all about it!" Penny suddenly became suspicious. "What are you keeping from me?"

Mr. Parker did not reply, for he was watching the man who had emerged from the alley. Joe seemed to debate for awhile, then crossed the street and entered the junk shop.

"Good!" exclaimed Mr. Parker. "Our bait seems to be working."

CHAPTER 9 - SALLY'S HELPER

"What are you talking about?" Penny demanded in exasperation. "Will you kindly explain?"

"You recall Mr. Gandiss asked me to help him solve the mystery of those brass thefts at the plant."

"Why, yes, but I didn't know you had begun to do anything about it."

"Our plan may not succeed. However, we're trying out a little idea of mine."

"Does it have anything to do with that junk shop?"

"Yes, the place was opened yesterday by Heiney Growski."

Penny's blue eyes opened wide for she knew the man well. A prominent detective in Riverview, he had won distinction by solving a number of difficult cases.

"Heiney is an expert at make-up and impersonation," Mr. Parker added. "We brought him here and installed him as the owner of the junk store across the street. His instructions are to buy brass and copper at above the prevailing market prices."

"You expect employes who may be pilfering metals to seek the highest price obtainable!"

"That's our idea. It may not work."

"It should," Penny cried jubilantly. "Sweeper Joe went in there not three minutes ago! I've suspected him from the first!"

"Aren't you jumping to pretty fast conclusions?"

"From what I heard him say to the gatekeeper Clayton, I'm sure he's mixed up in some underhanded scheme."

"You're not certain of it, Penny. Joe has been carefully investigated. He seems too stupid a fellow to have engineered such a clever, organized method of pilfering."

"He never appeared stupid to me. Dad, let's drift over to the junk shop, and learn what is happening."

"And give everything away? No, Heiney will report if anything of consequence develops. In the meantime, we must show no interest in the shop."

To Penny's disappointment, her father refused to remain longer in the vicinity of the factory. Without glancing toward the junk shop, they walked on to the riverfront. The motorboat they had expected to meet them had not yet arrived. While Mr. Parker purchased a newspaper and sat down on the dock to read, Penny sauntered along the shore.

A short distance away on a stretch of beach, a boat had been overturned. Sally Barker, in blue overalls rolled to the knees, was painting it with deft, sure strokes. Penny walked over to watch the work.

Glancing up, Sally smiled, but did not speak. A smudge of blue paint stained her cheek. She had sanded the bottom of the *Cat's Paw*, and now was slapping on a final coat of paint.

"Will it dry in time for the race tomorrow?" Penny inquired, making conversation.

"The finish won't be hard, but that's the way I want it," Sally said, dipping her brush. "It makes a faster racing bottom."

"Then you're all ready for competition?"

"The boat is ready." Sally hesitated, then added. "But I may not enter the race after all."

"Not enter? Why?"

Having finished painting, Sally carefully cleaned her brush, and tightly closed the paint and varnish cans. She wiped her hands on her faded overalls.

"The boy who was racing with me served notice this morning that he had changed his mind. I haven't asked anyone else, because I didn't want to be turned down."

"But I should think anyone who likes to sail would be crazy for the chance—" Penny began. Then as she met Sally's gaze, her voice trailed off.

"You know what I mean," said Sally quietly.

"Not the factory episode?"

"Yes, word traveled around."

"Jack didn't tell?"

"I don't think so, but I don't know," Sally replied honestly. "Anyway, everyone learned why I was discharged. Pop is furious."

"Your mother too, I suppose?"

"I have no mother. She died when I was ten. Since then, Pop and I have lived aboard the *Queen*. Pop always taught me to speak my mind, never to be afraid, and above all to be honest. To be accused of something one didn't do and to be branded as a thief is the limit!"

Penny nodded sympathetically. "About the race," she said, reverting to the previous subject, "you aren't really serious about not entering?"

"It means everything to me," Sally admitted soberly. "But I can't race alone. The rules call for two persons in each boat."

"You need an expert sailor?"

"Not necessarily. Of course, the person would have to know how to handle ropes and carry out orders. Also, not lose his head in an emergency. To balance the *Cat's Paw* right I need someone about my own weight."

"It has to be a boy?"

"Mercy, no! I would prefer a girl if I knew whom to ask." Sally suddenly caught the drift of Penny's conversation, and a look of amazed delight came upon her face. "Not you!" she exclaimed. "You don't mean you would be willing—"

"If you want or could use me. I'm a long way from an expert, but I do know a little about sailboats. We have one in Riverview. However, I never competed in a race."

"I'd be tickled pink to have you!"

"Then it's settled."

"But what about the Gandiss family? You are their guest."

"That part is a bit awkward," Penny admitted. "But they are all good sports. I'm sure no one will hold it against me."

"After I was discharged from the factory?"

"That really wasn't Mr. Gandiss' doing, Sally. The plant is so large he scarcely knows what goes on in some departments. You were discharged by the personnel manager."

"I realize that."

"Didn't Mr. Gandiss write you a letter asking you to come in for a personal interview?"

"Yes, he did," Sally acknowledged reluctantly. "I was angry and I tore it up."

"Then you shouldn't blame Mr. Gandiss."

"I'm not blaming him, Penny. I like Mr. Gandiss very much. In fact, I like him so well I never could bear to accept favors from him."

"Not even to clear your name?"

Sally washed her hands at the river's edge, and rolled down the legs of her overalls. "The person who put that brass in my locker hasn't been caught?" she inquired softly.

"Not to my knowledge."

"Then all Mr. Gandiss could do would be to offer me another chance," Sally said bitterly. "I'll never work in the factory on that basis. If I am cleared completely, then I am willing to go back."

"Mr. Gandiss is trying to solve the mystery of those thefts," Penny declared. "I know that to be a fact. Have you any idea who the guilty parties might be?"

Sally straightened up, digging at paint which had lodged beneath her fingernails. She did not answer.

"You do have a clue!" Penny cried.

"Maybe." Sally smiled mysteriously.

"Tell me what it is."

"No, I intend to work by myself until I'm sure that I'm on the right track. I've not even told Pop."

"Does it have anything to do with Sweeper Joe?"

Sally's expression became blank. "I don't know much about him," she dismissed the subject. "My information concerns a certain house upriver. But don't ask me to tell you more."

Hastily she gathered up paint cans and brush, turning to leave. "Are you really serious about racing with me tomorrow?" she demanded.

"Of course!"

"Then you're elected first mate of the *Cat's Paw*! Meet me at the yacht club dock at six in the morning for a trial workout. The preliminary race is at two."

"I'll be there without fail."

CHAPTER 9 - SALLY'S HELPER

"And bring a little luck with you," Sally added with a grin. "We may need it to defeat the *Spindrift*."

CHAPTER 10 - OVERTURNED

When Penny reached the dock next morning she found that Sally had preceded her by many hours. The varnished wood of the *Cat's Paw* shone in the sunlight. Below the waterline, the boat was as smooth and slippery as glass.

"Isn't she beautiful?" Sally asked proudly, squeezing water from a sponge she had been using. "The rigging has been overhauled, and Pop came through at the last minute with a new jib sail. Every rope has been changed too."

"It looks grand," Penny praised. "You must have worked like a galley slave getting everything ready for the race."

"I have, but I want to win. This race means everything to me."

"Are you sure you want me to sail with you?" Penny asked dubiously. "After all, I am not an expert. I might handicap you."

"Nonsense! There's no one I would rather have—that is, if you still want to do it. Was Jack angry when you told him?"

Penny confessed that she had not spoken to any of the Gandiss family of her intention to take part in the race. "But it will be all right," she added. "Jack really isn't such a bad sport when you get to know him. I only hope we win!"

"Oh, we'll come in among the leading five—that's certain," Sally said carelessly. "This is only a preliminary race today. The five winning boats will compete next week in the finals."

"If you lose today must you give up the trophy?"

"Not until after the final race." Sally laughed goodnaturedly. "But don't put such ideas in my head. We can't lose! I'm grimly determined that Jack mustn't beat me!"

"I do believe the race is a personal feud between you two! Why does it mean so much to defeat him?"

Sally stepped nimbly aboard the scrubbed deck, stowing away the sponge under one of the seats. "Jack and I always have been rivals," she admitted. "We went to grade school together. He used to make fun of me because I lived on a ferryboat."

"Jack was only a kid then."

"I know. But we always were in each other's hair. We competed in everything—debates, literary competitions, sports. Jack usually defeated me too. In sailing, due to Pop's coaching, I may have a slight edge over him."

"Do you really dislike Jack?"

"Why, no." Sally's tone indicated she never had given the matter previous thought. "If he weren't around to fight with, I suppose I'd miss him terribly."

Penny sat down on the dock to lace up a pair of soft-soled tennis shoes. By the time she had them on, Sally was ready to shove off for the trial run.

"Suppose we take about an hour's work-out, and then rest until time for the race," she suggested. "You'll quickly learn the tricks of this little boat. She's a sweet sailer."

The *Cat's Paw* had been tied to the dock with a stiff wind blowing across it, and larger boats were berthed on either side. To get away smoothly without endangering the other craft would be no easy task. As the girls ran up the mainsail, a few loiterers gathered to watch the departure.

"All set, mate?" grinned Sally. "Let's go."

CHAPTER 10 - OVERTURNED

With a speed that amazed Penny, she trimmed the main and jib sheets flat amidships, placing the tiller a little to starboard.

"Haul up the centerboard!" she instructed.

Penny pulled up the board, feeling a trifle awkward and inadept.

Sally leaped out onto the dock, and casting off, held the boat's head steady into the eye of the wind. With a tremendous shove which delighted the spectators, she sent the *Cat's Paw* straight aft, and made a flying leap aboard.

With sails flat amidships, the boat shot straight backwards. As they started to clear the stern of the boat that was to starboard, Sally let the tiller move over to that side. The bow of the *Cat's Paw* began to swing to starboard.

Not until then, did Penny observe that the *Spindrift* was tied up only a few boat-lengths away. Jack, armed with several bottles of pop, came hurriedly from the clubhouse. Noting Sally's spectacular departure, he joined the throng at the railing.

"We'll give the crowd a real thrill," Sally muttered, keeping her voice low so that it would not carry over the water. "If this trick works, it should be good."

Even Penny was worried. The bow of the *Cat's Paw* had swung rapidly to starboard. But Sally, calm and cool, still hung on to the sheets.

"Put your tiller the other way!" Jack shouted from the dock. "Let your sheet run!"

Enjoying the boy's excitement, Sally pretended to be deaf. Wind had struck the sails, but the *Cat's Paw* continued to sail backwards. A crash seemed impossible to avert. Then at the last instant, the bow swung clear of the neighboring boats.

Grinning triumphantly, Sally put the tiller to port and started the sheets. They sailed briskly away.

"Beautifully done!" praised Penny. "Not one sailor in a hundred could pull that off. It took nerve!"

"Pop taught me that trick. It's risky, of course. If the sails should decide to take charge, or the tiller should fail to go to starboard, one probably would collide with the other boats."

"You surprised Jack. He expected you to crash."

"We'll surprise him this afternoon too," Sally declared confidently, steering out into mid-stream. "If this breeze holds, it's just what the doctor ordered!"

For an hour the girls practiced maneuvers until Penny was thoroughly adept at handling the ropes and carrying out orders. Although the rules of the race did not allow them to sail the actual course, Sally pointed it out.

"We start near the clubhouse," she explained. "Then, taking a triangular route we sail past Hat Island to the first marker. After rounding it, we keep on to the marker near the eastern river shore, and sail back to our starting point."

Sally was in high spirits, for she declared that if the breeze held, *Cat's Paw* would perform at her best. Though no one knew exactly what Jack's new boat, *Spindrift* could do, observation had convinced most sailing enthusiasts that it would be favored in a light breeze.

"I hope it blows a gale this afternoon!" Sally chuckled as they moored at the dock. "Get some rest now, Penny, and meet me at the clubhouse about one o'clock. The race starts sharp at two."

Penny did not see Jack when she returned to Shadow Island, so had no chance to tell him of her plan to sail with Sally in the competition. Her father, whom she took into her confidence, was not entirely in favor of the decision.

"We are guests of Mr. and Mrs. Gandiss," he reproved mildly. "To sail against Jack is a tactless thing to do. Though actually you may do him a favor, for you'll likely be more of a handicap than a help in the race."

"That's what I figured," laughed Penny.

By chance, Mr. Gandiss overheard the conversation. Entering the living room, he declared that Penny must not hesitate to enter the competition.

"After all, the race is supposed to be for fun," he said emphatically. "Lately Jack and Sally have made it into a feud. I really think it would do the boy good to be defeated soundly."

Long before the hour of the race, Penny was at the yacht club docks, dressed in blue slacks, white polo shirt, and an added jacket for protection from wind and blistering sun rays.

Rowboats, canoes and small sailing craft plied lazily up and down the river, while motor yachts with flags flying, cruised past the clubhouse. Out in the main channel where the race was to be held, the judges' boat had been anchored. The shores were thronged with spectators, many of whom had enjoyed picnic lunches on the grassy banks.

Penny walked along the dock searching for the *Cat's Paw*. She came first to the *Spindrift* which was just preparing to get underway. Jack and a youth Penny did not know, were busy coiling ropes.

"Hi, Penny!" Jack greeted her, glancing up from his work. "You're going to see a real race today! Will I take Sally Barker for a breeze!"

Just at that moment, Sally herself appeared from inside the clubhouse. Seeing Penny, she waved and called: "Come on, mate, it's time we shove off!"

Jack's jaw dropped and he gazed at the two girls accusingly.

"What is this?" he demanded. "Penny, you're not racing in Sally's boat?"

"Yes, I am."

"Well, if that isn't something!" Jack said no more, but his tone had made it clear he considered Penny nothing short of a traitor.

The two boats presently sailed out from the protecting shores to join the other fifteen-footers which had entered the race. With the breeze blowing strong, the contestants tacked rapidly back and forth, jockeying for the best positions at the start of the contest.

Tensely Sally glanced at her wristwatch. "Five minutes until two," she observed. "The gun will go off any minute now."

Nineteen boats comprised the racing fleet, but in comparison to Jack and Sally, many of the youthful captains were mere novices. Experts were divided in opinion as to the winner, but nearly everyone agreed it would be either Jack or Sally, with the odds slightly in favor of the latter.

"There goes the signal!" cried Sally.

The boats made a bunched start with *Cat's Paw* and *Spindrift* in the best positions. In the sharp breeze, one of the craft carried away a stay, and with a broken mast, dropped out of the race. The others headed for the first marker.

At first Sally and Jack raced almost bow to bow, then gradually the *Cat's Paw* forged steadily ahead. Except for three or four boats, the others began to fall farther and farther behind.

"We'll win!" Penny cried jubilantly.

"It's too soon to crow yet," Sally warned. "While it looks as if this breeze will hold for the entire race, no one can tell. Anything might happen."

Penny glanced back at Jack's boat a good six to eight lengths behind. The boy deliberately turned his head, acting as if he did not see her.

The *Cat's Paw* hugged the marker as it made the turn at Hat Island. Rounding the body of land, the girls were annoyed to see a canoe with three children paddling directly across their course.

"Now how did they get out here?" Sally murmured with a worried frown. "They should know better!"

At first the children did not seem to realize that they were directly in the path of the racing boats. But as they saw the fleet rounding Hat Island in the wake of the *Cat's Paw* and the *Spindrift*, they suddenly became panic-stricken.

With frantic haste, they tried to get out of the way. In her confusion, one of the girls dropped a paddle, and as it floated away, she made a desperate lunge to recover it. Another of the occupants, heavy-set and awkward, leaned far over the same side in an attempt to help her.

"They'll upset if they aren't careful!" Penny groaned. "Yes, there they go!"

Even as she spoke, the canoe flipped over, tossing the three girls into the water. Two of them grasped the overturned craft and held on. The third, unable to swim, was too far away to reach the extended hand of her terrified companions.

Making inarticulate, strangled sounds in her throat, she frantically thrashed the water, trying desperately to save herself.

CHAPTER 11 - A QUESTION OF RULES

"Quick!" Sally cried, remaining at the tiller of the *Cat's Paw*. "The life preserver!"

Finding one under the seat, Penny took careful aim and hurled it in a high arc over the span of water. The throw was nearly perfect and the life preserver plopped heavily on the surface not two feet from the struggling girl. But she was too panic-stricken to reach out and grasp it.

The river current carried the preserver downstream. Sally knew then that to save the girl she must turn aside and abandon the race.

"Coming about!" she called sharply to warn Penny of the swinging boom.

Already beyond the girl, whose struggles were becoming weaker, they turned and sailed directly toward her. Penny kicked off her shoes, and before Sally could protest, dived over the gunwale.

A half dozen long strokes carried her directly behind the struggling girl. Hooking a hand beneath her chin, she pulled her into a firm, safe hold, then towed her to the *Cat's Paw* where Sally helped them both aboard.

Throughout the rescue, the other two children had clung to the overturned canoe. Sally saw that they were in no danger, for a motorboat from shore was plowing swiftly to the rescue. Standing by until the two were taken safely aboard, she then glanced toward the fleet of racing boats.

Nearly all of them had passed the *Cat's Paw* and were well on their way toward the second marker. The *Spindrift* led the field.

"We're out of the race," she said dismally.

"No! Don't give up!" Penny pleaded. "You still may have a chance. This girl is all right. I'll look after her while you sail."

Sally remained unconvinced. "We couldn't possibly overtake Jack now."

"But we do have a chance to come in among the five leaders! Then you would be able to race in the finals. You wouldn't lose the lantern trophy."

Sparkle came into Sally's eyes again. Her lips drew into a tight, determined line.

"All right, we'll keep on!" she decided. "But it will be nip and tuck to win even fifth place. See what you can do for our passenger."

The girl who had been hauled aboard was not more than thirteen years old. Although conscious, she had swallowed considerable water and was dazed from the experience. As she began to stir, Penny knelt beside her.

"Lie still," she said soothingly. "We'll have you at the dock soon."

Stripping off her own jacket, Penny tucked it about the shivering child.

"We're balanced badly," Sally commented, her eyes on the line of boats far ahead, "and overloaded too. It's foolish to try—"

"No, it isn't!" Penny said firmly. "We're sailing great guns, Sally! Look at the water boiling behind our rudder."

Almost as if it were driven by a motor, the *Cat's Paw* plowed through the waves, leaving a trail of foam and bubbles in her wake. Despite the handicap of an extra passenger, the boat was gaining on the contestants ahead.

"If only the course were longer!" Sally murmured, straining against the pull of the main sheet.

They rounded the second marker only a few feet behind a group of bunched boats. One by one they passed them until only seven remained ahead. But with the finish line close by, they could not seem to gain another inch.

"We can't make it," Sally said, turning to gaze at the shore with its crowd of excited spectators. "We're bound to finish seventh or eighth, out of the race."

"We're still footing faster than the other boats," Penny observed. "Don't give up yet."

A moment later, the crack of a revolver sounding over the water, told the girls that the *Spindrift* had crossed the finish line in first place.

To add to Sally's difficulties, the rescued girl began to stir and rock the boat. Each time she moved, the *Cat's Paw* lost pace. Though they passed the next two boats, they could not gain to any extent on the one which seemed destined to finish in fifth place.

Sally had been right, Penny realized. Barring a miracle, the *Cat's Paw* could not be among the winners. Although they were slowly gaining, the finish line was too close for them to overcome the lead of the remaining boats.

And then the miracle occurred. The *Elf*, directly ahead, seemed to falter and to turn slightly aside. The *Cat's Paw* seized the chance and forged even.

"Go to it, Sally!" her skipper, Tom Evans, a freckled youth, called. "You belong in the finals!"

Then the girls understood and were grateful. Deliberately, the boy had slowed his boat so that Sally might be among the winners.

"It was a fine thing to do!" Sally whispered. "But how I hate to win in such fashion!"

"Tom Evans knew he had no chance in the finals," Penny said. "As he said, you belong there for you are one of the best sailors in the fleet."

Sally crossed the finish line in fifth place, then sailed on to the dock by the clubhouse. As Penny leaped out to make the boat fast, willing hands assisted with the bedraggled passenger. The child was taken to the clubhouse for a change of clothes. Officials gathered about Penny and Sally, congratulating them upon the race.

"I didn't really win," the latter said, paying tribute to Tom Evans. "The *Elf* deliberately turned aside to give me a chance to pass."

Nearby, Jack Gandiss who had won the race, stood unnoticed. After awhile he walked over to the dock where Sally and Penny were collecting their belongings.

"That was a nice rescue," he said diffidently. "Of course it cost you second place, which was a pity."

Sally cocked an eyebrow. "*Second* place?" she repeated. "Well, I like that!"

"You never could have defeated the *Spindrift*."

"No? Well, if my memory serves me right, the *Cat's Paw* was leading when I had to turn aside. Not that I wasn't glad to do it."

"You may have been ahead, but I was coming up fast. I would have overtaken you at the second marker or sooner."

"Children! Children!" interposed Penny as she neatly folded a sail and slipped it into a snowy white cover. "Must you always claw at each other?"

"Why, we aren't fighting," Sally denied with a grin.

"Heck, no!" Jack agreed. He started away, then turned and came back. "By the way, Sally. How about the trophy?"

Sally did not understand what he meant.

"I won the race, so doesn't the brass lantern belong to me?" Jack pursued the subject.

"Well, it will if you win the final next week."

"That's in the bag."

"Like fun it is!" Sally said indignantly. "Jack, I hate to crush those delicate feelings of yours, but you're due for the worst defeat of your life!"

The argument might have started anew, but Jack reverted to the matter of the lantern trophy.

"I'm the winner now, and it should be turned over to me," he insisted.

Sally became annoyed. "That's not according to the rules of the competition," she returned. "The regulations governing the race say that the *final* winner is entitled to keep the trophy. I was last year's winner. The one this season hasn't yet been determined."

"It's not safe to keep the lantern aboard the *River Queen*."

"Don't be silly! There couldn't be a safer place! Pop and I chained the trophy to a beam. It can't be removed without cutting the chain."

"Someone could take the trophy by unlocking the padlock."

CHAPTER 11 - A QUESTION OF RULES

"Oh, no, they couldn't," Sally grinned provokingly. "You see, I've already lost the key. The only way that lantern can be removed is by cutting the chain."

Jack was enraged. "You've lost the key?" he demanded. "If that isn't the last straw!"

Hanson Brown, chairman of the racing committee, chanced to be passing, and Jack impulsively hailed him. To the chagrin of the girls, he asked for a ruling on the matter of the trophy's possession.

"Why, I don't recall that such a question ever came up before," the official replied. "My judgment is that Miss Barker has a right to retain the trophy until the final race."

"Ha!" chuckled Sally, enjoying Jack's discomfiture. "How do you like that?"

Jack turned to leave. But he could not refrain from one parting shot. "All right," he said, "you get to keep the trophy, but mind—if anything should happen to it—you alone will be responsible!"

CHAPTER 12 - NIGHT PROWLER

When Penny, her father, and the Gandiss family returned late that afternoon to Shadow Island, a strange motorboat was tied up at the dock. On the veranda a man sat waiting. Although his face appeared familiar, Penny did not recognize him.

Her father, however, spoke his name instantly. "Heiney Growski! Anything to report?"

Penny remembered then that he was the detective who had been placed in charge of the junk shop near the Gandiss factory.

The man arose, laying aside a newspaper he had been reading to pass the time. "I've learned a little," he replied to Mr. Parker's question. "Shall we talk here?"

"Go ahead," encouraged Mr. Gandiss carelessly. "This is my son, Jack, and our guest, Penny Parker. They know of the situation at the factory, and can be trusted not to talk."

Though seemingly reluctant to make a report in the presence of the two youngsters, the detective nevertheless obeyed instructions.

"Since opening up the shop, I've been approached twice by a man from the factory," he began.

"That sweeper, called Joe?" interposed Mr. Parker.

"Yes, the first time he merely came into the place, looked around a bit, and finally asked me what I paid for brass."

"You didn't appear too interested?" Mr. Parker inquired.

"No, I gave him a price just a little above the market."

"How did it strike him?"

"He didn't have much to say, but I could tell he was interested."

"Did he offer you any brass?"

"No, he hinted he might be able to get me a considerable quantity of it later on."

"Feeling you out."

"Yes, I figure he'll be back. That's why I came here for instructions. If he shows up with the brass, shall I have him arrested?"

Mr. Parker waited for the factory owner to answer the question.

"Make a record of every transaction," Mr. Gandiss said. "Encourage the man to talk, and he may reveal the names of others mixed up in the thefts. But make no arrests until we have more information."

"Very good, sir," the detective returned. "Unless the man is very crafty, I believe we may be able to trap him within a few weeks."

After Heiney had gone, Jack and Penny went down to the dock together to retie the *Spindrift*. The wind had shifted, and with the water level rising, the boat was bumping against its mooring post.

"By the way, Jack," said Penny as she unfastened one of the ropes to make it shorter, "I forgot to congratulate you upon winning the race this afternoon."

"Skip it," he replied grimly.

Penny glanced at him, wondering if her ears had deceived her.

"Why, I thought you were crazy-wild to win," she commented.

"Not that way." Jack kept his face averted as he tied a neat clove hitch. "I guess I made myself look like a heel, didn't I?"

For the first time Penny really felt sorry for the boy. Resisting a temptation to rub salt in his wounds, she said kindly:

CHAPTER 12 - NIGHT PROWLER

"Well, I suppose you felt justified in asking for the trophy."

"I wish I hadn't done that, Penny. It's just that Sally gets me sometimes. She's so blamed cocky!"

"And she feels the same way about you. On the whole, though, I wonder if Sally has had a square deal?"

Jack straightened, staring at the *Spindrift* which tugged impatiently at her shortened ropes. Waves were beginning to lap over the dock boards.

"You mean about the factory?" he asked in a subdued voice.

Penny nodded.

"I never did think Sally was a thief," Jack said slowly. "Judging from Heiney Growski's report, someone may have planted the brass in her locker. Probably that fellow Joe, the Sweeper."

"Don't you feel she should be cleared?"

"How can we do anything without proof? This fellow Joe isn't convicted yet. Besides, he's only one of a gang. Sally could be involved, though I doubt it."

"You're not really convinced then?" Penny gazed at him curiously.

"Yes, I am," Jack answered after a slight hesitation. "Sally's innocent. I know that."

"Then why don't we do something about it?"

"What? My father has employed the best detectives already."

"At least you could tell Sally how you feel about it."

Jack kicked at the dock post with the toe of his tennis shoe. "And have her tear into me like a wild cat?" he countered. "You don't know Sally."

"Are you so sure that you do?" Penny asked. Turning she walked swiftly away.

Jack came padding up the gravel path after her.

"Wait!" he commanded, grasping her by the arm. "So you think I've given Sally a raw deal?"

"I have no opinion in the matter," Penny returned, deliberately aloof.

"If I could do anything to prove Sally innocent you know I'd jump at the chance," Jack argued, trying to regain Penny's good graces.

"You really mean that?"

"Yes, I do."

"Then why don't you try to get a little evidence against this man Joe, the Sweeper?" Penny proposed eagerly. "You visit the factory nearly every day. Keep your eyes and ears open and see what you can learn."

"Everyone knows who I am," Jack argued. "There wouldn't be a chance—" Meeting Penny's steady, appraising gaze, he broke off and finished: "Oh, okay, I'll do what I can, but it's useless."

"Not if you have a plan."

Jack stared at Penny with sudden suspicion. "Say, what are you leading up to anyhow?" he demanded. "Do *you* have one?"

"Not exactly. It just occurred to me that by watching at the gate of the factory when the employes leave, one might spot some of the men who are carrying off brass in their clothing."

Jack gave an amused snort. "Oh, that's been done. Company detectives made any number of checks."

"That's just the point," Penny argued. "They were factory employes, probably known to some of the workers."

"I'm even more widely recognized," Jack said. "Besides, Clayton, our gateman, has instructions to be on the watch for anyone who might try to carry anything away. He's reported several persons. When they were searched, nothing was found."

"Your gateman is entirely trustworthy?"

"Why not? He's an old employee."

Penny said no more, though she was thinking of the conversation overheard while at the factory gatehouse. Even if Jack took no interest, she decided she would try to do what she could herself. But there really seemed no place to begin.

"If you get any good ideas, I'll be glad to help," Jack said as if reading her thoughts. "Just to barge ahead without any plan, doesn't make sense to me."

Penny knew that he was right. Much as she desired to help clear Sally, she had no definite scheme in mind.

As the pair turned to leave the docks, they heard a shout from across the water. The *Cat's Paw*, with canvas spread wide, was sailing before the wind, directly toward the island. Sally, at the tiller, signaled that she wanted to talk to them.

The boat came in like a house afire, but though the landing was fast, it was skillful. Sally looped a rope around the dock post, but did not bother to tie up.

"Penny," she said breathlessly. "I didn't get half a chance to thank you this afternoon for helping me in the race."

"I didn't do anything," Penny laughed. "I merely went along for the ride."

"That may be your story, but everyone who saw the race knows better. What I really came here for is to ask you to spend the night with me aboard the *River Queen*. We'll have a chance to get better acquainted."

The invitation caught Penny by surprise. Sally mistook her hesitation for reluctance.

"Probably you don't feel you want to leave here," she said quickly. "It was just one of those sudden ideas of mine."

"I want to come," Penny answered eagerly. "If Mr. and Mrs. Gandiss wouldn't mind. Wait and I'll ask."

Darting to the house, she talked over the matter with her father and then with her hostess. "By all means go," the latter urged. "I imagine you will enjoy the experience. Jack can pick you up in the motorboat in the morning."

Packing her pajamas and a few toilet articles into a tight roll, Penny ran back to the dock. Jack and Sally were arguing about details of the afternoon race, but they abandoned the battle as she hurried up.

"Jack, you're to pick me up tomorrow morning," she advised him as she climbed aboard the *Cat's Paw*, "Don't forget."

The *River Queen* already had been anchored for the night in a quiet cove half a mile down river. With darkness approaching, lights were winking all along the shore. Across the river, the Gandiss factory was a blaze of white illumination. Farther downstream, the colored lights of an amusement park with a high roller coaster, cut a bright pattern in the sky.

Sally glanced for a moment toward the factory but made no mention of her unpleasant experience there. "Pop and I stay alone at night on the *Queen*," she explained as they approached the ferry. "Our crew is made up of men who live in town, so usually they go home after the six o'clock run."

Skillfully bringing the *Cat's Paw* alongside the anchored *Queen*, she shouted for her father to help Penny up the ladder. Making the smaller craft secure for the night, she followed her to the deck.

"What's cooking, Pop?" she asked, sniffing the air.

"Catfish," the captain answered as he went aft. "Better get to the galley and tend to it, or we may not have any supper."

The catfish, sizzling in butter, was on the verge of scorching. Sally jerked the pan from the stove, and then with Penny's help, set a little built-in table which swung down from the cabin wall, and prepared the remainder of the meal.

Supper was not elaborate but Penny thought she had never tasted better food. The catfish was crisp and brown, and there were French fried potatoes and a salad to go with it. For dessert, Captain Barker brought a huge watermelon from the refrigerator, and they split it three ways.

"It's fun living on a ferryboat!" Penny declared enthusiastically as she and Sally washed the dishes. "I can't see why you ever would want to work in a factory when you can live such a carefree life here."

The remark was carelessly made. Penny regretted it instantly for she saw the smile leave Sally's face.

"I worked at the factory because I wanted to help make airplanes, and because Pop can't afford to give me much money," she explained quietly. "It was all a mistake. I realize that now."

"I'm sorry," Penny apologized, squeezing her hand. "I didn't mean to be so stupid. As far as your discharge is concerned, you'll be cleared."

"How?"

"Mr. Gandiss has detectives working on the case."

"Detectives!" Sally gave a snort of disgust. "Why, everyone in the plant knows who they are!"

After dishes were done, the girls went on deck. Protected from the night breezes by warm lap rugs, they sat listening to the lallup of the waves against the *River Queen*. Captain Barker's pipe kept the mosquitoes away and he talked reminiscently of his days as a boy on the waterfront.

CHAPTER 12 - NIGHT PROWLER

Presently, the blast of a motorboat engine cut the stillness of the night. Sally, straightening in her chair, listened intently.

"There goes Jack again!" she observed, glancing at her father. "To the Harpers', no doubt."

The light of the boat became visible and Sally followed it with her eyes as it slowly chugged upstream.

"I was right!" she exclaimed a moment later.

Penny's curiosity was aroused, for she knew that Jack absented himself from home nearly every night, and that his actions were a cause of worry to his parents. "Who are the Harpers?" she inquired.

"Oh! they live across the river where you see those red and blue lights," Sally said, pointing beyond the railing. "The house stands on stilts over the water, and is a meeting place for the scum of the city!"

"Sally!" her father reproved.

"Well, it's the truth! Ma Harper and her no-account husband, Claude, run an outdoor dance pavilion, but their income is derived from other sources too. Black market sales, for instance."

"Sally, your tongue is rattling like a chain!"

"Pop, you know very well the Harpers are trash."

"Nevertheless, don't make statements you can't prove."

Sally's outspoken remarks worried Penny because of their bearing upon Mr. Gandiss' son. "You don't think Jack is mixed up with the Harpers in black market dealings?" she asked.

"Oh, no!" Sally got up from the deck chair. "He goes there to have a good time. And if you ask me, Jack ought to stop being a playboy grasshopper!"

Captain Barker knocked ashes from his pipe and put it deep in his jacket pocket. "The shoe pinches," he told Penny with a wink. "Sally never learned to dance. I hear tell there's a girl who goes to the Harper shindigs that's an expert at jitter-bugging!"

"That has nothing to do with me!" Sally said furiously. "I'm going to bed!"

Captain Barker arose heavily from his chair. "How about the day's passenger receipts?" he asked. "Locked in the cabin safe?"

"Yes, we took in more than two hundred dollars today."

"That makes over five hundred in the safe," the captain said, frowning. "You'll have to take it to the bank first thing in the morning, I don't like to have so much cash aboard."

Going to the cabin they were to share, Sally and Penny undressed and tumbled into the double-deck beds. The gentle motion of the boat and the slap of waves on the *Queen's* hull quickly lulled them to sleep.

How long Penny slumbered she did not know. But toward morning she awoke in darkness to find Sally shaking her arm.

"What is it?" Penny mumbled drowsily. "Time to get up?"

"Sh!" Sally warned. "Don't make a sound!"

Penny sat up in the bunk. Her friend, she saw, had started to dress.

"I think someone is trying to get aboard!" Sally whispered. "Listen!"

Penny could hear no unusual sound, only the wash of the waves.

"I distinctly heard a boat grate against the *Queen* only a moment ago," Sally pulled on her slacks and thrust her feet into soft-soled slippers which would make no sound. "I'm going on deck to investigate!"

Penny was out of bed in a flash. "Wait!" she commanded. "I'm going with you!"

Dressing with nervous haste, she tiptoed to the cabin door with Sally. Stealing through the dark corridors to the companionway, they could hear no unusual sound. But midway up the steps, Sally's keen ears heard movement.

"Someone is in the lounge!" she whispered. "It may be Pop but I don't think so! Come on, and we'll see."

CHAPTER 13 - THE STOLEN TROPHY

Hand in hand the two girls tiptoed to the entranceway of the lounge. Distinctly they could hear someone moving about in the darkness, and the sound came from the direction of a small cabin which the Barkers used as an office room.

"Pop!" Sally called sharply. "Is that you?"

She was answered only by complete silence. Then a plank creaked. The prowler was stealing stealthily toward the girls!

"Pop!" shouted Sally at the top of her lungs, groping to find a light switch.

Before she could illuminate the room, a man brushed past the two girls. Penny seized him by the coat. A sharp object pierced her finger. She was thrust back against the wall so hard that it knocked the breath from her. The man twisted, and jerking his coat free, dashed up the stairs.

"Pop!" Sally called again.

Captain Barker, armed with revolver and flashlight, came out of his cabin. By this time, Sally had found and turned on the light switch.

"A prowler!" she cried. "He ran up on deck."

"Stay below!" ordered the captain. "I'll get him!"

Penny and Sally had no intention of missing any of the excitement. Close at Captain Barker's heels, they darted up the companionway to the deck. To the starboard, the trio heard a slight splash, then the sound of steady dipping oars.

"Someone's getting away in a rowboat!" Sally cried.

Captain Barker ran to the railing. "Halt!" he shouted. "Halt or I'll fire!"

The man, a mere shadow in the mist arising from the river, rowed faster. Captain Barker fired two shots, purposely high. The man ducked down into the boat, and a moment later switched on an outboard motor, which rapidly carried him beyond view.

"Did you see who the fellow was, Sally?" the captain demanded wrathfully.

"No, it was too dark. Do you think he got away with the money in the safe?"

Fearing the worst, the trio descended to an office room adjoining the passenger lounge. A chair had been overturned there, but the door of the safe remained locked.

"You girls must have surprised him before he had time to steal the money," Captain Barker declared in relief. "No harm done, but this is the first time in six years that anyone tried to sneak aboard the *Queen*. We'll have to keep a better watch from now on."

As the girls turned to leave the cabin, Sally saw that Penny was looking at the third finger of her right hand.

"Why, you're hurt!" she cried.

Penny's hand was smeared with blood which came from a tiny pin-prick wound on the finger.

"It's nothing," she insisted.

Sally ran to a cabinet for gauze, iodine and cotton. "How did it happen?" she asked.

"I tried to stop the prowler. As I grabbed his coat, something stuck my finger. It must have been a pin."

The wound was superficial and did not pain Penny. Sally wrapped the finger for her, and then after Captain Barker had said he would remain up for awhile, they returned to bed.

Throughout the night there were no further disturbances. At dawn the girls arose, feeling only a little tired as the result of their night's adventure. They had time for a quick swim in the river before breakfast and disgraced themselves by eating six pancakes each.

CHAPTER 13 - THE STOLEN TROPHY

"The crew will be coming aboard soon," Sally said, glancing at her watch. "I usually sweep out the lounge and straighten up a bit before we make our first passenger run."

Penny, who had nothing to do until Jack could come to take her back to the island, eagerly offered to help. Armed with brooms and dust rags, the girls went below.

In the doorway, Penny paused, staring at the overhead beam.

"Why, Sally," she commented in astonishment. "What did you do with the lantern trophy? Take it down?"

"No, it's still there."

Alarmed by Penny's question, Sally moved past her, gazing at the beam. Where the brass lantern had hung, there now was only a neatly severed chain.

"Why, it's gone!" she exclaimed in disbelief.

"Wasn't it here last night when we went to bed?"

"Of course."

"Then it was stolen last night!"

Dropping broom and dustpan, Sally brought a chair and inspected the chain. Obviously it had been cut by sharp metal scissors.

"That prowler who came aboard last night must have done it!" she exclaimed angrily. "Oh, what a mean, low trick!"

As the full realization of what the loss would mean came to her, Sally sank down on the chair, a picture of dejection.

"I'm responsible for the trophy, Penny! I'll be expected to produce it before the final race. Oh, what can we do?"

"Why do you suppose the thief took the lantern and nothing else?"

"Someone may have done it for pure spite. But I'm more inclined to think the person came aboard to steal our money in the office safe. The lantern hung here in a conspicuous place and he may have taken it on impulse."

Intending to notify Captain Barker of the loss, the girls started up the companionway. Abruptly, Penny paused, her attention drawn to an object lying on one of the steps. It was a circular badge with a picture and a number on it. No name. Such identifications, she knew, were used by many industrial plants.

"Where did this come from?" she murmured, picking it up.

The face on the badge was unfamiliar to her. The man had dark, bushy hair, sunken eyes and prominent cheekbones.

Sally turned to examine the identification pin. "Why, this badge came from the Gandiss factory!" she exclaimed, and studied the picture intently.

"Did you ever see the man before?"

"I can't place him, Penny. Yet I know I have seen him somewhere."

"The man should be easy to trace from this picture and number. When I caught hold of his clothing last night, I must have pulled off the pin. That was how my finger was pricked."

As the girls examined the pin, they heard a commotion on deck and the sound of voices. Before they could go up the steps to investigate, Jack Gandiss came clattering down to the lounge.

"I came to take you back to the island, Penny," he informed. "Ready?"

Then his gaze fastened upon the beam where the brass lantern had hung.

"Say, what became of the trophy?" he demanded sharply. "You decided to take it down after all?"

"It's gone," Sally said, misery in her voice. "Stolen!"

The two girls waited for the explosion, but strangely, Jack said nothing for a moment.

"You warned me," Sally hastened on. "Oh, it's all my fault. It was conceited and selfish of me to display the trophy here. I deserve everything you're going to say."

Still Jack remained mute, staring at the beam.

"Go on—tell me what you're thinking," Sally challenged miserably.

"It's a tough break," Jack said without rancor.

"This will practically ruin the race," Sally accused herself. "I can't replace the trophy for there's no other like it. An ordinary cup never would seem the same."

"That's so," Jack gloomily agreed. "Well, if it's gone, it's gone, and there's nothing more to be done."

The boy's calm acceptance of the calamity he had predicted, astonished Penny and Sally. Was this the Jack they knew? With a perfect opportunity to say, "I told you so," he had withheld blame.

Sally sank down on the lower step. "How will I face the racing committee?" she murmured. "What will the other contestants say? They'll feel like running me out of town."

"Maybe it won't be necessary to tell," Jack said slowly. "One of us is almost certain to win the race next Friday."

"Yes, that's true, but—"

"If you win, the lantern would be yours for keeps. Should I win, no one would need to know that you hadn't turned it over to me. You could make some excuse at the time of the presentation."

Sally gazed at Jack with a new light in her eyes. "I'm truly sorry for all the hateful things I've said to you in the past," she declared earnestly. "You're a true blue friend."

"Maybe I'm sorry about some of the cracks I made too," he grinned, extending his hand. "Shake?"

Sally sprang up and grasped the hand firmly, but her eyes were misty. She hastened to correct any wrong impression Jack might have gained.

"I'm glad you made the offer you did," she said, "but I never would dream of keeping the truth from the committee. I'll notify them today."

"Why be in such a hurry?" Penny asked. "The race is a week away. In that time we may be able to find the trophy. After all, we have a good clue."

"What clue?" asked Jack.

Penny showed him the pin. As he gazed at the picture on the face of the badge, a strange expression came into his eyes.

"You know the man?" Penny asked instantly.

"He works at our factory. But that's not where I've seen him."

"At the Harpers?" Sally asked.

"Yes," Jack admitted unwillingly. "I don't know his name, but he is a friend of Ma Harper and her husband."

"And of that no-account Joe, the Sweeper?"

"I don't know about that." The questioning had made Jack uncomfortable.

"The man should be arrested!"

"We have no proof, Sally," Penny pointed out. "While we're satisfied in our own minds that the man who took the lantern is the person who lost the badge, we can't be certain."

"The badge may have been dropped by a passenger yesterday," Jack added. "Let me find out this fellow's name first, and a few facts about him."

"I don't believe your friends, the Harpers, will tell you much," Sally said stiffly. "They're the scum of the waterfront. How you can go there—"

Penny, who saw that another storm was brewing, quickly intervened, saying it was time she and Jack started for the island. Sally, taking the hint, allowed the subject to drop.

But as she went on deck to see the pair off in Jack's motorboat, she whispered to Penny:

"See me this afternoon, if you can. I have an idea I don't want Jack to know about. If we work together, we may be able to trace the trophy."

CHAPTER 14 - TRAPPED

Jack had little to say about the theft as he and Penny returned to the Gandiss home. However, after lunch he offered to go to his father's factory to learn the identity of the employee who had lost the badge aboard the *River Queen*.

"Want to come along?" he invited.

Ordinarily, Penny would have welcomed the opportunity, but remembering that Sally had wished to see her, she regretfully turned down the invitation.

"I'll ride across the river if you don't mind," she said. "I have an errand in town."

By this time Penny was familiar with the daily route of the *River Queen* and knew where it would dock to pick up and unload passengers. Sally, she felt certain, would be aboard, expecting her.

They crossed the river in the motorboat, making an appointment to meet again at four o'clock. After Jack had gone, Penny set off for the *River Queen's* dock where a sizable group of passengers awaited the ferry.

Soon the *Queen* steamed in, her bell signaling a landing. Passengers crowded the railing, eager to be the first off. A crewman stood at the wheel, and Sally was nowhere to be seen.

As the boat brushed the dock, sailors leaped off to make fast to the dock posts. Captain Barker, annoyed because the passengers were pushing, bellowed impatient orders to his men: "All right, start that gangplank forward! Lively! Are you going to sleep over it all day?"

Then, seeing Penny, he raised his hand in friendly greeting.

"Is Sally aboard?" she called to him.

"No, she went up the shore a ways—didn't say where," the captain replied, waving his hand upriver. "Ought to be back here any minute."

Sally, however, did not appear, and the *Queen* pulled away without her. Penny loitered on the dock for twenty minutes. The sun was hot and with nothing to do, time lay heavy upon her. It lacked a half hour before the *River Queen* would return, and fully two hours before she was due to meet Jack. For lack of occupation, she walked upriver along the docks.

Buildings were few and far between. There were several fish houses, a boat rental place and the half-deserted amusement park. The beach beyond made easy walking, so Penny kept on. With quickening interest she saw that she was approaching a two-story building which appeared to stand on stilts over the water. Close by was a large, smoothly cemented area with overhead lights.

"That's the Harper place!" Penny recognized it. "With the dance area adjoining."

She moved on along the beach. Drawing closer to the building, she passed a clump of bushes fringing the sand. The leaves stirred slightly though there was no breeze. Penny failed to notice the movement.

But as she passed the bushes, a hand reached out and grasped her ankle.

Startled, Penny uttered a nervous cry.

"Be quiet, you goon!" a familiar voice bade.

It was Sally Barker crouched amid the foliage. Quickly she pulled Penny with her behind the bushes.

"Sally, what are you doing here?" Penny demanded.

"Watching that house. I saw you a long way down the beach."

"Anything doing?"

"A boat is coming in now. That's why I didn't want you to be seen."

A rowboat with an outboard, rapidly approached the Harper pier. Already it was making a wide sweep preparatory to a landing.

"Why, it's that fellow, Joe the Sweeper!" Penny exclaimed, peering out from the hiding place. "Who is steering the boat?"

"Claude Harper," Sally revealed. "Ma Harper's husband."

"Wonder what Joe would be doing here?"

"That's what I'd like to know myself," Sally returned grimly. "Joe isn't as stupid as he's given credit for being. He's crafty and mean, and being mixed up with the Harpers is no recommendation."

While the girls watched, the boat landed. The two men tied up the craft, and removing a burlap sack which apparently was filled with something heavy, carried it into the two-story house.

"I wish we knew what they brought here," Penny said. "Why not try to find out?"

"How?"

"Couldn't we sneak up to the house and peek in one of the windows?"

"We might be caught."

"True, but we'll learn nothing more here."

Debating a moment, the girls emerged from their hiding place. To reach the house they were compelled to cross an open stretch of beach. However, no one was to be seen outside the dwelling and their arrival appeared to attract no notice of anyone inside.

"How about that window at the east side?" Penny suggested.

The one she pointed out was half screened by bushes and at a level which would permit them to peer inside.

"Okay," agreed Sally, "but I'd hate to be caught at this business. The Harpers hate me and they would be mighty unpleasant if they came upon us snooping."

"What a harsh word!" chuckled Penny. "All this comes under the heading of investigation! The only difference is that Mr. Gandiss' detectives are paid and we aren't."

"If I could get the brass lantern back that would be pay enough for me," Sally returned.

Creeping to the window, the girls cautiously peeped into the house. The panes were so dirty it was hard to see inside. But they were able to distinguish three persons sitting at a living room table. Papers were spread out before them, and they were adding figures. There was no sign of the sack which had been carried into the house.

"Who are they?" Penny asked her companion.

"Joe the Sweeper, Ma Harper and her husband. Another woman is coming into the room now. But she's only a stupid houseworker Ma hires by the week."

Sally moved backwards, intending to give Penny her place at the window. Inadvertently, she stepped on a stick which broke in two with a snap. Though the sound was not loud, it apparently was heard by those inside the house.

For immediately Claude Harper shoved back his chair and started toward the window.

"What was that?" the girls heard him mutter. "I thought I heard someone outside."

"Quick! Crouch down or he'll see us!" Penny warned, pulling Sally to the ground.

Claude Harper, a sallow-faced man in dirty leather jacket, appeared at the window. To the alarm of the girls, he thrust up the sash. In plain view, should he peer down over the ledge, they held their breath.

The man, however, gazed toward the boat docks. "I don't see anyone," he reported to his companions. "I was sure I heard something—" he broke off, ending sharply: "And I did too!"

"What is it, Claude?" his wife called.

"Anyone been here this afternoon?" he demanded.

"Nary a soul until you came."

"Take a look at those shoetracks in the sand!"

Hearing the words, Penny and Sally gazed behind them. From the bush on the beach to the wall where they crouched, led a telltale trail.

"I'll go outside and look around!" Harper said to his wife. He slammed down the window.

"We're sunk!" Sally moaned. "We can't run across the beach without being seen, and we're certain to be caught here."

Keeping close to the wall, treading in firm earth which left no visible shoemarks, the girls crept around the building corner. The slamming of a door warned them that Claude Harper already was on their trail.

"Someone's been here by the window!" they heard him shout.

CHAPTER 14 - TRAPPED

Frantically, the girls looked about for a place to hide. There was no shrubbery nearby, only the waterfront. Penny's desperate gaze fastened upon the rowboat tied up at the pier nearby. In the bottom lay an old canvas sail.

"Quick! The boat!" she whispered to Sally.

"We'll be caught there sure!"

"It's even more certain if we stay here. Come on, it's our only chance."

Choosing the lesser of two evils, they tiptoed across the pier. Though many of the boards were rotten and loose, their shoes fortunately made no sound.

Scrambling down into the boat, the girls jerked the canvas sail over them. Barely had they hidden themselves, than their hearts sank, for they heard heavy footsteps approaching on the pier.

CHAPTER 15 - UNDER THE SAIL

That Claude Harper was searching for them, the girls did not doubt. But though he knew someone had been peering in the window, they were hopeful he had not actually seen them. Huddling beneath the sail in the bottom of the boat, they nervously waited.

The man came farther out on the pier, the boards creaking beneath his weight. At any instant the girls expected to have the sailcloth jerked from their heads. However, Harper's attention was diverted as Sweeper Joe came out of the house.

"Find anyone?" the factory worker asked.

"No, but tracks lead to the window. Someone's been spying."

"Kids probably."

"I don't know about that," Claude Harper returned gruffly. "I'd feel a lot safer if we didn't have all that stuff in the basement. What's our chances of getting rid of it tonight?"

"We can't do it. Tomorrow or next night maybe. Arrangements have got to be made, and if we try to push things, we'll end up in a jam."

The voices faded away, though not entirely. Presently daring to peep from beneath the canvas, Penny saw that the two men had seated themselves on the rear steps of the house at the edge of the river and within plain view of the tied-up boat.

"We're in a nice position now!" she whispered to Sally. "Suppose they sit there until they decide to leave in this boat?"

"We'll be caught. We're the same as trapped now unless they go back into the house."

The two men showed no inclination to leave. They talked earnestly together, evidently making plans of some sort. Though the girls tried hard to overhear, they could catch only an occasional word. After awhile, Ma Harper, a wiry, ugly woman with stringy black hair, came outdoors to join the men on the steps.

"It's getting late," she warned. "If you're goin' to tend to that job today, you'll have to be gettin' across the river. Ain't you due to show up for work at four o'clock, Joe?"

"That's right," the man yawned, getting up. "I'll be glad when I can chuck the whole business and live without workin'."

Though Penny and Sally did not hear much of the conversation, it was evident to them that the men were about ready to make use of the boat.

"We're sunk," Sally whispered fearfully. "Maybe we ought to climb out of here and make a dash for it."

Penny offered a better idea. "Why not untie the rope, and let the boat drift off?" she proposed. "The current is swift and should carry us downstream fairly fast."

"Any other boat around that they can use to follow us in?"

"I don't see any." Penny raised the sail a little higher as she gazed along the pier and nearby beach.

"All right, then do your stuff," Sally urged.

While she held the sail slightly above Penny's head so that no movement would be discernible to those on the house steps, the latter reached her hands from beneath the cloth and swiftly untied the rope. The boat began to drift away. Covered by the sail, the girls lay motionless and flat on the craft's bottom.

At first nothing happened. But as they began to hope that the men would not notice the drifting boat, they heard an explosive shout.

"Look!" Claude Harper exclaimed. "Our boat!"

"Jumpin' fish hooks!" Sweeper Joe muttered. "How did that happen? I tied 'er secure."

CHAPTER 15 - UNDER THE SAIL

"It looks like it," the other retorted sarcastically. "I can't afford to lose that boat."

The girls could hear running footsteps on the pier and boardwalk near the dance pavilion. Sally dared to peep from beneath the canvas again.

"They're after a motorboat!" she reported tensely. "Harper has one he keeps locked in a boathouse."

"How close are we to the bend in the river?"

"About twenty yards."

The swift current was doing its best for the girls, swinging their boat toward the bend. Once beyond it, they would be temporarily hidden from the pier. But the current also was tending to carry them farther and farther from shore.

"Do we dare row?" Penny asked nervously.

"Not yet. Harper is having trouble getting the engine of his boat started," Sally reported. "We'll be safe for a minute or two. We're getting closer to the bend."

To the nervous girls, the boat scarcely seemed to move. Then at last it passed the bend and they were screened by willow trees and bushes.

"Now!" Sally signalled in a tense whisper.

Throwing off the sail, they seized oars and paddled with all their strength.

"Quiet!" Sally warned as Penny's oar made a splash. "Sounds carry plainly over the water."

The blast of a motorboat engine told them that Harper and his companion had started in pursuit. Only a minute or two would be required for them to round the bend.

Throwing caution to the winds, Sally and Penny dug in with their oars, shooting their craft toward shore. The boat grated softly on the sand. Instantly, the girls leaped out, splashing through ankle-deep water.

As Sally was about to start across the beach, Penny seized her hand.

"We mustn't leave a trail of footprints this time!" she warned.

Treading a log at the water's edge, Penny walked its length to firm ground which took no visible shoe print. Sally followed her to a clump of bushes where they crouched and waited.

Barely had they taken cover when the motorboat came into view, heading for the little cove. There Claude Harper recaptured the runaway rowboat, tying it to the stern of the other craft.

Suddenly Penny was dismayed as she realized that in their flight, a most important detail had been overlooked.

"The oars!" she whispered. "They're wet!"

"Maybe the men won't see," Sally said hopefully. "We left them half covered by the canvas."

Intent only upon returning to the pier, Claude Harper and his companion failed to notice anything amiss. Apparently assuming the boat had been carelessly tied and had drifted away under its own power, they were not suspicious.

"That was a narrow squeak," Penny sighed in relief as the motorboat with the other craft in tow finally disappeared around the bend. "The oars will quickly dry in the sun, so I guess we're safe."

Now that they were well out of trouble, the adventure seemed fun. Penny glanced at her wristwatch, observing that it was past four o'clock.

"Jack will be waiting for me," she said to Sally. "I'll have to hurry."

"We'll have plenty of time," Sally returned carelessly. "You usually can count on Jack being half an hour late for appointments."

Walking swiftly along the deserted shore, the girls discussed what they had overheard at the Harpers.

"We stirred up a big fuss and didn't learn too much," Penny said regretfully. "All the same, it looks as if the Harpers and Sweeper Joe are mixed up in this brass business together."

"They spoke of having something stored in the basement. That is what interests me. Oh, Penny, if only we could go back there sometime when the Harpers are gone and really investigate!"

"Maybe we can."

Sally shook her head. "Ma Harper almost never goes away from home. But sometimes she has streams of visitors from Osage—mostly women. I've often wondered why."

"Factory girls?"

"No, they're housewives and every type of person. I think Mrs. Harper must be selling something to them, but I never could figure it out."

The *River Queen* was at the far side of the river, so Sally, for lack of occupation, walked on with Penny to the dock where she was to meet Jack. Greatly to their surprise, he was there ahead of them, and evidently had been waiting for some length of time.

Seeing the girls, he slowly arose to his feet.

"Well, Jack, what did you learn at the factory?" Penny asked eagerly.

"Why, not much of anything."

"You mean you weren't able to find out the name of the man who dropped his badge aboard the *Queen*?" Penny asked incredulously.

"Of course you learned the name if you really tried," Sally added. "Every single badge used at your factory would be recorded!"

Thus trapped, Jack said lamely: "Oh, I learned his name all right. Take it easy, and I'll tell you."

CHAPTER 16 - SILK STOCKINGS

Puzzled by Jack's behavior and his evident reluctance to reveal what he had learned, Penny and Sally sat down beside him on the dock. At their urging he said:

"Well, I traced the number through our employment office. The badge was issued to a worker named Adam Glowershick."

Neither of the girls ever had heard of the name, but Sally, upon studying the picture again, was sure she recalled having seen him as a passenger aboard the *River Queen*.

"He's a punch press operator," Jack added.

"And he's the man you thought you knew?" Penny asked curiously.

"Yes. As I told you, I've seen him at the Harpers." Jack acted ill at ease.

The girls exchanged a quick glance. But they did not tell Jack of their recent adventure.

"Well, why don't we have the fellow arrested?" Sally demanded after a moment of silence. "I'm satisfied he stole the brass lantern. He probably came aboard for money, and unable to get into the safe, took the trophy for meanness."

"Or he may be mixed up with the gang of factory brass thieves," Penny supplied.

"You can't prove a case against a man, because he might have dropped the badge anytime he happened to be a passenger aboard the ferry," Jack said. "It would do no good to have him booked on suspicion."

"Is he a friend of yours?" Sally asked significantly.

"Of course not!"

"Jack is right about it," Penny interposed hastily. "We need more information before we ask police to make an arrest. Any other news, Jack?"

"Nothing startling. But you know that detective your father brought here from Riverview?"

"Heiney?"

"Yes, he reported today that Sweeper Joe contacted him again, offering to sell a large quantity of brass. An appointment has been made for the delivery Friday night. If it proves to be stolen brass, then he's trapped himself."

"Can they prove it's the same brass?"

"Heiney numbers and records every piece he buys. He should be able to establish a case."

Knowing that her father had intended to keep the junkman's activities a secret, Penny was disturbed by Jack's talking in public. Evidently he had gleaned this latest information from his father. She was even more troubled by his attitude toward Adam Glowershick.

Presently saying goodbye to Sally, she and Jack returned to Shadow Island. A strange boat was tied up in the berth usually occupied by the *Spindrift*. Since the sailboat was nowhere along the dock, it was evident that Mr. Gandiss, his wife, and Mr. Parker had gone for an outing on the river.

"We seem to have a visitor," Penny remarked.

Jack said nothing, but intently studied the man who slouched near the boathouse, hat pulled low to shade his eyes from the sun glare.

"Why, isn't that the same fellow whose picture was on the factory badge!" Penny exclaimed. "Adam Glowershick!"

"Careful or he'll hear you," Jack warned, scowling. "I know this man. He's here to see me."

Penny gazed again at the stranger who had dark bushy hair and prominent cheekbones. "If that isn't Glowershick, it's his twin!" she thought, and asked Jack if he had the factory badge with him.

"No, I haven't," he answered irritably. "Furthermore, I wish you would cut out such wild speculation. He'll hear you."

Jack brought the boat in. Leaping ashore, he asked Penny to fasten the ropes. "I'll be back in a minute," he flung at her as he strode off.

It took time to make the craft secure. When Penny glanced up from her work, Jack and the stranger had disappeared behind the boathouse.

"Queer how fast Jack ducked out of here," she thought.

More than a little annoyed by the boy's behavior, Penny started up the gravel path to the house. Midway there she heard footsteps, and turning, saw Jack hastening after her.

"Penny—" he began diffidently.

She waited for him to go on.

"I hate to ask this," he said uncomfortably, "but how are you fixed for money?"

"I have a little. Dad gave me a fairly large sum to spend when we came here."

"Could you let me have twenty dollars? It would only be a loan for a few days. I—I wouldn't ask it, only I need it badly."

"Dad only gave me twenty-five, Jack."

"I'll pay you back in just a few days, Penny. Honest I will."

"I'll help you out of your jam," Penny agreed unwillingly, "but something tells me I shouldn't do it. Your parents—"

"Don't say anything to them about it," Jack pleaded. "My father gives me a good allowance, and if he knew I had spent all of it ahead, he'd have a fit."

Penny went to her room for the money, returning with four crisp five dollar bills. She had planned to buy a new dress but now it must wait.

"Thanks," Jack said gratefully, fairly snatching the money from her hand. "Oh, yes, another favor—please don't mention to my folks that anyone was here today."

"Who is the man, Jack?"

"Oh, just a fellow I met." The boy started moving away. Penny, however, pursued him down the path.

"Not so fast, Jack. Since I have a financial interest in your affairs now, it's only fair that I ask a few questions. Did you meet this man at the Harpers?"

"What if I did?"

"Now you're in debt to him and he's pressing you for money. You don't want your parents to know."

"Something like that," Jack muttered, avoiding her steady gaze.

"I don't like being a party to anything I fail to understand. Jack, if you expect me to keep quiet about this, you'll have to make a promise."

"What is it?"

"That you'll not go to the Harpers' again."

"Okay, I'll promise," Jack agreed promptly. "The truth is, I've had enough of the place. Now, is the lecture concluded?"

"Quite finished," Penny replied.

With troubled eyes she watched Jack return to the boathouse and hand her money to the bushy-haired stranger.

"Maybe that fellow isn't Glowershick," she thought, "but he certainly looks like the picture. If Jack should be mixed up with those brass thieves—"

Penny deliberately dismissed the idea from her mind. A guest of the Gandiss' family, she could not permit herself to distrust Jack. He was inclined to be wild, irresponsible and at times arrogant, yet she had never questioned his basic character. Even though it disturbed her to know that he had given money to the stranger, she refused to believe that he was dishonest or that he would betray his father's trust.

If Penny hoped that Jack would offer a complete explanation for his actions, she was disappointed. After the stranger had gone, he deliberately avoided her. And that night at dinner, he had very little to say.

When the meal was finished, Jack roved restlessly about the house, not knowing what to do with himself. "I hope you're planning on staying home tonight," his mother commented. "Lately, you've scarcely spent an evening here."

CHAPTER 16 - SILK STOCKINGS

"There's nothing to do on an island," Jack complained. "I thought I might run in to town for an hour or so."

He met Penny's gaze and amended hastily: "On second thought, I guess I won't. How about an exciting game of chess?"

The evening was dull, heightened only by Mr. Gandiss' discussion of the latest difficulties at the factory. Another large quantity of brass had disappeared, he revealed to Mr. Parker.

"Perhaps our detectives will solve the mystery eventually," he declared, "but I'm beginning to lose heart. The firm has lost $60,000 already, and the thieves become bolder each day. At the start, only a small ring operated. Now I am convinced at least ten or fifteen employes may be in on the scheme to defraud me."

"The brass must be smuggled past the gateman," Mr. Parker commented thoughtfully.

"We have three of them," Mr. Gandiss replied. "Several persons have been turned in, but nothing ever could be proved against any individual who was searched."

Deeply interested in her father's remark, Penny kept thinking about Clark Clayton, the night-shift gateman, and his apparent friendship with Sweeper Joe. Late the next afternoon when she knew he would be on duty, she purposely arrived at the factory just as a large group of employes was leaving.

Though at his usual post, Clark Clayton did not appear especially alert. As employes filed past him, he paid them no special heed. Several persons who carried bulky packages were not even stopped for inspection.

"Why, a person could carry a ton of brass through that gate and he wouldn't know the difference!" she thought.

Making no attempt to enter the grounds, Penny watched for a while. Then she hailed a taxi cab, and told the driver to take her to the river.

They were nearing the docks when the man, glancing back over his shoulder, said carelessly: "How would you like to buy some genuine silk stockings?"

"How would I like to stake out a claim to part of the moon!" Penny countered, scarcely knowing how to take the question.

"No, I'm serious," the cab driver went on, slowing the taxi to idling pace. "I know a woman along the river who has a pretty fair stock of genuine silk stockings. Beauties."

"Black market?" Penny asked with disapproval.

"Well, no, I wouldn't call it that," the man argued. "She had a supply of these stockings and wants to get rid of them. Nothing wrong in that. Five dollars a pair."

"Five dollars a pair!" Penny echoed, barely keeping her temper.

"If I took you there, she might let you have them for a dollar less."

Penny opened her lips to tell the black market "runner" what she thought of a person who would engage in such illegal business. Then she closed them again and did a little quick thinking. After all, it might be wise to learn where the place was and then report to the police.

"Well, I don't know," she said, pretending to hesitate. "I'd like to have a pair of silk stockings, but I haven't much money with me. Where is the place?"

"Not far from here along the river. I'll drive you there, and if you make a purchase, you needn't pay me any fare."

"All right, that's fair enough. Let's go," Penny agreed.

As they rattled along the street, she carefully memorized the cab's number, and took mental notes on the driver's appearance, intending to report him to police. No doubt he received a generous commission for bringing customers to the establishment, she reasoned.

The cab had not gone far when it began to slacken pace. Peering out, Penny was astonished to see that they were stopping in front of the Harper house, overlooking the river.

"Is this the place?" she gasped, as the driver swung open the door. "I—I don't believe I want to go in after all. I thought you were taking me to a shop."

"You can't get silk stockings anywhere else in the county," the driver said. "Not like the kind Ma Harper sells. Just go on in and tell her I brought you. She'll treat you right."

Taking Penny by the elbow, he half pulled her from the cab and started her toward the shabby, unpainted dwelling.

CHAPTER 17 - BASEMENT LOOT

While the cab driver waited, Penny crossed the sagging porch and rapped on the door. Evidently the taxi's approach had been noted, for almost at once Ma Harper appeared.

She was a tall, thin woman, sallow of face, and with a hard glint to her eyes. Penny was not in the least deceived by the smile that was bestowed upon her.

"Hello, deary," the woman greeted her, stepping aside for her to enter. "Did Ernst bring you to buy something?"

"He spoke of silk stockings," Penny returned cautiously. "I'm not sure that I'll care to purchase them."

"Oh, you will when you see them, deary," Ma Harper declared in a chirpy tone. "Just come in and I'll show them to you."

"Aren't genuine silk stockings hard to get now?"

"I don't know of any place they can be bought except here. I was lucky to lay in a good supply before the start of the war. Only one or two pairs are left now, but I'll let you have them, deary."

"That's very kind of you," returned Penny with dry humor.

"The stockings cost me plenty," went on the woman, motioning for the girl to seat herself on a sagging davenport. "I'll have to ask five dollars a pair."

She eyed Penny speculatively to note how the figure struck her. Penny had no intention of making a purchase at any price, but to keep the conversation rolling, she pretended to be interested.

"Five dollars ain't much when you consider you can't get stockings like these anywhere else," the woman added. "Just wait here, deary, and I'll bring 'em out." She went quickly from the room.

Left alone, Penny gazed with curiosity at the crude furnishings. Curtains hung at the windows, but they had not been washed in many months. The rug also was soiled and threadbare. The main piece of furniture, a table, stood in the center of the room.

Double doors opened out upon a balcony above the river. Wandering outside, Penny could see the *River Queen* plying its way far downstream. Closer by, a small boat with an outboard approached.

Due to the glare of a late afternoon sun on the water, she could not at first distinguish its two occupants. The boat, however, looked familiar.

"That's the same boat Sally and I escaped in yesterday!" she thought. "And it's coming here!"

Nearer and nearer the craft approached, until Penny could see the men's faces plainly. One was Sweeper Joe and the other, Clark Clayton, gateman at the Gandiss factory.

"If they see me here, they're certain to be suspicious!" Penny thought in panic. "They'll remember having seen me with Mr. Gandiss at the factory. I'll skip while the skipping is good!"

She turned to find Ma Harper standing in the doorway. "Anything wrong, deary?" the woman asked in a soft purr.

"Why, no," Penny stammered. "I—I was just admiring the river view."

"You were lookin' at that boat so funny-like I thought maybe you knew the men. Sure there ain't nothing wrong?"

"Of course not!" Penny was growing decidedly uncomfortable. She tried to slip through the doorway, but Ma Harper did not move aside.

"It's getting late," Penny said, glancing at her wrist watch. "Perhaps I should come some other time to look at the stockings. Shall we say tomorrow?"

"I have the hosiery right here, deary. Beauties, ain't they?"

CHAPTER 17 - BASEMENT LOOT

Ma Harper spread one of the filmy stockings over her rough, callous hand. The silk was fine and beautiful, unquestionably pre-war and of black market origin.

"Yes, they are lovely," Penny said nervously. "But the truth is, I haven't five dollars with me. I'll have to come back later."

Ma Harper's dark eyes snapped angrily.

"Then what you been takin' my time for?" she demanded. "Say—" she accused with sudden suspicion, her gaze roving to the boat which now was close to the pier, "—you seem in a mighty big hurry to get away from here all at once!"

"Why, no, it's just that the taxi man is waiting, and it's getting late."

"What's your name anyhow?"

"Penny Parker."

"Where do you live?"

"I am a summer vacationist."

The answers only partially satisfied Ma Harper. Evidently she was afraid that Penny might be an investigator, for she debated a moment. Then she said: "You wait here until I talk to someone."

"But I really must be leaving."

"You wait here, I said!" Ma Harper snapped. "Maybe you're okay, but I ain't takin' no chances on you getting me into trouble about these stockings. Wait until I talk to Joe."

Leaving Penny on the balcony, she went out by way of the front living room door. After it had closed, there was a sharp little click which made the girl fear she had been locked in.

The truth was quickly ascertained. The door was locked. For an instant, Penny was frightened, but she told herself she was not really a prisoner. There were windows she could unfasten, and another door at the rear of the house.

Intending to test it, she went quickly through the kitchen. Voices reached her ears. Evidently Ma Harper and the two men were standing close to the door, and although speaking in low tones she could hear most of the conversation.

"The girl may be all right, but I think she was sent here to spy!" Ma reported. "If we let her go, she may bring the police down on us!"

"And if you try to hold her here, you'll soon be in trouble!" one of the men answered. Penny thought the voice was that of Clark Clayton. "You and this petty stocking business of yours! We warned you to lay off it."

"Sure, blame me!" Ma's voice rose angrily. "The truth is, you're getting scared of your own racket. I was sellin' stockings and makin' a good, safe income until you come along and talked my husband into lettin' you store your loot in our basement. Well, I've made up my mind! You're gettin' the stuff out of here tonight, and you're not bringing any more in!"

"Okay, okay," growled Sweeper Joe. "Just take it easy, and quit your yippin'. We'll move the stuff as soon as it gets dark. Fact is, we've made a deal with a guy that runs a junk shop near the factory. He's offered us a good price. We had to play along slow and easy to be sure he wasn't tied up with the cops."

"What about the girl?" Ma demanded. "If I let her go, she's apt to get me into hot water about those stockings."

"That's your funeral," Joe the Sweeper retorted. "If you'd handled her right, she wouldn't have become suspicious."

The discussion went on, in lower tones. Then Penny heard Ma say:

"Okay, that's the way we'll do it. I'll think up some story to convince the girl. But that brass must be out of here tonight! Another thing, you can't sell the lantern that simpleton, Adam Glowershick, stole from the *River Queen*."

"Why not?" Sweeper Joe demanded. "There's good brass in it."

"You stupid lout!" Ma exclaimed, losing patience. "That lantern is known to practically every person along the waterfront. Let it show up in a pawnshop or second hand store, and the police would trace it straight to us. You'll have to heave it into the river."

"Okay, maybe you're right," the factory worker admitted.

Penny had learned enough to feel certain that brass, stolen piecemeal from the Gandiss factory, had been stored in the Harper basement. Even more astonishing was the information that the trophy taken from the *River Queen* also was somewhere in the house.

"If the lantern is thrown into the river, no one ever be able to recover it," she thought. "If only I could get it now and sneak away through a window!"

Penny's pulse stepped up a pace, for she knew that to venture into the basement was foolhardy. She listened again at the door. Ma and the men still were talking, but how long they would continue to do so, she could not guess.

"I'll risk it," she decided.

The basement door opened from an inside wall of the kitchen. Penny groped her way down the steep, dark stairs but could find no light switch.

The cellar room was damp and dirty. As her eyes became accustomed to the dim light which filtered in through two small windows, she saw a furnace surrounded by buckets of ashes and boxes of papers and trash. A clothes line was hung with stockings and silk underwear.

Penny poked into several of the boxes and barrels. All were empty. Then her gaze focused upon another door, which apparently led into a fruit or storage room. It was padlocked.

"The brass is locked in there!" she thought, her heart sinking. "The lantern too! How stupid of me not to expect it."

Without tools, Penny could not hope to break into the locked room. There was only one thing to do. She must get away from the house, and bring the police!

Starting up the stairs, she stopped short. An outside door had slammed. In the room above she heard footsteps, but no voices.

Frightened, Penny remained motionless on the basement stairs. She could hear Ma Harper tramping about, evidently in search of her, for the woman muttered angrily to herself.

"I don't dare stay here," the girl thought. "I'll have to make a dash for it."

Penny reasoned that in reentering the house, Ma Harper probably had left the front door unlocked. What had become of the two men she did not know, but she would have to take a chance on their whereabouts.

Noiselessly, she crept up the stairs to the kitchen door, opening it a tiny crack. Though she could not see Ma, footsteps told her that the woman had stepped out onto the balcony overlooking the river.

"This will be as good a chance as I may get," she reasoned.

The door squeaked as she opened it wide enough to slip through. Unnerved by the sound, Penny moved swiftly across the kitchen to the living room.

"So there you are!" cried Ma Harper from the balcony.

Penny threw caution to the winds. Darting across the room, she jerked at the outside door. It opened, but on the porch, facing her, stood Sweeper Joe and Clark Clayton!

CHAPTER 18 - OVER THE BALCONY

Panic-stricken, Penny's first thought was to try to dart past the men. But she realized that to do so would be impossible. Warned by Ma Harper's excited cries, they had moved into position to completely block her path.

"Stop that girl!" shouted Ma Harper, bearing down, upon her from the direction of the river balcony. "She's from the police and sent here to get evidence!"

Whirling around, Penny ran back toward the kitchen, with the woman in pursuit. She did not waste time testing the rear door, for she already knew it to be locked.

However, opening from the kitchen was another closed door which appeared to give exit. With no time to debate, Penny jerked it open and darted inside.

Instantly, she saw that she had made a serious mistake. She had entered a small washroom and had trapped herself. And Ma Harper was practically upon her.

Penny did the only possible thing. She slammed the door and turned the key in the lock. For a moment at least, she was beyond reach.

"I've really trapped myself now!" she thought, recapturing her breath. "What a mess! If I had used my head this wouldn't have happened."

Penny sat down on the edge of the bathtub to think. Already Ma Harper was pounding and thumping on the flimsy wooden door panel. The door rattled on its hinges.

"You open up or I'll break down the door!" the woman shouted furiously. "You hear me?"

Penny did not answer. There was no escape from the washroom for it had no window. The tub upon which she sat was ringed with dirt, evidently having seen no use in many weeks. Above her head stretched a short clothesline upon which hung a row of Ma Harper's stockings.

"You let me in!" Ma Harper shouted again. "If I ever lay hands on you, you'll pay for this!"

The threat left Penny entirely unmoved. She had no intention of opening the door, no matter what the woman might say or do.

Realizing that her tactics were gaining nothing, Ma tried another approach.

"Please let me in," she coaxed in a falsely sweet voice. "We won't hurt you. If you come out now, we'll let you go home just as you want to do."

Penny was not to be so easily taken in. She remained silent.

Ma Harper lost her temper completely then. She kicked at the door and shouted for the two men.

"Joe! Clark! Come and help me get this brat out of here!"

Penny, certain that her moments of freedom were limited, heard the two men approach. A heavy body heaved itself against the door, but still the lock held.

"I don't want my door smashed," she heard Ma Harper whine. "Can't you get a screwdriver and take off the hinges? There ain't no other key in the house."

The reply of the men was inaudible, but Penny heard their retreating footsteps. The door knob kept rattling, so she decided Ma Harper had been left there to keep watch.

"This probably is my only chance to escape!" Penny reasoned. "I might unlock the door and take a chance on overpowering Ma Harper. But she's a strong woman!"

Her roving gaze fastened upon the line of drying stockings, and suddenly she had an idea! Jerking one of the stockings down, she seized a thick bar of soap from the dish above the bathtub, and crammed it deep into the toe of the stocking.

"This will make a superb weapon!" she thought gleefully. "Almost as good as a blackjack!"

Taking a firm grip on the stocking, Penny swung it several times to be certain of its possibilities. Then she was ready.

Quickly she unlocked the door and stepped back.

For a moment nothing happened. Then Ma Harper pushed it open, just as she had expected.

"Now I'll get you!" she screamed, springing at Penny.

Penny kept the stocking behind her back. "I hate to do this," she thought, "but she's asking for it!"

As Ma reached out to seize her, she swung the stocking. The encased cake of soap cut a neat arc through the air and clipped the woman sharply on the head.

More startled than hurt, she stumbled backwards and collapsed into the bathtub.

Pausing only long enough to see that Ma was not really injured, Penny made a dash for safety. But her escape was cut off.

Sweeper Joe and Clayton the gateman were just entering the front door of the living room, armed with tools to use in taking down the washroom door.

Seeing Penny, they again blocked the exit. Desperate, she ran in the only possible direction—to the balcony overlooking the river.

The docks were directly beneath the house, and waves lapped the posts of the two-story porch. It was at least a fifteen-foot drop and the water was shallow. But Penny had no time to calculate the risk.

Leaping to the railing of the balcony, she poised there an instant, staring down at the rocks plainly visible in the still water.

Then, as Sweeper Joe reached out to grasp her by the shoulder, she jumped.

She struck the water head foremost in a shallow dive which wrenched her back but kept her from striking the river bottom. Brushing wet hair from her eyes, she began to stroke. Her shoes were heavy as lead and impeded her.

The force of Penny's dive had carried her many feet from shore into deep water, and the river current swept her farther away from the docks. Weighted down by the shoes, she knew she did not have sufficient strength to swim to shore with them on.

Burying her face in the water, she doubled up, and groping down, untied them, one at a time.

"Those were good shoes," she thought with regret as she kicked them off and saw them settle into the river.

Penny struck out with smooth crawl strokes for the nearby pier. Her skirt kept wrapping itself about her legs. Unwilling to discard it, she tucked it high about her waist which made swimming much easier.

Reaching the pier, she was pulling herself out onto it, when Ma Harper and the two men came running out of the house to intercept her.

"Oh! Oh!" thought Penny. "It's not going to be as easy as I assumed."

Joe ran out on the pier, while Ma and the other man separated, one starting upstream and the other down. No matter which way she turned, Penny saw that her escape would be cut off.

The river was wide, the current swift. Although an excellent swimmer, she had no desire to attempt such a contest of endurance. But there seemed no other way.

Deliberately pushing off from the pier, she swam directly away from shore, After a dozen strokes she rolled over on her back for a moment to see what was happening. Ma Harper had shouted to Joe, and the words carried plainly over the water.

"Take after her in the boat! We don't dare let her get away now! She knows too much!"

Penny had forgotten the motorboat tied up at the pier. Now as she saw Joe and Clark Clayton run toward it, her heart sank.

Though the race seemed hopeless, she flopped over onto her face again, and swam with all her strength. Going with the current, her feet churned the water behind her.

Several times, the men tried without success to start the motorboat engine. Penny grew hopeful. Then she heard the blast as the motor caught, and knew that in just a minute the men would overtake her.

Frantically, she glanced about for help. Already late afternoon, there were no fishing boats on the river. Save for Ma Harper, who stood ready to seize her should she try to swim in to the beach, no other persons were visible on either shore. The *River Queen* apparently was at the far end of her run, hidden beyond the bend.

CHAPTER 18 - OVER THE BALCONY

A hundred yards away, in shallow water, lay a large patch of tall river grass and cat-tails. Seeing it, Penny took new hope. The area was large enough to offer a temporary refuge if she could reach it! Not only would the dense mat of high grass protect her from view, but a boat would not be able to follow.

Starting to swim again, she put everything she had into each stroke. It would be pinch and go to reach the grass patch! Aware of her intention, Sweeper Joe and Clark Clayton had changed course, hoping to intercept her.

CHAPTER 19 - FLIGHT

The high water grass loomed up and Penny's feet struck a muddy bottom. With the boat almost upon her, she plunged into the morass. The water came to armpit level. Pushing aside the thick stalks which wrapped themselves about her arms and body, she waded far into the patch before she paused.

Hidden by the dense growth, she could not at first see the pursuing boat. She knew, however, that it had halted at the edge of the patch, for the motor had been cut off.

And after awhile she heard voices, low spoken, but nevertheless clear, for the slightest sound carried over water.

"She's over there somewhere in the center of the patch!" one of the men muttered. "I could tell where she went by the way the grass moved. Shall we let her go?"

"No, we got to get her or she'll tell everything she knows to old man Gandiss and the police!" the other answered.

With the motor shut off, the two men then took out paddles, and began to force the boat through the jungle of grass. Observing that they were coming straight toward her, Penny noiselessly waded on, taking every precaution not to move the stalks unnecessarily. Noting the direction of the wind, she went with it, hoping that any movement of the grass would appear to be caused by the stiff breeze.

But she hoped in vain. For suddenly Joe the Sweeper shouted hoarsely:

"There she is! Over there!" He pointed with his paddle blade.

The men pushed the boat on, smashing the grass ahead of them. In despair, Penny saw that wherever she went she was leaving a trail of trampled, broken grass behind her.

No longer trying to prevent splashes, she waded in a wide half-circle. Then quickly she back-tracked, this time making not a sound. Slipping into the dense growth just beside the trail she had made, she breathlessly waited.

The boat came into view. Taking a deep breath, Penny ducked under water. Opening her eyes, she could see the blurred, dark bottom of the craft moving slowly toward her, so close she could have reached out and touched it.

Her breath began to grow short. The boat barely seemed to move. Penny's lungs felt as if they were ready to burst, but still she remained under water.

Then the men had passed, and she dared raise her head for an instant to gulp in air. The boat reached the end of the trail through the grass that Penny herself had made. There it halted, as Sweeper Joe and his companion, realizing they had lost their quarry, debated their next move.

"She was here a minute ago!" Sweeper Joe growled. "I caught a glimpse of her clothes, and saw the grass move. Where did she go?"

"She must have doubled back."

With difficulty the men turned the boat around and rowed toward Penny again. When she dared wait no longer, she submerged again.

They passed her and she came up for air. A water snake slithered through the grass, almost touching her hand.

Startled, Penny leaped backwards, making an ugly, loud splash in the water. Slight as was the sound, it told the men where she hid. Turning in the boat, they saw her through the grass, and bore toward her again.

By this time, Penny actually enjoyed the desperate game of hide and seek, for so far, the advantage had been hers. She stood watching the boat until it came very close.

CHAPTER 19 - FLIGHT

Then she dived, coming up directly underneath the craft. Getting her shoulder squarely under one side, she raised up, and with an ease that surprised her, upset the boat.

The two men went sprawling into the water. Unable to swim, they made animal noises and clutched desperately at the grass for support. But as their feet found solid footing, they started furiously toward Penny. Taking her time, and deliberately seeking deeper water, she waded away.

"That will hold them for a few minutes," she thought gleefully. "I'll get out of this jungle now, and swim ashore."

One more the girl's hopes were rudely dashed. As she reached the edge of the grass area, she was disconcerted to see another rowboat approaching from the direction of the Harper place. With shadows deepening on the water, she could not at first distinguish the man. Then she recognized Claude Harper.

"He must have come home, and Ma sent him here to help capture me!" she thought. "If I swim out now, I'll certainly be caught."

Crouching down so that her nose was just above the water, she waited. Claude Harper rowed on, resting upon his oars when perhaps ten yards away.

"Joe!" he called.

There was an answering shout from the center of the grass patch.

"That gal's somewhere close by!" Sweeper Joe shouted in warning. "She upset our boat. Stay where you are, and see that she doesn't slip past you!"

Thus warned, Claude Harper began to survey the grass patch intently. He looked hard at the place where Penny stood. She was certain he had seen her, but after a moment, he turned slightly, and his eyes roved on.

As she hesitated, not knowing what to do, Sweeper Joe and Clark Clayton, who had bailed out their boat, came paddling out to meet Harper. Wet and plastered with mud, they had lost one of the paddles.

"If you ain't sights!" Harper cackled upon seeing them. He slapped his thigh in glee. "You look like a couple o' stupid mud turtles!"

"Fool!" rasped Sweeper Joe. "Don't you have sense enough to figure what will happen if that girl gets away from us?"

"You ain't goin' back to no job at the Gandiss factory. Nor Clayton neither!"

"It's a lot more serious than that!" Joe snapped. He guided the boat alongside Harper's craft. "Why do you think I took that job in the first place, and spent better than two years studyin' the Gandiss factory layout? I lined up the employes we could get to go along with us, got everything organized—and now this gal has to bust up the show just as the profits begin to roll in!"

"Better pipe down," Harper warned curtly. "She can hear you, and so can everyone else on the river."

"What's the difference?" Joe argued in disgust. "We're through. I'm gettin' out of this town tonight!"

"Me with you," added Clark Clayton. "Ever since Gandiss put detectives on the job, I figured the game was gettin' too dangerous."

Now it was Claude Harper who lost his temper. "Hold on," he said warningly. "It's all right for you guys to blow town, but what about me and the wife?"

"You can do what you please," Joe retorted.

"We got your brass cached in our basement. If the cops should find it there, we'd take the rap."

"Get rid of it."

"That's a lot easier said than done. Besides, that brass is worth a tidy sum o' money."

"Then why not sell it tonight?" Joe proposed suddenly. "If we can get it to the junkman who has a place across from the factory, he'll pay us a good price. We can complete the deal, and still get out of town before midnight."

"That's okay for you," Harper argued, "but Ma and I own property here, and we got a good business."

"It was your stupid wife's stocking business that got us into this jam!" Clark Clayton snarled.

"I ain't talkin' about that. I mean our dance hall. We clean up about a hundred bucks every Saturday night."

"You should have thought about that before you went in with us," Joe retorted. "You knew the risks you were taking. Anyway, this mess was your wife's making."

A silence fell, and then Clark Clayton said: "We ain't gettin' nowhere. We got to decide what we're goin' to do, and we got to make sure that gal don't get out o' this weed patch until we've arranged our escape."

849

In whispers, the men conferred. Though Penny strained her ears, she could not catch a single word. However, a plan satisfactory to the three seemed to have been formulated, for presently, the two boats separated.

Sweeper Joe and Clark Clayton paddled off, heading for the pier at the Harpers'. The other man remained in his rowboat, unquestionably detailed to keep watch of the grass patch and prevent the girl's escape.

To amuse himself, he began to call out to her, though he could not see her or know where she was.

"You think you're a clever one!" he taunted. "But you jest wait! We'll get you out o' there, and when we do, you ain't goin' to like it!"

Lest a movement of the grass or a splash betray her, Penny remained perfectly still. Shadows deepened on the river for night was fast coming on. Her muscles became stiff and cramped. The wind chilled her to the very bone, and the water which at first had not seemed unbearably cold, made her teeth chatter and dance. Each minute became an hour as the torture increased.

"I'll have to do something," she thought desperately. "I can't endure this much longer."

CHAPTER 20 - A DESPERATE PLIGHT

In the rowboat, Claude Harper slowly patrolled the area, keeping an alert watch for the slightest movement amid the grass. Once as a crane arose from the dense growth into the darkening sky, he focused a flashlight beam on the spot.

"He's prepared to stay here half the night if necessary," Penny thought, shivering.

She could think of no means of escape. When it became completely dark, she might be able to swim away without being detected. But long exposure in cold water had weakened her, and she was none too certain of her ability to reach shore.

Her absence at the island surely must have been noticed by this time, she reasoned. Why was not a boat sent in search of her?

"I hope they don't assume I am staying with Sally for the night," she worried.

Penny's thoughts were momentarily distracted as she heard indistinct voices from the direction of the Harper dock. Lights had been turned on in the house and basement.

"Those men are getting rid of the stolen brass," she reasoned. "If they try to sell it to Heiney, they still may be caught."

Presently the motorboat moved away from the Harper dock, its engine laboring. The craft was sunk low in the water as if from a heavy load.

The boat did not turn down stream as Penny expected. Instead, it crossed the river at right angles, stopping in mid-stream at the deepest part of the channel. There the engine was cut off.

"Now what?" thought Penny.

Claude Harper likewise seemed puzzled by the action, for he turned to stare, muttering to himself.

Though Penny could not see what the men were doing aboard the boat, she heard a loud splash as something heavy was dropped overboard.

"The fools!" Claude Harper exclaimed. "The fools!"

Another splash and still another followed. Then the boat turned and came toward the grass patch. Claude Harper hailed the men with an angry exclamation.

"You idiots! After all the risk we've taken, you dump our profits in the river!"

"Keep your shirt on!" Sweeper Joe retorted. "It was the only thing to do. Glowershick just phoned from town."

"What'd he have to report?"

"Nothing good. You know that junk shop where we arranged to sell our stuff? Where the owner offered us a higher price than any other place in town?"

"Well?"

"He was a dick, planted there by old man Gandiss himself. They've already got wind of who's in on the deal."

"Then if we try to sell the brass anywhere else, we'll be pinched."

"You're catching on, Harper."

"Have you dumped all the stuff in the river?"

"It will take two more trips at least. And there's the brass lantern to get rid of," Joe added. "As soon as the job is done, Clark and me are gettin' out of the city."

"What are Ma and me gonna do?" Harper whined. "We've got property here."

"That's up to you," Joe snapped. "If it wasn't for the gal you'd be safe enough. Seen anything of her?"

"Nary a sign."

"She may have slipped away under water. The gal swims like an eel."

"I don't think she got away. I been watchin' like a hawk."

"She's sure to spill everything, and she's seen plenty," Joe muttered. "Even though the cops don't find any evidence, they could make it plenty tough for you and the missus."

"We got to leave town," Harper admitted. "After takin' all this risk and bein' all set to cash in big, it's a dirty break. It ain't fair."

"Squawkin' won't do no good," Joe said shortly. "The question is, what are we goin' to do about the gal?"

"We got to make sure she won't carry no tales until we're safely out of town."

"Then we'll have to flush her out of this bird nest," Joe decided. "There's a way we can do it."

The manner in which she was to be caught, soon became apparent to Penny. Systematically, the men began to flatten all of the grass with their paddles and oars. Foot by foot, she retreated. Their strategy was discouragingly clear. The flattened grass no longer offered protection. Soon it all would be level with the water, and she would have no screen.

So cold that her limbs were nearly paralyzed, Penny considered giving herself up. In any case, the outcome would be the same. The only other recourse was to scream for help, and hope that someone along the shore would hear her and investigate.

With only the Harper house close by, the prospect that anyone would come to her aid was practically nil.

Angered at not finding the girl, Harper and his companions swung their paddles viciously. Penny retreated further, still reluctant to abandon freedom.

Then far downstream, she saw the *River Queen*, recognizing it by the pattern its lights made above the water. The ferry had finished its passenger run, and now apparently was coming upstream to anchor for the night.

As Penny watched the boat, she took new hope. If only she could signal Captain Barker or Sally! Unless the ferry changed course, it was almost certain to pass the grass patch. However, with the water shallow there, it would give the area a wide berth.

"Even if I shouted for help, no one aboard would hear me," she reasoned. "But I'll have to try something! I'm finished if I stay here."

Straight up the river came the *Queen*. Penny could see a man in the lighted pilot house, but no one was visible on the decks. The ferry was traveling at a rapid speed.

Penny decided to wait no longer. Creeping to the very edge of the grass, she ducked under water, and started to swim. Her strength had gone even more than she realized. Arms and legs were so stiff they barely could press against the water as she stroked. A few feet and she was forced to come to the surface.

"There she is!" shouted Sweeper Joe. Bringing the boat around, he started directly for her.

Penny swam with all the power at her command, stroking deep and fast. Not daring to look back, she could hear the dip of Sweeper Joe's oars.

Straight toward the deepest part of the channel, she propelled herself. Her crawl strokes were jerky, but they carried her along. And she had calculated well. Aided by the current, she would intercept the path of the oncoming *River Queen*.

From the water, the ferryboat looked like an immense monster as it steamed majestically up the river. Not wishing to attract attention to himself or his companions, Joe shipped his oars and temporarily gave up the chase. But he remained close by, watching alertly. Should the ferryboat fail to see or pick up Penny, he would be after her upon the instant.

Treading water, the girl shouted for help and waved an arm. Her voice was weak even to her own ears, and could not possibly carry to the pilot house of the *Queen*. Would her frantic signals be seen? The night was dark, and she was not yet in the arc of the vessel's lights.

Penny swam a few more strokes, then treaded water again, and signaled frantically. The *River Queen* did not slacken speed.

"They haven't seen me!" she thought desperately. "It's useless."

Now a new danger presented itself. The *Queen* had swerved slightly so that Penny was directly in its path. Still she had not been seen. Looming up in gigantic proportions above her, the ferry threatened to run her down.

CHAPTER 21 - RESCUE

Fearful that she would be killed, Penny screamed and waved. Straight on steamed the *River Queen*, so close now that she could see Sally Barker on the starboard deck. But the girl was gazing away from her, toward Sweeper Joe and the other drifting boat.

"Help! Help!" screamed Penny in one last desperate attempt to save herself.

Her cry carried, for she saw Sally whirl around and stare intently at the dark water ahead. Then she shouted an order to her father. There came a clanging of bells, and the *Queen* swerved to port, missing Penny by a scant ten feet.

Great waves engulfed her, and she fought to keep above the surface. Her strength was practically gone. She rolled over on her back, gasping for breath.

Then she saw that the *Queen* had greatly reduced speed and was turning back on her course. A lifeboat also was being lowered.

"They're going to pick me up!" Penny thought, nearly overcome by relief.

The next minute Sally and a sailor were pulling her into the boat.

"Why, it's Penny! And she's half drowned!" she heard her friend exclaim.

Then she knew no more.

When she opened her eyes, Penny found herself in a warm, comfortable bed. Sally stood beside her with a cup of steaming hot soup.

"You're coming around fine," she praised. "Drink this! Then you'll feel better."

Penny pulled herself up on an elbow and took a swallow of the soup. It was good and warmed her chilled body. She gulped the cupful down.

"Sally—"

"Better not try to talk too much now," Sally advised kindly. "How did you get into the water?"

The question aroused Penny, bringing back a flood of memories. She suddenly realized that she was in Sally's cabin on the *River Queen* and the ferry was moving.

"Where are we?" she asked.

"You're safe," Sally said soothingly. "You were swimming in the river. We nearly ran you down. Lucky I saw you just in time and we picked you up."

"Yes, I know," Penny agreed. "But *where* are we? Near the Harpers?"

"Oh, no, we passed their place long ago. We're far upriver."

Penny struggled up, swinging her feet out of the bunk. She saw then that she was wearing a pair of Sally's pajamas, and that her own wet garments hung over a chair.

"We must turn back!" she cried. "Tell Captain Barker, please! Oh, it's vitally important, Sally!"

Sally was maddeningly deliberate.

"Now don't get excited, Penny," she advised. "Everything will be all right."

Penny resisted as Sally tried to push her back into bed. "You don't understand!" she protested. "Sweeper Joe, Claude Harper, and Clark Clayton are expecting to make their get-away tonight. They're the ones who have been stealing brass from the Gandiss factory. It's all cached in the basement of the Harper house—or was unless they've dumped it."

"Penny, are you straight in your head? You know what you're saying?"

"I certainly do! I went there this afternoon. When I learned too much, they tried to hold me prisoner. I escaped by the river—hid in the grass patch. But they followed me there, and were about to get me, when the *River Queen* steamed by."

"I did see two small boats there. Just before you shouted I wondered what they would be doing at this time of night."

"Sweeper Joe and Clark Clayton have been dumping the stolen brass! Unless police stop them before they dispose of it all, not a scrap of evidence will be left! All those men expect to leave town tonight!"

"Thank heavens, we have a ship-to-shore radio telephone!" Sally cried, thoroughly aroused. "I'll have Pop call the police right away!"

She bolted out the cabin door.

Every muscle and joint in Penny's body ached, but there was no time to think of her misery. Her own clothes could not be put on. Searching in Sally's wardrobe, she found a sweater and a skirt, and undergarments she needed. By the time her friend returned, she was dressed.

"Penny, you shouldn't have gotten up!" Sally protested quickly.

"I can't afford to miss the excitement," Penny grinned. "Hope you don't mind lending me some of your clothes."

"Of course not, and if you must stay up, you'll need a pair of shoes." Sally found a pair of sandals, which although too large, would serve. After Penny had put them on, she said: "Let's go to the pilot house, because I want you to tell Pop exactly what happened."

"Did you notify police?"

"Pop sent the message. It may take a little while, but police should be at the Harpers' almost anytime now."

"Those men saw me taken aboard this boat," Penny worried. "I'm afraid they'll get away before the police arrive."

The girls climbed to the pilot house where Captain Barker had just turned the wheel over to a helmsman. All members of the crew remained aboard, for with the *Queen* late on her run, there had been no opportunity as yet to put the men ashore.

"We may need all our hands tonight," Captain Barker predicted. "No telling what may develop. I have one of those feelings."

"Now Pop!" reproved Sally. "The last time you made a remark like that, we smashed a rudder. Remember?"

"Aye, I remember all too well," he rejoined grimly.

Urged by Sally, Penny related everything that had happened at the Harpers', and told of her endurance contest in the grass patch.

"We'll head back that direction and see what's doing," Captain Barker offered to satisfy her. "Maybe we'll catch sight of those rascals in their boats."

Although the *Queen* cruised slowly near the shoal area where Penny had encountered adventure, there was no sign of any small boat. The ferry crept dangerously close to the grass patch.

"Watch 'er like a cat!" Captain Barker warned the helmsman. "Cramp her! Cramp her!"

When the man did not react speedily enough, he seized the wheel and helped spin it hard down. The *Queen* responded readily, moving into deeper waters.

Satisfied that there were no small boats in the vicinity, Captain Barker, headed upstream toward the Harpers'. Across the water, lights were to be seen on both floors of the two-story river house, but so far as could be discerned, no boats were tied up at the pier or docks.

"The place isn't deserted, that's certain," Penny declared, peering into the wall of darkness. "How long should it take the police to get there?"

"If the radio message we sent was properly transmitted, they should be on their way now," the captain replied.

Sally, impatient for action, was all for taking a crew and descending upon the house and its occupants. Puffing thoughtfully at his pipe, her father considered the proposal, but shook his head.

"We have no authority to make a search," he pointed out. "Any such action would make us liable for court action. Just be patient and you'll see fireworks."

Knowing that to stand by near the Harpers' pier would warn the house occupants they were being watched, Captain Barker ordered the *Queen* to turn downriver toward the main freight and passenger docks.

CHAPTER 21 - RESCUE

An excursion boat, the *Florence*, passed them, her railings lined with women and children who had enjoyed an all-day outing and were returning home. The steamer tied up at the Ninth Street dock and began to disgorge passengers.

Then it happened. Penny saw a sudden flash of flame which seemed to come from the hold of the excursion ship. The next instant fire shot from the portholes and began to spread.

Captain Barker gave a hoarse shout which sent a chill down her spine.

"The *Florence*!" he exclaimed huskily. "Her oil tanks must have exploded! She'll go up like matchwood, and with all those women and children aboard!"

CHAPTER 22 - CAPTAIN BARKER'S COURAGE

Never did a fire seem to spread so rapidly. In less than three minutes, as those aboard the *River Queen* watched in helpless horror, the *Florence* became a mass of flames from stem to stern. Terrified passengers jammed the gangplank as they tried to crowd ashore. Some of them leaped from the excursion boat's high railings to the dock below.

"Her mooring lines are ablaze!" Captain Barker shouted a moment later.

"And the freight sheds are catching afire," Penny added, observing a telltale line of flame starting from the flimsy wooden buildings along the wharf, directly back of the dock where the *Florence* had moored.

The blazing sheds worried Captain Barker far less than the fact that the mooring lines had caught fire. If the *Florence* should be cut loose from the dock, helpless women and children would be carried out onto the river in a flaming inferno.

"Why don't the fire boats get here!" Sally murmured nervously. "Oh, this is going to be a dreadful disaster if something isn't done to save those helpless people!"

At the bridge leading to the pilot house, Captain Barker stood tensely watching, his hand on the signal ropes.

"There go the mooring lines!" he shouted. "The current should bring her this way!"

As the *Florence* slowly drifted away from the blazing wharf, men and women began to leap over the railings into the dark waters.

"Man the lifeboats!" Captain Barker ordered his crew tersely. "I'm going to try to get a tow line on 'er!" He signaled the engine room, and the *River Queen* began to back rapidly toward the flaming excursion boat.

Penny and Sally ran to help launch the lifeboats. With the *River Queen* desperately short handed, they would be needed to handle oars. A fireman, an engineer, Captain Barker and a helmsman must remain at their posts, which left only three sailors to pick up passengers.

Leaping into the first boat launched, the girls rowed into the path of the blazing vessel. In its bright glow against the sky, they could see panic-stricken passengers running about the decks. An increasing number were leaping into the water, and many could not swim.

Ignoring the cries of those who had life belts or were swimming strongly, they rapidly picked up survivors. To pull children aboard was a comparatively easy task. But many of the women were heavy, and the combined strength of the girls barely was sufficient to get them into the boat without upsetting.

Finally the lifeboat was filled beyond capacity, and they turned to land their cargo aboard the *Queen*. Only then did they see what Captain Barker intended to do.

His men had succeeded in making a line fast to the *Florence's* stern. By this time the excursion boat was a flaming inferno, with only a few passengers, the captain, and crew remaining aboard.

"Pop's going to tow the *Florence* downstream away from the freight sheds!" Sally cried. "Some of those buildings are filled with war materials awaiting shipment—coal, oil and I don't know what all! If a fire once gets going there, nothing will stop it!"

Working feverishly, the girls unloaded their passengers and went back for more. Motorboats had set out from shore, and they too aided in the rescue work. Some of the survivors were taken to land, and others were put aboard the *Queen*.

Aided by a sailor they had picked up, the girls worked until they no longer could see bobbing heads in the swirling waters.

"We've done all we can," Sally gasped, as they helped the last of the passengers aboard the *Queen*. "The captain and most of his men will stay on the *Florence* as long as they are able."

CHAPTER 22 - CAPTAIN BARKER'S COURAGE

Though exhausted by their work, the girls did what they could for those aboard. Sally distributed all the blankets she could find, and Penny helped a sailor revive two women who were unconscious from having swallowed too much water.

Suddenly there came a loud report like the crack of a pistol.

The tow line to the *Florence* had parted! Once more the excursion boat, now a roaring furnace, was adrift in mid-stream.

In an instant it was apparent to Penny what would happen. The cross-current was strong, and in a minute or two would carry the burning vessel into the wharves and sheds. When the boat struck, flying sparks would ignite the dry wood for a considerable distance, and soon the entire waterfront would be ablaze.

Though outwardly calm, Captain Barker was beset as he appraised the situation. It would not be possible to get another tow line onto the *Florence* for already her decks had become untenable for the crew. The blazing vessel was drifting rapidly.

"We could ram her," he muttered. "She might be nosed out into the channel again, and headed away from the freight docks."

"Wouldn't that be dangerous?" Sally asked anxiously. "We have at least fifty passengers aboard. In this high wind, the *Queen* would be almost certain to catch fire."

"There's nothing else to do," Captain Barker decided grimly, signaling the engine room. "The *Florence* is drifting fast, and before the fire boats can get here, half the waterfront will be ablaze. Have the passengers wet down the decks and stand by with buckets!"

Penny and Sally worked feverishly carrying out orders. The deck hose was attached, and buckets were brought from below and filled with water. All survivors who were able to help, cooperated to the fullest extent, helping wet down the decks and assisting women and children to the stern of the ferryboat.

Captain Barker had given an order for the *Queen* to move full speed ahead.

In a moment the two boats made jarring contact. Penny was thrown from her feet. Scrambling up, she saw that blazing timbers from the *Florence* had crashed directly onto the *River Queen's* deck. Sparks were falling everywhere. The ferryboat had caught fire in a dozen places.

Seizing a bucket of water, she doused out the flames nearest her. Heat from the *Florence* was intense, and many of the men who had volunteered to help, began to retreat.

Penny and Sally stuck at their post, knowing that the lives of all depended upon extinguishing the flames quickly. Crew members of the *Florence* worked beside them with quiet, determined efficiency.

In the midst of the excitement, the final boatload of picked-up survivors had to be taken aboard. Captain Jamison, one of the last to leave the *Florence*, collapsed as he reached the deck. Severely burned, he was carried below to receive first-aid treatment.

Undaunted, Captain Barker shouted terse orders, goading the men to greater activity when the flames showed signs of getting beyond control. After the first contact with the Florence, only occasional sparks ignited the *Queen's* decks, but the heat was terrific. Women and children became hysterical, fearful that the ferryboat would become a flaming torch.

"The worst is over now," Sally sighed as she and Penny refilled water buckets. "Pop knows what he's doing. He's saved the waterfront."

"But this ferryboat?"

"It still may go up in smoke, but I don't think so," Sally replied calmly. "Pop is heading so that the wind will carry the flames away from us. He'll beach the *Florence* on Horseshoe Shoal and let the wreck burn to the water's edge."

For the next fifteen minutes, there was no lessening of worry aboard the *River Queen*. The ferryboat clung grimly to the blazing excursion boat, losing contact at times, then picking her up again, and pushing on toward the shoal.

Fire fighting activities aboard the ferryboat became better organized; the passengers, observing that Captain Barker knew what he was about, became calm and easily managed. By the time fire boats arrived to spray the *Florence* with streams of pressured water, the situation was well in hand.

Collapsing on the deck from sheer exhaustion, Penny and Sally gazed toward the warehouses and docks on the opposite shore. Only one fire of any size was visible there.

"The fire boats will quickly put it out," Sally said confidently. "But I hate to think what would have happened if the wind and current had driven the *Florence* along those wharves."

Penny wiped her cheek and saw that her hand was covered with black soot. Sally too was a sight. She had ripped the hem from her skirt, her hair was an untidy mess, everything about her was pungent with smoke.

"Where were we when all this excitement started?" Penny asked presently. "If my memory serves me correctly, we had sent out a police call for Claude Harper and his pals to be arrested. It all seems vague in my mind, as if it occurred a million years ago."

"Why, I had forgotten too!" Sally gasped. "I hope the police went there and caught those men before they made a get-away."

Scrambling to their feet, the girls moved to the starboard side of the *Queen*, which permitted a view of the Harper house far upriver. They were startled and dismayed to see tongues of flame shooting from a window.

"That place has caught on fire too!" Sally exclaimed, then corrected herself. "But sparks from the *Florence* never could have been carried so far!"

"The house has been set afire on purpose!" Penny cried. "Oh, Sally, don't you see? It's a trick to destroy all the evidence hidden there! The Harpers intend to skip town tonight, and they're taking advantage of this fire to make it appear that destruction of the house is accidental!"

CHAPTER 23 - FIRE!

Sick at heart, the two girls realized with the Harper house aflame, their last chance of proving the guilt of the brass thieves might be gone. As they stood at the railing of the *Queen*, gloomily watching the spreading, creeping line of fire, a motorboat chugged up.

"Ahoy!" shouted a familiar voice. "Can you take aboard three more survivors? They're the very last we can find on the river."

"It's Jack!" Penny cried, recognizing his voice though unable to see his face in the dark. "After we get the passengers aboard, perhaps he'll take us upriver to the Harpers!"

The girls ran to help with the new arrivals, but sailors already had lifted them from the boat and carried them aboard the *Queen*.

"This is my last load," Jack called out. "Nearly everyone was saved. Coast Guard boats are patrolling now, and if there are other survivors, they'll be taken ashore."

"Jack!" Penny called down to him.

"That you, Penny?" he demanded in astonishment. "Why didn't you come back to Shadow Island this afternoon? We've all been worried about you!"

"It's a long story, and there's no time to tell it now! Jack, will you take us to the Harpers' in your motorboat?"

"Now?"

"Yes, the house is on fire."

Helping the girls into the boat, Jack turned to gaze upstream. "That's strange!" he exclaimed. "How could sparks from the *Florence* have carried so far?"

"The answer is, they didn't," Penny said grimly. "The house was set afire on purpose. Just get us to the pier as quickly as you can."

Somewhere along the shore a big city clock struck the hour of midnight. The young people did not notice. As the boat raced over the water, bouncing as it struck each high wave, they discussed what had happened just prior to the outbreak of fire aboard the *Florence*.

"I know part of the stolen brass was dumped into the river by Sweeper Joe," Penny revealed excitedly. "The remainder was locked in the basement of the Harper house the last I knew. And I'm satisfied the brass lantern taken from the *Queen* by Adam Glowershick is among the loot. All the thieves expect to skip town tonight. Probably they're gone by this time."

Beaching the boat some distance from the burning house, the three young people ran up the slope. Firemen had not yet reached the scene, and the few persons who had gathered, were watching the flames but making no effort to battle them.

"It's a hopeless proposition," Jack commented. "This far from the city, there's no water pressure. The house will burn to the ground."

"And all the evidence with it," Penny added gloomily. "What miserable luck!"

No boats were tied up at the dock, nor was there any sign of the Harpers or their friends in the crowd. Obviously, the entire party had fled.

"Isn't there some place where we can telephone the police?" Penny suggested impatiently. "If they act quickly, these men still may be caught. They can't be very far away."

"The nearest house is up the beach about an eighth of a mile," Jack informed. "Maybe we can telephone from there."

"You two go," Sally said casually. "I want to stay here."

At the moment, Jack and Penny, intent only upon their mission, thought nothing about the remark. Following the paved road which made walking easy, they hastened as fast as they could.

"Jack," Penny said, puffing to keep pace with him. "There's something I want to ask you."

"Shoot!"

"Why have you felt so friendly toward that crook, Glowershick?"

Jack's eyebrows jerked upward and he gave a snort of disgust. "Whatever gave you that crazy idea?"

"Well, he came to the island, and you borrowed money from me to give him—"

"So you recognized him that day?"

"Yes," Penny answered quietly. "You tried to hide his identity, so I said nothing more. I kept thinking you would explain."

"I'm prepared to pay you what I owe, Penny."

"Oh, Jack, it's not the money. Don't you understand—"

"You think I've had a finger in lifting the brass lantern from the *Queen*," Jack said stiffly.

"Gracious, no! But shouldn't you explain?"

Jack was silent for a moment. Then he said, "Thanks, Penny, for having a little faith in me. I know I've been an awful sap."

"Suppose you tell me all about it."

"There's nothing to tell. I went to the Harpers a number of times—attended their dances, and spent a lot of money. I got into debt to that fellow Glowershick and he pressed me for it."

"There was nothing more to it?"

"Not a thing, except that I didn't want my folks to hear about it. That's why I pretended I didn't know Glowershick. I was afraid you would tell them. Don't you believe me?"

"Oh, I do, Jack. I'm so relieved. And the jitterbug girl at Harpers'—"

"Oh, *her*!" Jack said scornfully. "She was a stupid thing, and I don't see how I stood her silly chatter. Most of the money I borrowed from Glowershick was spent on her. As I've said, I was a complete chump."

Reaching a house some distance back from the river, they found the owner at home, and were given permission to telephone the police. Jack was promised by an inspector that all police cruisers would be ordered to watch for the escaped brass thieves. Railroad terminals, bus depots and all roads leading from the city would be guarded.

"Watch the riverfront too," Jack urged. "The men may have gone by boat to Tate's Beach, intending to catch a train from there."

Satisfied they had done everything possible, Penny and Jack hastened back to the Harpers'. The sky was tinted pink and flames now shot from the roof of the house. A large crowd had gathered, and there was excited talk and gesturing.

"Something's wrong!" Penny observed anxiously.

Pushing through the crowd, they sought vainly to find Sally.

A woman was talking excitedly, pointed toward the flaming building.

"I tell you, I saw a girl run in there only a few minutes ago!" she insisted. "And she didn't come out! She must be in there now!"

The words shocked Penny and Jack as the same thought came to them. Could it be that reckless Sally had ventured into the basement of the house, hoping to recover the brass lantern or other evidence which would incriminate the thieves?

"She acted funny when we left her here," Penny whispered in horror. "Oh, Jack! If she's inside the building—"

Pushing through the crowd, she grasped the arm of the woman who was talking. "Who was the girl? What was she wearing?" she demanded tensely.

"A blue sweater," the woman recalled. "Her hair was flying wild and her face was streaked with dirt as if she'd already been in the fire. I thought maybe she lived here."

"It was Sally," Penny murmured, her heart sinking to her shoe tops. "Why hasn't someone brought her out?"

"No human being could get into that house now," declared a man who stood close by. "The firemen aren't here yet. Anyway, we ain't sure there's anyone inside."

CHAPTER 23 - FIRE!

"I saw the girl run in, I tell you!" the woman insisted.

To debate over such a vital matter infuriated Penny and Jack. Sally was nowhere in the crowd and they were convinced she had entered the blazing building. Flames were blowing from some of the lower windows and smoke was dense. It was obvious that no man present was willing to risk his life to ascertain if the girl were inside.

"She must have tried to reach the basement!" Penny cried. "Oh, Jack, we've got to bring her out!"

Nodding grimly, Jack stripped off his coat. Throwing it over his head as a shield, he darted into the burning building. Penny, close at his heels, had no protection.

Inside the house, smoke was so black they could not see three feet ahead. Choking, gasping for breath, they groped their way through the living room to the kitchen. Penny jerked open the door leading into the cellar.

Flames roared into her face. The entire basement was an inferno of heat. No human being could descend the stairs and return. If Sally were below, she was beyond help.

Closing the door, Penny staggered backwards. Her head was spinning and she could not get her breath.

"It's no use!" Jack shouted in her ear. "We've got to get out of here! The walls or floor may collapse."

Clutching Penny's arm, he pulled her along. In the black smoke swirling about them, they missed the kitchen door.

Frantically, they crept along a scorching hot wall, seeking to find an exit.

Then Penny stumbled over an object on the floor and fell. As she tried to get up, her hand touched something soft and yielding. A body lay sprawled in a heap beside her on the floor.

"It's Sally!" she cried. "Oh, Jack, help me get her up!"

CHAPTER 24 - DREDGING THE RIVER

Sally moaned softly but did not stir as Penny tried to pull her to a sitting position. The heat now was almost unbearably intense, with flying brands dropping everywhere. But near the floor, the air was better, and Penny drew it in by deep gulps.

Jack's groping hand encountered the sink. Soaking his coat with water from one of the taps, he gave it to Penny to protect her head and shoulders.

"Help me get Sally onto my back in a Fireman's carry," he gasped. "We can make it."

The confidence in Jack's voice gave Penny new courage and strength. As he knelt down on the floor, she dragged Sally onto his back. Holding the inert body high on his shoulders, he staggered across the kitchen.

Penny guided him to the door. Flames had eaten into the living room, and a small portion of the floor had fallen through. To reach the exit was impossible.

"A window!" Jack directed.

Penny could see none, so dense was the smoke, but she remembered how the room had been laid out, and pulled Jack to an outer wall. Her exploring hand encountered a window sill, but she could not get the sash up.

In desperation, she kicked out the glass. A rush of cool, sweet air struck her face. Filling her lungs, she turned to help Jack with his burden. Before she could grasp him, he sagged slowly to the floor.

Thrusting her head through the broken window, Penny shouted for help.

Willing hands lifted her to safety, and two men climbed through the window to bring out Jack and Sally. Both were carried some distance from the blazing building to an automobile where they were revived.

However, Sally was in need of medical attention. Hair and eyebrows had been singed half away, and more serious, her hands and arms were severely burned. Jack and Penny rode with her to the hospital when the ambulance finally came.

Not until hours later, after Captain Barker had been summoned, did Sally know anyone. Heavily bandaged, with her father, Jack, and Penny at her bedside, she opened her eyes and gave them a half-hearted grin.

"The *Florence*?" she whispered.

"Safely beached on a shoal," Captain Barker assured her tenderly. "There's nothing to worry about. All the passengers have been taken to hospitals or to their homes. A preliminary check has shown only one man lost, an engineer who was trapped at his post when the explosion occurred aboard the *Florence*."

"Pop, you were marvelous," Sally whispered. "You saved the waterfront."

"And nearly lost a daughter. Sally, why did you try to get into that burning building?"

Sally drew a deep, tired sigh.

"Never mind," said Penny kindly. "We know why you went in—it was to find the brass lantern."

Sally nodded. "When I got to the basement, flames were shooting up everywhere," she recalled with a shudder. "I realized then that I couldn't possibly find the lantern or anything else. I tried to get back, but smoke was everywhere. That was the last I remembered."

"It was Jack who saved you," Penny said, but he cut in to insist that the credit belonged to her rather than to him.

In the midst of a good-natured argument over the subject, a nurse came to say that Penny and Jack both were wanted on the telephone.

"The police department calling," she explained.

CHAPTER 24 - DREDGING THE RIVER

They were down the hall in a flash to take the call. Captain Brown of the city police force informed them they were wanted immediately at police headquarters to identify Sweeper Joe, the Harpers, and Clark Clayton who had been arrested at the railroad station. Adam Glowershick also had been taken into custody.

At headquarters fifteen minutes later, the young people found Mr. Gandiss, Penny's father, and Heiney Growski already there. Questioned by police, the young people revealed everything they knew about the case.

"We can hold these men for a while," Chief Bailey promised Mr. Gandiss, "but to make charges stick, we'll have to have more evidence."

Penny had told of the cache of brass in the Harper basement, and also of seeing Sweeper Joe and Clark Clayton dump much of the loot in the river. She was assured that the ruins of the house would be searched in the morning and that a dredge would be assigned to try to locate the brass which had been thrown overboard into the deepest part of the channel.

Heiney Growski produced records he had kept, showing a list of Gandiss factory employes known to be implicated in the plot.

"Most of the persons involved are new employes who smuggled small pieces of brass out of the factory and turned them over to Sweeper Joe for pin money," he revealed. "The leaders are Joe, Clayton, and Glowershick. With them behind bars, the ring will dissolve."

"There's one thing I want to know," Penny declared feelingly. "Who planted the brass in Sally's locker while she was working at the factory?"

No one could answer the question at the moment, but the following day, after police had repeatedly questioned the prisoners, the entire story became known. Sweeper Joe, the real instigator of the plot, had slipped into the locker room himself, and had placed the incriminating piece of evidence in Sally's locker, using a master key. He had disliked her because several times she had resented his attempts to become friendly.

Although police had obtained signed confessions, tangible evidence also was needed, for as Chief Bailey pointed out to Mr. Gandiss, the men might repudiate their statements when they appeared in court. Accordingly, police squads were sent to the Harpers' to search the ashes for evidence, and also to the river to supervise dredging operations.

Throughout the day, between trips to the hospital to see Sally, Jack and Penny watched the dredge boat make its trips back and forth over the area where the loot had been dropped.

"I hope I wasn't mistaken in the location," Penny remarked anxiously as the vessel made repeated excursions without success. "After all, the night was dark, and I had no way of taking accurate bearings."

Across the river and barely visible, the blackened, smoking skeleton of the *Florence* lay stranded on a sandbar. Throughout the night, a fireboat had steadily pumped water into the burning vessel, but even so, fires had not been entirely extinguished.

Morning papers had carried the encouraging information that there was only one known casualty as a result of the disaster. That many lives had not been lost was credited entirely to the courageous action of Captain Barker.

Becoming weary of watching the monotonous dredging operations, Jack and Penny joined a throng of curious bystanders at the Harper property. Police had taken complete charge and were raking the smoldering ruins.

"Find anything?" Jack asked a policeman he knew.

The man pointed to a small heap of charred metal which had been taken from the basement. There were many pieces of brass, but the missing lantern was not to be found in the pile.

However, from a member of the arson squad, they learned that enough evidence had been found to prove conclusively that the fire had been started with gasoline.

"Ma Harper spilled the whole story," one of the policemen related. "She and her husband were fairly straight until they became mixed up with Sweeper Joe, who has a police record of long standing. Ma had a black market business in silk stockings that didn't amount to much. So far as we've been able to learn, she and a taxi driver whom we've caught, were the only ones involved. Her husband and the other men considered the stocking racket small potatoes for them."

After talking with the policemen for awhile, the young people wandered down to the river's edge to see how dredging operations progressed.

"They're hauling something out of the water now!" Jack exclaimed. "By George! It looks like brass to me!"

Finding a boat tied up at the dock, they borrowed it and rowed rapidly out to the dredge. There they saw that some of the metal which Sweeper Joe had dumped, had indeed been recovered.

Prodding in the muddy pile in the bottom of the dredge net, Penny uttered a little scream of joy. "The brass lantern is here, Jack! What wonderful luck!"

Seizing the slime-covered object, she washed it in the river. "Let's take it straight to Sally at the hospital!" she urged.

Because the lantern would be important evidence in the case against Glowershick, police aboard the dredge were unwilling for it to be removed. However, the young people carried the news to Sally.

"Oh, I'm so glad the lantern has been recovered!" she cried happily. "Jack, you'll win it in the race Friday."

Jack and Penny exchanged a quick, stricken glance. Temporarily, they had forgotten the race and all it meant to Sally. With her hands bandaged from painful burns, she never would be able to compete.

"We'll postpone the race," Jack said gruffly. "It would be no competition if we held it without you."

"Nonsense," replied Sally. "It will be weeks before I can use my hands well, so it would be stupid to postpone the race that long. Fortunately, the doctor says I may leave the hospital tomorrow, and I'll not be scarred."

"If you can't race, I won't either," declared Jack stubbornly.

"Jack, you must!" Agitated, Sally raised herself on an elbow. "I'd feel dreadful if you didn't compete. The race has meant everything to you."

"Not any more. Winning doesn't seem important now. I'll not sail in the race unless the *Cat's Paw* is entered, and that's final!"

"Oh, Jack, you're such an old mule!" Sally tossed her head impatiently on the pillow. Then she grinned. "If my *Cat* is in the race, you'll sail?"

"Sure," he agreed, suspecting no trick.

Sally laughed gleefully. "Then it's settled! Penny will represent me in the race!"

"I'll do what?" demanded Penny.

"You'll skipper the boat in my stead!"

"But I lack experience."

"You'll win the trophy easily," chuckled Sally. "Why, the *Cat's Paw* is by far the fastest boat on the river."

"Says who?" demanded Jack, but without his old fire.

"But I couldn't race alone," said Penny, decidedly worried. "Sally, would you be able to ride along as adviser and captain bold?"

"I certainly would jump at the chance if the doctor would give permission. Oh, Penny, if only he would!"

"The race isn't until Friday," Jack said encouragingly. "You can make it, Sally."

The girl pulled herself to a sitting posture, staring at her bandaged hands.

"Yes, I can," she agreed with quiet finality. "Why, I feel better already. Even if I have to be carried to the dock in a wheel chair, I'll be in that race!"

CHAPTER 25 - THE RACE

A mid-afternoon sun beat down upon the wharves as a group of sailboats tacked slowly toward the starting line for the annual Hat Island trophy race. The shores were lined with spectators, and from the clubhouse where a band played, music carried over the water.

At the tiller of the *Cat's Paw*, Penny, in white blouse and slacks, hair bound tightly to keep it from blowing, sat nervous and tense. Sally, lounging on a cushion in the bow, seemed thoroughly relaxed. Though her arms remained in bandages, otherwise she had completely recovered from her unpleasant experience.

"Isn't the wind dying?" Penny asked anxiously. "Oh, Sally, I was hoping we'd have a good stiff breeze for the race! Handicapped as we are—"

"We're not handicapped," Sally corrected. "Of course, I can't handle the ropes or do much to help, but we have a wonderful boat that will prove more than a match for Jack's *Spindrift*."

"You're only saying that to give me confidence."

"No, I'm not," Sally denied, turning to study the group of racing boats. "We'll win the trophy! Just wait and see."

"If we do, it will be because of your brain and my brawn," Penny chuckled. "I'll admit I'm scared silly. I never was in an important race before."

Conversation ceased, for the boats now were bunching close to the starting line, maneuvering for position. Jack drifted by in the *Spindrift*, raising his hand in friendly greeting. As he passed, he actually glanced anxiously toward Sally, as if worried lest the girl overtax herself.

"I hope he doesn't try to throw the race just to be gallant," Penny thought. "But I don't believe he will, for then the victory would be a hollow one."

The change apparent in Jack so amazed Penny that she had to pinch herself to realize it was true. Since the night of the fire, he had visited Sally every day. In a brief span of hours, he had grown from a selfish, arrogant youth into a steady, dependable man. And it now was evident to everyone that he liked Sally in more than a friendly way.

"Better come about now, Penny," Sally broke in upon her thoughts. "Head for the starting line. The signal should be given any minute now."

The boats started in a close, tight group. Jack was over the line first, but with *Cat's Paw* directly behind.

In the first leg of the race, the two boats kept fairly even, with the others lagging. As the initial marker was rounded, there was a noticeable fall-off in the wind.

"It's going to be a drifting race," Sally confirmed, raising troubled eyes to the wrinkled sail. "We're barely drawing now and Jack's boat has the edge in a calm."

The *Spindrift* skimmed merrily along, now in the lead by many yards. Though Penny held the tiller delicately, taking advantage of every breath of wind, the distance between the two boats rapidly increased.

"We're out of it," she sighed. "We can't hope to overtake Jack now."

Sally nodded gloomily. Shading her eyes against the glare of the sun, she gazed across the river, studying the triangular course. Far off-shore, well beyond the line the *Spindrift* and their own boat was taking, the surface of the water appeared rippled. Ahead of them there was only a smooth surface.

"Penny," she said quietly. "I believe there's more breeze out there."

Penny nodded and headed the *Cat's Paw* on the longer course out into the river. To many spectators ashore it appeared that the girls deliberately had abandoned the race, but aboard the *River Queen*, Captain Barker grinned proudly at his guests, Mr. Parker, and Mr. and Mrs. Gandiss.

"Those gals are using their heads!" he praised. "Well, Mr. Gandiss, it looks as if the Barkers will keep the trophy another year!"

"The race isn't over yet," Mr. Gandiss rumbled goodnaturedly.

Aboard the *Cat's Paw*, Penny and Sally were none too jubilant. Although sails curved with wind and they were footing much faster than the other boats, the course they had chosen would force them to sail a much longer distance. Could they cross the finish line ahead of the *Spindrift*?

"Shouldn't we turn now?" Penny asked impatiently. "Jack's so much closer than we."

"Not yet," Sally said calmly. "We must make it in one long tack. He will be forced to make several. That's our only chance. If we misjudge the distance, we're sunk."

Tensely, they watched the moving line of boats close along shore. The *Spindrift* seemed almost at the finish line, though her sails barely were drawing and she moved through the water at a snail's pace.

Again Penny glanced anxiously at her companion.

"Now!" Sally gave the signal.

Instantly Penny swung the *Cat's Paw* onto the homeward tack. Every inch of her sails drawing, she swept toward the finish line.

"We're so much farther away than the *Spindrift*," Penny groaned, crouching low so that her body would not deflect the wind. "Oh, Sally, will we make it?"

"Can't tell yet. It will be nip and tuck. But if we can keep this breeze—"

The wind held, and the *Cat's Paw*, sailing to windward of the finish line, moved along faster and faster. On the other hand, the *Spindrift* was forced to make several short tacks, losing distance each time. The boats drew even.

Suddenly Sally relaxed, and slumped down on the cushions.

"Just hold the old girl steady on her course," she grinned. "That brass lantern is the same as ours!"

"Then we'll win?"

"We can't lose now unless some disaster should overtake us."

Even as Sally spoke, boat whistles began to toot. Sailing experts nodded their heads in a pleased way, for it was a race to their liking.

A minute later, sweeping in like a house afire, the *Cat's Paw* crossed the finish line well in advance of the *Spindrift*. Jack's boat placed second with other craft far behind.

Friendly hands assisted the girls ashore where they were spirited away to the clubhouse for rest and refreshments. As everyone crowded about to congratulate them upon victory, Jack joined the throng.

"It was a dandy race," he said with sincerity. "I tried hard to win, but you outsmarted me."

"Why, Jack!" teased Sally. "Imagine admitting a thing like that!"

"Now don't try to rub it in," he pleaded. "I know I've been an awful heel. You probably won't believe me, but I'm sorry about the way I acted—"

"For goodness sakes, don't apologize," Sally cut him short. "I enjoyed every one of those squabbles we had. I hope we have a lot more of them."

"We probably will," Jack warned, "because I expect to be underfoot quite a bit of the time."

Later in the afternoon, the brass lantern which had been turned over to the club by the police, was formally presented to Sally. She was warned however, that the trophy would have to be returned later for use in court as evidence against Adam Glowershick.

The nicest surprise of all was yet to come. Captain Barker was requested by a committee chairman to kindly step forward into full view of the spectators.

"Now what's this?" he rumbled, edging away.

But he could not escape. Speaking into a loudspeaker, the committee chairman informed the captain and delighted spectators, that in appreciation of what he had done to save the waterfront, a thousand dollar purse had been raised. Mr. Gandiss, whose factory certainly would have faced destruction had wharves caught fire, had contributed half the sum himself.

"Why, beaching the *Florence* was nothing," the captain protested, deeply embarrassed. "I can repair the damage done to the *Queen* with less than a hundred dollars."

"The money is yours, and you must keep it," he was told. "You must have a use for it."

CHAPTER 25 - THE RACE

"I have that," Captain Barker admitted, winking at his daughter. "There's a certain young lady of my acquaintance who has been hankerin' to go away to college."

"Oh, Pop." Sally's eyes danced. "How wonderful! I know where I want to go too!"

"So you've been studying the school catalogues?" her father teased.

Sally shook her head. Reaching for Penny's hand, she drew her close.

"I don't need a catalogue," she laughed. "I only know I'm scheduled for the same place Penny selects! She's been my good luck star, and I'll set my future course by her!"

SIGNAL IN THE DARK

PENNY UTTERED A LITTLE CRY

CHAPTER 1 - HELP WANTED

"The situation is getting worse instead of better, Penny. Three of our reporters are sick, and we're trying to run the paper with only a third of our normal editorial staff." Anthony Parker, publisher of the *Riverview Star*, whirled around in the swivel chair to face his daughter who sat opposite him in the private office of the newspaper. "Frankly, I'm up against it," he added gloomily.

Penny, a slim girl with deep, intelligent blue eyes, uncurled herself from the window ledge. Carefully, she dusted her brown wool skirt which had picked up a cobweb and streaks of dirt.

"You could use a janitor around here too," she hinted teasingly. "How about hiring me?"

"As queen of the dustmop brigade?"

"As a reporter," Penny corrected. "I'm serious, Dad. You're desperate for employes. I'm desperate for spending money. I have three weeks school vacation coming up, so why not strike a bargain?"

"The paper needs experienced workers, Penny."

"Precisely."

"You're a very good writer," Mr. Parker admitted. "In fact, in months past you turned in some of the best feature stories the *Star* ever printed. But always they were special assignments. We must have a reporter who can work a daily, eight-hour grind and be depended upon to handle routine stories with speed, accuracy and efficiency."

"And you think I am not what the doctor ordered?"

"I think," corrected Mr. Parker, "that you would blow your pretty little top by the end of the second day. For instance, it's not easy nor pleasant to write obituaries. Yet it must be done, and accurately. On this paper, a new reporter is expected to do rewrites and other tedious work. You wouldn't like it, Penny."

"I'd take it neatly in my stride, Dad. Why not try me and see?"

Mr. Parker shook his head and began to read the three-star edition of the paper, its ink still damp from the press.

"Give me one sound, logical reason for turning me down," Penny persisted.

"Very well. You are my daughter. Our editors might feel that they were compelled to treat you with special consideration—give you the best assignments—handle you with kid gloves."

"You could take care of that matter easily enough."

"If they took my instructions seriously, you might not like it," the newspaper owner warned. "A reporter learns hard and bitter lessons. Mr. DeWitt, for instance, is a fine editor—our best, but he has a temper and—"

The frosted glass door swung open and an elderly, slightly bald man in shirt sleeves slouched in. Seeing Penny, he would have retreated, had not Mr. Parker called him back.

"What's on your mind, DeWitt?"

"Trouble," growled the editor. "That no-good, addle-brained boy we hired as night police reporter, just blew up! Said it was too confining to sit in a police station all night waiting for something to happen! So he gets himself a job in a canning factory! Now we're another employee short."

"Dad, let me take over the night police job!" Penny pleaded.

Both her father and Mr. DeWitt smiled as if suffering from intense pain. "Penny," Mr. Parker explained gently. "Night police work isn't suitable for a girl. Furthermore, it is one of the most undesirable jobs on a paper."

"But I want to work somewhere, and you're so stubborn!"

SIGNAL IN THE DARK

Mr. DeWitt studied Penny with concentrated interest. Hope flickered in his eyes. Turning abruptly to Mr. Parker he asked: "Why not, Chief? We could use her on the desk for rewrite. We're mighty hard up, and that's a fact."

"What about the personnel problem?" Mr. Parker frowned. "How would the staff take it?"

"Some of the reporters might not like it," Mr. DeWitt admitted, "but who's running this paper anyhow?"

"I often wonder," sighed Mr. Parker.

Detecting signs of a weakening, Penny appealed to Mr. DeWitt. "Wouldn't I be a help to you if I were on the staff?" she urged.

"Why, sure," he agreed cautiously.

"There, you see, Dad! Mr. DeWitt wants me!"

"Penny, it's a personnel problem," her father explained with growing impatience. "The other reporters might not consider you a welcome addition to the staff. You would expect favors."

"I never would!"

"We need her," said Mr. DeWitt significantly. "We really do."

With two against him, Mr. Parker suddenly gave in.

"All right," he agreed. "Penny, we'll put you on as a cub reporter. That means you'll start as a beginner with a beginner's salary and do routine work until you've proved your merit. You'll expect no special consideration. Is that understood?"

"Perfectly!" Grinning from ear to ear, Penny would have agreed to anything.

"Furthermore, if the work gets you down, I won't have you coming to me asking for a change."

"I'll never darken your office door, Dad. Just one question. How much money does a beginner get?"

"Twenty-five dollars."

Penny's face was a blank.

"It will be more than you are worth the first few weeks," Mr. Parker said.

"I'll take it," Penny declared hastily. "When do I start?"

"Right now," decided her father. "DeWitt, introduce her to the staff, and put her to work."

Feeling highly elated but a trifle self-conscious, Penny followed Editor DeWitt past the photography studio and the A.P. wire room to the main newsroom where reporters were tapping at their typewriters.

"Gang," said Mr. DeWitt in an all inclusive introduction. "This is Penny Parker. She'll be working here for a few weeks."

Heads lifted and appraising eyes focused upon her. Nearly everyone nodded and smiled, but one girl who sat at the far end of a long typewriter table regarded her with an intent, almost hostile stare. And as luck would have it, Mr. DeWitt assigned Penny to the typewriter adjoining hers.

"This is Elda Hunt," he introduced her. "Show Penny the ropes, will you?"

The girl, a blonde, with heavily-rouged cheeks, patted the rigid rolls of her hair into place. Staring at Mr. DeWitt, she answered not a word.

"I'll have a lot to learn," Penny said, trying to make friendly conversation.

Elda shrugged. "You're the publisher's daughter, aren't you?" she inquired.

"Yes."

"Then I don't think you'll have too hard a time," the girl drawled.

Penny started to reply, but thought better of it. Seating herself beside Elda, she unhooded the typewriter, rolled a sheet of copy paper into it, and experimented with the keys.

The main newsroom was a confusion of sound. Although work was being handled with dispatch, there was an air of tension, for press time on the five-star edition was drawing close. Telephones were ringing, and Editor DeWitt, who sat at the head of the big rectangular desk, tersely assigned reporters to take the incoming calls. Not far from Penny's ear, the police shortwave radio blared. Copy boys ran to and fro.

Benny Jewell, the assistant editor, tossed her a handful of typewritten sheets.

"Take these handouts and make 'em into shorts," he instructed briefly.

"Handouts?" Penny asked in bewilderment. "Shorts?"

"Cut the stories to a paragraph or two each."

"Oh," said Penny, catching on. "You want me to rewrite them."

At her elbow, Elda openly snickered.

CHAPTER 1 - HELP WANTED

Color stained Penny's cheeks, but she quietly read the first sheet, which was an account of a meeting to be held the following week. Picking out the most important facts, she boiled the story down to two short paragraphs, and dropped the finished copy into the editor's wire basket.

Only then did Elda speak. "You're supposed to make two carbons of every story you write," she said pityingly.

The girl might have told her sooner, Penny thought. However, she thanked her politely, and finding carbon paper, rewrote the story. In her nervousness she inserted one of the carbons upside down, ruining the impression. As she removed the sheets from the machine, she saw what she had done. Elda saw too, and smiled in a superior way.

"She dislikes me intensely," Penny thought. "I wonder why? I've not done a thing to her."

Aware that she had wasted paper and valuable time, Penny recopied the story a third time and turned it in to the editor. After that, she rewrote the additional stories with fairly good speed. By watching other reporters she learned that the carbon copies were speared on spindles which at intervals a copy boy collected and carried away.

A telephone rang, and this time, Mr. DeWitt, looking straight at Penny, said: "An obituary. Will you take it?"

She went to the phone and copied down the facts carefully, knowing that while death notices were routine, they were of vital interest to readers of the paper. Any mistake of fact could prove serious.

Returning to her typewriter, she wrote the item. But after she had turned it in, Mr. DeWitt called her to his desk. He was pleasant but firm.

"What day are services to be held?" he asked. "Who are the survivors? Where did the woman die? Furthermore, we never use the word 'Funeral Home'. Instead, we say 'mortuary'."

Penny telephoned for more information, and finally after rewriting the notice twice more, succeeded in getting it past Mr. DeWitt. But as he tossed the story to a copy reader, she saw that he had pencilled several changes.

"There's more to writing routine stories than I thought," she reflected. "I'll really have to dig in unless I want to disgrace Dad."

Penny was given another obituary to write which proved nearly as difficult as the first. Hopelessly discouraged, she started for the rest room to get a drink and wash her hands.

As she entered the lounge, voices reached her ears, and instantly she realized that Elda Hunt was talking to another girl reporter about her.

"The publisher's daughter!" she heard her say scathingly. "As if we aren't having a hard enough time here, without having to coddle her along!"

"I didn't think she seemed so bad," the other replied. "She'll catch on."

"She'll be promoted over all our heads if that's what you mean!" Elda retorted bitterly. "I know for a fact, she's starting at fifty a week, and no experience! If you ask me, it's unfair! We should walk out of here, and see how those fine editors would like that!"

CHAPTER 2 - EXPLOSION!

Penny's first thought was to accost the two girls and correct the misstatements. But sober reflection convinced her she could make no graver mistake. Far better, she reasoned, to ignore the entire matter.

She quickly washed her hands, purposely making enough noise to draw attention to her presence. Elda and her friend became silent. A moment later, coming through the inner door of the powder room, they saw her, but offered no comment. Penny hastily returned to the newsroom.

For the remainder of the day she worked with deep concentration, only dimly aware of what went on about her. Seemingly there were endless numbers of obituaries to write. Telephones rang constantly. Work was never finished, for as soon as one edition was off the press, another was in the making.

Now and then Penny caught herself glancing toward an empty desk at the far corner of the room. Jerry Livingston had sat there until a year ago when he had been granted a leave of absence to join the Army Air Force. Unquestionably the *Star's* most talented reporter, he had been Penny's best friend.

"I wish Jerry were here," she thought wistfully. "But if he were, he'd tell me to buckle down and not let this job lick me! Dad warned me it would be hard, monotonous work."

Penny worked with renewed energy. After awhile she began to feel that she was making definite progress. Mr. Jewell, the assistant editor, made fewer corrections as he read over her copy, and now and then she actually saw him nod approvingly. Once when she turned in a rewritten "hand-out"—a publicity story which had been sent to the paper in unusable form—he praised her for giving it a fresh touch.

"Good lead," he commented. "You're coming along all right."

Elda heard the praise and her eyes snapped angrily. At her typewriter, she slammed the carriage. No one noticed except Penny. A moment later, Mr. DeWitt called Elda to his desk, saying severely:

"Watch the spelling of names, Elda. This is the third one we've checked you on today. Don't you ever consult the city directory?"

"Of course I do!" Elda was indignant.

"Well, watch it," Mr. DeWitt said again. "We must have accuracy."

With a swish of skirts, Elda went back to her desk. Her face was as dark as a thunder cloud. Deliberately she dawdled over her next piece of copy. After she had turned it in, she returned to the editor's desk to take it from the wire basket and make additional corrections.

"Just being extra careful of names," she said arrogantly as the assistant editor shot her a quick, inquiring glance.

Thinking no more of the incident, Penny kept on with her own work. She took special care with names, even looking up in the city directory those of which she was almost certain. When she turned in a piece of copy, she was satisfied that not a name or fact was inaccurate.

Late in the afternoon, she noticed that Mr. DeWitt and Mr. Jewell appeared displeased about a story they had found in the Five Star edition of the paper. After reading it, they talked together, and then sorted through a roll of discarded copy, evidently searching for the original. Finally, Mr. DeWitt called:

"Miss Parker!"

Wondering what she had done wrong, Penny went quickly to his desk.

"You wrote this story?" he asked, jabbing a pencil at one of the printed obituaries.

"Why, yes," Penny acknowledged. "Is anything wrong with it?"

"Only that you've buried the wrong man," DeWitt said sarcastically. "Where did you get that name?"

CHAPTER 2 - EXPLOSION!

Penny felt actually sick, and her skin prickled with heat. She stared at the story in print. It said that John Gorman had died that morning in Mercy Hospital.

"The man who died was John Borman," DeWitt said grimly. "It happens that John Gorman is one of the city's most prominent industrialists. We've made the correction, but it was too late to catch two-thirds of the papers."

Penny stared again at the name, her mind working slowly.

"But Mr. DeWitt," she protested. "I don't think I wrote it that way. I knew the correct name was Borman. I'm sure that was how I turned it in."

"Maybe you hit a wrong letter on the typewriter," the editor said less severely. "That's why one always should read over a story after it's written."

"But I did that too," Penny said, and then bit her lip, because she realized she was arguing about the matter.

"We'll look at the carbons," decided Mr. DeWitt.

They had been taken from the spindles by copy boys, but the editor ordered the entire day's work returned to his desk. Pawing through the sheets, he came to the one Penny had written. Swiftly he compared it with the original copy.

"You're right!" he exclaimed in amazement. "The carbons show you wrote the name John Borman, not Gorman."

"I knew I did!"

"But the copy that was turned into the basket said John Gorman. Didn't you change it on the first sheet?"

"Indeed I didn't, Mr. DeWitt."

Scowling, the editor compared the two copies. Obviously on the original sheet, a neat erasure had been made, and a typewritten letter *G* had been substituted for *B*.

"There's something funny about this," Mr. DeWitt said. "Mighty funny!" His gaze roved about the typewriter table, focusing for an instant upon Elda who had been listening intently to the conversation. "Never mind," he added to Penny. "We'll look into this."

Later, she saw him showing the copy sheets to the assistant editor. Seemingly, the two men were deeply puzzled as to how the error had been made. Penny had her own opinion.

"Elda did it," she thought resentfully. "I'll wager she removed the sheet from the wire basket when she pretended to be making a correction on her own story!"

Having no proof, Penny wisely kept her thoughts to herself. But she knew that in the future she must take double precautions to guard against other tricks to discredit her.

At the end of the day, the newsroom rapidly emptied. One by one, reporters covered their typewriters and left the building. A few of the girls remained, among them, Penny and Elda. Editor DeWitt was putting on his hat when the telephone rang.

Absently he reached for it and then straightened to alert attention. Grabbing a sheet of copy paper, he scrawled a few words. Eyes focused upon him, for instinctively everyone knew that something important had happened.

DeWitt hung up the receiver, his eyes staring into space for an instant. Then he seized the telephone again and called the composing room.

"Hold the paper!" he ordered tersely. "We're making over the front page!"

The news was electrifying, for only a story of the greatest importance would bring an order to stop the thundering presses once they had started to roll.

Calling the photography room, DeWitt demanded: "Is Salt Sommers still there? Tell him to grab his camera and get over to the Conway Steel Plant in double-quick time! There's been a big explosion! They think it's sabotage!"

The editor's harassed gaze then wandered over the little group of remaining reporters. Elda pushed toward the desk.

"You want me to go over there, Chief?" she demanded eagerly.

DeWitt did not appear to hear her. Seizing the telephone once more, he tried without success to get two of the men reporters who had left the office only a few minutes earlier.

Slamming down the receiver, his gloomy gaze focused upon Elda for an instant. But he passed her by.

"Miss Parker!"

Penny was beside him in a flash.

"Ride with Salt Sommers to the Conway Plant!" he ordered tersely. "Two men have been reported killed in the explosion! Get everything you can and hold on until relieved!"

Seizing hat and purse, Penny made a dash for the stairway. No need for DeWitt to tell her that this was a big story! Because all the other reporters except Elda were gone, she had been given the assignment! But could she make good?

"This is my chance!" she thought jubilantly. "DeWitt probably thinks I'll fold up, but I'll prove to him I can get the facts as well as one of his seasoned reporters."

Penny was well acquainted with Salt Sommers, who next to Jerry Livingston was her best friend. Reaching the ground floor, she saw his battered car starting away from the curb.

"Salt!" she shouted. "Wait!"

The photographer halted and swung open the car door. She slid in beside him.

"What are you doing here, Penny?" he demanded, shifting gears.

"I'm your little assistant," Penny broke the news gently. "I just started to work on the paper."

"And DeWitt assigned you to this story?"

"He couldn't help himself. Nearly everyone else had left the office."

The car whirled around a corner and raced through a traffic light just as it turned amber. Suddenly from far away, there came a dull explosion which rocked the pavement. Salt and Penny stared at each other with alert comprehension.

"That was at the Conway Plant!" the photographer exclaimed, pushing his foot hard on the gas pedal. "Penny, we've got a real assignment ahead of us!"

CHAPTER 3 - SPECIAL ASSIGNMENT

Darkness shrouded the streets as the press car careened toward the outskirts of the city where the Conway Steel Plant was situated. Rattling over the river bridge, Salt and Penny caught their first glimpse of the factory.

Flames were shooting high into the sky from one of the buildings, and employes poured in panic through the main gate. No policemen were yet in evidence, nor had the fire department arrived.

Pulling up at the curb, Salt seized his camera and stuffed a handful of flashbulbs into his pockets. Grabbing Penny's elbow, he steered her toward the gate. To get through the barrier, they fought their way past the out-surging, panic-stricken tide of fleeing employes.

"Scared?" Salt asked as they paused to stare at the shooting flames.

"A little," Penny admitted truthfully. "Will there be any more explosions?"

"That's the chance we're taking. DeWitt shouldn't have sent you on this assignment!"

"He couldn't know there would be other explosions," Penny replied. "Besides, someone had to cover the story, and no one else was there. I can handle it."

"I think you can too," said Salt quietly. "But you'll have to work alone. My job is to take pictures."

"I'll meet you at the car," Penny threw over her shoulder as she left him.

Scarcely knowing how or where to begin, she ran toward the burning building. One of the smaller storage structures of the factory, it was not connected with the main office. The larger building remained intact. Workmen with an inadequate hose were making a frantic effort to keep the flames from spreading to the other structures.

Penny ran up to one of the men, plucking at his sleeve to command attention.

"What set off the explosion?" she shouted in his ear.

"Don't know," he replied above the roar of the flames.

"Anyone killed?"

"Two workmen. They're over there." The man waved his hand vaguely toward another building.

Unable to gain more information, Penny ran toward the nearby structure. The wind, she noted, was carrying flames in the opposite direction. Unless there were further explosions, danger of the fire spreading was not great.

Entering the building, she met several men who appeared to be officials of the company.

"I'm looking for Mr. Conway!" she accosted them. "Is he here?"

"Who are you?" one of the men asked bluntly.

"I'm Penny Parker from the *Star*."

"My name is Conway. What do you want to know?"

"How many killed and injured?"

"Two killed. Three or four injured. Perhaps more. We don't know yet."

Penny asked for names which were given her. But when she inquired how the explosion had occurred, Mr. Conway suddenly became uncommunicative.

"I have no statement to make," he said curtly. "We don't know what caused the trouble."

As if fearing that Penny would ask questions he did not wish to answer, the factory owner eluded her and disappeared into the darkness.

Running back to the burning building, Penny caught a glimpse of Salt taking a picture. From another workman she sought to glean additional details of the disaster.

"I was in the foundry when the first blast went off!" he revealed. "Just a minute before the explosion, I seen a man in a light overcoat and a dark hat, run from the building."

"Who was he?"

"No one I ever saw workin' at this plant. But I'll warrant, he touched off that explosion!"

"Then you think he was a saboteur?"

"Sure."

Penny did not place too much stock in the story, but as she wandered about among the excited employes, she heard others saying that they too had seen the strange man running from the building. No one knew his name nor could they provide an accurate description.

Sirens screamed, proclaiming the arrival of fire engines. As the ladders went up, and streams of water began to play on the blazing structure, Salt snapped several more pictures. His hat was gone, and his face had become streaked with soot.

"I got some good shots!" he told Penny enthusiastically as he sought her at the fringe of the crowd. "What luck you having?"

Penny told him everything she had learned.

"We'll talk with the Fire Chief and then let's head for a telephone and call the office," Salt declared.

As they started toward the fire lines, a strange sound accosted their ears. Hearing it, Salt stopped short to listen. From the gates outside the factory came the rumbling murmur of an angry crowd.

"A mob must be forming!" Salt exclaimed. "Something's up!"

He started for the gate with Penny hard at his heels.

At first they could not see what had caused the commotion. But as the group of angry employes swept nearer the gate, a man in a light overcoat who apparently was fleeing for his life, leaped into a car which waited at the curb.

"Quick!" Penny cried. "Take a picture!"

Salt already had his camera into position. As the car started up, the flash bulb went off.

"Got it!" Salt exclaimed triumphantly.

Penny tried to note the license number of the automobile, but the plate was so covered with mud she could not read a single figure. The car whirled around a corner and was lost to view.

"Salt, that man may have been the one who set off the explosion!" Penny cried. "The mob is of that opinion at least!"

Angry employes now were bearing directly toward Penny and Salt. Suddenly a woman in the crowd pointed toward the photographer, shouting: "There he is! Get him!"

Dismayed, Penny saw then that Salt wore a light overcoat which bore a striking resemblance to the garment of the fleeing stranger. Their builds too were somewhat similar, for both were thin and angular. In the darkness, the mob had failed to see the car roll away, and had mistaken Salt for the saboteur.

"Let's get out of here!" Salt muttered. "One thing you can't do is argue with a mob!"

He and Penny started in the opposite direction, only to be faced by a smaller group of workmen who had swarmed from another factory gate. Escape was cut off.

"Tell them we're from the *Star*!" Penny urged, but as she beheld the angry faces, she realized how futile were her words.

"They'll wreck my equipment before I can explain anything!" Salt said swiftly. He thrust the camera into her hands. "Here, take this and try to keep it safe! And these plates!"

Empty-handed, Salt turned to face the mob. Not knowing what to do, Penny tried to cut across the street. But the crowd evidently had taken her for a companion of the saboteur, and was determined she should not escape.

"Don't let her get away!" shouted a woman in slacks, her voice shrill with excitement. "Get her!"

A car was coming slowly down the street. Its driver, a woman, was watching the flaming building, and had rolled down the window glass to see better. The window of the rear seat also was halfway down.

As the women of the mob bore down upon Penny, she acted impulsively to save Salt's camera and the precious plates. Without thinking of the ultimate consequence, she tossed them through the open rear window onto the back seat of the moving car.

CHAPTER 3 - SPECIAL ASSIGNMENT

The driver, her attention focused upon the blazing factory, apparently did not observe the act, for she continued slowly on down the street.

"D F 3005," Penny noted the license number. "If only I can remember!"

The factory women were upon the girl, seizing her roughly by the shoulders and shouting accusations. Penny's jacket was ripped as she jerked free.

"I'm a reporter for the *Star*!" she cried desperately. "Sent here to cover the story!"

The words made not the slightest impression upon the women. But before they could lay hands upon her again, she fled across the street. The women did not pursue her, for just then two police cars rolled up to the curb.

Penny, greatly relieved, ran to summon help.

"Quick!" she urged the policemen. "That crazy mob has mistaken a reporter for one of the saboteurs who escaped in a car!"

With drawn clubs, the policemen battled their way through the crowd. Already Salt had been roughly handled. But arrival of the police saved him from further mistreatment, and fearful of arrest, the mob began to scatter. In another moment the photographer was free, although a bit battered. His coat had been torn to shreds, one eye had been blackened, and blood trickled from a cut on his lower lip.

"Are you all right?" he asked anxiously as Penny rushed to him.

"Oh, yes! But you're a sight, Salt. They half killed you!"

"I'm okay," Salt insisted. "The important thing is we've got a whale of a story, and we saved the camera and pictures."

A stricken look came over Penny's face.

"Salt—" she stammered. "Your camera—"

"It was smashed?"

"No, I tossed it into a car, but the car went on down the street. How we'll ever find it again I don't know!"

CHAPTER 4 - THE MISSING PLATES

Salt did not criticise Penny when he learned exactly what had happened.

"I'd rather lose a dozen pictures than have my camera smashed," he declared to cheer her. "Anyway, we may be able to trace the car and get everything back. Remember the license number?"

"D F 3005," Penny said promptly, and wrote it down lest she forget.

"Let's call the license bureau and get the owner's name," the photographer proposed, steering her toward a corner drugstore. "Gosh, it's late!" he added, noticing a clock in a store window. "And they're holding the paper for our story and pictures!"

"I certainly messed everything up," Penny said dismally. "At the moment, it seemed the thing to do. When those women started for me, I thought it was the only way to save the camera."

"Don't worry about it," Salt comforted. "I'll get the camera back."

"But how will we catch the edition with your pictures?"

"That's a horse of a different color," Salt admitted ruefully. "Anyway, it's my funeral. I'll tell DeWitt something."

"I'll tell him myself," Penny said firmly. "I lost the pictures, and I expect to take responsibility for it."

"Let's not worry ahead. Maybe we can trace that car if we have luck."

Entering the drugstore, Penny immediately telephoned Editor DeWitt at the *Star*, reporting all the facts she had picked up.

"Okay, that's fine," he praised. "One of our men reporters, Art Bailey, is on his way out there now. He'll take over. Tell Salt Sommers to get in here fast with his pictures!"

"He'll call you in just a minute or two," Penny said weakly.

From another phone, Salt had been in touch with the license bureau. As Penny left the booth to join him, she saw by the look of his face that he had had no luck.

"Couldn't you get the name of the owner?" she asked.

"It's worse than that, Penny. The license was made out to a man by the name of A. B. Bettenridge. He lives at Silbus City."

"Silbus City! At the far end of the state!"

"That's the size of it."

"But how did the car happen to be in Riverview?"

"The man or his wife probably is visiting relatives here, or possibly just passing through the city."

"And there's no way to trace them," Penny said, aghast. "Oh, Salt, I've not only lost your pictures, but your camera as well!"

"Cheer up," Salt said brusquely. "It's not that bad. We're sunk on the pictures, that's sure. But unless the people are dishonest, I'll get the camera again. I'll write a letter to Silbus City, or if necessary, go there myself."

Penny had little to say as she rode back to the *Star* office with the photographer. Editor DeWitt was not in the newsroom when they returned, but they found him in the composing room, shouting at the printers who were "making up the paper" to include the explosion story.

Seeing Penny and Salt, he whirled around to face them. "Get any good pictures?" he demanded.

"We lost all of 'em," Salt confessed, his face long.

"You what?"

"Lost the pictures. The mob tore into us, and we were lucky to get back alive."

CHAPTER 4 - THE MISSING PLATES

DeWitt's stony gaze fastened briefly upon Salt's scratched face and torn clothing, "One of the biggest stories of the year, and you lose the pictures!" he commented.

"It was my fault," Penny broke in. "I tossed the camera and plates into a passing car. I was trying to save them, but it didn't work out that way."

DeWitt's eyebrows jerked upward and he listened without comment as Penny told the story. Then he said grimly: "That's fine! That's just dandy!" and stalked out of the composing room.

Penny gazed despairingly at Salt.

"If you hadn't told him it was your fault, he'd have taken it okay," Salt sighed. "Oh, well, it was the only thing to do. Anyway, there's one consolation. He can't fire you."

"I wish he would. Salt, I feel worse than a worm."

"Oh, buck up, Penny! Things like this happen. One has to learn to take the breaks."

"Nothing like this ever happened before—I'm sure of that," Penny said dismally. "What ought I to do, Salt?"

"Not a thing," he assured her. "Just show up for work tomorrow the same as ever and don't think any more about it. I'll get the camera back, and by tomorrow DeWitt will have forgotten everything."

"You're very optimistic," Penny returned. "Very optimistic indeed."

Not wishing to return through the newsroom, she slipped down the back stairs and took a bus home. The Parker house stood on a knoll high above the winding river and was situated in a lovely district of Riverview. Only a few blocks away lived Louise Sidell, who was Penny's closest friend.

Reluctant to face her father, Penny lingered for a while in the dark garden, snipping a few roses. But presently a kitchen window flew up, and Mrs. Maude Weems, the family housekeeper called impatiently:

"Penny Parker, is that you prowling around out there? We had our dinner three hours ago. Will you please come in and explain what kept you so long?"

Penny drew a deep sigh and went in out of the night. Mrs. Weems stared at her in dismay as she entered the kitchen.

"Why, what have you done to yourself!" she exclaimed.

"Nothing."

"You look dreadful! Your hair isn't combed—your face is dirty—and your clothes! Why, they smell of smoke!"

"Didn't Dad tell you I started to work for the *Star* today?" Penny inquired innocently.

"The very idea of you coming home three hours late, and looking as if you had gone through the rollers of my washing machine! I'll tell your father a thing or two!"

Mrs. Weems had cared for Penny since the death of Mrs. Parker many years before. Although employed as a housekeeper, salary was no consideration, and she loved the girl as her own child. Penny and Mr. Parker regarded Mrs. Weems almost as a member of the family.

"Where is Dad?" Penny asked uneasily.

"In the study."

"Let's not disturb him now, Mrs. Weems. I'll just have a bite to eat and slip off to bed."

"So you don't want to see your father?" the housekeeper demanded alertly. "Why, may I ask? Is there more to this little escapade than meets the eye?"

"Maybe," Penny admitted. Then she added earnestly: "Believe me, Mrs. Weems, I've had a wretched day. Tomorrow I'll tell you everything. Tonight I just want to get a hot bath and go to bed."

Mrs. Weems instantly became solicitous. "You poor thing," she murmured sympathetically. "I'll get you some hot food right away."

Without asking another question, the housekeeper scurried about the kitchen, preparing supper. When it was set before her, Penny discovered she was not as hungry as she had thought. But because Mrs. Weems was watching her anxiously, she ate as much as she could.

After she had finished, she started upstairs. In passing her father's study, she saw his eyes upon her. Before she could move on up the steps, he came to the doorway, noting her disheveled appearance.

"A hard day at the office?" he inquired evenly.

Penny could not know how much her father already had learned, but from the twinkle of his eyes she suspected that DeWitt had telephoned him the details of her disgrace.

"Oh, just a little overtime work," she flung carelessly over her shoulder. "See you in the morning."

Penny took a hot bath and climbed into bed. Then she climbed out again and carefully set the clock alarm for eight o'clock. Snuggling down once more, she went almost instantly to sleep.

It seemed that she scarcely had closed her eyes when the alarm jangled in her ear. Drowsily, Penny reached and turned it off. She rolled over to go to sleep again, then suddenly realized she was a working woman and leaped from bed.

She dressed hurriedly and joined her father at the breakfast table. He had two papers spread before him, the *Star*, and its rival, the *Daily Times*. Penny knew from her father's expression that he had been comparing the explosion stories of the two papers, and was not pleased.

"Any news this morning?" she inquired a bit too innocently.

Her father shot back a quick, quizzical look, but gave no further indication that he suspected she might have had any connection with the Conway Steel Plant story.

"Oh, they did a little dynamiting last night," he replied, shoving the papers toward her. "The *Times* had very good pictures."

Penny scanned the front pages. The story in the *Star* was well written, with her own facts used, and a great many more supplied by other reporters. But in comparison to the *Times*, the story seemed colorless. Pictures, she realized, made the difference. The *Times* had published two of them which half covered the page.

"Can't see how DeWitt slipped up," Mr. Parker said, shaking his head sadly. "He should have sent one of our photographers out there."

"Dad—"

Mr. Parker, who had finished his breakfast, hastily shoved back his chair. "Well, I must be getting to the office," he said. "Don't be late, Penny."

"Dad, about that story last night—"

"No time now," he interposed. "On a newspaper, yesterday's stories are best forgotten."

Penny understood then that her father already knew all the details of her downfall. Relieved that there was no need to explain, she grinned and hurriedly ate her breakfast.

Because her father had taken the car and gone on, she was compelled to battle the crowd on the bus. The trip took longer than she had expected. Determined not to be late for work, she ran most of the way from the bus stop to the office. By the time she had climbed the stairs to the newsroom, she was almost breathless.

As she came hurriedly through the swinging door, Elda Hunt, cool and serene, looked up from her typewriter.

"Why the rush?" she drawled, but in a voice which carried clearly to everyone in the room. "Are you going to another fire?"

CHAPTER 5 - SHADOW ON THE SKYLIGHT

Ignoring the thrust, Penny hung up her hat and coat and went to work. Neither Editor DeWitt nor his assistant, Mr. Jewell, made any reference to the explosion story of the previous day.

Another reporter had written the "follow-up" on it which Penny read with interest. Cause of the explosion, responsible for more than $40,000 damages, had not yet been determined. However, Fire Chief Schirr had stated that there was evidence the explosion had not been accidental. Several witnesses had reported seeing a man in light overcoat flee from the building only a few minutes before the disaster.

"He must have been the fellow who leaped into that waiting car and escaped!" Penny thought. "And to think, Salt's picture might actually be evidence in the case, if I hadn't thrown it away!"

She was staring glumly at the story when DeWitt motioned for her to take a telephone call. It was another obituary.

"After muffing a good story, I'll probably be assigned to these things for the rest of my time on the paper," Penny thought as she mechanically scribbled notes.

All morning the obituaries kept coming in, and then there were the hospitals to call for accident reports, and the weather bureau. After lunch, a reporter was needed to interview a famous actress who had arrived in Riverview for a personal appearance. It was just the story Penny wanted to try. She knew she could do it well, for in months past, she frequently had contributed special feature stories to the paper.

Mr. DeWitt's gaze focused upon her for an instant, but he passed her by.

"Elda," he said, and she went quickly to his desk to receive instructions.

Elda was gone a long while on the assignment. When she returned in the afternoon, she spent nearly two hours typing the interview. Several times Editor DeWitt glanced impatiently at her, and finally he said: "Let's have a start on that story, Elda. You've been fussing with it long enough."

She gave it to him. As Mr. DeWitt read, he used his pencil to mark out large blocks of what had been written. But as he gave the story to a copy reader who would write the headline, he said: "Give her a byline."

Elda heard and grinned from ear to ear. A byline meant that a caption directly under the headline would proclaim: "By Elda Hunt."

Penny, who also heard, could not know that Mr. DeWitt had granted the byline only because it was customary with a personal interview story. She felt even more depressed than before.

"See if you can find a picture of this actress in the photography room," DeWitt instructed Elda. "Salt Sommers took one this morning, but it hasn't come up yet."

With a swishing of skirts, for she now was in a fine mood, Elda disappeared down the corridor. Fifteen minutes elapsed. Penny, busy writing hand-outs and obituaries, had forgotten about her entirely, until Mr. DeWitt summoned her to his desk.

"See if you can find out what became of Elda," he said in exasperation. "Tell her we'd like to have that picture for today's paper."

Penny went quickly toward the photography room. The door was closed. As she opened it, she was startled half out of her wits by hearing a shrill scream. The cry unmistakably came from an inner room of the photography studio and was Elda's voice. At the same instant, a gust of cool air struck Penny's face.

"Elda!" she called in alarm.

"Here," came the girl's muffled voice from the inner room.

Fearing the worst, Penny darted through the doorway. Elda had collapsed in a chair, her face white with terror. Wordlessly, she pointed toward the ceiling.

Penny gazed up but could see nothing amiss. Warm sunshine was pouring through the closed skylight which covered half the ceiling area.

"What ails you, Elda?" she asked. "Why did you scream?"

"The skylight!"

"What about the skylight?" Penny demanded with increasing impatience. "I can't see anything wrong with it."

"Only a moment ago I saw a shadow there," Elda whispered in awe.

"A shadow!" Penny was tempted to laugh. "What sort of shadow?"

"I—I can't describe it. But it must have been a human shadow. I think a man was crouching there."

"Nonsense, you must have imagined it."

"But I didn't," Elda insisted indignantly. "I saw it just before you opened the door."

"Did the skylight open?"

"Not that I saw."

Recalling the cool gust of wind that had struck her face, Penny took thought. Was it possible that Elda actually had seen someone crouching on the skylight? However, the idea seemed fantastic. She could think of no reason why any person would hide on the roof above the photography room.

"Oh, snap out of it, Elda," she said carelessly. "Even if you did see a shadow, what of it?"

"It was a man, I tell you!"

"A workman perhaps. Mr. DeWitt sent me to tell you he was in a hurry for that picture."

"Oh, tell Mr. DeWitt to jump in an ink well!" Elda retorted angrily. "He's always in a hurry."

"You haven't been watching a shadow all this time, I judge," Penny commented.

"Of course not. I went downstairs to get a candy bar."

With a sigh, Elda pulled herself from the chair. She really did look as if she had undergone a bad fright, Penny observed. Feeling a trifle sorry for the girl, she helped her find the photograph, and they started with it to the newsroom.

"I'd not say anything about the shadow if I were you, Elda," Penny remarked.

"Why not, pray?"

"Well, it sounds rather silly."

"Oh, so I'm silly, am I?"

"I didn't say that, Elda. I said the idea of a shadow on the skylight struck me that way. Of course, if you want to be teased about it, why tell everyone."

"At least I didn't make a mess of an important story," Elda retorted, tossing her head.

"Elda, why do you dislike me?" Penny demanded suddenly.

The question was so unexpected that it threw the girl off guard. "Did I say I did?" she countered.

"It's obvious that you do."

"I'll tell you what I dislike," Elda said sharply. "The rest of us here have to work for our promotions. You'll get yours without even turning a hair—just because you're Mr. Parker's one and only daughter."

"But that's not true, Elda. I'm expected to earn my way the same as you. I'm working at a beginner's salary."

"You can't expect me to believe that!"

"Was it because you thought I was making more money than you, that you changed the name on the Borman obituary?"

Elda stopped short. She tried to register indignation, but instead, only looked frightened. Penny was certain of her guilt.

"I haven't told Mr. DeWitt, and I don't intend to," she said quietly. "But I'm warning you! If anything like that happens again, you'll answer for it!"

"Well, of all the nerve!" Elda exploded, but her voice lacked fire. "Of all the nerve!"

Penny deliberately walked away from her.

The day dragged on. At five-thirty Penny covered her typewriter and telephoned Mrs. Weems.

"I'll be late coming home tonight," she said apologetically. "I thought I might get dinner downtown and perhaps go to a show."

"Another hard day?" the housekeeper asked sympathetically.

CHAPTER 5 - SHADOW ON THE SKYLIGHT

"Much easier than yesterday," Penny said, making her voice sound cheerful. "Don't worry about me. I'll be home no later than nine."

Though she would not have confessed it even to herself, Penny was reluctant to meet her father at dinner time. He might not ask questions, but his all-knowing, all-seeing eyes would read her secrets. At a glance he could tell that newspaper work was not going well for her, and that she disliked it.

"I certainly won't give him an opportunity to even think, 'I told you so,'" she reflected. "Even if it kills me, I'll stick here, and I'll pretend to like it too!"

Because it was too early to dine, Penny walked aimlessly toward the river. She paused at a dock to watch two boys fishing, and then sauntered on toward the passenger wharves.

A young man in an unpressed suit, and shoes badly in need of a shine, leaned against one of the freight buildings. Seeing Penny, he pulled his hat low over his eyes, and became engrossed in lighting a cigarette.

She would have passed him by without a second glance, save that he deliberately turned his back to shield his face. The hunch of his shoulders struck her as strangely familiar.

Involuntarily, she exclaimed: "Ben! Ben Bartell!"

He turned then and she saw that she had not been mistaken. The young man indeed was a former reporter for the *Riverview Mirror*, a news magazine published weekly. Ben had not shaved that day, and he looked years older than when she last had seen him.

"Hello, Penny," he said uncomfortably.

"Ben, what has happened to you?" she asked. "Why were you trying to avoid me?"

Ben did not reply for a moment. Then he said quietly: "Why should I want to see any of my old friends now? Just look at me and you have your answer."

"Why, Ben! You were one of the best reporters the *Mirror* ever had!"

"*Were* is right," returned Ben with a grim smile. "Haven't worked there for six months now. The truth is, I'm down and out."

"Why, that's ridiculous, Ben! Nearly every paper in town needs a good man."

"They don't need me."

"Ben, you sound so bitter! What has happened to you?"

"It's a long story, sister, and not for your dainty little ears."

Penny now was deeply troubled, for she had known Ben well and liked him.

"Ben, you must tell me," she urged, taking his arm. "We're going into a restaurant, and while we have dinner together, you must explain why you left the *Mirror*."

CHAPTER 6 - BEN'S STORY

Ben held back.

"Thanks," he said uncomfortably, "but I think I ought to be moving on."

"Have you had your dinner?" Penny asked.

"Not yet."

"Then do come with me, Ben. Or don't you want to tell me what happened at the *Mirror*?"

"It's not that, Penny. The truth is—well—"

"You haven't the price of a dinner?" Penny supplied. "Is that it, Ben?"

"I'm practically broke," he acknowledged ruefully. "Sounds screwy in a day and age like this, but I'm not strong enough for factory work. Was rejected from the Army on account of my health. Tomorrow I guess I'll take a desk job somewhere, but I've held off, not wanting to get stuck on it."

"You're a newspaper man, Ben. Reporting is all you've ever done, isn't it?"

"Yes, but I'm finished now. Can't get a job anywhere." The young man started to move away, but Penny caught his arm again.

"Ben, you *are* having dinner with me," she insisted. "I have plenty of money, and this is my treat. I really want to talk to you."

"I can't let you pay for my dinner," Ben protested, though with less vigor.

"Silly! You can take me somewhere as soon as you get your job."

"Well, if you put it that way," Ben agreed, falling willingly into step. "There's a place here on the waterfront that serves good meals, but it's not stylish."

"All the better. Lead on, Ben."

He took her to a small, crowded little restaurant only a block away. In the front window, a revolving spit upon which were impaled several roasting chickens, captured all eyes. Ben's glands began to work as he watched the birds browning over the charcoal.

"Ben, how long has it been since you've had a real meal?" Penny asked, picking up the menu.

"Oh, a week. I've mostly kept going on pancakes. But it's my own funeral. I could have had jobs of a sort if I had been willing to take them."

Penny gave her order to the waitress, taking double what she really wanted so that her companion would not feel backward about placing a similar order. Then she said:

"Ben, you remarked awhile ago that you can't get a newspaper job anywhere."

"That's true. I'm blacklisted."

"Did you try my father's paper, the *Star*?"

"I did. I couldn't even get past his secretary."

"That's not like Dad," Penny said with troubled eyes. "Did you really do something dreadful?"

"It was Jason Cordell who put the bee on me."

"Jason Cordell?" Penny repeated thoughtfully. "He's the editor of the *Mirror*, and has an office in the building adjoining the *Star*."

"Right. Well, he fired me."

"Lots of reporters are discharged, Ben, but they aren't necessarily blacklisted."

Ben squirmed uncomfortably in his chair.

"You needn't tell me if you don't wish," Penny said kindly. "I don't mean to pry into your personal affairs. I only thought that I might be able to help you."

CHAPTER 6 - BEN'S STORY

"I want to tell you, Penny. I really do. But I don't dare reveal some of the facts, because I haven't sufficient proof. I'll tell you this much. I stumbled into a story—a big one—and it discredited Jason Cordell."

"You didn't publish it?"

"Naturally not." Ben laughed shortly. "I doubt if any newspaper would touch it with a ten-foot pole. Cordell is supposed to be one of our substantial, respectable citizens."

"Actually?"

"He's as dishonorable as they come."

Knowing that Ben was bitter because of his discharge, Penny discredited some of the remarks, but she waited expectantly for him to continue. A waitress brought the dinner, and for awhile, as the reporter ate ravenously, he had little to say.

"You'll have to excuse me," he finally apologized. "I haven't tasted such fine food in a year! Now what is it you want to know, Penny? I'm in a mood to tell almost anything."

"What was this scandal you uncovered about Mr. Cordell?"

"That's the one thing I can't reveal, but it concerned the owner of the Conway Steel Plant. They're bitter enemies you know."

Penny had not known, and the information interested her greatly.

"Did you talk it over with Mr. Cordell?" she asked.

"That was the mistake I made." Ben slowly stirred his coffee. "Cordell didn't have much to say, but the next thing I knew, I was out of a job and on the street."

"Are you sure that was why he discharged you?"

"What else?"

Penny hesitated, not wishing to hurt Ben's feelings. There were several things she had heard about him—that he was undependable and that he drank heavily.

"Most of the things you've been told about me aren't true," Ben said quietly, reading her thoughts. "Jason Cordell started a lot of stories intended to discredit me. He told editors that I had walked off a job and left an important story uncovered. He pictured me as a drunkard and a trouble maker."

"I'll talk to my father," Penny promised. "As short as the *Star* is of employes, I'm sure there must be a place for you."

"You're swell," Ben said feelingly. "But I'm not asking for charity. I'll get along."

Refusing to talk longer about himself, he told Penny of amusing happenings along the waterfront. After dessert had been finished, she slipped a bill into his hand, and they left the restaurant.

Outside, the streets were dark, for in this section of the city, lights were few and far between. Ben offered to escort Penny back to the *Star* office or wherever she wished to go.

"This isn't too safe a part of the city for a girl," he declared. "Especially after night."

"All the same, to me the waterfront is the most fascinating part of Riverview," Penny declared. "You seem to know this part of town well, Ben."

"I should. I've lived here for the past six months."

"You have a room?"

"I'll show you where I live," Ben offered. "Wait until we reach the next corner."

They walked on along the river docks, passing warehouses and vessels tied up at the wharves. Twice they passed guards who gazed at them with intent scrutiny. However, Ben was recognized, and with a friendly salute, the men allowed him to pass unchallenged.

"The waterfront is strictly guarded now," the reporter told Penny. "Even so, plenty goes on here that shouldn't."

"Meaning?"

Ben did not answer for they had reached the corner. Beyond, on a vacant lot which Penny suspected might also be a dumping ground, stood three or four dilapidated shacks.

"See the third one," Ben indicated. "Well, that's my little mansion."

"Oh, Ben!"

"It's not bad inside. A little cold when the wind blows through the chinks, but otherwise, fairly comfortable."

"Ben, haven't you any friends or relatives?"

"Not here. I thought I had a few friends, but they dropped me like a hot potato when I ran into trouble."

"This is no life for you, Ben. I'll certainly talk to my father tomorrow."

Ben smiled and said nothing. From his silence, Penny gathered that he had no faith she would be able to do anything for him.

They walked on, and as they approached a small freighter tied up at the wharf, Ben pointed it out.

"That's the *Snark*," he informed her.

The name meant nothing to Penny. "Who owns her?" she inquired carelessly.

"I wish I knew, Penny. There's plenty goes on aboard that vessel, but it's strictly hush-hush. I have my suspicions that—"

Ben suddenly broke off, for several men had appeared on the deck of the *Snark*. The vessel was some distance away, and in the darkness only shadowy forms were visible.

Seizing Penny's arm, Ben pulled her flat against a warehouse.

Amazed by his action, she started to protest. Then she understood. Aboard the *Snark* there was some sort of disturbance or disagreement. The men, although speaking in low, almost inaudible tones, were arguing. Penny caught only one phrase: "Heave him overboard!"

"Ben, what's happening there?" she whispered anxiously.

"Don't know!" he answered. "But nothing good."

"Where are the guards?"

"Probably at the far end of their beats."

Aboard the *Snark*, there was a brief scuffle, as someone was dragged across the deck to the rail.

"That'll teach you!" they heard one of the men mutter.

Then the helpless victim was raised and dropped over the rail. Shrieking in terror, he fell with a great splash into the inky waters. Frantically, he began to struggle.

"Those fiends!" Penny cried. "They deliberately threw the man overboard, and he can't swim!"

CHAPTER 7 - MAN OVERBOARD!

Penny and Ben ran to the edge of the dock, peering into the dark, oily waters. On the deck of the *Snark* there was a murmur of voices, then silence.

Casting a quick glance upward, Penny was angered to see that the men who had been standing there had vanished into a cabin or companionway. Obviously, they had no intention of trying to aid the unfortunate man.

"There he is!" Ben exclaimed, suddenly catching another glimpse of the bobbing head. "About done in too!"

Kicking off his shoes and stripping off his coat, the reporter dived from the dock. He struck the water with an awkward splash, but Penny was relieved to see that he really could swim well. He struck out for the drowning man, but before he could reach him, the fellow slipped quietly beneath the surface.

Close by were two barges lashed together, and the current would take a body in that direction. Ben jackknifed and went down into the inky waters in a surface dive. Unable to find the man, he came up, filled his lungs in a noisy gulp, and went down again. He was under such a long time that Penny became frantic with anxiety.

She decided to turn in an alarm for the city rescue squad. But before she could act, Ben surfaced again, and this time she saw that he held the other man by the hair.

As Ben slowly towed the fellow toward the dock, Penny realized that she must find some way to get them both out of the river. She could expect no help from anyone aboard the *Snark*. Gazing upward again, she thought she saw a man watching her from the vessel's bow, but as her gaze focused upon him, he retreated into deeper shadow, beyond view.

No guards were anywhere near, and the entire waterfront seemed deserted. Penny's eyes fastened upon a rope which hung loosely over a dock post. It was long enough to serve her purpose, and finding it unattached, she hurled one end toward Ben.

He caught it on the second try and made a loop fast about the body of the man he towed. Penny then pulled them both to the dock.

"You can't haul us up," Ben instructed from below. "Just hold on, and I think I can get out of here by myself."

He swam off in the darkness and was lost to view. Penny clung desperately to the rope, knowing that if she relaxed for an instant, the man, already half drowned, would submerge for good. Her arms began to ache. It seemed to her she could not hold on another instant.

Then Ben, his clothes plastered to his thin body, came running across the planks.

Without a word he seized the rope, and together they raised the man to the dock. In the darkness Penny saw only that he was slender, and in civilian clothes.

Stretching him out on the dock boards, they prepared to give artificial resuscitation. But it was unnecessary. For at the first pressure on his back, the man rolled over and muttered: "Cut it out. I'm okay."

Then he lay still, exhausted, but breathing evenly.

"You were lucky to get him, Ben," Penny said as she knelt beside the stranger. "If the current had carried him beneath those barges, he never would have been taken out alive."

"I had to dive deep," Ben admitted. "Found him plastered right against the side of the first barge. Yeah, I was lucky, and so is he."

The man stirred again, and sat up. Penny tried to support him, but he moved away, revealing that he wanted no help.

"Who pushed you overboard?" Ben asked.

The man stared at him and did not answer.

Observing that Ben was shivering from cold, and that the stranger too was severely chilled, Penny proposed calling either the rescue squad or an ambulance.

"Not on your life," muttered the rescued man, trying to get up. "I'm okay, and I'm getting out of here."

With Ben's help, he managed to struggle to his feet, but they buckled under him when he tried to walk.

The man looked surprised.

"We'll have to call the rescue squad," Penny decided firmly.

"I have a better idea," Ben supplied. "We can take him to my shack."

Penny thought that the man should have hospital treatment. However, he sided with Ben, insisting he could walk to the nearby shack.

"I'm okay," he repeated again. "All I need is some dry clothes."

Supported on either side, the man managed to walk to the shack. Ben unlatched the door and hastily lighting an oil lamp, helped the fellow to the bed where he collapsed.

"Ben, I think we should have a doctor—" Penny began again, but Ben silenced her with a quick look.

Drawing her to the door he whispered: "Let him have his way. He's not badly off, and he has reason for not wanting anyone to know what happened. If we call the rescue squad or a doctor, he'll have to answer to a lot of questions."

"There are some things I'd like to know myself."

"We'll get the answers if we're patient. Now stay outside for a minute or two until I can get his clothes changed, and into dry ones myself."

Penny stepped outside the shack. A chill wind blew from the direction of the river, but with its freshness was blended the disagreeable odor of factory smoke, fish houses and dumpings of refuse.

"Poor Ben!" she thought. "He never should be living in such a place as this! No matter what he's done, he deserves another chance."

Exactly what she believed about the reporter, Penny could not have said. His courageous act had aroused her deep admiration. On the other hand, she was aware that his story regarding Jason Cordell might have been highly colored to cover his own shortcomings.

Within a few minutes Ben opened the door to let her in again. The stranger had been put to bed in a pair of the reporter's pajamas which were much too small for him. In the dim light from the oil lamp, she saw that he had a large, square-shaped face, with a tiny scar above his right eye. It was not a pleasant face. Gazing at him, Penny felt a tiny chill pass over her.

Ben also had changed his clothes. He busied himself starting a fire in the rusty old stove, and once he had a feeble blaze, hung up all the garments to dry.

The room was so barren that Penny tried not to give an appearance of noticing. There was only a table, one chair, the sagging bed, and a shelf with a few cracked dishes.

"I'll get along with him all right," Ben said, obviously expecting Penny to leave.

She refused to take the hint. Instead she said: "This man will either have to go to a hospital or stay here all night. He's in no condition to walk anywhere."

"He can have my bed tonight," Ben said. "I'll manage."

The stranger's intent eyes fastened first upon Penny and then Ben. But not a word of gratitude did he speak.

"You'll need more blankets and food," Penny said, thinking aloud. "I can get them from Mrs. Weems."

"Please don't bother," Ben said stiffly. "We'll get along."

Though rebuffed, Penny went over to the bedside. Instantly she saw a bruise on the stranger's forehead and a sizeable swollen place.

"Why, he must have struck his head!" she exclaimed, then corrected herself. "But he didn't strike anything that we saw. Ben, he must have been slugged while aboard the *Snark*!"

The stranger turned so that he looked directly into the girl's clear blue eyes. "Nuts!" he said emphatically.

"Our guest doesn't seem to care to discuss the little affair," Ben commented dryly. "I wonder why? He escaped drowning by only a few breaths."

"Listen," said the stranger, hitching up on an elbow. "You fished me out of the water, but that don't give you no right to put me through the third degree. My business is my business—see!"

"Who are you?" demanded Penny.

CHAPTER 7 - MAN OVERBOARD!

She thought he would refuse to answer, but after a moment he said curtly: "James Webster."

Both Penny and Ben were certain that the man had given a fictitious name.

"You work aboard the *Snark*?" Ben resumed the questioning.

"No."

"Then what were you doing there?"

"And why were you pushed overboard?" Penny demanded as the man failed to answer the first question.

"I wasn't pushed," he said sullenly.

"Then how did you get into the water?" Penny pursued the subject ruthlessly.

"I tripped and fell."

Penny and Ben looked at each other, and the latter shrugged, indicating that it would do no good to question the man. Determined to keep the truth from them, he would tell only lies.

"You can't expect us to believe that," Penny said coldly. "We happened to see you when you went overboard. There was a scuffle. Then the men who threw you in, disappeared. For the life of me, I can't see why you would wish to protect them."

"There are a lot of things you can't see, sister," he retorted. "Now will you go away, and let me sleep?"

"Better go," Ben urged in a low tone. "Anyone as savage as this egg, doesn't need a doctor. I'll let him stay here tonight, then send him on his way tomorrow morning."

"You really think that is best?"

"Yes, I do, Penny. We could call the police, but how far would we get? This bird would deny he was pushed off the boat, and we would look silly. We couldn't prove a thing."

"I suppose you're right," Penny sighed. "Well, I hope everything goes well tonight."

Moving to the door, she paused there, for some reason reluctant to leave.

"I'll take you home," Ben offered.

"No, stay here," Penny said firmly. "I'm not afraid to go alone. I only hope you get along all right with your guest."

Ben followed her outside the shack.

"Don't worry," he said, once beyond hearing of the stranger. "This fellow is a tough hombre, but I know how to handle him. If he tries to get rough, I'll heave him out."

"I never saw such ingratitude, Ben. After you risked your life to save him—"

"He's just a dock rat," the reporter said carelessly.

"Even so, why should he refuse to answer questions?"

"Obviously, he's mixed up in some mess and doesn't dare talk, Penny. I've always had my suspicions about the *Snark* and her owners."

"What do you mean, Ben?"

Before the reporter could answer, there came a thumping from inside the shack. Welcoming the interruption, Ben turned quickly to re-enter.

"Can't tell you now," he said hurriedly. "We'll talk some other time. So long, and don't worry about anything."

Firmly, he closed the door.

Penny stood there a moment until satisfied that there was no further disturbance inside the shack. Then with a puzzled shake of her head, she crossed the vacant lot to the docks.

"Those men aboard the *Snark* should be arrested," she thought indignantly. "I wish I could learn more about them."

She stood for a moment lost in deep reflection. Then with sudden decision, she turned and walked toward the *Snark*.

CHAPTER 8 - A SWINGING CHAIN

Approaching the *Snark*, Penny saw several men moving about on the unlighted decks. But as she drew nearer, their forms melted into the darkness. When she reached the dock, the vessel appeared deserted.

Yet, peering upward at the towering vessel, the girl had a feeling that she was being watched. She was satisfied that the rescue of the man who called himself James Webster had been observed. She was equally certain that those aboard the *Snark* were aware of her presence now.

"Ahoy, the *Snark*!" she called impulsively.

There was no answer from aboard the tied-up vessel, but footsteps pounded down the dock. Penny whirled around to find herself the target for a flashlight. Momentarily blinded, she could see nothing. Then, the light shifted away from her face, and she recognized a wharf guard.

"What you doing here?" he demanded gruffly.

Though tempted to tell the entire story, Penny held her tongue. "Just looking," she mumbled.

"Didn't I hear you call out?"

"Yes."

"Know anyone aboard the *Snark?*"

"No."

"Then move along," the guard ordered curtly.

Penny did not argue. Slipping quietly away, she sought a brightly lighted street which led toward the newspaper office. Midway there, she stopped at a corner drugstore to call home and inquire for her father. Mrs. Weems told her that so far as she knew Mr. Parker had returned to the *Star* office to do a little extra work.

"Then I'll catch him there," Penny declared.

"Is anything wrong?" the housekeeper inquired anxiously.

"Just something in connection with a news story," Penny reassured her. "I'll be home soon."

Hanging up the receiver before the housekeeper could ask any more questions, she walked swiftly on to the *Star* building. The front door was locked, but Penny had her own key. Letting herself in through the darkened advertising room, she climbed the stairs to the news floor.

A few members of the Sunday staff were working at their desks, but otherwise the room was deserted. Typewriters, like hooded ghosts, stood in rigid ranks.

Pausing to chat for a moment with the Sunday editor, Penny asked if her father were in the building.

"He was in his office a few minutes ago," the man replied. "I don't know if he left or not."

Going on through the long newsroom, Penny saw that her father's office was dark. The door remained locked.

Disappointed, she started to turn back when she noticed a light burning in the photography room. At this hour she knew no one would be working there, unless Salt Sommers or one of the other photographers had decided to develop and print a few of his own pictures.

"Dad, are you there?" she called.

No one answered, but Penny heard a scurry of footsteps.

"Salt!" she called, thinking it must be one of the photographers.

Again there was no reply, but a gust of wind came suddenly down the corridor. The door of the photography room slammed shut.

Startled, Penny decided to investigate. She pushed open the door. The light was on, but no one was in the room.

CHAPTER 8 - A SWINGING CHAIN

"Salt!" she called again, thinking that the photographer might be in the darkroom.

He did not reply. As she started forward to investigate, the swinging chain of the skylight drew her attention. The glass panels were closed and there was no breeze in the room. Yet the brass chain swung back and forth as if it had been agitated only a moment before.

"Queer!" thought Penny, staring upward. "Could anyone have come in here through that skylight?"

The idea seemed fantastic. She could think of no reason why anyone should seek such a difficult means of entering the newspaper office. To her knowledge, nothing of great value was kept in the photography rooms.

Yet, the fact remained that the light was on, the chain was swaying back and forth, and a door had slammed as if from a gust of wind.

Studying the skylight with keen interest, Penny decided that it would be possible and not too difficult for a person on the roof to raise the glass panels, and by means of the chain, drop down to the floor. But could a prowler reverse the process?

Penny would have dismissed the feat as impossible, had not her gaze focused upon an old filing cabinet which stood against the wall, almost directly beneath the skylight. Inspecting it, she was disturbed to find imprints of a man's shoe on its top surface.

"Someone was in here!" Penny thought. "To get out, he climbed up on this cabinet!"

The brass handles of the cabinet drawers offered convenient steps. As she tried them, the cabinet nearly toppled over, but she reached the top without catastrophe. By standing on tiptoe, her head and shoulders would just pass through the skylight.

Pulling the brass chain, she opened it, and peered out onto the dark roof. No one was in sight. In the adjoining building, lights burned in a number of offices.

Suddenly the door of the photography room opened. Startled, Penny ducked down so fast that she bumped her head.

"Well, for Pete's sake!" exclaimed a familiar voice. "What are you doing up there?"

Penny was relieved to recognize Salt. She closed the skylight and dropped lightly to the floor.

"Looking for termites?" the photographer asked.

"Two legged ones! Salt, someone has been prowling about in here! Whoever he was, he came in through this skylight."

"What makes you think so, kitten?" Salt looked mildly amused and not in the least convinced.

Penny told him what had happened and showed him the footprints on the filing cabinet. Only then did the photographer take her seriously.

"Well, this is something!" he exclaimed. "But who would sneak in here and for what reason?"

"Do you have anything valuable in the darkroom?"

"Only our cameras. Let's see if they're missing."

Striding across the room, Salt flung open the door of the inner darkroom, and snapped on a light. One glance assured him that the cameras remained untouched. But several old films were scattered on the floor. Picking them up, he examined them briefly, and tossed them into a paper basket.

"Someone has been here all right," he said softly. "But what was the fellow after?"

"Films perhaps."

"We haven't anything of value here, Penny. If we get a good picture we use it right away."

Methodically, Salt examined the room, but could find nothing missing.

"Perhaps the person, whoever he was, didn't get what he was after," Penny speculated. "I'm inclined to think this isn't his first visit here."

Questioned by Salt, she revealed Elda Hunt's recent experience in the photography room.

"That dizzy dame!" he dismissed the subject. "She wouldn't know whether she saw anything or not."

"Something frightened her," Penny insisted. "It may have been this same man trying to get in. Can't the skylight be locked?"

"Why, I suppose so," Salt agreed. "The only trouble is that this room gets pretty stuffy in the daytime. We need the fresh air."

"At least it should be locked when no one is here."

"I'll see that it is," Salt promised. "But it's not likely the prowler will come back again—especially as you nearly caught him."

It was growing late. Convinced that her father had left the *Star* building, Penny decided to take a bus home. As she turned to leave, she asked Salt carelessly:

"By the way, did you know Ben Bartell?"

"Fairly well," he returned. "Why?"

"Oh, I met him tonight. He's had a run of hard luck."

"So I hear."

"Salt, what did Ben do, that caused him to be blacklisted with all the newspapers?"

"Well, for one thing, he socked an editor on the jaw."

"Jason Cordell of the *Mirror*?"

"Yes, they got into a fight of some sort. Ben was discharged, and he didn't take it very well."

"Was he a hard drinker?"

"Ben? Not that I ever heard. I used to think he was a pretty fair reporter, but he made enemies."

Penny nodded, and without explaining why the information interested her, bade Salt goodnight. Leaving the *Star* building by the back stairway, she walked slowly toward the bus stop.

As she reached the corner, she heard the scream of a police car siren. Down the street came the ambulance, pulling up only a short distance away. Observing that a crowd had gathered, Penny quickened her step to see who had been injured.

Pushing her way through the throng of curious pedestrians, she saw a heavy-set man lying unconscious on the pavement. Policemen were lifting him onto a stretcher.

"What happened?" Penny asked the man nearest her.

"Just a drunk," he said with a shrug. "The fellow was weaving all over the street, and finally collapsed. A storekeeper called the ambulance crew."

Penny nodded and started to move away. Just then, the ambulance men pushed past her, and she caught a clear glimpse of the man on the stretcher. She recognized him as Edward McClusky, a deep water diver for the Evirude Salvage Company. She knew too that under no circumstances did he ever touch intoxicating liquors.

"Wait!" she exclaimed to the startled ambulance crew. "I know that man! Where are you taking him?"

CHAPTER 9 - THE METAL DISC

"We're taking this man to the lockup," the policemen told Penny. "He'll be okay as soon as he sobers up."

"But he's not drunk," she protested earnestly. "Edward McClusky is a diver for the Evirude Salvage Co. Whatever ails him must be serious!"

The policeman stared at Penny and then down at the unconscious man on the stretcher. "A deep sea diver!" he exclaimed. "Well, that's different!"

Deftly he loosened the man's collar, and at once his hand encountered a small disc of metal fastened on a string about his neck. He bent down to read what was engraved on it.

"Edward McClusky, 125 West Newell street," he repeated aloud. "In case of illness or unconsciousness, rush this man with all speed to the nearest decompression lock."

"You see!" cried Penny. "He's had an attack of the bends!"

"You're right!" exclaimed the policeman. He consulted his companions. "Where is the nearest decompression chamber?"

"Aboard the *Yarmouth* in the harbor."

"Then we'll rush him there." The policeman turned again to Penny. "You say you know this man and his family?"

"Not well, but they live only a few blocks from us."

"Then ride along in the ambulance," the policeman suggested.

Penny rode in front with the driver, who during the speedy dash to the river, questioned her regarding her knowledge of the unconscious man.

"I don't know much about him," she confessed. "Mrs. Weems, our housekeeper, is acquainted with his wife. I've heard her say that Mr. McClusky is subject to the bends. Once on an important diving job he stayed under water too long and wasn't properly put through a decompression lock when he came out. He is supposed to have regular check-ups from a doctor, but he is careless about it."

"Being careless this time might have cost him his life," the driver replied. "When a fellow is in his condition, he'll pass out quick if he isn't rushed to a lock. A night in jail would have finished him."

"Will he be all right now?"

"Can't tell," was the answer. "Even if he does come out of it, he may be paralyzed for life."

"Do you know what causes bends?" Penny inquired curiously.

"Nitrogen forms in bubbles in the blood stream," the driver answered, and drew up at the waterfront.

Penny followed the stretcher aboard the *Yarmouth*. In the emergency of offering quick treatment to McClusky, no one heeded her. The man was rushed into the air lock and placed on a long wooden bench.

A doctor went into the chamber with him, signaling for the pressure to be turned on. Bends could be cured, Penny knew, only by reproducing the deep water conditions under which the man previously had worked. Pressure would be raised, and then reduced by stages.

"How long will it take?" she asked a man who controlled the pressure gauges.

"Ordinarily only about twenty minutes," he replied. "But it will take at least two hours with this fellow."

"Will he come out of it all right?"

"Probably," was the answer. "Too soon to tell yet."

To wait two hours was out of the question for Penny. After discussing the matter with police, she agreed to notify Mrs. McClusky of her husband's difficulty. Glad to be rid of the duty, they dropped her off at the house on West Newell street.

Mrs. McClusky, a stout, red-faced woman with two small children clinging to her skirts, seemed stunned by the news.

"Oh, I knew this would happen!" she cried. "Ed has been so careless lately. Thank heavens, he was taken to the decompression chamber instead of the police station! A good friend of Ed's lost his life because no one understood what was wrong with him."

Penny called a taxicab for Mrs. McClusky while she excitedly bundled up the children.

"Bless you, for letting me know and for helping Ed," the woman murmured gratefully as she climbed into the cab. "Will you tell me your name?"

"Oh, I'm just a reporter at the *Star*," Penny returned carelessly. "I do hope your husband suffers no ill effects."

The taxi rattled away. With a tired sigh, Penny hastened on home. Lights burned downstairs, and both her father and Mrs. Weems had waited up for her.

"Now don't ask me where I've been," the girl pleaded, as she tossed her hat into a chair and collapsed on the sofa. "What a night! I've had enough adventures to fill a book."

Despite her admonition, both Mrs. Weems and her father plied her with questions. Penny told them about the deep sea diver and then worked back to the story of what had happened in the photography room.

"Are you certain anyone came through the skylight?" her father asked dubiously. "It doesn't sound convincing to me."

"Footprints don't lie, Dad. They were on top of the cabinet."

"The janitor may have stood on it to fix a light bulb or something."

Penny became slightly nettled. "I'm sure someone was sneaking around in that room tonight!" she declared flatly. "And it wasn't the janitor either!"

"I'll order the skylight kept locked except during office hours," Mr. Parker declared, yawning. "Any further adventures?"

"Plenty," Penny said, "but they'll keep until morning. There's just one thing I want to ask you. Are you in need of a good male reporter?"

Mr. Parker came instantly to life. "Just lead me to him," he said. "I'm desperate."

"Then why not hire Ben Bartell?"

Mr. Parker's face lost all animation. "I couldn't do that," he commented.

"Why not?"

"He's not the type of reporter I want on my paper."

"Exactly what do you mean?"

"Oh, Penny, I don't like to go into all this with you. Ben has a bad reputation. He's hot tempered and unreliable."

"Because he got into a fist fight with Jason Cordell?"

"Yes, and he foments trouble among employes. I have enough problems without adding him to the list."

"Ben didn't strike me as a trouble maker. Who told you about him?"

"Why, I don't remember—Jason Cordell, I suppose."

"That's just the point!" Penny cried. "Cordell hated him because Ben gained damaging evidence against him! Then to protect himself, Cordell told lies about Ben and got all of Riverview's publishers to blacklist him!"

"What gave you that idea, Penny?"

"I talked to Ben tonight."

"It strikes me he filled you with hot air," the newspaper owner commented dryly. "Penny, you must learn not to believe everything you hear."

"Then you'll not consider hiring Ben?"

"Afraid not," her father declined. "I've no special liking for Jason Cordell, who always impressed me as a stubborn, unscrupulous fellow, but I certainly can't employ Ben without more evidence in his favor than you have presented."

"There is more," said Penny, "but I'm too tired to tell you tonight."

CHAPTER 9 - THE METAL DISC

She went wearily to bed, and though she slept hard, still felt tired when the alarm went off the next morning. Hastening through breakfast, she rode with her father to the office, and en route related to him how Ben had rescued the stranger from the river.

"Commendable," nodded her father, "but it still doesn't prove he isn't a trouble maker."

"Oh, Dad, I think you're being unfair to him."

"And I think you have been unduly influenced," Mr. Parker returned. "However, I'll tell you what I'll do. I'll have Mr. DeWitt investigate the young man. If his findings are good, we'll give him another chance."

"Oh, Dad! That's grand!" Penny cried, squeezing his arm.

At the office, Penny found a letter tucked behind the roller of her typewriter. Although addressed to her, it had been sent to the *Star*. Instantly she knew the reason, for it was from Jerry Livingston, who had worked for the paper many years.

Eagerly, she ripped open the envelope and read the message. Jerry, in an Army camp in the west, expected to pilot a big bomber to Hawaii within the next few weeks. "Best regards to the newspaper gang," he concluded.

"Any news from Jerry?" inquired Mr. DeWitt, who had recognized the handwriting.

Penny gave him the letter to read.

"Let's tack it on the bulletin board," the editor suggested. "Jerry has a lot of friends here."

Penny allowed him to keep the letter and thought no more of it. Soon she became absorbed in the morning's work. There were obituaries to write as usual, but now and then Mr. DeWitt gave her a more interesting task. Seemingly he had forgotten about her unfortunate experience at the fire.

But Penny had not forgotten. It troubled her that Salt's camera remained missing. When he came to the desk to drop a handful of finished pictures, she asked him what he had learned.

"Haven't been able to trace the car yet," he answered. "But we'll locate it eventually. Don't worry about it, Penny."

The morning wore on. She saw Elda Hunt read Jerry's letter on the bulletin board, and later giggle and laugh as she talked with other girls in the office.

"That little witch said something uncomplimentary about me!" Penny thought. "If I weren't the publisher's daughter, I certainly would tangle with her! Maybe I will yet!"

At twelve o'clock, she put on her hat, intending to go to lunch. As she turned toward the wooden barrier gate, she saw that the receptionist was talking to a male visitor.

"I don't know the name of the girl," she heard him say distinctly, "but she saved my life. I know she works on the *Star* and I want to thank her."

He turned then and saw her. "Why, she looks like the one my wife described!" he exclaimed.

"Mr. McClusky!" Penny greeted him, extending her hand. "I'm so glad you're up and around today. How do you feel?"

"Fine!" he boomed in a voice which carried to every desk in the room. "Thanks to you. Aren't you the girl who saved my life?"

"I asked the police to take you to the *Yarmouth* if that's what you mean," Penny said self-consciously. "As for saving your life—"

"You certainly did, and the doc will say the same thing. Another ten minutes and I'd have been too far gone to have pulled out of it. Now I'll be okay—at least unless I have another attack of bends."

"I'm very glad you're feeling better," Penny said, edging away. She was painfully conscious that all of the reporters were listening to the conversation. All noise in the office had ceased.

"If there's anything I can do for you, just let me know!" the diver offered heartily.

"Sometime when I need a good waterfront story, I may call on you," Penny said jokingly.

"If I can give you a tip on anything, I sure will," he promised. "I know every inch of the river, and most of the folks that live along 'er."

"Have you heard of a boat called the *Snark*?" Penny asked impulsively.

McClusky's expression changed. He lowered his voice. "Sure, I know the *Snark*," he nodded soberly. "And here's a little tip. If you want a story—a good hot one with plenty o' trouble hooked up to it, then just go hunting around her berth. Maybe sometime I can help you."

With a friendly nod, he was gone.

CHAPTER 10 - COUNTRY SKIES

No more was said to Penny about her unfortunate experience at the Conway Steel Plant explosion, but she considered herself responsible for Salt's lost camera. Although the plates no longer would have picture value from the newspaper standpoint, she thought that they might provide a clue to the identity of the man who had escaped by automobile.

Police had been unsuccessful in apprehending any of the persons responsible for the explosion, and the story had died out of the newspapers.

After working for a week at the *Star*, Penny was tired in body and worn in mind. However, she was beginning to enjoy the routine. To receive her first hard-earned pay check gave her a real thrill of pleasure.

Louise Sidell, a school girl friend who lived near the Parker home, asked Penny how she planned to spend the money.

"I think I'll have the check framed," Penny laughed.

She and Louise were sitting on the front steps of the Parker home, watching a chattering squirrel on the lawn. It was a warm, sunny day with scarcely a cloud coasting around in the azure sky.

"Wish we could have a picnic or go to the country," Louise commented wistfully.

"Why not?" Penny asked, getting up. "I intended to drive to the waterfront this morning and see how Ben Bartell is making out. Then we could go out into the country from there."

"Who is Ben Bartell?" Louise inquired with interest.

Penny related her experience near the *Snark*, telling of the stranger who had been given shelter by the newspaper reporter.

"Ben probably has learned all about him by this time," she added. "Shall we stop there?"

"Let's," agreed Louise enthusiastically.

Dressed in comfortable slacks, the chums prepared sandwiches, and then, in Penny's battered old car, drove to the waterfront.

"I haven't much gasoline, so we can't go far," she warned as they parked not far from the vacant lot where Ben's shack stood. "Wonder if anyone will be here?"

Walking across the lot which was strewn with tin cans and rocks, they tapped lightly on the sagging door of the shack. Almost at once it was opened by Ben who looked even less cheerful than when Penny last had seen him.

"Well, how is your patient this morning?" she inquired brightly.

"He's gone," replied Ben flatly. "My watch with him!"

"Your watch!"

Ben nodded glumly. "That's the thanks a fellow gets! I saved his life, took him in and gave him my bed. Then he repays me by stealing my watch and my only good sweater. It makes me sick!"

"Oh, Ben, that is a shame! You didn't learn who the man was?"

"He wouldn't put out a thing. All I know is that his first name was Webb."

"Did you try to find him at the *Snark*?" Penny questioned.

"Sure, but there they just raise their eyebrows, and say they never heard of such a person. So far as anyone aboard that tub is concerned, no one ever fell into the brink either!"

"Ben, why not report to police?"

"I considered it, but what good would it do?" Ben shrugged. "The watch is gone. That's all I care about."

"But those men aboard the *Snark* must be criminals! We know they pushed Webb off the boat."

CHAPTER 10 - COUNTRY SKIES

"Probably had good reason for doing it too," Ben growled. "But we can't prove anything—no use to try."

"Ben, you're just discouraged."

"Who wouldn't be? I had planned on pawning that watch. It would have kept me going for a couple of weeks at least. I'd join the Army, only they've turned me down three times already."

Penny and Louise had not expected to stay long, but with the reporter in such a black mood, they thought they should do something to restore his spirits. Entering the dingy little shack, Penny talked cheerfully of her newspaper experiences, and told him that she had spoken to her father about adding him to the editorial staff.

"What'd he say?" the reporter demanded quickly.

"He promised to look into the matter."

"Which means he doesn't want me."

"Not necessarily. My father takes his time in arriving at a decision. But it always is a just one."

"Well, thanks anyhow," Ben said gloomily. "I appreciate how you've tried to help, Penny. It's just no use. Maybe I'll pull out of here and go to another city where I'm not known."

"Don't do that," Penny pleaded. "Sit tight for a few days, and something will break. I'm sure of it."

Knowing that Ben was too proud to take money, she did not offer any. But before leaving, she gave him a generous supply of their picnic food, and invited him to ride along into the country.

"No, thanks," he declined. "I would only spoil the fun. I'm in no mood today for anything except grouching."

The visit, brief as it was, tended to depress the girls. However, once they were speeding along the country road, their spirits began to revive. By the time they had reached a little town just beyond the state line, they had forgotten Ben and his troubles.

"Let's stop somewhere near Blue Hole Lake," Penny proposed. "This locality is as pretty as we'll find anywhere. Besides, I haven't much gasoline."

"Suits me," agreed Louise, amiable as always.

Finding a grove within view of the tiny lake, they spread out their picnic lunch. Afterwards, they stretched flat on their backs beneath the trees and relaxed.

"It's getting late," Penny finally remarked regretfully. "Time we're starting home."

"I want a drink of water first," Louise declared. "Pass me the thermos, will you please?"

"It's empty." Penny uncorked the bottle and held it upside down. "But we can stop at a farmhouse. I see one just up the road."

Returning to the car, they drove a few hundred yards down the highway, pulling up near a large two-story frame house which bore a sign in the front yard: "Tourist rooms."

In response to their knock on the side door, a pleasant, tired-faced woman of mid-fifty came to admit them.

"I'm full up," she said, assuming that they wished to rent a room. "My last suite was taken by the professor and his wife."

Penny explained that all they wanted was a drink of water.

"Goodness, just help yourselves at the well!" the woman exclaimed. "Wait, I'll fetch a clean glass."

The deep well, which operated with a chain and a crank, was situated in a vine-covered summer house only a few yards away. The farm woman, who said her name was Mrs. Herman Leonard, showed them how to operate it. The water, coming from deep in the earth, was cool and sweet.

"It must keep you quite busy, running a tourist home," Penny said to make conversation.

"Indeed, it does," sighed the woman. "Most of my roomers aren't so bad, but this last couple runs me ragged. They seem to expect hotel service."

"The professor and his wife?"

"Yes, Professor and Mrs. Bettenridge."

"Bettenridge," Penny repeated alertly. "I've heard that name before. Does the professor come from Silbus City?"

"He never said. But he's an inventor, and he brought his invention with him."

"What sort of invention is it?"

"A light ray machine which explodes mines on land or sea. The affair is very complicated."

At Penny's expression of doubt, Mrs. Leonard added: "It really works too! The first night the professor came here, he exploded a mine out in the lake. Such a splash as it made! I saw it with my own eyes! The professor expects to sell it to the Army or Navy for a lot of money."

"If it will do all he claims, why hasn't the government taken it over before this?"

"Oh, it takes a long while to complete negotiations," Mrs. Leonard replied. "The professor is expecting an officer here tomorrow to witness another demonstration."

"Where is the machine kept? In your house?"

"Oh, dear no! The professor has it in a little shack down by the lake. You can see the place from here."

Mrs. Leonard led the girls a short distance from the summer house, pointing through the trees to a knoll at the edge of Blue Hole Lake.

"The professor and his wife went down there a few minutes ago," she revealed. "Why don't you ask them to show you the invention? They might do it."

"I doubt if we have time."

"Oh, let's take time," Louise urged. "It sounds so interesting, Penny."

Thus urged, Penny agreed, and with her chum, walked down the hill toward the lake.

"It sounds fishy to me," she declared skeptically. "Probably this professor is just a crack-pot who thinks he has a wonderful invention, but hasn't."

"Mrs. Leonard said she saw a successful demonstration."

"I know, Lou. But how could a light ray machine explode mines that were under water? Why, if it could be done, military warfare would be revolutionized!"

"Unbelievable changes are coming every day."

"This one certainly is unbelievable! I'll take no stock in it unless I see the machine work with my own eyes!"

Approaching the shack, the girls saw no one. The door was closed. And it was locked, Penny discovered, upon testing it.

"No one here," she said in disappointment.

"They must be around somewhere," Louise declared, unwilling to give up. "Maybe that car belongs to them."

A sedan stood in a weed-grown lane not far away. Penny, turning to gaze carelessly at it, suddenly became excited.

"Lou, this trip has been worth while!" she cried. "Look at the license number of that auto! It's D F 3005!"

CHAPTER 11 - A FAMILIAR CAR

Louise gazed again at the automobile parked in the lane and at its mud-splattered license number.

"D F 3005," she read aloud. "What about it, Penny?"

"Why, that is the number of the car that went off with Salt Sommers' camera and plates the night of the big explosion," her chum explained excitedly.

"You're sure it's the same auto?"

"It certainly looks like it. Now I remember! Salt traced the license to an owner named Bettenridge!"

Hopeful of recovering the lost property, Penny, with Louise close at her side, tramped through the high grass to the deserted lane. Apparently the car owner had not gone far, for the doors had not been locked.

Penny climbed boldly in. A glance assured her that the camera or plates were not on the back seat where they had been tossed. As Penny ran her hands beneath the cushions, Louise plucked nervously at her skirt.

"Someone is coming, Penny! A man and a woman! They're heading straight toward this car."

"All the better," declared Penny, undisturbed. "If they own the car, we may be able to learn what became of Salt's property."

The man, middle-aged, was tall and thin and wore rimless glasses. He walked with a very slight limp. His wife, a striking brunette, who appeared many years his junior, might have been attractive had she not resorted to exaggerated make-up.

"Good afternoon," the professor said, eyeing the girls sharply. "My car seems to interest you."

"I was searching for something I thought might be on the back seat," Penny explained.

"Indeed? I'm afraid I don't understand."

"I was looking for a camera and plates."

"I regret I still fail to follow you," the man said stiffly. "Why should our car contain a camera? My wife and I take no interest in photography."

"Aren't you Professor Bettenridge?"

"I am."

Penny gazed again at the car. "This must be the automobile," she said, deeply troubled. "On the night of the Conway Steel Plant explosion, I tossed a camera and photographic plates into the back seat to prevent them being destroyed by a mob."

"Not this car," said the professor with quiet finality. "I have not been in Riverview for nearly a month."

"A woman who resembled your wife was driving the car."

"Are you accusing me of stealing a camera?" the woman demanded angrily.

"Oh, no! Certainly not! I just thought—" Penny became confused and finished: "The camera was expensive and didn't belong to me."

"I know nothing about the matter! You certainly have your nerve accusing me!"

"Come, come," said the professor, giving his wife a significant, warning glance. "There is no need for disagreement. The young ladies are quite welcome to search the car."

"We've already looked," Penny admitted. "The camera isn't there."

"Isn't it possible you were mistaken in the automobile?"

"I may have jotted down a wrong license number," Penny acknowledged reluctantly. "I'm sorry."

She turned to leave.

"That's quite all right," the professor assured her, his tone now becoming more friendly. "Do you girls live near here?"

"In Riverview," Louise supplied eagerly. "We drove over for a picnic. Mrs. Leonard told us about your light ray machine!"

"Indeed." Professor Bettenridge looked none too pleased.

"She said you might be willing to show it to us."

"Mrs. Leonard displays a remarkable interest in our affairs," Mrs. Bettenridge commented sarcastically.

Again her husband shot her a warning glance.

"My dear, it is only natural that she should be interested in such an amazing machine as ours," he said. "I see no reason why the young ladies should not view it."

"Oh, may we?" Louise cried eagerly.

Although his wife scowled with displeasure, the professor bade the girls follow him to the nearby shack. The door was padlocked and he opened it with a key.

Inside, the room was bare of furniture. There were a few boxes and a large table upon which rested a sizeable object covered with canvas.

"My secret ray machine is expected to revolutionize warfare," the professor said proudly. "Behold the product of fifteen years of faithful work!"

Dramatically he jerked aside the canvas cover, revealing a complicated mechanism of convex and concave mirrors which rotated on their bases. In the center of the machine was a small crystal ball.

"How does it operate?" Louise asked, deeply impressed.

"I am afraid a technical explanation would be too involved for you to understand. Briefly, a musical note produced on the crystal globe, is carried by ultra violet ray to the scene of the mine. The vibration will cause any unstable substance such as melinite to explode."

"And you claim you actually can explode mines with this machine?" Penny asked.

"I not only claim it, I have demonstrated the machine's powers," Professor Bettenridge replied. "How I do it, of course, is my own secret."

"Will you explode a mine for us now?" Louise questioned eagerly.

Professor Bettenridge looked mildly amused. "My dear young lady," he said. "Do you realize that mines are very expensive? I have been able to obtain only a few, and naturally I must save them for official tests."

"Of course," stammered Louise. "I hadn't thought of that."

"Besides, the demonstrations have a certain element of danger," the professor resumed. "I never give one without my assistant."

Penny, who had been studying the machine with increasing interest, remarked that a story about it might make an interesting feature for the *Star*. To her surprise, the professor did not seem to favor the idea.

"You are employed by a newspaper?" he inquired.

"Yes, the *Star*."

"I must ask you to say nothing about this matter," the professor directed. "Under no circumstance could I permit a story to be written about my work."

"But why?"

"Publicity at this time might rob me of an opportunity to sell the machine. A very prominent man, James Johnson, is now considering its purchase."

"But I thought you were expecting to sell your invention to the government," Penny said, puzzled.

Professor Bettenridge bit his lip. Obviously, he was beginning to share his wife's annoyance at the girls.

"I regret I can't tell you all the details of my negotiations," he said. "My wife and I are very tired, so if you will excuse us—"

"Certainly," said Penny, taking the hint. "Louise and I must be on our way to Riverview."

They started to leave, but before they could reach the door, someone tapped lightly on it. Professor Bettenridge and his wife exchanged a quick glance which Penny could not fathom. For a fleeting instant, she thought they both looked frightened.

Then the professor went to the door and opened it. A little man in a derby hat and with an apologetic manner stood on the threshold.

"Mr. Johnson!" exclaimed the professor, extending his hand. "My wife and I did not expect you until tomorrow."

CHAPTER 11 - A FAMILIAR CAR

"I came a little sooner than I planned," the newcomer admitted. "A business conference I had expected to attend was postponed until tomorrow. Naturally, that has upset my schedule. I had hoped you might consent to a demonstration of your machine tonight."

"Tonight?" The professor seemed caught off guard. "But that is impossible!"

"Impossible?" inquired Mr. Johnson. "Why?"

"For one thing, my assistant is not here."

"Can't you get in touch with him?"

"I doubt it. Besides, I have another engagement." The professor hesitated and added: "Officials of the Navy have invited me to confer with them tonight at the Gables Hotel in Riverview. I rather expect them to make me a very attractive offer for my invention."

"But you promised me first option on it!" Mr. Johnson protested. "If necessary, I can wait for the demonstration tomorrow night, though it will greatly inconvenience me."

"Tomorrow at eight o'clock," the professor nodded. "If you should care to put up a small sum of money as a guarantee of your intentions, I promise to make no final deal with the Navy until after that time."

"Why, yes," Mr. Johnson agreed, taking out his check book. "Any amount you say."

Feeling themselves no longer welcome by the Bettenridges, Penny and Louise slipped quietly away. As they climbed the hill they could hear the professor and Mr. Johnson discussing the amount to be paid.

"It's a graft, if you ask me," Penny declared. "Poor Mr. Johnson seems hypnotized."

"I wish we could see that test tomorrow night!"

"So do I. In fact, I'd be willing to bet the machine won't work."

"What makes you think so?"

"Just my doubting nature, I suppose. No, there's more to it than that, Lou. Didn't you notice how startled the Bettenridges were when their star customer appeared?"

"They did look a bit upset."

"And the professor refused to give a demonstration tonight, although obviously it would have been to his advantage."

"He explained he had an engagement with Navy men."

"Which I suspect was all a made-up story. No, Lou, there must be another reason why the professor was unwilling to give the demonstration. He probably knows his machine won't work."

"You're convinced he's a fraud."

"Yes, I am," Penny said. "Furthermore, I believe he knows what became of Salt's camera."

"We can't prove anything."

"No, but if he would steal a camera he might also take to swindle in a big way."

"There's nothing we can do unless we want to report him to the police."

"I have a little idea," Penny confessed. "As soon as we reach Riverview I propose to check the Gables Hotel and learn if any Navy men have registered there. By talking to them, we may get at the truth."

CHAPTER 12 - THE PROFESSOR'S HELPER

Climbing the hill, Penny and Louise sought their parked car. The day had been an interesting one, replete with surprises, and yet another surprise was in store.

As they were ready to drive away, a man came slowly down the road, cut across the Leonard yard and vanished down a path which led toward Blue Hole Lake.

"See that fellow!" Penny exclaimed.

"Why, yes," agreed Louise, surprised by her chum's tense manner. "What about him?"

"I'm sure he's Webb!"

"Webb?"

"The man who was pushed off the *Snark* and who stole Ben's watch!"

"What would he be doing here?"

"That's exactly what I want to learn! I'd like to get Ben's watch back for him!" Quickly Penny pushed open the car door and jumped out.

"What are you going to do, Penny?" Louise asked anxiously.

"Follow that man and learn for certain who he is!"

"But it's late," Louise protested. "Besides, he looks like an unpleasant sort of individual."

Penny paid no heed, but started off in pursuit of the stranger. He had already disappeared among the trees and was well on his way toward the lake. Not wishing to be deserted, Louise quickly followed her chum.

"He's going to the professor's shack!" Penny observed a moment later.

"Perhaps he is another prospective buyer of the secret ray machine," Louise speculated. "Business seems to be rushing today."

Penny was not convinced. "I'm sure it is Webb," she declared. "If we can force him to admit his identity, we may get Ben's watch back."

Not wishing to attract attention, the girls paused behind a large rock on the hillside. From there they could watch the man without being seen.

He walked directly to the shack and tapped on the door. In a moment it was opened by the professor, who looked anything but pleased to see the new arrival. Closing the door behind him as if fearful that Mr. Johnson would hear, he stepped out of doors.

The girls were too far away to overhear the conversation, but they saw the two men talk earnestly together for a moment. Then the man they believed to be Webb, walked on down the hill toward the lake's edge. Professor Bettenridge reentered the shack.

"Now what?" inquired Louise, straightening up from a cramped position behind the rock.

"Let's follow Webb. I have a hunch he may be the assistant Professor Bettenridge told Mr. Johnson about."

"But the man wasn't expected here until tomorrow."

"Which may or may not have been true, Lou. There's more to this deal than meets the eye. Let's see what we can learn."

Already the man had disappeared from view, so the girls walked swiftly after him. Reaching the lake's edge, they saw him striding along the sandy beach. Apparently he had no suspicion that he was being trailed, for he did not glance backward.

Presently the girls noticed another shack which had been erected in a clump of trees a few yards back from the beach. It was much smaller than the other little house, a mere box-like structure with a flat, low roof.

Walking directly toward it, the man unfastened a padlock and went inside. He closed the door behind him.

CHAPTER 12 - THE PROFESSOR'S HELPER

"Now what is he doing in there?" Penny fretted, as minutes elapsed and the man remained inside the building. "Listen!"

Both girls could hear a peculiar grinding sound as if from machinery turning inside the shack. The building was windowless, so it was impossible to see what was going on.

"This is maddening!" Penny muttered with increasing impatience. "I wonder—?" She broke off, and gazed thoughtfully at the flat roof of the shack.

"Lou, how is that building lighted?" she demanded.

"From here it looks as if there might be double panels of glass in the roof—a make-shift skylight."

"Lou, if we could get up there, we might be able to see what is going on!"

"And get caught too!"

"Not if we're careful. We can climb that tree which brushes against it, and perhaps see from there."

"What if we should be caught?"

"We'll decide that part when the time comes," Penny chuckled. "This should be fun."

Circling the shack, they climbed into the low-hanging boughs of a giant, scraggly maple tree. Inch by inch lest they make a sound which would betray them, they climbed out on the heavy branches.

"Penny, we're taking an awful chance," her chum murmured nervously. "If that man should look up—"

"He won't," Penny whispered confidently. "He's too busy with whatever he's doing."

Lying flat on the branch, she could look directly through the glass. In the room below she saw at least four large, oval-shaped mines without detonators, made of steel.

Evidently the man had finished whatever work had brought him to the shack, for he laid aside a tool, and then went out the door, carefully locking it behind him again.

"We were too late," Penny whispered in disgust after the man was a safe distance down the beach. "I wish I knew why he came here! One thing is certain, he's mixed up with Professor Bettenridge on this secret ray invention."

"Do you still believe the man is the one who was pushed off the *Snark*?"

"Yes, I do, and that part we can learn!" Realizing that much valuable time was being wasted, Penny slid down from the tree, snagging a stocking in the process. She helped Louise to reach the ground.

"What's the plan now?" her chum asked.

"Webb evidently is returning either to Professor Bettenridge's shack or to town. Let's overtake him and I'll ask a few questions. After helping fish him out of the river, I certainly have the right."

The man walked directly toward the shack which contained the secret ray apparatus, but when he drew close, paused and whistled twice as if in signal. No response came from within the cabin. Seemingly the man expected none, for he turned and selected a trail which led toward the road.

At that moment, the shack door opened. Professor Bettenridge, his wife, and Mr. Johnson came out together, chatting pleasantly. Without paying the slightest heed to Webb, they walked toward the farmhouse.

"What do you make of all that?" Louise asked in perplexity.

"I'm not sure," Penny admitted. "But I have a suspicion the professor doesn't want Mr. Johnson to know Webb is here today. He might insist on a test of the secret ray machine."

"Why all the mystery? Professor Bettenridge certainly can't expect to sell the invention unless he can give a successful demonstration."

"I suspect that may be the point, Lou. Things aren't properly set for a successful test today. Tomorrow night may be a different story."

"But if the machine is as good as the professor claims, it should explode mines as well one time as another."

"It should," Penny agreed, "but whether or not it does, is a horse of a different color. My guess is that the professor is a fraud, and that Webb helps him in his scheme."

The man believed to be Webb walked so rapidly that the girls realized they would lose sight of him unless they hastened on. Cutting across a field, they were able to get ahead of him.

"Yes, it's Webb," Penny whispered as they waited for the man to approach. "I'm certain."

Not until he was quite close did the man see the girls. Momentarily startled at recognizing Penny, he ignored her, and would have passed without a word.

"Webb!" she exclaimed. "Don't you remember me?"

The man halted, gazing at her with ice-cold, unfriendly eyes.

"Webb ain't my name," he said gruffly. "I never saw you before."

"You may not remember. I helped pull you out of the river after you had fallen from the deck of the *Snark*."

"Are you coo-coo?" the man demanded. "I don't know what you're talking about."

"I think you do," Penny said, losing patience. "You stayed with Ben Bartell at his shack by the river. For saving your life, you repaid him by stealing his watch!"

"Say, young lady, better be careful what you're sayin'!" the man snapped. "No one can accuse me of being a thief!"

"I want Ben's watch."

The man started on down the road, but Louise and Penny stood their ground, blocking his way.

"I want the watch!" Penny repeated firmly. "If you won't give it up, I'll report you to the police."

"Oh, you will, eh?" The man whirled toward her, his face convulsed with anger. "You'll get no watch from me, but here's something to teach you to mind your own business!"

With a cruel laugh, he pushed her so hard that she sprawled backwards into the ditch.

CHAPTER 13 - BEHIND OFFICE DOORS

"Are you hurt, Penny?" Rushing to her chum, Louise helped her out of the ditch where she had fallen.

"No!" Angrily, Penny brushed dust from her slacks. "But I'm as mad as a hornet! If that man thinks he can push me around—"

Already Webb was well down the road, walking at a leisurely but arrogant pace.

"Forget it, forget it," Louise soothed. "We'd get no place picking a quarrel with a man like that. Anyway, you more or less accused him of thievery."

"And a thief is exactly what he is!" Penny retorted. "There isn't a doubt in my mind that he's the one who stole Ben's watch!"

"Then the thing for us to do is report him to the police. We'll get nowhere talking to him ourselves."

"We'll stop in town—I think the place is called Newhall—and notify the sheriff," Penny decided. "I certainly shall ask for the man's arrest."

Returning to the car, she turned it around, and they drove toward the town, less than a half mile away. Soon they approached Webb who was walking at the side of the pavement. Deliberately, he ignored them as they passed.

At Newhall, the girls found the sheriff, and rather excitedly, poured out their story. Although the official took a few notes, he seemed somewhat bored by it all.

"You don't know the last name of the man," he recited. "You think he may be employed by Professor Bettenridge, but you are not sure. You believe he may be a thief, but you are not positive of that either."

"One thing I am sure of!" Penny exclaimed. "He pushed me into a ditch. So at least he's guilty of that!"

"Are you willing to sign charges and appear against the man?"

"You mean I would have to come back here later on?"

"Certainly."

Penny's enthusiasm waned. "Maybe I couldn't get here," she said, thinking of her newspaper work. "Oh, well, let it go."

"I'll keep an eye on the man anyhow," the sheriff promised. "Think you have the situation sized up wrong though. We've already investigated Professor Bettenridge. He has fine credentials, and his invention seems to have merit."

"You believe it actually will explode mines?" Penny asked incredulously.

"I saw it done. Fact is, Professor Bettenridge invited me to the first demonstration he gave at the lake."

"What happened?" Louise questioned eagerly.

"A mine was dumped into the lake. Then the professor exploded it with his machine. I didn't understand how it was done, but I saw the flames shoot up when it went off. It was the real thing."

Decidedly let-down, Penny and Louise took leave of the sheriff and drove to Riverview. But as they passed through the downtown section, Penny suddenly stopped in front of the Gables Hotel.

"I suppose I'm silly," she acknowledged, "but I still doubt the honesty of Professor Bettenridge. Just for the fun of it, I intend to run in here and learn if those Navy officials are registered."

Leaving her chum in the car, Penny was gone nearly fifteen minutes. When she returned, her face had taken on animation, so Louise knew she had interesting news.

"Just as I thought!" Penny exclaimed, sliding behind the steering wheel. "Not a Navy officer registered in the hotel, and none expected! So how could Professor Bettenridge have an appointment here tonight? He merely told Mr. Johnson that to impress him."

"It does look that way. Still, it's possible the officers might have registered at another hotel."

"Possible but hardly probable. Lou, I believe Professor Bettenridge is a crook. I wish we could witness that demonstration of his tomorrow night!"

"I'll never be able to go," Louise said regretfully. "I'm playing in a recital—worse luck."

"I might get Salt to ride over with me," Penny thought aloud. "Well, we'll see."

The following morning she took time from her work to seek the photographer. He was in the darkroom, but the door was open. As she stepped inside, he whirled around, his face startled.

"Oh, it's you!" he chuckled in relief.

"Why, Salt!" Penny teased. "You acted as if you thought I might be a holdup man. Why so jumpy?"

"Was I?" the photographer asked, his tone queer.

"You certainly were. Anything wrong?"

"This place was entered again last night," Salt said reluctantly. "I can't figure it out."

"Anything taken?"

"Not a thing so far as I can discover. That's the strange part of it. But the films were disturbed, as if someone had searched through them."

"How did the person get in?"

"Apparently through the skylight. It was ordered locked, but it got hot in here yesterday. One of the boys opened it up, and then forgot to snap the lock."

"Did you search the roof?"

"Yes, we found footprints leading to a hall window of the next building. That was as far as they could be traced."

"Do you suppose it could be anyone from the adjoining building, Salt?"

"Not necessarily. The person may have entered it from the street. We know he stepped out onto the roof from the hall window rather than from one of the office rooms."

Before returning to the newsroom, Penny told Salt about yesterday's adventure in the country.

"I sure would like a chance to go there with you tonight," he declared promptly. "Maybe we can get my camera back, even if those birds deny having seen it."

The morning passed slowly, and Penny found it difficult to keep her mind on her work. Elda, however, no longer bothered her. With more important problems to worry about, Penny was not the least bit wounded by the little slurring remarks the girl made.

At noon she lunched on a sandwich and chocolate at a corner drugstore close to the *Star* building. With half an hour to spend, she suddenly was struck by an idea.

"Why don't I talk to Jason Cordell, the *Mirror* editor, about Ben?" she thought. "Perhaps their difficulties are based on misunderstanding."

Crossing the street to the *Mirror* building, she found Mr. Cordell's office on the third floor. There, a secretary asked her to wait a few minutes.

Apparently an argument was in progress within the inner room, for she heard angry voices. Then a door slammed. Presently, Penny was told that she might go in.

Mr. Cordell sat at his desk, a scowl on his face. He was busy writing and barely glanced up as she entered. Finally he looked straight at her, demanding: "Well?" in a tone which sapped Penny's courage.

She wished she might retreat, but it now was too late.

"I—I am Miss Parker," she stammered. "My father is publisher of the *Star*."

"Oh, yes, yes indeed," the editor now became more friendly, and Penny took heart.

"I came to talk to you about one of your former employes—Ben Bartell."

A mask-like expression came over Mr. Cordell's face. He waited for Penny to continue.

"You discharged Ben, I believe. He's had a very hard time ever since."

"Indeed? Is he a friend of yours?"

"In a way. I feel sorry for him and I want to find newspaper work for him."

"Then why doesn't your father give him a job on the *Star*?"

Penny was prepared for the question. "I think my father would if he were assured that Ben had done nothing so very dishonorable. That's why I came to you. Why was he discharged?"

CHAPTER 13 - BEHIND OFFICE DOORS

"Unfortunately, I can't reply to that question. Nor can I assure you that Ben was discharged on a trivial offense. The opposite is true."

"But what did he do?"

Mr. Cordell arose. "I am sorry, I can't discuss it, Miss Parker. If you will excuse me for saying so, I think the matter really is not your concern. My advice would be to leave Ben Bartell entirely alone. He sent you here, I suppose?"

"Indeed, he didn't."

"Where is Ben now?"

"Living in a shack on the waterfront. Because you blacklisted him, he has been unable to get a newspaper job anywhere."

Mr. Cordell's smile was hard and triumphant. Penny knew then that she had made a grave error in thinking she might appeal to the man's sympathies. Obviously, he was highly pleased to learn of Ben's difficulties.

"I am sorry I can't help you," the editor said coldly. "Do drop in again sometime."

He opened the door for her, a pointed hint that she was to go.

As she stepped out into the outer waiting room, a man who evidently expected to see the editor, arose. He had entered the outer office only a few minutes before, and this was the first time that Penny had seen him. Upon recognizing him, she stopped short, for it was Webb.

"You can go in now, Mr. Nelson," the secretary told Webb.

Bestowing a sneering smile upon her, he entered the private office.

Then the door closed.

CHAPTER 14 - A NOTE FROM BEN

After Webb had gone into Mr. Cordell's office, Penny debated her next action. Could Webb and Cordell be friends? Or was this merely a business call? In any case, the two men were obviously of such different type and personality that she failed to understand what basis there might be for a friendship.

Deciding she could accomplish nothing by waiting and questioning Mr. Cordell, she left the office. As she passed down the corridor, an open window at its far end, drew her attention.

Pausing for an instant, she glanced out upon the rooftop of the *Riverview Star* building. The tin flooring, only a few feet below the level of the sill, easily could be reached by anyone climbing through the window.

Tempted to take a short cut to the office, Penny impulsively stepped through the opening. From the rooftop she could see the city spread out below in rigid pattern, and to the eastward, the winding river.

Crossing the dusty floor to the skylight above the *Star* photography room, Penny peered curiously down. No one was visible below.

"I wonder if a person really could get through that skylight," she speculated. "It would be quite a feat, but I believe it could be done."

A star athlete in high school, Penny felt a challenge. Giving no thought to her clothes, she squeezed through the narrow opening and snagged her sweater. As she freed herself, she noticed a tiny bit of blue cloth that had impaled itself on the nail.

The cloth was not from Penny's garments, and looked as if it might have been torn from a man's wool suit. Freeing it from the nail, she slipped it into her pocket for later examination.

Now, with her feet dangling into space, she considered how she was to get down into the room below. No longer was it possible to swing from the opening to the top of a filing cabinet, for Salt had carefully moved the heavy case to the far side of the room.

Seizing the skylight chain, Penny swung downward. The tiny brass rings cut into her hands and half-way down, she was forced to let go, dropping to the floor with a loud thump.

From the inner photography room came a terrified scream. Elda Hunt, her face white with fear, appeared in the doorway.

"You!" she exclaimed, recovering from the shock of Penny's unexpected entry.

"Now take it easy, Elda," Penny advised, brushing dirt from her sweater. "I was only experimenting."

"Experimenting!"

"I wanted to see if it would be possible for a person to get into this room through the skylight. It is possible!"

"You don't say!" Elda commented sarcastically. "I'll bet you were the one who pulled that stunt in the first place!"

"How ridiculous!" Penny was irritated. Not wishing to discuss the matter, she turned and walked out of the photography room.

In the corridor she met Salt Sommers who stopped her to ask when they were to visit Professor Bettenridge in the country.

"Eight o'clock tonight, if you're willing to go," Penny said eagerly. "I very much want to see the professor demonstrate his ray machine for Mr. Johnson."

"And I want to find out what became of my camera," Salt added grimly. "Is it a date?"

Penny nodded.

"Then suppose we start right after dinner. Can you meet me here at seven o'clock?"

CHAPTER 14 - A NOTE FROM BEN

"Let's make it a little earlier," Penny suggested. "I have a hunch that by getting there before the start of the demonstration we may learn more."

"Okay," agreed Salt. "Make it six-thirty."

Having over-stayed her lunch hour, Penny quickly washed her grimy hands and returned to her desk. As she sat down at the typewriter, she noticed a sealed letter thrust behind the roller. Addressed to her, the writing was in a bold scrawl she did not recognize.

Curiously, she scanned the message. It was written on cheap tablet paper and had been signed with Ben Bartell's name.

"See me if you can," was all it said. "I have a little information about the *Snark*."

Tucking the note into her pocketbook, Penny began to plan how she could visit Ben that day. She would not be off until five o'clock, and she had promised to meet Salt at six-thirty. If she were to get any dinner and see Ben at the waterfront, it would mean fast stepping.

Only by an effort of will could Penny keep her mind on the work before her. There were rewrites to do, and an interesting feature. At four-thirty with two stories yet to be done, she became panicky that she could not finish on time. But by really digging in, she completed the stories exactly on the dot of five, and with a tired sigh of relief, dropped them into Editor DeWitt's wire copy basket.

"You're just like a trained race horse, Penny," he said jokingly. "But your work is okay. You're improving."

Penny brightened at the praise, for Editor DeWitt was not given to complimentary words as a rule. Hurriedly washing carbon paper stains from her hands, she caught a bus which took her within a block of Ben's shack.

Smoke curled from the chimney, and as she thumped on the sagging door, she detected the odor of cooking bacon.

"Come in, come in!" Ben greeted her heartily. "You're just in time to share my supper. You got my note?"

"Yes, I did, Ben. What's up?"

Without answering, the former reporter stepped aside for her to enter. The room was much cleaner than when Penny last had visited it. Ben looked better too. Although his clothes remained unpressed, his hair had been cut, and there was a brightness to his eyes which she instantly noted.

"You've found work?" she surmised.

"Odd jobs," Ben answered briefly. "After talking to you I made up my mind I'd better snap out of it. If I can't find newspaper work, I'll try something else."

"I was thinking—" Penny sat down in a rickety chair, "—couldn't you do free lance work? Write stories for newspapers out of town?"

"Without a typewriter? I put mine in hock months ago, and it finally was sold for charges."

"I have a typewriter at home, Ben. I'll lend it to you."

Ben's face brightened, but he hesitated. "I've sure been lost without a machine," he declared. "But I hate to take yours. You know what happened to my watch. This shack isn't safe. Anyone might come in here and steal it."

"It's only an old typewriter, Ben. I'm willing to take a chance. I'll see that you get the machine within a day or so."

The former reporter stepped to the stove to turn the bacon. He kept his face averted as he said: "Penny, you've been a real friend—the only one. That day when you met me—well, I didn't give a darn. I was only one step from walking off a dock."

"Don't say such things, Ben!" Penny warned. "You've had a run of hard luck, but it's changing now. Suppose you tell me what you learned about the *Snark*."

"Nothing too startling, so don't get your hopes up," Ben grinned.

He set out two cracked plates on the battered table, two cups for coffee, and then dished up the bacon and a few fried potatoes. It was a meagre supper, but not for the world would Penny have offended Ben by refusing to share it.

"Now tell me about the *Snark*," she urged again, as Ben poured the coffee.

"I've been watching the boat at night, Penny. Queer things go on there."

"We suspected that after seeing Webb pitched overboard."

"I've seen a lot of men come and go from that vessel," Ben resumed. "It's a cinch they couldn't all be employed on her, because the *Snark* has been out of service for months."

"What do you make of it?"

"Oh, the *Snark* is being used as a meeting place—that's obvious. Just for the fun of it, I sneaked aboard last night."

"What did you learn, Ben?"

"The men were having a confab in one of the cabins. I couldn't hear much, but enough to gather that they are afraid Webb will talk to the police."

"About what, Ben?"

"Didn't learn that part. I aim to keep tab on the place for a while."

Penny told of seeing Webb that afternoon and also of his association with Professor Bettenridge.

"A secret ray machine, my eye!" Ben exploded. "You may be sure it's a fake if Webb has anything to do with it! Penny, this is no business for you to be mixed up in. Webb is a dock rat and as surly an egg as I ever met. You ought to give him a wide berth."

"I'll certainly be careful," Penny promised, arising. "Sorry to leave you with the dishes, Ben, but I must run or I'll be late for another appointment."

She really hated to go, for she saw that her companionship had made the young man more cheerful. Ben walked with her through the waterfront district, and then reluctantly said goodbye.

Hastening along the shadowy street, Penny noticed the large electric sign on top of the Gables Hotel.

Impulsively, she stopped at the hotel.

"That Navy official Professor Bettenridge spoke of may have arrived," she thought. "Just to make certain, I'll inquire again."

CHAPTER 15 - THE DEMONSTRATION

Penny was due to meet Salt Sommers in ten minutes, but if she were late, she knew he would not leave without her.

Entering the crowded hotel, she waited her turn at the desk and then inquired if any Navy officers had registered.

"Not to my knowledge," the clerk replied, consulting the register. "No, we've not had a Navy man in for at least a week."

"Any Army officers?"

"The last was a sergeant who checked out two weeks ago. Most of our guests rent on a monthly basis. We have only a few rooms for transient guests."

"Can you tell me if a Professor Bettenridge has called here in the last few days?"

"Not while I've been at the desk."

The information convinced Penny she had not misjudged the professor. She now was satisfied he never had arranged with Navy officers to inspect his ray machine. Instead, he had misinformed Mr. Johnson, no doubt hoping to impress him that others were interested in the invention.

Quickly leaving the hotel, Penny hastened on to the news office. As she passed near the loading platform, Salt hailed her from a car parked there.

"Here I am," he called.

Penny slid into the front seat beside him, apologizing for being late.

"That's okay," returned Salt, shifting into gear. "But we haven't much time unless we hurry. You know the way, don't you?"

"I do by daylight. And I think I can find the farmhouse, even if it should get dark before we reach there."

Salt was a fast and very skillful driver. He chose the less frequented streets and soon they were in the open. They made excellent time, reaching their destination just as it began to grow dark.

"How shall we explain to the professor?" Penny inquired dubiously as the photographer parked the car under an oak tree along the highway. "He may think it strange that I returned."

"Let him," said Salt, unconcerned. "I'm here to get my camera."

"Don't go at him too hard," Penny pleaded. "After all, there is a chance I was mistaken about the license number. In my excitement the night of the explosion, I may have remembered a wrong figure."

"That's so," Salt acknowledged gloomily. "Well, we'll see."

"Why not pretend we're here to get a feature story for the *Star*?" Penny suggested impulsively. "That way, I could ask him all the questions I like about the secret ray machine."

"Any way you want to do it," Salt agreed amiably.

He locked the car and they walked to the farmhouse. Learning that the professor and his wife were at the lake, they trudged down the lane.

"Wait!" Penny suddenly warned in a whisper.

Clutching Salt's arm, she drew him into the shadow of a tree. At first he could not understand the need for caution. Then as Penny pointed, he saw a hunched figure with a lighted lantern, walking along the lake shore away from the cabin where Professor Bettenridge's ray machine was kept.

"There goes Webb now!" Penny whispered. "He's evidently going to the shack where the mines are stored."

"What's he carrying?" Salt inquired.

Although too far away to see plainly, they thought that he had a small satchel tucked under his arm. As he drew closer they discerned that it was leather, and apparently used as a container for a long cylinder-shaped object.

Passing a short distance away, the man did not see Salt or Penny. They watched until they saw the red glow of his lantern vanish over a hillock.

"That's the foot-path to the shack where the mines are stored," Penny commented. "I wonder what's inside the satchel?"

"Shall we try to find out?"

"Let's talk to Professor Bettenridge first," Penny proposed, going down the lane.

The door of the cabin stood slightly ajar. Inside the lighted room were the professor, his wife, Mr. Johnson, and several other persons Penny had never seen before. However, she took them to be town residents who had heard of the test and were eager to see it.

"Well, professor," they heard Mr. Johnson say jovially. "We're all here, so why not go ahead? Show us what the machine will do."

"All in good time, all in good time," the professor rejoined. "You must give my assistant an opportunity to drop the mine into the lake. He will signal us by lantern when he is ready."

Penny tapped on the door. The professor whirled around, decidedly startled. Then, observing Salt and Penny, he abruptly came over to speak to them.

"Well?" he asked in a tone which was not friendly.

"We came to see the demonstration," Penny said brightly.

"Glad to have you," the professor replied, though without cordiality.

"We want to write a feature story about your machine too," Penny continued. "For the newspaper."

The request displeased the professor. Scowling, he said curtly:

"I am sorry, but there must be no publicity at this time—orders of the Navy, you know."

"The Navy is interested in buying your machine?" Penny asked, hoping to lead him on.

"The deal is concluded except for my signature," the professor said, darting a quick glance at Mr. Johnson. "I should have signed at once, but I promised Mr. Johnson first chance to buy the machine."

"I suppose the Navy men are in town now?" Penny inquired.

"In Riverview."

"At the Gables Hotel?" Penny pursued the subject.

The professor looked at her sharply, for the first time suspecting that she was inducing him to reveal far too much.

Without answering, he turned his back, and began to talk to Mr. Johnson about technical details of the machine.

"I am convinced it is a wonderful invention," the latter declared. "But before I invest $200,000, I must be absolutely certain that it will do everything you claim."

"You shall not be disappointed," reassured the professor. "Only be patient for a few minutes, and you will witness a demonstration that will convince you beyond a shadow of a doubt."

Ignored by the professor and his wife, Penny and Salt did not enter the cabin. Instead, they walked a short distance away to discuss their next move.

"The demonstration won't start for a few minutes," the photographer said. "Suppose we ankle down to the lake and find out what Webb is doing."

Proceeding down the path which led around the lake shore, they soon sighted the man's glowing lantern. He had set it down on the ground while he trundled out one of the heavy mines from the shack. As they watched from a distance, he loaded it into a boat, picked up the lantern, and slowly rowed out into the lake.

"Apparently he's going to drop it overboard for the test," Salt said. "While he's out there, let's take a look in the shack."

He tried the door. It was locked.

"I don't know how it's done, but I'm sure those mines are doctored in some way," Penny declared. "Louise and I saw Webb working on one when we were here yesterday, but what he did I couldn't guess."

"We'll learn nothing here," Salt said. "Let's go back to the cabin and see how the professor pulls off the demonstration. Apparently he has Mr. Johnson two-thirds convinced already."

CHAPTER 15 - THE DEMONSTRATION

"Whatever you do, don't get into an argument with the professor about your camera until after the test," Penny pleaded as they started up the slope again. "I want to watch the demonstration. If you accuse him of deliberately keeping the camera, he may throw us out."

"Okay, I'll wait," Salt promised.

Reaching the cabin, the pair became instantly aware of a tenseness in the attitude of the professor and his wife. Although they did not tell the newcomers they were unwelcome, it was evident by their expressions that they distrusted Penny and Salt.

Professor Bettenridge stood behind his machine, explaining its many parts to the awed spectators. Penny could make nothing of the technical jargon.

"The demonstration will soon start," the professor declared, looking at his watch. "I will turn on the motors now, as they must heat for several minutes."

He turned several switches and the room was filled with a low humming sound. Two tiny lights buried deep in the complicated mechanism began to glow a cherry red. The professor bent low over the machine, frowning thoughtfully. He adjusted three of the concave mirrors, and switched on another motor.

Despite a dubious attitude, Penny found herself becoming deeply impressed. Was it possible, she wondered, that she had misjudged the professor and his machine? She dismissed the thought. The mine never would explode unless it had been tampered with—she was certain of that.

"Watch closely now," the professor directed. "At any moment my assistant will signal with his lantern that he has dropped the mine and is safely away from the area."

The professor's wife had gone to the doorway. Tensely she watched the lake. Minutes passed. Then from out on the water, there came a moving circle of red—the signal from Webb.

"Now!" exclaimed the professor's wife.

Everyone in the little cabin held his breath. Dramatically, Professor Bettenridge took a metal tuning fork and struck it sharply against the crystal ball in the center of his machine.

"It will take a moment for the sound to reach the lake," he said softly. "But only a moment. Watch closely."

All persons in the room crowded to the door and the windows. Suddenly a huge burst of flame appeared on the lake, fanning out on the surface of the water. A moment later came the dull boom of a terrific explosion.

CHAPTER 16 - SUSPICION

Everyone who witnessed the spectacular demonstration was awed by the sight of the flames rising above the lake. As they died away, Professor Bettenridge, strutting a bit, walked back to his machine and covered it with the canvas hood.

"Now are you satisfied?" he inquired triumphantly. "Is there anyone here who doubts the remarkable possibilities of my invention?"

"It was a fine demonstration! Magnificent!" approved Mr. Johnson, fairly beside himself with excitement. "I am convinced of the machine's worth and if we can agree upon terms I will write you a check tonight."

Professor Bettenridge's expression did not change, but the brief glance he flashed his wife was not lost upon Penny or Salt.

"You understand, of course," he said smoothly, "that the Navy probably will insist upon ultimate purchase of the machine even if I relinquish ownership?"

"Certainly," agreed Mr. Johnson. "I should expect to make such a sale. The machine would have no practical use except in warfare."

Penny was tempted to ask the man if he considered it patriotic to try to obtain control of a machine in the hope of selling it to the government at a high profit to himself. But she wisely remained silent.

Salt, however, had a few pointed remarks to offer.

"How come," he observed, "that if this invention is so remarkable, the Navy hasn't already snapped it up?"

Professor Bettenridge froze him with a glance. "Young man," he said cuttingly, "you evidently do not understand how government business is conducted. Negotiations take months to complete. My wife and I need cash, so for that reason, we are willing to sell the machine quickly."

"Yesterday I understood you to say that Navy men were ready to complete the deal," Penny interposed innocently. "Did they change their minds?"

"Certainly not!" Professor Bettenridge's dark eyes flashed, and only by great effort did he maintain control of his temper. "You understand that while their recommendation would eventually be acted upon, a sale still would take many months to complete."

"Will your machine explode mines on land as well as in the water?" Salt inquired.

"Of course!"

"Then why not give us a land demonstration?"

"Us!" the professor mocked, his patience at an end. "Young man, you were not invited here, and I might add that your presence irritates me! Are you in any way associated with Mr. Johnson?"

"I am not."

"Then kindly do not inject yourself into our negotiations."

"The young man raises an interesting point," Mr. Johnson interposed, frowning thoughtfully. "Perhaps we should have a land demonstration before I pay over the money."

"So you doubt my honesty?" the professor demanded.

"Not at all. It's only that I must be very careful before I purchase such an expensive machine. I must satisfy myself that it will do everything you claim for it."

"You have just witnessed a successful demonstration. What more do you ask?"

"A successful water test," Salt remarked softly, "does not necessarily mean a successful land test."

"I think we should have a land test," Mr. Johnson decided. "If you convince me that the machine will work equally well under such circumstances, I will write the check instantly."

CHAPTER 16 - SUSPICION

"A land test is impossible," the professor said stiffly.

"But why?" inquired Mr. Johnson.

"The dangers are too great. Windows would be smashed for many miles around. Authorities would not permit such a test. Only with the greater difficulty did I obtain permission to discharge the mines under water."

"I had not thought of that," Mr. Johnson acknowledged. He hesitated, and it was evident that in another moment he would decide to purchase the machine without further tests.

"Mr. Johnson, I suppose you have witnessed tests made with your own mines," Penny interposed. "Or have they all been made with those supplied by the professor?"

The remark infuriated Mr. and Mrs. Bettenridge, as she had expected it would.

"You and this young man are trying to discredit my machine!" he exclaimed wrathfully. "Please leave."

"Why, certainly," agreed Penny, but made no move to depart.

Seeds of suspicion already had been implanted in Mr. Johnson's mind.

"The young lady is right," he said. "I should request a test on a mine which I provide myself."

"Ridiculous!" snapped the professor. "The machine will work equally well on any mine."

"Then surely you should not object to one further test?"

"The delay is unnecessary."

"I am certain I can provide a mine within two days," insisted Mr. Johnson. "Suppose we set the next test for Thursday night at this same hour?"

Thus trapped, Professor Bettenridge could not refuse without losing the sale. Scowling, he gave in.

"Very well. But this will be the final demonstration. If you are not satisfied Thursday night, the deal is off."

"Agreed," said Mr. Johnson.

Bowing to the Bettenridges, he departed. Others who had witnessed the demonstration began to melt away. Only Salt and Penny remained.

Professor Bettenridge closed the door so that the conversation would not be overheard. Then he turned angrily to the pair.

"Now what's your little game?" he demanded. "You deliberately tried to queer my sale? Why?"

"Mr. Johnson seems like such an innocent little rabbit, maybe we thought he ought to be protected," Salt drawled.

"Protected! Why, he's being given the opportunity of a lifetime! How much is it worth to you to keep out of my affairs?"

"Not a cent," Salt retorted. "We don't want any part of your deal. But there's something I did come here for—my camera."

"I've already told the young lady I know nothing about it. If you were stupid enough to throw it into a passing automobile, then you deserve to lose it. Now get out!"

Salt was tempted to argue the matter, but Penny took his arm, pulling him toward the door. The professor slammed it hard behind them as they went out into the night.

"That fellow is a crook!" Salt exploded. "I'll bet a cookie he has my camera too!"

"Well, we can't prove it," Penny sighed. "After all, we did act in a high-handed way. We may have queered his sale to Mr. Johnson."

"A good thing if we have."

"But we have no proof the machine is a fake. With our own eyes we saw the mine explode. Of course, we think Webb tampered with it in some fashion, but we're not certain of that either."

"The proof of the pudding will come Thursday night when and if the old boy explodes Mr. Johnson's mine."

"He's just clever enough to do it, too," Penny said gloomily.

The couple had walked only a short distance up the lane when they were startled to hear a shrill whistle in the darkness. It came from the beach.

Halting, they waited. In a moment the sound was repeated. Then to their surprise, came an answering whistle from inside Professor Bettenridge's cabin.

"That must be Webb," Salt whispered, observing a shadowy form approaching. "The whistle evidently is a signal to make certain the coast is clear."

As they watched, the hunched figure emerged from the darkness, was silhouetted momentarily in the light which came from the cabin, then disappeared inside.

"I wish we knew what they were talking about in there," Penny said. "It might clear up some of the mystery."

"Why not see what we can learn?" proposed Salt. "It's safe enough."

Taking care to walk softly, the pair stole back to the cabin. Crouching by the window, they could hear a low murmur of voices inside. At first it was difficult to catch the trend of the conversation, but gradually Professor Bettenridge's voice grew louder.

"I don't like it any better than you do," Salt and Penny heard him say, "but that's the way it is. If we're to finish the deal, we've got to explode one of Johnson's mines Thursday night. The question is, can we do it?"

"Depends on the type of mine," Webb replied gruffly. "How soon can we have it ahead of the test?"

"I'll insist that he deliver it here at least by afternoon. Will that give you time enough?"

"Sure, it won't take more than a half hour to fix 'er for the test, providing it can be done. But I ain't makin' no promises until I see the mine."

"It's a chance we have to take," Professor Bettenridge said. "The deal would have gone through tonight if it hadn't been for a couple of young newspaper fools who came nosing around here. They may make us trouble Thursday night too."

"I ain't aimin' to get mixed with the police," Webb said uneasily. "If this deal don't go through Thursday night, I'm quitting. We're in a mighty risky business."

"But we stand to make at least $200,000," the professor reminded him. "You'll get a third cut. If Johnson holds off Thursday night, I'll drop to $100,000. The thing we've got to do is to pull off that test okay and clear out."

Penny and Salt had heard enough to be certain that the men with whom they were dealing were crooks of the first rank. Slipping noiselessly away, they trudged to the car.

"Now what do we do?" Penny questioned. "Notify the police?"

"We could," Salt debated, "but so far, it's only our word against Professor Bettenridge's. He'd probably convince the police he was only a crack-pot inventor who thought he had a wonderful machine. They might let him go."

"Any other ideas?"

"A slick trick would be to fix that mine so it won't explode. That automatically would cause complications and probably delay the deal with Mr. Johnson."

"Just how do you propose to fix Mr. Johnson's mine?" Penny inquired. "It would take some doing."

"The mines are all kept in that shack on the beach?"

"Yes, Louise and I saw Webb working on one of them there. Evidently it was the one the professor exploded tonight."

"He must have doctored it in some special way. Probably an untampered mine won't explode."

"He'll fix Mr. Johnson's mine the same way, and then the test will appear successful."

Salt nodded gloomily. He was lost in thought for several minutes, and then he grinned.

"Maybe I have an idea!"

"What is it, Salt?"

The photographer switched on the car ignition. "Wait until Thursday night," he replied. "Can you get away from the office early?"

"Well, I really shouldn't—"

"I'll take care of that part," Salt said briskly. "Just sit tight, Penny. You and I will have some fun out of this affair yet, and maybe we'll save Mr. Johnson a tidy sum of money."

CHAPTER 17 - MAJOR BRYAN

It was nearly midnight by the time Penny reached home. Mrs. Weems had gone to bed, but a light still burned in the study where Mr. Parker was working on a speech he expected to deliver the following day before the Chamber of Commerce.

"Well, I'm glad you finally decided to come home," he remarked severely. "Since my little daughter became Tillie the Toiler, she seems to have developed independent hours."

"Wait until you hear where I've been," Penny said, sinking into an easy chair beside his desk. "Dad, you won't blame me for staying out late when I tell you what I saw and heard."

Eagerly she related all that had occurred, and was pleased to note that the story interested her father.

"Tell me more about Professor Bettenridge," he urged. "Describe him."

"He looks very scholarly, but his language doesn't fit the part," Penny recalled. "He's tall and thin and his nose is very pointed. Middle aged, which might mean forty-five or maybe fifty. That's about all I noticed except that he has a quick way of darting his eyes about. And he wears glasses."

"From your description, he sounds like the same person I heard about this afternoon," Mr. Parker commented.

"Someone told you of his experiments at the lake?"

"Quite the contrary. An Army officer, Major Alfred Bryan called at my office this afternoon, seeking information about a man who may be Professor Bettenridge."

"Was he interested in buying the machine for the Army, Dad?"

Mr. Parker dipped his pen in ink, wrote a few lines, and then looked up again. "No, Major Bryan was sent here to trace a man who has several charges against him. At one time he impersonated an officer and in recent months has been swindling persons by various schemes. He pretends to sell Army or Navy surplus war goods."

"That doesn't sound like Professor Bettenridge, Dad."

"Perhaps not, but from your description it could be the same man. This secret ray machine business sounds phoney to me. Most crooks try more than one game—the mine exploding trick may be his latest scheme to fleece gullible victims."

"Do you think we should report the professor to the police, Dad?"

"It might be a better idea to send Major Bryan to see him," Mr. Parker returned thoughtfully. "If the professor should prove to be the man he's after, then the Army would take over."

"Where is Major Bryan now, Dad?"

"He didn't mention the name of his hotel, because at the time he called at my office, I had no thought I could assist him in any way. However, he expected to stay in Riverview several days. It shouldn't be so hard to trace him. I'll get busy tomorrow."

Tired from her adventures of the night, Penny soon went to bed. The next day Mr. DeWitt gave her several interesting assignments, and when one of the stories appeared in the final edition of the *Star*, it bore a neat little "By Penny Parker," under the headline.

"Getting on in the world, I see," Elda Hunt observed sarcastically.

Not even the unkind remark could dull Penny's pleasure. She had earned her way on the newspaper by hard, routine work. The by-line meant that she had turned in an excellent well-written story. Elda, whose writing lacked crispness and originality, only once had seen her own name appear in the *Star*. Penny felt a trifle sorry for her.

"There's no fairness around here," Elda complained in a whine. "I've worked over a year. What do I have to show for it? Not even a raise."

Penny did not try to tell the girl it was her own fault, that her attitude toward her work was entirely wrong. Elda must learn for herself.

Not until Wednesday did Penny have a chance to ask her father if he had traced Major Bryan.

"To tell you the truth, the matter slipped my mind," he confessed ruefully. "I've had one conference after another all day long. Tomorrow I'll certainly try to find him."

Penny reminded him of his promise on the following day. Mr. Parker, after telephoning several places, found the major registered at the St. Regis Hotel, not far from the Parker home. However, the army officer had left for the day, and was not expected to return before nightfall.

"Oh, dear," fretted Penny, "that may be too late. If Professor Bettenridge is successful in his demonstration tonight, he may rake in Mr. Johnson's money and skip town before the major even sees him."

"It's unlikely the professor will leave without cashing the check, Penny. And banks will not be open until nine o'clock tomorrow."

"I'd feel safer to have police take over," Penny sighed. "If only we could prove charges against Bettenridge!"

"He hasn't swindled anyone yet," her father reminded her. "Learn what you can tonight, and if the sale goes through, we'll then turn him over to the police."

"It may be too late then."

"I think not," smiled her father. "You always were a little impatient, Penny."

Eagerly Penny awaited the arrival of evening and another adventure at Blue Hole Lake. She and Salt arranged to leave the office at four o'clock, hoping to reach the farmhouse early enough to observe what preparations Webb made for exploding Mr. Johnson's mine.

But at three, Salt was sent on an important assignment.

"I'll get back as soon as I can," he promised Penny, pausing beside her desk. "I may be a little late, but we'll still make it."

"I'll be right here waiting," Penny grinned.

At ten minutes past four Salt returned. Thinking he might have pictures to develop before he would be free to leave, Penny did not rush him by going back to the photography room right away. When she had typed her last story of the day and brought it to the editor's desk for inspection, she gathered up her purse and hat.

"Leaving early, aren't you?" Elda inquired in a loud voice so that everyone would notice.

"That's right," Penny replied, without explaining her special mission.

Not wishing to leave the city without ample funds, she first went downstairs to cash a pay check at the company treasurer's window. He gave her the crisp five dollar bills, joking with her about skipping town with so much money.

Penny tucked the bills into her purse and was turning to go back upstairs again, when through the window she saw a man coming down the alley from the rear of the *Star* building. Recognizing him as Mr. McClusky, the deep sea diver she had assisted, she darted to the window and rapped to attract his attention.

Not hearing her, he walked hurriedly on, and was lost in the crowd of the street.

"Wonder what he was doing here?" she thought as she slowly climbed the stairs. "Perhaps he came to see me. But in that case, he probably would have come up the front way."

Dismissing the matter from her mind, she sought Salt in the photography room. The outside gallery was empty, though the photographer's hat and coat hung on a hook by the window.

"Salt!" she called, thinking he must be in the darkroom.

No one answered. Nevertheless, a strange feeling Penny could not have explained, took possession of her. She sensed a presence somewhere near as if she were being watched.

Nervously Penny stepped to the door of the darkroom. She tapped lightly on it, but there was no answer.

Suddenly fearful, she jerked open the door and groped for a light. As the tiny room blazed with illumination, she uttered a startled gasp.

Almost at her feet, cheek against the floor, lay Salt Sommers.

CHAPTER 18 - A SECOND TEST

As Penny knelt beside Salt, he stirred slightly and raised a hand to his head. She saw then that there was a tiny break in the skin which also was slightly discolored. Either the photographer had fallen or he had been slugged.

Before she could go for help, he sat up, staring at her in a bewildered manner. Penny assisted him to a chair, and dampening a handkerchief with water from the tap above the developer trays, applied it to his forehead.

"What happened?" she inquired anxiously when Salt seemed able to speak.

"Slugged," he answered in disgust.

"By whom?"

"Don't know. The fellow must have been in the darkroom when I came here to develop my films. Fact is, I thought I heard someone moving around. I stepped to the door to see, and bing! That's the last I knew."

"Has anything been taken, I wonder?" Switching on another light, Penny glanced over the room. The drawer of a filing cabinet where old films, and plates were kept, remained open.

"Someone may have been looking in there!" she commented. "Salt, whoever he is, he must be searching for a film he is afraid we'll publish in the paper."

"Maybe so," Salt agreed, holding a hand to his throbbing forehead. "But I don't know of any picture we have that would damage anyone."

Penny stepped to the doorway of the darkroom. In the larger room, the skylight remained closed. It was impossible to tell if anyone had entered the building in that way.

Some distance down the hall was a seldom-used stairway which led to the roof. Finding a door opening into it, Penny climbed the steps to look about. The rooftop was deserted, but in the building directly across from the *Star*, a corridor window remained open.

"How easy it would be for a man to step out onto the roof from there," she thought. "If the skylight or the stairway door were unlocked, he easily could enter the *Star* photography room without being seen."

Across the way, in the adjoining building, a man stood at an office window, watching Penny curiously. Sun glared on the panes so his face was distorted. But from the location of the window, she felt certain it was Mr. Cordell.

After a moment, Penny turned and went back down the stairs. The exit at its base was barred by a door with a rusty key in the lock.

Passing through, Penny locked it, and slipped the key into her purse.

"That should stop our prowler for a few days," she thought.

In the photography room again, she checked the skylight, and finding it locked, was convinced that this time the mysterious visitor had entered the building by means of the stairs. She knew the door was usually kept locked, but undoubtedly the janitor had been careless.

By this time Salt was feeling much better. While Penny waited, he explained to the editor why the photos would not be ready until morning, then declared he was ready to start for Blue Hole Lake.

"Do you really feel like going?" Penny asked dubiously.

"Sure thing," the photographer insisted. "It takes more than a little tap on the head to put me out of running."

Salt walked a trifle unsteadily as they went down the back stairs together, but once they were in the press car, he seemed his usual jovial self.

"Now tell me about that plan of yours for tonight," Penny urged as they jounced along the country road.

"It's not much of a plan," the photographer confessed ruefully. "First, we've got to learn exactly what Webb does to those mines to make them explode. Then somehow we'll have to undo the work to cause the demonstration to turn out a flop."

"It sounds like a big order," Penny sighed. "We'll need plenty of luck to carry it out. Especially as we're arriving rather late."

Having no intention of announcing their presence, the pair drew up about a quarter of a mile from the lake, parking in a side road.

Shadows were casting long arms over the ground as they started hurriedly across the fields toward the beach. They had covered two thirds of the distance when Penny suddenly caught Salt's arm, pointing toward the lake.

"Look!" she exclaimed. "There they are now!"

Out on the lake a barge-type boat was being steered toward the beach near the shack where Professor Bettenridge stored the mines. The watching couple recognized three persons aboard the craft, the professor, Mr. Johnson and Webb. The barge also bore a large mine, similar in type to those Penny had seen inside the shack.

"That must be the mine Mr. Johnson is supplying for the test tonight," she whispered.

Hand in hand, Penny and Salt crept closer to the shore. The boat grated on the sand and Webb, with the professor helping him, carried the heavy mine toward the building.

"If the mine is to be exploded tonight, wouldn't it be easier to leave it on the barge ready to drop into the lake?" Penny commented. "Webb and the professor must have a special reason for hauling it ashore."

"I think you have something there," Salt observed. "Obviously, they're going to doctor it in some way. We'll see what happens."

Webb unlocked the door of the shack and the two men carried the mine inside. Creeping still closer to the building, Salt and Penny heard Mr. Johnson say:

"Just a minute. I see you have other mines stored here. How am I to be sure that the one exploded will be the mine I have provided?"

"You may mark it if you wish," the professor replied. "In fact, we prefer that you do, so there can be no possible doubt in your mind. Take this pocket knife and scratch your initials on the covering of the mine. Then tonight, before it is dumped in the lake, you may check again to see there has been no substitution."

"You understand, I don't distrust you," Mr. Johnson said, ill at ease. "But so much money is at stake—"

"I understand your attitude perfectly," the professor replied. "Certainly you are entitled to take every precaution."

A silence ensued, and Penny and Salt assumed that Mr. Johnson was scratching his initials on the mine.

"Now suppose we have dinner at the village inn," the professor presently suggested. "Then we will have the demonstration."

"Must we wait so long before setting off the mine?" Mr. Johnson inquired.

"Yes, village authorities gave permission for the test to be held at nine o'clock," the professor explained. "My own preference would be to get it over immediately, but I dare not disobey their orders."

Mr. Johnson made no reply, and a few minutes later, the three men walked away. No sooner had they disappeared up the lake than Penny and Salt came out of hiding from among the trees.

"You have to hand it to Professor Bettenridge," commented the photographer with grudging praise. "He's a smooth talker. I'll bet a frosted cookie the test could be held at one time as well as another so far as the village authorities are concerned. He has a special reason for wanting it at nine o'clock."

"Probably to give Webb time enough to work on the mine or exchange them," Penny said, and then frowned thoughtfully. "But what if the machine actually should work? After all, the professor agreed to explode Mr. Johnson's mine, and apparently he's marked it with his initials. It won't be easy to substitute another one now."

"All the same, if I'm any good at guessing, it will be done. Now what shall we do until nine o'clock? Grab ourselves something to eat?"

Penny was about to suggest that they drive to a village cafe, when she noticed Webb returning alone from up the beach. Barely did the pair have time to duck out of sight behind a boulder before he approached.

Walking directly to the shack, he unlocked the door, and entered.

"Now this must be where the hocus-pocus begins!" Salt whispered. "We've got to find out what he does to that mine."

CHAPTER 18 - A SECOND TEST

"Louise and I climbed up in that tree the other day and looked through the glass in the top."

"Then that's the trick for us! Come on!"

Making no sound, the pair climbed the tree close beside the shack. Noiselessly, they inched their way toward the skylight, and lying flat, peered down into the dark interior.

Webb had lighted a lantern which he hung on a wall nail. Unaware that he was being watched, he squatted in front of the mine which bore Mr. Johnson's initials, studying it thoughtfully.

Muttering to himself, he next took a powerful ratchet drill, and for a long time worked with it on the mine, boring a tiny but deep hole.

"I'm getting stiff in this position," Penny whispered. "What is he doing, Salt?"

"Don't know," the photographer admitted, puzzled. "Apparently, he's doctoring Mr. Johnson's mine so it will explode tonight, but I'm not smart enough to figure how the trick will be accomplished."

By now it was so dark that the pair in the tree no longer feared they would be seen. Keeping perfectly still, they watched the work in the room below.

"It's clear why Professor Bettenridge set nine o'clock for the demonstration," Salt whispered. "Webb needed all this time to get the mine ready."

"And that's why they brought it here instead of dumping it into the lake," Penny added. "But how can they make the mine explode at exactly the right moment?"

After Webb had worked for a while longer, he arose and stretched his cramped muscles. Going to a cupboard, he removed a white powder from a glass tube, and carefully inserted it in the hole he had just made in the mine. As a final act, he sealed the tiny hole with another material, and polished the surface so that the place did not show.

"Slick work!" Salt commented. "By the time he's through, no one ever could tell the mine has been touched! Certainly not that thick-skulled Johnson."

Apparently satisfied with his work, Webb put away his tools, made a final inspection of the mine, and then left the shack. After carefully locking the door, he disappeared into the night.

"Now what's our move?" Penny asked as she and Salt finally slid down from their uncomfortable perch. "Shall we tell Mr. Johnson what we just saw?"

"We could, but he might not believe us. Penny, I have a better idea! If we can get inside the shack—"

"But it's locked!"

"The skylight may be open." Salt climbed up on the roof to investigate, but to his disappointment, the roof window was tightly fastened from inside.

"We could smash the glass," Penny suggested dubiously.

Salt shook his head. "That would give the whole thing away. No, I think we can get inside another way, but we'll have to work fast! Now that Webb has the mine ready for the demonstration, the professor and Mr. Johnson may show up here at any minute."

CHAPTER 19 - THE LANTERN SIGNAL

Salt explained that he intended to pick the lock of the shack door.

"When I worked the police beat, a detective taught me this trick," he explained. "You keep watch while I work."

Now that Webb had disappeared no one was to be seen near the beach. To Penny's relief, not a person appeared, and Salt, working swiftly, soon had the door open.

To make certain they would not be taken unawares, Salt relocked the door on the inside. Groping about, he found the lantern Webb had left behind, and lighted it.

Three mines lay on the floor. "Which is the right one?" Penny asked. "They all look alike!"

"Mr. Johnson's initials must be on the one Webb tampered with."

Salt turned over one of the mines, inspecting it.

"That thing might go off any minute," Penny said, edging away. "Do be careful, Salt."

Salt chuckled. "If it should go off, we'd never know what hit us," he said. "This is the one Webb tampered with all right. Penny, how are you at forging?"

"Forging?" she repeated, not understanding what he meant.

"Can you duplicate Mr. Johnson's initials on another mine?"

"Oh, I don't think so. Not so it would look the same."

"Sure, you can," Salt said, thrusting his pocket knife into her hand. "It will be dark and no one will look too carefully."

"But why do you want me to do it? You mean to substitute Mr. Johnson's mine for one of the others?"

"That's the ticket," chuckled the photographer. "Maybe my guess is wrong, but I have a sneaking suspicion if we use one of the professor's own mines, it will fail to explode."

"The mine has to be doctored with that powder we saw Webb use!"

"That's my theory, Penny."

"But maybe the other mines have already been treated."

"That's a possibility," Salt admitted thoughtfully. "No way of telling that, because the hole would be covered so skillfully. We'll have to take a chance on it."

While Salt held the lantern, Penny scratched Mr. Johnson's initials on the metal covering of the mine. Skilled in art, she was able to copy them fairly well.

"They don't look exactly the same," Salt said, comparing the two, "but they're good enough to get by unless Mr. Johnson becomes very critical."

Quickly they moved the two mines, placing Mr. Johnson's well to the back of the room, and leaving the substitute exactly where the other had been.

"Well, that job is done," Salt chuckled. "Unless I miss my guess—"

He broke off, startled to hear a murmur of voices from a short distance down the beach. Quick as a flash he blew out the lantern and hung it in its accustomed place on the wall nail.

"Salt! Those men are coming!" Penny whispered fearfully. "We're trapped here!"

It was too late to slip out the door, for already the men were very close, and unmistakably, one of the voices was that of Professor Bettenridge.

The only available hiding place was a storage closet. Barely in time, Salt and Penny squeezed into it, closing the door and flattening themselves against the wall.

The door of the shack swung open to admit the professor, Webb, and Mr. Johnson.

CHAPTER 19 - THE LANTERN SIGNAL

"Dark as pitch in here," Webb muttered. "Wait and I'll light the lantern."

In a moment the yellow glow illuminated the dingy little room.

"Which is my mine?" Mr. Johnson asked. "They all look alike."

"And for all practical purposes they are exactly alike," said the professor smoothly. "So far as my machine is concerned, it makes not a particle of difference. Webb, which is the mine that Mr. Johnson supplied?"

"Here it is," the assistant said, tapping the one Salt and Penny had substituted. "See your initials, Mr. Johnson?"

"Yes, yes," agreed the man.

Inside the closet, Penny and Salt breathed easier.

"Let's get on with the demonstration," the professor urged with sudden impatience. "Load the mine onto the boat, Webb. Go out to the center of the lake. Then when you have dropped it, give the usual signal."

"When everything is okay, I'll wave my lantern three times," Webb agreed.

The mine was trundled out and the shack became dark. However, Salt and Penny did not dare come out of hiding until they heard Webb start the motor of the boat.

"The coast is clear," the photographer then reported, peering out a crack of the outer door. "Webb has gone, and the professor and Mr. Johnson are walking up to the cabin."

From the beach, Penny and Salt watched the boat moving slowly across the water. Presently the craft stopped, and the mine was heaved overboard. The pair waited, but there was no signal from Webb. Nor did his boat move away from the locality where the mine had been dropped.

"Why doesn't he wave the lantern?" Penny fretted.

"He's waiting deliberately, and for a purpose," Salt declared. "Why not amble up the hill and watch the professor perform?"

"Not a bad idea," agreed Penny.

Walking rapidly, they arrived at the cabin quite breathless. As they tapped lightly on the door, Professor Bettenridge appeared visibly startled. He stiffened to alert, guarded attention, but relaxed slightly as his wife admitted the pair.

"Oh, it's you two again," he said none too pleasantly. "You are just in time to witness my final demonstration. We are waiting now for my assistant's signal."

"It seems to take a long while," Mr. Johnson commented, glancing at his watch.

"Webb may have had trouble getting the mine overboard," the professor soothed. "Besides, he has to move out of the danger zone."

Penny and Salt looked at each other but said nothing. They were certain that Webb had been in no haste to return to shore.

"What are you two smirking about?" the professor demanded irritably. "I suppose you think my machine won't work?"

"I'll be surprised if it does," Salt agreed, unruffled.

Mrs. Bettenridge, who stood at the window, suddenly cried: "There is the signal!"

Professor Bettenridge snapped on a switch and the ray machine began to hum. He turned on another motor and lights began to glow. Then he struck the crystal ball, producing a musical vibration.

Assuming a confident pose, he waited.

Nothing happened.

As the seconds ticked by and still there was no explosion, the professor began to wilt. He gazed desperately at his wife who looked as dismayed as he.

"My dear, something seems to be wrong. Are you sure you saw the signal? Perhaps Webb has not yet dropped the mine."

"I saw the signal. The lantern was waved three times."

The professor made several adjustments on his machine, and again struck the musical note. But there was no explosion. Enjoying his discomfiture, Salt and Penny grinned from ear to ear.

"You did something to the machine!" the professor accused them furiously. "You came here and tampered!"

"We've not been near this place tonight until a moment ago," Penny retorted. "The truth is, you weren't able to explode Mr. Johnson's mine!"

"That's not so!" The professor's face now was red with anger. "Something has gone wrong, but that doesn't prove my machine is a failure. We'll have another test."

"I'm not sure that I shall be interested," Mr. Johnson said quietly. "I've been thinking the matter over and there are so many hazards—"

"I'll make you an especially good offer," the professor declared, flipping the canvas cover over his machine. "Furthermore, we will have the test tonight. I guarantee to explode the mine before you leave here."

"But the mine I supplied is at the bottom of the lake and it failed to go off," Mr. Johnson said.

"First, we will talk to Webb and learn exactly what happened," the professor said, taking him by the arm. "I know there is a logical explanation for the failure."

Glaring at Penny and Salt, he shooed everyone out of the cabin, locking the door.

"My dear," he said to his wife, giving her a significant look, "take Mr. Johnson to the house while I find Webb. I'll be with you in just a minute."

The professor went hurriedly down the beach while Mrs. Bettenridge and Mr. Johnson walked slowly toward the rooming house. Penny and Salt remained beside the cabin until everyone was beyond hearing.

"Well, our trick worked," Salt chuckled, "but if we aren't careful, the professor will pull off a successful test yet and ruin all our plans."

"He and Webb are certain to examine the mines and discover the one with Mr. Johnson's initials still in the shack. Then they may convince Mr. Johnson there was a mix-up, and go ahead with another test which will be successful."

"We've got to do something," Salt muttered. "But what?"

"I know!" Penny exclaimed. "I'll telephone Dad and have him come here right away with Major Bryan!"

"Good!" approved Salt. "I'll stay here and hold the fort while you telephone. Tell your father to step on the gas, because we've got to move fast to queer Professor Bettenridge's game."

CHAPTER 20 - A CROOK EXPOSED

Eager to carry out Salt Sommers' bidding, Penny ran up the hill in search of a telephone. She considered using the one at the house where Professor and Mrs. Bettenridge roomed, but decided against it, fearing that the conversation might be overheard or reported to them by the farm woman.

Hastening on, she saw a light farther down the road, and recalled having noticed a house there. Five minutes later, completely winded, she pounded on the door. A man in shirtsleeves, the evening newspaper in his hand, answered her knock.

"Please, may I use your telephone?" Penny gasped.

"Why, sure," he agreed, stepping aside for her to enter. "Anything wrong?"

Penny knew better than to mention what was happening at the lake. "I want to telephone my father in Riverview," she explained.

"The phone is in the other room," the man said, switching on a light.

Placing the call, Penny waited impatiently for it to be put through. She was uncertain whether her father would be at home. If she failed to reach him, then the only other thing was to notify the sheriff.

"Here is your party. Go ahead, please," came the long distance operator's voice. The next moment Penny heard her father's clear tones at the other end of the line.

"Dad, I'm at Blue Hole Lake with Salt," she explained hurriedly. "Can you drive here right away?"

"I suppose so," he answered, knowing from her voice that something serious was wrong. "What's up?"

"We've learned plenty about Professor Bettenridge, Dad. Unless something is done quickly, he may sell his fake machine to Mr. Johnson."

"But what can *I* do about it?" the publisher asked.

"Can you get hold of the Major and bring him with you?" Penny pleaded. "Professor Bettenridge may be the man he's after!"

"Maybe I can reach him!" Mr. Parker agreed. "If I have luck I'll be out there within twenty or thirty minutes. I'll come as fast as I can."

Before hanging up the receiver, Penny gave her father detailed instructions for reaching the lake and told him where to park. Leaving a dollar bill to pay for the call, she then hastened back to find Salt.

The photographer was nowhere near the cabin and she was afraid to call his name lest she be overheard by the Bettenridges.

As she stood in the shadow of the building, she heard voices from the beach. Someone with a lighted lantern was coming up the trail, and soon she distinguished two figures—Professor Bettenridge and Webb.

"That's the story you'll have to tell Johnson," she heard the professor say. "Tell him that somehow you got the two mines mixed up as you were loading them onto the boat and dumped one that was never meant to explode."

"But he saw us load the mine."

"It was dark and he may not be sure. Anyway, the mine with Johnson's initials is still in the shack. We'll show it to him."

"What bothers me is how did the mistake happen?" Webb muttered. "I know the mine I loaded on the boat had Johnson's initials. It should have gone off."

"Someone is onto our game, and tampered with the mines. It may have been a trick of that newspaper pair."

"In that case, we're in a dangerous spot. We ought to clear out while the clearing is good. If the authorities get onto what we're doing—"

"They won't—at least not tonight," the professor said confidently. "The sheriff is as dumb as they come, and is convinced I am a genius second only to Thomas Edison. We'll have to pull off a successful test tonight with Johnson's mine, collect what we can, and clear out."

"Okay," Webb agreed, "but this is my last job. The game is too dangerous. I served one stretch in the pen and I don't look forward to another."

"If we can explode Johnson's mine tonight, we'll collect the money and be away from here as soon as we cash the check. Can you pull off the job without any blunder?"

"Sure I can unless someone tampers with the mine! This time I'll make sure they don't!"

"Okay," the professor agreed. "Now I want you to talk to Johnson. Put up a good story, and get him to look at the mine that has his initials on it. If he refuses, we're licked, but it's worth a final try."

"I'd like to find the guy who broke into the shack!" Webb muttered.

"We may have time for that later. Just now our most important job is to convince Johnson we have something to sell."

The two men now were very close. Penny flattened herself against the building wall, fearful of being seen. The light from their lantern illuminated her for an instant, but the men were so absorbed in their discussion, they failed to see her. Going on up the hillside path, they vanished into the farmhouse.

What had become of Salt, Penny did not know. Thinking he might have gone down to the lake, she walked rapidly in that direction. As she approached the shack where the mines were stored, she heard a low whistle.

"Is that you, Salt?" she called softly.

He came from behind a clump of bushes to join her. Quickly they compared notes. Salt had overheard no conversation, but he had watched Professor Bettenridge and Webb as they reexamined the mines in the shack.

"They're onto our game, and it won't work twice," he said. "We've got to delay the test, but how?"

"Maybe we could cut the boat loose!"

"A capital idea!" Salt approved, chuckling. "Penny, you really have a brain!"

As they scurried over the stones to the water's edge, Penny suddenly stopped short.

"Listen!" she commanded.

"I didn't hear anything," Salt said.

"An automobile stopped by the roadside. I'm sure of it. Maybe it's my father!"

"He couldn't have reached here so soon."

"You don't know Dad," Penny chuckled. "He drives like the wind. It certainly sounded like the engine of our car."

"Let's have a look before we cut the boat loose," Salt said, slipping a knife back into his pocket.

"I'll go," Penny offered. "You wait here."

Before Salt could stop her, she darted away into the darkness. Crawling under a barbed wire fence, she took a short cut to the road. Even before she saw the car, she heard a voice which she recognized as her father's.

"Dad!" she called softly.

He was with another man whom Penny hoped was Major Bryan. As the two came toward the fence, she saw that it was indeed the Army officer.

"Dad, how did you get here so quickly?" she greeted him. "Salt and I didn't expect you for at least another twenty minutes."

"I was lucky enough to get hold of Major Bryan right away," Mr. Parker answered, climbing over the fence. "Now I hope you haven't brought us on a wild chase, Penny. What's up?"

"Come with me and I'll show you," she offered. "That's easier than explaining everything."

Major Bryan, a well-built man of early middle age, asked Penny several questions about Professor Bettenridge as the three walked hurriedly toward the lake.

"From your description, he seems to be the man I'm after," he declared grimly. "If he's the same person, his real name is Claude Arkwright and he's wanted for impersonating an officer and on various other charges. He pulled a big job in New York three months ago, then vanished."

Salt was waiting at the lake. "What's our move?" he asked, after relating everything that had occurred that night. "Shall we cut the boat loose?"

"First, let me examine those mines," the major requested. "Can we get into the shack?"

"I can pick the lock, but it takes time," Salt offered.

CHAPTER 20 - A CROOK EXPOSED

"We'll break it," the major decided. "Those men may return here at any minute, so there's no time to lose."

The door was forced open and Penny was placed on guard to watch the hillside for Webb or anyone in the professor's party.

There was no light in the shack, but both Mr. Parker and the major had brought flashlights. Salt pointed out the mine which had been doctored by Webb. Carefully, the Army officer examined it.

"I can't tell much by looking at it for the work has been cleverly concealed," he admitted. "But from what you've told me, I am quite certain how the mine is made to explode."

"How is it done?" Salt demanded.

"After the hole is made, a chemical—probably sodium—is inserted. Then another substance which melts slowly in water is used to seal up the opening."

"Then that explains why Webb delayed so long in giving the signal after the mine had been dropped into the water!" Penny exclaimed from the doorway. "He was waiting for the substance to melt!"

"Exactly," agreed the major. "If my theory is correct, only the action of water is required to explode this mine. The professor's machine, of course, has nothing whatsoever to do with it."

"Why don't we explode the mine now?" Penny suddenly proposed. "That would put an end to the professor's little scheme."

"It might also prevent us from arresting him," the major said. He debated a moment. Then he exclaimed: "It's worth trying! We'll load the mine on the boat and dump 'er in the lake!"

The men would not permit Penny to help with the dangerous work. Carefully they transported the mine to the boat. Salt was about to start the motor, but the major stopped him.

"No, we don't want the sound of the engine to give us away," he said. "We'll row out into the lake."

Penny was eager to accompany the men, but they would not hear of it. To her disappointment, she was compelled to remain on the beach.

Sitting down on the sand, she nervously watched until the boat faded into the black of the night. Presently, she heard a splash which told her that the mine had been lowered overboard. Anxiously, she waited for the boat to return.

"Why don't they come?" she thought, straining to hear the sound of oars. "If the explosion should go off while they're still out there—"

Then she heard the boat coming and breathed in relief. Soon the craft grated on sand, and the three men leaped out.

"Perhaps my theory is wrong," the major commented, as they all huddled together, waiting. "The mine should have gone off by this time."

Several minutes elapsed and still nothing happened. And then, as the group became convinced their plan had failed, there came a terrific explosion which sent flame and water high above the lake's surface.

CHAPTER 21 - IN SEARCH OF WEBB

"Beautiful! Beautiful!" chuckled the major as the flames began to die away. "That proves our theory. No machine is required to set off the mines—only the action of water."

"Professor Bettenridge must have heard the explosion!" Penny exclaimed, fairly beside herself with excitement. "What will happen now?"

"If human nature runs true to form, he will soon come here to investigate," the major predicted.

The four stepped back into the dense growth of trees to wait. Within five minutes they observed two shadowy figures scurrying down the path toward the shack where the mines were stored. As they came closer, Penny recognized the professor and his wife.

"And someone is following them," she discerned. "It looks like Mr. Johnson."

Professor Bettenridge and his wife now were near the trees. Their voices, though low, carried to those in hiding.

"That stupid lout, Webb!" the professor muttered. "He has ruined everything now by setting off the mine too soon."

"But how could it have been Webb?" his wife protested. "He was at the farmhouse only five minutes ago. He wouldn't have had time."

"Then it was someone else—" Professor Bettenridge paused, and cast a quick alert glance about the lake shore. He noted that the boat was tied, but that the door of the shack was wide open.

"We've been exposed!" he muttered. "Our game is up, and we've got to get away from here before the authorities arrest us."

"But what about Johnson?" his wife demanded, glancing over her shoulder at the man who was following them down the hillside path.

"We can do nothing now. He had begun to catch on even before tonight, and this explosion finishes everything. Don't even stop to pack your clothes. We'll get our car and clear out."

"Webb?"

"He'll have to look out for himself. We're traveling alone and traveling fast."

Those in hiding suddenly stepped forth from the trees, blocking the path. Major Bryan moved directly in front of the professor, flashing a light into his face.

"Good evening, Claude Arkwright," he said distinctly.

The professor was startled, but recovered poise quickly. "You are mistaken," he said in a cold voice. "My name is Bettenridge."

"No doubt that is what you call yourself now. You are wanted by the Federal government for impersonating an officer."

"Ridiculous!"

"May I see your draft card?" the major requested curtly.

"Sorry, I haven't it with me. It is in my room."

"Then we will go there."

Nettled, Professor Bettenridge could think of no further excuse. Glancing significantly at his wife, he said: "My dear, will you go to the house and get the card for our inquisitors?"

"We will all go," corrected the major. "Your wife may be wanted as your accomplice in this latest secret ray machine fleece. We prefer that she does not escape."

"You are very trusting," sneered the professor.

CHAPTER 21 - IN SEARCH OF WEBB

By this time, Mr. Johnson had reached the hillside. Puffing from having hurried so fast, he gazed in bewilderment at the little group.

"What does this mean?" he inquired. "What caused the mine to explode?"

"It was set off by being dropped in the lake," explained the major.

"You mean the explosion was not touched off by Professor Bettenridge's invention?"

"The machine had nothing whatsoever to do with it," Penny explained. "Professor Bettenridge and his accomplice, Webb Nelson, have been doctoring the mines with a powder and an outer shield which dissolves in water. They hoped to sell the worthless machine to you before you discovered the truth."

The information stunned Mr. Johnson, but recovering, he turned furiously upon Professor Bettenridge.

"You cheap trickster!" he shouted. "I'll have you arrested for this!"

"Have you given the man any money?" Mr. Parker inquired.

"A thousand dollars for an option on the machine. The rest was to have been paid tonight."

"You're lucky to get off so easily," Mr. Parker said. "It's possible too, that we can get part of your deposit back."

"You can't hold me on any trumped-up charge," Professor Bettenridge said angrily. "You have no warrant."

He started away, but was brought up short as he felt the major's revolver pressing against his ribs.

"This will hold you, I think," said the Army man coolly. "Now lead the way up the hill to the other cabin. I want to see your remarkable invention."

With his wife clinging to his arm, the professor marched stiffly ahead of the group. He unlocked the cabin door and all went inside.

Jerking off the canvas which covered the secret ray machine, Major Bryan inspected it briefly.

"A worthless contraption!" he said contemptuously. "Utterly useless!"

"Where did you meet Webb Nelson?" Penny asked the professor. "And where is he now?"

"You'll have to find him for yourself," sneered the professor. "If he has the sense I think, he's probably miles away from here by now."

Determined that the man should not escape, Penny, Salt and Mr. Parker started for the farmhouse, leaving the major and Mr. Johnson to question the professor. As they rapped on the screen door, Mrs. Leonard came to let them in.

"What is going on here tonight, may I ask?" she demanded irritably. "People banging in and out of the house at all hours! Explosions! I declare, I wish I never had rented a room to that crazy professor and his wife!"

"Is Webb Nelson here?" Mr. Parker asked.

"The professor's helper? Why, no, right after the explosion he came, gathered a bag of things from the professor's room, and went off down the road."

"In a car?"

"He was afoot when he left here. Is anything wrong?"

"Considerable. Professor Bettenridge has just been exposed as an impostor. Webb must have realized the jig was up when he heard the mine go off."

"The professor an impostor!" Mrs. Leonard exclaimed. "Well, of all things!"

"Which way did Webb go?" Mr. Parker asked.

"Down the road toward town when I last saw him."

"Maybe we can catch him!" Mr. Parker cried.

"If he didn't get a lift," Salt added.

All piled into the Parker car which had been left a short distance down the road. But in the drive to Newhall, the man was not sighted. Nor did inquiry in the town reveal anyone who had seen him.

"Undoubtedly he expected to be followed, and cut across the fields or took a side road," Mr. Parker declared. "We'll have to depend upon the authorities to pick him up now."

Stopping at the sheriff's office, warrants for the man's arrest were sworn out, and the party then returned to Mrs. Leonard's. Professor Bettenridge and his wife had been brought to the farmhouse by Major Bryan who proposed to hold them there pending the arrival of federal authorities from Riverview.

"There's one thing I want to know," Penny whispered to her father. "How did Professor Bettenridge meet Webb? Perhaps he can explain the man's connection with the *Snark*."

The question was put to the professor who replied briefly that he knew nothing whatsoever about Webb Nelson.

"I met him only two weeks ago," he said. "He claimed to be an expert at handling explosives, so I hired him."

No one believed the professor was telling the truth. However, it was useless to question him further. Determined not to implicate himself, his wife, or his helper, he spoke as seldom as possible.

"The man has a room here," Mr. Parker suggested. "Suppose we see what we can find."

Mrs. Leonard led the way upstairs. The professor's room was locked, but she opened it with a master key.

Two suitcases had been packed as if for a hasty departure and everything was in disorder. All garments had been removed from the closets. The scrap basket was filled with torn letters which Mr. Parker promptly gathered together and placed in an envelope for future piecing together.

In one of the suitcases he found several newspaper clippings. One bore a picture of the professor, but the name beneath it was Claude Arkwright, and the story related that he was wanted in connection with a $10,000 hoax.

"Bettenridge is our man all right," the publisher declared. "We made no mistake in holding him for the sheriff."

Penny had been searching the larger of the two suitcases which seemed to contain only clothing. But as she reached the lower layer, she suddenly gave a jubilant cry.

"Salt! Dad!" she exclaimed. "It's here! See what I've found!"

CHAPTER 22 - SALT'S MISSING CAMERA

From the suitcase, Penny lifted Salt's camera. With a cry of pleasure, he snatched it from her hand and eagerly examined it.

"Is it damaged in any way?" Penny asked.

"It doesn't seem to be. So the professor had it all the time just as we thought!"

"And here are the plates I tossed into the car the night of the explosion!" Penny added, burrowing deeper into the pile of clothing. "They're probably ruined by now."

"Maybe not," said Salt, examining them. "The professor may have thought they were unexposed plates and kept them for use later on."

"Anyway, it was crooked of him to try to keep the camera," Penny declared. "Though I suppose such a small theft doesn't amount to much in comparison to the trick he nearly played on Mr. Johnson."

"It matters to me," the photographer chuckled. "Am I glad to get this camera back! The plates won't do us any good now they are outdated, but I'll take them along anyhow. I'm curious to see if they would have shown anything of significance."

"By all means develop them," urged Mr. Parker. "Anything else in the suitcase?"

In a pocket of the case Penny found several letters from Mr. Johnson which she gave to her father. Knowing they would be valuable in establishing a case of attempted fraud against the professor, he kept them.

"I wish Webb Nelson hadn't managed to escape," Penny remarked as the trio went downstairs again. "He must have started for Newhall, perhaps to catch a train."

"Any due at this time?" her father asked thoughtfully.

"I wouldn't know."

"Tell you what," Mr. Parker proposed. "We can do nothing more here. We may as well drive to the village again and press an inquiry for Webb."

Once more the car with Salt as driver careened over the bumpy country road to Newhall. They reached the town without sighting anyone who resembled the professor's helper.

"Drive to the station," Mr. Parker instructed Salt. "There's an outside chance Webb went there."

The depot was a drab little red building, deserted except for a sleepy-eyed station agent who told them there was no passenger train scheduled to leave Newhall before six o'clock the next morning.

"Any freight trains?" Mr. Parker inquired.

"A couple are overdue," the agent said. "No. 32 from the east, and No. 20, also westbound. No. 20's just coming into the block."

Although it seemed unlikely Webb would take a freight train out of town, Mr. Parker, Salt and Penny, decided to wait for it to come in. They went outside, standing in the shadow of the station.

"No sign of anyone around," Salt declared, looking carefully about. "We may as well go back to the lake."

"Let's wait," Penny urged.

No. 20 rumbled into the station, stirring up a whirlwind of dust and cinders. A trainman with a lantern over his arm, came into the station to get his orders from the agent. He chatted a moment, then went out again, swinging aboard one of the cars. A moment later, the train began to move.

"Shall we go?" Mr. Parker said impatiently.

Penny buttoned her coat as she stepped beyond the protection of the building, for the night air was cold and penetrated her thin clothing. Treading along behind her father and Salt to the car, she started to climb in, when her attention riveted upon a lone figure some distance from the railroad station. A man, who resembled Webb

Nelson in build, had emerged from behind a tool shed, and stood close to the tracks watching the slowly moving freight.

Then he ran along beside the train and suddenly leaped into one of the empty box cars.

"Dad! Salt!" she exclaimed. "I just saw someone leap into one of those cars! I'm sure it was Webb!"

"Where?" demanded her father. "Which car?"

"The yellow one. Oh, he'll get away unless we can have him arrested at the next town!"

"He won't escape if I can stop him!" Salt muttered.

Racing across the platform, he waited for the car Penny had indicated. Although the train was moving faster now, he leaped and swung himself to a sitting position in the open doorway.

"Look out! Look out!" Penny screamed in warning.

Behind Salt, the man who had taken refuge in the car, moved stealthily toward him, obviously intending to push him off the train. But the photographer knew what to expect and was prepared.

He whirled suddenly and scrambled to his feet. His attacker caught him slightly off balance, and they went down together, rolling over and over on the straw littered floor.

Worried for Salt, Penny and Mr. Parker ran along beside the train. The publisher tried to leap aboard to help the photographer, but lacking the younger man's athletic prowess, he could not make it. Already winded, he began to fall behind.

Penny kept on and managed to grasp the doorway of the car, but she instantly realized she could not swing herself through the opening. The train now was moving rapidly and gaining speed each moment.

Inside the box car, the two men were rolling over and over, each fighting desperately to gain the advantage. Penny could not see what was happening. Forced by the speed of the train, she let go her hold. Her feet were swept from beneath her, and she stumbled and fell along the right of way.

Before she could scramble to her feet, her father had caught up with her.

"Are you hurt?" he asked anxiously.

Penny's knees were skinned but the injury was so trifling she did not speak of it. Her one concern was for Salt.

"Oh, Dad," she said, grasping his arm nervously. "What are we going to do? That brute may kill him!"

Mr. Parker shared Penny's concern, but he said calmly: "There's only one thing we can do now. We'll have the station agent send a wire to the next station. Police will meet the train and take Webb into custody."

"He may not be on the train by the time it reaches the next town! Oh, Dad, Salt may be half killed before then!"

Penny and her father stared after the departing freight. The engineer whistled for a high trestle spanning a narrow river, and the train began to rumble over it.

Suddenly Penny stiffened into alert attention. In the doorway of the open boxcar, she could see the two struggling men. Mr. Parker, too, became tense.

As they watched fearfully, one of the men was pushed from the car. He rolled over and over down a steep embankment toward the creek bed.

The other man, poised in the doorway an instant, then just before the car reached the trestle, leaped.

CHAPTER 23 - ESCAPE BY NIGHT

Fearful for Salt, Penny and her father ran down the tracks toward the railroad trestle. Scrambling and sliding down the slippery embankment, they saw Salt lying in a heap near the edge of the creek.

Webb, his ankle injured, was trying to hobble toward a corn field just beyond the railroad right of way.

"Get him! Don't let him escape!" Salt cried, raising himself to his knees.

Although alarmed for the photographer who appeared to have been injured by his leap, Penny and her father pursued Webb. Handicapped as he was with an injured ankle, they overtook him by the barbed wire fence.

Already badly battered from the fight, and bruised as a result of his fall from the train, the man put up only a brief struggle as Mr. Parker pinned him to the ground.

"Quick!" the publisher directed Penny. "See what you can do for Salt. He may be badly injured."

The photographer, however, had struggled to his feet. He stood unsteadily, staring down at his torn clothing.

"Are you all right?" Penny asked anxiously, running to his side.

"Yes, I'm okay," he said, gingerly touching a bruised jaw. "Boy! Is that lad a scrapper? Did you see me push him out of the boxcar?"

"We certainly did, and we were frightened half to death! We thought you would be killed."

Hobbling over to the fence, Salt confronted his assailant. Webb's face was a sorry sight. His nose was crimson, both eyes were blackened and his lip was bleeding.

"You may as well come along without making any more trouble," Mr. Parker told him grimly. "Professor Bettenridge has been taken into custody, and the entire fraud has been exposed."

"I figured that out when I heard the mine go off," the man returned sullenly. "Okay, you got me, but I was only carrying out orders. I worked for Professor Bettenridge, but any deals he made were his business, not mine."

"That remains to be seen," replied Mr. Parker. "We'll let you talk to the sheriff. Move along, and no monkey business."

Having no weapon, Salt and the publisher walked on either side of the prisoner, while Penny brought up the rear.

"You don't need to hang onto me," he complained bitterly. "I ain't going to try to escape."

"We're sure you won't," returned Salt, "because we'll be watching you every step of the way."

At first, as the four tramped down the tracks toward the station, the prisoner showed no disposition to talk. But gradually his curiosity gained the better of him. He sought information about Professor Bettenridge's arrest, and then tried to build up a story that would convince his captors he had only been an employee hired on a weekly basis.

"I suppose you know nothing about the *Snark* either," Penny observed bitterly. "After Ben Bartell and I pulled you out of the river, you repaid us by stealing his watch."

To her astonishment, the man reached in his pocket and gave her the timepiece.

"Here," he said gruffly, "give it back to him. I won't need it where I'm going."

"Why did you take the watch when it didn't belong to you?" Penny pursued the subject. "Especially after Ben risked his life to pull you out of the river."

"Oh, I don't know," the man answered impatiently. "I needed a watch, so I took it. Quit askin' so many questions."

"Why were you pushed off the *Snark*?" Penny demanded, refusing to abandon the subject.

She did not expect Webb to answer the question as he had refused to explain at the time of his rescue. To her surprise, he replied grimly:

"They tried to get rid of me. We had a disagreement over a job they wanted me to pull."

"What job was that?" Mr. Parker interposed.

"Dynamiting the Conway Steel Plant."

The words produced a powerful effect upon the publisher, Salt, and Penny. At their stunned silence, Webb added hastily:

"You understand, I didn't do it. They got sore because I refused to pull the job."

"Why, that doesn't make sense," Penny protested. "Evidently, you are mixed up on your dates, because the Conway Plant explosion took place before the night we rescued you from the water."

"Sure, I know," the man muttered, trying to cover his slip of tongue. "They were afraid I'd squawk to the police and that was why they pitched me overboard."

"Who pulled the job?" Salt asked.

"I don't know. Someone was hired to set off the explosion."

Webb's story was accepted but not believed. Penny knew from previous experience that the man was more inclined to tell a lie than the truth. Convinced that he might have been implicated in the explosion, she suddenly recalled his visit to the office of Jason Cordell. Could his call there have any hidden significance?

"You're a friend of Mr. Cordell's, aren't you?" she inquired abruptly.

The question caught Webb off guard. He gave her a quick look but answered in an indifferent way: "Never heard of him."

"I'm certain I saw you in his office," Penny insisted.

Realizing that his loose talk was building up trouble for himself, Webb would say no more. At the sheriff's office, he repeated practically the same story, insisting that he had been hired by Professor Bettenridge on a wage basis, and that he was in no way implicated in the plot to defraud Mr. Johnson.

"Your story doesn't hang together," Mr. Parker said severely. "Naturally you knew that the professor's machine was worthless?"

"Not at first," Webb whined. "He only told me he wanted a mine exploded at a certain time. It was only by chance that I learned he intended to cheat Mr. Johnson."

"Considering the conversations I overheard between you and the professor, that is a little hard to believe," Penny contributed.

"It might go a little easier with you, if you come through with the truth," a deputy sheriff in charge of the office, added. "Anything you want to say before we lock you up?"

Webb hesitated a long while, and then in a subdued voice said: "Okay, I may as well tell you. Sure, I knew the professor and his wife were crooks. They offered me a split on the profits if Johnson bought the secret ray machine."

"Where did you obtain your mines?" Salt asked curiously.

"I don't know," Webb answered, and for once spoke the truth. "Professor Bettenridge had a friend hooked up in a munitions plant who supplied him with a few which were defective."

"Now tell us the truth about the *Snark*," Penny insisted. "You said those men were mixed up in the dynamiting of the Conway Steel Plant. Was that one of the professor's jobs?"

"No, he had nothing to do with it."

"His car was in the vicinity of the plant on the night of the explosion."

"It was just accident then," Webb maintained. "He had nothing to do with it."

"Then you do know the persons involved?"

"If I told you, you wouldn't believe me," Webb said sullenly. "Why not go to the *Snark* and get information first hand if you want it."

It was evident the man would reveal no more, so the deputy sheriff locked him up. Within a few minutes Professor Bettenridge and his wife were brought in, and although they indignantly demanded release, they too were placed in jail cells.

Mr. Johnson who had accompanied Major Bryan to the sheriff's office, seemed rather stunned by the events which had transpired. He shook Penny's hand and could not praise her enough for exposing the professor's trickery.

CHAPTER 23 - ESCAPE BY NIGHT

"What a fool I was," he acknowledged. "His smooth talk hypnotized me. Why, I might have paid a large sum of money to him, if it hadn't been for you. Now I shall prosecute charges vigorously."

The wealthy man tried to press money upon both Penny and Salt, who smilingly refused to accept it. They assured him that knowing the professor's trick had failed was ample reward.

By the time Penny, her father and Salt finally reached the Parker home it was nearly midnight. Somewhat to their surprise, Mrs. Weems was still waiting up.

"I'm so glad you came!" she exclaimed, before they could explain what had happened. "Nearly an hour ago someone telephoned, asking for Penny. I think the message may be important."

"Who was it?" Penny asked.

"A man named Edward McClusky."

"The river diver!" Penny exclaimed. "What did he want, Mrs. Weems?"

"At first he wouldn't tell me, saying he had to talk to you personally. However, I finally persuaded him to trust me with the message. He said: 'Tell Miss Parker that her friend Ben Bartell went aboard the *Snark* last night and hasn't been seen since.'"

CHAPTER 24 - A RAID ON THE SNARK

"Oh, why didn't Mr. McClusky call the police instead?" Penny cried anxiously. "Ben may be in serious trouble!" Turning to her father she added: "Dad, we must go there right away!"

"To the *Snark*?" Mr. Parker frowned and reached for the telephone. "The matter is one for the police, Penny. I'll call the night inspector."

Contacting the police station, the publisher explained why he believed it advisable to search the *Snark*. He was assured that a squad would be sent there at once to investigate.

"We've had other complaints about that vessel," the inspector said. "So far we've not been able to find anything out of the way."

Having notified the police, Mr. Parker felt that his duty was done, but not Penny.

"Dad, can't we go there too?" she pleaded. "Ben is in trouble and we may be able to help him."

"I don't see what we could do, Penny. Besides, you know how I feel about Ben."

"And you're dead wrong. You've done him a dreadful injustice. Tonight may prove it."

Mr. Parker wavered, then suddenly gave in. "All right, get your heavy coat," he instructed. "It will be cold along the waterfront."

Penny raced for the warm garment and joined her father and Salt as they were backing the press car out of the driveway.

"The *Snark* is tied up at Pier 23," Penny directed. "Straight down this street and turn at Jackson."

The car reached the docks, parking alongside a dark warehouse. There was no sign of the police. A short distance away, the *Snark* with only dim deck lights showing, and no one in view, tugged at her heavy ropes.

"We'll wait for the police," Mr. Parker decided.

Within five minutes, two cars glided noiselessly up to the pier and a dozen men in uniform leaped out. Captain Bricker, in charge of the squad, strode to the *Snark* and called loudly: "Ahoy, there!"

No one answered.

"Ahoy, the *Snark*!" he shouted again.

Still receiving no answer, he ordered his men aboard. Single file, they crawled cautiously up a ladder to the dark deck.

"Anyone aboard?" the captain called once more.

Salt, Mr. Parker and Penny, eager for first hand information, followed the policemen up the ladder.

"My men will search the vessel," Captain Bricker told them, "but no one appears to be aboard. Everything seems in order."

Spreading out over the ship, the policemen returned one by one to report they could find nothing amiss. Not even a watchman was aboard.

"This seems to be a wild-goose chase, Captain," Mr. Parker apologized. "Sorry to have bothered you. We considered our information reliable."

The policemen began to leave. Penny, lingering on deck until the last, was being helped onto the ladder by Captain Bricker, when they both heard a sound below decks.

"What was that?" the officer muttered, listening alertly.

"It sounded like someone thumping on a wall," Penny cried. "There it is again!"

The noise was not repeated a third time, but Captain Bricker had heard enough to make him believe that someone remained below. Drawing his revolver, and warning Penny to keep back, he started down the dark companionway.

CHAPTER 24 - A RAID ON THE SNARK

At a safe distance, Penny trailed him. His bright flashlight beam cut paths of light over the walls as he tried the doors.

"Anyone here?" he shouted.

A thumping noise came from a room on the right. Guided by the sound, Captain Bricker tried the door. It was locked.

A powerfully built man, the officer hurled his weight against the door, and the lock gave way. Keeping back, lest he become a target for a bullet, he kicked the door open. The room was empty! But, the flashlight beam caught the outline of a trapdoor in the floor. The officer flung it open. Below, in the hold, lay a man gagged and bound hand and foot.

Following the police officer into the room, Penny uttered a little cry as she recognized Ben Bartell. Blinking owlishly in the light which had been focused upon him, he was a deplorable sight. His face was bruised, his hair matted with blood, and one eye was swollen almost shut.

"Oh, Ben! What have they done to you?" Penny gasped in horror.

Captain Bricker cut the young man free, and pulled the gag from his mouth. He helped Ben into a chair and then went to another cabin for water.

"Who did this to you?" Penny asked, rubbing the reporter's hands to restore circulation.

He seemed too exhausted to reply so she did not urge him to speak. The captain brought water which Ben drank thirstily.

"He's evidently been tied up several hours," the officer commented.

"Since last night," Ben whispered, moistening his cracked lips.

"How did you get aboard?"

"I sneaked on when no one was looking—wanted to see what I could learn."

"Who were the men that tied you up?"

"Don't know. But before they caught me, I heard plenty. The men on this boat are mixed up in the dynamiting of the Conway Steel Plant."

Penny nodded, for this information correlated with what she already had learned.

"Was Webb Nelson involved in the plot?" she asked eagerly.

"He set off the dynamite according to what I overheard last night," Ben revealed. "But he got into a fight with the gang over his pay for the job. He tried to shake them down for a big sum, threatening to spill everything to the police if they didn't cough up. It ended up in a fight, and Webb was pushed overboard."

"Then we pulled him out of the river," Penny supplied. "But he refused to tell us a thing."

"He knew better than to spill the story because he would have implicated himself. And the gang aboard this boat had no fear either, because they figured he was only pulling a bluff."

"But who was behind the plot?" Penny asked, puzzled. "What did the men hope to gain by dynamiting the plant?"

"They did it on orders from a man higher up—a man who personally hates the owner of the Conway Steel Plant."

"Then it was a grudge matter?" Captain Bricker inquired dubiously.

"Not entirely," Ben returned. "Labor troubles are mixed up in it. This man, who represents a minor faction, has been trying to gain control over the employes without much success. By planning a series of accidents similar to the dynamiting, he thought he might bring the management around to his way of thinking."

"Who is the leader?" Penny demanded impatiently.

Ben hesitated. "I hate to say," he confessed, "because I'm not absolutely certain. In the conversation I overheard before I was caught, he wasn't mentioned by name. But by putting two and two together, I have a fairly good idea."

"Guessing won't do in this business," said Captain Bricker.

"I know that," admitted Ben. "But here is one bit of fact I gained. The big boss was at the factory on the night of the explosion. In fact, he was nearly caught, and a photographer snapped a picture of him as he fled."

"You're sure of that?" Penny demanded excitedly.

"Yes, I heard the men talking about it. The boss has been worried for fear that picture will show up and convict him."

"Now I'm beginning to understand," Penny murmured. "It explains why the *Star* photography room was broken into several times. Someone was after those plates which weren't there!"

"What became of the pictures?" Captain Bricker asked. "They'll prove valuable evidence."

"Why, Salt Sommers has the camera and plates in the press car. Of course, we don't know what the plates will show until they're developed."

"We must have them at once," the captain said. He turned again to Ben. "Now did you know any of the men who attacked you?"

"Not a one. But I can give you a fairly good description of most of them. They're waterfront riff-raff."

"In that case some of them may have their pictures in our files," the captain said. "I'll issue orders to round up all loiterers in this neighborhood. You should be able to identify most of them in a police line-up."

"I'm sure I can."

"Now about the higher-up, who engineered the scheme. You said you had an idea who he is."

"That's right," agreed Ben. "The men spoke of him as a publisher. I don't like to accuse him outright, because I'll be suspected of trying to get even with a man I hate."

Light came swiftly to Penny. Into her mind leaped many facts hitherto puzzling, but which now seemed suddenly clear. The open skylight—the building adjoining the *Star*—Webb Nelson's call upon the editor of the *Mirror*.

"Ben, you don't need to accuse anyone!" she cried. "I'll do it myself. The man is Jason Cordell, and I think we can prove it too!"

CHAPTER 25 - PICTURE PROOF

"Yes, Jason Cordell is the man responsible," Ben agreed soberly. "I can't prove it, but in my own mind I'm sure."

"You used to work for him, didn't you?" the police captain inquired, the inflection of his voice implying that he thought the former reporter might be prejudiced.

"I was fired," Ben admitted readily. "Cordell let me go and blacklisted me everywhere to prevent me from exposing him. He wanted to discredit me, so that anything I might say would carry no weight."

"Why were you really discharged, Ben?" Penny asked. "What did you learn about Mr. Cordell?"

"That he had pulled off no end of crooked deals and that he was mixed up with this outlaw labor group. Over a period of three or four years, Cordell has made a mint of money, and not from his paper either!"

"We'll question Cordell tonight," Captain Bricker promised. "The trick now is to get you to the station for first aid treatment. Then we'll want you to look through the police morgue and identify the pictures of as many of the *Snark's* crew as you can."

The officer turned to Penny. "As for those undeveloped plates, can you get them right away?"

"I think so," Penny returned. While Captain Bricker helped Ben up the companionway, she ran ahead to find her father and Salt and tell them of the latest developments.

The two were waiting in the press car. But when Mr. Parker learned how significant the pictures of the Conway Plant explosion might prove to be, he surprised Penny by declining to turn them over immediately to the police.

"We may want those plates for the *Star*," he declared. "If the police once get their hands on them, it might be a job to get them back again in time to be of any use to us."

"But Jason Cordell's arrest may depend upon them," Penny protested.

"We'll have the plates developed, and let police see them," Mr. Parker decided. "But the plates must remain in our hands. Come on, let's go!"

At a nod from the publisher, Salt started the press car, and without being instructed, headed for the *Star* building.

"How long will it take you to develop those plates?" Mr. Parker asked the photographer.

"Ten minutes."

"Good!" approved the publisher. "If they reveal anything, we'll telephone the police station at once."

As the car coasted to a standstill alongside the *Star* building, Penny's gaze roved to the darkened offices next door. All of the floors save one were without light. But in the suite occupied by the *Mirror*, a man plainly could be seen moving to and fro.

"There is Jason Cordell now!" she drew attention to him. "Why do you suppose he's at his office so late tonight?"

"There's no crime in that," replied Mr. Parker. "He may be guilty as Ben says, but I'll not believe it until I have the proof."

Letting themselves into the newspaper building, the three went up the back stairs to the photography studio. Salt immediately set about developing the plates.

"Something is coming up all right!" he declared jubilantly, as he rocked the developer tray back and forth.

In a few minutes, Salt had washed the plates and was able to examine them beneath the red light. One was blurred and revealed little. But the other plainly showed a man fleeing toward a waiting car.

"Why, the man is Webb Nelson!" Penny exclaimed, recognizing him.

"But notice the driver of the car," Salt said. "It's Jason Cordell! Ben was right."

"Then the man is guilty!" Penny cried. "Oh, Dad, I was certain of it!"

Mr. Parker scanned the plate carefully to ascertain there was no possible mistake.

"Yes, it's Jason Cordell," he agreed. "The truth is hard to believe. Why, I lunched with him only yesterday—"

"Dad, he's a criminal no matter how respectable he has acted."

"You're right," acknowledged Mr. Parker. "I'll notify the police at once and have him picked up for questioning."

Transmitting the important information to police headquarters, Mr. Parker talked with Captain Bricker who promised to take personal charge of the matter. As the publisher hung up the receiver, he was startled to have Penny grasp his arm. Excitedly, she pointed out the window.

"Now what?" he asked, failing to understand.

"The light just went off in Mr. Cordell's office! He's leaving!"

"Then we'll stop him," her father decided. "Salt, you stay here and rush that plate through! I'll detain Cordell by one means or another until the police arrive!"

With Penny close beside him, he ran down the back stairs to the street. Breathlessly they arrived at the next building. The elevator was not running, but they could hear someone coming down the stairway. Then Jason Cordell, a brief case tucked under his arm, came into view. He stopped short upon seeing Mr. Parker and his daughter.

"Working late?" Mr. Parker inquired pleasantly.

"That's right," agreed the other. He would have walked on, but the publisher barred the exit.

"By the way, I met a friend of yours tonight," Mr. Parker said, stalling for time.

"That so? Who was he?"

"Webb Nelson."

Mr. Cordell's face did not change expression, but his eyes narrowed guardedly.

"Not a friend of mine," he corrected carelessly.

"But I've seen him in your office," Penny said.

Mr. Cordell looked her straight in the eyes and smiled as if in amusement. "That may be," he admitted, "but all who come to my office are not my friends."

He tried to pass again, but Mr. Parker stood his ground. "Say, what is this?" Mr. Cordell demanded, suddenly suspicious.

"I'm afraid I'll have to ask you a few questions about your friend Webb Nelson. Suppose we go back to your office."

"Suppose we don't," Cordell retorted. "I'm tired and I'm going home. If you want to see me, come around tomorrow during business hours."

"Which may be too late."

"I don't know what you're talking about," the *Mirror* editor blustered. "Furthermore, I'm not interested. Get out of my way."

Instead, Mr. Parker grasped him firmly by the arm. Cordell tried to jerk free, and in so doing, dropped his brief case, which Penny promptly seized.

"Give that to me!" the man shouted furiously.

Penny smiled, for through the plate glass window she had observed the approach of a police car. Another moment and uniformed men were swarming about Mr. Cordell.

"What is the meaning of this?" the man demanded angrily. "I'll report you all to the Safety Director who is my friend!"

"You'll report to him all right," agreed Captain Bricker. "Now come along quietly. If you can answer a few questions satisfactorily, you'll be allowed to return home."

"What do you want to know?" Cordell asked sullenly.

"Where were you on the night of the 16th?"

"Now how should I know?" the man retorted sarcastically. "I can't remember that far back. But probably I was home in bed."

"You're wanted in connection with the Conway dynamiting," the officer informed him.

CHAPTER 25 - PICTURE PROOF

Mr. Cordell snorted with anger. "Of all the ridiculous charges! I know nothing about the affair."

Out of the door burst Salt Sommers. He was without a hat, but he carried a picture, still wet, in the palm of his hand.

"So you know nothing about the dynamiting," he mimicked. "Well, gentlemen, take a look at this!"

Mr. Cordell and the policemen gathered about him, studying the photograph. Plainly it showed Webb Nelson fleeing toward a car driven by the *Mirror* editor.

"What does this prove?" the man blustered. "I admit the car is mine. I was driving past the plant at the time of the explosion. This fellow, Nelson, leaped into my auto and ordered me to drive on."

"A moment ago you claimed you weren't even near the Conway Plant," Penny tripped him. "You knew Webb Nelson very well. Furthermore, you entered the *Star* offices several times trying to get your hands on this picture!"

"Ridiculous!"

"At least once when you found the stairway door locked, you went in through the skylight," Penny accused.

"Of all the crazy ideas!" The editor laughed jeeringly. "Imagine me crawling through a skylight!"

"I notice your coat has a torn place," Penny said, taking a scrap of blue wool from her purse. "This, I believe, is a perfect match."

Mr. Cordell gazed at the wool and shrugged. "All right," he admitted coolly. "I did crawl through the skylight twice to see if I could find the picture. I knew this fool photographer had snapped a picture of me, and I feared I might be falsely accused."

"Then you knew Nelson was mixed up in the dynamiting?" Captain Bricker questioned.

"I wasn't certain," Mr. Cordell said in confusion. "The reason I didn't report to the police was that I was afraid of being involved. After that night, Webb Nelson tried to blackmail me. Because of my position, I dared have no publicity."

The *Mirror* editor's explanation carried a certain amount of conviction, and Penny was dismayed to hear Captain Bricker assure him that if a mistake had been made he would be granted freedom immediately after he had talked to the police chief.

"I shall accompany you without protest," the *Mirror* editor returned stiffly. "Later I shall file charges against those who have tried to damage my character."

Captain Bricker asked Salt for the picture which he intended to take to police headquarters.

"May I see it a moment?" Penny requested.

He gave the picture to her. She studied it and her face brightened. "Captain Bricker, look at this!" she exclaimed, pointing to an object in the car which barely was noticeable.

Everyone gathered about Penny, peering at the photograph. On the rear seat of the car driven by Mr. Cordell was a box which plainly bore the printing: "Salvage Company—Explosives."

"Ed McClusky who works for the Salvage Company, told me that dynamite had been stolen from his firm," Penny declared. "And here it is in Mr. Cordell's automobile! Apparently, he wasn't just driving by the plant at the time of the explosion! This picture proves why he was there!"

"Right you are, young lady," chuckled Captain Bricker. "You've pinned the goods on him for fair." Prodding the *Mirror* editor with his stick, he ordered curtly: "Get along, you! This puts a different face on it. You'll be spending the rest of the night in the Safety building."

After Mr. Cordell, still protesting his innocence, had been taken away, Penny, her father, and Salt returned to the deserted newspaper building.

"Will Cordell manage to get free?" she asked anxiously.

"Not a chance of it," Mr. Parker answered. "That picture tags him right. With Ed McClusky and Ben to testify against him, he's the same as convicted now."

"Speaking of Ben, what's to be done about him, Dad?"

"We'll give him a job here. He's had unfair treatment, but we'll make it up to him. However, we'll have to let one employee go."

"Not me?" Penny asked anxiously.

"No," her father laughed. "It's your friend, Elda Hunt. Her attitude isn't right. We've tried to give her a chance, but over and over she has demonstrated that she isn't cut out to be a newspaper woman."

"She'll probably blame me for her discharge," Penny sighed. "Not that it matters. I ceased worrying about Elda a long while ago."

"She'll have no difficulty getting work elsewhere, and I hope she'll be better adjusted."

"How about the story of Mr. Cordell's arrest? And the picture?" Penny inquired. "Will the *Star* print them tomorrow?"

"On the front page of our first edition," Mr. Parker chuckled. "Salt didn't turn over the plate to the police, so we're all set. By morning, the story should be bigger and better than ever. By then, the guilt will be well pinned on Cordell, and some of the *Snark* gang may have been rounded up."

Curious to learn the very latest details, Salt called the police station. He was told that Ben Bartell had identified several of the *Snark's* crew from police pictures, and it was expected all would be arrested within twenty-four hours.

"Not a bad night's work," Mr. Parker chuckled, as he snapped off the photography room lights. "Everything locked?"

"How about the skylight?" asked Penny.

"Open again," reported Salt as he checked it. "It's just no use trying to get folks to cooperate around here. Too many fresh air fiends."

"Let it stay unlocked," Mr. Parker directed carelessly. "With our prowler safely behind bars, we've no further cause for worry." He looked at his watch. "Now, even though it is late, suppose we go and celebrate?"

"Oh, fine!" cried Penny. "And why not stop at the Safety building and ask Ben Bartell to go with us? I want to tell him about his new job."

"So do I," agreed her father heartily. "Where shall we go?"

Penny linked arms with Salt and her father, skipping as she piloted them down the dark hall.

"Just a quiet place where they serve big juicy steaks," she decided. "If I know Ben, that's what he would like best of all."

WHISPERING WALLS

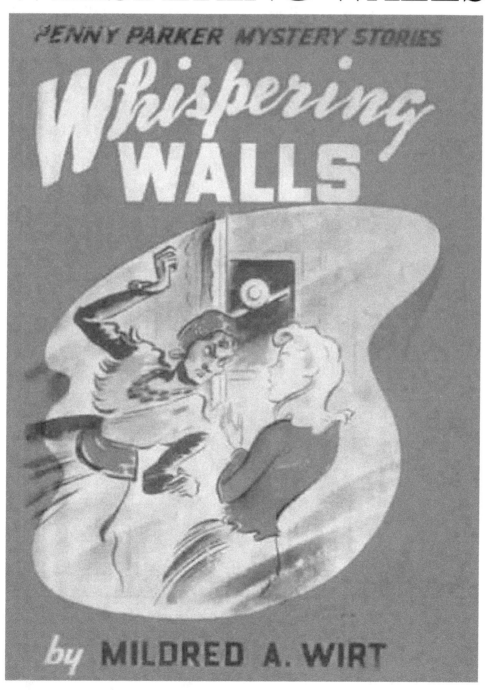

The floor beneath her feet suddenly gave way.

CHAPTER 1 - THE PLUMED SERPENT

Smoothly and with accurate aim, the slim girl in blue sweater and swinging skirt sent the heavy ball crashing down the polished floor of the bowling alley.

"Another strike, Penny!" cried her school companion, Louise Sidell, watching the tenpins topple helter skelter and vanish out of sight. "You're certainly going like a house afire today!"

"Lucky, that's all." Penny Parker's friendly grin widened as she chalked up the score. Brushing aside a sandy-gold lock of hair which had dropped over one eye, she suddenly squinted at the wall clock. "Ten minutes until four o'clock!" she exclaimed. "Lou, unless we call it a day, I'll be late for work!"

"You and your work!" scoffed Louise, but she quickly sat down to remove her bowling shoes. "Why spend all your spare time at that old newspaper?"

"The *Riverview Star* is the best daily in the city!" Penny shot back proudly. "Anyway, I like being a reporter."

"I'll give you no argument on that point, my pet. You love it! Especially poking that freckled little nose of yours into every big story or mystery that comes along! Confess now, isn't it the excitement you like, rather than the work?"

A twitch of Penny's lips acknowledged the truth of her chum's observation. Off and on for several years she had served in many capacities on the *Star*, a daily Riverview newspaper owned by her father, Anthony Parker.

Many of the publication's best stories had carried her name. Now that school had started again, she was unable to work full time, but on this particular Saturday afternoon she had promised Editor DeWitt she would report at two o'clock. She had no intention of being late.

"Let's go," she urged, picking up her coat.

Louise trailed Penny to a desk where the cashier was absently listening to a short wave radio. As they paid their bill, the instrument suddenly blared a police order:

"Patrol 34—First National Bank, Main and Front Streets. Repeating, First National Bank, Main and Front Streets. See complainant. Patrol 34 in service."

To Louise it was only a meaningless jumble of words but Penny instantly pricked up her ears.

"Front and Main is just around the corner! Maybe there's been a robbery, Lou!"

"I hope not," laughed Louise. "The First National's where I keep my money. All $28.50 of it!"

Sweeping her change from the counter, Penny glanced again at the clock and came to a quick decision. Doubtless, the *Star* office would send a reporter to check the police call, but considerable time might elapse before anyone reached the bank.

"Let's jog over there and see what's doing," she proposed.

Louise nodded, hastily pulling a tight-fitting hat over her dark curls. Penny was already out of the door, walking so fast that her chum was hard pressed to overtake her.

Rounding the corner at Main and Front Streets, the girls were just in time to see a patrol car park at the curb in front of the bank. A police sergeant was at the wheel, but before Penny could hail him, he and a companion vanished into the building. A third man posted himself at the door of the bank.

Penny walked over to him. "Anything doing?" she inquired in a friendly, off-hand way. "A robbery?"

"I wouldn't know," he replied curtly.

Fishing in a cluttered purse, Penny came up with a press card. "I'm from the *Star*," she added, waving her credentials before him.

"You'll have to talk to the sergeant if you want to get any information," he said, relaxing slightly. "Go on in, if you want to."

Louise kept close to Penny's side as they started into the bank. But the policeman brought her up short by saying: "Just a minute, sister. Where's your card?"

"She's with me," said Penny with careless assurance.

"So I see," observed the patrolman dryly. "She can't go in without a card."

Argument was useless. Decidedly crestfallen, Louise retreated to wait, while Penny went on into the darkened building. Curtains had been drawn in the big marble-floored bank, and the place appeared deserted. Teller cages were locked and empty, for the bank had closed to the public at noon.

Pausing, Penny heard the faint and distant hum of voices. She glanced upward to a second story gallery devoted to offices, and saw two policemen talking to a third man who leaned against the iron railing.

"Apparently this is no robbery," Penny thought, taking the marble steps two at a time. "Wonder what has happened?"

Breathlessly, she reached the top of the stairs. A short, thin man with glasses and a noticeably nervous manner stood talking to the two policemen. The sergeant, his back to Penny, started taking down notes.

"I'm Sergeant Gray," the policeman said. "What's your name?"

"Albert Potts," the man replied.

"A clerk here?"

"Secretary to Mr. Hamilton Rhett, the bank president. I called the police because a situation has developed which worries me. This afternoon I talked to Mrs. Rhett who gave me no satisfaction whatsoever. I said to myself, 'Albert Potts, this is a case for the police.' But there must be no publicity."

"What's wrong?" Sergeant Gray asked impatiently.

"Mr. Rhett has disappeared. Exactly nine days ago at three o'clock he put on his hat, walked out of the bank and hasn't been seen since."

Here indeed was news! Mr. Rhett was socially prominent and a very wealthy banker. His disappearance would be certain to create a sensation in Riverview.

"So Mr. Rhett walked out of here nine days ago," Sergeant Gray commented. "Why wasn't it reported earlier to the police?"

"Because at first we thought nothing of it. If you will excuse me for saying so, Mr. Rhett never has taken his bank duties very seriously. He comes and goes very much as he pleases. Some days he fails to show up until afternoon. On several occasions he has been absent for a week at a time."

"Then why does it seem so unusual now?"

"Yesterday I telephoned Mrs. Rhett. She said she had no idea what has become of her husband. I suggested notifying the police, but she discouraged it. In fact, she hung up the receiver while I was talking to her. Altogether, she acted in a most peculiar manner."

"That was yesterday, you say?"

"Yes, I told myself, 'Albert Potts, if Mrs. Rhett isn't worried about her husband's absence, it's none of your business.' I should have dismissed the matter thereupon, except that today I learned about the missing bonds."

"Missing bonds?" inquired the sergeant alertly. "Go on."

"Mr. Rhett handles securities for various trust funds. At the time of his disappearance, $250,000 in negotiable government bonds were in his possession."

"You're suggesting robbery?"

"I don't know what to think. Mr. Rhett should have returned the securities to our vault in the basement. I assumed he had done so, until this morning in making a thorough check, I learned not a single bond had been turned in. I can only conclude that Mr. Rhett had them in his portfolio when he walked out of the bank."

"So you decided to notify the police?"

"Exactly. It was my duty. Understand I wish to bring no embarrassment to Mrs. Rhett or to cast reflection upon my employer but—"

Albert Potts broke off, his gaze focusing upon Penny who had edged closer.

"Now who are you?" he demanded suspiciously.

Stepping forward, Penny introduced herself as a *Star* reporter.

CHAPTER 1 - THE PLUMED SERPENT

"You have no business here!" the secretary snapped. "If you overheard what I just said, you're not to print a line of it! Mrs. Rhett would never approve."

"I did hear what you told Sergeant Gray," replied Penny with dignity. "However, any report to the police is a matter of public record. It is for our editor to decide whether or not to use the story."

Behind thick glasses, Mr. Potts' watery eyes glinted angrily. He appeared on the verge of ordering the girl from the bank, but with an obvious effort regained control of his temper, and said curtly:

"If you must write a story, mind you keep the facts straight. Mr. Rhett hasn't been seen in nine days and that's all I know. He may return tomorrow. He may never appear."

"Then you believe he's been kidnapped?" Penny asked.

"I don't know. There's been no ransom demand."

"Perhaps he absconded with the $250,000 in bonds."

"Don't quote me as making such a statement even if it should prove true! Mr. Rhett is a wealthy man—or rather, he acquired a fortune when he married a rich widow who set him up here as bank president. But don't quote me on that either!" he exclaimed as Penny jotted down a few notes. "Leave my name out of it entirely!"

"Let's have a look at Mr. Rhett's office," proposed Sergeant Gray.

"Follow me, please."

His poise regained, Albert Potts led the way down the gallery to a large, spacious office room. On the polished mahogany desk rested a picture of an attractive woman in her early forties whom Penny guessed to be Mrs. Rhett. A door opened from the office into a directors' room, and another onto a narrow outdoor balcony overlooking Front Street.

Sergeant Gray and the patrolman made a thorough inspection of the two rooms and Mr. Rhett's desk.

"When last I saw the bonds, Mr. Rhett had them in the top drawer," the secretary volunteered eagerly. "He should have returned them to the vault, but he failed to do so. Now they're gone."

"Then you examined the desk?"

"Oh, yes, I considered it my duty."

While Penny remained in the background, Sergeant Gray asked Mr. Potts a number of questions about the bank president's habits, and particularly his recent visitors. The secretary, whose fund of information seemed inexhaustible, had ready answers at the tip of his tongue. He even produced a memo pad upon which the names of several persons had been written.

"These were Mr. Rhett's visitors on his last day here," he explained. "So far as I know, all were business acquaintances."

Writing down the names for future checking, Sergeant Gray inquired if Mr. Rhett had disagreed with any of the callers.

"A quarrel, you mean?" Mr. Potts hesitated, then answered with reluctance. "Only with his wife."

"Mrs. Rhett came to the bank the day your employer last was seen?"

"Yes, they were to have had lunch together. She came late and they quarreled about Mr. Rhett's work here in the bank. Finally she went away alone."

"You heard the conversation between them?"

"Well, no," Albert Potts said quickly. "Naturally I tried not to listen, but I did hear some of it."

"Mrs. Rhett may be able to explain her husband's absence," commented Sergeant Gray.

"She refused me any information when I telephoned. That was one reason I decided to notify the police. The loss of $250,000 could be very embarrassing to the bank."

"Who owns the bonds?"

"They belong to the Fred Harrington estate, 2756 Brightdale Avenue. If they aren't produced soon, there will be trouble. I've worked here for 15 years. You don't think anyone could possibly blame me, do you?"

The sergeant gave him a quick glance, but made no reply as he reexamined the mahogany desk. Finding nothing of interest, he slammed the top drawer shut.

From the back of the desk, a piece of paper fluttered to the floor, almost at Penny's feet. Evidently it had jarred from the rear side of an overflowing drawer, or had been held between desk and plaster wall.

Without thinking, Penny stooped to retrieve the sheet. She glanced at it carelessly, and then with a shock of surprise, really studied it. Drawn across the center of the paper in black and red ink was a crude but sinister-looking winged serpent.

Raising her eyes, Penny saw Albert Potts' cold gaze upon her. Was it imagination or did his shriveled face mirror fear?

"What have you there?" he demanded.

Penny gave the paper to Sergeant Gray. Mr. Potts moved quickly forward, to peer over the man's shoulder.

"A plumed serpent!" he exclaimed.

"And read the words beneath it," directed Penny.

Under the drawing in a cramped hand, had been scribbled: *"This shall be the end."*

CHAPTER 2 - AN UNEXPLAINED DISAPPEARANCE

Sergeant Gray studied the strange drawing for a moment and then said to Albert Potts: "Can you explain the meaning of this picture? And the words written beneath it?"

For the first time since the start of the interview, the bank secretary seemed at a loss for words. Finally he stammered: "Why, no—I've never seen the drawing before. I don't know how it got into Mr. Rhett's desk."

"You seemed to recognize the picture," interposed Penny. "At least you called it a plumed serpent."

"It is the symbol of an ancient cult, or at least that is what I take it to be. I've seen similar drawings in library books."

"And the writing beneath it?" probed the sergeant.

"I am not sure," the secretary murmured, ill at ease. "It slightly resembles Mr. Rhett's writing."

"You say you can't explain how the paper came to be in Mr. Rhett's desk?"

"My employer's private life is none of my concern."

"What do you mean—his private life?"

"Well, I hadn't intended to tell you this," Potts said unwillingly. "The truth is, Mr. Rhett was a strange man. He had queer interests and hobbies. I have been told he collects weird trophies of ancient cults."

"Then this drawing probably has a connection with your employer's hobby?"

"I wouldn't know," shrugged Potts. "If it weren't for the handwriting, I might think someone had sent a warning to him. As it is, I'm completely in the dark."

"Mr. Rhett had enemies?"

"He was a ruthless man and many persons disliked him. His friends were queer too. He preferred low class persons to people of culture and refinement. Why, only two days before his disappearance, he deliberately kept one of our largest stockholders waiting an hour while he chatted with a building porter! It was very humiliating! I had to tell Mrs. Biggs he was in conference, but I think she suspected the truth."

"Do you have a photograph of Mr. Rhett?" the sergeant asked.

"I deeply regret I haven't. For that matter, I never have seen a picture of him."

"But you can describe the man?"

"Oh, yes. He is forty-five, though he looks older. His hair is gray at the temples. He wore an expensive tailored suit—brown, I believe. One of the most distinguishing marks I should say, is a scar on his left cheek."

"I'll send one of the detectives around," Sergeant Gray promised. He had completed his investigation and with the other patrolman, started to leave the office.

Albert Potts drew a deep breath and seemed to relax. Only then did it occur to Penny that throughout the greater part of the interview he had stood in front of the outside balcony door, as if to shield it from attention.

Taking the plumed serpent drawing with them, Sergeant Gray and the patrolman left the office. Penny lingered, intending to ask Albert Potts a few questions about Mr. Rhett. But the man gave her no opportunity.

Barely had the others gone when he turned toward her, making no effort to mask his dislike.

"Now will you get out of here?" he demanded.

His tone annoyed Penny, and perversely made her determined to take her time in leaving. Deliberately she sidled over to the balcony door.

"Where does this lead?" she inquired.

"Outside."

Penny opened the door, but Potts immediately barred the way.

"There's nothing there except a balcony! Just get out of this office so I can lock up and go home! I've had a hard day, and you're making it worse!"

For a reason she could not have explained, Penny felt a deep urge to annoy the nervous little man further. Ignoring his protests, she pushed past him out onto the balcony.

Guarded by a high iron railing and fence, it extended for perhaps fifty feet along several offices. At each end, projecting from the sloping slate roof, was a grotesque decorative gargoyle.

"You see!" rasped Potts. "There's nothing here. Now are you satisfied?"

The gargoyle near the door had drawn Penny's attention. Its carved stone body angled out from the building, terminating in a horned animal head with massive open jaws.

"Will it bite?" Grinning impishly at Potts she started to thrust an arm between the stone teeth.

To her astonishment, he suddenly seized her and gave her a hard shove through the doorway into Mr. Rhett's office. She resisted and he immediately released her. But he locked the balcony door.

"You're driving me crazy!" he cried furiously. "Now get out of here! Unless you do—"

Potts was such a ridiculous little fellow that Penny could not be afraid of him. However, she decided that her joke had been carried a trifle too far.

"Okay, I'm going," she muttered. "Thanks for all your courtesy."

"Mind you print only the truth in your paper," Potts hurled after her as she went out the door. "If you don't, you may have a lawsuit on your hands!"

Penny reached the street to find that the police car had gone and Louise was nowhere to be seen. Deciding that her chum had grown tired of waiting, she hastened to a nearby drugstore to telephone the *Star* office.

Editor DeWitt answered, and Penny gave him the story straight and fast.

"Hamilton Rhett, the banker!" he exclaimed. "Sure you got the name right?"

"Positive!"

"This is apt to be a big story, especially if the man was kidnapped or walked off with the bonds! Grab a taxi and run out to the Rhett estate. Get all the dope you can from Mrs. Rhett, and don't forget pictures! We'll want one of Rhett. Better take all she has of him to keep the *Times* from getting them! Got that straight?"

"I think so."

"Okay, go right to town on the old gal and learn everything you can about her quarrel with Rhett! I'll send a photographer out there as soon as I can round one up."

Penny felt a trifle weak as she hung up the receiver. Editor DeWitt took it for granted she would bring in a bang-up story when she returned to the newspaper office. But from what she had learned of Mrs. Rhett, she surmised that an interview might not be granted willingly.

Looking up the address of the Rhett estate, Penny hailed a passing taxi. As the cab sped along the winding river boulevard, she speculated upon how best to approach Mrs. Rhett.

"I wish I were more experienced as a reporter," she thought, nervously examining her pocketbook to be certain she had paper and pencil. "Something tells me this story will be hard to get."

The only daughter of a distinguished newspaper owner and publisher, Penny considered herself an essential part of the *Star* office. Even as a youngster in pigtails, she had haunted the big noisy newsroom, pecking at the typewriters and making a pest of herself.

From her father, Editor DeWitt, Jerry Livingston, a star reporter, and the printers who adored her, the alert girl had gleaned much useful information. But there were yawning gaps in her newspaper experience. No one realized it better than she.

Gazing thoughtfully toward the river, Penny recalled the first story she ever had written, carried in the paper under the title, "Tale of the Witch Doll." Another yarn, "The Vanishing Houseboat," also had been bannered across the front page of the *Star*, but in acquiring that story Penny and Jerry had nearly lost their lives.

Slight wonder that Mrs. Maud Weems, the Parker housekeeper, was reluctant to see the girl she loved so dearly take up a journalistic career. Sadly she declared that Penny's nose for news and mystery would lead her into serious trouble. Mr. Parker, however, did not worry. "Penny has good horse sense," he said. "And she was born with printer's ink in her blood stream!"

The taxi stopped with a jerk in front of a large red brick mansion. Large acreage was enclosed by a wooden rail fence flanked by tall untrimmed bushes.

"Shall I wait?" inquired the cab driver as Penny alighted.

CHAPTER 2 - AN UNEXPLAINED DISAPPEARANCE

She shook her head, started to pay him, then thought of a better idea. "Charge this to the *Star*," she instructed.

The cab driver looked a trifle worried as if he were fearful of losing the fare, so Penny flashed her press card again. It worked like magic.

"Okay, a charge it is," he agreed. He shifted gears and drove away.

No sooner had Penny dismissed the cab than she regretted it. Although she expected to catch a ride with the *Star* photographer back to the paper, the mansion had a deserted look. As she walked up the gravel path, she noticed that many of the shades were drawn.

"There's no one here," she thought. "I've wasted my time coming."

Nevertheless, Penny walked on to the front door to ring the doorbell. Instead she found a brass knocker in the shape of an ugly carved face. She stared at it a moment, then let it fall against the brass plate.

As Penny had feared, no one came to admit her. She was turning away in defeat, when she fancied she saw a shade move in one of the upstairs rooms. Encouraged, she knocked again.

Still there was no answer, but distinctly she saw the curtain flutter. Stepping back a pace, she gazed upward.

A dark face was visible in a circular window of one of the tower rooms. For a moment appraising eyes focused upon her. Then the curtain jerked convulsively, and the man was gone.

CHAPTER 3 - A THATCHED ROOF COTTAGE

Satisfied that the house was not deserted, Penny hammered harder on the massive oaken door with the brass knocker. Still no one came to admit her.

"Someone is here," she thought, intensely annoyed. "Well, if he can be stubborn, so can I! I'll make such a nuisance of myself, they'll have to let me in."

She hammered steadily with the knocker for a half minute, then she experimented with pattern knocks, in interesting combinations of dots and dashes.

Suddenly, the window above her head flew open, and the same dark-faced man peered angrily down at her.

"What you want?" he demanded in an unpleasant voice.

"Why, I should like to see Mrs. Rhett," Penny replied politely. "She's here, isn't she?"

"Maybe she is, maybe she isn't," was the sharp retort. "Who are you?"

Resenting the man's unfriendly attitude, Penny nevertheless answered that she was from the *Riverview Star* and desired to interview Mrs. Rhett about her missing husband.

"Madam not seeing anyone. Go 'way now!"

The window slammed shut.

Convinced that the man, evidently a servant, had acted upon instructions from Mrs. Rhett, Penny wondered what to do. She considered returning to the *Star* office to explain to Editor DeWitt.

But in Mr. DeWitt's dictionary there was no such word as failure. He would cock an eyebrow at her, growl: "So you couldn't get in, eh?" and promptly send a more aggressive reporter to the mansion.

"I could force my way in, but that's trespassing," she reflected with deepening gloom. "If I were thrown into jail, Mr. DeWitt probably wouldn't even bother to bail me out! He'd say I didn't use my head in an emergency."

Penny decided to wait for the *Star* photographer, who also had been sent out. In a tight pinch, photographers nearly always could come up with a picture. Between them they might think of a means of getting into the mansion.

"I hope Salt Sommers is sent here," she thought. "He's a good scout. He'll help me get the story."

Penny glanced hopefully toward the highway, but the press car was not to be seen. With a sigh, she slowly circled the house.

The building, no longer new, once had been one of Riverview's finest homes. Now the red brick exterior had become discolored, and trees and bushes disclosed lack of skilled care. A hedge flanking the walk had been trimmed unevenly. The lawn was badly mowed, with many weeds going to seed.

Nevertheless, the estate was impressive, and Penny walked along a sloping path to a pool of water lilies. Seating herself on the cement rim, she dabbled her hand in the water. A moment later, raising her eyes, she caught a flash of color at one of the mansion windows.

"I'm being watched," she thought. "Perhaps if I poke around here long enough, Mrs. Rhett will decide to see me."

However, there was no further movement at the window, and presently Penny wandered around to the rear of the house. Two interesting architectural features drew her attention. At each side of the house were circular tower rooms, each with two tiny round windows which resembled human eyes.

From the rear of the mansion, several paths led in diverse directions. One, which was weed-choked, apparently angled toward the river beach. Years before, when the Heights Yacht Club had been in operation, many sailboats plied the waters at this particular point.

CHAPTER 3 - A THATCHED ROOF COTTAGE

Now, except for an occasional fisherman, few boats ever came so far upstream. As the once fine neighborhood had deteriorated, householders gradually had moved away. Penny judged that the Rhetts, isolated from their neighbors, probably were the only socially prominent people remaining.

Selecting a path which led away from the river, deeper into the grounds, Penny presently found herself some distance from the road and the boundary fences.

Hedging the cinder trail were high, untrimmed bushes which completely screened her view. After walking a short distance, she paused, uncertain whether to keep on or return to the road.

"This exploration isn't helping me get a story," she reflected. "If the *Star* photographer should come while I'm here, I might miss him."

However, the trail had a fascination for Penny and she was reluctant to turn back. In a tiny clearing a short distance ahead, she saw what appeared to be a thatched roof cottage. Only a moment or two would be required to investigate it, she thought. Then she would return to the road to await the photographer.

As Penny started eagerly on, she stubbed the toe of her shoe on a stone, and nearly tripped. By quick footwork, she saved herself a fall, but as she paused to recover breath, she plainly saw the bushes at the left hand side of the trail move convulsively. Only a slight breeze had rippled the tree leaves.

Penny was certain that someone stood behind the bush, watching her movements.

"Probably it's that dark skinned man who called to me from the window," she thought.

The knowledge that she was a trespasser on the Rhett property made Penny slightly uneasy. Likewise, it was unnerving to know that her every move was being watched. Admitting to herself that she should turn back, she nevertheless kept on down the path.

Without appearing to do so, she kept her eyes on the bushes at the left hand side of the trail. Now and then a slight jerk of the foliage convinced her that the one who watched was following and keeping pace with her.

Penny hastened her steps as she moved through a cool, densely shaded woodland. Frost had tinted many of the leaves with red and gold, but the arresting beauty of the foliage was completely lost upon her. She was only aware of those soft footsteps behind her.

Then unexpectedly, Penny came to the clearing. Scarcely seventy-five yards ahead, stood the thatched roof cottage which had attracted her interest from afar.

So quaint was the building that for a moment she gave it her entire attention, forgetting the one who watched from the bushes.

From where she stood, the cottage appeared to be about the size of a large room, and resembled a native hut. No windows were visible. The door was closed, and across it was painted in black and red a symbol which even from afar could be distinguished as a serpent-like figure.

The cottage fascinated Penny. At first glance she assumed it to be a large playhouse, but the serpent painting convinced her the building never had been intended for use of children.

A garden or tool house perhaps? She dismissed the thought as quickly as it came. Into her mind flashed a recollection of the drawing that had fallen from Mr. Rhett's desk in the First National Bank. The paper had borne a plumed serpent, apparently a counterpart of the painting on the door of the thatched roof cottage!

Forgetful of the person who crouched in the bushes, Penny started eagerly forward, intending to examine the strange drawing at close range. Something whizzed past her, to embed itself in a tree trunk six inches from her head.

Brought up short, she saw that it was an arrow which had narrowly missed her. Had it been shot from the bushes behind her, and by the person who had stealthily followed her along the trail?

In cold fury, Penny jerked the arrow from the tree. Only then did she notice a folded sheet of notebook paper attached to it with a bit of string. She broke the knot and freed the paper. Across its crumbled face had been penciled a message. The lead had smeared and the words were hard to read. But she made them out.

The warning note said: "Do not approach the thatched roof cottage. To do so is to endanger your life."

CHAPTER 4 - BEHIND THE BUSHES

Having read the warning message, Penny whirled around to gaze toward the bushes on the left side of the path. All now was still, with not the slightest movement of leaves to reveal the presence of the one who had shot the arrow.

"It's that man who talked so unpleasantly to me from the mansion window!" she thought. "Why, he might have struck me with the arrow! I'll put an end to his target practice!"

Acting impulsively, she made a sudden dive for the bushes, jerking them apart to expose the one who had followed her. No one was there.

The grass, however, was trampled, and some distance away, she heard a scurry of footsteps.

"Trying to get away!" she thought grimly. "Not if I can prevent it! I'll have it out with him and learn why he's warning me my life is endangered!"

The footsteps fast were dying away. Listening intently, Penny decided that the person who had shot the arrow was stealing through the bushes toward the river path.

Seeking the intersection of the two paths, the girl stole noiselessly down the cindered trail sloping toward the beach. She had guessed correctly. In a moment she heard an agitation in the bushes nearby and knew that the person she sought was struggling through a tangle of underbrush.

Soon the bushes parted and a thin girl in blue shirt and slacks stepped out onto the cindered path. In one hand she carried an Indian bow with a quiver of arrows, while with the other, she brushed dry leaves from her long, dark hair.

Having expected to see a man, Penny was startled. As she opened her lips to speak, the girl saw her and was brought up short. She gasped in dismay, turned, and with astonishing speed darted down the path leading to the beach.

"Wait!" called Penny.

Keeping her face down, the girl raced on.

Determining that she should not escape without an explanation, Penny gave chase. The runner had an excellent start, but on coming to a series of wooden steps, her heel caught in a small hole. Down she went, and before she could arise, Penny had overtaken her.

Observing that the fall had not injured the girl, she said sternly:

"Now little Miss Robin Hood, will you kindly explain why you tried to exterminate me with that arrow?"

Sitting up, the girl ruefully rubbed an ankle and gazed at Penny with hostile brown eyes.

"Don't be ridiculous!" she retorted. "I had no intention of hitting you. My aim is perfect."

"Modest, at any rate," observed Penny, smiling despite a determination to appear very stern. "You did write the warning note?"

"Naturally."

"Why, may I ask?"

"Because in the first place, you have no business being on our property. Secondly, I didn't want you to go to the thatched roof cottage."

"May I ask your name?"

"I'm Lorinda Rhett."

"Hamilton Rhett's daughter!"

"Stepdaughter," the girl corrected.

CHAPTER 4 - BEHIND THE BUSHES

"You're just the person I want to see!" exclaimed Penny, overjoyed at her good fortune. "Your stepfather—"

"I'll answer no questions about him," the girl interrupted. "You may as well spare your breath. Mother and I want no reporters here."

"So you know who I am?"

"How could one help knowing? You nearly broke our door down with your pounding, and I heard you talking to Antón."

"Your servant?"

"My stepfather's," Lorinda corrected with a slight inflection which suggested that she did not entirely approve of Antón. "Now will you stop asking questions and go away?"

"All in good time. First, I'm relieved to know that the thatched cottage isn't really dangerous. You only wrote that to be rid of me."

Lorinda gave her a long, steady look but said not a word.

"Or perhaps there is some mystery about the cottage," Penny went on. "After all, your stepfather's disappearance was very queer. But the police, no doubt, will get at the bottom of it when they come here."

Lorinda scrambled to her feet. "The police!" she gasped. "We'll not have them here prying around!"

"Whether or not you like it, I'm afraid you will have the police on your doorstep. A man of Mr. Rhett's prominence can't disappear without a few questions being asked."

Lorinda lost much of her defiance. "But this is our own private affair," she protested. "My stepfather will return—at least, I think he will."

"And the missing bonds?"

"Missing bonds?"

"Didn't Albert Potts, the bank secretary, inform your mother that $250,000 in negotiable securities also had disappeared?"

"Why, no! At least I knew nothing of it! Surely you don't think my stepfather would stoop to the theft of bank securities?"

"I have no opinion in the matter. I'm merely here to get the true story. For some reason you and your mother have been unwilling to cooperate."

Lorinda did not reply, but seemed to be thinking deeply.

"Do you have any idea where your stepfather is now?" Penny inquired, hoping that a direct approach might glean information.

"No, of course not."

"You haven't seen him for the past ten days?"

"That is true," Lorinda acknowledged with great reluctance. "But it's not so unusual. My stepfather frequently goes away on trips."

"Without telling anyone where he is going?"

"I'll not answer that question," Lorinda said with a proud uptilt of her chin.

"I'm afraid you don't like reporters very well," observed Penny pleasantly. "Nor do you seem especially fond of your stepfather."

"That's not true! I do like my stepfather. Why, he was the one who taught me how to shoot with a bow and arrow! He gave me this bow which is a valuable collector's item!"

She offered it to Penny who inspected the fine workmanship with keen interest.

"Mr. Rhett is a collector?" she inquired.

"Yes, he's traveled all over the world, but most of his time was spent in the jungles of Africa, Brazil, and other places in South America. That was before he married Mother, of course."

"Your stepfather was especially interested in ancient religious cults?"

"He made a study of it, and for a year gathered material by living in the jungle." Lorinda suddenly broke off, aware that she was warming to Penny and telling her entirely too much.

"Then it was your father who built the thatched roof cottage?"

"Please, let's not talk about it," Lorinda pleaded. "I don't like to be unfriendly or impolite, but you must understand there are things I can't tell you, and which must never be published."

Taking the ancient bow from Penny's hand, the girl started up the path, limping a trifle on her twisted ankle.

"Only one more question, Lorinda. Please tell me the truth. Why were you afraid to have me investigate the thatched roof cottage?"

The girl paused on the path, gazing at Penny quite pathetically.

"Don't ask me to tell you any more," she whispered. "The cottage is a place of evil omen. Truly, I did you a favor in warning you away."

"I saw a painting on the door—that of a winged or plumed serpent. Will you explain its significance?"

"I only know that my stepfather had it painted there when the cottage was built soon after his marriage to my mother. It is a symbol of one of the ancient cults he studied. Many of his trophies bear the same picture."

The information was a little disappointing to Penny. "Then I suppose the drawing that the police found in Mr. Rhett's office had no great significance," she remarked.

"Drawing?"

Penny described the serpent picture which had been found, adding: "On the sheet were written the words: 'This shall be the end.'"

"You are certain?"

"Oh, yes, I saw the paper myself."

Lorinda was visibly disturbed. "I must see that writing! It may mean—" she broke off and amended: "Tell me, where is the paper now?"

"The police have it."

"Oh!"

"Why do you seem to fear the police?" inquired Penny curiously.

"I am not afraid of them—certainly not. It's just that Mother and I prefer to keep our lives private. Facts can be so easily misinterpreted."

"Your reluctance to assist the police also can be misinterpreted," said Penny. "For instance, it seems strange to me that your stepfather's disappearance doesn't seem to disturb you."

"Oh, it does! It's only—well, there are things I can't tell you without my mother's permission. My stepfather is queer. Mother and I never liked his interest in weird cult practices. He had so many strange acquaintances and ties with the past. We always were afraid something dreadful might happen."

"Then he may have met foul play?"

"I don't know what to think," Lorinda said miserably. "A ten-day disappearance is not so serious. My stepfather occasionally went away before without telling us, though never for such a long period. If it weren't for the paper found in his desk, and the missing bonds, I would say it's much ado about nothing."

"As it is—?"

"The loss of $250,000 could be a very serious matter. Tell me, what is your name?"

"Penny Parker."

"You're here only to get a story for your paper?"

"That was why I came, but since meeting you I truthfully can say I also am very much interested in helping you if possible."

"I like you," Lorinda declared with a quick smile. "I'm sorry about the arrow. And I was very rude."

"Not at all. I deliberately egged you on, hoping you would tell me about your stepfather. I was sent here to get a picture of him, and I hate to fail."

"A picture? Mother has one, but I doubt that she would permit you to use it." Lorinda considered a moment, then added: "Tell you what! I'll take you to her, and perhaps, if you're a convincing talker, she'll agree to your request."

"Oh, Lorinda, that's fine!"

The Rhett girl linked arms with Penny as they trudged up the path to the house.

"Don't count your chickens just yet," she warned. "Mother doesn't like reporters. It will be sheer luck if she gives you the picture or any information you can use in the paper."

CHAPTER 5 - AN EVIL CHARM

"Mother has disliked reporters ever since she married my stepfather, two years ago," Lorinda confided as the girls approached the house. "We were in the Eastern part of the country at the time, and papers played up the story, suggesting that Mr. Rhett was a fortune hunter."

"Then he had no money of his own?"

"Not a great deal. You see, my stepfather loved travel, and until he met Mother he never really settled down. He made a little by writing magazine articles, and he spent it roving about the country and exploring far corners of the world."

"It must have been an interesting life," Penny commented politely. "Your mother enjoyed travel too?"

"Oh, mercy no! One hardly can get her away from Riverview. She and my stepfather never traveled together after they were married."

Penny gathered that Mr. and Mrs. Rhett were entirely different types of individuals, but she asked no additional questions, for by this time, the girls had reached the house.

Crossing a stone terrace at the rear of the dwelling, they entered a spacious living room furnished with elegant though formal furniture. Shades were partially drawn, giving the interior a gloomy atmosphere, despite the vases of brightly colored chrysanthemums which decorated the tables.

A woman with dark hair tinged with gray sat reading a book. She was immaculately groomed, every curl of an elaborate hair-do in place, but her face lacked tranquility. Her eyes were not on the page before her, Penny noted, and as the two girls came in, she visibly started.

"Oh, it's you, Lorinda," she murmured in relief. "I declare, I am getting jumpy! For a moment I thought it might be the police or that inquisitive reporter—"

"Mother," interposed Lorinda hastily, "allow me to present Penny Parker, from the *Riverview Star*."

Mrs. Rhett laid aside the book and stared at Penny, her face without expression. Her voice was cold as she spoke.

"From the *Star*? Lorinda, I am *very* sorry, but you know my feeling in this matter."

"Penny really is very nice, Mother," Lorinda said, flashing her companion an encouraging smile. "She didn't want to come out here and question us about father, but the editor sent her. He wants a picture, too."

Mrs. Rhett arose to terminate an interview which had never really begun. "I am sorry," she repeated with emphasis. "There are to be no pictures taken."

"The editor especially wanted a photograph of your husband," Penny said. "By publishing it in the paper, it may be easier to trace him."

"Miss Parker," replied Mrs. Rhett pleasantly but with no warmth, "if I need assistance in locating my husband I shall request it. Meanwhile, I do wish people would not concern themselves with our affairs."

"Mother, we may not be able to avoid publicity," Lorinda rushed on. "There's likely to be a scandal. You see, $250,000 in negotiable bonds disappeared from the bank."

For a moment, Mrs. Rhett did not speak. A dagger-type paper cutter lay on the polished table beside her. Nervously her fingers closed upon it, and unaware of the act, she jabbed the sharp point several times through a lace doily centerpiece.

"Mother, you're ruining that!"

Mrs. Rhett dropped the paper cutter, which clattered on the table and tumbled to the floor. Without picking it up, she moved restlessly to the window, only to return.

"What were you saying about $250,000 in bonds, Lorinda?" she asked. "Surely you didn't mean—"

"I only know what Penny told me. Soon after Father disappeared, Albert Potts discovered the bonds also were missing."

"There can be no connection. Why, even the suggestion that my husband would steal is ridiculous! It's preposterous!"

"No one has accused your husband," Penny said quietly. "Perhaps the bonds will be found. Now that the police have stepped into the case, there should be developments."

"The police," repeated Mrs. Rhett with a shiver. "Oh, dear, must we suffer their interference!"

A telephone in an adjoining room rang and Lorinda started to answer it. But her mother signalled to her.

"Let it go, Lorinda. It may be the police now, or another reporter. We'll have nothing to say."

The telephone rang again. Footsteps were heard down a hallway and a well-built, dark-skinned houseworker of middle age padded into the room. She gazed with intent curiosity at Penny as she started toward the library to answer the phone.

"No, let it ring, Celeste," Mrs. Rhett directed. "And if anyone comes to the door asking for me, remember, I am not at home."

"Yes'm," mumbled the housekeeper. She bent to pick up the paper cutter from the floor and as she did so an object which was tied about her neck with a cord and kept hidden beneath her starched uniform, swung into view.

Penny obtained only a fleeting glimpse of the curious article, for the woman hastily thrust it into her dress front again. However, it appeared to be a tiny packet of cloth.

Lorinda also had observed the object. Fixing the woman with a stern gaze she said: "Celeste, you're wearing one of those heathenish *ouange* charms again! You promised Mother you wouldn't!"

"This only keeps away bad sickness," the woman retorted, with a slight accent which nevertheless made her words hard to understand. "A good *ouange*. Now that my master is away, you are not to tell me what to do."

"Lorinda, don't plague her," Mrs. Rhett said wearily. "We have enough trouble as it is. Let her wear the charm, or a dozen of them, if it gives her any satisfaction."

Lorinda subsided into injured silence, while Celeste flashed a triumphant smile.

Mrs. Rhett turned again to Penny. In a tone which could be interpreted only as a final dismissal she said: "I am sorry, Miss Parker, that I cannot help you. At present I do not know my husband's whereabouts or why he went away. If you will excuse me now, I shall go to my room for a rest."

With dignity she crossed the living room to a handsome circular stairway with a railing of polished mahogany. Her head held proudly, she presented a regal figure as she slowly climbed the steps.

But half way up, she suddenly halted, her body jerking taut. Uttering a low cry which was almost a scream, she stared at an object lying on the step in front of her.

"Why, Mother! What's wrong?" cried Lorinda.

With Penny and Celeste, she hastened to the staircase. Mrs. Rhett's face was as colorless as if she had seen a ghost. Her lips trembled. Without speaking, she pointed to the stair carpet.

There at her feet lay two burnt match ends tied together with a bit of scarlet string.

"An *ouange*! An evil *ouange*!" whispered Celeste in horror.

Lorinda turned upon her angrily.

"Celeste, don't say such things! You know how nervous Mother is, and how easily she becomes upset! If this is one of your charms—"

"No! No!" the woman protested. She stared fixedly at the object on the floor. "This charm is not mine and it is not Antón's!"

"Then how did it get here?"

"I do not know. It is a sign of evil—a sign of death."

"Superstition!" exclaimed Lorinda.

Mrs. Rhett started on up the stairs, but as she would have stepped over the burned matches, Celeste seized her by the skirt, pulling her backwards. Frightened, the woman screamed and fell heavily against the wall.

Celeste kept her from collapsing, all the while muttering words Penny could not understand.

"Stop that gibberish!" Lorinda commanded.

Mrs. Rhett broke away from Celeste, and with an hysterical cry, moved down the stairway and into the library. Though she closed the door behind her, the girls could hear her sobs.

CHAPTER 5 - AN EVIL CHARM

"Now see what you've done!" Lorinda accused Celeste.

The woman paid no attention to her. Bending over the match sticks, she swayed back and forth as she muttered a strange chant. As Lorinda sought to pick up the charm, Celeste struck her wrist a sharp blow.

"Fool!" she exclaimed. "Would you let your mother die a slow and painful death? Do not touch this thing of evil until I have finished! If she had stepped over it, nothing would have saved her."

Celeste kept on with her mutterings until at last she was through. "I have done all I can," she said with a deep sigh. Gingerly she picked up the match ends and, dropping them into the living room fireplace, saw them consumed by flame.

"Now what is all this stupidity about Mother dying a slow death?" Lorinda demanded sternly. "How did that thing get into this house, and what does it mean?"

"How it came here I do not know," replied the woman. "Its meaning is simple. In the jungles such symbols are sometimes placed on new graves, that the departing spirit may kindle a little fire and warm its cold hands in the other world."

"That's enough!" interrupted Lorinda. "Don't tell me any more. It's all so silly."

"It is the truth."

"Well, true or false, Mother is not to be told such nonsense. She's upset enough as it is."

"Your mother already knows," said the housekeeper. "That is why she weeps. She fears that even now the spell is upon her."

"Celeste, you must be out of your mind!" Lorinda cried in exasperation. "You never said such dreadful things or acted like this when Father was here. What has taken possession of you?"

"I fear for the family. It bodes ill that my master should remain away. If only the Zudi drum were out of the house—destroyed—"

Lorinda's patience had been overtaxed. "The Zudi drum!" she cried. "Oh, Celeste, you're impossible! Go find Antón and if you must, talk such nonsense to him! But not another word of it before us! Do you understand?"

Celeste stood facing the two girls defiantly. Her eyes burned with an angry fire, and Penny expected her to make a bitter retort to Lorinda. Instead, she seemed to withdraw into herself, and with downcast head, scurried toward the kitchen.

CHAPTER 6 - MATCHES AND STRING

After Celeste had gone, Lorinda went quickly to the library. Speaking soothingly to her mother, she urged her to go upstairs and lie down.

"That dreadful thing on the steps!" Mrs. Rhett exclaimed with a shudder. "Celeste jerked me back to keep me from walking past it, didn't she? The charm has an evil significance—perhaps that I shall have a long lingering illness or die."

"You know better than that, Mother. It's all superstitious rot! What ever gave you such an idea?"

"Why, I don't really know, Lorinda. I suppose Hamilton told me about the charm long ago. When I saw it on the step it gave me a deep shock and I seemed to realize that it had been put there for me alone to find. Lorinda, what if it should be a native death charm?"

"Mother, I won't allow you to even think of such foolishness! You're just upset because Father isn't here."

"Yes, that must be it," Mrs. Rhett declared with a heavy sigh. "I have such a headache. I'll go to my room now and try to sleep."

Lorinda took her arm and helped her up the stairway. As they came to the step where the burnt matches had been, Mrs. Rhett glanced down and shivered. Then she laughed apologetically.

"It really is silly of me to let a little thing upset me so," she declared. "I'll be myself again as soon as I have slept."

After helping her mother into bed, Lorinda returned to the living room where Penny had waited.

"I do hope you won't put any of this in the paper," she began earnestly. "People wouldn't understand."

"I'm afraid I don't myself," said Penny. "For instance, what did Celeste mean when she spoke of the Zudi drum? And who is she anyhow?"

"Oh, I forgot to tell you! Celeste and her husband Antón, are a couple my stepfather brought to this country after spending a year studying ancient cult practices. Celeste befriended him, I believe, and helped him gain information about the tribesmen. Anyway, Father took a fancy to her, and persuaded the couple to come with him."

"That was before he married your mother?"

"Oh, yes. After the wedding, my stepfather was unwilling to let Celeste and Antón go, so Mother agreed that they might work here. Antón is a worthless servant. He allows the grounds to run down shamefully, and the only time he ever really works is when someone stands over him!"

"And Celeste?"

"Oh, she is a hard worker, but I confess I don't understand her," Lorinda replied. "We disliked each other on sight. In a way, I'm a little afraid of her."

"Why?"

"I can't explain." Lorinda stirred restlessly. "She makes me feel uneasy whenever I am near her—almost as if I were in the presence of Black Magic."

At Penny's expression of astonishment, she amended hastily: "Oh, I don't mean that exactly. Celeste is devoted to my stepfather and I'm sure only means to be helpful. But the truth is, she's steeped in a mysterious and not too wholesome past. Superstition is the breath of life to her."

"How did the match ends get on the stairway?"

"I wish I knew." Lorinda's forehead wrinkled with anxiety. "Celeste may have told the truth when she said neither she nor Antón had anything to do with it."

"Then how was the charm brought into the house?"

CHAPTER 6 - MATCHES AND STRING

"My stepfather had enemies. Something tells me all this may have a connection with the Zudi drum."

"Didn't Celeste suggest that idea to you? She hinted that the drum—whatever it is—should be removed from the house."

"I can see myself getting rid of the Zudi drum! Why, it is my stepfather's most prized trophy! He took it from a native tribe, and as you might imagine, there was plenty of trouble!"

"Your stepfather didn't steal the drum?"

"Not exactly, though tribesmen may have regarded it that way. The drum was used in ceremonials and was highly treasured by natives. Father tried to buy it. When he couldn't, he left money and trinkets and carried off the drum. Natives pursued him for more than a hundred miles, but he got away."

"And your stepfather has the drum now?"

"Yes, we keep it in the library wall safe. Want to see it?"

"I'd love to, if it's not too much trouble."

"The truth is I want to check to be certain the drum is still here," Lorinda replied, leading the way into the adjoining room. "What Celeste said made me uneasy."

"You think your stepfather may have removed the drum from the wall safe?"

"I can't imagine him doing that. However, his long absence is puzzling, and finding the burnt match charm gives the whole situation a sinister slant. It's barely possible some of those tribesmen followed him here, hoping to recover the Zudi drum."

"Why, that seems fantastic!"

"Not if you understand tribal customs. From all my stepfather told me of his experiences, I am sure members of the Zudi cult would stop at nothing in trying to recover their ceremonial drum."

Penny inquired if Mr. Rhett ever had received threats against his life.

"Oh, dozens of them, but that was years ago. Since he married Mother, I've not heard of any. But then, my stepfather was self-contained and rather strange in many ways. If he had received threats, he might not have told her."

Becoming more interested in the story minute by minute, Penny longed to ask if Mr. and Mrs. Rhett ever had had serious disagreements. However, the question was a difficult one, and she knew of no way to phrase it without risking offense to Lorinda.

"I'd never admit it to Celeste," the Rhett girl went on, carefully drawing heavy draperies across the arched doorway of the library and closing another door which opened toward the stairs. "But seeing that match and string *ouange* gave me an unpleasant moment. I'm afraid my stepfather's enemies may have picked up his trail. In that case—well, the charm really could become an omen of evil."

"You're becoming morbid," laughed Penny. "What is there to fear in two burnt matches tied with a string?"

"Nothing perhaps," replied Lorinda, though without firm conviction. "Let's hope the Zudi drum is still here. I wish it had never been brought into the house."

A large painting of a Dutch windmill hung low on the north library wall. To Penny's surprise, Lorinda gave one of its long gold cords a jerk. The picture swung back to disclose a cleverly hidden safe.

"Now I hope I haven't forgotten the combination," Lorinda murmured.

Thinking a moment, she whirled the dials with an expert touch. The safe failed to open. With an exclamation of annoyance, she tried again. This time there was a sharp little click and as she turned the handle, the circular door swung back.

Lorinda thrust her arm deep into the opening. "It's here all right!" she exclaimed.

From the safe she drew forth a bowl-shaped drum, perhaps eight inches in diameter at the opening. An animal skin was stretched over the framework and the sides were decorated with symbols.

"This probably is my stepfather's most valuable trophy," Lorinda declared. "He treasures it above all else, because there is no other exactly like it. But the drum never should have been taken from the native tribe."

With her fingers, the girl tapped out a rhythm on the drum. The first three notes were slow and heavy, with a series of triplets coming as a light splutter at the end.

. . . .
. . . .

WHISPERING WALLS

Penny, who had a keen sense of the ludicrous, began to sway to the jungle rhythm. Lorinda drummed with more energy, and they both burst into laughter.

But suddenly for no apparent reason, the mirth died from Lorinda's lips and abruptly she ended the tapping.

Tossing the Zudi drum into the wall safe, she closed the heavy door and spun the dials. With another swift movement, she swung the picture into place.

Penny started to speak, but a significant glance from her companion served as a warning to remain silent.

Lorinda darted across the room, and jerked aside the heavy brocade curtains which framed the arching doorway. Crouching behind the protective folds was the same dark-skinned servant who had talked to Penny from the upstairs window!

CHAPTER 7 - WHISPERING WALLS

"Antón!" Lorinda exclaimed in disapproval. "Why were you listening?"

The servant, a man of perhaps forty whose well-cut livery was worn in a sloppy manner, stared at her almost insolently and without the least embarrassment.

"Hear jungle drum," he said.

"I was showing the Zudi to Miss Parker," Lorinda replied stiffly.

"You keep him in wall safe?" inquired Antón.

Lorinda bit her lip with annoyance. She made no answer.

"Now that master gone, maybe much better you get rid of Zudi drum," Antón advised.

"Why do you say that?"

"Zudi drum bring trouble. Antón tell master so when he bring it to this country."

"And what do you suggest we do with the drum?"

"Antón take care of it," the servant offered eagerly. "Sink it deep in river."

Lorinda smiled and shook her head. "The Zudi drum is my stepfather's most cherished possession. He never would forgive me if I disposed of it while he's gone."

"Maybe master never come back."

"Antón!" Lorinda reproved. "You're not to make such remarks!"

"Yes'm," the man muttered, but as he retreated from the library doorway Penny fancied she saw him smile as if well pleased with himself.

After the servant had gone, Lorinda remarked in a whisper: "I wish he hadn't seen me put the drum away. Somehow I've never trusted Antón although he's always been devoted to my stepfather. Sometimes I feel that he hates me."

"You say he didn't know until just now where the drum was kept?"

"No, he may have suspected, but he never was certain. Antón always has been deeply interested in that drum, which as I understand, belonged to another tribe—sworn enemies of Antón's group. He and Celeste helped my stepfather obtain the drum, or rather they told him about its existence, so I suppose it's natural that they remain interested."

"Antón seemed to believe the drum might bring trouble on the household."

"Just stupid superstition! He's never worried about it before." Lorinda was thoughtful a moment, then added: "Of course, there is a possibility members of the Zudi tribe may have traced my stepfather here and intend to avenge themselves. But that hardly seems likely."

"What of the serpent drawing found in your stepfather's desk?" Penny reminded her. "And the words, 'This Shall be the End?'"

"I'd not venture an opinion until I have seen the handwriting," Lorinda returned.

As the girls were leaving the library, Penny heard an automobile rattle up to the front of the mansion. Peering from a window, she saw Salt Sommers climbing out of the car, camera and flashbulbs in his hand.

His arrival reminded her that she was here to get a story for the *Star*.

"The police aren't here?" Lorinda inquired tensely, moving to the window.

"No, it's one of our photographers. He'll need a picture of you and your mother. It will only take a minute."

Lorinda, who had been growing more and more friendly, now became cold and aloof.

"No picture," she said firmly. "I thought you understood. My mother and I wish no publicity whatsoever."

"But—"

"I am afraid I must ask you to leave now," Lorinda said.

Deeply chagrined by her failure to obtain a picture, Penny followed the Rhett girl to the front door.

"I'm sorry," Lorinda said, observing the proud tilt of Penny's chin. "It's nothing personal. I really like you very much and would like to help you—but I can't."

She opened the door and Penny went out. As the latch clicked behind her, Salt, a tall young man with an aggressive walk, came toward the porch.

"Hi, Penny!" he greeted her casually. "Sorry to be late, but I got tied up in a traffic jam at Fulton Bridge. Everything lined up for the pictures?"

Penny told him the bad news.

"Now see here, they can't do that to us," Salt said, knocking on the door of the old mansion. "I'll catch the dickens from DeWitt if I go back to the office without a picture. How about the story?"

"Not much we can use. I talked to Mrs. Rhett and her daughter, but they didn't give me any real information. Mr. Rhett's disappearance seems to be as puzzling to them as anyone else."

"You can hook your story onto that angle then. But me—I've got to come up with a picture." Salt knocked again on the door. "Say, are they all deaf in there?"

"It's no use," Penny said. "I doubt if anyone will answer."

Salt pounded a few more times, and then was forced to admit that he was only wasting his energy. "I might take a shot of the house," he said. "Gloomy old morgue, isn't it?"

"That's about all you can do under the circumstances."

"A picture of a house," Salt groaned. "DeWitt'll go for it like a ton o' brick. He'll probably throw a typewriter at me!"

"There's another place on the grounds that might be more interesting. It's a sort of thatched roof cottage."

Salt immediately brightened. "Let's have a look-see," he proposed. "Maybe we can round up a gardener or someone who'll pose."

Circling the house, Penny led the way down the graveled path. Salt took such long strides it was hard to keep up with him. He'd had a tough day, he told her. As if taking shots of society women at the Country Club hadn't been bad enough, right on top of it he'd been sent to the airport to catch a couple of prominent state officials. And then, before he'd had a chance to get the pictures printed, DeWitt had ordered him to the mansion.

"It's just one thing after another," he muttered. "I wish someone would tell me why I don't quit newspaper photography."

"Because, no matter what you say, you like the excitement," Penny supplied. "Remember those shots you took of the Governor that were printed in the rotogravure section?"

"Sure," grinned Salt, his good humor returning. "I also remember the time I was sent to a furniture store to take some pictures for the advertising department, and without me knowing it, the store closed for the night. I telephoned DeWitt I was locked in, and what did the old crow do? 'Just sit down and wait,' he says. 'I'll get hold of a watchman, and we'll have you right out of there.'"

Penny had heard the story several times but did not ruin the photographer's pleasure by saying so.

"DeWitt didn't do a doggone thing!" Salt went on. "He just told everyone in the office. I cooled my heels in that place until nine o'clock at night! A fire broke out across town then, and DeWitt needed another photographer, so finally he got me out!"

"Mr. DeWitt has a queer sense of humor," Penny acknowledged. "But he is a good editor."

"Best there is," Salt agreed loyally. "But wow! He's going to tear me apart limb from limb when I come in with nothing but a picture of a thatched roof cottage!"

Penny was tempted to tell the photographer of Lorinda's strange action in warning her not to approach the building. However, she felt sure he would make light of the entire matter, so she remained silent.

"Is that the place?" Glimpsing the thatched roof cottage through the trees, Salt paused to stare at it. "Looks like a jungle hut."

"A reproduction of one, I imagine," Penny said, "but it might be the genuine product. Mr. Rhett, I've been told, was a world traveler and brought home many relics and souvenirs of jungle and cult life."

They approached closer and Salt stopped again, this time to take two shots.

"What's inside?" he asked. "Let's take a look."

CHAPTER 7 - WHISPERING WALLS

Penny was curious to see the interior of the cottage despite Lorinda's warning. However, as she trotted along at Salt's heels, she experienced a strange, uneasy feeling, as if she were intruding upon forbidden ground.

The photographer was troubled by no such misgivings. Boldly he went to the door and tried to thrust it open. It was locked and would not budge.

Thwarted, he examined the painted plumed serpent which decorated the door.

"What's this thing?" he muttered.

Penny told him about the similar design which had been found on a paper in Mr. Rhett's office.

"I'll take a close-up of the door then," Salt decided. "It will tie in with your story, if you build up the mystery angle."

While the photographer took two pictures of the door, Penny wandered around to the back of the tiny cottage. Only one small window provided light. It had been cut in the wall high toward the sloping thatched roof, and to peer into the dark interior, Penny had to stand on tiptoe.

Inside the room, a spot of light and flame drew her gaze. And at the same instant, something jabbed her ribs from behind. With a startled cry, she whirled around.

Then she laughed, for it was Salt who had come up quietly.

"You frightened me out of a year's growth!" she exclaimed. "Don't ever do that again!"

"What do you see? Anything interesting?"

"It looks as if a lamp is burning inside. But the cottage must be deserted!"

Salt peeped through the window. "It is a light—an oil flame!" he exclaimed. "But there's no one in the room."

"Let's go," said Penny with a shiver. "It's getting late and we're due back at the office."

"Not scared, are you?" the photographer teased.

"Of course not! But the door is locked, and we're not supposed to be here."

Salt tested the window. Surprisingly, it raised easily.

"Here, I'll boost you in," he offered. "Up you go! Then you can unlock the door and let me in."

"Oh, Salt, should we?"

"Why not?" he argued. "We were sent to get a story and pictures, weren't we? Well, maybe what we're after is right here."

Only half convinced, Penny permitted herself to be boosted through the window. She dropped lightly onto a wooden floor. The interior of the cottage was gloomy, brightened only by a flickering flame which came from a floating wick in a cocoanut shell filled with oil.

The atmosphere of the room, was sombre, almost terrifying. Taking no time to look about, Penny scurried to unlock the door. She felt more at ease as Salt sauntered in.

"Well, this is a queer layout," he observed. "A regular jungle hut."

The room was bare of furniture except for a low wooden table upon which the cocoanut oil lamp burned. On one wall hung two black and red flags with serpentine symbols sewn with metallic beads.

Across the room, above the deep fireplace, two crossed machetes dangled from cords attached to the wall. Beneath the table was a small, crude wooden chest, and lying upon it was a rattle made from pebbles placed in a painted canister.

Salt shook the rattle several times. In the stillness of the room, the clatter of the pebbles seemed almost deafening to Penny's sensitive ears.

"Oh, please!" she pleaded.

"Don't you like it?" he teased.

Penny shook her head. With fascinated gaze, she stared at the flickering oil light.

"Do you suppose that thing burns all the time, Salt, or has someone just been here?"

"It couldn't burn very long, unless someone keeps refilling the shell with oil. Wonder what's in this chest?"

Salt stooped to raise the lid. As he did so, Penny, who stood close beside him, suddenly clutched his arm. At his look of surprise, she mumbled:

"I thought I heard something just then—like the rustling of silk!"

Salt listened a moment and chuckled. "That old imagination of yours is working overtime, Penny! Relax!"

"But I did hear a rustling sound as if someone were moving along the wall. Listen! There it is again!"

"No one could—" Salt began, and broke off. The queer look that came over his face told Penny that he too had heard the sound.

Then whispering began, and seemed to issue from the very cottage walls. At first the stunned pair could not distinguish a word. But gradually the words whispered in a throaty voice became audible.

"Go!" the warning voice commanded. "All is forbidden!"

CHAPTER 8 - GHOST OF THE DARK CORNERS

Salt was the first to recover from surprise at the whispered warning. Convinced that someone must be crouching beneath the open cottage window, he strode across the room to peer outside.

No one was in sight.

"The voice seemed to come from the wall itself!" Penny murmured. She added jokingly, "Maybe this place has a ghost who is annoyed because we climbed in through the window!"

"That whispered warning came from a very human ghost," the photographer muttered. "We'll do a little annoying ourselves if we can find the bird!"

Salt jerked open the door. Penny followed him outside. Behind them, the door swung shut again, but neither noticed.

Quickly they circled the cottage. No one was visible in the clearing nor were leaves stirring in the bushes close by.

Salt, however, remained convinced the warning had been whispered by someone standing close to the window who then had quickly retreated to the sheltering shrubbery.

"The warning seemed to come from the very inside of the walls," Penny repeated.

"How could it? The walls are only average thickness, so the only place a person could hide would be outside. It's a cinch no one was in the room with us!"

"Lorinda might have crept close to the cottage and whispered the warning," Penny said thoughtfully, "but I doubt it very much."

"Lorinda?"

"Mrs. Rhett's daughter. She tried to prevent me investigating the cottage before you arrived."

"Then she may have followed us here."

"The whispering voice didn't sound like hers," Penny insisted. "No, I can't believe it was Lorinda."

Salt started back toward the cottage. "Whoever it was, let's not be bluffed out, Penny. We'll see what's inside the wooden chest."

The cottage door was closed. To the photographer's annoyance, it refused to open even when he thrust his weight against it.

"Now what?" he demanded. "Did you close the door when you came out, Penny?"

"Not that I recall. The wind must have blown it shut."

"Wind? What wind? Look at the trees."

Scarcely a leaf was stirring.

"Then I'm afraid it must have been the jungle ghost," Penny said with a nervous giggle. She glanced at her wrist watch. "Salt, it's getting late. We must go."

"Not yet," retorted Salt grimly.

Again he circled the thatched cottage, with Penny tagging none too happily at his heels. As they saw the window, they both paused.

"Why, it's closed now!" Penny gasped. "How did we leave it?"

"Open. The cottage door may have blown shut by itself and locked with a spring catch, but this window is a horse of a different color. It couldn't have closed by itself."

"Who could have lowered it? How was it done without our knowledge?"

Salt had no explanation. Lifting Penny so that she could peer inside the room again, he asked her what she could see.

"Not a sign of anyone. But it's so dark—"

"See anything now?" Salt demanded impatiently as her voice trailed off.

"The cocoanut shell lamp! It's no longer burning!"

"Sure?"

"I couldn't see better if I wore bifocals! The room is dark."

"An experience like this shouldn't happen to a dog," muttered Salt. "We'll find out what's behind it! Raise the window and in we go."

Penny tugged at the sill. "Locked," she reported. "From the inside."

Disgusted, Salt allowed her to drop lightly to the ground. "Wait until I find a rock," he instructed. "We'll get in!"

Penny caught his arm. "No, Salt! We've already overstepped our rights. We mustn't damage the Rhett property."

"Well, someone is making a monkey of us," the photographer grumbled. "It burns me up!"

"There's more to it than meets the eyes, Salt. Even the atmosphere of this place is sinister."

"You say that, and yet you're willing to turn your back on an unsolved mystery? How times have changed!"

"Well—" Penny wavered, for it was true she loved mystery and adventure. But she finished in a firm voice: "We were sent here to get a story and picture for the *Star*! We'll miss the Green Streak edition if we don't get back to the office *pronto*."

She thrust her wrist watch beneath Salt's nose. He looked at the moving hands and muttered: "Jeepers! We've got just thirty-five minutes to catch our deadline! Let's go!"

Hurriedly, they went up the path toward the mansion and the road. As they approached the house, the rear door swung open and Lorinda came out on the flagstone terrace.

"There she is now!" Penny murmured in an undertone. "I don't believe she could have been the one who whispered the warning at the cottage! It must have been someone else."

"Is she the Rhett girl?" Salt demanded, starting to adjust his camera. "Maybe I can get a shot of her after all."

Lorinda came directly toward the pair, but she raised a hand squarely in front of her face as she saw that Salt meant to take her picture.

"Please don't!" she pleaded. "I can't pose. I only came to ask you to leave. Mother is so upset. The telephone is ringing constantly, and we expect the police any minute."

Lorinda obviously was on the verge of tears. Salt lowered his camera.

"I do want to help you," Lorinda hastened on. "That's why I am giving you this. Mother doesn't know about it, and she will be furious."

Into Penny's hand, she thrust a small but clear photograph of a middle-aged man who wore glasses. His left cheek was marred by a jagged though not particularly disfiguring scar.

"Your stepfather!" she exclaimed.

"Yes, this is the only picture we have of him. He never liked to have his photograph taken. If you use it, please take good care of the original and see that we get it back."

"Oh, we will!" Penny promised. "This photograph should help in tracing Mr. Rhett."

"Please go now," Lorinda urged again. She glanced uneasily down the path toward the thatched-roof cottage, but if she knew what had transpired there, she gave no sign.

Elated to have obtained the photograph, Penny and Salt hastened on to the parked press car. Starting the car with a jerk, Salt followed the winding river road.

Penny cast a glance over her shoulder. Through the trees she could see only the roof-top of the thatched cottage in the clearing.

The estate was bounded by a wooden rail fence, in many places fortified with dense, tall shrubbery. The fall weather had tinted many of the bushes scarlet, yellow or bronze. Gazing toward a patch of particularly brilliant-colored leaves, Penny detected movement behind them.

For a fleeting instant she thought she had seen a large, shaggy dog. Then she became certain it was a man who crouched behind the screen of leaves.

"Salt!" she exclaimed sharply. "Look at those bushes!"

The photographer slowed the car, turning his head.

CHAPTER 8 - GHOST OF THE DARK CORNERS

"What about 'em, Penny?"

"Someone is hiding there behind the fence! Perhaps it's the person who whispered a warning at the thatched cottage!"

"Oh, it's just a shadow," Salt began, only to change his mind. "You're right! Someone is crouching there!"

So suddenly that Penny was thrown sideways, the photographer swerved the car to the curb. He swung the door open.

"What are you going to do?" Penny demanded.

The photographer did not take time to reply. Already he was out of the car, running toward the hedge.

CHAPTER 9 - JERRY ENTERS THE CASE

As Salt ran toward him, the man who crouched behind the bushes began to move stealthily away. From the car Penny could not see his face which was screened by dense foliage.

"Salt, he's getting away!" she shouted.

Salt climbed over the fence. His clothing got snagged and by the time he had freed himself and struggled through a tangle of vines and bushes, the man he pursued had completely disappeared.

"Which way did he go, Penny?" he called.

"I lost sight of him after he ducked into a clump of shrubbery," she replied regretfully. "It's useless to try to find him now."

Salt came back to the car, and starting the engine, drove on.

"You didn't see who it was?" Penny asked hopefully.

"No, I think it was a man. Maybe the Rhett's gardener or a tramp."

"Whoever it was, I'm sure he stood there watching us drive away from the grounds," Penny declared.

Until the car was far down the street, she alertly watched the Rhett grounds. However, the one who had crouched by the fence now was well hidden and on guard. Not a movement of the bushes betrayed his presence.

As the Rhett mansion was lost completely from view, Penny's thoughts came back to the story which she must write. Nervously she glanced at her wrist watch.

"What's the bad news?" Salt asked, stepping hard on the gasoline pedal.

"Twenty-five minutes until deadline. Can you make it?"

Salt's lips compressed into a grim line and he concentrated on his driving, avoiding heavy traffic and red lights as they approached the center of town.

They came at last to the big stone building downtown which housed the *Riverview Star*. As Salt pulled up at the curb, Penny leaped out and ran inside. Without waiting for an elevator, she darted up the stairs to the busy newsroom.

Editor DeWitt was talking on a telephone, and, all about him, reporters were tapping typewriters at a furious pace.

Editor DeWitt held his hand over the phone mouthpiece and fixed Penny with a gloomy eye. "Time you got here," he observed. "Anything new? Did you get the pictures?"

Penny produced the photograph of Mr. Rhett which the editor studied an instant, then tossed to his assistant, with a terse: "Make it a one column—rush!"

Knowing that with a deadline practically at hand Mr. DeWitt was in no mood for a lengthy tale, Penny told him only such facts as were pertinent to Mr. Rhett's disappearance.

"So the family won't talk?" DeWitt growled. "Well, play up that angle. We've already set up everything you gave us over the phone. Make this an add and get it right out."

Penny nodded and slid into a chair behind the nearest typewriter. An "add" she knew, was an addition to a story already set up in type. It was easier to write than a "lead" which contained the main facts of all that had happened, but even so, she would be hard pressed to make the deadline.

For a moment she concentrated, but the noises of the room distracted her somewhat. Editor DeWitt was barking into the telephone again; a reporter on her left side was clicking a pencil against the desk; the short-wave radio blared a police call; and across the room someone bellowed: "Copy boy!"

CHAPTER 9 - JERRY ENTERS THE CASE

Then Penny began to write, and the noises blanked out, until she was aware only of the moving ribbon of words on the copy paper. She had written perhaps four paragraphs when DeWitt ordered tersely: "Give me a take."

Without looking up, Penny nodded, wrote a few more words, then jerked the copy from her machine. A boy snatched it from her hand and carried it to DeWitt, who read it rapidly. Pencilling a few minor corrections, he shot it to the copy desk.

Meanwhile, with another sheet of paper rolled in her machine, Penny was grinding out more of the story. Words flowed easily now, and she scarcely paused to think.

DeWitt called for more copy. Again she ripped it from the roller and gave it to the boy.

After the third "take," DeWitt called: "That's enough. Make her '30.'"

Penny understood the term. It signified the end of the story, and usually when reporters had completed an article, they wrote the figure at the bottom of the copy sheet.

Finishing the sentence she had started, she gave the last of her story to the boy, and settling back, took a deep breath. DeWitt's chair was empty. He had gone to the composing room, leaving his assistant to handle the final copy that came through before the presses rolled.

Penny knew that the last page she had written probably would not make the edition, but it did not matter. She had crammed all the important and most interesting of her information into the first part of the story. In any event, everything she had written would be used in the second edition, the Three Star, which followed the Green Streak by two hours. The final edition rolled from the presses later in the evening and was known as the Blue Streak.

A well-built, good looking reporter with a pencil tucked behind one ear, walked over to the desk.

"Big day, Penny?" he inquired affectionately.

Jerry Livingston, who rated as the *Star's* best reporter, also stood at the very top of Penny's long list of friends.

With Jerry, Penny always felt comfortable and at ease. Now she found herself telling him about the Rhett case, omitting few details of what had occurred in the thatched roof cottage. It took longer to relate all the events than Penny realized, for, before she had finished the story, the Green Streak edition was up, and a boy was distributing papers about the office. Penny reached eagerly for one, noting instantly that her article appeared in good position on the front page.

"Wonder who wrote the lead?" she asked. "You, Jerry?"

"Guilty," he laughed. "Any mistakes?"

Penny could find none. It was a perfect rewrite, based upon facts she had telephoned to the office after leaving the bank. The story had a professional swing she could not have achieved. Her own "add" went into it very smoothly, however, so that few persons reading the account ever would guess two reporters had contributed to the writing.

Mr. DeWitt had returned from the composing room, and with a relaxed air settled down to enjoy a cigarette. Now that the edition was rolling off the press, he no longer seemed nervous or irritable.

Presently he waved his hand toward Penny who went over to see what he wanted.

"This Rhett story is likely to develop into something," he said. "I'll want double coverage, so I'm assigning Jerry to help you. He'll handle the police angle."

Penny nodded, secretly glad it was Jerry who had been directed to help her instead of another reporter. Police work, particularly the checking of routine reports, was vitally important but uninteresting. She was pleased to escape it.

"You're to keep close tab on the Rhett mansion," Mr. DeWitt instructed. "Report everything of consequence that happens there. By tomorrow things may start popping."

The wire editor came swiftly to DeWitt's desk with a sheet of copy which had just been torn from an Associated Press teletype.

"Here's something," he said. "A few hours ago police published for all state banks the numbers of those bonds stolen from the First National Bank. According to this Culver City dispatch, one of the bonds, in $1,000 denomination, turned up there yesterday."

"Yesterday?" Penny inquired.

"Sure, a Culver City bank took the bond in, not knowing it was one of the missing ones. Late this afternoon, police sent out the numbers to every bank in the state."

DeWitt read the news item carefully his eyes glinting with interest.

"Too bad Albert Potts didn't notify the police several days ago. Rhett may be half way to the Mexican border by this time."

"Then you believe he walked off with the bonds?" asked Penny.

"Looks like it," shrugged the editor. "There's no other suspect. Or if there is, the police aren't talking. More of those missing bonds may show up. Jerry, get busy on the telephone!" he called to the reporter who sat nearby.

"What's doing?" Jerry inquired, getting up and coming to the desk.

DeWitt thrust the dispatch into his hand. "Get hold of that Culver City banker," he instructed. "Find out who turned the bond in, and if the description fits Rhett."

Jerry was occupied at the telephone for nearly fifteen minutes. He returned to report: "The bond was turned in by a woman, and the bank clerk didn't make a record of her name."

"Any description?"

"No, the clerk only remembers that she was a middle-aged woman."

DeWitt sighed heavily and turned his attention to other matters. Penny glanced at the clock. It was after six o'clock. Her father, she knew, would have left the office nearly an hour earlier. She could catch a bus home, but first a cup of coffee across the street might help to fortify her until she could enjoy a home-cooked dinner by Mrs. Weems.

As she started away from the office, Jerry followed her.

"Going across the way for a bite to eat?" he asked. "Mind if I tag along?"

"I wish you would," she replied eagerly. "We can talk about the Rhett case."

"Oh, let's bury that until tomorrow. I'd rather talk about a dozen other subjects—you, for instance."

"Me?"

"About that little curl behind your ear. Or the smudge of carbon on the end of your nose!"

"Oh! Why didn't you tell me before?" Indignantly, Penny peered at her reflection in a hand mirror and rubbed vigorously with her handkerchief.

Outside the *Star* building, newsboys were shouting their wares. As Penny and Jerry started to cross the street, one of the lads who had received a job through the girl's influence, spied the pair.

Approaching, he flashed a paper in front of their eyes.

"See this bird who robbed the bank!" he exclaimed, pointing to the picture of Hamilton Rhett.

"Tommy, I'm afraid your reading is inaccurate," Penny laughed. "The story doesn't say Mr. Rhett robbed a bank."

"He must have done it," the newsboy insisted. "What's the reward for his capture?"

"Mr. Rhett is not listed as a criminal," Penny explained. "There is no reward."

Tommy's face dropped an inch.

"What's the matter, son?" asked Jerry. "Figuring on cashing in?"

"Well, sort of," the boy admitted. "I saw the fellow not an hour ago!"

"He wasn't robbing another bank?" Jerry teased.

"He was going into a house on Fulton Street. I didn't take down the number 'cause when I saw him I didn't think nothin' of it. The Green Streak wasn't out then, and I hadn't seen his picture in the paper."

"Fulton Street?" repeated Penny, frowning. "What section?"

"It was at the corner of Fulton and Cherry. He went into an old three-story brick building with a sign: 'Rooms for rent—beds thirty cents.'"

"Why, Tommy means Riverview's cheapest flop house!" Jerry exclaimed. "I can't imagine a bank president luxuriating in a Fulton Street dump."

"All the same, I saw him. He wore old clothes, but it was the same bird."

"Tommy, you'll grow up to be a police detective some day," Jerry chuckled. He started to pull Penny along, but she held back.

"Wait, Jerry, if there should be anything to it—"

Jerry smiled indulgently.

CHAPTER 9 - JERRY ENTERS THE CASE

"Tell us more about the man you saw," Penny urged Tommy. "How was he dressed?"

"He wore old clothes and a floppy black hat. And there was a scar on his cheek."

"Jerry, Mr. Rhett had a similar scar!"

"And so have dozens of other people. Did I ever show you the one I got when I was a kid? Another boy socked me with a bottle and—"

"Be serious, Jerry! Tommy, are you sure the man you saw looked like the picture in the paper?"

"Cross my heart and hope to die. It was the spitten image! If you catch him, will you give me a reward?"

"We'll split fifty-fifty," grinned Jerry, pulling Penny on by brute force.

But across the street he met unexpected opposition. Stopping dead in her tracks, Penny announced: "This is where we part company. I'm going to investigate that place on Fulton Street!"

"Say, are you crazy? You can't go to a flop house alone!"

"That's exactly what I shall do, unless you come with me."

"It's a waste of time! You know these kids. Tommy read the story, and it fired his imagination."

"Maybe so," admitted Penny, unmoved. "All the same, I'm going there to make certain. How about you?"

Jerry looked longingly at the restaurant and drew a deep sigh.

"Okay," he gave in, "I learned years ago that it's no use arguing with a gal. Lead on, but don't say I didn't warn you!"

CHAPTER 10 - CHEAP LODGING

Street lights blinked on as Penny and Jerry reached the corner of Fulton and Cherry Streets, in the poorer section of Riverview.

"That must be the building," the reporter said, indicating an old, discolored brick building with a faded sign which proclaimed it a cheap rooming house of the type patronized by those who could afford only a few cents for a bed.

They crossed the street. Penny's courage faltered as she saw that they must climb a long, dark stairway. Dust was very thick; the air inside was stuffy.

"You still can change your mind, you know," said Jerry. "Why not wait outside, while I go up?"

Penny shook her head.

Climbing the stairs, they entered an open space from which branched narrow corridors. The landing was even dirtier and darker than the stairway, with a huge pasteboard carton standing in a corner filled with empty bottles.

In a little office room, behind a cage window, sat a plump middle-aged woman with reddish frizzled hair. She eyed the pair suspiciously. To her experienced eye, their manner and clothing immediately stamped them as "outsiders," perhaps investigators. She smiled ingratiatingly at Jerry.

"We're looking for a man," he said briefly.

"You're from the police, ain't you?" she demanded. "We got nothin' to hide. My husband and me run a respectable place for poor workin' men."

"May we see your room register?"

"Sure. Ever since that last copper was here I been keepin' it just like he told me I had to do."

Through the wooden slats of the cage, the woman thrust a grimy notebook which had been ruled off to provide spaces for names, addresses and date of registry.

Rapidly Jerry scanned the entries for several days back. No one by the name of Rhett had registered, but neither he nor Penny had expected the banker would be stupid enough to use his real name, if indeed he had come to such a place.

As Penny glanced about the dingy, smoke-stained room, it seemed impossible to her that Mr. Rhett, a man of culture and wealth, would voluntarily seek such quarters.

"The man we're looking for is middle-aged," Penny explained. "He wore glasses and may have been well dressed. We were told he was seen here earlier tonight."

"They all look alike to me," the woman said wearily. "Most of my rooms are empty now. We don't fill up until the coppers start runnin' loiterers off Cherry Street around ten o'clock. It's still warm enough outside so's a lot o' the cheap skates can sleep out on the river bank."

"Isn't anyone here?" inquired Jerry.

"Maybe one or two men. A fella name of Ben Smith came in about an hour or two ago. He signed up for one of the flops. Come to think of it, maybe he's the one you're after. He acted nervous like and I figured maybe he was dodgin' the police. Another thing, he acted like he was used to havin' money."

"Did he have much on him?"

"I couldn't see, but he paid me with a five dollar bill. And why would a fella with even that much dough sleep in a flop if he wasn't tryin' to dodge the cops?"

"Suppose you describe the man."

CHAPTER 10 - CHEAP LODGING

"He was about average height and middle-aged. No glasses, though. He couldn't have been down and out very long, because he still wore a ring."

"Describe it, please," requested Penny.

"It was a gold ring with a picture of a snake on it—some sort of order probably."

"The plumed serpent!" exclaimed Penny. "Jerry, perhaps Tommy was right!"

"Take us to this man," the reporter directed the landlady.

"How do I know if he's still here? The men come and go and so long as they're paid up, I don't pay no attention. What's he done anyhow?"

"Nothing very serious," Jerry replied. "Anyway, we're not from the police station."

The woman's pretended friendliness vanished. "Then what you pryin' around here for?" she demanded. "Who are you anyhow?"

"We're newspaper reporters."

"I don't want my name in the paper, and we don't want nothing written about this place!"

"Take it easy," Jerry advised. "Your name won't be in the paper. We're only looking for a man. Now lead us to him."

"When people take rooms or a bed in this place they got a right to privacy," the woman argued unpleasantly. "It ain't none o' my business what folks have done that come here."

"We want to talk to this man who registered as Smith. Either take us to him, or we'll have to call in the police. I'm a personal friend of Joe Grabey, the patrolman on this beat."

"I was only kiddin'," the woman said hastily. "You can talk to him if he's here."

Locking the office door behind her, the woman led the pair down a narrow corridor with rooms on either side. A door stood open. Penny caught a glimpse of a cell-like chamber, furnished only with a sagging bed, soiled blankets, and a rickety dresser. The dingy walls were lined with pegs.

"Those nails are for hanging up clothes, and symbolize a man's rise in the world," Jerry pointed out to her. "Men who patronize the flops usually have only the suit on their backs. But when they make a little money and get two suits, they need a safe place to keep the extra clothes during the day. So they rent one of these tiny rooms which can be locked."

Leading the way down a dark hall to the very end, the landlady opened a door. This room with paper-thin walls, sheltered perhaps twenty men, each cot jammed close to its neighbor. The air was disagreeable with the odor of strong disinfectant which had been used on the bare wood floor.

The room now was deserted save for a man in baggy black trousers who sat on one of the cots, reading a comic magazine. Other beds were made up, but empty.

"Is that man Ben Smith?" Penny asked in disappointment, for he bore not the slightest resemblance to the picture of Mr. Rhett.

"No, I don't know what became of Smith, if he ain't here," the landlady answered. She called to the man on the cot. "Jake, seen anyone in here during the last hour?"

He shook his head, staring curiously at the intruders.

To Jerry the woman said: "You'll have to come back later if you want to see Smith. Maybe after ten o'clock."

Jerry scribbled his name and telephone number on a sheet of notebook paper.

"If he does show up, will you telephone me?" he requested.

"Oh, sure," the woman replied, her careless tone making it clear she would never put herself to so much trouble.

Jerry gave her a five dollar bill. "This should make it worth your while," he said. "You'll earn another five if we find the man."

"I'll call you the minute he comes in," the woman promised with more enthusiasm.

Penny drew a deep breath as she and Jerry left the building, stepping out into the cool, sweet air of the street.

"I still doubt we're trailing the right man," remarked Jerry. "Why would Hamilton Rhett hole in at a place like this?"

"It does seem out of the picture. However, we know he wore a serpent ring at the time of his disappearance."

"The ring may not be the same. Also, if Rhett had been the victim of violence, a bum might have stolen it from him."

"I never thought of that. Should we report what we've learned to the police?"

"Not yet," advised Jerry. "Our clue is pretty flimsy. Let's watch and wait. The landlady may call us, and in any case I'll keep my eye on this place."

It now was so late that Penny decided to return home immediately. Bidding Jerry goodbye at the next corner, she boarded a bus and presently was slipping quietly into her own home.

If she had hoped to elude the watchful eye of Mrs. Maud Weems, the housekeeper, she was doomed to disappointment.

The plump, kindly lady who had looked after Penny since the death of Mrs. Parker many years before, had finished the dishes and was sweeping the kitchen. Fixing the girl with a stern eye, she observed:

"You're later than ever tonight, Penny. When your father came home nearly two hours ago, he had no idea what had become of you."

"Then Dad isn't keeping tab on his employes," chuckled Penny. "I've been working on a special story for the *Star*."

"I've heard that one before," sighed the housekeeper. "In fact, I suspect you charge a great many of your escapades to your work! If I had my way you would give it up."

"Oh, Mrs. Weems, don't be cross," Penny pleaded, giving her a squeeze. "Newspaper work is wonderful! Next time I'll telephone you if I know I'll be late."

"Have you had anything to eat?" the housekeeper asked in a softened tone. "Dinner was over an hour ago."

"I'll dig up something for myself from the refrigerator. Where's Dad?"

Even as Penny asked the question, Anthony Parker, a tall, lean man with graying hair, came to the arched doorway of the kitchen. "Now what's all this?" he inquired. "Penny off the reservation again?"

Mrs. Weems made no reply, knowing only too well that in almost any argument the publisher would support his daughter. Many times, and without success, she had told him she disapproved of his system of granting Penny almost unrestricted freedom.

No one doubted that Mr. Parker was an over-indulgent father, but the publisher had raised his daughter according to a strict code. He knew that she had writing talent and a flair for tracking down a story. Only because she had demonstrated that she could look after herself and think clearly in an emergency, did he allow her to make most of her own decisions.

Now, Penny eagerly poured out an account of her experiences in trying to get the Rhett story for the *Star*. Mr. Parker, who had read most of it in the Green Streak edition, listened attentively, offering little comment other than to say:

"I met Rhett once at a Chamber of Commerce luncheon. Not a bad fellow."

"What was he like?" Penny inquired eagerly.

"Quiet and rather bored by the meeting. I don't recall that he said a dozen words during the luncheon."

"Did he look like a man who would walk off with $250,000 in bonds?"

"Not that I noticed," commented the publisher dryly. "But then, nobody can judge character by external appearances."

Hat in hand, Mr. Parker moved toward the kitchen exit.

"Are you going back to the *Star* office?" his daughter asked with alert interest.

"No." Mr. Parker edged nearer the door, but Penny blocked the way.

"Then where are you going, Dad? You're holding out!"

"Must I give you a schedule of my life?"

"You're slipping off somewhere, and you don't want me to go!"

"If you must know, I thought I would drop in at the Gay Nineties, a new night club that is opening tonight. The proprietor is one of our best advertisers and he extended a special invitation to attend."

"Fine!" chuckled Penny. "I'll be with you in five minutes. Just give me time to wash my face and pull the snarls out of my hair."

"I was afraid of it," groaned the publisher. "Haven't you any school work to do?"

"Nary a bit. Besides, it's Saturday night and I haven't had any dinner. You can buy me a great big steak with all the trimmings. And perhaps you will dance with me."

CHAPTER 10 - CHEAP LODGING

Mr. Parker gazed helplessly at Mrs. Weems, but the housekeeper did not come to his rescue. Her shrug indicated that the problem was entirely his.

"Well, all right," he gave in. "But I'll warn you now, this is no party. We'll drop in for an hour or so, then come straight home."

Penny was off like a shot, bounding upstairs to her room. There was no time to change her dress, but she freshened up, and was ready by the time her father had backed the car from the garage.

The Gay Nineties on Euclid Avenue twinkled with lights, and many persons in evening dress were entering beneath the bright red street canopy.

"Looks like all the socialites of the city are here," Penny observed. "Maybe I should have worn my pearls."

"Or washed behind your ears," Mr. Parker chuckled, escorting her inside.

Penny and her father were given one of the best tables in the night club. Studying the menu, the girl was a trifle alarmed to note the prices.

"I'm dreadfully hungry too," she declared. "Dad, I hope you're not intending to charge this outing against my allowance."

"I know I'd have no chance to collect," he teased. "Just relax and select whatever you want. I can stand it this time."

After the order had been given, Penny glanced about the dimly lighted room. The floor show had not yet started. Everywhere she saw well-to-do and prominent persons who had turned out for the gala opening.

Suddenly her attention centered upon a couple who had just entered the door. The woman wore an obviously new white evening gown, and behind her came a short, stubby little man.

"Dad!" she whispered, giving him a kick with the toe of her slipper. "See that man who just came in?"

"Where?" he asked, turning his head.

"He's with the middle-aged woman in white."

"Oh, yes, who are they?" Mr. Parker commented, only mildly interested. "No one I know."

"The man is Albert Potts, secretary to Mr. Rhett at the First National Bank," Penny replied impressively. "How do you suppose he can afford to come to such an expensive night club? If you ask me, Dad, it looks odd!"

CHAPTER 11 - THE WOODEN DOLL

Mr. Parker studied the bank secretary and his wife with more interest. But he said mildly:

"I see nothing especially significant in Potts coming here, Penny. The club is public."

"It's expensive too. The cover charge is two dollars, and you can't touch a dinner for less than another four! How can Potts afford to pay such prices?"

"He may earn a good salary working for Mr. Rhett—probably does. Anyway, folks don't always spend their money wisely, even if they have very little of it."

Potts and his wife swept past the Parker table without noticing Penny or her father. A trifle self-consciously, as if unaccustomed to appearing in such places, they sat down and studied the menu with concentrated interest.

Penny tried but could not keep her eyes from the pair.

"Dad, I wonder if Potts has any more information about Mr. Rhett's disappearance," she presently remarked. "I have a notion to go over there and ask him."

Mr. Parker nodded absently, so Penny started across the room. She was only midway to Potts' table, when the bank secretary raised his eyes and saw her approaching.

A startled, almost dismayed expression came upon his face. He spoke hurriedly to his wife. She looked puzzled, but both arose and walked quickly toward the exit.

Penny started to follow, then thought better of it.

"Mr. Potts knows I'm a reporter," she reflected. "Probably he doesn't care to be annoyed by having to answer questions. On the other hand, is it possible he doesn't want to be recognized in this night club?"

Mr. and Mrs. Potts obtained their wraps at the checkroom and left the building. Somewhat crestfallen, Penny returned to her own table to find her father chatting with acquaintances.

Under the circumstance, she had no opportunity to speak of Mr. Potts' queer behavior. Soon, dinners were brought and after that the floor show began.

Not wishing to keep his daughter out late, Mr. Parker insisted that they leave in the middle of the entertainment. However, the drive home gave Penny time to tell him about the bank secretary. The incident did not seem to impress her father greatly.

"If I were you I wouldn't pester Potts too much," he advised. "He probably doesn't enjoy being the center of public attention."

Penny slept late the next morning, and because it was Sunday, did not visit the *Star* office. The paper that day was voluminous. But in going through it she could find no new facts about the Rhett case. No word had been received from the missing banker; there had been no ransom demand received; and neither had Albert Potts nor Mrs. Rhett shed the slightest light on what might have become of him.

After breakfast, Penny telephoned Jerry Livingston to inquire if he had heard from the Cherry Street landlady.

"Not a word," he reported. "I dropped back there late last night, but the man we're looking for apparently never returned."

Disappointed that the case had reached a dead end, Penny next telephoned the Rhett home. No one answered.

"I'm certain someone is there," she thought. "Mrs. Rhett probably has given orders not to answer the phone."

At a loss to know what to do, Penny spent the morning at home, had dinner, then went down the street to see Louise Sidell. However, her chum had gone to visit an aunt for the day.

CHAPTER 11 - THE WOODEN DOLL

"What miserable luck!" Penny muttered. "No one with whom I can talk over the Rhett case! Nothing to do!"

Suddenly it dawned upon her, that she might call on Albert Potts at his home, and perhaps induce him to reveal a few helpful facts about the missing banker.

From a telephone book she obtained the secretary's address. Thirty minutes later found her standing before a modest cottage on Berdan Avenue. In response to her knock, the same woman Penny had seen the previous night at the Gay Nineties, came to the door. Now she looked very plain and frowsy in a messy housedress, and her hair hung in untidy streamers.

The woman stared at Penny without recognition.

"Is Mr. Potts here?" the girl inquired.

"No, he's not," Mrs. Potts answered without cordiality, her voice coarse and unattractive. "Anything I can do?"

"I wanted to talk to him. Will he return soon?" Penny moved inside the door.

"When he goes off, I never know when he'll get back. He went to the bank, I guess."

"On Sunday?"

"Al's had a lot of work lately. I tell him he ought to let up. He's getting so jumpy he doesn't sleep at nights. Just tosses and keeps me awake."

Before Penny could ask another question, a boy of ten, who had Albert Potts' sharp features, came racing across the yard up to the door.

"Has the bicycle come yet, Ma?" he shouted.

"No, it hasn't, and I wish you'd quit pestering me!" she snapped. "There won't be any deliveries today."

To Penny, the woman explained: "My husband bought Eddie a new bicycle and he won't give us any peace until it comes. Deliveries take such a long time these days. None of the things we bought have come yet."

Penny did not mean to be inquisitive, but instantly it struck her as unusual that the Potts' family should be indulging in a sudden orgy of spending. Nor had she forgotten the couple's hasty departure from the Gay Nineties club.

"Eddie is getting quite a few new things, I take it," she observed casually.

The woman became more friendly. "Oh, yes, my husband ordered a trapeze set for him, and an electric train. But he bought me a lot too! A new piano and a living room rug. We have a new refrigerator on order, a vacuum cleaner and a bedroom suite!"

"Imagine!" exclaimed Penny. "Your husband must have come into a small fortune."

"He was given a raise last week at the bank. I don't know exactly how much, but it must have been a big one, because Al says we'll have enough now for everything we need."

"I think I've seen you before, Mrs. Potts," Penny remarked, seeking additional information. "Weren't you at the Gay Nineties last night?"

"Yes, we were! But we didn't stay long. Before we had ordered our dinner, my husband remembered an important appointment he had made. We had to leave suddenly. It was awfully disappointing. I never went to a night club before and I wanted to see the show!"

Mrs. Potts paused, obviously waiting for Penny to leave. "I'll tell my husband you called," she said. "You didn't give me your name."

Edging out of the door, Penny pretended not to hear the latter remark. Calling over her shoulder that she would try to see Mr. Potts at the bank next day, she retreated before the woman could learn her identity.

Walking toward the bus stop, the girl reflected upon what she had learned. The financial good fortune of the Potts' family was very puzzling. Apparently the bank secretary's salary had been increased since the disappearance of his employer, Mr. Rhett.

"It seems a queer time to raise the man," she mused. "If his duties have become so much heavier, I suppose the bank board may have granted a compensating wage increase. But it must have been an enormous one to enable him to buy everything in the stores!"

As Penny waited at the street corner for a home-bound bus, she saw one approaching which was headed for the outlying section near the Rhett estate area. Impulsively, she decided to go there to see Lorinda.

"I may not get into the house," she thought. "My luck is running badly today. Anyway, I'll give it a try."

It was nearly four o'clock by the time Penny alighted from the bus and walked to the Rhett estate. Her heart sank as she noticed that curtains were drawn in nearly all of the front windows of the house.

"No one here," she thought. "Lorinda and her mother may have left town to escape questioning by reporters and the police."

Because she had come so far, she knocked on the front door. No one came. Giving it up, she wandered around the house, into the garden.

Curiously she gazed toward the thatched roof cottage, wondering if anyone were there. The whispered warning she and Salt had heard the previous day, remained unexplained. She longed to investigate, yet hesitated to trespass.

As she debated, Penny observed a small column of black smoke rising from amid the shrubbery. Someone apparently had built a bonfire on the beach.

Seeking the steps which led down to the river, Penny presently saw that her guess was correct. A small fire of driftwood had been built on the sands. Lorinda, in slacks and an old sweater, was so engrossed in feeding the flames that she did not hear when her name was called.

Descending the steps, Penny hastened to the beach to join the Rhett girl. Lorinda did not hear the approaching footsteps. Deeply absorbed in what she was doing, she stirred the flames with a stick until they leaped merrily.

Then, from a paper sack she withdrew a queer wooden object which even from the distance Penny could see was a doll. Its body appeared to be tightly wound with scarlet thread.

Lorinda held the doll gingerly in her fingers. She stared at it a moment, shuddered, and then with a gesture of abhorrence, hurled it into the crackling flames.

CHAPTER 12 - SUPERSTITION

Penny quickened her step. "Lorinda!" she called again.

The girl at the bonfire whirled around. Seeing Penny, she gave the wooden doll a shove with the toe of her shoe, trying to bury it beneath a pile of burning wood.

Penny was not to be so easily deceived. Reaching the fire, she asked directly: "Lorinda, what in the world are you doing?"

"Why, nothing."

"You're burning something you don't want me to see!"

"It's nothing. Just an old doll."

The wooden object had not yet caught fire, and Penny could still see it plainly.

"Why, it's an effigy doll!" she exclaimed, then observing the face clearly, she added in a shocked voice: "A likeness of your mother!"

The scarlet string around the doll's body caught fire, and soon tongues of flame began to consume the wood. Only then did Lorinda speak.

"Now it is destroyed! But I cannot so easily destroy the evil that threatens my mother!"

"Why, Lorinda! What do you mean? Why are you burning this doll?"

Lorinda sank down on the sand, her eyes upon the fire. "I hadn't intended anyone to know. You swear you will never tell Mother?"

"Of course not."

"I found this doll in a downstairs coat closet. You saw for yourself that it was an effigy of Mother and that it was wrapped with string?"

"Yes, but I fail to understand its significance."

"That scarlet wool string is known as a life-thread. Each day a little of the thread is unwound until finally it all is gone. Then the person dies."

"Not your mother, Lorinda! Surely, you don't believe such a crazy superstition!"

"I don't," Lorinda answered, her voice barely above a whisper. "*But Mother will* if she learns about the doll. That is why she will die, unless I can do something to break the spell."

To Penny the words seemed fantastic, but she realized Lorinda was deadly in earnest and convinced that she was speaking the truth.

"Let's get to the bottom of this, Lorinda. How did the doll come into the house?"

"I only wish I knew. Obviously, it was brought by someone who hates my mother. The doll was carved in her image, and no doubt deadly *basiko* and *dayama* incantations were chanted as the string was wrapped tightly about the body."

"Who told you all this lingo?" Penny demanded suspiciously. "Your stepfather?"

"I learned a little of it from him," Lorinda admitted, "but most of my knowledge came from Celeste and Antón."

"Superstitious natives!"

"Laugh if you like, but this form of dark magic which is practiced in the jungles, is a sort of hypnotism. The victim weakens and dies because he *believes that he is doomed.*"

"Then the antidote is simple. Just don't put any stock in such rot."

"Easily said, but the victim *always believes.*"

"You think your mother will put faith in all this?" Penny scoffed.

Lorinda gave her a strange look. "I know she will, if she learns about the doll. That's why I'm burning it."

"A very sensible act. The doll is destroyed. We'll keep this strictly to ourselves, and the spell is broken!"

"You make it sound very easy."

"Your mother hasn't seen the doll?"

"No, I only found it a few minutes ago."

"Then she'll never hear about it. Haven't you any theory as to how the effigy got into the house?"

"No," Lorinda replied, after a slight hesitation.

"Would your stepfather have had a hand in it?"

"Oh, I don't think so! It would be such a vicious, wicked thing to do!"

"He and your mother always got on well together?"

"No, they had frequent disagreements," Lorinda admitted, squirming uncomfortably. "All the same, my stepfather was not a cruel man."

"Do you have utter confidence in Antón and Celeste?"

"They have been fairly efficient servants. Mother always has treated them well. What reason could they have for hating her?"

"I'm sure I can't see any. Yet someone brought the doll into the house after carving it in your mother's image." Penny thought a moment, and then asked: "Could the Zudi drum have anything to do with it?"

"That angle occurred to me," Lorinda nodded. "From the first, I've been afraid that natives would trail my stepfather here and try to revenge themselves upon him for taking the drum."

"Celeste and Antón are not members of the Zudi cult?"

"No, else they never would have aided my stepfather in acquiring the drum. I understand he never would have heard of it if Celeste hadn't told him of its existence."

"It's all a queer puzzle," Penny commented. "While I suppose it's possible natives could have followed your father to America and now seek revenge upon his wife, such a theory doesn't quite ring the gong."

"Celeste thinks we should get rid of the Zudi drum. Unless we do, she's convinced Mother will die a slow lingering death."

"Celeste seems to have implanted quite a few ideas in your mind," Penny observed dryly. "If you ask me, I should say she's a sinister influence on the household."

"Oh, Celeste means no harm. And the last few days since my stepfather disappeared, she's been very devoted to Mother, waiting on her as if she were a baby."

"Your mother must be terribly worried. You've heard nothing from your stepfather?"

"Not a word. Mother cries half the time, and this morning she refused to leave her room. Even now I'm afraid she is ill."

"Now Lorinda!" reproved Penny. "I'm afraid you're the one who has become hypnotized by that doll!"

"I hope it's just that I'm silly, and that there's nothing to it. But I'm afraid—terribly afraid."

Penny picked up a stick and poked the dying embers. She could find only a charred piece of the doll left on the fire. Flames soon consumed it.

"There, it's gone!" she exclaimed. "Take my advice, Lorinda, and forget this entire incident. Don't tell your mother, Celeste, or anyone."

Lorinda scrambled up, brushing sand from her slacks.

"All right, I'll do as you say," she agreed. "This shall be our secret. At any rate, by burning the doll, I should have put an end to its evil."

Extinguishing the few remaining flames by covering them with sand, the girls slowly climbed the steps. Penny inquired whether or not the police had called at the mansion. Lorinda told her that they had spent nearly two hours questioning Mrs. Rhett.

"By the way," Penny remarked as they approached the house, "do you know Albert Potts?"

"My stepfather's secretary? I've met him a few times. Why?"

"He was quite a favorite with your stepfather, I suppose?"

"A favorite?" Lorinda chuckled. "On the contrary, he couldn't stand him! Potts was always at his elbow, trying to tell him what to do, and what not to do. In his way he was efficient—too efficient, if you know what I mean."

CHAPTER 12 - SUPERSTITION

"I do," agreed Penny. "That was why I was surprised to learn he had been granted a substantial salary increase after your stepfather disappeared."

Lorinda turned her head quickly. "A pay raise? By the board, you mean?"

"I don't know who gave it to him."

"I can't imagine anyone giving old Potts a raise, certainly not the board. The members meet only once a month, on the fifteenth. Of course, it's possible a special session was called because of my stepfather's absence."

"That may have happened," agreed Penny. "At any rate, Mr. Potts seemingly has come into money."

Rounding a twist in the path, the girls came within view of the mansion terrace where Mrs. Rhett, in white, reclined.

"Why, Mother is downstairs!" Lorinda exclaimed in surprise.

The woman did not see the girls until they were very close. But as they reached the terrace, she raised her eyes, and smiled in a brief, sad manner. Penny instantly noted the pallor of her face.

"I appreciate your efforts, Lorinda," she said before either of the girls spoke. "But it is useless."

"What is useless, Mother?" inquired her daughter.

"I saw smoke rising from your fire on the beach."

Lorinda glanced quickly at Penny, laughed nervously and said: "Oh, that! I was burning a little driftwood."

Mrs. Rhett held her daughter's eyes in a steady, knowing gaze.

"It is useless to try to deceive me," she said quietly. "I know you burned the doll."

"Whatever gave you such an idea, Mother?"

"I know," replied the woman with quiet finality. "First the burnt match ends and now the doll! My life thread is reaching its end, and I shall slowly weaken and die."

CHAPTER 13 - MISSING FROM THE CHEST

"Mother, how did you learn about the wooden doll?" Lorinda gasped. "And where did you get such a crazy idea that you will weaken and die?"

"I have known it ever since my husband went away."

"But that's impossible!" cried Lorinda, fairly beside herself with anxiety. "I'm sure the doll wasn't in the house until today. Someone is putting these notions in your head! Is it Celeste?"

"Celeste is doing her best to help, but there is nothing she can do," Mrs. Rhett said sadly.

"Mother, snap out of this! You're worried about Father and it has made you morbid. Nothing will happen to you. The doll has been destroyed, and in any case, we know it's only a stupid effigy."

Dropping her head wearily on the chair back, Mrs. Rhett smiled and said nothing. Closing her eyes, she relaxed for a moment. Penny and Lorinda thought she might be dropping off to sleep, so they moved quietly away.

Mrs. Rhett's eyes opened then and she said: "Oh, Lorinda!"

"Yes, Mother."

"There's something I wish to mention—about my will."

"Your will?" the girl repeated with distaste. "Why talk about that—now of all times!"

"There may be no better time," Mrs. Rhett said. "As you know, my will is kept in the safe. It leaves this house and nearly all of my property to Hamilton."

"Let's not talk about it," Lorinda pleaded nervously. "At the time you made the will, we decided it was very fair."

"I thought so then, because you have substantial income in your own name. Hamilton, on the other hand, has nothing—scarcely a penny except his salary at the bank."

"You were right in leaving money to him, Mother. I never objected."

"The situation has changed now," Mrs. Rhett continued. "My husband may never return. If I should die suddenly, the estate would be left to him, but he might not appear to claim it. To my knowledge, he has no relatives. It could all become an awkward legal muddle."

"You certainly are borrowing trouble, Mother! Father will be found, and everything will be the same as before."

"I wish I could think so, Lorinda."

"Forget about the will."

Mrs. Rhett shook her head. "I think I shall change it. And soon. However, at this moment, I don't know how I wish to dispose of some of my property. Nearly everything I own is tied up in real estate."

The woman arose, and remarking that she had a severe headache, started into the house.

"I'll lie down for a little while," she murmured. "I feel so weak and tired."

Lorinda waited until her mother was well beyond hearing. Then she turned to Penny with stricken eyes.

"You heard what she said! She must have learned about that hideous doll from Celeste!"

"But how did Celeste know of it? You told her?"

"Oh, no! But Celeste has a way of knowing everything that goes on in this household. What ought I to do?"

"If I were in your place I would get rid of Celeste and Antón. Send them packing!"

The suggestion seemed almost shocking to Lorinda.

"Oh, I couldn't do that," she answered. "In the first place, my stepfather would be furious if he returned and found them gone. Secondly, I doubt that they would go on my orders. They're very independent."

CHAPTER 13 - MISSING FROM THE CHEST

"Then I don't see what you can do."

"If only my stepfather were here! Unless he returns soon I'm afraid something dreadful will happen to Mother. Did she look well to you?"

"Well—" Penny hesitated, and then said truthfully: "She seemed pale and listless. But one can understand that, considering what she has been through."

"I heard her give orders about her food this morning. She told Celeste she would have trays served in her room, and *no food is to be cooked with salt.*"

"Is that especially significant?"

"My stepfather once told me natives who believe a hex or *ouange* have been put on them are afraid to eat salted food. The salt is supposed to turn to poison in their bodies!"

Penny would have laughed had the matter not been so serious.

"Lorinda, you're as superstitious as a little savage!"

"I don't believe such a thing myself," the girl denied. "But Mother apparently does. She always was afraid of everything remotely connected with cult practices. She never wanted my stepfather to have books on the subject in the library, yet recently I saw her reading them."

"You said they disagreed about his interest in ancient cult practices?"

"Yes," Lorinda admitted. "Otherwise they got on quite well together. Perhaps I shouldn't tell you this, but two days before he went away, they had a violent disagreement. Mother wanted to discharge Antón and Celeste, and he refused. Then on the last day my stepfather was seen, Mother went to the bank to talk to him. She never told me what happened there."

"According to Albert Potts, they had another quarrel."

"I shouldn't wonder," Lorinda sighed. "And now Mother's attitude toward Celeste is so changed—she actually clings to her. Oh dear, it's all so upsetting."

"You're trying to take too much upon your shoulders," Penny said kindly.

Conversation lagged. Lorinda could not throw aside the deep mood of depression which possessed her. Penny knew she no longer had an excuse to linger, yet she was unwilling to leave without asking a few questions about the thatched roof cottage.

"Lorinda, why did you try to keep me from visiting it the other day?" she inquired.

"Well, I didn't know you then. My stepfather's trophies all are kept in the cottage, and I didn't want anyone prying about."

"Then actually it's not a place of evil?"

Lorinda hesitated and answered indirectly: "I almost never go to the cottage myself. Once I was badly frightened there—it was nothing—but for a silly reason, I've always dreaded going back."

"You didn't by chance hear whispering from within the walls?"

Lorinda gave her companion a quick, startled look. "Why do you ask, Penny?"

"Because I visited the cottage yesterday with Salt Sommers. We distinctly heard a voice which seemed to come from the wall itself. When we went outside to investigate, the door slammed shut and locked."

"It has an automatic catch," Lorinda explained. "I never heard voices there, but I had a strange feeling when I was in the room—as if the walls had eyes and I was being watched."

"The cottage always is kept locked?" Penny inquired.

"Yes, my stepfather's trophies are valuable, and we can't risk having them stolen. How did you get inside?"

Penny had the grace to blush. "Well, to make a long story short, we went in through the window," she admitted. "It was a dreadful thing to do, and I'm heartily ashamed."

"I don't blame you," Lorinda laughed. "Naturally you were curious after I tried so hard to keep you away. Would you like to see the cottage again?"

"Indeed, yes!"

"I'll get the key," Lorinda offered.

She vanished into the house and was gone so long that Penny wondered what could be delaying the girl. When she finally appeared on the veranda, her face was as dark as a rain cloud.

"The key is gone!" she exclaimed. "It's always been kept in the top drawer of the dresser in my stepfather's room. I couldn't find it anywhere."

"Perhaps he took it with him that last day he went to the bank," suggested Penny.

"Possibly," agreed Lorinda, though without conviction. "I hope nothing has been stolen from the cottage."

Alarmed at being unable to find the key, the girls walked hurriedly along the wooded path to the trophy house. From afar, Lorinda saw that the door was open a tiny crack.

"Either the place has been ransacked, or someone is there now!" she declared excitedly.

They approached swiftly but with noiseless tread. Lorinda suddenly flung open the cottage door.

The room was deserted. Trophies were exactly as Penny had seen them the previous day.

"That's funny," Lorinda commented, entering, "I was certain I'd find someone here. Perhaps you and your friend failed to lock the door after you left yesterday."

"It locked itself. We tried it, and couldn't get in. Anyway, even if we had left the door open, that still leaves the question of what became of the missing key."

Lorinda nodded thoughtfully as her gaze swept the room.

"Everything seems to be here," she remarked.

"What does the chest contain?" Penny inquired curiously. "Salt and I wanted to peek inside yesterday, but didn't have a chance."

"I'll show you," Lorinda offered.

Pulling out the chest, she raised the lid. The top compartment tray was empty. Looking a trifle puzzled, Lorinda jerked it from the wooden container. The lower section of the chest also was empty.

"Why, everything is gone!" she cried. "My stepfather kept an altar cloth, a feathered head dress, two carved knives, several rattles, and I don't know what all in this chest! They've been stolen!"

CHAPTER 14 - STORM WARNINGS

Penny dropped down on her knees beside Lorinda, peering into the empty wooden box.

"I hope you don't think Salt and I took anything when we were here," she murmured uncomfortably. "We never even opened the chest."

"Of course I know you didn't," Lorinda replied. "Such a thought never entered my mind. But it's disturbing to know these things are gone. Why weren't the other trophies taken also?"

"Possibly, because the person who stole them thought the objects inside the chest would not be so quickly missed."

Lorinda nodded as if in agreement, and closed the chest. As she straightened up, a tense, strained expression came over her face, and she stiffened.

"Listen!" she whispered.

From behind the walls of the house came a muffled dum—dum—dum of a drum. Even as the girls tensely listened, the sound died away.

"Could this cottage have a secret panel?" Penny asked in an excited voice.

"I don't think so." Badly frightened, Lorinda tried not to show it. "At least I never heard of one."

Penny began tapping the walls, none of which gave off a hollow sound. The section by the fireplace appeared somewhat thicker than the others. However, if it contained a moveable panel, she could not locate it.

Her gaze fell upon the cocoanut shell lamp, its bowl nearly exhausted of oil.

"Lorinda," she inquired, "is this room usually lighted?"

"Why, no."

"When Salt and I were here, we saw the cocoanut shell lamp burning. A little oil is left in it now."

"I can't imagine how it came to be there," Lorinda said in a hushed voice. "My stepfather may have filled it long ago, but he certainly never spoke of it."

Hurriedly the girls left the cottage, closing the door tightly behind them. Lorinda tested it twice to make certain the lock had caught.

"The sound of those drums—" she murmured. "Penny, did I imagine it?"

"I assure you, you didn't. I heard them too."

"Then the sound came from the beach," Lorinda declared firmly. "It couldn't have been otherwise. No one is anywhere around here."

"Let's go to the beach and look around," Penny proposed.

Almost at a run, they cut across the garden to the steps which led to the river's edge. Reaching the beach they paused to listen. No sound of drums could be heard and no one was in sight.

"It couldn't have come from here," Penny said. "Lorinda, that drumming definitely was tied up with the cottage."

"But the sound was muffled and far away."

"The cottage may have a passageway connection."

"I never heard of such a thing."

"How long ago was the cottage built, Lorinda?"

"The summer after Mother and my stepfather were married. I remember, Mother and I went away for a month to visit a cousin. When we returned, the cottage was finished. My stepfather ordered it done while we were away. Mother didn't like it one bit."

"Then you actually weren't here when the cottage was built? For all you know, a secret passageway or false panels in the walls, may have been put in?"

"I suppose it could have been done," Lorinda admitted reluctantly.

"Who would know about the cottage except your stepfather? Did you learn the builder's name?"

"I'm not sure there was one. I think my stepfather and Antón did most of the work themselves."

"Let's talk to Antón," suggested Penny. "Perhaps he can shed light on the mystery of those whispering, drum-pounding walls!"

Antón, however, was nowhere to be found. After searching for him in the house and on the grounds, the girls abandoned the search.

By this time it was growing late, so Penny regretfully bade her friend goodbye, and returned home.

Try as she would, she could not forget the strange events of the afternoon, nor Mrs. Rhett's obsession that she would have a long and fatal illness.

"Even now that woman is mentally ill," she thought. "I do hope Lorinda calls in a doctor without delay."

Although removed from the depressing mansion atmosphere, Penny found it impossible to forget the effigy and the conviction Lorinda had of its powers.

"Dad," she said abruptly that night when dinner was over. "Do you believe in black magic?"

"I don't believe in any kind of magic, black, red, pink or green," he answered absently. "What's on your mind now?"

Penny told him of her adventure at the Rhett estate. She confidently expected her father to make light of the entire affair, but to her surprise he listened with flattering attention and asked many questions.

"It's fantastic!" he exclaimed when she finished. "Utterly fantastic! Yet I've read of cases where natives have been taken ill and although doctors declared not a thing was the matter with them, they weakened and died. Is Mrs. Rhett an hysterical type of woman?"

"Yes, I think so."

"Then she may be in real danger! Obviously, something underhanded is going on at the mansion!"

Pulling himself out of a comfortable chair, Mr. Parker went to the hall closet for his hat, coat and cane.

"You're not going to the police station, are you, Dad?"

"No, I want to talk this over first with a man of my acquaintance who is better versed in cult practices and superstitions than anyone I know. He's Professor Kennedy of Riverview College. He spent many years in Africa, Egypt and along the Amazon river."

"May I go with you, Dad?"

"Come along," he invited. "You know all the facts, and I may get them mixed up."

Twenty minutes later Penny and her father were in the cozy study of Professor James Kennedy on Braemer Drive. An elderly man with a very soft voice, he greeted the Parkers cordially and displayed keen interest as they revealed the purpose of their call.

"I once met Mr. Rhett at a dinner party," Professor Kennedy remarked. "He is a highly intelligent gentleman and we had a very animated conversation."

"Did Rhett impress you as a man who might dabble in black magic practice to gain his ends?" Mr. Parker inquired.

Professor Kennedy dropped a log on the fire before he answered. Considering his words carefully, he said:

"Undoubtedly, Mr. Rhett would have the knowledge, but he struck me as a man of unusual character. Suppose you explain more fully what you have in mind."

Professor Kennedy listened soberly as Penny recounted her many observations while at the Rhett mansion. He frowned slightly as she told how Mrs. Rhett had found the burnt match ends tied with scarlet string. When she disclosed how Lorinda and she destroyed the wooden doll, he no longer could remain silent.

"Indeed, you are correct in thinking someone may be trying to practice a little jungle magic!" he exclaimed. "Mrs. Rhett may be in grave danger unless we take counter-measures."

"But why should anyone seek to harm her?" Penny inquired. "You don't think she'll actually be physically hurt?"

"Her mind will be influenced—poisoned," the professor explained. "Oh, I don't mean a drug will be used, but there are subtle and just as effective ways. Now those burned match ends and the doll are only symbols, harmless in themselves, yet they are a means by which Mrs. Rhett may be made seriously ill."

CHAPTER 14 - STORM WARNINGS

"Merely by the use of suggestion?"

"Yes."

"But it's all such nonsense!" Penny protested.

"To you—yes. But not to Mrs. Rhett. Tell me, does she know that the doll existed?"

"Yes, she learned about it—probably from Antón or Celeste."

The professor nodded. "The intended victim *always knows*," he declared. "By one means or another he is informed through those who seek his ruin. To be effective, the person must fear the mumbo-jumbo hocus-pocus."

"Mrs. Rhett does fear it," Penny confirmed. "What's worse, she already believes herself marked for long illness. She actually looked ill today."

"She is mentally sick, and the symptoms will develop, unless counter-measures quickly are adopted."

"What do you advise, Professor?" asked Mr. Parker. "Perhaps if Mrs. Rhett were sent away from Riverview for a short while—"

"It would be of no avail, for the basic belief that she is ill would remain in her mind. No, this thing, must be plucked out at the root. The doll has been burned. That is good! Now the one who seeks to will this sickness upon Mrs. Rhett must be found and confronted with his crime."

"We don't know who is behind it," said Mr. Parker.

"I read in the papers Mr. Rhett has vanished. However, I wonder, is it not possible he actually is still in Riverview?"

"But you said yourself, Mr. Rhett doesn't appear the type of man to do such a ghastly thing," broke in Mr. Parker.

"So I did, but we dare not close our eyes to such a possibility. I believe you mentioned two servants, Antón and Celeste, who also are versed in cult practices, no doubt."

"Celeste is the one I suspect!" cried Penny. "But she has no good reason for hating Mrs. Rhett who seemingly always has been kind to her."

"Regardless, my advice is that the two servants be watched closely. And when the guilty person is found, as he must be, ordinary threats or punishments are likely to prove useless in dealing with him. He must be fought with his own superstitious weapons."

Mr. Parker and Penny talked on and on with the professor whose discussion of the effects of auto-suggestion only served to heighten their anxiety regarding Mrs. Rhett. When they left the house at midnight, Penny was deeply depressed.

"It's all very well for the professor to say 'find the guilty party and fight him with his own weapons,'" she declared, "but how can we do it? In the first place, Lorinda is our only contact with the Rhett household."

"Secondly, we're not gifted in all this hocus-pocus. It's a case for the police," added her father.

"But we have no proof of anything," Penny pointed out.

"True," agreed her father. "I may talk to the police chief about it. Meanwhile, we're interested in keeping abreast of developments for the *Star*. If you're sent out there again, be watchfully alert, but say nothing to Lorinda or anyone else about your suspicions. The case could take an ugly turn. In that event, I don't want you involved."

"It's fun working on the story, Dad. But I also want to help Lorinda and especially her mother."

Penny realized her father had given excellent advice, and made up her mind to follow it. She became thoughtfully silent as they motored home.

"Wonder what the news is tonight?" Mr. Parker remarked, halting the car at a street corner to buy a newspaper.

Glaring headlines occupied the front page. Mr. Parker's first thought was that the missing banker had been found. He snapped on the interior car light to read the banner.

His stunned silence as he stared at it, caused Penny to peer over his shoulder. The lead story was not about Mr. Rhett's mysterious disappearance. Instead, the bold black type proclaimed:

"STORM WARNINGS POSTED. RIVERVIEW BELIEVED TO BE IN PATH OF APPROACHING HURRICANE!"

CHAPTER 15 - MRS. RHETT'S ILLNESS

News that a violent storm was sweeping toward Riverview held the front pages throughout Monday, and became almost the only topic of conversation on the streets.

Skies remained sunny, however, and presently fears were somewhat quieted by national wire service reports that the hurricane was believed to be veering eastward. Government observers now were quoted as predicting only the edge of the hurricane would strike the coast, and inland states might escape unscathed.

Accordingly, business went on much the same as usual. Lulled by the knowledge that never in the history of Riverview had a hurricane struck, the citizens now and then glanced at the falling barometer, but otherwise gave the matter little thought.

Although the disappearance of Hamilton Rhett had been crowded completely from the front pages, Penny did not lose interest in the case. Twice she telephoned the mansion, only to receive no response. She did not visit the estate, for Editor DeWitt kept her busy with special assignments.

After school Tuesday, Penny was sent to the Hanover Steamship Co. offices to interview a tugboat captain. Enroute she ran into Louise Sidell. Her chum regarded her accusingly.

"A great pal you turned out to be, Penny Parker! Remember—you left me standing at the door of the First National."

"I'm terribly sorry, Lou," Penny apologized. "I was inside much longer than I expected to be and when I came out, you were gone."

"You never even telephoned to tell me what happened, you egg! I read all about it in the papers."

"You may have read part of the story, but not all," Penny corrected. "I called for you on Sunday when you were out, and since then I've been busier than a hop toad. Right now I'm on my way to the steamship office. Want to come along?"

"I suppose it's the only way I'll get any information out of you," Louise grumbled, falling into step.

As they walked toward the docks, she asked leading questions and, by the time they reached the steamship offices, had gleaned most of the story.

"So you believe Mr. Rhett may be somewhere in Riverview?" she mused.

"Jerry and I thought so at first, but we've nearly abandoned the idea. The only clue we uncovered led to a dead end."

Pausing near the tugboat office, the girls stood for a moment watching waves pound against the docks. A chill, persistent wind had sprung up which penetrated their light clothing.

"B-r! It's getting colder!" Louise shivered, huddling close to Penny. "Maybe that storm the newspapers predicted is heading in this direction after all!"

Entering the tugboat office, the girls sought Captain Dolphin. The genial old fellow had been interviewed so many times that he knew the story of his life almost by heart and recited it with great gusto. Penny took a few notes and arose to leave.

"What do you think of the weather, captain?" she inquired casually.

His answer surprised her. "We don't like the look of 'er here," he said, frowning. "Barometer's been falling all day. I'm callin' in all my tugs off the river."

"Then you believe the storm actually may strike here?"

"We're not takin' any chances," replied the captain. "Once when I was a young twirp shippin' on a freighter, a hurricane struck us off the Florida Keys. We made port, but it was by the skin of a shark's tooth! Never want to see another storm like that one!"

CHAPTER 15 - MRS. RHETT'S ILLNESS

Penny pocketed her notebook, and the girls went outside into the rising wind. More conscious now of its icy bite, they huddled for a moment in the shelter of the office doorway.

Only a few doors away stood the Hartmann Steamship Company offices, whose large river boats plied up the Coast and on to distant world ports.

Through the plate glass window of the ticket office, Penny's attention was attracted to a slightly stooped man in rumpled clothing who was talking to the man in charge. He turned slightly, and as she saw his profile, she was struck by his remarkable resemblance to the newspaper photograph of Hamilton Rhett.

"Lou, see that man in the ticket office!" she exclaimed. "Doesn't he look like the missing banker?"

Louise studied the stranger a moment and replied: "How should I know? I've never seen him."

"Surely you saw the picture the *Star* published!"

"Yes, but I didn't pay much attention."

The man now was leaving the ticket office. Impulsively, Penny stepped forward to intercept him. "I beg your pardon—" she began.

Alert, wary eyes bore into her own as the stranger gazed straight at her for an instant. He said nothing, waiting for her to continue.

"Aren't you Hamilton Rhett?" Penny asked, deciding to make a direct approach.

"No, you are mistaken," the man replied.

Pushing past Penny, he went hurriedly on down the street.

"You see!" commented Louise. "That's what you get for jumping to such rash conclusions!"

Penny, however, was far from convinced that she had made a mistake.

"If that man wasn't Mr. Rhett, it was his double! Lou, did you notice if he wore a serpent ring?"

"He kept both hands in his pockets."

"That's so, he did!" agreed Penny. "Wait here for me! I'll ask the ticket agent a few questions!"

She was inside the office perhaps five minutes. When she returned, visibly excited, she glanced anxiously up the street. The stranger had vanished from view down the short street, apparently having turned at the first corner.

"We must overtake him!" Penny cried. "I have a hunch we let Mr. Rhett pull a fast one!"

Hurriedly, the girls walked to the corner. The stranger was nowhere to be seen. Whether he had disappeared into a building, down an alley or another street, they had no way of knowing. Penny stopped two pedestrians to inquire, but no one had noticed the man.

"We've lost him!" she exclaimed to Louise. "How disgusting!"

"What did the ticket man tell you, Penny?"

"That the man was inquiring about steamship accommodations to New Orleans, and on to South America. He didn't give his name."

"Then how can you be sure it was Mr. Rhett?"

"It's only a hunch. But the agent said the man was wearing a ring—he didn't notice the type."

"Any number of men wear rings," Louise scoffed. "Penny, aren't you indulging in a little wishful thinking? You want to find Mr. Rhett so badly you're letting your imagination run riot."

"Maybe you're right," Penny admitted with a sigh. "Anyway, we've lost the fellow, so we may as well forget it."

Saying goodbye to Louise, she hastened off to the *Star* office to write up the interview with the tugboat captain. However, she could not put her mind on her work, and after making three false starts, she decided to postpone the story until after dinner.

Fortified by a good meal, she wrote the story much easier, but Penny was far from satisfied when she turned her finished copy in at the desk.

"Guess I'm off the beam tonight," she remarked to Jerry. "It took me an age to write that story."

Penny glanced at the clock. Time had passed swiftly for it was now after nine.

"You look tired," observed the night editor. "There's nothing more for you to do. Why don't you skip out?"

"Guess I will," agreed Penny, reaching for her hat. "I have a geometry test coming up tomorrow."

She was through the swinging barrier, and half way down the hall when Jerry called to her: "Telephone for you, Penny."

With a sigh, she returned to take the call. Weariness vanished and she became wide-awake as she recognized Lorinda Rhett's voice at the other end of the line.

"Miss Parker?" the girl inquired in an agitated voice.

"Speaking."

"I'm sorry to bother you," Lorinda went on, "but could you possibly come to our house right away?"

"Why, I think so," Penny said, instantly divining that something was amiss at the mansion. "Is anything wrong?"

"Oh, yes! Everything! I can't tell you over the phone. Just come as quickly as you can. I need your help."

After hanging up the receiver, Penny related the conversation to the night editor. "I don't know exactly what the call means," she added. "Possibly, Lorinda has learned something about her missing stepfather. If so, it should make a good story!"

"Give us a ring from the mansion if any thing develops," the night editor instructed. "Better take Jerry along with you. No telling what may turn up."

Jerry already was on his feet, reaching for his hat. His car was parked on the street. Traffic flow had dwindled, enabling them to reach the mansion in record time.

The lower floor of the Rhett home was dark, but on the second floor, nearly all the rooms were ablaze with light.

"Wonder what's up!" mused Jerry, parking the car across the street.

"Lorinda is expecting me alone," Penny said. "Maybe it would be better for you to wait here until I have a chance to talk to her."

"Sure. Just signal if you need me."

Jerry switched off the car lights and settled himself for a lengthy vigil.

Penny ran up the walk and pounded on the door. In a moment, she heard footsteps; the living room light flashed on; then the door was opened by Lorinda.

"Is anything the matter?" Penny inquired anxiously.

"It's Mother," Lorinda explained. "She's very ill. We have the doctor now. I'm dreadfully worried."

Penny, at a loss to understand how she could be of help, nodded sympathetically.

"Come with me upstairs," Lorinda requested. "I want you to see and talk to Mother, and then tell me what you think."

"What seems to be the trouble?"

"She refuses food and she has rapidly failed since you last saw her. I've tried to reason with her, but it is useless. She is convinced she has a fatal illness and will die!"

Deeply troubled, Penny followed Lorinda upstairs to the luxuriously furnished bed chamber. Celeste, in white starched uniform, was hovering anxiously over the bed where Mrs. Rhett lay. Lorinda's mother looked ten years older than when Penny had last seen her. Her face was pale and shriveled, her eyes listless.

"I don't want the food!" she said peevishly to Celeste, pushing aside a spoonful of custard which was held to her lips. "It is useless to eat."

On the other side of the bed stood a stout, middle-aged man whom Lorinda introduced as Doctor Everett, a specialist.

"Mrs. Rhett," he said sternly, "you are acting very foolish in refusing food. I have made a careful examination and can find nothing whatsoever the matter."

"I didn't call you to this house," the woman retorted. "Please go away and leave me alone. One has a right to die in peace."

"You will not die," said the doctor patiently. "Your illness is only a fancy of the mind."

Mrs. Rhett tossed her head on the pillow. "Go away!" she ordered. "It was my daughter who called you here—not I. No doctor can be of the slightest aid to me."

"Not unless you are willing to cooperate. Now I suggest that a trained nurse be called in to—"

"A trained nurse!" cried Celeste, straightening from the bedside. "Only I will tend my mistress! We will have no stranger in the household!"

"I want Celeste," agreed Mrs. Rhett, clinging to the servant's hand. "She is the only one who understands my ailment. Celeste will take care of me—no one else."

CHAPTER 15 - MRS. RHETT'S ILLNESS

The doctor shrugged. "Very well, it was only a suggestion. I should like to help you, but under the circumstance, there is nothing I can do. Good evening."

As the doctor reached for his black bag, Lorinda moved quickly across the room. Her eyes pleaded with him to understand.

"Doctor Everett, you'll come again tomorrow?" she requested.

He smiled, but shook his head. "You might call Doctor Fellows, a psychiatrist," he advised. "There is nothing I can do."

While Lorinda accompanied the doctor to the front door, Penny remained in the bedroom. No sooner had the physician left than Celeste moved close to the bed, muttering:

"Good! He is gone! Only a fool would believe a doctor could help you. Until the *ouange* is broken, food will only turn to poison in your body! You will weaken and die. But Celeste will save you—Celeste will find a way to break the evil spell."

CHAPTER 16 - AN OPEN WINDOW

Unmindful of Penny, Celeste bent lower over her bed-ridden mistress, whispering words into her ear.

"Celeste! What are you saying?" Penny demanded. "Why, you're putting dangerous ideas into Mrs. Rhett's mind!"

The servant whirled toward her angrily. "Go away!" she ordered. "My mistress does not want you here!"

"Celeste!" reproved Mrs. Rhett, but in a mild voice.

Penny stood her ground, stubbornly determined that a servant should not order her away. For a moment she and Celeste measured each other with steady gaze. Nothing more was said. Mrs. Rhett sighed, closed her eyes, and seemed to drowse.

Lorinda came bounding up the stairs two at a time. Unaware that anything unpleasant had transpired during her absence, she said with forced cheerfulness:

"Now, Mother, let's have no more nonsense. You're to eat your food without fuss. Here, let's try the custard again."

Mrs. Rhett pushed away the spoon. "No, Lorinda, it is useless. But there is something you may do for me."

"Anything you wish, Mother."

"Bring pen and ink."

"Are you really strong enough to write a letter?"

"I intend to change my will. Lorinda, we spoke of this the other day. While I still have the strength I must revoke my former will and leave all my property to you."

"Oh, Mother, don't talk of such things! Why, the doctor says you're in perfect physical condition. You'll be up and around in another day or two. It's only worry about Father that has put you under the weather."

"I have made up my mind, Lorinda. The will must be changed—now—tonight, while I have the strength."

"Very well, if it will make you rest easier," Lorinda said reluctantly. "Celeste, bring ink, a pen and paper."

Celeste made no move to obey. "My mistress is not strong enough to write," she mumbled.

"Mother wishes to change the will. Please bring the materials."

"To change the will while one lies on a sick bed is to invite great trouble."

"Celeste! No more of such talk! Do as you are told!"

Penny thought the servant would refuse to obey, but she shuffled off. Many minutes passed before she returned with the requested materials.

Lorinda sat down at the bedside, and wrote at her Mother's dictation. It was a simple will in which Mrs. Rhett left all of her property to her daughter.

"If I thought my husband ever would return, I would want him to receive all my holdings," she said. "As it is, I think the money should go to you, Lorinda."

Penny was tempted to speak of her own belief that Mr. Rhett might be alive and in the city. However, realizing she had not a scrap of proof, she wisely remained silent.

Mrs. Rhett signed the will. Lorinda and Penny then added their names as witnesses to the document.

"Lock the will in the safe," Mrs. Rhett instructed her daughter. "Do it now, before you forget."

"Yes, Mother."

Seemingly relieved that the matter had been accomplished, Mrs. Rhett turned over in bed and tried to sleep. Leaving Celeste to look after her, Penny and Lorinda went downstairs to the study.

"Celeste seemed to be displeased because your mother changed the will," Penny remarked.

CHAPTER 16 - AN OPEN WINDOW

"Yes, Celeste has become a problem. I feel the doctor was right in suggesting a nurse for Mother. Celeste *may* mean well, but she is a distinct influence for the worse."

"Then why not get rid of her?"

"How?"

"Tell her to go."

Lorinda laughed shortly. "You don't know Celeste if you think she would take such an order from me!"

"Then have your mother dismiss her."

"I'm not sure she would do it. Furthermore, Celeste might defy her too. She has the idea she'll take orders only from my stepfather."

"I believe you're actually afraid of the woman," Penny commented.

"In a way I am," Lorinda admitted. "Mother used to dislike her intensely. Strangely, since she has become ill, she seems to depend more upon Celeste than she does upon me."

"Did it ever occur to you that Celeste might deliberately be planting ideas in your mother's mind?"

"Yes, I've thought of it. I don't believe Celeste would be evil enough to do it on purpose, but she is highly superstitious. I wish she were out of the house."

"You could get rid of her if you really wanted to. Just call in the police, and have them take over."

"I couldn't do that. Mother would never forgive me."

The girls entered the study, and Lorinda switched on a light. After pulling the blinds, she removed the wall picture, and prepared to open the safe.

Before she could spin the dials, footsteps padded on the stairway. Celeste appeared suddenly in the study doorway.

"Come quick!" she pleaded. "Mistress much worse!"

Lorinda dropped the will on the table, and with Penny close at her heels, followed Celeste up the stairway. Expecting the worst, they peered anxiously at Mrs. Rhett. She was tossing restlessly, but otherwise appeared the same as when they had seen her a few minutes ago.

"How do you feel, Mother?" Lorinda asked.

"Just the same," Mrs. Rhett replied listlessly.

Lorinda gazed questioningly at Celeste.

"Mistress much better now," the servant said. "She had sinking spell while you were downstairs."

"I'm afraid you imagined it, Celeste," Lorinda replied severely. "This really proves that we should have a trained nurse. Otherwise, you'll frighten us all out of our wits."

Celeste started to make a retort, but just then Mrs. Rhett spoke: "Lorinda, did you put the will in the safe?" she asked.

"I was doing it when Celeste called. I'll attend to it right away."

Lorinda stooped to kiss her mother and offer a glass of water which was declined. She then went downstairs once more with Penny.

"What do you suppose possessed Celeste to frighten me so?" she remarked thoughtfully. "Did Mother seem changed to you?"

"Not a particle."

Reaching the study, Lorinda went directly to the table where she had left the signed will. The paper was not there.

"Why, Penny, what did I do with it?" she demanded in bewilderment. "I was certain I left it here."

"I distinctly recall that you did," Penny replied, her gaze wandering to an open window where a curtain fluttered in the breeze. "Lorinda, I think while we were away, someone came in from outside and took the will!"

CHAPTER 17 - THE STOLEN WILL

Penny darted to the open window, peering out onto the dark street. No one was in sight, although Jerry's car with dimmed headlights still stood at the curb.

"Who could have taken the will?" Lorinda wailed. "I'm sure it didn't blow out the window and it didn't sprout legs and walk off either!"

"Perhaps Celeste—"

"She was upstairs all the time we were out of this room," Lorinda interrupted.

"It seemed odd she called us just at the moment she did—particularly when your mother had not suffered a relapse."

Lorinda did not appear to hear Penny's remark. Half doubting that the paper could be missing, she searched on the floor near the safe, under the window and in every corner of the room.

"I suspect someone deliberately stole that will!" Penny said with conviction. "Wait here! I may be able to learn more about it!"

Hastening outdoors, she gazed about the grounds. No one was in sight. She went directly to the press car. The automobile was deserted.

"Now what became of Jerry?" she asked herself impatiently. "Just when I need him!"

Disappointed, she turned toward the house again. Then she saw the reporter coming up a dark path from the direction of the beach.

"Jerry!" she called softly.

"Hi, Penny!" he returned. "Ready to go?"

"Oh, no! Everything is in a dreadful mess here. Lorinda's mother is very sick. She made a will, and Lorinda started to put it in the safe. Then we were called out of the room by the housekeeper, and when we returned, the paper was gone!"

"When did that happen, Penny?"

"Just now."

"Then that fellow I chased must have been the thief!"

"You saw someone take the will, Jerry?"

"I was sitting in the car," the reporter related. "A light was on in one of the downstairs rooms, but I was too sleepy to pay much attention. Suddenly though, I saw a man who apparently had been hiding in the shrubbery, rise up and climb through an open window."

"A man! Could you see who it was?"

"No, it was too dark. I jumped out of the car, but before I could cross the yard, the fellow climbed out through the window again, and started off. I called to him. He covered his face and ran. I chased him, but the fellow ducked down a path and I lost him."

"He must have stolen the will, Jerry! But how did he know about it, and why would it be of any value to him? Everything is so mixed up!"

"Maybe we ought to give the police a buzz."

Penny nodded. "I'll see what Lorinda wants to do," she replied. "Until now, the Rhetts have studiously avoided telling their troubles to the police—in fact, I am afraid Mrs. Rhett hasn't told everything she knows about her husband's disappearance."

"I'll wait in the car," Jerry said.

CHAPTER 17 - THE STOLEN WILL

Penny let herself into the house again and made her way through the dark living room to the library where a light burned.

"Lorinda—" she began, only to stop short.

For it was not Lorinda who stood with her back toward the door, awkwardly turning the dials of the wall safe. Instead, Celeste whirled around, plainly dismayed by the girl's unexpected appearance in the doorway.

"Celeste!" Penny said sharply. "What are you doing?"

"Nothing," the woman muttered, her mouth sullen.

"You were trying to get into that safe! Is it the will you want, or are you after the Zudi drum?"

Penny's words, shot blindly, struck the target. Celeste's eyes flashed and she advanced a step toward the girl.

"You go away from here! Never come back!" she ordered harshly.

"Sorry, I'm not taking orders from you, Celeste. Why do you hate Lorinda and Mrs. Rhett? What is your little game?"

Celeste glared at Penny. She drew in her breath and expelled it with a hissing sound through her yellow, crooked teeth. Her hand clutched at an object hidden beneath her uniform and worn around her neck on a dirty cord.

With no warning, she broke into a jargon which Penny could not understand. But the meaning was clear enough even if the words were unintelligible. Celeste was calling down all manner of evil upon her head!

"Go!" Celeste cried in English. "You come here again—harm befall you!"

"Celeste, all your jungle hocus-pocus doesn't impress me in the least. I'll leave when I feel in the mood—not before. What were you after in the safe?"

The woman's eyes met Penny's defiantly. She reached out as if to strike her, but at that moment footsteps padded on the stairway. Pushing past Penny, Celeste retreated to the kitchen.

Lorinda came into the library, gazing about curiously. "Thought I heard voices," she commented.

"You did. Celeste was here. Guess what? I found her tampering with the wall safe."

"She may have been trying to learn if the Zudi drum was stolen," Lorinda said absently. "I'm far more worried about the will. What became of it?"

Penny repeated what Jerry had witnessed, adding: "Obviously the will was taken by the man who climbed through the window. Could it have been Antón?"

"Antón? Why, I doubt that he even knew about the will, because Mother decided to change it at a moment's notice. What reason would he have for taking it? Neither he nor Celeste figured in the terms of either document."

"It seemed to me Celeste was tremendously interested," Penny said. "Oh, well, the loss shouldn't be of serious consequence. Your mother can draw up another will."

"That's exactly what she won't do. I told her about the will being taken, Penny. She immediately decided it was another omen—a sign that she should leave everything the way it is."

"How foolish! Celeste must have put those notions in her head!"

"I'm sure I don't know. As for the will, I never did encourage her to change it, because not for a moment do I believe she is sick enough to die. I don't want Mother's money. I only want her to get well and strong and be happy again. Penny, you don't think she is seriously ill?"

"The doctor said nothing is the matter with her."

"Yet we both know something dreadful is wrong." Lorinda's finger tips nervously tapped the table edge. "Oh, Penny, I'm scared—terribly scared. I don't explain it, but I just *feel* a sinister something in the air!"

"You shouldn't be here alone with Celeste and Antón. Why not override them and hire a nurse or companion for your mother?"

"Maybe I will," Lorinda agreed. "I'll think it over until tomorrow."

"You'll report the theft of the will to the police, of course?"

"No," Lorinda decided instantly. "They would only ask embarrassing questions."

"Why are you so reluctant to take anyone into your confidence?"

"We're in enough trouble now, Penny. Please, let's not talk about it any more until tomorrow."

Decidedly puzzled by Lorinda's attitude, Penny said goodbye and rejoined Jerry in the car. He had seen no more of the mysterious prowler and was convinced the man had fled the estate.

"Let's go," he said, starting the car.

As the automobile swung down the driveway, Penny peered intently at the roadside shrubbery. The bushes were crashing back and forth in the rising wind, but no one was visible anywhere near the estate. Chilled, she closed the car window.

"Do you think that hurricane really is heading our way?" she asked her companion.

"Didn't see the government report tonight," Jerry replied. "Probably at the last minute, the storm will veer off and we'll escape. Riverview never was struck by a hurricane. Too far inland."

The car purred smoothly on, following the road which curled toward the beach. Penny became silent. As they turned a corner, Jerry reached out to give her hand a friendly squeeze.

"Why so quiet, kitten?" he teased.

"Just thinking, Jerry. There are so many things about the Rhett case I can't understand."

"Why trouble your little brain?"

"Because this isn't just an ordinary story to me, Jerry. I like Lorinda, and I feel that unless something is done, her mother may die."

"Don't tell me you're becoming a superstitious little heathen!"

"Certainly not! But from what the professor told us, it's a mistake to underrate the power of suggestion. Mrs. Rhett is in real danger—"

Penny broke off, listening intently.

"What was that, Jerry?" she demanded.

"Didn't hear anything. Only the wind."

"No, I distinctly heard a sound like the throb of a drum!" Penny lowered the car window. "There it is again!"

This time Jerry, too, heard the sound, far away and indistinct. "You're right!" he exclaimed, slowing the car. "From down the beach!"

Penny grasped his arm excitedly. "Stop the car!" she exclaimed. "If we can find the drummer, we may be able to solve part of the mystery!"

CHAPTER 18 - THROUGH THE WINDOW

Jerry slammed on the foot brake and the car came to a jerky halt at the curb. Leaping out, they stood for a moment listening.

"Don't hear anything now!" the reporter muttered.

"Let's take a gander down the beach," Penny proposed. "The sound seemed to come from that direction."

Hand in hand they cut across a vacant lot where dead weeds came waist high, then followed a sloping path to the beach. The long stretch of sand was deserted.

"We must have imagined those drums," Jerry said, pausing. "Or maybe it was the Legion fife and drum corps having a night practice."

"It was the beat of a jungle drum." Penny turned to gaze toward the Rhett mansion on the wooded hillside. All the windows, save one in an upstairs bedroom, now were dark.

By the light of a three-quarters moon which was rising over the pines, she could see the wooden steps that led from the estate down to the beach. On either side extended tiers of twisted limestone rock. It occurred to Penny that somewhere among the crannies, a cave might be tucked away. She spoke of it to Jerry.

"Maybe," he agreed, "but I never heard of one around here."

A gust of wind caught Penny's felt hat, carrying it cartwheeling down the beach. She and Jerry raced in pursuit, colliding as they pounced on it together. They laughed, and as the reporter pulled the hat over Penny's flying hair, he kissed her quickly on the cheek.

Then before she could reprimand him, he exclaimed: "Wow! That wind really is getting strong! Let's get back to the car before we blow away!"

Penny liked Jerry and she liked the kiss. Best of all, she appreciated his consideration in never forcing serious attentions upon her. With a gay "I'll race you!", she ran ahead of him to the road.

Jerry took Penny directly home. Mrs. Weems had gone to bed while Mr. Parker had not returned from downtown.

"Will you come in and have a cup of chocolate?" Penny invited the reporter.

"Not tonight, thanks," he declined. "See you tomorrow at the office."

Penny went into the house, and after fixing herself a snack from the refrigerator, switched on the radio to catch the weather report. The news commentator, on a national hookup, warned that the hurricane continued to sweep toward the Atlantic coast, and that inland cities also were endangered.

"It really sounds serious," she thought, turning off the radio.

As she went upstairs, Mrs. Weems called to her in a sleepy voice, so Penny stepped into the housekeeper's bedroom for a moment.

"I'm glad you're home," Mrs. Weems said. "Is there any news about the approaching storm?"

"Nothing definite. The latest radio report said it's still heading this way."

"When will it strike?"

"Late tomorrow unless it veers off. It may be quite serious," Penny said.

Mrs. Weems sighed and settled beneath the covers again. "If it isn't one thing it's another! First thing in the morning we must get the awning down, and have all the shutters taken off."

"If the center of the hurricane should hit here, everything will go," Penny said cheerfully. "So why worry about shutters?"

"The storm may be a severe one, but I don't believe it will strike with hurricane force," Mrs. Weems insisted. "In any case, the shutters are coming down, and I'll need your help! So don't try to skip out in the morning!"

Penny went to her own room, but before she could undress, she heard her father's car on the driveway. He came into the house, locked the doors for the night, then climbed the stairs.

"Hello, Dad!" she called through the half open door of her bedroom. "Any news?"

"There will be by morning," he answered grimly. "The *Star* is coming out with front page headlines warning the city to prepare for the worst!"

Penny stepped quickly out into the hall.

"Then Riverview is in the path of the hurricane! Is there danger that the city will be destroyed?"

"Damage to property is almost certain to be extensive. I've just come from a meeting with the mayor and City Council. While there's an outside chance the city may be spared, it's folly not to prepare for the full brunt of the storm. The mayor has issued a proclamation declaring an emergency and advising everyone to keep off the streets after noon tomorrow. Most businesses will close."

"Then the *Star* will shut down too?"

"No. At such a time, folks depend more than ever upon their newspaper for accurate information. We'll publish as long as we have a plant and our trucks can keep delivering."

Mr. Parker's information brought home to Penny the true seriousness of the situation. However, as she peered out of her bedroom window a few minutes later, the clear sky and bright stars belied an approaching storm.

Undressed, Penny sat for a time propped up in bed with pillows, trying to read a book. The words held little meaning. Losing interest, she snapped off the light, and snuggled down.

But she could not sleep. The dark house was filled with many strange sounds. The stairway creaked, the shutters rattled, and in the bathroom, water dripped regularly from a faucet.

Thoughts raced rampant through Penny's mind. She squirmed and tossed and became increasingly aware of the rising wind.

Suddenly she was startled by a loud crash in the yard below. Leaping out of bed, she darted to the window. A large rotten tree limb had been ripped from the backyard maple and now lay across the driveway.

"Dad will have to move it before he can get the car out of the garage in the morning," she thought. "Some fun!"

Creeping back beneath the covers, she tried again to sleep. Instead, she found herself thinking over everything that had occurred at the Rhett mansion. Already the banker's disappearance was fading out of the newspapers, and with a hurricane in the offing, the story would be entirely forgotten.

"The police haven't shown much interest," she reflected. "Unless definite clues are obtained soon, Mr. Rhett may never be traced. The case will die."

Penny thought of the mysterious thatched roof cottage and the whispering voices.

"Those walls must have a secret panel," she reasoned. "I believe I might find it if I had an opportunity to make a thorough investigation!"

A flapping shutter reminded Penny once more of the storm. Then came the discouraging thought that even if only the tail-end of the hurricane struck Riverview, the flimsy thatched cottage undoubtedly would be carried away and destroyed.

"Unless I get out there tomorrow, I'll probably lose my chance!" she told herself. "Oh, dear, how will I make it when I have a thousand other things I'm supposed to do?"

Dancing tree limbs cast weird shadows on the rough plaster wall. Penny closed her eyes, but even then sleep would not come.

Suddenly the window pane crashed, and glass clattered onto the floor. Startled, Penny sat up and groped for the night table lamp. Her first thought was that a tree branch had hurtled against the pane, breaking it.

But as the light went on, she saw that only a small hole had been broken in the glass. On the floor, scarcely two feet from the bed, lay a small object wrapped in black cloth.

Penny rolled out of bed and gingerly picked it up. Carefully and with a feeling of revulsion, she untied the packet.

CHAPTER 18 - THROUGH THE WINDOW

Inside were two black feathers, the wing of a bird, herbs which Penny could not identify, a bit of bone, and a small amount of damp earth.

There was no warning message, nothing to identify the one who had thrown the packet, yet Penny instantly knew its significance and from whence it had come.

"Either Antón or Celeste hurled it because I've cramped their style!" she thought. "Well, their little hex won't work! I'll use this evil charm to fashion their own undoing!"

CHAPTER 19 - RISING WIND

The sound of crashing glass brought both Mrs. Weems and Mr. Parker to the bedroom. They found Penny standing at the window, the light off, peering down into the yard.

"What's coming off here?" Mr. Parker demanded, his voice cross because he had been aroused from sound slumber. "Did something blow against the window?"

"This was thrown," Penny revealed, holding up the packet. "Dad, can you see anyone hiding in the shrubbery?"

Mr. Parker moved to the window, gazing intently about the yard.

"I don't see anyone."

"Whoever it was, he's probably gone now." Penny carefully drew the blinds before snapping on the overhead light. She handed the packet to her father.

"What's this, Penny?"

"It was thrown through the window. I suspect it's intended as a bad luck omen, and to frighten me. Evidently my work on the Rhett case is not appreciated."

"A jungle charm!" exclaimed Mrs. Weems, horrified. "Oh, Penny, I knew no good would come of your having anything to do with that queer family! Here, give that horrid thing to me—I'll burn it in the furnace."

"Not so fast," chuckled Penny. "I intend to keep it as evidence."

"But it may bring you bad luck."

"Why, Mrs. Weems, I'm surprised at you," teased Penny. "Surely you're not superstitious?"

"No," the housekeeper denied, "but from what you've told me about those queer Rhett servants, I distrust them. I don't want you even to touch that ugly package!"

"These objects aren't harmful," Penny insisted, selecting the bit of bone and offering it to Mrs. Weems. "Why attach special significance to them?"

With a shudder, the housekeeper backed away.

"Penny is right," declared Mr. Parker. "The packet is silly and has no meaning unless we build it up in our own minds. That, of course, is exactly what the one who hurled it intends us to do."

"Penny mustn't go to that dreadful place again!"

"Oh, Mrs. Weems! Don't you see, that's just what Antón and Celeste hope to accomplish. If they can keep me away from the mansion merely by throwing one of their stupid charms through my window, their trick has been successful."

"I quite agree with Penny," Mr. Parker declared. "In fact, I may call at the mansion myself! I've become interested in Antón and Celeste—they're a very successful pair of bluffers."

"Oh, Dad! Will you go with me tomorrow?"

"Perhaps," he promised vaguely. "We'll see, when the time comes. I foresee any number of troubles far more serious than our concern with the Rhett family."

"With both of you against me, I'm only wasting my breath," Mrs. Weems sighed, drawing her robe tightly about her. "I may as well go to bed."

Penny put the black packet on the dresser after her father had finished inspecting it. "I intend to wear this charm around my neck the next time I go to the Rhetts'," she declared. "It will be fun to see how Celeste and Antón react."

"Don't carry your fun too far," her father advised. "While it's true this charm has no significance or supernatural power, Antón and Celeste may be dangerous characters. They'll bear watching."

CHAPTER 19 - RISING WIND

"And I'm the one to do it," Penny chuckled. "I'm not a bit afraid of them, Dad. As you said, they're a couple of bluffers."

"I may have used the word ill-advisedly," the publisher corrected. "Don't make the mistake of underrating them. The case, as you well know, has sinister aspects."

"I'll be careful," Penny promised soberly.

After her father had returned to his room, she went back to bed. A chill wind whistled in through the hole in the window, but she burrowed deep beneath the blankets and soon was sound asleep.

Next morning, as Mr. Parker had predicted, newspapers carried screaming headlines, announcing that the hurricane might reach Riverview by nightfall. Householders were advised to take every precaution to protect life and property.

School opened and was promptly dismissed at nine o'clock. At home, Penny helped Mrs. Weems carry in the porch awning, remove the shutters and all loose objects which were likely to be torn free by the wind.

By now, papers were blowing wildly, cluttering the yard. Each gust brought sticks or small limbs crashing down into the street.

Mrs. Weems, hovering near the radio to hear the last-minute reports, declared that the barometer continued to fall.

"The storm is steadily getting worse," she said nervously.

After lunch, Penny went to the newspaper office to inquire if Mr. DeWitt had any special assignment for her.

"Nothing right now," he said, rapidly scanning a page of copy. "But stick around. Anything may break."

Penny waited, growing increasingly restless. She was certain DeWitt had forgotten all about her, when he slammed down a telephone receiver and glanced in her direction.

"Go out on the street and see what's doing," he ordered. "Might check the police station, too, on your way in."

Penny nodded and went out through the barrier gate. The feel of the approaching hurricane was in the air. Walking toward the river, she saw blue-green water boiling into sinister white foam where it vaulted onto the docks.

Pedestrians were few in number and all hurrying. Business was at a standstill. Shutters were going up over plate glass windows, and street signs were being taken down.

Penny wandered about for a time and then, as a fine rain began to fall, sought the police station. Checking routine reports, she noted four injury cases caused by flying objects, several thefts of property, and more than the usual number of automobile accidents.

At the office once more, she wrote an impressionist account of what she had seen, then waited for another assignment.

"Penny, you may as well go home while you can get there," DeWitt said presently. "City Traction is shutting off service at six o'clock, and after that you won't be able to take a bus."

At another time Penny might have been disappointed to be sent home when exciting news was breaking, but dismissal now fitted neatly into her plans. She was determined to make one last investigation of the thatched roof cottage at the Rhett mansion. However, to beat the storm, she must move fast.

Going out the door, Penny met Jerry who had just come in from the river front. His felt hat was dripping wet.

"It's getting nasty outside," he remarked. "How are you going home, Penny? By bus?"

"Eventually, but not just now," she grinned. "First, I have a little errand at the Rhetts'."

"Better skip it," he advised. "This storm is the real McCoy."

"Can't afford to, Jerry. I want to look over that thatched cottage once more. If I don't do it now, it probably won't be there by tomorrow."

"If you're set on going out there, better make it a speedy trip," Jerry returned. "The storm is rolling in fast."

Reaching the mansion twenty minutes later, Penny was surprised to see an unfamiliar automobile parked on the Rhett driveway. As she went up the front walk, the door opened, and three men came outside. Without noticing the girl, they entered the car and drove away.

"Wonder who they are and what brought them here?" Penny mused.

WHISPERING WALLS

In response to her knock, Celeste opened the door. Seeing Penny, the woman tried to close it in her face, but the girl pushed boldly past her into the hallway.

Penny purposely had worn the black packet on a string around her neck. While Celeste was closing the door, she pulled it from her dress front, and then opened her raincoat so that the housekeeper could not fail to see the object.

Celeste's eyes instantly riveted upon the dangling packet.

"My good luck charm!" said Penny. "Someone gave it to me last night!"

Celeste's lips dropped apart to show her uneven teeth.

"It is an evil packet!" she hissed. "If you wear it, sickness and death will pursue you!"

"Not this cookie," chuckled Penny. "You see, I don't believe such nonsense. Whoever tossed this thing through my window went to a lot of trouble for nothing."

Celeste's face, an interesting study in mixed emotions, suddenly became a blank mask. Hearing footsteps, the woman mumbled something and scurried away.

Lorinda came down the stairway. "Oh, Penny!" she exclaimed, grasping her hand. "I'm so glad you came! We're in such trouble!"

"Your mother is worse?"

"Yes, she is failing rapidly, and the visit of those three bankers upset her dreadfully."

"The men I met on the walk?"

"Yes, they're members of the First National Bank board. They told Mother she must make up the $250,000 bond loss within forty-eight hours, or my stepfather will be exposed as a thief, and the estate sued! It seems Mr. Potts convinced them my stepfather had the bonds when he disappeared."

"What will your mother do?"

"What can she do? Nearly all of her property is in real estate. She might be able to raise $30,000 cash within the required time, but never the amount they demand."

"You've heard nothing from your stepfather?"

"Not a word. The police haven't contributed any worthwhile clues either. They didn't go deeply into the case."

"Can you blame them? You and your mother withheld facts and discouraged them at every turn."

"I know."

"Why did you do it?"

"I thought you understood," Lorinda answered in a low voice. "Mother and my stepfather quarreled violently on that last day at the bank. She didn't want the truth to get out, so she tried to keep from answering questions."

"Then your stepfather disappeared as a result of the quarrel?"

"I don't know. It is a possibility."

"You believe your stepfather may have stolen the bonds?"

"Oh, no! Never! He may have had them on his person when he went away or was spirited off, but I am sure he is no thief!"

Shutters were flapping in the wind. The porch furniture had not been brought into the house, and through the window, Penny saw that many loose, breakable objects remained in the garden. Abruptly changing the subject, she said:

"Lorinda, the storm is getting worse every minute. Can't we bring in the porch furniture?"

"I told Antón to do it early this morning. He went off somewhere. Celeste has been no help either. They're both acting so independent."

"We don't need their help. Come! We can do it together."

Lorinda put on her rain cape and they went out onto the porch. Already the rug was rain soaked. They rolled it up and carried it to the basement, where they also took the furniture. Deciding it was too late to do anything about nailing down the shutters or taking them off, they brought in loose objects from the yard.

In passing the library, Penny noticed that a window was open. The curtain was drenched and rain was pouring in upon the floor.

With a cry of dismay, she ran to close it. As she turned around, she saw at once that the wall safe was exposed to view, and open.

CHAPTER 19 - RISING WIND

"Lorinda!" she called.

Her friend came quickly to the doorway. "Anything wrong?" she inquired.

Penny directed her gaze toward the safe. "Did you leave it open?" she asked.

"No!" With a startled exclamation, Lorinda darted across the room. She thrust her arm into the circular opening, and withdrew it empty.

"The Zudi drum is gone!" she announced. "It's been stolen!"

CHAPTER 20 - TWELVE STEPS DOWN

The news did not astonish Penny for she had anticipated it. She said quietly:
"Lorinda, surely now you'll call in the police? The Zudi drum must be a very valuable trophy."
"It is. Yes, I suppose the only thing to do is notify police headquarters."
Lorinda went to a telephone, but although she tried many times, she was unable to contact the operator. "The line must be down," she reported. "The wire sounds dead."
"Then we're isolated here until after the storm. Lorinda, why don't you question Celeste and Antón?"
"It would be useless."
"Let me do it."
"Go ahead, but they'll not tell you anything," Lorinda said despairingly. "Antón and Celeste have been interested in the Zudi drum ever since they came here, but I've never known them to steal."
"Did they know the safe combination?"
"Not unless they learned it the last few days. I noticed that Celeste watches lately whenever anyone enters or leaves the library."
"Then she may have obtained the combination. I know she was tampering with the dial yesterday. Where is she now?"
"In the kitchen, I suppose."
Celeste, however, was not to be found there, nor was she in any of the upstairs bedrooms, or in her own room on the first floor adjoining the garage.
"I don't know where she and Antón went," Lorinda declared, deeply troubled. "I hate to accuse them without proof, but it does look as if they're the only ones who could have stolen the drum!"
"How about the trophies at the thatched roof cottage? Are they safe?"
"Let's find out," Lorinda proposed. "Wait, I'll get the key. Incidentally, it was mysteriously returned to my stepfather's room yesterday."
She returned with the key in a moment, and the girls ran down the slippery path through the falling rain. The whine of a steadily rising wind was in their ears as they opened the cottage door and stepped inside.
Lorinda looked carefully about. "Everything seems to be here—" she began, only to correct herself. "No, the crossed machetes which were on the wall! They're gone!"
"And the rattle!" exclaimed Penny. "Where is it?"
Lorinda pulled out the wooden chest and raised the lid. "The altar cloth is missing and any number of things! Almost everything has been taken!"
In the midst of checking over the few remaining objects in the chest, Lorinda suddenly raised her head.
"Listen!" she commanded.
At first, Penny could distinguish only the whistle of the wind, then she became aware of a low rumbling murmur which seemed to come from the very walls of the cottage.
"It's a chant!" whispered Lorinda. "I can hear drums too, as if from a long distance away!"
A little frightened, neither girl spoke for a while. The strange sound died away, then was resumed. This time they distinctly could hear the thumping of drums.
Penny went to the door of the cottage to listen. Outside there was only the whine of the wind and the crashing of tree branches.
"Lorinda, this cottage must have a secret passage!" she declared excitedly. "I thought so before, and now I'm certain of it!"

CHAPTER 20 - TWELVE STEPS DOWN

Already Lorinda was down on hands and knees before the fireplace, tapping the tiles. They gave forth a hollow sound. However, she could find no opening.

Penny removed a huge black kettle from hanging chains, and peered up into the chimney. Her groping hand encountered a rod which she assumed controlled the draft. She pulled on it. The floor beneath her feet suddenly gave way, and she would have pitched through the opening had not Lorinda seized her arms and held her.

Scrambling back to solid flooring, Penny peered down into the dark opening where the hearth had been. The tiles were only a sham, she saw now, fastened to a hinged rectangle of wood, which had fallen back like a trap door.

Steep stone steps led down into inky darkness.

"Why, I never dreamed this was here!" Lorinda whispered. "It must have been built that summer Mother and I were away!"

The sound of drums and incantations came plainly now. Neither Penny nor Lorinda was eager to investigate the passage. They feared that they might encounter something with which they would be unable to cope. But to retreat was equally unthinkable.

Penny found the cocoanut shell lamp and lit the floating wick. Moving ahead, she cautiously descended the stone steps. Lorinda kept close beside her.

Twelve steps led almost straight down. There the girls found themselves in a bricked-over passageway, so narrow they could barely squeeze through. However, after they had gone a few yards, it widened a little.

"Where do you suppose this leads?" Penny whispered. "To the river?"

"Probably. It seems to me the sound of the drums came from that direction."

The weird noises no longer could be heard and the silence disturbed the girls. Could it be that in entering the tunnel they had revealed their presence? Nervous and tense, they moved forward at a snail's pace, feeling their way along the wall and taking care to make no betraying sound.

The tunnel led downhill. In places the roof was so low the girls were forced to bend double to pass through. The walls were damp and crumbly and, at points near the roof, water dripped steadily.

Then presently Penny halted, shifting the lamp to her other hand. The passage had widened into a tiny room from which two tunnels branched.

"Which shall we take?" she asked Lorinda.

They selected the wider of the two, which soon proved a deception. Scarcely had they left the little dugout than it narrowed until they were barely able to edge through.

"Shall we turn back and try the other?" Penny suggested.

Lorinda wanted to keep on. "We're moving uphill now," she pointed out. "I suspect this must lead either to the house or the road."

Her guess proved to be correct. Another twenty yards and the tunnel terminated abruptly in front of a door. It opened readily. A dozen roughly carved steps led upward to a trap door. Penny pushed it aside and blinking owlishly, climbed out into a bedroom.

She saw then that the trap door had been cut in the center of the room floor, hidden from view by a large rag rug which now lay in an untidy heap.

"Why, we're in Celeste's room!" Lorinda exclaimed as she too emerged. "Adjoining the garage!"

"This explains quite a few things to me," remarked Penny.

"And to me! Celeste must have known about this passage all the time, but she never hinted of it to Mother or me!"

"If you ask my opinion, Celeste not only has known about the passage, she's been using it regularly," declared Penny, gazing curiously about the room.

The bed had been carelessly made, and a red bandana handkerchief had been left hanging on one of the wooden posts. On the dresser were a number of objects which drew the girls' attention. From the pin tray Penny picked up a tiny black feather and there were strips of torn black cloth which exactly matched the packet she wore about her neck.

"This proves it!" she exclaimed. "Celeste made the evil charm which was thrown through my window last night!"

"Charm?" Lorinda inquired. "Penny, what are you talking about?"

Penny showed her the packet and explained how it had been hurled through the window pane. "I'm sure Celeste had Antón do it or perhaps she tossed it herself. At any rate, she made the packet to frighten me, only it didn't work."

"Unless Celeste can explain matters satisfactorily, I'll turn her over to the police!" Lorinda said angrily.

"Finding her may not be so easy now. Also getting her into police custody may take a little doing. I'm afraid we've waited too long, Lorinda."

"No, we'll find her!" Lorinda announced with determination. "After all, she doesn't know how much we have learned. Let's investigate the other passageway."

"All right," Penny agreed, "but this lamp isn't much good. We need a flashlight."

"I have one in my room. I'll get it, see if Mother is all right, and be right back."

Lorinda was gone less than five minutes. "Mother is sleeping, so it's safe to leave her," she reported. "Here's the flash, but I couldn't find an extra battery."

Descending into the passageway, the girls retraced their steps to the tiny dugout midway between the thatched roof cottage and the mansion. As they entered the other tunnel, they again heard the throb of jungle drums, and the weird incantation of many guttural voices.

"A chant to the Serpent God!" whispered Lorinda. "Do you hear that high-pitched drum which sounds above the others?"

Penny nodded as she moved forward in the dark, narrow passage.

"It is the Zudi," Lorinda added. "I would know its tone anywhere! We must recover it, but if what I think is so, it will be a dangerous task!"

CHAPTER 21 - CEREMONIAL CAVE

The tunnel sloped gently downward, apparently toward the river beach. As the girls moved along, the pulsing of the drums came with increasing crescendo. They could hear the wailing chant plainly now, an incantation in which many voices were united.

"Better switch off the light," Lorinda advised in a whisper. "We're getting close."

Penny darkened the flashlight, groping her way along the damp, rocky wall. The passage now had widened, and suddenly ahead, she saw the flickering flame of a torch.

In the shadowy light swayed a half dozen celebrants of the weird rites. The room was circular, a cavern carved from the rocks years before by the action of water.

Penny's gaze focused upon the dancing figures. Antón, barefooted and grotesque with a red turban wound about his head, led the procession, beating out a rhythm and shaking the gourd rattle which had been stolen from the thatched cottage.

Behind him came a drummer Penny did not recognize, and three other dancers, who carried aloft a banner upon which were metallic, glittering serpentine symbols.

But it was Celeste, garbed in scarlet with an embroidered stole over her shoulders, who dominated the scene. Seated before an altar where two tall candles burned, she pounded out the basic rhythm on a long, narrow drum.

"The Zudi!" whispered Lorinda. "She stole it from the safe!"

"Let's make her give it up!"

"No! No!" Lorinda grasped Penny's arm, holding her back. "It would be folly to show ourselves now. Antón, Celeste and their stupid converts are hypnotized by their own music. If they knew we were watching their rites, there's no telling what they would do."

"Celeste is a cruel, dangerous woman."

"We'll turn her over to the police. I realize now it's the only thing to do."

Fascinated, the girls watched the strange sight. The drums were beating faster now, and at each boom of the Zudi, Antón leaped with frenzied glee rigid as an arrow into the air.

"Who are the others?" Penny whispered.

Lorinda shook her head. "No-good friends of Antón and Celeste probably," she returned. "Recruits from the slums of Riverview."

On the altar were many objects, a basket of bread, a basin of cooked fish, a carved wooden serpent and a wreath of feathers. A kettle contained a brew from which the dancers at intervals dipped with a gourd cup and drank.

Outside the cave, the wind howled an accompaniment to the wild ceremony, covering the shrill shrieks and savage laughter.

"We've seen enough of this!" whispered Penny. "Let's get the police and break it up!"

"All right," agreed Lorinda. "I hate to turn Antón and Celeste over to the authorities, but I'm convinced now they have reverted to heathen ways, and may even be responsible for Mother's sickness."

They started to retreat, making no sound. In the darkness Lorinda stumbled over a small rock. She made no outcry as she saved herself from a fall, but her shoes scuffed noisily and her body thudded heavily against the wall.

Instantly the Zudi drum ceased its rhythm. "What was that?" they heard Celeste ask sharply.

The girls huddled against the wall. An instant later, Antón, a torch in his hand, peered down the tunnel.

His cry told the girls they had been seen. In panic, they started down the passageway with Antón in hot pursuit. And close at his heels came Celeste and her followers.

Escape was impossible. Before the girls had gone a half dozen yards they were overtaken. Though they struggled to free themselves, Antón's grasp was like a steel bracelet upon their arms. They were half dragged back to the cave.

"Antón! Celeste! What is the meaning of this?" Lorinda demanded, seeking to regain control of the servants by sheer power of will.

She tried to shake herself free, but Antón did not release her. He awaited the word of his wife.

"Tie them up!" said Celeste harshly.

"Celeste, have you lost your mind!" Lorinda cried.

In the flickering light of the torch, the woman's face was like a rigid mask. Eyes burned with hatred; cheeks were deeply indrawn. Lorinda felt as if she were gazing upon a stranger, and suddenly was afraid.

"You dared to steal Father's drum!" she challenged.

"It is now my drum," retorted Celeste.

"You spied upon me many times until you learned the combination of the safe!" Lorinda accused.

Celeste did not deny the charge. She was burrowing behind the low altar and from the box-like structure drew forth a long stout cord. Severing it with the blade of a sharp knife, she handed the two pieces to Antón who attempted to tie Lorinda's hands behind her.

The girl fought like a wild cat, and Penny, held by one of Celeste's followers, sought to free herself, but it was useless. She too was tightly bound and thrown down on the floor of the cave.

"Celeste, why are you doing this cruel thing?" Lorinda asked in a pleading tone. "Does it mean nothing to you that Father brought you here, fed you, clothed you—gave you many advantages?"

For a moment Celeste softened and seemed to hesitate. Lorinda was quick to press the advantage.

"My father and my mother have been very kind to you—"

Mention of her mother's name proved unfortunate. Celeste's face hardened into rigid lines again and she said furiously:

"I hate her! May her flesh rot away and her bones be torn asunder!"

"Celeste! And to think we ever trusted you! Mother is ill because you have willed it so—it was you who made the wicked effigy doll—you who kept planting in her mind the idea that she would become ill and die!"

"And I have the will too!" the woman said gleefully. "I told Antón to get it from the library! Then I called you to your mother's room so he could snatch it from the table!"

"But why did you do it, Celeste? What have you gained?"

"You will not steal my master's money! The will is destroyed—burned!"

"Steal my stepfather's money? Indeed, you are out of your mind, Celeste! My stepfather has disappeared and may never be seen again."

"He lives."

"How do you know?" Lorinda cried eagerly.

"Celeste know—feel it here." The woman touched her breast.

"You've seen him—talked to him since he went away!" Lorinda accused.

"No!"

"Then unless you've had a message from him, you couldn't know whether he is alive or dead."

"Celeste know," the woman replied stubbornly. "We save the money for him."

"If my stepfather returns I'll be perfectly happy for him to have Mother's estate. You're all mixed up, Celeste. Now let's put an end to this nonsense. Free us!"

"No," retorted the grim woman. "Celeste and Antón go away now. Perhaps find master. You will stay in cave."

"Celeste, how did you know about this passage and cave?" Lorinda asked, stalling for time.

"Antón help build it."

"But why should my stepfather build the passageway?" Lorinda murmured. "It doesn't seem like him."

Celeste did not answer. Gathering up the machete, the Zudi drum, the embroidered altar cloth and other stolen treasures, she prepared to leave.

CHAPTER 21 - CEREMONIAL CAVE

"It was you who whispered the warning at the thatched cottage!" accused Penny. "You wanted to prevent discovery of this cave!"

Celeste's cruel smile acknowledged the truth. Saying something to Antón in their own language, she padded off down the passageway.

All save Antón now had gone. He blew out the altar candles, picked up the pine torch and would have blown out the cocoanut shell lamp, had Penny not said pleadingly:

"Please leave us a tiny light, Antón. It will be so dark here in the cave."

The man hesitated, glancing down the passage as if fearful Celeste would punish him for such a display of weakness. But he did as Penny requested. First, however, he noted that the lamp was nearly empty of oil and could not burn many minutes. Without extinguishing it, he disappeared into the tunnel.

Waiting only until she was certain Celeste, Antón and their converts were out of the passage, Lorinda said excitedly:

"They forgot to gag us! We can shout for help!"

"With a hurricane roaring outside, it's a waste of breath," replied Penny. "No one will be on the beach tonight, and our voices wouldn't carry a dozen yards."

"Then what are we to do? Antón and Celeste mean to run away now. The police never will be able to find them unless we act quickly."

"I have an idea, but it may not work."

Penny, her hands and feet securely tied, began to roll toward the cocoanut oil lamp.

"What are you trying to do?" Lorinda asked anxiously.

"Maybe I can burn the cords on my wrists. That's why I asked Antón to leave the lamp."

"Perhaps you can!" cried Lorinda, taking hope. "But it will be dangerous and very hard to do. The oil is almost gone. You'll have to work fast, Penny, or you'll lose your chance!"

CHAPTER 22 - STRANGER IN THE STORM

Penny squirmed and rolled until her hands were very close to the cocoanut oil lamp on the rocky floor of the cave.

"Be careful!" Lorinda cried fearfully. "If your clothing should catch fire, nothing could save you."

Penny held her hands, which were bound behind her back, over the flame. The heat seared her flesh and made her wince with pain.

"Keep it up, Penny!" encouraged her companion. "The cord is catching fire! But the lamp is almost out!"

Penny gritted her teeth and endured the pain. Then the lamp sputtered and went out, leaving the cave to darkness.

"Oh!" wailed Lorinda in bitter disappointment.

Penny tugged at the wrist cords. Although not severed, they were half burned through and weakened. A hard jerk freed her hands.

Only a moment then was required to untie the cords which held her feet. Next she freed Lorinda. As the girls started to leave through the passageway, Penny felt a cold blast of air upon her neck. Looking up, she was able to distinguish a small opening in the wall of the cave.

"Maybe we can get out there!" she exclaimed. "Give me a boost and I'll see!"

Lorinda lifted her up. Scrambling like a monkey, Penny secured a toe hold and crammed her head and shoulders through the opening. A moment later she ducked back to call to her friend:

"We can get out all right! But the storm is getting awful! I'll crawl out and then help you."

Scrambling through the narrow opening, Penny found herself amid the high rocks overlooking the beach. The wind was blowing in puffs, each so powerful that she nearly was dislodged from her precarious perch.

Reaching back through the hole, Penny offered her arms to Lorinda who succeeded in joining her. They huddled in the lee of an overhanging rock, rain driving into their faces.

"We must get word to the police!" Penny said breathlessly.

"And I must make certain Mother is safe!" Lorinda added. "She's been left too long alone. Antón and Celeste may have gone back there, and in that case, anything might happen!"

Slipping and sliding, the girls descended the rocks to the beach. The river, lashed by a sheet of rain, was dark and ugly. Much of the sand had been inundated and water bubbled at their heels as they ran toward the road.

A car swung toward them, its headlights blurred by the rain. It parked at the curb, and the driver tooted several times as if in signal.

"That looks like Jerry's car!" Penny cried hopefully.

It was, indeed, the reporter. He swung open the automobile door, and as they recognized him, they dashed across the road and gratefully slid into the shelter offered.

"Don't you girls know better than to be running around at a time like this?" Jerry demanded severely. "Lucky I saw you streaking up the beach!"

"What brought you here?" Penny gasped, taking several deep breaths.

"What brought me? Say, don't you realize we're in for a real storm, and it's almost here! The radio ten minutes ago reported that Oelwein, on the coast, has been completely destroyed! I knew you came here to do a little sleuthing, Penny, and I figured someone ought to look after you."

"Thanks, Jerry," she returned gratefully. "We were in trouble—plenty of it."

CHAPTER 22 - STRANGER IN THE STORM

As the reporter drove on toward the Rhett mansion, Penny quickly revealed what had happened. Jerry made little comment, but his expression was grim.

"Maybe Antón and Celeste are here," he said as the car reached the Rhett home. "If they are, we'll round 'em up."

Celeste and Antón, however, were not to be found in the mansion. Their rooms remained deserted and there was no indication that they had returned to the house after leaving the cave.

Lorinda lost not a moment in hastening to her mother's bedroom. To her relief, Mrs. Rhett was sleeping quietly and did not awaken.

"Thank goodness, she is safe," the girl murmured. "After what happened in the cave, I feared the worst."

"We ought to get the police on the trail of Antón and Celeste before they make their escape," Jerry urged. "Once the full force of this storm strikes, no one will be able to stir outside."

He tried the telephone but the line remained dead. "I'll drive to the police station," he decided. "Are you girls coming along?"

"I'll stay with Mother," Lorinda said. "She mustn't be left alone."

Penny hesitated, intending to remain with her friend, but Jerry seized her by the arm. "Your father sent me out here to round you up, so I'll take you to the newspaper office," he declared. "Let's go!"

As they opened the front door, rain poured in and a great blast of wind nearly swept the pair from their feet.

"Wow!" exclaimed the reporter, holding tight to Penny as with heads lowered, they ran for the car. "This is it!"

The air was filled with flying objects, and a shingle loosened from the mansion roof, hurtled against Penny. Jerry pulled the car door open. The wind seized it, nearly wrenching it off the hinges. Gusts were of greater velocity now, with the intervals much shorter.

For a dreadful moment, Penny and Jerry thought the car would not start. The reporter jammed his foot on the starter again and again and gave it the full choke. Suddenly, the motor caught.

As they drove off along the river road, the force of the wind was so great it required all of Jerry's strength to keep the car straight on the road.

"We'll be lucky if we reach the police station!" he exclaimed. "This is a lot worse than I figured."

"Jerry!"

Seizing the reporter's arm, Penny pointed to a crouched figure visible on the road ahead. The woman, hair flying in wild streamers, clutched a large object in her arms, and was bent almost double as she sought to move against the wind.

"It's Celeste!" Penny cried.

Jerry brought the car to the roadside almost beside the servant. Not until Penny and the reporter were out of the automobile and almost upon her, did she see them. Then with a startled cry, she turned to flee. But it was too late. Jerry seized her by the arm.

"You're coming with us!" he ordered sharply.

Battered and frightened by the force of the wind, Celeste, surprisingly, made no protest. Clutching the big Zudi drum, she allowed Jerry and Penny to pull her into the shelter of the car.

"Where is Antón?" the reporter demanded.

Celeste's answer was a shrug. She gazed toward the mansion grounds, and ignored the pair.

Jerry drove on. He glanced significantly at Penny who guessed that he intended to take Celeste directly to the police station.

However, as they approached the downtown section, the wind blew with even greater power. Not a vehicle was to be seen on the streets. The *Star* building loomed up, but the police station was six blocks away.

"We can't make it," Jerry decided. "I'm turning in here."

One of the double doors of the *Star* garage, where trucks were usually loaded with their papers, stood open. He drove inside, pulling up near the entrance to the newspaper pressroom on the ground floor.

Celeste stirred to life, and made a move to get out of the car.

"Oh, no you don't!" said Jerry, pushing her back. "You and that drum stay with us."

Celeste was of a different opinion. Glaring at Jerry, she slapped at him, and again tried to get her hand on the door handle.

"We can't hold her here," Jerry said. "But I have an idea! Penny, see if the pressroom door is unlocked."

Penny ran to test it and found it unlocked. Now that the extra was out, the pressmen had gathered in a far corner of the big room filled with giant rotary presses, to smoke and watch the storm.

Racing back to the car, Penny made her report.

"Good!" exclaimed Jerry.

With Penny's help, he got Celeste out of the car, separating her from the Zudi drum which they left in the automobile. The woman stubbornly refused to walk, so Jerry lifted her bodily and carried her kicking and struggling into the pressroom.

Near the door was a large storage closet where tools and oil for the presses were kept. Jerry shoved Celeste into this room and turned a key in the lock.

"That will hold her," he observed. "While you lock the Zudi drum in the car, I'll talk to the press foreman and tell him what we've done. Then Celeste can squawk her head off and it will do no good. We'll keep her here until the storm lets up and we can get a police squad to pick her up."

Penny ran back to the loading garage. It was deserted now save for a lone delivery truck which stood directly in front of the paper chute. Although his cargo was loaded, the driver hesitated to try to deliver until the storm abated.

Locking the car, Penny decided she would close the one big double garage door where rain was blowing in.

The hurricane now roared in full fury. Peering out into the deserted street, it seemed to Penny that no person could stand against its strength. Yet as she closed the doors, she was amazed to see a scurrying figure.

The man, his hat gone, overcoat whipped between his legs, grasped a corner of the building for support.

Seeing his face, Penny drew in her breath sharply. A small jagged scar disfigured one cheek. As he struggled past the door, she reached out and grasped his arm.

"Come in here out of the wind," she urged. As she gazed directly into his eyes, she added distinctly: "We have been looking for you a long while, Mr. Rhett!"

CHAPTER 23 - IN THE PRESSROOM

"You have made a mistake," the man mumbled. "I am not Mr. Rhett. My name is Brown—Edgar Brown."

Penny, none too certain of the identification, gazed at the man's hands. They were soft and white as if unaccustomed to hard work, but he wore no serpent ring on any of his fingers. She felt certain this was the man she had met at the steamship office.

The stranger pulled gently away from her grasp, ready to start out into the howling wind once more.

"You'll be swept off your feet if you try to battle that storm!" Penny protested. "You must stay here until the worst of it is over!"

"But I am not Mr. Rhett."

"Never mind about that," said Penny. "I mistook you for someone else. Just come inside and I'll close the doors."

The man peered outside once more, and noting the intensity of the storm, lost all desire to leave the shelter. He moved away from the entrance, and Penny closed the big, heavy door.

"Come along with me into the pressroom where it is warm," she invited.

Without comment, the man followed her across the cement toward the loading docks. At the other end of the drive, someone opened the doors for a moment to allow a truck to roll inside. A great gust of wind tore through the passage, and sent the stranger's hat careening into a corner.

He darted to recapture it. As he stooped to pick it up, an object on a string which he wore about his neck, swung from beneath his sport shirt. Quickly he pushed it out of sight again, but not before Penny had seen the ring and recognized the serpent design.

"He *is* Mr. Rhett!" she thought, her pulse pounding.

Wisely, she pretended to have observed nothing, and invited him into the pressroom where Jerry was waiting. Celeste, still locked in the storage closet, was rattling the door knob and kicking on the panel with all her strength.

"Jerry," said Penny, dropping her bombshell. "This is Mr. Rhett."

The reporter's mouth dropped agape, while the stranger plainly showed his annoyance.

"I told you I am not Mr. Rhett."

"Then kindly explain the significance of that ring you wear around your neck. I saw it only a moment ago."

The stranger became confused. "My ring—" he stammered. "Oh, that! An heirloom. I have had it for years."

"Please tell us the truth," pleaded Penny.

"I know nothing about this man you call Mr. Rhett," he replied, avoiding her direct gaze. "Evidently you have someone locked up here. Suppose you explain the meaning."

"Gladly," replied Penny. "We do have someone imprisoned in the storage room ready to turn over to the police as soon as the storm lets up. It is Celeste."

"Celeste!" The stranger's amazed expression betrayed him. Although he added: "And who is she?" it was unconvincing.

"Mr. Rhett, why pretend?" Penny demanded. "We know who you are."

"Very well," said the man, smiling faintly. "So I am Mr. Rhett! I assume you two are reporters for the *Star*."

"Right," agreed Jerry.

"And you want a story. Well, there's no story. Since you have me dead to rights as they say, I'll not deny I am Hamilton Rhett. However, my identity is my own affair. I stepped out of my old life—the bank and my home—because I was tired of a very boring existence. I never was cut to the cloth of a banker. I dislike being shut up indoors even for an hour. Probably I shall return to South America."

"You say it is your own affair," Penny remarked pointedly. "I am afraid it isn't. Aren't you forgetting a little matter of $250,000?"

"I don't know what you mean."

"I refer to that sum in negotiable bonds which you had in your possession at the time you left the bank."

Mr. Rhett did not seem to understand for a moment. Then he exclaimed: "Oh, the bonds! I was to have returned them to the vault, but it slipped my mind. You will find them in the top desk drawer in my office."

"The desk has been carefully searched. The bonds are not there."

"Not there?" For the first time Mr. Rhett seemed disturbed. "But they must be, unless they were stolen after I went away!"

"The bonds have not been found, and the bank trustees are pressing your family to make restitution. Furthermore, your wife is dangerously ill."

"My wife sick? What is wrong?"

"The doctors do not know. However, Lorinda burned an effigy doll made in your wife's image—she found it in the house. Two burned match sticks tied together also were found by Mrs. Rhett. For some reason she became obsessed with the idea she was doomed to a lingering fatal illness. She began to refuse food and since then has gone steadily downhill."

"The work of Celeste!"

"We think so. Tonight she stole the Zudi drum, and Lorinda and I found her with Antón and other followers celebrating their rites in a cave near the beach."

"Then they have reverted to their heathen ways!" the banker exclaimed. "My wife always said Celeste hated her, but I, like a blind fool, refused to see it. Once during the years I spent in the jungle, Celeste saved my life and I always felt grateful to her. Now I must forget that, for she is a dangerous woman if she seeks to practice her jungle magic."

"You don't actually believe Celeste could make your wife ill merely by suggestion?" Jerry inquired in amazement.

"In the jungles I have seen a native die from superficial wounds. If told the spear which struck him had been sung over by an enemy, the native would simply lie down, refuse food and pine away. My wife is in great danger!"

"Can nothing be done?" cried Penny.

Mr. Rhett's face tightened into hard, grim lines. "A great deal can be done," he said. "But Celeste must be fought with her own jungle weapons. To turn her over to the police will not be sufficient. She is inside the closet you say—let me talk to her."

"Okay," agreed Jerry, "but Celeste in her present mood is a pretty brisk customer. To make sure she doesn't get away, I'll lock the pressroom door before letting her out of her cage."

As the reporter went to the exit, Penny heard the pressmen at the other end of the room shout that the storm had abated.

"The hurricane has not passed," corrected Mr. Rhett quietly. "This lull merely marks the end of the first phase. The wind will return harder than ever in a few minutes from another quarter."

Jerry returned, and taking the key to the storage room from his pocket, cautiously unlocked the door. Celeste, blinking like an owl as she staggered out under the electric lights, gasped as she saw Mr. Rhett.

"Master!" she exclaimed worshipfully. "You come back!"

Mr. Rhett's face showed no trace of the affection he had felt for his servant. "Celeste," he said, "you've been dabbling in magic again! What's this nonsense about my wife being ill and going to die?"

"The truth, Master. Antón and I try hard to save her, but no use. She die next month. Maybe sooner."

"Get this through your head, Celeste. My wife will not die. She will be as well as you are within two days. All your incantations over the doll were wasted. You plotted to no avail. I am home now, and if you persist in your wickedness, I will meet your so-called magic with stronger magic of my own!"

"Celeste sorry," the old woman whimpered. "Do it only to get money for master."

"I need no money and want none. You have been very wicked, Celeste, and must be turned over to the police for safe keeping."

CHAPTER 23 - IN THE PRESSROOM

"Oh, no, Master! Not the police!"

"Yes, and now is the time to take you there during this lull in the storm."

Celeste's wild eyes darted about the room, searching for a means of escape. With a savage lunge, she reached the door only to find it locked.

As Jerry and Mr. Rhett bore down upon her, she scurried frantically along the outer room wall, coming to the metal paper chute through which packages of freshly-printed papers were tossed for delivery.

Quick as a cat, Celeste scrambled into the chute, crawling through on all fours. At the chute's exit on the sheltered cement drive, stood the waiting paper truck, its rear door ajar. Already loaded, the driver awaited only this lull in the storm before setting off to deliver his cargo.

Even as Celeste crawled through the chute, the man started the truck engine. The woman did not hesitate. Leaping into the rear of the vehicle, she slammed the door.

Hearing it close, the driver assumed another workman had shut it as a signal for him to pull out. Shifting gears, he drove away with his cargo of papers—and Celeste.

CHAPTER 24 - THE GRINNING GARGOYLE

By the time Jerry, Penny and Mr. Rhett unlocked the pressroom door and reached the loading dock, the truck bearing Celeste was far down the street.

"Hey, where'd that truck go?" the reporter shouted to another workman at the far end of the drive.

"Docks at the end of Basset Street," he answered. "A batch o' papers go aboard the *Monclove* for shipment to Presque Isle."

Jerry's car stood close by. He sprang in, making room for Penny and Mr. Rhett.

The newspaper truck had disappeared by the time they drove out on the street. Jerry took a short-cut route to the Basset Street docks. Signs and debris of all description cluttered the roadway. Rain had ceased, but the ominous quiet, the heaviness of the air, was even more frightening than the wind had been.

In a distant section of the city they heard the high-pitched whistle of a police siren; otherwise, the streets were as silent as the tomb.

The car turned a corner, and directly ahead Penny glimpsed the newspaper truck.

"There it is!" she cried, but Jerry also had seen the vehicle.

He put on speed, and was close behind as the truck pulled up with a jerk at Dock 12. Green water whipped to foam, crashed with heavy impact against the dock posts and flooded out on the slippery planking.

"We won't have much time!" Mr. Rhett exclaimed. "When the next phase of the storm comes—and it's close now—the wind will be terrific!"

The men, with Penny close behind, leaped from the car. Quick as they were, Celeste was out of the truck before they could reach its door.

She stopped short as she saw the trio, then like a trapped animal, turned and fled in the opposite direction.

"Celeste!" Mr. Rhett shouted. "Wait!"

The woman paid no attention. Splashing ankle-deep through water that washed the dock planks, she ran precariously close to the river's edge.

A hoarse shout from behind caused Penny to turn. The driver of the truck was gesturing and pointing first to the dark sky and then to an open shed. For a moment she did not understand, but as he ran for the shelter, she heard the deep-throated roar of the hurricane as it returned for its final onslaught.

"Quick!" cried Mr. Rhett who also recognized the danger. "Inside!"

The three ran back to the shed where the truck-driver had taken shelter. Although they shouted again and again to Celeste, she ignored their warnings.

As the wind struck, they saw her at the very edge of the dock. She half turned toward the shed as if debating whether or not to seek its shelter, then took a step or two in the opposite direction.

A great gust lifted off a section of the shed roof and whirled it away. As the full impact of the wind swept around the building, Celeste clung to a dock post for an instant; then her fingers lost their grip, and with a scream, she toppled over the edge into the churning water.

Jerry started toward the door, but Mr. Rhett seized his arm, dragging him back.

"Don't be a fool! Celeste is beyond help! You'll only lose your own life if you venture out there now!"

Already Celeste had disappeared beneath the turbulent waters, leaving no trace. Anxiously those in the shed watched but her head never appeared above the surface.

"Poor Celeste," said Mr. Rhett sadly. "She meant well, but she was superstitious and misguided. However, she would have pined away in captivity. Perhaps she went the best way."

CHAPTER 24 - THE GRINNING GARGOYLE

The servant's startling death placed a pall upon the four who huddled in the shed. Close together, they flattened themselves against the wall, expecting at any moment that the entire building would be lifted from its foundation and hurled into the river. The force of the wind was almost unbelievable.

After nearly a half hour, the gusts lost their strength and Mr. Rhett declared that the greatest danger had been passed.

"Tell me everything that happened while I was away," he requested Penny and Jerry.

"We will," promised Penny, "but first, suppose you explain why you went away."

"I thought I did tell you." Mr. Rhett drew a deep sigh. "For many months I considered retiring from the bank. I discussed it with my wife, but she failed to see my viewpoint and insisted that I remain. We became deadlocked, so to speak.

"I tried for her sake to force myself to like bank work, but it was utterly impossible. Each day I found myself longing for the old carefree adventurous days."

"So you quietly walked out?" Jerry supplied.

"Something like that. My actions weren't premeditated. One thing led to another. I had a quarrel with my wife over neglect of bank duties. As I sat thinking it over at my desk, it struck me that Lorinda and her mother probably would be happier if I removed myself from the picture."

"Did you write anything as you sat there?" Penny interposed eagerly.

"I'm not sure I know what you mean."

"Did you draw a picture of a plumed serpent?"

"Yes, I believe so, though it was only absent-minded doodling."

"And beneath the drawing you wrote, 'This shall be the end.'"

"Why, yes, I did," the man acknowledged. "I had decided to walk out and those words expressed the conclusion I reached. I wrote the thought absent-mindedly and never intended it to fall into anyone's hands. Did I leave the paper in the desk?"

"The police found it there."

"I must have been quite upset," Mr. Rhett said, frowning. "At any rate, I walked out with less than three dollars in my pocket, and didn't realize until later that I was without funds."

"So you took lodging in a cheap flop house on Cherry Street?" Jerry interposed.

"Yes, you seem to have followed my actions very closely. Although the lodgings were hardly deluxe, I did not mind the experience. I frequently have slept on the ground or in native huts."

"You stayed there only one night?" Penny inquired.

"Another lodger told me two persons had come to ask questions about a man who wore a serpent ring," Mr. Rhett said. "Not wishing to be found, I removed the ring from my finger, and found another lodging place. When my money ran out, I picked up a little work as a laborer at one of the mills."

"I saw you inquiring at one of the steamship ticket offices," Penny reminded him. "You remember that, I'm sure."

"I sought to work my passage on a boat going to South America," Mr. Rhett explained.

"All this time, didn't you read the newspapers?" Jerry asked curiously. "Didn't you know the bonds were missing and that your wife was ill?"

Mr. Rhett shook his head. "I purposely avoided looking at the newspapers. I was afraid if I did I might be tempted to return to my old life."

"And now?" asked Penny softly.

"I have no future, only the present. Before making any plans, I must return home to see that my wife frees her mind from Celeste's evil suggestions. I made a great mistake in bringing Celeste and Antón into the household. But once my wife knows Celeste is dead, I am confident she will quickly recover."

"You still love your wife?"

"I shall always love her," he returned quietly, "but she has no use for me. I've been a drag on her since the day we were married."

"She doesn't feel that way, I'm sure," Penny corrected. "Since you went away, she's been heartbroken. Lorinda needs you too."

"I can never return to the bank," Mr. Rhett repeated. "And there are the stolen bonds to be considered. Why, the police may even arrest me! I'm all mixed up."

"Matters will straighten out as soon as you see your wife," Penny declared. "However, I'll admit recovering the bonds may not be so easy. To my knowledge, the police haven't a single clue."

Jerry was peering out the open shed door. "The storm is letting up," he called. "We'll soon be able to get out of here."

Another half hour and the wind died sufficiently so that the party could safely leave the shelter. The truck driver returned to the newspaper office, while Jerry and Penny drove Mr. Rhett to his home.

The mansion yard was cluttered with uprooted trees, boards and debris. Penny ran down the path a short distance and returned to report that the thatched roof cottage had vanished without a trace.

"Perhaps it is just as well," said Mr. Rhett. "It was a mistake to build the cottage, but Celeste first put the idea in my head. I intended to use it only as a trophy room, but to Celeste it became a living symbol of the life she had left behind."

"Why did you build the passageway leading to the cave and to Celeste's room?" Penny inquired.

Mr. Rhett's blank expression told her that he did not understand. After she had explained, he said grimly: "Antón and Celeste must have dug the tunnel without my knowledge! Oh, they were a cunning pair!"

"And Antón still is on the loose," Jerry reminded the banker. "We'll have to notify the police to pick him up."

Mr. Rhett and the young people entered the house. Lorinda, startled by hearing the front door open, ran to the head of the stairway. Seeing her stepfather, she gave a cry of joy and raced to meet him.

"You've come back! Oh, Mother needs you so badly. Do go to her at once."

Mr. Rhett needed no urging. He was up the steps two at a time. Jerry and Penny, not wishing to intrude, remained in the living room, but a few minutes later, Lorinda called them.

"Oh, everything is wonderful!" she exclaimed. "Mother and Father have adjusted all their differences. And best of all, she's already half over the idea she is going to die. Why, he just told her Celeste was dead and that she could never do any further harm. Mother snapped right out of it!"

Lorinda insisted that Jerry and Penny go upstairs. Mrs. Rhett was sitting up in bed, and her eyes were shining.

"How silly I've been," she declared. "As I look back, I realize Celeste hated me and kept putting ideas in my mind. Why, I feel much better already."

"Hungry?" asked Lorinda.

"Indeed, I am. I must have a gigantic dinner tonight." Mrs. Rhett laughed and added: "With everything well salted!"

"About the bank—" began Mr. Rhett.

"Let's not talk about it now," his wife pleaded. "I was wrong about that too. I'll never ask you to go back there, for it isn't your type of life. Instead, perhaps we can go away somewhere on a long trip—South America, would that appeal to you, Hamilton?"

"Would it?" he chuckled. "Someone has been putting ideas in your head, and this time it wasn't Celeste!"

Anxious to return to the newspaper office and to stop at the police station, Jerry and Penny soon took leave of the Rhetts, after receiving urgent invitations to return later that night.

"Well, it appears everything is turning out hunkey dorey for the Rhetts," Jerry observed as he and Penny drove away from the mansion. "Antón is certain to be caught by the police, and those followers of his will be jailed too if they ever show their faces again."

"Everything *might* be fine for the Rhetts except for one thing," Penny returned. "Mrs. Rhett doesn't have much ready cash available, and there still remains a little matter of $250,000 in missing bonds."

"I'd forgotten about that. You're right, Rhett still is in an awkward spot."

The car drove into the downtown section where a few vehicles now were moving. Under the glow of the street lights, workmen were clearing the debris away.

As the car approached the First National Bank, Penny chanced to raise her eyes toward the second story balcony fronting the street. The grinning gargoyles stood out in dark relief, and as she gazed at them, she suddenly saw a shadowy figure moving stealthily toward the one nearest the open door leading from Mr. Rhett's private office.

"Why, that looks like Albert Potts!" she exclaimed.

CHAPTER 24 - THE GRINNING GARGOYLE

As she watched in amazement, the man approached the gargoyle. Reaching his hand far in between the open jaws, he removed something which he thrust into his overcoat pocket. Then, with a nervous glance down upon the deserted street, he stepped back into Mr. Rhett's office, and closed the door.

CHAPTER 25 - ON THE BALCONY

"Jerry, that was Albert Potts on the balcony!" Penny cried excitedly. "I'm sure I saw him remove an object from inside the gargoyle!"

"Maybe he was just looking to see what damage was done by the storm," commented the reporter.

"He took something out and put it in his overcoat pocket! Jerry, now that I think back, Potts acted queerly that first day when the police investigated Mr. Rhett's office. He didn't want anyone to go near the gargoyle! Another thing, he's been spending money as if it were rainwater!"

"You're suggesting—"

"That it was Albert Potts who stole the bonds! Weren't they left in Mr. Rhett's desk? Potts knew it and had a perfect chance to take them! He implied that Rhett walked off with them! Actually, he hid the bonds in the gargoyle, knowing that if they were found there, no blame would be likely to fall upon him. Whenever he needed money, he cashed a bond—that's why only a few have shown up at out of town banks!"

"Say, maybe you have something!" exclaimed Jerry, pulling up at the curb. "If he had hid the bonds in the gargoyle, it would be natural for him to wonder if they still were safe after this storm! He might have decided to shift them to another place."

"My idea exactly! Jerry, let's nab him and turn him over to the police!"

"Not quite so fast, my little chickadee. If we accuse Potts, and it turns out we're wrong, well, he could make it hot for us."

"We'll have to take a chance," Penny urged.

Leaving the car at the curb, the pair walked hurriedly to the bank. The building was dark and the lights were off inside.

"Sure you saw Potts on the balcony?" Jerry asked as they huddled against the wall for protection against the biting wind.

"Yes, and I think he's coming now!"

Penny was correct. They heard footsteps coming down the marble stairway, and a moment later, the bank secretary unlocked the door. The waiting couple made no move until he had locked himself out, but as he started away, Jerry tapped him on the shoulder.

Potts whirled around, obviously startled. His face blanched.

"Hello, Potts," said Jerry. "Working late, aren't you?"

"Why, yes," stammered the man, edging away.

"Can you spare a match?"

Potts half reached into his pocket as if to proffer one, then said testily: "I haven't any. Sorry."

"Sure now, you must have a match," said Jerry, brushing against him. "Maybe in your overcoat pocket."

Before Potts could prevent it, he had thrust his hands deep into each of the outside pockets. The bank clerk jerked angrily away. However, it was too late. Jerry triumphantly brought to light a heavy manila envelope.

"Give that to me!" Potts cried furiously.

Sidestepping him, Jerry pulled several bonds of large denomination from the envelope.

"The stolen bonds!" exclaimed Penny. "Mr. Potts, whatever possessed you to do it?"

The bank secretary never answered the question. Instead, he wheeled and started at a run down the street. As he reached the corner, a policeman who had just finished making a report to headquarters, turned from his phone box.

"Stop that man!" yelled Jerry.

CHAPTER 25 - ON THE BALCONY

The policeman grasped Potts, bringing him up short. After that, the bank secretary did his explaining to the desk sergeant at police headquarters. So unconvincing was his story, that he was immediately locked in a cell.

Meanwhile, Jerry and Penny related all they knew about the case. All scout cars were ordered to be on the alert to pick up Antón. Mr. Rhett was brought to the station within the hour, and promptly identified the recovered bonds as those he had left in his office desk.

At first, Potts firmly maintained his innocence, but after police had subjected him to a lie detector test, he realized his case was lost. When one of the detectives who was questioning him, remarked that his wife likely would be implicated in the theft, Potts broke completely:

"No! No! My wife had nothing to do with it," he insisted. "I wanted to give my family better things—that was why I took the bonds. I thought Mr. Rhett would never return and that he would be blamed for the theft."

"How did you cash the bonds?" he was asked.

"I was afraid to take them to a bank myself," Potts confessed. "Instead, I paid a woman in another town to do it for me. But she did it only as a favor, and had no idea the bonds were stolen. I alone am to blame."

A check by police revealed that Potts had spent only $2,000 of the total amount stolen. Mr. Rhett declared that this sum easily could be made up, so that the bank would sustain no loss. He was inclined to be lenient with his secretary, but police were insistent that the man be brought to trial.

Jerry and Penny, knowing that they had a big story to write, did not tarry long at the police station. However, the police desk sergeant promised to keep them informed of any new developments in the case. True to his word, he called them soon after they reached the *Star* office. His news was that Antón had been captured by the police and now was safely locked in a jail cell.

"Well, that rings the gong on the case," Jerry announced as he hung up the telephone. "Thanks to you, Penny, it's all wound up."

"And it's nearly edition time!" barked the city editor. "Let's get going on that story."

He looked at Jerry who was known as the best writer on the paper, and then his eyes moved on to Penny who waited with bated breath.

"This was her story from start to finish," said Jerry as the editor hesitated.

"Get going!" ordered the editor again, and now he looked straight at Penny. "Give it to me in takes."

Penny hurried to a typewriter. The lead, telling of Mr. Rhett's return, Potts' arrest and recovery of the stolen bonds, almost wrote itself. Keeping her own part and Jerry's entirely out of the story, she wrote smoothly and with speed.

When she had finished half a page, she called: "Copy boy!" and ripping the sheet of paper from the typewriter gave it to him to carry to the editor's desk.

With a fresh sheet in the machine, she wrote on until she had a second "take" ready. Again she called the copy boy and, as he snatched it from her hand, rolled still another sheet into the typewriter.

At last she was on the final page and glanced over it before she typed "30" at the end. The story had been well told, written tersely in the manner DeWitt liked. With a feeling of exultation, she realized she had done a good job.

Getting to her feet, she dropped the last page into the copy basket. Earlier sheets already had been copy-read and were in the process of being set into type. Any moment now, the edition would roll and papers would be on the street.

Penny turned from the desk to see Jerry sitting with his feet propped up on one of the tables. He was gazing at her quizzically and grinning.

"Well, you did it again, Penny!" he remarked.

"We did it together," she corrected.

"With the help of our silent partner," he added lightly.

"Silent partner?"

"The hurricane. It damaged a lot of Riverview property, but on the other side of the ledger, it helped write '30' to the Rhett case."

Penny nodded as she reached for her hat and raincoat. Just then, a copy boy ran up.

"Telephone for you," he said. "It's your housekeeper, Mrs. Weems. She wants to know if you're safe."

"Safe and sound and on my way home," laughed Penny. "Tell her I've already started."

"And that she's being driven by her faithful chauffeur," chuckled Jerry, as he reached for his hat. "Which reminds me, we have a little package to deliver to the Rhetts'."

"The Zudi drum! I forgot all about it!"

"Haven't you forgotten another important matter too?" teased Jerry, escorting her through the swinging gate. "Me, for instance."

"You?"

"My reward for tonight's work. Girl reporters, even cute little numbers like you, can't snatch my bylines without paying the piper!"

"And what fee do you require?" Penny asked with pretended innocence.

"We'll go into that later," he chuckled, pinning her neatly into a shadowy corner of the vestibule. "Just now, I'll take a little kiss on deposit!"

THE END

SWAMP ISLAND

SWAMP ISLAND

The boar had turned and was coming for her again.

CHAPTER 1 - THE BEARDED STRANGER

With slow, smooth strokes, Penny Parker sent the flat-bottomed skiff cutting through the still, sluggish water toward a small point of wooded land near the swamp's edge.

In the bottom of the boat, her dark-haired companion, Louise Sidell, sat with her hand resting carelessly on the collar of her dog, Bones, who drowsed beside her. The girl yawned and shifted cramped limbs.

"Let's go home, Penny," she pleaded. "We have all the flowers you'll need to decorate the banquet tables tonight."

"But not all I want," Penny corrected with a grin. "See those beautiful Cherokee roses growing over there on the island point? They're nicer than anything we have."

"Also harder to get."

Louise craned her neck to gaze at the wild, tangled growth which rose densely from the water's edge.

"Remember," she admonished, "when Trapper Joe rented us this boat his last words were: 'Don't go far, and stay in the skiff.'"

"After we gather the flowers, we'll start straight home, Lou. We're too near the edge of the swamp to lose our way."

Disregarding Louise's frown, Penny tossed a lock of auburn hair out of her eyes, and dug in again with the oars.

A giant crane, disturbed by the splash, flapped up from the tall water grass. As he trumpeted angrily, Bones stirred and scrambled to his feet.

"Quiet, Bones!" Louise ordered, giving him a reassuring pat. "It's only a saucy old crane."

The dog stretched out on the decking again, but through half-closed eyes watched the bird in flight.

"Lou, hasn't it been fun, coming here today?" Penny demanded in a sudden outbreak of enthusiasm. "I've loved every minute of it!"

"You certainly have! But it's getting late and we're both hot and tired. If you must have those flowers, let's get them quickly and start home."

The two girls, students at Riverview high school, had rented the skiff early that afternoon from Trapper Joe Scoville, a swamper who lived alone in a shack at the swamp's edge.

For three hours now, they had idled along the entrance channel, gathering water lilies, late-blooming Cherokee roses, yellow jessamine, and iris.

The excursion had been entirely Penny's idea. That night in a Riverview hotel, her father, Anthony Parker, publisher of the *Riverview Star*, was acting as host to a state newspapermen's convention. He had handed Penny twenty dollars, with instructions to buy flowers for the banquet tables.

Penny, with her usual flare for doing things differently, had decided to save the money by gathering swamp blooms.

"These flowers are nicer than anything we could have bought from a florist," she declared, gazing appreciatively at the mass of blooms which dripped water in the basket at her feet.

"And think what you can do with twenty dollars!" her chum teased.

"Seventeen. Remember, we owe Trapper Joe three dollars for boat rental."

"It will be four if we don't call it a day. Let's get the flowers, if we must, and start home."

"Fair enough," Penny agreed.

Squinting at the lowering sun, she guided the skiff to a point of the low-lying island. There she held it steady while her chum stepped out on the spongy ground.

Bones, eager to explore, leaped after her and was off in a flash before Louise could seize his collar.

Penny followed her chum ashore, beaching her skiff in a clump of water plants. "This place looks like a natural haunt for cottonmouths or moccasins," she remarked. "We'll have to watch out for snakes."

Already Louise was edging along in the soft muck, alertly keeping an eye upon all overhead limbs from which a poisonous reptile might drop.

Annoyed by thorny bushes which teethed into her jacket, she turned to protest to Penny that the roses were not worth the trouble it would take to gather them.

But the words never were spoken.

For just then, from some distance inland, came the sound of men's voices. Louise listened a moment and retreated toward the boat.

"Someone is here on the island," she whispered nervously. "Let's leave!"

All afternoon the girls had floated through the outer reaches of the swamp without seeing a single human being. Now to hear voices in this isolated area was slightly unnerving even to Penny. But she was not one to turn tail and run without good reason.

"Why should we leave?" she countered, careful to keep her voice low. "We have a perfect right to be here. They're probably fishermen from Riverview."

Louise was not so easily reassured.

"We have all the flowers you need, Penny. Please, let's go!"

"You wait for me in the boat, Lou. I'll slip over to the bank and get the roses. Only take a minute."

Stepping carefully across a half-decayed log, Penny started toward the roses, visible on a bank farther up shore.

Bones trotted a few feet ahead of her, his sensitive nose to the ground.

"Go back, Bones," Penny ordered softly. "Stay with Louise!"

Bones did not obey. As Penny overtook him and seized the trailing leash, she suddenly heard voices again.

Two men were talking several yards away, completely hidden by the bushes. Their words brought her up short.

"There hain't no reason to be afeared if we use our heads," the one was saying. "Maybe me and the boys will help if ye make it worth our while, but we hain't aimin' to tangle with no law."

The voice of the man who answered was low and husky.

"You'll help me all right, or I'll tell what I know! Only one thing brought me back here. I aim to get the guy who put me up! I was in town last night but didn't get sight of him. I'm going back soon's I leave here."

Penny had been listening so intently that she completely forgot Bones.

The dog tugged hard at the leash which slipped from the girl's hand. She scrambled for it, only to have Bones elude her and dart into the underbrush.

From the boat, Louise saw her pet escaping. Fearful that he would be lost, she called shrilly: "Bones! Bones! Come back here!"

The dog paid no heed. But Louise's cry had carried far and served to warn those inland that someone had landed on the point.

A moment of dead silence ensued. Then Penny heard one of the men demand sharply: "What was that?"

Waiting for no more, she backtracked toward the boat. Before she could reach it, the bushes behind her parted.

A tall, square-shouldered man whose jaw was covered with a jungle growth of red beard, peered out at her. He wore a wide-brimmed, floppy, felt hat and loose fitting work clothes with sturdy boots.

His eyes, fierce and hostile, fastened directly upon Penny.

"Git!" he said harshly.

Penny retreated a step, then held her ground.

"Please, sir, our dog is lost in the underbrush," she began. "We can't leave without him—"

"Git!" the man repeated. As he started toward her, Penny saw that he carried a gun in the crook of his arm.

CHAPTER 2 - ALERTING ALL CARS

Penny was no coward; neither was she foolhardy.

A second look at the bearded stranger, and her mind telegraphed the warning: "This man means business! Better play along."

The man fingered his gun. "Git goin' now!" he ordered sharply. "And don't come back!"

In the boat, Louise already had reached nervously for the oars. She wet her fingers and whistled for Bones, but the dog, off on a fascinating scent, had been completely swallowed up by the rank undergrowth.

"Ye heard me?" the stranger demanded. "I be a patient man, but I hain't speakin' agin."

Penny hesitated, half tempted to defy the swamper.

"Let Bones go," Louise called. "Come on."

Thus urged, Penny backed toward the skiff. Stumbling over a vine, she caught her balance and scrambled awkwardly into the boat.

Louise pushed off with the oars, stroking fast until they were well out into the channel. Only then did she give vent to anger.

"That mean man! Now we've lost Bones for good. We'll never get him back."

"Maybe we will."

"How? We'll never dare row back there today. He's still watching us."

Penny nodded, knowing that anything she might say would carry clearly over the water.

The stranger had not moved since the skiff had pulled away. Like a grim statue, he stood in the shadow of a towering oak, gazing straight before him.

"Who does he think he is anyhow?" Louise demanded, becoming bolder as they put greater distance between themselves and the island. "Does he own this swamp?"

"He seems to think he does—or at least this section of it. Don't feel too badly about Bones, Lou. We'll come back tomorrow and find him."

"Tomorrow may be too late. He'll be hopelessly lost, or maybe that man will shoot him! Oh, Penny, Bones was such a cute little dog. He always brought me the morning paper, and he knew so many clever tricks."

"It was all my fault for insisting upon landing there. Lou, I feel awful."

"You needn't."

Louise forced herself into a cheerful tone. "Maybe we'll find him again or he'll come home. If not—well—" her voice broke.

Both girls fell into a gloomy silence. Water swished gently against the skiff as Louise sent it forward with vicious stabs of the oars.

With growing distaste, Penny eyed the mass of flowers in the bottom of the boat. Already the blooms were wilting.

"I wish we never had come to the swamp today, Lou. It was a bum idea."

"No, we had a good time until we met that man. Please, Penny, it wasn't your fault."

Penny drew up her knees for a chin rest and gloomily watched her chum row. A big fish broke the surface of the still water. Across the channel, the sun had become a low-hanging, fiery-red disc. But Penny focused her eyes on the receding island.

"Lou," she said, "there were two men on the point. Did you hear what they were saying?"

"No, only a murmur of voices."

Her curiosity aroused, Louise waited patiently for more information. Penny plucked at a floating hyacinth plant and then added:

"I can't quite dope it out, Lou. One of those men seemed to be asking the other to hide him, and there was talk of evading the law—also a threat to 'get' someone."

"Us probably."

"No, until you called Bones, they apparently didn't know anyone was around. Who could those men be?"

"Crooks, I'll bet," Louise said grimly. "Thank goodness, we're almost out of the swamp now. I can see the clearing ahead and a little tumbledown house and barn."

"Not Trapper Joe's place?" Penny asked, straightening up to look.

The skiff had swung into faster water.

"We're not that far yet," Louise replied as she rested on the oars a moment. "Don't you remember—it's a house we passed just after we rented the boat."

"So it is. My mind is only hitting on half its cylinders today. Anyway, we're out of the swamp. Let's pull up and ask for a drink of cool water."

With a sigh of relief, Louise guided the skiff to a sagging, make-shift dock close to the farmhouse.

Some distance back from the river, enclosed by a broken fence, stood an unpainted, two-story frame house.

Beyond the woodshed rose a barn, its roof shingles badly curled. At the pump near the house, a middle-aged woman in loose-fitting faded blue dress, vigorously scrubbed a copper wash boiler.

She straightened quickly as the skiff grated against the dock.

"Howdy," she greeted the girls at their approach. Her tone lacked cordiality.

"Good afternoon," said Penny. "May we have a drink at the pump?"

"Help yourself."

The woman jerked a gnarled hand toward a gourd cup attached to the pump with a string. She studied the girls intently, almost suspiciously.

Louise and Penny drank only a few sips, for the water was warm and of unpleasant taste.

"You'uns be strangers hereabouts," the woman observed.

"Yes, we come from Riverview," Penny replied.

"You hain't been in the swamp?"

"Why, yes," answered Louise, eager to relate details of their adventure. "We gathered flowers, and then met a horrid man with red whiskers! He drove us away from the island before I could get my dog."

The woman gazed at the girls in an odd way.

"Sarved you'uns right to be driv off," she said in a grim voice. "The swamp's no place fer young gals. You might o' been et by a beast or bit by a snake."

"I don't believe the man we saw was much worried about that," Penny said dryly. "I wonder who he was?"

The farm woman shrugged and began to scour the copper boiler again. After a moment she looked up, fixing Penny with a stern and unfriendly eye.

"Let me give you a pocketful o' advice," she said. "Don't fret that purty head o' yourn about the swamp. And don't go pokin' yer nose into what ain't none o' your consarn. If I was you, I wouldn't come back. These here parts ain't none too health fer strangers, even young 'uns."

"But I want my dog," Louise insisted. "He's lost on the island."

"Hain't likely you'll ever see that dawg agin. And if you know what's good 'n smart, you'uns won't go back there agin."

Having delivered herself of this advice, the woman turned her back and went on with her work. Made increasingly aware of her hostility, Penny and Louise said goodbye and returned to the skiff.

As they shoved off, they could see that the woman was watching them.

"We're certainly popular today," Penny remarked when the skiff had floated on toward Trapper Joe's rental dock. "My, was she a sour pickle!"

Ten minutes later, as the girls brought up at Trapper Joe's place, they saw the lean old swamper standing near the dock, skinning a rabbit. His leathery, weather-beaten face crinkled into smiles.

"Sure am glad yer back safe an sound," he greeted them cheerfully. "After I let you take the skiff I got to worryin' fer fear you'd go too fur and git lost. 'Pears like you had good sense after all."

CHAPTER 2 - ALERTING ALL CARS

"The only thing we lost was my dog," Louise declared, stepping out on the dock. "Bones is gone for good, I guess."

She quickly told the old trapper what had happened on the island. He listened attentively, making no comment until she had finished.

"'Pears like you must have run afoul of Ezekiel Hawkins," he said then. "Leastwise, he's the only one hereabouts with a grizzly red beard."

"Is he a crook or a fugitive from the law?" Penny demanded.

"Not that nobody ever heard of. Ezekiel and his two boys, Hod and Coon, tend purty much to their own business. But they don't go fer strangers hangin' around."

"And do they own the island?"

"Not an inch of it—all that swamp's government land. Can't figure why, if 'twas Ezekiel, he'd drive you away from there. Unless—"

"Unless what?" Penny asked as the trapper fell silent.

"Jest a'thinkin'. Well, I'll keep an eye out fer the dog and maybe have a talk with Ezekiel."

Penny and Louise thanked the swamper and paid him for use of the boat. Gathering up the flowers they had picked, they started toward the road where they had parked Penny's coupe.

The trapper walked with them to the front gate.

"By the way," Penny remarked, "who is the woman on the farm just above here?"

"At the edge of the swamp? That's the Ezekiel Hawkins' place."

"Not the farm of that bearded man we met today!"

"Reckon so."

"We stopped there for a drink and talked to a tall, dark-haired woman. She was rather short with us."

"That would be Manthy, Ezekiel's wife. She's sharp-tongued, Manthy is, and not too friendly. Works hard slavin' and cookin' fer them two no-good boys of hers."

Penny and Louise asked no more questions, but again saying goodbye to Trapper Joe, went on down the dusty road.

Once they were beyond earshot, Penny observed: "What a joke on us, Lou! There we were, complaining to Mrs. Hawkins about her own husband! No wonder she was short with us."

"We had good reason to complain."

"Yes we did," Penny soberly agreed. "Of course, we can't be dead certain the bearded man was Ezekiel Hawkins. But Manthy did act unpleasant about it."

"If it weren't for Bones, I'd never set foot near this place again! Oh, I hope he finds his way home."

The girls had reached Penny's car, parked just off the sideroad. A clock on the dashboard warned them it was after five o'clock.

"Jeepers!" Penny exclaimed, snapping on the ignition. "I'll have to step on it to get dressed in time for the banquet! And I still have the tables to decorate!"

A fast drive over the bumpy sideroad brought the girls to the main paved highway. Much later, as they neared Riverview, Penny absently switched on the shortwave radio.

A number of routine police calls came through. Then the girls were startled to hear the dispatcher at headquarters say:

"Attention all scout cars! Be on the alert for escaped convict, Danny Deevers alias Spike Devons. Five-feet nine, blue eyes, brown hair. Last seen in state prison uniform. Believed heading for Riverview."

"Danny Deevers!" Penny whispered, and quickly turned the volume control. "I repeat," boomed the dispatcher's voice. "Be on lookout for Danny Deevers, a dangerous escaped criminal. Believed heading this way."

CHAPTER 3 - UNFINISHED BUSINESS

"Did you hear that?" Penny demanded of her chum as the police dispatcher went off the air. "Danny Deevers has escaped!"

The name rang no bell in Louise's memory.

"And who is Danny Deevers?" she inquired. "Anyone you know?"

"Not exactly. But Jerry Livingston has good reason to remember him."

"Jerry Livingston? That reporter you like so well?"

A quick grin brought confession from Penny. "Jerry is only one of my friends," she said. "But it's a known fact he's better looking and smarter than all the other *Star* reporters put together."

"It's a fact known to *you*," teased her chum. "Well, what about this escaped convict, Danny Deevers?"

Penny stopped for a red light. As it changed to green she replied:

"Don't you recall a series of stories Jerry wrote in our paper nearly a year ago? They exposed shortages which developed at the Third Federal Loan Bank. Jerry dug up a lot of evidence, and the result was, thefts were pinned on Danny Deevers. He was convicted and sent to the penitentiary for twenty years."

"Oh, yes, now I remember."

"At the time of his conviction, Deevers threatened if ever he went free, he would get even with Jerry."

"And now he's on the loose!"

"Not only that, but heading for Riverview, according to the police."

"You don't think he'd dare try to carry out his threat?"

Penny frowned and swerved to avoid hitting a cat which scuttled across the highway.

"Who knows, Lou? The police evidently are hot on Deevers' trail, but if they don't get him, he may try to seek revenge. It's odd he turns up today—and those men talking in the swamp—"

Louise's eyes opened wide. "Penny, you don't think Danny Deevers could have taken refuge in the swamp!"

"It's possible. Wouldn't it be a good hideout?"

"Only for a very courageous person," Louise shivered. "At night, all sorts of wild animals must prowl about. And one easily could be bitten by a poisonous snake and could die before help came."

"I'm not saying Danny Deevers was on the island today, Lou. But it's a thought. Maybe I'll pass it on to the police."

Penny fell into thoughtful silence as she reflected upon the strange snatch of conversation she had overheard between the two men in the underbrush. Had the bearded stranger really been Ezekiel Hawkins, and if so, with whom had he talked? The chance that the second man might have been Danny Deevers seemed slim, but it was a possibility.

When the car finally reached Riverview, Penny dropped Louise at the Sidell home and drove on to her own residence.

As she entered her own house, Mrs. Weems, the Parker family housekeeper, met the girl in the living room archway.

"Oh, Penny, where have you been!" she exclaimed. "Your father has telephoned twice. He's waiting for you now at the newspaper office."

"Do telephone him I'm practically on my way," Penny pleaded. "I'll grab a bath, dress, and be out of here in two shakes."

Midway up the stairs, the girl already had stripped off her sports shirt.

CHAPTER 3 - UNFINISHED BUSINESS

"I'll call your father," Mrs. Weems agreed, "but please, after this, pay more heed to time. You know how much the success of tonight's newspaper convention means to your father."

Penny's mumbled reply was blotted out by the slam of the bathroom door. The shower began to run full blast.

With a sigh, Mrs. Weems went to telephone Mr. Parker at the *Riverview Star* office.

For several years now, the housekeeper had efficiently supervised the motherless Parker home. She loved Penny, an only child, as her own, but there were times when she felt the girl was allowed too much freedom by an indulgent father.

Penny's active, alert mind was a never-ending source of amazement to Mrs. Weems. She had not entirely approved when Mr. Parker allowed the girl to spend her summers working as a reporter on the newspaper he owned.

Nevertheless, the housekeeper had been very proud because Penny had proved her ability. Not only had the girl written many fine stories which brought recognition, but also she had demonstrated a true "nose for news."

One of Penny's first lessons learned on the *Star* was that a deadline must always be met. Knowing now that she dared not be late, she hurriedly brushed her hair and wriggled into a long, full-skirted evening dress.

Almost before Mrs. Weems had completed the telephone call, she was downstairs again searching frantically for a beaded bag and gloves.

"Here they are, on the table," the housekeeper said. "Your father said he would wait just fifteen minutes."

"That's all I need, if the lights are green," Penny flung over her shoulder, as she ran to the parked car. "See you later, Mrs. Weems!"

Leaving an exhausted housekeeper behind, the girl made a quick trip to the downtown newspaper office.

As she reached the building, newsboys were on the streets crying the first edition, just off the press.

Upstairs, in the newsroom, reporters were relaxing at their desks, taking a few minutes' "breather" between editions.

Swinging through the entrance gate, Penny created a slight stir. At one of the desks under a neon light, Jerry Livingston, pencil behind one ear and hair slightly rumpled, tapped aimlessly at the keys of a typewriter. His quick eye appreciatively took in the long flowing skirt and the high heeled slippers.

"Well, if it isn't our little glamor girl!" he teased. "Cinderella ready for the ball!"

At another time, Penny would have paused to chat. Now she flashed a quick smile and clicked on toward the city desk.

Editor DeWitt, a quick-tempered, paunchy man of middle-age stood talking to her father, who looked more than ever distinguished in a new gray suit.

"Here she comes now," Mr. DeWitt said as Penny approached. "Your daughter never missed a deadline yet, Mr. Parker."

"Perhaps not," the publisher admitted, "but it always gives me heart failure, figuring she will."

"Dad, I'm sorry to have annoyed you," Penny said quickly before he could get in another word. "I was out at the swamp with Louise."

"The swamp!"

"Gathering flowers for the banquet table," Penny added hastily. "Oh, Dad, they're simply beautiful—so much nicer than any florist could have supplied."

"I can imagine." Mr. Parker smiled and looked at the wall clock. "We're due at the theater in ten minutes. I'm chairman of the program, unfortunately."

Penny gently broke the news. "Dad, I haven't had time to decorate the banquet table at the hotel. Will you drive me there?"

"I can't," Mr. Parker said, slightly exasperated. "I'm late now. Have one of the photographers take you. By the way, where's Salt Sommers?"

Hearing his name spoken, a young photographer whose clothes looked as if he had slept in them, moved out from behind a newspaper he had been reading.

"Coming right up, Chief," he answered.

"Run my daughter over to the Hillcrest Hotel," the publisher instructed. "Make it your job to see that she reaches the theater promptly."

"I guess I can handle her," Salt said, winking at Penny.

"And now, where is Jerry?" the publisher asked. "Has anyone seen him?"

"Relax, Dad," said Penny. "He's right here."

"I am jumpy tonight," Mr. Parker admitted, "but I have a lot on my mind. That stunt we've planned for the entertainment of our out-of-town men—is everything set?"

"Sure," DeWitt assured him. "There'll be no hitch. As the mayor winds up his address of welcome, the stage electrician turns off the stage lights. Jerry, in view of the audience, orders him to turn 'em on again. He refuses an' they argue over union rules. The fight gets hotter until finally the workman pulls a revolver and lets him have it full blast. Jerry falls, clutching his chest. Our newsboys gallop down the aisles with copies of the *Riverview Star* and screaming headlines telling all about the big murder. Everyone gets a swell laugh, figuring it's pretty snappy coverage."

"You certainly make it sound corny the way you tell it," Mr. Parker sighed. "Who thought up the idea anyhow?"

"Why, you did, Chief," grinned Salt. "Remember?"

"It was a poor idea. Maybe we ought to call it off."

"After we got the extras all printed an' everything?" Mr. DeWitt asked, looking injured. "The boys went to a lot of trouble."

"All right, we'll go ahead just as we planned, but I hope there is no slip-up. How about the revolver?"

"Right here," said Salt, whipping it from an inside pocket. "Loaded with blanks." He pointed it at a neon light, pulled the trigger and a loud bang resulted.

Jerry Livingston sauntered over. "So that's the lethal weapon," he observed. "Can I trust you guys not to slip a real bullet in when I'm not looking?"

"I've got to go," cut in Mr. Parker, looking again at the clock. "The program starts as soon as I get to the theater. Speeches should take about an hour. Then the stunt. And don't be late!"

"We'll be there," Salt promised. "Jerry, you riding with Penny and me?"

"I'll come later in my own car. Have a story to write first."

Going back to his typewriter, the reporter slipped carbons and paper into the machine and began pecking the keys.

At that moment a Western Union boy came through the newsroom. Catching Penny's eye, he pushed a telegram toward her and asked her to sign.

She wrote her name automatically, before noticing that the envelope bore Jerry's name.

"For you," she said, tossing it onto the roller of his typewriter. "More fan mail."

"It's probably a threat to bring suit if I don't pay my dry cleaning bill," Jerry chuckled.

He glanced at the envelope briefly, then slit it up the side. As he read the wire, his face became a study. His jaw tightened. Then he relaxed and laughed.

"This is a threat all right," he commented, "but not from the dry cleaners!"

Jerry reread the telegram, snorted with disgust, and then handed it to Penny.

In amazement she read: "ARRIVED IN TOWN TODAY TO TAKE CARE OF A LITTLE UNFINISHED BUSINESS. WILL BE SEEING YOU."

The telegram bore the signature, Danny Deevers.

CHAPTER 4 - A TRAFFIC ACCIDENT

As word spread through the office that Jerry had received a threat from the escaped convict, reporters gathered to read the telegram and comment upon it.

"Great stuff!" exclaimed Editor DeWitt, thinking in terms of headlines. "*Riverview Star* reporter threatened by Danny Deevers! We'll build it up—post a reward for his capture—provide you with a bodyguard."

"But I don't want a bodyguard," Jerry retorted. "Build up the story if you want to, but skip the kindergarten trimmings."

"You ought to have a bodyguard," DeWitt insisted seriously. "Danny Deevers is nobody's playboy. He may mean business. Reporters are hard to get these days. We can't risk having you bumped off."

"Oh, this telegram is pure bluff," Jerry replied, scrambling up the yellow sheet and hurling it into a tall metal scrap can. "I'll not be nursemaided by any bodyguard, and that's final!"

"Okay," DeWitt gave in, "but if you get bumped off, don't come crying to me!"

Jerry took a long drink at the fountain and then said thoughtfully: "You know, I have a hunch about Danny."

"Spill it," invited DeWitt.

"He didn't come back here to get even with me for those articles I wrote—or at least it's a secondary purpose."

"Then why did he head for Riverview?"

"I have an idea he may have come back to get $50,000."

"The money he stole from the Third Federal Bank?"

"Sure. The money disappeared, and when Danny took the rap, he refused to tell where he had hidden it. I'll bet the money is in a safe place somewhere in Riverview."

"You may be right at that," DeWitt agreed. "Anyway, it's a good story. Better write a couple pages before you go over to the theater—let that other stuff go."

Jerry nodded and with a quick glance at the clock, sat down at his typewriter.

"Ready, Penny?" called Salt, picking up his camera and heading for the door.

"In a minute."

Penny hesitated and then walked over to Jerry's desk.

"Jerry, you'll be careful, won't you?" she asked anxiously.

"Oh, sure," he agreed. "If I see Danny first, I'll start running."

"Do be serious, Jerry! You know, there's a chance Danny may be hiding in the swamp."

The carriage of Jerry's typewriter stopped with a jerk. He now gave Penny his full attention.

"What's that about Danny being in the swamp?"

"I didn't say he is for sure, but today when Louise and I were out there, we heard a very strange conversation."

Penny swiftly related everything that had occurred on the tiny island near the swamp entrance. She also described the bearded stranger who had ordered her away.

"That couldn't have been Danny," Jerry decided. "Not unless he's disguised his appearance."

"There was another man," Penny reminded him. "Louise and I never saw his face."

"Well, the swamp angle is worth investigating," the reporter assured her. "Personally, I doubt Danny would ever try living in the swamp—he's a city, slum-bred man—but I'll tell the police about it."

"Do be careful," Penny urged again, turning away.

Salt was waiting in the press car when she reached the street. Quickly transferring the flowers from her own automobile to his, she climbed in beside him.

"The Hillcrest?" he inquired, shifting gears.

"Yes, I'll decorate the tables. Then we'll drive to the theater."

With a complete disregard for speed laws, safety stops, and red lights, Salt toured the ten blocks to the hotel in record time. Pulling up at the entrance, he said:

"While you're in there, I'll amble across the street. Want to do a little inquiring at the Western Union office."

"About the telegram Danny Deevers sent Jerry?"

"Figured we might find from where it was sent."

"I should have thought of that myself! Do see what you can learn, Salt. It won't take me long to fix those tables."

Penny disappeared into the hotel but was back in fifteen minutes. A moment later, Salt sauntered across the street from the Western Union office.

"Learn anything?" Penny asked.

"A little. The manager told me a boy picked up the message from a rooming house on Clayton street. That's all they know about it."

"Did you get the address?"

"Sure—1497 Clayton Street—an apartment building. The clue may be a dud one though. Danny wouldn't likely be dumb enough to leave a wide open trail."

"All the same, oughtn't we to check into it?"

"We?"

"Naturally I'm included," grinned Penny. "By the way, aren't we near Clayton street now?"

"It's only a couple of blocks away."

"Then what's delaying us?"

"My conscience for one thing," Salt said, climbing into the car beside Penny. "Your father's expecting us at the theater. I'm supposed to take pictures of the visiting big-boys."

"We'll get there in time. This may be our only chance to trace Danny."

"You're a glutton for adventure," Salt said dubiously, studying his wristwatch. "Me—I'm not so sure."

"Danny probably won't be hiding out at the rooming house," Penny argued. "But someone may be able to tell us where he went."

"Okay," the photographer agreed, jamming his foot on the starter. "We got to make it snappy though."

The dingy old brick apartment house at 1497 Clayton Street stood jammed against other low-rent buildings in the downtown business section.

"You wait here," Salt advised as he pulled up near the dwelling. "If I don't come back in ten minutes, put in a call to the police. And arrange to give me a decent burial!"

The photographer disappeared into the building.

He was back almost at once. "It was a dud," he said in disgust. "The telegram was sent from here all right, but Danny's skipped."

"You talked to the building manager?"

Salt nodded. "A fellow that must have been Danny rented a room last night, but he pulled out early this morning."

"Why, the telegram didn't come until a few minutes ago!"

"Danny took care of that by having the janitor send it for him. He evidently escaped from the pen late yesterday, but authorities didn't give out the story until today."

Disappointed over their failure, Penny and Salt drove on toward the theater in glum silence.

Suddenly at the intersection of Jefferson and Huron Streets, a long black sedan driven by a woman, failed to observe a stop sign. Barging into a line of traffic, it spun unsteadily on two wheels and crashed into an ancient car in which two men were riding.

"Just another dumb woman driver," observed Salt. He brought up at the curb and reached for his camera.

"Nobody's hurt so it's hardly worth a picture. But if I don't grab it, DeWitt'll be asking me why I didn't."

CHAPTER 4 - A TRAFFIC ACCIDENT

Balancing the camera on the sill of the open car window, he snapped the shutter just as the two men climbed out of their ancient vehicle.

"Looks as if they're going to put up a big squawk," Salt observed with interest. "What they beefin' about? That old wreck isn't worth anything, and anyhow, the lady only bashed in a couple of fenders."

The driver of the black sedan took a quick glance at the two men and said hastily:

"Please don't call a policeman. I'll gladly pay for all the damage. I'm covered by insurance. Just give me your names and where you live. Or, if you prefer, I'll go with you now to a garage where your car can be repaired."

The two men paid her no heed. In fact, they appeared not to be listening. Instead, they were gazing across the street at Salt and his camera.

"Button up your lip, lady!" said one of the men rudely.

He was a heavy-set man, dressed in a new dark blue serge suit. His face was coarse, slightly pale, and his steel-blue eyes had a hard, calculating glint.

His companion, much younger, might have been a country boy for he wore a lumber jacket, corduroy pants, and heavy shoes caked with mud.

The older man crossed the street to Salt's car. He glanced at the "press" placard in the windshield and said curtly:

"Okay, buddy! I saw you take that picture! Hand over the plate!"

CHAPTER 5 - THE RED STAIN

"Hand over the plate, buddy!" the motorist repeated as Salt gave no hint that he had heard. "You're from a newspaper, and we don't want our pictures printed—see?"

"Sure, I see," retorted Salt. "I'm not turning over any pictures."

The man took a wallet from his suit pocket. "Here's a five spot to make it worth your while."

"No, thanks. Anyway, what's your kick? Your car didn't cause the accident. You're in the clear."

"Maybe we'll use the picture to collect damages," the man said. "Here, I'll give you ten."

"Nothing doing."

To put an end to the argument, Salt drove on.

"Wonder who those birds were?" he speculated.

Penny craned her neck to look back through the rear car window.

"Salt!" she exclaimed. "That man who argued with us is writing down our license plate number!"

"Let him!"

"He intends to find out who you are, Salt! He must want that picture badly."

"He'll get it all right—on the front page of the *Star* tomorrow! Maybe he's a police character and doesn't want any publicity. He looked like a bad egg."

"I wish we'd taken down *his* license number."

"We've got it," replied Salt. "It'll show up in the picture."

Penny settled back in the seat, paying no more attention to the traffic behind them. Neither she nor Salt noticed that they were being followed by the car with battered fenders.

At the theater, Salt parked in the alleyway.

"Go on in," he told Penny, opening the car door for her. "I want to collect some of my stuff and then I'll be along."

At the stagedoor, Penny was stopped by Old Jim, the doorman.

"You can't go in here without a pass, Miss," he said. "There's a newspaper convention on. My orders are not to let anyone in without a pass."

Penny flashed her press card.

"My mistake," the doorman mumbled.

Once inside, Penny wandered backstage in search of her father or Jerry. The program had started, but after listening a moment to a singer, she moved out of range of his voice.

Now and then, from the audience of newspapermen out front, came an occasional ripple of laughter or clapping of hands as they applauded a speaker.

"Sounds pretty dull," thought Penny. "Guess it's lucky Dad cooked up the shooting stunt. If everything goes off right, it should liven things up a bit."

Wandering on down a hall, she came to one of the dressing rooms. Stacked against the outside wall were hundreds of freshly printed newspapers ready for distribution.

Penny flipped one from the pile and read the headline: "REPORTER SHOT IN ARGUMENT WITH ELECTRICIAN!"

Beneath the banner followed a story of the staged stunt to take place. So convincingly was it written, Penny had to think twice to realize not a word was true. Other columns of the paper contained regular wire news stories and telephoto pictures. Much of the front page also was given over to an account of the convention itself.

CHAPTER 5 - THE RED STAIN

"This will make a nice souvenir edition," Penny thought. "Wonder where Jerry is? The stunt will be ruined if he doesn't get here."

Salt came down the corridor, loaded heavily with his camera, a tripod, a reflector, and other photographic equipment.

"Jerry here yet?" he inquired.

"I haven't seen him. It's getting late too."

"He'll be here," Salt said confidently. "Wonder where I'd better leave this revolver?"

Setting the photographic equipment on the floor, he took the revolver from his coat pocket, offering it to Penny.

"Don't give it to me," she protested.

"Put it in the dressing room," he advised. "I can't keep it, because I've got to go out front and shoot some pictures."

"Is the revolver loaded?" Penny asked, taking it unwillingly.

"Sure, with blanks. It's ready for the stunt."

Penny carried the weapon into the dressing room and deposited it on one of the tables. When she returned to the corridor, Salt had gathered up his equipment and was starting away.

However, before he could leave, an outside door slammed. Jim, the doorman, burst in upon them.

"Young feller, is that your car parked in the alley?"

"Yeah!" exclaimed Salt, startled. "Don't tell me the cops are handing me a ticket!"

"Some feller's out there, riflin' through your things!"

Salt dropped his camera and equipment, racing for the door. Penny was close behind.

Reaching the alley, they were just in time to see a man in a dark suit ducking around the corner of the building.

"Hey, you!" shouted Salt angrily.

The man turned slightly and vanished from view.

"Wasn't that the same fellow who was in the auto accident?" Penny demanded.

"Looked like him! Wonder if he got away with anything?"

"Didn't you lock the car, Salt?"

"Only the rear trunk compartment. Should have done it but I was in a hurry."

"Shall I call the police, Salt?"

"Why bother? That bird's gone now. Let's see if he stole anything first."

Salt muttered in disgust as he saw the interior of the car. A box of photographic equipment had been scattered over the back seat. The door of the glove compartment was open, its contents also helter-skelter.

"Anything missing?" Penny asked.

"Not that I can tell. Yes, there is! Some of the photographic plates!"

"Oh, Salt, I was afraid of it! The thief must have been one of those two men who were in the auto accident! You wouldn't sell them the picture they wanted so they followed you here and stole it!"

"They may have tried," the photographer corrected.

"You mean you still have it?"

"The plates that are missing are old ones, extras I exposed at a society tea and never bothered to develop."

"Then you have the one of the auto accident?"

"Right here in my pocket."

"Oh, Salt, how brilliant of you!" Penny laughed.

"It wasn't brilliancy on my part—just habit," Salt returned. "I wonder why that bird set such great store by the picture? Maybe for some reason he's afraid to have it come out in the paper."

"I can hardly wait to see it developed!"

As Penny and the photographer walked back to the theater entrance, a taxi skidded to a stop at the curb. Jerry alighted.

"Anything wrong?" he inquired, staring curiously at the pair.

Salt told him what had happened.

"Maybe you've got dynamite packed in that plate," Jerry commented when he had heard the story. "Better shoot it to the office and have it developed."

"I'm tied up here for half an hour at least."

"Send it back by the cab driver. He can deliver it to DeWitt."

"Good idea," agreed Salt.

He scribbled a note to accompany the plate and gave it to the cab driver, together with the holder.

"Take good care of this," he warned. "Don't turn it over to any one except the city editor."

After the cab had driven away, Salt, Jerry, and Penny re-entered the theater. Mr. Parker had come backstage and was talking earnestly to the doorman. Glimpsing the three, he exclaimed:

"There you are! And just in time too! The stunt goes on in five minutes."

"Are the newsboys here?" Jerry asked. "And Johnny Bates, the electrician?"

"The boys are out front. Johnny's waiting in the stage wings. Where's the revolver, Salt?"

"I'll get it," Penny volunteered, starting for the dressing room.

The revolver lay where she had left it. As she reached for the weapon, she suddenly sniffed the air. Plainly she could smell strong cigarette smoke.

Penny glanced swiftly about the room. No one was there and she had seen no one enter in the last few minutes.

"Someone must have been here," she thought. "Perhaps it was Old Jim, but he smokes a pipe."

"Penny!" her father called impatiently from outside. "We haven't much time."

Picking up the revolver, she hurriedly joined him.

"Dad, why not call the stunt off?" she began. "Something might go wrong—"

"We can't call it off now," her father cut in impatiently. Taking the revolver from her hand he gave it to Jerry. "Do your stuff, my boy, and don't be afraid to put plenty of heat into the argument. Remember your cue?"

"I'm to start talking just as soon as the Mayor finishes his speech."

"He's winding it up now. So get up there fast."

As Jerry started up the stairway, Penny trailed him.

"Someone must have been in the dressing room after I left the revolver there," she revealed nervously. "Be sure to check it before you turn it over to Mr. Bates."

The reporter nodded, scarcely hearing her words. His ears were tuned to the Mayor's closing lines. A ripple of applause from the audience told him the speech already had ended.

Taking the last few steps in a leap, Jerry reached the wings where John Bates was waiting. He gave him the revolver and at once plunged into his lines. So convincingly did he argue about the stage lights that Penny found herself almost believing the disagreement was genuine.

The argument waxed warmer, and the actors moved out on the stage in full view of the audience.

"Jerry's good," remarked Salt, who had joined Penny. "Didn't know he had that much ham in him!"

The quarrel now had reached its climax. As if in a sudden fit of rage, the electrician raised the revolver and pointed it at Jerry.

"Take that—and that—and that!" he shouted, thrice pulling the trigger.

Jerry staggered back, clutching in the region of his heart. Slowly, his face contorted, he crumpled to the floor.

Scarcely had he collapsed, than newsboys armed with their papers, began to rush through the aisles of the theater.

"Read all about it!" they shouted. "Reporter Shot in Argument! Extra! Extra!"

The newspapermen chuckled at the joke as they accepted the free papers.

On the stage, Jerry still lay where he had fallen. The electrician, his part ended, had disappeared to attend to regular duties.

"Come on, Jerry!" Salt called to him. "What are you waiting for? More applause? Break it up!"

The reporter did not stir. But on the floor beside him, a small red stain began to spread in a widening circle.

Penny and Salt saw it at the same instant and were frozen with horror.

"Ring down the curtain!" the photographer cried hoarsely. "Jerry's really been shot!"

CHAPTER 6 - AMBULANCE CALL

Penny ran across the stage to kneel beside Jerry, who lay limp on the floor. In horror, she saw that the red stain covered a jagged area on his shirt front.

"Oh, Jerry!" she cried frantically. "Speak to me!"

The reporter groaned loudly and stirred.

"Hold me in your arms," he whispered. "Let my last hours on this earth be happy ones."

Penny's hands dropped suddenly to her sides. She straightened up indignantly.

"You faker!" she accused. "I should think you'd be ashamed to frighten us so! That's not blood on your shirt! It's red ink!"

Jerry sat up, chuckling. "Ruined a good shirt too!"

"You shouldn't have done it," Penny said, still provoked.

"I wanted to put a little drama into the act. Also, I was curious to see how you would react."

Penny tossed her head, starting away. "You needn't be so smug about it, Jerry Livingston! And don't flatter yourself I was concerned about you! I was thinking what a scandal it would mean for Dad and the paper!"

"Oh, sure," Jerry agreed, pursuing her backstage and down a corridor. "Listen, Penny, it was only a joke—"

"Not a very funny one!"

"Penny, I'm sorry—I really am. I didn't realize anyone would get so worked up about it."

"I'm not worked up!" Penny denied, spinning on a heel to face him. "It just gave me a little shock, that's all. First, that threat from Danny Deevers. Then when I saw you flattened out, for a minute I thought someone had substituted a real bullet in the revolver and that you had been shot."

"It was a rummy joke—I realize that now. Forgive me, will you, Penny?"

"I suppose so. Just don't try anything like it again."

"I won't," Jerry promised. "Now that my part is finished here, suppose we go somewhere for a bite to eat?"

"With that blotch of red ink on your shirt front?"

"Oh, I'll change it. I brought an extra shirt along. Wait here and I'll be right with you."

Jerry stepped into the dressing room to make the change. Penny, while waiting, wandered back to the stage wings to talk to Salt. However, the photographer had gone out front and was busily engaged taking pictures of visiting celebrities.

After a few minutes, Penny went downstairs again. Jerry was nowhere to be seen.

The door of the dressing room stood slightly ajar. Penny tapped lightly on it, calling: "Get a move on, Jerry! You're slower than a snail!"

No answer came from inside.

Penny paced up and down the corridor and returned to listen at the door. She could hear no sound inside the room.

"Jerry, are you there?" she called again. "If you are, answer!"

Still there was no reply.

"Now where did he go?" Penny thought impatiently.

She hesitated a moment, then pushed open the door. Jerry's stained shirt lay on the floor where he had dropped it.

The reporter no longer was in the dressing room. Or so Penny thought at first glance.

But as her gaze roved slowly about, she was startled to see a pair of shoes protruding from a hinged decorative screen which stood in one corner of the room.

Jerry, very definitely was attached to the shoes. Stretched out on the floor again, his face remained hidden from view.

Penny resisted an impulse to run to his side.

"Jerry Livingston!" she exclaimed. "You've carried your stupid joke entirely too far! Our date is off!"

Turning her back, she started away. But in the doorway, something held her. She glanced back.

Jerry had not moved.

"Jerry, get up!" she commanded. "Please!"

The reporter made not the slightest response. Penny told herself that Jerry was only trying to plague her, yet she could not leave without being absolutely certain.

Though annoyed at herself for such weakness, she walked across the room to jerk aside the decorative screen.

Jerry lay flat on his back, eyelids closed. A slight gash was visible on the side of his head where the skin was bruised.

One glance convinced Penny that the reporter was not shamming this time. Obviously, he had been knocked unconscious, perhaps by a fall.

"Jerry!" she cried, seizing his hand which was cold to the touch.

Badly frightened, Penny darted to the door and called loudly for help.

Without waiting to learn if anyone had heard her cry, she rushed back to Jerry. On the dressing table nearby stood a pitcher of water and a glass.

Wetting a handkerchief, Penny pressed it to the reporter's forehead. It seemed to produce no effect. In desperation, she then poured half a glass of water over his face.

To her great relief, Jerry sputtered and his eyelids fluttered open.

"For crying out loud!" he muttered. "What you trying to do? Drown me?"

Raising a hand to his head, the reporter gingerly felt of a big bump which had risen there. He pulled himself to a sitting position.

"What happened, Jerry?" Penny asked after giving him a few minutes to recover his senses. "Did you trip and fall?"

The question seemed to revive Jerry completely. Without answering, he got to his feet, and walked unsteadily to the window overlooking the alley.

Penny then noticed for the first time that it was open. She also became aware of a heavy scent of tobacco smoke in the room—the same cigarette odor she had noticed earlier. Now however, it was much stronger.

Jerry peered out the window. "He's gone!" he mumbled.

"Who, Jerry? Tell me what happened."

"Things aren't too clear in my mind," the reporter admitted, sinking into a chair. "Wow! My head!"

"Did someone attack you?"

"With a blackjack. I came in here and changed my shirt. Had a queer feeling all the while, as if someone were in the room."

"Were you smoking a cigarette, Jerry?"

"Why, no."

"Did you notice smoke in the room? The odor still is here."

Jerry sniffed the air. "Neco's," he decided. "They're one of the strongest cigarettes on the market and not easy to get. Now that you mention it, the odor was in the room when I came in! But I didn't think about it at the time."

"Then whoever struck you must have been in here waiting!"

"Sure. Whoever it was, came in the window. He was hidden behind that screen. As I started to leave, he reared up and let me have it from behind! That's all I remember."

"Then you didn't see him?"

"No, it happened too fast."

"Jerry, it may have been Danny Deevers!"

"Maybe so," the reporter agreed. "But I always figured if he caught up with me, he wouldn't fool around with any rabbit punches."

CHAPTER 6 - AMBULANCE CALL

"He may have been frightened away, hearing me in the hall," Penny said. "Jerry, do you have other enemies besides Danny?"

"Dozens of them probably. Every reporter has. But I don't know of anyone who hates me enough to try to lay me out."

The dressing room door now swung open to admit Mr. Parker and several other newspapermen.

"Penny, did you call for help?" her father demanded. "What's wrong?"

"Jerry was slugged," Penny answered, and told what had happened.

"How do you feel, Jerry?" the publisher inquired. "That's a nasty looking bump on your head."

"I'm fit as a fiddle and ready for a dinner date," Jerry announced brightly, winking at Penny. "How about it?"

"Well, I don't know," she replied. "Are you sure you feel up to it?"

"I'm fine." To prove his words, Jerry got to his feet. He started across the room, weaving unsteadily.

Had not Mr. Parker and another man seized him by the arms, he would have slumped to the floor.

"Jerry, you're in no shape for anything except a hospital checkup," the publisher said firmly. "That's where you're going!"

"Oh, Chief, have a heart!"

Mr. Parker turned a deaf ear upon the appeal.

"For all we know, you may have a fractured skull," he said, helping to ease the reporter into a chair. "We'll have you X-rayed."

"I don't want to be X-rayed," Jerry protested. "I'm okay."

"Besides, with Danny Deevers still at large, a hospital is a nice safe place," Mr. Parker continued, thinking aloud. "Perhaps we can arrange for you to stay there a week."

"A week! Chief, I'm not going!"

"No arguments," said Mr. Parker. "You're the same as in Riverview Hospital now. Penny, telephone for an ambulance."

CHAPTER 7 - AN EMPTY BED

At Riverview hospital twenty minutes later, Jerry was given a complete physical check-up.

"The X-rays won't be developed for another half hour," an interne told him, "but you seem to be all right."

"I not only seem to be, I am," the reporter retorted. "Told you that when I came here! But would anyone listen to me?"

"Twenty-four hours rest will fix you right up. We have a nice private room waiting for you on the third floor. Bath and everything."

"Now listen!" exclaimed Jerry. "You said yourself I'm all right. I'm walking out of here now!"

"Sorry. Orders are you're in for twenty-four hours observation."

"Whose orders?"

"Dr. Bradley. He had a little talk with the publisher of your paper—"

"Oh, I get it! A conspiracy! They're keeping me here to keep me from checking up on Danny Deevers!"

"What's that?" the interne inquired curiously.

"Never mind," returned Jerry, closing up like a clam. "I'll slip you a fiver to get me out of here."

"Sorry. No can do."

The interne went to the door, motioning for two other internes who came in with a stretcher.

"Hop aboard," he told Jerry. "Better come peaceably."

Jerry considered resistance. Deciding it was useless, he rolled onto the stretcher and was transported via the elevator to the third floor. There he was deposited none too ceremoniously in a high bed.

"Just to make sure you stay here, I'm taking your clothes," said the interne. "Now just relax and take it easy."

"Relax!"

"Sure, what you got to kick about? Your bills are all being paid. You get twenty-four hours rest, a good looking nurse, and a radio. Also three meals thrown in."

Jerry settled back into the pillow. "Maybe you've got something after all," he agreed.

"That's the attitude, boy. Well, I'll be seeing you."

Satisfied that Jerry would make no more trouble, he took his clothes and went outside.

Penny and Salt, who had been waiting in the reception room below, stepped from the elevator at that moment.

"How is Jerry?" Penny inquired anxiously as she stopped the interne in the corridor.

"He's all right. Go on in if you want to talk to him."

"Which room?"

"Wait until I put these clothes away and I'll show you."

The interne hung Jerry's suit in a locker at the end of the corridor and then returned to escort Penny and Salt to Room 318.

Jerry, a picture of gloom, brightened as his friends entered.

"I'm sure glad you came!" he greeted them. "I want you to help me get out of here."

"Not a chance," said Salt, seating himself on the window ledge. "This is just the place for you—nice and quiet and safe."

Jerry snorted with disgust.

"Dad and Mr. DeWitt both think Danny Deevers means business," Penny added. "The paper is offering $10,000 reward for his capture."

CHAPTER 7 - AN EMPTY BED

"Ten thousand smackers! I could use that money myself. And I have a hunch about Danny—"

"Forget it," Salt advised. "This is a case for the police. Just lie down like a nice doggy and behave yourself. We'll keep you informed on the latest news."

"That reminds me," added Penny. "After the ambulance took you away, Dad had the theater searched and the alley. No clues."

Jerry lay still for several minutes, his eyes focused thoughtfully on the ceiling. "If it's the verdict that I stay here, I suppose I may as well give up and take my medicine."

"Now you're showing sense," approved Salt. "Penny and I have an idea that may help trace Deevers. We'll tell you about it later."

"Sure," retorted Jerry ironically, "spare me the shock now. By the way, did you meet an interne in the hall? He was carrying off my clothes."

"Yes, he brought us here," Penny nodded.

"You didn't happen to notice where he hid my clothes?"

"They're safe, Jerry," Penny assured him. "In a locker at the end of the hall."

The information seemed to satisfy Jerry. Wrapping himself like a cocoon in a blanket, he burrowed down and closed his eyes.

"I want to catch forty winks now," he said. "If you folks have a big idea that will lead to Danny's capture, don't let me detain you."

"Jerry, don't be cross with us," Penny pleaded. "We know how you feel, but honestly, you'll be so much safer here."

Jerry pretended not to hear.

After a moment, Salt and Penny quietly left the room.

"He's taking it hard," the photographer commented as they sped in the press car toward the *Riverview Star* building. "In a way, you can't blame him. Jerry's not the type to be shut up in a nice safe place."

"Dad wants to keep him in the hospital until Danny Deevers is captured, but it will be hard to do it."

Salt, driving with one hand, looked at his watch.

"It's after nine o'clock," he announced. "Penny, you've missed the dinner at the Hillcrest."

"I don't mind. So much has happened today, I've had no time to be hungry."

"Want me to drop you off there now?"

"No, the banquet will be nearly over. I couldn't bear to listen to speeches. Let's go straight to the office and find out what that traffic accident picture shows."

"Suits me, only I'm hungry." On impulse, Salt pulled up in front of a hamburger shop offering curb service. "Let's grab a bite before we really go to work to crack this case."

He tooted the horn and a uniformed girl came hurrying to take his order.

Fortified by sandwiches, coffee, and ice cream, the pair then drove on to the *Riverview Star* office.

Avoiding the busy newsroom, Salt and Penny went up the back stairs to the photographic studio. Bill Jones, a studio helper, was busy at the wire photo machine.

"Has that picture of the traffic accident I sent over come up yet?" Salt asked him.

"On the desk," the boy answered. "Not too sharp."

Salt picked up a dozen pictures which had been printed on glossy paper and rapidly ran through them until he found the one he sought.

Eagerly Penny peered over his shoulder. The two cars involved in the accident were plainly shown, the license numbers of both visible. In the ancient vehicle, the younger man had lowered his head so that his face was completely hidden. The camera had caught a profile view of the older man, also not clear.

"Lousy picture," said Salt contemptuously.

"It shows the license number of the car. Can't we trace the driver that way?"

"The Motor Vehicle Department is closed now. But I know a fellow who works there. Maybe he'll do us a favor and go back to the office tonight and look up the information."

Salt made the telephone call, and after ten minutes of argument, convinced his friend that the requested information was a matter of life and death.

"He'll do it," the photographer said, hanging up the receiver. "Soon's he gets the information, he'll telephone us here."

Penny had been studying the photograph again. She now was ready with a second suggestion. "Even if the faces aren't very clear, let's compare them with pictures of Danny Deevers in the morgue."

"Good idea," agreed Salt.

The newspaper morgue or library where photographs, cuts and newspaper clippings were carefully filed for reference, was just a few steps down the hall. Miss Adams, the librarian, had gone to lunch, so Salt obtained a key and they searched for their own information.

"Here's an envelope marked Danny Deevers!" Penny cried, pulling it from one of the long filing drawers. "All sorts of pictures of him too!"

Critically, the pair studied the photographs.

The escaped convict was a middle-aged, sullen looking man with hard, expressionless eyes. In one of the pictures, parted lips revealed a set of ugly, uneven teeth.

"This shot I took is so blurred, it's hard to tell if they're the same person or not," Salt complained. "But it looks like Danny."

"If it is, that would explain why he tried to make you give up the plate."

"Sure, he knew the car license number would be a tip-off to the police. But maybe the bird isn't Danny."

"I wish we were certain. Salt, couldn't Jerry identify him from the picture you took?"

"Maybe. Jerry saw Deevers several times before he was put away in the pen."

"Then why not take the picture to the hospital now?"

"Okay," agreed Salt. "Let's go."

Fifteen minutes later, at the hospital, they sought unsuccessfully to pass a receptionist who sat at a desk in the lobby.

"Sorry, visiting hours are over," she explained.

"We're from the *Star*," Salt insisted. "We have to see Jerry Livingston on an important business matter."

"That's different," the receptionist replied. "You may go up to his room, but please make the call brief."

An automatic elevator carried the pair to the third floor. Jerry's door near the end of the corridor stood slightly ajar. Salt tapped lightly on it, and hearing no answer, pushed it farther open.

"Well, what d'you know!" he exclaimed.

Penny, startled by his tone of voice, peered over his shoulder.

The room was deserted. Jerry's bed, unmade, stood empty.

CHAPTER 8 - IN SEARCH OF JERRY

"Now what could have become of Jerry?" Penny murmured as she and Salt gazed about the deserted room in amazement. "Surely we've made no mistake."

"He was assigned this room all right," the photographer declared. "But maybe they changed it later."

"That's it," agreed Penny in relief. "For a minute it gave me a shock seeing that empty bed. I thought perhaps he had taken a bad turn and been removed for emergency treatment."

The pair sought Miss Brent, a floor supervisor.

"Why, the patient in Room 318 hasn't been changed elsewhere," she replied. "At least, not to my knowledge. I've been off the floor for the last half hour."

Inspecting Room 318 to satisfy herself that the bed was empty, Miss Brent questioned several nurses and an interne. No one seemed to know what had become of the patient. There was a whispered conference and then Miss Brent made a call to the superintendent.

"Something has happened to Jerry!" Penny told Salt tensely. "He may have been abducted!"

A nurse came flying up the hall from the locker room.

"Mr. Livingston's clothes are gone!" she reported.

Light began to dawn on Penny. She recalled the seemingly innocent question Jerry had asked earlier that night as to the location of the clothes locker.

"He's probably walked out of the hospital!" she exclaimed.

"Impossible!" snapped Miss Brent, though her voice lacked conviction. "Nurses have been on duty here all the time. Mr. Livingston couldn't have obtained his clothes without being observed."

"The floor was deserted for about ten minutes," an interne recalled. "An emergency case came in and everyone was tied up."

Penny re-entered Jerry's room. The window remained closed and it was a straight drop of three stories to the yard below. She was satisfied the reporter had not taken that escape route.

A sheet of paper, propped against the mirror of the dresser attracted her eye. As she unfolded it, she saw at once that the handwriting was Jerry's.

"I'm too healthy a pup to stay in bed," he had scrawled. "Sorry, but I'm walking out."

Penny handed the note to Miss Brent who could not hide her annoyance as she read it.

"Nothing like this ever happened before!" she exclaimed. "How could the young man have left this floor and the building without being seen? He's in no condition to be wandering about the streets."

"Then Jerry really did need hospitalization?" inquired Penny.

"Certainly. He suffered shock and the doctor was afraid of brain injury. The patient should have been kept under observation for at least twenty-four hours. Wandering off this way is a very bad sign."

"We'll get him back here pronto!" Salt promised. "He can't have gone far."

In the lobby he and Penny paused to ask the receptionist if she had observed anyone answering Jerry's description leave the building.

"Why, no," she replied, only to correct herself. "Wait! A young man in a gray suit left here about twenty minutes ago. I didn't really notice his face."

"That must have been Jerry!" cried Penny. "Which way did he go?"

"I'm sorry, I haven't the slightest idea."

"Jerry may have gone to his room," Penny said hopefully. "Let's call his hotel."

Using a lobby telephone, they dialed the St. Agnes Hotel Apartments where the reporter lived. The desk clerk reported that Jerry had not been seen that night.

"Oh, where could he have gone?" Penny said as she and Salt left the hospital. "He may be wandering the streets in a dazed condition. Shouldn't we ask police to try to find him?"

"Guess it's all we can do," the photographer agreed. "Jerry sure will be sore at us though."

A taxi cab pulled up near the hospital steps.

"Taxi?" the driver inquired.

Salt shook his head. "We don't know where we want to go yet. We're looking for a friend of ours who left the hospital about twenty minutes ago."

"A girl?"

"No, a man in a gray suit," Penny supplied. "He probably wasn't wearing a hat."

"Say, he musta been the one that asked me about the fare to the swamp!"

At the pair's look of intense interest, the cab driver added: "I was waitin' here for a fare when some ladies came out of the hospital. I pulled up and took 'em aboard. Just then this young feller comes out.

"He didn't seem to notice I had my cab filled, and says: 'How much to take me to Caleb Corners?'"

"Caleb Corners?" Penny repeated, having never heard of the place.

"That's a long ways out, almost to the swamp. I says to him, 'Sorry, buddy, but I got a fare. If you can wait a few minutes I'll be right back and pick you up.'"

"What did Jerry say?" Salt asked.

"He said he wanted to get started right away. Reckon he picked up another cab."

Thanking the driver for the information, Penny and Salt retreated a few steps for a consultation.

"If Jerry started for the swamp at this time of night he must be wacky!" the photographer declared. "That knock on the head must have cracked him up and he doesn't know what he's doing!"

"Why would he start for the swamp? Maybe he remembers what I told him about seeing a stranger there today, and in his confusion, has an idea he'll find Danny Deevers!"

"Jerry can't have had much of a start, and we know he headed for Caleb Corners! I'll go after him."

"We'll both go," Penny said quickly. "Come on, let's get the car."

Before they could leave the hospital steps, the receptionist came hurrying outside.

"Oh, I'm glad you're still here!" she said breathlessly, looking at the photographer. "Aren't you Mr. Sommers?"

"That's me," agreed Salt.

"A telephone call for you."

"Say, maybe it's Jerry! Wait here, Penny. I'll be right back."

Salt was gone perhaps ten minutes. When he returned, his grim expression instantly informed Penny that the call had not been from Jerry.

"It was from my friend in the Motor Vehicle Department," he reported. "He traced the license number of the car that was in the accident."

"How did he know you were here, Salt?"

"Telephoned the office, and someone told him to try the hospital."

"Who owns the car, Salt?"

"A woman by the name of Sarah Jones, Route 3, Crissey Road."

"Crissey Road! Why, that's out near the swamp, not far from Trapper Joe's place! I recall seeing the name on a signpost when Louise and I were out there this afternoon."

"All roads lead to the swamp tonight," Salt commented. "I'm worried about Jerry. I called the office and he hasn't shown up there."

"Then he must have started for Caleb Corners! Salt, we're wasting time!"

"We sure are," he agreed. "Let's go!"

The press car had been parked in a circular area fifty yards from the hospital. Salt and Penny ran to it, and soon were on their way, speeding into the night on a deserted, narrow road.

CHAPTER 9 - THE WIDOW JONES

Caleb Corners scarcely was a stopping point on the narrow, dusty, county highway.

By night the crossroads were dark and gloomy, unlighted even by a traffic signal. To the right stood a filling station, and directly across from it, a little grocery store, long since closed for the day.

Salt turned in at the filling station, halting the press car almost at the doorway of the tiny office.

Inside, a young man who was counting change at a cash register, turned suddenly and reached for an object beneath the counter. As Salt came in, he kept his hand out of sight, regarding the photographer with suspicion.

"Relax, buddy," said Salt, guessing that the station owner feared robbery. "We're from the *Riverview Star* and need a little information."

"What do you want to know?" The young man still kept his hand beneath the counter.

"We're looking for a friend of ours who may have come out here a few minutes ago in a taxi."

"No cab's been through here in the last hour," the filling station man said. "This is a mighty lonesome corner at night. I should have closed up hours ago, only I'm expecting a truck to fill up here."

"Why not put that gun away?" Salt suggested pointedly. "We're not here to rob you. Do we look like crooks?"

"No, you don't," the man admitted, "but I've been taken in before. This station was broken into three times in the past six months. Only two weeks ago a man and woman stopped here about this same time of night—they looked okay and talked easy, but they got away with $48.50 of my hard earned cash."

"We really are from the *Star*," Penny assured him. "And we're worried about a friend of ours who slipped away from the hospital tonight. He was in an accident and wasn't entirely himself. He may get into serious trouble if we don't find him."

Her words seemed to convince the filling station man that he had nothing to fear. Dropping the revolver into the cash drawer, he said in a more friendly tone:

"I guess you folks are on the square. Anyway, you wouldn't get much if you robbed the till tonight. I only took in $37.50. Not enough to pay me for keeping open."

"You say a cab hasn't been through here tonight?" Salt asked impatiently.

"There's been cars through, but no taxi cabs."

"Where do these roads lead?"

"One takes you to Belle Plain and on to Three Forks. The other doesn't go much of anywhere—just on to the swamp."

"Any houses on the swamp road?" Salt inquired.

"An old trapper has a place up there, and the Hawkins' farm is on a piece. Closest house from here is the Widow Jones'."

"How far?"

"Oh, not more than three—four miles."

"Mrs. Jones drives a car?" Salt asked casually.

"Her?" The filling station man laughed. "Not on your life! She has an old rattle-trap her husband left her when he died, but she doesn't take it out of the shed often enough to keep air in the tires."

Penny and Salt inquired the way to the widow's home.

"You can't miss it," replied the station man. "Straight on down the swamp road about three miles. First house you come to on the right hand side of Crissey Road. But you won't likely find the widow up at this hour. She goes to bed with the chickens!"

SWAMP ISLAND

On the highway once more, Salt and Penny debated their next move. Jerry's failure to show up at Caleb Corners only partially relieved their anxiety. Now they could only speculate upon whether the reporter had remained in Riverview or had driven past the filling station without being seen.

"Since we've come this far, why not go on to the Widow Jones' place?" Salt proposed. "She may have seen Jerry. In any case, we can question her about that car she owns."

Bumping along on the rutty road, they presently rounded a bend and on a sideroad saw a small, square house which even in its desolation had a look of sturdy liveability.

"That must be the place," Salt decided, slowing the car. "No lights so I guess she's abed."

"I see one at the rear!" Penny exclaimed. "Someone is up!"

With a jerk, Salt halted the car beside a mailbox which stood on a high post. A brick walk, choked with weeds, led to the front door and around to a back porch.

Through an uncurtained window, the pair glimpsed a tall, wiry woman filling an oil lamp in the kitchen.

As Salt rapped on the door, they saw her start and reach quickly for a shotgun which stood in a corner of the room.

"Who's there?" she called sharply.

"We're from Riverview," answered Penny.

Reassured by a feminine voice, the woman opened the door. She towered above them, a quaint figure in white shirtwaist and a long flowing black skirt which swept the bare floor of the kitchen.

"Good evening," said Penny. "I hope we didn't startle you."

Slowly the widow's eyes traveled over the pair. She laid the shotgun aside and then said evenly:

"'Pears like you did. Hain't in the habit o' having visitors this time o' night. Whar be ye from and what do you want?"

Salt told of their search for Jerry, carefully describing the reporter.

"Hain't seen anyone like that," the Widow Jones said at once. "No one been by on this road since sundown 'cepting old Ezekiel Hawkins."

"By the way, do you drive a car?" Salt questioned.

"Not if I kin keep from it," the widow retorted. "Cars is the ruination o' civilization! Last time I tried to drive to town, backed square into a big sycamore and nigh onto knocked all my teeth out!"

"So you sold your car?" Salt interposed.

"It's a settin' out in the shed. That no-good young'un o' Ezekiel's, Coon Hawkins, tried to buy it off'en me a year ago, but I turned him down flat."

"Didn't he offer enough?" Penny asked curiously.

"'Twasn't that. Fust place, I don't think much o' Coon Hawkins! Second place, that car belonged to my departed husband, and I don't aim nobody else ever will drive it."

"Then you didn't have the car out today or loan it to anyone?"

"No, I didn't! Say, what you gittin' at anyway with all these questions?"

"Your car was involved in an accident this afternoon in Riverview," Salt explained.

"What you sayin'?" the woman demanded. "You must be out o' yer mind! My car ain't been out of the shed fer a month."

"We may have been mistaken," Penny admitted. "The license number of the car was K-4687."

"Why, that's the plate number of mine!" the Widow Jones exclaimed. "Leastwise, I recollect it is!"

"You're certain the car still is in the shed?" Salt asked.

"You got me all confused now, and I hain't cartain of anything. Come in while I get a lantern, and we'll look!"

Penny and Salt stepped into a clean kitchen, slightly fragrant with the odor of spicy catsup made that afternoon. On a table stood row upon row of sealed bottles ready to be carried to the cellar.

The Widow Jones lighted a lantern and threw a woolen shawl over her bony shoulders.

"Follow me," she bade.

At a swift pace, she led the way down a path to a rickety shed which stood far back from the road.

The woman unfastened the big door which swung back on creaking hinges. Raising her lantern, she flashed the light on the floor of the shed.

"Hit's gone!" she exclaimed. "Someone's stole the car!"

CHAPTER 9 - THE WIDOW JONES

Only a large blotch of oil on the cracked concrete floor revealed where the automobile had stood.

"Have you no idea who took the car?" Penny inquired.

Grimly the Widow Jones closed the shed door and slammed the hasp into place.

"Maybe I have an' maybe I han't! Leastwise, I larned forty years ago to keep my lips shut less I could back up my words with proof."

In silence the widow started back toward the house. Midway to the house, she suddenly paused, listening attentively.

From a nearby tree an owl hooted, but Penny and Salt sensed that was not the sound which had caught the woman's ear.

She blew out the lantern and wordlessly motioned for the pair to move back into the deep shadow of the tree.

Holding her shirt to keep it from blowing in the night breeze, the woman gazed intently toward a swamp road some distance from the boundary of her land. For the first time, Salt and Penny became aware of a muffled sound of a running truck motor.

"Sounds like a car or truck back there in the swamp," Salt commented. "Is there a road near here leading in?"

"There's a road yonder," the widow answered briefly.

"It goes into the swamp?"

"Only for a mile or so."

"What would a truck be doing in there at this time of night?" Penny probed.

"I wouldn't know," answered the widow dryly. "There's some things goes on in this swamp that smart folkses don't ask questions about."

Without relighting the lantern, she walked briskly on. Reaching the rear porch, she paused and turned once more to Salt and Penny.

"I be much obliged to ye comin' out here to tell me about my car being stole. Will ye come in and set a spell?"

"Thanks, we'll have to be getting back to Riverview," Salt declined the invitation. "It's late."

"You'll catch your death if you stay out in this damp swamp air," the woman said, her gaze resting disapprovingly on Penny's flimsy dress and low-cut slippers. "I'd advise you to git right back to town. 'Evenin' to you both."

She went inside and closed the door.

"Queer character," Salt commented as he and Penny made their way to the roadside, "Forthright to say the least."

"I rather liked her, Salt. She seemed genuine. And she has courage to live here alone at the edge of the swamp."

"Sure," the photographer agreed. "Plenty of iron in her soul. Wonder what she saw there at the edge of the swamp?"

"It seemed to me she was afraid we might try to investigate. Did you notice how she advised us to go directly to Riverview?"

"She did make the remark a little pointed. The Widow Jones is no dumbbell! You could tell she has a good idea who stole her auto, and she wasn't putting out anything about that truck."

Salt had started the car and was ready to turn around. Penny placed a detaining hand on the steering wheel.

"Let's go the other direction, Salt!"

"On into the swamp?"

"It's only a short distance to that other road. If the truck is still there, we might see something interesting."

Salt's lips parted in a wide grin.

"Sure thing," he agreed. "What have we got to lose?"

CHAPTER 10 - INSIDE THE WOODSHED

The throaty croak of frogs filled the night as Salt, car headlights darkened, brought up at a bend of the road near the swamp's edge.

Entrance to the pinelands could be gained in any one of three ways. A road, often mired with mud, had been built by a lumber mill, and led for nearly a mile into the higher section of the area. There it ended abruptly.

Half a mile away, near Trapper Joe's shack, lay the water course Penny and Louise had followed. From it branched a maze of confusing channels, one of which marked the way to the heart of the swamp. But only a few persons ever had ventured beyond Lookout Island, close to the exit.

The third entrance, also not far from Trapper Joe's, consisted of a narrow boardwalk path nailed to fallen trees and stumps just above the water level. The walk had fallen into decay and could be used for only five hundred feet.

"Seems like a funny time for a truck to be coming out of the swamp road," Salt remarked, peering into the gloom of the pine trees. "Hear anything?"

Penny listened intently and shook her head. But a moment later, she explained: "Now I do! The truck's coming this way."

"Let's get closer to the road exit," Salt proposed. "We'd better leave the car here, if we don't want to be seen."

Penny's high heels kept twisting on the rutty road, and finally in exasperation, she took them off, stripped away her stockings, and walked in her bare feet.

The truck now was very close and the pair could hear its laboring engine. Salt drew Penny back against the bottle-shaped trunk of a big tree at the road exitway. There they waited.

Presently the truck chugged into view, its headlights doused. On the main road, not ten yards from where Salt and Penny crouched, it came to a jerky halt.

The driver was a husky fellow who wore a heavy jacket and cap which shadowed his face. With him in the cab were two younger men of athletic build. Both wore homespun clothes and stout boots.

As the truck halted, the two younger men sprang to the ground.

Instantly Penny and Salt were certain they had seen one of the strangers before.

"He's the man who drove the accident car this afternoon!" Penny whispered. "The auto stolen from Widow Jones!"

Salt nodded, placing his hand over the girl's lips. He drew her back behind the tree.

The precaution was a wise one, for a moment later, a flashlight beam played over the spot where they had been standing.

"Thought I heard something!" one of the truckers muttered.

"Jest them frogs a-croakin'," his companion answered. "You're gettin' jumpy."

"Let's get a move on!" growled the driver of the truck. "I gotta get this load to Hartwell City before dawn. You keepin' any of the stuff?"

"A couple o' gallons will do us. Too durn heavy to carry."

From the rear end of the truck, the two young men who had alighted, pulled out a large wooden container with handles.

"When do you want me to stop by again?" the truck driver called above the rumble of the motor.

"Can't tell yet," one of the men answered, swinging the heavy container across his shoulder. "Pappy'll send word."

CHAPTER 10 - INSIDE THE WOODSHED

The truck pulled away, and the two young men started down the road in the opposite direction. Not until they were a considerable distance away, did Penny speak.

"What do you make of it all, Salt?"

"It's got me puzzled," he admitted. "If I'd have seen the truck come out of the swamp at any other time I wouldn't have thought much about it. But considering the way Mrs. Jones acted, some funny business seems to be going on here."

"I'm certain one of those young men was the driver of the accident car this afternoon!"

"It did look like him."

"They must be the Hawkins boys, Coon and Hod," Penny went on, thinking aloud. "What were they doing in the swamp so late at night? And what are they trucking?"

"Echo answers 'what'," Salt replied. "Well, shall we start for Riverview?"

"Without learning for certain who those two fellows are?"

"I would like to know. The only thing is, your father's going to be plenty annoyed when he finds how late I've kept you out."

"Leave Dad to me."

"Okay, but if we run into trouble tonight, we can figure we went out of our way to ask for it."

By this time, the two swampers had vanished into the darkness far up the road.

"They're heading toward Trapper Joe's place," Penny observed. "The Hawkins' farm is just beyond, on the waterway."

"We may as well give them a good start and then follow in the car," Salt decided.

They walked back to the parked automobile where Penny put on her shoes and stockings again. After giving the two strangers a good five minutes start, Salt drove slowly after them, keeping headlights turned off.

Trapper Joe's dismal shack loomed up dark and deserted.

"We'll have to park here," Penny instructed, "The road beyond is terrible and it plays out."

Alighting, the couple looked about for a glimpse of the two swampers. The nearby marsh seemed cold, unfriendly and menacing. Heavy dew lay on the earth and a thick mist was rising from among the trees.

From behind a shadowy bush, two gleaming eyes gazed steadily and unblinkingly at the pair. Penny drew back, nervously gripping Salt's hand.

"It's only a cat," he chuckled.

"A wild one, maybe," Penny shivered. "All sorts of animals live in the swamp, Trapper Joe told me."

"Want to stay in the car and spare those pretty shoes of yours?"

"No, let's go on." The gleaming eyes now had vanished and Penny felt courageous again. Nevertheless, she kept close beside Salt as they tramped along the dark road.

A pale moon was rising over the treetops, providing faint illumination. Penny and Salt no longer could see the pair they had followed, and were afraid they had lost them completely.

Then they spied the swampers crawling over a fence some distance away.

"There they are!" Penny whispered. Just as I thought! They're taking a short cut to the Hawkins' place."

Unaware that they were being followed, the two swampers crossed a plowed field, frequently shifting their heavy burden.

Coming at length to the Hawkins' farm, they vanished into the woodshed.

"Guess you were right, Penny," Salt acknowledged, pausing by the fence. "Evidently they're the Hawkins' boys."

The door of the house had opened and a light now glowed in the window. A bulky figure stood silhouetted on the threshold.

"Who's there?" the man called sharply. "That you, Coon?"

From inside the shed came a muffled reply: "Yep, it's me and Hod."

"How'd you make out, son?"

"She's all took care of an' on 'er way to Hartwell City. Ike says he'll fetch you the cash in a day or two."

"Git to bed soon's you kin," the older man said, apparently pleased by the information. "Your Ma's tired and wants to git to sleep 'for mawning."

He moved back into the house, closing the door.

"Guess we've learned all we can," Salt remarked. "We may as well get a little shut-eye ourselves."

Penny, however, was unwilling to leave so soon.

"I wish we could find out what is in that big container, Salt! After those Hawkins' boys leave, maybe we could sneak a peek."

"And get caught!"

"We can be careful. Salt, we've stumbled into a lot of information tonight that may prove very valuable. We'll never have another chance like it. Come on, Salt, it's worth a try."

Despite his better judgment, Salt allowed himself to be persuaded. For ten minutes the pair waited near the fence. Finally they saw Hod and Coon Hawkins emerge from the shed and enter the house.

Another ten minutes they waited. By that time the light had been extinguished inside the house.

"Everyone's abed now," Penny said in satisfaction. "Now for the woodshed!"

Crossing the field, the pair approached the tumbledown building from the side away from the house. The woodshed door was closed.

Penny groped for the knob and instead, her hand encountered a chain and padlock.

"Locked!" she muttered impatiently. "Just our luck!"

The rattle of the chain had disturbed a hound penned inside the shed. Before Salt and Penny could retreat, the animal's paws scratched against the door and he uttered a deep and prolonged bay.

"Jeepers!" exclaimed Salt. "We've got to get away from here—and fast!"

Already it was too late. A window on the second floor of the house flew up and Mrs. Hawkins in cotton nightdress and lace cap, peered down into the yard.

"Who's there?" she called sharply. "Answer up if you ain't hankerin' fer a bullet through yer innards!"

CHAPTER 11 - AN ABANDONED CAR

For Salt and Penny, the moment was a perilous one. In plain view of the upstairs window, they could not hope to escape detection.

But shrewdly, they reasoned that Mrs. Hawkins could not be certain they had been trying to break into the woodshed.

"Oh, is that you, Mrs. Hawkins?" Penny called as cheerily as if greeting an old friend. "I hope we didn't awaken you."

The farm woman leaned far out the window. "Who be ye folkses?" she demanded suspiciously. "What you doin' here?"

"Don't you remember me?" Penny asked. "I stopped here this afternoon with my girl friend. We had a drink at your pump."

"Humph! That ain't no gal with you now! Who is he?"

"Oh, just a friend who works at—" Penny was on the verge of saying the *Riverview Star*, but caught herself in time and finished—"a friend who works where I do."

"And what you spyin' around here for?"

"We're looking for another friend of ours."

"'Pears to me you got a heap o' friends," the woman said harshly. "This afternoon you was cryin' you lost a dog."

"It was Louise who lost the dog," said Penny, well realizing that her story would never convince the woman.

"Whatever you lost, man or beast, git off this property and don't come back!" Mrs. Hawkins ordered. "We hain't seen no dog, and we hain't seen none o' yer friends. Now git!"

Another face had appeared at the window—that of the bearded stranger Penny had seen earlier in the day on Lookout Point. No longer could she doubt that he was Ezekiel Hawkins, the man who a few minutes earlier had ordered his two sons to bed.

"We're leaving now," said Salt, before Penny had an opportunity to speak again of Louise's missing dog. "Sorry to have bothered you."

Taking Penny firmly by an elbow, he pulled her along. Not until they had reached the fence safely did they look back.

In the upper window of the Hawkins' house a light continued to burn dimly.

"We're still being watched," Salt commented. He helped Penny over the fence, disentangling her dress which snagged on a wire. "Whew! That was a close call! That old biddy would have enjoyed putting a bullet through us!"

"She dared to say Louise's dog hadn't been seen! All the while her husband stood right there! He's the one who refused to let us go after Bones this afternoon!"

"Sure?"

"Almost positive."

"Well, all I can say is the Hawkins' are mean customers," Salt sighed. "Stealing a dog probably is right in their line."

"They're up to other tricks too!"

"Oh, undoubtedly. Wish we could have learned what was in those cans they were trucking to the city."

In the press car, speeding toward Riverview, the pair discussed all phases of their night's adventure. Failure to learn anything about Jerry's whereabouts worried them.

Presently, worn out, Penny slumped against Salt's shoulder and fell asleep. She was awakened when the car stopped with a jerk.

"Where are we?" she mumbled drowsily. "Home?"

"Not yet, baby," he answered, shutting off the engine.

Penny straightened in the seat, brushing away a lock of hair which had tumbled over her left eye. Peering through the window she saw that they still were out in the country.

"What are we stopping here for, Salt?" she asked in astonishment. "Don't tell me we've run out of gas!"

"Nothing like that," he said easily. "Just go back to sleep. I'll be right back."

"You'll be right back! Where are you going, Salt Sommers?"

"Only down the road a ways. We passed a car, and I want to have a better look at it."

By now Penny was fully awake.

"I'm going with you," she announced.

Salt held the door open for her. "This probably is a waste of time," he admitted.

"Was it a car you saw in the ditch?" Penny questioned, walking fast to keep up with him. "An accident?"

"Don't think so. The car seemed to be parked back in the bushes on a road bisecting this one."

"What's so unusual in that?"

"Nothing perhaps. Only the car looked familiar."

"Not Jerry's coupe?"

"No. There it is now—see!" Salt pointed through the trees to an old upright vehicle of antiquated style. His flashlight picked up the numbers on the rear license plate.

"K-4687!" Penny read aloud. "Mrs. Jones' stolen auto!"

"It sure is," the photographer agreed in satisfaction. "Abandoned!"

"By whom? The Hawkins' boys?"

"Maybe. Let's have a closer look."

While Penny stood by, Salt made a thorough inspection of the old car. The battery was dead. Ignition keys, still in the lock, had been left turned on.

As the photographer flashed his light about, Penny noticed a package of cigarettes lying on the seat. She picked them up and sniffed.

"Necos," she declared. "Salt, one of the persons who rode in this car must have slugged Jerry at the theater!"

"Maybe, but we can't be sure. Necos aren't a common brand of cigarettes. On the other hand, I've known several fellows who smoke them."

A thorough inspection of the car revealed no other clues.

"We may as well get back to town," Salt said finally. "Mrs. Jones will be glad to learn her car has been recovered. We can let her know tomorrow after police have had a chance to inspect it."

Neither he nor Penny had much to say as they motored toward Riverview. Both were deeply discouraged by their failure to find any trace of Jerry.

"It's barely possible hospital officials were able to catch up with him," Penny said after a while, her eyes on the dark ribbon of highway ahead. "We might stop somewhere and telephone."

"Good idea," agreed Salt. "We're practically in the city now."

Already they could see the twinkling lights, laid out in rectangular street patterns. Directly ahead, at the corporation boundary, Penny saw the flashing electric sign of a hamburger hut operated by Mark Fiello, a genial old Italian.

"We might stop there," she suggested. "Mark will let us use his phone."

"Also, he has good hamburgers and coffee," Salt added. "I could go for some food!"

Mark, a stout, grizzled man in slightly soiled apron, was frying bacon and hamburgers at the grill as he shouted orders to a helper in the kitchen.

"You, Frankey!" he bellowed. "Git your nose outta dat ice cream and squeeze another quart of orange juice! What you think I pay you for—to eat me out of business?"

As Penny and Salt slid onto stools in front of the counter, he turned toward them to ask briskly: "What'll it be, folks?"

"Now Mark, don't give us the professional brush off," Salt joked. "Make mine a hamburger with everything on."

CHAPTER 11 - AN ABANDONED CAR

"And mine with everything off—especially onions," added Penny.

"Two hamburgers coming right up," chuckled Mark, flattening twin hunks of ground meat on the grill. "I giva you good beeg ones. One-a with, and one-a without. Haven't seen you folks in a long while. How you been?"

"Pretty well, Mark, until tonight," replied Penny. "May we use your phone?"

"It's your nickel, ain't it?" chuckled Mark. "Go right ahead."

"Looks as if we'll have to wait until your helper gets through using it," observed Salt.

"That worthless no-good!" Mark snorted. "I pay him thirty dolla a week to eat his head off and all the time calla dat girl of his! You, Frankey! Git off dat phone and git to work on them oranges!"

Frank, a youth of sallow complexion and unsteady gaze, dropped the telephone receiver as if it were a red hot coal.

He mumbled a "call you later," into the transmitter, hung up, and ducked into the kitchen.

"Such bad luck I have this summer," sighed Mark, expertly turning the hamburgers and salting them. "Six helpers I hire and fire. All no good. They talka big, eat big—but work? Naw!"

"It's a tough life," Salt agreed, fishing for a coin in his pocket. "Change for a dime, Mark?"

"Sure. Who you calla tonight? Big scoop for de paper, eh?"

"I wish it were," said Salt. "We've had a tough night."

"Jerry's missing," Penny added earnestly. "He was taken to the hospital this afternoon, but he walked out. We're trying to find him because he's in no condition to be wandering about."

Mark's jaw had dropped and for a moment he forgot the hamburgers sizzling on the grill.

"You looka for Jerry? Jerry Livingston?"

"Sure, you know him," Salt replied, starting for the telephone. "He used to be one of your favorite customers."

"Well, what do y'know!" mumbled Mark, obviously surprised. "What do y'know! Listen, I tell you something!"

"About Jerry?" Penny asked eagerly.

"You looka for your friend too late!"

"Too late? What do you mean, Mark? Jerry hasn't been hurt?"

"No! No! Your friend is all right like always. Twenty minutes ago, he eata three hamburgs on dis same stool where you sit now!"

"Jerry was here!" Penny cried joyfully. "Mark, are you sure?"

"Sure, I am sure! Jerry eata three beeg hamburgs, drinka two beeg cups of java, then go away."

"Did he seem dazed or confused?"

"Your friend the same as always. Make-a the joke."

On the grill, the hamburgers were beginning to burn at the edges. Mark flipped them between buns, adding generous quantities of mustard, pickle, catsup, and sliced onions to Salt's sandwich.

Penny now was so excited she scarcely could take time to eat.

"Which way did Jerry go when he left here?" she questioned eagerly.

"He crossa de street. After dat, I did not see."

"Jerry lives in the St. Agnes Apartments not far from here," Salt recalled. "Maybe he's there now!"

Quickly finishing their sandwiches, the pair gave Mark a dollar, refusing to accept change. As they started away, he followed them to the door.

"You know-a somebody who wanta good job, good pay?" he whispered. "Frankey is eating me outta all my profits. You know-a somebody?"

"Afraid we don't," Salt replied. "We'll keep it in mind though, and if we hear of anyone wanting work, we'll send him around."

From the hamburger hut, Penny and Salt drove directly to the St. Agnes Apartment Hotel. The clerk on duty could not tell them if Jerry were in his room or not.

"Go on up if you want to," he suggested. "Room 207."

Climbing the stairs, they pounded on the door. There was no answer. Salt tried again. Not a sound came from inside the room.

SWAMP ISLAND

"It's no use," the photographer said in disappointment. "Mark may have been mistaken. Anyway, Jerry's not here."

CHAPTER 12 - A JOB FOR PENNY

Penny gazed at Salt in grim despair. "I was so sure Jerry would be here," she murmured. "What can we do now?"

"We've run down every clue," he replied gloomily. "If he isn't at the hospital, I'm afraid it's a case for the police."

"But Mark was so sure he had seen Jerry tonight. Try once more, Salt."

"Okay, but it's useless. He's not here."

Again Salt hammered on the door with his fist. He was turning away when a sleepy voice called: "Who's there?"

"Jerry is in there!" Penny cried. "Thank goodness, he's safe!"

"Open up, you lug!" ordered Salt.

A bed creaked, footsteps padded across the carpet and the door swung back. Jerry, in silk dressing gown, blinked sleepily out at them.

"What do you want?" he mumbled. "Can't you let a fellow catch forty winks without sending out the riot squad?"

"How are you feeling, Jerry, my boy?" Salt inquired solicitously.

"Never felt better in my life, except I'm sleepy."

"Then what made you walk out of the hospital?"

"I don't like hospitals."

"We ought to punch you in the nose for making us so much trouble," Salt said affectionately. "Here we spent half the night searching the swamp for you!"

Jerry's face crinkled into a broad grin. "The swamp! That's good!"

"Didn't you ask a taximan at the hospital how much it would cost to go there?" Penny reminded him.

"Sure, but I decided not to go."

"You got a nerve!" Salt muttered. "Climb into your clothes and we'll take you back to your cell."

"Oh, no, you don't!" Jerry backed away from the door. "I'm no more sick than you are, and I'm not going back to the hospital!"

"You're an advanced case for a mental institution!" the photographer snapped. "Maybe you don't know Danny Deevers is out to get you and he means business!"

"I'm not worried about Danny."

"Maybe you don't think he cracked you on the head tonight at the theater?"

"I've been thinking it over," Jerry replied slowly. "Probably it was Danny, but I doubt he'll dare show his face again. Police are too hot on his trail."

"Says you!" snorted Salt. "By the way, why were you so interested in going to the swamp tonight? Any clues?"

"Only the information you and Penny gave me."

"We learned a little more this evening," Penny informed him eagerly. "And we have a photograph we want you to identify."

The story of their findings at Caleb Corners and beyond, was briefly told. Salt then showed Jerry the picture of the ancient car which had been involved in the traffic accident.

"This older man is Danny Deevers," Jerry positively identified him after studying the photograph a minute. "I don't recognize the driver of the car."

"We're almost sure he's one of the Hawkins' boys," Penny declared. "You know, the swamper we told you about."

Jerry nodded. "In that case, putting the finger on Deevers should be easy for the police. The Hawkins family could be arrested on suspicion. Like as not, Deevers is hiding in the swamp just as Penny suspected!"

"If he is, it won't be easy to capture him," commented Salt. "They say a man could hide there a year without being found. And if the Hawkins' boy is arrested, he'll naturally lie low."

Jerry thoughtfully studied the photograph again. "That's so," he admitted. "Anyway, our evidence is pretty weak. We couldn't pin anything on either of the Hawkins' boys on the strength of this photograph."

"It would only involve Mrs. Jones," contributed Penny. "Why turn it over to the police?"

"Well, it would relieve us of a lot of responsibility. Tell you what! I know the Chief pretty well. Suppose I give the picture to him and ask him to go easy on Mrs. Jones? I think he would play along with us."

"Sounds like a good idea to me," approved Salt. "The police can watch the Hawkins place and maybe learn Danny's hideout without tipping their hand."

The matter of the photograph settled, he and Penny turned to leave.

"We'll send the hospital ambulance after you, Jerry," Salt said by way of farewell. "Better get into some duds."

"I'm not going back there!"

"It's no use trying to make him," said Penny who knew from experience that the reporter could be stubborn. "But do be careful, won't you, Jerry?"

"Sure," he promised. "And thanks to both of you for all your trouble!"

The hour now was well past midnight. Saying goodbye to Jerry, Penny had Salt take her directly home.

Quietly she slipped into the house and upstairs to her own room without disturbing Mrs. Weems.

However, next morning, explanations were in order, and as was to be expected, the housekeeper did not look with approval upon the trip to the swamp.

"Your motives may have been excellent," she told Penny, "but your judgment was very poor. Even with Salt as an escort you shouldn't have gone."

To make amends, Penny stayed close at home that morning, helping with an ironing. At noon when her father came for luncheon, she eagerly plied him with questions about the Danny Deevers case.

"There's nothing new to report," Mr. Parker said. "He's still at large. The *Star* has posted a $10,000 reward for his capture."

"Ten thousand!" echoed Penny, her eyes sparkling. "I could use that money!"

Mr. Parker carefully laid down his knife and fork, fixing his daughter with a stern gaze.

"You're to forget Danny Deevers," he directed. "Just to make certain you do, I've arranged with Mr. DeWitt to give you a few days' work at the office. Kindly report at one-thirty this afternoon for your first assignment."

"Oh, Dad! Of all times—I had plans!"

"So I figured," her father replied dryly. "Mr. DeWitt, I trust, will keep you busy until after Danny Deevers has been rounded up by the police."

Penny knew that protests were quite useless, for when her father really set down his foot, he seldom changed his mind. At another time, she would have welcomed an opportunity to work at the *Star* office, but this day she regarded it as nothing less than punishment.

As her father had predicted, Penny was kept more than busy at the office. There were telephones to answer, obituaries to write, wire stories to redo, and a multitude of little writing jobs which kept her chained to a desk.

Penny pounded out page after page of routine copy, her face becoming longer and longer. Whenever the shortwave radio blared, she listened attentively. Never was there any news to suggest that police were even taking an interest in Danny Deevers' escape.

"Oh, they're working hard on the case," Jerry assured her when she talked it over with him. "You'll hear about it in good time."

"Everyone treats me as if I were a child!" Penny complained. "Just wait! If ever I get any more information, I'm keeping it under my hat!"

For two long days she worked and suffered in the newspaper office. Then late one afternoon, Mr. DeWitt beckoned her to his desk.

CHAPTER 12 - A JOB FOR PENNY

"You act as if you need a little fresh air," he said. "Take a run over to the Immigration Office. See a man named Trotsell. He'll tell you about a boy who entered this country illegally. They're looking for him now."

"I'll hippety-hop all the way!" Penny laughed, glad to escape from the office.

At the Immigration Building, Mr. Trotsell, an official of brisk manner and crisp speech, gave her the facts of the case in rapid-fire order.

"The boy is only sixteen," he said. "His name is Anthony Tienta and he was befriended by G.I.'s in Europe. Early in the war, his parents were killed. Anthony was put in an orphan's asylum by Fascists. He and another lad escaped to the mountains. For six months they lived in a cave on berries and what they could pilfer."

"Interesting," commented Penny, "but what is your connection with the case?"

"I'm coming to that. When G.I.'s entered Italy, Anthony left his mountain hideout to become a guide. He learned English and later joined an American division as a mascot. When the war ended, Anthony sought permission to come to this country and was turned down repeatedly."

"So he stowed aboard a troopship?"

"Yes, we don't know yet how he eluded Immigration officials in New York. Somehow he slipped into the country. Later he was traced to a farm in Michigan. We were closing in on him, when someone tipped him off and he fled. We know he's somewhere in this state."

"Near here?"

"It's very possible. We thought if a story appeared in the paper, someone who has seen the boy may report to us."

"Do you have a picture of him?"

"Unfortunately, no. He is sixteen, with dark eyes and dark, curly hair. The lad is athletic and very quick witted. His English is fairly good, heavily sprinkled with G.I. slang."

"I'll write the story for you," Penny promised as she arose to leave. "The truth is, though, my sympathy is with Anthony."

"So is mine," replied the official. "However, that does not change the law. He entered this country illegally and must be returned to Italy."

Penny left the office and was midway to the newspaper office when she bumped squarely into her friend, Louise Sidell, who had been downtown shopping.

"Oh, Lou!" she exclaimed. "I called you twice but you weren't at home. Did Bones ever find his way back?"

Louise shook her head. "He never will either. Those men probably kept him on the island. I'm going out there tomorrow."

"To the island?"

"If I can get Trapper Joe to take me. My father says I may offer him twenty-five dollars to help me get Bones back."

"It was entirely my fault, Lou. I'll pay the money."

"You needn't."

"I want to," said Penny firmly. "I've earned a little money the past two days at the newspaper office."

The two girls walked together to the next corner.

"What time are you starting for Trapper Joe's tomorrow?" Penny asked.

"I'd like to leave right after breakfast. Any chance you could take me in your car?"

"I was thinking the same thing," grinned Penny. "It may take a little doing—but yes, I'm sure you can count on me! I'm long overdue for a date myself with Old Man Swamp!"

CHAPTER 13 - INTO THE SWAMP

By eleven o'clock the next morning, the two girls were on their way to Caleb Corners in Penny's car. Both wore high boots, heavy shirts, and riding breeches, having dressed carefully for the swamp.

"I had one awful time convincing Dad and Mrs. Weems I should make this trip," Penny remarked as they parked the car under a giant oak not far from Trapper Joe's shack on the river creek. "If we hadn't had Bones for an excuse, they never would have allowed me to go."

Louise stared curiously at her chum.

"Why else would we make the trip?" she inquired.

"Oh, we're going there to find Bones," Penny assured her hastily. "But if we should meet Ezekiel Hawkins or whoever was on the island—"

"My parents made it very clear I'm not to go to the island unless Trapper Joe is with us."

"So did my father, unfortunately," sighed Penny.

As the girls approached Trapper Joe's shack, they saw smoke issuing in a straight column from the rear of the premises.

Investigating, they found the old guide roasting a fat turkey on a spit which slowly revolved above a fire of cherry red coals.

"Howdy," the old man greeted them. "You're jest in time fer some victuals."

"Lunch so early?" Louise asked in surprise.

"It hain't breakfast and it hain't lunch," the trapper chuckled. "I eat when I'm hongry, an' right now I feel a hankerin' fer food. Kin I give you a nice turkey leg?"

The girls looked at the delicately browned fowl and wavered.

"I'll fetch you'uns each a plate," the trapper offered.

From the shack he brought two cracked ones and forks with bent tines. To each of the girls he gave a generous helping, saving for himself a large slice of breast.

"What brings ye here today?" he presently asked. "Be ye aimin' to rent my boat again?"

"Providing your services go with it," Penny replied. "We want to search for Louise's dog."

"'Tain't likely you'll ever see him again."

"All the same, we've planned on searching the island thoroughly. Will you take us?"

Trapper Joe tossed away a turkey bone as he observed: "There's cottonmouths on that island and all manner o' varmints."

"That's why we want you to go with us," Penny urged. "We'll be safe with you."

"I hain't so sartain I'll be safe myself," Joe argued. "My gun's been stole. Some thieven scalawag made off with it late last night while I was skinnin' an animal. Left it a-settin' against a post down by the dock. The rascal took my gun and some salted meat I had in a crock!"

"Someone who came from the swamp?" Penny asked quickly.

"'Pears he must o' come from there."

"Could the thief have been one of the Hawkins family?"

"'Tain't likely," the guide replied. "They all got good guns o' their own. Anyhow, the Hawkins' hain't never stooped so low they'd steal from a neighbor."

"Will you take us in your boat?" Louise urged impatiently. "We'll pay you well for your time. If we find Bones, you'll receive an extra twenty-five dollars."

"It hain't the money. Lookin' fer that dog would be like lookin' fer a needle in a haystack."

CHAPTER 13 - INTO THE SWAMP

"You might accidentally run into the person who stole your gun," Penny suggested.

"Now, there'd be some sense to that," the trapper said with sudden interest. "I'd like to lay hands on him!"

"Then you'll go?" the girls demanded together.

"'Pears like I will," he said, his leathery face cracking into a smile. "'Tain't smart going into the swamp without a gun, but we kin trust to Providence an' our wits, I calculate."

Pleased that the trapper had consented, the girls leaped to their feet and started toward the skiff which was tied up at the dock.

"Not so fast!" the trapper brought them up short. "We got to take some water and some victuals with us."

"But we're not going far," Louise said in surprise. "We just ate."

"Ye can git mighty hongry and thirsty, rowin' in a broiling hot sun. When I go into the swamp, I always takes rations along jest in case."

"Surely you don't expect to lose your way," Penny said teasingly. "An old timer like you!"

"I'm an old timer 'cause I always prepares fer the wust," the trapper retorted witheringly. "Many a young punk's give his life being show-off and foolhardy in that swamp. I was lost there oncst years ago. I hain't never forgot my lesson."

Properly put in their places, Penny and Louise said no more as Trapper Joe prepared for the trip into the swamp. He wrapped the remains of the turkey in a paper, depositing it in a covered metal container in the bottom of the skiff.

Also, he dropped in a jug of water and an extra paddle.

"Tell us about the swamp," Louise urged as they finally shoved off. "Is it filled with wild and dangerous animals?"

"Bears mostly been killed off," the old trapper replied, sending the skiff along with powerful stabs of the oars. "The rooters are about the wust ye run into now."

"Rooters?" Louise repeated, puzzled.

"Wild hogs. They got a hide so tough even the rattlers can't kill 'em. It's most likely yer dogs been et by one."

"Oh, no!" Louise protested in horror.

"Rooters'll go straight fer a dog or a deer or a lamb. They'll attack a man too if they're hongry enough. Their tusks are sharp as daggers."

Penny quickly changed the subject by asking Trapper Joe if he thought Pretty Boy Danny Deevers might be hiding in the swamp.

"'Tain't likely," he replied briefly.

"Why do you think not?"

"City bred, waren't he?"

"That's what I was told."

"No city bred feller could live in the swamp many days. He wouldn't have sense enough to git his food; at night the sounds would drive him crazy, and he'd end up bein' bit by a snake."

"Yet someone stole your gun," Penny reminded him.

"It waren't Danny," said the old trapper with finality.

The skiff glided on. As the sun rose high overhead pouring down upon their backs, Penny and Louise began to feel drowsy. Repeatedly, they reached for Joe's jug of water.

As the channel became congested with floating plants and rotted logs, the trapper shipped the oars and used a paddle.

Presently they came within view of Lookout Island. In the bow, Penny leaned forward to peer at the jungle-like growth which grew densely to the water's edge.

"Someone's on the island!" she exclaimed in a low voice.

"Sure, it's Coon Hawkins doin' a little fishin'," agreed the trapper. "His boat's pulled up on the point."

Louise stirred uneasily. "Is anyone with him?" she whispered.

"Don't see no one 'cepting Coon. He won't hurt ye. Harmless, ole Coon is, an' mighty shiftless too."

"But is Coon really fishing?" Penny demanded suspiciously.

"He's got a pole and a string o' fish."

"Also, he's watching us very closely," whispered Penny. "I don't trust him one bit! He's hiding something on that island! I'll be surprised if he doesn't try to keep us from landing."

CHAPTER 14 - A CODE MESSAGE

The old trapper appeared not to have heard Penny's whispered observation. He paddled the skiff on until it drifted within ten yards of the point where Coon Hawkins sat fishing.

"Howdy!" called the trapper.

"Howdy," responded Coon, his gaze on the bobbing cork.

"Seen anything of a dog on the island?"

"Hain't no animal hereabouts," Coon replied.

"'Pears like the gals has lost a dog," said the old trapper, dipping his paddle again. "We're landin' to have a look around."

Coon's gaze shifted from the cork to the party in the boat. He scowled and then coldly turned his back.

"Suit yerself," he said indifferently. "You won't find no dawg here."

Trapper Joe beached the skiff very nearly where Penny had landed a few days earlier.

"Have a keer," he advised as the girls trod through the muck. "Watch out fer snakes."

"Here are Bones' tracks!" Louise cried a moment later, spying the prints which led away from the shore.

A short distance in, the tracks abruptly ended, but nearby were prints of a man's shoe and larger ones made from a heavy boot.

Trapper Joe noted them in silence, signaling for Penny and Louise to make no comment.

"Wait here while I look around," he instructed.

Penny and Louise sat down on a mossy log to wait. Coon paid them no heed, completely ignoring their presence. The sun climbed higher overhead.

Presently the old trapper returned, his clothing soaked with perspiration.

"Did you see anything of Bones?" Louise asked eagerly.

"Nary a sign. The dog hain't on the island."

"Told ye, didn't I?" Coon demanded triumphantly.

"That ye did, son," agreed Trapper Joe. "We'll be gittin' along." On his way to the skiff, he asked carelessly: "Come here offen, do ye?"

"When I feels like it," Coon retorted.

"Fishin' good?"

"Fair to middlin'."

The old trapper helped the girls into the skiff and shoved off.

"Please, must we turn back now?" Louise asked earnestly. "I hate to return without finding a trace of poor old Bones."

"'Tain't likely you'll ever see the dog again."

"We realize that," said Penny, "but it would be a satisfaction to keep looking."

"If the dog was still alive, it hain't likely he'd of swum away from the island."

"He could have been carried," Penny said, keeping her voice low.

The swamper stared steadily at her a moment, saying nothing.

"Besides, we'd like to go deeper into the swamp just to see it," Penny urged, sensing that he was hesitating. "It must be beautiful farther in."

"It is purty," the old guide agreed. "But you have to be mighty keerful."

"Do take us," Louise pleaded.

The old trapper raised his eyes to watch a giant crane, and then slowly turned the skiff. As he sought a sluggish channel leading deeper into the swamp, Penny noticed that Coon Hawkins had shifted his position on the point, the better to watch them.

The skiff moved on into gloomy water deeply shadowed by overhanging tree limbs. Only then did Penny ask the trapper what he thought really had happened to Louise's dog.

"'Tain't easy to say," he replied, resting on the paddle a moment and taking a chew of tobacco.

Penny sensed that the old man was unwilling to express his true opinion. He stared moodily at the sluggish water, lost in deep thought.

"The Hawkins' are up to something!" Penny declared. She was tempted to reveal what she and Salt had seen a few nights before on the swamp road, but held her tongue.

"After all, what do I know about Joe?" she reflected. "He may be a close friend of the Hawkins family for all his talk about them being a shiftless lot."

Penny remained silent. Sensing her disappointment because he had not talked more freely, Trapper Joe presently remarked:

"You know, things goes on in the swamp that it's best not to see. Sometimes it hain't healthy to know too much."

"What things do you mean?" Penny asked quickly.

Old Joe however, was not to be trapped by such a direct question.

"Jest things," he returned evasively. "Purty here, hain't it?"

The guide was now paddling along a sandy shore. Overhead on a bare tree branch, two racoons drowsed after their midday meal.

"In this swamp there's places where no man has ever set foot," the guide continued. "Beyond Black Island, in the heart o' the swamp, it's as wild as when everything belonged to the Indians."

"How does one reach Black Island?" Louise inquired.

"Only a few swampers that knows all the runs would dast go that far," said Old Joe. "If ye take a wrong turn, ye kin float around fer days without findin' yer way out."

"Is there only one exit—the way we came in?" Penny asked.

"No, oncst ye git to Black Island, there's a faster way out. Ye pick yer way through a maze o' channels 'till ye come to the main one which takes ye to the Door River."

"You've made the trip?"

"Did when I was young. Hain't been to Black Island in years lately."

"How long does the trip take?"

"Not many hours if ye know the trail. But if ye take a wrong twist, y'er apt to wind up anywheres. We're headin' toward Black Island now."

"Then why not go on?" cried Penny eagerly. "It's still early."

The old guide shook his head as he paddled into deeper water. "It's jest a long, hard row and there hain't nothin' there. I'm takin' ye to a place where some purty pink orchids grow. Then we'll turn back."

Penny suddenly sat up very straight, listening intently.

From some distance away came a faint, metallic pounding sound.

"What's that noise?" she asked, puzzled.

The old trapper also was listening alertly.

Again the strange noise was repeated. Bing-ping-ping! Ping-ping!

"It sounds like someone pounding on a sheet of metal!" exclaimed Penny. "I'd say it's coming from the edge of the swamp—perhaps Lookout Island!"

The trapper nodded, still listening.

Again they heard the pounding which seemed in a queer pattern of dots and dashes.

"It's a code!" Penny declared excitedly. "Perhaps a message is being sent to someone hiding here in the swamp!"

"In all the times I've been in these waters, I never before heard nothin' like that," the guide admitted. "I wonder—"

"Yes?" Penny prodded eagerly.

CHAPTER 14 - A CODE MESSAGE

But the old guide did not complete the thought. The boat now was drifting in a narrow run where boughs hung low over the water, causing the three occupants to lean far forward to avoid being brushed.

A tiny scream came from Louise's lips. The bow of the skiff where she sat had poked its nose against a protruding tree root.

Within inches of her face, staring unblinkingly into her eyes, was a large, ugly reptile!

CHAPTER 15 - BEYOND THE BOARDWALK

"Steady! Steady!" warned the old swamper as Louise shrank back in horror from the big snake. "Don't move or he'll strike!"

Digging his paddle into the slimy bed of the narrow run, Trapper Joe inched the skiff backwards. Should the boat jar against the tree root, he knew the snake almost certainly would strike its poisonous fangs into Louise's face.

"Hurry!" she whispered.

Slowly the skiff moved backwards through the still water, until at last it lay at a safe distance. The snake had not moved from its resting place.

Now that the danger was over, Louise collapsed with a shudder.

"You saved me!" she declared gratefully.

"It weren't nothin'," he replied as he sought another run. "There's thousands o' varmints like him in this swamp."

"And to think Penny and I dared come here by ourselves the other day! We didn't realize how dangerous it was!"

The incident had so unnerved both of the girls, that some minutes elapsed before they recalled the strange pounding sound which had previously held their attention.

"I don't hear it now," Penny said, listening intently. "Just before we ran into that snake, you were about to say something, Joe."

The guide stopped paddling a moment. "Was I now?" he asked. "I don't recollect."

"We were talking about the strange noise. You said you never had heard anything like it before in the swamp. Then you added—'I wonder—'"

"Jest a-thinkin'," Joe said, picking up the paddle once more. "One does a lot o' that in the swamp."

"And not much talking," rejoined Penny, slightly annoyed. "What do you think made the noise?"

"Couldn't rightly say."

Realizing it was useless to question the old man further, Penny dropped the subject. However, she was convinced that Joe had at least a theory as to the cause of the strange pounding sound.

"He knows a lot he isn't telling," she thought. "But I'll never get a word out of him by asking."

If Joe were unwilling to discuss the signal-like tappings, he showed no reluctance in telling the girls about the swamp itself.

Wild turkey, one of the wariest fowls in the area, could be found only on the islands far interior, they learned. Although there were more than a dozen species of snakes, only three needed to be feared, the rattlers, the coral snake, and the cottonmouth.

"Ye have to be keerful when yer passin' under tunnels o' overhanging limbs," Old Joe explained. "Sometimes they'll be hangin' solid with little snakes."

"Don't tell us any more," Louise pleaded. "I'm rapidly losing enthusiasm for this place!"

"Snakes mostly minds their own business 'less a feller goes botherin' 'em," Trapper Joe remarked. "Too bad more folks ain't that way."

The boat floated on, and the heat rising from the water became increasingly unpleasant. Penny mopped her face with a handkerchief and considered asking the old man to turn back.

Before she could speak, Joe who had been peering intently at the shore, veered the skiff in that direction.

"Are the orchids here?" Louise asked in surprise.

CHAPTER 15 - BEYOND THE BOARDWALK

Old Joe shook his head. "Jest want to look at something," he remarked.

He brought the skiff to shore, and looking carefully about for snakes, stepped out.

"May we go with you?" asked Penny, whose limbs had become cramped from sitting so long in one position.

"Kin if yer a mind to, but I only aim to look at that dead campfire."

"A campfire?" Penny questioned. "Where?"

The old trapper pointed to a barren, dry spot a few feet back from the water's edge, where a circle of ashes and a few charred pieces of wood lay.

"Why, I hadn't noticed it," Penny said. Wondering why the trapper should be interested in a campfire, she started to ask, but thought better of it. By remaining silent, she might learn—certainly not if she inquired directly.

Trapper Joe gazed briefly at the camp-site, kicking the dead embers with the toe of his heavy boot.

"Thet fire hain't very old—must have been built last night," he observed.

"By a swamper, I suppose," said Penny casually. "One of the Hawkins' family perhaps."

"It hain't likely they'd be comin' here after nightfall. An' that fire never was built by a swamper."

"Then a stranger must be hiding in the area!" Penny cried. "Danny Deevers!"

"Maybe so, but Danny was city-bred and never could survive long in the wilds. One night here would likely be his last."

"Supposing someone who knew the swamp were helping him?"

"Thet would make it easier, but it weren't Danny Deevers who built this fire."

"How can you be so positive?"

"Deevers was a big man, weren't he?"

"Why, fairly large, I guess."

"Then would he be leavin' little tracks?" Joe pointed to several shoeprints visible in the soft muck. "This man, whoever he be, didn't have anyone campin' with him. Leastwise, there hain't no tracks except from the one kind o' shoe."

"I guess you're right," agreed Penny, disappointed to have her theory exploded. "I wonder who did camp here?"

"I'm a-wonderin' myself," replied the old trapper. "If it's the feller thet stole my gun, I'd like pow'ful well to catch up with him."

Joe inspected the ground for some distance inland, satisfying himself that no one was about. As they returned to the boat, he said thoughtfully:

"Not in years heve I been as far as Black Island, but I've got an itch to go there now."

"Good!" chuckled Penny. "I want to see the place myself."

"It's a long, hard row. I couldn't rightly take you'uns."

"Why not?"

"Fer one thing, I hain't sure what I'll find at the island."

"All the better," laughed Penny.

But the old trapper was not to be persuaded. "The trip ain't one fer young'uns. Likewise, with three in a boat, it's hard goin'. Part o' the way, the run's so shallow, ye have to pole."

"In a polite way, he's telling us we're excess baggage," Louise said, grinning at Penny. "To me it sounds like a long, hot trip."

"I kin go another day," said the trapper. "There hain't no hurry."

"But you're well on your way there now," Penny remarked. "How long would it take to go and return here—that is, if you went alone?"

"Two hours if I made it fast."

"Then why not go?" Penny urged generously. "Isn't there somewhere Louise and I could wait?"

"Without a boat?" Louise interposed in alarm.

"I hain't suggestin' ye do it," said the old trapper. "But there is a safe place ye could wait."

"Where?" asked Penny.

"On the plank walk."

"Does it extend so far into the swamp?"

"This is a section of an old walk that was put in years ago," Joe explained. "It used to hook up with the planking at the entranceway, but it went to pieces. Folks never went to the trouble to rebuild this section."

"All right, take us there," Penny urged, ignoring Louise's worried frown. "If we're above the water, we should be safe enough."

The old trapper rowed the girls on a few yards to a series of shallow bays where water lilies and fragrant pink orchids grew in profusion. As they drew in their breath at the beautiful sight, he chuckled with pleasure.

"Purty, hain't it?" he asked. "Gatherin' posies should keep ye busy for awhile. The boardwalk's right here, and goes on fer quite a spell before it plays out. If ye stay on the walk, you'll be safe until I git back."

Louise gazed with misgiving at the old planks which were decayed and broken. As she and Penny alighted, the boards swayed at nearly every step.

"I'll pick ye up right here, soon's I can," the old guide promised. "If ye keep to the shade, ye won't git so much sunburn."

"What if you shouldn't get back before nightfall," Louise said nervously. "Wouldn't we be stranded here?"

"I'll git back."

"Where does the walk lead?" Penny asked.

"Nowheres in particular any more. Ye'd best not foller it far. Jest wait fer me purty close here, and I'll be back soon's I kin."

Reaching into the bottom of the skiff, the trapper tossed a parcel of lunch to Penny.

"Here's some meat if ye git hongry while I'm gone. Mind ye stay on the planks!"

With this final warning, Joe paddled away and soon was lost to view behind the tall bushes.

CHAPTER 16 - TREED BY A BOAR

Left to themselves, Penny and Louise walked a few steps on the sagging planks which had been nailed to tree stumps. The boards beneath them creaked protestingly and dipped nearly into the water.

"We must have been crazy!" Louise exclaimed. "We'll die of boredom waiting here. Two hours too!"

"It is a long time."

"And if Joe shouldn't come back, we're stranded—absolutely stranded."

"We did take a chance, Louise, but I'm sure Joe can be trusted."

"He seems all right, but what do we really know about him?" Louise argued. "If anything queer is going on here in the swamp, he may be mixed up in it!"

"I thought about that," Penny admitted. "Anyway, if we're to learn anything, we had to take a certain amount of chance. I'm sure everything will be all right."

Slowly they walked on along the rickety planks, now and then bending down to pluck a water lily. Louise quickly jerked back her hand as a water snake slithered past.

"Ugh!" she gasped. "Another one of those horrid things!"

Interested to learn where the planks led, the girls followed the bridge-like trail among the trees. Louise, however, soon grew tired. As they presently came to a stump which offered a perfect resting place, she sat down.

"This is as far as I'm going," she announced.

"But we have lots of time to explore, Louise. Don't you want to learn where this boardwalk goes?"

"Not at the risk of falling into the water! At any rate, I'm tired. If you want to explore, go on alone. I'll wait for you here."

Penny hesitated, reluctant to leave her chum alone.

"Sure you won't mind, Louise?"

"I'd much rather wait here. Please go on. I know you'll never rest until you reach the end of the walk."

Thus urged. Penny, with the package of lunch still tucked under her arm, picked her way carefully along.

The board path curved on between the trees for some distance only to end abruptly where boards had rotted and floated away. After a break of several yards, the walk picked up again for a short ways, but Penny had no intention of wading through water to follow it further.

Pausing to rest before starting back, she noticed beyond the water oaks a narrow stretch of higher land covered with dense, wild growth. Above the trees a huge buzzard soared lazily.

"Ugly bird!" she thought, watching its flight.

Penny was about to turn and retrace her steps, when she noticed something else—footsteps in the muck not far from the end of the boardwalk.

"Someone has been here recently," she reflected. "Those prints must have been made since the last rain."

Even from some distance away. Penny could see that the shoemarks were small ones.

"Probably the person who made them is the same fellow who built the campfire," she thought. "Wonder where the footprints lead?"

Penny tried to draw her eyes away, but the footprints fascinated and challenged her. She longed to investigate them further. However, she had not forgotten Trapper Joe's warning that it was unsafe to leave the boardwalk.

"If I watch out for snakes and only go a short ways, what harm can it do?" she reasoned.

A moment more and Penny was off the walk, treading her way cautiously along the muddy bank. She paused to listen.

All was very quiet—so still that it gave the girl an uneasy feeling, as if she were being watched by a multitude of hostile eyes.

The footprints led to a large tree in a fairly open area. On one of the low, overhanging bushes, a bit of dark wool had been snagged.

"Someone climbed up there either to rest or sleep," Penny thought.

In the bushes close by, the girl heard a faint, rustling sound.

"Who's there?" she called sharply.

No one answered. All was still for a moment. Then again she heard the whisper of disturbed leaves.

Penny's flesh began to creep. Suddenly losing all interest in the footprints, she decided to beat a hasty retreat to the boardwalk.

The decision came too late. Before she could move, a dozen big rooters led by an old gray boar, swarmed out of the bushes, surrounding her.

Too frightened and startled to cry out, Penny huddled back against the tree trunk. The rooters had spread out in a circle and slowly were coming closer.

Retreat to the safety of the boardwalk was completely cut off. The leader of the pack now was so near that she plainly could see his razor-sharp ivory tusks. In another moment, the animal would attack.

Throwing off the paralysis of fear which gripped her, Penny swung herself into the lowermost branch of the big trees. The package of lunch she had carried, dropped from her hand, falling at the base of the trunk.

Instantly, the rooters were upon it, tearing savagely at the meat and at each other. Sick with horror, Penny clung desperately to the tree limb.

"If I slip now, I'm a gonner!" she thought. "Those rooters are half starved. If I fall, they'll attack me!"

Penny considered shouting for Louise, but dismissed the thought as quickly as it came. Her chum probably was too far away to hear her cries. If she did come, unarmed as she was, she might leave the boardwalk only to endanger herself.

"Louise can't help me," Penny told herself. "I brought this on myself by not heeding Old Joe's warning. Now it's up to me to get out of the mess the best way I can."

The girl lay still on the limb, trying not to draw the attention of the rooters. Once they finished the meat, she was hopeful they would go away. Then she could make a dash for the walk.

Grunting and squealing, the rooters devoured the meat and looked about for more. To Penny's relief, they gradually wandered off—all except the old boar.

The leader of the pack stayed close to the big tree, eyeing the girl in the tree wickedly. Even in the dim light she could plainly see his evil little eyes and working jaws.

"Go away you big brute!" she muttered.

Penny's perch on the limb was a precarious one and her arms began to ache from the strain of holding on. Unsuccessfully, she tried to shift into a more comfortable position.

"I may be treed here for hours!" she thought. "Can I hold on that long?"

The old boar showed no disposition to move off, but kept circling the tree. It seemed to the now desperate Penny, that the animal sensed she was weakening and only awaited the moment when she would tumble down to the ground.

Breaking off a small tree branch she hurled it defiantly at the boar. The act caused her to lose her balance. Frantically, she clawed for a foothold but could not obtain it. Down she slipped to the base of the tree.

The old boar, quick to see his opportunity, charged. With a scream of terror, Penny leaped aside and the animal rushed past, squealing in rage at having missed his prey.

Even now, the boar stood between the girl and the plank walk. The tree from which she had fallen, offered her only refuge, and as she measured her chances, she realized that the probability of regaining the limb was a slim one.

The boar had turned and was coming for her again.

But at that instant, as Penny froze in terror, a shot was fired from somewhere in the bushes behind her. The bullet went straight and true, stopping the boar in his tracks. He grunted, rolled over, twitched twice, and lay still.

CHAPTER 17 - RESCUE

With a sob of relief, Penny whirled around to thank her rescuer. Through the thick leaves of the bushes she could see the shadowy figure of a man. But even as she watched, he retreated.

"Wait!" the girl cried.

There was no answer, and before she could call out a word of thanks for deliverance, the man had vanished.

His disappearance reminded her that though she had been snatched from the jaws of death, the danger by no means was over. At any moment the herd of rooters might return to attack.

Turning, Penny ran swiftly to the planked walk, in her haste not watching where she stepped. Her boots sank deeply in muck. Once on the planks well above the water level, she paused to catch her breath, and to gaze searchingly toward the bushes. All now was still.

"Who could my rescuer have been?" she mused. "Why didn't he wait for me to thank him?"

Penny called several times but received no reply. Finally, giving up, she started slowly back along the walk toward the bay where she had left Louise.

More than the girl realized, the adventure had unnerved her. She felt weak all over, and several times as she gazed steadily at the water, became dizzy and nearly lost her balance.

"Guess I'm not tough enough for swamp life," she reflected. "If ever I get out of here in one piece, I'm tempted to forget Danny Deevers and let the police do all the searching."

Footsteps became audible on the boardwalk some distance away.

Every sense now alert to danger, Penny halted to listen.

Someone was coming toward her, moving swiftly on the creaking planks.

"Penny!" called an agitated voice.

Penny relaxed as she knew that it was her chum. "Louise!" she answered, running to meet her.

Rounding a clump of bushes, and walking gingerly on the narrow boards, Louise stopped short as she beheld her friend.

"Why, you're as white as a ghost!" she exclaimed. "And I distinctly heard you shout! What happened? Did you see a snake?"

"A snake would be mild compared to what I've been through. Were you ever eaten alive?"

"Not that I recall."

"Well, I escaped it by the skin of my teeth," Penny said, rather relishing the adventure now that the story made such good telling. "I was saved by a mysterious stranger!"

Louise gazed at her chum anxiously and reached out to touch her forehead. "You're hot and feverish," she insisted. "This trip has been too much for you."

"I'm as cool as a piece of artificial ice!" Penny retorted. "Furthermore, I'm not touched by the heat!"

"Well, something is wrong with you."

"I've just had the fright of my life, that's all. If you'll give me a chance, I'll tell you what happened."

"The stage is all yours, sweet. But don't give me any tall tale about being rescued by a Prince Charming disguised as a frog!"

Penny's lips compressed into a tight line. "I can see you'll never believe the truth, Lou. So I'll prove it to you! Come with me, and I'll show you the animal that nearly made mince meat of me."

Treading single file, the girls returned the way Penny had come, to the end of the planks.

"Look over at the base of that big tree," Penny instructed, pointing. "What do you see?"

"Nothing."

"The boar that was shot—why, it should be there!" Penny scarcely could believe the sight of her own eyes. "But it's gone!"

"It's gone because it never was there. Penny, you're suffering from too much heat."

"I'm not! Neither am I imagining things! That old boar was there ten minutes ago. Either he came back to life and went off, or someone dragged him away."

"And your mysterious rescuer?" Louise teased. "What became of him?"

"I wish I knew! Lou, I'm not imagining any of this! Surely you must have heard the shot?"

"Well, I did hear something that sounded like one."

"Also, the lunch is gone. All that remains of it, is the paper lying over there by the tree."

"I do see a newspaper," Louise conceded.

"And that broken tree branch lying on the ground? I was up the tree and threw it at the boar. That's how I lost my balance and fell."

Louise now was convinced the story had solid foundation. "Start from the beginning," she urged.

Penny related what had occurred, rather building up the scene in which she had been delivered from death by the bullet shot from behind a bush.

"Whoever the man is, he must be somewhere close by," Louise said when she had finished. "Perhaps we can find him."

"Not a chance! He's deliberately hiding. Besides, I know better than to leave the walk again. It's dangerous!"

"In that case we may as well go back and wait for Joe," Louise said.

Treading their way carefully, the girls returned to the far end of the boardwalk. To their surprise, they saw a boat approaching.

"Why, it looks like Joe in the skiff!" Penny commented. "But he isn't due back for a long while yet."

Watching the oncoming boat for a moment, Louise said: "It's Joe all right, and he's coming fast. Something must be wrong."

Soon the guide brought the skiff alongside the sagging boardwalk.

"I heard a shot and started back," he explained. "I sure am glad to see both o' ye safe."

Before Penny could do so, Louise told Joe what had befallen her chum.

"Ye could have been kilt by that old boar," he said soberly. "It was the package o' meat that drew them rooters to the tree. They hain't likely to attack a human lest they're half starved."

"I wish I knew who saved me," Penny said. "Could it have been one of the Hawkins' boys?"

"From the sound, I'd say that shot weren't fired from their rifles. More'n likely it came from my own gun!"

"The stolen one?"

"That's what I'm a-thinkin'. If I could see the bullet that was fired, I could tell fer sure."

"The boar disappeared and the bullet with him," Penny said. "That's another queer thing."

"Whoever kilt the critter may have drug him off, or maybe the animal was only stunned." The guide squinted at the lowering sun. "I'd like powe'ful well to see the place, but it's gitten late. We gotta git back."

"What did you learn at Black Island?" Louise asked as she and Penny climbed into the skiff.

"Never got half way there," the guide said in disgust. "Since I went in last time, the main channel's clogged thick with hyacinths. To find yer way in now's a half day's job."

"Can't we try again tomorrow?" Penny asked eagerly.

The old guide gazed at her quizzically as he dipped his paddle. "Hain't ye had enough o' the swamp after today, young'un?"

"When that old boar came for me, I told myself if ever I got safely away, I'd never come again. But that was only a passing impulse. Black Island interests me."

"It's the most dangerous part of the swamp."

"Because of wild animals, you mean?"

"There's lots wuss things than animals," said the old guide soberly.

"For instance?"

Trapper Joe ignored Penny's question. Becoming as one deaf, he propelled the skiff with powerful strokes.

Penny waited patiently, but the guide showed no inclination to say more about Black Island.

"Shall we make it tomorrow?" she inquired presently.

CHAPTER 17 - RESCUE

"Make what?" Joe's wrinkled face was blank.

"Why, I mean, shall we visit Black Island!"

"I hate to disappoint ye, but we hain't a-goin'."

"You may be busy tomorrow. Later in the week perhaps?"

"Not tomorrer nor never. I hain't takin' the responsibility o' bringin' ye young'uns into the swamp agin."

"But why?" wailed Penny. "I wish now I hadn't told you about that old boar!"

"It hain't the boar that's got me worried."

"Then you must be afraid of something on Black Island—something you learned today and are keeping to yourself!"

"Maybe that's it," returned Joe briefly. "Anyhow, we hain't goin'. And it won't do no good to try coaxin' me with yer female wiles. My mind's made up!"

Having delivered himself of this ultimatum, the guide plied his paddle steadily.

The set of his jaw warned Penny it would be useless to tease. With a discouraged sigh, she settled down into the bottom of the skiff to think.

CHAPTER 18 - WANTED—A GUIDE

Since the eventful trip to the swamp, several days now had elapsed, and from Penny's viewpoint, nothing of consequence had happened.

Each day the *Riverview Star* carried a story giving details of the police search for Danny Deevers, and on each succeeding morning the account became shorter, with less new information.

Twice, it was rumored police were closing in on the escaped convict, and twice the rumor proved false.

At the request of Salt Sommers and Jerry Livingston, posses made several searches of the outer swamp area. However, no trace of the missing man was found, and investigators quickly switched their activities elsewhere.

Spurred by the *Star's* reward offer, clues, anonymous and otherwise, came to both the newspaper and police officials. All proved worthless.

"It begins to look as if Danny has pulled out of this territory," Mr. Parker remarked to Penny late one afternoon as she sat in his office at the plant. "At least he's made no further attempt to carry out his threat against Jerry."

"Maybe he's only lying low and waiting until the police search cools off a little."

"Quite possible," the publisher agreed, frowning as he fingered a paperweight. "In that case, Jerry is in real danger. I'll never feel entirely easy in my mind until Deevers is behind bars again."

"Speaking of me, Chief?" inquired a voice from the doorway.

Jerry stood there, a long streamer of pasted copy paper in his hand. He had written a story of a political squabble at city hall, and needed Mr. Parker's approval before handing it over to the typesetters.

The publisher quickly read the article, pencilled an "okay" at the top, and returned it to the reporter.

"Good stuff, Jerry," he approved. "By the way, any news of Danny Deevers?"

"Nothing new."

"Jerry, I can't help feeling he's hiding either in the swamp or somewhere close by," Penny interposed eagerly. "At least something queer is going on out there."

"That's what Salt thinks. We were out there last night."

"In the swamp?" Penny asked, caught by surprise.

"Not in it, but near the Hawkins' place."

"What did you learn, Jerry?"

"Frankly, nothing. You remember that swamp road where you and Salt saw the truck?"

"Yes, of course."

"We watched there for quite awhile around midnight."

"Did you see the truck stop there again?"

"No, but we thought we saw a couple of men at the edge of the swamp—apparently waiting for someone. We tried to sneak up close, but I'm afraid we gave ourselves away. Anyway, they vanished back among the trees."

"Did you notice or hear anything else unusual, Jerry?"

"Well, no. Not unless you'd call pounding on a dishpan out of the ordinary."

"A dishpan!" Penny exclaimed. "Who did it?"

"We couldn't tell. Salt and I heard the sound soon after we had passed the Hawkins' place on our way toward the swamp."

"What sort of sound was it?"

"Just a metallic tap-tap-tap. It may not have been on a dishpan."

CHAPTER 18 - WANTED—A GUIDE

"Were the taps in code, Jerry?"

"Couldn't have been a very complicated one for the pounding only lasted a minute or two. It was irregular though."

"Then I'm sure it was a code!" Penny cried. "Louise and I heard the same sound when we were with Trapper Joe in the boat!"

"Did the noise come from outside the swamp?"

"Inside, I'd say."

"Then we may not have heard the same thing. The pounding noise Salt and I noticed, came from the direction of the Hawkins' farm. It may have had no significance."

Before Jerry could say more, Editor DeWitt called him to the copy desk. Mr. Parker turned again to his daughter.

"Penny, if I were you, I'd try to forget Danny Deevers," he advised. "Whatever you do, don't go into the swamp again unless you're with Joe or another guide. Better still, don't go at all."

"Oh, Dad!"

"No good can come of it. Do I have your promise, Penny?"

"But I feel I should try to recover Louise's dog!"

"We'll buy her a new pet."

"It won't be Bones."

"The chance that the dog ever will be found is slim," Mr. Parker said. "In any case, he's not worth the risk of trying to find him. Your promise, Penny?"

"That I won't go in without a guide?" she asked, seizing upon the lesser of two evils. "All right, I promise."

The next day it rained, keeping Penny closely confined at home. However, the following morning gave promise of being sunny and pleasant.

Arising early, she packed a lunch for herself, dressed in hiking clothes with heavy boots, and was ready to leave the house by the time Mrs. Weems came downstairs for breakfast.

"Up so early, Penny?" she inquired.

"Just going on a little trip. Don't expect me back very early."

The housekeeper regarded her severely. "Penny Parker, you're not going to the swamp again!"

"Figured I might."

"Does your father know you're going?"

"We talked it over a day or so ago. He doesn't mind so long as I go with Trapper Joe or another guide."

"In that case I suppose I can't object," Mrs. Weems sighed. "Mind, you don't set foot in the swamp without someone along!"

"I've already given my promise to Dad."

"And do be careful," the housekeeper added. "I'll not feel easy until you're back."

Though neither she nor Penny knew it then, the girl's absence from home was to be a long one, and both were to have many uncomfortable moments before her return.

Reaching the swamp sometime later, Penny parked the car and walked to Trapper Joe's shack on the creek.

The old guide was sitting on the sagging porch, his feet propped on the railing. Catching sight of Penny he frowned slightly, but as she came up, greeted her in a friendly way.

"'Mawnin'," he said briefly. "What's on yer mind this time?"

"Can't you guess?" Penny asked, sitting down on a step at his feet.

"If yer wantin' me to take you into the swamp agin, yer only wastin' yer words. I hain't got the time."

"I'll pay you well."

"It hain't the money."

"Then why do you refuse to take me in?"

"Tole ye, didn't I? I got work to do."

Penny knew that Joe was only making excuses, for obviously, one day was very like another in his care-free life.

"What work do you have this morning that can't wait, Joe?"

"Well, fer one thing I gotta smoke out a swarm o' bees and git me a nice mess o' honey fer winter. Want to go with me?"

"Into the swamp?"

"No, this tree hain't in the swamp."

"Then I don't want to go. Joe, I think you're stubborn! You know how much this trip means to me."

"Reckon I do."

"Then why not take me? Tell me your reason for refusing."

Old Joe gazed steadily at Penny and for a moment seemed on the verge of making interesting revelations. But to her disappointment, he shook his head.

"Jest don't wanter go, thet's all."

"You learned something the other day when we were in the swamp!" Penny accused. "You're keeping it from me—probably to protect someone! Isn't that it?"

"Hain't saying."

"You know Danny Deevers is hidden somewhere in the swamp! You're helping to protect him!"

Old Joe's feet came down from the railing with a thump. "Now that hain't so!" he denied. "I got no time fer the likes o' Danny Deevers. If I knowed where he is, I'd give him up to the law."

"Well, someone is hiding there! I heard Ezekiel Hawkins talking on Lookout Point, didn't I? We found the dead campfire. Your gun was stolen, and later a mysterious person rescued me when I was treed by the boar."

"Could have been one o' the Hawkins."

"You don't honestly believe that, Joe."

"No, reckon I don't," the guide sighed. "You sure kin shoot questions at a feller faster'n these new Army rockets I hear tell about. I'd like to tell ye what ye want to know, but there's things best not talked about. Knowin' too much kin be dangerous."

Penny scarcely could hide her annoyance, for several times now the guide had made similar hints.

"I don't trust the Hawkins' family at all," she announced. "If they're not involved with Danny Deevers, they're up to something here in the swamp. Otherwise, why would they be so mean?"

"The Hawkins' family always has been mean an' ornery."

"Another thing—" Penny started to mention how she and Salt had seen large containers of some unknown product being removed from the swamp, but broke off as she decided to keep the information to herself.

"Yeah?" inquired the guide.

"Nothing," replied Penny. "If you won't take me into the swamp, is there anyone else who will?"

"Couldn't say fer sure," Joe replied, "but I reckon I'm the only guide herebouts fer maybe fifty miles."

"Won't you reconsider?"

"You put up a powe'ful strong argument, young'un, but I gotta say no fer yer own good."

"You've certainly ruined all my plans," Penny said crossly. "Well, since you won't help me, I'll say goodbye."

Back in the car once more, she could not bring herself to return home so early in the morning. Debating a moment, she drove to the homestead of the Widow Jones.

Dressed in a bright calico dress, the woman sat under a shade tree skillfully cutting up the meat of a turtle and dropping it into a pan of cold water.

As Penny walked across the weed-choked yard, she looked up in a startled way, but smiled as she recognized the girl.

"I'm fixin' to have me a nice soup," she explained. "Ye cook the turtle with diced carrots, potatoes, okra, and tomatoes and serve it piping hot. Ever et any?"

"No, I never have," Penny replied, watching the preparations with interest. "It sounds good."

"Ye kin stay and have dinner with me," the woman invited. "I'll fix some flour biscuits and we'll have a right nice meal."

"I'm afraid I'll have to get back home," Penny said regretfully. "My trip here today was a failure."

Because the Widow Jones gave her an inquiring look of sympathy, she explained that Trapper Joe had refused to take her into the swamp. She went on to tell why the trip meant so much to her, and of her belief that a clever investigator who knew the area might find clues which would lead to the capture of Danny Deevers.

"So Joe wouldn't take ye?" the Widow Jones inquired softly. "Why?"

"He says it's dangerous."

"And since when has Joe got so a-feared of his shadow?"

CHAPTER 18 - WANTED—A GUIDE

"It did sound like an excuse to me. I think he knows what is going on in the swamp, and wants no part of it."

"Ye say it means a lot to ye to make the trip?"

"Oh, yes, I'd do it in a minute, if I could find anyone who knows the channels. But Joe says he's the only guide for fifty miles around."

Mrs. Jones slapped the last piece of turtle meat into the water with a splash. She arose, gathering her long skirts about her.

"Joe's maybe fergettin' that as a gal, my paw taught me every crook and turn of the swamp. Hain't been in there fer quite a spell now, but I got a hankerin' to go agin."

Penny stared at her incredulously.

"You mean you'll take me?" she demanded. "Today? Now?"

"I've got a quilt I should be piecin' on this afternoon, but hit can wait. If you hain't afeared to place yerself in my hands, I'll take you."

"I'll jump at the chance! But do you have a boat?"

"We'll make Joe lend us his!" the widow said grimly. "And if he tries squirmin', well, I know how to handle him!"

CHAPTER 19 - PENNY'S PLAN

Making elaborate preparations for the trip into the swamp, Mrs. Jones packed a lunch, and donned a huge straw hat and stout boots.

However, she did not change the long, flowing skirt, which flopped about her ankles as she and Penny walked through the meadow to Trapper Joe's dock.

From the porch, the old guide saw the pair and watched them warily.

"We're takin' yer boat, Joe," the widow called to him from the creek's edge. "We're makin' a little trip into the swamp."

Joe pulled himself from the chair and came quickly to the dock.

"Hold on now!" he protested. "Two wimmin can't go alone into the swamp! Leastwise, not beyond Lookout Point."

"Says who?" retorted the widow, already untying the boat.

"That young 'un's talked you into goin' to Black Island! Ye can't do it. You'll git lost in one o' the false channels. The hyacinths are bad this year."

The widow hesitated, then tossed her head as she dropped the package of lunch into the skiff.

"Ye forgit I was swamp raised! Git me the paddles and a pole, Joe. Don't stand there gawkin'."

"No wimmin ever went as far as Black Island. It hain't safe!"

"My Paw took me there when I was a little girl. I hain't forgittin' the way."

"Ye'r stubborn as a mule!" Joe accused, glaring at her. "If you're dead set on goin', I see I'll have to give in and go with ye. But it's agin my best judgment."

"No one asked ye to go with us, Joe," the widow said tartly. "We aim to make this trip by ourselves. Jest git the paddles and pole."

Joe threw up his hands in a gesture of defeat and started slowly for the shack. "Wimmin!" he muttered. "There jest hain't no sense in 'em!"

He took his time inside the shack, but finally returned with the requested paddles and pole.

"There ye are!" he snapped. "But I'm warnin' ye, if ye git into trouble or lost, don't expect me to come after ye."

"Now I'll take the kicker motor," the widow ordered, paying no heed to his words.

"Not my motor!" Joe exclaimed defiantly. "I paid sixty dollars fer it secondhand and I hain't lettin' no female ruin it."

"Ye can't expect me to blister my hands rowin' all day," the widow replied. "We aim to make a quick trip."

"Ye can't use the motor in all them hyacinths!"

"Maybe not, but it'll take us through the open spots a heap faster. The motor, Joe."

Grumbling loudly, the guide went to the house once more. He came back with the motor which he attached and started for the widow.

"Thank ye kindly, Joe," she grinned at him as the boat pulled away from the dock. "I'll make ye one of my apple pies when I git back."

"*If ye get back*," the guide corrected morosely.

Propelled by the motor, the skiff sped steadily through the channel and came presently to the Hawkins' farm. The popping of the engine, which could be heard some distance, drew Mrs. Hawkins to the dock.

She signaled the boat as it drew near.

CHAPTER 19 - PENNY'S PLAN

"Howdy," the Widow Jones greeted her politely though with no warmth. She throttled down the engine and drifted in toward shore.

"Goin' in fer a little fishin', I take it," Mrs. Hawkins observed by way of inquiry. "But where's yer fishin' poles?"

"Left 'em ter home," the widow replied.

"Then you hain't fishin'."

"'Pears like yer right smart at usein' yer eyes," the widow agreed dryly.

A slight frown which did not escape Penny, puckered the farm woman's forehead. She seemed on the verge of speaking, then appeared to change her mind. As the boat drifted on, she watched stolidly.

"Never did like that woman," Mrs. Jones commented when the skiff had rounded a bend. "She's got sharp eyes, and she don't approve 'cause we're goin' inter the swamp together."

"Why should she care?" Penny asked.

"I wonder myself."

"I've noticed that she always seems to be watching the entrance channel into the swamp," Penny said thoughtfully. "Perhaps she is the one who taps out those signals!"

"Signals? What do you mean, young'un?"

Penny told of the strange pounding noises she had heard during her previous trip through the swamp.

"I could almost wager Mrs. Hawkins will wait until we're a safe distance away, and then signal!" the girl went on. "Don't I wish I could catch her though!"

"Maybe ye kin. We could shut off the motor and drift back and watch."

Penny's eyes began to sparkle with excitement. "I'd love to do it. But won't she be listening for the sound of our motor as we go deeper into the swamp? If she doesn't hear it, she's apt to suspect something."

"Ye've got a real head on yer shoulders," said the widow approvingly. "By the way, I don't like to keep callin' ye young'un now we're good friends. What's yer name?"

"I thought you knew. I'm sorry. It's Penny Parker."

"Penny! I never did hear o' a girl named after money."

"I wasn't exactly," Penny smiled. "My real name is Penelope, but no one ever liked it. So I'm called Penny."

"Penelope, hain't sich a bad name. That's what I'll call ye."

"About Mrs. Hawkins—" the girl reminded her.

"Oh, yes, now if ye was a mind to find out about her, it wouldn't be so hard."

"How?"

"We hain't gone fur into the swamp yet. I could let ye out here on the bank and ye could slip back afoot to the bend in the channel."

"Where I'd be able to watch the house!"

"Ye got the idea, Penelope. All the while, I would keep goin' on in the boat until the sound o' the motor jest naturally died out. Then I could row back here and pick ye up again."

"Mrs. Jones, you're the one who has a head on your shoulders!" Penny cried. "Let's do it!"

The widow brought the skiff alongside the bank, steadying it as the girl stepped ashore.

"Ye got a watch?" she asked.

"Yes."

"Then I'll meet ye right here in 'bout three-quarters of an hour. I kin keep track o' the time by lookin' at the sun."

"That may not give me enough time," Penny said anxiously.

"If yer late, I'll wait fer ye," the widow promised. "But try to be here. If ye hain't we may havter give up the trip, 'cause it hain't sensible startin' in late in the day."

"I'll be here," Penny assured her. "If nothing happens in three-quarters of an hour, I'll just give it up."

The boat, it's motor popping steadily, slipped away. Penny scrambled up the muddy bank, and finding a well-trod path, walked rapidly toward the Hawkins' place.

Soon she came to the bend in the creek, and there paused. From afar, she could hear the retreating sound of the skiff's motor.

Through a break in the bushes, the girl peered toward the distant farmhouse. To her disappointment, the yard was now deserted, and Mrs. Hawkins was nowhere in sight.

"Maybe I was wrong," Penny thought. "I'd hate to waste all this valuable time."

For a half hour she waited. Twice Mrs. Hawkins came out of the house, once to gather in clothes from the line and the second time to obtain a pail of water.

"I guess my hunch was crazy," Penny told herself. "I'll have to be starting back to meet Mrs. Jones."

The sound of the motorboat now had died out completely, so the girl knew the widow already was on her way to their appointed meeting place.

Turning away from the bushes, Penny paused for one last glance at the farmhouse. The yard remained deserted. But as she sighed in disappointment, the kitchen door again flew open.

Mrs. Hawkins came outside and walked rapidly to the shed. She listened attentively for a moment. Then from a peg on the outside wall, she took down a big tin dishpan and a huge wooden mixing spoon.

Penny watched with mounting excitement. This was the moment for which she had waited!

Carefully, the farm woman looked about to be certain no one was nearby. Then with firm precision, she beat out a tattoo on the dishpan.

"It's a signal to someone in the swamp!" guessed Penny. "In code she is tapping out that Mrs. Jones and I are on our way into the interior!"

CHAPTER 20 - TRAILING HOD HAWKINS

After Mrs. Hawkins had pounded out the signal, she hung the dishpan on its peg once more, and went to the door of the shed. Without opening it, she spoke to someone inside the building. Penny was too far away to hear what she said.

In a minute, the woman turned away and vanished into the house.

Penny waited a little while to be certain Mrs. Hawkins did not intend to come outside again. Then, with an uneasy glance at her wrist watch, she stole away to rejoin Mrs. Jones.

The skiff was drawn up to shore by the time she reached the appointed meeting place.

"I was jest about to give you up," the widow remarked as the girl scrambled into the boat. "Did ye learn what ye wanted to know?"

Penny told her what she had seen.

"'Pears you may be right about it bein' a signal," the widow agreed thoughtfully. "We may be able to learn more too, 'cause whoever had his'n ears tuned to Ma Hawkins' signal may figure we're deep in the swamp by this time."

"Let's keep on the alert as we near Lookout Point," Penny urged.

Mrs. Jones nodded and silently dipped the paddle.

Soon they came within view of the point. Passing beneath an overhanging tree branch, the widow grasped it with one hand, causing the skiff to swing sideways into a shelter of leaves.

"See anyone, Penelope?" she whispered.

"Not a soul."

"Then maybe we was wrong about Ma Hawkins signalling anyone."

"But I do see a boat beached on the point!" Penny added. "And see! Someone is coming out of the bush now!"

"Hod Hawkins!"

Keeping quiet, the pair in the skiff waited to see what would happen.

Hod came down to the water's edge, peering with a puzzled expression along the waterway. He did not see the skiff, shielded by leaves and dense shade.

"Hit's all-fired queer," they heard him mutter. "I shore didn't see no boat pass here this mawnin'. But Maw musta seen one go by or she wouldn't heve pounded the pan."

Hod sat down on a log, watching the channel. Penny and Mrs. Jones remained where they were. Once the current, sluggish as it was, swung the skiff against a projecting tree root. The resulting jar and scraping sound seemed very loud to their ears. But the Hawkins youth did not hear.

Penny and the widow were becoming weary of sitting in such cramped positions under the tree branch. To their relief, Hod arose after a few minutes. Reaching into the hollow log, he removed a tin pan somewhat smaller than the dishpan Mrs. Hawkins had used a few minutes earlier.

"He's going to signal!" Penny whispered excitedly. "Either to his mother, or someone deeper in the swamp!"

Already Hod was beating out a pattern on the pan, very similar to the one the girl had heard before.

After a few minutes, the swamper thrust the pan back into its hiding place. He hesitated, and then to the surprise of Penny and Mrs. Jones, stepped into his boat.

"If he comes this way, he's certain to see us!" Penny thought uneasily.

With never a glance toward the leafy hideout, Hod shoved off, rowing deeper into the swamp.

"Dare we follow him?" whispered Penny.

"That's what I aim to do," the Widow Jones rejoined grimly. "I hain't afeared o' the likes o' Hod Hawkins! Moreover, fer a long time, I been calculatin' to find out what takes him and Coon so offen into the swamp."

"You mean recently don't you, Mrs. Jones. Just since Danny Deevers escaped from prison?"

"I don't know nothin' about Danny Deevers," the widow replied as she picked up the paddle again. "I do know that the Hawkins' been up to mischief fer more'n a year."

"Then you must have an idea what that city truck was doing on the swamp road the other night."

"An idear—yes," agreed Mrs. Jones. "But I hain't sure, and until I am, I hain't makin' no accusations."

Now that Hod's boat was well away, the widow noiselessly sent the skiff forward.

"We kin follow close enough to jest about keep him in sight if we don't make no noise," she warned. "But we gotta be keerful."

Penny nodded and became silent.

Soon the channel was no more than a path through high water-grass and floating hyacinths. Hod propelled his boat with powerful muscles, alternating with forked pole and paddle. At times, when Penny took over to give the Widow Jones a "breather," she was hard pressed not to lose the trail.

"We're headin' straight fer Black Island, hit 'pears to me," Mrs. Jones whispered once. "The channel don't look the same though as when I was through here last. But I reckon if we git lost we kin find our way out somehow."

Soon the skiff was inching through a labyrinth of floating hyacinths; there were few stretches of open water. Shallow channels to confuse the unwary, radiated out in a dozen directions, many of them with no outlets.

Always, however, before the hyacinths closed in, the Widow Jones was able to pick up the path through which Hod had passed.

"From the way he's racin' along, he's been this way plenty o' times," she remarked. "We're headin' fer Black Island right enough."

The sun now was high overhead, beating down on Penny's back and shoulders with uncomfortable warmth. Mrs. Jones brought out the lunch and a jug of water. One ate while the other rowed.

"We're most to Black Island," the widow informed presently. "If ye look sharp through the grass, ye can see thet point o' high land. Thet's the beginnin' o' the island—biggest one in the swamp."

"But where is Hod?"

"He musta pulled up somewheres in the bushes. We'll have to be keerful and go slow now or we'll be caught."

"Listen!" whispered Penny.

Although she could as yet see no one on the island, voices floated out across the water.

"We heerd yer signal, Hod," a man said, "but we hain't seen no one."

"A boat musta come through, or Maw wouldn't heve beat the pan."

"Whoever 'twas, they probably went off somewheres else," the other man replied. "Glad yer here anyhow, Hod. We got a lot o' work to do and ye can help us."

Hod's reply was inaudible, for obviously the men were moving away into the interior of the island.

"Thet was old Ezekiel talkin' to his son," the Widow Jones declared, although Penny already had guessed as much. "They've gone off somewheres, so if we're a mind to land, now's our only chance."

Penny gazed at her companion in surprise and admiration.

"You're not afraid?" she inquired softly.

"Maybe I am," the Widow Jones admitted. "But that hain't no excuse fer me turnin' tail! This here's a free country ain't it?"

She poled the skiff around the point to a thick clump of bushes. There she pulled up, and with Penny's help made the skiff secure to a tree root hidden from sight by overhanging branches.

Scrambling up the muddy bank, the pair paused to take bearings. Voices now had died away and to all appearances the island might have been deserted.

Treading with utmost caution, Penny and the Widow Jones tramped along the shore until they came to a path. Abruptly, the girl halted, sniffing the air.

"I smell wood burning," she whispered. "From a campfire probably."

CHAPTER 20 - TRAILING HOD HAWKINS

"An' I smell somethin' more," added the Widow Jones grimly. "Cain't ye notice thet sickish, sweet odor in the air?"

"Yes, what is it?"

"We'll find out," replied Mrs. Jones. "But if we git cotched, I'm warnin' ye we won't never git away from here. Ye sure ye want to go on?"

"Very sure."

"Then come on. And be keerful not to crackle any leaves underfoot."

The path led to a low, tunnellike opening in the thicket. Penny, who again had taken the lead, crouched low, intending to crawl through.

Before she could do so, she heard a stifled cry behind her. Turning, she saw that Mrs. Jones had sagged to one knee, and her face was twisted with pain.

Penny ran to her. "You're hurt!" she whispered. "Bitten by a snake?"

Mrs. Jones shook her head, biting her lip to keep back the tears. She pointed to her ankle, caught beneath a tree root.

"I stumbled and wrenched it 'most off," she murmured. "Hit's a bad sprain and I'm afeared I can't go on."

CHAPTER 21 - THE TUNNEL OF LEAVES

Penny raised the woman to her feet, but as Mrs. Jones tried to take a step, she saw that the sprain indeed was a bad one.

Already the ankle was swelling and skin had been broken. At each attempted step, the widow winced with pain, suffering intensely.

"If I kin only git back to the boat, I'll be all right," she said, observing Penny's worried expression. "Drat it all! Jest when I wanted to find out what the Hawkins' are doin' on this island!"

Supporting much of the widow's weight on her shoulders, Penny helped her back to the skiff.

"I guess we may as well start back," she said, unable to hide her bitter disappointment.

The widow reached for an oar, then looked keenly at Penny and put it back again.

"'Course it would be a risky thing fer ye to go on by yerself while I wait here in the boat—"

Penny's slumped shoulders straightened. Her blue eyes began to dance.

"You mean you don't mind waiting here while I see where that tunnel of leaves leads?" she demanded.

"'Pears like we've come too fur not to find out what's goin' on. Think ye can git in there and back without being cotched?"

"I'm sure of it!"

The widow sighed. "I hain't sure of it, but you got more gumpshun than any other young'un I ever met. Go on if ye'r a-goin', and if anyone sees ye, light out fer the boat. I'll be ready to shove off."

"Mrs. Jones, you're a darling!" Penny whispered, giving the gnarled hand a quick pressure. "I'll make it all right!"

Moving directly to the thicket, she dropped on all fours and started through the leafy tunnel where Hod had disappeared. The sweetish odor now was much plainer than before.

She had crawled only a few feet, when a hand reached out of nowhere and grasped her shoulder.

Penny whirled around, expecting to see a member of the Hawkins' family. For a moment she saw no one, and then from the thicket beside the tunnel, a figure became visible. The hold on her shoulder relaxed.

"Who are you?" she demanded in a whisper.

"Friend."

"Then show yourself!"

The leaves rustled, and a dark-haired lad with tangled curls crawled into the tunnel beside her. His shoes were ripped, his clothing dirty and in tatters. A rifle was grasped in his hand.

"Bada men," he warned, jerking his head in the direction Penny had been crawling. "Mucha better go back boat."

"Who are you and why do you warn me?" Penny asked, deeply puzzled.

The boy did not reply.

Light dawned suddenly upon Penny. "You're the one who saved me from the boar!"

The boy's quick grin was acknowledgment he had fired the shot.

"But why did you run away?" Penny asked. "Why didn't you wait and let me thank you for saving my life?"

"You giva me to police maybe," replied the boy in broken English. "I staya here—starva first!"

"Who are you?"

"Name no matter."

CHAPTER 21 - THE TUNNEL OF LEAVES

Penny's mind had been working swiftly. She was convinced the boy who had saved her also was the one who had stolen Trapper Joe's gun. Evidently, he had needed it to survive in the swamp. He was thin and his eyes had a hungry look, she noted.

"How did you get to this island?" she inquired. "Do you have a boat?"

"Make-a raft." The boy's eyes darted down the leafy tunnel. "No good here," he said, seizing Penny's arm and pulling her back into the thicket. "Someone-a come!"

Scarcely had the pair flattened themselves on the ground than Ezekiel Hawkins crawled out through the tunnel, pushing his gun ahead of him. Standing upright not three feet from Penny and her companion, he gazed sharply about.

"Thought I heerd voices," he muttered.

Penny held her breath, knowing that if the swamper should walk down the shore even a dozen yards, he would see the Widow Jones waiting in the skiff.

To her great relief, Ezekiel moved in the opposite direction. After satisfying himself that no boat approached the island, he returned through the tunnel and disappeared.

"What's going on back in there?" Penny whispered as soon as it was safe to ask.

"Bada men," her companion said briefly.

"You're driving me to distraction!" Penny muttered, losing patience. "Do those swampers know you're here on the island?"

The boy shook his tangled curls, grinning broadly. "Chasa me once. No catch."

"You're Italian, aren't you?" Penny asked suddenly.

A guarded look came over the lad's sun-tanned face. His brown eyes lost some of their friendliness.

"Now I have it!" Penny exclaimed before he could speak. "You're Antonio Tienta, wanted by Immigration authorities for slipping into this country illegally!"

The boy did not deny the accusation, and the half-frightened, defiant look he gave her, confirmed that she had struck upon the truth.

"I no go back!" he muttered. "I starva first!"

"Don't become so excited, or those men will hear you and we'll both be caught," Penny warned. "Tell me about yourself, Tony. I already know a little."

"How mucha you know?" he asked cautiously.

"That you acted as a guide to G.I.'s in Italy and stowed aboard a troopship coming to this country. Even now, I guess authorities aren't certain how you slipped past New York officials."

"No trouble," boasted the lad. "On ship my friendsa the G.I.'s they feeda me. We dock New York; I hide under bunk; all G.I.'s leava boat. Boat go to other dock. Sailor friend giva me clothes. Sailors leave-a boat. I slippa out. No one geta wise."

"Then where did you go?"

"Stay in-a New York only two—three days. Go hitchhike into country. Work-a on farm. No like it. Hear Immigration men-a come, so I go. Come-a one day to swamp. Good place; I stay."

"You've not had an easy time keeping alive in this dismal place," Penny said sympathetically. "Isn't that Trapper Joe's gun?"

"Steal-a one night," the boy agreed. "Give back some-a time."

Penny studied the youth with growing concern. "Tony," she said, "you can't hope to stay here long. The only sensible thing is to give yourself up."

"No! I die first! American best country in all-a the world! No one ever take-a me back!"

"But you can't expect to elude Immigration officials very long. If you give yourself up, they might be lenient with you."

"They send-a me back," Tony said stubbornly. "I stay right-a here!"

"To starve? You're hungry now, aren't you?"

"Sure. But in Italy I hungry many times-a too."

"Tony, we'll talk about this later," Penny sighed. "Right now, I want to learn what's going on here at the island. Know anything about it?"

"Sure," the boy grinned. "Know plenty."

"Then suppose you tell me, Tony."

"I show-a you," the boy offered.

Avoiding the leafy tunnel, he led Penny in a half circle through another section of dense thicket.

Soon he motioned for her to drop on her knees.

The sickish odor rising through the trees now was very disagreeable again.

A few yards farther on, Tony halted. Still lying flat on his stomach, he carefully pulled aside the bushes so that his companion might see.

CHAPTER 22 - HELP FROM TONY

Through the leaves, Penny saw a fairly large clearing. Three men, Ezekiel Hawkins and his two sons, were squatted about a big hardwood fire over which was a large copper cooker.

A pipe extended above the cover, connected with a series of coils immersed in a barrel of cold water.

"A still!" the girl whispered. "They're making alcohol here and selling it in the city! That's what those containers held that were trucked away!"

"Make-a the stuff every day," volunteered Tony. "I watch—sometimes I steal-a the lunch. They very mad but no catch."

"They're probably afraid you'll tell revenue officers," Penny whispered.

From one of the barrels, Coon had taken a dipper filled with the pale fluid. As he drank deeply from it, his father said sharply:

"Thet's enough, Coon! We gotta git this stuff made an moved out o' here tonight, and ye won't be fitten."

"What's yer rush, Pappy? We got termorrer, hain't we?" Coon sat down, and bracing his back against a tree trunk, yawned drowsily.

"Ye want to be caught by them lousy revenooers?"

"There hain't no danger. Hain't we got a fool-proof system? If anyone starts this way, Maw'll spot 'em and give us the signal."

"Folkses is gittin' wise, and we hain't none too popular hereabouts. We're moving this stuff out tonight."

"Jest as you say, Pappy." Coon stirred reluctantly.

"An we hain't operatin' the still no more till things quiets down. I don't like it that gal snoopin' around here, claimin' to be lookin' fer her dawg."

"Ye should have kilt the dawg, stead o' keepin' him," Hod spoke up as he dumped a sack of mash into a tub. "Tole ye it would make us trouble."

"Yer always tellin' me!" Ezekiel retorted. "Thet dog's handy to heve here, an I never was one to kill a helpless animal without cause. Now git to yer work, and let me do the thinkin' fer this outfit!"

Penny's curiosity now had been fully satisfied as to the illegal business in which the Hawkins' family had engaged, but she also felt a little disappointed.

She had hoped the men would speak of Danny Deevers, perhaps revealing his hideout. The convict was nowhere to be seen, and there was no evidence he ever had been on Black Island.

Not wishing to leave Mrs. Jones too long alone in the boat, Penny presently motioned to Tony that she had seen and heard enough.

Inch by inch, they crept backwards away from the tiny clearing.

Then suddenly Penny stopped, for Ezekiel was speaking again:

"We gotta do something about Danny and git him off our hands."

Penny instantly became all ears, listening intently to Coon's reply:

"Now ye'r talkin', Pappy. Takin' him in was a big mistake. Hit's apt ter land us in jail if them city officers come snoopin' around here agin."

"There wouldn't have been no risk, if Hod and Danny hadn't taken the widder's car and drive into town. Didn't ye have no sense, Hod?"

"Danny wanted to go," Hod whined. "How was we ter know another car was goin' to smash into us? Thet fool newspaper camera man an' the girl had to be there!"

"That wasn't the wust," Ezekiel went on as he fed the fire with chips. "Then ye follered 'em to the theater!"

"Danny said we had ter git the picture or they'd print it in the newspaper."

"But did ye git the picture?"

"No," Hod growled.

"Instead o' that, ye let Danny git into a fight."

"'Twasn't no fight and nobody knew it was him. He seen an enemy o' his'n go into the building. I tried ter talk him out o' it, but he wouldn't listen. He crawled in through a window, and slugged the feller."

"He did have sense enough to git rid o' the car, but ye shouldn't have left it so close to our place," Ezekiel pointed out. "That newspaper gal's been out here twict now, and she's catchin' on!"

"She's only a gal," Hod said carelessly. "Ye do too much worryin', Pappy."

"I do the thinkin' fer this family. An' I say things is gittin' too hot fer comfort. We gotta git rid o' Danny tonight."

"How ye aimin' ter do it, Pappy?" inquired Coon. "Be ye fergittin' he's got $50,000 hid away somewheres an' he hain't give us our slice yet?"

"Fer all his promises, maybe he don't calculate ever to give us our cut! Ever think o' that?"

"Danny would double cross us if he got the chanst," Hod agreed. "Maybe ye'r right, Pappy!"

"Doggone tootin', I am! We git rid o' him tonight, soon's we git back from this island. But first we make him tell where he hid the money!"

"How we gonna do it, Pappy?" asked Coon.

"Hain't figured fer sure, but he's the same as our prisoner, ain't he? If we was to turn him over to the police, claimin' we found him hidin' out in the swamp, he couldn't prove no different."

"And we'd git $10,000 reward!" Hod added. "We could use thet money!"

"I hain't one to double cross a pal if it can be helped," Ezekiel amended hastily. "Now if Danny's a mind to tell where he hid the money, and split, we'll help him git out o' here tonight."

"And if he won't cough up?"

"We'll turn him over to police and claim the reward."

To Penny, it now was clear Hod Hawkins had been with Danny Deevers at the time Jerry was slugged. Also, the conversation made it evident the escaped convict had sought a hideout somewhere near if not in the swamp.

Tensely, the girl waited for further details of the escape plan, but none were forthcoming. The three men applied themselves to their work and said no more.

"My best bet is to get away from here fast and notify police!" Penny thought.

Noiselessly, she and Tony retreated through the thicket to a shoreline some distance away.

"Listen, Tony!" Penny said hurriedly. "I've got to go away for awhile! Will you stay here and keep watch of these men for me?"

"I stay," the boy promised soberly.

"I'll come back as soon as I can. And Tony! Please don't run away. I want to do something for you—perhaps I can."

"No go back to Italy," the boy said firmly. "Stay-a here—you come back. Then go far away. No trust poleese."

Penny dared not take time to try to convince the youth of the folly of fleeing from Immigration authorities. Saying goodbye, she ran to the boat where the Widow Jones anxiously awaited her.

"Shove off!" she ordered tersely. "I've seen plenty! I'll tell you about it, once we're away from here!"

Mrs. Jones gave a mighty push with her pole, and the skiff floated out of its hiding place into the hyacinth-clogged channel.

"How is your foot?" Penny inquired. "Better let me paddle."

"It hain't hurtin' so much now," the widow replied without giving up the paddle. "I'll steer until we're out o' these floatin' hyacinth beds."

"One place looks exactly like another to me," Penny said anxiously. "So many false channels!"

"Ye git a feel fer it after awhile. There's a current to follow, but it's mighty faint."

"We must get back as fast as we can," Penny urged, glancing nervously over her shoulder toward Black Island. In terse sentences she told of her meeting with Tony and all they had seen in the clearing.

"So the Hawkins' are runnin' a still!" commented the widow. "Humph! Jest as I figured, only I didn't dast say so without proof."

CHAPTER 22 - HELP FROM TONY

"The important thing is they're hiding Danny Deevers! Where they're keeping him will be for the police to discover as soon as they arrest Ezekiel and his sons."

"I'll git ye back fast," the widow promised grimly. "Soon's we git out o' these beds and away from the island, I kin switch on the motor."

Safely out of sight of the island, the couple found themselves in a labyrinth of floating hyacinths with no clearly defined channel. The Widow Jones tried a half dozen of them, each time being forced to return to a point she could identify as their starting place.

"Penelope, I can't seem to find the main channel," she confessed at last. "'Pears like we're lost."

"Oh, we can't be!" Penny exclaimed. "We must get back quickly!"

"I'm a-tryin' hard as I kin," the widow said doggedly.

"Let me paddle for awhile," Penny offered. "Your ankle is hurting and you're tired. Just tell me which way to go."

Mrs. Jones indicated a channel which opened in a wide sweep. But before Penny had paddled far, it played out. The sun, sinking lower in the sky, warned the pair how fast time was passing.

For another hour they sought desperately to find the exit channel. Although they took turns at paddling, and used the motor whenever the passageway was not too clogged, they soon became exhausted.

"It hain't no use," the widow said at last. "We're tuckered out, and we're goin' around in circles. We'll pull up on shore and take a little rest."

Penny nodded miserably.

Herons flew lazily over as the couple pulled the boat out on the soft muck. Seeking a high point of land, the widow flung herself flat on her back to rest.

For a time, Penny sat beside her, thinking over everything that had occurred. It was bitterly disappointing to realize that due purely to a stroke of bad luck, Danny Deevers undoubtedly would elude police.

"Mrs. Jones and I may not find our way out of here in twenty-four hours!" she thought. "By that time, the Hawkins' family will have helped him escape!"

Tormented by weariness, Penny stretched out beside the widow. Insects annoyed her for awhile. Then she dozed off.

Much later when the girl awoke, she saw that her companion still slept. The shadow of dusk already was heavy upon the swamp.

Sitting up, Penny gazed resentfully across the water at an almost solid sea of floating plants.

"Such miserable luck!" she muttered. "Of all times to be lost!"

Penny's gaze remained absently upon the hyacinth bed. The plants slowly were drifting westward. At first their movement signified nothing to the girl. Then suddenly, she sprang to her feet.

Excitedly she shook Mrs. Jones by the arm. "The channel!" she cried. "I can see it now! If we move fast, we still may get out of the swamp before night!"

CHAPTER 23 - LOST IN THE HYACINTHS

Mrs. Jones shaded her eyes from the slanting rays of the low-hung sun to gaze for a long moment at the almost motionless hyacinth bed blanketing the water.

"Right ye are, Penelope!" she exclaimed jubilantly. "The channel's plain to see now! Help me git to the boat, and we'll be out o' this tangle."

Once in the skiff, the widow again seized the paddle.

"We gotta inch our way along fer a little," she explained. "If we don't foller the drift o' the bed, we'll be lost agin and that hain't smart."

Steadily the widow shoved the little boat through the water plants, seldom hesitating in choice of the channel.

"I got the feel o' it agin!" she declared happily. "We'll be out o' this in no time!"

However, dark shadows were deepening to blackness when the boat finally came into water open enough to permit use of the motor. Propelled by the engine, the skiff presently approached Lookout Point.

"Let's paddle from here," proposed Penny. "Ezekiel and his sons may be out of the swamp by this time. We don't want them to see us or guess where we've been."

Mrs. Jones shut off the motor and with a tired sigh, offered the paddle to Penny. The channel now was plainly marked and easy to follow, even in semi-darkness. Whenever the girl hesitated, the widow told her which way to steer.

"We're out of it now," Mrs. Jones said as lights of the Hawkins' farmhouse twinkled through the trees. "Reckon Trapper Joe's fit to be tied, we been gone so long!"

Penny allowed the skiff to drift with the current. As it floated past the Hawkins' dock, loud voices came from the direction of the woodshed.

"Sounds like an argument goin' on," observed the widow.

Penny brought the skiff in and made fast to the dock.

"What ye aimin' to do?" the widow inquired in surprise.

"Wait here!" Penny whispered. "I have a hunch what's going on and I must find out!" Before Mrs. Jones could protest, she slipped away into the darkness.

Stealthily the girl approached the woodshed. A voice which she recognized as Ezekiel's, now plainly could be heard.

"Danny, we've fed ye and kept ye here fer days in this woodshed, and it hain't safe!" the speaker said. "Ye gotta git out tonight—now—through the swamp. The river'll take ye out the other end, and ye maybe kin git out o' the state."

"And maybe I'll be caught!" the other voice replied. Penny knew it was Danny Deevers who spoke. "I'm staying right here!"

"Coon and Hod'll guide ye through the swamp, so ye'll be safe enough till ye git to the other side," Ezekiel argued. "We hain't keepin' ye here another day. You got clothes and food and a good chanst to git away."

Penny crept close to the wall of the woodshed. Peering through a small, dirty window on the far side she saw four men seated on kegs in a room dimly lighted by a lantern.

The man facing her plainly was Danny Deevers. Opposite him were Ezekiel and his two sons, both armed with rifles.

"Hain't no use talkin' any more," Ezekiel said flatly. "Ye'r leavin' here tonight, Danny. Maw's fixin' ye a lunch to take."

CHAPTER 23 - LOST IN THE HYACINTHS

"Paw, hain't you forgittin' something?" Coon prodded his father.

"Hain't fergittin' nothin', Coon. Danny, 'fore you go, there's a matter o' money to be settled between us. Ye got $50,000 hid somewheres close, and we want our cut fer hidin' ye out from the police."

Danny laughed unpleasantly.

"You leeches won't get a penny! Not a penny! No one but me knows where that money is, and I'm not telling!"

"Then I calculate Hod and Coon cain't guide ye through the swamp tonight," Ezekiel said coolly. "We got word today the police got a hint ye'r here. We'll help 'em, by turning you in. Hod, git to the phone and call Sheriff Burtwell. Tell 'im we cotched this feller hidin' in the swamp."

"You betcha!" Hod said with alacrity.

"Wait!" Danny stopped him before he could reach the door. "How much of a cut do you dirty blackmailers want?"

"We don't like them words, Danny," Ezekiel said. "All we ask is a fair amount fer the risk we been takin' keepin' ye here."

"How much?"

"A third cut."

"I'll give you $10,000."

"'Tain't enough."

"You'll not get another cent. Take it or leave it. Turn me in if you want to! You'll involve yourself because I'll swear you hid me here."

"We hain't aimin' to be hard on ye, Danny," Ezekiel said hastily. "If we was to agree to the $10,000, kin ye deliver tonight?"

"In fifteen minutes!"

"Ye hain't got the money on ye or hid in the woodshed!"

"No."

"But it's somewheres close. I knowed that."

"If I give you $10,000, you'll guide me through the swamp and help me get away?"

"We will," Ezekiel promised.

"Then get a spade," Danny directed. "The money's buried under a fence post by the creek. I hid it there a year ago before they sent me up. Marked the post with a V-shaped slash of my jackknife."

"Git a spade, Hod," Ezekiel ordered.

Penny waited for no more. Stealing away, she ran to the boat where Mrs. Jones awaited her.

"No questions now!" she said tersely. "Just go as fast as you can and telephone the police! Also call my father, Anthony Parker at the *Riverview Star*! Ask him to come here right away and bring help!"

"You've found Danny Deevers!" the widow guessed, preparing to cast off.

"Yes, and maybe the stolen money! But there's not a second to lose! Let me have your knife, and go as fast as you can!"

Without questioning the odd request, Mrs. Jones gave her the knife and seized a paddle. Penny shoved the skiff far out into the stream.

Then she turned and with a quick glance toward the woodshed, darted to the nearby fence. Rapidly she examined the wooden posts, searching for a V-shaped mark. She could find no slashes of any kind. At any moment she knew the men might emerge from the woodshed and see her.

"Somehow I've got to keep them here until Mrs. Jones brings the police!" she thought. "But how?"

Suddenly an idea came to her. It might not work, but there was an outside chance it would. With desperate haste, she slashed several posts with V-shaped marks.

"That may confuse them for a few minutes," she reasoned. "But not for long."

The door of the woodshed now had opened. Penny dropped flat in the tall weeds near the fence.

Without seeing her, the four men came with a spade and began to inspect posts scarcely a dozen yards from where the girl lay.

"Here's a marked one!" called Hod as he found one of the posts Penny had slashed.

In the darkness the men did not notice that the cut was a fresh one. They began to dig. Silently the work went on until a large hole had been excavated.

"Where's the money?" Ezekiel demanded. "Danny, if ye'r pullin' a fast one—"

"I tell you I buried it under a post!" the other insisted. "Thought it was farther down the fence, but this one was marked."

Ezekiel flashed his lantern full on the post which now had been tilted far over on its side.

"The post's marked," he confirmed. "Fresh new slashes."

"Let's see!" Danny exclaimed. He examined the marking briefly and straightened up. "I never made those cuts! Someone's tricked me!"

Excited by the discovery, the men now moved from post to post. Other slashes were found.

"Here's the one with my mark!" Danny cried, pointing to a post close to where Penny lay hidden. "Who slashed these others? Someone must have learned where I buried the money!"

"It does look kinda bad," said Ezekiel. "But there hain't been no diggin' by this post. Git busy, boys!"

Taking turns, Coon and Hod fell to with the spade. Soon they had uncovered three large tin cans filled with bank notes.

"It's all here!" Danny said jubilantly. "Every dollar!"

Ezekiel blew out the lantern light, looking carefully about the yard. "There hain't no time to divide the money now," he said. "We gotta git you through the swamp, Danny, before them snoopin' police come around. Bring the cans and come on! We're moving out o' here right now!"

Hod shuffled off to get the boat ready as the others each picked up a can and followed quickly.

CHAPTER 24 - UNDER THE FENCE POST

Penny was tormented with worry as she saw the men walk hurriedly to the creek where they launched a flat-bottomed boat belonging to Ezekiel. Soon the craft was lost in the blackness of the swamp channel.

"There goes my chance to catch Danny and recover the stolen money!" she thought. "Oh, what can I do to prevent them from getting away?"

Another boat had been tied up at the dock, but Penny knew she never would dare enter the swamp alone at night. In any case, what chance would she have against four armed men?

"If only Mrs. Jones hadn't hurt her ankle!" she thought. "It will take her a long while to reach a telephone, and help may not get here for an hour!"

As Penny stood gazing gloomily toward the swamp, a shaft of light cut fleetingly across the water. The flash came from the headbeam of a car swinging up the lane to the Hawkins' house.

Not knowing who the arrivals might be, the girl stepped behind a tree to wait. Soon the car came closer, halting with a jerk.

From the sedan stepped Mr. Parker, Salt, and Jerry Livingston. Scarcely believing her eyes, Penny ran to meet them.

"Oh, Dad!" she cried. "You did get Mrs. Jones' message!"

"Message?" he inquired. "Why, no! We were worried because you had been gone so long, so we came out here to find you. What's this all about?"

Penny rapidly told of Danny's flight into the swamp with the stolen money.

"If Mrs. Jones reaches a phone, police should get here any minute!" she added.

"In the meantime, we can't let those men escape!" Mr. Parker exclaimed. "Salt, you stay here and wait for the police. If they don't come in ten minutes, go after them!"

"Sure, Chief!"

"Jerry, you come with me," the publisher directed, untying the boat at the dock. "We'll try to keep those men in sight and mark the way for police to follow."

As Penny followed Jerry into the boat, her father protested quickly:

"Penny, you know you can't go! Danny Deevers is a desperate character."

"If you expect to capture him, you'll have to take me, Dad. They'll probably follow the main channel to Black Island and beyond. You'll be lost before you've covered half the distance."

"All right, come along," Mr. Parker agreed unwillingly.

The boat shoved off into the cool night.

Fairly certain the Hawkins' boat would pass Lookout Point, Penny directed her father and Jerry to row toward it. Soon she caught a glimpse of a moving light through the trees.

"That's their boat!" she exclaimed. "Ezekiel must have lighted his lantern again!"

Scarcely had she spoken than those in the Parker craft were startled to hear a metallic pounding sound from the direction of the Hawkins' farmhouse.

"The dishpan signal!" Penny cried in dismay. "We forgot about Mrs. Hawkins! Evidently she saw us leave the dock and is warning her menfolks! Now they'll know someone is following them!"

Mr. Parker's face became very grave as the girl revealed the significance of the signal. Penny also told him what she and Mrs. Jones had learned on Black Island.

"Unarmed, we've no chance to capture those men," he commented. "Our best bet is to keep them in sight, marking the trail well for police to follow."

"And hope they do," Jerry added grimly.

Breaking overhanging tree limbs, and slashing trunks to blaze the trail, the party passed Lookout Point.

When they were perhaps twenty yards beyond the isle, a bullet suddenly whizzed through the trees, only a few feet above their heads. The shot had been fired from the island.

"Duck low!" Mr. Parker ordered. "They've taken refuge there!"

As the trio remained motionless, another bullet whined over their heads.

"Dad, it's only a trick to divert us!" Penny whispered. "One of the Hawkins' boys probably has stayed on the island, but the others have gone on! See through the trees!"

Jerry and Mr. Parker peered where she pointed and caught the brief flash of lantern light.

"You're right!" the publisher agreed. "Row on, Jerry! We're practically out of range of Lookout Point now."

The boat pushed on. A light mist was rising from the water and the night was very dark. Shielded by the blackness, the trio slipped away without becoming the target for another bullet.

"We've got to keep that other boat in sight!" Mr. Parker said grimly. "If we lose it, we may never find our way out of this place!"

"And if we catch up, we may never be allowed to get out!" Jerry observed.

Penny, who scarcely had taken her eyes from the moving point of light ahead, now exclaimed:

"They've blown out the lantern!"

"Then they may have seen us," Mr. Parker muttered. "If only we were armed!"

Cautiously, the party proceeded. A few minutes later as the boat passed a high point of land several hundred yards deeper in the swamp, another bullet whizzed dangerously close overhead.

"Where'd that come from?" Mr. Parker demanded, shielding Penny with his body.

Jerry pointed to the high point of land on the right hand side of the channel. "Those birds must have pulled up there and hope to pick us off!" he whispered.

Still another bullet whined close over their heads, splashing as it struck the water.

Hurriedly Jerry steered the boat into a clump of bushes. All remained motionless and silent.

Bullets kept splattering the water, though farther away.

"We're in a pocket!" Mr. Parker fumed. "They can pick us off almost at will if we stay here!"

"What's our move, Chief?" Jerry asked anxiously.

"Let's back-track to the farm and await police. It's the only thing we can do."

As a lull came in the firing, Jerry shoved off and rowed rapidly back toward Lookout Point. All crouched low in the boat, but no shots were fired at them.

"They're satisfied we've turned back," Mr. Parker said. "That was what they wanted."

However, as Lookout Point loomed up, the party was disconcerted to see a tall, lean figure silhouetted there.

"Stay where ye be, or I'll fire!" the man shouted. "If ye try to pass, I'll sink ye'r boat!"

"It's Ezekiel!" Penny whispered.

Mr. Parker signaled Jerry to row back out of range. "We've trapped ourselves between two fires!" he muttered in disgust. "Ezekiel stayed here on purpose to guard the channel while the others make their getaway."

"Danny could be captured easily if only we could get word to Salt and the police," Jerry added.

Penny and her father nodded gloomily. Salt, they knew, would follow their trail into the swamp as soon as police reached the Hawkins' farm. But Ezekiel from his point of vantage, would fire upon them before they realized they were running into danger.

"We could chance it and try to push through," Jerry proposed.

"Ezekiel's not bluffing," Mr. Parker replied. "Those first shots were a warning. If we attempt to pass now, he may shoot to kill."

"There's one way we might bring help," Jerry said, staring thoughtfully at the grim figure guarding the channel.

"How?" Penny demanded eagerly.

"You and your father would have to wait on the bank and let me take the boat."

"Too risky," Mr. Parker said. "You never could get through."

"I'd try an old trick," the reporter explained. "When Ezekiel starts shooting, I'll upset the boat and float beneath it until I'm past the point. I'm a good swimmer and can hold my breath a long while. Anyway, after the boat is upset, there will be a pocket of air beneath it."

CHAPTER 24 - UNDER THE FENCE POST

"It might not work."

"Let me try it. Unless we get word through, Danny Deevers is certain to escape."

After lengthy whispered debate, Mr. Parker reluctantly agreed to the plan. Retreating beyond Ezekiel's range of vision, the boat brought up on shore where Penny and her father alighted.

"Wait right here!" Jerry directed. "I'll be back for you in a few minutes!"

Boldly the reporter pushed off alone in the boat, drifting down channel. Before he had gone many yards, Ezekiel challenged him.

"Ye come another foot, and I'm lettin' ye have it!"

Jerry shouted an insult. But as Ezekiel's gun spat, he upset the boat, disappearing beneath it.

"Oh, Dad!" Penny murmured anxiously, watching the craft float slowly downstream past the point. "Was Jerry really hit?"

"I don't think so."

"What if Ezekiel fires again?"

"He can't harm Jerry now unless he's forced to come up for air."

Anxiously the trio watched the overturned boat. Unless Jerry had found the pocket of air, they knew not even an expert swimmer could remain so long underwater.

Finally the boat was beyond their range of vision, blotted out by darkness.

"Jerry has nerve!" Mr. Parker commented. "He's safely through now."

Nervously the publisher and Penny kept attentive watch of Lookout Point, fearful lest Ezekiel launch a boat and try to capture them. To their intense relief, the swamper made no such move. Occasionally, they caught brief glimpses of him as he shifted his position.

Directing all their attention upon Ezekiel, Penny and her father paid less heed to the channel. Near them was a passage so narrow a boatman could have reached out to touch bushes on either side.

A slight rustling sound close by suddenly startled Penny.

"What was that, Dad?" she whispered.

"Only the wind," he reassured her. "Ezekiel's still over there on the point. We're safe enough."

Even as he made the observation, a boat moved out from behind the screen of leaves. Penny and her father found themselves gazing directly into the barrel of a gun.

"Safe, are ye?" Coon Hawkins shouted in glee. "We got ye now, ye sneakin' snoopers! Ye won't do no more spyin' in this swamp!"

With him in the boat were his brother and Danny Deevers.

"Git in!" Coon ordered sharply.

"What will you do with us?" Mr. Parker asked, trying to stall for time.

"We're takin' ye to Black Island," Coon replied, prodding the publisher with his gun. "Move!"

One glance at the grim, determined faces of the men convinced Mr. Parker and Penny it would be folly to resist. Silently they entered the boat.

Hod pushed off and the craft moved noiselessly away into the night.

CHAPTER 25 - OUTWITTED

For an endless time, it seemed, the party moved deeper and deeper into the swamp. As the night became cool, Penny shivered and leaned close to her father.

Worn out, she slumped against his shoulder and finally dropped into a light sleep. When she opened her eyes, a pale moon had risen over the treetops, lighting the way.

At last, the boat brought up in a cove at Black Island.

"We're leavin' ye here," Coon informed the prisoners. "Maybe ye'll be found tomorrer or next week after we're safe away. If not, well hit's jest too bad!"

Penny and her father were hustled ashore. Despite vigorous struggles, Mr. Parker then was bound by Coon and Hod and lashed with his back to a tree. Before Penny could be treated likewise, a dog began to bark.

"It's Bones!" she cried. "You have him here on the island!"

"Sure, we got him," agreed Hod indifferently.

Penny loudly called the dog's name and he bounded through the brush toward her. His long hair was matted with burs, but he seemed in good health and well fed.

Before Penny could get her hands on him, Coon seized and tossed the dog into the boat.

"Please let me keep Bones!" she pleaded.

"Yeah, leave the dog on the island," growled Danny Deevers. "He'll be a bother to us."

"Git the dog then, gal," commanded Coon.

Penny scrambled aboard the Hawkins' boat. Bones had crawled far forward.

As she bent to gather him into her arms, her hand encountered a gunny sack. Inside were wrapped three hard, round objects.

"The cans of stolen money!" Penny thought, her pulse jumping.

Without considering the punishment that might be meted out to her, she seized the sack.

"Hey!" shouted Coon furiously. "Drop those cans!"

He sprang aboard, intending to strike her a stunning blow. Penny leaped for shore, but the boat shot from beneath her feet.

Misbalanced, it went over, tumbling Coon and herself into the water.

But as Penny went down, she clung fast to the cans of money. Fortunately, the muddy water was shallow. Her feet touched bottom and she came up sputtering.

Hod and Danny started for the boat on a run, intending to seize her. Suddenly, they halted, listening intently.

"What was that?" Danny demanded. "Thought I heard the splash of a paddle!"

"Two boats are coming!" Hod cried hoarsely. "Police!"

"Come on!" ordered Danny, seizing one end of the overturned boat. "Help me right this! We'll still get away! The girl goes with us as a hostage!"

Hod grasped Penny's arm, while his brother aided Danny with the boat.

"No go!" ordered a cool voice from the thicket. "I gotta you covered!"

As the three men whirled around, Tony, rifle in hand, came out of the deep shadows.

"Stand-a by tree!" he commanded, motioning with the gun. "Keep-a hands up!"

Sullenly the three men obeyed. Tony guarded them closely until policemen swarmed over the island.

In the first boat were Salt, Jerry and several officers. Behind came a second boat, also loaded with policemen.

CHAPTER 25 - OUTWITTED

Danny, Hod and Coon quickly were handcuffed and placed under heavy guard. Tony then helped Penny release her father.

"What about Ezekiel?" the publisher asked. "We ought to get him too!"

Jerry revealed that the swamper already had been taken prisoner at Lookout Island. Two policemen had remained behind to guard both him and his wife.

"Oh, Jerry! I'm so glad you got through safely!" Penny declared. "Did you have any trouble?"

"Not a bit," he replied. "When I reached the farmhouse, police already were there. Mrs. Jones had telephoned them."

"We arrested Mrs. Hawkins," Salt took up the story. "Then we captured Ezekiel at Lookout Point, and followed your boat here. Most of the time we had you in sight, though from a long distance."

Penny was greatly relieved to be able to turn over the three cans of stolen money to police officers. By lantern light a hasty count was made and it was disclosed that a sizeable portion of the funds were missing.

However, when Danny Deevers, Hod, and Coon were searched, a large roll of bills was found in the escaped convict's pocket.

"This should account for it all," said the police officer, taking charge of the money and adding it to the other. "So you were trying to double-cross your pals, Danny? Figured on keeping the lion's share!"

Danny glared at the officer, refusing to answer.

"So you got nothing to say, eh?" the officer prodded. "Maybe you'll be in a more talkative mood when we get you back to the pen. You'll do double time for skipping out!"

Danny's sullen gaze fastened briefly on Jerry Livingston.

"I got only one regret!" he muttered. "I wish I'd slugged that guy harder when I had the chance!"

"May I ask the prisoners a question or two?" Penny asked the officer in charge.

"Sure, go ahead," he nodded. "If you get anything out of 'em, you're good."

Penny knew that Danny, a hardened criminal, would never give her any information, so she centered her attention upon Hod and Coon.

At first, they only eyed her sullenly, refusing to speak. But after she had pointed out that a more cooperative attitude might bring a lighter sentence, they showed a little interest.

"How did you come to be mixed up with Danny?" she asked. "Were you all together in the big bank robbery?"

The question drew fire from Hod.

"No, we weren't!" he shouted. "We never even knowed where Danny hid the money until tonight!"

"Then why were you so willing to hide and help him?"

"'Cause him and Paw always was good friends! Danny come here, saying the cops was after him and would we give him some clothes and hide him fer a day or two? So like fools we was, we took him in and kept him in the woodshed. It would have been safe enough if you hadn't come snoopin' around!"

"No doubt you all would have gone free if you hadn't made the mistake of keeping Louise's dog," Penny retorted. "However, you seem to forget you were operating a still illegally."

"Anyone else in on that business?" the policeman cut in. "How'd they market the stuff?"

"Through a trucker at Hartwell City," Penny exclaimed. "I think they called him Ike."

"Too bad the bird will go free, while these eggs do a stretch in the pen," commented the policeman. "You can depend on it though, they'll never do the smart thing and turn him in."

"Oh, wouldn't we?" growled Hod. "He was no pal o' ourn!"

"Would it git us a lighter stretch if we was to turn him in?" asked Coon craftily.

"It might."

"His name's Ike Glanzy and he stays mostly at the Devon Club in Hartwell City," Hod volunteered.

"We'll pick him up," said the policeman. "Depend on it, he'll be behind bars before another twenty-four hours. Now let's get out of here!"

As the boats began to load for the return trip through the swamp, Penny glanced anxiously about the tiny clearing.

"Where's Tony?" she asked.

No one had seen the Italian lad in the last few minutes. Unnoticed, he had slipped away into the interior of the island.

"We can't leave without Tony!" Penny protested. "He's afraid he'll be sent back to Italy, so he's run off somewhere!"

"He can't have gone far," said Salt. "We should be able to find him."

However, an intensive search of the bushes nearby did not reveal the missing youth. At last, in desperation, Penny called his name several times.

"Please, Tony, give yourself up!" she pleaded. "You won't be sent back to Italy! I'm sure of it! Please come out of hiding!"

"If that appeal doesn't fetch him, nothing will," said Salt. "We've held up the party too long now, Penny. We've got to shove off."

Penny nodded disconsolately. When the photographer took her arm and started back toward the waiting boats, she did not resist.

But after they had gone a few yards, she abruptly halted.

"Tony *is* close by!" she insisted. "I can *feel* that he's watching us now! Listen! Don't you hear the bushes rustling?"

"I do hear something. Maybe it's only an animal."

"Tony," Penny made one last appeal, "if you're back there in the dark, please come out. Don't you understand? You were a hero tonight—you saved the day by popping out of the bushes at just the right moment. Please don't fail me now."

The leaves were stirring again. Then, to Penny's joy, the branches parted. Grinning sheepishly, Tony shuffled out.

"You call-a me?" he grinned.

"Oh, Tony!" Penny seized his arm and held fast. "We've practically torn out the lining of our lungs, trying to find you! Come on! You're going back with us!"

"Not to Immigration mens!"

"Oh, don't worry about that now, Tony! My father has a little influence and he'll help you all he can. Besides, you're almost certain to win a portion of the reward offered for Danny Deevers' capture."

"Money no good if they send-a me back to Italy!" Tony said stubbornly. "Want-a stay in America. I work-a hard. Go to school!"

"I think perhaps it can be arranged," Penny promised recklessly. With Salt's help, she kept steering the boy toward the boat. "After all you've done tonight, Immigration authorities couldn't be hard-hearted enough to refuse you citizenship."

Tony allowed himself to be persuaded and entered a boat with Penny and other members of the party. After a long and tiring but uneventful trip through the swamp, the Hawkins' farm finally was reached.

At the farmhouse, Mrs. Hawkins and her husband were being held prisoners by other policemen. Also waiting were the Widow Jones and Trapper Joe Scoville, whom she had summoned.

"Praises be! The police got to ye in time!" the widow exclaimed, giving Penny's hand an affectionate squeeze. "If harm had befallen ye this night, I never would have fergiven myself fer having taken ye into the swamp."

"Maybe what happened'll teach ye a lesson, but I got m' doubts," interposed the old trapper with a chuckle. "Wimmin is mighty stubborn critters!"

As Mrs. Hawkins and her husband were led out of the house, the woman caught sight of her two sons handcuffed to officers. "Hod! Coon!" she screamed hysterically.

She tried to break away from the policemen who held her, and would have attacked Danny Deevers had they not restrained her.

"Ye'r the one who got us into this mess!" she accused the convict. "I hope they lock ye up fer the rest o' y'er life!"

Much later, after all the prisoners had been confined in Riverview jail, Mr. Parker and Penny obtained custody of Tony. Arrangements were made so that the lad might remain in the Parker home while Immigration officials considered his case.

The Italian boy proved to be a perfect guest. Not only did he help about the house and yard, but he never overlooked an opportunity to improve his education. Many a time Penny or her father came upon him in the library, reading a book.

CHAPTER 25 - OUTWITTED

"If he doesn't get to stay, it will be a crime!" the girl declared. "Oh, why doesn't the Immigration department reach a decision?"

Despite Penny's fretting, weeks dragged on and still Tony's case hung fire. Many telegrams went back and forth between Riverview and Washington, D. C. So involved did the affair become that even Mr. Parker began to lose hope the boy could be kept in America.

But at last word came that the last bit of red tape had been cut. A high immigration official had ruled that although it was irregular, Tony might remain in Riverview, providing someone would guarantee his support.

Mr. Parker willingly signed the necessary papers. A job next was in order, but this Penny easily arranged through Mark Fiello, the hamburger shop man.

As for Danny Deevers, the convict promptly was returned to prison, and the stolen $50,000 turned over to the Third Federal Bank.

In due time, Ezekiel, Coon, Hod and Mrs. Hawkins were convicted on charges of harboring a fugitive from justice. At their trial, evidence also was introduced, showing they had operated a still illegally.

For many days the *Riverview Star* carried front page stories of the happenings. Penny wrote several of the articles, while others carried Jerry's byline.

"The best part of all is that with Danny behind bars, you'll no longer be in danger," the girl remarked one day to the reporter. "He really was out to get you."

"I suppose so," Jerry agreed, "but I never was much worried. Danny's real motive in coming back to Riverview was to recover the hidden $50,000. Running into me—and particularly you—proved his undoing."

In days that followed, Penny drove many times to the swamp to see Mrs. Jones and Trapper Joe. Both rejoiced that Danny Deevers and the Hawkins family could cause no more trouble.

One afternoon as the girl paid the widow a long call, they fell to talking over their swamp experiences.

"It was mighty excitin' out there—you and me in the boat," Mrs. Jones recalled. "Now that it's all over, I hain't ashamed to say I was plenty skeered we'd never git out o' the swamp alive."

"So was I," grinned Penny.

"Revenooers was in yesterday to smash up Ezekiel's still."

"They were!"

"Yep, and they got track o' that trucker who was in so thick with the Hawkins boys." The widow sighed and pulled aside a kitchen curtain to gaze thoughtfully toward the swamp. "Well, I reckon the last bit o' evil's been driv' away from Black Island. From now on, the land'll jest lie there and belong to the wind and the rain."

"And to us," Penny added softly.

The widow nodded as her gaze lingered long on the fringe of towering pines. "One o' these days, when the spirit moves us, we'll go back there," she promised. "The swamp always belongs to them that loves it!"

THE CRY AT MIDNIGHT

"Gaze deep into the glass. Deep—Deep...."

CHAPTER 1 - MIDNIGHT AT THE GATE

After a long, tiring climb, the two friends, Penny Parker and Jerry Livingston, had reached the summit of Knob Hill, far above the city of Riverview.

Now as they paused in the moonlight to catch their breath, the slim, golden-haired girl bent to adjust the irons of her skis before making a swift descent to the clearing below.

"We'll not have many more glorious skiing nights like this one," she said regretfully. "Anytime now, the weather is due to turn warm."

Jerry, a reporter at the *Riverview Star*, nodded as his gaze swept the snowy hillside, unmarked save for the herring-bone tracks made by their own skis.

Tall and muscular, he was several years older than Penny, who attended high school. The corners of his mouth turned up slightly, giving him the appearance of a semi-amused spectator of the world's goings-on.

"Jerry, it's getting late," she reminded him. "This will have to be our last run tonight. Ready?"

"Okay, I'll race you to the valley!" the reporter challenged. "Let's go!"

Digging in their poles, they flashed off down the hillside. Though they started together, Penny soon forged ahead, descending the steep slope in graceful, curving Christiania turns.

Beneath the mellow moon, snow crystals were brilliant with light. Every pine bristled with glowing icicles. Penny, feeling the rush of wind on her cheek, drew in her breath and was glad to be alive.

With effortless ease, she swung her hips for the sharp turns between the trees. Finally reaching the clearing, she brought up with a spectacular jump-turn and waited for Jerry who was close behind.

"You're getting faster every trip!" he praised. "I haven't a chance any more!"

Penny laughed, and with her arm linked in his, glided on to the fire where a group of noisy young people were roasting wieners and boiling coffee.

"Time you're getting back!" declared Louise Sidell, a dark-haired girl in heavy red woolen snowsuit. She was on her knees in the snow, feeding hickory chips to the cherry red fire.

Louise considered Penny her dearest friend. Though she would not have admitted it, she was slightly green-eyed whenever another person claimed any of her chum's attention.

"M—m! That coffee smells delicious!" Penny cried, sniffing the fragrant aroma. "I'm starved too!"

She and Jerry made their own sandwiches and poured the steaming beverage. After they had finished eating, the reporter suggested one last climb to Knob Hill.

"It's nearly midnight," said Louise, before Penny could accept. "Oughtn't we to be starting home?"

Immediately a loud chorus of protest arose from other members of the party. Penny looked at her wristwatch regretfully.

"I hate to break up the party," she said. "But I promised Dad I would be in fairly early tonight. Lou and I will run along, and the rest of you stay."

"I'll take you home if you must leave," Jerry offered.

"Oh, Penny has her car," said Louise quickly. "It's parked on the roadside just over the hill."

"Yes," Penny added, "we'll ski down there and be home in a few minutes."

"You're not afraid to go alone?" Jerry asked teasingly.

"Afraid?" The question caught Penny by surprise. "Why should we be?"

"You'll have to pass the old deserted Abbington Monastery to reach your car. It's a spooky place at night!"

Penny arose and slipped her wrists through the loops of her ski poles. "Now don't put ideas into our heads!" she chuckled. "It's just another building."

THE CRY AT MIDNIGHT

"Sure you don't want me to go along?" urged Jerry.

"Of course not! Louise and I can handle any ghost we'll meet tonight!"

The girls glided away, pausing at the top of the slope to wave goodbye to their friends. Then they shot down the hill on a trail which skirted a dense grove of pine.

Ahead loomed the gloomy old Abbington Monastery, a structure of moldy stone enclosed by a high brick wall. To the right, inside the enclosure, was an ancient graveyard, many of its white stones at rakish angles.

Penny studied the building with keen interest as she waited for Louise to catch up with her. Built generations earlier, the property first had been used by an order of Black Friars bound to the vows of poverty and obedience.

Later, the monastery had been taken over by an order of nuns, but as the buildings deteriorated, the property had been abandoned. For ten years now, it had stood unoccupied.

"Ugly old place!" puffed Louise, pausing beside her chum to catch her breath. "All the windows broken—why, that's funny!"

"What is?" demanded Penny.

"The windows aren't broken! They've been replaced!"

"Probably the owner did it to save his property from going completely to wreck and ruin. Wonder who owns the place anyhow?"

"The last I heard, it was sold at public auction for taxes. I think a real estate man bought it for a song."

"Then maybe he intends to fix it up for rent or sale," Penny remarked. "But who would want to live in that ancient shell? Somehow, the place gives me the creeps!"

Louise was staring hard at an upstairs window of the distant building.

"Penny!" she exclaimed. "I saw a moving light just then!"

"Where?"

Louise pointed to the window high on the stone wall of the monastery.

"I don't see anything," replied Penny. "You must have imagined it."

"I did not! The light is gone now. But I saw it plainly. It may have been from a lantern. Someone was moving from room to room!"

"Maybe it was a reflection of moonlight then." Undisturbed, Penny removed her skis. Carefully placing the running surfaces together, she threw them over her left shoulder.

Far away, in the city of Riverview, a tower clock began to chime the hour of midnight.

"Penny!" insisted Louise in a half-whisper. "I did see a light! Maybe the old monastery is haunted—"

"Now hush!" Penny silenced her. "What are you trying to do? Work up a case of nerves?"

"But—"

"Just climb out of those skis and come on, my pet." Penny moved briskly away. "We're late now."

"Wait for me!" Frantically, Louise fumbled with her ski irons. "Don't leave me here alone!"

"Then not another word about ghosts!" Penny chided.

However, she waited patiently until her chum had removed the skis. The two girls then walked rapidly toward the roadside where the car had been parked. No longer could they see the friendly campfire in the valley. As they drew closer to the monastery, towering pines blotted out the moonlight.

Like a powerful magnet, the old stone building drew their gaze.

Deep snow, glittering with an eerie blue lustre, lay heavy on the high boundary wall. In the deserted garden beyond the gatehouse, several statues also were covered with soft white shrouds.

Louise clutched her chum's hand and urged her to a faster pace.

Then suddenly, with one accord, the girls halted.

Directly ahead, at the front entrance to the monastery, a big rusty gate stood slightly ajar!

"It's open!" whispered Louise. "Why, never before have I seen that gate unlocked!"

For an instant, Penny too was slightly unnerved. But she replied steadily: "What of it? Perhaps someone has moved in."

While Louise watched uneasily, she walked to the gate, fingering the rusty chain which dangled in the snow.

Then boldly, she pushed the gate farther open.

"Don't go in there!" Louise warned, her voice sharp with anxiety. "Please come on."

CHAPTER 1 - MIDNIGHT AT THE GATE

Penny's ears were deaf to the plea. She stared intently at a trail of footprints which led from where she stood to a circular stone gatehouse only a few yards away. The marks were very large and had been made by a man's heavy boot.

"Lou—" she began, but the words froze on her lips.

From inside the monastery came a shrill, piercing scream. As the girls huddled together, the sound died slowly away.

Then a silence, even more terrifying, fell upon the grounds.

CHAPTER 2 - "NO TRESPASSING"

"Someone *is* inside that building!" Penny exclaimed, recovering from startled surprise.

Tensely, the girls waited, but the sound was not repeated.

"It was a woman's scream," Louise whispered after a moment. Nervously, she clung to her chum's hand as they stood in the shadow of the big iron gate. "What can be happening in there?"

Penny stared at the dark monastery, uncertain what to do. Nowhere was a light visible, yet she felt that not only was the building occupied, but also that alert eyes were watching them from somewhere in the gloomy interior.

"Someone may be in trouble and need help," she said in an unsteady voice. "Let's rap on the door and ask."

"At this time of night?" Louise tugged at her chum's hand, trying to pull her away. "Let's go, Penny! It's really none of our affair what goes on here."

"But someone may be ill and in need of a doctor."

"It wasn't that type of scream," Louise replied with a shiver. "That cry gave me the creeps!"

Penny allowed herself to be pulled from the gate, only to pause and gaze again at the darkened windows of the ancient monastery.

The only daughter of a newspaper owner, she had been trained to inquire the who, when, why, where, and how of anything unusual. Penny never willingly passed up an opportunity to obtain a good news story for the *Riverview Star*. She knew that if the old monastery were occupied after standing deserted so many years, the readers of her father's paper would be interested.

Furthermore, she reasoned, a scream from a darkened house, always called for investigation.

"Louise," she said with sudden decision. "We can't leave without trying to find out what's wrong here! I'm going inside!"

"Oh, Penny—please don't! This place is so far from other houses. If anything should happen—"

"Something *has* happened," replied Penny grimly. "You wait here, Lou. I'll be right back."

Despite her chum's protest, she returned to the big iron gate, and pushing it farther open, stepped inside the grounds.

Intuition warned Penny to proceed cautiously. She sensed rather than saw a dark figure crouching in the arched doorway of the circular stone gatehouse to the right of the snow-banked driveway.

Before she could decide whether the form was real or a product of her imagination, a large, savage dog darted from inside the gatehouse. His low growl warned her it might be dangerous to attempt to pass.

"Come back!" Louise called anxiously. "He'll tear you apart!"

Though no coward, a second glance at the dog convinced Penny that the animal had been trained to guard the property. Rapidly, she backed away.

Her hand was on the latch of the gate, when in the gatehouse doorway, she beheld a grotesque, deformed human figure.

The sight so startled Penny that for an instant she forgot the dog.

Plainly silhouetted against the gray stone was a hulk of a man with large head and twisted back made unsightly by a hump.

Though his eyes were full upon the girl, he remained motionless, speaking no word.

"Call off your dog!" Penny said sharply.

Only then did the figure move from the doorway into the moonlight.

"Quiet, Bruno!" he ordered in a rasping voice. "Lie down!"

CHAPTER 2 - "NO TRESPASSING"

As the dog obeyed, Penny caught her first plain glimpse of the deformed man's face. His skin was heavily lined and fell in deep folds at his stocky neck. But it was the dark, intent eyes which sent a shiver down her spine.

"Good evening," she said uneasily.

The gateman did not respond to the greeting. Instead, he demanded gruffly:

"What you doin' on this property?"

"Why, I was only investigating because the gate was unlocked," replied Penny. "I didn't know the house was occupied."

"You know it now. See that sign!" The gateman turned on his flashlight, focusing it upon a freshly painted placard tacked to a nearby tree.

The sign read, "No Trespassing."

"I'm sorry," Penny apologized, but stood her ground. "Are you the new owner of this place?"

"No, I ain't. I'm the gateman."

"Then who has taken over the building?"

"What's it to you?" the hunchback demanded unpleasantly.

"I'm interested, that's all."

"This place is being turned into an institution," the hunchback informed her. "The new owner moved in yesterday. Now git along, so I can lock the gate."

The gateman's eagerness to be rid of her made Penny all the more determined to remain until her curiosity was satisfied.

"Perhaps I fancied it," she remarked, "but a moment ago, I thought I heard a shrill scream from inside the building."

"You may have heard the howl of the wind."

"What wind?" Penny inquired pointedly. "It's a comparatively quiet night. I distinctly heard a scream."

"Then you got better ears than I have," the gateman muttered. "Will you go now, or do you want me to call the master?"

"I wish you would!"

Grumbling to himself, the hunchback stepped into the gatehouse and pressed a button which rang a bell inside the building.

A light went on in a downstairs room, and a moment later the front door opened. Framed on the threshold stood a very tall man in dark, hooded robe.

"What's wrong, Winkey?" he called. "You rang?"

"There's a girl here wants to see you," shouted the hunchback. "She says she heard a scream and wants to know how-come."

Treading lightly in the loose snow, the thin man came down the driveway to the gate. His long, brown robes were impressive, his demeanor pious. Penny suddenly felt very foolish indeed.

"Is anything wrong?" he asked in a kindly, silken-smooth voice.

"This girl's tryin' to get in," announced Winkey. "Says she heard a scream."

The hooded monk studied Penny with an intent gaze.

"You live near here?" he inquired.

"In Riverview. I was out skiing with a few friends when I passed this old building and heard the scream. Your gateman tried to tell me it was only the wind."

"My child, doubtlessly you did hear a scream," the monk replied. "It was Old Julia, a poor woman, who unfortunately sometimes becomes disturbed in her mind."

"This isn't a mental institution?" gasped Penny, regretting that her curiosity ever had taken her inside the grounds.

"No, my child," responded the monk. "Winkey should have explained. We have opened up the old monastery for the purpose of restoring an ancient order in which members dedicate themselves to a life of poverty, good will, and charity."

"The one you call Old Julia—she also is a member?"

The monk sighed deeply. "Old Julia is only an unfortunate whose twisted mind never can be healed by doctors. Because she had no home—no friends, I have taken her beneath my roof."

"I see," nodded Penny. "I'm very sorry to have troubled you."

"A natural mistake, my child. Is there anything else you wish to know? We have no secrets here—only serene faith and hope for a better world."

"I might inquire your name."

"Members of my flock call me Father Benedict. My baptismal name is Jay Highland. And yours?"

"Penny Parker. My father owns the *Riverview Star*."

"A newspaper?" The monk's inquiry was sharp.

"One of the best in the city," Penny said proudly.

"Your father sent you here, perhaps?"

"Oh, no! I was just passing by and noticed the buildings were occupied."

"To be sure," murmured the monk. "I trust you will use discretion in mentioning our work here. Should we become too well known, a path will be beaten to our door, and the privacy of our order will be no more."

"I'll scarcely mention it," Penny half-heartedly promised. "Good night."

Retreating through the gate, she closed it behind her.

A few paces away, Louise, who had heard only part of the conversation, waited in the darkness.

"Who were those men?" she demanded, falling into step with her chum. "What did you learn?"

Penny repeated everything Jay Highland had told her.

"He seemed rather nice," she added. "But when you sum it up, he didn't tell much about the order he is founding here."

"And the scream?"

"Oh, he explained that. It seems an old woman named Julia lives in the institution. She's demented."

"Must be a nice place!" The girls now had reached the car and Louise stood aside for her chum to unlock the door. Quickly they stowed their skis and poles in the rear and then Penny started the motor which popped and sputtered in the frosty air.

"It's snowing again," she observed, switching on the windshield wiper. "We didn't get started a minute too soon."

Before the girls had traveled a quarter of a mile, huge, wet flakes pelted the glass. Once as the wiper stuck, Penny had to get out and clear the windshield with a handkerchief.

"This is really getting awful!" she exclaimed, as they drove slowly on along the narrow, curving country road. "I can hardly see."

"Be careful," Louise warned a moment later. "You're close to the ditch."

Penny brought the wheels back onto the main track. But a dozen yards farther on, she saw directly in her path, a bent figure struggling along under the weight of a heavy suitcase. Her head was held low against the wind and snow.

Unaware of the approaching car, the pedestrian was walking almost in the center of the road.

"Look out, Penny!" screamed Louise as she too saw the girl with the heavy burden. "You'll run her down!"

CHAPTER 3 - STRANGER OF THE STORM

Penny swerved the steering wheel, missing the girl by inches. Somewhat shaken by the near-accident, she pulled up at the roadside.

"My, that was close!" exclaimed Louise. Lowering the side window of the coupe, she gazed curiously at the snowy figure, plodding through the drifts.

"Maybe we ought to offer her a lift to Riverview," said Penny. "Whoever she is, she shouldn't be walking alone at this time of night—and with a heavy suitcase too."

"But should we pick up a hitchhiker, Penny? It might not be safe."

"I don't like to do it as a rule, but this is different. It's storming hard and she looks about our age."

Debating no longer, Penny thrust her head through the window opening and called: "Want a ride?"

The girl with the suitcase had moved into the glare of the headlights. She turned toward the car with a startled expression. Penny and Louise saw that she was thinly clad in a light weight coat, and wore no galoshes.

To their astonishment, the girl shook her head and kept on walking.

"Well, what do you know!" exclaimed Penny. "She's more afraid to ride with us than we were to pick her up. She may not realize we're just a couple of school girls."

"She shouldn't be out in this storm dressed as she is," declared Louise, now concerned for the stranger. "Ask her again."

Penny shifted into low gear and pulled alongside. "Please, can't we give you a lift into the city?" she urged.

The girl stopped then, resting her suitcase in the roadway. A breath of wind swept a lock of dark hair across her thin face. Impatiently she brushed it aside and murmured: "No, no, thank you."

Penny would have driven on, but the voice held a hint of tears. It occurred to her that the girl might be running away from home—certainly she was bewildered and in trouble.

"Don't be foolish!" she exclaimed. "This snow is coming down heavier every minute. Of course, you want a ride." She flung the car door wide open.

A moment longer the girl hesitated. Then without a word, she swung the suitcase into the automobile and squeezed in beside Louise. However, she scarcely glanced at the girls, but centered her sober gaze on the snowflakes which danced across the windshield.

The car moved ahead. "Going far?" inquired Penny.

"I—I don't know."

"You don't know!" Penny twisted her head sideways to stare at the girl. She started to ask a question, then thinking better of it, remained silent.

Louise, however, could not allow the odd reply to pass unchallenged.

"Why, you must know where you're going!" she exclaimed. "Do you mean you have no home, or are running away?"

"I have a home," the girl replied shortly. "I only meant I haven't decided where I'll go or what I'll do when I reach Riverview. That's the name of the closest place, isn't it?"

Penny nodded. "Apparently, you come from some distance away," she remarked.

The girl made no reply.

"May we introduce ourselves?" said Louise, determined to learn the stranger's name. "This is Penny Parker, and I'm Louise Sidell."

Only by a brief nod did the girl acknowledge the introduction. She did not volunteer her own name. Her failure to do so, obviously was deliberate.

"Do you live near here?" Louise inquired.

The stranger squirmed uncomfortably. "I'm sorry," she said. "I don't feel like answering questions. That's why I didn't want to accept a ride."

Louise took the reply for a rebuke. "I certainly didn't mean to be personal," she returned stiffly. "Excuse it, please. Dreadful weather!"

The topic fell flat. No further attempt at conversation was made.

Penny kept close watch of the road, for the heavy, wet snow made visibility very poor. She was greatly relieved when they reached the outskirts of the city and a wide boulevard which followed the curve of the frozen river.

Seeing the lights of Riverview, the strange girl began to watch the streets intently.

"Just let me out anywhere," she said presently.

"Anywhere?" Penny repeated.

"Will we pass the river docks on this road?"

"Yes, at the next turn."

"Then let me off there, please."

"The river docks!" exclaimed Louise. "At this time of night? No boats are running and there are no houses or business places close by. Only deserted fish houses and the like."

"Please, that's where I want to get off."

Penny and Louise gave up trying to figure out their strange passenger. At the next turn in the road, they pulled up near a dimly lighted street corner.

The girl opened the car door and reached for her suitcase.

"Thanks for the ride," she said in a low voice. "I'm sorry if I seemed rude and unfriendly. There are things I can't explain."

Before Penny or Louise could answer, the car door closed firmly in their faces.

"Well, how do you like that?" the latter demanded furiously. "If she isn't a cool cucumber!"

"She may be running away from home," Penny said, frowning. "Why otherwise, would she refuse to tell her name?"

"And why did she insist in getting out on this corner, of all places?"

"It's a bad section of town, Louise. No one seems to be about, but even so, a girl shouldn't be wandering around here alone."

"We tried to warn her. She seemed to know what she wanted to do."

"All the same, I feel sort of responsible," Penny returned uneasily. "I hope nothing happens to her."

After leaving the car, the girl walked toward the river. Now at the corner, she paused beneath a street light, and glanced back.

"She's waiting for us to go on!" Penny guessed shrewdly. "For some reason, she doesn't want anyone to know where she's going!"

"Then let's wait and watch!"

"We'll learn nothing that way. She can tell we're keeping our eye on her." Penny threw in the clutch and the car rolled away from the curb. "Tell you what, Lou! We'll drive around the block."

"Good idea!" approved her chum. "That way she'll think we've gone and we can see where she really goes."

Penny turned at the first corner and made a quick trip around the block. As they again came within view of the ice-locked river, the girls looked quickly up and down the street for a glimpse of their former passenger.

"There she is!" Louise cried. "Why, she's walking straight to the docks!"

The two girls now were completely mystified and not a little worried. At this late hour, the waterfront was deserted.

Penny watched the retreating figure for a moment, and then swung the car door open.

"That girl can't know what she's doing!" she decided. "I'm going after her!"

"For our pains, we may be told to mind our own affairs."

"That's beside the point, Lou. Something's wrong."

Without taking time to lock the car, the two girls hurried down the dark street toward the docks. Far ahead they could see the one they pursued walking swiftly. Then in the blinding, whirling snow, they lost sight of her.

CHAPTER 3 - STRANGER OF THE STORM

Reaching the waterfront, Penny and Louise gazed about in disbelief and bewilderment. The girl had vanished.

"Now where could she have gone—" Penny murmured, only to break off as her gaze fell upon a trail of footsteps.

The prints led along the dock for a short distance, only to end at the river's edge.

CHAPTER 4 - VANISHING FOOTPRINTS

"That crazy girl must have jumped off here!" Louise exclaimed, as she too saw the footprints on the snowy planks.

"The river is solid ice—at least six inches thick," Penny pointed out. "She couldn't have crashed through."

"Then where did she go?"

Far upstream toward the Main Street Bridge, an iceboat could be seen tacking back and forth. Otherwise, the river was a gleaming ribbon of deserted ice.

"The only place she could have gone is under the dock," Penny said, her eyebrows knitting into a puzzled frown.

"*Under* it?"

"That's what she must have done," Penny insisted. "I suppose the planking would give some protection from the storm."

The snow was coming down harder now than ever, in huge flakes. Trailing the footprints to the dock's edge, Penny flattened herself on the planks and peered over the side.

"I can't see a thing!" she complained. "Dark as pitch!"

"Listen!" commanded Louise.

Both girls became quiet. Distinctly they could hear a faint creak of snow as someone walked beneath the dock, a long distance away.

"Hello, down there!" shouted Penny.

The creaking sound ceased. But no one answered the call.

"If she's down there, she'll never answer!" Louise said, thoroughly disgusted. "Should we go after her?"

Penny was sorely tempted. She studied the long, high dock only to shake her head.

"If once we get down there, we couldn't climb up again without walking a long distance, Lou."

"Then what should we do?"

"Let's call the police station," Penny urged. Scrambling to her feet, she brushed snow from her ski suit. "This is a case for them to investigate."

"That's what I think," agreed Louise, greatly relieved. "I know my parents wouldn't want me prowling under the docks at night."

Pelted by fast falling snow, the two friends returned to the parked car and then drove to a drugstore several blocks away. Penny telephoned Central Police Station, only to be informed a car could not be sent to the river for a few minutes. Heavy snow had snarled traffic, causing many accidents and tying up police personnel.

For twenty minutes the girls waited patiently in their car, but no one came to investigate. At last, giving up in disgust, they drove to their homes.

Try as she would, Penny could not forget the strange girl with the suitcase who had been so unwilling to answer questions. Who was she? And why had she taken refuge beneath the river docks?

She longed to talk the matter over with her father, but Mr. Parker had gone to bed early.

Penny kept thinking about the matter until she fell asleep and it was foremost in her thoughts when she awoke in the morning.

"Wonder if the *Riverview Star* carried any mention of a police investigation at the river?" she mused.

Dressing rapidly, she ran downstairs to bring the morning paper in from the porch. Eagerly she scanned the pages.

CHAPTER 4 - VANISHING FOOTPRINTS

"Not a single word here!" she exclaimed in disappointment. "Maybe the police didn't even bother to search the dock area."

To make certain, she telephoned Captain Brownell, a personal friend at Central Station. The officer explained that a police car had been dispatched to the river shortly after one o'clock. Footprints noted earlier by the two girls, had been blotted out by falling snow. No one had been found loitering in the area.

"Well, that's that," sighed Penny, turning away from the telephone. "I wish now, Lou and I had taken a chance and prowled under the dock."

From the breakfast alcove, Anthony Parker, a tall, lean man with iron gray hair and intelligent eyes, regarded his daughter in amusement.

"Talking to yourself again, Penny?" he teased.

"I am!" Penny slid into a chair beside her father and reached for a tall glass of orange juice. "The things I'm thinking about the police department aren't complimentary either! What this town needs is a larger force and at least a dozen extra patrol cars!"

"You could find plenty of work for them, I judge."

"Couldn't I? A nice situation when police are too busy to investigate an important call promptly!"

"So they gave you the run-around," teased Mr. Parker. "Suppose you tell me what happened."

Starting at the very beginning, Penny told of hearing the strange cry at the old monastery and later, the meeting with the unfriendly girl who had disappeared near the river docks.

While she related her odd experiences, Mrs. Maud Weems, the family housekeeper, came in bearing a platter of scrambled eggs. Since the death of Penny's mother, the woman had cared for the girl as her own daughter.

She listened attentively to the tale of adventure, and with obvious disapproval.

"In my opinion, that's what comes of midnight skiing parties!" she interrupted the story. "I hope you stay away from Knob Hill and the monastery after this."

"Oh, Mrs. Weems!" Penny's elfin face lost a little of its excited glow. "This wonderful skiing weather can't last many days! I simply must go back there!"

"To ski or to investigate the monastery?" asked the housekeeper. "If I know the signs, you're hot on the trail of another mystery!"

"Naturally I want to learn more about that strange cult," grinned Penny. "Who knows, I might track down a bang-up story for Dad's paper!"

"Skiing always seemed a wholesome sport to me," interposed Mr. Parker, winking slyly at his daughter. "Of course, I don't approve of late hours."

Mrs. Weems sighed as she set the egg platter down hard on the table. "You two always conspire against me!" she accused.

"Why, Mrs. Weems!" Penny observed innocently. "Don't you approve of skiing?"

"Skiing is only an excuse and you know it, Penelope Parker! Oh, dear, I try so hard to raise you properly."

"And you're doing a magnificent job, if I do say so myself," chuckled Penny. "Don't give the matter any further thought!"

"Penny always has proven she uses her head and knows how to take care of herself," added Mr. Parker. "An inquisitive mind is an asset—especially in the newspaper business."

With an injured sniff, Mrs. Weems retreated to the kitchen to wash the dishes.

Alone with her father, Penny grinned at him affectionately. His defense of her conduct meant only one thing! He did not disapprove of her interest in the monastery at Knob Hill.

"He's giving me the 'go' signal!" she thought jubilantly. Aloud she said. "Dad, don't you think Jay Highland and the monastery might be worth a feature story in the *Riverview Star*?"

"Possibly," he agreed, getting up from the table. "Well, I must move along to the office."

A little disappointed because her father had brushed the subject aside so lightly, Penny spent the morning helping Mrs. Weems with household tasks. However, directly after luncheon she packed her skis and prepared to set off for Knob Hill.

Unwilling to go alone, Penny stopped at the Sidell home. To her disappointment, Louise had gone shopping and was not expected back for several hours.

"Maybe I can induce Dad to go with me!" she thought. "He spends entirely too much time indoors. An outing will do him good!"

At the *Star* plant in the heart of downtown Riverview, Penny wandered through a nearly deserted editorial room to her father's office. For a morning paper the hour was early, and few reporters had as yet unhooded their typewriters.

Through the glass door Penny observed that her father had a visitor, a middle-aged, intelligent looking man she had never seen before. She would have slipped away had her father not motioned for her to enter.

"Penny, this is James Ayling, an investigator for the Barnes Mutual Insurance Co.," he said. "My daughter, Mr. Ayling."

The visitor arose to grasp the girl's hand firmly.

"Mr. Ayling is from Boston," explained the newspaper owner. He turned to the investigator. "Do you mind if I tell my daughter why you are here?"

"Not at all."

"Mr. Ayling is trying to locate an elderly woman whose family jewels are heavily insured with his company."

"Mrs. Hawthorne isn't actually our client," explained Mr. Ayling. "Originally, old Nathaniel Hawthorne, her late husband, insured a $100,000 star sapphire with us. The policy remains in effect until the gem becomes the possession of a granddaughter, Rhoda."

"Who has the sapphire now?" asked Penny, slightly puzzled.

"Mr. Hawthorne's will allows his wife the use of it during her lifetime. Upon her death it passes to the sixteen-year-old granddaughter, Rhoda Hawthorne."

"And you are searching for Mrs. Hawthorne now?" Penny inquired politely.

"Yes, so far as we know Mrs. Hawthorne has the gem. We are afraid it may be stolen from her or that she will dispose of it for a trifling sum. Mrs. Hawthorne hasn't been well and in her present state of mind she might act very foolishly."

"Tell Penny about the gem's history," suggested Mr. Parker.

"Oh, yes! The sapphire once was set in a necklace worn by a king who met violent death. Since then, there is a superstition that bad luck pursues the owner.

"The gem passed through many hands. Three times it was stolen. Several owners died strange or violent deaths."

"Not Mr. Hawthorne?"

"Well, he fell from a cliff while touring the West," explained the investigator. "Of course it was an accident, but Mrs. Hawthorne unfortunately became convinced his death resulted from ownership of the sapphire.

"She pleaded that the gem be sold for what it would bring, fearing that harm would come upon her grandchild when eventually the sapphire is turned over to her. According to terms of the will, the gem cannot be sold, and our firm must remain responsible for it in case of theft or loss."

"Mrs. Hawthorne still has the gem then?"

"We hope so," Mr. Ayling replied. "She went South on a vacation trip with her granddaughter, taking the sapphire with her. That was over a month ago. Nothing since has been heard from them."

"But what brings you to Riverview?" questioned Penny.

"I went South searching for Mrs. Hawthorne. At Miami only a week ago she bought two tickets for Riverview. From that point on, I've been unable to trace her."

"Does she have relatives or friends here?"

"Not so far as I've been able to learn. Perhaps our company is unduly concerned, but the truth is, Mrs. Hawthorne is a very foolish, gullible woman. Should she dispose of or lose the gem, our firm must pay a large sum of money."

"We'll be glad to run a picture of Mrs. Hawthorne in the paper," offered Mr. Parker. "If she has arrived in Riverview, someone will have seen her."

"I certainly appreciate your interest," said Mr. Ayling. "Unfortunately, I have no photograph of Mrs. Hawthorne with me. I'll wire my office tonight for one."

"In the meantime, we'll run a little story," the publisher promised. "No doubt you can describe the woman."

CHAPTER 4 - VANISHING FOOTPRINTS

"Oh, yes, in a general way. She's 68 years of age and walks with a cane. Her hair is white and she weighs about 150 pounds. She's deeply interested in art. Also in spiritualism and mystic cults, I regret to add."

"Mystic cults!" Penny's blue eyes began to dance with interest. She knew now why her father had made a point of calling her in to meet the investigator.

"Mrs. Hawthorne is very gullible and easily influenced. Since her husband died, she has been prey for one sharper after another. I judge a third of her fortune already has been squandered."

After a thoughtful pause, Penny hesitantly asked Mr. Ayling if he thought it possible Mrs. Hawthorne could have come to Riverview to join a cult.

"That's what I'm here to find out. Mrs. Hawthorne and her granddaughter have not registered at any of the leading hotels. Yet I know they came to the city."

"Have you tried the monastery at Knob Hill?" Penny suggested. "A new society has been established there in the last few days. I don't know much about the order yet, but its members are supposed to dedicate themselves to a life of charity and poverty."

"Why, that's exactly the sort of thing to attract Mrs. Hawthorne—for a few weeks," the investigator replied. "Then after the novelty wore off, she would flit on to something else. Where is this place?"

"I plan to drive out there in a few minutes," Penny told him eagerly. "Why not come with me, Mr. Ayling?"

The investigator glanced inquiringly at Mr. Parker.

"Go ahead if you think it's worth while," urged the publisher.

"I suppose the chance of finding Mrs. Hawthorne there is very remote," Mr. Ayling said, thinking aloud. "But I can't afford to overlook any possibility. Thanks, Miss Parker, I'll gladly accept your invitation."

"Want to come along, Dad?" Penny asked.

"No thanks," he declined. "I'm certain you'll be in good hands. Just let Mr. Ayling take the lead in any investigation."

"Why, Dad!" Penny protested. "You know me."

"I do, indeed," said Mr. Parker, smiling as he resumed his desk work. "That's why I feel confident Mr. Ayling may look forward to a very interesting afternoon."

CHAPTER 5 - A CRYSTAL BALL

Pine trees and bushes hung in frozen arches along the winding road which led to the ancient monastery.

Parking the automobile near the iron boundary fence, Penny was quick to note that the big ornamental gate now was locked and securely fastened with chain and padlock.

"Are you sure this place is occupied?" Mr. Ayling asked as he alighted and followed Penny to the gate. "Why, the property is a wreck!"

"The gate was unlocked last night," the girl replied. "We may have trouble getting inside."

Pressing her face against the rusty iron spikes, she gazed hopefully toward the gatehouse. The door was slightly ajar. Winkey, however, was nowhere to be seen.

Mr. Ayling rattled the gate chain several times.

"No one seems to be around," he said in disappointment.

"Yes, there is!" Penny corrected.

Just then she caught a fleeting glimpse of a face at the tiny circular window of the gatehouse. She was convinced it was Winkey, who for some reason, intended to ignore their presence at the gate.

"Let us in!" she called.

"Open up!" shouted Mr. Ayling.

Still there was no rustle of life from the gatehouse.

"Disgusting!" Penny muttered. "I know Winkey is watching us! He's only being contrary!"

Mr. Ayling's angular jaw tightened. "In that case," he said, "we'll have to get in the best way we can. I'll climb over the fence."

The words purposely were spoken loudly enough to be overheard in the gatehouse. Before the investigator could carry out his threat, the door of the circular, stone building swung back. Winkey, the hunchback, sauntered leisurely out.

"Want somethin'?" he inquired.

"Didn't you hear us trying to get in?" Mr. Ayling demanded.

"Sure," the hunchback shrugged, "but I was busy fixin' the bell that connects with the house. Anyhow, visitors ain't wanted here."

"So we observe," said Mr. Ayling. "Where is your master?"

"Inside."

"Then announce us," the investigator ordered. "We're here to ask a few questions."

Winkey's bird-like eyes blinked rapidly. He looked as if about to argue, then changed his mind.

"Go on to the house then," he said crossly. "I'll let 'em know by phone you're comin'."

The driveway curled through a large outer courtyard where a cluster of small and interesting buildings stood in various stages of ruin.

Near the gatehouse was the almonry, a shelter used in very early days to house visitors who sought free lodging.

Beyond were the ancient brewhouse, bakehouse, and granary. The latter two buildings now were little more than heaps of fallen brick. None of the structures was habitable.

In far better state of preservation was the central building with gabled roof and tall hooded chimneys. However, front steps long since had fallen away from the entrance doorway. Bridging the gap was a short ladder.

"What a place!" commented Mr. Ayling offering Penny his hand to help her across. "Looks as if it might cave in any day."

CHAPTER 5 - A CRYSTAL BALL

The visitors found themselves facing a weather-beaten but beautifully carved wooden doorway. Before they could knock, it opened on squeaky hinges.

A woman with heavily lined face, who wore a gray gown and white lace cap, peered out at them.

"Go away!" she murmured in a stage whisper. "Go quickly!"

"Julia!" said a voice directly behind her.

The woman whirled around and cringed as a brown-robed monk took her firmly by the arm.

"Go and light a fire in the parlor, Julia," her master directed. "I will greet our guests."

"Yes, Father Benedict," the woman muttered, scurrying away.

The master now turned apologetically to the visitors.

"I trust my servant was not rude," he said. "Poor creature! Her twisted mind causes her to believe that all persons who do not dwell within our walls are evil and to be feared."

As the monk spoke, he smiled in a kindly, friendly way, yet his keen eyes were appraising the two visitors. Though it was cold and windy on the door step, he did not hasten to invite Penny and Mr. Ayling inside. He stood holding the half-opened door in his hand.

"You must excuse our lack of hospitality," he said, fingering a gold chain which hung from his thin shoulders. "We have much cleaning and remodeling to do before we are ready to receive visitors."

Mr. Ayling explained that his call was one of business, adding that he represented the Barnes Mutual Insurance Co.

"Such matters must be discussed with me later," the monk said, slowly but firmly closing the door.

"I'm not selling insurance," Mr. Ayling assured him. Deliberately he leaned against the jamb, preventing the monk from shutting the door.

Father Benedict bit his lip in annoyance. "May I inquire your business with me?" he asked frostily.

"I'm seeking to trace a client—Mrs. Nathaniel Hawthorne."

"I know of no such person. Deeply I regret that I cannot help you, sir. If you will excuse me—"

"The woman may have used an assumed name," Mr. Ayling cut in. "She has a weakness—er, I mean a liking for cult practices."

"You are suggesting this woman may have joined my little flock?"

"That's the general idea."

"Absurd!" The monk's gaze rested briefly on Penny as he added: "I greatly fear you have been led astray by loose gossip as to the nature of the order I am founding here."

"I told Mr. Ayling about your work because I think it's so interesting," Penny said quickly. She slapped her mittened hands together. "My, it's cold today! May we warm ourselves at your fire before we start back to town?"

A frown puckered Father Benedict's eyebrows. Plainly the request displeased him. But with a show of hospitality, he said:

"Our abode is very humble and poorly furnished. Such as it is, you are welcome." Bowing slightly, he stepped aside to admit the visitors.

Penny and Mr. Ayling found themselves in a long, barren, and very cold hallway.

"Follow me, please," bade the monk.

Moving on the bare boards with noiseless tread, he led them through an arched doorway cut in the thick wall, across a wind-swept pillared cloister and into a parlor where a fire burned brightly in a huge, time-blackened fireplace.

The sheer comfort of the room surprised Penny. Underfoot was a thick velvet carpet. Other furnishings included a large mahogany desk, a sofa, two easy chairs, and a cabinet filled with fine glassware, gold and silver objects, and a blue glass decanter of wine.

Black velvet curtains were draped in heavy folds over an exit door, and similar hangings covered the windows. To Penny's astonishment, the ceiling, painted black, was studded with silver stars.

However, the object which held her roving gaze was a large crystal ball supported on the claws of a bronze dragon.

"You are a crystal gazer!" Mr. Ayling exclaimed as he too noted the curious globe.

"I have the power to read the future with reasonable accuracy," replied the monk. He dismissed the subject with a shrug, motioning for his guests to seat themselves before the fire.

"You spoke of searching for a Mrs. Rosenthorne—" he remarked, addressing the investigator.

"Mrs. Hawthorne," corrected Mr. Ayling.

"To be sure, Mrs. Hawthorne. Apparently you were under the misapprehension that she is in some way connected with this establishment."

"It was only a hope. My client has a deep interest in cults. I traced Mrs. Hawthorne and her granddaughter to Riverview, and thought possibly they might have been attracted to your place."

"My little flock is limited to only twelve members at present. All are very humble people who have sworn to live a life of poverty, devoted to charity and faith. We have no Mrs. Hawthorne here."

"Mightn't she have given another name?" suggested Penny. She stretched her cold fingers to the leaping flames on the hearth.

"I hardly think so." Father Benedict's lips curled in a superior smile. "Describe the woman, please."

Mr. Ayling repeated the description Penny had heard earlier that afternoon.

"We have no such person here," the monk said. "I regret I am unable to help you."

He arose, a plain hint that he considered the brief interview at an end. Somewhat reluctantly, Penny and her companion also turned their backs upon the crackling fire.

"You have made a comfortable place of this room," the girl said. Her gaze fastened admiringly upon a porcelain decanter in a wall cabinet. "And such interesting antiques!"

For the first time since the visitors had arrived, Father Benedict's eyes sparkled with warmth.

"Collecting art treasures is a hobby of mine," he revealed. Crossing to the cabinet, he removed the decanter.

"This is a piece of Ching-Hoa porcelain and very rare," he said. "And here is a Byzantine amulet—priceless. The golden goblets came from a European church destroyed a century ago."

"You're not afraid to keep such treasures in the monastery?" Mr. Ayling inquired.

"Afraid?" Father Benedict's dark eyes glittered with a strange light. "I must confess I know not the meaning of the word."

"You are so far out, I don't suppose you can expect much police protection," Mr. Ayling added.

"Winkey, my gateman, is quite dependable. While he is on duty, no thief or unwanted stranger will enter our grounds."

"Winkey is good at keeping folks out," agreed the investigator dryly. In walking toward the door, he paused to gaze again at the crystal ball.

"My glass interests you?" inquired the monk.

"I've seen those things before, but never took stock in them," rejoined Mr. Ayling. "One can't actually conjure up pictures by gazing into that globe?"

"Would you care to see for yourself?"

"Well, it's a little out of my line," Mr. Ayling laughed.

"I'd like to try it!" cried Penny. "May I?"

"Certainly. The principle is very simple. One merely gazes deeply into the glass until the optic nerve of the eye becomes fatigued. As it ceases to transmit impression from without, one sees events of the future."

"I've heard it explained a little differently," said Mr. Ayling. "As the optic nerve becomes paralyzed, it responds to the reflex action proceeding from the brain of the crystal gazer. One sees what one wishes to see."

"I do not agree!" Father Benedict's voice was sharp. "The ball accurately foretells the future. Shall we test and prove its powers?"

"Let me try it!" pleaded Penny again.

Smiling a bit grimly, the monk extinguished an overhead light and touched a match to the wick of two tall white candles.

Placing the crystal ball in front of a black screen, he set the burning tapers at either side. Penny suddenly began to lose zest for the adventure.

But before she could think of a graceful way to announce that she had changed her mind, the monk took her firmly by the arm.

"Place your hands on either side of the crystal ball," he directed. "Gaze deep into the glass. Deep—deep. And now my little one, what do you see?"

CHAPTER 6 - CREAKING WOOD

As Penny peered down into the highly polished surface of the crystal clear glass, a multitude of dancing points of light drew and held her attention.

"Gaze deep—deeper," intoned the monk. "Do you not see a picture forming?"

"The glass has become cloudy."

"Ah, yes. In a moment it will clear. Now what do you see?"

"Nothing. Nothing at all."

Father Benedict tapped the toe of his slipper impatiently. "You are resisting the glass," he muttered. "You do not believe."

Penny continued to stare fixedly into the crystal ball. "It's no use," she said finally, pulling her eyes away. "Guess I haven't enough of the witch in me!"

She stepped back from the dragon standard on which the globe stood, and for a minute was stone blind.

"I can't see a thing!" she gasped in alarm.

"The optic nerve is paralyzed," said the monk, steadying her as she swayed slightly. "Vision will be normal in a moment."

"I'm beginning to distinguish objects now," Penny admitted, reassured.

The monk released her arm. Seating himself before the crystal globe, he placed his hands on the polished surface.

"Now shall I try?" he suggested. "What would you like to know about the future?"

"You might find Mrs. Hawthorne for me," the investigator said in jest.

In the darkened room, Father Benedict's hooded face looked grotesque as light from the tall tapers flickered upon his angular jaw bones.

The moment was impressive. A tomb-like silence had fallen upon the three, and the only sound was the crackle of the fire.

Then, quite suddenly, Penny was certain she heard another noise. Though the occasion should not have been one for alarm, she felt her skin prickle. A tiny chill caused her to shiver.

Or was it a chill? Against her cheek she felt a breath of icy wind. Somewhere beyond the room a door had opened. Unmistakably, she heard the creak of old wood.

Penny's startled gaze roved to Mr. Ayling. Oblivious to all else, the investigator was watching Father Benedict closely.

Every sense now alert, the girl listened intently. Had someone stepped on a loose board as he crept along the passageway? Or had she merely heard the old house groaning to itself?

The creaking sound was not repeated.

Trying to throw off the pall which had fallen upon her, Penny centered her full attention upon the monk. As one hypnotized by the glass into which he peered, he mumbled words difficult to understand.

"Now the ball is clearing," he muttered. "What is this? I see a resort city on the sea coast—the rush and roar of waves. Ah, a beach! On the sand are two bathers—one a girl of perhaps sixteen or seventeen with dark hair. She wears a green bathing suit. Upon her third finger is a black cameo ring."

A startled look came upon Mr. Ayling's face, but he made no comment.

"Her companion is an elderly woman," continued the monk as if speaking in a trance. "Over her shoulders is flung a dark blue beach cape. The picture is fading now—I am losing the vision."

Penny's attention, wandering again, was drawn as if by a powerful magnet to the curtains covering the exit.

In fascination, she watched. An inch at a time, the door moved outward. Then a hand appeared between the black velvet draperies, cautiously pulling them apart.

Penny wondered if her eyes were playing tricks upon her. She felt an overpowering impulse to laugh or call out. Yet her throat was dry and tight.

The scene seemed fantastic. It couldn't be real, she told herself. Yet those curtains steadily were moving farther apart.

An arm came into view, then the side of a human figure. Last of all, a face, ghostly pale against the dark background, slowly emerged.

For one fleeting instant Penny saw a girl only a little older than herself, standing half wrapped in the folds of the velvet curtain. Their eyes met.

In that moment, through Penny's brain flashed the message that the one who crouched in the doorway was the same girl she and Louise had picked up on the road only the previous night.

"But that's crazy!" she thought. "It couldn't be the same person! I must be dreaming!"

The one behind the curtain had raised a finger to her lips as if commanding silence. Then the draperies were pulled together with a jerk and the figure was gone.

Another cold breath of air swept through the room, causing candles on either side of the crystal ball to flicker. Again Penny heard the soft *creak, creak* of wood as footsteps retreated.

She tried to speak, but the words stuck in her throat. Had her imagination played tricks upon her?

Slowly she turned her eyes upon Father Benedict, whose back had been toward the curtained door.

"Another picture is forming in the crystal ball," he muttered. "I see a man walking through a lonely wood. But what is this? Evil persons lie in wait behind the tall pine trees. Now they are waylaying him!

"They fall upon him and beat him with their cudgels. Woe is me! They leave him lying on the ground. The man is dying—dead. Oh, evil, evil! I can read no more in the glass today!"

Arising quickly, and brushing a hand over his glazed eyes, Father Benedict leaned for a moment against the damp plaster wall.

"Excuse me, please," he apologized. "What I saw was most unnerving."

The monk poured himself a drink of water and lighted a lamp on the center table.

"Now I can see again," he said in a more natural tone. "A reading always is an exhausting experience."

"Your demonstration was most impressive," said Mr. Ayling. "How would you interpret your vision of Mrs. Hawthorne?"

"I should say the woman and her granddaughter at this very moment are enjoying a pleasant vacation in a sunny climate. California perhaps, or Florida."

"Mrs. Hawthorne was in Florida, but she bought a ticket to Riverview."

"Obviously, she never arrived here," replied the monk. "You see, the crystal glass never lies."

"Then your advice would be to resume my search in Florida?" the investigator asked.

"I do not presume to advise you." From a cabinet, Father Benedict removed a black cloth which he used to polish away an imaginary speck on the crystal globe. Then he covered the standard with a cloth hood and added impressively: "However, I consider it my duty to warn you of danger."

"Warn me?" exclaimed Mr. Ayling. "Of what danger?"

"My second vision was most disturbing," Father Benedict said gravely. "As I interpret it, great harm—perhaps death, will pursue the man who walks alone in the woods, unless he alters his present course. You came to Riverview for a definite purpose, Mr. Ayling?"

"Why, yes, to find Mrs. Hawthorne."

"Mr. Ayling, for your own well being, you must abandon the search."

"Why?"

"Because," said the monk very low, "the vision was sent to me that you may be saved from disaster. The man attacked in the woods was yourself, Mr. Ayling!"

CHAPTER 7 - A WARNING

If Father Benedict's words disturbed the investigator, he gave no sign. Smiling, he said:

"I fear I am not a firm believer in the art of crystal gazing—all respect to your remarkable talent."

The monk frowned as he carefully laid another log on the dying fire. "You will be unwise to disregard the warning," he said. "Most unwise."

"Warning?"

"I should interpret the picture as such, dear Mr. Ayling. Apparently, if you pursue your present course, you are certain to meet misfortune."

"To what 'present course' do you refer?"

"That I would not know," replied the monk coldly. "Now may I thank you for coming to our humble abode and bid you good afternoon? I have a formal meeting soon with members of my little family of believers and must nap for a few minutes. You will excuse me?"

"We were just leaving," said Penny. "I'm really deeply interested in your society here. May I come sometime soon to watch a ceremony?"

The monk gazed at her sharply but answered in a polite voice:

"Later, when we are better organized and have our house in order, we shall be most happy to have you."

On the way out of the building, through the chilly cloister and gloomy hall, Penny looked carefully about for the girl who so stealthily had opened the door of the monk's study.

She saw no one. Mr. Ayling and Father Benedict, she was certain, were unaware of the incident which had so startled her.

"It wasn't imagination," she thought. "I did see the door open. But it may not have been that girl Louise and I met last night. Probably it was a member of Mr. Highland's cult."

Deeply puzzled, Penny decided that if an opportunity presented itself, she would revisit the monastery another day.

At the front door of the building, Father Benedict turned to bid his guests goodbye. Before he could retreat, a loud commotion was heard near the gatehouse.

The monk listened intently and with evident annoyance. "My! My! What now?" he sighed. "Are we to have no peace and quiet within our walls?"

Near the front gate, Winkey could be seen arguing with a stout, middle-aged man in a racoon coat who carried an easel and a palette under his arm.

"My orders are to keep folks out o' here!" Winkey shouted. "I don't care who you are! Ye ain't settin' foot inside here, unless the boss says so! Now get out!"

"Try to put me out!" the visitor challenged.

"Okay, I will!" retorted the hunchback.

He would have seized the visitor by the arm, had not Father Benedict called to him from the doorway: "Winkey!"

"Yes, Father," the hunchback mumbled.

"Now tell me what is wrong," the cult leader bade as he went down to the gate, followed by Penny and Mr. Ayling. "Who is this gentleman?"

"My name is Vernon Eckenrod," the visitor introduced himself. "I'm an artist. I live down the road a quarter of a mile."

"He wants to come in and paint a picture," interposed Winkey. "I told him nothin' doing."

"Your man doesn't understand," said Mr. Eckenrod, glaring at the hunchback. "I am doing a series of pictures of the monastery for a national magazine. The sketches are finished and now I'm starting to paint."

"You mean you wish to do exterior scenes?"

"Exterior and also interior. I want to do the arch to the chapter house today, and if I have time, either the stone-hooded chimneys or the window of the guest hall."

"You show remarkable familiarity with the monastery."

"I've been coming here for more than a year," the artist said, shifting his easel to a more comfortable position. "This building is one of the oldest in the state. See, I have a key." He held it before the startled gaze of the monk.

"Indeed!" Father Benedict's voice became less friendly. "And may I inquire how you came into possession of a key to my property?"

"Your property?"

"Certainly, I have rented these premises from the owner, with an option to buy."

"I've been trying to buy the place myself," the artist said, "but couldn't pay the amount asked. I'd like to restore the buildings and make it into a real show place."

"How did you obtain a key?" the monk reminded him.

"Oh, the owner gave me one. He lets me paint here whenever I like."

"The monastery now is exclusively mine," said Father Benedict. "Kindly turn the key over to me!"

"Surely," agreed Mr. Eckenrod, giving it up. "But you won't mind if I come here to finish my paintings? I'm under contract to complete the work by the fifteenth of the month."

Father Benedict secreted the key in the folds of his robe. "I appreciate your position," he said. "Nevertheless, we cannot have strangers intruding upon our privacy."

"Why, everyone around here knows me! Ask anyone about my character and work!"

"I do not question your character, my good man. But I must request you not to come here again."

"Now see here!" the artist exclaimed, losing his temper again. "You don't get the idea! My pictures are half done. If I don't complete the order, I'll stand to lose months of work."

"Complete them from the sketches."

"I can't do that—the color and feeling would be lost."

Father Benedict turned as if to leave. "I am sorry," he said firmly.

"Listen—" Mr. Eckenrod began furiously.

The monk coldly walked away, entering the house.

"You heard him!" cried Winkey, triumphantly. "Now git going and don't come back!"

"All right, I'll go," the artist retorted. "But I'll be here again. You can't get away with this even if you have rented the property!"

Scarcely aware of Penny and Mr. Ayling, who followed him to the gate, Mr. Eckenrod stomped off with easel and palette.

"They can't get away with it!" he stormed, addressing no one in particular. "I'll come back here with the sheriff!"

"I'm afraid Father Benedict is within his rights," remarked Mr. Ayling. "He's taken over the property."

"What's that?" the artist became aware of his presence. "Oh yes," he admitted grudgingly, "legally he is within his rights, I suppose. But what of justice?"

"It would seem only decent of him to allow you to complete your paintings."

"I've been coming to the monastery for months, off and on," the artist revealed in an aggrieved tone. "Always figured I'd buy the place. The owner, Peter Holden, picked it up at a foreclosure sale for a mere nothing. He'd have sold to me too, if this fellow hadn't come along. Who is he, anyhow?"

"I wonder myself," said Mr. Ayling.

"His gateman looks like a thug!"

"I'm afraid your unfortunate encounter with Winkey prejudiced you," smiled the investigator. "After all, the man apparently was acting under orders."

"I didn't like that monk either!" the artist scowled. "He acted as religious as my Aunt Sara!"

"His real name is Jay Highland," Penny contributed. "He's a crystal gazer."

"Humph! A fine calling! If the authorities are smart, they'll look into his business here!"

CHAPTER 7 - A WARNING

The trio now had reached the roadside where Penny's car was parked. Politely, she offered to give the artist a lift to his home.

"Thanks, but I'll walk," he declined the offer. "I live only a short distance. I'll just cut through the fields."

His dark eyes still snapping like firebrands, the artist strode off through the snow.

"Quite a character!" remarked Mr. Ayling, once he and Penny were in the car. "An eccentric!"

"I've heard Mr. Eckenrod really is a fine artist," Penny replied. "Too bad Father Benedict wouldn't let him complete his paintings. By the way, what did you think of him?"

"Well, if I'm any judge of character, he'll soon be back to make more trouble."

"No, I mean Father Benedict."

"He seemed pleasant enough," Mr. Ayling said slowly. "However, I can't say I went for the crystal ball demonstration."

"Oh, anyone could tell that was the bunk!"

"Frankly, it gave me quite a jolt."

"Oh, you mean the monk's warning!"

"Not that," replied Mr. Ayling. "His description of Mrs. Hawthorne and her daughter. Of course, I've never seen either of them, but the picture he conjured up seemed to fit them."

"Oh, he probably made it up." Penny started the car which rolled with creaking tires over the hilly, snow-packed road toward the city. "You described Mrs. Hawthorne to him earlier, you know."

"So I did. Except for one small detail, the reading would not have impressed me."

"And that detail?"

"In describing the girl on the beach, Father Benedict said she was wearing a black cameo ring."

"So he did! You certainly never mentioned that to him!"

"It rather jarred me," admitted Mr. Ayling. "Because, when Rhoda Hawthorne last was seen, she was wearing just such a cameo ring!"

CHAPTER 8 - INTO THE CREVASSE

Enroute to Riverview, Penny and Mr. Ayling discussed all phases of their strange interview with Father Benedict.

"The man may be all right," the investigator said. "Nevertheless, as a matter of routine I'll check on him. Where was he before he came to Riverview?"

"I never heard."

"And who are the members of his mysterious cult? Riverview people?"

"Not so far as I know. The only persons I've seen on the premises are Winkey, the one they call Julia, and a girl."

"A girl? Who is she?"

"I don't know. She peeped from behind a door while Father Benedict was giving the crystal ball reading. I started to speak and she motioned me to keep quiet. Then she slipped away."

"Odd."

"Yes, it was. For just a minute I thought she might be a girl I picked up on the road the other night in my car. The room was shadowy though, so I got no clear impression of her face."

"I'd like to meet the girl—also the other members of the cult."

"So would I! Why not visit there again soon?"

"We might try it tomorrow, say about this same time," proposed Mr. Ayling. "I don't plan to remain in Riverview longer than another twenty-four hours unless I obtain a clue to Mrs. Hawthorne's whereabouts."

"Maybe Winkey won't let us in," commented Penny dubiously.

"We'll worry about that when the time comes. Perhaps if he makes trouble, we can find ways to persuade him."

"Shall I pick you up at your hotel?" Penny offered.

"All right," the investigator agreed. "Meanwhile, I'll wire my office for photographs of Mrs. Hawthorne and her granddaughter which can be published in your father's paper. Also, I'll ask our company to check on Father Benedict's past. He may be operating a quick money racket here."

"Then you do distrust him!"

"Not exactly, but I've learned from past experience it pays to overlook nothing. Father Benedict is an eccentric. He may be all right and probably is. All the same, it will be interesting to learn more about him."

A little later, after agreeing to meet the next afternoon at two o'clock, Penny dropped Mr. Ayling at his hotel. In a high state of excitement, she then drove on home to report the day's adventure to Mrs. Weems and her father.

"Mr. Ayling's awfully nice and smart too!" she declared at the dinner table. "Together we'll find Mrs. Hawthorne and solve the mystery of the monastery!"

"What mystery?" teased her father.

"I don't know yet," Penny admitted with a chuckle. "But give me time! I'll find one! I can feel it bubbling in the air!"

Mrs. Weems, who came into the dining room with a platter of roast beef, observed: "If you take my advice, you'll stay away from that place!"

"Oh, Mrs. Weems!"

"You only invite trouble by going there," the housekeeper said severely. "Furthermore, it will distract you from your school work."

CHAPTER 8 - INTO THE CREVASSE

"School teachers' convention this week!" Penny reminded her. "We're off tomorrow and next day too! Don't worry about anything happening to me at the monastery, Mrs. Weems. Mr. Ayling makes a dandy chaperon."

"If you're going with him, I suppose I can't protest," the housekeeper gave in. "Mind, you're home before dark."

"I'll do my best," Penny grinned. "No rash promises though!"

The next afternoon, sharp at two o'clock, she drove to the front entranceway of the Riverview Hotel. Mr. Ayling was nowhere to be seen. After waiting ten minutes, she parked and went inside to inquire at the desk.

"Mr. Ayling has room 416," the clerk told her. "Doubt whether you'll find him in just now. He left here late last night and hasn't been back."

"That's queer," thought Penny. Aloud she asked if the investigator had left any message for her.

"Nothing," replied the clerk.

"He didn't say where he was going?"

"No, but he evidently intends to be back. His luggage is still here, and he hasn't paid his bill."

To satisfy herself, Penny telephoned Room 416. No one answered.

"Wonder if he could have thought he was to meet me at the monastery?" she mused. "Guess I may as well drive out there."

The sunshine was strong and the day slightly warm. Penny, who had worn heavy skiing clothes, shed her coat before she reached the monastery.

Pulling up at the barrier gate, she glanced hopefully about. Mr. Ayling was nowhere to be seen. If he had arrived ahead of her, undoubtedly he was inside the building.

As Penny hesitated, wondering what to do, Winkey's ugly face appeared behind the iron spokes of the gate.

"You again!" he observed with a scowl.

"Yes, I'm looking for a friend of mine, Mr. Ayling, who was here yesterday."

"You think we got him hid somewheres?" the gateman asked insolently.

"I thought he might have come here again."

"Well, he didn't. And Father Benedict ain't here either. So you can't come in."

Though annoyed by the hunchback's curt manners, Penny held her temper in check.

"I very much wanted to talk to your master," she said. "I may ask him to allow me to join the cult."

The hunchback's eyes opened wide, and, as was his habit, he then blinked rapidly.

"You ain't here just to snoop around?" he asked with distrust.

"Such an idea!" Penny hoped that her laughter sounded convincing.

"If ye want to join the cult, you can talk to Father Benedict later," the hunchback said grudgingly. "But unless you got something to contribute, it's no use trying to get in."

"Money you mean?"

"Either cash on the line or jewels."

"And what becomes of the money?"

"It goes for charity." Winkey fast was losing patience. "Now cut out the questions!" he said crossly. "If you want to join the society, talk to the boss."

"Are there any other girls staying here?" Penny had been leading up to this question.

"Talk to the boss, I said!" Winkey snapped. "Maybe he'll be here tomorrow. Now go away and stop botherin' me. I got work to do!"

Disappointed by her failure to find Mr. Ayling or extract information from Winkey, Penny returned to the car.

Driving along the road a few minutes later, she glimpsed, far over the hills, a skier who descended the steep slope at breakneck speed.

"It's a wonderful day for skiing!" she thought, recalling that all of her equipment was ready in the car. "Why don't I make the most of it?"

Pulling up, Penny got out skis and poles. Hastily waxing the runners, she put them on and set off across the fields toward the distant hill.

The loose snow had blown into deep banks and crevasses. Penny frequently had been warned by more experienced skiers that visible crevasses nearly always were a warning of hidden ones.

THE CRY AT MIDNIGHT

At first as she raced along, she kept alert watch for unexpected breaks or depressions in the snow. But as she drew near the hills to the rear of the old monastery, she frequently shifted her gaze toward the interesting old building.

Smoke curled lazily from the hooded chimneys. Otherwise, the premises appeared unoccupied.

Then, Penny saw a bent figure coming from the rear of the grounds, pulling a long sled behind him.

"Why, it's Winkey!" she recognized him. "Now what can he be doing with that sled? Surely at his age he isn't going coasting."

More than a little interested, the girl set her course the better to watch the hunchback. Soon she saw him striking off toward a pine woods and a large, two-story log cabin some distance away.

At the edge of the woods, not far from the cabin, had been stacked several cords of seasoned logs taken from the forest.

Pulling his sled alongside, Winkey began to pile it high with the cut firewood.

"I wonder if that's his wood?" thought Penny.

So absorbed had she become in Winkey's actions that she neglected to watch the drifts ahead. Too late, she saw that her singing skis were taking her directly into a wide, deep crevasse.

Desperately, Penny swerved and tried to check her speed. The break in the snow was extensive and could not be avoided.

Over the brink she shot. Poles flew from her hand and she clutched wildly for a hold on the bank. Failing, she tumbled over and over, landing in an ungainly heap of splintered skis at the base of the deep pit.

CHAPTER 9 - A CALL FOR HELP

After coming to a stop at the bottom of the crevasse, Penny momentarily was too stunned to move.

Gradually recovering her breath, she gingerly twisted first one leg, then the other. Though pains shot through them, no bones were broken.

Rolling over on her back, the girl gazed up at the narrow opening far above her.

"Served me right for being so careless!" she thought. "But the $64 question, is how am I going to get out?"

With fingers numb from cold, Penny removed her broken skis.

Walls of the hole into which she had fallen were sharp and firm with frozen ice, offering few if any handholds.

Unwilling to call attention to her plight unless absolutely necessary, she studied the sheer walls carefully, and then, grasping a projection, tried to raise herself to a ledge just over her head. The ice broke in her fingers, and she tumbled backwards again.

Penny now began to suffer from cold. Her clothes, damp from perspiration, were freezing to her body.

"This is no time to be proud!" she thought. "I'll have to shout for help and hope Winkey hears me. He's the last person in the world I'd ask voluntarily, but if he doesn't help me, I may be trapped here hours! I could freeze to death!"

Penny shouted for help and was alarmed by the sound of her own voice. Not only was it weak, but it seemed smothered by the walls of the crevasse. She knew the cry would not carry far.

But as she drew a deep breath preparatory to shouting again, she heard voices only a short distance away.

Her first thought was that her cry for help had been heard and someone was coming to her aid.

The next instant she knew better. Those who approached were arguing violently.

"You stole the wood from my land!" she heard the accuser shout. "I saw you pile it on your sled, and you're carrying it away now!"

Penny recognized the gruff voice of Vernon Eckenrod and guessed that he was talking to Winkey. Evidently the two were coming closer, for their argument was waxing louder.

Forgetting her own predicament, Penny listened intently. The pair were now almost at the brink of the crevasse.

"Say something!" Eckenrod roared. "What excuse have you got for stealing my wood?"

"Button your lip!" Winkey retorted. "The boss told me to get some wood for the fires at the monastery. So I done it."

"He told you to steal, did he?"

"You'll git your money."

"Money isn't the point! I cut that wood myself from my own land, and I want it for my own use! Here, give me that sled! You're hauling it straight back where you got it!"

"Keep your hands off!"

Penny heard the sound of scuffling, and then above her, at the mouth of the crevasse, she saw the two men struggling.

"Look out!" she called.

Startled by her voice, Eckenrod turned and looked down. At that instant, when he was off guard, the hunchback struck him. Reeling backwards, the artist tried to recover balance and could not. With a shriek of fright and rage, he fell into the chasm.

Penny attempted to break the man's fall with her body. She was not quick enough, and he rolled to the very bottom, ending up on a pile of broken skis. There he lay groaning.

If Penny had expected that Winkey would be aghast at his brutal act, she was to learn otherwise.

"That'll teach you!" he shouted in glee. "Don't never accuse me of stealing!"

"Help us out!" Penny called.

She knew Winkey heard her, for he stopped short and peered down into the crevasse to see who had appealed for help. Giving no sign he had seen her, he then disappeared.

"Maybe he's going for a rope!" Penny thought. "But I'd quicker think he's deserting us!"

Now thoroughly alarmed, the girl crept over the slippery ice to Vernon Eckenrod's side. He was conscious but stunned. Blood gushed from a cut on the back of his head and one leg remained crumpled beneath him.

With a handkerchief, Penny attempted to stop the flow of blood. She was relieved to note that the wound was a superficial one.

"Try to sit up," the girl urged. "If you lie on the ice your clothes will soon freeze fast."

Eckenrod's eyes opened and he stared blankly at her.

"Who are you?" he muttered. "How did you get down here?"

"I fell, the same as you. I'm Penny Parker, the girl you met yesterday at the monastery."

With her help, the artist pulled himself up on an elbow.

"I remember you now," he mumbled. "Did you see that hunchback push me down here?"

"Yes, I did. It was a brutal thing to do. I think now he may have gone for a rope."

"Don't you believe it!" Eckenrod said bitterly. "He wouldn't help us if we were freezing to death! The man is a thief! He was stealing my wood! I'll have the law on him!"

"First we have to get out of here," Penny reminded him. "That's not going to be easy."

Eckenrod became sober as he studied the sharp walls of the crevasse. The only possible handhold was a ledge well above their heads.

"If you can boost me up, I think I can make it," Penny said. "Then I'll go for help."

Eckenrod attempted to get to his feet, but his left leg crumbled beneath him. Pain and despair were in his eyes as he gazed at his companion.

"Broken," he said. "Now we are in a fix."

Trying not to disclose fright, Penny said the only thing to do was to call for help. However, after she had shouted until she was nearly hoarse, she too was filled with despair.

"Winkey isn't coming back," she acknowledged. "And no one else is close enough to hear our cries!"

In an attempt to ease Mr. Eckenrod's pain, Penny tore strips of cloth from her underskirt, and used the broken skis to make a splint.

"There's nothing wrong with my right leg," the artist insisted. "It's good and strong. If only I could get up on it, I think I could boost you to the ledge. We've got to do something!"

"Could you really do it?" Penny asked, hope reviving.

"I've got to," the artist replied grimly. "Night's coming on. We'll freeze if we're here an hour."

With Penny's help, Mr. Eckenrod after several attempts, managed to struggle upright on his good right leg. He weaved unsteadily a moment, then ordered:

"Now onto my shoulders!"

She scrambled up, grasping the icy ledge above. It broke in her fingers.

"Hurry!" muttered Mr. Eckenrod, gritting his teeth.

With desperate haste, Penny obtained another handhold which seemed fairly firm. She could feel Mr. Eckenrod sagging beneath her. Knowing it was then or never, she heaved herself up and rolled onto the ledge. Miraculously, it held her weight.

Relieved of the burden of the girl's weight, Mr. Eckenrod collapsed on the floor of the crevasse again, moaning with pain.

"Oh, Mr. Eckenrod!" Penny was aghast.

"Go on!" he urged in a stern voice. "You can make it now! Climb on out and bring help! And be quick about it!"

CHAPTER 10 - MR. ECKENROD'S SECRET

Thus urged, Penny scrambled up the slippery, sloping side of the wall and reached the top safely.

Completely spent, she lay there a moment resting.

"Don't give up!" she called to Mr. Eckenrod. "I'll get back as fast as I can!"

The closest house was the artist's own cabin in the woods. Plunging through the big drifts, the girl pounded on the door.

Almost at once it was opened by a middle-aged woman with graying hair and alert, blue eyes. Seeing the girl's rumpled hair and snow-caked skiing suit, she immediately understood that something was wrong.

"You're Mrs. Eckenrod?" Penny gasped.

"Yes, I am. What has happened?"

"Your husband has had a bad fall and his leg may be broken! We'll need a rope and a sled."

Mrs. Eckenrod won Penny's admiration by the cool manner with which she accepted the bad news. After the first quick intake of breath, she listened attentively as Penny told her what had happened.

"You'll find a long rope in the shed," she directed.

"And a sled?"

"The only one we have is a very small one my grandchildren use when they come here to play. It will have to do. You'll find it in the shed too. While you're getting the things, I'll telephone a doctor to come right out!"

"We'll need a man to help us!"

"No one lives within miles except those folks who moved into the monastery."

"We'll get no help from there!" Penny said bitterly.

"I'll call Riverview for men!"

"We don't dare wait, Mrs. Eckenrod. Your husband is half frozen now. We'll have to get him out ourselves somehow."

"If we must, we can," replied the woman quietly. "I'll telephone the doctor and be with you in a moment."

On her way to the shed, Penny looked hopefully across the darkening hills for a glimpse of the lone skier she had seen earlier in the afternoon. He was nowhere visible.

By the time Penny had found a rope and the sled, Mrs. Eckenrod joined her. The woman had put on a heavy coat, galoshes, and carried woolen blankets.

"How did the accident happen?" she asked, as they plodded through the drifts together.

Penny related the unfortunate argument involving the theft of firewood.

"Oh, dear! It's Vernon's dreadful temper again!" Mrs. Eckenrod exclaimed. "He is a wonderful man, but ready to quarrel if anyone crosses him!"

"In this case, I think he was in the right," Penny replied, helping her companion over a big drift. "I saw the hunchback take the wood, and I heard the argument."

"When those new people moved into the monastery, I was afraid we would have trouble with them. Something queer seems to be going on there."

"How do you mean?" Penny asked, recalling that she had expressed the identical thought at home.

"Well, the house is so quiet and deserted by day. Come night, one hears all sorts of weird noises and sees roving lights. Last night I distinctly heard a woman scream twice. It was most unnerving."

"Have you noticed anyone except the hunchback and his master leaving the building?"

"Only a young girl."

"Then I didn't imagine it!" Penny exclaimed.

Mrs. Eckenrod stared at her, puzzled by the remark.

Penny did not take time to explain, for they now had reached the crevasse. Anxiously, the rescuers peered down into the darkening hole.

"Vernon!" his wife cried.

At sound of her voice, he stirred and sat up.

Relieved that he was still conscious, Penny stretched out prone at the lip of the crevasse. Rapidly, she lowered the rope.

"Knot it around your waist!" she instructed.

Mr. Eckenrod obeyed and with a supreme effort, got up on his good leg.

"Now up you come!" Penny shouted encouragingly. "If you can help just a little, I think we can make it."

Mrs. Eckenrod was a solidly built, strong woman. Even so, it was all the two could do to pull the artist up onto the overhanging ledge. Completely spent, he lay there for a while as his rescuers recaptured their breath. Then, the remaining distance was made with less difficulty.

Penny and Mrs. Eckenrod rolled the man onto the sled, covering him with warm blankets. Even then, their troubles were not over. To pull the sled through the drifts to the cabin, took the last of their strength.

"We did it!" Penny cried jubilantly as they made a saddle of their arms to carry the artist into the warm living room.

Mrs. Eckenrod threw a log on the fire and went to brew hot coffee. Penny sponged the blood from the artist's head but did not attempt to bandage it, knowing a doctor was on the way.

Twenty minutes later, Dr. Wallace arrived from Riverview. After carefully examining the artist's leg, he placed it in a splint and bandaged it.

"You'll be on crutches for a few days," he told Mr. Eckenrod. "The bone may be cracked, but there is no break."

"That's the best news I've heard today!" Mr. Eckenrod declared in relief. "I've got some important business to take up with a certain party!"

"Vernon!" remonstrated his wife.

After the doctor had gone, Mr. Eckenrod was put to bed on the davenport. But he refused to remain still. As the pain in his leg eased, he experimented walking with the aid of a chair.

"I'll be using my pins in three days at the latest!" he predicted. "Just as soon as I can get around, I'm going to the monastery and punch that hunchback's nose!"

"Vernon!"

"Now don't 'Vernon' me," the artist glared at his wife. "The man richly deserves it! He's a thief and bully!"

Penny gathered up her mittens which had been drying by the hearth. "You may have trouble getting into the monastery," she remarked. "If Winkey sees you first, he'll probably lock the gate."

"You think that would stop me?"

"How else could you get in? Over the fence?"

"I know a way," the artist hinted mysteriously.

"Not another gate?"

"No."

"A secret entrance?"

Mr. Eckenrod's quick grin told Penny that her guess had been right.

"You did me a good turn today, so I'll let you into the secret," the artist said. "Help me hobble into the studio, and I'll show you something that will make your eyes pop!"

CHAPTER 11 - MAP OF THE MONASTERY

"Here, lend me a shoulder!" Mr. Eckenrod ordered as Penny hesitated. "Or aren't you interested?"

"Oh, I am—but your leg."

"Stuff and nonsense! The doc said it wasn't broken, didn't he? I'll be walking as well as ever in a few days."

Supported on one side by Penny and on the other by his wife, the artist hobbled to the adjoining studio.

On easels about the room were many half completed paintings. Several fine pictures, one of the artist's wife, hung on the walls. A paint-smeared smock had been draped carelessly over a statue.

"Vernon," sighed his wife, reaching to retrieve the garment, "you are so untidy."

"Without you, my dear, I should live like a pig in a sty and revel in it," chuckled the artist.

At a desk, amid a litter of letters and papers, were several large sheets of yellowed drawings.

"These are the original plans of the monastery," Mr. Eckenrod said, placing them in Penny's hands. "They show every detail of the old building before it was remodeled by later owners."

"How did you get these plans, Mr. Eckenrod?"

"The present owner of the building let me have them to study at the time I planned to buy the property. He would have sold the place to me too if that soft-talking fellow who calls himself Father Benedict hadn't come along!"

"Vernon, you mustn't speak that way of him!" reprimanded his wife in a shocked tone. "I'm sure he's a good, kind man of religion. Just because you had a quarrel with his servant—"

"Father Benedict has less religion than I've got in my little finger!" the artist growled. "You said yourself only last night that something's wrong at the place! What of those screams we heard?"

"It was explained to me that a simple-minded woman named Julia works at the monastery," Penny volunteered. "She is supposed to be easily upset."

"Humph!" muttered Mr. Eckenrod. "All I can say is, Father Benedict surrounds himself with mighty queer people."

"It's really none of our affair, Vernon," said his wife mildly.

"What goes on there is my business until the paintings are finished! But Father Benedict and ten hunchbacks can't keep me away! With these plans I can always outwit them!"

"What do they show?" Penny could not make much from the dim lines.

"The building is built on the pattern of Sherborne in England," Mr. Eckenrod explained. He pointed out the main part of the church with nave, south and north transepts, choir and chapel. "This section is a ruin now, but could be restored. Unfortunately, the roof has caved in and all paintings and statues were long ago destroyed."

"Show me the cloister," requested Penny.

"Here it is." The artist pointed with a stubby thumb. "Passages radiate from it. One leads to the old chapter house. North of the cloister is the refectory, used as a dining room. Behind is the abbey's kitchen."

"The sleeping rooms?"

"They're above the refectory and also to the west of the cloister. Under the refectory are the cellars. They also extend beneath the old chapel."

"Have you ever visited them, Mr. Eckenrod?"

"The cellars? I have. Also the burial crypt. A few of the old tombs remain in fairly good state of preservation."

"But where is the secret passageway?" asked Penny.

"Through the crypt. It leads into the churchyard to the west of the building."

"Do many people know about it?"

"I rather think I'm the only one. The building owner never bothered to study the plans, because he wasn't interested. Father Benedict may have learned the secret, but if so, he stumbled onto it by accident."

"Is the passageway well hidden?"

"Very cleverly. From the churchyard, one enters an empty tomb above ground. A passageway leads down to the crypt beneath the old chapel."

"Not a very pleasant way to enter or leave a building," said Penny with a shudder.

"But convenient in a pinch," chuckled Mr. Eckenrod. "If Father Benedict is stubborn about allowing me inside, I'll bide my time and slip in to finish my paintings one of these days when he is away."

Poring intently over the plans, Penny remarked that she would like to explore the passageway sometime.

"Wait a few days until my leg is strong and I'll take you through!" the artist offered.

"And if Father Benedict should catch us?"

"We can handle him!"

"Vernon, you shouldn't put Miss Parker up to such tricks!" his wife protested. "When it comes to playing pranks, or getting even with folks, you're just like a child!"

"It was no child's play pushing me into the crevasse!" the artist exclaimed. "As soon as I can hobble to town, I'll swear out a warrant for that hunchback's arrest!"

"And involve us in an endless feud with our neighbors," his wife sighed. "Vernon, you must forget it!"

The discussion was brought to an abrupt end by Penny who declared that she must leave immediately. The Eckenrods thanked her again for her timely assistance, urging her to visit them again soon.

"Don't forget our date!" the artist added with a chuckle. "I'll be walking in a day or two. Then we'll explore the crypt."

"I'll not forget," promised Penny.

Shadows were deepening into early darkness as she set off across the fields, guided by a flashlight Mrs. Eckenrod insisted she take.

The motor of her car was cold, the oil heavy. After two attempts she started it and soon was entering the outskirts of Riverview.

"Wonder if Dad's still at the office?" she thought. "If he is, I may as well give him a lift home."

By the time Penny had parked and climbed the stairs to the *Star* editorial room, the hands of her wristwatch were nosing six o'clock.

The first edition had rolled from the presses, and reporters, their feet on the desks, were relaxing for a few minutes.

Mr. DeWitt, the city editor, sat scanning the paper, noting corrections or changes to be made in the next edition.

"Hi, Mr. DeWitt!" Penny greeted him as she paused by the desk. "Dad here?"

"Hello there, Penny," the editor smiled at her. "He was a minute ago. Yes, here he comes now."

Mr. DeWitt jerked his head sideways toward the publisher's private office. Mr. Parker had on his hat and topcoat and would have left by the rear exit without having seen Penny had she not overtaken him.

"Want a lift home, Dad?" she inquired.

"Why, hello, Penny!" he said, pausing in surprise. "I certainly do. I left my car at home today."

Beside them, an unhooded Western Union teletype bell began to ring insistently.

"What's that for?" Penny inquired curiously.

"An incoming telegram," her father explained. "We have a direct wire with the Western Union office now. It saves sending so many messenger boys back and forth."

The carriage of the machine began to move and the telegram was typed on the long roll of yellow copy paper.

"Why, it's for you, Dad!" Penny said in surprise. "A wire from Chicago."

"Chicago?" Mr. Parker repeated. "Guess we'd better wait and see whom it's from. By the way, how did you and Mr. Ayling make out this afternoon at the monastery?"

"I haven't seen him since yesterday, Dad. When I went to the hotel to meet him, he wasn't there."

"Busy with other matters perhaps."

CHAPTER 11 - MAP OF THE MONASTERY

"I suppose so," Penny agreed, "but he might have notified me. He missed a lot of excitement by not going along."

Before she could tell her father about the skiing accident, the teletype message was completed. Mr. Parker ripped it from the machine. He whistled softly.

"Why, this wire is from Mr. Ayling!"

"Then he's in Chicago!"

"Apparently so. Listen to his message: 'CALLED HERE UNEXPECTEDLY BY TELEGRAM SIGNED MRS. HAWTHORNE. TELEGRAM PROVED A FAKE. RETURNING TO RIVERVIEW IMMEDIATELY TO RESUME SEARCH.'"

CHAPTER 12 - THE LOCKED DOOR

"Well, what d'you know!" Penny exclaimed as she peered over her father's shoulder to reread the telegram. "So that explains why Mr. Ayling didn't meet me today!"

"If he takes the first train back, he should get in early tomorrow," her father said. "I wonder who tricked him into going to Chicago?"

"Whoever did it probably figured he'd give up the search for Mrs. Hawthorne in disgust," Penny added excitedly. "Dad, this case is getting more interesting every minute!"

Mr. Parker smiled but made no comment as he pocketed the telegram. Together he and Penny went downstairs to the waiting car.

"Maybe I could help Mr. Ayling by inquiring around the city if anyone has seen Mrs. Hawthorne or her granddaughter," Penny suggested as she drove with skill through dense downtown traffic.

"I thought Mr. Ayling checked all hotels."

"Only the larger ones, I imagine. Anyhow, I might run into interesting information."

"Go ahead, if you like," her father encouraged her.

Early the next morning, Penny set off alone to visit a dozen hotels. At none of them had anyone by the name of Hawthorne registered.

"She may have used an assumed name," Penny thought, a trifle discouraged. "In that case, I'll never find her."

Hopeful that Mr. Ayling might arrive on the morning train, she went to the Union Railroad Station. Among those waiting on the platform for the incoming Chicago Express was Winkey, the hunchback.

He did not see Penny, and in the large crowd, she soon lost sight of him.

Finally, the train pulled in. But Mr. Ayling did not alight from either the coaches or pullmans. Feeling even more depressed, Penny went home for lunch.

Several times during the afternoon, she telephoned Mr. Ayling's hotel to inquire if he had arrived. Each time she was told he had not checked in.

"Wonder what's keeping him in Chicago?" Penny mused. "I hope he didn't change his mind about coming back here."

Throughout the day, she kept thinking about the monastery and its strange occupants. The skiing incident of the previous afternoon had convinced her that Winkey at least was cruel and dishonest. As to Father Benedict's character, she could not make up her mind.

"Possibly he doesn't know how surly and mean his servant acts," she thought. "Someone ought to tell him!"

Penny longed to return to the monastery, but hesitated to go there for the deliberate purpose of reporting Winkey's misbehavior.

"Mr. Ayling may return here tomorrow," she told herself. "Then perhaps we can drive out there together."

However, a check of the Riverview Hotel the following morning, disclosed that the investigator still had not arrived in the city.

Decidedly mystified by his failure to return, Penny clomped into the Parker kitchen after having spent an hour downtown. To her surprise she saw that during her absence a bulky package had been delivered.

"It came for you a half hour ago," Mrs. Weems explained.

"For me! Must be a mistake. I've ordered nothing from any store."

Plainly the package bore her name, so she tore off the heavy wrappings. Inside was a pair of new hickory skis.

CHAPTER 12 - THE LOCKED DOOR

"Dad must have sent them!" she exclaimed. "Just what I need."

However, the skis were not from her father. Among the wrappings she found a card with Mr. Eckenrod's name.

"Try these for size," the artist had scrawled in an almost illegible hand. "Thanks for pulling me out of a hole! My leg is mending rapidly, so don't forget our date!"

"Oh, the darling!" Penny cried. "Mighty decent of him to replace the skis I broke! Only I'm afraid I won't get to use them many times. It's thawing fast today."

Slipping her slim ankles through the leather bindings, she glided awkwardly about the polished linoleum.

"How soon's luncheon?" she asked impatiently. "I want to go skiing right away!"

"I'll put it on after I've telephoned Jake Cotton," the housekeeper promised. "He failed to show up here today."

"Jake Cotton, the carpenter?"

"Yes, your father ordered another bookcase for the den. Jake promised to build it last week. He's always putting other jobs ahead."

After telephoning, Mrs. Weems toasted sandwiches and made hot chocolate. Penny ate rapidly, as was her habit when thinking of other matters.

"You won't need any help with the dishes," she said hopefully when the meal was over.

"No, run along and ski," Mrs. Weems smiled. "In spirit you're already out there on the hills!"

Penny changed quickly into skiing outfit and telephoned Louise Sidell, inviting her to go along.

"Okay," her chum agreed half-heartedly, "but I'm still lame from the last time."

By the time the girls reached the hills near the Abbington Monastery, the weather had turned discouragingly warm.

Touring over the slopes, they discarded first their mittens, then their jackets. After Louise had fallen down several times, soaking her clothes in melted snow, she proposed that they abandon the sport.

"So early in the afternoon?" Penny protested. "Oh, we can't go home yet!"

"Then let's try something else. It's no fun skiing today."

Penny's gaze fastened speculatively upon the distant chimneys of the old monastery visible through the pine trees. "I have it, Lou!" she exclaimed.

"We're not going there!" cried Louise, reading the thought.

"Why not?" Already Penny was removing her skis. "I haven't learned half what I want to know about that place and the people who live there."

"It gives me the shivers to go near the property. Anyhow, that old hunchback never will let us inside!"

"Why don't we try, just for luck? Come on, Lou, at least we can talk to him."

Much against her will, Louise was induced to accompany Penny to the big grilled gate.

To their surprise, it stood slightly ajar as if in invitation for them to enter. The front grounds were deserted and so was the gatehouse.

"We're in luck!" chuckled Penny. "Winkey's gone off somewhere."

Louise's feet were reluctant as she followed her chum to the entrance door of the monastery. "Please—" she whispered, but already Penny had thumped the lion's head knocker against the brass plate.

Several moments elapsed and then a peephole panel just above their heads shot open. Old Julia, in white lace cap, her eyes dilated with wonder or fear, peered out at them.

Her lips moved in a gibberish they could not understand.

"She's telling us to go away!" Louise decided quickly. "And that's what we're doing!"

"No! Wait!" Penny held tight to her chum's arm. "Someone else is coming now."

Even as she spoke, the door opened and Father Benedict towered above them in his impressive robes.

"Yes?" he inquired. The word was mildly spoken but with no cordiality.

"Good afternoon, Father," said Penny brightly. "I hope you don't mind our coming here again. We're deeply interested in the work you're doing and would like to learn more about the cult."

"A story for newspaper publication?"

"Oh, no!" Penny assured him, reading displeasure in his eyes. "We're just interested on general principles. No one sent us."

The monk relaxed slightly but still did not invite the girls in. "I am very busy today," he said. "Perhaps another time—"

"Oh, but we'll be in school after this weekend, Father."

"We are preparing for a ceremonial to be held in the cloister," Father Benedict frowned. "I deeply regret—"

"Oh, a ceremonial!" Penny interrupted eagerly. "May we see it?"

"That is not allowed. Only members of our cult may take part or observe."

"Well, at least you don't mind if we come in and warm ourselves at your hospitable fire," Penny said, determined not to be turned away. "Since the organization is devoted to charity, shouldn't it begin with a couple of school girls?"

Father Benedict's thin lips cracked into a slight smile.

"My observation would lead me to believe that the day is a warm one and that neither of you are suffering from frost-bite. However, I admire perseverance and it shall be rewarded. You may come in—though only for a short while."

"Oh, thank you, Father!" Penny exclaimed, rather astonished by the decision.

In her eagerness to enter, she nearly stumbled over Old Julia, who huddled by the wall just inside the door. Angrily, the monk glared at his servant.

"Keep from underfoot, Julia!" he ordered. "Begone to the kitchen!"

The old woman, with a frightened glance directed at Louise and Penny, scurried away.

Once inside, the girls could understand why visitors were not welcome, for little had been done to make the place habitable since Penny's previous visit.

Through chilly halls the monk conducted the girls to the study beyond the cloister. There he motioned them to footstools before the fire. On the hearth a large log which Penny suspected had come from the Eckenrod property, had burned down to a cherry mass of coals.

"Now, suppose you tell me what you actually came here to learn?" Father Benedict asked, looking hard at Penny.

The abrupt question caught her slightly off guard. She could think of no ready reply. As she debated whether or not to tell him of Winkey's fight with Mr. Eckenrod, footsteps pounded down the corridor.

Suddenly the study door was flung open. The hunchback stood there, breathing hard from having hurried so fast.

"Come quick!" he said tersely to the monk.

"What's wrong, Winkey?"

"Trouble below!"

Preparing to follow the hunchback, Father Benedict briefly made his excuses to the girls. "I'll be gone only a minute," he said. "Warm yourselves until my return."

After the door had closed behind the pair, Penny said in a low tone: "Wonder what's up? So far as I know, the only rooms below are the storage cellars and crypt."

"Maybe some of the dead bodies are coming to life!" Louise joked feebly. "I hate this place worse every minute."

She arose and wandered slowly about the room. "Somehow, the air is oppressive. I feel as if doom were about to descend upon me!"

"Nerves!" chuckled Penny.

Louise paused beside the crystal ball. "What's this thing?" she asked suspiciously.

"Only Father Benedict's crystal globe. Take a look and see what's doing in the cellar!"

"You're joking!"

"Guess I am," Penny agreed. Arising, she joined Louise and for a long moment peered intently into the depths of the crystal ball. Seeing nothing in the glass she muttered in disgust: "Bunk!"

"How does one reach the basement and crypt?" Louise inquired.

"According to a plan I saw at Mr. Eckenrod's, a stairway leads down from the far end of the cloister. Say! Why not do a little exploring while Father Benedict is away?"

"He wouldn't like it."

"We'll never have a better chance." Crossing the room in long strides, Penny tried to open the door.

The knob turned readily, but the door would not open.

CHAPTER 12 - THE LOCKED DOOR

"Lou," she exclaimed in dismay, "Father Benedict certainly played a nice trick on us! We're locked in!"

CHAPTER 13 - OLD JULIA'S WARNING

Badly frightened, Louise came quickly to her chum's side.

"Are you sure the door is locked?" she asked nervously. "Maybe it's only stuck."

"It's locked all right. We'll do no exploring today."

"Let's scream for help! We've got to get out of here!"

"Father Benedict is in the basement and wouldn't hear us," Penny said.

"And he may have locked us in on purpose too! But I heard no key turn in the lock."

"Neither did I."

"The door may have an automatic catch."

"Probably that's so," Penny agreed to keep her chum from worrying. "Father Benedict should be back soon. Let's not let him know we even noticed the door was locked."

"Do you think he fastened it on purpose?"

"He may have," Penny said slowly. "Perhaps he didn't want us to wander about the monastery while he was gone."

"What if he doesn't come back?"

"He will, my pet. Now do stop worrying! The smart thing for us to do, is to learn what we can while we're here."

"A lot we can learn locked up in this stuffy room!"

Without replying, Penny wandered about the room, scrutinizing art objects and each piece of furniture.

"For a man who professes to live a life of poverty, Father Benedict shows quite a liking for luxury items," she remarked.

Coming to a battered desk cluttered with papers, she paused and eyed it thoughtfully.

"Penny, we wouldn't dare pry!" exclaimed Louise, guessing what was in her chum's mind.

"I suppose not," sighed Penny, "only I'm sure Mr. Ayling would do it if he were here. Those papers in the pigeon holes look as though they're unpaid bills—a whole stack of them too!"

On the desk lay an open account book and the girl gazed at it with keen interest. A long list of names had been written in ink. On one side of the ledger was a column marked "Contributions."

"Penny, you are snooping!" accused Louise, but she added with an excited laugh: "If you find anything worth while, let me know!"

"Then consider yourself officially notified!"

Startled, Louise went quickly to the desk. "What have you found?" she demanded.

Penny showed her the book in which were listed many names.

"This looks like a report covering donations made by cult members to the society!" she declared. "Do you suppose Mrs. Hawthorne's name is here?"

Hurriedly the girls examined the tiny ledger. First on the list was a Mrs. Carl Kingsley, who had contributed two diamond clips at estimated value of $650.

"Ever hear of her?" Penny asked, for the name was unfamiliar.

"Never. She may not be from Riverview."

Rapidly they scanned the entire list. There were many names, all of women. Contributions included cash, pearls, silver bracelets, gold wrist watches, an emerald pin, and other articles of jewelry.

However, the girls could not find Mrs. Hawthorne's name, nor that of her granddaughter.

CHAPTER 13 - OLD JULIA'S WARNING

"This list doesn't prove anything one way or the other," Penny said, carefully replacing the ledger on the desk where she had found it. "Mrs. Hawthorne could have joined the cult under a different name. Father Benedict might not even know who she is."

"Oh, Penny!" teased her companion. "You want to uncover a mystery so badly! Actually, there's not one bit of evidence that Mrs. Hawthorne ever came here."

"True," Penny acknowledged in a low tone, "but you will admit a lot of queer things have happened. For instance, who sent Mr. Ayling the fake telegram? And why hasn't he returned to Riverview as he said he would?"

"He's hardly had time yet. Anyway, what connection could his absence have with this monastery?"

"None, perhaps. Unless Mrs. Hawthorne should be here—"

"Oh, Penny! Father Benedict denied that she was, didn't he?"

"Yes, but that crystal ball reading he gave for Mr. Ayling's benefit was a strange affair. And Lou! The worst was, *he predicted harm would befall him*! Maybe it has!"

"So you're superstitious! Do you really believe in those crystal ball readings?"

"No, I'm not!" Penny denied hotly. "Not for a minute do I put any faith in that crystal ball! But—"

"Mr. Ayling is delayed in Chicago, so you start to worry," completed Louise. "Penny, you're certainly building up a case!"

"Maybe I am," Penny admitted with a shrug. "However, other things bother me too."

"For instance?"

"That scream we heard at midnight. Mr. Eckenrod and his wife told me they had been awakened by strange noises here."

"Didn't you understand from Father Benedict that Old Julia causes the commotion?"

"Yes, and it's plain to see she is a poor demented creature. Still, there's something about her—when we came in today, I had a feeling that she was trying to tell us something."

"She did warn us away. However, in her condition she might say anything. So I dismissed it."

"I wish I could talk to Old Julia when Father Benedict isn't around," Penny said soberly. "I have a hunch she could tell us interesting things about this place!"

"Then you do distrust Father Benedict!"

"Not exactly," Penny denied. "He's been pleasant enough to us, and I suppose he has a perfect right to start a crazy cult here if he chooses."

"It's not only crazy but profitable," Louise reminded her. "Those contributions listed total up to several thousand dollars!"

"According to Father Benedict, the money goes to charity. But what charity? It's a cinch he isn't spending much in supporting the members of his cult. This building is as barren as a barn, and I've not seen any supplies come into the place while we've been around!"

"And where are the cult members?"

"They must stay in their rooms."

"A fine life!"

"I'm sure there are people in this household who aren't listed in the ledger," Penny resumed thoughtfully. "For instance, that girl I saw when I came here with Mr. Ayling. Who is she, and where does she keep herself?"

"Why not ask Father Benedict—that is, if we ever get out of here."

"I can't quite bring myself to do it, Lou. If ever I started asking questions, I wouldn't know where to stop."

"There's only one that bothers me," Louise said, roving toward the door. "How are we going to get out of here? Let's call for help!"

"Okay," Penny agreed reluctantly. "I hate to do it though."

First testing the door again to be certain it was locked and not stuck, she pounded with her fists on the heavy oak paneling.

"Let us out!" Louise called loudly. "Let us out! We're locked in!"

"That ought to fetch someone!" chuckled Penny. "Listen! I think I hear footsteps now."

From down the corridor, the girls detected a soft patter and a creaking of boards. To attract attention to their plight, they again pounded on the oaken panel.

The footsteps approached the door and halted. Penny, her ear pressed to the panel, could hear the sound of breathing on the other side.

"Let us out!" she called. "We're locked in here!"

"Sh!" came the loud hiss.

"It must be Old Julia!" Penny whispered to Louise. "Do you suppose she'll have sense enough to help us?"

"I doubt it," Louise muttered, resigning herself to a long wait in the monk's study. "Maybe we can get across to her the idea that she should bring Father Benedict here."

"Listen, Julia," Penny began, speaking slowly and as clearly as she could. "We're locked in here and we need help. Can you bring your master?"

"No! No!" came the sharp answer.

"Then unlock the door," Penny urged.

"Key gone," the old woman mumbled.

"Can't you find it? Don't you know where your master keeps them?"

There was no answer, but the girls heard the old woman scurry away.

"Has she gone to find a key, or has she just gone?" Louise sighed. "Father Benedict probably still is in the basement with Winkey, so we can expect no help from that quarter."

Impatiently, Penny glanced at her wrist watch. Actually, they had been locked in the room less than twenty minutes, but it seemed three times that long.

"It's useless!" Louise said, seating herself by the fire again. "We're trapped here until Father Benedict gets around to letting us out!"

At the door, Penny's keen ears detected sound. Again the pad, pad of footsteps!

"Old Julia's coming back!" she exclaimed. "Maybe she's not as stupid as we thought!"

Anxiously the girls waited. To their great relief, they heard a key turn in the lock. Then, an inch at a time, the door was pushed open.

Old Julia, her eyes wild, and hair streaming down her face, stared blankly in at them.

"Thanks, Julia!" said Penny. She tried to touch the woman's hand in a gesture of friendship, only to have her shrink back.

"Why, we won't hurt you," Penny attempted to sooth her.

"Go!" the woman mumbled, her cracked lips quivering. "Go!"

Seeing us here always seems to upset her, Penny thought. Aloud she remarked: "Yes, we're leaving now. If Father Benedict wonders what became of us, I'm afraid he'll just have to guess."

The girls started toward the cloister with Old Julia following a step behind.

"Hurry! Hurry!" she muttered. "No time!"

"Oh, we have plenty of time, if that's what you mean," replied Penny, smiling at her in a friendly way. Suddenly she halted as the thought occurred to her that she might obtain useful information from the woman if only she phrased her questions skillfully.

"Julia, you must know everyone who lives here in the dormitory rooms," she began. "Do you often see a girl about my age?"

A strange light flickered for a moment in the old woman's watery gray eyes, then died. She merely stared at Penny.

"No soap!" commented Louise. "Let's get out of here."

Penny, however, was persistent.

"Julia, you must have seen her—a girl like me," she emphasized. "Does she sleep here?"

"Sleep—sleep—" the word seemingly had aroused an unpleasant chain of thought in the old woman's twisted mind.

"Where is the girl's room?" Penny probed.

Julia did not act as if she had heard the question. She was mumbling to herself, a look of horror upon her face.

"What's she saying?" Louise demanded, unable to catch a word.

Penny bent closer. Distinctly she heard the old woman mutter: "The canopied bed! In the chapel room—"

Then old Julia stiffened and she flattened herself against the wall of the passageway, her eyes wide with fear.

Directly ahead, in the doorway opening onto the cloister, stood Father Benedict.

CHAPTER 14 - AN ASSIGNMENT FOR PENNY

Father Benedict's face was as expressionless as a marble statue, but his dark eyes smoldered with anger.
Ignoring Penny and Louise for the moment, he fixed the cringing Julia with stern gaze.
"Did I not order you to remain in the kitchen?" he demanded. His voice was low, almost purring. Nevertheless, the woman acted as if she had been lashed with a whip.
Mumbling unintelligibly, she scurried off down the covered passageway along the side of the cloister, and disappeared through another doorway.
"Please, it wasn't Julia's fault that she was here," said Penny, feeling sorry for the unfortunate woman. "Louise and I called for help and she came to assist us."
"Yes, we were locked in the study," added Louise. "If she hadn't come to our rescue, we would have been there yet."
"Do I understand you to say you were *locked* in?" asked the monk, his shaggy eyebrows lifting in astonishment. "The door sticks sometimes."
"It was locked," interposed Penny quietly. "We tried several times to open it. Julia finally let us out with a key."
Having divulged this bit of information, she immediately regretted it. A shadow passed over the monk's countenance.
"A key?" he repeated. "How would Julia know—" Breaking off, he smiled and completed: "The locks here are very old and sadly in need of repair. I must have a locksmith in immediately."
Father Benedict fixed his gaze upon one of the twisted, weather-stained columns of the cloister, for the moment seeming to forget the girls. Becoming a little uncomfortable, they edged toward the exit.
"We'll be going now," said Penny to remind him of their presence. "That is, unless you'll permit us to witness the cult ceremony."
"The main hall has not yet been prepared," Father Benedict replied quickly. "We have postponed the ceremony until later tonight."
"Perhaps we could return then."
"It would be highly inadvisable." Father Benedict's deep frown plainly showed that he was becoming irritated. "The members of our sect are sensitive to visitors. I regret onlookers are not as yet welcome."
That's telling me in a nice way to mind my own business, thought Penny. Aloud she said: "I see. Well, later on, perhaps."
Politely, Father Benedict escorted the girls through the cloister. Penny noted that much of the dirt and debris had been swept away. A beautifully carved stone stairway, which she had failed to notice upon her previous visit, led up to a narrow balcony.
Observing that many doors opened from it, she inquired if the dormitories were above.
"They are," the monk replied in a brief tone which discouraged further questions.
"It's so still in here," remarked Louise as they walked on. "One never would dream many people are staying in the building."
"We lead a quiet life," the monk explained. "For the most part, my people spend their time reading or in meditation and prayer."
The three now had reached the front door, and Penny thought she detected an expression of relief upon Father Benedict's face as he opened it for them.
"By the way," she remarked, "was anything seriously wrong in the cellar?"

"Oh, no! Nothing at all! Merely a leaking pipe. A plumber will take care of it. Thank you, and good afternoon."

With no show of haste, but very firmly, the monk closed the door in their faces.

"Well, how do you like that!" Penny muttered. "I never received a smoother brush-off!"

Snow was melting fast and running in rivers down the brick walk as the girls sauntered toward the gate. Winkey was nowhere to be seen, but knowing he might be close by, they were careful not to discuss Father Benedict until they were well beyond the property boundaries.

"Well, I guess this puts an end to your visits here," remarked Louise as they walked toward the parked car. "Father Benedict seems determined not to let you witness one of the cult ceremonies."

"Which makes me all the more determined to see one!"

"I have a hunch he'll turn you away if you call at the monastery again. Why don't you forget the place, Penny?"

"I should say not! I have an idea—it just came to me!"

"I suppose you'll sneak back at night or something equally as dramatic," teased Louise.

Penny plucked an icicle from a roadside bush, nibbling at it thoughtfully as she replied: "Only as a last resort. No, I'll drop in at the newspaper office and get Mr. DeWitt, the city editor, to assign me to do a feature story on the ceremony tonight. If I officially represent the *Riverview Star*, Father Benedict can't so easily turn me away."

The girls had reached the car. Stowing their skiing equipment, they motored rapidly toward the city.

"What did you think of Old Julia?" Penny inquired as they neared Louise's home. "Especially her remark about the canopied bed in the chapel?"

"Whoever heard of a bed of any kind in a chapel?" Louise scoffed. "She's dizzy, that's all."

"From a map Mr. Eckenrod showed me, I know the chapel is just off the cloister above the crypt," Penny recalled, switching on the windshield wiper to clear the glass of melting snow. "I suppose it could have been converted into a bedroom."

"I don't think her remark meant a thing. She mumbles most of the time."

"True, but the thing I noticed was that she seemed so afraid of Father Benedict. Do you suppose he abuses her?"

"Oh, Penny! A man of his calling?"

"He's not a real monk. Apparently this cult is only an order that has been in existence a short time. Father Benedict doesn't impress me as a very religious man. Furthermore, all that crystal-glass-gazing business leads me to think he's more of a charlatan than anything else!"

"Do you think he runs the place to get money?"

"I'm wondering, that's all. We know he accepts very liberal contributions from his converts. Where does the money go?"

"If I were certain he locked us in that room today, I'd believe the worst!" Louise declared as the car stopped in front of the Sidell home. Opening the door to alight, she added: "He put up a good story though. I guess it must have been an accident."

Penny made no reply.

"Well, I'll see you tomorrow," Louise bade her goodbye. "If you arrange to see one of the cult ceremonies, be sure to let me know."

The afternoon now was late. Penny drove to the *Riverview Star* building. Girls who worked in the downstairs business office were leaving for the day, but upstairs the editorial staff was just swinging into action for a busy night.

At the city editor's desk a short wave radio blared routine police calls. Editor DeWitt, an eyeshade pulled low over his eyes, scowled as he rapidly scanned copy.

Seeing Penny, he looked up and smiled, which was the signal for her to explain the purpose of her call.

Going straight to the point, she asked to be assigned a feature story on the cult ceremony that night in the monastery.

"Think you can get it?" he demanded gruffly.

"Why not?"

CHAPTER 14 - AN ASSIGNMENT FOR PENNY

"Two of our reporters already have failed. The high monkey-monk out there won't allow any of our men in the building."

"Then you'd like a story?"

"Sure. We're interested in what's going on out there." Mr. DeWitt slashed a page of corrected copy in half with his long scissors. He dropped one section onto the floor and the other into the copy basket. "Learn anything worth while out there today?"

"Nothing worthy of print. If you'll assign me to the story I'll go back tonight. I think I can get inside again."

"Okay, give me a ring if you run into anything interesting. Your father know you're going?"

"Well, I haven't told him yet."

"Be sure you do," said Mr. DeWitt, looking her straight in the eyes. "I don't want to find myself sitting behind the eight ball!"

"Oh, I'll let Dad know," Penny assured him hastily. "I'll do it now."

However, her father was in conference, so after waiting around the office a little while, she decided to talk the matter over with him when he came home for dinner.

In the elevator, leaving the office, Penny ran into Jerry Livingston. Hearing of the assignment, he looked a little worried.

"Think you ought to go out to the monastery alone at night?" he inquired.

"I don't see why not, Jerry."

"I've not met Father Benedict myself," Jerry said, "but one of our reporters who was out there yesterday, didn't like his appearance. I'll bet a cent your father refuses to let you go."

"I hope not," Penny said anxiously. "I'll put up a big argument."

"What time you leaving?" Jerry asked as the elevator let them out on the main floor.

"Early. Maybe around seven o'clock."

"Well, good luck," Jerry said. "I suppose it's all right, or DeWitt wouldn't have given you the assignment."

Parting company with the reporter, Penny stopped briefly at the Riverview Hotel to inquire if Mr. Ayling had returned from Chicago. He had not checked in.

"Queer he doesn't come after sending that telegram," she thought. "I wonder what's delaying him?"

Arriving home a few minutes later, Penny heard the sound of pounding as she entered the kitchen. Mrs. Weems was scraping carrots at the sink.

"Did you have a good time skiing?" the housekeeper inquired.

"Fair." Penny stripped off her mittens and hung them on a radiator. "Snow's melting fast today. What's that awful pounding?"

"Jake Cotton finally came. He's building the bookcases in your father's study."

"Oh, yes," recalled Penny. "I thought from the sound the place was being torn down!"

After removing her heavy ski suit and putting her skiing equipment away, the girl wandered into the study.

Jake Cotton, a short, wiry old man, was gathering up his tools preparatory to leaving. Boards of various length were strewn over the carpet.

"Well, reckon I'll call it a day," he remarked. "It'll take me all tomorrow to finish the job. That is, if I can arrange to get back."

"You have another job?" Penny inquired.

"I've been doing a little work for them folks that moved into the monastery," the carpenter explained. "The man that owns the place pays well, but he's mighty fussy. Wants the work done the minute he says!"

"I suppose a great deal should be done out there, the building is so old."

"It's a wreck!" Jake Cotton said, picking up his tool kit. "A dozen workmen couldn't put it in liveable shape in two weeks! They want such trivial things done too, while they let more important repairs wait."

"For instance?"

"Well, the first job the monks had me do was fix the old freight lift into the cellar!"

"I didn't know the building had one," said Penny in surprise. "Is it on the first floor?"

"In the old chapel room off the cloister," Jake explained. "Least, that's what I took it to be. They're using it for a bedroom now. I ask you, what would any sensible person want with a freight lift in a bedroom?"

"It does seem unusual. Why was it originally installed in the chapel?"

"I heard it was done when the building was built," Mr. Cotton told her. "Years ago, they had burial services in the chapel, and caskets were lowered to the crypt below."

"How does the lift operate?"

"It's just a section of flooring that lowers when the machinery is turned on," the carpenter explained. "With a carpet over the boards, you wouldn't know it was there."

"And for what purpose is it to be used now?"

Mr. Cotton had started for the doorway. Penny trailed him to the front porch, eager to learn more.

"I couldn't figure out what the new owners aim to do with the lift," the carpenter replied, pausing on the steps. "Reckon they'll use it to lower heavy luggage and maybe unwanted furniture into the basement for storage."

"Did you see the crypt?"

"Didn't get down there. The monk had his own man, a hunchback, oil up the machinery and put it in working order. I only repaired the flooring."

"So the room is used as a bedroom now?"

"Looked that way to me. Leastwise, I saw a big bed in there. One of them old fashioned contraptions with a lot of dust-catching draperies over it."

"Not a canopied bed!"

"Reckon it was," Mr. Cotton answered carelessly. "Well, see you tomorrow if I'm not called back to the monastery to do another rush job! So long!"

Before the startled Penny could ask another question, he hurried off down the darkening street.

CHAPTER 15 - FOOTPRINTS IN THE SNOW

Jake Cotton's careless remark about the canopied bed at the monastery filled Penny with deep excitement.

"Perhaps Old Julia isn't as crazy as she seems!" she thought. "The place does have a canopied bed, and she may have been trying to tell me something about it!"

Now more than ever, Penny was determined to revisit the monastery that night. Many unanswered questions plagued her. Not only was she curious to witness a cult ceremony, but also she wished to learn the identity of the strange girl who lived on the premises. And she hoped to view the chapel room with the freight lift and if possible, to see the canopied bed of which Old Julia had prattled so unintelligibly.

Hastening into the house, Penny sought Mrs. Weems in the kitchen.

"Anything I can do to help with dinner?" she inquired.

The housekeeper, in the act of putting a kettle of potatoes on the fire to boil, eyed her with instant suspicion.

"And where do you plan to go when dinner is over, may I ask?" she inquired.

"Only out to the monastery."

"Again! You came from there not a half hour ago!"

"Oh, Mr. DeWitt assigned me to cover a cult meeting tonight," Penny assured her hastily.

"And your father approves?"

"Haven't seen him yet. He ought to be coming home any minute now."

"Your father telephoned he will be detained," Mrs. Weems explained. "I doubt he'll be home before nine o'clock. So the monastery expedition is out of the question!"

"Oh, Mrs. Weems!" Penny was aghast. "I promised Mr. DeWitt! He's depending on the story."

"That's neither here nor there," the housekeeper replied, though she softened a little. "I simply can't allow you to go to the monastery alone at night—"

"Oh, I'll start right away—just as soon as I can grab a bite of dinner," Penny broke in eagerly. "If Father Benedict refuses me permission to see the ceremony, then I can come back."

"You can, but will you?"

"Eventually, at least," Penny grinned. "Oh, Mrs. Weems, have a heart! Can't I telephone Dad somewhere?"

The housekeeper shook her head. "He's in an important meeting and can't be disturbed until it's over."

"But you will let me go? I won't be gone long."

"Oh, I suppose I'll have to give in," Mrs. Weems sighed. "I usually do. I'll hurry dinner along so you can get back early."

While the housekeeper fried pork chops, Penny set the table and prepared a salad. When the meal was ready she ate with a haste that shocked Mrs. Weems.

"I declare, your table manners become worse every day!" she protested. "Your mind isn't on what you are doing."

"It's on what I'm about to do!" Penny chuckled, getting up from the table. "I don't want any dessert tonight. See you later!"

Donning a heavy coat and slipping a flashlight into one of the deep pockets, she left the house.

The night was dark, for as yet there was no moon. Penny drove rapidly through Riverview and along the lonely road which led to the monastery.

Despite the speed of her car, she soon noted that another automobile was overtaking her. The girl pressed her foot a little more firmly on the gasoline pedal, but still the other car gained.

THE CRY AT MIDNIGHT

She was driving forty-five miles an hour when the big black car passed her traveling at least sixty. On the narrow road, Penny was crowded dangerously close to the ditch.

"The nerve of some people!" she muttered in disgust. "No wonder there are so many highway accidents!"

Penny caught only a fleeting glimpse of the black car's driver, a man hunched low over the steering wheel.

"Why, that looked like Winkey!" she thought. "And another man was with him in the front seat! I wonder if it was Father Benedict?"

Penny speeded up but found it impossible to keep the car in view. When she skidded at a curve, she wisely slowed down and abandoned the chase.

Approaching the monastery ten minutes later, the girl decided to park a short distance from the entrance gate. She left the car at the roadside beyond view of the gatehouse, and tramped on through the slush and snow.

Coming within sight of the ancient building, she paused.

The big gate stood ajar, and on the driveway stood the black automobile which had passed her car down the road.

"So it was Winkey!" she thought.

At the gateway Penny gazed carefully about the grounds. The hunchback was nowhere to be seen and the gatehouse remained deserted.

"So far, so good!" she encouraged herself. "Now if only Father Benedict doesn't refuse to let me into the house!"

Thinking over what she would say to the monk, Penny walked slowly up the driveway. Nearly all of the snow had melted, leaving large puddles to be avoided.

However, near where the black car had been parked, a section of yard was shadowed from the sun during the day. Here the damp snow remained in deep banks.

As Penny passed the car, she noticed a double set of men's footprints leading from the parked automobile toward the rear of the premises.

Also, she observed long marks which indicated the two men had dragged a heavy object over the snow.

"I suppose it was a sack of potatoes or supplies for the monastery," she mused. "It must be a job keeping this place in operation. Riverview stores never would make deliveries so far out."

Windows of the monastery were dark, though far inside the building dim lights could be seen. With a feeling akin to dread Penny went to the door and rapped with the brass knocker.

Now that she actually was embarked upon adventure, she rather regretted she had promised Mr. DeWitt a feature story. By night the monastery seemed more austere and unfriendly.

Minutes elapsed and no one came to answer the door. Impatiently, Penny clanged the knocker several times in rapid succession. Only then did she hear approaching footsteps.

At last the big door swung outward to reveal Father Benedict. His eyes narrowed with displeasure as he saw her.

"Well?" he inquired. Penny observed that he was a little breathless from having hastened.

"I don't suppose you expected to see me here again so soon!" she began with forced gaiety. "Do you mind if I witness the cult ceremony tonight?"

"We discussed that this afternoon. I am very sorry—" Father Benedict began to close the door.

"I want to write a little story about it for the newspaper," Penny went on, talking fast. "If you'll only—"

The door closed in her face. Distinctly she heard a key grate in the lock.

"Well, how do you like that?" Penny muttered angrily. "Who does he think he is, anyhow?"

She started away, only to pause and gaze thoughtfully back at the darkened windows. To return to the newspaper office without a story would be humiliating. A good reporter never failed.

"There must be some way to see that ceremony!" she reasoned. "Perhaps I can slip in through a rear door."

Penny circled the building, taking care to avoid snow patches where revealing footprints would be left behind. She crossed through the old church-yard with its toppled, weather-stained stones, passing close along the church wall.

Coming to a small arching door, she tried the knob.

"Locked!" she muttered in disgust. "One would think this place were a jail!"

Half way around the building Penny found another door which evidently opened into the kitchen. It too was locked.

CHAPTER 15 - FOOTPRINTS IN THE SNOW

"I'm out of luck!" she decided, losing heart.

As she turned away intending to return to her car, she noticed a window at shoulder level, opening from a kitchen wall. A ventilator screen had been inserted to permit free circulation of outside air.

Penny carefully studied the window. A crack between the screen and window frame encouraged her to hope that the mesh might be removed.

Obviously, the plan had disadvantages. In removing the screen, she might make too much noise and be detected.

Furthermore, a wide patch of snow separated her from the window. She could not reach the wall without leaving a trail of telltale footprints.

Then an idea flashed into Penny's mind. How easy it would be to make deceptive prints in the snow merely by walking *backwards*!

"If Father Benedict discovers my shoetracks, he'll think someone from inside the building crawled out the window!" she chuckled. "At least I hope he will!"

Now completely dedicated to the adventure, the girl carefully backed toward the window. She took each step slowly to make a distinct print.

Reaching the window, she tried the ventilator screen. To her delight, it folded like an accordian when she pushed one side against the edge of the window. Making no sound, she removed it.

Listening a moment to make certain no one was close by, Penny raised the window higher. Then on strong arms she swung herself up and over the ledge.

The girl found herself in a large kitchen lighted only by a smoldering log in a great cavern of a fireplace.

Rows of copper pans hung on the smoke-stained walls. In a huge black kettle, watery soup simmered over the fire.

Penny turned to close the window and stepped squarely on the tail of a drowsing cat.

"Ye-eow!" screeched the frightened animal.

Penny huddled against the wall, listening. Her heart sank as she heard heavy footsteps in the passageway. The howling cat had brought someone to investigate!

Frantically, the girl glanced about the room. Huge cupboards which rose from the floor to the ceiling offered the only possible hiding place in the otherwise barren kitchen.

Pulling open one of the doors, she saw an interior cluttered with greasy pans and dishes. With desperate haste, she tried the adjoining door. This cupboard was empty except for a few dusty newspapers.

Penny stepped inside, softly closing the door. Only then, as she heard someone enter the kitchen, did she realize that in her haste to hide, she had forgotten to close the window.

CHAPTER 16 - THE KITCHEN CUPBOARD

Into the kitchen lumbered Old Julia. She picked up the whimpering cat and began to croon endearments. Penny breathed easier. The next instant she became tense again as she heard another person enter the room.

"What was that noise, Julia?" a man demanded harshly.

Penny recognized Father Benedict's voice.

"Only the cat, Father."

"Why is the room so cold? Oh, I see! Against my orders you opened the window again!"

"No, I didn't!" Old Julia defended herself. "I hain't been near a door or window since you told me not to talk to nobody nor let 'em in. I don't talk to nobody—only Patsy, the cat. Nice Patsy!"

"You're a stupid old woman! What made the cat howl?"

"I dunno. She must've seen a mouse."

"Cats don't howl unless they are hurt! You opened the window!"

"No! No! I didn't!" the old woman cried. "Don't strike me! I'm telling you the truth."

Penny heard the monk walk to the window. Her heart skipped a beat when he said: "Perhaps you are, Julia! I can see footprints in the snow! Someone crawled out through this window! You helped that girl get away!"

"I didn't! I didn't!" whimpered Julia. "I dunno how the window got open."

The monk seemed to be talking to himself as he went on: "I knew that girl would make trouble the minute I set eyes on her! If it hadn't been for her interference, everything would have gone just as planned! Now she'll have to pay for her folly!"

For a moment Penny thought Father Benedict was speaking of her. Then it came to her that he must be referring to the dark-haired girl she had seen briefly on the day of her first visit to the monastery.

"This isn't the only time she's slipped out of here!" the monk went on angrily. "But it will be the last!"

Father Benedict rang a bell. While waiting for it to be answered, he slammed down the kitchen window.

Soon Winkey, the hunchback, appeared. "You called me, boss?" he inquired.

"I did," said the monk. "And kindly remember not to call me 'boss.' Father Benedict is a more respectful term."

"That's a laugh," rejoined Winkey rudely. "What did you call me for?"

"Look out the window and see for yourself."

"Footprints!"

"Going away from the monastery," Father Benedict added. "That girl has run off again! This time when she gets back, see that she is punished."

The command seemed to startle the gateman for he asked dubiously: "You don't mean—"

"I do." The monk's words dropped like chips of steel. "The usual punishment."

"But ain't it a little harsh for a girl? She's only a kid—"

"Only a kid!" Father Benedict's voice rose in mockery. "From the hour we came here she has been a thorn in my side. If it hadn't been for her interference, we would have been away from here yesterday!"

"Okay, if those are your orders. Are you sure the girl has skipped?"

"Certainly I am. I found the window open, and there are the footprints in the snow!"

"Maybe she won't be back."

"She will," Father Benedict said grimly. "You see, so long as we have her—"

He broke off to listen intently. From the direction of the cloister a silver bell had chimed.

"The signal for the processional!" Father Benedict exclaimed, interrupting himself. "I must go!"

CHAPTER 16 - THE KITCHEN CUPBOARD

In the doorway he apparently paused, for Penny heard him say to Julia:

"Start dishing up the soup ready to serve as soon as the ceremony is over! A bowl and four crackers to each person!"

"Is that all they're getting to eat?" Winkey inquired. "We're in for a lot of squawks!"

"You forget that the members of our sect have taken a vow of poverty and abstinence," retorted the monk with heavy sarcasm. "If there are any complaints, I know how to handle them."

"You sure do," agreed Winkey, his laughter crackling. "I'll hand you the gold plated medal for that!"

Voices of the two men died away, informing Penny that they had gone. As she huddled in the cramped quarters, she could hear Julia moving about the kitchen. The woman sighed heavily and once muttered: "Woe is me! Wisht I was dead, I do!"

Minutes elapsed and the girl became increasingly uncomfortable and impatient. Old Julia showed no inclination to leave the kitchen.

"I've got to get out of here or I'll miss the entire ceremony!" Penny told herself. "Well, here goes! If Julia screams, I'm a cooked goose!"

Opening the cupboard door a tiny crack, she peered out.

Old Julia had lighted candles. In their flickering light she could be seen with her back to Penny, stirring the soup. On the table beside her were ten wooden bowls.

"It's now or never!" the girl thought. "Julia may give me away, but I'll have to chance it!"

Opening the door wider, she moved noiselessly out and glided across the floor. A board creaked. But as Julia turned her head, Penny reached out and covered her mouth with her hand.

Seeing her, the old woman's eyes dilated with fear, but she could not speak.

"Don't try to scream! Don't say a word!" Penny warned. "I won't hurt you! I'm here to help you."

The old woman tried to break from the girl's grasp. Penny kept talking to her in a soothing tone until gradually she relaxed.

"Will you keep quiet if I release you?" she finally demanded.

The old woman's head bobbed up and down.

Penny removed her hand, expecting the worst. But Julia did not scream. Instead, she stared fixedly at the girl.

"Julia, I must see the ceremony, and Father Benedict isn't to know I am here," Penny whispered. "Will you keep my secret?"

Again Julia's head inclined, but the look of terror remained in her eyes.

"Go!" she whispered, pointing to the window. "Leave while there is time!"

"Not until I've seen the ceremony. Julia, I need a robe. Where can I find one?"

So stupidly did Julia stare at her that Penny was certain the woman did not understand. However, after a moment she shuffled to one of the storage cupboards where linen was kept. Returning with a white cotton robe, she placed it in the girl's hands.

Penny put the garment on over her coat, pulling the hood well down over her blond curls.

Then, with another whispered warning to Julia not to reveal her presence, she left the kitchen. The disguise gave her renewed confidence, for in the shadowy halls she felt that only at close range would anyone recognize her.

Three stone steps led up to the cloister. Approaching with great caution, Penny observed that it too had been lighted with candles.

In the center of the cloister near the old fountain, Father Benedict's crystal globe had been set up. On either side stood stately rows of tall candles.

Impressive as was the sight, Penny had no time to admire it, for a door had opened. Winkey came in, dragging a girl by the wrist.

With a shock Penny recognized her as the same girl she had seen while visiting the monastery with Mr. Ayling.

"And she's the same one Louise and I picked up in our car!" she thought.

The girl struggled to free herself from the hunchback's firm grasp.

"Let me go!" she cried, kicking at him. "Let me go!"

"Oh, no, you don't!" he taunted her. "This time you'll have to pay for sneaking out of the house and coming back!"

"I don't know what you're talking about!" the girl retorted. "I've not been out of this house tonight! If I could get away, I'd bring the police and have you arrested! You can't mistreat me! Let go my wrist!"

Before Winkey could answer, another door opened to admit Father Benedict. Walking straight toward the hunchback he exclaimed harshly:

"Fool! Don't bring her in here! The ceremony is starting! Lock her up and be quick about it!"

CHAPTER 17 - THE CULT CEREMONY

As Penny watched from behind a pillar in the cloister, Winkey pulled the struggling girl through a doorway and out of sight.

Father Benedict then adjusted his long robe and rang a silver bell. With stately tread he retired to a position behind the crystal globe.

An instant later from the far side of the cloister, a door was flung open. A procession of ten persons in white robes moved slowly into the shadowy room.

As far as Penny could tell, all who participated were women, many of advanced age. Leaders of the strange procession carried banners embroidered in silver and gold symbols.

The white robed figures moved slowly along the passageway, and Penny saw that they would pass the pillar where she stood.

Fearing detection, she shifted position slightly to avoid being seen.

But as the mumbling, chanting group passed her, she was overcome with a sudden impulse to join the procession.

"If I can get up close, I'll be able to hear what is said!" she thought. "Maybe I'll learn the secret of Father Benedict's strange power over these people!"

As the procession passed the pillar, Penny attached herself to the rear. With bowed head, she followed the others who formed a semicircle about the fountain.

The monk began a chant in Latin which Penny could not understand. However, his gestures were eloquent, and despite herself, she was impressed.

Presently he spoke in English, quoting the White Lady of Sir Walter Scott's "The Monastery."

"Mortal warp and mortal woof
Cannot brook this charmed roof;
All that mortal art hath wrought
In our cell returns to naught.
The molten gold returns to clay,
The polish'd diamond melts away;
All is alter'd, all is flown,
Naught stands fast but truth alone.
Not for that thy quest give o'er;
Courage! prove thy chance once more."

Eloquently, the monk then praised the frugal life, assuring his listeners that those who gave of their treasure to the cult society would receive untold spiritual values.

"As you file past the fountain cast your jewels into the basin," he bade the group. "You will be rewarded three-fold."

Slowly the robed women circled the fountain. The one leading the procession dropped a bracelet. The woman following fumbled beneath her robe and reluctantly gave a cameo broach.

"It was the last gift of my dear departed husband," she whispered tearfully. "I do so dislike to part with it—"

"You shall have your reward," the monk assured her. "Later, in the crystal globe, you will see the face of your husband!"

"So that's how he rules them!" thought Penny. "He plays upon their emotions and then pretends to conjure up visions of departed relatives!"

Another woman stripped a diamond ring from her finger, and cast it into the bowl of the fountain. The one who followed her, stood empty handed.

"Where is your contribution?" demanded the monk.

"I have none, O Master! At the last ceremony, I gave all!"

"Those who have no gift for the celestial spirits receive no rewards," Father Benedict said sharply.

"Please—"

"Pass on!" ordered the monk.

Realization now came to Penny that in another moment she too would be expected to drop her contribution into the fountain. What could she give?

On her third finger the girl wore a silver colored ring with a red glass stone. She had won it several days before at a church party fish pond, and despite the fact that it obviously had been bought in a dime store, had kept it.

As Penny's turn came she removed the cheap ring and let it fall into the basin of the fountain. Keeping the hood well over her face, she mumbled in a disguised voice: "I give my precious ruby ring!"

"Blessings upon you, my good woman!" said the monk approvingly. "The celestial spirits will remember your generosity."

Father Benedict now led the procession to the refectory where supper was to be served.

The room was drafty and barren except for one long table and benches. Old Julia had set out the wooden bowls of soup, and crackers, thoughtfully remembering to set an extra one for Penny. No other food was in evidence.

"Soup again?" asked one of the cult members in bitter disappointment. "We are hungry!"

"We've had little more than soup since we came here!" exclaimed another old lady plaintively.

"Are you so soon forgetting your vows?" chided Father Benedict. "Material things have no true meaning."

Grumbling a little, the women sat down at the table and began to eat. Penny took an empty place near the door. She tasted the soup and nearly gagged.

Father Benedict did not join the group. After lingering a few minutes he quietly slipped away. This offered Penny an opportunity to leave without arousing the monk's suspicions.

"I must learn more about that girl who is locked up here somewhere!" she thought. "Perhaps I can help her escape!"

Still wearing the white robe, Penny started back to the cloister. The cult ceremony which she had witnessed greatly disturbed her.

"Father Benedict is taking unfair advantage of these people," she told herself. "He accepts their jewels and gives nothing in return. Furthermore, he is cruel!"

Voices in the cloister directly ahead warned the girl to proceed cautiously. Keeping close to the wall and holding her robe tightly about her, she crept closer to the fountain.

The candles had all been extinguished. However, Father Benedict and Winkey were there, working by the light of a lantern.

"Fish out the jewels and be quick about it!" the monk ordered his servant. "We must be finished before they're through in the refectory."

The hunchback scrambled down into the bowl of the fountain, and groped with his hands for the trinkets the cult members had thrown away.

"Did the old lady kick in with the sapphire tonight?" Winkey asked as he worked.

"No!" the monk answered. "She sent word that she was too sick to leave her room! I suspect that girl put her up to it!"

"You goin' to let her get by with it?"

"I'll talk with her later tonight," Father Benedict said. "If she doesn't come across by tomorrow, we'll find ways to persuade her."

"You been saying that ever since she came here! If you ask me, we won't never have any luck with her until we get rid of the girl! She's been a wrench in the machinery from the start."

CHAPTER 17 - THE CULT CEREMONY

"I'm afraid you are correct, Winkey," sighed the monk. "But I do so dislike violence. Well, if it must be, so be it. You assigned her to the room with the canopied bed?"

"I locked her in like you said." Winkey, having gathered all of the trinkets, scrambled out of the stone basin onto the tiled cloister floor.

"What have we here?" asked the monk eagerly.

Winkey spread the contributions on a handkerchief. Father Benedict held the lantern closer to inspect the articles.

"Junk! Trash!" he exclaimed. "Only the diamond has any value."

"How about this ring?" demanded Winkey, picking up Penny's dime store contribution.

"Glass!" In fury, the monk hurled the ring across the cloister.

Penny suppressed a giggle. But Father Benedict's next words sent a shiver down her spine.

"This settles it!" he said. "I'll talk to the old lady now! If she refuses to give up the sapphire, then you know what to do with the girl!"

"I'm waiting for the chance!" growled the hunchback. "Just say when!"

"Once the girl is where she can't influence the old lady, we'll have no trouble," the monk continued. "However, we must work fast. After tonight, I have a feeling we will do well to move our institution elsewhere."

"The newspapers are sending reporters around to ask a lot of questions," agreed Winkey. "I don't like it! If anyone should find out about the crypt—"

"Let me do the worrying," interrupted Father Benedict. "We'll get the sapphire and be away before anyone even sets foot inside the place."

"What about that Parker girl?"

"She's only a child!" the monk scoffed. "A very annoying, nosey one, I grant you."

Taking the lantern with them, Father Benedict and Winkey disappeared in the direction of the monk's study. Left in darkness, Penny debated her next action.

If only she could telephone her father or Mr. DeWitt at the *Star* office! This, of course, was out of the question, for the ancient building obviously had no phone service.

"I might go for help," she reasoned, "but a full hour would be needed for me to reach Riverview and return with anyone. And what can I prove?"

Though Penny was convinced Father Benedict and Winkey were fleecing cult members, she knew the women voluntarily had given up their jewelry. In the event police tried to arrest Father Benedict, the cult members might rise to his defense.

"I'll have to have more evidence!" she decided. "The one person who should be able to tell me what goes on here is that girl who is locked in the chapel bedroom!"

Stealing across the dark cloister, Penny listened a moment at the passageway leading to the refectory. An undercurrent of conversation and the clatter of tin spoons told her that cult members had not yet finished the evening repast.

From the map Mr. Eckenrod had shown her, the girl knew the location of the chapel bedroom. Tiptoeing down a corridor opening from the cloister, she came to a massive oaken door.

"This must be the one," she decided.

Softly she tapped on the panel.

"Who is there?" called a startled voice. The words were so muffled, Penny barely could distinguish them.

"A friend," replied Penny.

Footsteps pattered across the room. "Help me get out!" the imprisoned girl pleaded.

Penny tried the door. As she had expected, it was locked.

"Where is the key?" she called through the panel. "If I can find it, I may be able to get you out of here."

"Speak louder!" the girl protested. "I can't hear you."

Penny dared raise her voice no higher. She realized that the heavy paneling deadened sound and made it impossible to carry on a satisfactory conversation.

"The key!" she called again. "Where is it?"

As she spoke the words, a board snapped directly behind her. Penny's heart jumped. Before she could turn to look over her shoulder, a bony hand reached out of the darkness and grasped her wrist.

CHAPTER 18 - ELEVEN BOWLS

Smothering a scream, Penny twisted around to see that it was Old Julia who had seized her arm.

"Oh!" she gasped in relief. "I thought it was Winkey or Father Benedict!"

"You go now!" the old woman urged her. "*Please!*"

"I can't until I've helped whoever is locked in here," Penny replied, gently prying away Julia's fingers which were cutting into her flesh. "Tell me, where is the key?"

Old Julia shook her head in a stupid sort of way.

"The key to this door," Penny explained patiently. "Where is it kept?"

"Father Benedict," Julia mumbled. "No other."

"Then it's impossible to help the girl without bringing police!" Penny exclaimed. "I'll have to get out of here and drive to Riverview! But can I prove anything?"

Old Julia stared blankly at Penny as if not understanding a word. But she reached out, and taking hold of the girl's hand, pulled her along the corridor.

Believing that the servant meant to show her a quick means of exit from the building, Penny willingly followed.

However, Old Julia led her only a few yards before pausing beside another door. Opening it, she motioned for Penny to step inside.

The girl saw with some misgiving that Old Julia expected her to enter what appeared to be a rather large, empty storage closet.

"Oh, I don't want to hide," Penny explained thinking that the old woman had misunderstood. "I must leave here now."

"Inside!" bade Julia insistently. "You see! Talk!"

She gave Penny a little shove into the room and closed the door.

Only then did the girl realize that she barely had escaped detection. For, in the corridor, heavy footsteps now were heard. Standing motionless against the closet door, she recognized Father Benedict's voice as he spoke to Julia:

"What are you doing here?" he asked the servant harshly. "Have I not told you never to come into this section of the building?"

Julia's reply was inaudible. The monk's next remark warned Penny that she courted detection if she remained longer in the building.

"I have just come from the refectory," he said. "I counted the soup bowls. There were ten empty and one barely touched. *Who was the eleventh person in this household that was served tonight?*"

"Don't ask me," moaned Old Julia. "I dunno nothing."

"Sometimes," said the master coldly, "I am inclined to think you know far more than you let on. Get to the dishes now! Go!"

Evidently Father Benedict struck or kicked the woman, for Old Julia uttered a sharp cry of pain. Her sobs died away as she retreated down the corridor.

After the old woman had gone, Father Benedict unlocked the door of the bedroom and stepped inside. By pressing her ear against the closet wall, Penny was able to hear every word of the ensuing conversation.

"Well, my dear," said Father Benedict to the imprisoned girl. "Are you ready to come to your senses?"

"If you mean, am I willing to sit quietly by and see you rob my grandmother, the answer is 'No!'"

CHAPTER 18 - ELEVEN BOWLS

"I do not care for your choice of words, my dear," replied the monk. "You are an impertinent child who must be disciplined."

"Wait until I get away from here!" the girl challenged. "People will learn exactly what's going on in this place!"

"Will they indeed? So you propose to make trouble?"

"I'll tell what I've seen. You're only a cheap trickster! Furthermore, you can't keep me a prisoner in this room."

"No?" Father Benedict's voice crackled with amusement. "In this house *I am the law*! Since you are in no mood to discuss matters reasonably, I shall leave you here. Your grandmother, I trust, will display a more sensible attitude."

"You leave my grandmother alone!" the imprisoned girl cried furiously. "You're only after her gems!"

"If you were to cooperate—"

"I'll never fall in with your schemes!" the girl exclaimed. "Let me out of here!"

Penny heard a scuffle and knew that an unsuccessful attempt had been made to reach the door. As her own hand groped along the closet wall, it suddenly encountered a small, circular panel of wood. As she pushed against it, a crack of light showed through.

"A peephole!" Penny thought. "Julia knew it was here! That was what she meant when she said I could see and listen!"

Stealthily, so as to make no sound, she slid the piece of wood aside.

Gazing into the semi-dark bedroom, she saw Father Benedict push the struggling girl backwards onto the canopied bed.

"You have settled your own fate!" he said angrily. "Now you'll stay here until I find a better place! Sweet dreams, my little wildcat!"

Quitting the room, he locked the heavy door. The girl on the bed buried her head in the dusty, scarlet draperies and began to cry.

Penny waited only until she was certain Father Benedict was far down the corridor. Then she rapped softly on the closet wall.

Through the peephole, she saw the girl start violently and look about the room.

"Hist!" Penny whispered. "Over here!"

She rapped again, and this time the girl saw the tiny hole in the wall. Leaping from bed, she came across the room.

"Who are you?" she demanded, unable to see Penny's face.

"A friend! I'm here to help you."

"Can you get me out of this room?"

"Father Benedict seems to have the only key," Penny told her. "I'll sneak out of here and telephone the police. But first, I must know exactly what case we have against Father Benedict."

"He's mean and cruel! He half starves the people who live here and takes all their money and jewels!"

"Why did he shut you up here?"

"Because I've opposed him. Though I tried hard to prevent it, he coaxed my grandmother to come to this horrible place."

"Have either of you been mistreated?" Penny asked.

"Until tonight, Father Benedict favored us above the other cult members. Of course, that was only because as yet he hasn't been able to get his thieving hands on the star sapphire!"

At mention of the gem, Penny's pulse leaped. No longer did she doubt that the girl was the missing Hawthorne heiress sought by Mr. Ayling.

"You're the one I picked up on the road," she said. "But you've never told me your name. Is it possible you're Rhoda—"

"Rhoda Hawthorne," the girl completed for her. "I refused to answer your questions before because I distrusted everyone."

"And now?"

"I realize you're a true friend—the only one I have. Oh, you must get me out of this room quickly! Please bring police at once!"

CHAPTER 19 - A DORMITORY ROOM

"I'll get you out of this room somehow," Penny promised through the peephole. "First, before I go for police, tell me more. Why were you carrying a suitcase that night Louise and I met you on the road?"

"I was running away," Rhoda Hawthorne replied.

"Yet you returned here."

"I had to. When I thought about Grandmother alone in the clutches of Father Benedict, I knew I couldn't desert her. She is putty in his hands!"

"But why didn't you bring police here yourself, Rhoda?"

"What could I prove? Until tonight when Father Benedict locked me up, I had no real evidence against him."

"Even now, we haven't very much," said Penny. "He'll deny he imprisoned you unless police take him by surprise and find you here."

"Grandmother will be worrying about me," Rhoda said anxiously. "She's in her room now, sick abed. I'm afraid it's from eating such vile food."

"What does the doctor think?"

"No doctor has seen her. Father Benedict won't allow anyone to call if he can prevent it. He has only one thought—to get his hands on the sapphire and leave here before police catch up with him."

"You're really convinced he is a crook?"

"I'm certain of it! Grandmother and I met him at a Florida resort. As soon as he learned about the star sapphire, he attached himself to us like a leech. Soon he found out Grandmother is superstitious about the gem, so he started playing upon her feelings. He told her about this wretched society of his and painted the monastery in such glowing colors that Grandmother became fascinated."

"So he talked her into coming here?"

"Yes," Rhoda said bitterly, "it was only supposed to be for a day's visit. But once we were inside the monastery, we became as prisoners. Letters are confiscated and there is no telephone."

"You did get away once."

"With Julia's help—yes. Only once though. The place is guarded by Winkey and he is very watchful."

"Tell me, have you seen Mr. Ayling, the insurance company investigator?"

"Mr. Ayling?" Rhoda was puzzled.

"I mean the man who was with me the day you peeped at us from behind the curtain in Father Benedict's study," Penny explained.

"Oh! No, only on that day."

"Mr. Ayling came here to find you and your grandmother. Then he went to Chicago and hasn't returned. I'm afraid something has happened to him."

"I've seen no one here except members of the society," Rhoda said. "Sometimes though, I wonder what goes on in the cellar. Once I heard a dreadful commotion! And the way Julia screams when she is upset!"

"She's a simple soul."

"Simple perhaps, but she knows more than anyone else about the real secrets of this house."

"Speaking of secrets," said Penny hesitantly, "I'm wondering what ever became of the star sapphire?"

"It's safe—at least I think so," Rhoda replied. "Not even Grandmother knows where I have hidden it."

"Then there's no chance Father Benedict can get his hands on it while I go for police?"

CHAPTER 19 - A DORMITORY ROOM

"Not unless he forces me to tell where the gem is hidden. And I'll die first! But I'm afraid he may torture Grandmother in an attempt to make her reveal what she doesn't know."

Penny prepared to close the peephole. "I'll go for the authorities now as fast as I can," she promised. "Keep up your courage until I return."

"Do be careful," Rhoda warned nervously. "If Father Benedict should catch you trying to escape, there's no guessing what he would do!"

Penny closed the peephole and stole out of the dark closet. The corridor was deserted.

Retracing her way to the cloister, the girl paused beside a wall niche a moment as she considered the safest way to attempt an escape.

"I'll try the kitchen window," she decided. "It worked well enough coming in."

On tiptoe she approached the kitchen, only to halt as she heard voices. Father Benedict was berating Old Julia again.

"There *were* eleven bowls of soup served!" she heard him insist. "Mrs. Hawthorne and her daughter were not in the dining room. So that makes one extra person unaccounted for. Julia, someone entered this house tonight to spy, and you know who the person is!"

"No! No! I dunno nothin'," the servant moaned. "Even if you strike me and break my bones I can't tell you no different!"

"We'll see about that," said the monk harshly. "After a few hours below, perhaps you'll be willing to talk!"

Julia uttered a squeal of terror. "Don't take me down into that awful place where the tombs are!" she pleaded. "Please!"

"Then tell me who entered this house tonight."

"I'll tell, if you quit twisting my arm," Julia sobbed. "Only I didn't want to get her into trouble. She didn't mean no harm."

"*She!*"

"It was just a girl."

"A blond?"

"I dunno. I guess so."

"It was that Parker girl!" Father Benedict muttered. "She represents the *Riverview Star*, worse luck!" Giving Julia a hard shake, he demanded: "She got in through the window?"

"I guess so. I dunno."

"You know nothing, especially when it suits your purpose!" Father Benedict accused her furiously. "Where is the girl now? Did she get away or is she still here?"

"I seen her a few minutes ago."

"Where?"

Penny's heart nearly failed her, for she was certain Old Julia would reveal that she had hidden in the closet with the peephole.

To her great relief, the woman replied that she had taken part in the cult ceremony and then had supped in the refectory.

"I knew that before, stupid!" Father Benedict shouted. "The girl must still be in the building. I'll find her, and when I do—"

Waiting to hear no more, Penny retreated to the cloister. All candles had been blown out and it was very dark.

"I must get out of here now or never!" she thought. "Father Benedict will start looking for me and he'll probably order Winkey to watch the gates."

Starting hurriedly along the cloister, she heard approaching footsteps. Momentarily confused, she started up a short, steep stairway to a balcony overlooking the court.

Belatedly, Penny realized she had turned toward the dormitories.

Opening from the balcony was a bedroom door which stood partly ajar.

After listening for a moment, and hearing no movement inside, she cautiously tiptoed into the room.

"A window here may be unlocked," she thought. "If the drop to the ground isn't too far, maybe I can get out this way."

As Penny crossed the room, an elderly woman she had failed to see, suddenly sat up in bed.

"Rhoda, is that you?" she asked in a whining voice. "Why have you been gone so long? Oh, I've been so worried!"

Penny hesitated, then went over to the bed.

"I'm not Rhoda, but a friend of hers," she explained. "Do you mind if I crawl out through the window?"

"It's nailed down and there are bars," the elderly woman replied. "Oh, this is a horrible place! Rhoda tried to tell me. I wouldn't listen!"

Scarcely hearing, Penny ran to the window. As she pulled aside the dusty velvet draperies, she saw for herself that the window was guarded by ancient rusty bars. Everywhere escape seemed cut off!

Turning to the bed again, she observed with some alarm that the old lady had fallen back on her pillow. Moonlight flooding in through the diamond-shaped panes of glass accentuated her pallor.

"You're Mrs. Hawthorne, aren't you?" she inquired gently.

The woman nodded. She coughed several times and pulled the one thin coverlet closer about her.

"Where is Rhoda?" she asked. "Why doesn't she come to me?"

Penny could not tell her the truth—that her granddaughter had been locked in the chapel bedroom by Father Benedict. Nor could she express the fear that an even worse fate was in store for the girl unless help came quickly to the monastery.

As she groped for words, Mrs. Hawthorne suddenly gasped. Her face became convulsed and she writhed in bed.

"Oh, those stomach cramps!" she moaned. "They're starting again! Please—please, a doctor!"

Never had Penny felt so helpless as she watched the poor woman suffer. Mrs. Hawthorne's wrinkled face broke out in perspiration. She gripped the girl's hand with a pressure that was painful.

When the cramp had passed, she lay limp and exhausted.

"I'll get a doctor here as soon as I can," Penny promised. "Until then, perhaps a hot water bottle will help."

"There's no hot water in the place," Mrs. Hawthorne mumbled. "Oh, if I ever get away from here alive—"

"Sh!" Penny suddenly interrupted. She placed her fingertips on the woman's lips.

Heavy footsteps warned her that someone approached.

"It may be Father Benedict!" Penny whispered. "Whatever you do, don't give me away! I must hide!"

Frantically, she looked about for a safe place. The room had no closet.

"Under the bed," urged Mrs. Hawthorne.

Penny wriggled beneath it. Barely had she secreted herself, than Father Benedict stamped into the bedroom.

CHAPTER 20 - TRICKERY

Lighting his way with a tall, flickering candle, Father Benedict walked directly to the bed where Mrs. Hawthorne lay.

"How are you feeling?" he inquired with a show of sympathy.

"Dreadful," the woman murmured. "I must have a doctor."

"Do you really believe that a doctor can help you, my good woman?"

The question startled Mrs. Hawthorne. She half-raised herself from the pillow to stare at the monk.

"Why, what do you mean?" she asked. "Surely a doctor can give me medicine to help these wretched pains. It is only a stomach disorder."

"My dear Mrs. Hawthorne, surely you must realize that your difficulty is not one that a man of medicine can cure."

"You don't mean I have a serious, incurable disease?" the woman gasped.

"You are indeed suffering from a most serious malady which may take your life," affirmed Father Benedict. "Is it not true that bad fortune has pursued every owner of the star sapphire?"

Mrs. Hawthorne remained silent.

"Is it not so?" prodded the monk. "Think back over the history of the gem. Even your husband met with misfortune."

"And now you believe my turn has come? Oh!"

"I dislike to distress you," resumed Father Benedict with malice, "but perhaps by warning you I may yet save your life. Tonight in the crystal globe I saw your face. A message came that you must dispose of the star sapphire immediately or you too will die!"

"I—I always have hated and feared the gem," Mrs. Hawthorne whispered, her lips trembling. "You are right. It has brought only misfortune upon our family."

"Then your way is clear. You must dispose of the sapphire at once—tonight."

"The gem is very valuable. You suggest that I give it to your society?"

"To our society," corrected the monk. "Once you have contributed the gem, you will become our most honored member."

"The gem was left to me in trust for my granddaughter."

"You told me yourself you desire that it never should fall into her hands."

"Only because I fear evil will befall her. I had planned to sell the gem and place the money in her name."

Father Benedict beat an impatient tattoo with his foot. "The curse would remain," he insisted. "Only by giving the gem to a worthy charity can evil be erased. For your own sake and that of your granddaughter, I beg of you, give us the sapphire."

"A few days ago, I might have considered it," said Mrs. Hawthorne peevishly. "Now I don't even like this place. It is too much on the order of a prison. The food is wretched! Tomorrow if I am stronger, I shall take my granddaughter and leave."

"Indeed?" Father Benedict sneered. "For you there will be no tomorrow. I have seen the face of a corpse in my glass!"

Penny knew that the words shocked Mrs. Hawthorne, for she heard her draw in her breath sharply. But the woman retorted with spirit:

"You cannot frighten me with your predictions! Rhoda insisted from the first that you are an imposter! She is right! You'll get no gem from me!"

"No?" Father Benedict's voice became mocking. "We shall see!"

Placing the candle on the floor close to the bed, he crossed the room to the old fashioned dresser. One by one, he began to paw through the drawers.

"Stop it!" cried Mrs. Hawthorne. "Don't dare touch my things!"

Father Benedict paid her not the slightest heed. Rapidly he emptied boxes and containers and tossed clothing in a heap on the floor.

With a supreme effort, Mrs. Hawthorne pulled herself from the bed. Staggering across the floor, she seized the man's arm.

Father Benedict pushed her backwards onto the bed.

"You are a cruel, heartless man!" Mrs. Hawthorne sobbed. The bed shook convulsively beneath her weight as she lay where Father Benedict had pushed her.

Penny was sorely tempted to go to the woman's assistance, but reason told her it would be sheer folly to betray her presence. Everything depended upon getting quickly and safely out of the monastery. If she failed, Father Benedict undoubtedly would escape, leaving them all locked in the building.

The monk now had finished searching the dresser and turned his attention to a suitcase. With professional skill and thoroughness, he ripped open the lining. Likewise, he explored every garment hem and pocket.

"To think that I ever trusted you!" Mrs. Hawthorne cried bitterly. "Oh, I see it all now! From the very first, you were after the sapphire!"

"And I have it too!" cried the man in triumph.

His sensitive, exploring fingers had come upon a small, hard object sewed into the hem of one of Mrs. Hawthorne's frocks.

"Don't you dare take the stone!" the woman screamed. "I'll have you arrested as a common thief!"

"You'll never get out of this room," chuckled the monk. "I intend to lock you in!"

The boast threw Penny into a panic. Not for an instant did she doubt that Father Benedict would carry out his threat. If he locked Mrs. Hawthorne in, she too would be a prisoner!

Penny had no time to plan strategy or reason out the best course. Already, Father Benedict had removed the gem from the hem of the garment.

Before he could examine it, or move toward the door, Penny, with a mighty "whoosh" blew out the candle.

Scrambling from beneath the bed, she darted to the door.

Taken by surprise, Father Benedict was too slow to intercept her. She slammed the door in his face, groping frantically for a key.

Finding none, she knew the monk must have the only one on his person.

"The fat's in the fire now for sure!" she thought in panic.

Penny raced across the balcony and down the stone steps to the cloister. In this emergency the pillars, though shadowed, offered no protection whatsoever. Nor was the dry fountain bed a safe place in which to hide.

Pounding footsteps warned that there was no time in which to search for a hideout. The only possible place was under an old tarpaulin which lay in a heap on the tiles beside the fountain.

Wriggling beneath the canvas, Penny pulled the folds over her head.

Barely had she flattened herself on the floor than Father Benedict pounded into the cloister. So close did he pass to where she lay, that Penny could hear his heavy breathing.

"Now where did that brat go?" he muttered. "She's here somewhere!"

The monk rang a bell which brought Winkey on the run.

"I've looked everywhere for that Parker girl," he reported before the master could speak. "She must have got away."

"Fool!" rasped the monk. "She has been hiding in Mrs. Hawthorne's room! She saw me take the sapphire!"

"You mean you got the gem, boss?"

"Here in my hand. Hold your lantern closer and see for yourself."

A long pause followed. Penny guessed that the two men were inspecting the gem beneath a light. She was unprepared for the next explosive comment of Father Benedict.

"I've been tricked!" he muttered. "This isn't the sapphire Mrs. Hawthorne showed me in Florida! It's only a cheap imitation!"

CHAPTER 20 - TRICKERY

"Maybe that girl sneaked in and took it herself!"

"If she did it will be the worse for her! I know Mrs. Hawthorne brought a genuine sapphire into this house. Either her granddaughter has it, or this Parker pest!"

"What'll we do, boss?"

"We're leaving here as quickly as we can get away," Father Benedict said decisively. "We've over-played our hand and our luck has run out."

"You mean we're going without the sapphire?" grumbled Winkey. "After all our work?"

"We'll get the sapphire. First, we must make certain that Parker girl doesn't slip out of the building."

"I let the dogs loose in the yard. And the windows and doors are all locked. If she tries to get out, they'll set up a yip."

"Good! She must be somewhere in the house and we'll soon find her."

"How much did she learn, boss?"

"I don't know, but enough to jail us both! Go to my study and destroy all the papers you find there. Then bring the car to the rear exit."

"How soon we leaving?"

"Fifteen minutes."

"Can you get the sapphire in that time?" Winkey asked doubtfully. "What if the old lady holds out?"

"I've locked her in her room. Also the other women. I'll not bother with Mrs. Hawthorne. There are quicker methods."

"Her granddaughter?"

"Exactly. We'll carry out my original plan. Miss Rhoda will be glad to talk when I have finished with her!"

"It's kinda harsh treatment—"

"Do as you are told!" Father Benedict cut in sharply.

"Okay, boss," agreed Winkey. "I'll sure be glad to shake the dust of this place off my feet. This cult racket never was in our line. We got in deeper than we figured."

"Do less talking and more thinking!" snapped the monk. "I'll take care of Rhoda and have the sapphire within fifteen minutes. She's asleep by this time, I hope."

"I looked in through the peephole a minute ago," the hunchback informed. "Sleeping like a babe!"

"Good!" Father Benedict approved. His final order sent an icy chill down Penny's spine. "Give me your lantern, Winkey. I'll go below now and turn on the machinery."

CHAPTER 21 - SNATCHED FROM THE FLAMES

From beneath the dusty tarpaulin, Penny had listened tensely as Father Benedict and Winkey planned their escape.

She knew that by morning they would be in another state, beyond reach of Riverview police.

Fifteen minutes! The time was so short—too short for her to summon authorities even if she could reach a telephone.

And what of Rhoda in the chapel bedroom? Father Benedict had spoken of turning on machinery in the cellar! What machinery did he mean?

A great fear arose within Penny. Rhoda was in great danger! She must make every effort to save her—but how?

Father Benedict and his servant now were leaving the cloister, walking directly toward the canvas under which the girl huddled.

Suddenly, to Penny's horror, the dust of the tarpaulin began to irritate her nose.

She fought against an impulse to sneeze but could not control it. Though she pressed both hands against her nose, a muffled ker-chew came from beneath the canvas.

Father Benedict halted, looking sharply about the darkened cloister.

"What was that?" he demanded.

"I didn't hear nothin'," replied Winkey, flashing his lantern on the pillars.

"I thought someone sneezed."

"You're getting jumpy, boss," insisted the hunchback. "I sure didn't hear nothing."

"What's that over there by the fountain?" Father Benedict demanded, noticing the tarpaulin.

"Only an old piece of canvas. I brought it up from the basement this afternoon."

"For a second, I thought I saw it moving!"

"You've sure got the jumps," said Winkey. "If you want me to look for that girl again, I'll give the place a good going over."

"No, there's no time!" the monk decided. "As long as the dogs are loose in the yard, she never can get out of here without them sounding an alarm. Then we'll nab her."

"I'll go after the car and have it at the rear exit before you're ready to leave," the hunchback promised. "Just be sure you get the sapphire!"

"Leave it to me," said Father Benedict grimly. His voice faded away and Penny knew that the two conspirators were at last leaving the cloister.

Waiting a moment longer to be certain they would not change their minds and return, she extricated herself from the folds of the grimy canvas.

"Wow! That was a close call!" she told herself. "If what Father Benedict said is true, then I'm trapped in this building along with the others! What a predicament!"

Penny groped for her flashlight and was reassured to find it still in her pocket. She tested it briefly, then switched it off again.

Tiptoeing down a long, damp-smelling corridor, she passed a window. Hopeful that it might be unlocked, she paused to test it.

Not only was the catch fastened, but the window also had been nailed. Peering out, she gazed hopefully toward the distant road. No cars were in sight. Nor was there a light gleaming in the windows of the Eckenrod cabin, over the hill.

CHAPTER 21 - SNATCHED FROM THE FLAMES

Instead, Penny saw an ugly hound circling the monastery grounds, his nose to the earth.

"Winkey already has turned the dogs loose!" she thought in dismay. "I haven't a chance to get out of here quickly!"

Switching on her flashlight for an instant, Penny looked at her wristwatch. In astonishment, she saw that it was only twenty minutes after nine. She had assumed the hour to be much later, so many events had transpired since her arrival at the monastery.

"If only I could let the *Star* office know of my predicament!" she thought. "Mr. DeWitt won't even wonder what's become of me before ten o'clock. By that time Father Benedict and Winkey will be miles from here!"

The main gate of the monastery had been closed and locked. Penny reasoned that even if she were able to get out of the building, the dogs would be upon her before she could scale the high boundary fence, and make her escape.

As she hesitated at the window, debating whether or not to smash the glass and take a chance, she heard the roar of an automobile motor.

For a moment she was hopeful a car was coming down the road. Then, with a sinking heart she realized that it was Winkey bringing the big black automobile from the front of the house to the rear exit.

"The minute he and Father Benedict get their thieving hands on the sapphire, they'll leave here!" she reasoned. "Oh, why can't I think of some way to stop them?"

Penny had left her own car parked on the road not far from the monastery. She was hopeful that should her father or anyone from the newspaper office seek her, they would see the car and deduct that she was somewhere inside the ancient building.

"But no one will come until it's too late," she thought. "Mrs. Weems probably went to bed early and didn't tell Dad I came here. Mr. DeWitt won't think about it until nearly deadline time at the *Star*."

Outside, the hounds kept roaming the grounds. Penny had never seen such vicious looking animals.

Abandoning all hope of getting away without risking being torn to pieces, she decided her wisest course would be to keep hidden until Father Benedict had driven away.

"Maybe by staying, I can help Rhoda," she reflected. "Father Benedict intends to force her to tell where the sapphire is hidden!"

With noiseless tread she started toward the chapel bedroom which adjoined the church ruins. In passing the monk's study she noticed that the door stood slightly ajar.

Peering cautiously in, she saw that the room was in disarray. All of Father Benedict's clothing, art treasures, and personal belongings had been removed. Drawers of the desk had been emptied of their contents.

In the fireplace, flames leaped merrily. Plainly, the monk had disposed of many papers by consigning them to the fire.

At the edge of the hearth lay several sheets torn from a notebook. One of the pages had caught fire and was burning slowly.

Recognizing it as a sheet listing society contributions, Penny darted forward and stamped out the flames.

Only half of the paper had been charred. Many of the names still could be read. Folding the good section, she placed it in her coat pocket.

Two other pages which had not caught fire proved to be blank.

Unable to rescue anything else from the flames, Penny quitted the study and moved hurriedly toward the chapel bedroom.

From the dormitories she now could hear muffled cries and poundings which told her cult members had discovered themselves locked in their rooms.

"I can't get them out without keys," Penny thought. "But if they make enough noise, someone may hear and come here to investigate."

The closing of a nearby door brought the girl up short. As she froze against the passageway wall, Father Benedict stepped from the closet adjoining the bedroom where Rhoda was imprisoned.

Instantly Penny guessed that he had been watching the girl through the peephole.

Father Benedict's satisfaction as he started toward the ruined church was frightening to behold. Thin lips were twisted into an ugly smile, and as he passed within a few feet of where Penny stood he muttered:

"Ah rest!—no rest but change of place and posture;
Ah sleep—no sleep but worn-out posture; Nature's swooning;

THE CRY AT MIDNIGHT

Ah bed!—no bed but cushion fill'd with stones."

CHAPTER 22 - THE CANOPIED BED

In the chapel bedroom Rhoda Hawthorne had been greatly cheered to realize that soon she might be freed from imprisonment.

The brief conversation with Penny through the closet peephole encouraged her to believe that almost at once help would come.

Penny is proving to be one of the best friends I ever had and I hardly know her, she thought. *I wish now I had told her everything, especially about the sapphire.*

With regret the girl recalled how she had rebuffed Penny and Louise on the occasion when they had offered her a ride into Riverview.

But at that time she had considered them strangers who only meant to pry into her affairs. *If I had told everything then, Grandmother and I might have been spared much suffering*, she reflected. *I should have asked them to take me to the police. The worst mistake of my life was coming back to this horrible place.*

Restlessly, Rhoda tramped about the chapel room. The air was very stuffy and the absence of windows distressed her. She felt oppressed, as if the four walls were pressing in upon her.

The room was scantily furnished with only the huge canopied bed, an old fashioned dresser, and a table. There were no chairs.

Groping on the dresser, the girl found a stub of a candle in a holder. At first she could discover no matches. However, after examining all the dresser drawers, she came upon one.

Shielding it carefully from draughts, she managed to light it and ignite the wick of the candle.

"It won't burn longer than twenty minutes," she estimated. "But by that time, perhaps Penny will be back here with help."

The dim light depressed rather than cheered the girl. Cold currents of air coming from the chinks of the walls caused the flame to flicker weirdly, and almost go out.

A grotesque figure weaved like a huge shadow-boxer on the expanse of smoky plaster. At first, watching it in fascination, Rhoda could not determine its cause. Then, with no little relief, she decided it was a shadow of the bed draperies, moving slightly with the draughts of cold air.

The room had no heat. Soon, against her will, Rhoda was driven by the chill to seek the warmth of the canopied bed.

With repugnance she eyed the strange, old-fashioned piece of furniture which dominated the room. The bed was wide enough to accommodate three or four persons comfortably. Tall posters of twisted wood supported a carved framework to which were attached dusty, scarlet draperies.

A moth-eaten carpet covered a section of floor directly beneath the bedstead. Rhoda gave it only a passing glance and did not think to look under its curling, frayed edges.

With a shiver of distaste, she pulled aside the draperies and crawled into the bed. No cover had been provided, but there were clean sheets. The damp-smelling spread offered a little relief from the cold.

For some time Rhoda lay staring at the beamed ceiling and trying in her mind to reconstruct the old chapel as it might have been in the days when the monastery was a religious center.

The girl had not the slightest intention of falling asleep. She felt wide awake, tense in every muscle. Not a sound escaped her, and every noise seemed intensified.

A board creaked.

It's nothing, she told herself. *All old houses make strange sounds, especially when a wind is blowing.*

THE CRY AT MIDNIGHT

Yet disturbing thoughts plagued the girl. What did Father Benedict intend to do with her? Why had he locked her in this particular room?

Suddenly Rhoda stiffened and clutched the sheet convulsively. Was it imagination or had she heard a low moan?

The sound had seemed to come from beneath the bed. Half tempted to look beneath the draperies, she resisted the impulse.

I did hear something, she thought. *It sounded as if someone were in pain. And the noise came from the cellar below!*

Now to torment the girl came reflections of unexplained happenings since her arrival at the monastery. On several nights she had heard disturbances from the cellar region. Winkey, she knew, made frequent trips to the crypt upon one pretext or another.

Suddenly Rhoda was startled by a light and repeated tapping on the wall near the closet peephole.

Certain that it was Penny who had returned, she leaped out of bed and bounded across the room.

The panel of wood moved back and two eyes peered in at her.

"Is that you, Penny?" Rhoda whispered eagerly.

"Julia!" was the answer.

"Oh," Rhoda murmured in bitter disappointment. "I hoped—"

"Master send you some supper," the servant mumbled. "Bread and coffee."

"I don't want them!"

"Better you eat and drink," Julia admonished. "But do not sleep. This room is evil—evil!"

"You're telling me!" retorted Rhoda, lapsing into slang. "All I want is to get out of here. Julia, let me free and I'll pay you well! I'll give you anything you want!"

"No key."

"But you know where it is kept?"

"The master keep keys on him always."

"He would! Can't you trick him or something?" Seeing the old woman's blank stare, Rhoda sighed and answered her own question. "No, it's too much to expect. But maybe you could slip away from here and bring help—"

"Master never let me out of the house. My place is in the kitchen. I must go there now—to the kitchen."

"Wait!" Rhoda checked her. "You say Father Benedict sent some food? On second thought, I'll take it. He may not give me anything again for a long while. I expect to be out of here soon, but something could go wrong."

Rhoda longed to ask Old Julia if she had seen Penny or if the girl had escaped. However, knowing that the old woman might divulge the secret to Father Benedict, she wisely did not bring up the subject.

Julia thrust a hard crust of bread in through the peephole, and then shoved a cup of steaming black coffee into her hand.

"Thanks, Julia," Rhoda said. "I know you mean well. Working in a place like this isn't your fault. How did you ever meet Father Benedict anyhow?"

The question was an unfortunate one. Apparently, unpleasant recollections stirred in the woman's brain, for her eyes became wild. She muttered gibberish Rhoda could not understand. Then she slammed shut the peephole.

A moment later, Rhoda heard her footsteps as she left the closet and retreated down the corridor.

"Poor old Julia," she sighed. "Wonder if I'll ever come to the same pass she's in? I'm sure I will if I have to spend a night in this torture chamber!"

Shivering, Rhoda climbed back into bed. She bit into the bread. Discovering it to be moldy, she hurled it into a far corner of the room.

Rhoda was cold and the hot coffee smelled good. She sipped it cautiously. The brew tasted peculiar, sweetish and unlike any coffee she ever had had before. Nevertheless, it was hot and would warm her chilled bones perhaps.

She drank the entire cupful and leaned back on the pillow.

What was it Julia said, she mused drowsily. *Oh, yes, I must stay awake. Must stay awake.*

CHAPTER 22 - THE CANOPIED BED

But the warmth of the bed was closing in on her, inviting her to shut her eyes. Though she fought against it, she could feel sleep taking possession of her.

She tried to raise her hand and found it too heavy to lift. Only then did the frightening truth seep into her mind. She had been drugged! Undoubtedly, Father Benedict had slipped a heavy sleeping powder into the coffee! And she stupidly had drunk all of the brew.

The sound of the peephole panel moving again, aroused her momentarily from the stupor into which she rapidly was falling.

Rhoda saw a face at the opening and recognized Father Benedict. He spoke no word, but gazed at her with an expression of evil gloating.

The girl tried to move but her limbs seemed paralyzed. She could not stir.

Then the panel closed and Father Benedict had gone.

Rhoda fell into a sleep only to be rudely awakened as the huge bed gave a slight jerk. The stupefied girl could not think where she was for a moment.

Her head was a-whirl and the room seemed to be spinning. Like a person taking ether, she felt as if she were slipping farther and farther away from reality with each breath.

The canopied bed had come to life and was moving slowly downward through an opening in the floor.

Rhoda stifled an impulse to laugh. Perspiration broke out in every pore as she suddenly knew that it was not a dream nor a horrible imagining. *The bed actually was moving!*

As she realized her desperate plight, the girl struggled to free herself from the bed clothing. But her limbs refused to obey the commands of her mind. Paralyzed with fright, she tried to scream and made only a choking sound in her throat.

CHAPTER 23 - DESCENT INTO THE CRYPT

Meanwhile, a great fear had taken possession of Penny as she saw Father Benedict leave the chapel bedroom closet and disappear down a corridor leading into the ruins of the church.

The expression of his face and his evil mutterings warned her that the man thoroughly enjoyed his role, despite his insistence that he abhorred violence.

Fearing for Rhoda's safety, Penny waited only until he had vanished. Then she slipped into the closet of the bedroom and fumbled for the peephole opening.

She found it and peered anxiously into the darkened bed chamber. Rhoda was lying on the canopied bed, apparently sound asleep.

"Rhoda!" Penny called in a loud whisper.

The girl did not stir.

As Penny whispered the name still louder, she saw the bed jerk. The floor beneath it began to move slowly downward.

In horror, Penny recalled what Jake Cotton, the carpenter, had told her about repairing the ancient lift. Rhoda was being lowered into the crypt below!

"Rhoda!" she cried. "Wake up! Quick! Jump out of bed!"

The girl seemed to hear for she moved slightly and made a choking sound in her throat. But she could not extricate herself from the slowly descending bed.

Numb with despair, Penny saw the girl disappear beyond view. There was a whine of machinery as the bed apparently came to a standstill on the subterranean floor below.

Then after a moment, she heard movement again. The bed slowly ascended. A glance sufficed to show Penny that it was empty.

"I've got to help her!" she thought. "That fiend will torture her into telling where the sapphire is hidden if I don't think of some scheme for saving her. But how?"

Quitting the closet, Penny sought the same passageway Father Benedict had taken into the ruined church.

As she cautiously opened the squeaky door, she saw before her shattered Gothic columns which once had supported a magnificent roof. Now dim stars cast a ghostly light over a mass of piled-up rubble.

Walls, however, had proved remarkably sturdy, rising to a height Penny could not hope to scale. There were no visible exits.

"Where did Father Benedict go?" she speculated. "Steps must lead down to the crypt."

Penny flashed her light about, seeking an opening. Investigating a pile of stone which had tumbled from an archway, she was elated to find her search at an end. Behind the piled up rocks, cleverly concealed, was a vaulted stone passage and stairway leading down.

Though Penny knew it was highly dangerous to venture below, she did not hesitate. A step at a time, and pausing frequently to listen, she stole down toward the inky blackness of the crypt.

The stone walls on either side of the narrow, curving stairway were cold and clammy to the touch. Water dripped from overhead.

Ahead, in a sunken recess amid the stones, the girl suddenly saw a shadowy figure. Startled, she jerked to a standstill. Then, observing that the object was not a human being but a rusty coat of armor, she breathed easier and went on.

A minute later, as she crept around a turn of the stairway, terror gripped her at first glimpse of the dimly lighted burial crypt.

CHAPTER 23 - DESCENT INTO THE CRYPT

In grim, orderly rows were the elaborately carved stone sarcophaguses of former residents of the monastery.

Beyond the tombs, backed against a wall, sat Rhoda. Sleepy-eyed, her hair in disarray, she faced Father Benedict who held a lighted lantern close to her face.

Jay Highland had doffed his long robes and stood revealed in ordinary gray business suit. In his coat pocket, within easy reach of his right hand, was a revolver.

"Wake up!" he said, giving Rhoda a hard shake. "You're only pretending now! The drug in the coffee was not strong enough to keep you asleep. Wake up!"

Rhoda stared at him and her eyes widened in horror.

"You fiend!" she accused him. "Don't you dare touch me! I'll scream!"

"Scream at the top of your lungs, my dear. Only the dead will hear you."

"The dead! Oh!" A shudder wracked Rhoda's thin body as she became aware of the tombs in the crypt. "Why did you bring me here?"

"For one purpose. I want the sapphire. Hand it over and you will not be harmed."

"I haven't the gem."

"But you know where it is."

Rhoda remained silent.

"You'll tell," Highland rasped, losing all patience. "I haven't all day! You tricked me with that cheap substitute, and you induced your grandmother to hold out against me. Now we are through playing."

"You're nothing but a cheap crook!"

"A crook perhaps," said the man, "but hardly cheap. The sapphire should be worth $50,000 at a conservative estimate. Now where is it?"

"You'll never learn from me!" Rhoda cried defiantly. "I'll die before I'll tell!"

"My! My! Such heroics! However, I think you will change your mind. Let me show you something, my dear."

Setting the lantern on the floor, Highland grasped Rhoda roughly by the arm and led her to a small doorway at the far side of the crypt.

"Tell me what you see," he purred.

Rhoda drew in her breath sharply and recoiled from the sight. She was speechless with fright.

"My dear, I was not thinking of mistreating you—certainly not," Highland purred. "No, instead we will bring your aged grandmother down here."

"You wouldn't dare!" Rhoda gasped. "Why, she's sick."

"The damp and cold will be bad for her, no doubt," agreed the imposter. "When I saw her tonight, she seemed to have developed a severe cough. The onset of pneumonia perhaps."

"Oh!"

"You could so easily spare her suffering," continued the man wickedly. "Merely by telling me where you hid the sapphire. I know your grandmother had it when she came into this house. But you made off with it, substituting a paste gem."

"It's true, I did hide the gem," Rhoda confessed. "Punish me—not Grandmother."

"Unless you tell me where the sapphire is hidden she shall be brought down here and treated as those others who defied me." The man jerked his head toward the room beyond Penny's view. "What do you say?"

"Let me think about it for a few minutes."

"You're stalling for time, hoping that Parker girl will bring help!" the man accused. From his pocket he took a stout cord with which he securely bound Rhoda's hands and feet.

Bracing her back against the wall, he likewise whipped a handkerchief gag from his clothing.

"This is your last chance," he warned. "Will you tell, or shall I go for your grandmother?"

"I'll tell," Rhoda whispered. "The gem is a long ways from here."

"Where?"

"Down by the river docks."

"By the river docks! A likely story!"

"You remember I ran away?" Rhoda asked hurriedly. "I took my suitcase, intending not to come back. Then for Grandmother's sake I returned. I was afraid I might never get a chance to sneak my clothes out again, so I hid the suitcase under a dock by the river."

"And the gem?"

"I took it with me when I ran away. It was sewed in the hem of a blue skirt packed in the suitcase."

"Fool!" Highland exclaimed furiously. "Of all the stupid tricks! Where is the suitcase now?"

"Still under the dock unless someone has found it. But it should be there, because I pushed it up high out of sight beneath the underpinning."

"Which dock?" the man rasped.

"It was just at the edge of Riverview. Dock Fourteen."

"At least you remember the number!" he snapped. "If I fail to find the gem, I'll come back here and make you pay! You may be certain of that!"

"I hope you do come back and that the police are waiting at the gate!" Rhoda retorted. "I hope they put you in prison for the rest of your life!"

Picking up the lantern, Jay Highland started toward the stairway where Penny crouched. She moved hurriedly behind the door which opened into the crypt.

Slight as was the sound she made, Highland detected it.

"Who is there?" he called, holding his lantern high. "Answer or I'll shoot!"

Penny did not doubt that the man would carry out his threat. Her hand closed on a stone which lay on a ledge directly behind her.

"Don't shoot," she said, exposing herself to view.

"So it's you again!" hissed Highland. "I might have known!"

Penny let fly the stone. It struck the lantern. The light went out and oil and flame splattered over the stone floor.

Knowing it was her only chance to escape, Penny made a wild dash up the stairs. But she could not climb swiftly enough.

Jay Highland pounded hard after her. As she neared the top of the circular steps, he seized her arm and pulled her backwards.

Penny fought like a tiger to free herself. Together they stumbled and rolled down the wide stones to the floor of the crypt. There the man pressed his revolver hard into the girl's ribs, and she knew the game was up.

"Get in there!" he said, giving her a hard push. "This time you'll stay!"

As Penny reeled backwards into a wall, she heard the door of the crypt close and lock. With despair she realized that she too was a prisoner in the chamber of the dead.

CHAPTER 24 - CHAMBER OF THE DEAD

Furious at herself because she had been so careless, Penny quickly tested the door. Finding it securely fastened as she had known it would be, she reached for her flashlight. It was missing from her pocket.

Though she groped about in the darkness, she could not find it. Giving up, she next turned her attention to Rhoda Hawthorne.

Thongs about the girl's wrists and ankles had been loosely tied. In a minute, Penny had set her free.

"Now to find a way out of here!" she exclaimed. "Highland and Winkey probably are driving to the river dock by this time!"

"It's no use trying to get out," Rhoda said despairingly as she rubbed her bruised wrists. "I'm sure this door is the only exit. Look in the adjoining room and you'll see what I mean."

Even as Penny started for the inner doorway, she heard a low moan of pain from someone imprisoned there.

"Who is it?" she asked tensely.

"I don't know," Rhoda admitted, huddling close beside Penny. "Two men, one of them in frightful condition."

"Can't we set them free? Rhoda, try to find my flashlight. It fell somewhere near the stairway."

While Rhoda groped for the flashlight, Penny entered the inner prison room. Not until she was very close could she see two men who were chained to a supporting pillar. Gags covered the mouths of both victims.

Penny untied the cloths. The first man she thus freed was someone she never before had seen. But as she jerked the gag from the lips of the second prisoner, she was startled to recognize Mr. Ayling.

"You!" she exclaimed.

"In the flesh, or what's left of it," the investigator attempted to banter. "Nice fix for an investigator, eh? The company probably will give me a merit award for this!"

"How were you enticed here?"

"It's a long story," sighed Mr. Ayling. "I've not been chained here long, fortunately. My companion, Joseph Merkill, is in much worse shape. He's been here a couple of days."

"I'll set him free first," Penny offered. She groped along the chains which fastened the man to the stone column. "Handcuffs? How can I get them off?"

"You can't, without a key," replied Mr. Ayling. "You'll have to go for help, or if there's no escape, wait until someone finds us here."

"That may not be before morning! Even if police should come here tonight, they might not see the stairway to the crypt."

"Any chance to break down the door?"

"I doubt it. Rhoda and I can try though."

"Rhoda Hawthorne! So it was her voice I heard! She and her grandmother are imprisoned also?"

"Yes, Rhoda's with me. Her grandmother, seriously ill, is locked in a bedroom upstairs. Who is Mr. Merkill?"

"His wife is an inmate here," the investigator explained. "Jay Highland—I know now he's a notorious jewel thief—induced Mrs. Merkill to come to the monastery. After he fleeced her of a diamond necklace, she smuggled a note out, telling how she was being mistreated. Her husband, from whom she had been estranged, decided to investigate. He came here alone. Discovering what was going on, he threatened to expose Highland to the police."

"Highland tricked me," Mr. Merkill added. "He promised I could take my former wife away and he would close the monastery. To show there were no hard feelings, he suggested we have coffee together. I drank it and became so sleepy I had to go to bed. That's all I remember until I woke up here, chained to a post!"

"I should have been more suspicious of Highland the first time I met him," Mr. Ayling blamed himself.

"Why did you go to Chicago?" Penny asked as she worked at the chains.

"I know now it was Highland who sent me the fake telegram. He wanted to get me away from here. While in Chicago, I contacted my home office and obtained information which convinced me Highland was a gem thief. So I came here, intending to demand a police investigation."

"I met one train," said Penny. "You weren't on it."

"I didn't arrive until early tonight. When the train came in, Winkey and Mr. Highland were waiting at the station."

"For you, obviously?"

"Yes, they told me Mrs. Hawthorne was at the monastery, seriously sick and wanted to see me at once. The story fitted with my own conclusion that despite Highland's previous statements, Mrs. Hawthorne was here. So I foolishly agreed to accompany them."

"Then what happened?"

"In the car, speeding out here, I realized I was being foolhardy to return to the monastery without police escort. At an intersection I tried to get out. Winkey slugged me. That's the last I knew until I found myself in this crypt."

Rhoda now groped her way to the door of the inner prison room.

"I found the flashlight but it's broken," she reported.

"With or without a light, we must get out of here and bring the police!" Penny exclaimed. "We haven't a chance to free Mr. Ayling and Mr. Merkill ourselves."

"And you haven't a chance to get out of here either—not until someone breaks into the house," Mr. Ayling added. "The only door is the one Highland locked."

"There is another exit!" Penny recalled. "Mr. Eckenrod showed it to me on the map of this old building. If only we can find it!"

Filled with hope, she began to grope about the walls of the inner room. In the semi-darkness, she could find no break anywhere on the rough stone surface.

"According to the map, the opening should be along this wall," she told Rhoda who joined her in the search. "But there's nothing here."

"Maybe the opening was sealed up years ago."

Though half convinced Rhoda was right, Penny would not give up. Even after her friend had abandoned the search, she kept tapping the walls.

One section, adjoining a large stone tomb, gave off a hollow sound. But try as she would, Penny could not find a moveable section of wall.

"It's no use," she admitted, "unless—"

"Unless what?" Rhoda demanded as Penny's voice trailed off.

"What a dud I am! I remember now, Mr. Eckenrod said the hidden passage comes out through a tomb in the churchyard! So the entrance to the tunnel may be through this tomb which stands against the wall!"

"The wall did give off a hollow sound when you tapped it," Rhoda declared, hope reviving.

"See if you can open the door of the tomb!" Mr. Ayling urged, becoming excited. "I have a hunch you're on the right track!"

Thus urged, Penny overcame her own reluctance. The latch on the big stone door appeared to be locked. She experimented with it for awhile, and was rewarded to hear a sharp click. As she pulled on the door with all her strength, it slowly swung backwards.

Peering in, she saw that the tomb was empty. Also, the back wall was missing.

"The entrance to the passageway!" she cried. "We've found it!"

As Rhoda sprang to her feet, Penny hesitated. She felt it would be cruel to abandon the two men who remained chained to the column.

"Go as fast as you can!" Mr. Ayling urged. "It's our only hope! If you get out safely, send the police after Highland and Winkey! Then bring help."

CHAPTER 24 - CHAMBER OF THE DEAD

"We'll hurry!" Penny promised.

She grasped Rhoda's trembling hand and started through the opening into a narrow, low passageway vaulted over with brick.

"You say we'll come out in the churchyard?" Rhoda gasped, huddling close behind her friend.

"I imagine so. This passage can't be very long. I only hope it isn't blocked by a cave-in."

Their anxiety increased as they inched their way along. Frequently they were forced to climb over piles of brick which had fallen from the ceiling.

Once they were certain the passage was completely blocked. However, Penny pulled aside a mass of debris, enabling them to climb through and go on.

Then at last the tunnel began to ascend over wet, slippery ground.

"We're coming out!" Penny announced jubilantly. "I can see a crack of light ahead!"

A few feet farther and the passageway was blocked by a small stone door. However, dim light shone beneath it and the girls could feel cold night air on their cheeks.

Penny tugged at the door and it opened readily. The pair emerged into another empty tomb. Closing the stone door carefully behind them, they made their way out into the night.

"We're still on the grounds!" Penny observed in a hushed voice as she looked alertly about. "In the old graveyard."

"Any sign of Father Benedict or the dogs?" Rhoda whispered nervously.

"Nary a trace. The car at the rear of the monastery is gone! We must get to a telephone as quickly as we can!"

Alternately stumbling over fragments of stone and mounds of earth, the girls raced for the front gate. Even as they reached it, a car skidded to a standstill close beside the fence.

"It's someone from the *Star* office!" Penny cried, recognizing one of the newspaper-owned automobiles.

As she struggled with the latch of the big gate, her father, Jerry Livingston, and Salt Sommers leaped from the car.

"That you, Penny?" called Mr. Parker anxiously. "We were getting mighty worried about you. What kept you here so long?"

"This and that," replied Penny, opening the gate. "It will take too long to tell. We need help and need it fast!"

As rapidly as she could, she related the essential facts of Jay Highland's flight, apparently to the river docks.

"Salt, streak for the nearest phone and turn in a police alarm!" Mr. Parker ordered.

"It may be too late to overtake Highland," Penny said anxiously. "But if we don't catch him, the Hawthorne sapphire will be lost!"

"Don't bother about the suitcase under the dock," Rhoda interposed. "Just get Mr. Ayling, my grandmother and all those poor folks out of the monastery. That's the important thing."

"Salt can come back here and wait until police open up the monastery," Mr. Parker said, thinking fast. "Jerry and I will try to pick up Highland's trail!"

"I'll send another squad to the river," Salt promised, starting off at a run toward Vernon Eckenrod's cabin across the fields.

"Highland and Winkey are heading for Dock Fourteen," Penny said. "Dad, I'll go with you to point it out."

"The suitcase really doesn't matter," Rhoda interrupted again. "You see, the sapphire—"

Jerry, Mr. Parker and Penny were not listening. Already they were running to the press car. The publisher started the engine with a roar, and the automobile raced off to make a quick turn and speed toward the city.

Disregarding the icy road, Mr. Parker drove at high speed. Once the car skidded dangerously and barely missed a ditch.

Soon they approached the outskirts of the city. Penny watched the riverfront intently. She was the first to glimpse the familiar long, black automobile parked close to the dock where Rhoda had hidden her suitcase.

"There's Highland's car!" she cried. "He and Winkey must be here! Probably they're under the dock now! Highland is armed, Dad."

"Then our best bet is to try to keep the men in sight until police catch up with us," Mr. Parker said, pulling up beside the other car. "We're unarmed and can put up no fight."

"If those birds are under the dock on the ice, they're taking their lives in hand," observed Jerry quietly. "All day, the river's been on the verge of breaking up. When she goes, it will be with a bang!"

Penny opened the car door and leaped out. "I can't see anyone down there," she said anxiously. "Do you suppose they abandoned the car after getting the suitcase?"

Fearful that they had arrived too late, the trio ran down a boardwalk to the docks.

Suddenly, Mr. Parker caught Penny by the arm, restraining her.

"There they are!" he whispered. "See! Just coming out from under the dock!"

Two men, easily recognized as Jay Highland and Winkey, climbed from beneath the long dock. The hunchback was burdened with a suitcase.

"What will we do?" Penny whispered. "We can't let them escape with the sapphire!"

"Listen!" commanded Jerry. "I have a hunch we won't need to do anything except wait!"

Even as he spoke, a loud crack not unlike the report of a gun, sounded along the riverfront. The ice was breaking up!

Jay Highland and his companion, well aware of their danger, began to run. Frantically, they sought a place at which to climb up over the high docks. But too late. Already the river ice was clearing away. A great crack appeared directly in front of the two men.

In panic, they started the other way, only to see water on all sides. Then the block on which they stood, began to drift slowly off.

"Help!" shouted Winkey hoarsely. "Help!"

In panic, the hunchback turned his eyes shoreward. Seeing Penny, her father and Jerry on the planking above, he realized that only arrest faced him if he were rescued. Fear gave way to blind rage.

"You'll never get the sapphire!" he shouted. "I'll see it in the bottom of the river first!"

Raising the case high over his head, he hurled it into the churning water. The next instant the ice beneath his feet gave way, and both he and his master plunged into the river!

CHAPTER 25 - THE STAR SAPPHIRE

In a moment, the two men reappeared above the surface of the water, struggling frantically for grips on the floating cakes of ice.

Coiled around a dock post lay an old rope which had not been taken in for the winter. Jerry and Mr. Parker quickly obtained it and tossed it squarely between the two men.

Both grasped it and were pulled slowly toward shore.

Just then a police car drove up at high speed, parking close by.

"Salt's telephone call went through!" Penny cried, signaling to the officers who piled out of the car. "The police arrived just when we need them!"

The shivering pair had no opportunity to attempt escape. As they were pulled out of the water, officers placed them under arrest.

"All right! You've got us!" snarled Winkey. "But you'll never find the suitcase! It's at the bottom of the river!"

"Quiet!" Jay Highland warned him. "Anything you say will be used against us!"

Gazing gloomily at the churning water where the suitcase had been lost, Penny asked if the river might not be dragged after the ice had gone out.

"We'll mark the place," an officer promised. "Don't count on the case being found though. The current is fast here. Objects could be carried a long distance."

Sullen and silent, the two prisoners were removed to the police car. After consulting with Mr. Parker, officers agreed to take Highland and Winkey to the monastery enroute to the lockup. By confronting them with their victims, it was hoped Winkey at least, might make damaging statements.

Penny, Jerry, and Mr. Parker followed close behind as the police car sped to the monastery. Other policemen had arrived there, summoned by Salt. The front door had been broken in, and a search was being made of the building.

Spying Salt at the gate, Penny ran to ask if Mr. Ayling, Mr. Merkill, and Rhoda's grandmother had been released.

"Rhoda's inside now, showing the officers the different rooms," the photographer explained. "Why don't you go on in?"

"Guess I will," Penny agreed, starting up the driveway. "I certainly hate to tell her the bad news though. The sapphire has been lost in the river! It was in her suitcase."

Jerry and Mr. Parker overtook the girl as she entered the monastery. Hearing voices in Mr. Highland's study, they all went there.

A fire had been rebuilt in the grate, and cult members, released from their rooms, were being herded into the chamber. Mrs. Hawthorne, looking very ill, lay on a couch, covered by coats. Beside her, Rhoda hovered anxiously.

Seeing Penny, the girl crossed the room to whisper: "Grandmother is very sick, but Captain Duveen of the police force says she will pull through all right. We've sent for an ambulance to take her to the hospital."

"Have Mr. Ayling and Mr. Merkill been freed yet?"

"Police are down in the crypt now. Did you catch Winkey and that cruel Jay Highland?"

"We did," Penny replied, "but the story is too long to tell now. I'm afraid though, I have bad news."

"How do you mean?"

"The sapphire is gone. Winkey hurled your suitcase into the river."

Rhoda's tense face relaxed into a little smile. "Has that been worrying you?" she asked.

"Naturally."

"But I tried to tell you—you were in such a hurry you wouldn't listen!"

"You tried to tell me what?"

"Why, the sapphire wasn't in the suitcase. It's here in the house."

"But I thought you said you took it with you when you ran away!"

"I did. Then when I decided to leave my suitcase under the dock for a quick getaway should I try to escape from this place later on, I brought the sapphire back with me. I was afraid to leave it, even sewed up in a dress hem, for fear someone would find the suitcase."

"Yet you substituted a fake gem for the real one."

"I did," Rhoda agreed, "because I was certain Highland sooner or later would attempt to steal the gem."

"Then what became of the real sapphire? Is it safe?"

"I hope so," Rhoda said earnestly. "Let's see if we can find it."

Taking Penny by the hand, she led her down the hall to the cloister. At a niche in the wall, she abruptly paused.

"It should be here, beneath this broken statuette," she declared. "I found a tiny crack in the stone, just large enough to insert the gem. Lend me a hairpin, please."

Penny gave her a bobbypin. Rhoda pried beneath the statuette and presently found the small object for which she searched.

"It's here!" she announced triumphantly. "See!"

Into Penny's hand she dropped a star-shaped gem which under artificial light had taken on a violet hue.

"By daylight it's even more beautiful," Rhoda explained. "It looks sky blue then."

"Never have I seen anything so gorgeous," Penny murmured in awe. "And to think Jay Highland nearly made off with it! How clever of you to let him believe it was hidden in the suitcase!"

"I was desperate," Rhoda chuckled. "Grandfather willed the sapphire to me, and I intend to keep it always."

"Then you're not afraid of the old superstition, that harm will befall the owner?"

"I should say not!" grinned Rhoda. "That was only Grandmother's idea. If ordinary precautions are taken, the gem always will be safe. After all, it's highly insured."

"As Mr. Ayling now realizes to his sorrow," added Penny. "Let's see if he and Mr. Merkill are out of the crypt."

Before the girls could find the stairway leading down, policemen appeared, assisting the two men to the first floor of the monastery. Mr. Ayling, who had been imprisoned only a short time, was able to walk. However, it was necessary for officers to carry Mr. Merkill.

"Save my wife," he pleaded. "She is here somewhere. That crook stole a diamond necklace from her too!"

"Your wife is safe and in good health," the officer assured him. "We've found no jewelry though. Describe the necklace."

While he was being carried outside on an improvised stretcher, Mr. Merkill gave police a detailed description of the missing jewelry.

Other persons, members of the cult, also gathered around to press claims for articles Mr. Highland had taken from them.

Under guard, the former master of the monastery and Winkey, were removed from the patrol car to be confronted with victims they had fleeced. Jay Highland arrogantly denied he had accepted or stolen any object of value.

"You have no evidence against me," he defied the group. "True, I established a cult here, but entirely within the law. Not even the sapphire was found in my possession! These people lie if they say I took jewelry from them. They were not charged a penny, even for room and lodging."

"You say you took nothing from them?" Penny inquired. "Look at this!"

From her pocket, she removed the charred sheet of paper rescued from the fireplace. Taking care that Highland should not get his hands on it, she gave it to one of the policemen.

"This is good evidence!" the officer declared. "These birds will talk all right after we get them to the station!"

Highland and Winkey were escorted back to the police car.